DEBORAH HARKNESS

The Book of Life

PENGUIN BOOKS

PENGUIN BOOKS
Published by the Penguin Group
Penguin Group (USA) LLC
375 Hudson Street
New York, New York 10014

USA | Canada | UK | Ireland | Australia | New Zealand | India | South Africa | China
penguin.com
A Penguin Random House Company

First published in the United States of America by Viking Penguin,
a member of Penguin Group (USA) LLC, 2014
Published in Penguin Books 2015

THE LIBRARY OF CONGRESS HAS CATALOGED THE
HARDCOVER EDITION AS FOLLOWS:
Harkness, Deborah E.
The book of life : a novel / Deborah Harkness.
pages cm.—(All souls trilogy; 3)
ISBN 978-0-670-02559-6 (hc.)
ISBN 978-0-14-312752-9 (pbk.)
1. Witches—Fiction. 2. Women historians—Fiction. 3. Vampires—Fiction.
4. Science and magic—Fiction. 5. Time travel—Fiction. I. Title.
PS3608.A7436B66 2014
813'.6—dc23 2014004495

Printed in the United States of America
3 5 7 9 10 8 6 4 2

Set in Adobe Garamond Pro
Designed by Francesca Belanger

This is a work of fiction. Names, characters, places, and incidents either are the product of the author's imagination or are used fictitiously, and any resemblance to actual persons, living or dead, businesses, companies, events, or locales is entirely coincidental.

Praise for *The Book of Life*

"The nail-biting, long-awaited finale of the All Souls trilogy . . . With this series, Harkness has woven a one-of-a-kind web of magic, science, history, and fiction. This story, which centers around the search for a magical book, is infinitely rich and multifaceted. . . . Weaving an extraordinarily rich story of magic and science, history and fiction, passion and power, secrets and truths, Harkness delivers an unforgettable and spellbinding finale that's not to be missed. Diana and Matthew's epic adventure proves that love, empathy, and fearless determination have the true power to change everything."
—*USA Today*

"Juicy and action packed . . . Even at 561 pages, this is one book no one will mind lugging to the beach."
—*People*

"The epic and erudite vampire-witch romance comes to a thoroughly satisfying conclusion in the action-packed All Souls trilogy ender."
—*Entertainment Weekly*

"A stirring, poignant saga."
—*Us Weekly*

"This trilogy is a superlative example in a subgenre you could call realistic fantasy—think *Harry Potter* but for grown-ups or Susanna Clarke's *Jonathan Strange & Mr. Norrell.* Witches, vampires, and daemons exist, along with time travel. But this world also is recognizably ours, not a wholly made-up setting like George R. R. Martin's Westeros. When done well, as it is here, this sort of fiction provides characters who are recognizably human in their desires and actions even if most of them are creatures with supernatural powers. Through them, Harkness succeeds at the hardest part of writing fantasy: she makes this world so real that you believe it exists—or at the very least that you wish that it did."
—*The Miami Herald*

"The charm in Deborah Harkness's wildly successful All Souls trilogy lies not merely in the spells that its creature characters cast as they lurk pretty much in plain sight of humans, but in the adroit way Harkness has insinuated her world of daemons, witches, and vampires into ours. . . . From the novel's poignant opening, Harkness casts her own indelible spell of enchantment, heartbreak, and resilience. . . . She is terrific at bringing her magic world to life, maintaining a fast-paced, page-turning narrative."
—*The Boston Globe*

"Where Harkness excels is with her charmingly offbeat details of witches and witchcraft, especially whenever Diana and her aunt Sarah take center stage. At their best, these scenes can stand beside J. K Rowling's depictions of life at Hogwarts. A noted scholar of the history of science, Harkness also does a deft job of weaving in details relating to alchemy, herb lore, and a few tongue-in-cheek references to Elizabethan historical figures. . . . While this volume may mark the end of the All Souls trilogy, its immortal characters seem disposed to live on and on as well." —*The Washington Post*

"Harkness has immersed and spellbound readers with her alternative universe. . . . Her ambitious melding of scientific and historical detail is inventive and brings surprising depth. . . . *The Book of Life* brims with sensuality, intrigue, violence, and much-welcome humor." —*Los Angeles Times*

"There is no shortage of action in this sprawling sequel, and nearly every chapter brings a wrinkle to the tale. The storytelling is lively and energetic, and Diana remains an appealing heroine even as her life becomes ever more extraordinary. A delightful wrap-up to the trilogy." —*Publishers Weekly*

"Harkness herself proves to be quite the alchemist as she combines elements of magic, history, romance, and science, transforming them into a compelling journey through time, space, and geography. By bridging the gaps between *Harry Potter*, *Twilight*, and *Outlander* fans, Harkness artfully appeals to a broad range of fantasy lovers." —*Booklist*

"The witch Diana's and the vampire Matthew's quests to discover their origins and confront the threats to their star-crossed union tie up as neatly as one of Diana's magical weaver's knots. . . . As in the previous two installments, there are healthy doses of action, colorful magic, angsty romance, and emotional epiphany, plus mansion-hopping across the globe, historical tidbits, and name-dropping of famous artworks and manuscripts. . . . It's still satisfying to travel with these characters toward their more-than-well-earned happy ending." —*Kirkus Reviews*

"The adventure never lets up. . . . History, science, and the unpredictable actions of paranormal characters with hidden agendas all swirl together to create a not-to-be-missed finale to a stellar series." —*Library Journal*

PENGUIN BOOKS

THE BOOK OF LIFE

Deborah Harkness is the number one *New York Times* bestselling author of *A Discovery of Witches* and *Shadow of Night*, the first two volumes in her All Souls trilogy. A professor of history at the University of Southern California, Harkness has received Fulbright, Guggenheim, and National Humanities Center fellowships.

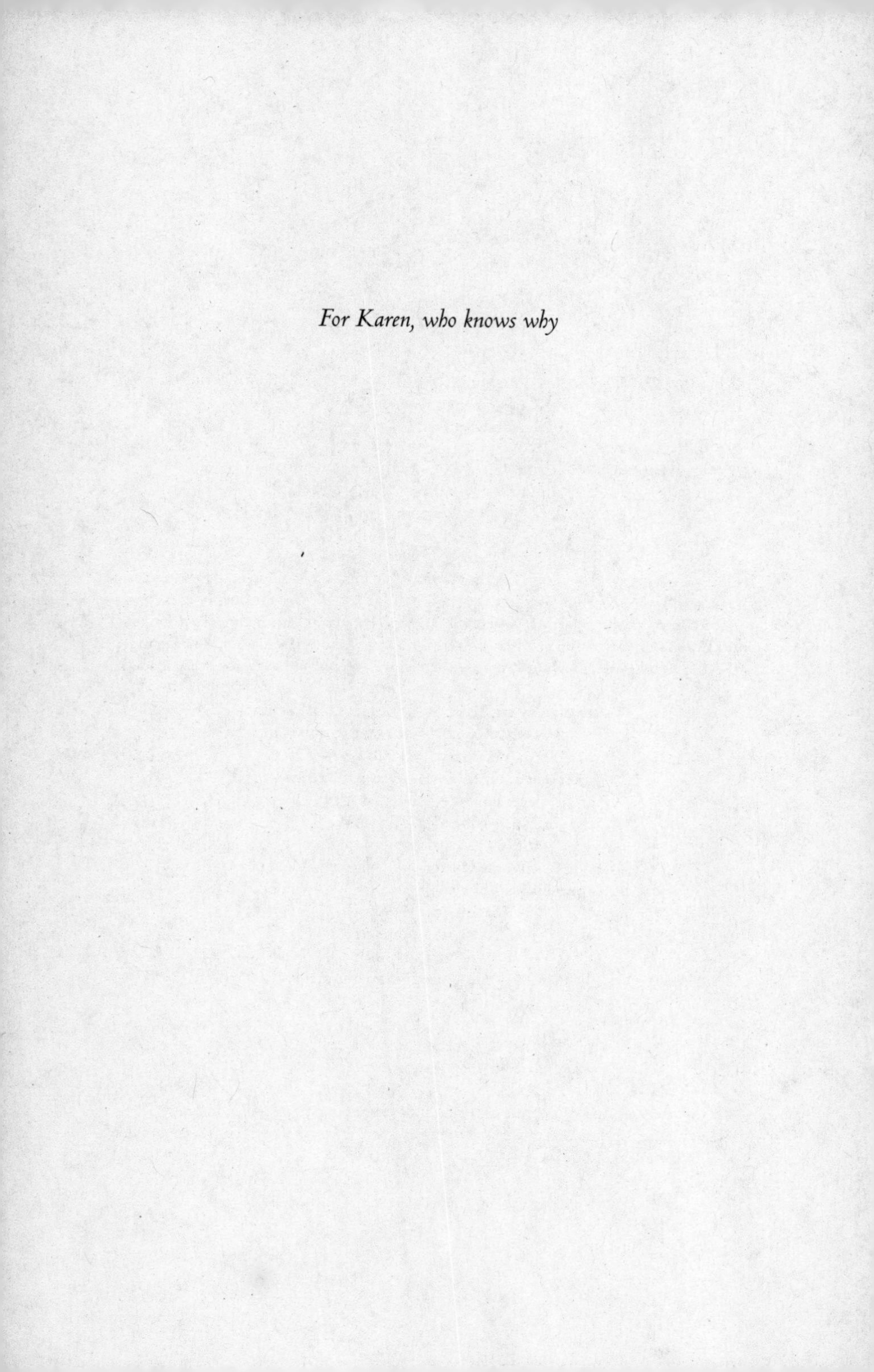

For Karen, who knows why

It is not the strongest of the species that survives, nor the most intelligent that survives. It is the one that is most adaptable to change.

—Philippe de Clermont,
often attributed to Charles Darwin

Sol in Cancer

The signe of the Crabbe pertains to houses, lands, treasures, and whatever is hidden. It is the fourth house of the Zodiak. It signifies death and the end of thinges.

—*Anonymous English Commonplace Book, c. 1590, Gonçalves MS 4890, f. 8*[r]

1

Ghosts didn't have much substance. All they were composed of was memories and heart. Atop one of Sept-Tours' round towers, Emily Mather pressed a diaphanous hand against the spot in the center of her chest that even now was heavy with dread.

Does it ever get easier? Her voice, like the rest of her, was almost imperceptible. *The watching? The waiting? The knowing?*

Not that I've noticed, Philippe de Clermont replied shortly. He was perched nearby, studying his own transparent fingers. Of all the things Philippe disliked about being dead—the inability to touch his wife, Ysabeau; his lack of smell or taste; the fact that he had no muscles for a good sparring match—invisibility topped the list. It was a constant reminder of how inconsequential he had become.

Emily's face fell, and Philippe silently cursed himself. Since she'd died, the witch had been his constant companion, cutting his loneliness in two. What was he thinking, barking at her as if she were a servant?

Perhaps it will be easier when they don't need us anymore, Philippe said in a gentler tone. He might be the more experienced ghost, but it was Emily who understood the metaphysics of their situation. What the witch had told him went against everything Philippe believed about the afterworld. He thought the living saw the dead *because* they needed something from them: assistance, forgiveness, retribution. Emily insisted these were nothing more than human myths, and it was only when the living moved on and let go that the dead could appear to them.

This information made Ysabeau's failure to notice him somewhat easier to bear, but not much.

"I can't wait to see Em's reaction. She's going to be so surprised." Diana's warm alto floated up to the battlements.

Diana and Matthew, Emily and Philippe said in unison, peering down to the cobbled courtyard that surrounded the château.

There, Philippe said, pointing at the drive. Even dead, he had vampire sight that was sharper than any human's. He was also still handsomer than any man had a right to be, with his broad shoulders and devilish grin. He turned the latter on Emily, who couldn't help grinning back. *They are a fine couple, are they not? Look how much my son has changed.*

Vampires weren't supposed to be altered by the passing of time, and therefore Emily expected to see the same black hair, so dark it glinted blue; the same mutable gray-green eyes, cool and remote as a winter sea; the same pale skin and wide mouth. There were a few subtle differences, though, as Philippe suggested. Matthew's hair was shorter, and he had a beard that made him look even more dangerous, like a pirate. She gasped.

Is Matthew . . . bigger?

He is. I fattened him up when he and Diana were here in 1590. Books were making him soft. Matthew needed to fight more and read less. Philippe had always contended there was such a thing as too much education. Matthew was living proof of it.

Diana looks different, too. More like her mother, with that long, coppery hair, Em said, acknowledging the most obvious change in her niece.

Diana stumbled on a cobblestone, and Matthew's hand shot out to steady her. Once, Emily had seen Matthew's incessant hovering as a sign of vampire overprotectiveness. Now, with the perspicacity of a ghost, she realized that this tendency stemmed from his preternatural awareness of every change in Diana's expression, every shift of mood, every sign of fatigue or hunger. Today, however, Matthew's concern seemed even more focused and acute.

It's not just Diana's hair that has changed. Philippe's face had a look of wonder. *Diana is with child—Matthew's child.*

Emily examined her niece more carefully, using the enhanced grasp of truth that death afforded. Philippe was right—in part. *You mean "with* children.*" Diana is having twins.*

Twins, Philippe said in an awed voice. He looked away, distracted by the appearance of his wife. *Look, here are Ysabeau and Sarah with Sophie and Margaret.*

What will happen now, Philippe? Emily asked, her heart growing heavier with anticipation.

Endings. Beginnings, Philippe said with deliberate vagueness. *Change.*

Diana has never liked change, Emily said.

That is because Diana is afraid of what she must become, Philippe replied.

Marcus Whitmore had faced horrors aplenty since the night in 1781 when Matthew de Clermont made him a vampire. None had prepared him for today's ordeal: telling Diana Bishop that her beloved aunt, Emily Mather, was dead.

Marcus had received the phone call from Ysabeau while he and Nathaniel Wilson were watching the television news in the family library. Sophie, Nathaniel's wife, and their baby, Margaret, were dozing on a nearby sofa.

"The temple," Ysabeau had said breathlessly, her tone frantic. "Come. At once."

Marcus had obeyed his grandmother without question, only taking time to shout for his cousin, Gallowglass, and his Aunt Verin on his way out the door.

The summer half-light of evening had lightened further as he approached the clearing at the top of the mountain, brightened by the otherworldly power that Marcus glimpsed through the trees. His hair stood at attention at the magic in the air.

Then he scented the presence of a vampire, Gerbert of Aurillac. And someone else—a witch.

A light, purposeful step sounded down the stone corridor, drawing Marcus out of the past and back into the present. The heavy door opened, creaking as it always did.

"Hello, sweetheart." Marcus turned from the view of the Auvergne countryside and drew a deep breath. Phoebe Taylor's scent reminded him of the thicket of lilac bushes that had grown outside the red-painted door of his family's farm. Delicate and resolute, the fragrance had symbolized the hope of spring after a long Massachusetts winter and conjured up his long-dead mother's understanding smile. Now it only made Marcus think of the petite, iron-willed woman before him.

"Everything will be all right." Phoebe reached up and straightened his collar, her olive eyes full of concern. Marcus had taken to wearing more formal clothes than concert T-shirts around the same time he'd started to sign his letters Marcus de Clermont instead of Marcus Whitmore—the name she'd first known him by, before he had told her about vampires, fifteen-hundred-year-old fathers, French castles full of forbidding relatives, and a witch named Diana Bishop. It was, in Marcus's opinion, nothing short of miraculous that Phoebe had remained at his side.

"No. It won't." He caught one of her hands and planted a kiss on the palm. Phoebe didn't know Matthew. "Stay here with Nathaniel and the rest of them. Please."

"For the final time, Marcus Whitmore, I will be standing beside you when you greet your father and his wife. I don't believe we need discuss it further." Phoebe held out her hand. "Shall we?"

Marcus put his hand in Phoebe's, but instead of following her out the door as she expected, he tugged her toward him. Phoebe came to rest against his chest, one hand clasped in his and the other pressed to his heart. She looked at him with surprise.

"Very well. But if you come down with me, Phoebe, there are conditions. First, you are with me or with Ysabeau at all times."

Phoebe opened her mouth to protest, but Marcus's serious look silenced her.

"Second, if I tell you to leave the room, you will do so. No delay. No questions. Go straight to Fernando. He'll be in the chapel or the kitchen." Marcus searched her face and saw a wary acceptance. "Third, do not, under any circumstances, get within arm's reach of my father. Agreed?"

Phoebe nodded. Like any good diplomat, she was prepared to follow Marcus's rules—for now. But if Marcus's father was the monster some in the house seemed to think he was, Phoebe would do what she must.

Fernando Gonçalves poured beaten eggs into the hot skillet, blanketing the browned potatoes already in the pan. His tortilla española was one of the few dishes Sarah Bishop would eat, and today of all days the widow needed sustenance.

Gallowglass sat at the kitchen table, picking drops of wax out of a crack in the ancient boards. With his collar-length blond hair and muscular build, he looked like a morose bear. Tattoos snaked around his forearms and biceps in bright swirls of color. Their subject matter revealed whatever was on Gallowglass's mind at the moment, for a tattoo lasted only a few months on a vampire. Right now he seemed to be thinking about his roots, for his arms were covered with Celtic knotwork, runes, and fabulous beasts drawn from Norse and Gaelic myths and legends.

"Stop worrying." Fernando's voice was as warm and cultured as sherry aged in oak barrels.

Gallowglass looked up for a moment, then returned his attention to the wax.

"No one will prevent Matthew from doing what he must, Gallowglass. Avenging Emily's death is a matter of honor." Fernando turned off the heat and joined Gallowglass at the table, bare feet moving silently across the flagstone floors. As he walked, he rolled down the sleeves of his white shirt. It was pristine, in spite of the hours he'd spent in the kitchen that day. He tucked the shirt into the waistband of his jeans and ran his fingers through his dark, wavy hair.

"Marcus is going to try to take the blame, you know," Gallowglass said. "But Emily's death wasn't the boy's fault."

The scene on the mountain had been oddly peaceful, considering the circumstances. Gallowglass had arrived at the temple a few moments after Marcus. There had been nothing but silence and the sight of Emily Mather kneeling inside a circle marked out with pale rocks. The witch Peter Knox had been with her, his hands on her head and a look of anticipation—even hunger—on his face. Gerbert of Aurillac, the de Clermonts' nearest vampire neighbor, was looking on with interest.

"Emily!" Sarah's anguished cry had torn through the silence with such force that even Gerbert stepped back.

Startled, Knox released Emily. She crumpled to the ground, unconscious. Sarah beat the other witch back with a single, powerful spell that sent Knox flying across the clearing.

"No, Marcus didn't kill her," Fernando said, drawing Gallowglass's attention. "But his negligence—"

"Inexperience," Gallowglass interjected.

"Negligence," Fernando repeated, "did play a role in the tragedy. Marcus knows that and accepts responsibility for it."

"Marcus didn't ask to be in charge," Gallowglass grumbled.

"No. I nominated him for the position, and Matthew agreed it was the right decision." Fernando pressed Gallowglass's shoulder briefly and returned to the stove.

"Is that why you came? Because you felt guilty about refusing to lead the brotherhood when Matthew asked for your help?" No one had been more surprised than Gallowglass when Fernando turned up at Sept-Tours. Fernando had avoided the place ever since Gallowglass's father, Hugh de Clermont, died in the fourteenth century.

"I am here because Matthew was there for me after the French king executed Hugh. I was alone in all the world then, except for my grief." Fernando's tone was harsh. "And I refused to lead the Knights of Lazarus because I am not a de Clermont."

"You were Father's mate!" Gallowglass protested. "You are as much a de Clermont as Ysabeau or her children!"

Fernando carefully shut the oven door. "I *am* Hugh's mate," he said, his back still turned. "Your father will never be past tense to me."

"Sorry, Fernando," Gallowglass said, stricken. Though Hugh had been dead for nearly seven centuries, Fernando had never recovered from the loss. Gallowglass doubted he ever would.

"As for my being a de Clermont," Fernando continued, still staring at the wall over the stove, "Philippe disagreed."

Gallowglass resumed his nervous picking at the wax. Fernando poured two glasses of red wine and carried them to the table.

"Here," he said, thrusting one at Gallowglass. "You'll need your strength today, too."

Marthe bustled into the kitchen. Ysabeau's housekeeper ruled over this part of the château and was not pleased to see intruders in it. After giving Fernando and Gallowglass sour looks, she sniffed and wrested the oven door open.

"That is my best pan!" she said accusingly.

"I know. That's why I'm using it," Fernando replied, taking a sip of wine.

"You do not belong in the kitchen, Dom Fernando. Go upstairs. Take Gallowglass with you." Marthe took a packet of tea and a teapot from the shelf by the sink. Then she noticed the towel-wrapped pot sitting on a tray next to cups, saucers, milk, and sugar. Her frown deepened.

"What is wrong with my being here?" Fernando demanded.

"You are not a servant," Marthe said. She picked the lid off the top of the pot and sniffed suspiciously at its contents.

"It's Diana's favorite. You told me what she liked, remember?" Fernando smiled sadly. "And everyone in this house serves the de Clermonts, Marthe. The only difference is that you, Alain, and Victoire are paid handsomely to do so. The rest of us are expected to be grateful for the privilege."

"With good reason. Other *manjasang* dream of being part of this family. See that you remember that in future—and the lemon, Dom Fernando," Marthe said, placing emphasis on his lordly title. She picked up the tea tray. "By the way, your eggs are burning."

Fernando leaped up to rescue them.

"As for you," Marthe said, fixing her black eyes on Gallowglass, "you did not tell us everything you should have about Matthew and his wife."

Gallowglass looked down into his wine with a guilty expression.

"*Madame* your grandmother will deal with you later." On that bone-chilling note, Marthe stalked out of the room.

"What have you done now?" asked Fernando, putting his tortilla—which was not ruined, *Alhamdulillah*—on the stove. Long experience had taught him that whatever the mess, Gallowglass had made it with good intentions and complete disregard for possible disaster.

"Weeell," Gallowglass said, drawing out the vowels as only a Scot could, "I might have left one or two things out of the tale."

"Like what?" Fernando said, catching a whiff of catastrophe among the kitchen's homely scents.

"Like the fact that Auntie is pregnant—and by none other than Matthew. And the fact that Granddad adopted her as a daughter. Lord, his blood vow was deafening." Gallowglass looked reflective. "Do you think we'll still be able to hear it?"

Fernando stood, openmouthed and silent.

"Don't look at me that way. It didn't seem right to share the news about the babe. Women can be funny about such things. And Philippe told Auntie Verin about the blood vow before he died in 1945, and she never said a word either!" Gallowglass said defensively.

A concussion tore the air, as if a silent bomb had been detonated. Something green and fiery streaked past the kitchen window.

"What the hell was that?" Fernando flung the door open and shielded his eyes against the bright sunlight.

"One pissed-off witch, I imagine." Gallowglass's tone was glum. "Sarah must have told Diana and Matthew the news about Emily."

"Not the explosion. That!" Fernando pointed to Saint-Lucien's bell tower, which was being circled by a winged, two-legged, fire-breathing creature. Gallowglass rose for a better look.

"That's Corra. She goes where Auntie goes," Gallowglass said matter-of-factly.

"But that's a *dragon.*" Fernando turned wild eyes on his stepson.

"Bah! That's no dragon. Can't you see she's only got two legs? Corra is a firedrake." Gallowglass twisted his arm to show off a tattoo of a winged creature that strongly resembled the airborne beast. "Like this. I might have left out one or two details, but I did warn everybody that Auntie Diana wasn't going to be the same witch she was before."

"It's true, honey. Em is dead." The stress of telling Diana and Matthew was clearly too much for her. Sarah could have sworn that she saw a dragon. Fernando was right. She needed to cut back on the whiskey.

"I don't believe you." Diana's voice was high and sharp with panic. She searched Ysabeau's grand salon as though she expected to find Emily hiding behind one of the ornate settees.

"Emily's not here, Diana." Matthew's hushed voice was infused with regret and tenderness as he stepped before her. "She's gone."

"No." Diana tried to push past him and continue her search, but Matthew drew her into his arms.

"I'm so sorry, Sarah," Matthew said, holding Diana tight to his body.

"Don't say you're sorry!" Diana cried, struggling to free herself from the vampire's unbreakable hold. She pounded on Matthew's shoulder with her fist. "Em isn't dead! This is a nightmare. Wake me up, Matthew—please! I want to wake up and find we're still in 1591."

"This isn't a nightmare," Sarah said. The long weeks had convinced her that Em's death was horribly real.

"Then I took a wrong turn—or tied a bad knot in the timewalking spell. This can't be where we were supposed to end up!" Diana was shaking from head to toe with grief and shock. "Em promised she would never leave without saying good-bye."

"Em didn't have time to say good-bye—to anyone. But that doesn't mean she didn't love you." Sarah reminded herself of this a hundred times a day.

"Diana should sit," Marcus said, pulling a chair closer to Sarah. In many ways Matthew's son looked like the same twenty-something surfer who had walked into the Bishop house last October. His leather cord, with its strange assortment of objects gathered over the centuries, was still tangled in the blond hair at the nape of his neck. The Converse sneakers he loved remained on his feet. The guarded, sad look in his eyes was new, however.

Sarah was grateful for the presence of Marcus and Ysabeau, but the person she really wanted at her side at this moment was Fernando. He'd been her rock during this ordeal.

"Thank you, Marcus," Matthew said, settling Diana in the seat. Phoebe tried to press a glass of water into Diana's hand. When Diana just stared at it blankly, Matthew took it and placed it on a nearby table.

All eyes alighted on Sarah.

Sarah was no good at this kind of thing. Diana was the historian in the family. She would know where to start and how to string the confusing events into a coherent story with a beginning, a middle, and an end, and perhaps even a plausible explanation of why Emily had died.

"There's no easy way to tell you this," Diana's aunt began.

"You don't have to tell us anything," Matthew said, his eyes filled with compassion and sympathy. "The explanations can wait."

"No. You both need to know." Sarah reached for the glass of whiskey that usually sat at her side, but there was nothing there. She looked to Marcus in mute appeal.

"Emily died up at the old temple," Marcus said, taking up the role of storyteller.

"The temple dedicated to the goddess?" Diana whispered, her brow creasing with the effort to concentrate.

"Yes," Sarah croaked, coughing to dislodge the lump in her throat. "Emily was spending more and more time up there."

"Was she alone?" Matthew's expression was no longer warm and understanding, and his tone was frosty.

Silence descended again, this one heavy and awkward.

"Emily wouldn't let anyone go with her," Sarah said, steeling herself to be honest. Diana was a witch, too, and would know if she strayed from the truth. "Marcus tried to convince her to take someone with her, but Emily refused."

"Why did she want to be alone?" Diana said, picking up on Sarah's own uneasiness. "What was going on, Sarah?"

"Since January, Em had been turning to the higher magics for guidance." Sarah looked away from Diana's shocked face. "She was having terrible premonitions of death and disaster and thought they might help her figure out why."

"But Em always said higher magics were too dark for witches to handle safely," Diana said, her voice rising again. "She said any witch who thought she was immune to their dangers would find out the hard way just how powerful they were."

"She spoke from experience," Sarah said. "They can be addictive. Emily didn't want you to know she'd felt their lure, honey. She hadn't touched a scrying stone or tried to summon a spirit for decades."

"Summon spirits?" Matthew's eyes narrowed into slits. With his dark beard, he looked truly terrifying.

"I think she was trying to reach Rebecca. If I'd realized how far she'd gone in her attempts, I would have tried harder to stop her." Sarah's eyes brimmed with tears. "Peter Knox must have sensed the power Emily was working with, and the higher magics have always fascinated him. Once he found her—"

"Knox?" Matthew spoke softly, but the hairs on the back of Sarah's neck rose in warning.

"When we found Em, Knox and Gerbert were there, too," Marcus explained, looking miserable at the admission. "She'd suffered a heart attack. Emily must have been under enormous stress trying to resist whatever Knox was doing. She was barely conscious. I tried to revive her. So did Sarah. But there was nothing either of us could do."

"Why were Gerbert and Knox here? And what in the world did Knox hope to gain from killing Em?" Diana cried.

"I don't think Knox was trying to kill her, honey," Sarah replied. "Knox was reading Emily's thoughts, or trying his best to. Her last words were, 'I know the secret of Ashmole 782, and you will never possess it.'"

"Ashmole 782?" Diana looked stunned. "Are you sure?"

"Positive." Sarah wished her niece had never found that damned manuscript in the Bodleian Library. It was the cause of most of their present problems.

"Knox insisted that the de Clermonts had missing pages from Diana's manuscript and knew its secrets," Ysabeau chimed in. "Verin and I told Knox he was mistaken, but the only thing that distracted him from the subject was the baby. Margaret."

"Nathaniel and Sophie followed us to the temple. Margaret was with them," Marcus explained in answer to Matthew's astonished stare. "Before Emily fell unconscious, Knox saw Margaret and demanded to know how two daemons had given birth to a baby witch. Knox invoked the covenant. He threatened to take Margaret to the Congregation pending investigation into what he called 'serious breaches' of law. While we were trying to revive Emily and get the baby to safety, Gerbert and Knox slipped away."

Until recently Sarah had always seen the Congregation and the covenant as necessary evils. It was not easy for the three otherworldly species—daemons, vampires, and witches—to live among humans. All had been targets of human fear and violence at some point in history, and creatures had long ago agreed to a covenant to minimize the risk of their world's coming to human attention. It limited fraternization between species as well as any participation in human religion or politics. The nine-member Congregation enforced the covenant and made sure that creatures abided by its terms. Now that Diana and Matthew were home, the Congregation could go to hell and take their covenant with them as far as Sarah was concerned.

Diana's head swung around, and a look of disbelief passed over her face.

"Gallowglass?" she breathed as the salon filled with the scent of the sea.

"Welcome home, Auntie." Gallowglass stepped forward, his golden beard gleaming where the sunlight struck it. Diana stared at him in astonishment before a sob broke free.

"There, there." Gallowglass lifted her into a bear hug. "It's been some time since the sight of me brought a woman to tears. Besides, it really should be me weeping at our reunion. As far as you're concerned, it's been only a few days since we spoke. By my reckoning it's been centuries."

Something numinous flickered around the edges of Diana's body, like a candle slowly catching light. Sarah blinked. She really was going to have to lay off the booze.

Matthew and his nephew exchanged glances. Matthew's expression grew even more concerned as Diana's tears increased and the glow surrounding her intensified.

"Let Matthew take you upstairs." Gallowglass reached into a pocket and pulled out a crumpled yellow bandanna. He offered this to Diana, carefully shielding her from view.

"Is she all right?" Sarah asked.

"Just a wee bit tired," Gallowglass said as he and Matthew hustled Diana off toward Matthew's remote tower rooms.

Once Diana and Matthew were gone, Sarah's fragile composure cracked, and she began to weep. Reliving the events of Em's death was a daily occurrence, but having to do so with Diana was even more painful. Fernando appeared, his expression concerned.

"It's all right, Sarah. Let it out," Fernando murmured, drawing her close.

"Where were you when I needed you?" Sarah demanded as her weeping turned to sobs.

"I'm here now," Fernando said, rocking her gently. "And Diana and Matthew are safely home."

"I can't stop shaking." Diana's teeth were chattering, and her limbs were jerking as if pulled by invisible strings. Gallowglass pressed his lips together, standing back while Matthew wrapped a blanket tight around his wife.

"That's the shock, *mon coeur,*" Matthew murmured, pressing a kiss to her cheek. It wasn't just the death of Emily but the memories of the earlier, traumatic loss of her parents that were causing her distress. He rubbed her arms, the blanket moving against her flesh. "Can you get some wine, Gallowglass?"

"I shouldn't. The babies . . ." Diana began. Her expression turned wild and her tears returned. "They'll never know Em. Our children will grow up not knowing Em."

"Here." Gallowglass thrust a silver flask in Matthew's direction. His uncle looked at him gratefully.

"Even better," Matthew said, pulling the stopper free. "Just a sip, Diana. It won't hurt the twins, and it will help calm you. I'll have Marthe bring up some black tea with plenty of sugar."

"I'm going to kill Peter Knox," Diana said fiercely after she'd taken a sip of whiskey. The light around her grew brighter.

"Not today you're not," Matthew said firmly, handing the flask back to Gallowglass.

"Has Auntie's *glaem* been this bright since you returned?" Gallowglass hadn't seen Diana Bishop since 1591, but he didn't recall it being this noticeable.

"Yes. She's been wearing a disguising spell. The shock must have knocked it out of place," Matthew said, lowering her onto the sofa. "Diana wanted Emily and Sarah to enjoy the fact that they were going to be grandmothers before they started asking questions about her increased power."

Gallowglass bit back an oath.

"Better?" Matthew asked, drawing Diana's fingers to his lips.

Diana nodded. Her teeth were still chattering, Gallowglass noted. It made him ache to think about the effort it must be taking for her to control herself.

"I am so sorry about Emily," Matthew said, cupping her face between his hands.

"Is it our fault? Did we stay in the past too long, like Dad said?" Diana spoke so softly it was hard for even Gallowglass to hear.

"Of course not," Gallowglass replied, his voice brusque. "Peter Knox did this. Nobody else is to blame."

"Let's not worry about who's to blame," Matthew said, but his eyes were angry.

Gallowglass gave him a nod of understanding. Matthew would have plenty to say about Knox and Gerbert—later. Right now he was concerned with his wife.

"Emily would want you to focus on taking care of yourself and Sarah. That's enough for now." Matthew brushed back the coppery strands that were stuck to Diana's cheeks by the salt from her tears.

"I should go back downstairs," Diana said, drawing Gallowglass's bright yellow bandanna to her eyes. "Sarah needs me."

"Let's stay up here a bit longer. Wait for Marthe to bring the tea," Matthew said, sitting down next to her. Diana slumped against him, her breath hiccupping in and out as she tried to hold back the tears.

"I'll leave you two," Gallowglass said gruffly.

Matthew nodded in silent thanks.

"Thank you, Gallowglass," Diana said, holding out the bandanna.

"Keep it," he said, turning for the stairs.

"We're alone. You don't have to be strong now," Matthew murmured to Diana as Gallowglass descended the twisting staircase.

Gallowglass left Matthew and Diana twined together in an unbreakable knot, their faces twisted with pain and sorrow, each giving the other the comfort they could not find for themselves.

I should never have summoned you here. I should have found another way to get my answers. Emily turned to face her closest friend. *You should be with Stephen.*

I'd rather be here with my daughter than anywhere else, Rebecca Bishop said. *Stephen understands.* She turned back to the sight of Diana and Matthew, still locked in their sorrowful embrace.

Do not fear. Matthew will take care of her, Philippe said. He was still trying to figure out Rebecca Bishop—she was an unusually challenging creature, and as skilled at keeping secrets as any vampire.

They'll take care of each other, Rebecca said, her hand over her heart, *just as I knew they would.*

Matthew raced down the curving stone staircase that wound between his tower rooms at Sept-Tours and the main floor of the château. He avoided the slippery spot on the thirtieth tread and the rough patch on the seventeenth where Baldwin's sword had bashed the edge during one of their arguments.

Matthew had built the tower addition as his private refuge, a place apart from the relentless busyness that always surrounded Philippe and Ysabeau. Vampire families were large and noisy, with two or more bloodlines coming uncomfortably together and trying to live as one happy pack. This seldom happened with predators, even those who walked on two legs and lived in fine houses. As a result, Matthew's tower was designed primarily for defense. It had no doors to muffle a vampire's stealthy approach and no way out except for the way you came in. His careful arrangements spoke volumes about his relationships with his brothers and sisters.

Tonight his tower's isolation seemed confining, a far cry from the busy life he and Diana had created in Elizabethan London, surrounded by family and friends. Matthew's job as a spy for the queen had been challenging but rewarding. From his former seat on the Congregation, he had managed to save a few witches from hanging. Diana had begun the lifelong process of growing into her powers as a witch. They'd even taken in two orphaned children and given them a chance at a better future. Their life in the sixteenth century had not always been easy, but their days had been filled with love and the sense of hope that followed Diana wherever she went. Here at Sept-Tours, they seemed surrounded on all sides by death and de Clermonts.

The combination made Matthew restless, and the anger he kept so carefully in check whenever Diana was near him was dangerously close to the surface. Blood rage—the sickness that Matthew had inherited from Ysabeau when she'd made him—could take over a vampire's mind and body quickly, leaving no room for reason or control. In an effort to keep the blood rage in check, Matthew had reluctantly agreed to leave Diana in Ysabeau's care while he walked around the castle grounds with his dogs, Fallon and Hector, trying to clear his head.

Gallowglass was crooning a sea chantey in the château's great hall. For reasons Matthew couldn't fathom, every other verse was punctuated by expletives and ultimatums. After a moment of indecision, Matthew's curiosity won out.

"Fucking firedrake." Gallowglass had one of the pikes down from the cache of weapons by the entrance and was waving it slowly in the air. "*'Farewell and adieu to you, ladies of Spain.'* Get your arse down here, or Granny will poach you in white wine and feed you to the dogs. *'For we've received orders for to sail for old England.'* What are you thinking, flying around the house like a demented parakeet? *'And we may never see you fair ladies again.'*"

"What the hell are you doing?" Matthew demanded.

Gallowglass turned wide blue eyes on Matthew. The younger man was wearing a black T-shirt adorned with a skull and crossbones. Something had slashed the back, rending it from left shoulder to right hip. The holes in his nephew's jeans looked to be the result of wear, not war, and his hair was shaggy even by Gallowglassian standards. Ysabeau had taken to calling him "Sir Vagabond," but this had done little to improve his grooming.

"Trying to catch your wife's wee beastie." Gallowglass made a sudden upward thrust with the pike. There was a shriek of surprise, followed by a hail of pale green scales that shattered like isinglass when they hit the floor. The blond hair on Gallowglass's forearms shimmered with their iridescent green dust. He sneezed.

Corra, Diana's familiar, was clinging to the minstrels' gallery with her talons, chattering madly and clacking her tongue. She waved hello to Matthew with her barbed tail, piercing a priceless tapestry depicting a unicorn in a garden. Matthew winced.

"I had her cornered in the chapel, up by the altar, but Corra is a cunning lass," Gallowglass said with a touch of pride. "She was hiding atop Granddad's tomb, her wings spread wide. I mistook her for an effigy. Now look at her. Up in the rafters, vainglorious as the devil and twice as much trouble. Why, she's put her tail through one of Ysabeau's favorite draperies. Granny is going to have a stroke."

"If Corra is anything like her mistress, cornering her won't end well," Matthew said mildly. "Try reasoning with her instead."

"Oh, aye. That works very well with Auntie Diana." Gallowglass sniffed. "Whatever possessed you to let Corra out of your sight?"

"The more active the firedrake is, the calmer Diana seems," Matthew said.

"Perhaps, but Corra is hell on the decor. She broke one of Granny's Sèvres vases this afternoon."

"So long as it wasn't one of the blue ones with the lion heads that Philippe gave her, I shouldn't worry." Matthew groaned when he saw Gallowglass's expression. *"Merde."*

"That was Alain's response, too." Gallowglass leaned on his pike.

"Ysabeau will have to make do with one less piece of pottery," Matthew said. "Corra may be a nuisance, but Diana is sleeping soundly for the first time since we came home."

"Oh, well, that's all right, then. Just tell Ysabeau that Corra's clumsiness is good for the grandbabies. Granny will hand over her vases as sacrificial offerings. Meanwhile I'll try to keep the flying termagant entertained so Auntie can sleep."

"How are you going to do that?" Matthew asked with skepticism.

"Sing to her, of course." Gallowglass looked up. Corra cooed at his renewed attention, stretching her wings a bit farther so that they caught the light from the torches stuck into brackets along the walls. Taking this as an encouraging sign, Gallowglass drew a deep breath and began another booming ballad.

"'My head turns round, I'm in a flame, / I love like any dragon. / Say would you know my mistress's name?'"

Corra clacked her teeth in approval. Gallowglass grinned and began to move the pike like a metronome. He waggled his eyebrows at Matthew before singing his next lines.

"'I sent her trinkets without end,
Gems, pearls, to make her civil,
Till having nothing more to send,
I sent her—to the devil.'"

"Good luck," Matthew murmured, sincerely hoping that Corra didn't understand the lyrics.

Matthew scanned the nearby rooms, cataloging their occupants. Hamish was in the family library doing paperwork, based on the sound of pen scratching against paper and the faint scent of lavender and peppermint he detected. Matthew hesitated for a moment, then pushed the door open.

"Time for an old friend?" he asked.

"I was beginning to think you were avoiding me." Hamish Osborne put down his pen and loosened his tie, which was covered in a summery floral print most men wouldn't have had the courage to wear. Even in the French countryside, Hamish was dressed as if for a meeting with members of Parliament in a navy pin-striped suit with a lavender shirt. It made him look like a dapper throwback to Edwardian days.

Matthew knew that the daemon was trying to provoke an argument. He and Hamish had been friends for decades, ever since the two of them were at Oxford. Their friendship was based on mutual respect and had been kept strong because of their compatible, razor-sharp intellects. Between Hamish and Matthew, even simple exchanges could be as complicated and strategic as a chess game between two masters. But it was too soon in their conversation to let Hamish put him at a disadvantage.

"How is Diana?" Hamish had noted Matthew's deliberate refusal to take the bait.

"As well as can be expected."

"I would have asked her myself, of course, but your nephew told me to go away." Hamish picked up a wineglass and took a sip. "Wine?"

"Did it come from my cellar or Baldwin's?" Matthew's seemingly innocuous question served as a subtle reminder that now that he and Diana were back, Hamish might have to choose between Matthew and the rest of the de Clermonts.

"It's claret." Hamish swirled the contents in the glass while he waited for Matthew's reaction. "Expensive. Old. Fine."

Matthew's lip curled. "Thank you, no. I've never had the same fondness for the stuff as most of my family." He'd rather fill the fountains in the garden with Baldwin's store of precious Bordeaux than drink it.

"What's the story with the dragon?" A muscle in Hamish's jaws twitched, whether from amusement or anger, Matthew couldn't tell. "Gallowglass says Diana brought it back as a souvenir, but nobody believes him."

"She belongs to Diana," Matthew said. "You'll have to ask her."

"You've got everybody at Sept-Tours quaking in their boots, you know." With this abrupt change of topic, Hamish approached. "The rest of them haven't realized yet that the most terrified person in the château is *you.*"

"And how is William?" Matthew could make a dizzying change in subject as effectively as any daemon.

"Sweet William has planted his affections elsewhere." Hamish's mouth twisted, and he turned away, his obvious distress bringing their game to an unexpected close.

"I'm so sorry, Hamish." Matthew had thought the relationship would last. "William loved you."

"Not enough." Hamish shrugged but couldn't hide the pain in his eyes. "You'll have to pin your romantic hopes on Marcus and Phoebe, I'm afraid."

"I've barely spoken to the girl," Matthew said. He sighed and poured himself a glass of Baldwin's claret. "What can you tell me about her?"

"Young Miss Taylor works at one of the auction houses in London—Sotheby's or Christie's. I never can keep them straight," Hamish said, sinking into a leather armchair in front of the cold fireplace. "Marcus met her when he was picking up something for Ysabeau. I think it's serious."

"It is." Matthew took his wine and prowled along the bookshelves that lined the walls. "Marcus's scent is all over her. He's mated."

"I suspected as much." Hamish sipped and watched his friend's restless movements. "Nobody has said anything, of course. Your family really could teach MI6 a thing or two about secrets."

"Ysabeau should have stopped it. Phoebe is too young for a relationship with a vampire," Matthew said. "She can't be more than twenty-two, yet Marcus has entangled her in an irrevocable bond."

"Oh, yes, forbidding Marcus to fall in love would have gone down a treat," Hamish said, his Scots burr increasing with his amusement. "Marcus is just as pigheaded as you are when it comes to love, it turns out."

"Maybe if he'd been thinking about his job as the leader of the Knights of Lazarus—"

"Stop right there, Matt, before you say something so unfair I might never forgive you for it." Hamish's voice lashed at him. "You know how difficult it is to be the brotherhood's grand master. Marcus was expected to fill some pretty big shoes—and vampire or not, he isn't much older than Phoebe."

The Knights of Lazarus had been founded during the Crusades, a chivalric order established to protect vampire interests in a world that was increasingly dominated by humans. Philippe de Clermont, Ysabeau's mate, had been the first grand master. But he was a legendary figure, not just among vampires but among other creatures as well. It was an impossible task for any man to live up to the standard he'd set.

"I know, but to fall in love—" Matthew protested, his anger mounting.

"Marcus has done a brilliant job, no buts about it," Hamish interrupted. "He's recruited new members and overseen every financial detail of our operations. He demanded that the Congregation punish Knox for his actions here in May and has formally requested the covenant be revoked. Nobody could have done more. Not even you."

"Punishing Knox doesn't begin to address what happened. He and Gerbert violated my home. Knox murdered a woman who was like a mother to my wife." Matthew gulped down his wine in an effort to drown his anger.

"Emily had a heart attack," Hamish cautioned. "Marcus said there's no way to know the cause."

"I know enough," Matthew said with sudden fury, hurling his empty glass across the room. It smashed against the edge of one of the bookshelves, sending shards of glass into the thick carpet. Hamish's eyes widened. "Our children will never have the chance to know Emily now. And Gerbert, who's been on intimate terms with this family for centuries, stood by and watched Knox do it, knowing that Diana was my mate."

"Everyone in the house said you wouldn't let Congregation justice take its course. I didn't believe them." Hamish didn't like the changes he was seeing in his friend. It was as though being in the sixteenth century had ripped the scab off some old, forgotten wound.

"I should have dealt with Gerbert and Knox after they helped Satu Järvinen kidnap Diana and held her at La Pierre. If I had, Emily would still be alive." Matthew's shoulders stiffened with remorse. "But Baldwin forbade it. He said the Congregation had enough trouble on its hands."

"You mean the vampire murders?" Hamish asked.

"Yes. He said if I challenged Gerbert and Knox, I would only make matters worse." News of these murders—with the severed arteries, the absence of blood evidence, the almost animalistic attacks on human bodies—had been in newspapers from London to Moscow. Every story had focused on the murderer's strange method of killing and had threatened to expose vampires to human notice.

"I won't make the mistake of remaining silent again," Matthew continued. "The Knights of Lazarus and the de Clermonts might not be able to protect my wife and her family, but I certainly can."

"You're not a killer, Matt," Hamish insisted. "Don't let your anger blind you."

When Matthew turned black eyes to him, Hamish blanched. Though he knew that Matthew was a few steps closer to the animal kingdom than most creatures who walked on two legs, Hamish had never seen him look quite so wolflike and dangerous.

"Are you sure, Hamish?" Matthew's obsidian eyes blinked, and he turned and stalked from the room.

Following the distinctive licorice-root scent of Marcus Whitmore, mixed tonight with the heady aroma of lilacs, Matthew was easily able to track his son to the family apartments on the second floor of the château. His conscience pricked at the thought of what Marcus might have overheard during this heated exchange, given his son's keen vampire hearing. Matthew pressed his lips together when his nose led him to a door just off the stairs, and he tamped down the flicker of anger that accompanied his realization that Marcus was using Philippe's old office.

Matthew knocked and pushed at the heavy slab of wood without waiting for a response. With the exception of the shiny silver laptop on the desk where the blotter used to be, the room looked exactly as it had on the day Philippe de Clermont died in 1945. The same Bakelite telephone was on a table by the window. Stacks of thin envelopes and curling, yellowed paper stood at the ready for Philippe to write to one of his many correspondents. Tacked to the wall was an old map of Europe, which Philippe had used to track the positions of Hitler's army.

Matthew closed his eyes against the sudden, sharp pain. What Philippe had *not* foreseen was that he would fall into the Nazis' hands. One of the unexpected gifts of their timewalk had been the chance to see Philippe again and be reconciled with him. The price Matthew had to pay was the renewed sense of loss as he once more faced a world without Philippe de Clermont in it.

When Matthew's eyes opened again, he was confronted with the furious face of Phoebe Taylor. It took only a fraction of a second for Marcus to angle his body between Matthew and the warmblooded woman. Matthew was gratified to see that his son hadn't lost all his wits when he took a mate, though if Matthew had wanted to harm Phoebe, the girl would already be dead.

"Marcus." Matthew briefly acknowledged his son before looking beyond him. Phoebe was not Marcus's usual type at all. He had always preferred redheads. "There was no time for a proper introduction when we first met. I'm Matthew Clairmont. Marcus's father."

"I know who you are." Phoebe's proper British accent was the one common to public schools, country houses, and decaying aristocratic families. Marcus, the family's democratic idealist, had fallen for a blueblood.

"Welcome to the family, Miss Taylor." Matthew bowed to hide his smile.

"Phoebe, please." Phoebe stepped around Marcus in a blink, her right hand extended. Matthew ignored it. "In most polite circles, Professor Clairmont, this is where you would take my hand and shake it." Phoebe's expression was more than a little annoyed, her hand still outstretched.

"You're surrounded by vampires. Whatever made you think you would find civilization here?" Matthew studied her with unblinking eyes. Uncomfortable, Phoebe looked away. "You may think my greeting unnecessarily formal, Phoebe, but no vampire touches another's mate—or even his betrothed—without permission." He glanced down at the large emerald on the third finger of her left hand. Marcus had won the stone in a card game in Paris centuries ago. Then and now it was worth a small fortune.

"Oh. Marcus didn't tell me that," Phoebe said with a frown.

"No, but I did give you a few simple rules. Perhaps it's time to review them," Marcus murmured to his fiancée. "We'll rehearse our wedding vows while we're at it."

"Why? You still won't find the word 'obey' in them," Phoebe said crisply.

Before the argument could get off the ground, Matthew coughed again.

"I came to apologize for my outburst in the library," Matthew said. "I am too quick to anger at the moment. Forgive me for my temper."

It was more than temper, but Marcus—like Hamish—didn't know that.

"What outburst?" Phoebe frowned.

"It was nothing," Marcus responded, though his expression suggested otherwise.

"I was also wondering if you would be willing to examine Diana? As you no doubt know, she is carrying twins. I believe she's in the beginning of her second trimester, but we've been out of reach of proper medical care, and I'd like to be sure." Matthew's proffered olive branch, like Phoebe's hand, remained in the air for several long moments before it was acknowledged.

"Of c-course," Marcus stammered. "Thank you for trusting Diana to my care. I won't let you down. And Hamish is right," he added. "Even if I'd performed an autopsy on Emily—which Sarah didn't want—there would have been no way to determine if she was killed by magic or by natural causes. We may never know."

Matthew didn't bother to argue. He would find out the precise role that Knox had played in Emily's death, for the answer would determine how quickly Matthew killed him and how much the witch suffered first.

"Phoebe, it has been a pleasure," Matthew said instead.

"Likewise." The girl lied politely and convincingly. She would be a useful addition to the de Clermont pack.

"Come to Diana in the morning, Marcus. We'll be expecting you." With a final smile and another shallow bow to the fascinating Phoebe Taylor, Matthew left the room.

Matthew's nocturnal prowl around Sept-Tours had not lessened his restlessness or his anger. If anything, the cracks in his control had widened. Frustrated, he took a route back to his rooms that passed by the château's keep and the chapel. Memorials to most of the departed de Clermonts were there—Philippe; Louisa; her twin brother, Louis; Godfrey; Hugh—as well as some of their children and beloved friends and servants.

"Good morning, Matthew." The scent of saffron and bitter orange filled the air.

Fernando. After a long pause, Matthew forced himself to turn.

Usually the chapel's ancient wooden door was closed, as only Matthew spent time there. Tonight it stood open in welcome, and the figure of a man was silhouetted against the warm candlelight inside.

"I hoped I might see you." Fernando swept his arm wide in invitation.

Fernando watched as his brother-in-law made his way toward him, searching his features for the warning signs that Matthew was in trouble:

the enlargement of his pupils, the ripple in his shoulders reminiscent of a wolf's hackles, a roughness deep in his throat.

"Do I pass inspection?" Matthew asked, unable to keep the defensive note from his tone.

"You'll do." Fernando closed the door firmly behind them. "Barely."

Matthew ran his fingers lightly along Philippe's massive sarcophagus in the center of the chapel and moved restlessly around the chamber while Fernando's deep brown eyes followed him.

"Congratulations on your marriage, Matthew," Fernando said. "Though I haven't met Diana yet, Sarah has told me so many stories about her that I feel we are very old friends."

"I'm sorry, Fernando, it's just—" Matthew began, his expression guilty.

Fernando stopped him with a raised hand. "There is no need for apology."

"Thank you for taking care of Diana's aunt," Matthew said. "I know how difficult it is for you to be here."

"The widow needed somebody to think of her pain first. Just as you did for me when Hugh died," Fernando said simply.

At Sept-Tours everybody from Gallowglass and the gardener to Victoire and Ysabeau referred to Sarah by her status relative to Emily rather than by her name, when she was not in the room. It was a title of respect as well as a constant reminder of Sarah's loss.

"I must ask you, Matthew: Does Diana know about your blood rage?" Fernando kept his voice low. The chapel walls were thick, and not much sound escaped, but it was wise to take precautions.

"Of course she knows." Matthew dropped to his knees in front of a small pile of armor and weapons arranged in one of the chapel's carved niches. The space was big enough to hold a coffin, but Hugh de Clermont had been burned at the stake, leaving no body to bury. Matthew had created a memorial to his favorite brother out of painted wood and metal instead: his shield, his gauntlets, his mail hauberk and coat of plates, his sword, his helm.

"Forgive me for insulting you with the suggestion that you would keep something so important from one you love." Fernando boxed him on the ear. "I'm glad you told your wife, but you deserve a whipping for not telling Marcus or Hamish—or Sarah."

"You're welcome to try." Matthew's response carried a threat that would drive off any other member of his family—but not Fernando.

"You'd like a straightforward punishment, wouldn't you? But you aren't getting off so easy. Not this time." Fernando knelt beside him.

There was a long silence while Fernando waited for Matthew to lower his guard.

"The blood rage. It's gotten worse." Matthew hung his head over his clasped hands in an attitude of prayer.

"Of course it has. You're mated now. What did you expect?"

The chemical and emotional responses that accompanied mating were intense, and even perfectly healthy vampires found it difficult to let their mates out of their sight. On those occasions when being together was impossible, it led to irritation, aggression, anxiety, and, in rare cases, madness. For a vampire with blood rage, both the mating impulse and the effects of separation were heightened.

"I expected to handle it." Matthew's forehead lowered until it was resting on his fingers. "I believed that the love I felt for Diana was stronger than the disease."

"Oh, Matthew. You can be more idealistic than Hugh on even his sunniest days." Fernando sighed and put a comforting hand on Matthew's shoulder.

Fernando always lent comfort and assistance to those who needed it—even when they didn't deserve it. He had sent Matthew to study with the surgeon Albucasis, back when he was trying to overcome the deadly rampages that marked his first centuries as a vampire. It was Fernando who kept Hugh—the brother whom Matthew had worshipped—safe from harm as he made his way from battlefield to book and back to the battlefield again. Without Fernando's care Hugh would have shown up to fight with nothing but a volume of poetry, a dull sword, and one gauntlet. And it was Fernando who told Philippe that ordering Matthew back to Jerusalem would be a terrible mistake. Unfortunately, neither Philippe nor Matthew had listened to him.

"I had to force myself to leave her side tonight." Matthew's eyes darted around the chapel. "I can't sit still, I want to kill something—badly—and even so it was almost impossible for me to venture beyond the sound of her breathing."

Fernando listened in silent sympathy, though he wondered why Matthew sounded surprised. Fernando had to remind himself that newly mated vampires often underestimated how strongly the bond could affect them.

"Right now Diana wants to stay close to Sarah and me. But when the grief over Emily's death has subsided, she's going to want to resume her own life," Matthew said, clearly worried.

"Well, she can't. Not with you standing by her elbow." Fernando never minced words with Matthew. Idealists like him needed plain speech or they lost their way. "If Diana loves you, she'll adapt."

"She won't have to adapt," Matthew said through gritted teeth. "I won't take her freedom—no matter what it costs me. I wasn't with Diana at every moment in the sixteenth century. There's no reason for that to change in the twenty-first."

"You managed your feelings in the past because whenever you weren't at her side, Gallowglass was. Oh, he told me all about your life in London and Prague," Fernando said when Matthew turned a startled face his way. "And if not Gallowglass, Diana was with someone else: Philippe, Davy, another witch, Mary, Henry. Do you honestly think that mobile phones are going to give you a comparable sense of connection and control?"

Matthew still looked angry, the blood rage just beneath the surface, but he looked miserable, too. Fernando thought it was a step in the right direction.

"Ysabeau should have stopped you from getting involved with Diana Bishop as soon as it was clear you were feeling a mating bond," Fernando said sternly. Had Matthew been his child, Fernando would have locked him in a steel tower to prevent it.

"She did stop me." Matthew's expression grew even more miserable. "I wasn't fully mated to Diana until we came to Sept-Tours in 1590. Philippe gave us his blessing."

Fernando's mouth filled with bitterness. "That man's arrogance knew no bounds. No doubt he planned to fix everything when you returned to the present."

"Philippe knew he wouldn't be here," Matthew confessed. Fernando's eyes widened. "I didn't tell him about his death. Philippe figured it out for himself."

Fernando swore a blistering oath. He was sure that Matthew's god would forgive the blasphemy, since it was so richly deserved in this case.

"And did your mating with Diana take place before or after Philippe marked her with his blood vow?" Even after the timewalking, Philippe's blood vow was audible and, according to Verin de Clermont and Gallowglass, still deafening. Happily, Fernando was not a full-blooded de Clermont, so Philippe's bloodsong registered as nothing more than a persistent hum.

"After."

"Of course. Philippe's blood vow ensured her safety. *'Noli me tangere,'*" Fernando said with a shake of his head. "Gallowglass was wasting his time watching Diana so closely."

"'Touch me not, for Caesar's I am,'" Matthew echoed softly. "It's true. No vampire meddled with her after that. Except Louisa."

"Louisa was as mad as a March hare to ignore your father's wishes on this," Fernando commented. "I take it that's why Philippe sent Louisa packing to the outer reaches of the known world in 1591." The decision had always seemed abrupt, and Philippe hadn't stirred a finger to avenge her later death. Fernando filed away the information for future consideration.

The door swung open. Sarah's cat, Tabitha, shot into the chapel in a streak of gray fur and feline indignation. Gallowglass followed her, bearing a pack of cigarettes in one hand and a silver flask in the other. Tabitha wound her way around Matthew's legs, begging for his attention.

"Sarah's moggy is nearly as troublesome as Auntie's firedrake." Gallowglass thrust the flask in Matthew's direction. "Have some. It's not blood, but it's none of Granny's French stuff either. What she serves makes fine cologne, but it's no good for anything else."

Matthew refused the offering with a shake of the head. Baldwin's wine was already souring his stomach.

"And you call yourself a vampire," Fernando scolded Gallowglass. "Driven to drink by *um pequeno dragão.*"

"*You* try taming Corra if you think it's so bloody easy." Gallowglass removed a cigarette from his pack and put it to his lips. "Or we can vote on what to do with her."

"Vote?" Matthew said, incredulous. "Since when did we vote in this family?"

"Since Marcus took over the Knights of Lazarus," Gallowglass replied, drawing a silver lighter from his pocket. "We've been choking on democracy since the day you left."

Fernando looked at him pointedly.

"What?" Gallowglass said, swinging the lighter open.

"This is a holy place, Gallowglass. And you know how Marcus feels about smoking when there are warmbloods in the house," Fernando said reprovingly.

"And you can imagine my own thoughts on the matter, with my pregnant wife upstairs." Matthew snatched the cigarette from Gallowglass's mouth.

"This family was more fun when we had fewer medical degrees," Gallowglass said darkly. "I remember the good old days, when we sewed ourselves up if we were wounded in battle and didn't give a tinker's dam about our iron levels and vitamin D."

"Oh, yes." Fernando held up his hand, displaying a ragged scar. "Those days were glorious indeed. And your skills with the needle were legendary, *Bife*."

"I got better," Gallowglass said defensively. "I was never as good as Matthew or Marcus, of course. But we can't all go to university."

"Not so long as Philippe was head of the family," Fernando murmured. "He preferred that his children and grandchildren wield swords rather than ideas. It made you all so much more pliable."

There was a grain of truth in the remark, and an ocean of pain behind it.

"I should get back to Diana." Matthew rocked to his feet and rested his hand on Fernando's shoulder for a brief moment before turning to leave.

"Waiting will not make it any easier to tell Marcus and Hamish about the blood rage, my friend," Fernando warned, stopping him.

"I thought after all these years my secret was safe," Matthew said.

"Secrets, like the dead, do not always stay buried," Fernando said sadly. "Tell them. Soon."

Matthew returned to his tower more agitated than when he'd left.

Ysabeau frowned at the sight of him.

"Thank you for watching Diana, *Maman,*" he said, kissing Ysabeau's cheek.

"And you, my son?" Ysabeau put her palm to his cheek, searching as Fernando had for signs of blood rage. "Should I be watching over you instead?"

"I'm fine. Truly," Matthew said.

"Of course," Ysabeau replied. This phrase meant many things in his mother's private lexicon. What it never meant was that she agreed with you. "I will be in my room if you need me."

When the sound of his mother's quiet footfalls had faded, Matthew flung wide the windows and pulled his chair close to the open casement. He drank in the intense summer scents of catchfly and the last of the gillyflowers. The sound of Diana's even breathing upstairs blended into the other night songs that only vampires could hear—the clack of stag beetles locking horns as they competed for females, the loirs' wheezing as they ran across the battlements, the high-pitched squeaks of the death's-head hawkmoth, the scrabbling of pine martens climbing the trees. Based on the grunts and snuffles Matthew heard in the garden, Gallowglass had been no more successful catching the wild boar uprooting Marthe's vegetables than he had been in catching Corra.

Normally Matthew relished this quiet hour equidistant from midnight and dawn when the owls had stopped their hooting and even the most disciplined early risers had not yet peeled back the bedcovers. Tonight not even the familiar scents and sounds of home could work their magic.

Only one thing could.

Matthew climbed the stairs to the tower's top floor. There he looked down at Diana's sleeping form. He smoothed her hair, smiling when his wife instinctively pressed her skull deeper into his waiting hand. Impossible as it was, they fit: vampire and witch, man and woman, husband and wife. The hard fist around his heart loosened a few precious millimeters.

Silently Matthew shucked off his clothes and slid into bed. The sheets were tangled around Diana's legs, and he pulled the linen free, settling it over their bodies. Matthew tucked his knees behind Diana's and drew her hips back into his. He drank in the soft, pleasing scent of her—honey and chamomile and willow sap—and feathered a kiss against her bright hair.

After only a few breaths, Matthew's heart calmed and his restlessness seeped away as Diana provided the peace that was eluding him. Here, within the circle of his arms, was all that he had ever wanted. A wife. Children. A family of his own. He let the powerful rightness that he always felt in Diana's presence sink into his soul.

"Matthew?" Diana asked sleepily.

"I'm here," he murmured against her ear, holding her closer. "Go back to sleep. The sun hasn't risen yet."

Instead Diana turned to face him, burrowing into his neck.

"What is it, *mon coeur*?" Matthew frowned and pulled back to study her expression. Her skin was puffy and red from the crying, and the fine lines around her eyes were deepened by worry and grief. It destroyed him to see her this way. "Tell me," he said gently.

"There's no point. No one can fix it," she said sadly.

Matthew smiled. "At least let me try."

"Can you make time stand still?" Diana whispered after a moment of hesitation. "Just for a little while?"

Matthew was an ancient vampire, not a timewalking witch. But he was also a man, and he knew of one way to achieve this magical feat. His head told him that it was too soon after Emily's death, but his body sent other, more persuasive messages.

He lowered his mouth deliberately, giving Diana time to push him away. Instead she threaded her fingers through his cropped hair, returning his kiss with an intensity that stole his breath.

Her fine linen shift had traveled with them from the past, and though practically transparent, it was still a barrier between their flesh. He lifted the cloth, exposing the soft swell of her belly where his children grew, the curve of her breasts that every day ripened with fertile promise. They had not made love since London, and Matthew noticed the additional tightness of Diana's abdomen—a sign that the babies were continuing to develop—as well as the heightened blood flow to her breasts and her sex.

He took his fill of her with his eyes, his fingers, his mouth. But instead of being sated, his hunger for her only increased. Matthew lowered Diana back onto the bed and trailed kisses down her body until he reached the hidden places only he knew. Her hands tried to press his mouth more firmly against her, and he nipped her thigh in a silent reproach.

Once Diana began to fight his control in earnest, demanding softly that he take her, Matthew turned her in his arms and drew one cool hand down her spine.

"You wanted time to stand still," he reminded her.

"It has," Diana insisted, pressing against him in invitation.

"Then why are you rushing me?" Matthew traced the star-shaped scar between her shoulder blades and the crescent moon that swooped from one side of her ribs to the other. He frowned. There was a shadow on her lower back. It was deep within her skin, a pearly gray outline that looked a bit like a firedrake, its jaws biting into the crescent moon above, the wings covering Diana's rib cage, and a tail that disappeared around her hips.

"Why have you stopped?" Diana pushed her hair out of her eyes and craned her neck over her shoulder. "I want time to stand still—not you."

"There's something on your back." Matthew traced the firedrake's wings.

"You mean something else?" she asked with a nervous laugh. She still worried that her healed wounds were blemishes.

"With your other scars, it reminds me of a painting in Mary Sidney's laboratory, the one of the firedrake capturing the moon in its mouth." He wondered if it would be visible to others or if only his vampire eyes could detect it. "It's beautiful. Another sign of your courage."

"You told me I was reckless," Diana said breathlessly as his mouth descended to the dragon's head.

"You are." Matthew traced the swirling path of the dragon's tail with his lips and tongue. His mouth drifted lower, deeper. "It drives me crazy."

He battened his mouth on her, keeping Diana on the edge of desire, stopping his attentions to whisper an endearment or a promise before resuming, never allowing her to be swept away. She wanted satisfaction and the peace that came with forgetting, but he wanted this moment—filled with safety and intimacy—to last forever. Matthew turned Diana to face him. Her lips were soft and full, her eyes dreamy, as he slid slowly inside her. He continued his gentle movements until the upward tick in his wife's heartbeat told him that her climax was near.

Diana cried his name, weaving a spell that put them in the center of the world.

Afterward they lay twined together in the final rose-tinged moments of darkness before dawn. Diana drew Matthew's head to her breast. He gave her a questioning look, and his wife nodded. Matthew lowered his mouth to the silvery moon over a prominent blue vein.

This was the ancient way for a vampire to know his mate, the sacred moment of communion when thoughts and emotions were exchanged honestly and without judgment. Vampires were secretive creatures, but when a vampire took blood from his mate's heart vein, there was a moment of perfect peace and understanding that quieted the constant, dull need to hunt and possess.

Diana's skin parted underneath his teeth, and Matthew drank in a few precious ounces of her blood. With it came a flood of impressions and feelings: joy mixed with sorrow, delight in being back with friends and family tempered with grief, rage over Emily's death held in check by Diana's concern for him and their children.

"I would have spared you this loss if I could have," Matthew murmured, kissing the mark his mouth left on her skin. He rolled them over so that he was on his back and Diana was draped over his recumbent form. She looked down into his eyes.

"I know. Just don't ever leave me, Matthew. Not without saying goodbye."

"I will never leave you," he promised.

Diana touched her lips to Matthew's forehead. She pressed them into the skin between his eyes. Most warmblooded mates could not share in the vampire's ritual of togetherness, but his wife had found a way around the limitation, as she did with most obstacles in her path. Diana had discovered that when she kissed him just here, she also caught glimpses of his innermost thoughts and the dark places where his fears and secrets hid.

Matthew felt nothing more than a tingle of her power as she gave him her witch's kiss and remained as still as possible, wanting Diana to take her fill of him. He forced himself to relax so that his feelings and thoughts could flow unimpeded.

"Welcome home, *sister*." The unexpected scent of wood fires and saddle leather flooded the room, as Baldwin ripped the sheet from the bed.

Diana let out a startled cry. Matthew tried to pull her naked body behind him, but it was too late. His wife was already in the grip of another.

"I could hear my father's blood vow halfway up the drive. You're pregnant, too." Baldwin de Clermont's face was coldly furious under his fiery hair as his eyes dropped to Diana's rounded belly. He twisted her arm so that he could sniff her wrist. "And only Matthew's scent upon you. Well, well."

Baldwin released Diana, and Matthew caught her.

"Get up. Both of you," Baldwin commanded, his fury evident.

"You have no authority over me, Baldwin!" Diana cried, her eyes narrowing.

She couldn't have calculated a response that would have angered Matthew's brother more. Without warning, Baldwin swooped until his face was inches away. Only the firm pressure of Matthew's hand around Baldwin's throat kept the vampire from getting even closer.

"My father's blood vow says I do, witch." Baldwin stared into Diana's eyes, trying to force her through sheer will to look away. When she did not, Baldwin's eyes flickered. "Your wife lacks manners, Matthew. School her, or I will."

"School me?" Diana's eyes widened. Her fingers splayed, and the wind in the room circled her feet, ready to answer her call. High above, Corra shrieked to let her mistress know she was on the way.

"No magic and no dragon," Matthew murmured against her ear, praying that just this once his wife would obey him. He didn't want Baldwin or anyone else in the family to know how much Diana's abilities had grown while they were in London.

Miraculously, Diana nodded.

"What is the meaning of this?" Ysabeau's frosty voice cracked through the room. "The only excuse for your presence here, Baldwin, is that you have lost your senses."

"Careful, Ysabeau. Your claws are showing." Baldwin stalked toward the stairs. "And you forget: I'm the head of the de Clermont family. I don't need an excuse. Meet me in the family library, Matthew. You, too, Diana."

Baldwin turned to level his strange golden-brown eyes at Matthew.

"Don't keep me waiting."

3

The de Clermont family library was bathed in a gentle predawn light that made everything in it appear in soft focus: the edges of the books, the strong lines of the wooden bookcases that lined the room, the warm golden and blue hues of the Aubusson rug.

What it could not blunt was my anger.

For three days I had thought that nothing could displace my grief over Emily's death, but three minutes in Baldwin's company had proved me wrong.

"Come in, Diana." Baldwin sat in a thronelike Savonarola chair by the tall windows. His burnished red-gold hair gleamed in the lamplight, its color reminding me of the feathers on Augusta, the eagle that Emperor Rudolf hunted with in Prague. Every inch of Baldwin's muscular frame was taut with anger and banked strength.

I looked around the room. We were not the only ones to have been summoned to Baldwin's impromptu meeting. Waiting by the fireplace was a waif of a young woman with skin the color of skim milk and black, spiky hair. Her eyes were deep gray and enormous, fringed with thick lashes. She sniffed the air as though scenting a storm.

"Verin." Matthew had warned me about Philippe's daughters, who were so terrifying that the family asked him to stop making them. But she didn't look very frightening. Verin's face was smooth and serene, her posture easy, and her eyes sparkled with energy and intelligence. Were it not for her unrelieved black clothing, you might mistake her for an elf.

Then I noticed a knife hilt peeking out from her high-heeled black boots.

"Wölfling," Verin replied. It was a cold greeting for a sister to give her brother, but the look she gave me was even more frigid. "Witch."

"It's Diana," I said, my anger flaring.

"I told you there was no way to mistake it," Verin said, turning to Baldwin without acknowledging my reply.

"Why are you here, Baldwin?" Matthew asked.

"I wasn't aware I needed an invitation to come to my father's house," he replied. "But as it happens, I came from Venice to see Marcus."

The eyes of the two men locked.

"Imagine my surprise at finding you here," Baldwin continued. "Nor did I expect to discover that your *mate* is now my sister. Philippe died in 1945. So how is it that I can feel my father's blood vow? Smell it? Hear it?"

"Someone else can catch you up on the news." Matthew took me by the hand and turned to go back upstairs.

"Neither of you is leaving my sight until I find out how that witch tricked a blood vow from a dead vampire." Baldwin's voice was low with menace.

"It was no trick," I said, indignant.

"Was it necromancy, then? Some foul resurrection spell?" Baldwin asked. "Or did you conjure his spirit and force him to give you his vow?"

"What happened between Philippe and me had nothing to do with my magic and everything to do with his generosity." My own anger burned hotter.

"You make it sound as though you knew him," Baldwin said. "That's impossible."

"Not for a timewalker," I replied.

"Timewalker?" Baldwin was stunned.

"Diana and I have been in the past," Matthew explained. "In 1590, to be exact. We were here at Sept-Tours just before Christmas."

"You saw Philippe?" Baldwin asked.

"We did. Philippe was alone that winter. He sent a coin and ordered me home," Matthew said. The de Clermonts present understood their father's private code: When a command was sent along with one of Philippe's ancient silver coins, the recipient was to obey without question.

"December? That means we have to endure five more months of Philippe's bloodsong," Verin muttered, her fingers pinching the bridge of her nose as though her head ached. I frowned.

"Why five months?" I asked.

"According to our legends, a vampire's blood vow sings for a year and a day. All vampires can hear it, but the song is particularly loud and clear to those who carry Philippe's blood in their veins," Baldwin said.

"Philippe said he wanted there to be no doubt I was a de Clermont," I said, looking up at Matthew. All the vampires who had met me in the sixteenth century must have heard Philippe's bloodsong and known I was not only Matthew's mate but also Philippe de Clermont's daughter. Philippe had been protecting me during every step of our journey through the past.

"No witch will ever be recognized as a de Clermont." Baldwin's voice was flat and final.

"I already am." I held up my left hand so he could see my wedding ring. "Matthew and I are married as well as mated. Your father hosted the ceremony. If Saint-Lucien's parish registers survive, you'll find our wedding took place on the seventh of December, 1590."

"What we will likely find, should we go to the village, is that a single page has been torn out of the priest's book," Verin said under her breath. "*Atta* always covered his tracks."

"Whether you and Matthew are married is of no consequence, for Matthew is not a true de Clermont either," Baldwin said coldly. "He is merely the child of my father's mate."

"That's ridiculous," I protested. "Philippe considered Matthew his son. Matthew calls you brother and Verin sister."

"I am not that whelp's sister. We share no blood, only a name," Verin said. "And thank God for it."

"You will find, Diana, that marriage and mating don't count for much with most of the de Clermonts," said a quiet voice with a marked Spanish or Portuguese accent. It came from the mouth of a stranger standing just inside the door. His dark hair and espresso-colored eyes set off his pale golden skin and light shirt.

"Your presence wasn't requested, Fernando," Baldwin said angrily.

"As you know, I come when I'm needed, not when I'm called." Fernando bowed slightly in my direction. "Fernando Gonçalves. I am very sorry for your loss."

The man's name pricked at my memory. I'd heard it somewhere before.

"You're the man Matthew asked to lead the Knights of Lazarus when he gave up the position of grand master," I said, finally placing him. Fernando Gonçalves was reputed to be one of the brotherhood's most formidable warriors. Judging by the breadth of his shoulders and his overall fitness, I had no doubt this was true.

"He did." Like that of all vampires, Fernando's voice was warm and rich, filling the room with otherworldly sound. "But Hugh de Clermont is my mate. Ever since he died alongside the Templars, I have had little to do with chivalric orders, for even the bravest knights lack the courage to keep their promises." Fernando fixed his dark eyes on Matthew's brother. "Isn't that right, Baldwin?"

"Are you challenging me?" Baldwin said, standing.

"Do I need to?" Fernando smiled. He was shorter than Baldwin, but something told me he would not be easy to best in battle. "I would not have thought you would ignore your father's blood vow, Baldwin."

"We have no idea what Philippe wanted from the witch. He might have been trying to learn more about her power. Or she could have used magic to coerce him," Baldwin said, his chin jutting out at a stubborn angle.

"Don't be daft. Auntie didn't use any magic on Granddad." Gallowglass breezed into the room, as relaxed as if the de Clermonts always met at half past four in the morning to discuss urgent business.

"Now that Gallowglass is here, I'll leave the de Clermonts to their own devices." Fernando nodded to Matthew. "Call if you need me, Matthew."

"We'll be just fine. We're family, after all." Gallowglass blinked innocently at Verin and Baldwin as Fernando departed. "As for what Philippe wanted, it's quite simple, Uncle: He wanted you to formally acknowledge Diana as his daughter. Ask Verin."

"What does he mean?" Baldwin demanded of his sister.

"*Atta* summoned me a few days before he died," Verin said, her voice low and her expression miserable. The word "*Atta*" was unfamiliar, but it was clearly a daughterly endearment. "Philippe was worried that you might ignore his blood vow. He made me swear to acknowledge it, no matter what."

"Philippe's oath was private—something between him and me. It doesn't need to be acknowledged. Not by you or anyone else." I didn't want my memories of Philippe—or that moment—damaged by Baldwin and Verin.

"Nothing is more public than adopting a warmblood into a vampire clan," Verin told me. She looked at Matthew. "Didn't you take the time to teach the witch our vampire customs before you rushed into this forbidden affair?"

"Time was a luxury we didn't have," I replied instead. From the very beginning of our relationship, Ysabeau had warned me that I had a lot to learn about vampires. After this conversation, the topic of blood vows was moving to the head of my research agenda.

"Then let me explain it to you," Verin said, her voice sharper than any schoolmarm's. "Before Philippe's bloodsong fades, one of his full-blooded children must acknowledge it. Unless that happens, you are not truly a de Clermont and no other vampire is obligated to honor you as such."

"Is that all? I don't care about vampire honor. Being Matthew's wife is enough for me." The more I heard about becoming a de Clermont, the less I liked it.

"If that were true, then my father wouldn't have adopted you," Verin observed.

"We will compromise," Baldwin said. "Surely Philippe would be satisfied if, when the witch's children are born, their names are listed among my kin on the de Clermont family pedigree." His words sounded magnanimous, but I was sure there was some darker purpose to them.

"My children are not your kin." Matthew's voice sounded like thunder.

"They are if Diana is a de Clermont as she claims," Baldwin said with a smile.

"Wait. What pedigree?" I needed to back up a step in the argument.

"The Congregation maintains official pedigrees of all vampire families," Baldwin said. "Some no longer observe the tradition. The de Clermonts do. The pedigrees include information about rebirths, deaths, and the names of mates and their offspring."

My hand automatically covered my belly. I wanted the Congregation to remain unaware of my children for as long as possible. Based on the wary look in Matthew's eyes, he felt the same way.

"Maybe your timewalking will be enough to satisfy questions about the blood vow, but only the blackest of magics—or infidelity—can explain this pregnancy," Baldwin said, relishing his brother's discomfort. "The children cannot be yours, Matthew."

"Diana is carrying *my* children," Matthew said, his eyes dangerously dark.

"Impossible," Baldwin stated flatly.

"True," Matthew retorted.

"If so, they'll be the most hated—and the most hunted—children the world has ever known. Creatures will be baying for their blood. And yours," Baldwin said.

I registered Matthew's sudden departure from my side at the same moment that I heard Baldwin's chair break. When the blur of movement ceased, Matthew stood behind his brother with his arm locked around Baldwin's throat, pressing a knife into the skin over his brother's heart.

Verin looked down at her boot in amazement and found nothing but an empty scabbard. She swore.

"You may be head of the family, Baldwin, but never forget that I am its assassin," Matthew growled.

"Assassin?" I tried to hide my confusion as another hidden side of Matthew was brought to light.

Scientist. Vampire. Warrior. Spy. Prince.

Assassin.

Matthew had told me he was a killer—repeatedly—but I had always considered this part and parcel of being a vampire. I knew he'd killed in self-defense, in battle, and to survive. I'd never dreamed that Matthew committed murder at his family's behest.

"Surely you knew this?" Verin asked in a voice tinged with malice, her cold eyes studying me closely. "If Matthew weren't so good at it, one of us would have put him down long ago."

"We all have a role in this family, Verin." Matthew's voice dripped with bitterness. "Does Ernst know yours—how it begins between soft sheets and a man's thighs?"

Verin moved like lightning, her fingers bent into lethal claws as she went for Matthew.

Vampires were fast, but magic was faster.

I pushed Verin against a wall with a blast of witchwind, keeping her away from my husband and Baldwin long enough for Matthew to exact some promise from his brother and release him.

"Thank you, *ma lionne.*" It was Matthew's usual endearment when I'd done something brave—or incredibly stupid. He handed me Verin's knife. "Hold on to this."

Matthew lifted Verin to her feet while Gallowglass moved closer to stand at my elbow.

"Well, well," Verin murmured when she was standing upright again. "I see why *Atta* was drawn to your wife, but I wouldn't have thought you had the stones for such a woman, Matthew."

"Things change," Matthew said shortly.

"Apparently." Verin gave me an appraising look.

"You'll be keeping your promise to Granddad, then?" Gallowglass asked Verin.

"We'll see," she said cautiously. "I have months to decide."

"Time will pass, but nothing will change." Baldwin looked at me with barely concealed loathing. "Recognizing Matthew's wife will have catastrophic consequences, Verin."

"I honored *Atta*'s wishes while he lived," Verin said. "I cannot ignore them now that he is dead."

"We must take comfort from the fact that the Congregation is already looking for Matthew and his mate," Baldwin said. "Who knows? They may both be dead before December."

After giving us a final, contemptuous look, Baldwin stalked from the room. Verin stole an apologetic glance at Gallowglass and trailed after him.

"So . . . that went well," Gallowglass muttered "Are you all right, Auntie? You've gone a bit shiny."

"The witchwind blew my disguising spell out of place." I tried to tug it around me again.

"Given what happened here this morning, I think you'd better keep it on while Baldwin is at home," Gallowglass suggested.

"Baldwin cannot know of Diana's power. I'd appreciate your help with that, Gallowglass. Fernando's, too." Matthew didn't specify what form this assistance would take.

"Of course. I've been watching over Auntie her whole life," Gallowglass said, matter-of-fact. "I'll not be stopping now."

At these words parts of my past that I had never understood slid into place like jagged puzzle pieces. As a child I'd often felt other creatures watching me, their eyes nudging and tingling and freezing my skin. One had been Peter Knox, my father's enemy and the same witch who had come to Sept-Tours looking for Matthew and me only to kill Em. Could another have been this giant bear of a man, whom I now loved like a brother but had not even met until we traveled back to the sixteenth century?

"You were watching me?" My eyes filled, and I blinked back the tears.

"I promised Granddad I'd keep you safe. For Matthew's sake." Gallowglass's blue eyes softened. "And it's a good thing, too. You were a right hellion: climbing trees, running after bicycles in the street, and heading into the forest without a hint as to where you were going. How your parents managed is beyond me."

"Did Daddy know?" I had to ask. My father had met the big Gael in Elizabethan London, when he'd unexpectedly run into Matthew and me on one of his regular timewalks. Even in modern-day Massachusetts, my father would have recognized Gallowglass on sight. The man was unmistakable.

"I did my best not to show myself."

"That's not what I asked, Gallowglass." I was getting better at ferreting out a vampire's half-truths. "Did my father know you were watching over me?"

"I made sure Stephen saw me just before he and your mother left for Africa that last time," Gallowglass confessed, his voice little more than a whisper. "I thought it might help him to know, when the end came, that I was nearby. You were still such a wee thing. Stephen must have been beside himself with worry thinking about how long it would be before you were with Matthew."

Unbeknownst to Matthew or me, the Bishops and the de Clermonts had been working for years, even centuries, to bring us safely together: Philippe, Gallowglass, my father, Emily, my mother.

"Thank you, Gallowglass," Matthew said hoarsely. Like me, he was surprised by the morning's revelations.

"No need, Uncle. I did it gladly." Gallowglass cleared the emotion from his throat and departed.

An awkward silence fell.

"Christ." Matthew raked his fingers through his hair. It was the usual sign he'd been driven to the end of his patience.

"What are we going to do?" I said, still trying to regain my equilibrium after Baldwin's sudden appearance.

A gentle cough announced a new presence in the room and kept Matthew from responding.

"I am sorry to interrupt, *milord*." Alain Le Merle, Philippe de Clermont's onetime squire, stood in the doorway to the library. He was holding an ancient coffer with the initials P.C. picked out on the top in silver studs and a small ledger bound in green buckram. His salt-and-pepper hair and kind expression were the same as when I'd first met him in 1590. Like Matthew and Gallowglass, he was a fixed star in my universe of change.

"What is it, Alain?" Matthew asked.

"I have business with Madame de Clermont," Alain replied.

"Business?" Matthew frowned. "Can it wait?"

"I'm afraid not," Alain said apologetically. "This is a difficult time I know, *milord*, but *Sieur* Philippe was adamant that Madame de Clermont be given her things as soon as possible."

Alain ushered us back up to our tower. What I saw on Matthew's desk drove the events of the past hour completely from my mind and left me breathless.

A small book bound in brown leather.

An embroidered sleeve, threadbare with age.

Priceless jewels—pearls and diamonds and sapphires.

A golden arrowhead on a long chain.

A pair of miniatures, their bright surfaces as fresh as the day they were painted.

Letters, tied with a faded carnation ribbon.

A silver rat trap, tarnish clinging to the fine engraving.

A gilded astronomical instrument fit for an emperor.

A wooden box carved by a wizard out of a branch from a rowan tree.

The collection of objects didn't look like much, but they held enormous significance, for they represented the past eight months of our lives.

I picked up the small book with a trembling hand and flipped it open. Matthew had given it to me soon after we'd arrived at his mansion in Woodstock. In the autumn of 1590, the book's binding had been fresh and the pages creamy. Today the leather was speckled and the paper yellowed with age. In the past I'd tucked the book away on a high shelf in the Old Lodge, but a bookplate inside told me that it was now the property of a library in Seville. The call mark, *"Manuscrito Gonçalves 4890,"* was inked onto the flyleaf. Someone—Gallowglass, no doubt—had removed the first page. Once it had been covered with my tentative attempts to record my name. The blots from that missing leaf had seeped through to the page below, but the list I'd made of the Elizabethan coins in circulation in 1590 was still legible.

I flipped through the rest of the pages, remembering the headache cure I'd attempted to master in a futile attempt to appear a proper Elizabethan housewife. My diary of daily happenings brought back bittersweet memories of our time with the School of Night. I'd dedicated a handful of pages to an overview of the twelve signs of the zodiac, copied down a few more recipes, and scribbled a packing list for our journey to Sept-Tours in the back. I heard the gentle chime as past and present rubbed against each other, and I spotted the blue and amber threads that were barely visible in the corners of the fireplace.

"How did you get this?" I said, focusing on the here and now.

"Master Gallowglass gave it to Dom Fernando long ago. When he arrived at Sept-Tours in May, Dom Fernando asked me to return it to you," Alain explained.

"It's a miracle anything survived. How did you manage to keep all this hidden from me for so many years?" Matthew picked up the silver rat trap. He had teased me when I'd commissioned one of London's most expensive clockmakers to make the mechanism to catch the rats prowling our attics in the Blackfriars. Monsieur Vallin had designed it to resemble a cat, with ears set on the crossbars and a little mouse perched on the fierce feline's nose. Matthew deliberately sprang the mechanism, and the cat's sharp teeth dug into the flesh of his finger.

"We did as we must, *milord.* We waited. We kept silent. We never lost faith that time would bring Madame de Clermont back to us." A sad smile played at the corners of Alain's mouth. "If only *Sieur* Philippe could have lived to see this day."

At the thought of Philippe, my heart skittered. He must have known how badly his children would react to having me as a sister. Why had he put me in such an impossible situation?

"All right, Diana?" Matthew gently laid his hand over mine.

"Yes. Just a bit overwhelmed." I took up the portraits of Matthew and me wearing fine Elizabethan clothing. Nicholas Hilliard had painted them at the Countess of Pembroke's request. She and the Earl of Northumberland had given the tiny likenesses to us as wedding gifts. The two of them had been Matthew's friends at first—along with the other members of the School of Night: Walter Raleigh, George Chapman, Thomas Harriot, and Christopher Marlowe. In time most of them became my friends, too.

"It was Madame Ysabeau who found the miniatures," Alain explained. "She scoured the newspapers every day looking for traces of you—anomalies that stood out from the rest of the day's events. When Madame Ysabeau saw these in an auction notice, she sent Master Marcus to London. It's how he met Mademoiselle Phoebe."

"This sleeve came from your wedding dress." Matthew touched the fragile fabric, tracing the outlines of a cornucopia, the traditional symbol of abundance. "I will never forget the sight of you, coming down the hill to the village with the torches blazing and the children clearing the way through the snow." His smile was full of love and a pleased pride.

"After the wedding many men in the village offered to pay Madame de Clermont court, should you tire of her." Alain chuckled.

"Thank you for keeping all of these memories for me." I looked down at the desk. "It's much too easy to think I somehow imagined everything—that we were never really there in 1590. This makes that time seem real again."

"*Sieur* Philippe thought you might feel that way. Alas, there are two more items that require your attention, Madame de Clermont." Alain held out the ledger. A tied string kept it from being opened, and a blob of wax sealed the knot to the cover.

"What's this?" I frowned and took the ledger. It was far thinner than the ones here in Matthew's study that contained the financial records of the Knights of Lazarus.

"Your accounts, *madame*."

"I thought Hamish was keeping my finances." He'd left piles of documents for me, all of them awaiting my signature.

"Mr. Osborne took charge of your marriage settlement from *milord*. These are the funds you received from *Sieur* Philippe." Alain's attention lingered for a moment on my forehead, where Philippe had placed his blood to claim me as his daughter.

Curious, I cracked the seal and opened the covers. The little account book had been rebound periodically when more pages were required. The first entries were made on thick sixteenth-century paper and dated from the year 1591. One accounted for the deposit of the dowry that Philippe had provided when I married Matthew: 20,000 Venetian zecchini and 30,000 silver Reichsthaler. Every subsequent investment of that money—such as the roll-over of any interest paid on the funds and the houses and land purchased with the proceeds—was meticulously accounted for in Alain's neat hand. I flipped through to the final pages of the book. The last entry, made on sparkling white bond, was dated 4 July 2010, the day we had arrived back at Sept-Tours. My eyes popped at the amount indicated in the assets column.

"I am sorry it is not more," Alain said hastily, mistaking my reaction for alarm. "I invested your money as I did my own, but the more lucrative, and therefore riskier, opportunities would have required *Sieur* Baldwin's approval, and of course he could not know of your existence."

"It's more than I could ever imagine possessing, Alain." Matthew had settled a substantial amount of property on me when he drew up our marriage agreement, but this was a vast sum. Philippe had wanted me to have financial independence like the rest of the de Clermont women. And as I had learned this morning, my father-in-law, whether dead or alive, got what he wanted. I put the ledger aside. "Thank you."

"It was my pleasure," Alain said with a bow. He drew something from his pocket. "Finally, *Sieur* Philippe instructed me to give you this."

Alain handed me an envelope made from cheap, thin stock. My name was on the front. Though the poor adhesive had long since dried up, the envelope had been sealed with a swirl of black and red waxes. An ancient coin was embedded in it: Philippe's special signal.

"*Sieur* Philippe worked on this letter for over an hour. He made me read it back to him when he finished, to be sure that it captured what he wanted to say."

"When?" Matthew asked hoarsely.

"The day he died." Alain's expression was haunted.

The shaky handwriting belonged to someone too old or infirm to hold a pen properly. It was a vivid reminder of how much Philippe had suffered. I traced my name. When my fingertips reached the final letter, I dragged them across the surface of the envelope, pulling at the letters so that they unraveled. First there was a pool of black on the envelope, and then the ink resolved into the image of a man's face. It was still beautiful, though ravaged with pain and marred by a deep, empty socket where once a tawny eye had shimmered with intelligence and humor.

"You didn't tell me the Nazis had blinded him." I knew that my father-in-law had been tortured, but I had never imagined his captors had inflicted this much damage. I studied the other wounds on Philippe's face. Mercifully, there weren't enough letters in my name to draw a detailed portrait. I touched my father-in-law's cheek gently, and the image dissolved, leaving an ink stain on the envelope. With a flick of my fingers, the stain lifted into a small black tornado. When the whirling stopped, the letters dropped back into their proper place.

"*Sieur* Philippe often spoke with you about his troubles, Madame de Clermont," Alain continued softly, "when the pain was very bad."

"Spoke with her?" Matthew repeated numbly.

"Almost every day," Alain said with a nod. "He would bid me to send everyone from that part of the château, for fear someone would overhear. Madame de Clermont brought *Sieur* Philippe comfort when no one else could."

I turned the envelope over, tracing the raised markings on the ancient silver coin. "Philippe expected his coins to be returned to him. In person. How can I, if he's dead?"

"Perhaps the answer is inside," Matthew suggested.

I slid my finger under the envelope's seal, freeing the coin from the wax. I carefully removed the fragile sheet of paper, which crackled ominously as it was unfolded.

Philippe's faint scent of bay, figs, and rosemary tickled my nose.

Looking down at the paper, I was grateful for my expertise in deciphering difficult handwriting. After a close look, I began to read the letter aloud.

Diana—

Do not let the ghosts of the past steal the joy from the future.
Thank you for holding my hand.
You can let go now.
Your father, in blood and vow,
Philippe

P.S. The coin is for the ferryman. Tell Matthew I will see you safe on the other side.

I choked on the last few words. They echoed in the silent room.

"So Philippe does expect me to return his coin." He would be sitting on the banks of the river Styx waiting for Charon's boat to bring me across. Perhaps Emily waited with him, and my parents, too. I closed my eyes, hoping to block out the painful images.

"What did he mean, '*Thank you for holding my hand*'?" Matthew asked.

"I promised him he wouldn't be alone in the dark times. That I'd be there, with him." My eyes brimmed with tears. "How can I have no memory of doing so?"

"I don't know, my love. But somehow you managed to keep your promise." Matthew leaned down and kissed me. He looked over my shoulder. "And Philippe made sure he got the last word, as usual."

"What do you mean?" I asked, wiping at my cheeks.

"He left written proof that he freely and gladly wanted you for his daughter." Matthew's long white finger touched the page.

"That is why *Sieur* Philippe wanted Madame de Clermont to have these as soon as possible," Alain admitted.

"I don't understand," I said, looking at Matthew.

"Between the jewels, your dowry, and this letter, it will be impossible for any of Philippe's children—or even the Congregation—to suggest he was somehow forced to bestow a blood vow on you," Matthew explained.

"*Sieur* Philippe knew his children well. He often foresaw their future as easily as any witch," Alain said, nodding. "I will leave you to your memories."

"Thank you, Alain." Matthew waited until the sound of Alain's footsteps faded before saying anything more. He looked down at me with concern. "All right, *mon coeur*?"

"Of course," I murmured, staring at the desk. The past was strewn across it, and a clear future was nowhere to be found.

"I'm going upstairs to change. I won't be long," Matthew said, giving me a kiss. "Then we can go down to breakfast."

"Take your time," I said, mustering what I hoped was a genuine smile.

Once Matthew was gone, I reached for the golden arrowhead that Philippe gave me to wear at my wedding. Its weight was comforting, and the metal warmed quickly to my touch. I slipped its chain over my head.

The arrowhead's point nestled between my breasts, its edges too soft and worn to nick my skin.

I felt a squirming sensation in the pocket of my jeans and drew out a clutch of silk ribbons. My weaver's cords had come with me from the past, and unlike the sleeve from my wedding dress or the faded silk that bound my letters, these strands were fresh and shiny. They twined and danced around my wrists and one another like a handful of brightly colored snakes, merging into new colors for a moment before separating into their original strands and hues. The cords snaked up my arms and wormed their way into my hair as if they were looking for something. I pulled them free and tucked the silks away.

I was supposed to be the weaver. But would I ever comprehend the tangled web that Philippe de Clermont had been spinning when he made me his blood-sworn daughter?

4

Were you ever going to tell me you were the de Clermont family's assassin?" I asked, reaching for the grapefruit juice.

Matthew looked at me in silence across the kitchen table where Marthe had laid out my morning meal. He had sneaked Hector and Fallon inside, and they were following our conversation—and my selection of foods—with interest.

"And Fernando's relationship with your brother Hugh?" I asked. "I was raised by two women. You couldn't possibly have been withholding that piece of information because you thought I might disapprove."

Hector and Fallon looked to Matthew for an answer. When none was forthcoming, the dogs looked back at me.

"Verin seems nice," I said, deliberately trying to provoke him.

"Nice?" Matthew beetled his eyebrows at me.

"Well, except for the fact she was armed with a knife," I admitted mildly, pleased that my strategy had worked.

"Knives," Matthew corrected me. "She had one in her boot, one in her waistband, and one in her bra."

"Was Verin ever a Girl Scout?" It was my turn to lift my brows.

Before Matthew could answer, Gallowglass shot through the kitchen in a streak of blue and black, followed by Fernando. Matthew scrambled to his feet. When the dogs got up to follow, he pointed to the floor and they immediately sat down again.

"Finish your breakfast, then go to the tower," Matthew ordered just before he vanished. "Take the dogs with you. And don't come down until I come and get you."

"What's going on?" I asked Marthe, blinking at the suddenly vacant room.

"Baldwin is home," she replied, as though this were a sufficient answer.

"Marcus," I said, remembering that Baldwin had returned to see Matthew's son. The dogs and I jumped up. "Where is he?"

"Philippe's office." Marthe frowned. "I do not think Matthew wants you there. There may be bloodshed."

"Story of my life." I was looking over my shoulder when I said it and ran smack into Verin as a result. A dignified older gentleman who had a tall, gaunt frame and kind eyes was with her. I tried to get around them. "Excuse me."

"Where do you think you're going?" Verin asked, blocking my way.

"Philippe's office."

"Matthew told you to go to his tower." Verin's eyes narrowed. "He is your mate, and you're supposed to obey him like a proper vampire wife." Her accent was softly Germanic—not quite German, or Austrian, or Swiss, but something that borrowed from all three.

"What a pity for all of you that I'm a witch." I stuck my hand out to the gentleman, who was watching our conversation with thinly veiled amusement. "Diana Bishop."

"Ernst Neumann. I'm Verin's husband." Ernst's accent placed his origins squarely in the neighborhood of Berlin. "Why not let Diana go after him, *Schatz*? That way you can follow. I know how you hate to miss a good argument. I will wait in the salon for the others."

"Good idea, my love. They can hardly fault me if the witch escapes from the kitchen." Verin regarded him with open admiration and gave him a lingering kiss. Though she looked young enough to be his granddaughter, it was obvious that she and Ernst were deeply in love.

"I have them occasionally," he said with a definite twinkle in his eye. "Now, before Diana runs off and you give chase, tell me: Shall I take a knife or a gun with me in case one of your brothers goes on a rampage?"

Verin considered the matter. "I think Marthe's cleaver should be sufficient. It was enough to slow down Gerbert, and his hide is far thicker than Baldwin's—or Matthew's."

"You took a cleaver to Gerbert?" I liked Ernst more and more.

"That would be an exaggeration," Ernst said, turning slightly pink with embarrassment.

"I fear that Phoebe is trying diplomacy," Verin interrupted, turning me around and facing me in the direction of the tussle. "That never works with Baldwin. We must go."

"If Ernst is taking a knife, I'm taking the dogs." I clicked my fingers at

Hector and Fallon and set off at a fast trot, the dogs following near my heels barking and wagging as though we were playing a grand game.

The second-floor landing that led to the family apartments was crowded with concerned onlookers when we arrived: Nathaniel, a round-eyed Sophie with Margaret in her arms, Hamish in a splendid silk paisley bathrobe and only one side of his face shaved, and Sarah, who appeared to have been woken up by the fracas. Ysabeau exuded ennui as if to say this sort of thing happened all the time.

"Everybody in the salon," I said, drawing Sarah in the direction of the stairs. "Ernst will join you there."

"I don't know what set Marcus off," Hamish said, wiping the shaving cream from his chin with a towel. "Baldwin called for him, and it all seemed fine at first. Then they started shouting."

The small room that Philippe used to conduct his business was filled with vampires and testosterone as Matthew, Fernando, and Gallowglass all jostled for the best position. Baldwin sat in a Windsor chair that was tipped back so he could cross his feet on the desk. Marcus leaned on the other side of the desk, his color high. Marcus's mate—for the petite young woman standing nearby was the one I dimly remembered from our first day back, Phoebe Taylor—was trying to referee the dispute between the head of the de Clermont family and the grand master of the Knights of Lazarus.

"This strange household of witches and daemons you've gathered must disband immediately," Baldwin said, trying without success to rein in his temper. His chair dropped to the floor with a bang.

"Sept-Tours belongs to the Knights of Lazarus! I am the grand master, not you. I say what happens here!" Marcus shouted back.

"Leave it, Marcus." Matthew had his son by the elbow.

"If you don't do exactly what I say, there will *be* no Knights of Lazarus!" Baldwin stood, so that the two vampires were nose to nose.

"Stop threatening me, Baldwin," Marcus said. "You aren't my father, and you aren't my master."

"No, but I am the head of this family." Baldwin's fist met the wooden desk with a resounding crash. "You will listen to me, Marcus, or accept the consequences for your disobedience."

"Why can't the two of you sit down and talk about this reasonably?"

Phoebe said, making a rather courageous effort to separate the two vampires.

Baldwin snarled at her in warning, and Marcus lunged for his uncle's throat.

Matthew grabbed Phoebe and pulled her out of the way. She was shaking, though more from anger than fear. Fernando spun Marcus around and pinned his arms to his sides. Gallowglass clamped his hand on Baldwin's shoulder.

"Do not challenge him," Fernando said sharply, when Marcus tried to worm his way free. "Not unless you are prepared to walk out of this house and never return."

After a few long moments, Marcus nodded. Fernando released him but remained close.

"These threats are absurd," Marcus said in a slightly more measured tone. "The Knights of Lazarus and the Congregation have been in bed with each other for years. We oversee their financial affairs, not to mention help them enforce order among the vampires. Surely—"

"Surely the Congregation wouldn't risk de Clermont family retaliation? Wouldn't violate the sanctuary that has always been afforded to Sept-Tours?" Baldwin shook his head. "They already have, Marcus. The Congregation is not playing games this time. They've been looking for a reason to disband the Knights of Lazarus for years."

"They're doing so now because I brought official charges against Knox for Emily's death?" Marcus asked.

"Only in part. It was your insistence on having the covenant set aside that the Congregation couldn't stomach." Baldwin thrust a roll of parchment at Marcus. Three wax seals hung from the bottom, swaying slightly due to the rough treatment. "We considered your request—again. It's been denied. Again."

That one word—"we"—solved a long-standing mystery. Since the covenant had been signed and the Congregation had been formed in the twelfth century, there had always been a de Clermont among the three vampires at the meeting table. Until now I had not known that creature's present identity: Baldwin.

"It was bad enough that a vampire interfered in a dispute between two witches," he continued. "Demanding reparations for Emily Mather's death was foolish, Marcus. But continuing to challenge the covenant was unforgivably naïve."

"What happened?" Matthew asked. He passed Phoebe into my care, though his look suggested he was none too happy to see me.

"Marcus and the other participants in his little rebellion called for an end to the covenant in April. Marcus declared that the Bishop family was under the direct protection of the Knights of Lazarus, thereby involving the brotherhood."

Matthew looked at Marcus sharply. I didn't know whether to kiss Matthew's son for his efforts to protect my family or chide him for his optimism.

"In May . . . well, you know what happened in May," Baldwin said. "Marcus characterized Emily's death as a hostile act undertaken by members of the Congregation intent on provoking open conflict between creatures. He thought that the Congregation might want to reconsider his earlier request to abandon the covenant in exchange for a truce with the Knights of Lazarus."

"It was an entirely reasonable request." Marcus unrolled the document and scanned the lines.

"Reasonable or not, the measure went down: two in favor and seven opposed," Baldwin reported. "Never allow a vote whose outcome you can't predict in advance, Marcus. You should have discovered that unpleasant truth about democracy by now."

"It's not possible. That means only you and Nathaniel's mother voted in favor of my proposal," Marcus said, bewildered. Agatha Wilson, mother to Marcus's friend Nathaniel, was one of the three daemons who were members of the Congregation.

"Another daemon sided with Agatha," Baldwin said coldly.

"You voted against it?" Clearly Marcus had counted on his family's support. Given my few dealings with Baldwin, I could have told him this was unduly hopeful.

"Let me see that," Matthew said, plucking the parchment from Marcus's fingers. His look demanded that Baldwin explain his actions.

"I had no choice," Baldwin told Matthew. "Do you know how much damage your son has done? From now on there will be whispers about how a young upstart from an inferior branch of the de Clermont family tree tried to mount an insurrection against a thousand years of tradition."

"Inferior?" I was aghast at the insult to Ysabeau. My mother-in-law didn't look at all surprised, however. If anything, she looked even more bored, studying her perfectly manicured long nails.

"You go too far, Baldwin," Gallowglass growled. "You weren't here. The rogue members of the Congregation who came here in May and killed Emily—"

"Gerbert and Knox aren't rogue members!" Baldwin said, his voice rising again. "They belong to a two-thirds majority."

"I don't care. Telling witches, vampires, and daemons to keep to themselves no longer makes sense—if it ever did," Marcus insisted, stony-faced. "Abandoning the covenant is the right thing to do."

"Since when has that mattered?" Baldwin sounded tired.

"It says here that Peter Knox has been censured," Matthew said, looking up from the document.

"More than that, Knox was forced to resign. Gerbert and Satu argued that he was provoked to take action against Emily, but the Congregation couldn't deny he played some role in the witch's death." Baldwin reclaimed his seat behind his father's desk. Though a large man, he did not seem of sufficient stature to occupy Philippe's place.

"So Knox did kill my aunt." My anger—and my power—was rising.

"He claims all he was doing was questioning her about Matthew's whereabouts and the location of a Bodleian Library manuscript—which sounded very much like the sacred text we vampires call the Book of Life," said Baldwin. "Knox said Emily became agitated when he discovered that the Wilsons' daughter was a witch but had two daemon parents. He blames her heart attack on stress."

"Emily was healthy as a horse," I retorted.

"And what price will Knox pay for killing a member of my mate's family?" Matthew asked quietly, his hand on my shoulder.

"Knox has been stripped of his seat and banned from ever serving on the Congregation again," Baldwin said. "Marcus got his way on that at least, but I'm not sure we won't regret it in the end." He and Matthew exchanged another long look. I was missing something vital.

"Who will take his place?" Matthew asked.

"It's too soon to say. The witches insist on a Scottish replacement, on the grounds that Knox hadn't finished out his term. Janet Gowdie is obviously too old to serve again, so my money would be on one of the McNivens—Kate, perhaps. Or possibly Jenny Horne," Baldwin replied.

"The Scots produce powerful witches," Gallowglass said somberly, "and the Gowdies, the Hornes, and the McNivens are the most respected families in the north."

"They may not be as easy to handle as Knox. And one thing is clear: The witches are determined to have the Book of Life," Baldwin said.

"They've always wanted it," Matthew said.

"Not like this. Knox found a letter in Prague. He says it provides proof that you either have or once had the book of origins—or the witches' original book of spells, if you prefer his version of the tale," Baldwin explained. "I told the Congregation this was nothing more than a power-hungry wizard's fantasy, but they didn't believe me. They've ordered a full inquiry."

There were many legends about the contents of the ancient book now hidden in Oxford's Bodleian Library under the call number Ashmole Manuscript 782. The witches believed that it contained the first spells ever cast, the vampires that it told the story of how they were first made. Daemons thought the book held secrets about their kind, too. I had possessed the book too briefly to know which, if any, of these stories were true—but Matthew, Gallowglass, and I knew that whatever else the Book of Life contained paled in comparison to the genetic information bound within its covers. For the Book of Life had been fashioned from the remains of once-living creatures: The parchment was made from their skin, the inks contained their blood, the pages were held together with creature hair and binding glue extracted from their bones.

"Knox said the Book of Life was damaged by a daemon named Edward Kelley, who removed three of its pages in sixteenth-century Prague. He claims you know where those pages are, Matthew." Baldwin looked at him with open curiosity. "Is that true?"

"No," Matthew said honestly, meeting Baldwin's eyes.

Like many of Matthew's answers, this was only a partial truth. He did not know the location of two of the missing pages from the Book of Life. But one of them was safely tucked into a locked drawer of his desk.

"Thank God for that," Baldwin said, satisfied with the answer. "I swore on Philippe's soul that such a charge could not be true."

Gallowglass eyed Fernando blandly. Matthew gazed out the window. Ysabeau, who could smell a lie as easily as any witch, narrowed her eyes at me.

"And the Congregation took you at your word?" Matthew asked.

"Not entirely," Baldwin said with reluctance.

"What other assurances did you make, little viper?" Ysabeau asked lazily. "You hiss so prettily, Baldwin, but there's a sting somewhere."

"I promised the Congregation that Marcus and the Knights of Lazarus would continue to uphold the covenant." Baldwin paused. "Then the Congregation selected an impartial delegation—one witch and one vampire—and charged them with inspecting Sept-Tours from top to bottom. They will make sure there are no witches or daemons or even a scrap of paper from the Book of Life within its walls. Gerbert and Satu Järvinen will be here in one week's time."

The silence was deafening.

"How was I to know that Matthew and Diana were here?" Baldwin said. "But it's no matter. The Congregation's delegation will not find a single irregularity during their visit. That means Diana must go, too."

"What else?" Matthew demanded.

"Is abandoning our friends and families not enough?" Marcus asked. Phoebe slid an arm around his waist in a gesture of comfort.

"Your uncle always delivers the good news first, Marcus," Fernando explained. "And if the prospect of a visit with Gerbert is the good news, the bad news must be very bad."

"The Congregation wants insurance." Matthew swore. "Something that will keep the de Clermonts and the Knights of Lazarus on their best behavior."

"Not something. Someone," Baldwin said flatly.

"Who?" I asked.

"Me, of course," Ysabeau said, sounding unconcerned.

"Absolutely not!" Matthew beheld Baldwin in horror.

"I'm afraid so. I offered them Verin first, but they refused," Baldwin said. Verin appeared mildly affronted.

"The Congregation may be small-minded, but they're not complete fools," Ysabeau murmured. "No one could hold Verin hostage for more than twenty-four hours."

"The witches said it had to be someone who could force Matthew out of hiding. Verin wasn't considered sufficient inducement," Baldwin explained.

"The last time I was held against my will, you were my jailer, Baldwin," Ysabeau said in a syrupy voice. "Will you do the honors again?"

"Not this time," Baldwin said. "Knox and Järvinen wanted you held in Venice, where the Congregation could keep an eye on you, but I refused."

"Why Venice?" I knew that Baldwin had come from there, but I couldn't imagine why the Congregation would prefer it to any other location.

"Venice has been the Congregation's headquarters since the fifteenth century, when we were forced out of Constantinople," Matthew explained quickly. "Nothing happens in the city without the Congregation knowing of it. And Venice is home to scores of creatures who have long-standing relationships with the council—including Domenico's brood."

"A repulsive gathering of ingrates and sycophants," Ysabeau murmured with a delicate shudder. "I'm very glad not to be going there. Even without Domenico's clan, Venice is unbearable this time of year. So many tourists. And the mosquitoes are impossible."

The thought of what vampire blood might do to the mosquito population was deeply disturbing.

"Your comfort was not the Congregation's chief concern, Ysabeau." Baldwin gave her a forbidding look.

"Where am I to go, then?" Ysabeau asked.

"After expressing appropriate initial reluctance given his long-standing friendship with the family, Gerbert has generously agreed to keep you at his home. The Congregation could hardly refuse him," Baldwin replied. "That won't pose a problem, will it?"

Ysabeau lifted her shoulders in an expressive Gallic shrug. "Not for me."

"Gerbert cannot be trusted." Matthew turned on his brother with almost as much anger as Marcus had shown. "Christ, Baldwin. He stood by and watched while Knox worked his magic on Emily!"

"I do hope Gerbert has managed to retain his butcher," Ysabeau mused as though her son had not spoken. "Marthe will have to come with me, of course. You will see to it, Baldwin."

"You're not going," Matthew said. "I'll give myself up first."

Before I could protest, Ysabeau spoke. "No, my son. Gerbert and I have done this before, as you know. I will be back in no time—a few months at most."

"Why is this necessary at all?" Marcus said. "Once the Congregation inspects Sept-Tours and finds nothing objectionable, they should leave us alone."

"The Congregation must have a hostage to demonstrate that they are greater than the de Clermonts," Phoebe explained, showing a remarkable grasp of the situation.

"But, *Grand-mère,*" Marcus began, looking stricken, "it should be me, not you. This is my fault."

"I may be your grandmother, but I am not so old and fragile as you think," Ysabeau said with a touch of frostiness. "My blood, inferior though it might be, does not shrink from its duty."

"Surely there's another way," I protested.

"No, Diana," Ysabeau answered. "We all have our roles in this family. Baldwin will bully us. Marcus will look after the brotherhood. Matthew will look after you, and you will look after my grandchildren. As for me, I find that I am invigorated at the prospect of being held for ransom once more."

My mother-in-law's feral smile made me believe her.

Having helped Baldwin and Marcus to reach a fragile state of détente, Matthew and I returned to our rooms on the other side of the château. Matthew switched on the sound system as soon as we'd passed through the doorway, flooding the room with the intricate strains of Bach. The music made it more difficult for the other vampires in the house to overhear our conversations, so Matthew invariably had something playing in the background.

"It's a good thing we know more about Ashmole 782 than Knox does," I said quietly. "Once I retrieve the book from the Bodleian Library, the Congregation will have to stop handing out ultimatums from Venice and start dealing with us directly. Then we can hold Knox accountable for Emily's death."

Matthew studied me silently for a moment, then poured himself some wine and drank it down in one gulp. He offered me water, but I shook my head. The only thing I craved at this hour was tea. Marcus had urged me to avoid caffeine during the pregnancy, however, and herbal blends were a poor substitute.

"What do you know about the Congregation's vampire pedigrees?" I took a seat on the sofa.

"Not much," Matthew replied, pouring another glass of wine. I frowned. There was no chance of a vampire getting intoxicated by drinking wine from a bottle—the only way that one could feel the influence was to consume blood from an inebriated source—but it wasn't usual for him to drink like this.

"Does the Congregation keep witch and daemon genealogies, too?" I asked, hoping to distract him.

"I don't know. The affairs of witches and daemons never concerned me." Matthew moved across the room and stood facing the fireplace.

"Well, it doesn't matter," I said, all business. "Our top priority has to be Ashmole 782. I'll need to go to Oxford as quickly as possible."

"And what will you do then, *ma lionne*?"

"Figure out a way to recall it." I thought for a moment of the conditions my father had woven through the spell that bound the book to the library. "My father made sure that the Book of Life would come to me if I need it. Our present circumstances certainly qualify."

"So the safety of Ashmole 782 is your chief concern," Matthew said with dangerous softness.

"Of course. That and finding its missing pages," I said. "Without them the Book of Life will never reveal its secrets."

When the daemon alchemist Edward Kelley removed three of its pages in sixteenth-century Prague, he had damaged whatever magic had been used in the making of the book. For protection, the text had burrowed into the parchment, creating a magical palimpsest, and the words chased one another through the pages as if looking for the missing letters. It wasn't possible to read what remained.

"After I recover it, you might be able to figure out which creatures are bound into it, perhaps even date it, by analyzing its genetic information in your lab," I continued. Matthew's scientific work focused on issues of species origins and extinction. "When I locate the two missing pages—"

Matthew turned, his face a calm mask. "You mean when *we* recover Ashmole 782 and when *we* locate the other pages."

"Matthew, be reasonable. Nothing would anger the Congregation more than the news that we were seen together at the Bodleian."

His voice got even softer, his face calmer. "You are more than three months pregnant, Diana. Members of the Congregation have already invaded my home and killed your aunt. Peter Knox is desperate to get his hands on Ashmole 782 and knows that you have the power to do it. Somehow he knows about the Book of Life's missing pages, too. You will not be going to the Bodleian Library or anywhere else without me."

"I have to put the Book of Life back together again," I said, my voice rising.

"Then *we* will, Diana. Right now Ashmole 782 is safely in the library. Leave it there and let this business with the Congregation settle down." Matthew was relying—perhaps too much—on the idea that I was the only witch who could release the spell my father had placed on the book.

"How long will that take?"

"Perhaps until after the babies are born," Matthew said.

"That may be six more months," I said, reining in my anger. "So I'm supposed to wait and gestate. And your plan is to twiddle your thumbs and watch the calendar with me?"

"I will do whatever Baldwin commands," Matthew said, drinking the last of his wine.

"You cannot be serious!" I exclaimed. "Why do you put up with his autocratic nonsense?"

"Because a strong head of the family prevents chaos, unnecessary bloodshed, and worse," Matthew explained. "You forget that I was reborn in a very different time, Diana, when most creatures were expected to obey someone else without question—your lord, your priest, your father, your husband. Carrying out Baldwin's orders is not as difficult for me as it will be for you."

"For me? I'm not a vampire," I retorted. "I don't have to listen to him."

"You do if you're a de Clermont." Matthew gripped my elbows. "The Congregation and vampire tradition have left us with precious few options. By the middle of December, you will be a fully fledged member of Baldwin's family. I know Verin, and she would never renege on a promise made to Philippe."

"I don't need Baldwin's help," I said. "I'm a weaver and have power of my own."

"Baldwin mustn't know about that," Matthew said, holding me tighter. "Not yet. And no one can offer you or our children the security that Baldwin and the rest of the de Clermonts can."

"*You* are a de Clermont," I said, jabbing a finger into his chest. "Philippe made that perfectly clear."

"Not in the eyes of other vampires." Matthew took my hand in his. "I may be Philippe de Clermont's kin, but I am not his blood. You are. For that reason alone, I will do whatever Baldwin asks me to do."

"Even kill Knox?"

Matthew looked surprised.

"You're Baldwin's assassin. Knox trespassed on de Clermont land, which is a direct challenge to the family's honor. I assume that makes Knox your problem." I kept my tone matter-of-fact, but it took effort. I knew that Matthew had killed men before, but somehow the word "assassin" made those deaths more disturbing.

"As I said, I'll follow Baldwin's orders." Matthew's gray eyes had taken on a greenish cast and were cold and lifeless.

"I don't care what Baldwin commands. You can't go after a witch, Matthew—certainly not one who was once a member of the Congregation," I said. "It will only make matters worse."

"After what he did to Emily, Knox is already a dead man," Matthew said. He released me and strode to the window.

The threads around him flashed red and black. The fabric of the world wasn't visible to every witch, but as a weaver—a maker of spells, like my father—I could see it plainly.

I joined Matthew at the window. The sun was up now, highlighting the green hills with gold. It looked so pastoral and serene, but I knew that rocks lay below the surface, as hard and forbidding as the man I loved. I slid my arms around Matthew's waist and rested my head against him. This was how he held me when I needed to feel safe.

"You don't have to go after Knox for me," I told him, "or for Baldwin."

"No," he said softly. "I have to do it for Emily."

They'd laid Em to rest within the ruins of the ancient nearby temple consecrated to the goddess. I'd been there before with Philippe, and Matthew had insisted I see the grave shortly after our return so that I would have to face that my aunt was gone—forever. Since then I'd visited it a few times when I needed quiet and some time to think. Matthew had asked me not to go alone. Today Ysabeau was my escort, as I needed time away from my husband, as well as from Baldwin and the troubles that had soured the air at Sept-Tours.

The place was as beautiful as I remembered, with the cypress trees standing like sentinels around broken columns that were barely visible now. Today the ground was not snow-covered, as it had been in December of 1590, but lush and green—except for the rectangular brown slash that marked Em's final resting place. There were hoofprints in the soft earth and a faint depression on the top.

"A white hart has taken to sleeping on the grave," Ysabeau explained, following my glance. "They are very rare."

"A white buck appeared when Philippe and I came here before my wedding to make offerings to the goddess." I'd felt her power then, ebbing and flowing under my feet. I felt it now, but said nothing. Matthew had been adamant that no one must know about my magic.

"Philippe told me he met you," Ysabeau said. "He left a note for me in the binding of one of Godfrey's alchemical books." Through the notes Philippe and Ysabeau had shared the tiny details of everyday life that would otherwise be easily forgotten.

"How you must miss him." I swallowed down the lump that threatened to choke me. "He was extraordinary, Ysabeau."

"Yes," she said softly. "We shall never see another one such as him."

The two of us stood near the grave, silent and reflective.

"What happened this morning will change everything," Ysabeau said. "The Congregation's inquiry will make it more difficult to keep our secrets. And Matthew has more to hide than most of us."

"Like the fact that he's the family's assassin?" I asked.

"Yes," Ysabeau said. "Many vampire families would dearly like to know which member of the de Clermont clan is responsible for the deaths of their loved ones."

"When we were here with Philippe, I thought I'd uncovered most of Matthew's secrets. I know about his attempted suicide. And what he did for his father." It had been the hardest secret for my husband to reveal—that he had helped Philippe to his death.

"With vampires there is no end to them," Ysabeau said. "But secrets are unreliable allies. They allow us to believe we are safe, yet all the while they are destroying us."

I wondered if I was one of the destructive secrets lying at the heart of the de Clermont family. I drew an envelope from my pocket and handed it to Ysabeau. She saw the crabbed handwriting, and her face froze.

"Alain gave me this note. Philippe wrote it on the day he died," I explained. "I'd like you to read it. I think the message was meant for all of us."

Ysabeau's hand trembled as she unfolded the single sheet. She opened it carefully and read the few lines aloud. One of the lines struck me with renewed force: *"Do not let the ghosts of the past rob the future of its joys."*

"Oh, Philippe," she said sadly. Ysabeau handed back the note and reached for my forehead. For one unguarded moment, I saw the woman she had once been: formidable but capable of joy. She stopped, her finger withdrawing.

I caught her hand. She was colder even than her son. I gently set her icy fingers on the skin between my eyebrows, giving her silent permission to examine the place where Philippe de Clermont had marked me. The pressure of Ysabeau's fingers changed infinitesimally while she explored my forehead. When she stepped away, I could see her throat working.

"I do feel . . . something. A presence, some hint of Philippe." Ysabeau's eyes were shining.

"I wish he were here," I confessed. "He would know what to do about this mess: Baldwin, the blood vow, the Congregation, Knox, even Ashmole 782."

"My husband never *did* anything unless it was absolutely necessary," Ysabeau replied.

"But he was always doing something." I thought of how he'd orchestrated our trip to Sept-Tours in 1590, in spite of the weather and Matthew's reluctance.

"Not so. He watched. He waited. Philippe let others take the risks while he gathered their secrets and stored them up for future use. It is why he survived so long," Ysabeau said.

Ysabeau's words reminded me of the job Philippe had given me in 1590, after he made me his blood-sworn daughter: *Think—and stay alive.*

"Remember that, before you rush back to Oxford for your book," Ysabeau continued, dropping her voice to a whisper. "Remember that in the difficult days to come, as the darkest de Clermont family secrets are exposed to the light. Remember that and you will show them all that you are Philippe de Clermont's daughter in more than name."

5

After two days with Baldwin in residence at Sept-Tours, I not only understood why Matthew had built a tower onto the house, I wished he'd located it in another province—if not another country.

Baldwin made it clear that no matter who legally owned the château, Sept-Tours was his home. He presided over every meal. Alain saw him first thing each morning to receive his orders and periodically throughout the day to report on his progress. The mayor of Saint-Lucien came to call and sat in the salon with him, talking about local affairs. Baldwin examined Marthe's provisioning of the household and grudgingly acknowledged it to be outstanding. He also entered rooms without knocking, took Marcus and Matthew to task for slights real and imagined, and needled Ysabeau about everything from the salon decor to the dust in the great hall.

Nathaniel, Sophie, and Margaret were the first lucky creatures to leave the château. They said a tearful good-bye to Marcus and Phoebe and promised to be in touch once they were settled. Baldwin had urged them to go to Australia and put on a show of solidarity with Nathaniel's mother, who was not only a daemon but also a member of the Congregation. Nathaniel had protested at first, arguing that they would be fine back in North Carolina, but cooler heads—Phoebe's in particular—had prevailed.

When questioned later as to why she'd backed Baldwin in this matter, Phoebe explained that Marcus was worried about Margaret's safety and she would not permit Marcus to take on the responsibility for the baby's well-being. Therefore Nathaniel was going to do what Baldwin thought best. Phoebe's expression warned me that if I had a different opinion on the matter, I could keep it to myself.

Even after this initial wave of departures, Sept-Tours felt crowded with Baldwin, Matthew, and Marcus in it—not to mention Verin, Ysabeau, and Gallowglass. Fernando was less obtrusive, spending much of his time with Sarah or Hamish. We all found hideaways where we could retreat for some much-needed peace and quiet. So it was something of a surprise when Ysabeau burst into Matthew's study with an announcement about Marcus's present whereabouts.

"Marcus is in the Round Tower with Sarah," Ysabeau said, two spots of color brightening her usually pale complexion. "Phoebe and Hamish are with them. They've found the old family pedigrees."

I couldn't imagine why this news had Matthew flinging down his pen and leaping from his chair. When Ysabeau caught my curious look, she gave me a sad smile in return.

"Marcus is about to find out one of his father's secrets," Ysabeau explained.

That got me moving, too.

I had never set foot in the Round Tower, which stood opposite Matthew's and was separated from it by the main part of the château. As soon as we reached it, I comprehended why no one had included it on my château tour.

A round metal grate was sunk into the center of the tower floor. A familiar, damp smell of age, death, and despair emanated from the deep hole it covered.

"An oubliette," I said, temporarily frozen by the sight. Matthew heard me and clattered back down the stairs.

"Philippe built it for a prison. He seldom used it." Matthew's forehead creased with worry.

"Go," I said, waving him and the bad memories away. "We'll be right behind you."

The oubliette on the Round Tower's ground floor was a place of forgetting, but the tower's second floor was a place of remembering. It was stuffed with boxes, papers, documents, and artifacts. This must be the de Clermont family archives.

"No wonder Emily spent so much time up here," Sarah said. She was bent over a long, partially unrolled scroll on a battered worktable, Phoebe at her side. Half a dozen more scrolls lay on the table, waiting to be studied. "She was a genealogy nut."

"Hi!" Marcus waved happily from a high catwalk that circled the room and supported still more boxes and stacks. The dire revelations that Ysabeau feared apparently hadn't happened yet. "Hamish was just about to come and get you."

Marcus vaulted over the catwalk railing and landed softly next to Phoebe. With no ladder or staircase in sight, there was no way to get to that level of storage except to climb using the rough stones for handholds and no way to get down except to jump. Vampire security at its finest.

"What are you looking for?" Matthew said with just the right touch of curiosity. Marcus would never suspect that he had been tipped off.

"A way to get Baldwin off our backs, of course," Marcus said. He handed a worn notebook to Hamish. "There you go. Godfrey's notes on vampire law."

Hamish turned the pages, clearly searching for some useful piece of legal information. Godfrey had been the youngest of Philippe's three male children, known for his formidable, devious intellect. A sense of foreboding began to take root.

"And have you found it?" Matthew said, glancing at the scroll.

"Come and see." Marcus beckoned us toward the table.

"You'll love this, Diana," Sarah said, adjusting her reading glasses. "Marcus said it's a de Clermont family tree. It looks really old."

"It is," I said. The genealogy was medieval, with brightly colored likenesses of Philippe and Ysabeau standing in separate square boxes at the top of the page. Their hands were clasped across the space that divided them. Ribbons of color connected them to the roundels below. Each bubble contained a name. Some were familiar to me—Hugh, Baldwin, Godfrey, Matthew, Verin, Freyja, Stasia. Many were not.

"Twelfth century. French. In the style of the workshop at Saint-Sever," Phoebe said, confirming my sense of the age of the work.

"It all started when I complained to Gallowglass about Baldwin's interference. He told me that Philippe was nearly as bad and that when Hugh got fed up, he struck out on his own with Fernando," Marcus explained. "Gallowglass called their family a scion and said sometimes scions were the only way to keep the peace."

The look of suppressed fury on Matthew's face suggested that peace was the last thing Gallowglass was going to enjoy once his uncle found him.

"I remembered reading something about scions back when Grandfather hoped I would turn to law and take on Godfrey's old duties," Marcus said.

"Found it," Hamish said, his finger tapping against the page. "*'Any male with full-blooded children of his own can establish a scion, provided he has the approval of his sire or the head of his clan. The new scion will be considered a branch of the original family, but in all other ways the new scion's sire shall exercise his will and power freely.'* That sounds straightforward enough, but since Godfrey was involved, there must be more to it."

"Forming a scion—a distinct branch of the de Clermont family under your authority—will solve all of our problems!" Marcus said.

"Not all clan leaders welcome scions, Marcus," Matthew warned.

"Once a rebel, always a rebel," Marcus said with a shrug. "You knew that when you made me."

"And Phoebe?" Matthew's brows lifted. "Does your fiancée share your revolutionary sentiments? She might not like the idea of being cast out of Sept-Tours without a penny after all of your assets are seized by your uncle."

"What do you mean?" Marcus said, uneasy.

"Hamish can correct me if I'm wrong, but I believe the next section of Godfrey's book lays out the penalties associated with establishing a scion without your sire's permission," Matthew replied.

"You're my sire," Marcus said, his chin set in stubborn lines.

"Only in the biological sense: I provided you with my blood so you could be reborn a vampire." Matthew rammed his hands through his hair, a sign that his own frustration was mounting. "And you know how I detest the term 'sire' used in that context. I consider myself your father—not your blood donor."

"I'm asking you to be more than that," Marcus said. "Baldwin is wrong about the covenant and wrong about the Congregation. If you establish a scion, we could chart our own path, make our own decisions."

"Is there some problem with you establishing your own scion, Matt?" Hamish asked. "Now that Diana's pregnant, I would think you'd be eager to get out from under Baldwin's thumb."

"It's not as simple as you think," Matthew told him. "And Baldwin may have reservations."

"What's this, Phoebe?" Sarah's finger pointed to a rough patch in the parchment under Matthew's name. She was more interested in the genealogy than the legal complexities.

Phoebe took a closer look. "It's an erasure of some sort. There used to be another roundel there. I can almost make out the name. Beia—oh, it must be Benjamin. They've used common medieval abbreviations and substituted an *i* for a *j*."

"They scratched out the circle but forgot to get rid of the little red line that connects him to Matthew. Based on that, this Benjamin is one of Matthew's children," Sarah said.

The mention of Benjamin's name made my blood run cold. Matthew did have a son of that name. He was a terrifying creature.

Phoebe unrolled another scroll. This genealogy looked ancient, too, though not quite as old as the one we'd all been studying. She frowned.

"This looks to be from a century later." Phoebe put the parchment on the table. "There's no erasure on this one and no mention of a Benjamin either. He just disappears without a trace."

"Who's Benjamin?" asked Marcus, though I couldn't imagine why. Surely he must know the identities of Matthew's other children.

"Benjamin does not exist." Ysabeau's expression was guarded, and she had chosen her words carefully.

My brain tried to process the implications of Marcus's question and Ysabeau's odd response. If Matthew's son didn't know about Benjamin . . .

"Is that why his name is erased?" Phoebe asked. "Did someone make a mistake?"

"Yes, he was a mistake," Matthew said, his voice hollow.

"But Benjamin does exist," I said, meeting Matthew's gray-green eyes. They were shuttered and remote. "I met him in sixteenth-century Prague."

"Is he alive now?" Hamish asked.

"I don't know. I thought he was dead shortly after I made him in the twelfth century," Matthew replied. "Hundreds of years later, Philippe heard of someone who fit Benjamin's description, but he dropped out of sight again before we could be sure. There were rumors of Benjamin in the nineteenth century, but I never saw any proof."

"I don't understand," Marcus said. "Even if he's dead, Benjamin should still appear in the genealogy."

"I disavowed him. So did Philippe." Matthew closed his eyes rather than meet our curious looks. "Just as a creature can be made part of your family with a blood vow, he can be formally cast out to fend for himself without family or the protection of vampire law. You know how important a pedigree is among vampires, Marcus. Not having an acknowledged bloodline is as serious a stain among vampires as being spellbound is for witches."

It was becoming clearer to me why Baldwin might not want me included in the de Clermont family tree as one of Philippe's children.

"So Benjamin *is* dead," Hamish said. "Legally at least."

"And the dead sometimes rise up to haunt us," Ysabeau murmured, earning a dark look from her son.

"I can't imagine what Benjamin did to make you turn away from your own blood, Matthew." Marcus still sounded confused. "I was a holy terror in my early years, and you didn't abandon me."

"Benjamin was one of the German crusaders who marched with Count Emicho's army toward the Holy Land. When they were beaten in Hungary, he joined up with my brother Godfrey's forces," Matthew began. "Benjamin's mother was the daughter of a prominent merchant in the Levant, and he had learned some Hebrew and even Arabic because of the family's business operations. He was a valuable ally—at first."

"So Benjamin was Godfrey's son?" Sarah asked.

"No," Matthew replied. "He was mine. Benjamin began to trade in de Clermont family secrets. He swore he would expose the existence of creatures—not just vampires but witches and daemons—to the humans in Jerusalem. When I discovered his betrayal, I lost control. Philippe dreamed of creating a safe haven for us all in the Holy Land, a place where we could live without fear. Benjamin had the power to crush Philippe's hopes, and I had given him that power."

I knew my husband well enough to imagine the depth of his guilt and remorse.

"Why didn't you kill him?" Marcus demanded.

"Death was too quick. I wanted to punish Benjamin for being a false friend. I wanted him to suffer as we creatures suffered. I made him a vampire so that if he exposed the de Clermonts, he would have to expose himself." Matthew paused. "Then I abandoned him to fend for himself."

"Who taught him how to survive?" Marcus said, his voice hushed.

"Benjamin taught himself. That was part of his punishment." Matthew held his son's gaze. "It became part of mine, too—God's way of making me atone for my sin. Because I abandoned Benjamin, I didn't know that I had given him the same blood rage that was in my own veins. It was years before I found out what a monster Benjamin had become."

"Blood rage?" Marcus looked at his father incredulously. "That's impossible. It turns you into a cold-blooded killer, without reason or compassion. There hasn't been a case of it for nearly two millennia. You told me so yourself."

"I lied." Matthew's voice cracked at the admission.

"You can't have blood rage, Matt," Hamish said. "There was a mention of it in the family papers. Its symptoms include blind fury, the inability to reason, and an overwhelming instinct to kill. You've never shown any sign of the disease."

"I've learned to control it," Matthew said. "Most of the time."

"If the Congregation were to find out, there would be a price on your head. According to what I've read here, other creatures would have carte blanche to destroy you," Hamish observed, clearly concerned.

"Not just me." Matthew's glance flickered over my rounding abdomen. "My children, too."

Sarah's expression was stricken. "The babies . . ."

"And Marcus?" Phoebe's knuckles showed white on the edge of the table though her voice was calm.

"Marcus is only a carrier," Matthew tried to reassure her. "The symptoms manifest immediately."

Phoebe looked relieved.

Matthew looked his son squarely in the eye. "When I made you, I genuinely believed that I was cured. It had been almost a century since I'd had an episode. It was the Age of Reason. In our pride we believed that all sorts of past evils had been eradicated, from smallpox to superstition. Then you went to New Orleans."

"My own children." Marcus looked wild, and then understanding dawned. "You and Juliette Durand came to the city, and they started turning up dead. I thought Juliette killed them. But it was you. You killed them because of their blood rage."

"Your father had no choice," Ysabeau said. "The Congregation knew there was trouble in New Orleans. Philippe ordered Matthew to deal with it before the vampires found out the cause. Had Matthew refused, you all would have died."

"The other vampires on the Congregation were convinced that the old scourge of blood rage had returned," Matthew said. "They wanted to raze the city and burn it out of existence, but I argued that the madness was a result of youth and inexperience, not blood rage. I was supposed to kill them all. I was supposed to kill you, too, Marcus."

Marcus looked surprised. Ysabeau did not.

"Philippe was furious with me, but I destroyed only those who were symptomatic. I killed them quickly, without pain or fear," Matthew said, his voice dead. I hated the secrets he kept and the lies he told to cover them up, but my heart hurt for him nonetheless. "I explained away the rest of my grandchildren's excesses however I could—poverty, inebriation, greed. Then I took responsibility for what happened in New Orleans, resigned my seat on the Congregation, and swore that you would make no more children until you were older and wiser."

"You told me I was a failure—a disgrace to the family." Marcus was hoarse with suppressed emotion.

"I had to make you stop. I didn't know what else to do." Matthew confessed his sins without asking for forgiveness.

"Who else knows your secret, Matthew?" Sarah asked.

"Verin, Baldwin, Stasia, and Freyja. Fernando and Gallowglass. Miriam. Marthe. Alain." Matthew extended his fingers one by one as the names tumbled from his mouth. "So did Hugh, Godfrey, Hancock, Louisa, and Louis."

Marcus looked at his father bitterly. "I want to know everything. From the beginning."

"Matthew cannot tell you the beginning of this tale," Ysabeau said softly. "Only I can."

"No, *Maman,*" Matthew said, shaking his head. "That's not necessary."

"Of course it is," Ysabeau said. "I brought the disease into the family. I am a carrier, like Marcus."

"You?" Sarah looked stunned.

"The disease was in my sire. He believed it was a great blessing for a lamia to carry his blood, for it made you truly terrifying and nearly impossible to kill." The contempt and loathing with which Ysabeau said the word "sire" made me understand why Matthew disliked the term.

"There was constant warfare between vampires then, and any possible advantage was seized. But I was a disappointment," Ysabeau continued. "My maker's blood did not work in me as he had hoped, though the blood rage was strong in his other children. As a punishment—"

Ysabeau stopped and drew a shaky breath.

"As a punishment," she repeated slowly, "I was locked in a cage to provide my brothers and sisters with a source of entertainment, as well as a creature on whom they could practice killing. My sire did not expect me to survive."

Ysabeau touched her fingers to her lips, unable for a moment to go on.

"I lived for a very long time in that tiny, barred prison—filthy, starving, wounded inside and out, unable to die though I longed for it. But the more I fought and the longer I survived, the more interesting I became. My sire—my father—took me against my will, as did my brothers. Everything that was done to me stemmed from a morbid curiosity to see what might finally tame me. But I was fast—and smart. My sire began to think I might be useful to him after all."

"That's not the story Philippe told," Marcus said numbly. "Grandfather said he rescued you from a fortress—that your maker had kidnapped you and made you a vampire against your will because you were so beautiful he couldn't bear to let anyone else have you. Philippe said your sire made you to serve as his wife."

"All of that was the truth—just not the whole truth." Ysabeau met Marcus's eyes squarely. "Philippe did find me in a fortress and rescued me from that terrible place. But I was no beauty then, no matter what romantic stories your grandfather told later. I'd shorn my head with a broken shell that a bird had dropped on the window ledge, so that they couldn't use my hair to hold me down. I still have the scars, though they are hidden now. One of my legs was broken. An arm, too, I think," Ysabeau said vaguely. "Marthe will remember."

No wonder Ysabeau and Marthe had treated me so tenderly after La Pierre. One had been tortured, and the other had put her back together again after the ordeal. But Ysabeau's tale was not yet finished.

"When Philippe and his soldiers came, they were the answer to my prayers," Ysabeau said. "They killed my sire straightaway. Philippe's men demanded all of my sire's children be put to death so that the evil poison in our blood would not spread. One morning they came and took my brothers and sisters away. Philippe kept me behind. He would not let them touch me. Your grandfather lied and said that I had not been infected with my maker's disease—that someone else had made me and I had killed only to survive. There was no one left to dispute it."

Ysabeau looked at her grandson. "It is why Philippe forgave Matthew for not killing you, Marcus, though he had ordered him to do so. Philippe knew what it was to love someone too much to see him perish unjustly."

But Ysabeau's words did not lift the shadows from Marcus's eyes.

"We kept my secret—Philippe and Marthe and I—for centuries. I made many children before we came to France, and I thought that blood rage was a horror we had left behind. My children all lived long lives and never showed a trace of the illness. Then came Matthew . . ." Ysabeau trailed off. A drop of red formed along her lower lid. She blinked away the blood tear before it could fall.

"By the time I made Matthew, my sire was nothing more than a dark legend among vampires. He was held up as an example of what would happen to us if we gave in to our desires for blood and power. Any vampire even suspected of having blood rage was immediately put down, as was his sire and any offspring," Ysabeau said dispassionately. "But I could not kill my child, and I would not let anyone else do so either. It was not Matthew's fault that he was sick."

"It was no one's fault, *Maman,*" Matthew said. "It's a genetic disease—one that we still don't understand. Because of Philippe's initial ruthlessness, and all the family has done to hide the truth, the Congregation doesn't know that the sickness is in my veins."

"They may not know for sure," Ysabeau warned, "but some of the Congregation suspect it. There were vampires who believed that your sister's illness was not madness, as we claimed, but blood rage."

"Gerbert," I whispered.

Ysabeau nodded. "Domenico, too."

"Don't borrow trouble," Matthew said, trying to comfort her. "I've sat at the council table while the disease was discussed, and no one had the slightest inkling I was afflicted with it. So long as they believe blood rage is extinct, our secret is safe."

"I'm afraid I have bad news, then. The Congregation fears that blood rage is back," Marcus said.

"What do you mean?" Matthew asked.

"The vampire murders," Marcus explained.

I'd seen the press clippings Matthew had collected back in his Oxford laboratory last year. The mysterious killings were widespread and had taken place over a number of months. Investigators had been stymied, and the murders had captured human attention.

"The killings seemed to stop this winter, but the Congregation is still dealing with the sensational headlines," Marcus continued. "The perpetrator was never caught, so the Congregation is braced for the killings to resume at any moment. Gerbert told me so in April, when I made my initial request that the covenant be repealed."

"No wonder Baldwin is reluctant to acknowledge me as his sister," I said. "With all the attention Philippe's blood vow would bring to the de Clermont family, someone might start asking questions. You might all become murder suspects."

"The Congregation's official pedigree contains no mention of Benjamin. What Phoebe and Marcus have discovered are only family copies," Ysabeau said. "Philippe said there was no need to share Matthew's . . . indiscretion. When Benjamin was made, the Congregation's pedigrees were in Constantinople. We were in faraway Outremer, struggling to hold our territory in the Holy Land. Who would know if we left him out?"

"But surely other vampires in the Crusader colonies knew about Benjamin?" Hamish asked.

"Very few of those vampires survive. Even fewer would dare to question Philippe's official story," Matthew said. Hamish looked skeptical.

"Hamish is right to worry. When Matthew's marriage to Diana becomes common knowledge—not to mention Philippe's blood vow and the existence of the twins—some who have remained silent about my past may not be willing to do so any longer," Ysabeau said.

This time it was Sarah who repeated the name we were all thinking. "Gerbert."

Ysabeau nodded. "Someone will remember Louisa's escapades. And then another vampire may recall what happened among Marcus's children in New Orleans. Gerbert might remind the Congregation that once, long ago, Matthew showed signs of madness, though he seemed to grow out of them. The de Clermonts will be vulnerable as they have never been before."

"And one or both of the twins might have the disease," Hamish said. "A six-month-old killer is a terrifying prospect. No creature would blame the Congregation for taking action."

"Perhaps a witch's blood will somehow prevent the disease from taking root," Ysabeau said.

"Wait." Marcus's face was still as he concentrated. "When exactly was Benjamin made?"

"In the early twelfth century," Matthew replied, frowning. "After the First Crusade."

"And when did the witch in Jerusalem give birth to a vampire baby?"

"What vampire baby?" Matthew's voice echoed through the room like a gunshot.

"The one that Ysabeau told us about in January," Sarah said. "It turns out you and Diana aren't the only special creatures in the world. This has all happened before."

"I've always thought it was nothing more than a rumor spread to turn creatures against one another," Ysabeau said, her voice shaking. "But Philippe believed the tale. And now Diana has come home pregnant. . . ."

"Tell me, *Maman,*" Matthew said. "Everything."

"A vampire raped a witch in Jerusalem. She conceived his child," Ysabeau said, the words coming out in a rush. "We never knew who the vampire was. The witch refused to identify him."

Only weavers could carry a vampire's child—not ordinary witches. Goody Alsop had told me as much in London.

"When?" Matthew's tone was hushed.

Ysabeau looked thoughtful. "Just before the Congregation was formed and the covenant was signed."

"Just after I made Benjamin," Matthew said.

"Perhaps Benjamin inherited more than blood rage from you," Hamish said.

"And the child?" Matthew asked.

"Died of starvation," Ysabeau whispered. "The babe refused her mother's breast."

Matthew shot to his feet.

"Many newborns will not take their mother's milk," Ysabeau protested.

"Did the baby drink blood?" Matthew demanded.

"The mother claimed she did." Ysabeau winced when Matthew's fist struck the table. "But Philippe was not sure. By the time he held the child, she was on the brink of death and would not take any nourishment at all."

"Philippe should have told me about this when he met Diana." Matthew pointed an accusatory finger at Ysabeau. "Failing that, *you* should have told me when I first brought her home."

"And if we all did what we should, we would wake to find ourselves in paradise," Ysabeau said, her temper rising.

"Stop it. Both of you. You can't hate your father or Ysabeau for something you've done yourself, Matthew," Sarah observed quietly. "Besides, we have enough problems in the present without worrying about what happened in the past."

Sarah's words immediately lowered the tension in the room.

"What are we going to do?" Marcus asked his father.

Matthew seemed surprised by the question.

"We're a family," Marcus said, "whether the Congregation recognizes us or not, just as you and Diana are husband and wife no matter what those idiots in Venice believe."

"We'll let Baldwin have his way—for now," Matthew replied after thinking for a moment. "I'll take Sarah and Diana to Oxford. If what you say is true, and another vampire—possibly Benjamin—fathered a child on a witch, we need to know how and why some witches and some vampires can reproduce."

"I'll let Miriam know," Marcus said. "She'll be glad to have you back in the lab again. While you're there, you can try to figure out how blood rage works."

"What do you think I've been doing all these years?" Matthew asked softly.

"Your research," I said, thinking of Matthew's study of creature evolution and genetics. "You haven't been looking solely for creature origins.

You've been trying to figure out how blood rage is contracted and how to cure it."

"No matter what else Miriam and I are doing in the lab, we're always hoping to make some discovery that will lead to a cure," Matthew admitted.

"What can I do?" Hamish asked, capturing Matthew's attention.

"You'll have to leave Sept-Tours, too. I need you to study the covenant—whatever you can find out about early Congregation debates, anything that might shed light on what happened in Jerusalem between the end of the First Crusade and the date the covenant became law." Matthew looked about the Round Tower. "It's too bad you can't work here."

"I'll help with that research if you'd like," said Phoebe.

"Surely you'll go back to London," Hamish said.

"I will stay here, with Marcus," Phoebe said, her chin rising. "I'm not a witch or a daemon. There's no Congregation rule that bars me from remaining at Sept-Tours."

"These restrictions are only temporary," Matthew said. "Once the members of the Congregation satisfy themselves that everything is as it should be at Sept-Tours, Gerbert will take Ysabeau to his house in the Cantal. After that drama Baldwin will soon grow bored and return to New York. Then we can all meet back here. Hopefully by then we'll know more and can make a better plan."

Marcus nodded, though he didn't look pleased. "Of course, if you formed a scion . . ."

"Impossible," Matthew said.

"*'Impossible' n'est pas français,*" Ysabeau said, her tone as tart as vinegar. "And it certainly was not a word in your father's vocabulary."

"The only thing that sounds out of the question to me is remaining within Baldwin's clan and under his direct control," Marcus said, nodding at his grandmother.

"After all the secrets that have been exposed today, you still think my name and blood are something you should be proud to possess?" Matthew asked Marcus.

"Rather you than Baldwin," Marcus said, meeting his father's gaze.

"I don't know how you can bear to have me in your presence," Matthew said softly, turning away, "never mind forgive me."

"I haven't forgiven you," Marcus said evenly. "Find the cure for blood rage. Fight to have the covenant repealed, and refuse to support a Congregation that upholds such unjust laws. Form a scion, so that we can live without Baldwin breathing down our necks."

"And then?" Matthew said, a sardonic lift to his eyebrow.

"Then not only will I forgive you, I'll be the first to offer you my allegiance," Marcus said, "not only as my father but as my sire."

6

Most evenings at Sept-Tours, dinner was a slapdash affair. All of us ate when—and what—we liked. But tonight was our last at the château, and Baldwin had commanded the entire family's presence to give thanks that all of the other creatures were gone and to bid Sarah, Matthew, and me adieu.

I had been given the dubious honor of making the arrangements. If Baldwin expected to cow me, he was going to be disappointed. Having provided meals for the inhabitants of Sept-Tours in 1590, I could surely manage it in modern times. I'd sent out invitations to every vampire, witch, and warmblood still in residence and hoped for the best.

At the moment I was regretting my request that everyone dress formally for dinner. I looped Philippe's pearls around my neck to accompany the golden arrow that I'd taken to wearing, but they skimmed the tops of my thighs and were too long to suit trousers. I returned the pearls to the velvet-lined jewelry box that arrived from Ysabeau, along with a sparkling pair of earrings that brushed my jawline and caught the light. I stabbed the posts through the holes in my ears.

"I've never known you to fuss so much over your jewelry." Matthew came out of the bathroom and studied my reflection in the mirror as he slid a pair of gold cuff links through the buttonholes at his wrists. They were emblazoned with the New College crest, a gesture of fealty to me and to one of his many alma maters.

"Matthew! You've shaved." It had been some time since I'd seen him without his Elizabethan beard and mustache. Though Matthew's appearance would be striking no matter the era or its fashions, this was the clean-cut, elegant man I'd fallen in love with last year.

"Since we're going back to Oxford, I thought I might as well look the part of the university don," he said, his fingers moving over his smooth chin. "It's a relief, actually. Beards really do itch like the devil."

"I love having my handsome professor back, in place of my dangerous prince," I said softly.

Matthew shrugged a charcoal-colored jacket made of fine wool over his shoulders and pulled at his pearl gray cuffs, looking adorably self-conscious. His smile was shy but became more appreciative when I stood up.

"You look beautiful," he said with an admiring whistle. "With or without the pearls."

"Victoire is a miracle worker," I said. Victoire, my vampire seamstress and Alain's wife, had made me a midnight blue pair of trousers and a matching silk blouse with an open neckline that skimmed the edges of my shoulders and fell in soft pleats around my hips. The full shirt hid my swelling midriff without making me look like I was wearing a maternity smock.

"You are especially irresistible in blue," Matthew said.

"What a sweet talker you are." I smoothed his lapels and adjusted his collar. It was completely unnecessary—the jacket fit perfectly, and not a stitch was out of place—but the gestures satisfied my proprietary feelings. I lifted onto my toes to kiss him.

Matthew returned my embrace with enthusiasm, threading his fingers through the coppery strands that fell down my back. My answering sigh was soft and satisfied.

"Oh, I like that sound." Matthew deepened the kiss, and when I made a low, throaty hum, he grinned. "I like that one even more."

"After a kiss like that, a woman should be excused if she's late to dinner," I said, my hands sliding between the waistband of his trousers and his neatly tucked shirt.

"Temptress." Matthew nipped softly at my lip before pulling away.

I took a final look in the mirror. Given Matthew's recent attentions, it was a good thing Victoire hadn't curled and twisted my hair into a more elaborate arrangement, since I'd never have been able to set it to rights again. Happily, I was able to tighten the low ponytail and brush a few hairs back into place.

Finally I wove a disguising spell around me. The effect was like pulling sheer curtains over a sunny window. The spell dulled my coloring and softened my features. I had resorted to wearing it in London and had kept doing so when we returned to the present. No one would look at me twice now—except Matthew, who was scowling at the transformation.

"After we get to Oxford, I want you to stop wearing your disguising spell." Matthew crossed his arms. "I hate that thing."

"I can't go around the university shimmering."

"And I can't go around killing people, even though I have blood rage," Matthew said. "We all have our crosses to bear."

"I thought you didn't want anyone to know how much stronger my power is." At this point I was worried that even casual observers would be drawn to me because of it. In another time, when there were more weavers about, I might not have been so conspicuous.

"I still don't want Baldwin to know, or the rest of the de Clermonts. But please tell Sarah as soon as possible," he said. "You shouldn't have to hide your magic at home."

"It's annoying to weave a disguising spell in the morning and then take it off at night only to weave it again the next day. It's easier to just keep it on." That way I'd never be caught off guard by unexpected visitors or eruptions of undisciplined power.

"Our children are going to know who their mother truly is. They are not going to be brought up in the dark as you were." Matthew's tone brooked no argument.

"And is that sauce good for the gander as well as the goose?" I shot back. "Will the twins know their father has blood rage, or will you keep them in the dark like Marcus?"

"It's not the same. Your magic is a gift. Blood rage is a curse."

"It's exactly the same, and you know it." I took his hands in mine. "We've grown used to hiding what we're ashamed of, you and I. It has to end now, before the children are born. And after this latest crisis with the Congregation is resolved, we are going to sit down—as a family—and discuss the scion business." Marcus was right: If forming a scion meant we wouldn't have to obey Baldwin, it was worth considering.

"Forming a scion comes with responsibilities and obligations. You would be expected to behave like a vampire and function as my consort, helping me control the rest of the family." Matthew shook his head. "You aren't suited to that life, and I won't ask it of you."

"You're not asking," I replied. "I'm offering. And Ysabeau will teach me what I need to know."

"Ysabeau will be the first to try to dissuade you. The pressure she was under as Philippe's mate was inconceivable," Matthew said. "When my father called Ysabeau his general, only the humans laughed. Every vampire knew he was telling the gospel truth. Ysabeau forced, flattered, and cajoled us into doing Philippe's bidding. He could run the whole world because Ysabeau managed his family with an iron fist. Her decisions were absolute and her retribution swift. No one crossed her."

"That sounds challenging but not impossible," I replied mildly.

"It's a full-time job, Diana." Matthew's irritation continued to climb. "Are you ready to give up being Professor Bishop in order to be Mrs. Clairmont?"

"Maybe it's escaped your attention, but *I already have.*"

Matthew blinked.

"I haven't advised a student, stood in front of a classroom, read an academic journal, or published an article in more than a year," I continued.

"That's temporary," Matthew said sharply.

"Really?" My eyebrows shot up. "You're ready to sacrifice your fellowship at All Souls in order to be Mr. Mom? Or are we going to hire a nanny to take care of our doubtless exceptionally challenging children while I go back to work?"

Matthew's silence was telling. This issue had clearly never occurred to him. He'd simply assumed I would somehow juggle teaching and child care with no trouble at all. *Typical,* I thought, before plunging on.

"Except for a brief moment when you ran back to Oxford last year thinking you could play knight in shining armor and this moment of nerves, which I forgive you for, we've faced our troubles together. What makes you think that would change?" I demanded.

"These aren't your troubles," Matthew replied.

"When I took you on, they became my troubles. We already share responsibility for our own children—why not yours as well?"

Matthew stared at me in silence for so long that I became concerned he'd been struck dumb.

"Never again," he finally murmured with a shake of his head. "After today I will never make this mistake again."

"The word 'never' is not in our family vocabulary, Matthew." My anger with him boiled over and I dug my fingers into his shoulders. "Ysabeau says 'impossible' isn't French? Well, 'never' is not Bishop-Clairmont. Don't ever use it again. As for mistakes, how dare you—"

Matthew stole my next words with a kiss. I pounded on his shoulders until my strength—and my interest in beating him to a pulp—subsided. He pulled away with a wry smile.

"You must try to allow me to finish my thoughts. Never"—he caught my fist before it made contact with his shoulder—"never again will I make the mistake of underestimating you."

Matthew took advantage of my astonishment to kiss me more thoroughly than before.

"No wonder Philippe always looked so exhausted," he said ruefully when he was through. "It's very fatiguing pretending you're in charge when your wife actually rules the roost."

"Hmph," I said, finding his analysis of the dynamics of our relationship somewhat suspect.

"While I have your attention, let me make myself clear: I want you to tell Sarah about being a weaver and what happened in London." Matthew's tone was stern. "After that, there will be no more disguising spells at home. Agreed?"

"Agreed." I hoped he didn't notice my crossed fingers.

Alain was waiting for us at the bottom of the stairs, wearing his usual look of circumspection and a dark suit.

"Is everything ready?" I asked him.

"Of course," he murmured, handing me the final menu.

My eyes darted over it. "Perfect. The place cards are arranged? The wine was brought up and decanted? And you found the silver cups?"

Alain's mouth twitched. "All of your instructions were followed to the letter, Madame de Clermont."

"There you are. I was beginning to think you two were going to leave me to the lions." Gallowglass's efforts to dress for dinner had yielded only combed hair and something leather in place of his worn denims, though I supposed cowboy boots qualified as formalwear of a sort. He was, alas, still wearing a T-shirt. This particular garment instructed us to KEEP CALM AND HARLEY ON. It also revealed a staggering number of tattoos.

"Sorry about the shirt, Auntie. It is black," Gallowglass apologized, tracking my glances. "Matthew sent over one of his shirts, but it split down the back when I did up the buttons."

"You look very dashing." I searched the hall for signs of our other guests.

I found Corra instead, perched on the statue of a nymph like an oddly shaped hat. She'd spent the whole day flying around Sept-Tours and Saint-Lucien in exchange for promises of good behavior tomorrow while we were traveling.

"What were you two doing up there all this time?" Sarah emerged from the salon and gave Matthew a suspicious once-over. Like Gallowglass, Sarah took a limited view of formalwear. She was wearing a long lavender shirt that extended past her hips and a pair of ankle-length beige trousers. "We thought we were going to have to send up a search party."

"Diana couldn't find her shoes," Matthew said smoothly. He slid an apologetic glance toward Victoire, who was standing by with a tray of drinks. She had, of course, left my shoes next to the bed.

"That doesn't sound like Victoire." Sarah's eyes narrowed.

Corra squawked and chattered her teeth in agreement, blowing her breath through her nose so that a rain of sparks fell down onto the stone floors. Thankfully, there was no rug.

"Honestly, Diana, couldn't you have brought home something from Elizabethan England that wasn't so much trouble?" Sarah looked at Corra with a sour expression.

"Like what? A snow globe?" I asked.

"First I was subjected to witchwater falling from the tower. Now there is a dragon in my hallway. This is what comes of having witches in the family." Ysabeau appeared in a pale silk suit that perfectly matched the color of the Champagne in the glass she took from Victoire. "There are days when I cannot help thinking the Congregation is right to keep us apart."

"Drink, Madame de Clermont?" Victoire turned to me, rescuing me from the need to respond.

"Thank you," I replied. Her tray held not only wine but also glasses filled with ice cubes containing blue borage flowers and mint leaves, topped up with sparkling water.

"Hello, sister." Verin sauntered out of the salon behind Ysabeau wearing knee-high black boots and an exceedingly short, sleeveless black dress that left more than a few inches of her pearly white legs exposed, as well as the tip of the scabbard strapped to her thigh.

Wondering why Verin thought she needed to dine armed, I reached up with nervous fingers and drew the golden arrowhead from where it had fallen inside the neck of my blouse. It felt like a talisman, and it reminded me of Philippe. Ysabeau's cold eyes latched on to it.

"I thought that arrowhead was lost forever," she said quietly.

"Philippe gave it to me on my wedding day." I started to lift the chain from my neck, thinking it must belong to her.

"No. Philippe wanted you to have it, and it was his to bestow." Ysabeau gently closed my fingers around the worn metal. "You must keep this safe, my child. It is very old and not easily replaced."

"Is dinner ready?" Baldwin boomed, arriving at my side with the suddenness of an earthquake and his usual disregard for a warmblood's nervous system.

"It is," Alain whispered in my ear.

"It is," I said brightly, plastering a smile on my face.

Baldwin offered me his arm.

"Let us go in, *Matthieu*," Ysabeau murmured, taking her son by the hand.

"Diana?" Baldwin prompted, his arm still extended.

I stared up at him with loathing, ignored his proffered arm, and marched toward the door behind Matthew and Ysabeau.

"This is an order, not a request. Defy me and I will turn you and Matthew over to the Congregation without a second thought." Baldwin's voice was menacing.

For a few moments, I considered resisting and to hell with the consequences. If I did, Baldwin would win. *Think,* I reminded myself. *And stay alive.* Then I rested my hand atop his rather than taking his elbow like a modern woman. Baldwin's eyes widened slightly.

"Why so surprised, *brother*?" I demanded. "You've been positively feudal since the moment you arrived. If you're determined to play the role of king, we should do it properly."

"Very well, *sister.*" Baldwin's fist tightened under my fingers. It was a reminder of his authority, as well as his power.

Baldwin and I entered the dining room as though it were the audience chamber at Greenwich and we were the king and queen of England. Fernando's mouth twitched at the sight, and Baldwin glowered at him in response.

"Does that little cup have blood in it?" Sarah, seemingly oblivious to the tension, bent over and sniffed at Gallowglass's plate.

"I did not know we still had these," Ysabeau said, holding up one of the engraved silver beakers. She gave me a smile as Marcus settled her into the spot to his left while Matthew rounded the table and did the honors for Phoebe, who sat opposite.

"I had Alain and Marthe search for them. Philippe used them at our wedding feast." I fingered the golden arrowhead. Courtly Ernst pulled out my chair. "Please. Everybody sit."

"The table is beautifully arranged, Diana," Phoebe said appreciatively. But she wasn't looking at the crystal, the precious porcelain, or the fine silver. Instead Phoebe was taking careful note of the arrangement of creatures around the gleaming expanse of rosewood.

Mary Sidney had once told me that the order of table precedence at a banquet was no less complex than the arrangement of troops before a battle. I had observed the rules I'd learned in Elizabethan England as strictly as possible while minimizing the risk of outright war.

"Thank you, Phoebe, but it was all Marthe and Victoire's doing. They picked out the china," I said, deliberately misunderstanding her.

Verin and Fernando stared at the plates before them and exchanged a look. Marthe adored the eye-popping Bleu Celeste pattern Ysabeau had commissioned in the eighteenth century, and Victoire's first choice had been an ostentatious gilded service decorated with swans. I couldn't imagine eating off either and had selected dignified black-and-white neoclassical place settings with the de Clermont ouroboros surrounding a crowned letter *C*.

"I believe we are in danger of being civilized," Verin muttered. "And by warmbloods, too."

"Not a moment too soon," Fernando said, picking up his napkin and spreading it on his lap.

"A toast," Matthew said, raising his glass. "To lost loved ones. May their spirits be with us tonight and always."

There were murmurs of agreement and echoes of his first line as glasses were lifted. Sarah dashed a tear from her eye, and Gallowglass took her hand and gave it a gentle kiss. I choked back my own sorrow and gave Gallowglass a grateful smile.

"Another toast to the health of my sister Diana and to Marcus's fiancée—the newest members of my family." Baldwin raised his glass once more.

"Diana and Phoebe," Marcus said, joining in.

Glasses were lifted around the table, although I thought for a moment that Matthew might direct the contents of his at Baldwin. Sarah took a hesitant sip of her sparkling wine and made a face.

"Let's eat," she said, putting the glass down hastily. "Emily hated it when the food got cold, and I don't imagine Marthe will be any more forgiving."

Dinner proceeded seamlessly. There was cold soup for the warmbloods and tiny silver beakers of blood for the vampires. The trout served for the fish course had been swimming along in the nearby river without a care in the world only a few hours before. Roast chicken came next out of deference to Sarah, who couldn't abide the taste of game birds. Some at the table then had venison, though I abstained. At the end of the meal, Marthe and Alain put footed compotes draped with fruit on the table, along with bowls of nuts and platters of cheese.

"What an excellent meal," Ernst said, sitting back in his chair and patting his lean stomach.

There was a gratifying amount of agreement around the room. Despite the rocky start, we'd enjoyed a perfectly pleasant evening as a family. I relaxed into my chair.

"Since we're all here, we have some news to share," Marcus said, smiling across the table at Phoebe. "As you know, Phoebe has agreed to marry me."

"Have you set a date?" Ysabeau asked.

"Not yet. We've decided to do things the old-fashioned way, you see," Marcus replied.

All the de Clermonts in the room turned to Matthew, their faces frozen.

"I'm not sure old-fashioned is an option," Sarah commented drily, "given the fact the two of you are already sharing a room."

"Vampires have different traditions, Sarah," Phoebe explained. "Marcus asked if I would like to be with him for the rest of his life. I said yes."

"Oh," Sarah said with a puzzled frown.

"You can't mean . . ." I trailed off, my eyes on Matthew.

"I've decided to become a vampire." Phoebe's eyes shone with happiness as she looked at her once-and-forever husband. "Marcus insists that I get used to that before we marry, so yes, our engagement may be a bit longer than we'd like."

Phoebe sounded as though she were contemplating minor plastic surgery or a change of hairstyle, rather than a complete biological transformation.

"I don't want her to have any regrets," Marcus said softly, his face split into a wide grin.

"Phoebe will not become a vampire. I forbid it." Matthew's voice was quiet, but it seemed to echo in the crowded room.

"You don't get a vote. This is our decision—Phoebe's and mine," Marcus said. Then he threw down the gauntlet. "And of course Baldwin's. He is head of the family."

Baldwin tented his fingers in front of his face as though considering the question, while Matthew looked at his son in disbelief. Marcus returned his father's stare with a challenging one of his own.

"All I've ever wanted is a traditional marriage, like Grandfather and Ysabeau enjoyed," Marcus said. "When it comes to love, you're the family revolutionary, Matthew. Not me."

"Even if Phoebe were to become a vampire, it could never be traditional. Because of the blood rage, she should never take blood from your heart vein," Matthew said.

"I'm sure Grandfather took Ysabeau's blood." Marcus looked to his grandmother. "Isn't that right?"

"Do you want to take that risk, knowing what we know now about blood-borne diseases?" Matthew said. "If you truly love her, Marcus, don't change her."

Matthew's phone rang, and he reluctantly looked at the display. "It's Miriam," he said, frowning.

"She wouldn't call at this hour unless something important had come up in the lab," Marcus said.

Matthew switched on the phone's speaker so the warmbloods could hear as well as the vampires and answered the call. "Miriam?"

"No, Father. It's your son. Benjamin."

The voice on the other end of the line was both alien and familiar, as the voices in nightmares often were.

Ysabeau rose to her feet, her face the color of snow.

"Where is Miriam?" Matthew demanded.

"I don't know," Benjamin replied, his tone lazy. "Perhaps with someone named Jason. He's called a few times. Or someone named Amira. She called twice. Miriam is your bitch, Father. Perhaps if you snap your fingers, she will come running."

Marcus opened his mouth, and Baldwin hissed a warning that made his nephew's jaws snap shut.

"I'm told there was trouble at Sept-Tours. Something about a witch," Benjamin said.

Matthew refused to take the bait.

"The witch had discovered a de Clermont secret, I understand, but died before she could reveal it. Such a shame." Benjamin made a sound of mocking sympathy. "Was she anything like the one you were holding in thrall in Prague? A fascinating creature."

Matthew swung his head around, automatically checking that I was safe.

"You always said I was the black sheep of the family, but we're more alike than you want to admit," Benjamin continued. "I've even come to share your appreciation for the company of witches."

I felt the change in the air as the rage surged through Matthew's veins. My skin prickled, and a dull throbbing started in my left thumb.

"Nothing you do interests me," Matthew said coldly.

"Not even if it involves the Book of Life?" Benjamin waited for a few moments. "I know you're looking for it. Does it have some relevance to your research? Difficult subject, genetics."

"What do you want?" Matthew asked.

"Your attention." Benjamin laughed.

Matthew fell silent once more.

"You're not often at a loss for words, Matthew," Benjamin said. "Happily, it's your turn to listen. At last I've found a way to destroy you and the rest of the de Clermonts. Neither the Book of Life nor your pathetic vision of science can help you now."

"I'm going to enjoy making a liar out of you," Matthew promised.

"Oh, I don't think so." Benjamin's voice dropped, as though he were imparting a great secret. "You see, I know what the witches discovered all those years ago. Do you?"

Matthew's eyes locked on mine.

"I'll be in touch," Benjamin said. The line went dead.

"Call the lab," I said urgently, thinking only of Miriam.

Matthew's fingers raced to make the call.

"It's about time you phoned, Matthew. Exactly what am I supposed to be looking for in your DNA? Marcus said to look for reproductive markers. What is that supposed to mean?" Miriam sounded sharp, annoyed, and utterly like herself. "Your in-box is overflowing, and I'm due a vacation, by the way."

"Are you safe?" Matthew's voice was hoarse.

"Yes. Why?"

"Do you know where your phone is?" Matthew asked.

"No. I left it somewhere today. A shop, probably. I'm sure whoever has it will call me."

"He called me instead." Matthew swore. "Benjamin has your phone, Miriam."

The line went silent.

"*Your* Benjamin?" Miriam asked, horrified. "I thought he was dead."

"Alas, he's not," Fernando said with real regret.

"Fernando?" His name came out of Miriam's mouth with a whoosh of relief.

"Sim, Miriam. Tudo bem contigo?" Fernando asked gently.

"Thank God you're there. Yes, yes, I'm fine." Miriam's voice shook, but she made a valiant effort to control it. "When was the last time anyone heard from Benjamin?"

"Centuries ago," Baldwin said. "And yet Matthew has been home for only a few weeks, and Benjamin has already found a way to contact him."

"That means Benjamin has been watching and waiting for him," Miriam whispered. "Oh, God."

"Was there anything about our research on your phone, Miriam?" Matthew asked. "Stored e-mails? Data?"

"No. You know I delete my e-mails after I read them." She paused. "My address book. Benjamin has your phone numbers now."

"We'll get new ones," Matthew said briskly. "Don't go home. Stay with Amira at the Old Lodge. I don't want either of you alone. Benjamin mentioned Amira by name." Matthew hesitated. "Jason, too."

Miriam sucked in her breath. "Bertrand's son?"

"It's all right, Miriam," Matthew said, trying to be soothing. I was glad she couldn't see the expression in his eyes. "Benjamin noticed he'd called you a few times, that's all."

"Jason's picture is in my photos. Now Benjamin will be able to recognize him!" Miriam said, clearly rattled. "Jason is all that I have left of my mate, Matthew. If anything were to happen to him—"

"I'll make sure Jason is aware of the danger." Matthew looked to Gallowglass, who immediately picked up his phone.

"Jace?" Gallowglass murmured as he left the room, shutting the door softly behind him.

"Why has Benjamin reappeared now?" Miriam asked numbly.

"I don't know." Matthew looked in my direction. "He knew about Emily's death and mentioned our genetics research and the Book of Life."

I could sense some crucial piece in a larger puzzle fall into place.

"Benjamin was in Prague in 1591," I said slowly. "That must be where Benjamin heard about the Book of Life. Emperor Rudolf had it."

Matthew gave me a warning look. When he spoke, his tone had turned brisk. "Don't worry, Miriam. We'll figure out what Benjamin's after, I promise." Matthew urged Miriam to be careful and told her he'd call her once we reached Oxford. After he hung up, the silence was deafening.

Gallowglass slipped back into the room. "Jace hasn't seen anything out of the ordinary, but he promised to be on guard. So. What do we do now?"

"We?" Baldwin said, brows arched.

"Benjamin is my responsibility," Matthew said grimly.

"Yes, he is," Baldwin agreed. "It's high time you acknowledged that and dealt with the chaos you've caused, instead of hiding behind Ysabeau's skirts and indulging in these intellectual fantasies about curing blood rage and discovering the secret of life."

"You may have waited too long, Matthew," Verin added. "It would have been easy to destroy Benjamin in Jerusalem after he was first reborn, but it won't be now. Benjamin couldn't have remained hidden for so long without having children and allies around him."

"Matthew will manage somehow. He is the family assassin, isn't he?" Baldwin said mockingly.

"I'll help," Marcus said to Matthew.

"You aren't going anywhere, Marcus. You'll stay here, at my side, and welcome the Congregation's delegation. So will Gallowglass and Verin. We need a show of family solidarity." Baldwin studied Phoebe closely. She returned his look with an indignant one of her own.

"I've considered your wish to become a vampire, Phoebe," Baldwin reported when his inspection of her was complete, "and I'm prepared to support it, irrespective of Matthew's feelings. Marcus's desire for a traditional mate will demonstrate that the de Clermonts still honor the old ways. You will stay here, too."

"If Marcus wishes me to do so, I would be delighted to remain here in Ysabeau's house. Would that be all right, Ysabeau?" Phoebe used courtesy as both a weapon and a crutch, as only the British could.

"Of course," Ysabeau said, sitting down at last. She gathered her composure and smiled weakly at her grandson's fiancée. "You are always welcome, Phoebe."

"Thank you, Ysabeau," Phoebe replied, giving Baldwin a pointed look.

Baldwin turned his attention to me. "All that's left to decide is what to do with Diana."

"My wife—like my son—is my concern," said Matthew.

"You cannot return to Oxford now." Baldwin ignored his brother's interruption. "Benjamin might still be there."

"We'll go to Amsterdam," Matthew said promptly.

"Also out of the question," Baldwin said. "The house is indefensible. If you cannot ensure her safety, Matthew, Diana will stay with my daughter Miyako."

"Diana would hate Hachiōji," Gallowglass stated with conviction.

"Not to mention Miyako," Verin murmured.

"Then Matthew had better do his duty." Baldwin stood. "Quickly." Matthew's brother left the room so fast he seemed to vanish. Verin and Ernst quickly said their good-nights and followed. Once they'd gone, Ysabeau suggested we adjourn to the salon. There was an ancient stereo there and enough Brahms to muffle the lengthiest of conversations.

"What will you do, Matthew?" Ysabeau still looked shattered. "You cannot let Diana go to Japan. Miyako would eat her alive."

"We're going to the Bishop house in Madison," I said. It was hard to know who was most surprised by this revelation we were going to New York: Ysabeau, Matthew, or Sarah.

"I'm not sure that's a good idea," Matthew said cautiously.

"Em discovered something important here at Sept-Tours—something she'd rather die than reveal." I marveled at how calm I sounded.

"What makes you think so?" Matthew asked.

"Sarah said Em had been poking through things in the Round Tower, where all the de Clermont family records are kept. If she knew about the witch's baby in Jerusalem, she would have wanted to know more," I replied.

"Ysabeau told both of us about the baby," Sarah said, looking at Ysabeau for confirmation. "Then we told Marcus. I still don't see why this means we should go to Madison."

"Because whatever it was that Emily discovered drove her to summon up spirits," I said. "Sarah thinks Emily was trying to reach Mom. Maybe Mom knew something, too. If that's true, we might be able to find out more about it in Madison."

"That's a lot of thinks, mights, and maybes, Auntie," Gallowglass said with a frown.

I looked at my husband, who had not responded to my suggestion but was instead staring absently into his wineglass. "What do you think, Matthew?"

"We can go to Madison," he said. "For now."

"I'll go with you," Fernando murmured. "Keep Sarah company." She smiled at him gratefully.

"There's more going on here than meets the eye—and it involves Knox and Gerbert. Knox came to Sept-Tours because of a letter he'd found in Prague that mentioned Ashmole 782." Matthew looked somber. "It can't be a coincidence that Knox's discovery of that letter coincides with Emily's death and Benjamin's reappearance."

"You were in Prague. The Book of Life was in Prague. Benjamin was in Prague. Knox found something in Prague," Fernando said slowly. "You're right, Matthew. That's more than a coincidence. It's a pattern."

"There's something else—something we haven't told you about the Book of Life," Matthew said. "It's written on parchment made from the skins of daemons, vampires, and witches."

Marcus's eyes widened. "That means it contains genetic information."

"That's right," Matthew said. "We can't let it fall into Knox's hands—or, God forbid, Benjamin's."

"Finding the Book of Life and its missing pages still has to be our top priority," I agreed.

"Not only could it tell us about creature origins and evolution, it may help us understand blood rage," Marcus said. "Still, we might not be able to gather any useful genetic information from it."

"The Bishop house returned the page with the chemical wedding to Diana shortly after we came back," Matthew said. The house was known among the area's witches for its magical misbehavior and often took cherished items for safekeeping, only to restore them to their owners at a later date. "If we can get to a lab, we could test it."

"Unfortunately, it isn't easy to talk your way into state-of-the-art genetics laboratories." Marcus shook his head. "And Baldwin is right. You can't go to Oxford."

"Maybe Chris could find you something at Yale. He's a biochemist, too. Would his lab have the right equipment?" My understanding of laboratory practices petered out around 1715.

"I'm not analyzing a page from the Book of Life in a college laboratory," Matthew said. "I'll look for a private laboratory. There must be something I can hire out."

"Ancient DNA is fragile. We'll need more than a single page to work with if we want reliable results," Marcus warned.

"Another reason to get Ashmole 782 out of the Bodleian," I said.

"It's safe where it is, Diana," Matthew assured me.

"For the moment," I replied.

"Aren't there two more loose pages out there in the world?" Marcus said. "We could look for them first."

"Maybe I can help," Phoebe offered.

"Thanks, Phoebe." I'd seen Marcus's mate in research mode in the Round Tower. I'd be happy to have her skills at my disposal.

"And Benjamin?" Ysabeau asked. "Do you know what he meant when he said he had come to share your appreciation for witches, Matthew?"

Matthew shook his head.

My witch's sixth sense told me that finding out the answer to Ysabeau's question might well be the key to everything.

Sol in Leo

She who is born when the sun is in Leo shall be naturally subtle and witty, and desirous of learning. Whatsoever she heareth or seeth if it seems to comprise any difficulty of matter immediately will she desire to know it. The magic sciences will do her great stead. She shall be familiar to and well beloved by princes. Her first child shall be a female, and the second a male. During her life she shall sustain many troubles and perils.

—*Anonymous English Commonplace Book*, c. 1590,
Gonçalves MS 4890, f. 8v

7

I stood in Sarah's stillroom and stared through the dust on the surface of the window's wavy glass. The whole house needed a good airing. The stiff brass latch on the sash resisted my attempts at first, but the swollen frame finally gave up the fight and the window rocketed upward, quivering with indignation at the rough treatment.

"Deal with it," I said crossly, turning away and surveying the room before me. It was a familiarly strange place, this room where my aunts had spent so much of their time and I so little. Sarah left her usual disorderly ways at the threshold. In here all was neat and tidy, surfaces clear, mason jars lined up on the shelves, and wooden drawers labeled with their contents.

CONEFLOWER, FEVERFEW, MILK THISTLE, SKULLCAP, BONESET, YARROW, MOONWORT.

Though the ingredients for Sarah's craft were not arranged alphabetically, I was sure some witchy principle governed their placement, since she was always able to reach instantly for the herb or seed she needed.

Sarah had taken the Bishop grimoire with her to Sept-Tours, but now it was back where it belonged: resting on what remained of an old pulpit that Em had bought in one of Bouckville's antique shops. She and Sarah had sawed off its supporting pillar, and now the lectern sat on the old kitchen table that had come here with the first Bishops at the end of the eighteenth century. One of the table's legs was markedly shorter than the other—nobody knew why—but the unevenness of the floorboards meant that its surface was surprisingly level and solid. As a child I'd thought it was magic. As an adult I knew it was dumb luck.

Various old appliances and a battered electrical-outlet strip were strewn around Sarah's work surface. There was an avocado green slow cooker, a venerable coffeemaker, two coffee grinders, and a blender. These were the tools of the modern witch, though Sarah kept a big black cauldron by the fireplace for old times' sake. My aunts used the slow cooker for making oils and potions, the coffee grinders and blender for preparing incense and pulverizing herbs, and the coffee machine for brewing infusions. In the corner stood a shining white specimen fridge with a red cross on the door, unplugged and unused.

"Maybe Matthew can find something more high-tech for Sarah," I mused aloud. A Bunsen burner. A few alembics, perhaps. Suddenly I longed for Mary Sidney's well-equipped sixteenth-century laboratory. I looked up, half hoping to see the splendid murals of alchemical processes that decorated her walls at Baynard's Castle.

Instead dried herbs and flowers hung from twine strung up between the exposed rafters. I could identify some of them: the swollen pods of nigella, bursting with tiny seeds; prickly topped milk thistle; long-stemmed mullein crowned with the bright yellow flowers that earned them the name of witches' candles; stalks of fennel. Sarah knew every one of them by sight, touch, taste, and smell. With them she cast spells and manufactured charms. The dried plants were gray with dust, but I knew better than to disturb them. Sarah would never forgive me if she came into her stillroom and discovered nothing but stems.

The stillroom had once been the farmhouse's kitchen. One wall was occupied by a huge fireplace complete with a wide hearth and a pair of ovens. Above it was a storage loft accessible by a rickety old ladder. I'd spent many a rainy afternoon there, curled up with a book listening to the rain patter against the roof. Corra was up there now, one eye open in lazy interest.

I sighed and set the dust motes dancing. It was going to take water—and lots of elbow grease—to make this room welcoming again. And if my mother had known something that might help us find the Book of Life, this is where I would find it.

A soft chime sounded. Then another.

Goody Alsop had taught me how to discern the threads that bound the world and pull on them to weave spells that were not in any grimoire. The threads were around me all the time, and when they brushed together, they made a sort of music. I reached out and snagged a few strands on my fingers. Blue and amber—the colors that connected the past to the present and the future. I'd seen them before, but only in corners where unsuspecting creatures wouldn't be caught in time's warp and weft.

Not surprisingly, time was not behaving as it should in the Bishop house. I twisted the blue and amber threads into a knot and tried to push them back where they belonged, but they sprang back, weighting the air with memories and regret. A weaver's knot wouldn't fix what was wrong here.

My body was damp with perspiration, even though all I'd done was displace the dust and dirt from one location to another. I'd forgotten how hot Madison could be at this time of year. Picking up a bucket full of dingy water, I pushed against the stillroom door. It didn't budge.

"Move, Tabitha," I said, nudging the door another inch in hopes of dislodging the cat.

Tabitha yowled. She refused to join me in the stillroom. It was Sarah and Em's domain, and she considered me an invader.

"I'll set Corra on you," I threatened.

Tabitha shifted. One paw stretched forward past the crack, then the other as she slipped away. Sarah's cat had no wish to battle my familiar, but her dignity forbade a hurried retreat.

I pushed open the back door. Outside, a drone of insects and an unrelenting pounding filled the air. I flung the dirty water off the deck, and Tabitha shot outside to join Fernando. He was standing with a foot propped up on a stump we used to split wood, watching Matthew drive fence posts into the field.

"Is he still at it?" I asked, swinging the empty bucket. The pounding had been going on for days: first replacing loose shingles on the roof, then hammering the trellises into place in the garden, and now mending fences.

"Matthew's mind is quieter when he is working with his hands," Fernando said. "Carving stone, fighting with his sword, sailing a boat, writing a poem, doing an experiment—it doesn't really matter."

"He's thinking about Benjamin." If so, it was no wonder Matthew was seeking distractions.

Fernando's cool attention turned to me. "The more Matthew thinks about his son, the more he is taken back to a time when he did not like himself or the choices he made."

"Matthew doesn't often talk about Jerusalem. He showed me his pilgrim's badge and told me about Eleanor." It wasn't a lot, given how much time Matthew must have spent there. And such ancient memories didn't often reveal themselves to my witch's kiss.

"Ah. Fair Eleanor. Her death was another preventable mistake," Fernando said bitterly. "Matthew should never have gone to the Holy Land the first time, never mind the second. The politics and bloodshed were too much for any young vampire to handle, especially one with blood rage. But Philippe needed every weapon at his disposal if he hoped to succeed in Outremer."

Medieval history was not my area of expertise, but the Crusader colonies brought back hazy memories of bloody conflicts and the deadly siege of Jerusalem.

"Philippe dreamed of setting up a *manjasang* kingdom there, but it was not to be. For once in his life, he underestimated the avarice of the warmbloods, not to mention their religious fanaticism. Philippe should have left Matthew in Córdoba with Hugh and me, for Matthew was no help to him in Jerusalem or Acre or any of the other places his father sent him." Fernando gave the stump a savage kick, dislodging a bit of moss clinging to the old wood. "Blood rage can be an asset, it seems, when what you want is a killer."

"I don't think you liked Philippe," I said softly.

"In time I came to respect him. But like him?" Fernando shook his head. "No."

Recently, I'd experienced twinges of dislike where Philippe was concerned. He had given Matthew the job of family assassin, after all. Sometimes I looked at my husband, standing alone in the lengthening summer shadows or silhouetted against the light from the window, and saw the heaviness of that responsibility weighing on his shoulders.

Matthew fitted a fence post into the ground and looked up. "Do you need something?" he shouted.

"Nope. Just getting some water," I called back.

"Have Fernando help you." Matthew pointed to the empty bucket. He didn't approve of pregnant women doing heavy lifting.

"Of course," I said noncommittally as Matthew went back to his work.

"You have no intention of letting me carry your bucket." Fernando put a hand over his heart in mock dismay. "You wound me. How will I hold up my head in the de Clermont family if you don't allow me to put you on a pedestal as a proper knight would do?"

"If you keep Matthew from renting that steel roller he's been talking about to resurface the driveway, I'll let you wear shining armor for the rest of the summer." I gave Fernando a peck on the cheek and departed.

Feeling restless and uncomfortable in the heat, I abandoned the empty bucket in the kitchen sink and went in search of my aunt. It wasn't hard to find her. Sarah had taken to sitting in my grandmother's rocking chair in the keeping room and staring at the ebonized tree growing out of the fireplace. In coming back to Madison, Sarah was being forced to confront the loss of Emily in an entirely new way. It had left her subdued and remote.

"It's too hot to clean. I'm going into town to run errands. Do you want to come?" I asked.

"No. I'm okay here," Sarah said, rocking back and forth.

"Hannah O'Neil called again. She's invited us to her Lughnasadh potluck." Since our return we'd received a stream of phone calls from members of the Madison coven. Sarah had told the high priestess, Vivian Harrison, that she was perfectly fine and was being well taken care of by family. After that, she refused to talk to anyone.

Sarah ignored my mention of Hannah's invitation and continued to study the tree. "The ghosts are bound to come back eventually, don't you think?"

The house had been remarkably free of spectral visitors since our return. Matthew blamed Corra, but Sarah and I knew better. With Em so recently gone, the rest of the ghosts were staying away so that we didn't pester them with questions about how she was faring.

"Sure," I said, "but it's probably going to be a while."

"The house is so quiet without them. I never saw them like you did, but you could tell they were around." Sarah rocked with more energy, as if this would somehow bring the ghosts closer.

"Have you decided what to do about the Blasted Tree?" It had been waiting for Matthew and me when we returned from 1591, the gnarled black trunk taking up most of the chimney and its roots and branches extending into the room. Though it seemed devoid of life, the tree did occasionally produce strange fruit: car keys, as well as the image of the chemical wedding that had been torn from Ashmole 782. More recently it had offered up a recipe for rhubarb compote circa 1875 and a pair of false eyelashes circa 1973. Fernando and I thought the tree should be removed, the chimney repaired, and the paneling patched and painted. Sarah and Matthew were less convinced.

"I don't know," Sarah said with a sigh. "I'm getting used to it. We can always decorate it for the holidays."

"The snow is going to blow straight through those cracks come winter," I said, picking up my purse.

"What did I teach you about magical objects?" Sarah asked, and I heard a trace of her normal sharpness.

"Don't touch them until you understand them," I intoned in the voice of a six-year-old.

"Cutting down a magically produced tree certainly qualifies as 'touching,' don't you agree?" Sarah motioned Tabitha away from the hearth, where she was sitting staring at the bark. "We need milk. And eggs. And Fernando wants some kind of fancy rice. He promised to make paella."

"Milk. Eggs. Rice. Got it." I gave Sarah one last worried look. "Tell Matthew I won't be long."

The floorboards in the front hall creaked out a brief complaint as I crossed to the door. I paused, my foot glued in place. The Bishop house was not an ordinary home and had a history of making its feelings known on a variety of issues, from who had a right to occupy it to whether or not it approved of the new paint color on the shutters.

But there was no further response from the house. Like the ghosts, it was waiting.

Outside, Sarah's new car was parked by the front door. Her old Honda Civic had met with a mishap during its return from Montreal, where Matthew and I had left it. A de Clermont functionary had been tasked to drive it back to Madison, but the engine had fallen out somewhere between Bouckville and Watertown. To console Sarah, Matthew had presented her with a metallic purple Mini Cooper, complete with white racing stripes edged with black and silver and a personalized license plate that said NEW BROOM. Matthew hoped this witchy message would obviate Sarah's need to put bumper stickers all over the vehicle, but I feared it was only a matter of time before this car looked like the old one.

In case anyone thought Sarah's new car and her lack of slogans meant her paganism was wavering, Matthew purchased a witch antenna ball. She had red hair and was wearing a pointy hat and sunglasses. No matter where Sarah parked, someone stole it. He kept a box of replacements in the mudroom cupboard.

I waited until Matthew was hammering in his next fence post before jumping into Sarah's Mini. I reversed it and sped away from the house. Matthew hadn't gone so far as to forbid me from leaving the farm unaccompanied, and Sarah knew where I was going. Happy to be getting away, I opened the sunroof to catch the July breezes on my way into town.

My first stop was at the post office. Mrs. Hutchinson eyed the tight swell under the hem of my T-shirt with interest but said nothing. The only other people in the post office were two antiques dealers and Smitty, Matthew's new best friend from the hardware store.

"How is that post maul working out for Mr. Clairmont?" Smitty asked, tapping his sheaf of junk mail against the brim of his John Deere hat. "Haven't sold one of them in ages. Most people want post pounders these days."

"Matthew seems quite happy with it." *Most people aren't six-foot-three vampires,* I thought, chucking the sales flyer for the local grocery store and the offers for new tires into the recycling bin.

"You've caught a good one there," Smitty said, eyeing my wedding ring. "And he seems to be getting along with Miz Bishop, too." This last was said in a slightly awed tone.

My mouth twitched. I picked up the stack of catalogs and bills that remained and put them in my bag. "You take care, Smitty."

"Bye, Mrs. Clairmont. Tell Mr. Clairmont to let me know when he decides about that roller for the driveway."

"It's not Mrs. Clairmont. I still use—Oh, never mind," I said, catching Smitty's confused expression. I opened the door and stepped aside to let two children enter. The kids were in hot pursuit of lollipops, which Mrs. Hutchinson kept on the counter. I was almost out the door when I heard Smitty whispering to the postmistress.

"Have you met Mr. Clairmont, Annie? Nice guy. I was beginning to think Diana was going to be a spinster like Miz Bishop, if you know what I mean," Smitty said, giving Mrs. Hutchinson a meaningful wink.

I turned west onto Route 20, through green fields and past old farmsteads that had once provided food to the area's residents. Many of the properties had been subdivided and their land turned to different purposes. There were schools and offices, a granite yard, a yarn shop in a converted barn.

When I pulled in to the parking lot of the supermarket in nearby Hamilton, it was practically deserted. Even when college was in session, it was never more than half full.

I maneuvered Sarah's car into one of the plentiful open spaces near the doors, parking next to one of the vans that people bought when they had children. It had sliding doors to allow for the easy installation of car seats, lots of cup holders, and beige carpets to hide the cereal that got flung on the floor. My future life flashed before my eyes.

Sarah's zippy little car was a welcome reminder that there were other options, though Matthew would probably insist on a Panzer tank once the twins were born. I eyed the silly green witch on the antenna. As I murmured a few words, the wires in the antenna rerouted themselves through the soft foam ball and the witch's hat. No one would be stealing Sarah's mascot on my watch.

"Nice binding spell," a dry voice said from behind me. "I don't believe I know that one."

I whirled around. The woman standing there was fiftyish with shoulder-length hair that had gone prematurely silver and emerald green eyes. A low hum of power surrounded her—not showy, but solid. This was the high priestess of Madison's coven.

"Hello, Mrs. Harrison." The Harrisons were an old Hamilton family. They'd come from Connecticut, and, like the Bishops, the women kept the family name regardless of marriage. Vivian's husband, Roger, had taken the radical step of changing his last name from Barker to Harrison when the two wed, earning him a revered spot in the coven annals for his willingness to honor tradition and a fair amount of ribbing from the other husbands.

"I think you're old enough to call me Vivian, don't you?" Her eyes dropped to my abdomen. "Going shopping?"

"Uh-huh." No witch could lie to a fellow witch. Under the circumstances it was best to keep my responses brief.

"What a coincidence. So am I." Behind Vivian two shopping carts detached themselves from the stack and rolled out of their corral.

"So you're due in January?" she asked once we were inside. I fumbled and nearly dropped the paper bag of apples grown on a nearby farm.

"Only if I carry the babies to full term. I'm expecting twins."

"Twins are a handful," Vivian said ruefully. "Just ask Abby." She waved at a woman holding two cartons of eggs.

"Hi, Diana. I don't think we've met." Abby put one of the cartons in the section of the cart designed for toddlers. She buckled the eggs into place using the flimsy seat belt. "Once the babies are born, you'll have to come up with a different way to keep them from getting broken. I've got some zucchini for you in the car, so don't even think of buying any."

"Does everybody in the county know that I'm pregnant?" I asked. Not to mention what I was shopping for today.

"Only the witches," Abby said. "And anybody who talks to Smitty." A four-year-old boy in a striped shirt and wearing a Spider-Man mask sped by. "John Pratt! Stop chasing your sister!"

"Not to worry. I found Grace in the cookie aisle," said a handsome man in shorts and a gray and maroon Colgate University T-shirt. He was holding a squirming toddler whose face was smeared with chocolate and cookie crumbs. "Hi, Diana. I'm Abby's husband, Caleb Pratt. I teach here." Caleb's voice was easy, but there was a crackle of energy around him. Could he have a touch of elemental magic?

My question highlighted the fine threads that surrounded him, but Vivian distracted me before I could be certain.

"Caleb is a professor in the anthropology department," Vivian said with pride. "He and Abby have been a welcome addition to the community."

"Nice to meet you," I murmured. The whole coven must shop at the Cost Cutter on Thursday.

"Only when we need to talk business," Abby said, reading my mind with ease. So far as I could tell, she had considerably less magical talent than Vivian or Caleb, but there was obviously some power in her blood. "We expected to see Sarah today, but she's avoiding us. Is she okay?"

"Not really." I hesitated. Once the Madison coven had represented everything I wanted to deny about myself and about being a Bishop. But the witches of London had taught me that there was a price to pay for living cut off from other witches. And the simple truth was that Matthew and I couldn't manage on our own. Not after everything that had transpired at Sept-Tours.

"Something you want to say, Diana?" Vivian looked at me shrewdly.

"I think we need your help." The words slipped out easily. My astonishment must have shown, for the three witches all started to laugh.

"Good. That's what we're here for," she said, casting an approving smile at me. "What's the problem?"

"Sarah's stuck," I said bluntly. "And Matthew and I are in trouble."

"I know. My thumbs have been bothering me for days," Caleb said, bouncing Grace on his hip. "At first I thought it was just the vampires."

"It's more than that." My voice was grim. "It involves witches, too. And the Congregation. My mother may have had a premonition about it, but I don't know where to begin searching for more information."

"What does Sarah say?" Vivian asked.

"Not much. She's mourning Emily all over again. Sarah sits by the fireplace, watches the tree growing out of the hearth, and waits for the ghosts to come back."

"And your husband?" Caleb's eyebrows lifted.

"Matthew's replacing fence posts." I pushed a hand through my hair, lifting the damp strands from my neck. If it got any warmer, you'd be able to fry an egg on Sarah's car.

"A classic example of displaced aggression," Caleb said thoughtfully, "as well as a need to establish firm boundaries."

"What kind of magic is that?" I was astonished that he could know so much about Matthew from my few words.

"It's anthropology." Caleb grinned.

"Maybe we should talk about this somewhere else." Vivian smiled warmly at the growing crowd of onlookers in the produce section. The few humans in the store couldn't help noticing the gathering of four otherworldly creatures, and several were openly listening in on our conversation while pretending to judge the ripeness of cantaloupes and watermelons.

"I'll meet you back at Sarah's in twenty minutes," I said, eager to get away.

"The arborio rice is in aisle five," Caleb said helpfully, handing Grace back to Abby. "It's the closest thing to paella rice in Hamilton. If that's not good enough, you can stop by and see Maureen at the health-food store. She'll special-order some Spanish rice for you. Otherwise you'll have to drive to Syracuse."

"Thanks," I said weakly. There would be no stops at the health-food store, which was the local hangout for witches when they weren't at the Cost Cutter. I pushed my cart in the direction of aisle five. "Good idea."

"Don't forget the milk!" Abby called after me.

When I got back home, Matthew and Fernando were standing in the field, deep in conversation. I put the groceries away and found the bucket in the sink where I'd left it. My fingers automatically reached for the tap, ready to twist it open so that the water flowed.

"What the hell is wrong with me?" I muttered, pulling the empty bucket out of the sink. I carried it back to the stillroom and let the door swing shut.

This room had seen some of my greatest humiliations as a witch. Even though I understood that my past difficulties with magic had come about because I was a weaver and spellbound to boot, it was still difficult to leave the memories of failure behind.

But it was time to try.

Placing the bucket on the hearth, I felt for the tide that always flowed through me. Thanks to my father, not only was I a weaver, but my blood was full of water. Crouching next to the pail, I directed my hand into the shape of a spout and focused on my desires.

Clean. Fresh. New.

Within moments my hand looked like metal rather than flesh and water poured from my fingers, hitting the plastic with a dull thud. Once the bucket was full, my hand was just a hand again. I smiled and sat back on my heels, pleased that I'd been able to work magic in the Bishop house. All around me the air sparkled with colored threads. It no longer felt thick and heavy but bright and full of potential. A cool breeze blew through the open window. Maybe I couldn't solve all of our problems with a single knot, but if I wanted to find out what Emily and my mother knew, I had to start somewhere.

"With knot of one, the spell's begun," I whispered, snagging a silver thread and knotting it securely.

Out of the corner of my eye, I glimpsed the full skirts and a brightly embroidered bodice that belonged to my ancestor Bridget Bishop.

Welcome home, granddaughter, said her ghostly voice.

8

Matthew swung the maul and lowered it onto the head of the wooden post. It landed with a satisfying *thwack* that reverberated up his arms, across his shoulders, and down his back. He lifted the maul again.

"I don't believe you need to strike the post a third time," Fernando drawled from behind him. "It should still be standing straight and tall when the next ice age comes."

Matthew rested the business end of the maul on the ground and propped his arms on the shaft. He was not sweaty or winded. He was, however, annoyed at the interruption.

"What is it, Fernando?"

"I heard you speaking to Baldwin last night," he replied.

Matthew picked up the posthole digger without responding.

"I take it he told you to stay here and not to cause any trouble—for now," Fernando continued.

Matthew thrust the two sharp blades into the earth. They descended quite a bit farther into the soil than they would have if a human had been wielding the tool. He gave the implement a twist, withdrew it from the ground, and picked up a wooden post.

"Come, *Mateus.* Fixing Sarah's fence is hardly the most useful way to spend your time."

"The most *useful* way to spend my time would be to find Benjamin and rid the family of the monster once and for all." Matthew held the seven-foot fence post in one hand as easily as though it weighed no more than a pencil and drove the tip into the soft earth. "Instead I'm waiting for Baldwin to give me permission to do what I should have done long ago."

"Hmm." Fernando studied the fence post. "Why don't you go, then? To hell with Baldwin and his dictatorial ways. See to Benjamin. It will be no trouble for me to look after Diana as well as Sarah."

Matthew turned a scathing glance on Fernando. "I am not going to leave my pregnant mate in the middle of nowhere—not even with you."

"So your plan is to stay here, fixing whatever you can find that is broken, until the happy moment when Baldwin rings to authorize you to kill your own child. Then you will drag Diana along to whatever godforsaken hole Benjamin occupies and eviscerate him in front of your wife?" Fernando flung his hands up in disgust. "Don't be absurd."

"Baldwin won't tolerate anything but obedience, Fernando. He made that very clear at Sept-Tours."

Baldwin had dragged the de Clermont men and Fernando out into the night and explained in brutal and detailed terms just what would befall each and every one of them if he detected a whisper of protest or a glimmer of insurrection. Afterward even Gallowglass had looked shaken.

"There was a time when you enjoyed outflanking Baldwin. But since your father died, you have let your brother treat you abominably." Fernando snagged the post maul before Matthew could get his hands on it.

"I couldn't lose Sept-Tours. *Maman* wouldn't have survived it—not after Philippe's death." Matthew's mother had been far from invincible then. She had been as fragile as blown glass. "The château might technically belong to the Knights of Lazarus, but everyone knows that the brotherhood belongs to the de Clermonts. If Baldwin wanted to challenge Philippe's will and claim Sept-Tours, he would have succeeded, and Ysabeau would have been out in the cold."

"Ysabeau seems to have recovered from Philippe's death. What is your excuse now?"

"Now my wife is a de Clermont." Matthew gave Fernando a level look.

"I see." Fernando snorted. "Marriage has turned your mind to mush and bent your spine like a willow twig, my friend."

"I won't do anything to jeopardize her position. She might not yet understand what it means, but you and I both know how important it is to be counted among Philippe's children," Matthew said. "The de Clermont name will protect her from all sorts of threats."

"And for this tenuous toehold in the family, you would sell your soul to that devil?" Fernando was genuinely surprised.

"For Diana's sake?" Matthew turned away. "I would do anything. Pay any price."

"Your love for her borders on obsession." Fernando stood his ground when Matthew whirled back around, his eyes black. "It is not healthy, *Mateus.* Not for you. Nor for her."

"So Sarah's been filling your ears with my shortcomings, has she? Diana's aunts never really did approve of me." Matthew glared at the house. It may have been a trick of the light, but the house appeared to be shaking on its foundations with laughter.

"Now that I see you with their niece, I understand why," Fernando said mildly. "The blood rage has always made you prone to excessive behavior. Being mated has made it worse."

"I have thirty years with her, Fernando. Forty or fifty, if I'm lucky. How many centuries did you share with Hugh?"

"Six," Fernando bit out.

"And was that enough?" Matthew exploded. "Before you judge me for being consumed with my mate's well-being, put yourself in my shoes and imagine how you would have behaved had you known that your time with Hugh would be so brief."

"Loss is loss, Matthew, and a vampire's soul is as fragile as that of any warmblood. Six hundred years or sixty or six—it doesn't matter. When your mate dies, a part of your soul dies with him. Or her," Fernando said gently. "And you will have your children—Marcus as well as the twins—to comfort you."

"How will any of that matter if Diana is not here to share it?" Matthew looked desperate.

"No wonder you were so hard on Marcus and Phoebe," Fernando said with dawning understanding. "Turning Diana into a vampire is your greatest desire—"

"Never," Matthew interrupted, his voice savage.

"And your greatest horror," Fernando finished.

"If she became a vampire, she would no longer be my Diana," Matthew said. "She would be something—someone—else."

"You might love her just the same," Fernando said.

"How could I, when I love Diana for all that she is?" Matthew replied.

Fernando had no answer for this. He could not imagine Hugh as anything but a vampire. It had defined him, given him the unique combination of fierce courage and dreamy idealism that had made Fernando fall in love with him.

"Your children will change Diana. What will happen to your love when they are born?"

"Nothing," Matthew said roughly, snatching at the maul. Fernando tossed the heavy tool easily from one hand to the other to keep it out of his reach.

"That is the blood rage talking. I can hear it in your voice." The maul went sailing through the air at ninety miles an hour and landed in the O'Neils' yard. Fernando grabbed Matthew by the throat. "I am frightened for your children. It pains me to say it—to even think it—but I have seen you kill someone you loved."

"Diana. Is. Not. Eleanor." Matthew ground out the words one at a time.

"No. What you felt for Eleanor is nothing compared to what you feel for Diana. Yet all it took was a casual touch from Baldwin, a mere suggestion that Eleanor might agree with him rather than you, and you were ready to tear them both apart." Fernando searched Matthew's face. "What will you do if Diana sees to the babies' needs before yours?"

"I'm in control now, Fernando."

"Blood rage heightens all the instincts a vampire has until they are as keen as honed steel. Your possessiveness is already dangerous. How can you be sure you will keep it in check?"

"Christ, Fernando. I can't be sure. Is that what you want me to say?" Matthew drove his fingers through his hair.

"I want you to listen to Marcus instead of building fences and seeing to the gutters," Fernando replied.

"Not you, too. It's madness to even think of branching out on my own with Benjamin on the loose and the Congregation up in arms," Matthew snapped.

"I was not talking about forming a scion." Fernando thought Marcus's idea was excellent, but he knew when to keep his own counsel.

"What, then?" Matthew said with a frown.

"Your work. If you were to focus on the blood rage, you might be able to stop whatever plans Benjamin is setting into motion without striking a single blow." Fernando let this sink in before he continued. "Even Gallowglass thinks you should be in a laboratory analyzing that page you have from the Book of Life, and he doesn't understand the first thing about science."

"None of the local colleges have sufficient laboratories for my needs," Matthew said. "I haven't only been buying new downspouts, you see. I've been making inquiries, too. And you're right. Gallowglass has no idea what my research entails."

Nor did Fernando. Not really. But he knew who did.

"Surely Miriam has been doing *something* while you were gone. She's hardly the type to sit around idly. Can you not go over her most recent findings?" Fernando asked.

"I told her they could wait," Matthew said gruffly.

"Even previously gathered data might prove useful, now that you have Diana and the twins to consider." Fernando would use anything—even Diana—to bait this hook if it would get Matthew acting instead of simply reacting. "Perhaps it's not only the blood rage that explains her pregnancy. Perhaps she and the witch in Jerusalem both inherited an ability to conceive a vampire's child."

"It's possible," Matthew said slowly. Then his attention was caught by Sarah's purple Mini Cooper skidding and slipping along on the loose gravel. Matthew's shoulders lowered, and some of the darkness disappeared from his eyes. "I really have to resurface the driveway," he said absently, watching the car's progress.

Diana got out of the car and waved in their direction. Matthew smiled and waved back.

"You have to start thinking again," Fernando retorted.

Matthew's phone rang. "What is it, Miriam?"

"I've been thinking." Miriam never bothered with pleasantries. Not even the recent scare with Benjamin had changed that.

"What a coincidence," Matthew said drily. "Fernando's just been urging me to do the same."

"Do you remember when someone broke in to Diana's rooms last October? We feared at the time that whoever it was might be looking for genetic information about her—hair, nail clippings, bits of skin."

"Of course I remember," Matthew said, wiping his hand over his face.

"You were sure it was Knox and the American witch Gillian Chamberlain. What if *Benjamin* was involved?" Miriam paused. "I have a really bad feeling about all this, Matthew—like I've woken up from a pleasant dream only to discover that a spider has snared me in his web."

"He wasn't in her rooms. I would have caught the scent." Matthew sounded sure, but there was a trace of worry in his voice as well.

"Benjamin is too smart to have gone himself. He would have sent a lackey—or one of his children. As his sire, you can sniff him out, but you know that the scent signature is practically undetectable in grandchildren." Miriam sighed with exasperation. "Benjamin mentioned witches and your genetics research. You don't believe in coincidences, remember?"

Matthew did remember saying something like that once—long before he'd met Diana. He made an involuntary check on the house. It was a combination of instinct and reflex now, this need to protect his wife. Matthew pushed away Fernando's earlier warning about his obsessiveness.

"Have you had a chance to delve further into Diana's DNA?" He had taken the blood samples and cheek swabs last year.

"What do you think I've been doing all this while? Crocheting blankets in case you came home with babies and weeping about your absence? And yes, I know as much about the twins as the rest—which is to say not nearly enough."

Matthew shook his head ruefully. "I've missed you, Miriam."

"Don't. Because the next time I see you, I'm going to bite you so hard you'll have the scar for years." Miriam's voice shook. "You should have killed Benjamin long ago. You knew he was a monster."

"Even monsters can change," Matthew said softly. "Look at me."

"You were never a monster," she said. "That was a lie you told to keep the rest of us away."

Matthew disagreed, but he let the matter drop. "So what did you learn about Diana?"

"I learned that what we think we know about your wife is minuscule compared to what we don't know. Her nuclear DNA is like a labyrinth: If you go wandering in it, you're likely to get lost," Miriam said, referring to Diana's unique genetic fingerprint. "And her mtDNA is equally perplexing."

"Let's put aside the mtDNA for the moment. All that will tell us is what Diana has in common with her female ancestors." Matthew would get back to Diana's mitochondrial DNA later. "I want to understand what makes her unique."

"What's worrying you?" Miriam knew Matthew well enough to hear what he wasn't saying.

"Her ability to conceive my children, for a start." Matthew drew a deep breath. "And Diana picked up a sort of dragon while she was in the sixteenth century. Corra is a firedrake. And her familiar."

"Familiar? I thought that business about witches and familiars was a human myth. No wonder her transmogrification gene is so strange," Miriam muttered. "A firedrake. Just what we need. Wait a minute. Is it on a leash or something? Can we get a blood sample?"

"Perhaps," Matthew said dubiously. "I'm not sure Corra would cooperate for a cheek swab, though."

"I wonder if she and Diana are genetically related. . . ." Miriam trailed off, intrigued by the possibilities.

"Have you found anything in Diana's witch chromosome that leads you to believe it controls fertility?" Matthew asked.

"That's an entirely new request, and you know that scientists usually don't find anything unless they're looking for it," Miriam said tartly. "Give me a few days, and I'll see what I can uncover. There are so many unidentified genes in Diana's witch chromosome that some days I wonder if she *is* a witch." Miriam laughed.

Matthew remained silent. He couldn't very well tell her that Diana was a weaver when not even Sarah knew.

"You're keeping something from me," Miriam said, a note of accusation in her voice.

"Send me a report on whatever else you've managed to identify," he said. "We'll discuss it more in a few days. Take a look at my DNA profile, too. Focus on whatever genes we haven't identified yet, especially if they're near the blood-rage gene. See if anything strikes you."

"Ooo-kay," Miriam said deliberately. "You have a secure Internet connection, right?"

"As secure as Baldwin's money can buy."

"Pretty damn secure, then," she said under her breath. "Talk to you later. And, Matthew?"

"Yes?" he said, frowning.

"I'm still going to bite you for not killing Benjamin when you had a chance."

"You'll have to catch me first."

"That's easy. All I have to do is catch Diana. You'll walk right into my arms then," she said just before she disconnected.

"Miriam's back in top form," Fernando said.

"She always was able to recover from a crisis with amazing speed," Matthew said fondly. "Do you remember when Bertrand—"

An unfamiliar car turned in to the driveway.

Matthew sprinted toward it, Fernando at his heels.

The gray-haired woman driving a dented navy Volvo didn't seem a bit surprised to be confronted by two vampires, one of them exceptionally tall. Instead she rolled down the window.

"You must be Matthew," the woman said. "I'm Vivian Harrison. Diana asked me to stop by and see Sarah. She's worried about the tree in the keeping room."

"What is that scent?" Fernando asked Matthew.

"Bergamot," Matthew replied, his eyes narrowing.

"It's a common scent! Besides, I'm an accountant," Vivian said indignantly, "not just the coven's high priestess. What do you expect me to smell of—fire and brimstone?"

"Vivian?" Sarah stood at the front door and squinted into the sunlight. "Is someone sick?"

Vivian climbed out of the car. "Nobody's sick. I ran into Diana at the store."

"I see you've met Matthew and Fernando," Sarah said.

"I have." Vivian looked the two of them over. "Goddess preserve us from handsome vampires." She started walking toward the house. "Diana said you've got a bit of trouble."

"Nothing we can't handle," Matthew said with a scowl.

"He always says that. Sometimes he's even right." Sarah beckoned to Vivian. "Come inside. Diana's got iced tea made."

"Everything is fine, Ms. Harrison," Matthew said, stalking alongside the witch.

Diana appeared behind Sarah. She looked at Matthew in fury, her hands on her hips.

"Fine?" she demanded. "Peter Knox murdered Em. There's a tree growing out of the fireplace. I'm pregnant with your children. We've been evicted from Sept-Tours. And the Congregation could show up at any minute and force us to separate. Does that sound fine to you, Vivian?"

"The Peter Knox who had a crush on Diana's mother? Isn't he a member of the Congregation?" Vivian asked.

"Not anymore," Matthew replied.

Vivian shook her finger at Sarah. "You told me Em had a heart attack."

"She did," Sarah said defensively. Vivian's lips curled in disgust. "It's the truth! Matthew's son said that was the cause of death."

"You're awfully good at telling the truth and lying at the same time, Sarah." Vivian's tone softened. "Emily was a big part of our community. So are you. We need to know what really happened in France."

"Knowing whether it's Knox's fault or not won't change anything. Emily will still be dead." Sarah's eyes brimmed with tears. She dashed them away. "And I don't want the coven involved. It's too dangerous."

"We're your friends. We're already involved." Vivian rubbed her hands together. "Sunday is Lughnasadh."

"Lughnasadh?" Sarah said suspiciously. "The Madison coven hasn't celebrated Lughnasadh for decades."

"We don't normally have a big celebration, it's true, but this year Hannah O'Neil is pulling out all the stops to welcome you back home. And to give us all a chance to say good-bye to Em."

"But Matthew—Fernando." Sarah dropped her voice. "The covenant."

Vivian shouted with laughter. "Diana's pregnant. It's a little late to worry about breaking the rules. Besides, the coven knows all about Matthew. Fernando, too."

"They do?" Sarah said, startled.

"They do," Diana said firmly. "Smitty has bonded with Matthew over hand tools, and you know what a gossip he can be." The indulgent smile she gave Matthew took some of the sting out of her words.

"We're known as a progressive coven. If we're lucky, maybe Diana will trust us with whatever is wrapped up inside her disguising spell. See you Sunday." With a smile at Matthew and a wave to Fernando, Vivian got into her car and pulled away.

"Vivian Harrison is a bulldozer," Sarah grumbled.

"Observant, too," Matthew said thoughtfully.

"She is." Sarah studied Diana. "Vivian's right. You are wearing a disguising spell—a good one. Who cast it for you?"

"Nobody. I—" Unable to lie, and still unwilling to tell her aunt the truth, Diana snapped her mouth shut. Matthew scowled.

"Fine. Don't tell me." Sarah stomped back to the keeping room. "And I'm not going to that potluck. The whole coven is on some vegetarian kick. There will be nothing to eat but zucchini and Hannah's famously inedible Key lime pudding pie."

"The widow is feeling more herself," Fernando whispered, giving Diana a thumbs-up as he followed Sarah into the house. "Returning to Madison was a good idea."

"You promised you'd tell Sarah you're a weaver once we were settled here at the Bishop house," Matthew said when he and Diana were alone. "Why haven't you?"

"I'm not the only one keeping secrets. And I'm not just talking about the blood-vow business or even the fact that vampires kill other vampires with blood rage. You should have told me that Hugh and Fernando were a couple. And you definitely should have told me that Philippe had been using your illness as a weapon all these years."

"Does Sarah know that Corra is your familiar, not a souvenir? And what about meeting your father in London?" Matthew crossed his arms.

"It wasn't the right moment," Diana said with a sniff.

"Ah, yes, the elusive right moment." Matthew snorted. "It never comes, Diana. Sometimes we just have to throw caution to the wind and trust the people we love."

"I do trust Sarah." Diana bit her lip. She didn't have to finish. Matthew knew that the real problem was she didn't trust herself or her magic. Not completely.

"Take a walk with me," he said, holding out his hand. "We can talk about this later."

"It's too hot," Diana protested, though she still put her hand in his.

"I'll cool you off," he promised with a smile.

Diana looked at him with interest. Matthew's smile broadened.

His wife—his heart, his mate, his life—stepped down off the porch and into his arms. Diana's eyes were the blue and gold of a summer sky, and Matthew wanted nothing more than to fall headlong into their bright depths, not to lose himself but to be found.

No wonder we don't celebrate Lughnasadh," Sarah muttered, pushing open the front door. "All those awful songs about the end of summer and the coming of winter—not to mention Mary Bassett's tambourine accompaniment."

"The music wasn't *that* bad," I protested. Matthew's grimace indicated that Sarah had a right to complain.

"Do you have more of that temperamental wine, Fernando?" Sarah flicked on the hall lights. "I need a drink. My head is pounding."

"Tempranillo." Fernando tossed the picnic blankets on the hall bench. "Tempranillo. Remember: It's Spanish."

"French, Spanish, whatever—I need some," she said, sounding desperate.

I stood aside so Abby and Caleb could get in the door. John was conked out in Caleb's arms, but Grace was wide awake. She squirmed to get down.

"Let her go, Abby. She can't hurt anything," Sarah said, heading for the kitchen.

Abby put Grace down, and the child toddled straight toward the stairs. Matthew laughed.

"She has the most amazing instincts when it comes to trouble. No stairs, Grace." Abby swooped in and swung Grace up in the air before depositing her back on the floor and pointing her in the direction of the family room.

"Why don't you put John in the keeping room?" I suggested. John had abandoned his Spider-Man mask and was wearing a T-shirt with the superhero on it instead.

"Thanks, Diana." Caleb whistled. "I see what you mean about the tree, Matthew. So it just sprang up out of the hearth?"

"We think some fire and a bit of blood might have been involved," Matthew explained, shaking out one of the blankets and following Caleb. The two had been chatting all evening about everything from academic politics to Matthew's hospital work at the John Radcliffe to the fate of the polar bears. Matthew arranged a blanket on the floor for John, while Caleb ran his fingers over the bark on the Blasted Tree.

This is what Matthew needs, I realized. *Home. Family. Pack.* Without other people to take care of, he retreated to that dark place where his past deeds haunted him. And he was especially prone to brooding now, given Benjamin's recent reappearance.

I needed this, too. Living in the sixteenth century, in households rather than simply in houses, I had grown accustomed to being surrounded by other people. My fear of being discovered had receded, and in its place had grown a wish to belong.

As a result I'd found the coven potluck surprisingly enjoyable. The Madison witches had occupied an intimidating place in my imagination, but tonight the assembled witches were pleasant and, except for my high-school nemeses Cassie and Lydia, welcoming. They were also surprisingly powerless when compared to the witches I'd known in London. One or two of them had some elemental magic at their disposal, but none were as formidable as the firewitches or waterwitches of the past. And the Madison witches who *could* work the craft couldn't hold a candle to Sarah.

"Wine, Abby?" Fernando offered her a glass.

"Sure." Abby giggled. "I'm surprised you made it out of the potluck alive, Fernando. I was positive that someone was going to work a bit of love magic on you."

"Fernando shouldn't have encouraged them," I said with mock severity. "There was no need to both bow *and* kiss Betty Eastey's hand."

"Her poor husband is going to hear nothing but 'Fernando this' and 'Fernando that' for days," Abby said with another giggle.

"The ladies will be very disappointed when they discover they are trying to saddle the wrong horse," Fernando replied. "Your friends told me the most charming stories, Diana. Did you know that vampires are really quite cuddly, once we find our true love?"

"Matthew hasn't exactly been transformed into a teddy bear," I said drily.

"Ah, but you didn't know him before." Fernando's smile was wicked.

"Fernando!" Sarah called from the kitchen. "Come help me light this stupid fire. I can't get it to catch."

Why she felt it was necessary to light a fire in this kind of heat was beyond me, but Sarah said Em had always lit a fire on Lughnasadh, and that was that.

"Duty calls," Fernando murmured, giving Abby a little bow. Like Betty Eastey, she blushed.

"We'll go with you." Caleb took Grace by the hand. "Come on, sprout."

Matthew watched the Pratts troop off to the kitchen, a smile playing at the corner of his mouth.

"That will be us soon," I said, slipping my arms around him.

"That's just what I was thinking." Matthew kissed me. "Are you ready to tell your aunt about being a weaver?"

"As soon as the Pratts leave." Every morning I promised to tell Sarah about all that I'd learned from the London coven, but with every passing day it got harder to share my news.

"You don't have to tell her everything all at once," Matthew said, running his hands over my shoulders. "Just tell her you're a weaver so you can stop wearing this shroud."

We joined the others in the kitchen. Sarah's fire was now crackling merrily in the stillroom, adding to the warmth of the summer evening. We sat around the table, comparing notes on the party and gossiping about the latest coven happenings. Then the talk turned to baseball. Caleb was a Red Sox fan, just like my dad.

"What is it about Harvard men and the Red Sox?" I got up to make some tea.

A flicker of white caught my eye. I smiled and put the kettle on the stove, thinking it was one of the house's missing ghosts. Sarah would be so happy if one of them were ready to apparate again.

That was no ghost.

Grace tottered in front of the stillroom fireplace on unsteady, two-year-old legs. "Pretty," she cooed.

"Grace!"

Startled by my cry, Grace turned her head. That was enough to upset her balance, and she tipped toward the fire.

I'd never reach her in time—not with a kitchen island and twenty-five feet between us. I reached into the pocket of my shorts and pulled out my weaver's cords. They snaked through my fingers and twisted around my wrists just as Grace's scream pierced the air.

But there was no time for spells, either. Instead I acted on pure instinct and rooted my feet into the floor. Water was all around us, trickling through deep arteries that crisscrossed the Bishop land. It was within me, too, and in an effort to focus its raw, elemental power I isolated the filaments of blue, green, and silver that highlighted everything in the kitchen and the still-room that was tied to water.

In a quicksilver flash, I directed a bolt of water at the fireplace. A spout of steam erupted, coals hissed, and Grace hit the slurry of ash and water on the hearth with a thud.

"Grace!" Abby ran past me, followed by Caleb.

Matthew drew me into his arms. I was soaked to the skin and shivering. He rubbed my back, trying to restore some warmth.

"Thank God you have so much power over water, Diana," Abby said, holding a tearful Grace.

"Is she okay?" I asked. "She reached out to steady herself, but she was awfully close to the flames."

"Her hand is a little pink," Caleb said, examining her small fingers. "What do you think, Matthew?"

Matthew took Grace's hand.

"Pretty," she said, her lower lip trembling.

"I know," Matthew murmured. "Fire is very pretty. Very hot, too." He blew on her fingers, and she laughed. Fernando handed him a damp cloth and an ice cube.

"'Gain," she commanded, thrusting her hand in Matthew's face.

"Nothing seems to be damaged, and there are no blisters," Matthew said after obeying the tiny tyrant's command to blow on her fingers once more. He wrapped the cloth carefully around her hand and held the ice cube to it. "She should be fine."

"I didn't know you could wield waterbolts." Sarah looked at me sharply. "Are you okay? You look different—shiny."

"I'm fine." I pulled away from Matthew, trying to draw the tattered remains of my disguising spell around me. I searched the floor surrounding the kitchen island, looking for my dropped weaver's cords in case some surreptitious patching was required.

"What did you get all over yourself?" Sarah grabbed my hand and turned it palm up. What I saw made me gasp.

Each finger bore a strip of color down its center. My pinkie was streaked with brown, my ring finger yellow. A vivid blue marked my middle finger, and red blazed down my index finger in an imperious slash. The colored lines joined together on my palm, continuing on to the fleshy mound at its base in a braided, multicolored rope. There the rope met up with a strand of green that wandered down from my thumb—ironic, given the fate of most of my houseplants. The five-colored twist traveled the short distance to my wrist and formed a knot with five crossings—the pentacle.

"My weaver's cords. They're . . . inside me." I looked up at Matthew in disbelief.

But most weavers used nine cords, not five. I turned over my left palm and discovered the missing strands: black on my thumb, white on my pinkie, gold on my ring finger, and silver on my middle finger. The pointer finger bore no color at all. And the colors that twisted down to my left wrist created an ouroboros, a circle with no beginning and no end that looked like a snake with its tail in its mouth. It was the de Clermont family emblem.

"Is Diana . . . shimmering?" Abby asked.

Still staring at my hands, I flexed my fingers. An explosion of colored threads illuminated the air.

"What was that?" Sarah's eyes were round.

"Threads. They bind the worlds and govern magic," I explained.

Corra chose that moment to return from her hunting. She swooped down the stillroom chimney and landed in the damp pile of wood. Coughing and wheezing, she lurched to her feet.

"Is that . . . a dragon?" Caleb asked.

"No, it's a souvenir," Sarah said. "Diana brought it back with her from Elizabethan England."

"Corra's not a souvenir. She's my familiar," I whispered.

Sarah snorted. "Witches don't have familiars."

"Weavers do," I said. Matthew's hand rested on my lower back, lending quiet support. "You'd better call Vivian. I need to tell you something."

"So the dragon—" Vivian began, her hands wrapped tight around a steaming mug of coffee.

"Firedrake," I interrupted.

"So it—"

"She. Corra is a female."

"—is your familiar?" Vivian finished.

"Yes. Corra appeared when I wove my first spell in London."

"Are all familiars dragons . . . er, firedrakes?" Abby shifted her legs on the family-room couch. We were all settled around the television, except for John, who had slept peacefully through the excitement.

"No. My teacher, Goody Alsop, had a fetch—a shadow self. She was inclined toward air, you see, and a weaver's familiar takes shape according to a witch's elemental predisposition." It was probably the longest utterance I'd ever made on the subject of magic. It was also largely unintelligible to any of the witches present, who didn't know a thing about weavers.

"I have an affinity for water as well as fire," I explained, plunging on. "Unlike dragons, firedrakes are as comfortable in the sea as in the flames."

"They're also able to fly," Vivian said. "Firedrakes actually represent a triplicity of elemental power."

Sarah looked at her in astonishment.

Vivian shrugged. "I have a master's degree in medieval literature. Wyverns—or firedrakes, if you prefer—were once common in European mythology and legends."

"But you . . . you're my accountant," Sarah sputtered.

"Do you have any idea how many English majors are accountants?" Vivian asked with raised eyebrows. She returned her attention to me. "Can you fly, Diana?"

"Yes," I admitted reluctantly. Flight was not a common talent among witches. It was showy, and therefore undesirable if you wanted to live quietly among humans.

"Do other weavers shimmer like you?" Abby asked, tilting her head.

"I don't know if there *are* other weavers. There weren't many left, even in the sixteenth century. Goody Alsop was the only one in the British Isles after the Scottish weaver was executed. There was a weaver in Prague. And my father was a weaver, too. It runs in families."

"Stephen Proctor was not a weaver," Sarah said tartly. "He never shimmered and had no familiar. Your father was a perfectly ordinary witch."

"The Proctors haven't produced a really first-rate witch for generations," Vivian said apologetically.

"Most weavers aren't first-rate at anything—not by traditional standards." It was even true at a genetic level, where Matthew's tests had revealed all sorts of contradictory markers in my blood. "That's why I was never any good with the craft. Sarah can teach anybody how to work a spell—but not me. I was a disaster." My laugh was shaky. "Daddy told me I should have let the spells go in one ear and out the other and then make up my own."

"When did Stephen tell you that?" Sarah's voice cracked across the room.

"In London. Daddy was there in 1591, too. I got my timewalking abilities from him, after all." In spite of Matthew's insistence that I didn't have to tell Sarah everything at once, that's how the story was coming out.

"Did you see Rebecca?" Sarah was wide-eyed.

"No. Just Daddy." Like meeting Philippe de Clermont, seeing my own father again had been an unexpected gift on our journey.

"I'll be damned," Sarah murmured.

"He wasn't there long, but for a few days, there were three weavers in London. We were the talk of the town." And not only because my father kept feeding plot points and lines of dialogue to William Shakespeare.

Sarah opened her mouth to fire off another question, but Vivian held her hand up for quiet.

"If weaving runs in families, why are there so few of you?" Vivian asked.

"Because a long time ago, other witches set out to destroy us." My fingers tightened on the towel that Matthew had wrapped around my shoulders.

"Goody Alsop told us that whole families were murdered to ensure that no children carried on the legacy." Matthew's fingers pressed into the tense muscles in my neck. "Those who survived went into hiding. War, disease, and infant mortality would have put considerable stress on those few remaining bloodlines."

"Why eradicate weavers? New spells would be highly desirable in any coven," Caleb asked.

"I'd kill for a spell that would unfreeze my computer when John jams the keys," Abby added. "I've tried everything: the charm for stuck wheels, the spell for broken locks, the blessing for new endeavors. None of them seem to work with these modern electronics."

"Maybe weavers were too powerful and other witches were jealous. Maybe it was just fear. When it comes right down to it, I don't think creatures are any more accepting of difference than humans are. . . ." My words faded into silence.

"New spells." Caleb whistled. "Where do you start?"

"That depends on the weaver. With me it's a question or a desire. I focus on that, and my cords do the rest." I held my hands up. "I guess my fingers will have to do it now."

"Let me see your hands, Diana," Sarah said. I rose and stood before her, palms outstretched.

Sarah looked closely at the colors. Her fingers traced the pentacle-shaped knot with five crossings on my right wrist.

"That's the fifth knot," I explained while Sarah continued her examination. "Weavers use it to cast spells to overcome challenges or heighten experiences."

"The pentacle represents the elements." Sarah tapped my palm where the brown, yellow, blue, and red streaks twined together. "Here are the four colors that traditionally represent earth, air, water, and fire. And the green on your thumb is associated with the goddess—the goddess as mother in particular."

"Your hand is a magical primer, Diana," Vivian observed, "with the four elements, the pentacle, and the goddess all inscribed on it. It's everything a witch needs to work the craft."

"And this must be the tenth knot." Sarah gently released my right hand to take up my left. She studied the loop around the pulse at my wrist. "It looks like the symbol on the flag flying over Sept-Tours."

"It is. Not all weavers can make the tenth knot, even though it looks so simple." I took a deep breath. "It's the knot of creation. And destruction."

Sarah closed my fingers into a fist and folded her own hand around mine. She and Vivian exchanged a worried look.

"Why is one of my fingers missing a color?" I asked, suddenly uneasy.

"Let's talk about that tomorrow," Sarah said. "It's late. And it's been a long evening."

"We should get these kids into bed." Abby climbed to her feet, careful not to disturb her daughter. "Wait until the rest of the coven hears that Diana can make new spells. Cassie and Lydia will have a fit."

"We can't tell the coven," Sarah said firmly. "Not until we figure out what it all means."

"Diana really is awfully shiny," Abby pointed out. "I didn't notice it before, but even the humans are going to see it."

"I was wearing a disguising spell. I can cast another." One glimpse of Matthew's forbidding expression had me hastily adding, "I wouldn't wear it at home, of course."

"Disguising spell or no, the O'Neils are bound to know something is going on," Vivian said.

Caleb looked somber. "We don't have to inform the whole coven, Sarah, but we can't keep everybody in the dark either. We should choose who to tell and what to tell them."

"It will be far harder to explain Diana's pregnancy than it will be to come up with a good reason for her shimmering," Sarah said, stating the obvious. "She's just starting to show, but with twins the pregnancy is going to be impossible to ignore very soon."

"Which is exactly why we need to be completely honest," Abby argued. "Witches can smell a half-truth just as easily as a lie."

"This will be a test of the coven's loyalty and open-mindedness," Caleb said thoughtfully.

"And if we fail this test?" Sarah asked.

"That would divide us forever," he replied.

"Maybe we should leave." I'd experienced what such divisiveness could do firsthand, and I still had nightmares about what had happened in Scotland when witch turned against witch and the Berwick trials began. I didn't want to be responsible for destroying the Madison coven, forcing people to uproot themselves from houses and farms their families had owned for generations.

"Vivian?" Caleb turned to the coven's leader.

"The decision should be left to Sarah," Vivian said.

"Once I would have believed that all this weaving business should be shared. But I've seen witches do terrible things to each other, and I'm not talking solely about Emily." Sarah glanced in my direction but didn't elaborate.

"I can keep Corra indoors—mostly. I can even avoid going into town. But I'm not going to be able to hide my differences forever, no matter how good my disguising spell," I warned the assembled witches.

"I realize that," Vivian said calmly. "But this isn't just a test—it's an opportunity. When witches set out to destroy the weavers those many years ago, we lost more than lives. We lost bloodlines, expertise, knowledge—all because we feared a power we didn't understand. This is our chance to begin again."

"'*For storms will rage and oceans roar,*'" I whispered. "'*When Gabriel stands on sea and shore. / And as he blows his wondrous horn, / Old worlds die and new be born.*'" Were we in the midst of just such a change?

"Where did you learn that?" Sarah's voice was sharp.

"Goody Alsop shared it with me. It was her teacher's prophecy—Mother Ursula."

"I know whose prophecy it is, Diana," Sarah said. "Mother Ursula was a famous cunning woman and a powerful seer."

"She was?" I wondered why Goody Alsop hadn't told me.

"Yes, she was. For a historian you really are appallingly ignorant of witches' lore," Sarah replied. "I'll be damned. You learned how to weave spells from one of Ursula Shipton's apprentices." Sarah's voice held a note of real respect.

"Then we haven't lost everything," Vivian said softly, "so long as we don't lose you."

Abby and Caleb packed their van with chairs, leftovers, and children. I was on the driveway, waving good-bye, when Vivian approached me, a container of potato salad in one hand.

"If you want Sarah to snap out of her funk and stop staring at that tree, tell her more about weaving. Show her how you do it—insofar as you can."

"I'm still not very good at it, Vivian."

"All the more reason to enlist Sarah's help. She may not be a weaver, but Sarah knows more about the architecture of spells than any witch I've ever met. It will give her a purpose, now that Emily is gone." Vivian gave my hand an encouraging squeeze.

"And the coven?"

"Caleb says this is a test," she replied. "Let's see if we can pass it."

Vivian pulled down the driveway, her car's headlights sweeping the old fence. I returned to the house, turned off the lights, and climbed the stairs to my husband.

"Did you lock the front door?" Matthew asked, putting down his book. He was stretched out on the bed, which was barely long enough to contain him.

"I couldn't. It's a dead bolt, and Sarah lost the key." My eyes strayed to the key to our bedroom door, which the house had helpfully supplied on an earlier occasion. The memories of that night pushed my lips up into a smile.

"Dr. Bishop, are you feeling wanton?" Matthew's tone was as seductive as a caress.

"We're married." I shucked off my shoes and reached for the top button on my seersucker shirt. "It's my wifely duty to have carnal desires where you're concerned."

"And it's my husbandly obligation to satisfy them." Matthew moved from the bed to the bureau at the speed of light. He gently replaced my fingers with his own and slid the button through its hole. Then he moved on to the next, and the next. Each inch of revealed flesh earned a kiss, a soft press of teeth. Five buttons later I was shivering slightly in the humid summer air.

"How strange that you're shivering," he murmured, sliding his hands around to release the clasp on my bra. Matthew brushed his lips over the crescent-shaped scar near my heart. "You don't feel cold."

"It's all relative, vampire." I tightened my fingers in his hair, and he chuckled. "Now, are you going to love me, or do you just want to take my temperature?"

Later I held my hand up before me, turning it this way and that in the silver light. The middle and ring fingers on my left hand each bore a colored line, one the shade of a moonbeam and the other as gold as the sun. The vestiges of the other cords had faded slightly, though a pearly knot was still barely visible on the pale flesh of each wrist.

"What do you think it all means?" Matthew asked, his lips moving against my hair while his fingers traced figure eights and circles on my shoulders.

"That you've married the tattooed lady—or someone possessed by aliens." Between the new lives rooting within me, Corra, and now my weaver's cords, I was beginning to feel crowded inside my own skin.

"I was proud of you tonight. You thought of a way to save Grace so quickly."

"I didn't think at all. When Grace screamed, it flipped some switch in me. I was all instinct then." I twisted in his arms. "Is that dragon thing still on my back?"

"Yes. And it's darker than it was before." Matthew's hands slid around my waist, and he turned me back to face him. "Any theories as to why?"

"Not yet." The answer was just out of my reach. I could feel it, waiting for me.

"Perhaps it has something to do with your power. It's stronger now than it's ever been." Matthew carried my wrist to his mouth. He drank in my scent, then pressed his lips to my veins. "You still give off the scent of summer lightning, but now there's also a note like dynamite when the lit fuse first touches the powder."

"I have enough power. I don't want any more," I said, burrowing into Matthew.

But since we'd returned to Madison, a dark desire was stirring in my blood.

Liar, whispered a familiar voice.

My skin prickled as if a thousand witches were looking at me. But it was only one creature who watched me now: *the goddess.*

I stole a glance around the room, but there was no sign of her. If Matthew were to detect the goddess's presence, he'd start asking questions I didn't want to answer. And he might uncover one secret I was still hiding.

"Thank goodness," I said under my breath.

"Did you say something?" Matthew asked.

"No," I lied again, and crept closer to Matthew. "You must be hearing things."

10

I stumbled downstairs the next morning, exhausted from my encounter with witchwater and the vivid dreams that had followed.

"The house was awfully quiet last night." Sarah stood behind the old pulpit with her reading glasses perched on the end of her nose, red hair wild around her face, and the Bishop grimoire open in front of her. The sight would have given Emily's Puritan ancestor, Cotton Mather, fits.

"Really? I didn't notice." I yawned, trailing my fingers through the old wooden dough trough that held fresh-picked lavender. Soon the herbs would be hanging upside down to dry from the twine running between the rafters. A spider was adding to that serviceable web with a silken version of her own.

"You've certainly been busy this morning," I said, changing the subject. The milk-thistle heads were in the sieve, ready to be shaken to free the seeds from their downy surround. Bunches of yellow-flowered rue and button-centered feverfew were tied with string and ready for hanging. Sarah had dragged out her heavy flower press, and there was a tray of long, aromatic leaves waiting to go into it. Bouquets of newly harvested flowers and herbs sat on the counter, their purpose not yet clear.

"There's lots of work to do," Sarah said. "Someone's been tending to the garden while we were gone, but they have their own plots to take care of, and the winter and spring seeds never got into the ground."

Several anonymous "someones" must have been involved, given the size of the witch's garden at the Bishop house. Thinking to help, I reached for a bunch of rue. The scent of it would always remind me of Satu and the horrors that I'd experienced after she took me from the garden at Sept-Tours to La Pierre. Sarah's hand shot out and intercepted mine.

"Pregnant women don't touch rue, Diana. If you want to help me, go to the garden and cut some moonwort. Use that." She pointed to her white-handled knife. The last time I'd held it, I'd used it to open my own vein and save Matthew. Neither of us had forgotten it. Neither of us mentioned it either.

"Moonwort's that plant with the pods on it, right?"

"Purple flowers. Long stalks. Papery-looking flat disks," Sarah instructed with more patience than usual. "Cut the stems down to the base of the plant. We'll separate the flowers from the rest before we hang them up to dry."

Sarah's garden was tucked into a far corner of the orchard where the apple trees thinned out and the cypresses and oaks of the forest didn't yet overshadow the soil. It was surrounded by palisades of fencing made from metal posts, wire mesh, pickets, retooled pallets—if it could be used to keep out rabbits, voles, and skunks, Sarah had used it. For extra security the whole perimeter was smudged twice a year and warded with protection spells.

Inside the enclosure Sarah had re-created a bit of paradise. Some of the garden's wide paths led to shady glens where ferns and other tender plants found shelter in the shadows of the taller trees. Others bisected the raised vegetable beds that were closest to the house, with their trellises and beanpoles. Normally these would be covered with vegetation—sweet peas and snap peas and beans of every description—but they were skeletal this year.

I skirted Sarah's small teaching garden where she instructed the coven's children—and sometimes their parents—on the elemental associations of various flowers, plants, and herbs. Her young charges had put up their own fence, using paint stirrers, willow twigs, and Popsicle sticks to demarcate their sacred space from that of the larger garden. Easy-to-grow plants like elfwort and yarrow helped the children understand the seasonal cycle of birth, growth, decay, and fallowness that guided any witch's work in the craft. A hollow stump served as a container for mint and other invasive plants.

Two apple trees marked the center of the garden, and a hammock spanned the distance between them. It was wide enough to hold both Sarah and Em, and it had been their favorite spot for dreaming and talking late into the warm summer nights.

Beyond the apple trees, I passed through a second gate into the garden of a professional witch. Sarah's garden served the same purpose as one of my libraries: It provided a source of inspiration and refuge, as well as information and the tools to do her job.

I found the three-foot-high stems topped with purple flowers that Sarah wanted. Mindful to leave enough to self-seed for next year, I filled the wicker basket and returned to the house.

There my aunt and I worked in companionable silence. She chopped off the moonwort flowers, which she would use to make a fragrant oil, and returned the stems to me so that I could tie a bit of twine around each one—no bunches here, for fear of damaging the pods—and hang them to dry.

"How will you use the pods?" I asked, knotting the string.

"Protection charms. When school starts in a few weeks, there will be a demand for them. Moonwort pods are especially good for children, since they keep monsters and nightmares away."

Corra, who was napping in the stillroom loft, cocked her eye in Sarah's direction, and smoke billowed from her nose and mouth in a firedrake's harrumph.

"I've got something else in mind for *you,*" Sarah said, pointing her knife in the firedrake's direction.

Unconcerned, Corra turned her back. Her tail flopped over the edge of the loft and hung like a pendulum, its spade-shaped tip moving gently to and fro. Ducking past it, I tied another moonwort stem to the rafters, careful not to shake loose any of the papery ovals that clung to it.

"How long will they hang before they're dried?" I asked, returning to the table.

"A week," Sarah said, looking up briefly. "By then we'll be able to rub the skin from the pods. Underneath is a silver disk."

"Like the moon. Like a mirror," I said, nodding in understanding. "Reflecting the nightmare back on itself, so that it won't disturb the child."

Sarah nodded, too, pleased by my insight.

"Some witches scry with moonwort pods," Sarah continued after a few moments. "The witch in Hamilton who taught high-school chemistry told me that alchemists collected May dew on them to use as a base for the elixir of life."

"That would require a lot of moonwort," I said with a laugh, thinking of all the water Mary Sidney and I had used in our experiments. "I think we should stick to the protection charms."

"Okay, then." Sarah smiled. "For kids I put the charms in dream pillows. They're not as spooky as a poppet or a pentacle made of blackberry canes. If you were going to make one, what ingredients would you use for the stuffing?"

I took a deep breath and focused on the question. Dream pillows didn't have to be big, after all—the size of the palm of my hand would do.

The palm of my hand. Ordinarily I would have run my fingers through my weaver's cords, waiting for inspiration—and guidance—to strike. But the cords were inside me now. When I turned my hands and splayed the fingers wide, shimmering knots appeared over the tracery of veins at my wrist and the thumb and pinkie on my right hand gleamed green and brown in the colors of the craft.

Sarah's mason jars glinted in the light from the windows. I moved toward them, running my little finger down the labels until I felt resistance.

"Agrimony." I traveled along the shelf. "Mugwort."

Using it like the pointer on a Ouija board, I tilted my pinkie backward. "Aniseed." Down moved my finger. "Hops." Up it swooped in a diagonal line to the opposite side. "Valerian."

What was that going to smell like? Too pungent?

My thumb tingled.

"A bay leaf, a few pinches of rosemary, and some thyme," I said.

But what if the child woke up anyway and grabbed at the pillow?

"And five dried beans." It was an odd addition, but my weaver's instinct told me they would make all the difference.

"Well, I'll be damned." Sarah pushed her glasses onto her head. She looked at me in astonishment, then grinned. "It's like an old charm your great-grandmother collected, except hers had mullein and vervain in it, too—and no beans."

"I'd put the beans in the pillows first," I said. "They should rattle against one another if you shake it. You can tell the kids the noise will help with the monsters."

"Nice touch," Sarah admitted. "And the moonwort pods—would you powder them or leave them whole?"

"Whole," I replied, "sewn onto the front of the pillow."

But herbs were only the first half of a protection charm. Words were needed to go along with them. And if any other witch was going to be able to use it, those words had to be packed with potential. The London witches had taught me a great deal, but the spells I wrote tended to lie flat on the page, inert on anyone's tongue but mine. Most spells were written in rhyme, which made them easier to remember as well as livelier. But I was no poet, like Matthew or his friends. I hesitated.

"Something wrong?" Sarah said.

"My gramarye sucks," I confessed, lowering my voice.

"If I had the slightest idea what that was, I'd feel sorry for you," Sarah said drily.

"Gramarye is how a weaver puts magic into words. I can construct spells and perform them myself, but without gramarye they won't work for other witches." I pointed to the Bishop grimoire. "Hundreds and hundreds of weavers came up with the words for those spells, and other witches passed them down through the ages. Even now the spells retain their power. I'm lucky if *my* spells remain potent for an hour."

"What's the problem?" Sarah asked.

"I don't see spells in words but in shapes and colors." The underside of my thumb and pinkie were still slightly discolored. "Red ink helped my fire spell. So did arranging the words on the page so that they made a kind of picture."

"Show me," Sarah said, pushing a piece of scrap paper and a charred stick in my direction. "Witch hazel," she explained when I held it up for clarification. "I use it as a pencil when I'm trying to copy a spell for the first time. If something goes wrong, the aftereffects are less . . . er, permanent than with ink." She colored slightly. One of her unruly spells had caused a cyclone in the bathroom. For weeks we found spatters of suntan lotion and shampoo in the oddest places.

I wrote out the spell I'd devised to set things alight, careful not to say the words to myself and thereby work the magic. When I was through, the index finger of my right hand was glowing red.

"This was my first attempt at gramarye," I said, looking at it critically before handing it to Sarah. "A third-grader probably would have done a better job."

Fire
Ignite till
Roaring bright
Extinguishing night

"It's not *that* bad," Sarah said. When I looked crestfallen, she hastily added, "I've seen worse. Spelling out fire with the first letter of every line was clever. But why a triangle?"

"That's the structure of the spell. It's pretty simple, really—just a thrice-crossed knot." It was my turn to study my work. "Funny thing is, the triangle was a symbol many alchemists used for fire."

"A thrice-crossed knot?" Sarah looked over the frames of her glasses. "You're having one of your Yoda moments." This was her way of letting the air out of my vocabulary.

"I'm making it as plain as I can, Sarah. It would be easier to show you what I mean if my cords weren't inside my hands." I held them up and waggled my fingers at her.

Sarah murmured something, and the ball of twine rolled across the table. "Will ordinary string do, Yoda?"

I stopped the ball by saying my own spell to arrest its motion. It was heavy with the power of earth and had a thicket of thrice-crossed knots surrounding it. Sarah twitched in surprise.

"Of course," I said, pleased by my aunt's reaction. After giving the twine a whack with her knife, I picked up a length of string approximately nine inches long. "Every knot has a different number of crossings. You use two of them in your craft—the slipknot and the double slipknot. Those are the two weaver's knots that all witches know. It's when we come to the third knot that things get complicated."

I wasn't sure if kitchen twine was up to showing what I meant, though. Knots made with my weaver's cords were three-dimensional, but given that I was working with ordinary string, I decided to work on the flat. Holding one end of the length in my left hand, I made a loop to the right, pulled the string loosely under one side of the loop and over the other, and joined the ends together. The result was a trefoil-shaped knot that resembled a triangle.

"See, three crossings," I said. "You try."

When I took my hands off the string, it sprang up into a familiar pyramid with the ends properly fused together into an unbreakable knot. Sarah gasped.

"Cool," I said. "Plain old string works just fine."

"You sound just like your father." Sarah poked at the knot with her finger. "There's one of those hidden in every spell?"

"At least one. Really complicated spells might have two or three knots, each one tying into the threads you saw last night in the keeping room—the ones that bind the world." I smiled. "I guess gramarye is a disguising spell of sorts—one that hides magic's inner workings."

"And when you say the words, it reveals them," Sarah said thoughtfully. "Let's give yours a go."

Before I could warn her, Sarah read the words of my spell aloud. The paper burst into flame in her hands. She dropped it on the table, and I doused it with a shower of conjured water.

"I thought that was a spell for lighting a candle—not setting a house on fire!" she exclaimed, looking at the charred mess.

"Sorry. The spell is still pretty new. It will settle down eventually. Gramarye can't hold a spell together forever, so its magic weakens over time. It's why spells stop working," I explained.

"Really? Then you should be able to figure out the relative ages of spells." Sarah's eyes gleamed. She was a great believer in tradition, and the older a piece of magic was, the more she liked it.

"Maybe," I said doubtfully, "but there are other reasons that spells fail. Weavers have different abilities, for one thing. And if words were left out or changed when later witches copied them, that will compromise the magic, too."

But Sarah was already in front of her spell book, leafing through the pages.

"Here, look at this one." She beckoned me toward her. "I always suspected this was the oldest spell in the Bishop grimoire."

"'*An exceeding great charm for drawing clean air into any place,*'" I read aloud, "'*one handed down from old Maude Bishop and proven by me, Charity Bishop, in the year 1705.*'" In the margins were notes made by other witches, including my grandmother, who had later mastered the spell. A caustic annotation by Sarah proclaimed, *"utterly worthless."*

"Well?" Sarah demanded.

"It's dated 1705," I pointed out.

"Yes, but its genealogy goes back beyond that. Em never could find out who Maude Bishop was—a relative of Bridget's from England, perhaps?" This unfinished genealogical research project provided Sarah her first opportunity to mention Em's name without sorrow. Vivian was right. Sarah needed me in her stillroom just as much as I needed to be there.

"Perhaps," I said again, trying not to raise unrealistic hopes.

"Do that thing you did with the jars. Read with your fingers," Sarah said, pushing the pulpit toward me.

I ran my fingertips lightly over the words of the spell. My skin tingled in recognition as they encountered the ingredients woven into it: the air blowing around my ring finger, the sensation of liquid coursing under the nail of my middle finger, and the explosion of scents that clung to my little finger.

"Hyssop, marjoram, and lots of salt," I said thoughtfully. These were common ingredients found in every witch's house and garden.

"So why won't it work?" Sarah was staring at my upraised right hand as though it were an oracle.

"I'm not sure," I admitted. "And you know I could repeat it a thousand times and it will never work for me." Sarah and her friends in the coven were going to have to figure out what was wrong with Maude Bishop's spell themselves. That, or buy a can of air freshener.

"Maybe you can stitch it back together, or weave a patch, or whatever it is that witches like you do."

Witches like you. Sarah didn't mean to do it, but her words left me feeling uneasy and isolated. Staring down at the page from the grimoire, I wondered if an inability to perform magic on command was one reason that weavers had been targeted by their communities.

"It doesn't work that way." I folded my hands atop the open book and pressed my lips together, withdrawing like a crab into its shell.

"You said weaving started with a question. Ask the spell what's wrong," Sarah suggested.

I wished I'd never seen Maude Bishop's cleansing spell. Even more, I wished Sarah had never seen it.

"What are you doing?" Sarah pointed to the Bishop grimoire in horror.

Underneath my hands the writing was unspooling from its neat curlicues. Leftover splatters of ink marred the otherwise blank page. Within moments there was no trace of Maude Bishop's spell except for a small, tight blue-and-yellow knot. I stared at it in fascination and had the sudden urge to—

"Don't touch it!" Sarah cried, waking Corra from her slumber. I jumped away from the book, and Sarah swooped down on it, trapping the knot under a mason jar.

We both peered at the UMO—unfamiliar magical object.

"Now what do we do?" I always thought of spells as living, breathing creations. It seemed unkind to keep it contained.

"I'm not sure there's much we *can* do." Sarah took my left hand and flipped it over, revealing a black-stained thumb.

"I got ink on it," I said.

Sarah shook her head. "That's not ink. That's the color of death. You killed the spell."

"What do you mean, killed it?" I snatched my hand away, holding it behind me like a child caught raiding the cookie jar.

"Don't panic," Sarah said. "Rebecca learned to control it. You can, too."

"My mother?" I thought of the long look that Sarah and Vivian had exchanged last night. "You knew something like this might happen."

"Only after I saw your left hand. It bears all the colors of the higher magics, like exorcism and auguries, just as your right hand shows the colors of the craft." Sarah paused. "It bears the colors of the darker magics, too."

"Good thing I'm right-handed." It was an attempt at humor, but the tremor in my voice gave me away.

"You're not right-handed. You're ambidextrous. You only favor your right hand because that horrible first-grade teacher said left-handed children were demonic." Sarah had seen to it that the woman was formally censured. After experiencing her first Halloween in Madison, Miss Somerton had resigned her position.

I wanted to say I wasn't interested in the higher magics either, but nothing came out.

Sarah looked at me sadly. "You can't lie to another witch, Diana. Especially not a whopper like that."

"No dark magic." Emily had died trying to summon and bind a spirit—probably my mother. Peter Knox was interested in the darker aspects of the craft, too. And dark magic was bound up in Ashmole 782 as well—not to mention more than one thumb's worth of death.

"Dark doesn't have to mean evil," Sarah said. "Is the new moon evil?"

I shook my head. "The dark of the moon is a time for new beginnings."

"Owls? Spiders? Bats? Dragons?" Sarah was using her teacher voice.

"No," I admitted.

"No. They are not. Humans made up those stories about the moon and nocturnal creatures because they represent the unknown. It's no coincidence that they also symbolize wisdom. There is nothing more powerful than knowledge. That's why we're so careful when we teach someone dark magic." Sarah took my hand. "Black is the color of the goddess as crone, plus the color of concealment, bad omens, and death."

"And these?" I wiggled the three other fingers.

"Here we have the color of the goddess as maiden and huntress," she said, folding in my silver middle finger. Now I knew why the goddess's voice sounded as it did. "And here is the color of worldly power." She folded in my golden ring finger. "As for your pinkie, white is the color of divination and prophecy. It's also used to break curses and banish unwanted spirits."

"Except for the death, that doesn't sound so terrible."

"Like I said, dark doesn't necessarily mean evil," Sarah said. "Think about worldly power. In beneficent hands it's a force for good. But if someone abuses it for personal gain or to harm others, it can be terribly destructive. The darkness depends on the witch."

"You said Emily wasn't very good at the higher magics. What about Mom?"

"Rebecca excelled at them. She went straight from bell, book, and candle to calling down the moon," Sarah said wistfully.

Some of what I'd witnessed my mother do when I was a child made sense now, like the night she'd conjured wraiths out of a bowl of water. So, too, did Peter Knox's preoccupation with her.

"Rebecca seemed to lose interest in higher magics once she met your father, though. The only subjects that appealed to her then were anthropology and Stephen. And you, of course," Sarah said. "I don't think she worked much higher magic after you were born."

Not where anybody but Dad or I could see, I thought. "Why didn't you tell me?" I said aloud.

"You didn't want anything to do with magic, remember?" Sarah's hazel gaze held mine. "I saved some of Rebecca's things, just in case you ever showed any ability. The house took the rest."

Sarah murmured a spell—an opening spell, based on the threads that suddenly illuminated the room with shades of red, yellow, and green. A cabinet and drawers appeared to the left of the old fireplace, built into the ancient masonry. The room filled with the scent of lily of the valley and something heavy and exotic that stirred sharp, uncomfortable feelings within me: emptiness and yearning, familiarity and dread. Sarah opened a drawer and took out a chunk of something red and resinous.

"Dragon's blood. I can't smell it without thinking of Rebecca." Sarah sniffed it. "The stuff you can get now isn't as good as this, and it costs an absolute fortune. I wanted to sell this and use the proceeds to fix the roof when it collapsed in the blizzard of '93, but Em wouldn't let me."

"What did Mom use it for?" I said around the lump in my throat.

"Rebecca made ink from it. When she used that ink to copy out a charm, the force of it could suck the power out of half the town. There were lots of blackouts in Madison during your mother's teen years." Sarah chuckled. "Her spell book should be here somewhere—unless the house ate it while I was gone. That will tell you more."

"Spell book?" I frowned. "What was wrong with the Bishop grimoire?"

"Most witches who practice the higher, darker magics keep their own grimoire. It's tradition," Sarah said, rummaging around in the cupboard. "Nope. It doesn't seem to be here."

Despite the pang of disappointment that accompanied Sarah's announcement, I was relieved. I already had one mysterious book in my life. I wasn't sure I wanted another—even if it might shed light on why Emily had been trying to summon my mother's spirit at Sept-Tours.

"Oh, no." Sarah backed away from the cupboard, a look of horror on her face.

"Is there a rat?" My experiences in London had conditioned me to believe that they lurked in every dusty corner. I peered into the cupboard's depths but saw only a collection of grimy jars containing herbs and roots and an ancient clock radio. Its brown cord hung down from the shelf like Corra's tail, waving gently in the breeze. I sneezed.

As if on cue, a strange metallic clinking and rolling started in the walls, like coins being fed into a jukebox. The musical grinding that followed, reminiscent of an old record player set to 33 rpm instead of 45 rpm, soon gave way to a recognizable song.

I cocked my head. "Is that . . . Fleetwood Mac?"

"No. Not again!" Sarah looked as if she'd seen a ghost. I glanced around, but the only invisible presence in the room was Stevie Nicks and a Welsh witch named Rhiannon. In the seventies the song had been a coming-out anthem for scores of witches and wizards.

"I guess the house is waking up." Maybe that was what was upsetting Sarah.

Sarah darted to the door and lifted the latch, but it wouldn't budge. She banged on the wooden panels. The music got louder.

"This isn't my favorite Stevie Nicks tune either," I said, trying to calm her, "but it won't last forever. Maybe you'll like the next song better."

"The next song is 'Over My Head.' I know the whole damn album by heart. Your mother listened to it all through her pregnancy. It went on for months. Just when Rebecca seemed to get over her obsession, Fleetwood Mac's next album came out. It was hell." Sarah tore at her hair.

"Really?" I was always hungry for details about my parents. "Fleetwood Mac seems more like Dad's kind of band."

"We have to stop the music." Sarah went to the window, but the sash wouldn't move. She thumped on the frame in frustration.

"Let me try." The harder I pushed, the louder the music got. There was a momentary pause after Stevie Nicks stopped warbling about Rhiannon. A few seconds later, Christine McVie informed us how nice it was to be in over your head. The window remained closed.

"This is a nightmare!" Sarah exploded. She jammed her hands over her ears to block the sound, then raced to the grimoire and flipped through the pages. "Prudence Willard's dog-bite cure. Patience Severance's method for sweetening sour milk." She flipped some more. "Clara Bishop's spell for stopping up a drafty chimney! That might work."

"But it's music, not smoke," I said, peering over Sarah's shoulder at the lines of text.

"Both are carried on the air." Sarah rolled up her sleeves. "If it doesn't do the trick, we'll try something else. Maybe thunder. I'm good with thunder. That might interrupt the energy and drive the sound away."

I started to hum along to the song. It was catchy, in a 1970s kind of way.

"Don't you start." Sarah's eyes were wild. She turned back to the grimoire. "Get me some eyebright, please. And plug in the coffeemaker."

I dutifully went to the ancient outlet strip and shoved the coffeemaker's cord into it. Electricity leaped from the socket in orange and blue arcs. I jumped back.

"You need a surge protector—preferably one bought in the last decade—or you're going to burn the whole house down," I told Sarah.

She kept muttering as she put a paper filter into the swing-out basket in the coffeemaker, followed by an extensive selection of herbs.

Since we were trapped inside the stillroom and Sarah didn't seem to want my help, I might as well work on the words to accompany my anti-nightmare spell for the children. I went to my mother's cabinet and found some black ink, a quill pen, and a slip of paper.

Matthew knocked on the windowpane. "Are you two all right? I smelled something burning."

"A minor electrical problem!" I shouted, waving my quill pen in the air. Then I remembered that Matthew was a vampire and could hear me perfectly well through stone, brick, wood, and yes, single panes of glass. I lowered my voice. "Nothing to worry about."

"Over My Head" screeched to a halt, and "You Make Loving Fun" began. *Nice choice,* I thought, smiling at Matthew. Who needed a deejay when you had magical radio?

"Oh, God. The house has moved on to their second album," Sarah groaned. "I hate *Rumours.*"

"Where is that music coming from?" Matthew frowned.

"Mom's old clock radio." I pointed with the feather. "She liked Fleetwood Mac." I glanced at my aunt, who was reciting the words to Clara Bishop's spell with her hands clapped over her ears. "Sarah doesn't."

"Ah." Matthew's brow cleared. "I'll leave you to it, then." He pressed his hand against the glass in a silent gesture of farewell.

My heart filled. Loving Matthew wasn't *all* I wanted to do, but he was definitely the only one for me. I wished there wasn't a pane of glass between us so that I could tell him so.

Glass is only sand and fire. One puff of smoke later, a pile of sand lay on the windowsill. I reached through the empty square in the window frame and clasped his hand.

"Thanks for checking on us. It's been an interesting afternoon. I have a lot to tell you."

Matthew blinked at our twined hands.

"You make me very happy, you know."

"I try," he said with a shy grin.

"You succeed. Do you think Fernando could rescue Sarah?" I lowered my voice. "The house has jammed the stillroom doors and windows shut, and she's about to blow. She's going to need a cigarette when she gets out, and a stiff drink."

"Fernando hasn't rescued a woman in distress for some time, but I'm sure he remembers how," Matthew assured me. "Will the house let him?"

"Give it five minutes or until the music stops, whichever comes first." I pulled free and blew him a kiss. It had rather more fire and water than usual, and enough air behind it to land with a decided smack on his cheek.

I returned to the worktable and dipped my mother's quill pen into the ink. It smelled of blackberries and walnuts. Thanks to my experience with Elizabethan writing implements, I was able to write out the charm for Sarah's dream pillows without a single splotch.

Mirror
Shimmers
Monsters Shake
Banish Nightmares
Until We
Wake

I blew on it gently to set the ink. Very respectable, I decided. It was much better than my spell for conjuring fire, and easy enough for children to remember. When the pods were dry and the papery covering rubbed off, I'd write the charm in tiny letters right on their silvery surface.

Eager to show my work to Sarah, I slid down from the stool. One look at her face convinced me to put it off until my aunt had had her whiskey and a smoke. She'd been hoping for decades that I'd show an interest in magic. I could wait another twenty minutes for my grade in Sleeping Charms 101.

A slight tingle behind me alerted me to a ghostly presence a moment before a hug as soft as down settled around my shoulders.

"Nice job, peanut," whispered a familiar voice. *"Excellent taste in music, too."*

When I turned my head, there was nothing except a faint smudge of green, but I didn't need to see my father to know that he was there.

"Thanks, Dad," I said softly.

11

Matthew took the news about my mother's proficiency with higher magic better than expected. He had long suspected that something existed between the homely work of the craft and the bright spectacles of elemental magic. He was not at all surprised that I, in another mark of in-betweenness, could practice such a magic. What shocked him was that this talent came through my mother's blood.

"I'll have to take a closer look at your mtDNA workup after all," he said, giving one of my mother's inks a sniff.

"Sounds good." It was the first time Matthew had shown any desire to return to his genetic research. Days had gone by without any mention of Oxford, Baldwin, the Book of Life, or blood rage. And while he might have forgotten that there was genetic information bound up in Ashmole 782, I had not. Once we had the manuscript back in our hands, we were going to need his scientific skills to decipher it.

"You're right. There's definitely blood in it, as well as resin and acacia." Matthew swirled the ink around. Acacia, I'd learned this morning, was the source of gum arabic, which made the ink less runny.

"I thought as much. The inks used in Ashmole 782 had blood in them, too. It must be a more common practice than I thought," I said.

"There's some frankincense in it, too." Matthew said, ignoring my mention of the Book of Life.

"Ah. That's what gives it that exotic scent." I rummaged through the remaining bottles, hoping to find something else to catch his biochemical curiosity.

"That and the blood, of course," Matthew said drily.

"If it's my mother's blood, that could shed even more light on my DNA," I remarked. "My talent for higher magic, too."

"Hmm," Matthew said noncommittally.

"What about this one?" I drew the stopper out of a bottle of blue-green liquid, and the scent of a summer garden filled the air.

"That's made from iris," Matthew said. "Remember your search for green ink in London?"

"So this is what Master Platt's fantastically expensive ink looked like!" I laughed.

"Made from roots imported from Florence. Or so he said." Matthew surveyed the table and its blue, red, black, green, purple, and magenta pots of liquid. "It looks like you have enough ink to keep you going for some time."

He was right: I had enough to get me through the next few weeks. And that was as far as I was willing to project, even if my left pinkie *was* throbbing in anticipation of the future.

"This should be plenty, even with all the jobs Sarah has for me," I agreed. Each of the open jars on the table had a small slip of paper underneath with a note in her sprawling handwriting. *"Mosquito bites,"* read one. *"Better cellphone reception,"* read another. Her requests made me feel like a server at a fast-food restaurant. "Thanks for your help."

"Anytime," Matthew said, kissing me good-bye.

Over the next few days, the routines of daily life began to anchor us to the Bishop house and to each other—even without the steadying presence of Em, who had always been the house's center of gravity.

Fernando was a domestic tyrant—far worse than Em ever was—and his changes to Sarah's diet and exercise plan were radical and inflexible. He signed my aunt up for a CSA program that delivered a box of exotic vegetables like kale and chard every week, and he walked the property's fence line with her whenever she tried to sneak a cigarette. Fernando cooked and cleaned and even plumped cushions—all of which had me wondering about his life with Hugh.

"When we didn't have servants—and that was often the case—I kept the house," he explained, hanging up clothes on the line. "If I'd waited for Hugh to do it, we'd have lived in squalor. He didn't pay attention to such mundane matters as clean sheets or whether we had run out of wine. Hugh was either writing poetry or planning a three-month siege. There was no time in his day for domestic chores."

"And Gallowglass?" I asked, handing him a clothespin.

"Gallowglass is worse. Not even the furniture—or lack of it—matters to him. We came home one night to find our house robbed and Gallowglass sleeping on the table like a Viking warrior ready to be sent out to sea." Fernando shook his head. "Besides, I enjoy the work. Keeping house is like preparing weapons for battle. It's repetitive and very soothing." His confession made me feel less guilty about letting him do all the cooking.

Fernando's other domain, aside from the kitchen, was the toolshed. He'd cleared out what was broken, cleaned and sharpened what remained, and bought items he felt were missing, like a scythe. The edges on the rose secateurs were now so keen you could slice a tomato with them. I was reminded of all the wars that had been fought using common household implements and wondered if Fernando were quietly arming us for combat.

Sarah, for her part, grumbled at the new regime but went along with it. When she got cranky—which was often—she took it out on the house. It was still not fully awake, but periodic rumblings of activity reminded us that its self-imposed hibernation was drawing to a close. Most of its energy was directed at Sarah. One morning we woke to find that all the liquor in the house had been dumped down the sink and a makeshift mobile of empty bottles and silverware was attached to the kitchen light fixture. Matthew and I laughed, but as far as Sarah was concerned, this was war. From that moment my aunt and the house were in an all-out battle for supremacy.

The house was winning, thanks to its chief weapon: Fleetwood Mac. Sarah had bashed Mom's old radio to bits two days after we found it during a never-ending concert of "The Chain." The house retaliated by removing all the toilet-paper rolls from the bathroom cabinets and replacing them with a variety of electronic gadgets capable of playing music. It made for a rousing morning alarm.

Nothing deterred the house from playing selections from the band's first two albums—not even Sarah's defenestration of three record players, an eight-track tape machine, and an ancient Dictaphone. The house simply diverted the music through the furnace, the bass notes reverberating in the ductwork while the treble wafted from the heating vents.

With all her ire directed at the house, Sarah was surprisingly patient and gentle with me. We had turned the stillroom inside out looking for Mom's spell book, going so far as to remove all the drawers and shelves from the cabinet. We'd found some surprisingly graphic love letters from the 1820s hidden beneath one drawer's false bottom and a macabre collection of rodent skulls tacked in orderly rows behind a sliding panel at the back of the shelving, but no spell book. The house would present it when it was ready.

When the music and memories of Emily and my parents became too overwhelming, Sarah and I escaped to the garden or the woods. Today my aunt had offered to show me where baneful plants could be found. The moon would be full dark tonight, the beginning of a new cycle of growth. It would be a propitious time for gathering up the materials for higher magic. Matthew followed us like a shadow as we wended our way through the vegetable patch and the teaching garden. When we reached her witch's garden, Sarah kept walking. A giant moonflower vine marked the boundary between the garden and the woods. It sprawled in every direction, obscuring the fence and the gate underneath.

"Allow me, Sarah." Matthew stepped forward to spring the latch. Until now he'd been sauntering behind us, seemingly interested in the flowers. But I knew that bringing up the rear placed him in the perfect defensive position. He stepped through the gate, made sure nothing dangerous lurked there, and pulled the vine away so Sarah and I could pass through into another world.

There were many magical places on the Bishop homestead—oak groves dedicated to the goddess, long avenues between yew trees that were once old roads and still showed the deep ruts of wagons laden with wood and produce for the markets, even the old Bishop graveyard. But this little grove between the garden and the forest was my favorite.

Dappled sunlight broke through its center, moving through the cypress that surrounded the place. In ages past, it might have been called a fairy ring, because the ground was thick with toadstools and mushrooms. As a child I'd been forbidden to pick anything that grew there. Now I understood why: Every plant here was either baneful or associated with the darker aspects of the craft. Two paths intersected in the middle of the grove.

"A crossroads." I froze.

"The crossroads have been here longer than the house. Some say these pathways were made by the Oneida before the English settled here." Sarah beckoned me forward. "Come and look at this plant. Is it deadly nightshade or black nightshade?"

Instead of listening, I was completely mesmerized by the X in the middle of the grove.

There was power there. Knowledge, too. I felt the familiar push and pull of desire and fear as I saw the clearing through the eyes of those who had walked these paths before.

"What is it?" Matthew asked, his instincts warning him that something was wrong.

But other voices, though faint, had captured my attention: my mother and Emily, my father and my grandmother, and others unknown to me. *Wolfsbane,* the voices whispered. *Skullcap. Devil's bit. Adder's tongue. Witch's broom.* Their chant was punctuated with warnings and suggestions, and their litany of spells included plants that featured in fairy tales.

Gather cinquefoil when the moon is full to extend the reach of your power.

Hellebore makes any disguising spell more effective.

Mistletoe will bring you love and many children.

To see the future more clearly, use black henbane.

"Diana?" Sarah straightened, hands on hips.

"Coming," I murmured, dragging my attention away from the faint voices and going obediently to my aunt's side.

Sarah gave me all sorts of instructions about the plants in the grove. Her words went in one ear and out the other, flowing through me in a way that would have made my father proud. My aunt could recite all the common and botanical names for every wildflower, weed, root, and herb as well as their uses, both benign and baneful. But her mastery was born of reading and study. I had learned the limits of book-based knowledge in Mary Sidney's alchemical laboratory, when I was confronted for the first time with the challenges of doing what I'd spent years reading and writing about as a scholar. There I had discovered that being able to cite alchemical texts was nothing when weighed against experience. But my mother and Emily were no longer here to help me. If I was going to walk the dark paths of higher magic, I was going to have to do it alone.

The prospect terrified me.

Just before moonrise Sarah invited me to go back out with her to gather the plants she would need for this month's work.

I begged off, claiming I was too tired to go along. But it was the insistent call of the voices at the crossroads that made me refuse.

"Does your reluctance to go to the woods tonight have something to do with your trip there this afternoon?" Matthew asked.

"Perhaps," I said, staring out the window. "Sarah and Fernando are back."

My aunt was carrying a basket full of greenery. The kitchen screen slammed shut behind her, and then the stillroom door creaked open. A few minutes later, she and Fernando climbed the stairs. Sarah was wheezing less than she had last week. Fernando's health regime was working.

"Come to bed," Matthew said, turning back the covers.

The night was dark, illuminated only by the stars. Soon it would be midnight, the moment between night and day. The voices at the crossroads grew louder.

"I have to go." I pushed past Matthew and headed downstairs.

"*We* have to go," he said, following me. "I won't stop you or interfere. But you are not going to the woods by yourself."

"There's power there, Matthew. Dark power. I could feel it. And it's been calling to me since the sun set!"

He took me by the elbow and propelled me out the front door. He didn't want anyone to hear the rest of this conversation.

"Then answer its call," he snapped. "Say yes or say no, but don't expect me to sit here and wait quietly for you to return."

"And if I say yes?" I demanded.

"We'll face it. Together."

"I don't believe you. You told me before that you don't want me meddling with life and death. That's the kind of power that's waiting for me where the paths cross in the woods. And I want it!" I wrested my elbow from his grip and jabbed a finger in his chest. "I hate myself for wanting it, but I do!"

I turned from the revulsion that I knew would be in his eyes. Matthew turned my face back toward him.

"I've known that the darkness was in you since I found you in the Bodleian, hiding from the other witches on Mabon."

My breath caught. His eyes held mine.

"I felt its allure, and the darkness in me responded to it. Should I loathe myself, then?" Matthew's voice dropped to a barely audible whisper. "Should you?"

"But you said—"

"I said I didn't want you to meddle with life and death, not that you couldn't do so." Matthew took my hands in his. "I've been covered in blood, held a man's future in my hands, decided if a woman's heart would beat again. Something in your own soul dies each time you make the choice for another. I saw what Juliette's death did to you, and Champier's, too."

"I didn't have a choice in those cases. Not really." Champier would have taken all my memories and hurt the people who were trying to help me. Juliette had been trying to kill Matthew—and would have succeeded had I not called on the goddess.

"Yes you did." Matthew pressed a kiss on my knuckles. "You chose death for them, just as you chose life for me, life for Louisa and Kit even though they tried to harm you, life for Jack when you brought him to our house in the Blackfriars instead of leaving him on the street to starve, life for baby Grace when you rescued her from the fire. Whether you realize it or not, you paid a price every time."

I knew the price I'd paid for Matthew's survival, though he did not: My life belonged to the goddess for as long as she saw fit.

"Philippe was the only other creature I've ever known who made life-or-death decisions as quickly and instinctively as you. The price that Philippe paid was terrible loneliness, one that grew over time. Not even Ysabeau could banish it." Matthew rested his forehead against mine. "I don't want that to be your fate."

But my fate was not my own. It was time to tell Matthew so.

"The night I saved you. Do you remember it?" I asked.

Matthew nodded. He didn't like to talk about the night we'd both almost lost our lives.

"The maiden and the crone were there—two aspects of the goddess." My heart was hammering. "We called Ysabeau after you fixed me up, and I told her I'd seen them." I searched his face for signs of understanding, but he still looked bewildered. "I didn't save you, Matthew. The goddess did. I asked her to do it."

His fingers dug into my arm. "Tell me you didn't strike a bargain with her in exchange."

"You were dying, and I didn't have enough power to heal you." I gripped his shirt. "My blood wouldn't have been enough. But the goddess drew the life out of that ancient oak tree so I could feed it to you through my veins."

"And in return?" Matthew's hands tightened, lifting me until my feet were barely touching the ground. "Your gods and goddesses don't grant boons without getting something back. Philippe taught me that."

"I told her to take anyone, anything, so long as she saved you."

Matthew let go abruptly. "Emily?"

"No." I shook my head. "The goddess wanted a life for a life—not a death for a life. She chose mine." My eyes filled with tears at the look of betrayal I saw on his face. "I didn't know her decision until I wove my first spell. I saw her then. The goddess said she still had work for me to do."

"We're going to fix this." Matthew practically dragged me in the direction of the garden gate. Under the dark sky, the moonflowers that covered it were the only signposts to illuminate our way. We reached the crossroads quickly. Matthew pushed me to the center.

"We can't," I protested.

"If you can weave the tenth knot, you can dissolve whatever promise you made to the goddess," he said roughly.

"No!" My stomach clenched, and my chest started to burn. "I can't just wave my hand and make our agreement disappear."

The dead branches of an ancient oak, the one the goddess had sacrificed so that Matthew would live, were barely visible. Under my feet the earth seemed to shift. I looked down and saw that I was straddling the center of the crossroads. The burning sensation in my heart extended down my arms and into my fingers.

"You will not bind your future to some capricious deity. Not for my sake," Matthew said, his voice shaking with fury.

"Don't speak ill of the goddess here," I warned. "I didn't go to your church and mock your god."

"If you won't break your promise to the goddess, then use your magic to summon her." Matthew joined me where the paths converged.

"Get out of the crossroads, Matthew." The wind was swirling around my feet in a magical storm. Corra shrieked through the night sky, trailing fire like a comet. She circled above us, crying out in warning.

"Not until you call her." Matthew's feet remained where they were. "You won't pay for my life with your own."

"It was my choice." My hair was crackling around my face, fiery tendrils writhing against my neck. "I chose you."

"I won't let you."

"It's already done." My heart thudded, and his heart echoed it. "If the goddess wants me to fulfill some purpose of hers, I'll do it—gladly. Because you're mine, and I'm not done with you yet."

My final words were almost identical to those the goddess had once said to me. They rang with power, quieting the wind and silencing Corra's cries. The fire in my veins subsided, the burning sensation becoming a smoldering heat as the connection between Matthew and me tightened, the links that bound us shining and strong.

"You cannot make me regret what I asked the goddess for, or any price I've paid because of it," I said. "Nor will I break my promise to her. Have you thought about what would happen if I did?"

Matthew remained silent, listening.

"Without you I would never have known Philippe or received his blood vow. I wouldn't be carrying your children. I wouldn't have seen my father or known I was a weaver. Don't you understand?" My hands rose to cradle his face. "In saving your life, I saved mine, too."

"What does she want you to do?" Matthew's voice was rough with emotion.

"I don't know. But there's one thing I'm sure of: The goddess needs me alive to do it."

Matthew's hand came to rest on the space between my hips where our children slept.

I felt a soft flutter. Another. I looked at him in alarm.

His hand flexed over my skin, pressing slightly, and there was a stronger flicker of movement in my belly.

"Is something wrong?" I asked.

"Not at all. The babies. They've quickened." Matthew's expression was awed as well as relieved.

We waited together for the next flurry of activity within me. When it came, Matthew and I both laughed, caught up in the unexpected joy. I tilted back my head. The stars seemed brighter, keeping the darkness of the new moon in balance with the light.

The crossroads was silent, and the sharp need I had felt to be out under the dark moon had passed. It was not death that had brought me here, but life. Hand in hand, Matthew and I went back to the house. When I turned on the kitchen light, something unexpected was waiting for me.

"It's a bit soon for someone to leave me a birthday present," I said, eyeing the strangely wrapped parcel. When Matthew moved forward to examine it more closely, I put out a hand and stopped him. "Don't touch it."

He looked at me in confusion.

"It's got enough magical wards on it to repel an army," I explained.

The package was thin and rectangular. An odd assortment of wrapping paper had been patched together to cover it: pink paper with storks, paper covered with primary-colored inchworms forming the shape of the number four, garish Christmas-tree wrapping paper, and silver foil with embossed wedding bells. A bouquet of bright bows covered its surface.

"Where did it come from?" Matthew asked.

"The house, I think." I poked it with my finger. "I recognize some of the wrapping paper from birthdays past."

"Are you sure it's for you?" He looked dubious.

I nodded. The package was definitely for me. Gingerly I picked it up. The bows, all of which had been used before and therefore lacked adhesive, slipped off and rained down on the kitchen island.

"Shall I get Sarah?" Matthew asked.

"No. I've got it covered." My hands were tingling, and every rainbow stripe was in evidence as I removed the wrapping paper.

Inside was a composition book—the kind with a black-and-white cover and pages sewn together with thick string. Someone had glued a magenta daisy over the white box for your name, and WIDE RULE had been edited to read WITCHES RULE.

"*Rebecca Bishop's Book of Shadows,*'" I said, reading aloud from the words written in thick black ink on the daisy. "This is my mother's missing spell book—the one she used for the higher magics."

I cracked open the cover. After all our problems with Ashmole 782, I was braced for anything from mysterious illustrations to encoded script. Instead I found my mother's round, childish handwriting.

"*To summon a spirit recently dead and question it*" was the first spell in the book.

"Mom certainly believed in starting with a bang," I said, showing Matthew the words on the page. The notes beneath the spell recorded the dates when she and Emily had tried to work the magic, as well as the results. Their first three attempts had failed. On the fourth try, they succeeded.

Both of them were thirteen at the time.

"Christ," Matthew said. "They were babes. What business did they have with the dead?"

"Apparently they wanted to know if Bobby Woodruff liked Mary Bassett," I said, peering at the cramped script.

"Why didn't they just ask Bobby Woodruff?" Matthew wondered.

I flipped through the pages. Binding spells, banishing spells, protection spells, charms to summon the elemental powers—they were all in there, along with love magic and other coercive enchantments. My fingers stopped. Matthew sniffed.

Something thin and almost transparent was pressed onto a page inserted in the back of the book. Scrawled above it in a more mature version of the same round hand were the words:

Diana:

Happy Birthday!

I kept this for you. It was our first indication that you were going to be a great witch.

Maybe you'll need it one day.

Lots of love, Mom

"It's my caul." I looked up at Matthew. "Do you think it's meaningful that I got it back on the same day the babies quickened?"

"No," Matthew said. "It's far more likely that the house gave it back to you tonight because you finally stopped running from what your mother and father knew since the very beginning."

"What's that?" I frowned.

"That you were going to possess an extraordinary combination of your parents' very different magical abilities," he replied.

The tenth knot burned on my wrist. I turned over my hand and looked at its writhing shape.

"That's why I can tie the tenth knot," I said, understanding for the first time where the power came from. "I can create because my father was a weaver, and I can destroy because my mother had the talent for higher, darker magics."

"A union of opposites," Matthew said. "Your parents were an alchemical wedding, too. One that produced a marvelous child."

I closed the spell book carefully. It would take me months—years, perhaps—to learn from my mother's mistakes and create spells of my own that would achieve the same ends. With one hand pressing my mother's spell book to my sternum and the other pressed against my abdomen, I leaned back and listened to the slow beating of Matthew's heart.

"*'Do not refuse me because I am dark and shadowed,'*" I whispered, remembering a passage from an alchemical text I'd studied in Matthew's library. "That line from the *Aurora Consurgens* used to remind me of you, but now it makes me think of my parents, as well as my own magic and how hard I resisted it."

Matthew's thumb stroked my wrist, bringing the tenth knot to brilliant, colorful life.

"This reminds me of another part of the *Aurora Consurgens,*" he murmured. "*'As I am the end, so my lover is the beginning. I encompass the whole work of creation, and all knowledge is hidden in me.'*"

"What do you think it means?" I turned my head so I could see his expression.

He smiled, and his arms circled my waist, one hand now resting on the babies. They moved as if recognizing their father's touch.

"That I am a very lucky man," Matthew replied.

12

I woke up to Matthew's cool hands sliding under my pajama top, his lips soothing against my damp neck.

"Happy birthday," he murmured.

"My own private air conditioner," I said, snuggling against him. A vampire husband brought welcome relief in tropical conditions. "What a thoughtful present."

"There are more," he said, giving me a slow, wicked kiss.

"Fernando and Sarah?" I was almost past caring who might hear our lovemaking, but not quite.

"Outside. In the garden hammock. With the paper."

"We'll have to be quick, then." The local papers were short on news and long on advertisements. They took ten minutes to read—fifteen if you were shopping the back-to-school sales or wanted to know which of the three grocery chains had the best deal on bleach.

"I went out for the *New York Times* this morning," he said.

"Always prepared, aren't you?" I reached down and touched him. Matthew swore. In French. "You're just like Verin. Such a Boy Scout."

"Not always," he said, closing his eyes. "Not now, certainly."

"Awfully sure of yourself, too." My mouth slid along his in a teasing kiss. "The *New York Times.* What if I were tired? Cranky? Or hormonal? The Albany paper would have been more than enough to keep them busy then."

"I was relying on my presents to sweeten you up."

"Well, I don't know." A sinuous twist of my hand elicited another French curse. "Why don't I finish unwrapping this one? Then you can show me what else you've got."

By eleven o'clock on my birthday morning, the mercury had already climbed above ninety degrees. The August heat wave showed no signs of breaking.

Worried about Sarah's garden, I spliced together four hoses using a new binding spell and some duct tape so that I could reach all the flower beds.

My headphones were jammed into my ears, and I was listening to Fleetwood Mac. The house had fallen eerily silent, as if it were waiting for something to happen, and I found myself missing the beat of my parents' favorite band.

While dragging the hose across the lawn, my attention was momentarily caught by the large iron weather vane sprouting from the top of the hop barn. It hadn't been there yesterday. I wondered why the house was tinkering with the outbuildings. While I considered the question, two more weather vanes popped out of the ridgepole. They quivered for a moment like newly emerged plants, then whirled madly. When the motion stopped, they all pointed north. Hopefully, their position was an indication that rain was on the way. Until then, the hose was going to have to suffice.

I was giving the plants a good soaking when someone engulfed me in an embrace.

"Thank God! I've been so worried about you." The deep voice was muted by the sound of guitars and drums, but I recognized it nonetheless. I ripped the headphones from my ears and turned to face my best friend. His deep brown eyes were full of concern.

"Chris!" I flung my arms around his broad shoulders. "What are you doing here?" I searched his features for changes but found none. Still the same close-cropped curly hair, still the same walnut skin, still the same high cheekbones angled under straight brows, still the same wide mouth.

"I'm looking for you!" Chris replied. "What the hell is going on? You totally disappeared last November. You don't answer your phone or your e-mail. Then I see the fall teaching schedule and you're not on it! I had to get the chair of the history department drunk before he spilled that you were on medical leave. I thought you were dying—not pregnant."

Well, that was one less thing I'd have to tell him.

"I'm sorry, Chris. There was no cell-phone reception where I was. Or Internet."

"You could have called me from here," he said, not yet ready to let me off the hook. "I've left messages for your aunts, sent letters. Nobody responded."

I could feel Matthew's gaze, cold and demanding. I felt Fernando's attention, too.

"Who is this, Diana?" Matthew asked quietly, coming to my side.

"Chris Roberts. Who the hell are *you*?" Chris demanded.

"This is Matthew Clairmont, fellow of All Souls College, Oxford University." I hesitated. "My husband."

Chris's mouth dropped open.

"Chris!" Sarah waved from the back porch. "Come here and give me a hug!"

"Hi, Sarah!" Chris's hand rose in greeting. He turned and gave me an accusatory look. "You got married?"

"You're here for the weekend, right?" Sarah called.

"That depends, Sarah." Chris's shrewd glance moved from me to Matthew and back.

"On?" Matthew's brow rose in aristocratic disdain.

"On how long it takes me to figure out why Diana married somebody like you, Clairmont, and whether you deserve her. And don't waste your lord-of-the-manor act on me. I come from a long line of field hands. I am *not* impressed," Chris said, stalking toward the house. "Where's Em?"

Sarah froze, her face white. Fernando leaped up the porch steps to join her.

"Why don't we go inside?" he murmured, trying to steer her away from Chris.

"Can I have a word?" Matthew asked, putting his hand on Chris's arm.

"It's all right, Matthew. I had to tell Diana. I can tell Chris, too." Sarah's throat worked. "Emily had a heart attack. She died in May."

"God, Sarah. I'm so sorry." Chris enveloped her in a less bone-crushing version of the hug he'd given me. He rocked slightly on his feet, his eyes screwed tightly shut. Sarah moved with him, her body relaxed and open rather than tight and full of grief. My aunt had not yet gotten over Emily's death—like Fernando, she might never get over that fundamental loss—but there were small signs that she was beginning the slow process of learning to live again.

Chris's dark eyes opened and sought me out over Sarah's shoulder. They held anger and hurt, as well as sorrow and unanswered questions. *Why didn't you tell me? Where have you been? Why didn't you let me help?*

"I'd like to talk to Chris," I said softly. "Alone."

"You'll be most comfortable in the keeping room." Sarah drew away from Chris and wiped her eyes. The nod she gave me encouraged me to tell him our family's secret. Based on the tightness of his jaw, Matthew was not feeling as generous.

"Call if you need me." Matthew raised my hand to his lips. There was a warning squeeze, a tiny nip on the knuckle of my ring finger as if to remind me—and him—that we were husband and wife. Matthew reluctantly released me.

Chris and I passed through the house to the keeping room. Once we were inside, I slid the doors shut.

"You're married to Matthew Clairmont?" Chris exploded. "Since when?"

"About ten months. It all happened very quickly," I said apologetically.

"I'll say!" Chris lowered his voice. "I warned you about his reputation with women. Clairmont may be a great scientist, but he's also a notorious asshole! Besides, he's too old for you."

"He's only thirty-seven, Chris." Give or take fifteen hundred years. "And I should warn you, Matthew and Fernando are listening to every word we say." With vampires around, a closed door was no guarantee of privacy.

"How? Did your boyfriend—husband—bug the house?" Chris's tone was sharp.

"No. He's a vampire. They have exceptional hearing." Sometimes honesty really was the best policy.

A heavy pot crashed in the kitchen.

"A vampire." Chris's look suggested I had lost my mind. "Like on TV?"

"Not exactly," I said, proceeding with caution. Telling humans how the world really worked tended to unsettle them. I'd done it only once before—and it had been a huge mistake. My freshman roommate, Melanie, had passed out.

"A vampire," Chris repeated slowly, as if he were thinking it all through.

"You'd better sit down." I gestured toward the sofa. If he fell, I didn't want him to hit his head.

Ignoring my suggestion, Chris plopped himself in the wing chair instead. It was more comfortable, to be sure, but had been known to forcibly eject visitors it didn't like. I eyed it warily.

"Are you a vampire, too?" Chris demanded.

"No." I perched gingerly on the edge of my grandmother's rocking chair.

"Are you absolutely sure that Clairmont is? That's his child you're carrying, right?" Chris sat forward, as though a great deal depended on the answer.

"Children." I held two fingers in the air. "Twins."

Chris threw his hands in the air. "Well, no vampire ever knocked up a girl on *Buffy*. Not even Spike. And God knows he never practiced safe sex."

Bewitched had provided my mother's generation with their supernatural primer. For mine it was *Buffy the Vampire Slayer*. Whichever creatures had introduced Joss Whedon to our world had a lot to answer for. I sighed.

"I'm absolutely positive that Matthew is the father."

Chris's attention drifted to my neck.

"That's not where he bites me."

His eyes widened. "Where . . . ?" He shook his head. "No, don't tell me."

It was, I thought, a strange place to draw the line. Chris wasn't normally squeamish—or prudish. Still, he hadn't passed out. That was encouraging.

"You're taking this very well," I said, grateful for his equanimity.

"I'm a scientist. I'm trained to suspend disbelief and remain open-minded until something is disproved." Chris was now staring at the Blasted Tree. "Why is there a tree in the fireplace?"

"Good question. We don't really know. Maybe you have other questions I could answer, though." It was an awkward invitation, but I was still worried he might faint.

"A few." Once again Chris fixed his dark eyes on mine. He wasn't a witch, but it had been very difficult to lie to him for all these years. "You say Clairmont's a vampire, but you're not. What are *you*, Diana? I've known for some time that you aren't like other people."

I didn't know what to say. How do you explain to someone you love that you've failed to mention a defining characteristic of yourself?

"I'm your best friend—or I was until Clairmont came along. Surely you trust me enough to come out to me," Chris said. "No matter what it is, it won't change anything between us."

Beyond Chris's shoulder a green smudge trailed off toward the Blasted Tree. The green smudge became the indistinct form of Bridget Bishop, with her embroidered bodice and full skirts.

Be canny, daughter. The wind blows from the north, a sign of a battle to come. Who will stand with you, and who will stand against you?

I had plenty of enemies. I couldn't afford to lose a single friend.

"Maybe you don't trust me enough," Chris said softly when I didn't immediately respond.

"I'm a witch." My words were barely audible.

"Okay." Chris waited. "And?"

"And what?"

"That's it? That's what you've been afraid to tell me?"

"I'm not talking neo-pagan, Chris—though I am pagan, of course. I'm talking an abracadabra, spell-casting, potion-making witch." In this case Chris's love of prime-time TV might actually prove useful.

"Do you have a wand?"

"No. But I do have a firedrake. That's a kind of dragon."

"Cool." Chris grinned. "Very, very cool. Is that why you've stayed out of New Haven? Were you taking it to dragon obedience class or something?"

"Matthew and I had to get out of town quickly, that's all. I'm sorry I didn't tell you."

"Where were you?"

"In 1590."

"Did you get any research done?" Chris looked thoughtful. "I suppose that would cause all kinds of citation problems. What would you put in your footnotes? 'Personal conversation with William Shakespeare'?" He laughed.

"I never met Shakespeare. Matthew's friends didn't approve of him." I paused. "I did meet the queen."

"Even better," Chris said, nodding. "Equally impossible to footnote, however."

"You're supposed to be shocked!" This was not at all what I'd expected. "Don't you want proof?"

"I haven't been shocked by anything since the MacArthur Foundation called me. If that can happen, anything is possible." Chris shook his head. "Vampires and witches. Wow."

"There are daemons, too. But their eyes don't glow and they're not evil. Well, no more so than any other species."

"Other species?" Chris's tone sharpened with interest. "Are there werewolves?"

"Absolutely not!" Matthew shouted in the distance.

"Touchy subject." I gave Chris a tentative smile. "So you're really fine with this?"

"Why wouldn't I be? The government spends millions searching for aliens in outer space, and it turns out you're right here. Think of all the grant money this could free up." Chris was always looking for a way to diminish the importance of the physics department.

"You can't tell anybody," I said hastily. "Not many humans know about us, and we need to keep it that way."

"We're bound to find out eventually," Chris said. "Besides, most people would be thrilled."

"You think? The dean of Yale College would be thrilled to know that they'd tenured a witch?" I raised my eyebrows. "My students' parents would be happy to discover that their beloved children are learning about the Scientific Revolution from a witch?"

"Well, maybe not the dean." Chris's voice dropped. "Matthew isn't going to bite me to keep me quiet?"

"No," I assured him.

Fernando inserted his foot between the keeping-room doors and nudged them open.

"I'd be happy to bite you instead, but only if you ask very nicely." Fernando put a tray on the table. "Sarah thought you might like coffee. Or something stronger. Call me if you need anything else. No need to shout." He gave Chris the kind of dazzling smile he'd bestowed on the coven's female membership at the Lughnasadh potluck.

"Saddling the wrong horse, Fernando," I warned as he departed.

"He's a vampire, too?" Chris whispered.

"Yep. Matthew's brother-in-law." I held up the whiskey bottle and the coffeepot. "Coffee? Whiskey?"

"Both," said Chris, reaching for a mug. He looked at me in alarm. "You haven't kept this witch business from your aunt, have you?"

"Sarah's a witch, too. So was Em." I poured a healthy slug of whiskey in his mug and topped it off with a bit of coffee. "This is the third or fourth pot of the day, so it's mostly decaf. Otherwise we have to scrape Sarah off the ceiling."

"Coffee makes her fly?" Chris took a sip, considered a moment, and added more whiskey.

"In a manner of speaking," I said, uncapping the water and taking a swig. The babies fluttered, and I gave my abdomen a gentle pat.

"I can't believe you're pregnant." For the first time, Chris sounded amazed.

"You've just learned that I spent most of last year in the sixteenth century, I have a pet dragon, and that you're surrounded by daemons, vampires, and witches, but it's my pregnancy that you find implausible?"

"Trust me, honey," Chris said, pulling out his best Alabama drawl. "It's way more implausible."

13

When the phone rang, it was pitch black outside. I shook myself from sleep, reaching across the bed to jostle Matthew awake. He wasn't there.

I rolled over and picked up his mobile from the bedside table. The name MIRIAM was displayed, along with the time. Three o'clock Monday morning. My heart thudded in alarm. Only an emergency would have induced her to call at such an hour.

"Miriam?" I said after pushing the answer button.

"Where is he?" Miriam's voice shook. "I need to speak with Matthew."

"I'll find him. He must be downstairs, or outside hunting." I threw off the covers. "Is something wrong?"

"Yes," Miriam said abruptly. Then she switched to another language, one I didn't understand. The cadence was unmistakable, though. Miriam Shephard was praying.

Matthew burst through the door, Fernando behind him.

"Here's Matthew." I hit the speaker button and handed him the phone. He was not going to have this conversation in private.

"What is it, Miriam?" Matthew said.

"There was a note. In the mailbox. A Web address was typed on it." There was a curse, a jagged sob, and Miriam's prayer resumed.

"Text me the address, Miriam," Matthew said calmly.

"It's him, Matthew. It's Benjamin," Miriam whispered. "And there was no stamp on the envelope. He must still be here. In Oxford."

I leaped out of bed, shivering in the predawn darkness.

"Text me the address," Matthew repeated.

A light came on in the hallway.

"What's going on?" Chris joined Fernando at the threshold, rubbing the sleep from his eyes.

"It's one of Matthew's colleagues from Oxford, Miriam Shephard. Something's happened at the lab," I told him.

"Oh," Chris said with a yawn. He shook his head to clear the cobwebs and frowned. "Not the Miriam Shephard who wrote the classic article about how inbreeding among zoo animals leads to a loss of heterozygosity?" I'd spent a lot of time around scientists, but it seldom helped me to understand what they were talking about.

"The same," Matthew murmured.

"I thought she was dead," Chris said.

"Not quite," said Miriam in her piercing soprano. "To whom am I speaking?"

"Chris—Christopher Roberts. Yale University," Chris stammered. He sounded like a graduate student introducing himself at his first conference.

"Oh. I liked your last piece in *Science*. Your research model is impressive, even though the conclusions are all wrong." Miriam sounded more like herself now that she was criticizing a fellow researcher. Matthew noticed the positive change, too.

"Keep her talking," Matthew encouraged Chris before issuing a quiet command to Fernando.

"Is that Miriam?" Sarah asked, shoving her arms through the sleeves of her bathrobe. "Don't vampires have clocks? It's three in the morning!"

"What's wrong with my conclusions?" Chris asked, his expression thunderous.

Fernando was back, and he handed Matthew his laptop. It was already on, the screen's glow illuminating the room. Sarah reached around the door frame and flicked the light switch, banishing the remaining darkness. Even so I could feel the shadows pressing down on the house.

Matthew perched on the edge of the bed, his laptop on his knee. Fernando tossed him another cell phone, and Matthew tethered it to the computer.

"Have you seen Benjamin's message?" Miriam sounded calmer than before, but fear kept her voice keen.

"I'm calling it up now," Matthew said.

"Don't use Sarah's Internet connection!" Her agitation was palpable. "He's monitoring traffic to the site. He might be able to locate you from your IP address."

"It's all right, Miriam," Matthew said, his voice soothing. "I'm using Fernando's mobile. And Baldwin's computer people made sure that no one can trace my location from it."

Now I understood why Baldwin had supplied us with new cell phones when we left Sept-Tours, changed all our phone plans, and canceled Sarah's Internet service.

An image of an empty room appeared on the screen. It was white-tiled and barren except for an old sink with exposed plumbing and an examination table. There was a drain in the floor. The date and time were in the lower left corner, the numbers on the clock whirring forward as each second passed.

"What's that lump?" Chris pointed to a pile of rags on the floor. It stirred.

"A woman," Miriam said. "She's been lying there since I got on the site ten minutes ago." As soon as Miriam said it, I could make out her thin arms and legs, the curve of her breast and belly. The scrap of cloth over her wasn't large enough to protect her from the cold. She shivered and whimpered.

"And Benjamin?" Matthew said, his eyes glued to the screen.

"He walked through the room and said something to her. Then he looked straight at the camera—and smiled."

"Did he say anything else?" Matthew asked.

"Yes. 'Hello, Miriam.'"

Chris leaned over Matthew's shoulder and touched the computer's trackpad. The image grew larger.

"There's blood on the floor. And she's chained to the wall." Chris stared at me. "Who's Benjamin?"

"My son." Matthew's glance flickered to Chris, then returned to the screen.

Chris crossed his arms over his chest and stared, unblinking, at the image.

Soft strains of music came out of the computer speakers. The woman shrank against the wall, her eyes wide.

"No," she moaned. "Not again. Please. No." She stared straight at the camera. "Help me."

My hands flashed with colors, and the knots on my wrists burned. I felt a tingle, dull but unmistakable.

"She's a witch. That woman is a witch." I touched the screen. When I drew my finger away, a thin green thread was attached to the tip.

The thread snapped.

"Can she hear us?" I asked Matthew.

"No," Matthew said grimly. "I don't believe so. Benjamin wants me to listen to him."

"No talking to our guests." There was no sign of Matthew's son, but I knew that cold voice. The woman instantly subsided, hugging her arms around her body.

Benjamin approached the camera until his face filled most of the screen. The woman was still visible over his shoulder. He'd staged this performance carefully.

"Another visitor has joined us—Matthew, no doubt. How clever of you to mask your location. And dear Miriam is still with us, I see." Benjamin smiled again. No wonder Miriam was shaken. It was a horrifying sight: those curved lips and the dead eyes I remembered from Prague. Even after more than four centuries, Benjamin was recognizable as the man whom Rabbi Loew had called Herr Fuchs.

"How do you like my laboratory?" Benjamin's arm swept the room. "Not as well equipped as yours, Matthew, but I don't need much. Experience is really the best teacher. All I require is a cooperative research subject. And warmbloods are so much more revealing than animals."

"Christ," Matthew murmured.

"I'd hoped the next time we talked it would be to discuss my latest successful experiment. But things haven't worked out quite as planned." Benjamin turned his head, and his voice became menacing. "Have they?"

The music grew louder, and the woman on the floor moaned and tried to block her ears.

"She used to love Bach," Benjamin reported with mock sadness. "The St. Matthew Passion in particular. I'm careful to play it whenever I take her. Now the witch becomes unaccountably distressed as soon as she hears the first strains." He hummed along with the next bars of music.

"Does he mean what I think he means?" Sarah asked uneasily.

"Benjamin is repeatedly raping that woman," Fernando said with barely controlled fury. It was the first time I'd seen the vampire beneath his easygoing façade.

"Why?" Chris asked. Before anyone could answer, Benjamin resumed.

"As soon as she shows signs of being pregnant, the music stops. It's the witch's reward for doing her job and pleasing me. Sometimes nature has other ideas, though."

The implications of Benjamin's words sank in. As in long-ago Jerusalem, this witch had to be a weaver. I covered my mouth as the bile rose.

The glint in Benjamin's eye intensified. He adjusted the angle of the camera and zoomed in on the blood that stained the woman's legs and the floor.

"Unfortunately, the witch miscarried." Benjamin's voice had the detachment of any scientist reporting his research findings. "It was the fourth month—the longest she's been able to sustain a pregnancy. So far. My son impregnated her last December, but that time she miscarried in the eighth week."

Matthew and I had conceived our first child in December, too. I'd miscarried early in that pregnancy, around the same time as Benjamin's witch. I started to shake at this new connection between me and the woman on the floor. Matthew's arm hooked around my hips, steadying me.

"I was so sure my ability to father a child was linked to the blood rage you gave me—a gift that I've shared with many of my own children. After the witch miscarried the first time, my sons and I tried impregnating daemons and humans without success. I concluded there must be some special reproductive affinity between vampires with blood rage and witches. But these failures mean I'll have to reexamine my hypothesis." Benjamin pulled a stool up to the camera and sat, oblivious to the growing agitation of the woman behind him. In the background the Bach continued to play.

"And there is another piece of information that I'll also have to factor into my deliberations: your marriage. Has your new wife replaced Eleanor in your affections? Mad Juliette? Poor Celia? That fascinating witch I met in Prague?" Benjamin snapped his fingers as if trying to remember something. "What was her name? Diana?"

Fernando hissed. Chris's skin broke out in raised bumps. He stared at Fernando and stepped away.

"I'm told your new wife is a witch, too. Why don't you ever share your ideas with me? You must know I'd understand." Benjamin leaned closer as if sharing a confidence. "We're both driven by the same things, after all: a lust for power, an unquenchable thirst for blood, a desire for revenge."

The music reached a crescendo, and the woman began to rock back and forth in an attempt to soothe herself.

"I can't help wondering how long you've known about the power in our blood. The witches surely knew. What other secret could the Book of Life possibly contain?" Benjamin paused as if waiting for an answer. "Not going to tell me, eh? Well, then. I have no choice but to go back to my own experiment. Don't worry. I'll figure out how to breed this witch eventually—or kill her trying. Then I'll look for a new witch. Maybe yours will suit."

Benjamin smiled. I drew away from Matthew, not wanting him to sense my fear. But his expression told me that he knew.

"Bye for now." Benjamin gave a jaunty wave. "Sometimes I let people watch me work, but I'm not in the mood for an audience today. I'll be sure to let you know if anything interesting develops. Meanwhile you might want to think about sharing what you know. It might save me from having to ask your wife."

With that, Benjamin switched off the lens and the sound. It left a black screen, with the clock still ticking down the seconds in the corner.

"What are we going to do?" Miriam asked.

"Rescue that woman," Matthew said, his fury evident, "for a start."

"Benjamin wants you to rush into the open and expose yourself," Fernando warned. "Your attack will have to be well planned and perfectly executed."

"Fernando's right," Miriam said. "You can't go after Benjamin until you're sure you can destroy him. Otherwise you put Diana at risk."

"That witch won't survive much longer!" Matthew exclaimed.

"If you are hasty and fail to bring Benjamin to heel, he will simply take another and the nightmare will begin again for some other unsuspecting creature," Fernando said, his hand clasped around Matthew's arm.

"You're right." Matthew dragged his eyes away from the screen. "Can you warn Amira, Miriam? She needs to know that Benjamin has one witch already and is likely to kidnap again."

"Amira isn't a weaver. She wouldn't be able to conceive Benjamin's child," I observed.

"I don't think Benjamin knows about weavers. Yet." Matthew rubbed at his jaw.

"What's a weaver?" Miriam and Chris said at the same moment. I opened my mouth to reply, but the slight shake of Matthew's head made me close it again.

"I'll tell you later, Miriam. Will you do what I asked?"

"Sure, Matthew," Miriam agreed.

"Call me later and check in." Matthew's worried glance settled on me.

"Stifle Diana with your excessive attention if you must, but I don't need a babysitter. Besides, I've got work to do." Miriam hung up.

A second later Chris delivered a powerful uppercut to Matthew's jaw. He followed it with a left hook. Matthew intercepted that blow with a raised palm.

"I took one punch, for Diana's sake." Matthew closed his fist around Chris's clenched hand. "My wife does, after all, bring out the protective instincts in people. But don't press your luck."

Chris didn't budge. Fernando sighed.

"Let it go, Roberts. You will not win a physical contest with a vampire." Fernando put his hand on Chris's shoulder, prepared to pull him away if necessary.

"If you let that bastard within fifty miles of Diana, you won't see another sunrise—vampire or no vampire. Are we clear on that?" Chris demanded, his attention locked on Matthew.

"Crystal," Matthew replied. Chris pulled his arm back, and Matthew released his fist.

"Nobody's getting any more sleep tonight. Not after this," Sarah said. "We need to talk. And lots of coffee—and don't you dare use decaf, Diana. But first I'm going outside to have a cigarette, no matter what Fernando says." Sarah marched out of the room. "See you in the kitchen," she shot over her shoulder.

"Keep that site online. When Benjamin is turning on the camera, he might do or say something that will give his location away." Matthew handed his laptop and the still-attached mobile to Fernando. There was still nothing but a black screen and that horrible clock marking the passage of time. Matthew angled his head toward the door, and Fernando followed Sarah.

"So let me get this straight. Matthew's Bad Seed is engaged in some down-home genetics research involving a hereditary condition, a kidnapped witch, and some half-baked ideas about eugenics." Chris folded his arms over his chest. There were a few details missing, but he had sized up the situation in no time at all. "You left some important plot twists out of the fairy tale you told me yesterday, Diana."

"She didn't know about Benjamin's scientific interests. None of us knew." Matthew stood.

"You must have known that the Bad Seed was as crazy as a shit-house rat. He is your son." Chris's eyes narrowed. "According to him you both share this blood-rage thing. That means you're both a danger to Diana."

"I knew he was unstable, yes. And his name is Benjamin." Matthew chose not to respond to the second half of Chris's remarks.

"Unstable? The man is a psychopath. He's trying to engineer a master race of vampire-witches. So why isn't the Bad—Benjamin locked up? That way he couldn't kidnap and rape his way onto the roster of scientific madmen alongside Sims, Verschuer, Mengele, and Stanley."

"Let's go to the kitchen." I urged them both in the direction of the stairs.

"After you," Matthew murmured, putting his hand on the small of my back. Relieved by his easy acquiescence, I began my descent.

There was a thud, a muffled curse.

Chris was pinned against the door, Matthew's hand wrapped around his windpipe.

"Based on the profanity that's come out of your mouth in the past twenty-four hours, I can only conclude that you think of Diana as one of the guys." Matthew gave me a warning look when I backed up to intervene. "She's not. She's my wife. I would appreciate it if you limited your vulgarity in her presence. Are we clear?"

"Crystal." Chris looked at him with loathing.

"I'm glad to hear it." Matthew was at my side in a flash, his hand once more on the dip in my spine where the shadowy firedrake had appeared. "Watch the stairs, *mon coeur,*" he murmured.

When we reached the ground floor, I sneaked a backward glance at Chris. He was studying Matthew as though he were a strange new life-form—which I suppose he was. My heart sank. Matthew might have won the first few battles, but the war between my best friend and my husband was far from over.

By the time Sarah joined us in the kitchen, her hair exuded the scents of tobacco and the hop vine that was planted against the porch railings. I waved my hand in front of my nose—cigarette smoke was one of the few things that still triggered nausea this late in my pregnancy—and made coffee.

When it was ready, I poured the pot's steaming contents into mugs for Sarah, Chris, and Fernando. Matthew and I stuck to ordinary water. Chris was the first to break the silence.

"So, Matthew, you and Dr. Shephard have been studying vampire genetics for decades in an effort to understand blood rage."

"Matthew knew Darwin. He's been studying creature origins and evolution for more than a few decades." I wasn't going to tell Chris how much more, but I didn't want him to be blindsided by Matthew's age, as I had been.

"We have. My son has been working with us." Matthew gave me a quelling look.

"Yes, I saw that," Chris said, a muscle ticking in his cheek. "Not something I'd boast about, myself."

"Not Benjamin. My other son, Marcus Whitmore."

"Marcus Whitmore." Chris made an amused sound. "Covering all the bases, I see. You handle the evolutionary biology and neuroscience, Miriam Shephard is an expert on population genetics, and Marcus Whitmore is known for his study of functional morphology and efforts to debunk phenotypic plasticity. That's a hell of a research team you've assembled, Clairmont."

"I'm very fortunate," Matthew said mildly.

"Wait a minute." Chris looked at Matthew in amazement. "Evolutionary biology. Evolutionary physiology. Population genetics. Figuring out how blood rage is transmitted isn't your only research objective. You're trying to diagram evolutionary descent. You're working on the Tree of Life—and not just the human branches."

"Is that what the tree in the fireplace is called?" Sarah asked.

"I don't think so." Matthew patted her hand.

"Evolution. I'll be damned." Chris pushed away from the island. "So have you discovered the common ancestor for humans and you guys?" He waved in our direction.

"If by 'you guys' you mean creatures—daemons, vampires, and witches—then no." Matthew's brow arched.

"Okay. What are the crucial genetic differences separating us?"

"Vampires and witches have an extra chromosome pair," Matthew explained. "Daemons have a single extra chromosome."

"You've got a genetic map for these creature chromosomes?"

"Yes," Matthew said.

"Then you've probably been working on this little project since before 1990, just to keep up with the humans."

"That's right," Matthew said. "And I've been working since 1968 on how blood rage is inherited, if you must know."

"Of course. You adapted Donahue's use of family pedigrees to determine gene transmission between generations." Chris nodded. "Good call. How far along are you with sequencing? Have you located the blood-rage gene?"

Matthew stared at him without replying.

"Well?" Chris demanded.

"I had a teacher like you once," Matthew said coldly. "He drove me insane."

"And I have students like you. They don't last long in my lab." Chris leaned across the table. "I take it that not every vampire on the planet has your condition. Have you determined exactly how blood rage is inherited, and why some contract it and some don't?"

"Not entirely," Matthew admitted. "It's a bit more complicated with vampires, considering we have three parents."

"You need to pick up the pace, my friend. Diana is pregnant. With twins." Chris looked at me pointedly. "I assume you've drawn up full genetic profiles for the two of you and made predictions for inheritance patterns among your offspring, including but not limited to blood rage?"

"I've been in the sixteenth century for the best part of a year." Matthew really disliked being questioned. "I lacked the opportunity."

"High time we started, then," Chris remarked blandly.

"Matthew was working on something." I looked to Matthew for confirmation. "Remember? I found that paper covered with X's and O's."

"X's and O's? Lord God Almighty." This seemed to confirm Chris's worst fears. "You tell me you have three parents, but you remain married to a Mendelian inheritance model. I suppose that's what happens when you're as old as dirt and knew Darwin."

"I met Mendel once, too," Matthew said crisply, sounding like an irritated professor himself. "Besides, blood rage may be a Mendelian trait. We can't rule that out."

"Highly unlikely," Chris said. "And not just because of this three-parent problem—which I'll have to consider in more detail. It must create havoc in the data."

"Explain." Matthew tented his fingers in front of his face.

"I have to give an overview of non-Mendelian inheritance to a fellow of All Souls?" Chris's eyebrows rose. "Somebody needs to look at the appointment policies at Oxford University."

"Do you understand a word they're saying?" Sarah whispered.

"One in three," I said apologetically.

"I mean gene conversion. Infectious heredity. Genomic imprinting. Mosaicism." Chris ticked them off on his finger. "Ring any bells, Professor Clairmont, or would you like me to continue with the lecture I give to my undergraduates?"

"Isn't mosaicism a form of chimerism?" It was the only word I'd recognized.

Chris nodded at me approvingly.

"I'm a chimera—if that helps."

"Diana," Matthew growled.

"Chris is my best friend, Matthew," I said. "And if he's going to help you figure out how vampires and witches can reproduce—not to mention find a cure for the disease—he needs to know everything. That includes my genetic test results, by the way."

"That information can be deadly in the wrong hands," Matthew said.

"Matthew is right," Chris agreed.

"I'm so glad you think so." Matthew's words dripped acid.

"Don't patronize me, Clairmont. I know the dangers of human-subject research. I'm a black man from Alabama and grew up in the shadow of Tuskegee." Chris turned to me. "Don't hand over your genetic information to anybody outside this room—even if they're wearing a white coat. Especially if they're wearing a white coat, come to think of it."

"Thanks for your input, Christopher," Matthew said stiffly. "I'll be sure to pass your ideas on to the rest of my team."

"So what are we going to do about all this?" Fernando asked. "There may not have been any urgency before, but now . . ." He looked to Matthew for guidance.

"The Bad Seed's breeding program changes everything," Chris proclaimed before Matthew could speak. "First we have to figure out if blood rage really is what makes conception possible or if it's a combination of factors. And we need to know the likelihood of Diana's children contracting the disease. We'll need the witch and the vampire genetic maps for that."

"You'll need my DNA, too," I said quietly. "Not all witches can reproduce."

"Do you need to be a good witch? A bad witch?" Chris's silly jokes usually made me smile, but not tonight.

"You need to be a weaver," I replied. "You're going to need to sequence my genome in particular and compare it to that of other witches. And you'll need to do the same for Matthew and vampires who don't have blood rage. We have to understand blood rage well enough to cure it, or Benjamin and his children will continue to be a threat."

"Okay, then." Chris slapped his thighs. "We need a lab. And help. Plenty of data and computer time, too. I can put my people on this."

"Absolutely not." Matthew shot to his feet. "I have a lab, too. Miriam has been working on the problems of blood rage and the creature genomes for some time."

"Then she should come here immediately and bring her work with her. My students are good, Matthew. The best. They'll see things you and I have been conditioned not to see."

"Yes. Like vampires. And witches." Matthew ran his fingers through his hair. Chris looked alarmed at the transformation in his tidy appearance. "I don't like the idea of more humans knowing about us."

Matthew's words reminded me who *did* need to know about Benjamin's latest message. "Marcus. We need to tell Marcus."

Matthew dialed his number.

"Matthew? Is everything all right?" Marcus said as soon as he picked up the call.

"Not really. We have a situation." Matthew quickly told him about Benjamin and the witch he was keeping hostage. Then he told Marcus why.

"If I send you the Web address, will you have Nathaniel Wilson figure out how to monitor Benjamin's feed 24/7? And if he could find where the signal is originating from, that would save a lot of time," Matthew said.

"Consider it done," Marcus replied.

No sooner had Matthew disconnected than my own cell phone rang.

"Who now?" I said, glancing at the clock. The sun had barely risen. "Hello?"

"Thank God you're awake," Vivian Harrison said, relieved.

"What's wrong?" My black thumb prickled.

"We've got trouble," she said grimly.

"What kind of trouble?" I asked. Sarah pressed her ear against the receiver next to mine. I tried to flap her away.

"I received a message from Sidonie von Borcke," Vivian said.

"Who is Sidonie von Borcke?" I'd never heard the name before.

"One of the Congregation's witches," Vivian and Sarah said in unison.

14

"The coven failed the test." Vivian flung her satchel-size purse onto the kitchen island and poured herself a cup of coffee.

"Is she a witch, too?" Chris asked me in a whisper.

"I am," Vivian replied instead, noticing Chris for the first time.

"Oh." He looked at her appraisingly. "Can I take a cheek swab? It's painless."

"Maybe later." Vivian did a double take. "I'm sorry, but who are you?"

"This is Chris Roberts, Vivian, my colleague from Yale. He's a molecular biologist." I passed the sugar and gave Chris a pinch on the arm to keep him quiet. "Can we possibly talk in the family room? My head is killing me—and my feet are swelling up like balloons."

"Somebody complained to the Congregation about covenant violations in Madison County," Vivian told us when we were comfortably ensconced in the sofas and armchairs arranged in front of the TV.

"Do you know who it was?" Sarah asked.

"Cassie and Lydia." Vivian stared morosely into her coffee.

"The *cheerleaders* narked us out?" Sarah was dumbfounded.

"Figures," I said. They'd been inseparable since childhood, insufferable since adolescence, and indistinguishable since high school with their softly curling blond hair and blue eyes. Neither Cassie nor Lydia had let her witchy ancestry keep her in the shadows. Together they had co-captained the cheerleading squad and witches credited them with giving Madison its most successful football season in history by inserting victory spells into every chant and routine.

"And what are the charges—exactly?" Matthew had switched into lawyer mode.

"That Diana and Sarah have been consorting with vampires," Vivian muttered.

"Consorting?" Sarah's outrage was clear.

Vivian flung her hands up in the air. "I know, I know. It sounds positively lewd, but I assure you those were Sidonie's exact words. Happily, Sidonie is in Las Vegas and can't come in person to investigate. The Clark County covens are too heavily invested in real estate, and they're using spells to try to shore up the housing market."

"So what happens now?" I asked Vivian.

"I have to respond. In writing."

"Thank goodness. That means you can lie," I said, relieved.

"No way, Diana. She's too smart. I saw Sidonie question the SoHo coven two years ago when they opened up that haunted house on Spring Street, right where the Halloween parade lineup begins. It was masterful." Vivian shuddered. "She even got them to divulge how they suspended a bubbling cauldron over their parade float for six hours. After Sidonie's visit the coven was grounded for a full year—no flying, no apparating, and positively no exorcisms. They still haven't recovered."

"What kind of witch is she?" I asked.

"A powerful one," Vivian said with a snort. But that's not what I meant.

"Is her power elemental or based in the craft?"

"She's got a good grasp of spells, from what I hear," Sarah said.

"Sidonie can fly, and she's a respected seer, too," Vivian added.

Chris raised his hand.

"Yes, Chris?" Sarah sounded like a schoolmarm.

"Smart, powerful, flying—it doesn't matter. You can't let her find out about Diana's children, what with the Bad Seed's latest research project and this covenant you're all worried about."

"Bad Seed?" Vivian stared at Chris blankly.

"Matthew's son knocked up a witch. It seems that reproductive abilities run in the Clairmont family." Chris glared at Matthew. "And about this covenant you've all agreed to. I take it that witches aren't supposed to hang out with vampires?"

"Or with daemons. It makes humans uncomfortable," Matthew said.

"Uncomfortable?" Chris looked dubious. "So did blacks sitting on buses next to white people. Segregation isn't the answer."

"Humans notice creatures if we're in mixed groups," I said, hoping to placate Chris.

"We notice you, Diana, even when you're walking down Temple Street by yourself at ten o'clock in the morning," Chris said, shattering my last, fragile hope that I appeared to be just like everybody else.

"The Congregation was established to enforce the covenant, to keep us safe from human attention and interference," I said, sticking to my guns nonetheless. "In exchange we all stay out of human politics and religion."

"Think what you want, but forced segregation—or the covenant if you want to be fancy about it—is often about concerns for racial purity." Chris propped his legs on the coffee table. "Your covenant probably came into being because witches were having vampire babies. Making humans more 'comfortable' was just a convenient excuse."

Fernando and Matthew exchanged glances.

"I assumed that Diana's ability to conceive was unique—that this was the goddess at work, not part of some broader pattern." Vivian was aghast. "Scores of long-lived creatures with supernatural powers would be terrifying."

"Not if you want to engineer a super race. Then such a creature would be quite a genetic coup," Chris observed. "Do we happen to know of any megalomaniacs with an interest in vampire genetics? Oh, wait. We know two of them."

"I prefer to leave such things to God, Christopher." A dark vein pulsed in Matthew's forehead. "I have no interest in eugenics."

"I forgot. You're obsessed with species evolution—in other words, history and chemistry. Those are Diana's research interests. What a coincidence." Chris's eyes narrowed. "Based on what I've overheard, I have two questions, Professor Clairmont. Is it just vampires who are dying out, or are witches and daemons going extinct, too? And which of these so-called species cares the most about racial purity?"

Chris really *was* a genius. With every insightful question he was delving deeper into the mysteries bound up in the Book of Life, the de Clermont family's secrets, and the mysteries in my own—and Matthew's—blood.

"Chris is right," Matthew said with suspicious speed. "We can't risk the Congregation discovering Diana's pregnancy. If you have no objection, *mon coeur,* I think we should go to Fernando's house in Seville without delay. Sarah can come with us, of course. Then the coven's reputation won't be brought into disrepute."

"I said you can't let the Wicked Witch find out about Diana, not that she should run away," Chris said, disgusted. "Have you forgotten Benjamin?"

"Let's fight this war on one front at a time, Christopher." Matthew's expression must have matched his tone, because Chris immediately subsided.

"Okay. I'll go to Seville." I didn't want to, but I didn't want the Madison witches to suffer either.

"No, it's not okay," Sarah said, her voice rising. "The Congregation wants answers? Well, I want answers, too. You tell Sidonie von Borcke that I have been *consorting* with vampires since last October, ever since Satu Järvinen kidnapped and tortured my niece while Peter Knox stood by and did nothing. If that means I've violated the covenant, that's too damn bad. Without the de Clermonts, Diana would be dead—or worse."

"Those are serious allegations," Vivian said. "You're sure you want to make them?"

"Yes," Sarah said stubbornly. "Knox has already been banished from the Congregation. I want Satu's ass kicked off, too."

"They're looking for Knox's replacement now," Vivian reported. "It's rumored that Janet Gowdie is going to come out of retirement to fill the chair."

"Janet Gowdie is ninety if she's a day," Sarah said. "She can't possibly be up to the job."

"Knox insists that it be a witch known for her spell-casting abilities, as he was. No one—not even Janet Gowdie—ever bested him when it came to performing spells," Vivian said.

"Yet," said Sarah succinctly.

"There's something else, Sarah—and it might make you pause before you go after the witches of the Congregation." Vivian hesitated. "Sidonie has asked for a report on Diana. She says it's standard procedure to check on witches who haven't developed their magical talents to see if anything manifested later in life."

"If it's my power the Congregation is interested in, then Sidonie's request really has nothing to do with Sarah and me consorting with vampires," I said.

"Sidonie claims that she has a childhood assessment of Diana that indicated she was not expected to manifest any of the normal powers traditionally associated with witches," Vivian went on, looking miserable. "Peter Knox conducted it. Rebecca and Stephen agreed to his findings and signed off on it."

"Tell the Congregation that Rebecca and Stephen's assessment of their daughter's magical abilities was absolutely correct, down to the last detail." Sarah's eyes glittered with anger. "My niece has no normal powers."

"Well done, Sarah," Matthew said, his admiration of her careful truth evident. "That answer was worthy of my brother Godfrey."

"Thank you, Matthew," Sarah said with a little nod.

"Knox knows something—or suspects something—about me. He has since I was a child." I expected Matthew to argue. He didn't. "I thought we'd discovered what my parents were hiding: that I'm a weaver, like Dad. But now that I know about Mom's interest in higher magics, I wonder if that doesn't have something to do with Knox's interest as well."

"He's a dedicated practitioner of higher magics," Vivian mused. "And if you were able to devise new dark spells? I imagine that Knox would be willing to do almost anything to get his hands on them."

The house moaned, and the sound of a guitar filled the room with a recognizable melody. Of all the songs on my mother's favorite album, "Landslide" was the one that most tugged at my heart. Whenever I heard it, I remembered her holding me on her lap and humming.

"Mom loved this song," I said. "She knew that change was coming, and she was afraid of it, just like the woman in the song. But we can't afford fear anymore."

"What are you saying, Diana?" Vivian asked.

"The change my mom was expecting? It's here," I said simply.

"And even more change is on the way," Chris said. "You're not going to be able to keep the existence of creatures secret from humans for much longer. You're one autopsy, one genetic-counseling session, one home genetic-testing kit away from being outed."

"Nonsense," Matthew declared.

"Gospel. You have two choices. Do you want to be in control of the situation when it happens, Matthew, or do you want to get smacked upside the head with it?" Chris waited. "Based on our limited acquaintance, I'm guessing you'd prefer option A."

Matthew ran his fingers over his scalp and glared at Chris.

"I thought so." Chris tipped back his chair. "So. Given your predicament, what can Yale University do for you, Professor Clairmont?"

"No." Matthew shook his head. "You are not using research students and postgraduates to analyze creature DNA."

"It's scary as hell, I know," Chris continued in a gentler tone. "We'd all rather hide somewhere safe and let someone else make the tough decisions. But somebody is going to have to stand up and fight for what's right. Fernando tells me you're a pretty impressive warrior."

Matthew stared at Chris, unblinking.

"I'll stand with you, if that helps," Chris added, "provided you meet me halfway."

Matthew was not only an impressive warrior but an experienced one. He knew when he was beaten.

"You win, Chris," he said quietly.

"Good. Let's get started, then. I want to see the creature genetic maps. Then I want to sequence and reassemble the three creature genomes so they can be compared to the human genome." Chris ticked off one item after another. "I want to be sure that you've correctly identified the gene responsible for blood rage. And I want the gene that makes it possible for Diana to conceive your child isolated. I don't believe you've even started to look for that yet."

"Is there anything else I can help you with?" Matthew's brows rose.

"As a matter of fact, there is." Chris's chair thudded to the ground. "Tell Miriam Shephard I want her ass in Kline Biology Tower on Monday morning. It's on Science Hill. You can't miss it. My lab is on the fifth floor. I'd like her to explain how my conclusions in *Science* were wrong before she joins us for our first team meeting at eleven."

"I'll pass that message along." Matthew and Fernando glanced at each other, and Fernando shrugged as if to say, *His funeral.* "Just a reminder, Chris. The research you've outlined thus far will take years to complete. We won't be at Yale for very long. Diana and I will have to be back in Europe by October, if we want the twins born there. Diana shouldn't travel long distances after that."

"All the more reason to have as many people as possible working on the project." Chris stood up and put out his hand. "Deal?"

After a long pause, Matthew took it.

"Smart decision," Chris said, giving it a shake. "I hope you brought your checkbook, Clairmont. The Yale Center for Genome Analysis and the DNA Analysis Facility both charge steep fees, but they're fast and accurate." He looked at his watch. "My bag is already in the car. How long before you two can hit the road?"

"We'll be a few hours behind you," Matthew said.

Chris kissed Sarah on the cheek and gave me a hug. Then his finger rose in a gesture of warning. "Eleven A.M. on Monday, Matthew. Don't be late."

On that note he left.

"What have I done?" Matthew muttered when the front door slammed shut. He looked a bit shell-shocked.

"It will be fine, Matthew," Sarah said with surprising optimism. "I have a good feeling about all this."

A few hours later, we climbed into the car. I waved to Sarah and Fernando from the passenger seat, blinking back the tears. Sarah was smiling, but her arms were wrapped so tightly around herself that the knuckles were white. Fernando exchanged a few words with Matthew and clasped him briefly, hand to elbow, in the familiar de Clermont fashion.

Matthew slid behind the wheel. "All set?"

I nodded. His finger pressed the switch, and the engine turned over.

Keyboard and drums flooded out of the sound system, accompanied by piercing guitars. Matthew fumbled with the controls, trying to turn the music down. When that failed, he tried to turn it off. But no matter what he did, Fleetwood Mac warned us not to stop thinking about tomorrow. Finally he flung up his hands in defeat.

"The house is sending us off in style, I see." He shook his head and put the car in drive.

"Don't worry. It won't be able to keep the song going once we leave the property."

We drove down the long driveway toward the road, the bumps all but imperceptible thanks to the Range Rover's shock absorbers.

I twisted in the seat when Matthew flicked on the turn signal to leave the Bishop farm, but the last words of the song made me face forward again.

"Don't look back," I whispered.

Sol in Virgo

When the sun is in Virgo, send children to school.

This signe signifieth a change of place.

—*Anonymous English Commonplace Book*, c. 1590,
Gonçalves MS 4890, f. 9r

More tea, Professor Bishop?"

"Hmm?" I looked up at the preppy young man with the expectant expression. "Oh. Yes. Of course. Thank you."

"Right away." He whisked the white porcelain teapot from the table.

I looked toward the door, but there was still no sign of Matthew. He was at Human Resources getting his identification badge while I waited for him in the rarefied atmosphere of the nearby New Haven Lawn Club. The hushed confines of the main building dampened the distinctive *plonk* of tennis balls and the screaming children enjoying the pool during the last week of summer vacation. Three brides-to-be and their mothers had been escorted through the room where I was sitting to view the facilities they would enjoy should they be married here.

This might be New Haven, but it was not my New Haven.

"Here you are, Professor." My attentive waiter was back, accompanied by the fresh scent of mint leaves. "Peppermint tea."

Living in New Haven with Matthew was going to require some adjustment. My little row house on the tree-lined, pedestrians-only stretch of Court Street was far more spartan than any of the residences we'd occupied over the last year, whether in the present or the past. It was furnished simply with flea-market finds, cheap pine furniture left over from my graduate-student days, and shelf upon shelf of books and journals. My bed didn't have a footboard or a headboard, never mind a canopy. But the mattress was wide and welcoming, and at the end of our long drive from Madison the two of us had collapsed into it with groans of relief.

We'd spent most of the weekend stocking the house with essentials like any normal New Haven couple: wine from the store on Whitney Avenue for Matthew, groceries for me, and enough electronics to outfit a computer lab. Matthew was horrified that I owned only a laptop. We left the computer store on Broadway with two of everything—one for him and one for me. Afterward we strolled the paths of the residential colleges while the carillon played in Harkness Tower. College and town were just beginning to swell with returning students who shouted greetings across the quad and shared complaints about reading lists and class schedules.

"It's good to be back," I had whispered, my hand hooked through his arm. It felt like we were embarking on a new adventure, just the two of us.

But today was different. I felt out of step and out of sorts.

"There you are." Matthew appeared at my elbow and gave me a lingering kiss. "I missed you."

I laughed. "We've been apart for an hour and a half."

"Exactly. Far too long." His attention wandered over the table, taking in the untouched pot of tea, my blank yellow legal pad, and the unopened copy of the latest *American Historical Review* that we'd rescued from my overstuffed department mailbox on our way to Science Hill. "How was your morning?"

"They've taken very good care of me."

"So they should." On our way into the grand brick building, Matthew had explained that Marcus was one of the founding members of the private club and that the facility was built on land he'd once owned.

"Can I get you something, Professor Clairmont?"

I pressed my lips together. A small crease appeared in the smooth skin between my husband's keen eyes.

"Thank you, Chip, but I believe we're ready to go."

It was not a moment too soon. I stood and gathered my things, slipping them into the large messenger bag at my feet.

"Can you put the charges on Dr. Whitmore's account?" Matthew murmured, pulling out my chair.

"Absolutely," Chip said. "No problem. Always a pleasure to welcome a member of Dr. Whitmore's family."

For once I beat Matthew outside.

"Where's the car?" I said, searching the parking lot.

"It's parked in the shade." Matthew lifted the messenger bag from my shoulder. "We're walking to the lab, not driving. Members are free to leave their cars here, and it's very close to the lab." He looked sympathetic. "This is strange for both of us, but the oddness will pass."

I took a deep breath and nodded. Matthew carried my bag, holding it by the short handle on top.

"It will be better once I'm in the library," I said, as much for my benefit as his. "Shall we get to work?"

Matthew held out his free hand. I took it, and his expression softened. "Lead the way," he said.

We crossed Whitney Avenue by the garden filled with dinosaur statuary, cut behind the Peabody, and approached the tall tower where Chris's labs were located. My steps slowed. Matthew looked up, and up some more.

"No. Please not there. It's worse than the Beinecke." His eyes were glued to the unappealing outlines of Kline Biology Tower, or KBT as it was known on campus. He'd likened the Beinecke, with its white marble walls carved into square hollows, to a giant ice-cube tray. "It reminds me of—"

"Your lab in Oxford was no great beauty either, as I recall," I said, cutting him off before he could give me another vivid analogy that would stay with me forever. "Let's go."

It was Matthew's turn to be reluctant now. He grumbled as we walked into the building, refused to put his blue-and-white Yale lanyard with its magnetized plastic ID card around his neck when the security guard asked him to, continued to complain in the elevator, and was glowering as we looked for the door to Chris's lab.

"It's going to be fine, Matthew. Chris's students will be thrilled to meet you," I assured him. Matthew was an internationally renowned scholar and a member of the Oxford University faculty. There were few institutions that impressed Yale, but that was one of them.

"The last time I was around students was when Hamish and I were fellows at All Souls." Matthew looked away in an effort to hide his nervousness. "I'm better suited to a research lab."

I pulled on his arm, forcing him to stop. Finally he met my eyes.

"You taught Jack all sorts of things. Annie, too," I reminded him, remembering how he'd been with the two children who had lived with us in Elizabethan London.

"That was different. They were . . ." Matthew trailed off, a shadow flitting through his eyes.

"Family?"

I waited for his response. He nodded reluctantly.

"Students want the same things Annie and Jack did: your attention, your honesty, and your faith in them. You're going to be brilliant at this. I promise."

"I'll settle for adequate," Matthew muttered. He scanned the hallway. "There's Christopher's lab. We should go. If I'm late, he's threatened to repossess my ID."

Chris pushed the door open, clearly frazzled. Matthew caught it and propped it open with his foot.

"Another minute, Clairmont, and I would have started without you. Hey, Diana," Chris said, kissing me on the cheek. "I didn't expect to see you here. Why aren't you at the Beinecke?"

"Special delivery." I motioned toward the messenger bag, and Matthew handed it over. "The page from Ashmole 782, remember?"

"Oh. Right." Chris didn't sound the least bit interested. He and Matthew were clearly focused on other questions.

"You two promised," I said.

"Right. Ashmole 782." Chris crossed his arms. "Where's Miriam?"

"I gave Miriam your invitation and will spare you her response. She will be here when—and if—she chooses." Matthew held up his ID card. Even the employment office couldn't take a bad picture of him. He looked like a model. "I'm official, or so they tell me."

"Good. Let's go." Chris took a white lab coat off the nearby rack and shrugged it over his shoulders. He held another out to Matthew.

Matthew looked at it dubiously. "I'm not wearing one of those."

"Suit yourself. No coat, no contact with the equipment. Up to you." Chris turned and marched off.

A woman approached him with a sheaf of papers. She was wearing a lab coat with the name CONNELLY embroidered on it and "Beaker" written above it in red marker.

"Thanks, Beaker." Chris looked them over. "Good. Nobody refused."

"What are those?" I asked.

"Nondisclosure forms. Chris said neither of you has to sign them." Beaker looked at Matthew and nodded in greeting. "We're honored to have you here, Professor Clairmont. I'm Joy Connelly, Chris's second in command. We're short a lab manager at the moment, so I'm filling in until Chris finds either Mother Teresa or Mussolini. Would you please swipe in so that we have a record of when you arrived? And you have to swipe out to leave. It keeps the records straight." She pointed to the reader by the door.

"Thank you, Dr. Connelly." Matthew obediently swiped his card. He was still not wearing a lab coat, though.

"Professor Bishop needs to swipe in, too. Lab protocol. And please call me Beaker. Everybody else does."

"Why?" Matthew asked while I fished my ID out of my bag. As usual, it had settled to the bottom.

"Chris finds nicknames easier to remember," Beaker said.

"He had seventeen Amys and twelve Jareds in his first undergraduate lecture," I added. "I don't think he'll ever recover."

"Happily, my memory is excellent, Dr. Connelly. So is your work on catalytic RNA, by the way." Matthew smiled. Dr. Connelly looked pleased.

"Beaker!" Chris bellowed.

"Coming!" Beaker called. "I sure hope he finds Mother Teresa soon," she muttered to me. "We don't need another Mussolini."

"Mother Teresa is dead," I whispered, running my card through the reader.

"I know. When Chris wrote the job description for the new lab manager, it listed 'Mother Teresa or Mussolini' under qualifications. We rewrote it, of course. Human Resources wouldn't have approved the posting otherwise."

"What did Chris call his last lab manager?" I was almost afraid to ask.

"Caligula." Beaker sighed. "We really miss her."

Matthew waited for us to enter before releasing the door. Beaker looked nonplussed by the courtesy. The door swooshed closed behind us.

A gaggle of white-coated researchers of all ages and descriptions waited for us inside, including senior researchers like Beaker, some exhausted-looking postdoctoral fellows, and a bevy of graduate students. Most sat on stools pulled up to the lab benches; a few lounged against sinks or cabinets. One sink bore a hand-lettered sign over it that said rather ominously THIS SINK RESERVED FOR HAZMAT. Tina, Chris's perpetually harried administrative assistant, was trying to extricate the filled-out nondisclosure forms from beneath a can of soda without disturbing the laptop that Chris was booting up. The hum of conversation stopped when we entered.

"Oh. My. God. That's—" A woman stared at Matthew and clapped a hand over her mouth. Matthew had been recognized.

"Hey, Professor Bishop!" A graduate student stood up, smoothing out his lab coat. He looked more nervous than Matthew. "Jonathan Garcia. Remember me? History of Chemistry? Two years ago?"

"Of course. How are you, Jonathan?" I felt several nudging looks as the attention in the room swung in my direction. There were daemons in Chris's lab. I looked around, trying to figure out who they were. Then I caught the cold stare of a vampire. He was standing by a locked cabinet with Beaker and another woman. Matthew had already noticed him.

"Richard," Matthew said with a cool nod. "I didn't know you'd left Berkeley."

"Last year." Richard's expression never wavered.

It had never occurred to me that there would already be creatures in Chris's lab. I'd visited him only once or twice, when he was working alone. My messenger bag suddenly felt heavy with secrets and possible disaster.

"There will be time for your reunion with Clairmont later, Shotgun," Chris said, hooking the laptop to a projector. There was a wave of appreciative laughter. "Lights please, Beaker."

The laughter quieted as the lights dimmed. Chris's research team leaned forward to see what he had projected on the whiteboard. Black-and-white bars marched across the top of the page, and the overflow was arranged underneath. Each bar—or ideogram, as Matthew had explained to me last night—represented a chromosome.

"This semester we have an all-new research project." Chris leaned against the whiteboard, his dark skin and white lab coat making him look like another ideogram on the display. "Here's our subject. Who wants to tell me what it is?"

"Is it alive or dead?" a cool female voice asked.

"Good question, Scully." Chris grinned.

"Why do you ask?" Matthew looked at the student sharply. Scully squirmed.

"Because," she explained, "if he's deceased—oh, the subject is male, by the way—the cause of death might have a genetic component."

The graduate students, eager to prove their worth, started tossing out rare and deadly genetic disorders faster than they could record them on their laptops.

"All right, all right." Chris held up his hand. "Our zoo has no more room for zebras. Back to basics, please."

Matthew's eyes danced with amusement. When I looked at him in confusion, he explained.

"Students tend to go for exotic explanations rather than the more obvious ones—like thinking a patient has SARS rather than a common cold. We call them 'zebras,' because they're hearing hoofbeats and concluding zebras rather than horses."

"Thanks." Between the nicknames and the wildlife, I was understandably disoriented.

"Stop trying to impress one another and look at the screen. What do you see?" Chris said, calling a halt to the escalating competition.

"It's male," said a weedy-looking young man in a bow tie, who was using a traditional laboratory notebook rather than a computer. Shotgun and Beaker rolled their eyes at each other and shook their heads.

"Scully already deduced that." Chris looked at them impatiently. He snapped his fingers. "Do *not* embarrass me in front of Oxford University, or you will all lift weights with me for the entire month of September."

Everybody groaned. Chris's level of physical fitness was legendary, as was his habit of wearing his old Harvard football jersey whenever Yale had a game. He was the only professor who was publicly, and routinely, booed in class.

"Whatever he is, he's not human," Jonathan said. "He has twenty-four chromosome pairs."

Chris looked down at his watch. "Four and a half minutes. Two minutes longer than I thought it would take, but much quicker than Professor Clairmont expected."

"Touché, Professor Roberts," Matthew said mildly. Chris's team slid glances in Matthew's direction, still trying to figure out what an Oxford professor was doing in a Yale research lab.

"Wait a minute. Rice has twenty-four chromosomes. We're studying *rice*?" asked a young woman I'd seen dining at Branford College.

"Of course we're not studying rice," Chris said with exasperation. "Since when did rice have a sex, Hazmat?" She must be the owner of the specially labeled sink.

"Chimps?" The young man who offered up this suggestion was handsome, in a studious sort of way, with his blue oxford shirt and wavy brown hair.

Chris circled one of the ideograms at the top of the display with a red Magic Marker. "Does that look like chromosome 2A for a chimp?"

"No," the young man replied, crestfallen. "The upper arm is too long. That looks like human chromosome 2."

"It is human chromosome 2." Chris erased his red mark and started to number the ideograms. When he got to the twenty-fourth, he circled it. "This is what we'll be focusing on this semester. Chromosome 24, known henceforward as CC so that the research team studying genetically modified rice over in Osborn doesn't get the heebie-jeebies. We have a lot of work to do. The DNA has been sequenced, but very few gene functions have been identified."

"How many base pairs?" Shotgun asked.

"Somewhere in the neighborhood of forty million," replied Chris.

"Thank God," Shotgun murmured, looking straight at Matthew. It sounded like an awful lot to me, but I was glad he was pleased.

"What does CC stand for?" asked a petite Asian woman.

"Before I answer that, I want to remind you that every person here has given Tina a signed nondisclosure agreement," Chris said.

"Are we working with something that will result in a patent?" A graduate student rubbed his hands together. "Excellent."

"We are working on a highly sensitive, highly confidential research project with far-reaching implications. What happens in this lab stays in this lab. No talking to your friends. No telling your parents. No boasting in the library. If you talk, you walk. Got it?"

Heads nodded.

"No personal laptops, no cell phones, no photographs. One lab terminal will have Internet access, but only Beaker, Shotgun, and Sherlock will have the access code," Chris continued, pointing to the senior researchers. "We'll be keeping lab notebooks the old-fashioned way, written in longhand on paper, and they will all be turned in to Beaker before you swipe out. For those who have forgotten how to use a pen, Bones will show you."

Bones, the weedy young man with the paper notebook, looked smug. A bit reluctantly the students parted with their cell phones, depositing them in a plastic bucket that Beaker carried around the room. Meanwhile Shotgun gathered up the laptops and locked them in a cabinet. Once the laboratory had been cleared of contraband electronics, Chris continued.

"When, in the fullness of time, we decide to go public with our findings—and yes, Professor Clairmont, they will one day be published, because that's what scientists do," Chris said, looking at Matthew sharply, "—none of you will have to worry about your careers ever again."

There were smiles all around.

"CC stands for 'creature chromosome.'"

The formerly smiling faces went blank.

"C-c-creature?" Bones asked.

"I told you there were aliens," said a man sitting next to Hazmat.

"He's not from outer space, Mulder," Chris said.

"Good name," I told Matthew, who looked bewildered. He didn't own a TV, after all. "I'll tell you why later."

"A werewolf?" Mulder said hopefully. Matthew scowled.

"No more guesses," Chris said hastily. "Okay, team. Hands up if you're a daemon."

Matthew's jaw dropped.

"What are you doing?" I whispered to Chris.

"Research," he replied, looking around the room. After a few moments of stunned silence, Chris snapped his fingers. "Come on. Don't be shy."

The Asian woman raised her hand. So did a young man who resembled a giraffe with his ginger-colored hair and long neck.

"Should have guessed it would be Game Boy and Xbox," Chris murmured. "Anyone else?"

"Daisy," the woman said, pointing to a dreamy-eyed creature wearing bright yellow and white clothes who was humming and staring out the window.

"Are you sure, Game Boy?" Chris sounded incredulous. "She's so . . . um, organized. And precise. She's nothing like you and Xbox."

"Daisy doesn't know it yet," Game Boy whispered, her forehead creased with concern, "so go easy on her. Finding out what you really are can freak you out."

"Perfectly understandable," Chris replied.

"What's a daemon?" Scully asked.

"A highly valued member of this research team who colors outside the lines." Chris's response was lightning quick. Shotgun pressed his lips together in amusement.

"Oh" was Scully's mild response.

"I must be a daemon, too, then," Bones claimed.

"Wannabe," Game Boy muttered.

Matthew's lips twitched.

"Wow. Daemons. I knew Yale was a better choice than Johns Hopkins," Mulder said. "Is this Xbox's DNA?"

Xbox looked at Matthew in silent entreaty. Daisy stopped humming and was now paying guarded attention to the conversation.

Matthew, Shotgun, and I were the grown-ups in this situation. Telling humans about creatures shouldn't be left to the students. I opened my mouth to reply, but Matthew put a hand on my shoulder.

"It's not your colleague's DNA," Matthew said. "It's mine."

"You're a daemon, too?" Mulder looked at Matthew with interest.

"No, I'm a vampire." Matthew stepped forward, joining Chris under the projector's light. "And before you ask, I can go outside during the day and my hair won't catch fire in the sunlight. I'm Catholic and have a crucifix. When I sleep, which is not often, I prefer a bed to a coffin. If you try to stake me, the wood will likely splinter before it enters my skin."

He bared his teeth. "No fangs either. And one last thing: I do not, nor have I ever, sparkled." Matthew's face darkened to emphasize the point.

I had been proud of Matthew on many previous occasions. I'd seen him stand up to a queen, a spoiled emperor, and his own awe-inspiring father. His courage—whether fighting with swords or struggling with his own daemons—was bone-deep. But nothing compared to how I felt watching him stand before a group of students and his scientific peers and own up to what he was.

"How old are you?" Mulder asked breathlessly. Like his namesake, Mulder was a true believer in all things wondrous and strange.

"Thirty-seven."

I heard exclamations of disappointment. Matthew took pity on them.

"Give or take about fifteen hundred years."

"Holy shit!" Scully blurted, looking as though her rational world had been turned inside out. "That's older than old. I just can't believe there's a vampire at Yale."

"You've obviously never been to the astronomy department," Game Boy said. "There are four vampires on the faculty there. And that new professor in economics—the woman they hired away from MIT—is definitely a vamp. Rumor has it there are a few in the chemistry department, but they keep to themselves."

"There are witches at Yale, too." My voice was quiet, and I avoided Shotgun's eyes. "We've lived alongside humans for millennia. Surely you'll want to study all three creature chromosomes, Professor Roberts?"

"I will." Chris's smile was slow and heartfelt. "Are you volunteering your DNA, Professor Bishop?"

"Let's take one creature chromosome at a time." Matthew gave Chris a warning look. He might be willing to let students pore over *his* genetic information, but Matthew remained unconvinced about letting them pry into mine.

Jonathan looked at me appraisingly. "So it's witches who sparkle?"

"It's really more of a glimmer," I said. "Not all witches have it. I'm one of the lucky ones, I guess." Saying the words felt freeing, and when nobody ran screaming from the room, I was flooded with a wave of relief and hope. I also had an insane urge to giggle.

"Lights, please," Chris said.

The lights came up gradually.

"You said we were working on several projects?" Beaker prompted.

"You'll be analyzing this, too." I reached into my messenger bag and drew out a large manila envelope. It was stiffened with cardboard inserts so that the contents wouldn't be bent and damaged. I untied the strings and pulled out the page from the Book of Life. The brightly colored illustration of the mystical union of Sol and Luna shone in the lab's fluorescent lights. Someone whistled. Shotgun straightened, his eyes fixed on the page.

"Hey, that's the chemical wedding of mercury and sulfur," Jonathan said. "I remember seeing something like that in class, Professor Bishop."

I gave my former student an approving nod.

"Shouldn't that be in the Beinecke?" Shotgun asked Matthew. "Or somewhere else that's safe?" The emphasis he placed on "safe" was so slight that I thought I might have imagined it. The expression on Matthew's face told me I hadn't.

"Surely it's safe here, Richard?" The prince-assassin was back in Matthew's smile. It made me uncomfortable to see Matthew's lethal personae among the flasks and test tubes.

"What are we supposed to do with it?" Mulder asked, openly curious.

"Analyze its DNA," I replied. "The illumination is on skin. I'd like to know how old the skin is—and the type of creature it came from."

"I just read about this kind of research," Jonathan said. "They're doing mtDNA analysis on medieval books. They hope it will help to date them and determine where they were made." Mitochondrial DNA recorded what an organism had inherited from all its maternal ancestors.

"Maybe you could pull those articles for your colleagues, in case they're not as well read as you are." Matthew looked pleased that Jonathan was up to date on the literature. "But we'll be extracting nuclear DNA as well as mtDNA."

"That's impossible," Shotgun protested. "The parchment has gone through a chemical process to turn skin into a writing surface. Both its age and the changes it underwent during manufacture would damage the DNA—if you could even extract enough to work with."

"It's difficult, but not impossible," Matthew corrected. "I've worked extensively with old, fragile, and damaged DNA. My methods should work with this sample, too."

There were excited looks around the room as the implications of the two research plans sank in. Both projects represented the kind of work that all scientists hoped to do, no matter what stage of their career they were in.

"You don't think cows or goats gave their hide for that page, do you, Dr. Bishop?" Beaker's uneasy voice quieted the room.

"No. I think it was a daemon, a human, a vampire, or a witch." I was pretty sure it wasn't human skin but couldn't rule it out entirely.

"Human?" Scully's eyes popped at the idea. The prospect of other creatures being flayed to make a book didn't seem to alarm her.

"Anthropodermic bibliopegy," Mulder whispered. "I thought it was a myth."

"Technically it's not anthropodermic bibliopegy," I said. "The book this came from isn't just bound in creature remains—it's completely constructed from it."

"Why?" Bones asked.

"Why not?" Daisy replied enigmatically. "Desperate times call for desperate measures."

"Let's not get ahead of ourselves," Matthew said, plucking the page from my fingers. "We're scientists. The whys come after the whats."

"I think that's enough for today," Chris said. "You all look like you need a break."

"I need a beer," Jonathan muttered.

"It's a bit early in the day, but I completely understand. Just remember—you talk, you walk," Chris said sternly. "That means no talking to each other outside these walls either. I don't want anyone to overhear."

"If someone did overhear us talking about witches and vampires, they'd just think we were playing D&D," Xbox said. Game Boy nodded.

"No. Talking," Chris repeated.

The door swooshed open. A tiny woman in a purple miniskirt, red boots, and a black T-shirt that read STAND BACK—I'M GOING TO TRY SCIENCE walked through.

Miriam Shephard had arrived.

"Who are you?" Chris demanded.

"Your worst nightmare—and new lab manager. Hi, Diana." Miriam pointed to the can of soda. "Whose is that?"

"Mine," Chris said.

"No food or drink in the lab. That goes double for you, Roberts," Miriam said, jabbing her finger in Chris's direction.

"Human Resources didn't tell me they were sending an applicant," Beaker said, confused.

"I'm not an applicant. I filled out the paperwork this morning, was hired, and got my dog tags." Miriam held up her ID card, which was, as mandated, attached to her lanyard.

"But I'm supposed to interview . . ." Chris began. "Who did you say you are?"

"Miriam Shephard. And HR waived the interview after I showed them this." Miriam pulled her cell phone out of her waistband. "I quote: 'Have your ass in my lab at nine A.M., and be prepared to explain my mistakes in two hours—no excuses.'" Miriam removed two sheets of paper from her messenger bag, which was stuffed with laptops and paper files. "Who is Tina?"

"I am." A smiling Tina stepped forward. "Hello, Dr. Shephard."

"Hello. I've got my hiring manifest or health-insurance waiver or something for you. And this is Roberts's formal reprimand for his inappropriate text message. File it." Miriam handed over the papers. She slung the bag from her shoulder and tossed it to Matthew. "I brought everything you asked for, Matthew."

The entire lab watched, openmouthed, as the bag full of computers sailed through the air. Matthew caught it without damaging a single laptop, and Chris looked at Miriam's throwing arm with naked admiration.

"Thank you, Miriam," Matthew murmured. "I trust you had an uneventful journey." His tone and choice of words were formal, but there was no disguising his relief at seeing her.

"I'm here, aren't I?" she said caustically. Miriam pulled another piece of paper out of the back pocket on her miniskirt. After examining it she looked up. "Which one of you is Beaker?"

"Here." Beaker walked toward Miriam, her hand extended. "Joy Connelly."

"Oh. Sorry. All I have is a ridiculous list of nicknames drawn from the dregs of popular culture, along with some acronyms." Miriam shook Beaker's hand, drew a pen out of her boot, and crossed something out. She scribbled something next to it. "Nice to meet you. I like your RNA work. Sound stuff. Very helpful. Let's go get coffee and figure out what needs to be done to whip this place into compliance."

"The closest decent coffee is a bit of a hike," Beaker said apologetically.

"Unacceptable." Miriam made another note on her paper. "We need a café in the basement as soon as possible. I toured the building on my way up here, and that space is wasted now."

"Should I come with you?" Chris asked, shifting on his feet.

"Not now," Miriam told him. "Surely you have something more important to do. I'll be back at one o'clock. That's when I want to see"—she paused and scrutinized her list—"Sherlock, Game Boy, and Scully."

"What about me, Miriam?" Shotgun asked.

"We'll catch up later, Richard. Nice to see a familiar face." She looked down at her list. "What does Roberts call you?"

"Shotgun." Richard's mouth twitched.

"I trust it's because of your speedy sequencing, not because you've taken to hunting like humans." Miriam's eyes narrowed. "Is what we're doing here going to be a problem, Richard?"

"Can't imagine why," Richard said with a small shrug. "The Congregation and its concerns are way above my pay grade."

"Good." Miriam surveyed her openly curious new charges. "Well? What are you waiting for? If you want something to do, you can always run some gels. Or unpack supply boxes. There are plenty of them stacked up in the corridor."

Everyone in the lab scattered.

"Thought so." She smiled at Chris. He looked nervous. "As for you, Roberts, I'll see you at two o'clock. We have your article to discuss. And your protocols to review. After that, you can take me to dinner. Somewhere nice, with steak and a good wine list."

Chris looked dazed but nodded.

"Could you give us a minute?" I asked Chris and Beaker. They moved off to the side, Beaker grinning from ear to ear and Chris pinching the bridge of his nose. Matthew joined us.

"You look surprisingly well for someone who's been to the sixteenth century and back, Matthew. And Diana's obviously *enceinte,*" Miriam said, using the French word for "pregnant."

"Thanks. Are you at Marcus's place?" Matthew asked.

"That monstrosity on Orange Street? No chance. It's a convenient location, but it gives me the creeps." Miriam shivered. "Too much mahogany."

"You're welcome to stay with us on Court Street," I offered. "There's a spare bedroom on the third floor. You'd have privacy."

"Thanks, but I'm around the corner. At Gallowglass's condo," Miriam replied.

"What condo?" Matthew frowned.

"The one he bought on Wooster Square. Some converted church. It's very nice—a bit too Danish in decor, but far preferable to Marcus's dark-

and-gloomy period." Miriam looked at Matthew sharply. "Gallowglass did tell you he was coming with me?"

"No, he did not." Matthew ran his fingers through his hair.

I knew just how my husband felt: The de Clermonts had switched into overprotective mode. Only now they weren't protecting just me. They were protecting Matthew as well.

16

Bad news, I'm afraid." Lucy Meriweather's lips twisted in a sympathetic grimace. She was one of the Beinecke librarians, and she'd helped me for years, both with my own research and on the occasions when I brought my students to the library to use the rare books there. "If you want to look at Manuscript 408, you'll have to go into a private room with a curator. And there's a limit of thirty minutes. They won't let you sit in the reading room with it."

"Thirty minutes? With a curator?" I was stunned by the restrictions, having spent the last ten months with Matthew, who never paid any attention to rules and regulations. "I'm a Yale professor. Why does a curator have to babysit me?"

"Those are the rules for everybody—even our own faculty. The whole thing *is* online," Lucy reminded me.

But a computer image, no matter how high the resolution, wasn't going to give me the information I needed. I'd last seen the Voynich manuscript—now Beinecke Library MS 408—in 1591, when Matthew had carried the book from Dr. Dee's library to the court of Emperor Rudolf in Prague, hoping that we could swap it for the Book of Life. Now I hoped it would shed light on what Edward Kelley might have done with the Book of Life's missing pages.

I'd been searching for clues to their whereabouts since we went to Madison. One missing page had an image of two scaly, long-tailed creatures bleeding into a round vessel. The other image was a splendid rendering of a tree, its branches bearing an impossible combination of flowers, fruit, and leaves and its trunk made up of writhing human shapes. I'd hoped that locating the two pages would be fairly straightforward in the age of Internet searches and digitized images. So far that had not been the case.

"Maybe if you could explain why you need to see the physical book . . ." Lucy trailed off.

But how could I tell Lucy I needed the book so I could use magic on it?

This was the Beinecke Library, for heaven's sake.

If anyone found out, it would ruin my career.

"I'll look at the Voynich tomorrow." Hopefully, I would have another plan by then, since I couldn't very well haul out my mother's book of shadows and devise new spells in front of a curator. Juggling my witch self and my scholar self was proving difficult. "Did the other books I requested arrive?"

"They did." Lucy's eyebrows lifted when she slid the collection of medieval magical texts across the desk, along with several early printed books. "Changing your research focus?"

In an effort to be prepared for any magical eventuality when finally it came time to recall Ashmole 782 and reunite it with its missing pages, I had called up books that might inspire my efforts to weave new higher-magic spells. Though my mother's spell book was a valuable resource, I knew from my own experience how far modern witches had fallen when compared to the witches of the past.

"Alchemy and magic aren't completely distinct," I told Lucy defensively. Sarah and Em had tried to get me to see that for years. At last I believed them.

Once I was settled in the reading room, the magical manuscripts were as intriguing as I'd hoped, with sigils that reminded me of weavers' knots and gramarye that was precise and potent. The early-modern books on witchcraft, most of which I knew only by title and reputation, were horrifying, however. Each one brimmed with hatred—for witches and anyone else who was different, rebellious, or refused to conform to societal expectations.

Hours later, still seething over Jean Bodin's vitriolic insistence that all foul opinions about witches and their evil deeds were warranted, I returned the books and manuscripts to Lucy and made an appointment for nine o'clock the next morning to view the Voynich manuscript with the head curator.

I tramped up the staircase to the main level of the library. Here, glass-encased books formed the Beinecke's spinal column, the core of knowledge and ideas around which the collection was built. Rows and rows of rare books were lined up on the shelves, bathed in light. It was a breathtaking sight, one that reminded me of my purpose as a historian: to rediscover the forgotten truths contained in those old, dusty volumes.

Matthew was waiting for me outside. He was lounging against the low wall overlooking the Beinecke's stark sculpture garden, his legs crossed at the ankles, thumbing through the messages on his phone. Sensing my presence, he looked up and smiled.

Not a creature alive could have resisted that smile or the look of concentration in those gray-green eyes.

"How was your day?" he asked after giving me a kiss. I'd asked him not to text me constantly, and he'd been unusually cooperative. As a result he genuinely didn't know.

"A bit frustrating. I suppose my research skills are bound to be rusty after so many months. Besides"—my voice dropped—"the books all look weird to me. They're so old and worn compared to how they looked in the sixteenth century."

Matthew put his head back and laughed. "I hadn't thought about that. Your surroundings have changed, too, since you last worked on alchemy at Baynard's Castle." He looked over his shoulder at the Beinecke. "I know the library is an architectural treasure, but I still think it looks like an ice-cube tray."

"So it does," I agreed with a smile. "I suppose if you'd built it, the Beinecke would look like a Norman keep or a Romanesque cloister."

"I was thinking of something Gothic—far more modern," Matthew teased. "Ready to go home?"

"More than ready," I said, wanting to leave Jean Bodin behind me.

He gestured at my book bag. "May I?"

Usually Matthew didn't ask. He was trying not to smother me, just as he was attempting to rein in his overprotectiveness. I rewarded him with a smile and handed it over without a word.

"Where's Roger?" I asked Lucy, looking down at my watch. I'd been granted exactly thirty minutes with the Voynich manuscript, and the curator was nowhere to be seen.

"Roger called in sick, just as he always does on the first day of classes. He hates the hysteria and all the freshmen asking for directions. You're stuck with me." Lucy picked up the box that held Beinecke MS 408.

"Sounds good." I tried to keep the excitement out of my voice. This might be exactly the break I needed.

Lucy led me to a small private room with windows overlooking the reading room, poor lighting, and a beat-up foam cradle. Security cameras mounted high on the walls would deter any reader from stealing or damaging one of the Beinecke's priceless books.

"I won't start the clock until you unwrap it." Lucy handed me the boxed manuscript. It was all she was carrying. There were no papers, reading materials, or even a cell phone to distract her from the job of monitoring me.

Though I normally flipped manuscripts open to look at the images, I wanted to take my time with the Voynich. I slid the manuscript's limp vellum binding—the early-modern equivalent of a paperback—through my fingers. Images flooded my mind, my witch's touch revealing that the present cover was put on the book several centuries after it was written and at least fifty years after I'd held it in Dee's library. I could see the bookbinder's face and seventeenth-century hairstyle when I touched the spine.

I carefully laid the Voynich in the waiting foam cradle and opened the book. I lowered my nose until it practically touched the first, stained page.

"What are you doing, Diana? Smelling it?" Lucy laughed softly.

"As a matter of fact, I am." If Lucy was going to cooperate with my strange requests this morning, I needed to be as honest as possible.

Openly curious, Lucy came around the table. She gave the Voynich a good sniff, too.

"Smells like an old manuscript to me. Lots of bookworm damage." She swung her reading glasses down and took an even closer look.

"Robert Hooke examined bookworms under his microscope in the seventeenth century. He called them 'the teeth of time.'" Looking at the first page of the Voynich, I could see why. It was riddled with holes in the upper right corner and the bottom margin, both of which were stained. "I think the bookworms must have been drawn to the oils that readers' fingers transferred to the parchment."

"What makes you say that?" Lucy asked. It was just the response I'd hoped for.

"The damage is worst where a reader would have touched to turn to the next folio." I rested my finger on the corner of the page, as if I were pointing to something.

That brief contact set off another explosion of faces, one morphing into another: Emperor Rudolf's avaricious expression; a series of unknown men dressed in clothing from different periods, two of them clerics; a woman taking careful notes; another woman packing up a box of books. And the daemon Edward Kelley, furtively tucking something into the Voynich's cover.

"There is a lot of damage on the bottom edge, too, where the manuscript would have rested against the body if you were carrying it." Ignorant of the slide show playing before my witch's third eye, Lucy peered down at the page. "The clothes of the time were probably pretty oily. Didn't most people wear wool?"

"Wool and silk." I hesitated, then decided to risk everything—my library card, my reputation, perhaps even my job. "Can I ask a favor, Lucy?"

She looked at me warily. "That depends."

"I want to rest my hand flat on the page. It will be only for a moment." I watched her carefully to gauge whether she was planning to call in the security guards for reinforcement.

"You can't touch the pages, Diana. You know that. If I let you, I would be fired."

I nodded. "I know. I'm sorry to put you in such a tough spot."

"Why do you need to touch it?" Lucy asked after a moment of silence, her curiosity aroused.

"I have a sixth sense when it comes to old books. Sometimes I can detect information about them that's not visible to the naked eye." That sounded weirder than I'd anticipated.

"Are you some kind of book witch?" Lucy's eyes narrowed.

"That's exactly what I am," I said with a laugh.

"I'd like to help you, Diana, but we're on camera—though there's no sound, thank God. Everything that happens in this room is taped, and someone is supposed to be watching the monitor whenever the room is occupied." She shook her head. "It's too risky."

"What if nobody could see what I was doing?"

"If you cut off the camera or put chewing gum on the lens—and yes, someone did try that—security will be here in five seconds," Lucy replied.

"I wasn't going to use chewing gum, but something like this." I pulled my familiar disguising spell around me. It would make any magic I worked all but invisible. Then I turned my right hand over and touched the tip of my ring finger to my thumb, pinching the green and yellow threads that filled the room into a tiny bundle. Together the two colors blended into the unnatural yellow-green that was good for disorientation and deception spells. I planned on tying them up in the fifth knot—since the security cameras definitely qualified as a challenge. The fifth knot's image burned at my right wrist in anticipation.

"Nice tats," Lucy commented, peering at my hands. "Why did you choose gray ink?"

Gray? When magic was in the air, my hands were every color of the rainbow. My disguising spell must be working.

"Because gray goes with everything." It was the first thing to cross my mind.

"Oh. Good thinking." She still looked puzzled.

I returned to my spell. It needed some black in it, as well as the yellow and green. I snagged the fine black threads that surrounded me on my left thumb and then slid them through a loop made by my right thumb and ring finger. The result looked like an unorthodox mudra—one of the hand positions in yoga.

"With knot of five, the spell will thrive," I murmured, envisioning the completed weaving with my third eye. The twist of yellow-green and black tied itself into an unbreakable knot with five crossings.

"Did you just bewitch the Voynich?" Lucy whispered with alarm.

"Of course not." After my experiences with bewitched manuscripts, I wouldn't do such a thing lightly. "I bewitched the air around it."

To show Lucy what I meant, I moved my hand over the first page, hovering about two inches above the surface. The spell made it appear that my fingers stopped at the bottom of the book.

"Um, Diana? Whatever you were trying to do didn't work. You're just touching the edge of the page like you're supposed to," Lucy said.

"Actually my hand is over here." I wiggled my fingers so that they peeked out over the top edge of the book. It was a bit like the old magician's trick where a woman was put in a box and the box was sawed in half. "Try it. Don't touch the page yet—just move your hand so that it covers the text."

I slid my hand out to give Lucy room. She followed my directions and slid her hand between the Voynich and the deception spell. Her hand appeared to stop when it reached the edge of the book, but if you looked carefully, you could see that her forearm was getting shorter. She withdrew quickly, as though she'd touched a hot pan. She turned to me and stared.

"You are a witch." Lucy swallowed, then smiled. "What a relief. I always suspected you were hiding something, and I was afraid it might be something unsavory—or even illegal." Like Chris, she didn't seem remotely surprised to discover that there really *were* witches.

"Will you let me break the rules?" I glanced down at the Voynich.

"Only if you tell me what you learn. This damned manuscript is the bane of our existence. We get ten requests a day to see it and turn down almost every one." Lucy returned to her seat and adopted a watchful position. "But be careful. If someone sees you, you'll lose your library privileges. And I don't think you would survive if you were banned from the Beinecke."

I took a deep breath and stared down at the open book. The key to activating my magic was curiosity. But if I wanted more than a dizzying display of faces, I would need to formulate a careful question before putting hand to parchment. I was more certain than ever that the Voynich held important clues about the Book of Life and its missing pages. But I was only going to get one chance to find out what they were.

"What did Edward Kelley place inside the Voynich, and what happened to it?" I whispered before looking down and gently resting my hand on the first folio of the manuscript.

One of the missing pages from the Book of Life appeared before my eyes: the illumination of the tree with its trunk full of writhing, human shapes. It was gray and ghostly, transparent enough that I could see through it to my hand and the writing on the Voynich's first folio.

A second shadowy page appeared atop the first: two dragons shedding their blood so that it fell into a vessel below.

A third insubstantial page layered over the previous two: the illumination of the alchemical wedding.

For a moment the layers of text and image remained stacked in a magical palimpsest atop the Voynich's stained parchment. Then, the alchemical wedding dissolved, followed by the picture of the two dragons. But the page with the tree remained.

Hopeful that the image had become real, I lifted my hand from the page and withdrew it. I gathered up the knot at the heart of the spell and jammed it over my pencil eraser, rendering it temporarily invisible and revealing Beinecke MS 408. My heart sank. There was no missing page from the Book of Life there.

"Not what you expected to see?" Lucy looked at me sympathetically.

"No. Something was here once—a few pages from another manuscript—but they're long gone." I pinched the bridge of my nose.

"Maybe the sale records mention them. We have boxes of paperwork on the Voynich's acquisition. Do you want to see them?" she asked.

The dates of book sales and the names of the people who bought and sold the books could be assembled into a genealogy that described a book's history and descent right down to the present. In this case it might also provide clues as to who might once have owned the pictures of the tree and the dragons that Kelley removed from the Book of Life.

"Absolutely!" I replied.

Lucy boxed up the Voynich and returned it to the locked hold. She returned shortly thereafter with a trolley loaded with folders, boxes, various notebooks, and a tube.

"Here's everything on the Voynich, in all its confusing glory. It's been picked through thousands of times by researchers, but nobody was looking for three missing manuscript pages." She headed toward our private room. "Come on. I'll help you sort through it all."

It took thirty minutes simply to organize the materials on the long table. Some of it would be no use at all: the tube and the scrapbook full of newspaper clippings, the old photostats, and lectures and articles written about the manuscript after the collector Wilfrid Voynich purchased it in 1912. That still left folders full of correspondence, handwritten notes, and a clutch of notebooks kept by Wilfrid's wife, Ethel.

"Here's a copy of the chemical analysis of the manuscript, a printout of the cataloging information, and a list of everyone granted access to the manuscript in the past three years." Lucy handed me a sheaf of papers. "You can keep them. Don't tell anyone I gave you that list of library patrons, though."

Matthew would have to go over the chemistry with me—it was all about the inks used in the manuscript, a subject that interested both of us. The list of people who'd seen the manuscript was surprisingly short. Hardly anyone got to look at it anymore. Those who had been granted access were mostly academics—a historian of science from the University of Southern California and another from Cal State Fullerton, a mathematician-cryptographer from Princeton, another from Australia. I'd had coffee with one of the visitors before leaving for Oxford: a writer of popular fiction who was interested in alchemy. One name jumped off the page, though.

Peter Knox had seen the Voynich this past May, before Emily died.

"That bastard." My fingers tingled, and the knots on my wrists burned in warning.

"Something wrong?" Lucy asked.

"There was a name on the list I didn't expect to see."

"Ah. A scholarly rival." She nodded sagely.

"I guess you could say that." But my difficulty with Knox was more than an argument over competing historical interpretations. This was war. And if I were going to win it, I would need to pull ahead of him for a change.

The problem was that I had little experience tracking down manuscripts and establishing their provenance. The papers I knew best had belonged to the chemist Robert Boyle. All seventy-four volumes of them had been presented to the Royal Society in 1769, and, like everything else in the Royal Society archives, they were meticulously cataloged, indexed, and cross-referenced.

"If I want to trace the Voynich's chain of ownership, where do I start?" I mused aloud, staring at the materials.

"The fastest way would be for one of us to start at the manuscript's origins and work forward while the other starts at the Beinecke's acquisition of it and works backward. With luck we'll meet at the middle." Lucy handed me a folder. "You're the historian. You take the old stuff."

I opened the folder, expecting to see something relating to Rudolf II. Instead I found a letter from a mathematician in Prague, Johannes Marcus Marci. It was written in Latin, dated 1665, and sent to someone in Rome addressed as *"Reverende et Eximie Domine in Christo Pater."* The recipient was a cleric then, perhaps one of the men I'd seen when I touched the corner of the Voynich's first page.

I quickly scanned the rest of the text, noting that the cleric was a Father Athanasius and that Marci's letter was accompanied by a mysterious book that needed deciphering. The Book of Life, perhaps?

Marci said that attempts had been made to contact Father Athanasius before, but the letters had been met with silence. Excited, I kept reading. When the third paragraph revealed the identity of Father Athanasius, however, my excitement turned to dismay.

"The Voynich manuscript once belonged to Athanasius Kircher?" If the missing pages had passed into Kircher's hands, they could be anywhere.

"I'm afraid so," Lucy replied. "I understand he was quite . . . er, wide-ranging in his interests."

"That's an understatement," I said. Athanasius Kircher's modest goal had been nothing less than universal knowledge. He had published forty books and was an internationally bestselling author as well as an inventor. Kircher's museum of rare and ancient objects was a famous stop on early European grand tours, his range of correspondents extensive, and his library vast. I didn't have the language skills to work through Kircher's oeuvre. More important, I lacked the time.

My phone vibrated in my pocket, making me jump.

"Excuse me, Lucy." I slid the phone out and checked the display. On it was a text message from Matthew.

Where are you? Gallowglass is waiting for you. We have a doctor's appointment in ninety minutes.

I cursed silently.

I'm just leaving the Beinecke, I typed back.

"My husband and I have a date, Lucy. I'm going to have to pick up with this again tomorrow," I said, closing the folder containing Marci's letter to Kircher.

"A reliable source told me you were on campus with someone tall, dark, and handsome." Lucy grinned.

"That's my husband, all right," I said. "Can I look through this stuff tomorrow?"

"Leave everything with me. Things are pretty slow around here at the moment. I'll see what I can piece together."

"Thanks for your help, Lucy. I'm under a tight—and nonnegotiable—deadline." I scooped up pencil, laptop, and pad of paper and rushed to meet Gallowglass. Matthew had seconded his nephew to act as my security detail. Gallowglass was also responsible for monitoring Benjamin's Internet feed, but so far the screen had remained blank.

"Hello, Auntie. You're looking bonny." He kissed me on the cheek.

"I'm sorry. I'm late."

"Of course you're late. You were with your books. I didn't expect you for another hour at least," Gallowglass said, dismissing my apology.

When we got to the lab, Matthew had the image of the alchemical wedding from Ashmole 782 in front of him and was so absorbed that he didn't even look up when the door pinged. Chris and Sherlock were standing at his shoulder, watching intently. Scully sat on a rolling stool nearby. Game Boy had a tiny instrument in her hand and was holding it dangerously close to the manuscript page.

"You get scruffier all the time, Gallowglass. When did you last comb your hair?" Miriam swiped a card through the reader at the door. It was marked VISITOR. Chris was taking security seriously.

"Yesterday." Gallowglass patted the back and sides of his head. "Why? Is a bird nesting in it?"

"One might well be." Miriam nodded in my direction. "Hi, Diana. Matthew will be with you soon."

"What's he doing?" I asked.

"Trying to teach a postgraduate student with no knowledge of biology or proper laboratory procedures how to remove DNA samples from parchment." Miriam looked at the group surrounding Matthew with disapproval. "I don't know why Roberts funds creatures who don't even know how to run agarose gels, but I'm just the lab manager."

Across the room Game Boy let out a frustrated expletive.

"Pull up a stool. This could be a while." Miriam rolled her eyes.

"Don't worry. It takes practice," Matthew told Game Boy, his voice soothing. "I'm nothing but thumbs with that computer game of yours. Try again."

Again? My mouth dried up. Making repeated stabs at the page from Ashmole 782 might damage the palimpsest. I started toward my husband, and Chris spotted me.

"Hey, Diana." He intercepted me with a hug. He looked at Gallowglass. "I'm Chris Roberts. Diana's friend."

"Gallowglass. Matthew's nephew." Gallowglass surveyed the room, and his nose wrinkled. "Something stinks."

"The grad students played a little joke on Matthew." Chris pointed to the computer terminal, which was festooned with wreaths of garlic bulbs. A crucifix designed for a car dashboard was attached to the mouse pad with a suction cup. Chris turned his attention to Gallowglass's neck with an intensity that was practically vampiric. "Do you wrestle?"

"Weeell, I have been known to do so for sport." Gallowglass looked down shyly, his cheeks dimpled.

"Not Greco-Roman by any chance?" Chris asked. "My partner injured his knee and will be in rehab for months. I'm looking for a temporary replacement."

"It must be Greek. I'm not sure about the Roman part."

"Where did you learn?" Chris asked.

"My grandfather taught me." Gallowglass scrunched up his face as his concentration deepened. "I think he wrestled a giant once. He was a fierce fighter."

"Is this a vampire grandfather?" Chris asked.

Gallowglass nodded.

"Vampire wrestling must be fun to watch." Chris grinned. "Like alligator wrestling, but without the tail."

"No wrestling. I'm serious, Chris." I wanted no responsibility, no matter how indirect, for causing bodily harm to a MacArthur genius.

"Spoilsport." Chris let out a piercing whistle. "Wolfman! Your wife is here."

Wolfman?

"I was aware of that, Christopher." Matthew's tone was frosty, but he gave me a warm smile that made my toes curl. "Hello, Diana. I'll be with you as soon as I'm finished with Janette."

"Game Boy's name is Janette?" Chris murmured. "Who knew?"

"I did. So did Matthew. Perhaps you could tell me why she's in my lab?" Miriam asked. "Janette's Ph.D. will be in computational bioinformatics. She belongs in a room full of terminals, not test tubes."

"I like the way her brain works," Chris said with a shrug. "She's a gamer and sees patterns in lab results that the rest of us miss. So she never did advanced work in biology. Who cares? I'm up to my eyeballs in biologists already."

Chris looked at Matthew and Game Boy working together and shook his head.

"What's wrong?" I asked.

"Matthew is wasted in a research laboratory. Your husband belongs in a classroom. He's a born teacher." Chris tapped Gallowglass on the arm. "Call me if you want to meet up in the gym. Diana has my number."

Chris went back to his work and I turned my attention to Matthew. I'd only seen flashes of this side of my husband, when he was interacting with Annie or Jack in London, but Chris was right. Matthew was using all the tools in a teacher's bag of tricks: modeling, positive reinforcement, patience, just the right amount of praise, and a touch of humor.

"Why can't we just swab the surface again?" Game Boy asked. "I know it came up with mouse DNA, but if we picked a fresh spot, it might be different."

"Maybe," Matthew said, "but there were a lot of mice in medieval libraries. Still, you should feel free to swab it again after you've taken this sample."

Game Boy sighed and steadied her hand.

"Deep breath, Janette." Matthew gave her an encouraging nod. "Take your time."

With great care Game Boy inserted a needle so fine it was almost invisible into the very edge of the parchment.

"There you go," Matthew said softly. "Slow and steady."

"I did it!" Game Boy shouted. You would have thought she'd split the atom. There were whoops of support, a high five, and a muttered "About time" from Miriam. But it was Matthew's response that mattered. Game Boy turned to him expectantly.

"Eureka," Matthew said, his hands spread wide. Game Boy grinned broadly. "Well done, Janette. We'll make a geneticist out of you yet."

"No way. I'd rather build a computer from spare parts than do that again." Game Boy stripped her gloves off quickly.

"Hello, darling. How was your day?" Matthew rose and kissed me on the cheek. One eyebrow lifted as he looked at Gallowglass, who silently conveyed that all was well.

"Let's see . . . I worked some magic in the Beinecke."

"Should I worry?" Matthew asked, clearly thinking of the havoc that witchwind and witchfire might cause.

"Nope," I said. "And I have a lead on one of the missing pages from Ashmole 782."

"That was quick. You can tell me about it on our way to the doctor's office," he said, swiping his card through the reader.

"By all means take your time with Diana. There's nothing pressing here.

One hundred and twenty-five vampire genes identified and only four hundred to go," Miriam called as we left. "Chris will be counting the minutes."

"Five hundred genes to go!" Chris shouted.

"Your gene prediction is way off," Miriam replied.

"A hundred bucks says it's not." Chris glanced up from a report.

"That the best you can do?" Miriam pursed her lips.

"I'll empty my piggy bank when I get home and let you know, Miriam," Chris said. Miriam's lips twitched.

"Let's go," said Matthew, "before they start arguing about something else."

"Oh, they're not arguing," Gallowglass said, holding the door open for us. "They're flirting."

My jaw dropped. "What makes you say that?"

"Chris likes to give people nicknames." Gallowglass turned to Matthew. "Chris called you Wolfman. What does he call Miriam?"

Matthew thought for a moment. "Miriam."

"Exactly." Gallowglass grinned from ear to ear.

Matthew swore.

"Don't fret, Uncle. Miriam hasn't given any man a tumble since Bertrand was killed."

"Miriam . . . and a human?" Matthew sounded stunned.

"Nothing will come of it," Gallowglass said soothingly as the elevator doors opened. "She will break Chris's heart, of course, but there's naught we can do about it."

I was deeply grateful to Miriam. Now Matthew and Gallowglass had someone to worry about besides me.

"Poor lad." Gallowglass sighed, pushing the button that closed the elevator doors. As we descended, he cracked his knuckles. "Perhaps I will wrestle with him after all. A good thrashing always clears the mind."

A few days ago, I'd worried whether the vampires would survive being at Yale once the students and faculty were around.

Now I wondered whether Yale would survive the vampires.

17

I stood in front of the refrigerator, staring at the images of our children with my hands curved around my belly. Where had the month of September gone?

The three-dimensional ultrasound pictures of Baby A and Baby B—Matthew and I had elected not to learn the sexes of our two children—were uncanny. Instead of the familiar ghostly silhouette I'd seen in friends' pregnancy scans, these revealed detailed images of faces with crinkled brows, thumbs rammed into mouths, perfectly bowed lips. My finger reached out, and I touched Baby B's nose.

Cool hands slid around me from behind, and a tall, muscular body provided a strong pillar for me to rest against. Matthew pressed lightly on a spot a few inches above my pubic bone.

"B's nose is just there in that picture," he said softly. His other hand rested a bit higher on the swell of my belly. "Baby A was here."

We stood silently as the chain that had always joined me to Matthew extended to accommodate these two bright, fragile links. For months I had *known* that Matthew's children—our children—were growing inside me. But I had not *felt* it. Everything was different now that I'd seen their faces, crumpled in concentration as they did the hard work of becoming.

"What are you thinking?" Matthew asked, curious about my extended silence.

"I'm not thinking. I'm feeling." And what I was feeling was impossible to describe.

His laugh was soft, as though he didn't want to disturb the babies' sleep.

"They're both all right," I assured myself. "Normal. Perfect."

"They are perfectly healthy. But none of our children will ever be normal. And thank God for that." He kissed me. "What's on your schedule for today?"

"More work at the library." My initial, magical lead that had promised to reveal the fate of at least one of the Book of Life's missing pages had turned into weeks of hard, scholarly slogging. Lucy and I had been working steadily to discover just how the Voynich manuscript came into Athanasius Kircher's hands and later into Yale's possession, hoping to catch a trace of the mysterious tree image that had remained superimposed on the Voynich for a few precious moments. We'd set up camp in the same small private room where I'd worked my spell so that we could talk without disturbing the growing number of students and faculty using the Beinecke's adjacent reading room. There we'd pored over library lists and indexes of Kircher's correspondence, and we'd written dozens of letters to various experts in the United States and abroad—with no concrete results.

"You're remembering what the doctor said about taking breaks?" Matthew asked. With the exception of the ultrasound, our trip to the doctor's office had been sobering. She had drummed into me the dangers of premature labor and preeclampsia, the necessity of staying hydrated, my body's additional need for rest.

"My blood pressure is fine." This, I understood, was one of the biggest risks: that through a combination of dehydration, fatigue, and stress, my blood pressure would suddenly spike.

"I know." Monitoring my blood pressure was my vampire husband's responsibility, and Matthew took it seriously. "But it won't remain that way if you push yourself."

"This is my twenty-fifth week of pregnancy, Matthew. It's almost October."

"I know that, too."

After October 1 the doctor was grounding me. If we remained in New Haven where we could continue working, the only way to get to the Bodleian Library would be by some combination of boat, plane, and automobile. Even now I was restricted to flights of no more than three hours.

"We can still get you to Oxford by plane." Matthew knew of my concerns. "It will have to stop in Montreal, and then Newfoundland, Iceland, and Ireland, but if you *must* get to London, we can manage it." His expression suggested that he and I might have different ideas about what circumstances would justify my crossing the Atlantic in this hopscotch fashion. "Of course, if you'd prefer we can go to Europe now."

"Let's not borrow trouble." I pulled away from him. "Tell me about your day."

"Chris and Miriam think they have a new approach to understanding the blood-rage gene," he said. "They're planning to trawl through my genome using one of Marcus's theories about noncoding DNA. Their current hypothesis is that it might contain triggers that control how and to what extent blood rage manifests in a given individual."

"This is Marcus's junk DNA—the ninety-eight percent of the genome that doesn't code proteins, right?" I took a bottle of water out of the fridge and popped the cap off to show my commitment to hydration.

"That's right. I'm still resistant to the notion, but the evidence they're pulling together is convincing." Matthew looked wry. "I really am an old Mendelian fossil, just as Chris said."

"Yes, but you're *my* Mendelian fossil," I said. Matthew laughed. "And if Marcus's hypothesis is correct, what will that mean in terms of finding a cure?"

His smile died. "It may mean that there is no cure—that blood rage is a hereditary genetic condition that develops in response to a multitude of factors. It can be far easier to cure a disease with a single, unequivocal cause, like a germ or a single gene mutation."

"Can the contents of my genome help?" There had been much discussion of the babies since I'd had my ultrasound, and speculation as to what effect a witch's blood—a weaver's in particular—might have on the blood-rage gene. I didn't want my children to end up as science experiments, especially after seeing Benjamin's horrific laboratory, but I had no objection to doing my bit for scientific progress.

"I don't want your DNA to be the subject of further scientific research." Matthew stalked to the window. "I should never have taken that sample from you back in Oxford."

I smothered a sigh. With every hard-won freedom Matthew granted me and each conscious effort he made not to smother me with overpossessiveness, his authoritarian traits had to find a new outlet. It was like watching someone try to dam up a raging river. And Matthew's inability to locate Benjamin and release his captive witch were only making it worse. Every lead Matthew received about Benjamin's current location turned into a dead end, just like my attempts to trace Ashmole 782's missing pages. Before I could try to reason with him, my phone rang. It was a distinctive ringtone—the opening bars of "Sympathy for the Devil"—which I had not yet managed to change. When the phone was programmed, someone had irrevocably attached it to one of my contacts.

"Your brother is calling." Matthew's tone was capable of freezing Old Faithful.

"What do you want, Baldwin?" There was no need for polite preamble.

"Your lack of faith wounds me, sister." Baldwin laughed. "I'm in New York. I thought I might come to New Haven and make sure that your accommodations are suitable."

Matthew's vampire hearing made my conversation with Baldwin completely audible. The oath he uttered in response to his brother's words was blistering.

"Matthew is with me. Gallowglass and Miriam are one block away. Mind your own business." I drew the phone from my ear, eager to disconnect.

"Diana." Baldwin's voice managed to extend to even my limited human hearing.

I returned the phone to my ear.

"There is another vampire working in Matthew's lab—Richard Bellingham is the name he goes by now."

"Yes." My eyes went to Matthew, who was standing in a deceptively relaxed position in front of the window—legs spread slightly, hands clasped behind his back. It was a stance of readiness.

"Be careful around him." Baldwin's voice flattened. "You don't want me to have to order Matthew to get rid of Bellingham. But I will do that, without hesitation, should I think he possesses information that could prove . . . difficult . . . for the family."

"He knows I'm a witch. And that I'm pregnant." It was evident that Baldwin knew a great deal about our life in New Haven already. There was no point in hiding the truth.

"Every vampire in that provincial town knows. And they travel to New York. Often." Baldwin paused. "In my family if you create a mess, you clean it up—or Matthew does. Those are your options."

"It's always such a pleasure to hear from you, *brother*."

Baldwin merely laughed.

"Is that all, *milord*?"

"It's '*sieur*.' Do you need me to refresh your memory of vampire law and etiquette?"

"No," I said, spitting out the word.

"Good. Tell Matthew to stop blocking my calls, and we won't have to repeat this conversation." The line went dead.

"That f—" I began.

Matthew wrenched the phone out of my hand and flung it across the room. It made a satisfying sound of breaking glass when it hit the mantel of the defunct fireplace. Then his hands were cradling my face as though the violent moment that came before had been a mirage.

"Now I'll have to get another phone." I looked into Matthew's stormy eyes. They were a reliable indication of his state of mind: clear gray when he was at ease, appearing green when his pupils enlarged with emotion and blotted out all but the bright rim around his iris. At the moment, the gray and green were battling for supremacy.

"Baldwin will no doubt have one here before the day is done." Matthew's attention fixed on the pulse at my throat.

"Let's hope your brother doesn't feel he needs to deliver it himself."

Matthew's eyes drifted to my lips. "He's not my brother. He's *your* brother."

"Hello the house!" Gallowglass's booming, cheerful voice rose up from the downstairs hall.

Matthew's kiss was hard and demanding. I gave him what he needed, deliberately softening my spine and my mouth so that he could feel, in this moment at least, that he was in charge.

"Oh. Sorry. Shall I come back?" Gallowglass said from the stairs. Then his nostrils flared as he detected my husband's overpowering clove scent. "Something wrong, Matthew?"

"Nothing that Baldwin's sudden and seemingly accidental death wouldn't fix," Matthew said darkly.

"Business as usual, then. I thought you might want me to walk Auntie to the library."

"Why?" Matthew asked.

"Miriam called. She's in a mood and wants you to 'get out of Diana's knickers and into my lab.'" Gallowglass consulted the palm of his hand. It was covered in writing. "Yep. That's exactly what she said."

"I'll get my bag," I murmured, pulling away from Matthew.

"Hello, Apple and Bean." Gallowglass stared, besotted, at the images on the fridge. He thought calling them Baby A and Baby B was beneath their dignity and so had bestowed nicknames upon them. "Bean has Granny's fingers. Did you notice, Matthew?"

Gallowglass kept the mood light and the banter flowing on our walk to campus. Matthew accompanied us to the Beinecke, as though he expected Baldwin to rise up out of the sidewalk before us with a new phone and another dire warning.

Leaving the de Clermonts behind, it was with relief that I opened the door into our research room.

"I've never seen such a tangled provenance!" Lucy exclaimed the moment I appeared. "So John Dee *did* own the Voynich?"

"That's right." I put down my pad of paper and my pencil. Other than my magic, they were the only items I carried. Happily, my power didn't set off the metal detectors. "Dee gave the Voynich to Emperor Rudolf in exchange for Ashmole 782." It was, in truth, a bit more complicated than that, as was often the case when Gallowglass and Matthew were involved in the transfer of property.

"The Bodleian Library manuscript that's missing three pages?" Lucy held her head in her hands and stared down at the notes, clippings, and correspondence littering the table.

"Edward Kelley removed those pages before Ashmole 782 was sent back to England. Kelley temporarily put them inside the Voynich for safekeeping. At some point he gave two of the pages away. But he kept one for himself—the page with the illumination of a tree on it." It really was impossibly tangled.

"So it must have been Kelley who gave the Voynich manuscript—along with the picture of the tree—to Emperor Rudolf's botanist, the Jacobus de Tepenecz whose signature is on the back of the first folio." Time had faded the ink, but Lucy had shown me photographs taken under ultraviolet light.

"Probably," I said.

"And after the botanist, an alchemist owned it?" She made some annotations on her Voynich timeline. It was looking a bit messy with our constant deletions and additions.

"Georg Baresch. I haven't been able to find out much about him." I studied my own notes. "Baresch was friends with de Tepenecz, and Marci acquired the Voynich from him."

"The Voynich manuscript's illustrations of strange flora would certainly intrigue a botanist—not to mention the illumination of a tree from Ashmole 782. But why would an alchemist be interested in them?" Lucy asked.

"Because some of the Voynich's illustrations resemble alchemical apparatus. The ingredients and processes needed to make the philosopher's stone were jealously guarded secrets, and alchemists often hid them in symbols: plants, animals, even people." The Book of Life contained the same potent blend of the real and the symbolic.

"And Athanasius Kircher was interested in words and symbols, too. That's why you think he would have been interested in the illumination of the tree as well as the Voynich," Lucy said slowly.

"Yes. It's why the missing letter that Georg Baresch claims he sent to Kircher in 1637 is so significant." I slid a folder in her direction. "The Kircher expert I know from Stanford is in Rome. She volunteered to go to the Pontifical Gregorian University archives, where the bulk of Kircher's correspondence is kept, and nose around. She sent me a transcription of the later letter from Baresch to Kircher written in 1639. It refers back to their exchange, but the Jesuits told her the original letter can't be found."

"When librarians say 'it's lost,' I always wonder if that's really true," she grumbled.

"Me, too." I thought wryly of my experiences with Ashmole 782.

Lucy opened the folder and groaned. "This is in Latin, Diana. You're going to have to tell me what it says."

"Baresch thought Kircher might be able to decipher the Voynich's secrets. Kircher had been working on Egyptian hieroglyphs. It made him an international celebrity, and people sent him mysterious texts and writings from far and wide," I explained. "To better hook Kircher's interest, Baresch forwarded partial transcripts of the Voynich to Rome in 1637 and again in 1639."

"There's no specific mention of a picture of a tree, though," Lucy said.

"No. But it's still possible that Baresch sent it to Kircher as an additional lure. It's of a much higher quality than the Voynich's pictures." I sat back in my chair. "I'm afraid that's as far as I've been able to get. What have you found out about the book sale where Wilfrid Voynich acquired the manuscript?"

Just as Lucy opened her mouth to reply, a librarian rapped on the door and entered.

"Your husband is on the phone, Professor Bishop." He looked at me in disapproval. "Please tell him that we aren't a hotel switchboard and don't usually take calls for our patrons."

"Sorry," I said, getting out of my chair. "I had an accident with my phone this morning. My husband is a bit . . . er, overprotective." I gestured apologetically at my rounded form.

The librarian looked slightly mollified and pointed to a phone on the wall that had a single flashing light. "Use that."

"How did Baldwin get here so fast?" I asked Matthew when we were connected. It was the only thing I could think of that would make Matthew call the library's main number. "Did he come by helicopter?"

"It's not Baldwin. We've discovered something strange about the picture of the chemical wedding from Ashmole 782."

"Strange how?"

"Come and see. I'd rather not talk about it on the phone."

"Be right there." I hung up and turned to Lucy. "I'm so sorry, Lucy, but I have to go. My husband wants me to help with a problem in his lab. Can we continue later?"

"Sure," she said.

I hesitated. "Would you like to come with me? You could meet Matthew—and see a page from Ashmole 782."

"One of the fugitive sheets?" Lucy was out of her chair in an instant. "Give me a minute and I'll meet you upstairs."

Rushing outside, we ran smack into my bodyguard.

"Slow down, Auntie. You don't want to joggle the babes." Gallowglass gripped my elbow until I was steady on my feet, then gazed down at my petite companion. "Are you all right, miss?"

"M-me?" Lucy stammered, craning her neck to make eye contact with the big Gael. "I'm fine."

"Just checking," Gallowglass said kindly. "I'm as big as a galleon under full sail. Running into me has bruised men far bigger than you."

"This is my husband's nephew, Gallowglass. Gallowglass, Lucy Meriweather. She's coming with us." After that hasty introduction, I dashed in the direction of Kline Biology Tower, my bag banging against my hip. After a few clumsy strides, Gallowglass took the bag and transferred it to his own arm.

"He carries your books?" Lucy whispered.

"And groceries," I whispered back. "He would carry me, too, if I let him."

Gallowglass snorted.

"Hurry," I said, my worn sneakers squeaking on the polished floors of the building where Matthew and Chris worked.

At the doorway to Chris's lab, I swiped my ID card and the doors opened. Miriam was waiting for us inside, looking at her watch.

"Time!" she called. "I won. Again. That's ten dollars, Roberts."

Chris groaned. "I was sure Gallowglass would slow her down." The lab was quiet today, with only a handful of people working. I waved at Beaker. Scully was there, too, standing next to Mulder and a digital scale.

"Sorry to interrupt your research, but we wanted you to know straightaway what we discovered." Matthew glanced at Lucy.

"Matthew, this is Lucy Meriweather. I thought Lucy should see the page from Ashmole 782, since she's spending so much time searching for its lost siblings," I explained.

"A pleasure, Lucy. Come see what you're helping Diana to find." Matthew's expression went from wary to welcoming, and he gestured toward Mulder and Scully. "Miriam, can you log Lucy in as a guest?"

"Already done." Miriam tapped Chris on the shoulder. "Staring at that genetic map isn't getting you anywhere, Roberts. Take a break."

Chris flung down his pen. "We need more data."

"We're scientists. Of course we need more data." The air between Chris and Miriam hummed with tension. "Come and look at the pretty picture anyway."

"Oh, okay," Chris grumbled, giving Miriam a sheepish smile.

The illumination of the alchemical wedding rested on a wooden book stand. No matter how often I saw it, the image always amazed me—and not just because the personifications of sulfur and quicksilver looked like Matthew and me. So much detail surrounded the chemical couple: the rocky landscape, the wedding guests, the mythical and symbolic beasts who witnessed the ceremony, the phoenix who encompassed the scene within flaming wings. Next to the page was something that looked like a flat metal postal scale with a blank sheet of parchment in the tray.

"Scully will tell us what she discovered." Matthew gave the student the floor.

"This illuminated page is too heavy," Scully said, blinking her eyes behind a pair of thick lenses. "Heavier than a single page should be, I mean."

"Sarah and I both thought it felt heavy." I looked at Matthew. "Remember when the house first gave us the page in Madison?" I reminded him in a whisper.

He nodded. "Perhaps it's something a vampire can't perceive. Even now that I've seen Scully's evidence, the page feels entirely normal to me."

"I ordered some vellum online from a traditional parchment maker," Scully said. "It arrived this morning. I cut the sheet to the same size—nine inches by eleven and a half inches—and weighed it. You can have the leftovers, Professor Clairmont. We can all use some practice with that probe you've developed."

"Thank you, Scully. Good idea. And we'll run some core samples of the modern vellum for comparison's sake," Matthew said with a smile.

"As you can see," Scully resumed, "the new vellum weighed a little over an ounce and a half. When I weighed Professor Bishop's page the first time, it weighed thirteen ounces—as much as approximately nine sheets of ordinary vellum." Scully removed the fresh sheet of calfskin and put the page from Ashmole 782 in its place.

"The weight of the ink can't account for that discrepancy." Lucy put on her own glasses to take a closer look at the digital readout. "And the parchment used in Ashmole 782 looks like it's thinner, too."

"It's about half the thickness of the vellum. I measured it." Scully pushed her glasses back into place.

"But the Book of Life had more than a hundred pages—probably close to two hundred." I did some rapid calculations. "If a single page weighs thirteen ounces, the whole book would weigh close to a hundred and fifty pounds."

"That's not all. The page isn't always the same weight," Mulder said. He pointed to the scale's digital readout. "Look, Professor Clairmont. The weight's dropped again. Now it's down to seven ounces." He took up a clipboard and noted the time and weight on it.

"It's been fluctuating randomly all morning," Matthew said. "Thankfully, Scully had the good sense to leave the page on the scale. If she'd removed it immediately, we would have missed it."

"That wasn't deliberate." Scully flushed and lowered her voice. "I had to use the restroom. When I came back, the weight had risen to a full pound."

"What's your conclusion, Scully?" Chris asked in his teacher voice.

"I don't have one," she said, clearly frustrated. "Vellum can't lose weight and gain it again. It's dead. Nothing I'm observing is possible!"

"Welcome to the world of science, my friend," Chris said with a laugh. He turned to Scully's companion. "How about you, Mulder?"

"The page is clearly some sort of magical container. There are other pages inside it. Its weight changes because it's still somehow connected to the rest of the manuscript." Mulder slid a glance in my direction.

"I think you're right, Mulder," I said, smiling.

"We should leave it where it is and record its weight every fifteen minutes. Maybe there will be a pattern," Mulder suggested.

"Sounds like a plan." Chris looked at Mulder approvingly.

"So, Professor Bishop," Mulder said cautiously, "do you think there really are other pages inside this one?"

"If so, that would make Ashmole 782 a palimpsest," Lucy said, her imagination sparking. "A magical palimpsest."

My conclusion from today's events in the lab was that humans are much cleverer than we creatures give them credit for.

"It *is* a palimpsest," I confirmed. "But I never thought of Ashmole 782 as—what did you call it, Mulder?"

"A magical container," he repeated, looking pleased.

We already knew that Ashmole 782 was valuable because of its text and its genetic information. If Mulder was correct, there was no telling what else might be in it.

"Have the DNA results come back from the sample you took a few weeks ago, Matthew?" Maybe if we knew what creature the vellum came from, it would shed some light on the situation.

"Wait. You removed a piece of this manuscript and ran a chemical analysis on it?" Lucy looked horrified.

"Only a very small piece from the core of the page. We inserted a microscopic probe into the edge. You can't see the hole it made—not even with a magnifying glass," Matthew assured her.

"I've never heard of such a thing," Lucy said.

"That's because Professor Clairmont developed the technology, and he hasn't shared it with the rest of the class." Chris cast a disapproving look at Matthew. "But we're going to change that, aren't we, Matthew?"

"Apparently," said Matthew.

Miriam shrugged. "Give it up, Matthew. We've used it for years to remove DNA from all sorts of soft tissue samples. It's time somebody else had fun with it," she said.

"We'll leave the page to you, Scully." Chris inclined his head toward the other end of the lab in a clear request for a conversation.

"Can I touch it?" Lucy asked, her eyes glued to the page.

"Of course. It's survived all these years, after all," Matthew said. "Mulder, Scully, can you help Ms. Meriweather? Let us know when you're ready to leave, Lucy, and we'll get you back to work."

Based on Lucy's avid expression, we had plenty of time to talk.

"What is it?" I asked Chris. Now that we were away from his students, Chris looked as if he had bad news.

"If we're going to learn anything more about blood rage, we need more data," Chris said. "And before you say anything, Miriam, I'm not criticizing what you and Matthew have managed to figure out. It's as good as it could possibly be, given that most of your DNA samples come from the long dead—or the undead. But DNA deteriorates over time. And we need to develop the genetic maps for daemons and witches and sequence their genomes if we want to reach accurate conclusions about what makes you distinct."

"So we get more data," I said, relieved. "I thought this was serious."

"It is," Matthew said grimly. "One of the reasons the genetic maps for witches and daemons are less complete is that I had no good way to acquire DNA samples from living donors. Amira and Hamish were happy to volunteer theirs, of course, as were some of the regulars at Amira's yoga classes at the Old Lodge."

"But if you were to ask for samples from a broader cross section of creatures, you'd have to answer their questions about how the material was going to be used." Now I understood.

"We've got another problem," Chris said. "We simply don't have enough DNA from Matthew's bloodline to establish a pedigree that can tell us how blood rage is inherited. There are samples from Matthew, his mother, and Marcus Whitmore—that's all."

"Why not send Marcus to New Orleans?" Miriam asked Matthew.

"What's in New Orleans?" Chris asked sharply.

"Marcus's children," Gallowglass said.

"Whitmore has children?" Chris looked at Matthew incredulously. "How many?"

"A fair few," Gallowglass said, cocking his head to the side. "Grandchildren, too. And Mad Myra's got more than her fair share of blood rage, doesn't she? You'd be wanting her DNA, for sure."

Chris thumped a lab bench, the rack of empty test tubes rattling like bones.

"Goddamn it, Matthew! You told me you had no other living offspring. I've been wasting my time with results based on three family samples while your grandchildren and great-grandchildren are running up and down Bourbon Street?"

"I didn't want to bother Marcus," Matthew said shortly. "He has other concerns."

"Like what? Another psychotic brother? There's been nothing on the Bad Seed's video feed for weeks, but that's not going to continue indefinitely. When Benjamin pops up again, we'll need more than predictive modeling and hunches to outsmart him!" Chris exclaimed.

"Calm down, Chris," Miriam said, putting a hand on his arm. "The vampire genome already includes better data than either the witch or the daemon genome."

"But it's still shaky in places," Chris argued, "especially now that we're looking at the junk DNA. I need more witch, daemon, and vampire DNA—stat."

"Game Boy, Xbox, and Daisy all volunteered to be swabbed," Miriam said. "It violates modern research protocols, but I don't think it's an insurmountable problem provided you're transparent about it later, Chris."

"Xbox mentioned a club on Crown Street where the daemons hang out." Chris wiped at his tired eyes. "I'll go down and recruit some volunteers."

"You can't go there. You'll stick out as a human—and a professor," Miriam said firmly. "I'll do it. I'm far scarier."

"Only after dark." Chris shot her a slow smile.

"Good idea, Miriam," I said hastily. I wanted no further information about what Miriam was like when the sun went down.

"You can swab me," Gallowglass said. "I'm not Matthew's bloodline, but it could help. And there are plenty of other vampires in New Haven. Give Eva Jäeger a ring."

"Baldwin's Eva?" Matthew was stunned. "I haven't seen Eva since she discovered Baldwin's role in the German stock market crash of 1911 and left him."

"I don't think either of them would appreciate your being so indiscreet, Matthew," Gallowglass chided.

"Let me guess: She's the new hire in the economics department," I said. "Wonderful. Baldwin's ex. That's just what we need."

"And have you run into more of these New Haven vampires?" Matthew demanded.

"A few," Gallowglass said vaguely.

As Matthew opened his mouth to inquire further, Lucy interrupted us.

"The page from Ashmole 782 changed its weight three times while I was standing there." She shook her head in amazement. "If I hadn't seen it myself, I wouldn't have believed it. I'm sorry to break this up, but I have to get back to the Beinecke."

"I'll go with you, Lucy," I said. "You still haven't told me what you've learned about the Voynich."

"After all this science, it's not very exciting," she said apologetically.

"It is to me." I kissed Matthew. "See you at home."

"I should be there by late afternoon." He hooked me into his arm and pressed his mouth against my ear. His next words were low so that the other vampires would have to strain to hear them. "Don't stay too long at the library. Remember what the doctor said."

"I remember, Matthew," I promised him. "Bye, Chris."

"See you soon." Chris gave me a hug and released me quickly. He looked down at my protruding stomach reproachfully. "One of your kids just elbowed me."

"Or kneed you." I laughed, smoothing a hand over the bump. "They're both pretty active these days."

Matthew's gaze rested on me: proud, tender, a shade worried. It felt like falling into a pile of freshly fallen snow—crisp and soft at the same time. If we had been at home, he would have pulled me into his arms so that he, too, could feel the kicks, or knelt before me to watch the bulges of feet and hands and elbows.

I smiled at him shyly. Miriam cleared her throat.

"Take care, Gallowglass," Matthew murmured. It was no casual farewell, but an order.

His nephew nodded. "As if your wife were my own."

We returned to the Beinecke at a statelier pace, chatting about the Voynich and Ashmole 782. Lucy was even more caught up in the mystery now. Gallowglass insisted we pick up something to eat, so we stopped at the pizza place on Wall Street. I waved to a fellow historian who was sitting in one of the scarred booths with stacks of index cards and an enormous soft drink, but she was so absorbed in her work she barely acknowledged me.

Leaving Gallowglass at his post outside the Beinecke, we went to the staff room with our late lunch. Everybody else had already eaten, so we had the place to ourselves. In between bites Lucy gave me an overview of her findings.

"Wilfrid Voynich bought Yale's mysterious manuscript from the Jesuits in 1912," she said, munching on a cucumber from her healthy salad. "They were quietly liquidating their collections at the Villa Mondragone outside Rome."

"Mondragone?" I shook my head, thinking of Corra.

"Yep. It got its name from the heraldic device of Pope Gregory XIII—the guy who reformed the calendar. But you probably know more about that than I do."

I nodded. Crossing Europe in the late sixteenth century had required familiarity with Gregory's reforms if I had wanted to know what day it was.

"More than three hundred volumes from the Jesuit College in Rome were moved to the Villa Mondragone sometime in the late nineteenth century. I'm still a bit fuzzy on the details, but there was some sort of confiscation of church property during Italian unification." Lucy stabbed an anemic cherry tomato with her fork. "The books sent to Villa Mondragone were reportedly the most treasured volumes in the Jesuit library."

"Hmm. I wonder if I could get a list." I'd owe my friend from Stanford even more, but it might lead to one of the missing pages.

"It's worth a shot. Voynich wasn't the only interested collector, of course. The Villa Mondragone sale was one of the greatest private book auctions of the twentieth century. Voynich almost lost the manuscript to two other buyers."

"Do you know who they were?" I asked.

"Not yet, but I'm working on it. One was from Prague. That's all I've been able to discover."

"Prague?" I felt faint.

"You don't look well," Lucy said. "You should go home and rest. I'll keep working on it and see you tomorrow," she added, closing up her empty Styrofoam container.

"Auntie. You're early," Gallowglass said when I exited the building.

"Ran into a research snag." I sighed. "The whole day has been a few bits of progress sandwiched between two thick slices of frustration. Hopefully, Matthew and Chris will make further discoveries in the lab, because we're running out of time. Or perhaps I should say *I'm* running out of time."

"It will all work out in the end," Gallowglass said with a sage nod. "It always does."

We cut across the green and through the gap between the courthouse and City Hall. On Court Street we crossed the railroad tracks and headed toward my house.

"When did you buy your condo on Wooster Square, Gallowglass?" I asked, finally getting around to one of many questions about the de Clermonts and their relationship to New Haven.

"After you came here as a teacher," Gallowglass said. "I wanted to be sure you were all right in your new job, and Marcus was always telling stories about a robbery at his house or that his car had been vandalized."

"I take it Marcus wasn't living in his house at the time," I said, raising an eyebrow.

"Lord no. He hasn't been in New Haven for decades."

"Well, we're perfectly safe here." I looked down the pedestrians-only length of Court Street, a tree-lined, residential enclave in the heart of the city. As usual, it was deserted, except for a black cat and some potted plants.

"Perhaps," Gallowglass said dubiously.

We had just reached the stairs leading to the front door when a dark car pulled up to the intersection of Court and Olive Streets where we had been only moments before. The car idled while a lanky young man with sandy blond hair unfolded from the passenger seat. He was all legs and arms, with surprisingly broad shoulders for someone so slender. I thought he must be an undergraduate, because he wore one of the standard Yale student uniforms:

dark jeans and a black T-shirt. Sunglasses shielded his eyes, and he bent over and spoke to the driver.

"Good God." Gallowglass looked as though he'd seen a ghost. "It can't be."

I studied the undergraduate without recognition. "Do you know him?"

The young man's eyes met mine. Mirrored lenses could not block the effects of a vampire's cold stare. He took the glasses off and gave me a lop-sided smile.

"You're a hard woman to find, Mistress Roydon."

That voice. When I'd last heard it, it was higher, without the low rumble at the back of his throat.

Those eyes. Golden brown shot through with gold and leafy green. They still looked older than his years.

His smile. The left corner had always lifted higher than the right.

"Jack?" I choked on the name as my heart constricted.

A hundred pounds of white dog pawed out of the backseat of the car, hopping over the gearshift and through the open door, long hair flying and pink tongue lolling out of his mouth. Jack grabbed him by the collar.

"Stay, Lobero." Jack ruffled the hair atop the dog's shaggy head, revealing glimpses of black button eyes. The dog gazed at him adoringly, thumped his tail, and sat panting to await further instruction.

"Hello, Gallowglass." Jack walked slowly toward us.

"Jackie." Gallowglass's voice was thick with emotion. "I thought you were dead."

"I was. Then I wasn't." Jack looked down at me, unsure of his welcome. Leaving no room for doubt, I flung my arms around him.

"Oh, Jack." Jack smelled of coal fires and foggy mornings rather than warm bread, as he had when he was a child. After a moment of hesitation, he enfolded me within long, lean arms. He was older and taller, but he still felt fragile, as though his mature appearance were nothing more than a shell.

"I missed you," Jack whispered.

"Diana!" Matthew was still more than two blocks away, but he'd spotted the car blocking the entrance into Court Street, as well as the strange man who held me. From his perspective I must have looked trapped, even with Gallowglass standing nearby. Instinct took over, and Matthew ran, his body a blur.

Lobero raised an alarm with a booming bark. Komondors were a lot like vampires: bred to protect those they loved, loyal to family, large enough to take down wolves and bears, and ready to die rather than yield to another creature.

Jack sensed the threat, without seeing its source. He transformed before my eyes into a creature from nightmares, teeth bared and eyes glassy and black. He grabbed me and held me tight, shielding me from whatever loomed behind. But he was restricting the flow of air into my lungs as well.

"No! Not you, too," I gasped, wasting the last of my breath. Now there was no way for me to warn Matthew that someone had given our bright, vulnerable boy blood rage.

Before Matthew could hurtle over the car's hood, a man climbed out of the driver's seat and grabbed him. He must be a vampire, too, I thought dizzily, if he had the strength to stop Matthew.

"Stop, Matthew. It's Jack." The man's deep, rumbling voice and distinctive London accent conjured up unwelcome memories of a single drop of blood falling into a vampire's waiting mouth.

Andrew Hubbard. The vampire king of London was in New Haven. Stars flickered at the edges of my vision.

Matthew snarled and twisted. Hubbard's spine met the metal frame of the car with a bone-crushing thud.

"It's Jack," Hubbard repeated, gripping Matthew by the neck and forcing him to listen.

This time the message got through. Matthew's eyes widened, and he looked in our direction.

"Jack?" Matthew's voice was hoarse.

"Master Roydon?" Without turning, Jack cocked his head to the side as Matthew's voice penetrated the black haze of the blood rage. His grip loosened.

I drew in a lungful of air, struggling to push back the star-filled darkness. My hand went instinctively to my belly, where I felt a reassuring poke, then another. Lobero sniffed at my feet and hands as if trying to figure out my relationship to his master, then sat before me and growled at Matthew.

"Is this another dream?" There was a trace of the lost child he had once been in his bass voice, and Jack squeezed his eyes shut rather than risk waking up.

"It's no dream, Jack," Gallowglass said softly. "Step away from Mistress Roydon now. Matthew poses no danger to his mate."

"Oh, God. I touched her." Jack sounded horrified. Slowly he turned and held up his hands in surrender, willing to accept whatever punishment Matthew saw fit to mete out. Jack's eyes, which had been returning to normal, darkened again. But he wasn't angry. So why was the blood rage resurfacing?

"Hush," I said, gently lowering his arm. "You've touched me a thousand times. Matthew doesn't care."

"I wasn't . . . this . . . before." Jack's voice was taut with self-loathing.

Matthew drew closer slowly so as not to startle Jack. Andrew Hubbard slammed the car door and followed him. The centuries had done little to change the London vampire famous for his priestly ways and his brood of adopted creatures of all species and ages. He looked the same: clean-shaven, pale of face, and blond of hair. Only Hubbard's slate-colored eyes and somber clothing provided notes of contrast to his otherwise pallid appearance. And his body was still tall and thin, with slightly stooped, broad shoulders.

As the two vampires approached, the dog's growl turned more menacing and his lips peeled back from his teeth.

"Come, Lobero," Matthew commanded. He crouched down and waited patiently while the dog considered his options.

"He's a one-man dog," Hubbard warned. "The only creature he'll listen to is Jack."

Lobero's wet nose pushed into my hand, and then he sniffed his master. The dog's muzzle lifted to take in the other scents before he moved toward Matthew and Hubbard. Lobero recognized Father Hubbard, but Matthew received a more thorough evaluation. When he was through, Lobero's tail shifted from left to right. It wasn't exactly a wag, but the dog had instinctively acknowledged the alpha in this pack.

"Good boy." Matthew stood and pointed to his heel. Lobero obediently swung around and followed as Matthew joined Jack, Gallowglass, and me.

"All right, *mon coeur*?" Matthew murmured.

"Of course," I said, still a bit short of breath.

"And you, Jack?" Matthew rested a hand on Jack's shoulder. It was not the typical de Clermont embrace. This was a father greeting his son after a long separation—a father who feared that his child had been through hell.

"I'm better now." Jack could always be relied upon to tell the truth when asked a direct question. "I overreact when I'm surprised."

"So do I." Matthew's grip on him tightened a fraction. "I'm sorry. You had your back turned, and I wasn't expecting ever to see you again."

"It's been . . . difficult. To stay away." The faint vibration in Jack's voice suggested it had been more than difficult.

"I can imagine. Why don't we go inside and you can tell us your tale?" This was not a casual invitation; Matthew was asking Jack to bare his soul. Jack looked worried at the prospect.

"What you say is your choice, Jack," Matthew assured him. "Tell us nothing, tell us everything, but let's go inside while you do it. Your latest Lobero is no quieter than your first. He'll have the neighbors calling the police if he keeps barking."

Jack nodded.

Matthew's head cocked to the side. The gesture made him look a bit like Jack. He smiled. "Where has our little boy gone? I don't have to crouch down anymore to meet your eyes."

The remaining tension left Jack's body with Matthew's gentle teasing. He grinned shyly and scratched Lobero's ears.

"Father Hubbard will come with us. Could you take the car, Gallowglass, and park it somewhere where it's not blocking the road?" Matthew asked.

Gallowglass held out his hand, and Hubbard put the keys into it.

"There's a briefcase in the trunk," Hubbard said. "Bring it back with you."

Gallowglass nodded, his lips pressed into a thin line. He gave Hubbard a blistering look before stalking toward the car.

"He never has liked me." Hubbard straightened the lapels on his austere black jacket, which he wore over a black shirt. Even after more than six hundred years, the vampire remained a cleric at heart. He nodded to me, acknowledging my presence for the first time. "Mistress Roydon."

"My name is Bishop." I wanted to remind him of the last time we'd seen each other and the agreement that he'd made—and broken, based on the evidence before me.

"Dr. Bishop, then." Hubbard's strange, multicolored eyes narrowed.

"You didn't keep your promise," I hissed. Jack's agitated stare settled on my neck.

"What promise?" Jack demanded from behind me.

Damn. Jack had always had excellent hearing but I'd forgotten he was now gifted with preternatural senses, too.

"I swore that I'd take care of you and Annie for Mistress Roydon," Hubbard said.

"Father Hubbard kept his word, mistress," Jack said quietly. "I wouldn't be here otherwise."

"And we're grateful to him." Matthew looked anything but. He tossed me the keys to the house. Gallowglass still had my bag, and without its contents I had no way to open the door.

Hubbard caught them instead and turned the key in the lock.

"Take Lobero upstairs and get him some water, Jack. The kitchen's on the first floor." Matthew plucked the keys from Hubbard's grasp as he went past and put them in a bowl on the hall table.

Jack called to Lobero and obediently started up the worn, painted treads.

"You're a dead man, Hubbard—and so is the one who made Jack a vampire." Matthew's voice was no more than a hollow murmur. Jack heard it nonetheless.

"You can't kill him, Master Roydon." Jack stood at the top of the stairs, his fingers wrapped tightly around Lobero's collar. "Father Hubbard is your grandson. He's my maker, too."

Jack turned away, and we heard the cabinet doors open, then water running from an open tap. The sounds were oddly homely considering that a conversational bomb had just gone off.

"My grandson?" Matthew looked at Hubbard in shock. "But that means . . ."

"Benjamin Fox is my sire." Andrew Hubbard's origins had always been shrouded in obscurity. London legends said that he had been a priest when the Black Death first visited England in 1349. After Hubbard's parishioners all succumbed to the illness, Hubbard had dug his own grave and climbed into it. Some mysterious vampire had brought Hubbard back from the brink of death—but no one seemed to know who.

"As far as your son was concerned, I was only a tool—someone he made to further his aims in England. Benjamin hoped I would have blood rage," Hubbard continued. "He also hoped I would help him organize an army to stand against the de Clermonts and their allies. But he was disappointed on both counts, and I've managed to keep him away from me and my flock. Until now."

"What's happened?" Matthew asked brusquely.

"Benjamin wants Jack. I can't let him have the boy again," was Hubbard's equally abrupt reply.

"Again?" That madman had been with Jack. I turned blindly toward the stairs, but Matthew caught me by the wrists and trapped me against his chest.

"Wait," he commanded.

Gallowglass came through the door with a large black briefcase and my book bag. He surveyed the scene and dropped what he was carrying.

"What's happened now?" he asked, looking from Matthew to Hubbard.

"Father Hubbard made Jack a vampire," I said as neutrally as I could. Jack was listening after all.

Gallowglass slammed Hubbard against the wall. "You bastard. I could smell your scent all over him. I thought—"

It was Gallowglass's turn to be tossed against something—in his case it was the floor. Hubbard pressed one polished black shoe against the big Gael's sternum. I was astonished that someone who looked so skeletal could be so strong.

"Thought what, Gallowglass?" Hubbard's tone was menacing. "That I'd violated a child?"

Upstairs, Jack's rising agitation soured the air. He'd learned from an early age how quickly ordinary quarrels could turn violent. As a boy he'd found even a hint of disagreement between Matthew and me distressing.

"Corra!" I cried, instinctively wanting her support.

By the time my firedrake swooped down from our bedroom and landed on the newel post, Matthew had averted any potential bloodshed by picking up Gallowglass and Hubbard by the scruffs of their necks, prying them apart, and shaking them until their teeth rattled.

Corra gave an irritated bleat and fixed a malevolent stare on Father Hubbard, suspecting quite rightly that he was to blame for her interrupted nap.

"I'll be damned." Jack's fair head peeked over the railing. "Didn't I tell you Corra would survive the timewalking, Father H?" He gave a hoot of delight and pounded on the painted wood. Jack's behavior reminded me so strongly of the joyous boy he had once been that I had to fight back the tears.

Corra let out an answering cry of welcome, followed by a stream of fire and song that filled the entrance with happiness. She took flight, zooming up and latching her wings around Jack. Then she tucked her head atop his and began to croon, her tail encircling his ribs so that the spade-shaped tip could gently pat his back. Lobero padded over to his master and gave Corra a suspicious sniff. She must have smelled like family, and therefore a creature to be included among his many responsibilities. He dropped down at Jack's side, head on his paws but eyes still watchful.

"Your tongue is even longer than Lobero's," Jack said, trying not to giggle as Corra tickled his neck. "I can't believe she remembers me."

"Of course she remembers you! How could she forget someone who spoiled her with currant buns?" I said with a smile.

By the time we were settled in the living room overlooking Court Street, the blood rage had receded from Jack's veins. Aware of his low position in the house's pecking order, he waited until everyone else took a chair before choosing his own seat. He was ready to join the dog on the floor when Matthew patted the sofa cushion.

"Sit with me, Jack." Matthew's invitation held a note of command. Jack sat, pulling at the knees of his jeans.

"You look to be about twenty," Matthew observed, hoping to draw him into conversation.

"Twenty, maybe twenty-one," Jack said. "Leonard and I—You remember Leonard?" Matthew nodded. "We figured it out because of my memories of the Armada. Nothing specific, you understand, just the fear of the Spanish invasion in the streets, the lighting of the beacons, and the victory celebrations. I must have been at least five in 1588 to remember that."

I did some rapid calculations. That meant Jack was made a vampire in 1603. "The plague."

The disease had swept through London with a vengeance that year. I noticed a mottled patch on his neck, just under his ear. It looked like a bruise, but it must be a mark left by a plague sore. For it to have remained visible even after Jack became a vampire suggested that he had been moments from death when Hubbard transformed him.

"Aye," Jack said, looking down at his hands. He turned them this way and that. "Annie died from it ten years earlier, soon after Master Marlowe was killed in Deptford."

I'd wondered what had happened to our Annie. I had imagined her a prosperous seamstress with her own business. I'd hoped she would have married a good man and had children. But she'd died while still a teenager, her life snuffed out before it truly began.

"That was a dreadful year, 1593, Mistress Roydon. The dead were everywhere. By the time Father Hubbard and I learned she was sick, it was too late," Jack said, his expression bereft.

"You're old enough to call me Diana," I said gently.

Jack plucked at his jeans without replying. "Father Hubbard took me in when you . . . left," he continued. "Sir Walter was in trouble, and Lord Northumberland was too busy at court to look after me." Jack smiled at Hubbard with obvious affection. "Those were good times, running about London with the gang."

"I was on very intimate terms with the sheriff during your so-called good times," Hubbard said drily. "You and Leonard got into more mischief than any two boys who ever lived."

"Nah," Jack said, grinning. "The only really serious trouble was when we snuck into the Tower to take Sir Walter his books and stayed on to pass a letter from him to Lady Raleigh."

"You did—" Matthew shuddered and shook his head. "Christ, Jack. You never could distinguish between a petty crime and a hanging offense."

"I can now," Jack said cheerfully. Then his expression became nervous once more. Lobero's head rose, and he rested his muzzle on Jack's knee.

"Don't be mad at Father Hubbard. He only did what I asked, Master Roydon. Leonard explained creatures to me long before I became one, so I knew what you and Gallowglass and Davy were. Things made better sense after that." Jack paused. "I should have had the courage to face death and accept it, but I couldn't go to my grave without seeing you again. My life felt . . . unfinished."

"And how does it feel now?" Matthew asked.

"Long. Lonely. And hard—harder than I ever imagined." Jack twisted Lobero's hair, rolling the strands until they formed a tight rope. He cleared his throat. "But it was all worth it for today," he continued softly. "Every bit of it."

Matthew's long arm reached for Jack's shoulder. He squeezed it, then quickly let go again. For a moment I saw desolation and grief on my husband's face before he donned his composed mask once more. It was the vampire version of a disguising spell.

"Father Hubbard told me his blood might make me ill, Master Roydon." Jack shrugged. "But I was already sick. What difference would it make to change one illness for another?"

No difference at all, I thought, except that one killed you and the other could make you a killer.

"Andrew was right to tell you," Matthew said. Father Hubbard looked surprised by this admission. "I don't imagine your grandsire gave him the same consideration." Matthew was careful to use the terms that Hubbard and Jack used to describe their relationship to Benjamin.

"No. He wouldn't have done. My grandsire doesn't believe that he owes anyone an explanation for any of his actions." Jack shot to his feet and traveled aimlessly around the room, Lobero following. He examined the moldings around the door, running his fingers along the wood. "You have the sickness in your blood, too, Master Roydon. I remember it from Greenwich. But it doesn't control you, like it does my grandsire. And me."

"It did once." Matthew looked at Gallowglass and gave him a slight nod.

"I remember when Matthew was as wild as the devil and nigh invincible with a sword in his hand. Even the bravest men ran in terror." Gallowglass leaned forward, hands clasped and knees spread wide.

"My grandsire told me about Master—Matthew's past." Jack shuddered. "He said that Matthew's talent for killing was in me, too, and I had to be true to it or you would never recognize me as your blood."

I'd seen Benjamin's unspeakable cruelty on camera, how he twisted hopes and fears into a weapon to destroy a creature's sense of self. That he'd done so with Jack's feelings for Matthew made me blind with fury. I clenched my hands into fists, tightening the cords in my fingers until the magic threatened to burst through my skin.

"Benjamin doesn't know me as well as he thinks." Anger was building in Matthew, too, his spicy scent growing sharper. "I would recognize you as mine before the entire world, and proudly—even if you weren't my blood."

Hubbard looked uneasy. His attention shifted from Matthew to Jack.

"You would make me your blood-sworn son?" Jack slowly turned to Matthew. "Like Philippe did with Mistress Roydon—I mean, Diana?"

Matthew's eyes widened slightly as he nodded, trying to absorb the fact that Philippe had known of Matthew's grandchildren when Matthew had not. A look of betrayal crossed his face.

"Philippe visited me whenever he came to London," Jack explained, oblivious to the changes in Matthew. "He told me to listen for his blood vow, because it was loud and I would probably hear Mistress Roydon before I saw her. And you were right, Mis—Diana. Matthew's father really was as big as the emperor's bear."

"If you met my father, then I'm sure you heard plenty of tales about my bad behavior." The muscle in Matthew's jaw had started ticking as betrayal turned to bitterness, his pupils growing larger by the second as his rage continued to gain ground.

"No," Jack said, confusion wrinkling his brow. "Philippe spoke only of his admiration and said you would teach me to ignore what my blood was telling me to do."

Matthew jerked as though he'd been hit.

"Philippe always made me feel closer to you and Mistress Roydon. Calmer, too." Jack looked nervous again. "But it has been a long time since I saw Philippe."

"He was captured in the war," Matthew explained, "and died as a result of what he suffered."

It was a careful half-truth.

"Father Hubbard told me. I'm glad Philippe didn't live to see—" This time the shudder traveled through Jack from the marrow of his bones to the surface of his skin. His eyes went full black without warning, filled with horror and dread.

Jack's present suffering was far worse than what Matthew had to endure. With Matthew it was only bitter fury that brought the blood rage to the surface. With Jack a wider range of emotions triggered it.

"It's all right." Matthew was with him in an instant, one hand clamped around his neck and the other resting on his cheek. Lobero pawed at Matthew's foot as if to say, *Do something.*

"Don't touch me when I'm like this," Jack snarled, pushing at Matthew's chest. But he might as well have tried to move a mountain. "You'll make it worse."

"You think you can order me about, pup?" Matthew's eyebrow arched. "Whatever you think is so terrible, just say it. You'll feel better once you do."

With Matthew's encouragement Jack's confession tumbled from some dark place inside where he stored up everything that was evil and terrifying.

"Benjamin found me a few years ago. He said he'd been waiting for me. My grandsire promised to take me to you, but only after I'd proved that I was really one of Matthew de Clermont's blood."

Gallowglass swore. Jack's eyes darted to him, and a snarl broke free.

"Keep your eyes on me, Jack." Matthew's tone made it clear that any resistance would be met with a swift and harsh reprisal. My husband was performing an impossible balancing act, one that required unconditional love along with a steady assertion of dominance. Pack dynamics were always fraught. With blood rage they could turn deadly in an instant.

Jack dragged his attention from Gallowglass, and his shoulders lowered a fraction.

"Then what happened?" Matthew prompted.

"I killed. Again and again. The more I killed, the more I wanted to kill. The blood did more than feed me—it fed the blood rage, too."

"It was clever of you to understand that so quickly," Matthew said approvingly.

"Sometimes I came to my senses long enough to realize that what I was doing was wrong. I tried to save the warmbloods then, but I couldn't stop drinking," Jack confessed. "I managed to turn two of my prey into vampires. Benjamin was pleased with me then."

"Only two?" A shadow flitted across Matthew's features.

"Benjamin wanted me to save more, but it took too much control. No matter what I did, most of them died." Jack's inky eyes filled with blood tears, the pupils taking on a red sheen.

"Where did these deaths occur?" Matthew sounded only mildly curious, but my sixth sense told me the question was crucial to understanding what had happened to Jack.

"Everywhere. I had to keep moving. There was so much blood. I had to get away from the police, and the newspapers. . . ." Jack shuddered.

VAMPIRE ON THE LOOSE IN LONDON. I remembered the vivid headline and all the clippings of the "vampire murders" that Matthew had collected from around the world. I bowed my head, not wanting Jack to realize I knew that he was the murderer whom European authorities were seeking.

"But it's the ones that lived who suffered the most," Jack continued, his voice deadening further with every word. "My grandsire took my children from me and said he would make sure they were raised properly."

"Benjamin used you." Matthew looked deep into his eyes, trying to make a connection. Jack shook his head.

"When I made those children, I broke my vow to Father Hubbard. He said the world didn't need more vampires—there were plenty already—and if I was lonely, I could take care of creatures whose families didn't want them anymore. All Father Hubbard asked was that I not make children, but I failed him again and again. After that, I couldn't go back to London—not with so much blood on my hands. And I couldn't stay with my grandsire. When I told Benjamin I wanted to leave, he went into a terrible rage and killed one of my children in retaliation. His sons held me down and forced me to watch." Jack bit back a harsh sound. "And my daughter. My daughter. They—"

He retched. He clamped a hand over his mouth, but it was too late to keep the blood from escaping as he vomited. It streamed over his chin, soaking into his dark shirt. Lobero leaped up, barking sharply and pawing at his back.

Unable to stay away a moment longer, I rushed to Jack's side.

"Diana!" Gallowglass cried. "You must not—"

"Don't tell me what to do. Get me a towel!" I snapped.

Jack fell to his hands and knees, his landing softened by Matthew's strong arms. I knelt beside him as he continued to purge his stomach of its contents. Gallowglass handed me a towel. I used it to mop Jack's face and hands, which were covered with blood. The towel was soon sodden and icy cold from my frantic efforts to stanch the flow, the contact with so much vampire blood making my hands numb and clumsy.

"The force of the vomiting must have broken some blood vessels in his stomach and throat," Matthew said. "Andrew, can you get a pitcher of water? Put plenty of ice in it."

Hubbard went to the kitchen and was back in moments.

"Here," he said, thrusting the pitcher at Matthew.

"Raise his head, Diana," Matthew instructed. "Keep hold of him, Andrew. His body is screaming for blood, and he'll fight against taking water."

"What can I do?" Gallowglass said, his voice gruff.

"Wipe off Lobero's paws before he tracks blood all over the house. Jack won't need any reminders of what's happened." Matthew gripped Jack's chin. "Jack!"

Jack's glassy black eyes swiveled toward Matthew.

"Drink this," Matthew commanded, raising Jack's chin a few inches. Jack spluttered and snapped in an attempt to throw him off. But Hubbard kept Jack immobilized long enough to empty the pitcher.

Jack hiccupped, and Hubbard loosened his hold.

"Well done, Jackie," Gallowglass said.

I smoothed Jack's hair away from his forehead as he bent forward again, clutching at his visibly heaving stomach.

"I got blood on you," he whispered. My shirt was streaked with it.

"So you did," I said. "It's not the first time a vampire's bled on me, Jack."

"Try to rest now," Matthew told him. "You're exhausted."

"I don't want to sleep." Jack swallowed hard as the gorge rose again in his throat.

"Shh." I rubbed his neck. "I can promise there will be no nightmares."

"How can you be sure?" Jack asked.

"Magic." I traced the pattern of the fifth knot on his forehead and lowered my voice to a whisper. "Mirror shimmers, monsters shake, banish nightmares until he wakes."

Jack's eyes slowly closed. After a few minutes, he was curled on his side, sleeping peacefully.

I wove another spell—one that was meant just for him. It required no words, for no one would ever use it but me. The threads surrounding Jack were a furious snarl of red, black, and yellow. I pulled on the healing green threads that surrounded me, as well as the white threads that helped break curses and establish new beginnings. I twisted them together and tied them around Jack's wrist, fixing the braid with a secure, six-crossed knot.

"There's a guest room upstairs," I said. "We'll put Jack to bed there. Corra and Lobero will let us know if he stirs."

"Would that be all right?" Matthew asked Hubbard.

"When it comes to Jack, you don't need my permission," Hubbard replied.

"Yes I do. You're his father," Matthew said.

"I'm only his sire," Hubbard said softly. "You're Jack's father, Matthew. You always have been."

Matthew carried Jack up to the third floor, cradling his body as if he were a baby. Lobero and Corra accompanied us, both beasts aware of the job they had to do. While Matthew stripped off Jack's blood-soaked shirt, I rummaged in our bedroom closet for something he could wear instead. Jack was easily six feet tall, but he had a much rangier frame than Matthew. I found an oversize Yale men's crew team shirt that I sometimes slept in, hoping it would do. Matthew slipped Jack's seemingly boneless arms into it and pulled it over his lolling head. My spell had knocked him out cold.

Together we settled him on the bed, neither of us speaking unless it was absolutely necessary. I drew the sheet up around Jack's shoulders while Lobero watched my every move from the floor. Corra perched on the lamp, attentive and unblinking, her weight bending the shade to an alarming degree.

I touched Jack's sandy hair and the dark mark on his neck, then pressed my hand over his heart. Even though he was asleep, I could feel the parts of him warring for control: mind, body, soul. Though Hubbard had ensured that Jack would be twenty-one forever, he had a weariness that made him seem like a man three times that age.

Jack had been through so much. Too much, thanks to Benjamin. I wanted that madman obliterated from the face of the earth. The fingers on my left hand splayed wide, my wrist stinging where the knot circled my pulse. Magic was nothing more than desire made real, and the power in my veins responded to my unspoken wishes for revenge.

"Jack was our responsibility, and we weren't there for him." My voice was low and fierce. "And Annie . . ."

"We're here for Jack now." Matthew's eyes held the same sorrow and anger that I knew were in my own. "There's nothing we can do for Annie, except pray that her soul found rest."

I nodded, controlling my emotions with difficulty.

"Take a shower, *ma lionne.* Hubbard's touch and Jack's blood . . ."

Matthew couldn't abide it when my skin carried the scent of another creature. "I'll stay with him while you do. Then you and I will go downstairs and talk to . . . my grandson." His final words were slow and deliberate, as though he were getting his tongue used to them.

I squeezed his hand, kissed Jack lightly on the forehead, and reluctantly headed into the bathroom in a futile effort to wash myself clean of the evening's events.

Thirty minutes later we found Gallowglass and Hubbard sitting opposite each other at the simple pine dining table. They glared. They stared. They growled. I was glad Jack wasn't awake to witness it.

Matthew dropped my hand and walked the few steps to the kitchen. He pulled out a bottle of sparkling water for me and three bottles of wine. After distributing them he went back for a corkscrew and four glasses.

"You may be my cousin, but I still don't like you, Hubbard." Gallowglass's growl subsided into an inhuman sound that was far more disturbing.

"It's mutual." Hubbard hoisted his black briefcase onto the table and left it within easy reach.

Matthew worked the corkscrew into his bottle, watching his nephew and Hubbard jockey for position without comment. He poured himself a glass of wine and drank it down in two gulps.

"You're not fit to be a parent," Gallowglass said, eyes narrowing.

"Who is?" Hubbard shot back.

"Enough." Matthew didn't raise his voice, but there was a timbre in it that lifted the hairs on my neck and instantly silenced Gallowglass and Hubbard. "Has the blood rage always affected Jack this way, Andrew, or has it worsened since he met Benjamin?"

Hubbard sat back in his chair with a sardonic smile. "That's where you want to start, is it?"

"How about *you* start by explaining why you made Jack a vampire when you knew it could give him blood rage!" My anger had burned straight through any courtesy I might once have extended to him.

"I gave him a choice, Diana," Hubbard retorted, "not to mention a chance."

"Jack was dying of plague!" I cried. "He wasn't capable of making a clear decision. You were the grown-up. Jack was a child."

"Jack was full on twenty years—a man, not the boy you left with Lord Northumberland. And he'd been through hell waiting in vain for your return!" Hubbard said.

Afraid we might wake Jack, I lowered my voice. "I left you with plenty of money to keep both Jack and Annie out of harm's way. Neither of them should have wanted for anything."

"You think a warm bed and food in his belly could mend Jack's broken heart?" Hubbard's otherworldly eyes were cold. "He looked for you every day for *twelve years.* That's twelve years of going to the docks to meet the ships from Europe in hopes that you would be aboard; twelve years interviewing every foreigner he could find in London to inquire if you had been seen in Amsterdam, or Lübeck, or Prague; and twelve years walking up to anyone he suspected of being a witch to show that person a picture he'd drawn of the famous sorceress Diana Roydon. It's a miracle the plague took his life and not the queen's justices!"

I blanched.

"You had a choice, too," Hubbard reminded me. "So if you want to cast blame for Jack's becoming a vampire, blame yourself or blame Matthew. He was your responsibility. You made him mine."

"That wasn't our bargain, and you know it!" The words slipped out of my mouth before I could stop them. I froze, a look of horror on my face. This was another secret I'd kept from Matthew, one that I'd thought was safely behind me.

Gallowglass's breath hissed in surprise. Matthew's icy gaze splintered against my skin. Then the room fell utterly silent.

"I need to speak to my wife and my grandson, Gallowglass. Alone," Matthew said. The emphasis he placed on "my wife" and "my grandson" was subtle but unmistakable.

Gallowglass stood, his face set in lines of disapproval. "I'll be upstairs with Jack."

Matthew shook his head. "Go home and wait for Miriam. I'll call when Andrew and Jack are ready to join you."

"Jack will stay here," I said, my voice rising again, "with us. Where he belongs."

The forbidding look Matthew directed my way silenced me immediately, even though the twenty-first century was no place for a Renaissance prince and a year ago I would have protested his high-handedness. Now I knew that my husband was hanging on to his control by a very slender thread.

"I'm not staying under the same roof as a de Clermont. Especially not him," Hubbard said, pointing in Gallowglass's direction.

"You forget, Andrew," Matthew said, "*you* are a de Clermont. So is Jack."

"I was never a de Clermont," Hubbard said viciously.

"Once you drank Benjamin's blood, you were never anything else." Matthew's voice was clipped. "In this family you do what I say."

"Family?" Hubbard scoffed. "You were part of Philippe's pack, and now you answer to Baldwin. You don't have a family of your own."

"Apparently I do." Matthew's mouth twisted with regret. "Time to go, Gallowglass."

"Very well, Matthew. I'll let you send me off—this time—but I'll not go far. And if my instincts tell me there's trouble, I'm coming back and to hell with vampire custom and law." Gallowglass got up and kissed me on the cheek. "Holler if you need me, Auntie."

Matthew waited until the front door closed before he turned on Hubbard. "Exactly what deal did you strike with my mate?" he demanded.

"It's my fault, Matthew. I went to Hubbard—" I began, wanting to confess and get it over with.

The table reverberated under the force of Matthew's blow. "Answer me, Andrew."

"I agreed to protect anyone who belonged to her, even you," Hubbard said shortly. In this respect he was a de Clermont to the bone—volunteering nothing, only giving away what he must.

"And in exchange?" Matthew asked sharply. "You wouldn't make such a vow without getting something equally precious in return."

"Your *mate* gave me one drop of blood—one single drop," Hubbard said, his tone resentful. I'd tricked him, abiding to the letter of his request rather than its spirit. Apparently Andrew Hubbard held grudges.

"Did you know then that I was your grandfather?" Matthew asked. I couldn't imagine why this was important.

"Yes," Andrew said, looking slightly green.

Matthew hauled him across the table so that they were nose to nose. "And what did you learn from that one drop of blood?"

"Her true name—Diana Bishop. Nothing more, I swear. The witch used her magic to make sure of it." On Hubbard's tongue the word "witch" sounded filthy and obscene.

"Never take advantage of my wife's protective instincts again, Andrew. If you do, I'll have your head." Matthew's grip tightened. "Given your prurience, there isn't a vampire alive who would fault me for doing so."

"I don't care what the two of you get up to behind closed doors—though others will, since your mate is obviously pregnant and there isn't a hint of another man's scent on her." Hubbard pursed his lips in disapproval.

At last I understood Matthew's earlier question. By knowingly taking my blood and seeking out my thoughts and memories, Andrew Hubbard had done the vampire equivalent of watching his grandparents have sex. Had I not found a way to slow its flow so he got only the drop he asked for and nothing more, Hubbard would have seen into our private lives and might have learned Matthew's secrets as well as my own. My eyes closed tight against the realization of the damage that would have resulted.

A distracting murmur came from Andrew's briefcase. It reminded me of the noise I sometimes heard during a lecture, when a student's phone went off unexpectedly.

"You left your phone on speaker," I said, my attention drawn to the low chatter. "Someone is leaving a message."

Matthew and Andrew both frowned.

"I don't hear anything," Matthew said.

"And I don't own a mobile phone," Hubbard added.

"Where is it coming from, then?" I asked, looking around. "Did someone turn on the radio?"

"The only thing in my briefcase is this." Hubbard released its two brass clasps and withdrew something.

The chattering grew louder as a jolt of power entered my body. Every sense I had was heightened, and the threads that bound the world chimed in sudden agitation, coiling and twisting in the space between me and the sheet of vellum that Andrew Hubbard held in his fingers. My blood responded to the faint vestiges of magic that clung to this solitary page from the Book of Life, and my wrists burned as a faint, familiar scent of must and age filled the room.

Hubbard turned the page so that it faced me, but I already knew what I would see there: two alchemical dragons locked together, the blood from their wounds falling into a basin from which naked, pale figures rose. It depicted the stage in the alchemical process after the chemical marriage of the moon queen and the sun king: *conceptio,* when a new and powerful substance sprang forth from the union of opposites—male and female, light and dark, sun and moon.

After spending weeks in the Beinecke looking for Ashmole 782's missing pages, I'd unexpectedly encountered one of them in my own dining room.

"Edward Kelley sent it to me the autumn after you left. He told me not to let it out of my sight." Hubbard slid the page toward me.

We had only caught a glimpse of this illumination in Rudolf's palace. Later Matthew and I had speculated that what we thought were two dragons might actually be a firedrake and an ouroboros. One of the alchemical dragons was indeed a firedrake, with two legs and wings, and the other was a snake with its tail in its mouth. The ouroboros at my wrist writhed in recognition, its colors shining with possibility. The image was mesmerizing, and now that I had time to study it properly, small things struck me: the dragons' rapt expressions as they gazed into each other's eyes, the look of wonder on their progeny's faces as they emerged from the basin where they'd been born, the striking balance between two such powerful creatures.

"Jack made sure Edward's picture was safe no matter what. Plague, fire, war—the boy never let anything touch it. He claimed it belonged to you, Mistress Roydon," Hubbard said, interrupting my reveries.

"To me?" I touched the corner of the vellum, and one of the twins gave a strong kick. "No. It belongs to all of us."

"And yet you have some kind of special connection to it. You're the only one who has ever heard it speak," Andrew said. "Long ago, a witch in my care said he thought it came from the witches' first spell book. But an old vampire passing through London said it was a page from the Book of Life. I pray to God that neither tale is true."

"What do you know about the Book of Life?" Matthew's voice was a peal of thunder.

"I know that Benjamin wants it," Hubbard said. "He told Jack as much. But that wasn't the first time my sire mentioned the book. Benjamin looked for it in Oxford long ago—before he made me a vampire."

That meant Benjamin had been looking for the Book of Life since before the middle of the fourteenth century—far longer than Matthew had been interested in it.

"My sire thought he might find it in the library of an Oxford sorcerer. Benjamin took the witch a gift in exchange for the book: a brass head that supposedly spoke oracles." Hubbard's face filled with sadness. "It is always a pity to see such a wise man taken in by superstition. *'Do not turn to idols or make for yourselves any gods of cast metal,'* sayeth the Lord."

Gerbert of Aurillac had reputedly owned just such a miraculous device. I had thought Peter Knox was the member of the Congregation who was most interested in Ashmole 782. Was it possible that Gerbert had been in league with Benjamin all these years and it was he who sought out Peter Knox's help?

"The witch in Oxford took the brass head but wouldn't relinquish the book," Hubbard continued. "Decades later my sire still cursed him for his duplicity. I never did discover the witch's name."

"I believe it was Roger Bacon—an alchemist and a philosopher as well as a witch." Matthew looked at me. Bacon once owned the Book of Life, and had called it the "true secret of secrets."

"Alchemy is one of the witches' many vanities," Hubbard said with disdain. His expression turned anxious. "My children tell me Benjamin has been back in England."

"He has. Benjamin has been watching my lab in Oxford." Matthew made no mention of the fact that the Book of Life was currently a few blocks away from that very laboratory. Hubbard might be his grandson, but that didn't mean Matthew trusted him.

"If Benjamin is in England, how will we keep him away from Jack?" I asked Matthew urgently.

"Jack will return to London. My sire is no more welcome there than you are, Matthew." Hubbard stood. "So long as he is with me, Jack will be safe."

"No one is safe from Benjamin. Jack is not going back to London." The note of command was back in Matthew's voice. "Nor are you, Andrew. Not yet."

"We've done very well without your interference," Hubbard retorted. "It's a bit late for you to decide you want to lord it over your children like some ancient Roman father."

"The paterfamilias. A fascinating tradition." Matthew settled back in his chair, his wineglass cupped in his hand. He looked no longer like a prince but a king. "Imagine giving one man the power of life and death over his wife, his children, his servants, anyone he adopted into his family, and even his close relatives who lacked a strong father of their own. It reminds me a bit of what you tried to accomplish in London."

Matthew sipped at his wine. Hubbard looked more uncomfortable with each passing moment.

"My children obey me willingly," Hubbard said stiffly. "They honor me, as godly children should."

"Such an idealist," Matthew said, softly mocking. "You know who came up with the paterfamilias, of course."

"The Romans, as I said," Hubbard replied sharply. "I am educated, Matthew, in spite of your doubts on this score."

"No, it was Philippe." Matthew's eyes gleamed with amusement. "Philippe thought Roman society could benefit from a healthy dose of vampire family discipline, and a reminder of the father's importance."

"Philippe de Clermont was guilty of the sin of pride. God is the only true Father. You are a Christian, Matthew. Surely you agree." Hubbard's expression held the fervency of a true believer.

"Perhaps," Matthew said, as though he were seriously considering his grandson's argument. "But until God calls us to Him, I will have to suffice. Like it or not, Andrew, in the eyes of other vampires I am your paterfamilias, the head of your clan, your alpha—call it what you like. And all your children—including Jack and all the other strays you've adopted be they daemon, vampire, or witch—are *mine* under vampire law."

"No." Hubbard shook his head. "I never wanted any part of the de Clermont family."

"What you want doesn't matter. Not anymore." Matthew put down his wine and took my hand in his.

"To command my loyalty, you would have to recognize my sire—Benjamin—as your son. And you will *never* do that," Hubbard said savagely. "As head of the de Clermonts, Baldwin takes the family's honor and position seriously. He won't permit you to branch out on your own given the scourge in your blood."

Before Matthew could respond to Andrew's challenge, Corra uttered a warning squawk. Realizing that Jack must have awoken, I rose from my seat to go to him. Unfamiliar rooms had terrified him as a child.

"Stay here," Matthew said, his grip on my hand tightening.

"He needs me!" I protested.

"Jack needs a strong hand and consistent boundaries," Matthew said softly. "He knows you love him. But he can't handle such strong feelings at the moment."

"I trust him." My voice quavered with anger and hurt.

"I don't," Matthew said sharply. "It's not just anger that sets off the blood rage in him. Love and loyalty do, too."

"Don't ask me to ignore him." I wanted Matthew to stop acting the role of paterfamilias long enough to behave like a true father.

"I'm sorry, Diana." A shadow settled in Matthew's eyes, one that I thought was gone forever. "I have to put Jack's needs first."

"What needs?" Jack stood in the door. He yawned, tufts of hair standing up in apparent alarm. Lobero pushed past his master and went straight to Matthew, looking for acknowledgment of a job well done.

"You need to hunt. The moon is bright, alas, but not even I can control the heavens." Matthew's lie flowed from his tongue like honey. He ruffled Lobero's ears. "We're all going—you, me, your father, even Gallowglass. Lobero can come, too."

Jack's nose wrinkled. "Not hungry."

"Don't feed, then. But you're hunting nevertheless. Be ready at midnight. I'll pick you up."

"Pick me up?" Jack looked from me to Hubbard. "I thought we would stay here."

"You'll be just around the corner with Gallowglass and Miriam. Andrew will be there with you," Matthew assured him. "This house isn't large enough for a witch and three vampires. We're nocturnal creatures, and Diana and the babies need their sleep."

Jack looked at my belly wistfully. "I always wanted a baby brother."

"You may well get two sisters instead," Matthew said, chuckling.

My hand lowered automatically over my belly as one of the twins gave another strong kick. They had been unusually active ever since Jack showed up.

"Are they moving?" Jack asked me, his face eager. "Can I touch them?"

I looked at Matthew. Jack's glance slid in the same direction.

"Let me show you how." Matthew's tone was easy, though his eyes were sharp. He took Jack's hand and pressed it into the side of my belly.

"I don't feel anything," Jack said, frowning with concentration.

A particularly strong kick, followed by a sharp elbow, thudded against the wall of my uterus.

"Whoa!" Jack's face was inches from mine, his eyes full of wonder. "Do they kick like that all day?"

"It feels like it." I wanted to smooth down the mess of Jack's hair. I wanted to take him into my arms and promise him that no one was ever going to hurt him again. But I could offer him neither of these comforts.

Sensing the maternal turn my mood had taken, Matthew lifted Jack's hand away. Jack's face fell, experiencing it as rejection. Furious with Matthew, I reached to jerk Jack's hand back. Before I could, Matthew put his hand at my waist and pulled me against his side. It was an unmistakable gesture of possession.

Jack's eyes went black.

Hubbard pitched forward to intervene, and Matthew froze him in place with a look.

In the space of five heartbeats, Jack's eyes returned to normal. When they were brown and green once more, Matthew gave him an approving smile.

"Your instinct to protect Diana is entirely appropriate," Matthew told him. "Believing you have to shield her from me is not."

"I'm sorry, Matthew," Jack whispered. "It won't happen again."

"I accept your apology. Sadly, it *will* happen again. Learning to control your illness isn't going to be easy—or quick." Matthew's tone turned brisk. "Kiss Diana good night, Jack, and get settled at Gallowglass's house. It's a former church around the corner. You'll feel right at home."

"Hear that, Father H?" Jack grinned. "Wonder if it has bats in its belfry, like yours."

"I no longer have a bat problem," Hubbard said sourly.

"Father H still lives in a church in the city," Jack explained, suddenly animated. "It's not the same one you visited. That old heap burned down. Most of this one did, too, come to think of it."

I laughed. Jack had always loved telling stories and had a talent for it, too.

"Now just the tower remains. Father H did it up so nicely you hardly notice it's just a pile of rubbish." Jack grinned at Hubbard and gave me a perfunctory kiss on the cheek, his mood swinging from blood rage to happiness in a remarkably short period of time. He sped down the stairs. "Come on, Lobero. Let's go wrestle with Gallowglass."

"Midnight," Matthew called after him. "Be ready. And be nice to Miriam, Jack. If you don't, she'll make you wish you'd never been reborn."

"Don't worry, I'm used to dealing with difficult females!" Jack replied. Lobero barked with excitement and orbited Jack's legs to encourage him outside.

"Keep the picture, Mistress Roydon. If both Matthew and Benjamin covet it, then I wish to be as far away from it as possible," Andrew said.

"How generous, Andrew." Matthew's hand shot out and closed around Hubbard's throat. "Stay in New Haven until I give you leave to go."

Their eyes clashed, slate and gray-green. Andrew was the first to look away.

"Come on, Father H!" Jack bellowed. "I want to see Gallowglass's church, and Lobero needs a walk."

"Midnight, Andrew." Matthew's words were perfectly cordial, but there was a warning in them.

The door closed, and the sound of Lobero's barking faded. When it had faded completely, I turned on Matthew.

"How could you—"

The sight of Matthew, his head buried in his hands, brought me to an abrupt stop. My anger, which had been blazing, slowly fizzled. He looked up, his face ravaged with guilt and sorrow.

"Jack . . . Benjamin . . ." Matthew shuddered. "God help me, what have I done?"

20

Matthew sat in the broken-down easy chair opposite the bed where Diana was sleeping, plowing through another inconclusive set of test results so that he and Chris could reevaluate their research strategy at tomorrow's meeting. Given the late hour, he was taken by surprise when his phone's screen lit up.

Moving carefully so as not to wake his wife, Matthew padded silently out of the room and down the stairs to the kitchen, where he could speak without being overheard.

"You need to come," Gallowglass said, his voice gruff and low. "Now."

Matthew's flesh prickled, and his eyes rose to the ceiling as though he could see through the plaster and floorboards into the bedroom. His first instinct was always to protect her, even though it was clear that the danger was elsewhere.

"Leave Auntie at home," Gallowglass said flatly, as though he could witness Matthew's actions. "Miriam's on her way." The phone went dead.

Matthew stared down at the display for a moment, its bright colors bringing a note of false cheer to the early-morning hours before they faded to black.

The front door creaked open.

Matthew was at the top of the stairs by the time Miriam walked through it. He studied her closely. There was not a drop of blood on her, thank God. Even so, Miriam's eyes were wide and her face bore a haunted expression. Very little frightened his longtime friend and colleague, but she was clearly terrified. Matthew swore.

"What's wrong?" Diana descended from the third floor, her coppery hair seeming to capture all the available light in the house. "Is it Jack?"

Matthew nodded. Gallowglass wouldn't have called otherwise.

"I'll only be a minute," Diana said, reversing her direction to get dressed.

"No, Diana," Miriam said quietly.

Diana froze, her hand on the banister. She twisted her body around and met Miriam's eyes.

"Is he d-dead?" she whispered numbly. Matthew was at her side in the space of a human heartbeat.

"No, *mon coeur.* He's not dead." Matthew knew this was Diana's worst nightmare: that someone she loved would be taken from her before the two of them could say a proper farewell. But whatever was taking place in the house on Wooster Square might somehow be worse.

"Stay with Miriam." Matthew pressed a kiss against her stiff lips. "I'll be home soon."

"He's been doing so well," Diana said. Jack had been in New Haven for a week, and his blood rage had diminished in both frequency and intensity. Matthew's strict boundaries and consistent expectations had already made a difference.

"We knew there would be setbacks," Matthew said, tucking a silky strand of hair behind Diana's ear. "I know you won't sleep, but try to rest at least." He was worried she'd do nothing but pace and stare out the window until he returned with news.

"You can read these while you wait." Miriam drew a thick stack of articles out of her bag. She was making an effort to sound brisk and matter-of-fact, her bittersweet scent of galbanum and pomegranate stronger now. "This is everything you asked for, and I added some other articles you might be interested in: all of Matthew's studies on wolves, as well as some classic pieces on wolf parenting and pack behavior. It's basically Dr. Spock for the modern vampire parent."

Matthew turned to Diana in amazement. Once again, his wife had surprised him. Her cheeks reddened, and she took the articles from Miriam.

"I need to understand how this vampire family stuff works. Go. Tell Jack I love him." Diana's voice broke. "If you can."

Matthew squeezed her hand without replying. He would make no promises on that score. Jack had to understand that his access to Diana depended on his behavior—and Matthew's approval.

"Prepare yourself," Miriam murmured when he passed her. "And I don't care if Benjamin is your son. If you don't kill him after seeing this, I will."

* * *

In spite of the late hour, Gallowglass's house was not the only one in the neighborhood that was still illuminated. New Haven was a college town, after all. Most of Wooster Square's night owls sought a strange companionship, working in full view with curtains and blinds open. What distinguished the vampire's house was that the drapes were tightly closed and only cracks of golden light around the edges of the windows betrayed the fact that someone was still awake.

Inside the house pools of lamplight cast a warm glow over a few personal belongings. Otherwise it was sparsely decorated with Danish Modern furniture made from blond wood accented with occasional antiques and splashes of bold color. One of Gallowglass's most treasured possessions—a tattered eighteenth-century Red Ensign that he and Davy Hancock had stripped from their beloved cargo ship the *Earl of Pembroke* before it was refitted and renamed *Endeavour*—was balled up on the floor.

Matthew sniffed. The house was filled with the bitter, acrid scent that Diana had likened to a coal fire, and faint strains of Bach filled the air. The St. Matthew Passion—the same music that Benjamin played in his laboratory to torture his captive witch. Matthew's stomach twisted into a heavy knot.

He rounded the corner of the living room. What he saw brought him to an immediate stop. Stark murals in shades of black and gray covered every inch of the canvas-hued walls. Jack stood atop a makeshift scaffold constructed from pieces of furniture, wielding a soft artist's pencil. The floor was littered with pencil stubs and the paper peelings that Jack had torn away to reveal fresh charcoal.

Matthew's eyes swept the walls from floor to ceiling. Detailed landscapes, studies of animals and plants that were almost microscopic in their precision, and sensitive portraits were linked together with breathtaking swaths of line and form that defied painterly logic. The overall effect was beautiful yet disturbing, as if Sir Anthony van Dyck had painted Picasso's *Guernica*.

"Christ." Matthew's right hand automatically made the sign of the cross.

"Jack ran out of paper two hours ago," Gallowglass said grimly, pointing to the easels in the front window. Each now bore a single sheet, but the drifts of paper surrounding their tripod supports suggested that these were merely a selection from a larger series of drawings.

"Matthew." Chris came from the kitchen, sipping a cup of black coffee, the aroma of the roasted beans blending with Jack's bitter scent.

"This is no place for a warmblood, Chris," Matthew said, keeping a wary eye on Jack.

"I promised Miriam I'd stay." Chris settled into a worn plantation chair and placed his coffee mug on the wide arms. When he moved, the woven seat underneath him creaked like a ship under sail. "So Jack's another one of your grandchildren?"

"Not now, Chris. Where's Andrew?" Matthew said, continuing to observe Jack at work.

"He's upstairs getting more pencils." Chris had a sip of coffee, his dark eyes taking in the details of what Jack was sketching now: a naked woman, her head thrown back in agony. "I wish like hell he would go back to drawing daffodils."

Matthew wiped his hand across his mouth, hoping to remove the sourness that rose up from his stomach. Thank God that Diana hadn't come with him. Jack would never be able to look her in the eyes again if he knew she'd seen this.

Moments later Hubbard returned to the living room. He put a box of fresh supplies on the stepladder where Jack balanced. Utterly absorbed in his work, Jack didn't react to Hubbard's presence any more than he had to Matthew's arrival.

"You should have called me sooner." Matthew kept his voice deliberately calm. In spite of his efforts, Jack turned glassy, unseeing eyes toward him as his blood rage responded to the tension in the air.

"Jack's done this before," Hubbard said. "He's drawn on his bedroom walls and on the walls in the church undercroft. But he's never made so many images so quickly. And never . . . him." He looked up.

Benjamin's eyes, nose, and mouth dominated one wall, looking down on Jack with an expression that was equal parts avarice and malice. His features were unmistakable in their cruelty, and somehow more ominous for not being contained within the outlines of a human face.

Jack had moved a few feet along from Benjamin's portrait and was now working on the last empty stretch of wall. The pictures around the room followed a rough sequence of events leading from Jack's time in London before Hubbard had made him a vampire all the way to the present day.

The easels in the window were the starting point for Jack's troubling image cycle.

Matthew examined them. Each held what artists called a study—a single element of a larger scene that helped them to understand particular problems of composition or perspective. The first was a drawing of a man's hand, skin cracked and coarsened through poverty and manual labor. The image of a cruel mouth with missing teeth occupied another easel. The third showed the crisscrossing laces on a man's breeches, along with a finger hooked and ready to pull them free. The last was of a knife, pressing against a boy's prominent hip bone until the tip slid into the skin.

Matthew put the solitary images together in his mind—hand, mouth, breeches, knife—while the St. Matthew Passion thundered in the background. He swore at the abusive scene that instantly sprang to mind.

"One of Jack's earliest memories," Hubbard said.

Matthew was reminded of his first encounter with Jack, when he would have taken the boy's ear if not for Diana's intervention. He had been yet another creature to offer Jack violence instead of compassion.

"If not for his art and music, Jack would have destroyed himself. We have often thanked God for Philippe's gift." Andrew gestured toward the cello propped up in the corner.

Matthew had recognized the instrument's distinctive scroll the moment he clapped eyes on it. He and Signor Montagnana, the instrument's Venetian maker, had dubbed the cello "the Duchess of Marlborough" for its generous, yet still elegant, curves. Matthew had learned to play on Duchess back when lutes fell out of favor and were replaced by violins, violas, and cellos. Duchess had mysteriously disappeared while he was in New Orleans disciplining Marcus's brood of children. When Matthew returned, he had asked Philippe what had happened to the instrument. His father had shrugged and muttered something about Napoleon and the English that had made no sense at all.

"Does Jack always listen to Bach when he draws?" Matthew murmured.

"He prefers Beethoven. Jack started listening to Bach after . . . you know." Hubbard's mouth twisted.

"Perhaps his drawings can help us find Benjamin," Gallowglass said.

Matthew's eyes darted over the many faces and places that might provide vital clues.

"Chris already took pictures," Gallowglass assured him.

"And a video," Chris added, "once he got to . . . er, him." Chris, too, avoided saying Benjamin's name and simply waved to where Jack was still sketching and crooning something under his breath.

Matthew held his hand up for silence.

"'All the king's horses and all the king's men / Couldn't put Jack back together again.'" He shuddered and dropped what little remained of his pencil. Andrew handed him a replacement, and Jack began another detailed study of a male hand, this one reaching out in a gesture of entreaty.

"Thanks be to God. He's nearing the end of his frenzy." Some of the tension in Hubbard's shoulders dissipated. "Soon Jack will be back in his right mind."

Wanting to take advantage of the moment, Matthew moved silently to the cello. He gripped it by the neck and picked the bow off the floor where Jack had carelessly dropped it.

Matthew sat on the edge of a wooden chair, holding his ear near the instrument while he plucked and worked the bow over the strings, still able to hear the cello's round tones over the Bach that blared from the speakers on a nearby bookcase.

"Shut that noise off," he told Gallowglass, making a final adjustment to the tuning pegs before he began to play. For a few measures, the cello's music clashed with the choir and orchestra. Then Bach's great choral work fell silent. Into the void, Matthew poured music that was an intermediary step between the histrionic strains of the Passion and something that he hoped would help Jack regain his emotional bearing.

Matthew had chosen the piece carefully: the Lacrimosa from Johann Christian Bach's Requiem. Even so, Jack startled at the change in musical accompaniment, his hand stilling against the wall. As the music washed through him, his breathing became slower and more regular. When he resumed sketching, it was to draw the outlines of Westminster Abbey instead of another creature in pain.

While he played, Matthew bent his head in supplication. Had a choir been present, as the composer intended, they would have been singing the Latin mass for the dead. Since he was alone, Matthew made the cello's mournful tones imitate the absent human voices.

Lacrimosa dies illa, Matthew's cello sang. *"Tearful will be that day, / On which from the ash arises / The guilty man who is to be judged."*

Spare him therefore, God, Matthew prayed as he played the next line of music, putting his faith and anguish into every stroke of the bow.

When he reached the end of the Lacrimosa, Matthew took up the strains of Beethoven's Cello Sonata no. 1 in F Major. Beethoven had written the piece for piano as well as for cello, but Matthew hoped Jack was familiar enough with the music to fill in the missing notes.

The strokes of Jack's charcoal pencil slowed further, becoming gentler with each passing measure. Matthew recognized the torch of the Statue of Liberty, the steeple of the Center Church in New Haven.

Jack's temporary madness might be slowing to a close as he moved toward the present day, but Matthew knew he was not free of it yet.

One image was missing.

To help nudge Jack along, Matthew turned to one of his favorite pieces of music: Fauré's inspiring, hopeful Requiem. Long before he'd met Diana, one of his great joys had been to go to New College and listen to the choir perform the piece. It was not until the strains of the last section, In Paradisum, that the image Matthew had been waiting for took shape under Jack's hand. By that point Jack was sketching in time to the stately music, his body swaying to the cello's peaceful song.

"May the ranks of angels receive you, and with Lazarus, / Once a poor man, may you have eternal rest." Matthew knew these verses by heart, for they accompanied the corpse from church to grave—a place of peace that was too often denied to a creature like him. Matthew had sung these same words over Philippe's body, wept through them when Hugh had died, punished himself with them when Eleanor and Celia had perished, and repeated them for fifteen centuries as he mourned Blanca and Lucas, his warmblooded wife and child.

Tonight, however, the familiar words led Jack—and Matthew with him—to a place of second chances. Matthew watched, riveted, as Jack brought Diana's familiar, lovely face to life against the wall's creamy surface. Her eyes were wide and full of joy, her lips parted in astonishment and lifting into the beginning of a smile. Matthew had missed the precious moments when Diana first recognized Jack. He witnessed them now.

Seeing her portrait confirmed what Matthew already suspected: that it was Diana who had the power to bring Jack's life full circle. Matthew might make Jack feel safe the way a father should, but it was Diana who made him feel loved.

Matthew continued to move the bow against the strings, his fingers pressing and plucking to draw the music out. At last Jack stopped, the pencil dropping from his nerveless hands and clattering to the floor.

"You are one hell of an artist, Jack," Chris said, leaning forward in his seat to better view Diana's image.

Jack's shoulders slumped in exhaustion, and he looked around for Chris. Though they were hazy with exhaustion, there was no sign of blood rage in his eyes. They were once again brown and green.

"Matthew." Jack jumped off the top of the scaffold, soaring through the air and landing with the silence of a cat.

"Good morning, Jack." Matthew put the cello aside.

"The music—was it you?" Jack asked with a confused frown.

"I thought you might benefit from something less Baroque," Matthew said, rising to his feet. "The seventeenth century can be a bit florid for vampires. It's best taken in small doses." His glance flickered to the wall, and Jack drew a shaking hand across his forehead as he realized what he'd done.

"I'm sorry," he said, stricken. "I'll paint over it, Gallowglass. Today. I promise."

"No!" Matthew, Gallowglass, Hubbard, and Chris said in unison.

"But the walls," Jack protested. "I've ruined them."

"No more so than da Vinci or Michelangelo did," Gallowglass said mildly. "Or Matthew, come to think of it, with his doodles on the emperor's palace in Prague." Humor illuminated Jack's eyes for a moment before the light dimmed once more.

"A running deer is one thing. But nobody could possibly want to see these pictures—not even me," Jack said, staring at a particularly gruesome drawing of a decaying corpse floating faceup in the river.

"Art and music must come from the heart," Matthew said, gripping his great-grandson by the shoulder. "Even the darkest places need to be brought into the light of day, or else they'll grow until they swallow a man whole."

Jack's expression was bleak. "What if they already have?"

"You wouldn't have tried to save that woman if you were dark through and through." Matthew pointed to a desolate figure looking up at an outstretched hand. The hand matched Jack's, right down to the scar at the base of the thumb.

"But I didn't save her. She was too frightened to let me help her. Afraid of me!" Jack tried to jerk away, his elbow cracking with the strain, but Matthew refused to let him go.

"It was *her* darkness that stopped her—*her* fear—not yours," Matthew insisted.

"I don't believe you," Jack said, stubbornly holding on to the notion that his blood rage made him guilty, no matter what. Matthew got a small taste of what Philippe and Ysabeau had endured with his own steadfast refusals to accept absolution.

"That's because you've got two wolves fighting inside you. We all do." Chris joined Matthew.

"What do you mean?" Jack asked, his expression wary.

"It's an old Cherokee legend—one that my grandmother, Nana Bets, learned from her grandmother."

"You don't look like a Cherokee," Jack said, eyes narrowing.

"You'd be surprised by what's in my blood. I'm mostly French and African, with a little bit of English, Scottish, Spanish, and Native American thrown into the mix. I'm a lot like you, really. Phenotype can be misleading," Chris said with a smile. Jack looked confused, and Matthew made a mental note to buy him a basic biology textbook.

"Uh-huh," Jack said skeptically, and Chris laughed. "And the wolves?"

"According to my grandmother's people, two wolves live inside every creature: one evil and the other good. They spend all their time trying to destroy each other."

It was, Matthew thought, as good a description of blood rage as he was ever likely to hear from someone not afflicted with the disease.

"My bad wolf is winning." Jack looked sad.

"He doesn't have to," Chris promised. "Nana Bets said the wolf who wins is the wolf you feed. The evil wolf feeds on anger, guilt, sorrow, lies, and regret. The good wolf needs a diet of love and honesty, spiced up with big spoonfuls of compassion and faith. So if you want the good wolf to win, you're going to have to starve the other one."

"What if I can't stop feeding the bad wolf?" Jack looked worried. "What if I fail?"

"You won't fail," Matthew said firmly.

"We won't let you," Chris said, nodding in agreement. "There are five of us in this room. Your big bad wolf doesn't stand a chance."

"Five?" Jack whispered, looking around at Matthew and Gallowglass, Hubbard and Chris. "You're all going to help me?"

"Every last one of us," Chris promised, taking Jack's hand. When Chris jerked his head at him, Matthew obediently rested his own hand on top.

"All for one and all that jazz." Chris turned to Gallowglass. "What are you waiting for? Get over here and join us."

"Bah. The Musketeers were all tossers," Gallowglass said, scowling as he stalked toward them. In spite of his dismissive words, Matthew's nephew laid his huge paw atop theirs. "Don't be telling Baldwin about this, young Jack, or I'll give your evil wolf a double helping of dinner."

"What about you, Andrew?" Chris called across the room.

"I believe the saying is *'Un pour tous, tous pour un,'* not 'All for one and all that jazz.'"

Matthew winced. The words were right enough, but Hubbard's Cockney accent made them practically unintelligible. Philippe should have delivered a French tutor along with the cello.

Hubbard's gaunt hand was the last to join the pile. Matthew saw his thumb move top to bottom, then right to left, as the priest bestowed his blessing on their strange pact. They were an unlikely band, Matthew thought: three creatures related by blood, a fourth bound by loyalty, and a fifth who had joined them for no apparent reason other than that he was a good man.

He hoped that, together, they would be enough to help Jack heal.

In the aftermath of his furious activity, Jack had wanted to talk. He sat with Matthew and Hubbard in the living room, surrounded by his past, and shifted the burden of some of his harrowing experiences onto Matthew's shoulders. On the subject of Benjamin, however, he was mute. Matthew wasn't surprised. How could words convey the horror Jack had endured at Benjamin's hands?

"Come on, Jackie," Gallowglass interrupted, holding up Lobero's leash. "Mop needs a walk."

"I'd like a bit of fresh air, too." Andrew unfolded from a strange red chair that looked like a piece of modern sculpture but that Matthew had discovered was surprisingly comfortable.

As the front door closed, Chris sauntered into the living room with a fresh cup of coffee. Matthew didn't know how the man survived with so much caffeine in his veins.

"I talked to your son tonight—your other son, Marcus." Chris took up his usual seat in the plantation chair. "Nice guy. Smart, too. You must be proud of him."

"I am," Matthew said warily. "Why did Marcus call?"

"We called him." Chris sipped at his coffee. "Miriam thought he should see the video. Once he had, Marcus agreed we should take some more blood from Jack. We took two samples."

"You *what?*" Matthew was aghast.

"Hubbard gave me permission. He is Jack's next of kin," Chris replied calmly.

"You think I'm worried about informed consent?" Matthew was barely able to keep his temper in check. "Drawing blood from a vampire in the grip of blood rage—you could have been killed."

"It was a perfect opportunity to monitor the changes that take place in a vampire's body chemistry at the onset of blood rage," Chris said. "We'll need that information if we want to have a shot at coming up with a medicine that might lessen the symptoms."

Matthew frowned. "Lessen the symptoms? We're looking for a cure."

Chris reached down and picked up a folder. He offered it to Matthew. "The latest findings."

Both Hubbard and Jack had been swabbed and given blood samples. They'd been rushed through processing, and their genome report was due any day. Matthew took the folder with nerveless fingers, afraid of what he might find inside it.

"I'm sorry, Matthew," Chris said with heartfelt regret.

Matthew's eyes raced over the results, flipping the pages.

"Marcus identified them. No one else would have. We weren't looking in the right place," Chris said.

Matthew couldn't absorb what he was seeing. It changed . . . everything.

"Jack has more of the triggers in his noncoding DNA than you do." Chris paused. "I have to ask, Matthew. Are you sure you can trust Jack around Diana?"

Before Matthew could respond, the front door opened. There was none of the usual chatter that accompanied Jack's appearance, or Gallowglass's cheerful whistling, or Andrew's pious sermonizing. The only sound was Lobero's low whine.

Matthew's nostrils flared, and he leaped to his feet, the test results scattering around him. Then he was gone, moving to the doorway in a flash.

"What the hell?" Chris said behind him.

"We met someone while we were out walking," Gallowglass said, leading a reluctant Lobero into the house.

21

Move," Baldwin commanded, holding Jack by the scruff of his neck. Matthew had seen that hand tear another vampire's head clean off.

Jack hadn't witnessed that brutal episode, but he knew he was at Baldwin's mercy just the same. The boy was white-skinned and wide-eyed, with enormous black pupils. Not surprisingly, he obeyed Baldwin without hesitation.

Lobero knew it, too. Gallowglass still held the leash, but the dog circled the Gael's feet with eyes fixed on his master.

"It's okay, Mop," Jack assured his dog in a whisper, but Lobero was having none of it.

"Trouble, Matthew?" Chris was so close that Matthew could feel his breath.

"There's always trouble," Matthew said grimly.

"Go home," Jack urged Chris. "Take Mop, too, and—" Jack stopped with a wince. Blood suffused the skin on his neck where Baldwin's fingertips were leaving a dark bruise.

"They're staying," Baldwin hissed.

Jack had made a strategic error. Baldwin delighted in destroying what other people loved. Some experience in his past must have shaped the impulse, but Matthew had never discovered what it was. Baldwin would never let Chris or Mop go now. Not until he got what he came for.

"And you don't give orders. You take them." Baldwin was careful to keep the boy between him and Matthew as he pushed him toward the living room. It was a devastatingly simple and effective tactic, one that brought back painful memories.

Jack is not Eleanor, Matthew told himself. Jack was a vampire, too. But he was Matthew's blood, and Baldwin could use him to bring Matthew to heel.

"That stunt you pulled in the square will be the last time you challenge me, mongrel." Baldwin's shirt showed teeth marks at the shoulder, and there were beads of blood around the torn fabric.

Christ. Jack had bitten Baldwin.

"But I'm not yours." Jack sounded desperate. "Tell him that I belong to you, Matthew!"

"And who do you think Matthew belongs to?" Baldwin whispered in his ear, quietly menacing.

"Diana," Jack snarled, turning on his captor.

"Diana?" Baldwin's laugh was mocking, and the blow he gave Jack would have flattened a warmblood twice his size and weight. Jack's knees met the hard wooden floors. "Get in here, Matthew. And shut that dog up."

"Disavow Jack before the de Clermont sire and I'll see you to hell personally," Hubbard hissed, grabbing at Matthew's sleeve as he went past.

Matthew looked at him coldly, and Hubbard dropped his arm.

"Let him go. He's my blood," Matthew said, stalking into the room. "Then go back to Manhattan where you belong, Baldwin."

"Oh," Chris said in a tone that suggested he finally saw the light. "Of course. You live on Central Park, don't you?"

Baldwin didn't reply. In fact, he owned most of that stretch of Fifth Avenue and liked to keep a close eye on his investments. Recently he had been developing his hunting ground in the Meatpacking District, filling it with nightclubs to complement the butcher shops, but as a rule he preferred not to reside where he fed.

"No wonder you're such an entitled bastard," Chris said. "Well, buddy, you're in New Haven now. We play by different rules here."

"Rules?" Baldwin drawled. "In New Haven?"

"Yeah. All for one and all that jazz." It was Chris's call to arms.

Matthew was so close that he could feel Chris's muscles bunch and was prepared when the small knife went past his ear. The thin blade was so insignificant that it would barely have damaged a human's skin, never mind Baldwin's tough hide. Matthew reached up and pinched it between his fingertips before it could reach its target. Chris scowled at him reproachfully, and Matthew shook his head.

"Don't." Matthew might have let Chris get in a solid punch, but Baldwin had narrower views when it came to the privileges that should be afforded to warmbloods. He turned to Baldwin. "Leave. Jack is my blood and my problem."

"And miss all the fun?" Baldwin bent Jack's head to the side. Jack looked up at Baldwin, his expression black and deadly. "Quite a resemblance, Matthew."

"I like to think so," Matthew said coolly, giving Jack a tight smile. He took Lobero's lead from Gallowglass. The dog quieted immediately. "Baldwin might be thirsty. Offer him a drink, Gallowglass."

Maybe that would sweeten Baldwin's mood long enough to get Jack safely away. Matthew could send him to Marcus's house with Hubbard. It was a better alternative than Diana's house on Court Street. If his wife got wind of Baldwin's presence, she'd be on Wooster Square with a firedrake and a lightning bolt.

"I've got a full larder," Gallowglass said. "Coffee, wine, water, blood. I'm sure I could scare up some hemlock and honey if you'd prefer that, Uncle."

"What I require only the boy can provide." Without warning or preamble, Baldwin's teeth ripped into Jack's neck. His bite was savage, deliberately so.

This was vampire justice—swift, unbending, remorseless. For minor infractions the sire's punishment would consist only of this public show of submission. Through that blood the sire received a thin trickle of his progeny's innermost thoughts and memories. The ritual stripped a vampire's soul bare, making him shamefully vulnerable. Acquiring another creature's secrets, by whatever means, sustained a vampire in much the same way the hunt did, nourishing that part of his soul that forever sought to possess more.

If the offenses were more significant, the ritual of submission would be followed by death. Killing another vampire was physically taxing, emotionally draining, and spiritually devastating. It was why most vampire sires appointed one of their kin to do it for them. Though Philippe and Hugh had polished the de Clermonts' façade to a high sheen over the centuries, it was Matthew who had performed all of the house's dirty maintenance.

There were hundreds of ways to kill a vampire, and Matthew knew them all. You could drink a vampire dry as he had Philippe. You could weaken a vampire physically by releasing his blood slowly and putting him in the dreaded state of suspension known as thrall. Unable to fight back, the vampire could be tortured into a confession or mercifully allowed to die. There was beheading and evisceration, though some preferred the more old-fashioned method of punching through the rib cage and wrenching out the heart. You could sever the carotid and the aorta, a method that Gerbert's lovely assassin, Juliette, had tried and failed to use on him.

Matthew prayed that taking Jack's blood and his memories would suffice for Baldwin tonight.

Too late, he remembered that Jack's memories held tales best left untold.

Too late, he caught the scent of honeysuckle and summer storms.

Too late, he saw Diana release Corra.

Diana's firedrake rose up from her mistress's shoulders and into the air. Corra swooped down on Baldwin with a shriek, talons extended and wings aflame. Baldwin grabbed the firedrake by the foot with his free hand, wresting her body away. Corra hurtled into the wall, her wing crumpling at the impact. Diana bent double, grabbing at her own arm in sudden pain, but it didn't shake her resolve.

"Take your hands. Off. My. Son." Diana's skin was gleaming, the subtle nimbus that was always visible without her disguising spell now appearing as a distinctive, prismatic light. Rainbows of color shot under her skin—not just the hands but up her arms, along the tendons of her neck, twisting and spiraling as though the cords in her fingers had extended through her whole body.

When Lobero lunged at the end of his lead, trying to get to Corra, Matthew let the dog go. Lobero crouched over the firedrake, licking at her face and nudging her with his nose as she struggled to get up and go to Diana's aid.

But Diana didn't need help—not from Matthew, not from Lobero, not even from Corra. His wife straightened, splayed out her left hand with the palm facing down, and directed her fingers at the floor. The wooden planks shattered and split, re-forming into thick canes that rose up and wound themselves around Baldwin's feet, keeping him in place. Lethally long, sharp thorns sprang out of the shoots, digging through his clothes and into flesh.

Diana fixed her gaze on Baldwin, reached out with her right hand, and pulled. Jack's wrist jerked out and to the side as if he were tethered to her. The rest of him followed, and in moments he was lying in a heap on the floor, out of Baldwin's reach.

Matthew adopted a similar pose to Lobero's, standing over Jack's body to shield him.

"Enough, Baldwin." Matthew's hand sliced through the air.

"I'm sorry, Matthew," Jack whispered, remaining on the floor. "He came out of nowhere and went straight for Gallowglass. When I'm surprised—" He stopped with a shudder, his knees drawing close to his chest. "I didn't know who he was."

Miriam came into the room. After studying the scene, she took charge. She pointed Gallowglass and Hubbard in Jack's direction and cast a worried look at Diana, who stood unmoving and unblinking, as though she had taken root in the living room.

"Is Jack okay?" Chris asked, his voice strained.

"He'll be fine. Every vampire alive has been bitten by their sire at least once," Miriam said, trying to put his mind at rest. Chris didn't seem comforted by this revelation about creature family life.

Matthew helped Jack up. The bite mark on his neck was shallow and would heal quickly, but at the moment it looked gruesome. Matthew touched it briefly, hoping to reassure Jack that he would, as Miriam promised, be fine.

"Can you see to Corra?" Matthew asked Miriam as he handed Jack off to Gallowglass and Hubbard.

Miriam nodded.

Matthew was already crossing the room, his hands wrapping around Baldwin's throat.

"I want your word that if Diana lets you go, you will not touch her for what happened here tonight." Matthew's fingers tightened. "If not, I will kill you, Baldwin. Make no mistake about that."

"We're not finished here, Matthew," Baldwin warned.

"I know." Matthew locked his eyes on his brother until the man nodded.

Then he turned to Diana. The colors pulsing beneath her skin reminded him of the shining ball of energy she had gifted him in Madison before either of them knew she was a weaver. The colors were brightest at her fingertips, as though her magic were waiting there, ready to be released. Matthew knew how unpredictable his own blood rage could be when it was that close to the surface, and he treated his wife with caution.

"Diana?" Matthew smoothed the hair back from her face, searching her blue-and-gold irises for signs of recognition. Instead he saw infinity, her eyes fixed on some invisible vista. He changed tack, trying to bring her back to the here and now.

"Jack is with Gallowglass and Andrew, *ma lionne.* Baldwin will not harm him tonight." Matthew's words were carefully chosen. "You should take him back home."

Chris started, ready to voice a protest.

"Perhaps Chris will go with you," Matthew continued smoothly. "Corra and Lobero, too."

"Corra," Diana croaked. Her eyes flickered, but not even concern for her firedrake could break her mesmerized stare. Matthew wondered what she saw that the rest of them did not and why it held such a powerful attraction for her. He felt a disturbing pang of jealousy.

"Miriam is with Corra." Matthew found himself unable to look away from the navy depths of her eyes.

"Baldwin . . . hurt her." Diana sounded confused, as though she had forgotten that vampires were not like other creatures. She rubbed absently at her arm.

Just when Matthew thought whatever it was that held her might give way to reason, Diana's anger caught again. He could smell it—taste it.

"He hurt Jack." Diana's fingers opened wide in a sudden spasm. No longer concerned with the wisdom of getting between a weaver and her power, Matthew caught them before they could work magic.

"Baldwin will let you take Jack home. In return you have to release Baldwin. We can't have the two of you at war. The family wouldn't survive it." Based on what he'd seen tonight, Diana was as single-minded as Baldwin when it came to destroying the obstacles in her way.

Matthew lifted her hands and brushed the knuckles with his lips. "Remember when we talked about our children in London? We spoke then about what they would need."

That got Diana's attention. *At last.* Her eyes focused on him.

"Love," she whispered. "A grown-up to take responsibility for them. A soft place to land."

"That's right." Matthew smiled. "Jack needs you. Release Baldwin from your spell."

Diana's magic gave way in a shudder that passed through her from feet to head. She flicked her fingers in Baldwin's direction. The thorns withdrew from his skin. The canes loosened, retracting back into the splintered floorboards surrounding the vampire. Soon he was free and Gallowglass's house was returned to its normal, disenchanted state.

While her spell slowly unraveled, Diana went to Jack and cupped his face. The skin on his neck was already starting to knit together, but it would take several days to heal completely. Her generous mouth became a thin line.

"Don't worry," Jack told her, covering the wound self-consciously.

"Come on, Jackie. Diana and I will take you to Court Street. You must be famished." Gallowglass clapped his hand on Jack's shoulder. Jack was exhausted but tried to look less wan for Diana's sake.

"Corra," Diana said, beckoning to her firedrake. Corra limped toward her, gaining strength as she drew closer to her mistress. When the weaver and the firedrake were nearly touching, Corra faded into invisibility as she and Diana became one.

"Let Chris help you home," Matthew said, careful to keep his broad frame between his wife and the disturbing images on the walls. She was, thankfully, too tired to do more than glance at them.

Matthew was pleased to see that Miriam had rounded up everyone in the house except Baldwin. They were huddled in the entrance—Chris, Andrew, Lobero, and Miriam—waiting for Diana, Gallowglass, and Jack. The more creatures there to support the boy, the better.

Watching them go took every ounce of control Matthew had. He forced himself to wave encouragingly at Diana when she turned for one more glimpse of him. Once they disappeared between the houses on Court Street, he returned to Baldwin.

His brother was staring up at the last section of the murals, his shirt dotted with dark stains where Jack's teeth and Diana's briars had pierced the skin.

"Jack is the vampire murderer. I saw it in his thoughts, and now I see it here on the walls. We've been looking for him for more than a year. How has he evaded the Congregation all this time?" Baldwin asked.

"He was with Benjamin. Then he was on the run." Matthew deliberately avoided looking at the horrifying images that surrounded Benjamin's disembodied features. They were, he supposed, no more hideous than other brutal acts that vampires had perpetrated over the years. What made them so unbearable was that Jack had done them.

"Jack has to be stopped." Baldwin's tone was matter-of-fact.

"God forgive me." Matthew lowered his head.

"Philippe was right. Your Christianity really does make you perfect for your job." Baldwin snorted. "What other faith promises to wash away your sins if only you confess them?"

Sadly, Baldwin had never grasped the concept of atonement. His view of Matthew's faith was purely transactional—you went to church, confessed, and walked out a clean man. But salvation was more complicated. Philippe had come to understand that in the end, although he had long found Matthew's constant search for forgiveness irritating and irrational.

"You know very well there's no place for him among the de Clermonts—not if his disease is as serious as these pictures suggest." Baldwin saw in Jack what Benjamin had seen: a dangerous weapon, one that could be shaped and twisted to make it as deadly as possible. Unlike Benjamin, Baldwin had a conscience. He would not use the weapon that had come so unexpectedly into his hand, but neither would he allow it to be used by another.

Matthew's head remained bowed, weighted down with memories and regret. Baldwin's next words were expected, but Matthew felt them as a blow nevertheless.

"Kill him," commanded the head of the de Clermont family.

When Matthew returned home to the brightly painted red door with the white trim and the black pediment, it opened wide.

Diana had been waiting. She had changed into something that would ward off the chill and was bundled into one of his old cardigans, lessening the scent of the others she'd come into contact with that night. Even so, Matthew's kiss of greeting was rough and possessive, and he only reluctantly drew away.

"What's wrong?" Diana's fingers went to Philippe's arrowhead. It had become a reliable signal that her anxiety was climbing. The smudges of color on their tips told the same tale, growing more visible with every passing moment.

Matthew looked heavenward, hoping to find some guidance. What he saw instead was a sky totally devoid of stars. The reasonable, human part of him knew that this was due to the city's bright lights and tonight's full moon. But the vampire within was instinctively alarmed. There was nothing to orient him in such a place, no markers to guide his way.

"Come." Matthew picked up Diana's coat from the chair in the front hall, took his wife's hand, and led her down the steps.

"Where are we going?" she said, struggling to keep up.

"To a place where I can see the stars," Matthew replied.

22

Matthew headed north and west and out of the city with Diana beside him. He drove uncharacteristically fast, and in less than fifteen minutes they were on a quiet lane tucked into the shadow of the peaks known locally as the Sleeping Giant. Matthew pulled in to an otherwise dark driveway and shut off the car's ignition. A porch light came on, and an elderly man peered into the darkness.

"That you, Mr. Clairmont?" The man's voice was faint and thready but there was still a sharp intelligence in his eyes.

"It is, Mr. Phelps," Matthew said with a nod. He circled the car and helped Diana down. "My wife and I are going up to the cottage."

"Nice to meet you, ma'am," Mr. Phelps said, touching his forehead with his hand. "Mr. Gallowglass called to warn me you might be stopping by to check on things. He said not to worry if I heard somebody out here."

"I'm sorry we woke you," Diana said.

"I'm an old man, Mrs. Clairmont. I don't get much shut-eye these days. I figure I'll sleep when I'm dead," Mr. Phelps said with a wheezing laugh. "You'll find everything you need up on the mountain."

"Thank you for watching over the place," Matthew said.

"It's a family tradition," Mr. Phelps replied. "You'll find Mr. Whitmore's Ranger by the shed, if you don't want to use my old Gator. I don't imagine your wife will want to walk all that way. The park gates are closed, but you know how to get in. Have a nice night."

Mr. Phelps went back inside, the screen hitting the door frame with a snap of aluminum and mesh.

Matthew took Diana by the elbow and steered her toward what looked like a cross between a golf cart with unusually rugged tires and a dune buggy. He let go of her only long enough to round the vehicle and climb in.

The gate into the park was so well hidden it was all but invisible, and the dirt trail that served as a road was unlit and unmarked, but Matthew found both with ease. He navigated a few sharp turns, climbing steadily as they traveled up the side of the mountain, passing through the edges of heavy forest until they reached an open field with a small wooden house tucked under the trees. The lights were on inside, making it as golden and inviting as a cottage in a fairy tale.

Matthew stopped Marcus's Ranger and engaged the brake. He took a deep breath to drink in the night scents of mountain pine and dew-touched grass. Below, the valley looked bleak. He wondered if it was his mood or the silvered moonlight that rendered it so unwelcoming.

"The ground is uneven. I don't want you to fall." Matthew held out his hand, giving Diana the choice whether to take it or not.

After a concerned look, she put her hand in his. Matthew scanned the horizon, unable to stop searching for new threats. Then his attention turned skyward.

"The moon is bright tonight," he mused. "Even here it's hard to see the stars."

"That's because it's Mabon," Diana said quietly.

"Mabon?" Matthew looked startled.

She nodded. "One year ago you walked into the Bodleian Library and straight into my heart. As soon as that wicked mouth of yours smiled, the moment your eyes lightened with recognition even though we'd never met before, I knew that my life would never be the same."

Diana's words gave Matthew a momentary reprieve from the relentless agitation that Baldwin's order and Chris's news had set off in him, and for a brief moment the world was poised between absence and desire, between blood and fear, between the warmth of summer and the icy depths of winter.

"What's wrong?" Diana searched his face. "Is it Jack? The blood rage? Baldwin?"

"Yes. No. In a way." Matthew drove his hands through his hair and whirled around to avoid her keen gaze. "Baldwin knows that Jack killed those warmbloods in Europe. He knows that Jack is the vampire murderer."

"Surely this isn't the first time a vampire's thirst for blood has resulted in unexpected deaths," Diana said, trying to defuse the situation.

"This time it's different." There was no easy way to say it. "Baldwin ordered me to kill Jack."

"No. I forbid it." Diana's words echoed, and a wind kicked up from the east. She whirled around, and Matthew caught her. She struggled in his grip, sending a gray-and-brown twist of air howling around his feet.

"Don't walk away from me." He wasn't sure he could control himself if she did. "You must listen to reason."

"No." Still she tried to avoid him. "You can't give up on him. Jack won't always have blood rage. You're going to find a cure."

"Blood rage has no cure." Matthew would have given his life to change that fact.

"What?" Diana's shock was evident.

"We've been running the new DNA samples. For the first time, we're able to chart a multigenerational pedigree that extends beyond Marcus. Chris and Miriam traced the blood-rage gene from Ysabeau through me and Andrew down to Jack." Matthew had Diana's complete attention now.

"Blood rage is a developmental anomaly," he continued. "There's a genetic component, but the blood-rage gene appears to be triggered by something in our noncoding DNA. Jack and I have that something. *Maman*, Marcus, and Andrew don't."

"I don't understand," Diana whispered.

"During my rebirth something already in my noncoding, human DNA reacted to the new genetic information flooding my system," Matthew said patiently. "We know that vampire genes are brutal—they push aside what's human in order to dominate the newly modified cells. But they don't replace everything. If they did, my genome and Ysabeau's would be identical. Instead I am her child—a combination of the genetic ingredients I inherited from my human parents as well as what I inherited from her."

"So you had blood rage *before* Ysabeau made you a vampire?" Diana was understandably confused.

"No. But I possessed the triggers the blood-rage gene needed to express itself," Matthew said. "Marcus has identified specific noncoding DNA that he believes plays a role."

"In what he calls junk DNA?" Diana asked.

Matthew nodded.

"Then a cure is still possible," she insisted. "In a few years—"

"No, *mon coeur*." He couldn't allow her hopes to rise. "The more we understand the blood-rage gene and learn about the noncoding genes, the better the treatment might become, but this is not a disease we can cure. Our only hope is to prevent it and, God willing, lessen its symptoms."

"Until you do, you can teach Jack how to control it." Diana's face remained set in stubborn lines. "There's no need to kill him."

"Jack's symptoms are far worse than mine. The genetic factors that appear to trigger the disease are present at much higher levels in him." Matthew blinked back the blood tears that he could feel forming. "He won't suffer. I promise you."

"But *you* will. You say I pay a price for dealing with matters of life and death? So do you. Jack will be gone, but you will live on, hating yourself," Diana said. "Think of what Philippe's death has cost you."

Matthew could think of little else. He had killed other creatures since his father's death, but only to settle his own scores. Until tonight the last de Clermont sire to command him to kill had been Philippe. And the death Philippe had ordered was his own.

"Jack is suffering, Diana. This would mean an end to it." Matthew used the same words Philippe had to convince his wife to admit the inevitable.

"For him maybe. Not for us." Diana's hand strayed to the round swell of her belly. "The twins could have blood rage. Will you kill them, too?"

She waited for him to deny it, to tell her that she was insane to even think of such a thing. But he didn't.

"When the Congregation discovers what Jack has done—and it's only a matter of time before they do—they will kill him. And they won't care how frightened he is or how much pain they cause. Baldwin will try to kill Jack before it comes to that, to keep the Congregation out of the family business. If he tries to run, Jack could fall into Benjamin's hands. If he does, Benjamin will exact a terrible revenge for Jack's betrayal. Death would be a blessing then." Matthew's face and voice were impassive, but the agony that flashed through Diana's eyes would haunt him forever.

"Then Jack will disappear. He'll go far away, where nobody can find him."

Matthew smothered his impatience. He'd known that Diana was stubborn when he first met her. It was one of the reasons he loved her—even though at times it drove him to distraction. "A lone vampire cannot survive. Like wolves, we have to be part of a pack or we go mad. Think of Benjamin, Diana, and what happened when I abandoned him."

"We'll go with him," she said, grasping at straws in her efforts to save Jack.

"That would only make it easier for Benjamin or the Congregation to hunt him down."

"Then you must establish a scion immediately, as Marcus suggested," Diana said. "Jack will have a whole family to protect him."

"If I do, I'll have to acknowledge Benjamin. That would expose not only Jack's blood rage but my own. It would put Ysabeau and Marcus in terrible danger—the twins, too. And it's not just they who will suffer if we stand against the Congregation without Baldwin's support." Matthew drew a ragged breath. "If you're at my side—my consort—the Congregation will demand your submission as well as mine."

"Submission?" Diana said faintly.

"This is war, Diana. That's what happens to women who fight. You heard my mother's tale. Do you think your fate would be any different at the vampires' hands?"

She shook her head.

"You must believe me: We are far better off remaining in Baldwin's family than striking out on our own," he insisted.

"You're wrong. The twins and I will never be entirely safe under Baldwin's rule. Neither will Jack. Standing our ground is the only possible way forward. Every other road just leads back into the past," Diana said. "And we know from experience that the past is never more than a temporary reprieve."

"You don't understand the forces that would gather against us if I do this. Everything my children and grandchildren have done or will ever do is laid at my doorstep under vampire law. The vampire murders? I committed them. Benjamin's evil deeds? I am guilty of them." Matthew had to make Diana see what this decision might cost.

"They can't blame you for what Benjamin and Jack did," Diana protested.

"But they can." Matthew cradled her hands between his. "I made Benjamin. If I hadn't, none of these crimes would have taken place. It was my job, as Benjamin's sire and Jack's grandsire, to curb them if possible or to kill them if not."

"That's barbaric." Diana tugged at her hands. He could feel the power burning under her skin.

"No, that's vampire honor. Vampires can survive among warmbloods because of three systems of belief: law, honor, and justice. You saw vampire justice at work tonight," Matthew said. "It's swift—and brutal. If I stand as sire of my own scion, I'll have to mete it out, too."

"Rather you than Baldwin," Diana retorted. "If he's in charge, I'll always wonder if this is the day he will grow tired of protecting me and the twins and order our deaths."

His wife had a point. But it put Matthew in an impossible situation. To save Jack, Matthew would have to disobey Baldwin. If he disobeyed Baldwin, he would have no choice but to become the sire of his own scion. That would require convincing a pack of rebellious vampires to accept his leadership and risk their own extermination by exposing the blood rage in their ranks. It would be a bloody, violent, and complicated process.

"Please, Matthew," Diana whispered. "I beg you: Do not follow Baldwin's order."

Matthew examined his wife's face. He took into account the pain and desperation he saw in her eyes. It was impossible to say no.

"Very well," Matthew replied reluctantly. "I'll go to New Orleans—on one condition."

Diana's relief was evident. "Anything. Name it."

"You don't come with me." Matthew kept his voice even, though the mere mention of being away from his mate was enough to send the blood rage surging through his veins.

"Don't you dare order me to stay here!" Diana said, her own anger flaring.

"You can't be anywhere near me while I do this." Centuries of practice made it possible for Matthew to keep his own feelings in check, in spite of his wife's agitation. "I don't want to go anywhere without you. Christ, I can barely let you out of my sight. But having you in New Orleans while I battle my own grandchildren would put you in terrible danger. And it wouldn't be Baldwin or the Congregation who would be putting your safety at risk. It would be me."

"You would never hurt me." Diana had clung to this belief from the beginning of their relationship. It was time to tell her the truth.

"Eleanor thought that—once. Then I killed her in a moment of madness and jealousy. Jack's not the only vampire in this family whose blood rage is set off by love and loyalty." Matthew met his wife's eyes. "So is mine."

"And you and Eleanor were merely lovers. We're mates." Diana's expression revealed her dawning understanding. "All along you've said I shouldn't trust you. You swore you would kill me yourself before you let anyone else touch me."

"I told you the truth." Matthew's fingertips traced the line of Diana's cheekbone, sweeping up to catch the tear that threatened to fall from the corner of her eye.

"But not the whole truth. Why didn't you tell me that our mating bond was going to make your blood rage worse?" Diana cried.

"I thought I could find a cure. Until then, I thought I could manage my feelings," Matthew replied. "But you have become as vital to me as breath and blood. My heart no longer knows where I end and you begin. I knew that you were a powerful witch from the moment I saw you, but how could I have imagined that you would have so much power over me?"

Diana answered him not with words but with a kiss that was startling in its intensity. Matthew's response matched it. When they drew apart they were both shaken. Diana touched her lips with trembling fingers. Matthew rested his head atop hers, his heart—her heart—thudding with emotion.

"Founding a new scion will require my complete attention, as well as complete control," Matthew said when at last he was able to speak. "If I succeed—"

"You must," Diana said firmly. "You will."

"Very well, *ma lionne. When* I succeed, there will still be times when I'll have to handle matters on my own," Matthew explained. "It isn't that I distrust you, but I cannot trust myself."

"Like you've handled Jack," Diana said. Matthew nodded.

"Being apart from you will be a living hell, but being distracted would be unspeakably dangerous. As for my control . . . well, I think we know just how little I have when you are around." He brushed her lips with another kiss, this one seductive. Diana's cheeks reddened.

"What will I do while you're in New Orleans?" Diana asked. "There must be some way I can help you."

"Find that missing page from Ashmole 782," Matthew replied. "We'll need the Book of Life for leverage—no matter what happens between me and Marcus's children." The fact that the search would keep Diana from being directly involved in the disaster should this harebrained scheme fail was an added benefit. "Phoebe will help you look for the third illumination. Go to Sept-Tours. Wait there for me."

"How will I know you're all right?" Diana asked. The reality of their impending separation was beginning to sink in.

"I'll find a way. But no phone calls. No e-mails. We can't leave a trail of evidence for the Congregation to follow if Baldwin—or one of my own blood—turns me in," Matthew said. "You have to remain in his good graces, at least until you are recognized as a de Clermont."

"But that's months away!" Diana's expression turned desperate. "What if the children are born early?"

"Marthe and Sarah will deliver them," he said gently. "There's no telling how long this will take, Diana." *It could be years,* Matthew thought.

"How will I make the children understand why their father isn't with them?" she asked, somehow hearing his unspoken words.

"You will tell the twins I had to stay away because I loved them—and their mother—with all my heart." Matthew's voice broke. He pulled her into his arms, holding her as though that might delay her inevitable departure.

"Matthew?" The familiar voice came out of the darkness.

"Marcus?" Diana had not heard his approach, though Matthew had picked up first his scent and then the soft sound of his son's footsteps as he climbed the mountain.

"Hello, Diana." Marcus stepped out of the shadows and into a patch of moonlight.

She frowned with concern. "Is something wrong at Sept-Tours?"

"Everything in France is fine. I thought Matthew needed me here," Marcus said.

"And Phoebe?" Diana asked.

"With Alain and Marthe." Marcus sounded tired. "I couldn't help but overhear your plans. There will be no turning back once we put them in motion. Are you sure about forming a scion, Matthew?"

"No," Matthew said, unable to lie. "But Diana is." He looked at his wife. "Chris and Gallowglass are waiting for you down the path. Go now, *mon coeur.*"

"This minute?" For a moment Diana looked frightened at the enormity of what they were about to do.

"It will never be any easier. You're going to have to walk away from me.

Don't look back. And for God's sake don't run." Matthew would never be able to control himself if she did.

"But—" Diana pressed her lips together. She nodded and dashed the back of her hand against her cheek, brushing away sudden tears.

Matthew put more than a thousand years of longing into one last kiss.

"I'll never—" Diana began.

"Hush." He silenced her with another touch of his lips. "No nevers for us, remember?"

Matthew set her away from him. It was only a few inches, but it might have been a thousand leagues. As soon as he did, his blood howled. He turned her so she could see the two faint circles of light from their friends' flashlights.

"Don't make this harder on him," Marcus told Diana softly. "Go now. Slowly."

For a few seconds, Matthew wasn't sure she would be able to do it. He could see the gold and silver threads hanging from her fingertips, sparking and shimmering as if trying to fuse together something that had been suddenly, horribly broken. She took a tentative step. Then another. Matthew saw the muscles in her back trembling as she struggled to keep her composure. Her head dropped. Then she squared her shoulders and slowly walked in the opposite direction.

"I knew from the goddamn beginning you were going to break her heart," Chris called to Matthew when she reached him. He drew Diana into his arms.

But it was Matthew's heart that was breaking, taking with it his composure, his sanity, and his last traces of humanity.

Marcus watched him without blinking as Gallowglass and Chris led Diana away. When they disappeared from sight, Matthew leaped forward. Marcus caught him.

"Are you going to make it without her?" Marcus asked his father. He had been away from Phoebe for less than twelve hours and already he was uneasy at their separation.

"I have to," Matthew said, though at the moment he couldn't imagine how.

"Does Diana know what being apart will do to you?" Marcus still had nightmares about Ysabeau and how much she had suffered during Philippe's capture and death. It had been like watching someone go through the worst withdrawal imaginable—the shaking, the irrational behavior, the physical pain. And his grandparents were among the fortunate few vampires who, though mated, could be separated for periods of time. Matthew's blood rage made that impossible. Even before Matthew and Diana were fully mated, Ysabeau had warned Marcus that his father was not to be trusted if something were to happen to Diana.

"Does she know?" Marcus repeated.

"Not entirely. She knows what will happen to me if I stay here and obey my brother, though." Matthew shook off his son's arm. "You don't have to go along with this—with me. You still have a choice. Baldwin will take you in, so long as you beg for his forgiveness."

"I made my choice in 1781, remember?" Marcus's eyes were silver in the moonlight. "Tonight you've proved it was the right one."

"There are no guarantees this will work," Matthew warned. "Baldwin might refuse to sanction the scion. The Congregation could get wind of what we're doing before we're through. God knows your own children have reason to oppose it."

"They're not going to make it easy for you, but my children will do what I tell them to do. Eventually. Besides," Marcus said, "you're under my protection now."

Matthew looked at him in surprise.

"The safety of you, your mate, and those twins she's carrying is now the Knights of Lazarus's top priority," Marcus explained. "Baldwin can threaten all he wants, but I have more than a thousand vampires, daemons, and yes, even witches, under my command."

"They'll never obey you," Matthew said, "not when they find out what you're asking them to fight for."

"How do you think I recruited them in the first place?" Marcus shook his head. "Do you really think you're the only two creatures on the planet who have reason to dislike the covenant's restrictions?"

But Matthew was too distracted to respond. He already felt the first, restless impulse to go after Diana. Soon he wouldn't be able to sit still for more than a few moments before his instincts demanded he go to her. And it would only get worse from there.

"Come on." Marcus put his arm across his father's shoulders. "Jack and Andrew are waiting for us. I suppose the damn dog will have to come to New Orleans, too."

Still Matthew didn't respond. He was listening for Diana's voice, her distinctive step, the rhythm of her heartbeat.

There was only silence, and stars too faint to show him the way home.

Sol in Libra

When the sun passeth through Libra, it is a good time for journeys. Beware of open enemies, war, and opposition.

—*Anonymous English Commonplace Book, c. 1590, Gonçalves MS 4890, f. 9^r*

23

Let me in, Miriam, before I break down the damn door." Gallowglass wasn't in the mood for games.

Miriam flung the door open. "Matthew may be gone, but don't try anything funny. I'm still watching you."

That was no surprise to Gallowglass. Jason had once told him that learning how to be a vampire under Miriam's guidance had convinced him that there was indeed an all-knowing, all-seeing, and vengeful deity. Contrary to biblical teachings, however, She was female and sarcastic.

"Did Matthew and the others get off safely?" Diana asked quietly from the top of the stairs. She was ghostly pale, and a small suitcase sat at her feet. Gallowglass cursed and leaped up the steps.

"They did," he said, grabbing the case before she did something daft and tried to carry it herself. Gallowglass found it more mysterious with every passing hour that Diana didn't simply topple over given the burden of the twins.

"Why did you pack a suitcase?" Chris asked. "What's going on?"

"Auntie is going on a journey." Gallowglass still thought leaving New Haven was a bad idea, but Diana had informed him that she was going—with him or without him.

"Where?" Chris demanded. Gallowglass shrugged.

"Promise me you'll keep working on the DNA samples from Ashmole 782 as well as the blood-rage problem, Chris," Diana said as she descended the stairs.

"You know I don't leave research problems unfinished." Chris turned on Miriam. "Did you know that Diana was leaving?"

"How could I not? She made enough noise getting her suitcase out of the closet and calling the pilot." Miriam grabbed Chris's coffee. She took a sip and grimaced. "Too sweet."

"Get your coat, Auntie." Gallowglass didn't know what Diana had planned—she said she would tell him once they were in the air—but he doubted they were headed for a Caribbean island with swaying palms and warm breezes.

For once Diana didn't protest at his hovering.

"Lock the door when you leave, Chris. And make sure the coffeepot is unplugged." She stood on her toes and kissed her friend on the cheek. "Take care of Miriam. Don't let her walk across New Haven Green at night, even if she is a vampire."

"Here," Miriam said, handing over a large manila envelope. "As requested."

Diana peeked inside. "Are you sure you don't need them?"

"We have plenty of samples," she replied.

Chris looked deep into Diana's eyes. "Call if you need me. No matter why, no matter when, no matter where—I'll be on the next flight."

"Thank you," she whispered, "I'll be fine. Gallowglass is with me."

To his surprise, the words brought Gallowglass no joy.

How could they, when they were uttered with such resignation?

The de Clermont jet lifted off from the New Haven airport. Gallowglass stared out the window, tapping his phone against his leg. The plane banked, and he sniffed the air. North by northeast.

Diana was sitting next to him, eyes closed and lips white. One hand was resting lightly on Apple and Bean as though she were comforting them. There was a trace of moisture on her cheeks.

"Don't cry. I cannot bear it," Gallowglass said gruffly.

"I'm sorry. I can't seem to help it." Diana turned in her seat so that she faced the opposite side of the cabin. Her shoulders trembled.

"Hell, Auntie. Looking the other way does no good." Gallowglass unclipped his seat belt and crouched by her leather recliner. He patted Diana on the knee. She grasped his hand. The power pulsed under her skin. It had abated somewhat since the astonishing moment when she'd wrapped the sire of the de Clermont family in a briar patch, but it was still all too visible. Gallowglass had even seen it through the disguising spell Diana wore until she boarded the jet.

"How was Marcus with Jack?" she asked, her eyes still closed.

"Marcus greeted him as an uncle should and distracted him with tales of his children and their antics. Lord knows they're an entertaining bunch,"

Gallowglass said under his breath. But this wasn't what Diana really wanted to know.

"Matthew was bearing up as well as could be expected," he continued more gently. There had been a moment when it appeared Matthew was going to strangle Hubbard, but Gallowglass wasn't going to worry about something that was, on the face of it, an excellent notion.

"I'm glad you and Chris called Marcus," Diana whispered.

"That was Miriam's idea," Gallowglass admitted. Miriam had been protecting Matthew for centuries, just as he had been looking after Diana. "As soon as she saw the test results Miriam knew that Matthew would need his son at his side."

"Poor Phoebe," Diana said, a note of worry creeping into her voice. "Marcus couldn't have had time to give her much of an explanation."

"Don't fret about Phoebe." Gallowglass had spent two months with the girl and had taken her measure. "She's got a strong spine and a stout heart, just like you."

Gallowglass insisted Diana sleep. The aircraft's cabin was outfitted with seats that converted to beds. He made sure Diana had drifted off before he marched into the cockpit and demanded to know their destination.

"Europe," the pilot told him.

"What do you mean 'Europe'?" That could be anywhere from Amsterdam to the Auvergne to Oxford.

"Madame de Clermont hasn't chosen her final destination. She told me to head to Europe. So I'm headed for Europe."

"She must be going to Sept-Tours. Go to Gander, then," Gallowglass instructed.

"That was my plan, sir," the pilot said drily. "Do you want to fly her?"

"Yes. No." What Gallowglass wanted was to hit something. "Hell, man. You do your job and I'll do mine."

There were times Gallowglass wished with all his heart he'd fallen in battle to someone other than Hugh de Clermont.

After landing safely at the airport in Gander, Gallowglass helped Diana down the stairs so that she could do as the doctor had ordered and stretch her legs.

"You're not dressed for Newfoundland," he observed, settling a worn leather jacket over her shoulders. "The wind will shred that pitiful excuse for a coat to ribbons."

"Thank you, Gallowglass," Diana said, shivering.

"What's your final destination, Auntie?" he asked after their second lap of the tiny airstrip.

"Does it matter?" Diana's voice had gone from resigned to weary to something worse.

Hopeless.

"No, Auntie. It's Nar-SAR-s'wauk—not NUR-sar-squawk," Gallowglass explained, tucking one of the down-filled blankets around Diana's shoulder. Narsarsuaq, on the southern tip of Greenland, was colder even than Gander. Diana had insisted on taking a brisk walk anyway.

"How do you know?" she asked peevishly, her lips slightly blue.

"I just know." Gallowglass motioned to the flight attendant, who brought him a steaming mug of tea. He poured a dollop of whiskey into it.

"No caffeine. Or alcohol," Diana said, waving the tea away.

"My own mam drank whiskey every day of her pregnancy—and look how hale and hearty I turned out," Gallowglass said, holding the mug in her direction. His voice turned wheedling. "Come on, now. A wee nip won't do you any harm. Besides, it can't be as bad for Apple and Bean as frostbite."

"They're fine," Diana said sharply.

"Oh, aye. Finer than frog's hair." Gallowglass extended his hand farther and hoped that the tea's aroma would persuade her to indulge. "It's Scottish Breakfast tea. One of your favorites."

"Get thee behind me, Satan," Diana grumbled, taking the mug. "And your mam couldn't have been drinking whiskey while she carried you. There's no evidence of whiskey distillation in Scotland or Ireland before the fifteenth century. You're older than that."

Gallowglass smothered a sigh of relief at her historical nitpicking.

Diana drew out a phone.

"Who are you calling, Auntie?" Gallowglass asked warily.

"Hamish."

When Matthew's best friend picked up the call, his words were exactly what Gallowglass expected them to be.

"Diana? What's wrong? Where are you?"

"I can't remember where my house is," she said in lieu of explanation.

"Your house?" Hamish sounded confused.

"My house," Diana repeated patiently. "The one Matthew gave me in London. You made me sign off on the maintenance bills when we were at Sept-Tours."

London? Being a vampire was no help at all in his present situation, Gallowglass realized. It would be far better to have been born a witch. Perhaps then he could have divined how this woman's mind worked.

"It's in Mayfair, on a little street near the Connaught. Why?"

"I need the key. And the address." Diana paused for a moment, mulling something over before she spoke. "I'll need a driver, too, to get around the city. Daemons like the Underground, and vampires own all the major cab companies."

Of course they owned the cab companies. Who else had the time to memorize the three hundred twenty routes, twenty-five thousand streets, and twenty thousand landmarks within six miles of Charing Cross that were required in order to get a license?

"A driver?" Hamish sputtered.

"Yes. And does that fancy Coutts account I have come with a bank card—one with a high spending limit?"

Gallowglass swore. She looked at him frostily.

"Yes." Hamish's wariness increased.

"Good. I need to buy some books. Everything Athanasius Kircher ever wrote. First or second editions. Do you think you could send out a few inquiries before the weekend?" Diana studiously avoided Gallowglass's piercing gaze.

"Athanasius who?" Hamish asked. Gallowglass could hear a pen scratching on paper.

"Kircher." She spelled it out for him, letter by letter. "You'll have to go to the rare-book dealers. There must be copies floating around London. I don't care how much they cost."

"You sound like Granny," Gallowglass muttered. That alone was reason for concern.

"If you can't get me copies by the end of next week, I suppose I'll have to go to the British Library. But fall term has started, and the rare-book room is bound to be full of witches. I'm sure it would be better if I stayed at home."

"Could I talk to Matthew?" Hamish said a trifle breathlessly.

"He's not here."

"You're alone?" He sounded shocked.

"Of course not. Gallowglass is with me," Diana replied.

"And Gallowglass knows about your plan to sit in the public reading rooms of the British Library and read these books by—what's his name? Athanasius Kircher? Have you gone completely mad? The whole Congregation is looking for you!" Hamish's voice rose steadily with each sentence.

"I am aware of the Congregation's interest, Hamish. That's why I asked you to buy the books," Diana said mildly.

"Where is Matthew?" Hamish demanded.

"I don't know." Diana crossed her fingers when she told the lie.

There was a long silence.

"I'll meet you at the airport. Let me know when you're an hour away," Hamish said.

"That's not necessary," she said.

"One hour before you land, call me." Hamish paused. "And Diana? I don't know what the hell is going on, but of one thing I'm sure: Matthew loves you. More than his own life."

"I know," Diana whispered before she hung up.

Now she'd gone from hopeless to dead-sounding.

The plane turned south and east. The vampire at the controls had overheard the conversation and acted accordingly.

"What is that oaf doing?" Gallowglass growled, shooting to his feet and upsetting the tea tray so that the shortbread biscuits scattered all over the floor. "You cannot head directly for London!" he shouted into the cockpit. "That's a four-hour flight, and she's not to be in the air for more than three."

"Where to, then?" came the pilot's muffled reply as the plane changed course.

"Put in at Stornoway. It's a straight shot, and less than three hours. From there it will be an easy jump to London," Gallowglass replied.

That settled it. Marcus's ride with Matthew, Jack, Hubbard, and Lobero, no matter how hellish, couldn't possibly compare to this.

* * *

"It's beautiful." Diana held her hair away from her face. It was dawn, and the sun was just rising over the Minch. Gallowglass filled his lungs with the familiar air of home and set about remembering a sight he had often dreamed of: Diana Bishop standing here, on the land of his ancestors.

"Aye." He turned and marched toward the jet. It was waiting on the taxiway, lights on and ready to depart.

"I'll be there in a minute." Diana scanned the horizon. Autumn had painted the hills with umber and golden strokes among the green. The wind carried the witch's red hair out in a streak that glowed like embers.

Gallowglass wondered what had captured her attention. There was nothing to see but a misguided gray heron, his long, bright yellow legs too insubstantial to hold up the rest of his body.

"Come, Auntie. You'll freeze to death out here." Ever since he'd parted with his leather jacket, Gallowglass had worn nothing more than his habitual uniform of T-shirt and torn jeans. He no longer felt the cold, but he remembered how the early-morning air in this part of the world could cut to the bone.

The heron stared at Diana for a moment. He ducked his head up and down, stretching his wings and crying out. The bird took flight, soaring away toward the sea.

"Diana?"

She turned blue-gold eyes in Gallowglass's direction. His hackles rose. There was something otherworldly in her gaze that made him recall his childhood, and a dark room where his grandfather cast runes and uttered prophecies.

Even after the plane took to the skies, Diana remained fixed on some unseen, distant view. Gallowglass stared out the window and prayed for a strong tailwind.

"Will we ever stop running, do you think?" Her voice startled him.

Gallowglass didn't know the answer and couldn't bear to lie to her. He remained silent.

Diana buried her face in her hands.

"There, there." He rocked her against his chest. "You mustn't think the worst, Auntie. It's not like you."

"I'm just so tired, Gallowglass."

"With good reason. Between past and present, you've had a hell of a year." Gallowglass tucked her head under his chin. She might be Matthew's lion, but even lions had to close their eyes and rest occasionally.

"Is that Corra?" Diana's fingers traced the outlines of the firedrake on his forearm. Gallowglass shivered. "Where does her tail go?"

She lifted his sleeve before he could stop her. Her eyes widened.

"You weren't meant to see that," Gallowglass said. He released her and tugged the soft fabric back into place.

"Show me."

"Auntie, I think it's best—"

"Show me," Diana repeated. "Please."

He grasped the hem of his shirt and pulled it over his head. His tattoos told a complicated tale, but only a few chapters would be of interest to Matthew's wife. Diana's hand went to her mouth.

"Oh, Gallowglass."

A siren sat on a rock above his heart, her arm extended so that her hand reached over to his left bicep. She held a clutch of cords. The cords snaked down his arm, falling and twisting to become Corra's sinuous tail, which swirled around his elbow until it met with the firedrake's body.

The siren had Diana's face.

"You're a hard woman to find, but you're an even harder one to forget." Gallowglass pulled his shirt back over his head.

"How long?" Diana's eyes were blue with regret and sympathy.

"Four months." He didn't tell her that it was the latest in a series of similar images that had been inked over his heart.

"That's not what I meant," Diana said softly.

"Oh." Gallowglass stared between his knees at the carpeted floor. "Four hundred years. More or less."

"I'm so sor—"

"I won't have you feeling sorry for something you couldn't prevent," Gallowglass said, silencing her with a slash of his hand. "I knew you could never be mine. It didn't matter."

"Before I was Matthew's, I was yours," Diana said simply.

"Only because I was watching you grow into Matthew's wife," he said roughly. "Granddad always did have an unholy ability to give us jobs we could neither refuse nor perform without losing some piece of our souls." Gallowglass took a deep breath.

"Until I saw the newspaper story about Lady Pembroke's laboratory book," he continued, "a small part of me hoped fate might have another surprise up her sleeve. I wondered if you might come back different, or without Matthew, or without loving him as much as he loves you."

Diana listened without saying a word.

"So I went to Sept-Tours to wait for you, like I promised Granddad I would. Emily and Sarah were always going on about the changes your time-walking might have wrought. Miniatures and telescopes are one thing. But there was only ever one man for you, Diana. And God knows there was only ever one woman for Matthew."

"It's strange to hear you say my name," Diana said softly.

"So long as I call you Auntie, I never forget who really owns your heart," Gallowglass said gruffly.

"Philippe shouldn't have expected you to watch over me. It was cruel," she said.

"No crueler than what Philippe expected from you," Gallowglass replied. "And far less so than what Granddad demanded of himself."

Seeing her confusion, Gallowglass continued.

"Philippe always put his own needs last," Gallowglass said. "Vampires are creatures ruled by their desire, with instincts for self-preservation that are much stronger than any warmblood's. But Philippe was never like the rest of us. It broke his heart every time Granny got restless and went away. Then I didn't understand why Ysabeau felt it necessary to leave. Now that I've heard her tale, I think Philippe's love frightened her. It was so deep and selfless that Granny simply couldn't trust it—not after what her sire put her through. Part of her was always braced for Philippe to turn on her, to demand something for himself that she couldn't give."

Diana looked thoughtful.

"Whenever I see Matthew struggle to give you the freedom you need—to let you do something without him that you think is minor but that is an agony of worrying and waiting for him—it reminds me of Philippe," Gallowglass said, drawing his tale to a close.

"What are we going to do now?" She didn't mean when they got to London, but he pretended she did.

"Now we wait for Matthew," Gallowglass said flatly. "You wanted him to establish a family. He's off doing it."

Under the surface of her skin, Diana's magic pulsed again in iridescent agitation. It reminded Gallowglass of long nights watching the aurora borealis from the sandy stretch of coastline beneath the cliffs where his father and grandfather had once lived.

"Don't worry. Matthew won't be able to stay away for long. It's one thing to wander in the darkness because you know no different, but it's quite another to enjoy the light only to have it taken from you," Gallowglass said.

"You sound so sure," she whispered.

"I am. Marcus's children are a handful, but he'll make them heel." Gallowglass lowered his voice. "I assume there's a good reason you chose London?"

Her glance flickered.

"I thought so. You're not just looking for the last missing page. You're going after Ashmole 782. And I'm not talking nonsense," Gallowglass said, raising his hand when Diana opened her mouth to protest. "You'll be wanting people around you, then. People you can trust unto death, like Granny and Sarah and Fernando." He drew out his phone.

"Sarah already knows I'm on my way to Europe. I told her I'd let her know where I was once I was settled." Diana frowned at the phone. "And Ysabeau is still Gerbert's prisoner. She's not in touch with the outside world."

"Oh, Granny has her ways," Gallowglass said serenely, his fingers racing across the keys. "I'll just send her a message and tell her where we're headed. Then I'll tell Fernando. You can't do this alone, Auntie. Not what you've got planned."

"You're taking this very well, Gallowglass," Diana said gratefully. "Matthew would be trying to talk me out of it."

"That's what you get for falling in love with the wrong man," he said under his breath, slipping the phone back into his pocket.

Ysabeau de Clermont picked up her sleek red phone and looked at the illuminated display. She noted the time—7:37 A.M. Then she read the waiting message. It began with three repetitions of a single word:

Mayday
Mayday
Mayday

She'd been expecting Gallowglass to get in touch ever since Phoebe had notified her that Marcus had departed in the middle of the night, mysteriously and suddenly, to go off and join Matthew.

Ysabeau and Gallowglass had decided early on that they needed a way to notify each other when things went "pear-shaped," to use her grandson's expression. Their system had changed over the years, from beacons and secret messages written in onion juice to codes and ciphers, then to objects sent through the mail without explanation. Now they used the phone.

At first Ysabeau had been dubious about owning one of these cellular contraptions, but given recent events she was glad to have it restored to her. Gerbert had confiscated it shortly after her arrival in Aurillac, in the vain hope that being without it would make her more malleable.

Gerbert had returned the phone to Ysabeau several weeks ago. She had been taken hostage to satisfy the witches and to make a public show of the Congregation's power and influence. Gerbert was under no illusion that his prisoner would part with a scrap of information that would help them find Matthew. He was, however, grateful that Ysabeau was willing to play along with the charade. Since arriving at Gerbert's home, she had been a model prisoner. He claimed that having her phone back was a reward for good behavior, but she knew it was largely due to the fact that Gerbert could not figure out how to silence the many alarms that sounded throughout the day.

Ysabeau liked these reminders of events that had altered her world: just before midday, when Philippe and his men had burst into her prison and she felt the first glimmers of hope; two hours before sunrise, when Philippe had first admitted that he loved her; three in the afternoon, the hour she had found Matthew's broken body in the half-built church in Saint-Lucien; 1:23 P.M., when Matthew drew the last drops of blood from Philippe's pain-ravaged body. Other alarms marked the hour of Hugh's death and Godfrey's, the hour when Louisa had first exhibited signs of blood rage, the hour when Marcus had demonstrated definitively that the same disease had not touched him. The rest of her daily alarms were reserved for significant historical events, such as the births of kings and queens whom Ysabeau had called friends, wars that she had fought in and won, and battles that she had unaccountably lost in spite of her careful plans.

The alarms rang day and night, each one a different, carefully chosen song. Gerbert had particularly objected to the alarm that blasted "Chant de Guerre pour l'Armée du Rhin" at 5:30 P.M.—the precise moment when the revolutionary mob swept through the gates of the Bastille in 1789. But these tunes served as aide-mémoire, conjuring up faces and places that might otherwise have faded away over time.

Ysabeau read the rest of Gallowglass's message. To anyone else it would have appeared nothing more than a garbled combination of shipping forecast, aeronautical distress signal, and horoscope, with its references to shadows, the moon, Gemini, Libra, and a series of longitude and latitude coordinates. Ysabeau reread the message twice: once to make sure she had correctly ascertained its meaning and a second time to memorize Gallowglass's instructions. Then she typed her reply.

Je Viens

"I am afraid it is time for me to go, Gerbert," Ysabeau said without a trace of regret. She looked across the faux-Gothic horror of a room to where her jailer sat before a computer at the foot of an ornate carved table. At the opposite end, a heavy Bible rested on a raised stand flanked by thick white candles, as though Gerbert's work space were an altar. Ysabeau's lip curled at the pretension, which was matched by the room's heavy nineteenth-century woodwork, pews converted to settees, and garish green-and-blue silk wallpaper ornamented with chivalric shields. The only authentic items in the room were the enormous stone fireplace and the monumental chess set before it.

Gerbert peered at his computer screen and hit a key on the keyboard. He groaned.

"Jean-Luc will come from Saint-Lucien and help if you are still having trouble with your computer," Ysabeau said.

Gerbert had hired the nice young man to set up a home computer network after Ysabeau had shared two morsels of Sept-Tours gossip gleaned from conversations around the dinner table: Nathaniel Wilson's belief that future wars would be fought on the Internet and Marcus's plan to handle a majority of the Knights of Lazarus's banking through online channels.

Baldwin and Hamish had overruled her grandson's extraordinary idea, but Gerbert didn't need to know that.

While installing the components of Gerbert's hastily purchased system, Jean-Luc had needed to call back to the office several times for advice. Marcus's dear friend Nathaniel had set up the small business in Saint-Lucien to bring the villagers into the modern age, and though he was now in Australia, he was happy to help his former employee whenever his greater experience was required. On this occasion Nathaniel had walked Jean-Luc through the various security configurations that Gerbert requested.

Nathaniel added a few modifications of his own, too.

The end result was that Ysabeau and Nathaniel knew more about Gerbert of Aurillac than she had dreamed was possible, or indeed had ever wanted, to know. It was astonishing how much a person's online shopping habits revealed about his character and activities.

Ysabeau had made sure Jean-Luc signed Gerbert up for various social-media services to keep the vampire occupied and out of her way. She could not imagine why these companies all chose shades of blue for their logos. Blue had always struck her as such a serene, soothing color, yet all social media offered was endless agitation and posturing. It was worse than the court of Versailles. Come to think of it, Ysabeau reflected, Louis-Dieudonné had quite liked blue as well.

Gerbert's only complaint about his new virtual existence was that he had been unable to secure "Pontifex Maximus" as a user name. Ysabeau told him that it was probably for the best, since it might constitute a violation of the covenant in the eyes of some creatures.

Sadly for Gerbert—though happily for Ysabeau—an addiction to the Internet and an understanding of how best to use it did not always go hand in hand. Because of the sites he frequented, Gerbert was plagued by computer viruses. He also tended to pick overly complex passwords and lose track of which sites he'd visited and how he had found them. This led to many phone calls with Jean-Luc, who unfailingly bailed Gerbert out of his difficulties and thereby kept up to date on how to access all Gerbert's online information.

With Gerbert thus engaged, Ysabeau was free to wander around his castle, going through his belongings and copying down the surprising entries in the vampire's many address books.

Life as Gerbert's hostage had been most illuminating.

"It is time for me to go," Ysabeau repeated when Gerbert finally tore his eyes away from the screen. "There is no reason to keep me here any longer. The Congregation won. I have just received word from the family that Matthew and Diana are no longer together. I imagine that the strain was too much for her, poor girl. You must be very pleased."

"I hadn't heard. And you?" Gerbert's expression was suspicious. "Are you pleased?"

"Of course. I have always despised witches." Gerbert had no need to know how completely Ysabeau's feelings had changed.

"Hmm." He still looked wary. "Has Matthew's witch gone to Madison? Surely Diana Bishop will want to be with her aunt if she has left your son."

"I am sure she longs for home," Ysabeau said vaguely. "It is typical, after heartbreak, to seek out what is familiar."

Ysabeau thought it was a promising sign, therefore, that Diana had chosen to return to the place where she and Matthew had enjoyed a life together. As for heartbreak, there were many ways to ease the pain and loneliness that went along with being mated to the sire of a great vampire clan—which Matthew would soon be. Ysabeau looked forward to sharing them with her daughter-in-law, who was made of sterner stuff than most vampires would have expected.

"Do you need to clear my departure with someone? Domenico? Satu, perhaps?" Ysabeau asked solicitously.

"They dance to my tune, Ysabeau," Gerbert said with a scowl.

It was pathetically easy to manipulate Gerbert if his ego was involved. And it was always involved. Ysabeau hid her satisfied smile.

"If I release you, you will go back to Sept-Tours and stay there?" Gerbert asked.

"Of course," she said promptly.

"Ysabeau," he growled.

"I have not left de Clermont territory since shortly after the war," she said with a touch of impatience. "Unless the Congregation decides to take me prisoner again, I will remain in de Clermont territory. Only Philippe himself could persuade me to do otherwise."

"Happily, not even Philippe de Clermont is capable of ordering us about from the grave," Gerbert said, "though I am sure he would dearly love to do so."

You would be surprised, you toad, Ysabeau thought.

"Very well, then. You are free to go." Gerbert sighed. "But do try to remember we are at war, Ysabeau. To keep up appearances."

"Oh, I would never forget we are at war, Gerbert." Unable to maintain her countenance for another moment, and afraid she might find a creative use for the iron poker that was propped up by the fireplace, Ysabeau went to find Marthe.

Her trusted companion was downstairs in the meticulous kitchen, sitting by the fireplace with a battered copy of *Tinker Tailor Soldier Spy* and a steaming cup of mulled wine. Gerbert's butcher stood at the nearby chopping block, dismembering a rabbit for his master's breakfast. The Delft tile on the walls provided an oddly cheerful note.

"We are going home, Marthe," Ysabeau said.

"Finally." Marthe got to her feet with a groan. "I hate Aurillac. The air here is bad. *Adiu siatz,* Theo."

"*Adiu siatz,* Marthe," Theo grunted, whacking the unfortunate rabbit.

Gerbert met them at the front door to bid them farewell. He kissed Ysabeau on both cheeks, his actions supervised by a dead boar that Philippe had killed, the head of which had been preserved and mounted on a plaque over the fire. "Shall I have Enzo drive you?"

"I think we will walk." It would give her and Marthe the opportunity to make plans. After so many weeks conducting espionage under Gerbert's roof, it was going to be difficult to let go of her excessive caution.

"It's eighty miles," Gerbert pointed out.

"We shall stop in Allanche for lunch. A large herd of deer once roamed the woods there." They would not make it so far, for Ysabeau had already sent Alain a message to meet them outside Murat. Alain would drive them from there to Clermont-Ferrand, where they would board one of Baldwin's infernal flying machines and proceed to London. Marthe abhorred air travel, which she believed was unnatural, but they could not allow Diana to arrive at a cold house. Ysabeau slipped Jean-Luc's card into Gerbert's hand. "Until next time."

Arm in arm, Ysabeau and Marthe walked out into the crisp dawn. The towers of Château des Anges Déchus grew smaller and smaller behind them until they disappeared from sight.

"I must set a new alarm, Marthe. Seven thirty-seven A.M. Do not let me forget. "Marche Henri IV' would be most appropriate for it, I think," Ysabeau whispered as their feet moved quickly north toward the dormant peaks of the ancient volcanoes and onward to their future.

24

This cannot be my house, Leonard." The palatial brick mansion's expansive five-windowed frontage and towering four stories in one of London's toniest neighborhoods made it inconceivable. I felt a pang of regret, though. The tall windows were trimmed in white to stand out against the warm brick, their old glass winking in the midday sunshine. Inside, I imagined that the house would be flooded with light. It would be warm, too, for there were not the usual two chimneys but three. And there was enough polished brass on the front door to start a marching band. It would be a glorious bit of history to call home.

"This is where I was told to go, Mistress . . . er, Mrs. . . . um, Diana." Leonard Shoreditch, Jack's erstwhile friend and another of Hubbard's disreputable gang of lost boys, had been waiting—with Hamish—in the private arrivals area at London City Airport in the Docklands. Leonard now parked the Mercedes and craned his neck over the seat, awaiting further instructions.

"I promise you it's your house, Auntie. If you don't like it, we'll swap it for a new one. But let's discuss future real-estate transactions inside, please—not sitting in the street where any creature might see us. Get the luggage, lad." Gallowglass clambered out of the front passenger seat and slammed the door behind him. He was still angry not to have been the one to drive us to Mayfair. But I'd been ferried around London by Gallowglass before and preferred to take my chances with Leonard.

I gave the mansion another dubious look.

"Don't worry, Diana. Clairmont House isn't half so grand inside as it is out. There is the staircase, of course. And some of the plasterwork is ornate," Hamish said as he opened the car door. "Come to think of it, the whole house *is* rather grand."

Leonard rooted around in the car trunk and removed my small suitcase and the large, hand-lettered sign he'd been holding when he met us. Leonard had wanted to do things properly, he said, and the sign bore the name CLAIRMONT in blocky capitals. When Hamish had told him we needed to be discreet, Leonard had drawn a line through the name and scrawled ROYDON underneath it in even darker characters using a felt-tip marker.

"How did you know to call Leonard?" I asked Hamish as he helped me out of the car. When last seen in 1591, Leonard had been in the company of another boy with the strangely fitting name of Amen Corner. As I recalled, Matthew had thrown a dagger at the two simply for delivering a message from Father Hubbard. I couldn't imagine that my husband had stayed in touch with either young man.

"Gallowglass texted me his number. He said we should keep our affairs in the family as much as possible." Hamish turned curious eyes on me. "I wasn't aware Matthew owned a private car-hire business."

"The company belongs to Matthew's grandson." I'd spent most of the journey from the airport staring at the promotional leaflets in the pocket behind the driver's seat, which advertised the services of Hubbards of Houndsditch, Ltd., "proudly meeting London's most discriminating transportation needs since 1917."

Before I could explain further, a small, aged woman with ample hips and a familiar scowl pulled open the arched blue door. I stared in shock.

"You're looking bonny, Marthe." Gallowglass stooped and kissed her. Then he turned and frowned down the short flight of stairs that rose from the sidewalk. "Why are you still out on the curb, Auntie?"

"Why is Marthe here?" My throat was dry and the question came out in a croak.

"Is that Diana?" Ysabeau's bell-like voice cut through the quiet murmur of city sounds. "Marthe and I are here to help, of course."

Gallowglass whistled. "Being held against your will agreed with you, Granny. You haven't looked so lively since Victoria was crowned."

"Flatterer." Ysabeau patted her grandson on the cheek. Then she looked at me and gasped. "Diana is as white as snow, Marthe. Get her inside, Gallowglass. At once."

"You heard her, Auntie," he said, sweeping me off my feet and onto the top step.

Ysabeau and Marthe propelled me through the airy entrance with its gleaming black-and-white marble floor and a curved staircase so splendid it made my eyes widen. The four flights of stairs were topped with a domed skylight that let in the sunshine and picked out the details in the moldings.

From there I was ushered into a tranquil reception room. Long drapes in gray figured silk hung at the windows, their color a pleasing contrast to the creamy walls. The upholstery pulled in shades of slate blue, terra-cotta, cream, and black to accent the gray, and the faint fragrance of cinnamon and cloves clung to all of it. Matthew's taste was everywhere, too: in a small orrery, its brass wires gleaming; a piece of Japanese porcelain; the warmly colored rug.

"Hello, Diana. I thought you might need tea." Phoebe Taylor arrived, accompanied by the scent of lilacs and the gentle clatter of silver and porcelain.

"Why aren't you at Sept-Tours?" I asked, equally astonished to see her.

"Ysabeau told me I was needed here." Phoebe's neat black heels clicked against the polished wood. She eyed Leonard as she put the tea tray down on a graceful table that was polished to such a high sheen that I could see her reflection in it. "I'm so sorry, but I don't believe we've met. Would you like some tea?"

"Leonard Shoreditch, ma-madam, at your service," Leonard said, stammering slightly. He bent in a stiff bow. "And thank you. I would dearly love some tea. White. Four sugars."

Phoebe poured steaming liquid into a cup and put only three cubes of sugar in it before she handed it off to Leonard. Marthe snorted and sat down in a straight-backed chair next to the tea table, obviously intent on supervising Phoebe—and Leonard—like a hawk.

"That will rot your teeth, Leonard," I said, unable to stop the maternal intervention.

"Vampires don't worry much about tooth decay, Mistress . . . er, Mrs. . . . um, Diana." Leonard's hand shook alarmingly, making the tiny cup and saucer with its red Japanese-style decoration clatter. Phoebe blanched.

"That's Chelsea porcelain, and quite early, too. Everything in the house should be in display cases at the V&A Museum." Phoebe handed me an identical cup and saucer with a beautiful silver spoon balanced on the edge. "If anything is broken, I'll never forgive myself. They're irreplaceable."

If Phoebe were going to marry Marcus as she planned, she would have to get used to being surrounded by museum-quality objects.

I took a sip of the scalding hot, sweet, milky tea and sighed with pleasure.

Silence fell. I took another sip and looked around the room. Gallowglass was stuffed into a Queen Anne corner chair, his muscular legs splayed wide. Ysabeau was enthroned in the most ornate chair in the room: high-backed, its frame covered in silver leaf, and upholstered in damask. Hamish shared a mahogany settee with Phoebe. Leonard nervously perched on one of the side chairs that flanked the tea table.

They were all waiting. Since Matthew wasn't present, our friends and family were looking to me for guidance. The burden of responsibility settled on my shoulders. It was uncomfortable, just as Matthew had predicted.

"When did the Congregation set you free, Ysabeau?" I asked, my mouth still dry in spite of the tea.

"Gerbert and I came to an agreement shortly after you arrived in Scotland," she replied breezily, though her smile told me there was more to the story.

"Does Marcus know you're here, Phoebe?" Something told me he had no idea.

"My resignation from Sotheby's takes effect on Monday. He knew I had to clear out my desk." Phoebe's words were carefully chosen, but the underlying response to my question was clearly no. Marcus was still under the impression that his fiancée was in a heavily fortified castle in France, not an airy town house in London.

"Resignation?" I was surprised.

"If I want to go back to work at Sotheby's, I'll have centuries to do so." Phoebe looked around her. "Though properly cataloging the de Clermont family's possessions could take me several lifetimes."

"Then you are still set on becoming a vampire?" I asked.

Phoebe nodded. I should sit down with her and try to talk her out of it. Matthew would have her blood on his hands if anything went wrong. And something always went wrong in this family.

"Who's gonna make her a vamp?" Leonard whispered to Gallowglass. "Father H?"

"I think Father Hubbard has enough children. Don't you, Leonard?" Come to think of it, I needed to know that number as soon as possible—and how many were witches and daemons.

"I suppose so, Mistress . . . er, Mrs. . . . er—"

"The proper form of address for *Sieur* Matthew's mate is '*Madame*.' From now on, you will use that title when speaking to Diana," Ysabeau said briskly. "It simplifies matters."

Marthe and Gallowglass turned in Ysabeau's direction, their faces registering surprise.

"*Sieur* Matthew," I repeated softly. Until now Matthew had been "*Milord*" to his family. But Philippe had been called "*Sieur*" in 1590. *"Everyone here calls me either 'sire' or 'Father,'"* Philippe had told me when I asked how he should be addressed. At the time I'd thought the title was nothing more than an antiquated French honorific. Now I knew better. To call Matthew "*Sieur*"—the vampire sire—marked him head of a vampire clan.

As far as Ysabeau was concerned, Matthew's new scion was a fait accompli.

"*Madame* what?" Leonard asked, confused.

"Just *Madame*," Ysabeau replied serenely. "You may call me Madame Ysabeau. When Phoebe marries Milord Marcus, she will be Madame de Clermont. Until then you may call her Miss Phoebe."

"Oh." Leonard's look of intense concentration indicated he was chewing on these morsels of vampire etiquette.

Silence fell again. Ysabeau stood.

"Marthe put you in the Forest Room, Diana. It is next to Matthew's bedchamber," she said. "If you are finished with the tea, I will take you upstairs. You should rest for a few hours before you tell us what you require."

"Thank you, Ysabeau." I put the cup and saucer on the small round table at my elbow. I wasn't finished with my tea, but its heat had quickly dissipated through the fragile porcelain. As for what I required, where to start?

Together Ysabeau and I crossed the foyer, climbed the graceful staircase up to the first floor, and kept going.

"You will have your privacy on the second floor," Ysabeau explained. "There are only two bedrooms on that level, as well as Matthew's study and a small sitting room. Now that the house is yours, you may arrange things as you like, of course."

"Where are the rest of you sleeping?" I asked as Ysabeau turned onto the second-floor landing.

"Phoebe and I have rooms on the floor above you. Marthe prefers to sleep on the lower ground floor, in the housekeeper's rooms. If you feel crowded, Phoebe and I can move into Marcus's home. It is near St. James's Palace, and once belonged to Matthew."

"I can't imagine that will be necessary," I said, thinking of the size of the house.

"We'll see. Your bedchamber." Ysabeau pushed open a wide, paneled door with a gleaming brass knob. I gasped.

Everything in the room was in shades of green, silver, pale gray, and white. The walls were papered with hand-painted depictions of branches and leaves against a pale gray background. Silver accents gave the effect of moonlight, the mirrored moon in the center of the ceiling's plasterwork appearing to be the source of the light. A ghostly female face looked down from the mirror with a serene smile. Four depictions of Nyx, the personification of night, anchored the four quadrants of the room's ceiling, her veil billowing out in a smoky black drapery that was painted so realistically it looked like actual fabric. Silver stars were entangled in the veiling, catching the light from the windows and the mirror's reflection.

"It is extraordinary, I agree," Ysabeau said, pleased by my reaction. "Matthew wanted to create the effect of being outside in the forest, under a moonlit sky. Once this bedchamber was decorated, he said it was too beautiful to use and moved to the room next door."

Ysabeau went to the windows and drew the curtains open. The bright light revealed an ancient four-poster canopied bed set into a recess in the wall, which slightly minimized its considerable size. The bed hangings were silk and bore the same design as the wallpaper. Another large-scale mirror topped the fireplace, trapping images of trees on the wallpaper and sending them back into the room. The shining surface reflected the room's furniture, too: the small dressing table between the large windows, the chaise by the fire, the gleaming flowers and leaves inlaid into the low walnut chest of drawers. The room's decoration and furnishings must have cost Matthew a fortune.

My eyes fell on a vast canvas of a sorceress sitting on the ground and sketching magical symbols. It hung on the wall opposite the bed, between the tall windows. A veiled woman had interrupted the sorceress's work, her outstretched hand suggesting that she wanted the witch's help. It was an odd choice of subject for a vampire's house.

"Whose room was this, Ysabeau?"

"I think Matthew made it for you—only he did not realize it at the time." Ysabeau twitched open another pair of curtains.

"Has another woman slept here?" There was no way I could rest in a room that Juliette Durand had once occupied.

"Matthew took his lovers elsewhere," Ysabeau answered, equally blunt. When she saw my expression, she softened her tone. "He has many houses. Most of them mean nothing to him. Some do. This is one of them. He would not have given you a gift he didn't value himself."

"I never believed that being separated from him would be so hard." My voice was muted.

"Being the consort in a vampire family is never easy," Ysabeau said with a sad smile. "And sometimes being apart is the only way to stay together. Matthew had no choice but to leave you this time."

"Did Philippe ever banish you from his side?" I studied my composed mother-in-law with open curiosity.

"Of course. Mostly Philippe sent me away when I was an unwelcome distraction. On other occasions to keep me from being implicated if disaster struck—and in his family it struck more often than not." She smiled. "My husband always commanded me to go when he knew I would not be able to resist meddling and was worried for my safety."

"So Matthew learned how to be overprotective from Philippe?" I asked, thinking of all the times he had stepped into harm's way to keep me from it.

"Matthew had mastered the art of fussing over the woman he loved long before he became a vampire," Ysabeau replied softly. "You know that."

"And did you always obey Philippe's orders?"

"No more than you obey Matthew." Ysabeau's voice dropped conspiratorially. "And you will quickly discover that you are never so free to make your own decisions as when Matthew is off being patriarchal with someone else. Like me, you might even come to look forward to these moments apart."

"I doubt it." I pressed a fist into the small of my back in an effort to work out the kinks. It was something Matthew usually did. "I should tell you what happened in New Haven."

"You must never explain Matthew's actions to anyone," Ysabeau said sharply. "Vampires don't tell tales for a reason. Knowledge is power in our world."

"You're Matthew's mother. Surely I'm not supposed to keep secrets from you." I sifted through the events of the past few days. "Matthew discovered the identity of one of Benjamin's children—and met a great-grandson he didn't know he had." Of all the strange twists and turns our lives had taken, meeting up with Jack and his father had to be the most significant, not least because we were now in Father Hubbard's city. "His name is Jack Blackfriars, and he lived in our household in 1591."

"So my son knows at last about Andrew Hubbard," Ysabeau said, her face devoid of emotion.

"You *knew?*" I cried.

Ysabeau's smile would have terrified me—once. "And do you still think I deserve your complete honesty, daughter?"

Matthew had warned me that I wasn't equipped to lead a pack of vampires.

"You are a sire's consort, Diana. You must learn to tell others only what they need to know, and nothing more," she instructed.

Here was my first lesson learned, but there were sure to be more.

"Will you teach me, Ysabeau?"

"Yes." Her one-word response was more trustworthy than any lengthy vow. "First you must be careful, Diana. Even though you are Matthew's mate and his consort, you are a de Clermont and must remain so until this matter of a scion is settled. Your status in Philippe's family will protect Matthew."

"Matthew said the Congregation will try to kill him—and Jack, too—once they find out about Benjamin and the blood rage," I said.

"They will try. We will not let them. But for now you must rest." Ysabeau pulled back the bed's silk coverlet and plumped the pillows.

I circled the enormous bed, wrapping my hand around one of the posts that supported the canopy. The carving under my fingers felt familiar. *I've slept in this bed before,* I realized. This was not another woman's bed. It was mine. It had been in our house in the Blackfriars in 1590 and had somehow survived all these centuries to end up in a chamber that Matthew had dedicated to moonlight and enchantment.

After a whispered word of thanks to Ysabeau, I rested my head on the soft pillows and drifted off into troubled sleep.

* * *

I slept for nearly twenty-four hours, and it might have been longer but for a loud car alarm that pulled me out of my dreams and plunged me into an unfamiliar, green-tinged darkness. It was only then that other sounds penetrated my consciousness: the bustle of traffic on the street outside my windows, a door closing somewhere in the house, a quickly hushed conversation in the hallway.

Hoping that a pounding flow of hot water would ease my stiff muscles and clear my head, I explored the warren of small rooms beyond a white door. I found not only a shower but also my suitcase resting on a folding stand designed for much grander pieces of luggage. From it I pulled out the two pages from Ashmole 782 and my laptop. The rest of my packing had left a great deal to be desired. Except for some underwear, several tank tops, yoga tights that no longer fit me, a pair of mismatched shoes, and black maternity pants, there was nothing else in the bag. Happily, Matthew's closet held plenty of pressed shirts. I slid one made of gray broadcloth over my arms and shoulders and avoided the closed door that surely led to his bedroom.

I padded downstairs in bare feet, my computer and the large envelope with the pages from the Book of Life in my arms. The grand first-floor rooms were empty—an echoing ballroom with enough crystal and gold paint to renovate Versailles, a smaller music room with a piano and other instruments, a formal salon that looked to have been decorated by Ysabeau, an equally formal dining room with an endless stretch of mahogany table and seating for twenty-four, a library full of eighteenth-century books, and a games room with green-felted card tables that looked as if it had been plucked from a Jane Austen novel.

Longing for a homier atmosphere, I descended to the ground floor. No one was in the sitting room, so I poked around in office spaces, parlors, and morning rooms until I found a more intimate dining room than the one upstairs. It was located at the rear of the house, its bowed window looking out over a small private garden. The walls were painted to resemble brick, lending the space a warm, inviting air. Another mahogany table—this one round rather than rectangular—was encircled by only eight chairs. On its surface was an assortment of carefully arranged old books.

Phoebe entered the room and put a tray bearing tea and toast on a small sideboard. "Marthe told me you would be up at any moment. She said that this was what you would need first thing and that if you were still hungry, you could go down to the kitchen for eggs and sausage. We don't eat up here as a rule. By the time the food makes it up the stairs, it's stone cold."

"What is all this?" I gestured at the table.

"The books you requested from Hamish," Phoebe explained, straightening a volume that was slightly off kilter. "We're still waiting for a few items. You're a historian, so I put them in chronological order. I hope that's all right."

"But I only asked for them on Thursday," I said, bewildered. It was now Sunday morning. How could she have managed such a feat? One of the sheets of paper bore a title and date—*Arca Noë* 1675—in a neat, feminine hand, along with a price and the name and address of a book dealer.

"Ysabeau knows every dealer in London." Phoebe's mouth lifted into a mischievous smile, changing her face from attractive to beautiful. "And no wonder. The phrase 'the price isn't important' will galvanize any auction house, no matter the lateness of the hour, even on the weekend."

I picked up another volume—Kircher's *Obeliscus Pamphilius*—and opened the cover. Matthew's sprawling signature was on the flyleaf.

"I had a rummage through the libraries here and at Pickering Place first. There didn't seem much point in purchasing something that was already in your possession," Phoebe explained. "Matthew has wide-ranging tastes when it comes to books. There's a first edition of *Paradise Lost* at Pickering Place and a first edition of *Poor Richard's Almanack* signed by Franklin upstairs."

"Pickering Place?" Unable to stop myself, I traced the letters of Matthew's signature with my finger.

"Marcus's house over by St. James's Palace. It was a gift from Matthew, I understand. He lived there before he built Clairmont House," Phoebe said. Her lips pursed. "Marcus may be fascinated by politics, but I don't think it's appropriate for the Magna Carta and one of the original copies of the Declaration of Independence to remain in private hands. I'm sure you agree."

My finger rose from the page. Matthew's likeness hovered for a moment above the blank spot where his signature had been. Phoebe's eyes widened.

"I'm sorry," I said, releasing the ink back onto the paper. It swirled back onto the surface, re-forming into my husband's signature. "I shouldn't practice magic in front of warmbloods."

"But you didn't say any words or write down a charm." Phoebe looked confused.

"Some witches don't need to recite spells to make magic." Remembering Ysabeau's words, I kept my explanation as brief as possible.

"Oh." She nodded. "I still have a great deal to learn about creatures."

"Me, too." I smiled warmly at her, and Phoebe gave me a tentative smile in return.

"I assume you're interested in Kircher's imagery?" Phoebe asked, carefully opening another of the thick tomes. It was his book on magnetism, *Magnes sive De Arte Magnetica*. The engraved title page showed a tall tree, its wide branches bearing the fruits of knowledge. These were chained together to suggest their common bond. In the center God's divine eye looked out from the eternal world of archetypes and truth. A ribbon wove among the tree's branches and fruits. It bore a Latin motto: *Omnia nodis arcanis connexa quiescunt*. Translating mottoes was a tricky business, since their meanings were deliberately enigmatic, but most scholars agreed that it referred to the hidden magnetic influences that Kircher believed gave unity to the world: *"All things are at rest, connected by secret knots."*

"'*They all wait silently, connected by secret knots,*'" Phoebe murmured. "Who are 'they'? And what are they waiting for?"

With no detailed knowledge of Kircher's ideas about magnetism, Phoebe had read an entirely different meaning in the inscription.

"And why are these four disks larger?" she continued, pointing to the center of the page. Three of the disks were arranged in a triangular fashion around one containing an unblinking eye.

"I'm not sure," I confessed, reading the Latin descriptions that accompanied the images. "The eye represents the world of archetypes."

"Oh. The origin of all things." Phoebe looked at the image more closely.

"What did you say?" My own third eye opened, suddenly interested in what Phoebe Taylor had to say.

"Archetypes are original patterns. See, here are the sublunar world, the heavens, and man," she said, tapping in succession each of the three disks surrounding the archetypal eye. "Each one of them is linked to the world of archetypes—their point of origin—as well as to one another. The motto suggests we should see the chains as knots, though. I'm not sure if that's relevant."

"Oh, I think it's relevant," I said under my breath, more certain than ever that Athanasius Kircher and the Villa Mondragone sale were crucial links in the series of events that led from Edward Kelley in Prague to the final missing page. Somehow, Father Athanasius must have learned about the world of creatures. Either that or he was one himself.

"The Tree of Life is a powerful archetype in its own right, of course," Phoebe mused, "one that also describes the relationships between parts of the created world. There's a reason genealogists use family trees to show lines of descent."

Having an art historian in the family was going to be an unexpected boon—from both a research standpoint and a conversational one. Finally I had someone to talk to about arcane imagery.

"And you already know how important trees of knowledge are in scientific imagery. Not all of them are this representational, though," Phoebe said with regret. "Most are just simple branching diagrams, like Darwin's Tree of Life from *On the Origin of Species.* It was the only image in the whole book. Too bad Darwin didn't think to hire a proper artist like Kircher did—someone who could produce something truly splendid."

The knotted threads that had been waiting silently all around me began to chime. There was something I was missing. Some powerful connection that was nearly within my grasp, if only . . .

"Where is everybody?" Hamish poked his head into the room.

"Good morning, Hamish," Phoebe said with a warm smile. "Leonard has gone to pick up Sarah and Fernando. Everybody else is here somewhere."

"Hullo, Hamish." Gallowglass waved from the garden window. "Feeling better after your sleep, Auntie?"

"Much, thank you." But my attention was fixed on Hamish.

"He hasn't called," Hamish said gently in response to my silent question.

I wasn't surprised. Nevertheless, I stared down at my new books to hide my disappointment.

"Good morning, Diana. Hello, Hamish." Ysabeau sailed into the room and offered her cheek to the daemon. He kissed it obediently. "Has Phoebe located the books you need, Diana, or should she keep looking?"

"Phoebe has done an amazing job—and quickly, too. I'm afraid I still need help, though."

"Well, that is what we are here for." Ysabeau beckoned her grandson inside and gave me a steadying look. "Your tea has gone cold. Marthe will bring more, and then you will tell us what must be done."

After Marthe dutifully appeared (this time with something minty and decaffeinated rather than the strong black brew that Phoebe had poured) and Gallowglass joined us, I brought out the two pages from Ashmole 782. Hamish whistled.

"These are two illuminations removed from the Book of Life in the sixteenth century—the manuscript known today as Ashmole 782. One has yet to be found: an image of a tree. It looks a little like this." I showed them the frontispiece from Kircher's book on magnestism. "We have to find it before anyone else does, and that includes Knox, Benjamin, and the Congregation."

"Why do they all want the Book of Life so badly?" Phoebe's shrewd, olive-colored eyes were guileless. I wondered how long they would stay that way after she became a de Clermont and a vampire.

"None of us really know," I admitted. "Is it a grimoire? A story of our origins? A record of some kind? I've held it in my hands twice: once in its damaged state at the Bodleian in Oxford and once in Emperor Rudolf's cabinet of curiosities when it was whole and complete. I'm still not sure why so many creatures are seeking the book. All I can say with certainty is that the Book of Life is full of power—power and secrets."

"No wonder the witches and vampires are so keen to acquire it," Hamish said drily.

"The daemons as well, Hamish," I said. "Just ask Nathaniel's mother, Agatha Wilson. She wants it, too."

"Wherever did you find this second page?" He touched the picture of the dragons.

"Someone brought it to New Haven."

"Who?" Hamish asked.

"Andrew Hubbard." After Ysabeau's warnings I wasn't sure how much to reveal. But Hamish was our lawyer. I couldn't keep secrets from him. "He's a vampire."

"Oh, I'm well aware of who—and what—Andrew Hubbard is. I'm a daemon and work in the City, after all," Hamish said with a laugh. "But I'm surprised Matthew let him get near. He despises the man."

I could have explained how much things had changed, and why, but the tale of Jack Blackfriars was Matthew's to tell.

"What does the missing picture of the tree have to do with Athanasius Kircher?" Phoebe asked, bringing our attention back to the matter at hand.

"While I was in New Haven, my colleague Lucy Meriweather helped me track down what might have happened to the Book of Life. One of Rudolf's mysterious manuscripts ended up in Kircher's hands. We thought that the illumination of the tree might have been included with it." I gestured at the frontispiece to *Magnes sive De Arte Magnetica*. "I'm more certain than ever that Kircher had at least seen the image, based solely on that illustration."

"Can't you just look through Kircher's books and papers?" Hamish asked.

"I can," I replied with a smile, "provided the books and papers can still be located. Kircher's personal collection was sent to an old papal residence for safekeeping—Villa Mondragone in Italy. In the early twentieth century, the Jesuits began to discreetly sell off some of the books to raise revenue. Lucy and I think they sold the page then."

"In that case there should be records of the sale," Phoebe said thoughtfully. "Have you contacted the Jesuits?"

"Yes." I nodded. "They have no records of it—or if they do, they aren't sharing them. Lucy wrote to the major auction houses, too."

"Well, she wouldn't have got very far. Sales information is confidential," Phoebe said.

"So we were told." I hesitated just long enough for Phoebe to offer what I was afraid to ask for.

"I'll e-mail Sylvia today and tell her that I won't be able to clear out my desk tomorrow as planned," Phoebe said. "I can't hold Sotheby's off indefinitely, but there are other resources I can check and people who might talk to me if approached in the right way."

Before I could respond, the doorbell rang. After a momentary pause, it rang again. And again. The fourth time the ringing went on and on as though the visitor had jammed a finger into the button and left it there.

"Diana!" shouted a familiar voice. The ringing was replaced by pounding.

"Sarah!" I cried, rising to my feet.

A fresh October breeze swept into the house, carrying with it the scents of brimstone and saffron. I rushed into the hall. Sarah was there, her face white and her hair floating around her shoulders in a mad tangle of red. Fernando stood behind her, carrying two suitcases as though their collective weight were no more than a first-class letter.

Sarah's red-rimmed eyes met mine, and she dropped Tabitha's cat carrier on the marble floor with a thud. She held her arms wide, and I moved into them. Em had always offered me comfort when I felt alone and frightened as a child, but right now Sarah was exactly who I needed.

"It will be all right, honey," she whispered, holding me tight.

"I just spoke to Father H, and he said I'm to follow your instructions to the letter, Mistress . . . Madame," Leonard Shoreditch said cheerfully, pushing past Sarah and me on his way into the house. He gave me a jaunty salute.

"Did Andrew say anything else?" I asked, drawing away from my aunt. Perhaps Hubbard had shared news of Jack—or Matthew.

"Let's see." Leonard pulled on the end of his long nose. "Father H said to make sure you know where London begins and ends, and if there's trouble, go straight to St. Paul's and help will be along presently."

Hearty slaps indicated that Fernando and Gallowglass had been reunited.

"No problems?" Gallowglass murmured.

"None, except that I had to persuade Sarah not to disable the smoke detector in the first-class lavatory so she could sneak a cigarette," Fernando said mildly. "Next time she needs to fly internationally, send a de Clermont plane. We'll wait."

"Thank you for getting her here so quickly, Fernando," I said with a grateful smile. "You must be wishing you'd never met me and Sarah. All the Bishops seem to do is get you more entangled with the de Clermonts and their problems."

"On the contrary," he said softly, "you are freeing me from them." To my astonishment, Fernando dropped the bags and knelt before me.

"Get up. Please." I tried to lift him.

"The last time I fell to my knees before a woman, I had lost one of Isabella of Castile's ships. Two of her guards forced me to do so at sword point, so that I might beg for her forgiveness," Fernando said with a sardonic lift to his mouth. "As I'm doing so voluntarily on this occasion, I will get up when I am through."

Marthe appeared, taken aback by the sight of Fernando in such an abject position.

"I am without kith or kin. My maker is gone. My mate is gone. I have no children of my own." Fernando bit into his wrist and clenched his fist. The blood welled up from the wound, streaming over his arm and splashing onto the black-and-white floor. "I dedicate my blood and body to the service and honor of your family."

"Blimey," Leonard breathed. "That's not how Father H does it." I had seen Andrew Hubbard induct a creature into his flock, and though the two ceremonies weren't identical, they were similar in tone and intent.

Once again everyone in the house waited for my response. There were probably rules and precedents to follow, but at that moment I neither knew nor cared what they were. I took Fernando's bloody hand in mine.

"Thank you for putting your trust in Matthew," I said simply.

"I have always trusted him," Fernando said, looking up at me with sharp eyes. "Now it is time for Matthew to trust himself."

I found it." Phoebe put a printed e-mail before me on the Georgian writing desk's tooled-leather surface. The fact that she hadn't first knocked politely on the door to the sitting room told me that something exciting had happened.

"Already?" I regarded her in amazement.

"I told my former supervisor that I was looking for an item for the de Clermont family—a picture of a tree drawn by Athanasius Kircher." Phoebe glanced around the room, her connoisseur's eye caught by the black-and-gold chinoiserie chest on a stand, the faux bamboo carvings on a chair, the colorful silk cushions splashed across the chaise longue by the window. She peered at the walls, muttering the name Jean Pillement and words like "impossible" and "priceless" and "museum."

"But the illustrations in the Book of Life weren't drawn by Kircher." Frowning, I picked up the e-mail. "And it's not a picture. It's a page torn out of a manuscript."

"Attribution and provenance are crucial to a good sale," Phoebe explained. "The temptation to link the picture to Kircher would have been irresistible. And if the edges of the parchment were cleaned up and the text was invisible, it would have commanded a higher price as a stand-alone drawing or painting."

I scanned the message. It began with a tart reference to Phoebe's resignation and future marital state. But it was the next lines that caught my attention:

I do find record of the sale and purchase of "an allegory of the Tree of Life believed to have once been displayed in the museum of Athanasius Kircher, SJ, in Rome." Could this be the image the de Clermonts are seeking?

"Who bought it?" I whispered, hardly daring to breathe.

"Sylvia wouldn't tell me," Phoebe said, pointing to the final lines of the e-mail. "The sale was recent, and the details are confidential. She revealed the purchase price: sixteen hundred and fifty pounds."

"That's all?" I exclaimed. Most of the books Phoebe had purchased for me cost far more than that.

"The possible Kircher provenance wasn't firm enough to convince potential buyers to spend more," she said.

"Is there really no way to discover the buyer's identity?" I began to imagine how I might use magic to find out more.

"Sotheby's can't afford to tell their clients' secrets." Phoebe shook her head. "Imagine how Ysabeau would react if her privacy was violated."

"Did you call me, Phoebe?" My mother-in-law was standing in the arched doorway before the seed of my plan could put out its first shoots.

"Phoebe's discovered that a recent sale at Sotheby's describes a picture very like the one I'm looking for," I explained to Ysabeau. "They won't tell us who bought it."

"I know where the sales records are kept," Phoebe said. "When I go to Sotheby's to hand in my keys, I could take a look."

"No, Phoebe. It's too risky. If you can tell me exactly where they are, I may be able to figure out a way to get access to them." Some combination of my magic and Hubbard's gang of thieves and lost boys could manage it. But my mother-in-law had her own ideas.

"Ysabeau de Clermont calling for Lord Sutton." The clear voice echoed against the room's high ceilings.

Phoebe looked shocked. "You can't just call the director of Sotheby's and expect him to do your bidding."

Apparently Ysabeau could—and did.

"Charles. It's been too long." Ysabeau draped herself over a chair and let her pearls fall through her fingers. "You've been so busy, I've had to rely on Matthew for news. And the refinancing he helped you arrange—did it achieve what you had hoped?"

Ysabeau made soft, encouraging sounds of interest and expressions of appreciation at his cleverness. If I had to describe her behavior, I would be tempted to call it kittenish—provided the kitten were a baby Bengal tiger.

"Oh, I am so glad, Charles. Matthew felt sure it would work." Ysabeau ran a delicate finger over her lips. "I was wondering if you could help with a little situation. Marcus is getting married, you see—to one of your employees. They met when Marcus picked up those miniatures you were so kind as to procure for me in January."

Lord Sutton's precise reply was inaudible, but the warm hum of contentment in his voice was unmistakable.

"The art of matchmaking." Ysabeau's laugh was crystalline. "How witty you are, Charles. Marcus has his heart set on buying Phoebe a special gift, something he remembers seeing long ago—a picture of a family tree."

My eyes widened. "Psst!" I waved. "It's not a family tree. It's—"

Ysabeau's hand made a dismissive gesture as the murmurs on the other end of the line turned eager.

"I believe Sylvia was able to track the item down to a recent sale. But of course she is too discreet to tell me who bought it." Ysabeau nodded through the apologetic response for a few moments. Then the kitten pounced. "You will contact the owner for me, Charles. I cannot bear to see my grandson disappointed at such a happy time."

Lord Sutton was reduced to utter silence.

"The de Clermonts are fortunate to have such a long and happy relationship with Sotheby's. Matthew's tower would have collapsed under the weight of his books if not for meeting Samuel Baker."

"Good Lord." Phoebe's jaw dropped.

"And you managed to clear out most of Matthew's house in Amsterdam. I never liked that fellow or his pictures. You know the one I mean. What was his name? The one whose paintings all look unfinished?"

"Frans Hals," Phoebe whispered, eyes round.

"Frans Hals." Ysabeau nodded approvingly at her future granddaughter-in-law. "Now you and I must convince him to let go of the portrait of that gloomy minister he has hanging over the fireplace in the upstairs parlor."

Phoebe squeaked. I suspected that a trip to Amsterdam would be included in one of her upcoming cataloging adventures.

Lord Sutton made some assurances, but Ysabeau was having none of it.

"I trust you completely, Charles," she interrupted—though it was clear to everyone, Lord Sutton in particular, that she did not. "We can discuss this over coffee tomorrow."

It was Lord Sutton's turn to squeak. A rapid stream of explanations and justifications followed.

"You don't need to come to France. I'm in London. Quite close to your offices on Bond Street, as a matter of fact." Ysabeau tapped her cheek with her finger. "Eleven o'clock? Good. Give my regards to Henrietta. Until tomorrow."

She hung up. "What?" she demanded, looking at Phoebe and me in turn.

"You just manhandled Lord Sutton!" Phoebe exclaimed. "I thought you said diplomacy was required."

"Diplomacy, yes. Elaborate schemes, no. Simple is often best." Ysabeau smiled her tiger smile. "Charles owes Matthew a great deal. In time, Phoebe, you will have many creatures in your debt, too. Then you will see how easy it is to achieve your desires." Ysabeau eyed me sharply. "You look pale, Diana. Aren't you happy that you will soon have all three missing pages from the Book of Life?"

"Yes," I said.

"Then what is the problem?" Ysabeau's eyebrow lifted.

The problem? Once I had the three missing pages, there would be nothing standing between me and the need to steal a manuscript from the Bodleian Library. I was about to become a book thief.

"Nothing," I said faintly.

Back at the desk in the aptly named Chinese Room, I looked again at Kircher's engravings, trying not to think what might happen should Phoebe and Ysabeau find the last missing page. Unable to concentrate on my efforts to locate every engraving of a tree in Kircher's substantial body of work, I rose and went to the window. The street below was quiet, with only the occasional parent leading a child down the sidewalk or a tourist holding a map.

Matthew could always jostle me out of my worries with a snatch of song, or a joke, or (even better) a kiss. Needing to feel closer to him, I prowled down the vacant second-floor hallway until I reached his study. My hand hovered over the knob. After a moment of indecision, I twisted it and went inside.

The aroma of cinnamon and cloves washed over me. Matthew could not have been here in the past twelve months, yet his absence—and my pregnancy—had made me more sensitive to his scent.

Whichever decorator had designed my opulent bedchamber and the confection of a sitting room where I'd spent the morning had not been allowed in here. This room was masculine and unfussy, its walls lined with bookshelves and windows. Splendid globes—one celestial, the other terrestrial—sat in wooden stands, ready to be consulted should a question of astronomy or geography present itself. Natural curiosities were scattered here and there on small tables. I trod a clockwise path around the room as though weaving a spell to bring Matthew back, stopping occasionally to examine a book or to give the celestial globe a spin. The oddest chair I'd ever seen required a longer pause. Its high, deeply curved back had a leather-covered book stand mounted on it, and the seat was shaped rather like a saddle. The only way to occupy the chair would be to sit astride it, as Gallowglass did whenever he turned a chair at the dining-room table. Someone sitting astride the seat and facing the book stand would have the contraption at the perfect height for holding a book or some writing equipment. I tried out the theory by swinging my leg over the padded seat. It was surprisingly comfortable, and I imagined Matthew sitting here, reading for hours in the ample light from the windows.

I dismounted the chair and turned. What I saw hanging over the fireplace made me gasp: a life-size double portrait of Philippe and Ysabeau.

Matthew's mother and father wore splendid clothes from the middle of the eighteenth century, that happy period of fashion when women's gowns did not yet resemble birdcages and men had abandoned the long curls and high heels of the previous century. My fingers itched to touch the surface of the painting, convinced that they would be met with silks and lace rather than canvas.

What was most striking about the portrait was not the vividness of their features (though it would be impossible not to recognize Ysabeau) but the way the artist had captured the relationship between Philippe and his wife.

Philippe de Clermont faced the viewer in a cream-and-blue silk suit, his broad shoulders square to the canvas and his right hand extended toward Ysabeau as if he were about to introduce her. A smile played at his lips, the hint of softness accentuating the stern lines of his face and the long sword that hung from his belt. Philippe's eyes, however, did not meet mine as his position suggested they should. Instead they were directed in a sidelong glance at Ysabeau. Nothing, it seemed, could drag his attention away from the woman he loved. Ysabeau was painted in three-quarter profile, one hand resting lightly in her husband's fingers and the other holding up the folds of her cream-and-gold silk dress as though she were stepping forward to be closer to Philippe. Instead of looking up at her husband, however, Ysabeau stared boldly at the viewer, her lips parted as if surprised to be interrupted in such a private moment.

I heard footsteps behind me and felt the tingling touch of a witch's glance.

"Is that Matthew's father?" Sarah asked, standing at my shoulder and looking up at the grand canvas.

"Yes. It's an amazing likeness," I said with a nod.

"I figured as much, given how perfectly the artist captured Ysabeau." Sarah's attention turned to me. "You don't look well, Diana."

"That's not surprising, is it?" I said. "Matthew is out there, trying to stitch together a family. It may get him killed, and I asked him to do it."

"Not even you could make Matthew do something he didn't want to do," Sarah said bluntly.

"You don't know what happened in New Haven, Sarah. Matthew discovered he had a grandson he didn't know about—Benjamin's son—and a great-grandson, too."

"Fernando told me all about Andrew Hubbard, and Jack, and the blood rage," Sarah replied. "He told me that Baldwin ordered Matthew to kill the boy, too—but you wouldn't let him do it."

I looked up at Philippe, wishing that I understood why he had appointed Matthew the official de Clermont family executioner. "Jack was like a child to us, Sarah. And if Matthew killed Jack, what would stop him from killing the twins if they, too, turn out to have blood rage?"

"Baldwin would never ask Matthew to kill his own flesh and blood," Sarah said.

"Yes," I said sadly. "He would."

"Then it sounds as though Matthew is doing what he has to do," she said firmly. "You need to do your job, too."

"I am," I said, sounding defensive. "My job is to find the missing pages from the Book of Life and then put it back together so that we can use it as leverage—with Baldwin, with Benjamin, even the Congregation."

"You have to take care of the twins, too," Sarah pointed out. "Mooning around up here on your own isn't going to do you—or them—any good."

"Don't you dare play the baby card with me," I said, coldly furious. "I'm trying very hard not to hate my own children—not to mention Jack—right now." It wasn't fair, nor was it logical, but I was blaming them for our separation, even though I had been the one to insist upon it.

"I hated you for a while." Sarah's tone was matter-of-fact. "If not for you, Rebecca would still be alive. Or so I told myself."

Her words came as no surprise. Children always know what grown-ups are thinking. Em had never made me feel that it was my fault that my parents were dead. Of course, she'd known what they were planning—and why. But Sarah was a different story.

"Then I got over it," Sarah continued quietly. "You will, too. One day you'll see the twins and you'll realize that Matthew is right there, staring out at you from an eight-year-old's eyes."

"My life doesn't make sense without Matthew," I said.

"He can't be your whole world, Diana."

"He already is," I whispered. "And if he succeeds in breaking free of the de Clermonts, he's going to need me to be at his side like Ysabeau was for Philippe. I'll never be able to fill her shoes."

"Bullshit." Sarah jammed her hands onto her hips. "And if you think Matthew wants you to be like his mother, you're crazy."

"You have a lot to learn about vampires." Somehow the line didn't sound as convincing when a witch delivered it.

"Oh. Now I see the problem." Sarah's eyes narrowed. "Em said you'd come back to us different—whole. But you're still trying to be something you're not." She pointed an accusatory finger at me. "You've gone all vampire again."

"Stop it, Sarah."

"If Matthew had wanted a vampire bride, he could have his pick. Hell, he could have turned you into a vampire last October in Madison," she said. "You'd willingly given him most of your blood."

"Matthew wouldn't change me," I said.

"I know. He promised me as much the morning before you left." Sarah looked daggers at me. "Matthew doesn't mind that you're a witch. Why do you?" When I didn't reply, she grabbed my hand.

"Where are we going?" I asked as my aunt dragged me down the stairs.

"Out." Sarah stopped in front of the gaggle of vampires standing in the front hall. "Diana needs to remember who she is. You're coming, too, Gallowglass."

"Ooo-kaaay," Gallowglass said uneasily, drawing out the two syllables. "Are we going far?"

"How the hell do I know?" Sarah retorted. "This is my first time in London. We're going to Diana's old house—the one she and Matthew shared in Elizabethan times."

"My house is gone—it burned down in the Great Fire," I said, trying to escape.

"We're going anyway."

"Oh, Christ." Gallowglass threw a set of car keys at Leonard. "Get the car, Lenny. We're going for a Sunday drive."

Leonard grinned. "Right."

"Why is that boy always hanging around?" Sarah asked, watching as the gangly vampire bolted toward the back of the house.

"He belongs to Andrew," I explained.

"In other words he belongs to you," she said with a nod. My jaw dropped. "Oh, yes. I know all about vampires and their crazy ways." Apparently, Fernando didn't have the same reluctance as Matthew and Ysabeau did to tell vampire tales.

Leonard pulled up to the front door with a squeal of tires. He was out of the car and had the rear door opened in a blink. "Where to, madame?"

I did a double take. It was the first time Leonard hadn't stumbled over my name.

"Diana's house, Lenny," Sarah answered. "Her real house, not this overdecorated dust-bunny sanctuary."

"I'm sorry, but it's not there anymore, miss," Leonard said, as though the Great Fire of London had been his fault. Knowing Leonard, this was entirely possible.

"Don't vampires have any imagination?" Sarah asked tartly. "Take me where the house *used* to be."

"Oh." Leonard looked at Gallowglass, wide-eyed.

Gallowglass shrugged. "You heard the lady," my nephew said.

We rocketed across London, heading east. When we passed Temple Bar and moved onto Fleet Street, Leonard turned south toward the river.

"This isn't the way," I said.

"One-way streets, madame," he said. "Things have changed a bit since you were last here." He made a sharp left in front of the Blackfriars Station. I put my hand on the door handle to get out and heard a click as the child-proof locks engaged.

"Stay in the car, Auntie," Gallowglass said.

Leonard jerked the steering wheel to the left once more, and we jostled over pavement and rough road surfaces.

"Blackfriars Lane," I said reading the sign that zipped past. I jiggled the door handle. "Let me out."

The car stopped abruptly, blocking the entrance to a loading dock.

"Your house, madame," Leonard said, sounding like a tour guide and waving at the red-and-cream brick office building that loomed above us. He released the door locks. "It's safe to walk about. Please mind the uneven pavement. Don't want to have to explain to Father H how you broke your leg, do I?"

I stepped out onto the stone sidewalk. It was firmer footing than the usual mud and muck of Water Lane, as we'd called the street in the past. Automatically I headed in the general direction of St. Paul's Cathedral. I felt a hand on my elbow, holding me back.

"You know how Uncle feels about you wandering around town unaccompanied." Gallowglass bowed, and for a moment I saw him in doublet and hose. "At your service, Madame Roydon."

"Where exactly are we?" Sarah asked, scanning the nearby alleys. "This doesn't look like a residential area."

"The Blackfriars. Once upon a time, hundreds of people lived here." It took me only a few steps to reach a narrow cobbled street that used to lead to the inner precincts of the old Blackfriars Priory. I frowned and pointed. "Wasn't the Cardinal's Hat in there?" It was one of Kit Marlowe's watering holes.

"Good memory, Auntie. They call it Playhouse Yard now."

Our house had backed up to that part of the former monastery. Gallowglass and Sarah followed me into the cul-de-sac. Once it had been filled to bursting with merchants, craftsmen, housewives, apprentices, and children—not to mention carts, dogs, and chickens. Today it was deserted.

"Slow down," Sarah said peevishly, struggling to keep up.

It didn't matter how much the old neighborhood had changed. My heart had provided the necessary directions, and my feet followed, swift and sure. In 1591 I would have been surrounded by the ramshackle tenement and entertainment complex that had sprung up within the former priory. Now there were office buildings, a small residence serving well-heeled business executives, more office buildings, and the headquarters of London's apothecaries. I crossed Playhouse Yard and slipped between two buildings.

"Where is she going now?" Sarah asked Gallowglass, her irritation mounting.

"Unless I miss my guess, Auntie's looking for the back way to Baynard's Castle."

At the foot of a narrow thoroughfare called Church Entry, I stopped to get my bearings. If only I could orient myself properly, I could find my way to Mary's house. Where had the Fields' printing shop been? I shut my eyes to avoid the distraction of the incongruous modern buildings.

"Just there," I pointed. "That's where the Fields' shop was. The apothecary lived a few houses along the lane. This way led down to the docks." I kept turning, my arms tracing the line of buildings I saw in my mind. "The door to Monsieur Vallin's silver shop stood here. You could see our back garden from this spot. And here was the old gate that I took to get to Baynard's Castle." I stood for a moment, soaking in the familiar feeling of my former home and wishing I could open my eyes and find myself in the Countess of Pembroke's solar. Mary would have understood my current predicament perfectly and been generous with advice on matters dynastic and political.

"Holy shit," Sarah gasped.

My eyes flew open. A transparent wooden door was a few yards away, set into a crumbling, equally transparent stone wall. Mesmerized, I tried to take a step toward it but was prevented from doing so by the blue and amber threads that swirled tightly around my legs.

"Don't move!" Sarah sounded panicked.

"Why?" I could see her through a scrim of Elizabethan shop fronts.

"You've cast a counterclock. It rewinds images from past times, like a movie," Sarah said, peering at me through the windows of Master Prior's pastry shop.

"Magic," Gallowglass moaned. "Just what we need."

An elderly woman in a neat navy blue cardigan and a pale blue shirt-waist dress who was very much of the here and now came out of the nearby apartment building.

"You'll find this part of London can be a bit tricky, magically speaking," she called out in that authoritative, cheerful tone that only British women of a certain age and social status could produce. "You'll want to take some precautions if you plan on doing any more spell casting."

As the woman approached, I was struck by a sense of déjà vu. She reminded me of one of the witches I'd known in 1591—an earthwitch called Marjorie Cooper, who had helped me to weave my first spell.

"I'm Linda Crosby." She smiled, and the resemblance to Marjorie became more pronounced. "Welcome home, Diana Bishop. We've been expecting you."

I stared at her, dumbfounded.

"I'm Diana's aunt," Sarah said, wading into the silence. "Sarah Bishop."

"Pleasure," Linda said warmly, shaking Sarah's hand. Both witches stared down at my feet. During our brief introductions, time's blue and amber bindings had loosened somewhat, fading away one by one as they were absorbed back into the fabric of the Blackfriars. Monsieur Vallin's front door was still all too evident, however.

"I'd give it a few more minutes. You are a timewalker, after all," Linda said, perching on one of the curved benches that surrounded a circular brick planter. It occupied the same spot as had the wellhead in the Cardinal's Hat yard.

"Are you one of Hubbard's family?" Sarah asked, reaching into her pocket. Out came her forbidden cigarettes. She offered one to Linda.

"I'm a witch," Linda said, taking the cigarette. "And I live in the City of London. So, yes—I am a member of Father Hubbard's family. Proudly so."

Gallowglass lit the witches' cigarettes and then his own. The three puffed away like chimneys, careful to direct the smoke so it didn't waft toward me.

"I haven't met Hubbard yet," Sarah confessed. "Most of the vampires I know don't think much of him."

"Really?" Linda asked with interest. "How very odd. Father Hubbard is a beloved figure here. He protects everybody's interests, be they daemon, vampire, or witch. So many creatures have wanted to move into his territory that it's led to a housing crisis. He can't buy property fast enough to satisfy the demand."

"He's still a wanker," Gallowglass muttered.

"Language!" Linda said, shocked.

"How many witches are there in the city?" Sarah asked.

"Three dozen," Linda responded. "We limit the numbers, of course, or it would be madness in the Square Mile."

"The Madison coven is the same size," Sarah said approvingly. "Makes it easier to hold the meetings, that's for sure."

"We gather once a month in Father Hubbard's crypt. He lives in what's left of the Greyfriars Priory, just over there." Linda aimed her cigarette at a point north of Playhouse Yard. "These days most of the creatures in the City proper are vampires—financiers and hedge-fund managers and such. They don't like to hire out their meeting rooms to witches. No offense, sir."

"None taken," Gallowglass said mildly.

"The Greyfriars? Has Lady Agnes moved on?" I asked, surprised. The ghost's antics had been the talk of the town when I lived here.

"Oh, no. Lady Agnes is still there. With Father Hubbard's help, we were able to broker an agreement between her and Queen Isabella. They seem to be on friendly terms now—which is more than I can say for the ghost of Elizabeth Barton. Ever since that novel about Cromwell came out, she's been impossible." Linda eyed my belly speculatively. "At our Mabon tea this year, Elizabeth Barton said you're having twins."

"I am." Even the ghosts of London knew my business.

"It's so difficult to tell which of Elizabeth's prophecies are to be taken seriously when every one of them is accompanied by shrieking. It's all so . . . vulgar." Linda pursed her lips in disapproval, and Sarah nodded sympathetically.

"Um, I hate to break this up, but I think my spell for the counterclock thingy expired." Not only could I see my own ankle (provided I lifted my leg up—otherwise the babies were in the way), but Monsieur Vallin's door had utterly vanished.

"Expired?" Linda laughed. "You make it sound as though your magic has a sell-by date."

"I certainly didn't tell it to stop," I grumbled. Then again, I had never told it to start either.

"It stopped because you didn't wind it up tight enough," Sarah said. "If you don't give a counterclock a good crank, it runs down."

"And we do recommend that you not stand on top of the counterclock once you cast it," Linda said, sounding a bit like my middle-school gym teacher. "You want to address the spell without blinking, then step away from it at the last minute."

"My mistake," I murmured. "Can I move now?"

Linda surveyed Playhouse Yard with a crinkled brow. "Yes, I do believe it's perfectly safe now," she proclaimed.

I groaned and rubbed at my back. Standing still for so long had made it ache, and my feet felt like they were going to explode. I propped one of them upon the bench where Sarah and Linda were sitting and bent to loosen the ties on my sneakers.

"What's that?" I said, peering through the bench's slats. I reached down and retrieved a scroll of paper tied up with a red ribbon. The fingers on my right hand tingled when I touched it, and the pentacle at my wrist swirled with color.

"It's tradition for people to leave requests for magic in the yard. There's always been a concentration of power associated with this spot." Linda's voice softened. "A great witch lived here once, you see. Legend says she'll return one day, to remind us of all we once were and could be again. We haven't forgotten her and trust that she will not forget us."

The Blackfriars was haunted by my past self. Part of me had died when we left London. It was the part that had once been able to juggle being Matthew's wife, Annie and Jack's mother, Mary Sidney's alchemical assistant, and a weaver-in-training. And another part of me had joined it in the grave when I walked away from Matthew on the mountain outside New Haven. I buried my head in my hands.

"I've made a mess of things," I whispered.

"No, you dove into the deep end and got in over your head," Sarah replied. "This is what Em and I worried about when you and Matthew first got involved. You both moved so fast, and we knew that neither of you had thought about what this relationship was going to require."

"We knew we would face plenty of opposition."

"Oh, you two had the star-crossed-lovers part down—and I understand how romantic it can be to feel it's just the two of you against the world." Sarah chuckled. "Em and I were star-crossed lovers, after all. In upstate New York in the 1970s, nothing was more star-crossed than two women falling in love."

Her tone grew serious. "But the sun always rises the next morning. Fairy tales don't tell you much about what happens to star-crossed lovers in the bright light of day, but somehow you have to figure out how to be happy."

"We were happy here," I said quietly. "Weren't we, Gallowglass?"

"Aye, Auntie, you were—even with Matthew's spymaster breathing down his neck and the whole country on the lookout for witches." Gallowglass shook his head. "How you managed it, I've never understood."

"You managed it because neither of you were trying to be something you weren't. Matthew wasn't trying to be civilized, and you weren't trying to be human," Sarah said. "You weren't trying to be Rebecca's perfect daughter, or Matthew's perfect wife, or a tenured professor at Yale either."

She took my hands in hers, scroll and all, and turned them so the palms faced up. My weaver's cords stood out bright against the pale flesh.

"You're a witch, Diana. A weaver. Don't deny your power. Use it." Sarah looked pointedly at my left hand. "All of it."

My phone pinged in the pocket of my jacket. I scrambled for it, hoping against hope it was some kind of message from Matthew. He'd promised to let me know how he was doing. The display indicated there was a text waiting from him. I opened it eagerly.

The message contained no words that the Congregation could use against us, only a picture of Jack. He was sitting on a porch, his face split into a wide grin as he listened to someone—a man, though his back was to the camera and I could see nothing more than the black hair curling around his collar—tell a story as only a southerner could. Marcus stood behind Jack, one hand draped casually over his shoulder. Like Jack, he was grinning.

They looked like two ordinary young men enjoying a laugh over the weekend. Jack fit perfectly into Marcus's family, as though he belonged.

"Who's that with Marcus?" Sarah said, looking over my shoulder.

"Jack." I touched his face. "I'm not sure who the other man is."

"That's Ransome." Gallowglass sniffed. "Marcus's eldest, and he puts Lucifer to shame. Not the best role model for young Jack, but I reckon Matthew knows best."

"Look at the lad," Linda said fondly, standing so she could get a look at the picture, too. "I've never seen Jack look so happy—except when he was telling stories about Diana, of course."

St. Paul's bells rang the hour. I pushed the button on my phone, dimming the display. I would look at the picture again later, in private.

"See, honey. Matthew is doing just fine," Sarah said, her voice soothing.

But without seeing his eyes, gauging the set of his shoulders, hearing the tone of his voice, I couldn't be sure.

"Matthew's doing his job," I reminded myself, standing up. "I need to get back to mine."

"Does that mean you're ready to do whatever it takes to keep your family together like you did in 1591—even if higher magics are involved?" Sarah's eyebrow shot up in open query.

"Yes." I sounded more convinced than I felt.

"Higher magics? How deliciously dark." Linda beamed. "Can I help?"

"No," I said quickly.

"Possibly," Sarah said at the same time.

"Well, if you need us, give a ring. Leonard knows how to reach me," Linda said. "The London coven is at your disposal. And if you were to come to one of our meetings, it would be quite a boost to morale."

"We'll see," I said vaguely, not wanting to make a promise I couldn't keep. "The situation is complicated, and I wouldn't want to get anyone into trouble."

"Vampires are always trouble," Linda said with a primly disapproving look, "holding grudges and going off half-cocked on some vendetta or other. It's really very trying. Still, we are all one big family, as Father Hubbard reminds us."

"One big family." I looked at our old neighborhood. "Maybe Father Hubbard was on the right track all along."

"Well, we think so. Do consider coming to our next meeting. Doris makes a divine Battenberg cake."

Sarah and Linda swapped telephone numbers just in case, and Gallowglass went to Apothecaries' Hall and let out an earsplitting whistle to call Leonard around with the car. I took the opportunity to snap a picture of Playhouse Yard and sent it to Matthew without a comment or a caption.

Magic was nothing more than desire made real, after all.

The October breeze came off the Thames and carried my unspoken wishes into the sky, where they wove a spell to bring Matthew safely back to me.

A slice of Battenberg cake with a moist pink-and-yellow checkerboard interior and canary-colored icing sat before me at our secluded table at the Wolseley, along with still more contraband black tea. I lifted the lid on the teapot and drank in its malty aroma, sighing happily. I'd been craving tea and cake ever since our unexpected meeting with Linda Crosby at the Blackfriars.

Hamish, who was a breakfast regular there, had commandeered a large table at the bustling Piccadilly restaurant for the entire morning and proceeded to treat the space—and the staff—as though they were his office. Thus far he'd taken a dozen phone calls, made several lunch engagements (three of them for the same day next week, I noted with alarm), and read every London daily in its entirety. He had also, bless him, wheedled my cake out of the pastry chef hours before it was normally served, citing my condition as justification. The speed with which the request was met was either an additional indication of Hamish's importance or a sign that the young man who wielded the whisks and rolling pins understood the special relationship between pregnant women and sugar.

"This is taking forever," Sarah grumbled. She'd bolted down a soft-boiled egg with toast batons, consumed an ocean of black coffee, and had been dividing her attention between her wristwatch and the door ever since.

"When it comes to extortion, Granny doesn't like to rush." Gallowglass smiled affably at the ladies at a nearby table, who were casting admiring glances at his muscular, tattooed arms.

"If they don't arrive soon, I'll be walking back to Westminster under my own steam thanks to all the caffeine." Hamish waved down the manager. "Another cappuccino, Adam. Better make it a decaf."

"Of course, sir. More toast and jam?"

"Please," Hamish said, handing Adam the empty toast rack. "Strawberry. You know I can't resist the strawberry."

"And why is it again that we couldn't wait for Granny and Phoebe at the house?" Gallowglass shifted nervously on his tiny seat. The chair was not designed for a man of his size, but rather for MPs, socialites, morning-television personalities, and other such insubstantial persons.

"Diana's neighbors are wealthy and paranoid. There hasn't been any activity at the house for nearly a year. Suddenly there are people around at all hours and Allens of Mayfair is making daily deliveries." Hamish made room on the table for his fresh cappuccino. "We don't want them thinking you're an international drug cartel and calling the police. West End Central station is full of witches, especially the CID. And don't forget: You're not under Hubbard's protection outside the City limits."

"Hmph. You're not worried about the coppers. You just didn't want to miss anything." Gallowglass wagged a finger at him. "I'm on to you, Hamish."

"Here's Fernando," Sarah said in a tone suggesting that deliverance had come at last.

Fernando tried to hold open the door for Ysabeau, but Adam beat him to it. My mother-in-law looked like a youthful film star, and every male head in the room turned as she entered with Phoebe in her wake. Fernando hung back, his dark coat the perfect backdrop for Ysabeau's off-white and taupe ensemble.

"No wonder Ysabeau prefers to stay at home," I said. She stood out like a beacon on a foggy day.

"Philippe always said it was easier to withstand a siege than to cross a room at Ysabeau's side. He had to fend off her admirers with more than a stick, I can tell you." Gallowglass rose as his grandmother approached. "Hello, Granny. Did they give in to your demands?"

Ysabeau offered her cheek to be kissed. "Of course."

"In part," Phoebe said hastily.

"Was there trouble?" Gallowglass asked Fernando.

"None worth mentioning." Fernando pulled out a chair. Ysabeau slid onto it gracefully, crossing her slim ankles.

"Charles was most accommodating when you consider how many company policies I expected him to violate," she said, refusing the menu Adam offered her with a little moue of distaste. "Champagne, please."

"The hideous painting you took off his hands will more than compensate for it," Fernando said, installing Phoebe into her place at the table. "Whatever made you buy it, Ysabeau?"

"It is not hideous, though abstract expressionism is an acquired taste," she admitted. "The painting is raw, mysterious—sensual. I will give it to the Louvre and force Parisians to expand their minds. Mark my words: This time next year, Clyfford Still will be at the top of every museum's wish list."

"Expect a call from Coutts," Phoebe murmured to Hamish. "She wouldn't haggle."

"There is no need to worry. Both Sotheby's and Coutts know I am good for it." Ysabeau extracted a slip of paper from her sleek leather bag and extended it to me. "Voilà."

"T. J. Weston, Esquire." I looked up from the slip. "This is who bought the page from Ashmole 782?"

"Possibly." Phoebe's reply was terse. "The file contained nothing but a sales slip—he paid cash—and six pieces of misdirected correspondence. Not a single address we have for Weston is valid."

"It shouldn't be that hard to locate him. How many T. J. Westons can there be?" I wondered.

"More than three hundred," Phoebe replied. "I checked the national directory. And don't assume that T. J. Weston is a man. We don't know the buyer's sex or nationality. One of the addresses is in Denmark."

"Do not be so negative, Phoebe. We will make calls. Use Hamish's connections. And Leonard is outside. He will drive us where we need to go." Ysabeau looked unconcerned.

"My connections?" Hamish buried his head in his hands and groaned. "This could take weeks. I might as well live at the Wolseley, given all the coffees I'm going to have with people."

"It won't take weeks, and you don't need to worry about your caffeine intake." I put the paper in my pocket, slung my messenger bag over my shoulder, and hoisted myself to my feet, almost upsetting the table in the process.

"Lord bless us, Auntie. You get bigger by the hour."

"Thank you for noticing, Gallowglass." I'd managed to wedge myself between a coatrack, the wall, and my chair. He leaped up to extricate me.

"How can you be so sure?" Sarah asked me, looking as doubtful as Phoebe.

Wordlessly I held up my hands. They were multicolored and shining.

"Ah. Let us get Diana home," Ysabeau said. "I do not think the proprietor would appreciate having a dragon in his restaurant any more than I did having one in my house."

"Put your hands in your pockets," Sarah hissed. They really were rather bright.

I was not yet at the waddling stage of pregnancy, but it was still a challenge to make my way through the close tables, especially with my hands jammed into my raincoat.

"Please clear the way for my daughter-in-law," Ysabeau said imperiously, taking my elbow and tugging me along. Men stood, pulled their chairs in, and fawned as she passed.

"My husband's stepmother," I whispered to one outraged woman who was gripping her fork like a weapon. She was appropriately disturbed by the notion that I had married a boy of twelve and gotten pregnant by him, for Ysabeau was far too young to have children older than that. "Second marriage. Younger wife. You know how it is."

"So much for blending in," Hamish muttered. "Every creature in W1 will know that Ysabeau de Clermont is in town after this. Can't you control her, Gallowglass?"

"Control Granny?" Gallowglass roared with laughter and slapped Hamish on the back.

"This is a nightmare," Hamish said as more heads turned. He reached the front door. "See you tomorrow, Adam."

"Your usual table for one, sir?" Adam asked, offering Hamish his umbrella.

"Yes. Thank God."

Hamish stepped into a waiting car and headed back to his office in the City. Leonard tucked me into the rear of the Mercedes with Phoebe, and Ysabeau and Fernando took the passenger seat. Gallowglass lit a cigarette and ambled along the sidewalk, emitting more smoke than a Mississippi steamboat. We lost sight of him outside the Coach and Horses, where Gallowglass indicated through a series of silent gestures that he was going in for a drink.

"Coward," Fernando said, shaking his head.

* * *

"Now what?" Sarah asked after we were back at Clairmont House in the cozy morning room. Though the front parlor was comfortable and welcoming, this snug spot was my favorite room in the house. It contained a ragtag assemblage of furniture, including a stool that I was certain had been in our house in the Blackfriars, which made the room feel as if it had been lived in rather than decorated.

"Now we find T. J. Weston, Esquire, whoever she or he may be." I propped up my feet on the age-blackened Elizabethan stool with a groan, letting the warmth from the crackling fire seep into my aching bones.

"It will be like finding a needle in a haystack," Phoebe said, allowing herself the small discourtesy of a sigh.

"Not if Diana uses her magic it won't," Sarah said confidently.

"Magic?" Ysabeau's head swung around, and her eyes sparkled.

"I thought you didn't approve of witches?" My mother-in-law had made her feelings on this matter known from the very beginning of my relationship with Matthew.

"Ysabeau might not like witches, but she's got nothing except admiration for magic," Fernando said.

"You draw a mighty fine line, Ysabeau," Sarah said with a shake of her head.

"What kind of magic?" Gallowglass had returned, unnoticed, and was standing in the hall, his hair and coat dripping with moisture. He rather resembled Lobero after a long run in the emperor's Stag Moat.

"A candle spell can work when you're searching for a lost object," Sarah said thoughtfully. She was something of an expert on candle spells, since Em had been famous for leaving her things all around the house—and Madison.

"I remember a witch who used some earth and a knotted piece of linen," Ysabeau said. Sarah and I turned to her, mouths open in astonishment. She drew herself straight and regarded us with hauteur. "You need not look so surprised. I have known a great many witches over the years."

Fernando ignored Ysabeau and spoke to Phoebe instead. "You said one of the addresses for T. J. Weston was in Denmark. What about the others?"

"All from the UK: four in England and one in Northern Ireland," Phoebe said. "In England the addresses were all in the south—Devon, Cornwall, Essex, Wiltshire."

"Do you really need to meddle with magic, Auntie?" Gallowglass looked concerned. "Surely there's a way for Nathaniel to use his computers and find this person. Did you write the addresses down, Phoebe?"

"Of course." She produced a crumpled Boots receipt covered with handwriting. Gallowglass looked at it dubiously. "I couldn't very well take a notebook into the file room. It would have been suspicious."

"Very clever," Ysabeau assured her. "I will send the addresses on to Nathaniel so he can get to work on them."

"I still think magic would be faster—so long as I can figure out what spell to use," I said. "I'll need something visual. I'm better with visuals than with candles."

"What about a map?" Gallowglass suggested. "Matthew must have a map or two in his library upstairs. If not, I could go around to Hatchards and see what they've got." He had only just returned, but Gallowglass was clearly eager to be outdoors in the frigid downpour. It was, I supposed, as close to the weather in the middle of the Atlantic as he was likely to find.

"A map might work—if it were big enough," I said. "We'll be no better off if the spell is only able to pinpoint that T. J. Weston's location is in Wiltshire." I wondered if it would be possible for Leonard to drive me around the county with a box of candles.

"There's a lovely map shop just by Shoreditch," Leonard said proudly, as though he were personally responsible for its location. "They make big maps what hang on walls. I'll give them a ring."

"What will you need besides the map?" Sarah asked. "A compass?"

"It's too bad I don't have the mathematical instrument Emperor Rudolf gave me," I said. "It was always whirring around as though it were trying to find something." At first I'd thought its movements indicated that somebody was searching for Matthew and me. Over time I'd wondered if the compendium swung into action whenever someone was searching for the Book of Life.

Phoebe and Ysabeau exchanged a look.

"Excuse me." Phoebe slipped out of the room.

"That brass gadget that Annie and Jack called a witch's clock?" Gallowglass chuckled. "I doubt that would be much help, Auntie. It couldn't even keep proper time, and Master Habermel's latitude charts were a bit . . . er, fanciful." Habermel had been utterly defeated by my request to include a reference to the New World and had simply picked a coordinate that for all I knew would have put me in Tierra del Fuego.

"Divination is the way to go," Sarah said. "We'll put candles on the four cardinal points of north, east, south, and west, then sit you in the center with a bowl of water and see what develops."

"If I'm going to divine by water, I'll need more space than this." The breakfast room would fill up with witchwater at an alarming speed.

"We could use the garden," Ysabeau suggested. "Or the ballroom upstairs. I never did think the Trojan War was a suitable subject for the frescoes, so it would be no great loss if they were damaged."

"We might want to tune up your third eye before you start, too," Sarah said, looking critically at my forehead as though it were a radio.

Phoebe returned with a small box. She handed it to Ysabeau.

"Perhaps we should see if this can help first." Ysabeau drew Master Habermel's compendium from the cardboard container. "Alain packed up some of your things from Sept-Tours. He thought they would make you feel more at home here."

The compendium was a beautiful instrument, expertly fashioned from brass, gilded and silvered to make it shine, and loaded with everything from a storage slot for paper and pencil to a compass, latitude tables, and a small clock. At the moment the instrument appeared to be going haywire, for the dials on the face of the compendium were spinning around. We could hear the steady whir of the gears.

Sarah peered at the instrument. "Definitely enchanted."

"It's going to wear itself out." Gallowglass extended a thick finger, ready to give the hands on the clock a poke to slow them down.

"No touching," Sarah said sharply. "You can never anticipate how a bewitched object will respond to unwanted interference."

"Did you ever put it near the picture of the chemical wedding, Auntie?" Gallowglass asked. "If you're right, and Master Habermel's toy acts up when someone is looking for the Book of Life, then maybe seeing the page will quiet it."

"Good idea. The picture of the chemical wedding is in the Chinese Room along with the picture of the dragons." I lumbered to my feet. "I left them on the card table."

Ysabeau was gone before I could straighten up. She was back quickly, holding the two pages as though they were glass and might shatter at any moment. As soon as I laid them on the table, the hand on the compendium dial began to swing slowly from left to right instead of revolving around its central pin. When I picked the pages up, the compendium began to spin again—though slower than it had before.

"I do not think the compendium registers when someone is looking for the Book of Life," Fernando said. "The instrument itself seems to be searching for the book. Now that it senses some of the pages are nearby, it is narrowing its focus."

"How strange." I put the pages back on the table and watched in fascination as the hand slowed and resumed its pendulum swing.

"Can you use it to find the last missing page?" Ysabeau said, staring at the compendium with equal fascination.

"Only if I drive all over England, Wales, and Scotland with it." I wondered how long it would take me to damage the delicate, priceless instrument, holding it on my lap while Gallowglass or Leonard sped up the M40.

"Or you could devise a locator spell. With a map and that contraption, you might be able to triangulate the missing page's position," Sarah said thoughtfully, tapping her lips with her finger.

"What kind of locator spell do you have in mind?" This went well beyond bell, book, and candle or writing a charm on a moonwort pod.

"We'd have to try a few and see—test them to figure out which is best," Sarah mused. "Then you'd need to perform it under the right conditions, with plenty of magical support so the spell doesn't get bent out of shape."

"Where are you going to find magical support in Mayfair?" Fernando asked.

"Linda Crosby," my aunt and I said at the same time.

Sarah and I spent more than a week testing and retesting spells in the basement of the house in Mayfair as well as the tiny kitchen of Linda's flat in the Blackfriars. After nearly drowning Tabitha and having the fire brigade show up twice in Playhouse Yard, I had finally managed to cobble together some knots and a handful of magically significant items into a locator spell that might—just might—work.

The London coven met in a portion of the medieval Greyfriars crypt that had survived a series of disasters over its long history, from the dissolution of the monasteries to the Blitz. Atop the crypt stood Andrew Hubbard's house: the church's former bell tower. It was twelve stories tall and had only one large room on each of its floors. Outside the tower he had planted a pleasant garden in the one corner of the old churchyard that had resisted urban renewal.

"What a strange house," Ysabeau murmured.

"Andrew is a very strange vampire," I replied with a shiver.

"Father H likes lofty spaces, that's all. He says they make him feel closer to God." Leonard rapped on the door again.

"I just felt a ghost go by," Sarah said, drawing her coat more closely around her. There was no mistaking the cold sensation.

"I don't feel anything," Leonard said with a vampire's cavalier disregard for something as corporeal as warmth. His rapping turned to pounding. "Come on, sunshine!"

"Patience, Leonard. We are not all twenty-year-old vampires!" Linda Crosby said crossly once she'd wrestled the door open. "There are a prodigious number of stairs to climb."

Happily, we had only to descend one floor from the main entrance level to reach the room that Hubbard had set aside for the use of the City of London's official coven.

"Welcome to our gathering!" Linda said as she led us down the staircase.

Halfway down, I stopped with a gasp.

"Is that . . . you?" Sarah stared at the walls in amazement.

The walls were covered with images of me—weaving my first spell, calling forth a rowan tree, watching Corra as she flew along the Thames, standing beside the witches who had taken me under their wing when I was first learning about my magic. There was Goody Alsop, the coven's elder, with her fine features and stooped shoulders; the midwife Susanna Norman; and the three remaining witches Catherine Streeter, Elizabeth Jackson, and Marjorie Cooper.

As for the artist, that was clear without a signature. Jack had painted these images, smearing the walls with wet plaster and adding the lines and color so that they became a permanent part of the building. Smoke-stained, mottled with damp, and cracked with age, they had somehow retained their beauty.

"We are fortunate to have such a room to work in," Linda said, beaming.

"Your journey has long been a source of inspiration for London's witches. Come and meet your sisters."

The three witches waiting at the bottom of the stairs studied me with interest, their glances snapping and crackling against my skin. They might not have the power of the Garlickhythe gathering in 1591, but these witches were not devoid of talent.

"Here is our Diana Bishop, come back to us once more," Linda said. "She has brought her aunt with her, Sarah Bishop, and her mother-in-law, who I trust needs no introduction."

"None at all," said the most elderly of the four witches. "We've all heard cautionary tales about Mélisande de Clermont."

Linda had warned me the coven had some doubts about tonight's proceedings. She had handpicked the witches who would help us: firewitch Sybil Bonewits, waterwitch Tamsin Soothtell, and windwitch Cassandra Kyteler. Linda's powers relied heavily on the element of earth. So, too, did Sarah's.

"Times change," Ysabeau said crisply. "If you would like me to leave . . ."

"Nonsense." Linda shot a warning glance at her fellow witch. "Diana asked for you to be here when she cast her spell. We will all muddle through somehow. Won't we, Cassandra?"

The elderly witch gave a curt nod.

"Make way for the maps if you please, ladies!" Leonard said, his arms full of tubes. He dumped them on a rickety table encrusted with wax and beat a fast retreat up the stairs. "Call me if you need anything." The door to the crypt slammed shut behind him.

Linda directed the placement of the maps, for after much fiddling we had found that the best results came from using a huge map of the British Isles surrounded by individual county maps. The map of Great Britain alone took up a section of floor that was around six feet by four feet.

"This looks like a bad elementary-school geography project," Sarah muttered as she straightened a map of Dorset.

"It may not be pretty, but it works," I replied, drawing Master Habermel's compendium from my bag. Fernando had devised a protective sleeve for it using one of Gallowglass's clean socks. It was miraculously undamaged. I got out my phone, too, and took a few shots of the murals on the wall. They made me feel closer to Jack—and to Matthew.

"Where should I put the pages from the Book of Life?" Ysabeau had been given custody of the precious sheets of vellum.

"Give the picture of the chemical wedding to Sarah. You hold on to the one with the two dragons," I said.

"Me?" Ysabeau's eyes widened. It had been a controversial decision, but I had prevailed against Sarah and Linda in the end.

"I hope you don't mind. The chemical-wedding picture came to me from my parents. The dragons belonged to Andrew Hubbard. I thought we could balance the spell by keeping them in witch and vampire hands." All my instincts told me this was the right decision.

"Of c-course." Ysabeau's tongue slipped on the familiar words.

"It will be all right. I promise." I gave her arm a squeeze. "Sarah will be standing opposite, and Linda and Tamsin will be on either side."

"You should be worrying about the spell. Ysabeau can take care of herself." Sarah handed me a pot of red ink and a quill pen made from a white feather with striking brown and gray markings.

"It's time, ladies," Linda said with a brisk clap. She distributed brown candles to the other members of the London coven. Brown was a propitious color for finding lost objects. It had the added benefit of grounding the spell—which I was sorely in need of, given my inexperience. Each witch took her place outside the ring of county maps, and they all lit their candles with whispered spells. The flames were unnaturally large and bright—true witch's candles.

Linda escorted Ysabeau to her place just below the south coast of England. Sarah stood across from her, as promised, above the north coast of Scotland. Linda walked clockwise three times around the carefully arranged witches, maps, and vampire, sprinkling salt to cast a protective circle.

Once everyone was in her proper place, I took the stopper out of the bottle of red ink. The distinctive scent of dragon's-blood resin filled the air. There were other ingredients in the ink, too, including more than a few drops of my own blood. Ysabeau's nostrils flared at the coppery tang. I dipped the quill pen into the ink and pressed the chiseled silver nib onto a narrow slip of parchment. It had taken me two days to find someone willing to make me a pen using a feather from a barn owl—far longer than it would have in Elizabethan London.

Letter by letter, working from the outside of the parchment to the center, I wrote the name of the person I sought.

T, N, J, O, W, T, E, S

T J WESTON

I folded the parchment carefully to hide the name. Now it was my turn to walk outside the sacred circle and work another binding. After slipping Master Habermel's compendium into the pocket of my sweater along with the parchment rectangle, I began a circular perambulation from the place between the firewitch and the waterwitch. I passed by Tamsin and Ysabeau, Linda and Cassandra, Sarah and Sybil.

When I arrived back at the place where I began, a shimmering line ran outside the salt, illuminating the witches' astonished faces. I turned my left hand palm up. For a moment there was a flicker of color on my index finger, but it was gone before I could determine what it had been. Even without the missing hue, my hand gleamed with gold, silver, black, and white lines of power that pulsed under the skin. The streaks twisted and twined into the orobouros-shaped tenth knot that surrounded the prominent blue veins at my wrist.

I stepped through a narrow gap in the shimmering line and drew the circle closed. The power roared through it, keening and crying out for release. Corra wanted out, too. She was restless, shifting and stretching inside me.

"Patience, Corra," I said, stepping carefully over the salt and onto the map of England. Each step took me closer to the spot that represented London. At last my feet rested on the City. Corra released her wings with a snap of skin and bone and a cry of frustration.

"Fly, Corra!" I commanded.

Free at last, Corra shot around the room, sparks streaming from her wings and tongues of flame escaping from her mouth. As she gained altitude and found air currents that would help to carry her where she wanted to go, the beating of her wings slowed. Corra caught sight of her portrait and cooed in approval, reaching out to pat the wall with her tail.

I pulled the compendium from my pocket and held it in my right hand. The folded slip of parchment went into my left. My arms stretched wide, and I waited while the threads that bound the world and filled the Greyfriars crypt snaked and slithered over me, seeking out the cords that had been absorbed into my hands. When they met, the cords lengthened and expanded, filling my whole body with power. They knotted around my joints, created a protective web around my womb and heart, and traveled along veins and the pathways forged by nerves and sinews.

I recited my spell:

Missing pages
Lost and found
Where is Weston
On this ground?

Then I blew on the slip of parchment, and Weston's name caught light, the red ink bursting into flame. I cupped the fiery words in my palm where they continued to burn bright. Overhead, Corra circled above the map watchfully, her keen eyes alert.

The compendium's gears whirred, and the hands on the main dial moved. A roaring filled my ears as a bright thread of gold shot out from the compendium. It spun outward until it met up with the two pages from the Book of Life. Another thread came from the compendium's gilded dial. It slithered off to a map at Linda's feet.

Corra swept down and pounced on the spot, crying out with triumph as though she had caught some unsuspecting prey. A town's name illuminated, a bright burst of flame leaving the charred outlines of letters.

The spell complete, the roaring diminished. Power receded from my body, loosening the knotted cords. But they did not recoil back into my hands. They stayed where they were, running through me as if they had formed a new bodily system.

When the power had retreated, I swayed slightly. Ysabeau started forward.

"No!" Sarah cried. "Don't break the circle, Ysabeau."

My mother-in-law clearly thought this was madness. Without Matthew here she was prepared to be overprotective in his stead. But Sarah was right: Nobody could break the circle but me. Feet dragging, I returned to the same spot where I'd started weaving my spell. Sybil and Tamsin smiled encouragingly as the fingers on my left hand flicked and furled, releasing the circle's hold. All that remained to do then was to trudge around the circle counterclockwise, unmaking the magic.

Linda was much quicker, briskly walking her own path in reverse. The moment she was through, both Ysabeau and Sarah rushed to my side. The London witches raced to the map that revealed Weston's location.

"*Dieu,* I have not seen magic like that for centuries. Matthew told me true when he said you were a formidable witch," Ysabeau said with admiration.

"Very nice spell casting, honey." Sarah was proud of me. "Not a single wobble of doubt or moment of hesitation."

"Did it work?" I certainly hoped so. Another spell of that magnitude would require weeks of rest first. I joined the witches at the map. "Oxfordshire?"

"Yes," Linda said doubtfully. "But I fear we may not have asked a specific enough question."

There, on the map, was the blackened outline of a very English-sounding village called Chipping Weston.

"The initials were on the paper, but I forgot to include them in the words of the spell." My heart sank.

"It is far too soon to admit defeat." Ysabeau already had her phone out and was dialing. "Phoebe? Does a T. J. Weston live in Chipping Weston?"

The possibility that T. J. Weston could live in a town called Weston had not occurred to any of us. We waited for Phoebe's reply.

Ysabeau's face relaxed in sudden relief. "Thank you. We will be home soon. Tell Marthe that Diana will need a compress for her head and cold cloths for her feet."

Both were aching, and my legs were more swollen with each passing minute. I looked at Ysabeau gratefully.

"Phoebe tells me there is a T. J. Weston in Chipping Weston," Ysabeau reported. "He lives in the Manor House."

"Oh, well done. Well done, Diana." Linda beamed at me. The other London witches clapped, as though I had just performed a particularly difficult piano solo without flubbing a note.

"This is not a night we will soon forget," Tamsin said, her voice shaking with emotion, "for tonight a weaver came back to London, bringing the past and future together so that old worlds might die and new be born."

"That's Mother Shipton's prophecy," I said, recognizing the words.

"Ursula Shipton was born Ursula Soothtell. Her aunt, Alice Soothtell, was my ancestor," Tamsin said. "She was a weaver, like you."

"*You* are related to Ursula Shipton!" Sarah exclaimed.

"I am," Tamsin replied. "The women in my family have kept the knowledge of weavers alive, even though we have had only one other weaver born into the family in more than five hundred years. But Ursula prophesied that the power was not lost forever. She foresaw the years of darkness, when witches would forget weavers and all they represent: hope, rebirth, change. Ursula saw this night, too."

"How so?" I thought of the few lines of Mother Shipton's prophecy that I knew. None of them seemed relevant to tonight's events.

"'*And those that live will ever fear / The dragon's tail for many year, / But time erases memory. / You think it strange. But it will be,*'" Tamsin recited. She nodded, and the other witches joined in, speaking in one voice.

And before the race is built anew,
A silver serpent comes to view
And spews out men of like unknown
To mingle with the earth now grown
Cold from its heat, and these men can
Enlighten the minds of future man.

"The dragon and the serpent?" I shivered.

"They foretell the advent of a new golden age for creatures," Linda said. "It has been too long in coming, but we all are pleased to have lived to see it."

It was too much responsibility. First the twins, then Matthew's scion, and now the future of the species? My hand covered the bump where our children grew. I felt pulled in too many directions, the parts of me that were witch battling with the parts that were scholar, wife, and now mother.

I looked at the walls. In 1591 every part of me had fit together. In 1591 I had been myself.

"Do not worry," Sybil said gently. "You will be whole once more. Your vampire will help you."

"We will all help you," Cassandra said.

27

Stop here," Gallowglass ordered. Leonard stepped on the Mercedes' brakes, and they engaged immediately and silently in front of the Old Lodge's gatehouse. Since no one was prepared to wait in London for news of the third page except for Hamish, who was busy saving the euro from collapse, my full entourage had come along, Fernando following in one of Matthew's inexhaustible supply of Range Rovers.

"No. Not here. Go on to the house," I told Leonard. The gatehouse would remind me too much of Matthew. As we passed down the drive, the Old Lodge's familiar outlines emerged from the Oxfordshire fog. It was strange to see it again without the surrounding fields filled with sheep and piles of hay, and only one chimney sending a thin plume of smoke into the sky. I rested my forehead against the car's cold window and let the black-and-white half-timbering and the diamond-shaped panes of glass remind me of other, happier times.

I sat back in the deep leather seat and reached for my phone. There was no new message from Matthew. I consoled myself with looking once more at the two pictures he'd already sent: Jack with Marcus and Jack sitting on his own with a sketch pad propped on his knee, utterly absorbed in what he was doing. This last picture had arrived after I sent Matthew my shot of the Greyfriars frescoes. Thanks to the magic of photography, I had captured the ghost of Queen Isabella as well, her face arranged in a look of haughty disdain.

Sarah's glance fell on me. She and Gallowglass had insisted we rest for a few hours here before traveling on to Chipping Weston. I had protested. Weaving spells always left me feeling hollow afterward, and I'd assured them that my paleness and lack of appetite were due entirely to magic. Sarah and Gallowglass had ignored me.

"Here, madame?" Leonard slowed in front of the clipped yew hedge that stood between the gravel driveway and the moat. In 1590 we'd simply ridden right into the house's central courtyard, but now neither automobile could make it over the narrow stone bridge.

Instead, we traveled around to the small courtyard at the rear of the house that had been used for deliveries and tradesmen when I lived here before. A small Fiat was parked there, along with a battered lorry that was clearly used for chores around the estate. Amira Chavan, Matthew's friend and tenant, was waiting for us.

"It is good to see you again, Diana," Amira said, her tingling glance familiar. "Where is Matthew?"

"Away on business," I said shortly, climbing out of the car. Amira gasped and hurried forward.

"You're pregnant," she said in the tone one would use to announce the discovery of life on Mars.

"Seven months," I said, arching my back. "I could use one of your yoga classes." Amira led extraordinary classes here at the Old Lodge—classes that catered to a mixed clientele of daemons, witches, and vampires.

"No tying yourself into a pretzel." Gallowglass took my elbow gently. "Come inside, Auntie, and rest a spell. You can put your feet up on the table while Fernando makes us all something to eat."

"I'm not lifting a pan—not with Amira here." Fernando kissed Amira on the cheek. "No incidents that I should worry about, *shona*?"

"I haven't seen or sensed anything." Amira smiled at Fernando with fondness. "It has been too long since we've seen each other."

"Make Diana some akuri on toast and I will forgive you," Fernando said with an answering grin. "The scent alone will transport me to heaven."

After a round of introductions, I found myself in the tiny room where we had taken our family meals in 1590. There was no map on the wall, but a fire burned cheerily, dispelling some of the dampness.

Amira put plates of scrambled eggs and toast before us, along with bowls of rice and lentils. Everything was fragrant with chilies, mustard seed, lime, and coriander. Fernando hovered over the dishes, inhaling the aromatic steam.

"Your kanda poha reminds me of that little stall we visited on our way to Gharapuri to see the caves, the one that had the chai made with coconut milk." He inhaled deeply.

"It should," Amira said, sticking a spoon in the lentils. "He was using my grandmother's recipe. And I ground the rice the traditional way, in an iron mortar and pestle, so it is very good for Diana's pregnancy."

In spite of my insistence that I was not hungry, there was something downright alchemical in the effect that cumin and lime had on my appetite. Soon I was looking down at an empty plate.

"That's more like it," Gallowglass said with satisfaction. "Now, why don't you lie on the settle and close your eyes. If you're not comfortable there, you can always rest on the bed in Pierre's old office, or your own bed, come to think of it."

The settle was oaken, heavily carved, and designed to discourage loafing. It had been in the formal parlor during my previous life in the house and had simply drifted a few rooms to provide a seat underneath the window. The stack of papers on the end of it suggested that this was where Amira sat in the mornings to catch up on the news.

I was beginning to understand how Matthew treated his houses. He lived in them, left them, and returned decades or centuries later without touching the contents other than to slightly rearrange the furniture. It meant he owned a series of museums, rather than proper homes. I thought of the memories that awaited me in the rest of the house—the great hall where I'd met George Chapman and Widow Beaton, the formal parlor where Walter Raleigh had discussed our predicament under the watchful eyes of Henry VIII and Elizabeth I, and the bedchamber where Matthew and I had first set foot in the sixteenth century.

"The settle will be fine," I said hastily. If Gallowglass would surrender his leather jacket and Fernando his long woolen coat, the carved roses on the backrest wouldn't jab into my side too sharply. To make my desire real, the pile of coats by the fireplace arranged themselves into a makeshift mattress. Surrounded by scents of bitter orange, sea spray, lilac, tobacco, and narcissus, I felt my eyes grow heavy and I drifted into sleep.

"No one has caught so much as a glimpse of him," Amira said, her low voice waking me from my nap.

"Still, you shouldn't be teaching classes so long as Benjamin poses a risk to your safety." Fernando sounded uncharacteristically firm. "What if he were to walk through the front door?"

"Benjamin would find himself facing two dozen furious daemons, vampires, and witches, that's what," Amira replied. "Matthew told me to stop, Fernando, but the work that I'm doing seems more important now than ever."

"It is." I swung my legs off the settle and sat up, rubbing the sleep from my eyes. According to the clock, forty-five minutes had passed. It was impossible to gauge the passage of time from the changing light, since we were still entombed in fog.

Sarah called to Marthe, who brought tea. It was mint and rose hips, with none of the caffeine that would have made me more alert, but it was blessedly hot. I'd forgotten how cold sixteenth-century homes could be.

Gallowglass made a spot for me close to the fire. It saddened me to think of all that concern directed at me. He was so worthy of being loved; I didn't want him to be alone. Something in my expression must have revealed what was on my mind.

"No pity, Auntie. The winds do not always blow as the ship desires," he murmured, tucking me into my chair.

"The winds do what I tell them to do."

"And I plot my own course. If you don't stop clucking over me, I'll tell Matthew what you're up to and you can deal with two royally pissed-off vampires instead of one."

It was a prudent time to change the subject.

"Matthew is establishing his own family, Amira," I said, turning to our host. "It will have all kinds of creatures in it. Who knows, we might even let in humans. We'll need all the yoga we can get if he succeeds." I paused as my right hand began to tingle and pulse with color. I studied it for a moment in silence, then came to a decision. I wished the stiff leather portfolio that Phoebe had bought to protect the pages from the Book of Life was here at the table and not across the room. Despite the nap, I was still exhausted.

The portfolio appeared on a nearby table.

"Abracadabra," Fernando murmured.

"Since you live at Matthew's house, it only seems right to explain why we've all descended on you," I said to Amira. "You've probably heard stories about the witches' first grimoire?"

Amira nodded. I handed her the two pages we'd already gathered.

"These come from that book—the same book the vampires call the

Book of Life. We think another page is in the possession of someone named T. J. Weston, living in Chipping Weston. Now that we're all fed and watered, Phoebe and I are going to see if he or she is amenable to selling it."

Ysabeau and Phoebe appeared right on cue. Phoebe was as white as a sheet. Ysabeau looked mildly bored.

"What's wrong, Phoebe?" I asked.

"There's a Holbein. In the bathroom." She pressed her hands against her cheeks. "A small oil painting of Thomas More's daughter, Margaret. It shouldn't be hung over a toilet!"

I was beginning to understand why Matthew found my constant objections to the way his family treated their library books tiresome.

"Stop being so prudish," Ysabeau said with mild irritation. "Margaret was not the kind of woman to be bothered by a bit of exposed flesh."

"You think—That is—" Phoebe sputtered. "It's not the decorum of the situation that troubles me, but the fact that Margaret More might tumble into the loo at any moment!"

"I understand, Phoebe." I tried to sound sympathetic. "Would it help to know that there are other, far larger and more important works by Holbein in the parlor?"

"And upstairs. The whole sainted family is in one of the attics." Ysabeau pointed heavenward. "Thomas More was an arrogant young man, and he did not grow more humble with age. Matthew did not seem to mind, but Thomas and Philippe nearly came to blows on several occasions. If his daughter drowns in the lavatory, it will serve him right."

Amira began to giggle. After a shocked look, Fernando joined in. Soon we were all laughing, even Phoebe.

"What is all this noise? What has happened now?" Marthe eyed us suspiciously from the door.

"Phoebe is adjusting to being a de Clermont," I said, wiping at my eyes.

"Bonne chance," Marthe said. This only made us laugh harder.

It was a welcome reminder that, different though we might be, we were a family of sorts—no stranger or more idiosyncratic than thousands that had come before us.

"And these pages you've brought—are they from Matthew's collections as well?" Amira said, picking up the conversation where we'd abandoned it.

"No. One of them was given to my parents, and the other was in the hands of Matthew's grandson Andrew Hubbard."

"Hmm. So much fear." Amira's eyes lost focus. She was a witch with significant insight and empathic powers.

"Amira?" I looked at her closely.

"Blood and fear." She shuddered, not seeming to hear me. "It's in the parchment itself, not just the words."

"Should I stop her?" I asked Sarah. In most situations it was best to let a witch's second sight play itself out, but Amira had slipped too quickly into her vision of another time and place. A witch might wander so far into a thicket of images and feelings that she couldn't find her way out of them.

"Absolutely not," Sarah said. "There are two of us to help her if she gets lost."

"A young woman—a mother. She was killed in front of her children," Amira murmured. My stomach flipped. "Their father was already dead. When the witches brought her husband's body to her, they dropped it at her feet and made her look at what they had done to him. It was she who first cursed the book. So much knowledge, lost forever." Amira's eyes drifted closed. When they opened again, they were shining with unshed tears. "This parchment was made from the skin that stretched over her ribs."

I knew that the Book of Life had dead creatures in it, but I never imagined I would know anything more about them than whatever their DNA was capable of revealing. I bolted for the door, stomach heaving. Corra flapped her wings in agitation, turning this way and that to stabilize her position, but there was little room for her to maneuver thanks to the growing presence of the twins.

"Shh. That will not be your fate. I promise you," Ysabeau said, catching me in her arms. She was cool and solid, her strength evident in spite of her graceful build.

"Am I doing the right thing to try to mend this broken book?" I asked once the roiling in my guts had stopped. "And to do it without Matthew?"

"Right or wrong, it must be done." Ysabeau smoothed back my hair, which had tumbled forward, obscuring my face. "Call him, Diana. He would not want you to suffer like this."

"No." I shook my head. "Matthew has his job to do. I have mine."

"Let us finish it then," Ysabeau said.

* * *

Chipping Weston was the type of picturesque English village where novelists liked to set murder mysteries. It looked like a postcard or a film set, but it was home to several hundred people who lived in thatched houses spread out over a handful of narrow lanes. The village green had retained its stocks for punishing its citizens found guilty of some wrongdoing, and there were two pubs so that even if you had a falling-out with half your neighbors, you'd still have a place to go where you could have your evening pint.

The Manor House was not difficult to find.

"The gates are open." Gallowglass cracked his knuckles.

"What is your plan, Gallowglass? Running at the front door and battering it down with your bare hands?" I climbed out of Leonard's car. "Come on, Phoebe. Let's go ring the bell."

Gallowglass was behind us as we walked straight through the open front gates and skirted the round stone planter that I suspected had been a fountain before it was filled in with soil. Standing in the middle were two box trees clipped to resemble dachshunds.

"How extraordinary," Phoebe murmured, eyeing the green sculptures.

The door to the manor was set in the middle of a bank of low windows. There was no bell, but an iron knocker—also shaped like a dachshund—had been inexpertly affixed to the stout Elizabethan panels. Before Phoebe could give me a lecture about the preservation of old houses, I lifted the dog and rapped sharply.

Silence.

I rapped again, putting a bit more weight into it.

"We are standing in plain view of the road," Gallowglass growled. "That's the sorriest excuse for a wall I've ever seen. A child could step over it."

"Not everybody can have a moat," I said. "I hardly think Benjamin has ever heard of Chipping Weston, never mind followed us here."

Gallowglass was unconvinced and continued to look around like an anxious owl.

I was about to rap again when the door was flung open. A man wearing goggles and a parachute slung around his shoulders like a cape stood in the entrance. Dogs swarmed around his feet, wriggling and barking.

"Whenever have you been?" The stranger engulfed me in a hug while I tried to sort out what his strange question meant. The dogs leaped and frolicked, excited to meet me now that their master had signaled his approval. He let me go and lifted his goggles, his nudging stare feeling like a buss of welcome.

"You're a daemon," I said unnecessarily.

"And you're a witch." With one green eye and one blue, he studied Gallowglass. "And he's a vampire. Not the same one you had with you before, but still big enough to replace the lightbulbs."

"I don't do lightbulbs," Gallowglass said.

"Wait. I know you," I said, sifting through the faces in my memory. This was one of the daemons I'd seen in the Bodleian last year when I'd first encountered Ashmole 782. He liked lattes and taking apart microfilm readers. He always wore earbuds, even when they weren't attached to anything. "Timothy?"

"The same." Timothy turned his eyes to me and cocked his fingers and thumbs so they looked like six-shooters. He was, I noticed, still wearing mismatched cowboy boots, but this time one was green and the other blue—to match his eyes, one presumed. He clicked his tongue against his teeth. "Told you, babe: You're the one."

"Are you T. J. Weston?" Phoebe asked, trying to make her voice heard above the din of yelping, wriggling dogs.

Timothy stuffed his fingers in his ears and mouthed, "I can't hear you."

"Oy!" Gallowglass shouted. "Shut your gobs, little yappers."

The barking stopped instantly. The dogs sat, jaws open and tongues lolling, and looked at Gallowglass adoringly. Timothy removed a finger from one of his ears.

"Nice," the daemon said with a low whistle of appreciation. The dogs immediately started barking again.

Gallowglass bundled us all inside, muttering darkly about sight lines and defensive positions and possible hearing damage to Apple and Bean. Peace was achieved once he got down on the floor in front of the fireplace and let the dogs scramble all over him, licking and burrowing as if their pack's alpha had been returned to them after a long absence.

"What are their names?" Phoebe inquired, trying to count the number of tails in the squirming mound.

"Hansel and Gretel, obviously." Timothy looked at Phoebe as though she were hopeless.

"And the other four?" Phoebe asked.

"Oscar. Molly. Rusty. And Puddles." Timothy pointed to each dog in turn.

"He likes to play outside in the rain?"

"No," Timothy replied. "She likes to piddle on the floor. Her name was Penelope, but everybody in the village calls her Puddles now."

A graceful segue from this subject to the Book of Life was impossible, so I plunged forward. "Did you buy a page from an illuminated manuscript that has a tree on it?"

"Yep." Timothy blinked.

"Would you be willing to sell it to me?" There was no point in being coy.

"Nope."

"We're prepared to pay handsomely for it." Phoebe might not like the de Clermonts' casual indifference to where pictures were hung, but she was beginning to see the benefits of their purchasing power.

"It's not for sale." Timothy ruffled the ears of one of the dogs who then returned to Gallowglass and began to gnaw on the toe of his boot.

"Can I see it?" Perhaps Timothy would let me borrow it, I thought.

"Sure." Timothy divested himself of the parachute and strode out of the room. We scrambled to keep up.

He led us through several rooms that had clearly been designed for different purposes from the ones they were now used for. A dining room had a battered drum kit set up in the center with DEREK AND THE DERANGERS painted on the bass-drum head, and another room looked like an electronics graveyard except for the chintz sofas and beribboned wallpaper.

"It's in there. Somewhere," Timothy said, gesturing at the next room.

"Holy Mother of God," Gallowglass said, astonished.

"There" was the former library. "Somewhere" covered a multitude of possible hiding places, including unopened shipping crates and mail, cardboard cartons full of sheet music going back to the 1920s, and stacks and stacks of old newspapers. There was a large collection of clock faces of all sizes, descriptions, and vintages, too.

And there were manuscripts. Thousands of manuscripts.

"I think it's in a blue folder," Timothy said, scratching his chin. He had obviously started shaving at some point earlier in the day but only partially completed the task, leaving two grizzled patches.

"How long have you been buying old books?" I asked, picking up the first one that came to hand. It was an eighteenth-century student science notebook, German, and of no particular value except to a scholar of Enlightenment education.

"Since I was thirteen. That's when my gran died and left me this place. My mom left when I was five, and my dad, Derek, died of an accidental overdose when I turned nine, so it was just me and Gran after that." Timothy looked around the room fondly. "I've been restoring it ever since. Do you want to see my paint chips for the gallery upstairs?"

"Maybe later," I said.

"Okay." His face fell.

"Why do manuscripts interest you?" When trying to get answers from daemons and undergraduates, it was best to ask genuinely open-ended questions.

"They're like the house—they remind me of something I shouldn't forget," Timothy said, as though that explained everything.

"With any luck one of them will remind him where he put the page from your book," Gallowglass said under his breath. "If not, it's going to take us weeks to go through all this rubbish."

We didn't have weeks. I wanted Ashmole 782 out of the Bodleian and stitched back together so that Matthew could come home. Without the Book of Life, we were vulnerable to the Congregation, Benjamin, and whatever private ambitions Knox and Gerbert might harbor. Once it was safely in our possession, they would all have to deal with us on our terms—scion or no scion. I pushed up my sleeves.

"Would it be all right with you, Timothy, if I used magic in your library?" It seemed polite to ask.

"Will it be loud?" Timothy asked. "The dogs don't like noise."

"No," I said, considering my options. "I think it will be completely silent."

"Oh, well, that's okay, then," he said, relieved. He put his goggles back on for additional security.

"More magic, Auntie?" Gallowglass's eyebrows lowered. "You've been using an awful lot of it lately."

"Wait until tomorrow," I murmured. If I got all three missing pages, I was going to the Bodleian. Then it was gloves-off time.

A flurry of papers rose from the floor.

"You've started already?" Gallowglass said, alarmed.

"No," I said.

"Then what's causing the ruckus?" Gallowglass moved toward the agitated pile.

A tail wagged from between a leather-bound folio and a box of pens.

"Puddles!" Timothy said.

The dog emerged, tail first, pulling a blue folder.

"Good doggy," Gallowglass crooned. He crouched down and held out his hand. "Bring it to me."

Puddles stood with the missing page from Ashmole 782 gripped in her teeth, looking very pleased with herself. She did not, however, take it to Gallowglass.

"She wants you to chase her," Timothy explained.

Gallowglass scowled. "I'm not chasing that dog."

In the end we all chased her. Puddles was the fastest, cleverest dachshund who'd ever lived, darting under furniture and feinting left and then right before dashing away again. Gallowglass was speedy, but he was not small. Puddles slipped through his fingers again and again, her glee evident.

Finally Puddles' need to pant meant that she had to drop the now slightly moist blue folder in front of her paws. Gallowglass took the opportunity to reach in and secure it.

"What a good girl!" Timothy picked up the squirming dog. "You're going to win the Great Dachshund Games this summer. No question." A slip of paper was attached to one of Puddles' claws. "Hey. There's my council tax bill."

Gallowglass handed me the folder.

"Phoebe should do the honors," I said. "If not for her, we wouldn't be here." I passed the folder on to her.

Phoebe cracked it open. The image inside was so vivid that it might have been painted yesterday, and its striking colors and the details of trunk and leaf only increased the sense of vibrancy that came from the page. There was power in it. That much was unmistakable.

"It's beautiful." Phoebe lifted her eyes. "Is this the page you've been looking for?"

"Aye," Gallowglass said. "That's it, all right."

Phoebe placed the page in my waiting hands. As soon as the parchment touched them, they brightened, shooting little sparks of color into the room. Filaments of power erupted from my fingertips, connecting to the parchment with an almost audible snap of electricity.

"There's a lot of energy on that page. Not all of it good," Timothy said, backing away. "It needs to go back into that book you discovered in the Bodleian."

"I know you don't want to sell the page," I said, "but could I borrow it? Just for a day?" I could go straight to the Bodleian, recall Ashmole 782, and have the page back tomorrow afternoon—provided the Book of Life let me remove it again, once I'd returned it to the binding.

"Nope." Timothy shook his head.

"You won't let me buy it. You won't let me borrow it," I said, exasperation mounting. "Do you have some sentimental attachment to it?"

"Of course I do. I mean, he's my ancestor, isn't he?"

Every eye in the room went to the illustration of the tree in my hands. Even Puddles looked at it with renewed interest, sniffing the air with her long, delicate nose.

"How do you know that?" I whispered.

"I see things—microchips, crossword puzzles, you, the guy whose skin made that parchment. I knew who you were from the moment you walked into Duke Humfrey's." Timothy looked sad. "I told you as much. But you didn't listen to me and left with the big vampire. You're the one."

"The one for what?" My throat closed. Daemon visions were bizarre and surreal, but they could be shockingly accurate.

"The one who will learn how it all began—the blood, the death, the fear. And the one who can put a stop to it, once and for all." Timothy sighed. "You can't buy my grandfather, and you can't borrow him. But if I give him to you, for safekeeping, you'll make his death mean something?"

"I can't promise you that, Timothy." There was no way I could swear to something so enormous and imprecise. "We don't know what the book will reveal. And I certainly can't guarantee that anything will change."

"Can you make sure his name won't be forgotten, once you learn what it is?" Timothy asked. "Names are important, you know."

A sense of the uncanny washed over me. Ysabeau had told me the same thing shortly after I met her. I saw Edward Kelley in my mind's eye. *"You will find your name in it, too,"* he had cried when Emperor Rudolf made him hand over the Book of Life. The hackles on my neck rose.

"I won't forget his name," I promised.

"Sometimes that's enough," Timothy said.

It was several hours past midnight, and any hope I had of sleep was gone. The fog had lifted slightly, and the brightness of the full moon pierced through the gray wisps that still clung to the trunks of trees and the low places in the park where the deer slept. One or two members of the herd were still out, picking over the grass in search of the last remaining fodder. A hard frost was coming; I could sense it. I was attuned to the rhythms of the earth and sky in ways that I had not been before I lived in a time when the day was organized around the height of the sun instead of the dial of a clock, and the season of the year determined everything from what you ate to the physic that you took.

I was in our bedchamber again, the one where Matthew and I had spent our first night in the sixteenth century. Only a few things had changed: the electricity that powered the lamps, the Victorian bellpull that hung by the fire to call the servants to tend to it or bring tea (though why this was necessary in a vampire household, I could not fathom), the closet that had been carved out of an adjoining room.

Our return to the Old Lodge after meeting Timothy Weston had been unexpectedly tense. Gallowglass had flatly refused to take me to Oxford after we located the final page of the Book of Life, though it was not yet the supper hour and Duke Humfrey's was open until seven o'clock during term time. When Leonard offered to drive, Gallowglass threatened to kill him in disturbingly detailed and graphic terms. Fernando and Gallowglass had departed, ostensibly to talk, and Gallowglass had returned with a rapidly healing split lip, a slightly bruised eye, and a mumbled apology to Leonard.

"You aren't going," Fernando said when I headed for the door. "I'll take you tomorrow, but not tonight. Gallowglass is right: You look like death."

"Stop coddling me," I said through gritted teeth, my hands still shooting out intermittent sparks.

"I'll coddle you until your mate—and my sire—returns," Fernando said. "The only creature on this earth who could make me take you to Oxford is Matthew. Feel free to call him." He held out his phone.

That had been the end of the discussion. I'd accepted Fernando's ultimatum with poor grace, though my head was pounding and I'd worked more magic in the past week than I had my whole life previous.

"So long as you have these three pages, no other creature can possess the book," Amira said, trying to comfort me. But it seemed like a poor consolation when the book was so close.

Not even the sight of the three pages, lined up on the long table in the great hall, had improved my mood. I'd been anticipating and dreading this moment since we left Madison, but now that it was here, it felt strangely anticlimactic.

Phoebe had arranged the images carefully, making sure they didn't touch. We'd learned the hard way that they seemed to have a magnetic affinity. When I'd arrived home and bundled them together in preparation for going to the Bodleian, a soft keening had come from the pages, followed by a chattering that everybody heard—even Phoebe.

"You can't just march into the Bodleian with these three pages and stuff them back into an enchanted book," Sarah said. "It's crazy. There are bound to be witches in the room. They'll come running."

"And who knows how the Book of Life will respond?" Ysabeau poked at the illustration of the tree with her finger. "What if it shrieks? Ghosts might be released. Or Diana might set off a rain of fire." After her experiences in London, Ysabeau had been doing some reading. She was now prepared to discuss a wide variety of topics, including spectral apparitions and the number of occult phenomena that had been observed in the British Isles over the past two years.

"You're going to have to steal it," Sarah said.

"I'm a tenured professor at Yale, Sarah! I can't! My life as a scholar—"

"Is probably over," Sarah said, finishing my sentence.

"Come now, Sarah," Fernando chided. "That is a bit extreme, even for you. Surely there is a way for Diana to check out Ashmole 782 and return it at some future date."

I tried to explain that you didn't borrow books from the Bodleian, but to no avail. With Ysabeau and Sarah in charge of logistics and Fernando and Gallowglass in charge of security, I was relegated to a position where

I could only advise, counsel, and warn. They were more high-handed than Matthew.

And so here I was at four o'clock in the morning, staring out the window and waiting for the sun to rise.

"What should I do?" I murmured, my forehead pressed against the cold, diamond-shaped panes.

As soon as I asked the question, my skin flared with awareness, as though I'd stuck a finger into an electrical socket. A shimmering figure dressed in white came from the forest, accompanied by a white deer. The otherworldly animal walked sedately at the woman's side, unafraid of the huntress who held a bow and a quiver of arrows in her hand. *The goddess.*

She stopped and looked up at my window. "Why so sad, daughter?" her silvery voice whispered. "Have you lost what you most desire?"

I had learned not to answer her questions. She smiled at my reluctance.

"Dare to join me under this full moon. Perhaps you will find it once more." The goddess rested her fingers on the deer's antlers and waited.

I slipped outside undetected. My feet crunched across the gravel paths of the knot gardens, then left dark impressions in the frost-touched grass. Soon, I stood in front of the goddess.

"Why are you here?" I asked.

"To help you." The goddess's eyes were silver and black in the moonlight. "You will have to give something up if you want to possess the Book of Life—something precious to you."

"I've given enough." My voice trembled. "My parents, then my first child, then my aunt. Not even my life is my own anymore. It belongs to you."

"And I do not abandon those who serve me." The goddess withdrew an arrow from her quiver. It was long and silver, with owl-feather fletches. She offered it to me. "Take it."

"No." I shook my head. "Not without knowing the price."

"No one refuses me." The goddess put the arrow shaft into her bow, aimed. It was then I noticed that her weapon lacked its pointed tip. Her hand drew back, the silver string pulled taut.

There was no time to react before the goddess released the shaft. It shot straight toward my breast. I felt a searing pain, a yank of the chain around my neck, and a tingling feeling of warmth between my left shoulder blade and my spine. The golden links that had held Philippe's arrowhead slithered down my body and landed at my feet. I felt the fabric that covered my chest for the telltale wetness of blood, but there was nothing except a small hole to indicate where the shaft had passed through.

"You cannot outrun my arrow. No creature can. It is part of you now," she said. "Even those born to strength should carry weapons."

I searched the ground around my feet, looking for Philippe's jewel. When I straightened, I could feel its point pressing into my ribs. I stared at the goddess in astonishment.

"My arrow never misses its target," the goddess said. "When you have need of it, do not hesitate. And aim true."

"They've been moved *where*?" This could not be happening. Not when we were so close to finding answers.

"The Radcliffe Science Library." Sean was apologetic, but his patience was wearing thin. "It's not the end of the world, Diana."

"But . . . that is . . ." I trailed off, the completed call slip for Ashmole 782 dangling from my fingers.

"Don't you read your e-mails? We've been sending out notices about the move for months," Sean said. "I'm happy to take the request and put it in the system, since you've been away and apparently out of reach of the Internet. But none of the Ashmole manuscripts are here, and you can't call them up to this reading room unless you have a bona fide intellectual reason that's related to the manuscripts and maps that are still here."

Of all the exigencies we had planned for this morning—and they were many and varied—the Bodleian Library's decision to move rare books and manuscripts from Duke Humfrey's to the Radcliffe Science Library had not been among them. We'd left Sarah and Amira at home with Leonard in case we needed magical backup. Gallowglass and Fernando were both outside, loafing around the statue of Mary Herbert's son William and being photographed by female visitors. Ysabeau had gained entrance to the library after enticing the head of development with a gift to rival the annual budget of Liechtenstein. She was now on a private tour of the facility. Phoebe, who had attended Christ Church and was therefore the only member of my book posse in possession of a library card, had accompanied me into Duke

Humfrey's and was now waiting patiently in a seat overlooking Exeter College's gardens.

"How aggravating." No matter how many rare books and precious manuscripts they'd relocated, I was absolutely sure Ashmole 782 was still here. My father had not bound the Book of Life to its call number after all, but to the library. In 1850 the Radcliffe Science Library didn't exist.

I looked at my watch. It was only ten-thirty. A swarm of children on a school trip were released into the quadrangle, their high-pitched voices echoing against the stone walls. How long would it take me to manufacture an excuse that would satisfy Sean? Phoebe and I needed to regroup. I tried to reach the spot on my lower back where the tip of the goddess's arrow was lodged. The shaft kept my posture ramrod straight, and if I slouched the slightest bit, I felt a warning prickle..

"And don't think it's going to be easy to come up with a good rationale for looking at your manuscript here," Sean warned, reading my mind. Humans never failed to activate their usually dormant sixth sense at the most inopportune moments. "Your friend has been sending requests of all sorts for weeks, and no matter how many times he asks to see manuscripts here, the requests keep getting redirected to Parks Road."

"Tweed jacket? Corduroy pants?" If Peter Knox was in Duke Humfrey's, I was going to throttle him.

"No. The guy who sits by the card catalogs." Sean jerked his thumb in the direction of the Selden End.

I backed carefully out of Sean's office across from the old call desk and felt the numbing sensation of a vampire's stare. *Gerbert?*

"Mistress Roydon."

Not Gerbert.

Benjamin's arm was draped over Phoebe's shoulders, and there were spots of red on the collar of her white blouse. For the first time since I'd met her, Phoebe looked terrified.

"Herr Fuchs." I spoke slightly louder than usual. Hopefully, Ysabeau or Gallowglass would hear his name over the din that the children were causing. I forced my feet to move toward him at an even pace.

"What a surprise to see you here—and looking so . . . fertile." Benjamin's eyes drifted slowly over my breasts to where the twins lay curled in my belly. One of them was kicking furiously, as though to make a break for freedom. Corra, too, twisted and snarled inside me.

No fire or flame. The oath I'd taken when I got my first reader's card floated through my mind.

"I expected Matthew. Instead I get his mate. And my brother's, too." Benjamin's nose went to the pulse under Phoebe's ear. His teeth grazed her flesh. She bit her lip to keep from crying out. "What a good boy Marcus is, always standing by his father. I wonder if he'll stand by you, pet, once I've made you mine."

"Let her go, Benjamin." Once the words were out of my mouth, the logical part of my brain registered their pointlessness. There was no chance that Benjamin was going to let Phoebe go.

"Don't worry. You won't be left out." His fingers stroked the place on Phoebe's neck where her pulse hammered. "I've got big plans for you, too, Mistress Roydon. You're a good breeder. I can see that."

Where was Ysabeau?

The arrow burned against my spine, inviting me to use its power. But how could I target Benjamin without running the risk of harming Phoebe? He had placed Phoebe slightly in front of him, like a shield.

"This one dreams of being a vampire." Benjamin's mouth lowered, brushed against Phoebe's neck. She whimpered. "I could make those dreams come true. With any luck I could send you back to Marcus with blood so strong you could bring him to his knees."

Philippe's voice rang in my mind: *Think—and stay alive.* That was the job he had given me. But my thoughts ran in disorganized circles. Snatches of spells and half-remembered warnings from Goody Alsop chased Benjamin's threats. I needed to concentrate.

Phoebe's eyes begged me to do *something.*

"Use your pitiful power, witch. I may not know what's in the Book of Life—yet—but I've learned that witches are no match for vampires."

I hesitated. Benjamin smiled. I stood at the crossroads between the life I'd always thought I wanted—scholarly, intellectual, free from the complicated messiness of magic—and the life I now had. If I worked magic here, in the Bodleian Library, there would be no turning back.

"Something wrong?" he drawled.

My back continued to burn, the pain spreading into my shoulder. I lifted my hands and separated them as though they held a bow, then aimed my left index finger at Benjamin to create a line of sight.

My hand was no longer colorless. A blaze of purple, thick and vivid, ran all the way down to the palm. I groaned inwardly. Of course my magic would decide to change *now.* Think. *What was the magical significance of purple?*

I felt the sensation of a rough string scraping against my cheek. I twisted my lips and directed a puff of air toward it. *No distractions. Think. Stay alive.*

When my focus returned to my hands, there was a bow in them—a real, tangible bow made of wood ornamented with silver and gold. I felt a strange tingle from the wood, one I recognized. *Rowan.* And there was an arrow between my fingers, too: silver-shafted and tipped with Philippe's golden arrowhead. Would it find its target as the goddess had promised? Benjamin twisted Phoebe so that she was directly in front of him.

"Take your best shot, witch. You'll kill Marcus's warmblood, but I'll still have everything I came for."

The image of Juliette's fiery death came to mind. I closed my eyes.

I hesitated, unable to shoot. The bow and arrow dissolved between my fingers. I'd done exactly what the goddess had instructed me not to do.

I heard the pages of the books lying open on nearby desks ruffle in a sudden breeze. The hair on the back of my neck rose. *Witchwind.*

There must be another witch in the library. I opened my eyes to see who it was.

It was a vampire.

Ysabeau stood before Benjamin, one hand wrapped around his throat and the other pushing Phoebe in my direction.

"Ysabeau." Benjamin looked at her sourly.

"Expecting someone else? Matthew, perhaps?" Blood welled from a small puncture wound on him that was filled with Ysabeau's finger. That pressure was enough to keep Benjamin where he was. Nausea swept over me in a wave. "He is otherwise engaged. Phoebe, dearest, you must take Diana down to Gallowglass and Fernando. At once." Without looking away from her prey, Ysabeau pointed in my direction with her free hand.

"Let's go," Phoebe murmured, pulling at my arm.

Ysabeau removed her finger from Benjamin's neck with an audible pop. His hand clamped over the spot.

"We're not finished, Ysabeau. Tell Matthew I'll be in touch. Soon."

"Oh, I will." Ysabeau gave him a terrifyingly toothy smile. She took two steps backward, took my other elbow, and jerked me around to face the exit.

"Diana?" Benjamin called.

I stopped but didn't turn around.

"I hope your children are both girls."

"Nobody speaks until we're in the car." Gallowglass let out a piercing whistle. "Disguising spell, Auntie."

I could feel that it had slipped out of shape but couldn't muster the energy to do much about it. The nausea I'd felt upstairs was getting worse.

Leonard squealed up to the gates of Hertford College.

"I hesitated. Just like with Juliette." Then it had almost cost Matthew his life. Today it was Phoebe who had paid for my fear.

"Mind your head," Gallowglass said, inserting me into the passenger seat.

"Thank God we used Matthew's bloody great car," Leonard muttered to Fernando as he slid in the front. "Back home?"

"Yes," I said.

"No," Ysabeau said at the same moment, appearing on the other side of the car. "To the airport. We are going to Sept-Tours. Call Baldwin, Gallowglass."

"I am *not* going to Sept-Tours," I said. Live under Baldwin's thumb? Never.

"What about Sarah?" Fernando asked from the front seat.

"Tell Amira to drive Sarah to London and meet us there." Ysabeau tapped Leonard on the shoulder. "If you do not put your foot on the gas pedal immediately, I cannot be held accountable for my actions."

"We're all in. Go!" Gallowglass closed the door of the cargo space just as Leonard squealed into reverse, narrowly missing a distinguished don on a bicycle.

"Bloody hell. I've not got the temperament for crime," Gallowglass said, huffing slightly. "Show us the book, Auntie."

"Diana does not have the book." Ysabeau's words caused Fernando to stop mid-conversation and look back at us.

"Then what is the rush?" Gallowglass demanded.

"We met Matthew's son." Phoebe sat forward and began to speak loudly in the direction of Fernando's cell phone. "Benjamin knows that Diana is pregnant, Sarah. You are not safe, nor is Amira. Leave. At once."

"Benjamin?" Sarah's voice was unmistakably horrified.

A large hand jerked Phoebe back. It twisted her head to the side.

"He bit you." Gallowglass's face whitened. He grabbed me and inspected every inch of my face and neck. "Christ. Why didn't you call for help?"

Thanks to Leonard's complete disregard for traffic restrictions or speed limits, we were nearly to the M40.

"He had Phoebe." I shrank into the seat, trying to stabilize my roiling stomach by clamping both arms over the twins.

"Where was Granny?" Gallowglass asked.

"Granny was listening to a horrible woman in a magenta blouse tell me about the library's building works while sixty children screamed in the quadrangle." Ysabeau glared at Gallowglass. "Where were *you*?"

"Both of you stop it. We were all exactly where we planned to be." As usual, Phoebe's voice was the only reasonable one. "And we all got out alive. Let's not lose sight of the big picture."

Leonard sped onto the M40, headed for Heathrow.

I held a cold hand to my forehead. "I'm so sorry, Phoebe." I pressed my lips together as the car swayed. "I couldn't think."

"Perfectly understandable," Phoebe said briskly. "May I please speak to Miriam?"

"Miriam?" Fernando asked.

"Yes. I know that I am not infected with blood rage, because I didn't ingest any of Benjamin's blood. But he did bite me, and she may wish to have a sample of my blood to see if his saliva has affected me."

We all stared at her, openmouthed.

"Later," Gallowglass said curtly. "We'll worry about science and that godforsaken manuscript later."

The countryside rushed by in a blur. I rested my forehead against the glass and wished with all my heart that Matthew was with me, that the day had ended differently, that Benjamin didn't know I was pregnant with twins.

His final words—and the prospect of the future they painted—taunted me as we drew closer to the airport.

I hope your children are both girls.

* * *

"Diana!" Ysabeau's voice interrupted my troubled sleep. "Matthew or Baldwin. Choose." Her tone was fierce. "One of them has to be told."

"Not Matthew." I winced and sat straighter. That damned arrow was still jabbing my shoulder. "He'll come running, and there's no reason for it. Phoebe is right. We're all alive."

Ysabeau swore like a sailor and pulled out her red phone. Before anyone could stop her, she was speaking to Baldwin in rapid French. I caught only half of it, but based on her awed response, Phoebe obviously understood more.

"Oh, Christ." Gallowglass shook his shaggy head.

"Baldwin wishes to speak with you." Ysabeau extended the phone in my direction.

"I understand you've seen Benjamin." Baldwin was as cool and composed as Phoebe.

"I did."

"He threatened the twins?"

"He did."

"I'm your brother, Diana, not your enemy," Baldwin said. "Ysabeau was right to call me."

"If you say so," I said. *"Sieur."*

"Do you know where Matthew is?" he demanded.

"No." I didn't know—not exactly. "Do you?"

"I presume he is off somewhere burying Jack Blackfriars."

The silence that followed Baldwin's words was lengthy.

"You are an utter bastard, Baldwin de Clermont." My voice shook.

"Jack was a necessary casualty of a dangerous and deadly war—one that you started, by the way." Baldwin sighed. "Come home, sister. That's an order. Lick your wounds and wait for him. It's what we've all learned to do when Matthew goes off to assuage his guilty conscience."

He hung up on me before I could manage a reply.

"I. Hate. Him." I spit out each word.

"So do I," Ysabeau said, taking back her phone.

"Baldwin is jealous of Matthew, that's all," Phoebe said. This time her reasonableness was irritating, and I felt the power rush through my body.

"I don't feel right." My anxiety spiked. "Is something wrong? Is someone following us?"

Gallowglass forced my head around. "You look hectic. How far are we from London?"

"London?" Leonard exclaimed. "You said Heathrow." He wrenched the wheel to head in a different direction off the roundabout.

My stomach proceeded on our previous route. I retched, trying to hold down the vomit. But it wasn't possible.

"Diana?" Ysabeau said, holding back my hair and wiping at my mouth with her silk scarf. "What is it?"

"I must have eaten something that didn't agree with me," I said, suppressing another urge to vomit. "I've felt funny for the last few days."

"Funny how?" Gallowglass's voice was urgent. "Do you have a headache, Diana? Are you having trouble breathing? Does your shoulder pain you?"

I nodded, the bile rising.

"You said she was anxious, Phoebe?"

"Of course Diana was anxious," Ysabeau retorted. She dumped the contents of her purse onto the seat and held it under my chin. I couldn't imagine throwing up into a Chanel bag, but at this point anything was possible. "She was preparing to do battle with Benjamin!"

"Anxiety is a symptom of some condition I can't pronounce. Diana had leaflets about it in New Haven. You hold on, Auntie!" Gallowglass sounded frantic.

I wondered dimly why he sounded so alarmed before I vomited again, right into Ysabeau's purse.

"Hamish? We need a doctor. A vampire doctor. Something's wrong with Diana."

Sol in Scorpio

When the sun is in the signe of Scorpio, expect death, feare, and poison. During this dangerous time, beware of serpents and all other venomous creatures. Scorpio rules over conception and childbirth, and children born under this sign are blessed with many gifts.

—Anonymous English Commonplace Book, c. 1590, Gonçalves MS 4890, f. 9r

29

Where is Matthew? He should be here," Fernando murmured, turning away from the view of Diana sitting in the small, sunny room where she spent most of her time since being put on a strict regime of bed rest.

Diana was still brooding over what happened in the Bodleian. She had not forgiven herself for allowing Benjamin to threaten Phoebe or for letting the opportunity to kill Matthew's son slip through her fingers. But Fernando feared that this would not be the last time her nerves would fail in the face of the enemy.

"Diana's fine." Gallowglass was propped up against the wall in the hallway opposite the door, his arms crossed. "The doctor said so this morning. Besides, Matthew can't return until he gets his new family sorted out."

Gallowglass had been their only link to Matthew for weeks. Fernando swore. He pounced, pressing his mouth tightly against Gallowglass's ear and his hand against his windpipe.

"You haven't told Matthew," Fernando said, lowering his voice so that no one else in the house could hear. "He has a right to know what's happened here, Gallowglass: the magic, finding that page from the Book of Life, Benjamin's appearance, Diana's condition—all of it."

"If Matthew wanted to know what was happening to his wife, he would be here and not bringing a pack of recalcitrant children to heel," Gallowglass choked out, grasping Fernando's wrist.

"And you believe this because *you* would have stayed?" Fernando released him. "You are more lost than the moon in winter. It does not matter where Matthew is. Diana belongs to him. She will never be yours."

"I know that." Gallowglass's blue eyes did not waver.

"Matthew may kill you for this." There was not a touch of histrionics in Fernando's pronouncement.

"There are worse things than my being killed," Gallowglass said evenly. "The doctor said no stress or the babes could die. So could Diana. Not even

Matthew will harm them while I have breath in my body. That's my job—and I do it well."

"When I next see Philippe de Clermont—and he is no doubt toasting his feet before the devil's fire—he will answer to me for asking this of you." Fernando knew that Philippe enjoyed making other people's decisions. He should have made a different one in this case.

"I would have done it regardless." Gallowglass stepped away. "I don't seem to have a choice."

"You always have a choice. And you deserve a chance to be happy." There had to be a woman out there for Gallowglass, Fernando thought—one who would make him forget Diana Bishop.

"Do I?" Gallowglass's expression turned wistful.

"Yes. Diana has a right to be happy, too." Fernando's words were deliberately blunt. "They've been apart long enough. It's time Matthew came home."

"Not unless his blood rage is under control. Being away from Diana so long will have made him unstable enough. If Matthew finds out the pregnancy is putting her life in peril, God only knows what he'll do." Gallowglass matched blunt with blunt. "Baldwin is right. The greatest danger we face is not Benjamin, and it isn't the Congregation—it's Matthew. Better fifty enemies outside the door than one within it."

"So Matthew is your enemy now?" Fernando spoke in a whisper. "And you think he's the one who has lost his senses?"

Gallowglass made no reply.

"If you know what is good for you, Gallowglass, you will walk out of this house the minute Matthew returns. Wherever you go—and the ends of the earth may not be far enough to keep you from his wrath—I advise you to spend time on your knees begging God for His protection."

The Domino Club on Royal Street hadn't changed much since Matthew had first walked through its doors almost two centuries ago. The three-story façade, gray walls, and crisp black-and-white–painted trim was the same, the height of the arched windows at street level suggesting an openness to the outside world that was belied by the closing of their heavy shutters. When the shutters were flung wide at five o'clock, the general public would be welcomed to a beautiful polished bar and to enjoy music provided by a variety of local performers.

But Matthew was not interested in tonight's entertainment. His eyes were fixed on an ornate iron railing wrapped around the second-floor balcony that provided a sheltering overhang for the pedestrians below. That floor and the one above were restricted to members. A significant portion of the Domino Club's membership roster had signed up when it was founded in 1839—two years before the Boston Club, officially the oldest gentlemen's club in New Orleans, opened its doors. The rest had been carefully selected according to their looks, breeding, and ability to lose large sums of money at the gambling tables.

Ransome Fayrweather, Marcus's eldest son and the club's owner, would be on the second floor in his office overlooking the corner. Matthew pushed open the black door and entered the cool, dark bar. The place smelled of bourbon and pheromones, the most familiar cocktail in the city. The heels of his shoes made a soft *snick* against the checkered marble floor.

It was four o'clock, and only Ransome and his staff were on the premises.

"Mr. Clairmont?" The vampire behind the bar looked as though he'd seen a ghost and took a step toward the cash register. One glance from Matthew and he froze.

"I'm here to see Ransome." Matthew stalked toward the stairs. No one stopped him.

Ransome's door was closed, and Matthew opened it without knocking.

A man sat with his back to the door and his feet propped up on the windowsill. He was wearing a black suit, and his hair was the same rich brown as the wood of the mahogany chair in which he sat.

"Well, well. Grandpa's home," Ransome said in a treacle-dipped drawl. He didn't turn to look at his visitor, and a worn ebony-and-ivory domino kept moving between his pale fingers. "What brings you to Royal Street?"

"I understand you wish to settle accounts." Matthew took a seat opposite, leaving the heavy desk between him and his grandson.

Ransome slowly turned. The man's eyes were cold chips of green glass in an otherwise handsome and relaxed face. Then his heavy lids dropped, hiding all that sharpness and suggesting a sensual somnolence that Matthew knew was nothing more than a front.

"As you're aware, I'm here to bring you to heel. Your brothers and sister have all agreed to support me and the new scion." Matthew sat back in his chair. "You're the last holdout, Ransome."

All of Marcus's other children had submitted quickly. When Matthew told them they carried the genetic marker for blood rage, they had been first stunned and then furious. After that had come fear. They were schooled enough in vampire law to know that their bloodline made them vulnerable, that if any other vampire found out about their condition, they could face immediate death. Marcus's children needed Matthew as much as he needed them. Without him, they would not survive.

"I have a better memory than they do," Ransome said. He opened his desk drawer and pulled out an old ledger.

With every day away from Diana, Matthew's temper shortened and his propensity for violence increased. It was vital to have Ransome on his side. And yet, at this moment, he wanted to throttle this grandson. The whole business of confessing and seeking atonement had taken much longer than he'd anticipated—and it was keeping him far from where he should be.

"I had no choice but to kill them, Ransome." It took an effort for Matthew to keep his voice even. "Even now Baldwin would rather I kill Jack than risk having him expose our secret. But Marcus convinced me I had other options."

"Marcus told you that last time. Yet you still culled us, one by one. What's changed?" Ransome asked.

"I have."

"Never try to con a con, Matthew," Ransome said in the same lazy drawl. "You've still got that look in your eye that warns creatures not to cross you. Had you lost it, your corpse would be laid out in my foyer. The barkeep was told to shoot you on sight."

"To give him credit, he did reach for the shotgun by the register." Matthew's attention never drifted from Ransome's face. "Tell him to pull the knife from his belt next time."

"I'll be sure to pass on that tip." Ransome's domino paused momentarily, caught between his middle and ring fingers. "What happened to Juliette Durand?"

The muscle in Matthew's jaw ticked. The last time he came to town, Juliette Durand had been with him. When the two left New Orleans, Marcus's boisterous family was significantly smaller. Juliette was Gerbert's creature and had been eager to prove her usefulness at a time when Matthew was growing tired of being the de Clermont family's problem solver. She had disposed of more vampires in New Orleans than Matthew had.

"My wife killed her." Matthew didn't elaborate.

"Sounds like you found yourself a good woman," Ransome said, snapping open the ledger before him. He took the cap off a nearby pen, the tip of which looked as if it had been chewed by a wild animal. "Care to play a game of chance with me, Matthew?"

Matthew's cool eyes met Ransome's brighter green gaze. Matthew's pupils were growing larger by the second. Ransome's lip curled in a scornful smile.

"Afraid?" Ransome asked. "Of me? I'm flattered."

"Whether I play the game or not depends on the stakes."

"My sworn allegiance if you win," Ransome replied, his smile foxy.

"And if I lose?" Matthew's drawl was not treacle-coated but was just as disarming.

"That's where the chance comes in." Ransome sent the domino spinning into the air.

Matthew caught it. "I'll take your wager."

"You don't know what the game is yet," Ransome said.

Matthew stared at him impassively.

Ransome's lips tipped up at the corners. "If you weren't such a bastard, I might grow to like you," he observed.

"Likewise," Matthew said crisply. "The game?"

Ransome drew the ledger closer. "If you can name every sister, brother, niece, nephew, and child of mine you killed in New Orleans all those years ago—as well as any other vampires you killed in the city along the way—I will throw myself in with the rest."

Matthew studied his grandson.

"Wish you'd asked for the terms sooner?" Ransome grinned.

"Malachi Smith. Crispin Jones. Suzette Boudrot. Claude Le Breton." Matthew paused as Ransome searched the ledger's entries for the names.

"You should have kept them in chronological order instead of alphabetical. That's how I remember them."

Ransome looked up in surprise. Matthew's smile was small and wolfish, the kind to make any fox run for the hills.

Matthew continued to recite names long after the downstairs bar opened for business. He finished just in time to see the first gamblers arrive at nine o'clock. Ransome had consumed a fifth of bourbon by then. Matthew was still sipping his first glass of 1775 Château Lafite, which he had given to Marcus in 1789 when the Constitution went into effect. Ransome had been storing it for his father since the Domino Club opened.

"I believe that settles matters, Ransome." Matthew stood and placed the domino on the desk.

Ransome looked dazed. "How can you possibly remember all of them?"

"How could I ever forget?" Matthew drank down the last of his wine. "You have potential, Ransome. I look forward to doing business with you in future. Thank you for the wine."

"Son of a bitch," Ransome muttered under his breath as the sire of his clan departed.

Matthew was weary to the bone and ready to murder something when he returned to the Garden District. He'd walked there from the French Quarter, hoping to burn off some excess emotion. The endless list of names had stirred up too many memories, none of them pleasant. Guilt had followed in their wake.

He took out his phone, hoping that Diana had sent him a photograph. The images she sent thus far were his lifeline. Though Matthew had been furious to discover from them that his wife was in London rather than Sept-Tours, there had been moments over the past weeks when the glimpses into her life there were all that kept him sane.

"Hello, Matthew." To his surprise, Fernando sat on the wide front steps of Marcus's house, waiting for him. Chris Roberts was perched nearby.

"Diana?" It was part howl, part accusation, and entirely terrifying. Behind Fernando the door opened.

"Fernando? Chris?" Marcus looked startled. "What are you doing here?"

"Waiting for Matthew," Fernando replied.

"Come inside. All of you." Marcus beckoned them forward. "Miss Davenport is watching." His neighbors were old, idle, and nosy.

Matthew, however, was beyond the reach of reason. He'd been nearly there several times, but the unexpected sight of Fernando and Chris had sent him over. Now that Marcus knew that his father had blood rage, he understood why Matthew always went away—alone—to recover when he got into this state.

"Who is with her?" Matthew's voice was like a musket firing: first a raspy sound of warning, then a loud report.

"Ysabeau, I expect," Marcus said. "Phoebe. And Sarah. And of course Gallowglass."

"Don't forget Leonard," Jack said, appearing behind Marcus. "He's my best friend, Matthew. Leonard would never let anything happen to Diana."

"You see, Matthew? Diana is just fine." Marcus had already heard from Ransome that Matthew had come from Royal Street, having achieved his goal of family solidarity. Marcus couldn't imagine what had put Matthew in such a foul mood, given his success.

Matthew's arm moved quickly and with enough power to pulverize a human's bones. Instead of choosing a soft target, however, he smashed his hand into one of the white Ionic pillars supporting the upper gallery of the house. Jack put a restraining hand on his other arm.

"If this keeps up, I'm going to have to move back to the Marigny," Marcus said mildly, eyeing a cannonball-size depression near the front door.

"Let me go," Matthew said. Jack's hand dropped to his side, and Matthew shot up the steps and stalked down the long hall to the back of the house. A door slammed in the distance.

"Well, that went better than I expected." Fernando stood.

"He's been worse since my mo—" Jack bit his lip and avoided Marcus's gaze.

"You must be Jack," Fernando said. He bowed, as though Jack were royalty and not a penniless orphan with a deadly disease. "It is an honor to meet you. *Madame* your mother speaks of you often, and with great pride."

"She's not my mother," Jack said, lightning quick. "It was a mistake."

"That was no mistake," Fernando said. "Blood may speak loudly, but I always prefer the tales told by the heart."

"Did you say '*madame*'?" Marcus's lungs felt tight, and his voice sounded strange. He hadn't let himself hope that Fernando would do such a selfless thing, and yet . . .

"Yes, *milord.*" Fernando bowed again.

"Why is he bowing to you?" Jack whispered to Marcus. "And who is '*milord*'?"

"Marcus is '*milord,*' because he is one of Matthew's children," Fernando explained. "And I bow to you both, because that is how family members who are not of the blood treat those who are—with respect and gratitude."

"Thank God. You've joined us." The air left Marcus's lungs in a whoosh of relief.

"I sure as hell hope there's enough bourbon in this house to wash down all the bullshit," Chris said. "'*Milord*' my ass. And I'm not bowing to anybody."

"Duly noted," Marcus said. "What brings you both to New Orleans?"

"Miriam sent me," Chris said. "I've got test results for Matthew, and she didn't want to send them electronically. Plus, Fernando didn't know how to find Matthew. Good thing Jack and I stayed in touch." He smiled at the young man. Jack grinned back.

"As for me, I am here to save your father from himself," Fernando bowed again, this time with a trace of mockery. "With your permission, *milord.*"

"Be my guest," Marcus said, stepping inside. "But if you call me '*milord*' or bow to me one more time, I'll put you in the bayou. And Chris will help me."

"I'll show you where Matthew is," Jack said, already eager to rejoin his idol.

"What about me? We need to catch up," Chris said, grabbing his arm. "Have you been sketching, Jack?"

"My sketchbook is upstairs. . . ." Jack cast a worried look toward the back garden. "Matthew isn't feeling well. He never leaves me when I'm like this. I should—"

Fernando rested his hands on the young man's tense shoulders. "You remind me of Matthew, back when he was a young vampire." It hurt Fernando's heart to see it, but it was true.

"I do?" Jack sounded awed.

"You do. Same compassion. Same courage, too." Fernando looked at Jack thoughtfully. "And you share Matthew's hope that if you shoulder the burdens of others, they will love you in spite of the sickness in your veins."

Jack looked at his feet.

"Did Matthew tell you that his brother Hugh was my mate?" Fernando asked.

"No," Jack murmured.

"Long ago Hugh told Matthew something very important. I am here to remind him of it." Fernando waited for Jack to meet his eyes.

"What?" Jack asked, unable to hide his curiosity.

"If you truly love someone, you will cherish what they despise most about themselves." Fernando's voice dropped. "Next time Matthew forgets that, you remind him. And if you forget, I'll remind you. Once. After that, I'm telling Diana that you are wallowing in self-hatred. And your mother is not nearly as forgiving as I am."

Fernando found Matthew in the narrow back garden, under the cover of a small gazebo. The rain that had been threatening all evening had finally started to fall. He was oddly preoccupied with his phone. Every minute or so, his thumb moved, followed by a fixed stare, then another movement of the thumb.

"You're as bad as Diana, staring at her phone all the time without ever sending a message." Fernando's laughter stopped abruptly. "It's you. You've been in touch with her all along."

"Just pictures. No words. I don't trust myself—or the Congregation—with words." Matthew's thumb moved.

Fernando had heard Diana say to Sarah, "Still no word from Matthew." Literally speaking, the witch had not lied, which had prevented the family from knowing her secret. And as long as Diana sent only pictures, there would be little way for Matthew to know how badly things had gone wrong in Oxford.

Matthew's breath was ragged. He steadied it with visible effort. His thumb moved.

"Do that one more time and I'll break it. And I'm not talking about the phone."

The sound that came out of Matthew's mouth was more bark than laugh, as if the human part of him had given up the fight and let the wolf win.

"What do you think Hugh would have done with a cell phone?" Matthew cradled his in both hands as though it were his last precious link to the world outside his own troubled mind.

"Not much. Hugh wouldn't remember to charge it, for a start. I loved your brother with all my heart, Matthew, but he was hopeless when it came to daily life."

This time Matthew's answering chuckle sounded less like a sound a wild animal might make.

"I take it that patriarchy has been more difficult than you anticipated?" Fernando didn't envy Matthew for having to assert his leadership over this pack.

"Not really. Marcus's children still hate me, and rightfully so." Matthew's fingers closed on the phone, his eyes straying to the screen like an addict's. "I just saw the last of them. Ransome made me account for every vampire death I was responsible for in New Orleans—even the ones that had nothing to do with purging the blood rage from the city."

"That must have taken some time," Fernando murmured.

"Five hours. Ransome was surprised I remembered them all by name," Matthew said.

Fernando was not.

"Now all of Marcus's children have agreed to support me and be included in the scion, but I wouldn't want to test their devotion," Matthew continued. "Mine is a family built on fear—fear of Benjamin, of the Congregation, of other vampires, even of me. It's not based on love or respect."

"Fear is easy to root. Love and respect take more time," Fernando told him.

The silence stretched, became leaden.

"Do you not want to ask me about your wife?"

"No." Matthew stared at an ax buried in a thick stump. There were piles of split logs all around it. He rose and picked up a fresh log. "Not until I'm well enough to go to her and see for myself. I couldn't bear it, Fernando. Not being able to hold her—to watch our children grow inside her—to know she is safe, it's been—"

Fernando waited until the ax thunked into the wood before he prompted Matthew to continue.

"It's been what, *Mateus?*"

Matthew pulled the ax free. He swung again.

Had Fernando not been a vampire, he wouldn't have heard the response.

"It's been like having my heart ripped out." Matthew's axhead cleaved the wood with a mighty crack. "Every single minute of every single day."

Fernando gave Matthew forty-eight hours to recover from the ordeal with Ransome. Confessions of past sins were never easy, and Matthew was particularly prone to brooding.

Fernando took advantage of that time to introduce himself to Marcus's children and grandchildren. He made sure they understood the family rules and who would punish those who disobeyed them, for Fernando had appointed himself Matthew's enforcer—and executioner. The New Orleans branch of the Bishop-Clairmont family was rather subdued afterward, and Fernando decided Matthew could now go home. Fernando was increasingly concerned about Diana. Ysabeau said her medical condition was unchanged, but Sarah was still worried. Something was not right, she told Fernando, and she suspected that only Matthew would be able to fix it.

Fernando found Matthew in the garden as he often was, eyes black and hackles raised. He was still in the grip of blood rage. Sadly, there was no more wood for him to chop in Orleans Parish.

"Here." Fernando dropped a bag at Matthew's feet.

Inside the bag Matthew found his small ax and chisel, T-handled augers of various sizes, a frame saw, and two of his precious planes. Alain had neatly wrapped the planes in oiled cloth to protect them during their travels. Matthew stared at his well-used tools, then at his hands.

"Those hands haven't always done bloody work," Fernando reminded him. "I remember when they healed, created, made music."

Matthew looked at him, mute.

"Will you make them on straight legs or with a curved base so they can be rocked?" Fernando asked conversationally.

Matthew frowned. "Make what?"

"The cradles. For the twins." Fernando let his words sink in. "I think oak is best—stout and strong—but Marcus tells me that cherry is traditional in America. Perhaps Diana would prefer that."

Matthew picked up his chisel. The worn handle filled his palm. "Rowan. I'll make them out of rowan for protection."

Fernando squeezed Matthew's shoulder with approval and departed.

Matthew dropped the chisel back into the bag. He took out his phone, hesitated, and snapped a photograph. Then he waited.

Diana's response was swift and made his bones hollow with longing. His wife was in the bath. He recognized the curves of the copper tub in the Mayfair house. But these were not the curves that interested him.

His wife—his clever, wicked wife—had propped the phone on her breastbone and taken a picture down the length of her naked body. All that was visible was the mound of her belly, the skin stretched impossibly tight, and the tips of her toes resting on the curled edge of the tub.

If he concentrated, Matthew could imagine her scent rising from the warm water, feel the silk of her hair between his fingers, trace the long, strong lines of her thigh and shoulder. Christ, he missed her.

"Fernando said you needed lumber." Marcus was standing before him, frowning.

Matthew dragged his eyes away from the phone. What he needed, only Diana could provide.

"Fernando also said if anyone woke him in the next forty-eight hours, there would be hell to pay," Marcus said, looking at the stacks of split logs. They certainly wouldn't lack firewood this winter. "You know how Ransome loves a challenge—not to mention a brush with the devil—so you can imagine his response."

"Do tell," Matthew said with a dry chuckle. He hadn't laughed in some time, so the sound was rusty and raw.

"Ransome has already been on the phone to the Krewe of Muses. I expect the Ninth Ward Marching Band will be here by suppertime. Vampire or no, they'll rouse Fernando for sure." Marcus looked down at his father's leather tool bag. "Are you finally going to teach Jack to carve?" The boy had been begging Matthew for lessons since he arrived.

Matthew shook his head. "I thought he might like to help me make cradles instead."

Matthew and Jack worked on the cradles for almost a week. Every cut of wood, every finely hewn dovetail that joined the pieces together, every swipe of the plane helped to reduce Matthew's blood rage. Working on a present for Diana made him feel connected to her again, and he began to talk about the children and his hopes.

Jack was a good pupil, and his skills as an artist proved handy when it came to carving decorative designs into the cradles. While they worked, Jack asked Matthew about his childhood and how he'd met Diana at the Bodleian. No one else would have gotten away with asking such direct, personal questions, but the rules were always slightly different where Jack was concerned.

When they were finished, the cradles were works of art. Matthew and Jack wrapped them carefully in soft blankets to protect them on the journey back to London.

It was only after the cradles were finished and ready to go that Fernando told Matthew about Diana's condition.

Matthew's response was entirely expected. First he went still and silent. Then he swung into action.

"Get the pilot on the phone. I'm not waiting until tomorrow. I want to be in London by morning," Matthew said, his tone clipped and precise. "Marcus!"

"What's wrong?" Marcus said.

"Diana isn't well." Matthew scowled ferociously at Fernando. "I should have been told."

"I thought you had been." Fernando didn't need to say anything else. Matthew knew who had kept this from him. Fernando suspected that Matthew knew why as well.

Matthew's usually mobile face turned to stone, and his normally expressive eyes were blank.

"What happened?" Marcus said. He told Jack where to find his medical bag and called for Ransome.

"Diana found the missing page from Ashmole 782." Fernando took Matthew by the shoulders. "There's more. She saw Benjamin at the Bodleian Library. He knows about the pregnancy. He attacked Phoebe."

"Phoebe?" Marcus was distraught. "Is she all right?"

"Benjamin?" Jack inhaled sharply.

"Phoebe is fine. And Benjamin is nowhere to be found," Fernando reassured them. "As for Diana, Hamish called Edward Garrett and Jane Sharp. They're overseeing her case."

"They're among the finest doctors in the city, Matthew," Marcus said. "Diana couldn't be in better care."

"She will be," Matthew said, picking up a cradle and heading out the door. "She'll be in mine."

30

You shouldn't have any problem with it now," I told the young witch sitting before me. She had come at the suggestion of Linda Crosby to see if I could figure out why her protection spell was no longer effective.

Working out of Clairmont House, I had become London's chief magical diagnostician, listening to accounts of failed exorcisms, spells gone bad, and elemental magic on the loose, and then helping the witches find solutions. As soon as Amanda cast her spell for me, I could see the problem: When she recited the words, the blue and green threads around her got tangled up with a single strand of red that pulled on the six-crossed knots at the core of the spell. The gramarye had become convoluted, the spell's intentions murky, and now instead of protecting Amanda it was the magical equivalent of an angry Chihuahua, snarling and snapping at everything that came close.

"Hello, Amanda," Sarah said, sticking her head in to see how we were faring. "Did you get what you needed?"

"Diana was brilliant, thanks," Amanda said.

"Wonderful. Let me show you out," Sarah said.

I leaned back on the cushions, sad to see Amanda go. Since the doctors from Harley Street had me on bed rest, my visitors were few.

The good news was that I didn't have preeclampsia—at least not as it usually develops in warmbloods. I had no protein in my urine, and my blood pressure was actually below normal. Nevertheless, swelling, nausea, and shoulder pain were not symptoms the jovial Dr. Garrett or his aptly named colleague, Dr. Sharp, wished to ignore—especially not after Ysabeau explained that I was Matthew Clairmont's mate.

The bad news was that they put me on modified bed rest nonetheless, and so I would remain until the twins were born—which Dr. Sharp hoped would not be for another four weeks at least, although her worried look suggested that this was an optimistic projection. I was allowed to do some gentle stretching under Amira's supervision and take two ten-minute walks around the garden per day. Stairs, standing, lifting were positively forbidden.

My phone buzzed on the side table. I picked it up, hoping for a text from Matthew.

A picture of the front door of Clairmont House was waiting for me.

It was then that I noticed how quiet it was, the only sound the ticking of the house's many clocks.

The creak of the front-door hinges and the soft scrape of wood against marble broke the silence. Without thinking I shot to my feet, teetering on legs that had grown weaker during my enforced inactivity.

And then Matthew was there.

All that either of us could do for the first long moments was to drink in the sight of the other. Matthew's hair was tousled and slightly wavy from the damp London air, and he was wearing a gray sweater and black jeans. Fine lines around his eyes showed the stress he'd been under.

He stalked toward me. I wanted to jump up and run at him, but something in his expression kept me glued to the spot.

When at last Matthew reached me, he cradled my neck with his fingertips and searched my eyes. His thumb brushed across my lips, bringing the blood to the surface. I saw the small changes in him: the firm set of his jaw, the unusual tightness of his mouth, the hooded expression caused by the lowering of his eyelids.

My lips parted as his thumb made another pass over my tingling mouth.

"I missed you, *mon coeur,*" Matthew said, his voice rough. He leaned down with the same deliberation as he had crossed the room, and he kissed me.

My head spun. He was *here.* My hands gripped his sweater as though that could keep him from disappearing. A raspy catch in the back of his throat that was almost a growl kept me quiet when I prepared to rise up and meet him in his embrace. Matthew's free hand roamed over my back, my hip, and settled on my belly. One of the babies gave a sharp, reproachful kick. He smiled against my mouth, the thumb that had first stroked my lip now featherlight on my pulse. Then he registered the books, flowers, and fruit.

"I'm absolutely fine. I was a bit nauseated and had a pain in my shoulder, that's all," I said quickly. His medical education would send his mind racing toward all sorts of terrible diagnoses. "My blood pressure is fine, and so are the babies."

"Fernando told me. I'm sorry I wasn't here," he murmured, his fingers rubbing my tense neck muscles. For the first time since New Haven, I let myself relax.

"I missed you, too." My heart was too full to let me say more.

But Matthew didn't want more words. The next thing I knew I was airborne, cradled in his arms with my feet dangling.

Upstairs, Matthew put me in the leafy surrounds of the bed we'd slept in so many lifetimes ago in the Blackfriars. Silently he undressed me, examining every inch of exposed flesh as though he had been given an unexpected glimpse of something rare and precious. He was utterly silent as he did so, letting his eyes and the gentleness of his touch speak for him.

Over the course of the next few hours, Matthew reclaimed me, his fingers erasing every trace of the other creatures I'd been in contact with since he departed. At some point he let me undress him, his body responding to mine with gratifying speed. Dr. Sharp had been absolutely clear on the risks associated with any contraction of my uterine muscles, however. There would be no release of sexual tension for me, but just because I had to deny my body's needs, that didn't mean Matthew did, too. When I reached for him, however, he stilled my hand and kissed me deeply.

Together, Matthew said without a word. *Together, or not at all.*

"Don't tell me you can't find him, Fernando," Matthew said, not even trying to sound reasonable. He was in the kitchen of Clairmont House, scrambling eggs and making toast. Diana was upstairs resting, unaware of the conference taking place on the lower ground floor.

"I still think we should ask Jack," Fernando said. "He could help us narrow down the options, at least."

"No. I don't want him involved." Matthew turned to Marcus. "Is Phoebe all right?"

"It was too close for comfort, Matthew," Marcus said grimly. "I know you don't approve of Phoebe's becoming a vampire, but—"

"You have my blessing," Matthew interrupted. "Just choose someone who will do it properly."

"Thank you. I already have." Marcus hesitated. "Jack has been asking to see Diana."

"Send him over this evening." Matthew flipped the eggs onto a plate. "Tell him to bring the cradles. Around seven. We'll be expecting him."

"I'll tell him," Marcus said. "Anything else?"

"Yes," Matthew said. "Someone must be feeding Benjamin information. Since you can't find Benjamin, you can look for him—or her."

"And then?" Fernando asked.

"Bring them to me," Matthew replied as he left the room.

We remained locked alone in the house for three days, twined together, talking little, never separated for more than the few moments when Matthew went downstairs to make me something to eat or to accept a meal dropped off by the Connaught's staff. The hotel had apparently worked out a food-for-wine scheme with Matthew. Several cases of 1961 Château Latour left the house in exchange for exquisite morsels of food, such as hard-boiled quail eggs in a nest of seaweed and delicate ravioli filled with tender cèpes that the chef assured Matthew had been flown in from France only that morning.

On the second day, Matthew and I trusted ourselves to talk, and similarly tiny mouthfuls of words were offered up and digested alongside the delicacies from a few streets away. He reported on Jack's efforts at self-governance in the thick of Marcus's sprawling brood. Matthew spoke with great admiration of Marcus's deft handling of his children and grandchildren, all of whom had names worthy of characters in a nineteenth-century penny dreadful. And, reluctantly, Matthew told me of his struggles not only with his blood rage but with his desire to be at my side.

"I would have gone mad without the pictures," he confessed, spooned up against my back with his long, cold nose buried in my neck. "The images of where we'd lived, or the flowers in the garden, or your toes on the edge of the bath kept my sanity from slipping entirely."

I shared my own tale with a slowness worthy of a vampire, gauging Matthew's reactions so that I could take a break when necessary and let him absorb what I'd experienced in London and Oxford. There was finding Timothy and the missing page, as well as meeting up with Amira and being back at the Old Lodge. I showed Matthew my purple finger and shared the goddess's proclamation that to possess the Book of Life I would have to give up something I cherished. And I spared no details from my account of meeting Benjamin—not my own failures as a witch, nor what he'd done to Phoebe, not even his final, parting threat.

"If I hadn't hesitated, Benjamin would be dead." I'd been over the event hundreds of times and still didn't understand why my nerve had failed. "First Juliette and now—"

"You cannot blame yourself for choosing not to kill someone," Matthew said, pressing a finger to my lips. "Death is a difficult business."

"Do you think Benjamin is still here, in England?" I asked.

"Not here," Matthew assured me, rolling me to face him. "Never again where you are."

Never is a long time. Philippe's admonishment came back to me clearly.

I pushed the worry away and pulled my husband closer.

"Benjamin has utterly vanished," Andrew Hubbard told Matthew. "That's what he does."

"That's not entirely true. Addie claims she saw him in Munich," Marcus said. "She alerted her fellow knights."

While Matthew was in the sixteenth century, Marcus had admitted women into the brotherhood. He began with Miriam, and she helped him name the rest. Matthew wasn't sure if this was madness or genius at work, but if it helped him locate Benjamin, he was prepared to remain agnostic. Matthew blamed Marcus's progressive ideas on his onetime neighbor Catherine Macaulay, who had occupied an important place in his son's life when he was first made a vampire and filled his ears with her bluestocking ideas.

"We could ask Baldwin," Fernando said. "He is in Berlin, after all."

"Not yet," Matthew said.

"Does Diana know you're looking for Benjamin?" Marcus asked.

"No," Matthew said as he headed back to his wife with a plate of food from the Connaught.

"Not yet," Andrew Hubbard muttered.

That evening it was difficult to determine who was more overjoyed at our reunion: Jack or Lobero. The pair got twisted in a tangle of legs and feet, but

Jack finally managed to extricate himself from the beast, who nevertheless beat him to my chaise longue in the Chinese Room and leaped onto the cushion with a triumphant bark.

"Down, Lobero. You'll make the thing collapse." Jack stooped and kissed me respectfully on the cheek. "Grandmother."

"Don't you dare!" I warned, taking his hand in mine. "Save your grandmotherly endearments for Ysabeau."

"I told you she wouldn't like it," Matthew said with a grin. He snapped his fingers at Lobero and pointed to the floor. The dog slid his forelegs off the chaise, leaving his backside planted firmly against me. It took another snap of the fingers for him to slide off entirely.

"Madame Ysabeau said she has standards to maintain, and I will have to do two extremely wicked things before she will let me call her Grandmother," Jack said.

"And yet you're still calling her Madame Ysabeau?" I looked at him in amazement. "What's keeping you? You've been back in London for days."

Jack looked down, his lips curved at the prospect of more delicious mischief to come. "Well, I've been on my best behavior, *madame.*"

"Madame?" I groaned and threw a pillow at him. "That's worse than calling me 'Grandmother.'"

Jack let the pillow hit him square in the face.

"Fernando's right," Matthew said. "Your heart knows what to call Diana, even if your thick head and vampire propriety are telling you different. Now, help me bring in your mother's present."

Under Lobero's careful supervision, Matthew and Jack carried in first one, then another cloth-wrapped bundle. They were tall and seemingly rectangular in shape, rather like small bookcases. Matthew had sent me a picture of a stack of wood and some tools. The two must have worked on the items together. I smiled at the sudden image of them, dark head and light bowed over a common project.

As Matthew and Jack gradually unwrapped the two objects, it became clear that they were not bookcases but cradles: two beautiful, identically carved and painted, wooden cradles. Their curved bases hung inside sturdy wooden stands that sat on level feet. This way the cradles could be rocked gently in the air or removed from their supports and put on the floor to be nudged with a foot. My eyes filled.

"We made them out of rowan wood. Ransome couldn't figure out where the hell we were going to find Scottish wood in Louisiana, but he obviously doesn't know Matthew." Jack ran his fingers along one of the smooth edges.

"The cradles are rowan, but the stand is made from oak—strong American white oak." Matthew regarded me with a touch of anxiety. "Do you like them?"

"I love them." I looked up at my husband, hoping my expression would tell him just how much. It must have, for he cupped the side of my face tenderly and his own expression was happier than I'd seen since we returned to the present.

"Matthew designed them. He said it's how cradles used to be made, so you could get them up off the floor and out of the way of the chickens," Jack explained.

"And the carving?" A tree had been incised into the wood at the foot of each cradle, its roots and branches intertwined. Carefully applied silver and gold paint highlighted the leaves and bark.

"That was Jack's idea," Matthew said, putting his hand on the younger man's shoulder. "He remembered the design on your spell box and thought the symbol was fitting for a baby's bed."

"Every part of the cradles has meaning," Jack said. "The rowan is a magical tree, you know, and white oak symbolizes strength and immortality. The finials on the four corners are shaped like acorns—that's for luck—and the rowanberries carved on the supports are supposed to protect them. Corra's on the cradles, too. Dragons guard rowan trees to keep humans from eating their fruit."

I looked more closely and saw that a firedrake's curving tail provided the arc for the cradles' rockers.

"These will be the two safest babies in all the world, then," I said, "not to mention the luckiest, sleeping in such beautiful beds."

His gifts having been given and gratefully received, Jack sat on the floor with Lobero and told animated tales about life in New Orleans. Matthew relaxed in one of the japanned easy chairs, watching the minutes tick by with Jack showing no sign of blood rage.

The clocks were striking ten when Jack left for Pickering Place, which he described as crowded but of good cheer.

"Is Gallowglass there?" I hadn't seen him since Matthew returned.

"He left right after we arrived back in London. Said he had somewhere to go and would be back when he was able." Jack shrugged.

Something must have flickered in my eyes, for Matthew was instantly watchful. He said nothing, however, until he'd seen Jack and Lobero downstairs and safely on their way.

"It's probably for the best," Matthew said when he returned. He arranged himself in the chaise longue behind me so that he could serve as my backrest. I settled into him with a sigh of contentment as he circled his arms around me.

"That all of our family and friends are at Marcus's house?" I snorted. "Of course you think that's for the best."

"No. That Gallowglass has decided to go away for a little while." Matthew pressed his lips against my hair. I stiffened.

"Matthew . . ." I needed to tell him about Gallowglass.

"I know, *mon coeur.* I've suspected it for some time, but when I saw him with you in New Haven, I was sure." Matthew rocked one of the cradles with a gentle push of his finger.

"Since when?" I asked.

"Maybe from the beginning. Certainly from the night Rudolf touched you in Prague," Matthew replied. The emperor had behaved so badly on Walpurgisnacht, the same night we'd seen the Book of Life whole and complete for the last time. "Even then it came as no surprise, simply a confirmation of something I already, on some level, understood."

"Gallowglass didn't do anything improper," I said quickly.

"I know that, too. Gallowglass is Hugh's son and incapable of dishonor." Matthew's throat moved as he cleared the emotion from his voice. "Perhaps once the babies are born, he will be able to move on with his life. I would like him to be happy."

"Me, too," I whispered, wondering how many knots and threads it would take to help Gallowglass find his mate.

"Where has Gallowglass gone?" Matthew glowered at Fernando, though they both knew that his nephew's sudden disappearance wasn't Fernando's fault.

"Wherever it is, he's better off there than here waiting for you and Diana to welcome your children into the world," Fernando said.

"Diana doesn't agree." Matthew flipped through his e-mail. He'd taken to reading it downstairs so that Diana didn't know about the intelligence he was gathering on Benjamin. "She's asking for him."

"Philippe was wrong to make Gallowglass watch over her." Fernando downed a cup of wine.

"You think so? It's what I would have done," Matthew said.

"Think, Matthew," Dr. Garrett said impatiently. "Your children have vampire blood in them—though how that is possible, I will leave between you and God. That means they have some vampire immunity at least. Wouldn't you rather your wife give birth at home, as women have done for centuries?"

Now that Matthew was back, he expected to play a significant role in determining how the twins would be brought into the world. As far as he was concerned, I should deliver in the hospital. My preference was to give birth at Clairmont House, with Marcus in attendance.

"Marcus hasn't practiced obstetrics for years," Matthew grumbled.

"Hell, man, you taught him anatomy. You taught *me* anatomy, come to think of it!" Dr. Garrett was clearly at the end of his rope. "Do you think the uterus has suddenly wandered off to a new location? Talk sense into him, Jane."

"Edward is right," Dr. Sharp said. "The four of us have dozens of medical degrees between us and more than two millennia of combined experience. Marthe has very likely delivered more babies than anyone now living, and Diana's aunt is a certified midwife. I suspect we'll manage."

I suspected she was right. So did Matthew, in the end. Having been overruled about the twins' delivery, he was eager to get out of the room when Fernando arrived. The two disappeared downstairs. They often closeted themselves together, talking family business.

"What did Matthew say when you told him you'd sworn your allegiance to the Bishop-Clairmont family?" I asked Fernando when he came upstairs later to say hello.

"He told me I was mad," Fernando replied with a twinkle in his eye. "I told Matthew that I expect to be made a godfather to your eldest child in return."

"I'm sure that can be arranged," I said, though I was beginning to worry at the number of godparents the children were going to have.

"I hope you're keeping track of all the promises you've made," I remarked to Matthew later that afternoon.

"I am," he said. "Chris wants the smartest and Fernando the eldest. Hamish wants the best-looking. Marcus wants a girl. Jack wants a brother. Gallowglass expressed an interest in being godfather to any blond babies before we left New Haven." Matthew ticked them off on his fingers.

"I'm having twins, not a litter of puppies," I said, staggered by the number of interested parties. "Besides, we're not royals. And I'm pagan! The twins don't need so many godparents."

"Do you want me to pick the godmothers, too?" Matthew's eyebrow rose.

"Miriam," I said hastily, before he could suggest any of his terrifying female relatives. "Phoebe, of course. Marthe. Sophie. Amira. I'd like to ask Vivian Harrison, too."

"See. Once you get started, they mount up quickly," Matthew said with a smile.

That left us with six godparents per child. We were going to be drowning in silver baby cups and teddy bears if the piles of tiny clothes, booties, and blankets Ysabeau and Sarah had already purchased were any indication.

Two of the twins' potential godparents joined us for dinner most evenings. Marcus and Phoebe were so obviously in love that it was impossible not to feel romantic in their presence. The air between them thrummed with tension. Phoebe, for her part, was as unflappable and self-possessed as ever. She didn't hesitate to lecture Matthew on the state of the frescoes in the ballroom and how shocked Angelica Kauffmann would be to find her work neglected in such a fashion. Nor did Phoebe plan on allowing the de Clermont family treasures to be kept from the eyes of the public indefinitely.

"There are ways to share them anonymously, and for a fixed period of time," she told Matthew.

"Expect to see the picture of Margaret More from the Old Lodge's upstairs loo on display at the National Portrait Gallery very soon." I squeezed Matthew's hand encouragingly.

"Why didn't someone warn me it would be so difficult to have historians in the family?" he asked Marcus, looking a trifle dazed. "And how did we end up with two?"

"Good taste," Marcus said, giving Phoebe a smoldering glance.

"Indeed." Matthew's mouth twitched at the obvious double entendre.

When it was just the four of us like this, Matthew and Marcus would talk for hours about the new scion—though Marcus preferred to call it "Matthew's clan" for reasons that had as much to do with his Scottish grandfather as with his dislike of applying botanical and zoological terms to vampire families.

"Members of the Bishop-Clairmont scion—or clan if you insist—will have to be especially careful when they mate or marry," Matthew said one evening over dinner. "The eyes of every vampire will be on us."

Marcus did a double take. "Bishop-Clairmont?"

"Of course," Matthew said with a frown. "What did you expect us to be called? Diana doesn't use my name, and our children will bear both. It's only right that a family composed of witches and vampires has a name that reflects that."

I was touched by his thoughtfulness. Matthew could be such a patriarchal, overprotective creature, but he had not forgotten my family's traditions.

"Why, Matthew de Clermont," Marcus said with a slow smile. "That's downright progressive for an old fossil like you."

"Hmph." Matthew sipped at his wine.

Marcus's phone buzzed, and he looked at his display. "Hamish is here. I'll go down and let him in."

Muted conversation floated up the stairs. Matthew rose. "Stay with Diana, Phoebe."

Phoebe and I exchanged worried looks.

"It will be so much more convenient when I'm a vampire, too," she said, trying in vain to hear what was being said downstairs. "At least then we'll know what's going on."

"Then they'll just take a walk," I said. "I need to devise a spell—one that will magnify the sound waves. Something using air and a bit of water, perhaps."

"Shh." Phoebe tilted her head and made an impatient sound. "Now they've lowered their voices. How maddening."

When Matthew and Marcus reappeared with Hamish in tow, their faces told me that something was seriously wrong.

"There's been another message from Benjamin." Matthew crouched before me, his eyes level with mine. "I don't want to keep this from you, Diana, but you must stay calm."

"Just tell me," I said, my heart in my throat.

"The witch that Benjamin captured is dead. Her child died with her." Matthew's eyes searched mine, which filled with tears. And not only for the young witch but for myself, and my own failure. *If I hadn't hesitated, Benjamin's witch might still be alive.*

"Why can't we have the time we need to sort things out and deal with this huge mess we seem to have made? And why do people have to keep dying while we do it?" I cried.

"There was no way to prevent this," Matthew said, stroking my hair away from my forehead. "Not this time."

"What about next time?" I demanded.

The men were grim and silent.

"Oh. Of course." I drew in a sharp lungful of air, and my fingers tingled. Corra burst out from my ribs with an agitated squawk and launched herself upward to perch on the chandelier. "You'll stop him. Because next time he's coming for me."

I felt a pop, a trickle of liquid.

Matthew looked down to my rounded belly in shock.

The babies were on their way.

31

Don't you dare tell me not to push." I was red-faced and sweating, and all I wanted was to get these babies out of me as quickly as possible.

"Do. Not. Push," Marthe repeated. She and Sarah had me walking around in an effort to ease the aching in my back and legs. The contractions were still around five minutes apart, but the pain was becoming excruciating, radiating from my spine around to my belly.

"I want to lie down." After weeks of resisting bed rest, now I just wanted to crawl back into the bed, with its rubber-covered mattress and sterilized sheets. The irony was not lost on me, nor on anyone else in the room.

"You're not lying down," Sarah said.

"Oh, God. Here comes another one." I stopped in my tracks and gripped their hands. The contraction lasted a long time. I had just straightened up and started breathing normally when another one hit. "I want Matthew!"

"I'm right here," Matthew said, taking Marthe's place. He nodded to Sarah. "That was fast."

"The book said the contractions are supposed to get gradually closer together." I sounded like a peevish schoolmarm.

"Babies don't read books, honey," Sarah said. "They have their own ideas about these things."

"And when they're of a mind to be born, babies make no bones about it," Dr. Sharp said, entering the room with a smile. Dr. Garrett had been called away to another delivery at the last minute, so Dr. Sharp had taken charge of my medical team. She pressed the stethoscope against my belly, moved it, and pressed again. "You're doing marvelously, Diana. So are the twins. No sign of distress. I'd recommend we try to deliver vaginally."

"I want to lie down," I said through gritted teeth as another band of steel shot out from my spine and threatened to cut me in two. "Where's Marcus?"

"He's just across the hall," Matthew said. I dimly remembered ejecting Marcus from the room when the contractions intensified.

"If I need a cesarean, can Marcus be here in time?" I demanded.

"You called?" Marcus said, entering the room in scrubs. His genial grin and unruffled demeanor calmed me instantly. Now that he'd returned, I couldn't remember why I'd kicked him out of the room.

"Who moved the damn bed?" I puffed my way through another contraction. The bed seemed to be in the same place, but this was clearly an illusion for it was taking forever for me to reach it.

"Matthew did," Sarah said breezily.

"I did no such thing," Matthew protested.

"In labor we blame absolutely everything on the husband. It keeps the mother from developing homicidal fantasies and reminds the men they aren't the center of attention," Sarah explained.

I laughed, thereby missing the rising wave of pain that accompanied the next fierce contraction.

"Fu—Sh—Godda—" I pressed my lips firmly together.

"You are *not* getting through tonight's main event without swearing, Diana," Marcus said.

"I don't want a string of profanity to be the first words the babies hear." Now I recalled the reason for Marcus's expulsion: He'd suggested I was being too prim in the midst of my agony.

"Matthew can sing—and he's loud. I'm sure he could drown you out."

"God—blasted—it hurts," I said, doubling over. "Move the fucking bed if you want to be helpful, but stop arguing with me, you asshole!"

My reply was met with shocked silence.

"Atta girl," Marcus said. "I knew you had it in you. Let's have a look."

Matthew helped me onto the bed, which had been stripped of its priceless silk coverlet and most of its curtains. The two cradles stood in front of the fire, waiting for the twins. I stared at them while Marcus conducted his examination.

Thus far this had been the most physically intrusive four hours of my life. I'd had more things jabbed into me and more stuff taken out of me than I thought possible. It was oddly dehumanizing, considering that I was responsible for bringing new life into the world.

"Still a little while to go," Marcus said, "but things are speeding up nicely."

"Easy for you to say." I would have hit him, but he was positioned between my thighs and the babies were in the way.

"This is your last chance for an epidural," Marcus said. "If you say no, and we have to do a C-section, we'll have to knock you out completely."

"There's no need for you to be heroic, *ma lionne,*" Matthew said.

"I'm not being heroic," I told him for the fourth or fifth time. "We have no idea what an epidural might do to the babies." I stopped, my face scrunched in an attempt to block the pain.

"You have to keep breathing, honey," Sarah pushed her way to my side. "You heard her, Matthew. She isn't taking the epidural, and there's no point in arguing with her about it. Now, about the pain. Laughter helps, Diana. So does focusing on something else."

"Pleasure helps, too," Marthe said, adjusting my feet on the mattress in such a way that my back immediately relaxed.

"Pleasure?" I said, confused. Marthe nodded. I looked at her in horror. "You can't mean *that.*"

"She does," Sarah said. "It can make a huge difference."

"No. How can you even suggest such a thing?" I couldn't think of a less erotically charged moment. Walking now seemed like a very good idea, and I swung my legs over the edge of the bed. That was as far as I got before another contraction seized me. When it was over, Matthew and I were alone.

"Don't even think about it," I said when he put his arms around me.

"I understand 'no' in two dozen languages." His steadiness was annoying.

"Don't you want to yell at me or *something*?" I asked.

Matthew took a moment to consider. "Yes."

"Oh." I'd expected a song and dance about the sanctity of pregnant women and how he would put up with anything for me. I giggled.

"Lie on your left side and I'll rub your back." Matthew pulled me down next to him.

"That's the only thing you're going to rub," I warned.

"So I understand," he said with more aggravating control. "Lie down. Now."

"That sounds more like you. I was beginning to think they'd given *you* the epidural by mistake." I turned and fitted my body into his.

"Witch," he said, nipping me on the shoulder.

It was a good thing I was lying down when the next contraction hit.

"We don't want you to push, because there's no telling how long this will take and the babies aren't ready to be born yet. It's been four hours and eighteen minutes since the contractions started. There could be another day of this ahead of you. You need to rest. That's one reason I wanted you to have the nerve blocker." Matthew used his thumbs to massage the small of my back.

"It's only been four hours and eighteen minutes?" My voice was faint.

"Nineteen minutes now, but yes." Matthew held me while my body was racked with another fierce contraction. When I was able to think straight, I groaned softly and pressed back into Matthew's hand.

"Your thumb is in an absolutely divine spot." I sighed with relief.

"And this spot?" Matthew's thumb traveled lower and closer to my spine.

"Heaven," I said, able to breathe through the next contraction a bit better.

"Your blood pressure is still normal, and the back rub seems to be helping. Let's do it properly." Matthew called for Marcus to bring in the oddly shaped, leather-padded chair with the reading stand from his library and had him set it up by the window, a pillow resting on the support that was designed to hold a book. Matthew helped me sit astride it, facing the pillow.

My belly swelled out and made contact with the back of the chair.

"What on earth is this chair really for?"

"Watching cockfights and playing all-night card games," Matthew said. "You'll find it's much easier on your lower back if you can lean forward a bit and rest your head on the pillow."

It was. Matthew began a thorough massage that started at my hips and moved up until he was loosening the muscles at the base of my skull. I had three more contractions while he was working, and though they were prolonged, Matthew's cool hands and strong fingers seemed to soften some of the pain.

"How many pregnant women have you helped this way?" I asked, mildly curious about where he had acquired this skill. Matthew's hands stilled.

"Only you." His soothing motions continued.

I turned my head and found him looking at me, though his fingers never stopped moving.

"Ysabeau said I'm the only one to sleep in this bedroom."

"Nobody I met seemed worthy of it. But I could envision you in this room—with me, of course—shortly after we met."

"Why do you love me so much, Matthew?" I couldn't see the attraction, especially not when I was rotund, facedown, and gasping with pain. His response was swift:

"To every question I have ever had, or ever will have, you are the answer." He pulled my hair away from my neck and kissed me on the soft flesh beneath the ear. "Do you feel like getting up for a bit?"

A sudden, sharper pain that coursed through my lower extremities kept me from responding. I gasped instead.

"That sounds like ten centimeters' dilation to me," Matthew murmured. "Marcus?"

"Good news, Diana," Marcus said cheerfully as he walked into the room. "You get to push now!"

Push I did. For what seemed like days.

I tried it the modern way first: lying down, with Matthew clasping my hand, a look of adoration on his face.

That didn't work well.

"It's not necessarily a sign of trouble," Dr. Sharp told us, looking at Matthew and me from her vantage point between my thighs. "Twins can take longer to get moving during this stage of labor. Right, Marthe?"

"She needs a stool," Marthe said with a frown.

"I brought mine," Dr. Sharp said. "It's in the hall." She jerked her head in that direction.

And so the babies that were conceived in the sixteenth century opted to eschew modern medical convention and be born the old-fashioned way: on a simple wooden chair with a horseshoe-shaped seat.

Instead of having a half dozen strangers share the birth experience, I was surrounded by the ones I loved: Matthew behind me, holding me up physically and emotionally; Jane and Marthe at my feet, congratulating me on having babies so considerate as to present themselves to the world headfirst; Marcus offering a gentle suggestion every now and then; Sarah at my side, telling me when to breathe and when to push; Ysabeau standing by the door, relaying messages to Phoebe, who waited in the hall and sent a constant stream of texts to Pickering Place, where Fernando, Jack, and Andrew were waiting for news.

It was excruciating.

It took forever.

When at 11:55 P.M. the first indignant cry was heard at long last, I started to weep and laugh. A fierce protective feeling took root where my child had been only moments before, filling me with purpose.

"Is it okay?" I asked, looking down.

"She is perfect," Marthe said, beaming at me proudly.

"She?" Matthew sounded dazed.

"It is a girl. Phoebe, tell them *Madame* has given birth to a girl," Ysabeau said with excitement.

Jane held the tiny creature up. She was blue and wrinkled and smeared with gruesome-looking substances that I'd read about but was inadequately prepared to see on my own child. Her hair was jet black, and there was plenty of it.

"Why is she blue? What's wrong with her? Is she dying?" I felt my anxiety climb.

"She'll turn as red as a beet in no time," Marcus said, looking down at his new sister. He held out a pair of scissors and a clamp to Matthew. "And there's certainly nothing wrong with her lungs. I think you should do the honors."

Matthew stood, motionless.

"If you faint, Matthew Clairmont, I will never let you forget it," Sarah said testily. "Get your ass over there and cut the cord."

"You do it, Sarah." Matthew's hands trembled on my shoulders.

"No. I want Matthew to do it," I said. If he didn't, he was going to regret it later.

My words got Matthew moving, and he was soon on his knees next to Dr. Sharp. In spite of his initial reluctance, once he was presented with a baby and the proper medical equipment, his movements were practiced and sure. After the cord was clamped and cut, Dr. Sharp quickly swaddled our daughter in a waiting blanket. Then she presented this bundle to Matthew.

He stood, dumbstruck, cradling the tiny body in his large hands. There was something miraculous in the juxtaposition of a father's strength with his daughter's vulnerability. She stopped crying for a moment, yawned, and resumed yelling at the cold indignity of her current situation.

"Hello, little stranger," Matthew whispered. He looked at me in awe. "She's beautiful."

"Lord, just listen to her," Marcus said. "A solid eight on the Apgar test, don't you think, Jane?"

"I agree. Why don't you weigh and measure her while we clean up a bit and get ready for the next one?"

Suddenly aware that my job was only half done, Matthew handed the baby into Marcus's care. He then gave me a long look, a deep kiss, and a nod.

"Ready, *ma lionne*?"

"As I'll ever be," I said, seized by another sharp pain.

Twenty minutes later, at 12:15 A.M., our son was born. He was larger than his sister, in both length and weight, but blessed with a similarly robust lung capacity. This, I was told, was a very good thing, though I did wonder if we would still feel that way in twelve hours. Unlike our firstborn, our son had reddish blond hair.

Matthew asked Sarah to cut the cord, since he was wholly absorbed in murmuring a stream of pleasant nonsense into my ear about how beautiful I was and how strong I'd been, all the while holding me upright.

It was after the second baby was born that I started to shake from head to foot.

"What's. Wrong?" I asked through chattering teeth.

Matthew had me out of the birthing stool and onto the bed in a blink.

"Get the babies over here," he ordered.

Marthe plopped one baby on me, and Sarah deposited the other. The babies' limbs were all hitched up and their faces puce with irritation. As soon as I felt the weight of my son and daughter on my chest, the shaking stopped.

"That's the one downside to a birthing stool when there are twins," Dr. Sharp said, beaming. "Mums can get a bit shaky from the sudden emptiness, and we don't get a chance to let you bond with the first child before the second one needs your attention."

Marthe pushed Matthew aside and wrapped both babies in blankets without ever seeming to disturb their position, a bit of vampire legerdemain that I was sure was beyond the capacity of most midwives, no matter how experienced. While Marthe tended to the babies, Sarah gently massaged my stomach until the afterbirth came free with a final, constrictive cramp.

Matthew held the babies for a few moments while Sarah gently cleaned me. A shower, she told me, could wait until I felt like getting up—which I was sure would be approximately never.

She and Marthe removed the sheets and replaced them with new ones, all without my being required to stir. In no time I was propped up against the bed's downy pillows, surrounded by fresh linen. Matthew put the babies back into my arms. The room was empty.

"I don't know how you women survive it," he said, pressing his lips against my forehead.

"Being turned inside out?" I looked at one tiny face, then the other. "I don't know either." My voice dropped. "I wish Mom and Dad were here. Philippe, too."

"If he were, Philippe would be shouting in the streets and waking the neighbors," Matthew said.

"I want to name him Philip, after your father," I said softly. At my words our son cracked one eye open. "Is that okay with you?"

"Only if we name our daughter Rebecca," Matthew said, his hand cupping her dark head. She screwed up her face tighter.

"I'm not sure she approves," I said, marveling that someone so tiny could be so opinionated.

"Rebecca will have plenty of other names to choose from if she continues to object," Matthew said. "Almost as many names as godparents, come to think of it."

"We're going to need a spreadsheet to figure that mess out," I said, hitching Philip higher in my arms. "He is definitely the heavy one."

"They're both a very good size. And Philip is eighteen inches long." Matthew looked at his son with pride.

"He's going to be tall, like his father." I settled more deeply into the pillows.

"And a redhead like his mother and grandmother," Matthew said. He rounded the bed, gave the fire a poke, then lay next to me, propped up on one elbow.

"We've spent all this time searching for ancient secrets and long-lost books of magic, but they're the true chemical wedding," I said, watching while Matthew put his finger in Philip's tiny hand. The baby gripped it with surprising strength.

"You're right." Matthew turned his son's hand this way and that. "A little bit of you, a little bit of me. Part vampire, part witch."

"And all ours," I said firmly, sealing his mouth with a kiss.

* * *

"I have a daughter and a son," Matthew told Baldwin. "Rebecca and Philip. Both are healthy and well."

"And their mother?" Baldwin asked.

"Diana got through it beautifully." Matthew's hands shook whenever he thought of what she'd been through.

"Congratulations, Matthew." Baldwin didn't sound happy.

"What is it?" Matthew frowned.

"The Congregation already knows about the birth."

"How?" Matthew demanded. Someone must be watching the house—either a vampire with very sharp eyes, or a witch with strong second sight.

"Who knows?" Baldwin said wearily. "They're willing to hold in abeyance the charges against you and Diana in exchange for an opportunity to examine the babies."

"Never." Matthew's anger caught light.

"The Congregation only wants to know what the twins are," Baldwin said shortly.

"Mine. Philip and Rebecca are mine," Matthew replied.

"No one seems to be disputing that—impossible though it supposedly is," Baldwin said.

"This is Gerbert's doing." Every instinct told him that the vampire was a crucial link between Benjamin and the search for the Book of Life. He had been manipulating Congregation politics for years, and in all likelihood pulled Knox, Satu, and Domenico into his schemes.

"Perhaps. Not every vampire in London is Hubbard's creature," Baldwin said. "Verin still intends to go to the Congregation on the sixth of December."

"The babies' birth doesn't change anything," Matthew said, though he knew that it did.

"Take care of my sister, Matthew," Baldwin said quietly. Matthew thought he detected a note of real worry in his brother's tone.

"Always," Matthew replied.

The grandmothers were the babies' first visitors. Sarah's grin stretched from ear to ear, and Ysabeau's face was shining with happiness. When we shared the babies' first names, they both were touched at the thought that the legacy of the children's absent grandparents would be carried into the future.

"Leave it to you two to have twins that aren't even born on the same day," Sarah said, swapping Rebecca for Philip, who had been staring at his grandmother with a fascinated frown. "See if you can get her to open her eyes, Ysabeau."

Ysabeau blew gently on Rebecca's face. Her eyes popped wide, and she began to scream, waving her mittened hands at her grandmother. "There. Now we can see you properly, my beauty."

"They're different signs of the zodiac, too," Sarah said, swaying gently with Philip in her arms. Unlike his sister, Philip was content to lie still and quietly observe his surroundings, his dark eyes wide.

"Who are?" I was feeling drowsy, and Sarah's chatter was too complicated for me to follow.

"The babies. Rebecca is a Scorpio, and Philip is a Sagittarius. The serpent and the archer," Sarah replied.

The de Clermonts and the Bishops. The tenth knot and the goddess. The arrow's owl-feather fletches tickled my shoulder, and the firedrake's tail tightened around my aching hips. A premonitory finger drew up my spine, leaving my nerves tingling.

Matthew frowned. "Something wrong, *mon coeur*?"

"No. Just a strange feeling." The urge to protect that had taken root in the aftermath of the babies' birth grew stronger. I didn't want Rebecca and Philip tied to some larger weaving, the design of which could never be understood by someone as small and insignificant as their mother. They were my children—our children—and I would make sure that they were allowed to find their own path, not follow the one that destiny and fate handed them.

"Hello, Father. Are you watching?"

Matthew stared at his computer screen, his phone tucked between his shoulder and his ear. This time Benjamin had called to deliver the message. He wanted to hear Matthew's reactions to what he was seeing on the screen.

"I understand that congratulations are in order." Benjamin's voice was pinched with fatigue. The body of a dead witch lay on an operating table behind him, cut open in a vain attempt to save the child she'd been carrying. "A girl. A boy, too."

"What do you want?" The question was expressed calmly, but Matthew was seething inside. Why could no one find his godforsaken son?

"Your wife and daughter, of course." Benjamin's eyes hardened. "Your witch is fertile. Why is that, Matthew?"

Matthew remained silent.

"I'll find out what makes that witch so special." Benjamin leaned forward and smiled. "You know I will. If you tell me what I want to know now, I won't have to extract it from her later."

"You will never touch her." Matthew's voice—and his control—broke. Upstairs a baby cried.

"Oh, but I will," Benjamin promised softly. "Over and over again, until Diana Bishop gives me what I want."

I couldn't have slept for more than thirty or forty minutes before Rebecca's furious cries woke me. When my bleary eyes focused, I saw that Matthew was walking her in front of the fireplace, murmuring endearments and words of comfort.

"I know. The world can be a harsh place, little one. It will be easier to bear in time. Can you hear the logs crackle? See the lights play on the wall? That's fire, Rebecca. You may have it in your veins, like your mother. Shh. It's just a shadow. Nothing but a shadow." Matthew cuddled the baby closer, crooning a French lullaby.

Chut! Plus de bruit,
C'est la ronde de nuit,
En diligence, faisons silence.
Marchons sans bruit,
C'est la ronde de nuit.

Matthew de Clermont was in love. I smiled at his adoring expression.

"Dr. Sharp said they'd be hungry," I told him from the bed, rubbing the sleep out of my eyes. My lip caught in my teeth. She had also explained that premature babies could be difficult to feed because the muscles they needed in order to suckle hadn't developed sufficiently.

"Shall I get Marthe?" Matthew asked above Rebecca's insistent cries. He knew that I was nervous about breast-feeding.

"Let's try it on our own," I said. Matthew positioned a pillow in my lap and handed me Rebecca. Then he woke Philip, who was sleeping soundly. Both Sarah and Marthe had drummed into me the importance of nursing both children at the same time, or else I would no sooner feed one than the other would be hungry.

"Philip is going to be the troublemaker," Matthew said contentedly, lifting him from the cradle. Philip frowned at his father, his huge eyes blinking.

"How can you tell?" I shifted Rebecca slightly to make room for Philip.

"He's too quiet," Matthew said with a grin.

It took several tries before Philip latched on. Rebecca, however, was impossible.

"She won't stop crying long enough to suck," I said in frustration.

Matthew put his finger in her mouth, and she obediently closed it around the tip. "Let's switch them. Maybe the scent of the colostrum—and her brother—will convince Rebecca to give it a try."

We made the necessary adjustments. Philip screamed like a banshee when Matthew moved him, and he hiccupped and huffed a bit on the other breast just to make sure we understood that such interruptions would not be tolerated in the future. There were a few snuffling moments of indecision while Rebecca rooted around to see what the fuss was about before she cautiously took my breast. After her first suck, her eyes popped wide.

"Ah. Now she understands. Didn't I tell you, little one?" Matthew murmured. "*Maman* is the answer for everything."

Sol in Sagittarius

Sagittarius governs faith, religion, writings, bookes, and the interpretation of dreames. Those born under the signe of the archer shall work great wonders and receive much honour and joye. While Sagittarius rules the heavens, consult with lawyers about thy business. It is a good season for making oaths and striking bargains.

Anonymous English Commonplace Book, c. 1590,
Gonçalves Manuscript 4890, f. 9^{v}

32

The twins are ten days old. Don't you think they're a bit young to be made members of a chivalric order?" I yawned and walked up and down the second-floor hallway with Rebecca, who was resentful of being removed from her cozy fireside cradle.

"All new members of the de Clermont family become knights as soon as possible," Matthew said, passing me with Philip. "It's tradition."

"Yes, but most new de Clermonts are grown women and men! And we have to do this at Sept-Tours?" My thought processes had slowed to a crawl. As he had promised, Matthew took care of the children during the night, but so long as I was breast-feeding, I was still awakened every few hours.

"There or Jerusalem," Matthew said.

"Not Jerusalem. In December? Are you mad?" Ysabeau appeared on the landing, silent as a ghost. "The pilgrims are twelve deep. Besides, the babies should be christened at home, in the church their father built, not in London. Both ceremonies can take place on the same day."

"Clairmont House is our home at the moment, *Maman*." Matthew scowled. He was growing weary of the grandmothers and their constant interference. "And Andrew has volunteered to christen them here, if need be."

Philip, who had already exhibited an uncanny sensitivity to his father's mercurial moods, arranged his features in a perfect imitation of Matthew's frown and waved one arm in the air as if calling for a sword so they could vanquish their enemies together.

"Sept-Tours it is, then," I said. While Andrew Hubbard was no longer a constant thorn in my side, I was not eager for him to take on the role of the children's spiritual adviser.

"If you're sure," Matthew said.

"Will Baldwin be invited?" I knew Matthew had told him about the twins. Baldwin had sent me a lavish bouquet of flowers and two teething rings made of silver and horn for Rebecca and Philip. Teething rings were a common gift for newborns, of course, but in this case I felt sure it was a none-too-subtle reminder of the vampire blood in their veins.

"Probably. But let's not worry about that now. Why don't you take a walk with Ysabeau and Sarah—get out of the house for a little while. There's plenty of milk if the babies get fussy," Matthew suggested.

I did as Matthew suggested, though I had the uncomfortable feeling that the babies and I were being positioned on a vast de Clermont chessboard by creatures who had been playing the game for centuries.

That feeling grew stronger with each passing day as we prepared to go to France. There were too many hushed conversations for my peace of mind. But my hands were full with the twins, and I had no time for family politics at the moment.

"Of course I invited Baldwin," Marcus said. "He has to be there."

"And Gallowglass?" Matthew asked. He had sent his nephew pictures of the twins, along with their full and rather imposing monikers. Matthew had hoped that Gallowglass might respond when he found out that he was Philip's godfather and that the baby bore one of his names, but he had been disappointed.

"Give him time," Marcus said.

But time had not been on Matthew's side lately, and he had no expectation it would cooperate now.

"There's been no further word from Benjamin," Fernando reported. "He's gone silent. Again."

"Where the hell is he?" Matthew drove his fingers through his hair.

"We're doing our best, Matthew. Even as a warmblood, Benjamin was devious to a fault."

"Fine. If we can't locate Benjamin, then let's turn our attention to Knox," Matthew said. "He'll be easier to smoke out than Gerbert—and the two of them are providing information to Benjamin. I'm sure of it. I want proof."

He wouldn't rest until every creature who posed a danger to Diana or the twins was found and destroyed.

"Ready to go?" Marcus chucked Rebecca under the chin, and her mouth made a perfect O of happiness. She adored her older brother.

"Where's Jack?" I said, frazzled. No sooner did I get one child situated than another wandered off. A simple leave-taking had become a logistical nightmare roughly equivalent to sending a battalion off to war.

"Going for a walk with the beast. Speaking of which, where is Corra?" Fernando asked.

"Safely tucked away." In fact, Corra and I were having a difficult time of it. She had been restless and moody since the twins' birth and didn't appreciate getting wedged back into me for a journey to France. I wasn't happy with the arrangement myself. Being in sole possession of my body again was glorious.

A series of loud barks and the sudden appearance of the world's largest floor sweeper heralded Jack's return.

"Come on, Jack. Don't keep us waiting," Marcus called. Jack trotted up to his side, and Marcus held out a set of keys. "Think you can manage to get Sarah, Marthe, and your grandmother to France?"

"Course I can," Jack said, grabbing at the key ring. He hit the buttons on the key fob, and they unlocked another large vehicle, this one outfitted with a dog bed rather than infant seats.

"How exciting to be setting off for home." Ysabeau slipped her arm through Jack's elbow. "I am reminded of the time Philippe asked me to take sixteen wagons from Constantinople to Antioch. The roads were terrible, and there were bandits all along the route. It was a most difficult journey, full of dangers and the threat of death. I had a splendid time."

"As I recall, you lost most of the wagons," Matthew said with a dark look. "The horses, too."

"Not to mention a fair amount of other people's money," Fernando recalled.

"Only ten wagons were lost. The other six arrived in perfect condition. As for the money, it was merely reinvested," Ysabeau said, her voice dripping with hauteur. "Pay no attention, Jack. I will tell you about my adventures as we drive. It will keep your mind off the traffic."

Phoebe and Marcus set out in one of his trademark blue sports cars—this one British and looking as though James Bond should be driving it. I was beginning to appreciate the value of two-seat automobiles and thought longingly of spending the next nine hours with only Matthew for company.

Given the speed at which Marcus and Phoebe traveled and the fact they wouldn't have to stop en route for bathroom breaks, diaper changes, and meals, it was not surprising that the couple was waiting for us when we arrived at Sept-Tours, standing at the top of the torchlit stairs along with Alain and Victoire, welcoming us home.

"Milord Marcus tells me we will have a full house for the ceremonies, Madame Ysabeau," Alain said, greeting his mistress. His wife, Victoire, danced with excitement when she spied the baby carriers and rushed over to lend a hand.

"It will be like the old days, Alain. We will set up cots in the barn for the men. Those who are vampires will not mind the cold, and the rest will get used to it." Ysabeau sounded unconcerned as she handed Marthe her gloves and turned to help with the babies. They were swaddled within an inch of their lives to protect them from the freezing temperatures. "Are not Milord Philip and Milady Rebecca the most beautiful creatures you have ever seen, Victoire?"

Victoire was incapable of more than oohs and aahs, but Ysabeau seemed to find her response sufficient.

"Shall I help with the babies' luggage?" Alain asked, surveying the contents of the overstuffed cargo space.

"That would be wonderful, Alain." Matthew directed him to the bags, totes, portable playpens, and stacks of disposable diapers.

Matthew took a baby carrier in each hand and, with much input from Marthe, Sarah, Ysabeau, and Victoire on the icy state of the stairs, climbed to the front door. Inside, the magnitude of where he was, and why, struck him. Matthew was bringing the latest in a long line of de Clermonts back to their ancestral home. It didn't matter if our family was only a lowly scion of that distinguished lineage. This was, and would always be, a place steeped in tradition for our children.

"Welcome home." I kissed him.

He kissed me back, then gave me one of his dazzling, slow smiles. "Thank you, *mon coeur.*"

Returning to Sept-Tours had been the right decision. Hopefully, no mishaps would darken our otherwise pleasant homecoming.

In the days leading up to the christening, it seemed as though my wishes would be granted.

Sept-Tours was so busy with the preparations for the twins' christening that I kept expecting Philippe to burst into the room, singing and telling jokes. But it was Marcus who was the life of the household now, roaming all over the place as if he owned it—which I suppose he technically did—and jollying everybody into a more festive mood. For the first time, I could see why Marcus reminded Fernando of Matthew's father.

When Marcus ordered that all the furniture in the great hall be replaced with long tables and benches capable of seating the expected hordes, I had a dizzying sense of déjà vu as Sept-Tours was transformed back to its medieval self. Only Matthew's rooms remained unchanged. Marcus had declared them off-limits, since the guests of honor were sleeping there. I retreated to Matthew's tower at regular intervals to feed, bathe, and change the babies—and to rest from the constant crush of people employed to clean, sort, and move furniture.

"Thank you, Marthe," I said upon my return from a brisk walk in the garden. She had happily left the crowded kitchen in favor of nanny duty and another of her beloved murder mysteries.

I gave my sleeping son a gentle pat on the back and picked Rebecca up from the cradle. My lips compressed into a thin line at her low weight relative to her brother's.

"She is hungry." Marthe's dark eyes met mine.

"I know." Rebecca was always hungry and never satisfied. My thoughts danced away from the implications. "Matthew said it's too early for concern." I buried my nose in Rebecca's neck and breathed in her sweet baby smell.

"What does Matthew know?" Marthe snorted. "You are her mother."

"He wouldn't like it," I warned.

"Matthew would like it less if she dies," Marthe said bluntly.

Still I hesitated. If I followed Marthe's broad hints without consulting him, Matthew would be furious. But if I asked Matthew for his input, he would tell me that Rebecca was in no immediate danger. That might be true, but she certainly wasn't brimming over with health and wellness. Her frustrated cries broke my heart.

"Is Matthew still hunting?" If I were going to do this, it had to be when Matthew wasn't around to fret.

"So far as I know."

"Shh, it's all right. Mommy's going to fix it," I murmured, sitting down by the fire and undoing my shirt with one hand. I put Rebecca to my right breast, and she latched on immediately, sucking with all her might. Milk dribbled out of the corner of her mouth, and her whimper turned into an outright wail. She had been easier to feed before my milk came in, as though colostrum were more tolerable to her system.

That was when I'd first started to worry.

"Here." Marthe held out a sharp, thin knife.

"I don't need it." I swung Rebecca onto my shoulder and patted her back. She let out a gassy belch, and a stream of white liquid followed.

"She cannot digest the milk properly," Marthe said.

"Let's see how she handles this, then." I rested Rebecca's head on my forearm, flicked my fingertips toward the soft, scarred skin at my left elbow where I'd tempted her father to take my blood, and waited while red, life-giving fluid swelled from the veins.

Rebecca was instantly alert.

"Is this what you want?" I curled my arm, pressing her mouth to my skin. I felt the same sense of suction that I did when she nursed at my breast, except that now the child wasn't fussy—she was ravenous.

Freely flowing venous blood was bound to be noticed in a house full of vampires. Ysabeau was there in moments. Fernando was nearly as quick. Then Matthew appeared like a tornado, his hair disheveled from the wind.

"Everyone. Out." He pointed to the stairs. Without waiting to see if they obeyed him, he dropped to his knees before me. "What are you doing?"

"I'm feeding your daughter." Tears stung my eyes.

Rebecca's contented swallowing was audible in the quiet room.

"Everybody's been wondering for months what the children would be. Well, here's one mystery solved: Rebecca needs blood to thrive." I inserted my pinkie gently between her mouth and my skin to break the suction and slow the flow of blood.

"And Philip?" Matthew asked, his face frozen.

"He seems satisfied with my milk," I said. "Maybe, in time, Rebecca will take to a more varied diet. But for now she needs blood, and she's going to get it."

"There are good reasons we don't turn children into vampires," Matthew said.

"We have not *turned* Rebecca into anything. She came to us this way.

And she's not a vampire. She's a vampitch. Or a wimpire." I wasn't trying to be ridiculous, though the names invited laughter.

"Others will want to know what kind of creature they're dealing with," Matthew said.

"Well, they're going to have to wait," I snapped. "It's too soon to tell, and I won't have people forcing Rebecca into a narrow box for their own convenience."

"And when her teeth come in? What then?" Matthew asked, his voice rising. "Have you forgotten Jack?"

Ah. So it was the blood rage, more than whether they were vampire or witch, that was worrying Matthew. I passed the soundly sleeping Rebecca to him and buttoned my shirt. When I was finished, he had her tucked tightly against his heart, her head cradled between his chin and shoulder. His eyes were closed, as if to block out what he had seen.

"If Rebecca or Philip has blood rage, then we will deal with it—together, as a family," I said, brushing the hair from where it had tumbled over his forehead. "Try not to worry so much."

"Deal with it? How? You can't reason with a two-year-old in a killing rage," Matthew said.

"Then I'll spellbind her." It wasn't something we'd discussed, but I'd do it without hesitation. "Just as I'd spellbind Jack, if that was the only way to protect him."

"You will not do to our children what your parents did to you, Diana. You would never forgive yourself."

The arrow resting along my spine pricked my shoulder, and the tenth knot writhed on my wrist as the cords within me snapped to attention. This time there was no hesitation.

"To save my family, I'll do what I must."

"It's done," Matthew said, putting down his phone.

It was the sixth of December, one year and one day since Philippe had marked Diana with his blood vow. On Isola della Stella, a small island in the Venetian lagoon, a sworn testament of her status as a de Clermont sat on the desk of a Congregation functionary waiting to be entered into the family pedigree.

"So Aunt Verin came through in the end," Marcus said.

"Perhaps she has been in touch with Gallowglass." Fernando hadn't given up hope that Hugh's son would return in time for the christening.

"Baldwin did it." Matthew sat back in his chair and wiped his hands over his face.

Alain appeared with an apology for the interruption, a stack of mail, and a glass of wine. He cast a worried glance at the three vampires huddled around the kitchen fire and left without comment.

Fernando and Marcus looked at each other, their consternation evident.

"Baldwin? But if Baldwin did it . . ." Marcus trailed off.

"He's more worried about Diana's safety than the de Clermonts' reputation," Matthew finished. "The question is, what does he know that we don't?"

The seventh of December was our anniversary, and Sarah and Ysabeau babysat the twins to give Matthew and me a few hours on our own. I prepared bottles of milk for Philip, mixed blood and a bit of milk for Rebecca, and brought the pair down to the family library. There Ysabeau and Sarah had constructed a wonderland of blankets, toys, and mobiles to entertain them and were looking forward to the evening with their grandchildren.

When I suggested we would simply have a quiet dinner in Matthew's tower so as to be within calling distance if there was a problem, Ysabeau handed me a set of keys.

"Dinner is waiting for you at Les Revenants," she said.

"Les Revenants?" It was not a place I'd heard of before.

"Philippe built the castle to house Crusaders coming home from the Holy Land," Matthew explained. "It belongs to *Maman.*"

"It's your house now. I'm giving it to you," Ysabeau said. "Happy anniversary."

"You can't give us a house. It's too much, Ysabeau," I protested.

"Les Revenants is better suited to a family than this place is. It is really quite cozy." Ysabeau's expression was touched with wistfulness. "And Philippe and I were happy there."

"Are you sure?" Matthew asked his mother.

"Yes. And you will like it, Diana," Ysabeau said with a lift of her eyebrows. "All the rooms have doors."

"How could anyone describe this as cozy?" I asked when we arrived at the house outside Limousin.

Les Revenants was smaller than Sept-Tours, but not by much. There were only four towers, Matthew pointed out, one on each corner of the square keep. But the moat that surrounded it was large enough to qualify as a lake, and the splendid stable complex and beautiful interior courtyard rather took away from any claims that this was more modest than the official de Clermont residence. Inside, however, there was an intimate feeling to the place, in spite of its large public rooms on the ground floor. Though the castle had been built in the twelfth century, it had been thoroughly renovated and was now fully updated with modern conveniences such as bathrooms, electricity, and even heat in some of the rooms. Despite all that, I was just winding myself up to reject the gift and any idea that we would ever live here when my clever husband showed me the library.

The Gothic Revival room with its beamed ceiling, carved woodwork, large fireplace, and decorative heraldic shields was tucked into the southwest corner of the main building. A large bank of windows overlooked the inner courtyard while another, smaller window framed the Limousin countryside. Bookcases lined the only two straight walls, rising to the ceiling. A curved walnut staircase led up to a gallery that gave access to the higher shelves. It reminded me a bit of Duke Humfrey's Reading Room, with its dark woodwork and hushed lighting.

"What is all this stuff?" The walnut shelves were filled with boxes and books arranged higgledy-piggledy.

"Philippe's personal papers," Matthew said. "*Maman* moved them here after the war. Anything having to do with official de Clermont family business or the Knights of Lazarus is still at Sept-Tours, of course."

This had to be the most extensive personal archive in the world. I sat with a thunk, suddenly sympathetic to Phoebe's plight among all the family's artistic treasures, and I covered my mouth with my hand.

"I suppose you'll want to sort through them, Dr. Bishop," Matthew said, planting a kiss on my head.

"Of course I do! They could tell us about the Book of Life and the early days of the Congregation. There may be letters here that refer to Benjamin and to the witch's child in Jerusalem." My mind reeled with the possibilities.

Matthew looked doubtful. "I think you're more likely to find Philippe's designs for siege engines and instructions about the care and feeding of horses than anything about Benjamin."

Every historical instinct told me that Matthew was grossly underestimating the significance of what was here. Two hours after he'd shown me into the room, I was still there, poking among the boxes while Matthew drank wine and humored me by translating texts when they were in ciphers or a language I didn't know. Poor Alain and Victoire ended up serving the romantic anniversary dinner they'd prepared for us on the library table rather than down in the dining room.

We moved into Les Revenants the next morning, along with the children, and with no further complaints from me about its size, heating bills, or the number of stairs I would be required to climb to take a bath. The last worry was moot in any event, since Philippe had installed a screw-drive elevator in the tall tower after a visit to Russia in 1811. Happily, the elevator had been electrified in 1896 and no longer required the strength of a vampire to turn the crank.

Only Marthe accompanied us to Les Revenants, though Alain and Victoire would have preferred to join us in Limousin and leave Marcus's house party in other, younger, hands. Marthe cooked and helped Matthew and me get used to the logistical demands of caring for two infants. As Sept-Tours filled up with knights, Fernando and Sarah would join us here—Jack, too, if he found the crush of strangers overwhelming—but for now we were on our own.

Though we rattled around Les Revenants, it gave us a chance to finally be a family. Rebecca was putting on weight now that we knew how to nourish her tiny body properly. And Philip weathered every change of routine and location with his usual thoughtful expression, staring at the light moving against the stone walls or listening with quiet contentment to the sound of me shuffling papers in the library.

Marthe watched over the children whenever we asked her to, giving Matthew and me a chance to reconnect after our weeks of separation and the stresses and joys of the twins' birth. During those precious moments on our own, we walked hand in hand along the moat and talked about our plans for the house, including where I would plant my witch's garden to take best advantage of the sunshine and the perfect spot for Matthew to build the twins a tree house.

No matter how wonderful it was to be alone, however, we spent every moment we could with the new lives we had created. We sat before the fire in our bedroom and watched Rebecca and Philip inch and squirm closer, staring at each other with rapt expressions as their hands clasped. The two were always happiest when they were touching, as though the months they'd spent together in my womb had accustomed them to constant contact. They would soon be too large to do so, but for now we put them to sleep in the same cradle. No matter how we arranged them, they always ended up with their tiny arms wrapped tightly around each other and their faces pressed together.

Every day Matthew and I worked in the library, looking for clues about Benjamin's present whereabouts, the mysterious witch in Jerusalem and her equally mysterious child, and the Book of Life. Philip and Rebecca were soon familiar with the smell of paper and parchment. Their heads turned to follow the sound of Matthew's voice reading aloud from documents written in Greek, Latin, Occitan, Old French, ancient German dialects, Old English, and Philippe's unique patois.

Philippe's linguistic idiosyncrasy was echoed in whatever organizational scheme he had used for storing his personal files and books. Concerted efforts to locate Crusade-era documents, for example, yielded a remarkable letter from Bishop Adhémar justifying the spiritual motives for the First Crusade, bizarrely accompanied by a 1930s shopping list that enumerated the items Philippe wanted Alain to send from Paris: new shoes from Berluti, a copy of *La Cuisine en Dix Minutes,* and the third volume of *The Science of Life* by H. G. Wells, Julian Huxley, and G. P. Wells.

Our time together as a family felt miraculous. There were opportunities for laughter and song, for marveling in the tiny perfection of our children, for confessing how anxious we had both been about the pregnancy and its possible complications.

Though our feelings for each other had never faltered, we reaffirmed them in those quiet, perfect days at Les Revenants even as we braced for the challenges the next weeks would bring.

* * *

"These are the knights who have agreed to attend." Marcus handed Matthew the guest list. His father's eyes raced down the page.

"Giles. Russell. Excellent." Matthew flipped the page over. "Addie. Verin. Miriam." He looked up. "Whenever did you make Chris a knight?"

"While we were in New Orleans. It seemed right," Marcus said a touch sheepishly.

"Well done, Marcus. Given who will be in attendance at the children's christening, I wouldn't imagine anyone from the Congregation would dare to cause trouble," Fernando said with a smile. "I think you can relax, Matthew. Diana should be able to enjoy the day as you'd hoped."

Matthew didn't feel relaxed, however.

"I wish we'd found Knox." Matthew gazed out the kitchen window at the snow. Like Benjamin, Knox had disappeared without a trace. What this suggested was too terrifying to put into words.

"Shall I question Gerbert?" Fernando asked. They had discussed the possible repercussions if they acted in a way to suggest that Gerbert was a traitor. It could bring the vampires in the southern half of France into open conflict for the first time in more than a millennium.

"Not yet," Matthew said, reluctant to add to their troubles. "I'll keep looking through Philippe's papers. There must be some clue there as to where Benjamin is hiding."

"Jesus, Mary, and Joseph. There cannot be anything more we need to pack for a thirty-minute drive to my mother's house." For the past week, Matthew had been making sacrilegious references to the Holy Family and their December journeys, but it was all the more striking today, when the twins were to be christened. Something was bothering him, but he refused to tell me what it was.

"I want to be sure Philip and Rebecca are completely comfortable, given the number of strangers they'll be meeting," I said, bouncing Philip up and down in an attempt to get him to burp now rather than spit up halfway through the trip.

"Maybe the cradle can stay?" Matthew said hopefully.

"We have plenty of room to take it with us, and they're going to need at least one nap. Besides, I've been reliably informed that this is the largest motorized vehicle in Limousin, with the exception of Claude Raynard's hay wagon." The local populace had bestowed upon Matthew the nickname Gaston Lagaffe after the lovably inept comic book character, and had gently teased him about his *grande guimbarde* ever since he ran to the store for bread and got the Range Rover wedged between a tiny Citroën and an even more minuscule Renault.

Matthew slammed the rear hatch shut without comment.

"Stop glowering, Matthew," Sarah said, joining us in front of the house. "Your children are going to grow up thinking you're a bear."

"Don't you look beautiful," I commented. Sarah was dressed to the nines in a deep green tailored suit and a luscious cream silk blouse that set off her red hair. She looked both glamorous and festive.

"Agatha made it for me. She knows her stuff," Sarah said, turning around so we could admire her further. "Oh, before I forget: Ysabeau called. Matthew should ignore all the cars parked along the drive and come straight up to the door. They've saved a place for you in the courtyard."

"Cars? Parked along the drive?" I looked at Matthew in shock.

"Marcus thought it might be a good idea to have some of the knights present," he said smoothly.

"Why?" My stomach somersaulted as my instincts warned me that all was not as it seemed.

"In case the Congregation decides to take exception to the event," Matthew said. His eyes met mine, cool and tranquil as a summer sea.

In spite of Ysabeau's warning, nothing could possibly have prepared me for the enthusiastic welcome we received. Marcus had transformed Sept-Tours into Camelot, with flags and banners twisting in the stiff December breeze, their bright colors standing out against both the snow and the dark local basalt. Atop the square keep, the de Clermont family's black-and-silver standard with the ouroboros on it had been topped by a large square flag bearing the great seal of the Knights of Lazarus. The two pieces of silk flapped on the same pole, extending the height of the already tall tower by nearly thirty feet.

"Well, if the Congregation didn't know something was happening before, they do now," I said, looking at the spectacle.

"There didn't seem much point in trying to be inconspicuous," Matthew said. "We shall start as we intend to go on. And that means we aren't going to hide the children from the truth—or the rest of the world."

I nodded and took his hand in mine.

When Matthew pulled in to the courtyard, it was filled with well-wishers. He carefully navigated the car among the throngs, occasionally stopping by an old friend who wanted to shake his hand and congratulate us on our good fortune. He slammed on the brakes hard, however, when he saw Chris Roberts standing with a large grin on his face and a silver tankard in his hand.

"Hey!" Chris banged on the window with the tankard. "I want to see my goddaughter. Now."

"Hello, Chris! I didn't realize you were coming," Sarah said, lowering the window and giving him a kiss.

"I'm a knight. I have to be here." Chris's grin grew.

"So I've been told," Sarah said. There had been other warmblooded members before Chris—Walter Raleigh and Henry Percy to name just two—but I had never thought to count my best friend among them.

"Yep. I'm going to make my students call me *Sir* Christopher next semester," Chris said.

"Better that than *St.* Christopher," said a piercing soprano voice. Miriam grinned, her hands on her hips. The pose showed off the T-shirt she was wearing under a demure navy blazer. It, too, was navy and had SCIENCE: RUINING EVERYTHING SINCE 1543 spelled out across the chest along with a unicorn, an Aristotelian depiction of the heavens, and the outline of God and Adam from Michelangelo's Sistine Chapel. A red bar sinister obliterated each image.

"Hello, Miriam!" I waved.

"Park the car so we can see the sprogs," she demanded.

Matthew obliged, but when a crowd started to form, he said that the babies needed to be out of the cold and beat a hasty retreat into the kitchen, armed with a diaper bag and using Philip as a shield.

"How many people are here?" I asked Fernando. We had passed dozens of parked cars.

"At least a hundred," he replied. "I haven't stopped to count."

Based on the feverish preparations in the kitchen, there were more than a few warmbloods in attendance. I saw a stuffed goose go into the oven and a pig come out of it, ready to be basted with wine and herbs. My mouth watered at the aromas.

Shortly before eleven in the morning, the church bells in Saint-Lucien pealed. By that time Sarah and I had changed the twins into matching white gowns made of silk and lace and little caps sewn by Marthe and Victoire. They looked every inch sixteenth-century babies. We bundled them into blankets and made our way downstairs.

It was then that the ceremonies took an unexpected turn. Sarah climbed into one of the family's ATVs with Ysabeau, and Marcus directed us to the Range Rover. Once we were strapped in, Marcus drove us not to the church but to the goddess's temple on the mountain.

My eyes filled at the sight of the well-wishers gathered beneath the oak and cypress. Only some of the faces were familiar to me, but Matthew recognized far more. I spotted Sophie and Margaret, with Nathaniel by their side. Agatha Wilson was there, too, looking at me vaguely as though she recognized but wasn't able to place me. Amira and Hamish stood together, both looking slightly overwhelmed by all the ceremony. But it was the dozens of unfamiliar vampires present who surprised me most. Their stares were cold and curious, but not malicious.

"What is this about?" I asked Matthew when he opened my door.

"I thought we should divide the ceremony into two parts: a pagan naming ceremony here, and a Christian baptism at the church," he explained. "That way Emily could be a part of the babies' day."

Matthew's thoughtfulness—and his efforts to remember Em—rendered me temporarily mute. I knew he was always hatching plans and conducting business while I slept. I hadn't imagined his nocturnal work included overseeing the arrangements for the christening.

"Is it all right, *mon coeur*?" he asked, anxious at my silence. "I wanted it to be a surprise."

"It's perfect," I said when I was able. "And it will mean so much to Sarah."

The guests formed a circle around the ancient altar dedicated to the goddess. Sarah, Matthew, and I took our places within it. My aunt had anticipated that I wouldn't remember a single word of any baby-naming ritual that I had ever witnessed or taken part in, and she was prepared to officiate. The ceremony was a simple but important moment in a young witch's life, since it was a formal welcome into the community. But there was more to it than that, as Sarah knew.

"Welcome, friends and family of Diana and Matthew," Sarah began, her cheeks pink with cold and excitement. "We are gathered here today to bestow upon their children the names that they will take with them as they go into the world. Among witches to call something by name is to recognize its power. By naming these children, we honor the goddess who entrusted them to our care and express gratitude for the gifts she has given them."

Matthew and I had used a formula to come up with the babies' names—and I had vetoed the vampire tradition of five first names in favor of an elemental foursome. With a hyphenated last name, that seemed ample. Each of the babies' first names came from a grandparent. Their second name honored a de Clermont tradition of bestowing the names of archangels on Matthew and members of his family. We took their third name from yet another grandparent. For the fourth and final name, we selected someone who had been important to their conception and birth.

No one knew the babies' full names until now—except for Matthew, Sarah, and me.

Sarah directed Matthew to hold Rebecca up so that her face was turned to the sky.

"Rebecca Arielle Emily Marthe," Sarah said, her voice ringing through the clearing, "we welcome you into the world and into our hearts. Go forth with the knowledge that all here will recognize you by this honorable name and hold your life sacred."

Rebecca Arielle Emily Marthe, the trees and the wind whispered back. I was not the only one to hear it. Amira's eyes widened, and Margaret Wilson cooed and waved her arms in joy.

Matthew lowered Rebecca, his expression full of love as he looked down on the daughter who resembled him so much. Rebecca reached up and touched his nose with her delicate finger in return, a gesture of connection that filled my heart to bursting.

When it was my turn, I lifted Philip to the sky, offering him to the goddess and the elements of fire, air, earth, and water.

"Philip Michael Addison Sorley," Sarah said, "we also welcome you into the world and into our hearts. Go forth knowing that all present will recognize you by this honorable name and hold your life sacred."

The vampires exchanged glances when they heard Philip's last given name and searched the crowd for Gallowglass. We had chosen Addison because it was my father's middle name, but Sorley belonged to the absent Gael. I wished he had been able to hear it echo through the trees.

"May Rebecca and Philip bear their names proudly, grow into their promise in the fullness of time, and trust that they will be cherished and protected by all those who have borne witness to the love their parents have for them. Blessed be," Sarah said, her eyes shining with unshed tears.

It was impossible to find a dry eye in the clearing or to know who was the most moved by the ceremony. Even my normally vocal daughter was awed by the occasion and sucked pensively on her lower lip.

From the clearing we decamped to the church. The vampires walked, beating everybody down the hill. The rest of us used a combination of ATVs and cars with four-wheel drive, which led to much self-congratulation on Matthew's part as to the wisdom of his automotive preferences.

At the church the crowd of witnesses swelled to include people from the village, and, as on the day of our marriage, the priest was waiting for us at the door with the godparents.

"Does every Catholic religious ceremony take place in the open air?" I asked, tucking Philip's blanket more firmly around him.

"A fair few of them," Fernando replied. "It never made any sense to me, but I am an infidel, after all."

"Shh," Marcus warned, eyeing the priest with concern. "Père Antoine is admirably ecumenical and agreed to pass lightly over the usual exorcisms, but let's not push him. Now, does anyone know the words of the ceremony?"

"I do," Jack said.

"Me, too," Miriam said.

"Good. Jack will take Philip, and Miriam will hold Rebecca. You two can do the talking. The rest of us will look attentive and nod when it seems appropriate," Marcus said, his bonhomie unwavering. He gave the priest a thumbs-up. *"Nous sommes prêts, Père Antoine!"*

Matthew took my arm and steered me inside.

"Are they going to be okay?" I whispered. The godparents included only one lonely Catholic, accompanied by a converso, a Baptist, two Presbyterians, one Anglican, three witches, a daemon, and three vampires of uncertain religious persuasion.

"This is a house of prayer, and I beseeched God to watch over them," Matthew murmured as we took our places near the altar. "Hopefully, He is listening."

But neither we—nor God—needed to worry. Jack and Miriam answered all the priest's questions about their faith and the state of the children's souls in perfect Latin. Philip chortled when the priest blew on his face to expel any evil spirits and objected strenuously when salt was put in his tiny mouth. Rebecca seemed more interested in Miriam's long curls, one of which was clenched in her fist.

As for the rest of the godparents, they were a formidable group. Fernando, Marcus, Chris, Marthe, and Sarah (in place of Vivian Harrison, who could not be there) served with Miriam as godparents for Rebecca. Jack, along with Hamish, Phoebe, Sophie, Amira, and Ysabeau (who stood up for her absent grandson Gallowglass) promised to guide and care for Philip. Even for a nonbeliever such as myself, the ancient words spoken by the priest made me feel that these children were going to be looked after and cared for, no matter what might happen.

The ceremony drew to a close, and Matthew visibly relaxed. Père Antoine asked Matthew and me to come forward and take Rebecca and Philip from their godparents. When we faced the congregation for the first time, there was one spontaneous cheer, then another.

"And there's an end to the covenant!" an unfamiliar vampire said in a loud voice. "About bloody time, too."

"Hear, hear, Russell," several murmured in reply.

The bells rang out overhead. My smile turned to laughter as we were caught up in the happiness of the moment.

As usual, that was when everything started to go wrong.

The south door opened, letting in a gust of cold air. A man stood silhouetted against the light. I squinted, trying to make out his features. Throughout the church, vampires seemed to vanish only to reappear in the nave, barring the new arrival from coming any farther inside.

I drew closer to Matthew, holding Rebecca tight. The bells fell silent, though the air still reverberated with their final echoes.

"Congratulations, sister." Baldwin's deep voice filled the space. "I've come to welcome your children into the de Clermont family."

Matthew drew himself up to his full height. Without a backward look, he handed Philip to Jack and marched down the aisle to his brother.

"Our children are not de Clermonts," Matthew said coldly. He reached into his jacket and thrust a folded document at Baldwin. "They belong to me."

33

The creatures gathered for the christening let out a collective gasp. Ysabeau signaled to Père Antoine, who quickly shepherded the villagers from the church. Then she and Fernando took up watchful positions on either side of Jack and me.

"Surely you don't expect me to acknowledge a corrupt, diseased branch of this family and give it my blessing and respect?" Baldwin crumpled the document in his fist.

Jack's eyes blackened at the insult.

"Matthew entrusted Philip to you. You are responsible for your godson," Ysabeau reminded Jack. "Do not let Baldwin's words provoke you to ignore your sire's wishes."

Jack drew a deep, shaky breath and nodded. Philip cooed for Jack's attention, and when he received it, he rewarded his godfather with a frown of concern. When Jack looked up again, his eyes were green and brown once again.

"This hardly seems like friendly behavior to me, Uncle Baldwin," Marcus said calmly. "Let's wait and discuss family business after the feast."

"No, Marcus. We'll discuss it now and get it over with," Matthew said, countermanding his son.

In another time and place, Henry VIII's courtiers had delivered the news of his fifth wife's infidelity in church so that the king would think twice before killing the messenger. Matthew apparently believed it might keep Baldwin from killing him, too.

When Matthew suddenly appeared behind his brother, having only a moment before been in front, I realized that his decision to remain here was actually intended to protect Baldwin. Matthew, like Henry, would not shed blood on holy ground.

That did not mean, however, that Matthew was going to be entirely merciful. He had his brother in an unbreakable hold, with one long arm wrapped around Baldwin's neck so that Matthew was grasping his own bicep. His right hand drove into Baldwin's shoulder blade with enough force to snap it in two, his expression devoid of emotion and his eyes balanced evenly between gray and black.

"And that is why you never let Matthew Clairmont come up behind you," one vampire murmured to another.

"Soon it will hurt like hell, too," his friend replied. "Unless Baldwin blacks out first."

Wordlessly I passed Rebecca to Miriam. My hands were itching with power, and I hid them in the pockets of my coat. The arrow's silver shaft felt heavy against my spine, and Corra was on high alert, her wings ready to spring open. After New Haven my familiar didn't trust Baldwin any more than I did.

Baldwin almost succeeded in overcoming Matthew—or at least I thought he had. Before I could cry out in warning, it became evident that Baldwin's seeming advantage was only a clever trick by Matthew to lull him into changing his position. When he did, Matthew used Baldwin's own weight and a quick, bone-cracking kick to his brother's leg to drop him to his knees. Baldwin let out a strangled grunt.

It was a vivid reminder that though Baldwin might be the bigger man, Matthew was the killer.

"Now, *sieur.*" Matthew's arm lifted slightly so that his brother hung by his chin, putting more pressure on his neck. "It would please me if you would reconsider my respectful request to establish a de Clermont scion."

"Never," Baldwin gurgled out. His lips were turning blue from lack of oxygen.

"My wife tells me that the word 'never' is not to be used where the Bishop-Clairmonts are concerned." Matthew's arm tightened, and Baldwin's eyes began to roll back into his head. "I'm not going to let you pass out, by the way, nor am I going to kill you. If you're unconscious or dead, you can't agree to my request. So if you're determined to keep saying no, you can look forward to many hours of this."

"Let. Me. Go." Baldwin struggled to get each word out. Deliberately Matthew let him take a short, gasping breath. It was enough to keep the vampire going but not to permit him to recover.

"Let *me* go, Baldwin. After all these years, I want to be something more than the de Clermont family's black sheep," Matthew murmured.

"No," Baldwin said thickly.

Matthew adjusted his arm so that his brother could get out more than a word or two at a time, though this still didn't remove the bluish cast from his lips. Matthew took the wise precaution of driving the heel of his shoe into his brother's ankle in case Baldwin planned on using the extra oxygen to fight back. Baldwin howled.

"Take Rebecca and Philip back to Sept-Tours," I told Miriam, pushing up my sleeves. I didn't want them to see their father like this. Nor did I want them to see their mother use magic against a member of their family. The wind picked up around my feet, swirling the dust in the church into miniature tornadoes. The flames in the candelabrum danced, ready to do my bidding, and the water in the baptismal font began to bubble.

"Release me and mine, Baldwin," Matthew said. "You don't want us anyway."

"Might . . . need . . . you. My . . . killer . . . after . . . all," Baldwin replied.

The church erupted into shocked exclamations and whispered exchanges as this de Clermont secret was openly mentioned, though I was sure that some present knew the role Matthew had played in the family.

"Do your own dirty work for a change," Matthew said. "God knows you're as capable of murder as I am."

"You. Different. Twins. Have blood rage. Too?" Baldwin bit out.

The assembled guests fell silent.

"Blood rage?" A vampire's voice cut through the quiet, his Irish accent slight but noticeable. "What is he talking about, Matthew?"

The vampires in the church traded worried glances as the murmur of conversation resumed. Blood rage was clearly more than they had bargained for when they'd accepted Marcus's invitation. Fighting the Congregation and protecting vampire-witch children was one thing. A disease that might transform you into a bloodthirsty monster was quite another.

"Baldwin told you true, Giles. My blood is tainted," Matthew said. His eyes locked with mine, the pupils slightly enlarged. *Leave while you can,* they silently urged.

But this time Matthew would not be alone. I pushed my way past Ysabeau and Fernando and headed for my husband's side.

"That means Marcus . . ." Giles trailed off. His eyes narrowed. "We cannot allow the Knights of Lazarus to be led by someone with blood rage. It is impossible."

"Don't be such a bloody lobcock," the vampire next to Giles said in a crisp British accent. "Matthew's already been grand master, and we were none the wiser. In fact, if memory serves, Matthew was an uncommonly good commander of the brotherhood in more than one tricky situation. I believe that Marcus, though a rebel and a traitor, shows promise as well." The vampire smiled, but his nod toward Marcus was respectful.

"Thank you, Russell," Marcus said. "Coming from you, that's a compliment."

"Terribly sorry about the brotherhood slip, Miriam," Russell said with a wink. "And I'm no physician, but I do believe that Matthew is about to render Baldwin unconscious."

Matthew adjusted his arm slightly, and Baldwin's eyeballs returned to their normal position.

"My father's blood rage is under control. There's no reason for us to act out of fear and superstition," Marcus said, addressing everyone in the church. "The Knights of Lazarus were founded to protect the vulnerable. Every member of the order swore an oath to defend his or her fellow knights to the death. I needn't remind anyone here that Matthew is a knight. From this moment, so, too, are his children."

The need for an infant investiture for Rebecca and Philip made sense now.

"So what do you say, Uncle?" Marcus strode down the aisle to stand before Baldwin and Matthew. "Are you still a knight, or have you become a coward in your old age?"

Baldwin turned purple—and not from lack of oxygen.

"Careful, Marcus," Matthew warned. "I will have to let him go eventually."

"Knight." Baldwin looked at Marcus with loathing.

"Then start behaving like one and treat my father with the respect he's earned." Marcus looked around the church. "Matthew and Diana want to establish a scion, and the Knights of Lazarus will support them when they do. Anybody who disagrees is welcome to formally challenge my leadership. Otherwise the matter is not up for discussion."

The church was absolutely silent.

Matthew's lips lifted into a smile. "Thank you."

"Don't thank me yet," Marcus said. "We've still got the Congregation to contend with."

"An unpleasant task, to be sure, but not an unmanageable one," Russell said drily. "Let Baldwin go, Matthew. Your brother has never been very fast, and Oliver is at your left elbow. He's been longing to teach Baldwin a lesson ever since your brother broke his daughter's heart."

Several of the guests chuckled and the winds of opinion began to blow in our favor.

Slowly Matthew did as Russell suggested. He made no attempt to get away from his brother or to shield me. Baldwin remained on his knees for a few moments, then climbed to his feet. As soon as he did, Matthew knelt before him.

"I place my trust in you, *sieur,*" Matthew said, bowing his head. "I ask for your trust in return. Neither I nor mine will dishonor the de Clermont family."

"You know I cannot, Matthew," Baldwin said. "A vampire with blood rage is never in control, not absolutely." His eyes flickered to Jack, but it was Benjamin he was thinking of—and Matthew.

"And if a vampire could be?" I demanded.

"Diana, this is no time for wishful thinking. I know that you and Matthew have been hoping for a cure, but—"

"If I gave you my word, as Philippe's blood-sworn daughter, that any of Matthew's kin with blood rage can be brought under control, would you recognize him as the head of his family?" I was inches away from Baldwin, and my power was humming. My suspicion that my disguising spell had burned away was borne out by the curious looks I received.

"You can't promise that," Baldwin said.

"Diana, don't—" Matthew began, but I cut him off with a look.

"I can and I do. We don't have to wait for science to come up with a solution when a magical one already exists. If any member of Matthew's family acts on their blood rage, I will spellbind them," I said. "Agreed?"

Matthew stared at me in shock. And with good reason. This time last year I was still clinging to the belief that science was superior to magic.

"No," Baldwin said with a shake of his head. "Your word is not good enough. You would have to prove it. Then we would all have to wait and see if your magic is as good as you think it is, witch."

"Very well," I said promptly. "Our probation starts now."

Baldwin's eyes narrowed. Matthew looked up at his brother.

"Queen checks king," Matthew said softly.

"Don't get ahead of yourself, brother." Baldwin hoisted Matthew to his feet. "Our game is far from over."

"It was left in Père Antoine's office," Fernando said hours after the last revelers had gone to their beds. "No one saw who brought it."

Matthew looked down at the preserved stillborn fetus. A girl.

"He's even more insane than I thought." Baldwin looked pale, and not just because of what had happened in the church.

Matthew read the note again.

"Congratulations on your children's birth," it said. *"I wanted you to have my daughter, since I will soon possess yours."* The note was signed simply *"Your son."*

"Someone is reporting your every move to Benjamin," Baldwin said.

"The question is who." Fernando put his hand on Matthew's arm. "We won't let him take Rebecca—or Diana."

The prospect was so chilling that Matthew could only nod.

In spite of Fernando's assurances, Matthew would not know another moment's peace until Benjamin was dead.

After the drama of the christening, the rest of the winter holiday was a quiet family affair. Our guests departed, except for the extended Wilson family, who remained at Sept-Tours to enjoy what Agatha Wilson described as "very merry mayhem." Chris and Miriam returned to Yale, still committed to reaching a better understanding of blood rage and its possible treatment. Baldwin took off for Venice at the earliest opportunity to try to manage the Congregation's response to any news trickling in from France.

Matthew flung himself into Christmas preparations, determined to banish any lingering sourness after the christening. He went off into the woods on the other side of the moat and came back with a tall fir tree for the great hall, which he draped with tiny white lights that shone like fireflies.

Remembering Philippe and his decorations for Yule, we cut moons and stars out of silver and gold paper. With the combination of a flying spell and a binding charm, I swirled them into the air and let them settle onto the branches, where they winked and sparkled in the firelight.

Matthew went to Saint-Lucien for mass on Christmas Eve. He and Jack were the only vampires in attendance, which pleased Père Antoine. After the christening he was understandably reluctant to have too many creatures in his pews.

The children were fed and sleeping soundly when Matthew returned, stomping the snow from his shoes. I was sitting by the fire in the great hall with a bottle of Matthew's favorite wine and two glasses. Marcus had assured me that a single glass every now and again wouldn't affect the babies, provided I waited a couple of hours before I nursed.

"Peace, perfect peace," Matthew said, cocking his head for signs that the babies were stirring.

"Silent night, holy night," I agreed with a grin, leaning over to switch off the baby monitor. Like blood-pressure cuffs and power tools, such equipment was optional in a vampire household.

While I fiddled with the controls, Matthew tackled me. Weeks of separation and standing up to Baldwin had brought out his playful side.

"Your nose is freezing," I said, giggling as he drew its tip along the warm skin of my neck. I gasped. "Your hands, too."

"Why do you think I took a warmblood for a wife?" Matthew's icy fingers rummaged around underneath my sweater.

"Wouldn't a hot-water bottle have been less trouble?" I teased. His fingers found what they sought, and I arched into his touch.

"Perhaps." Matthew kissed me. "But not nearly so much fun."

The wine forgotten, we marked the hours until midnight in heartbeats rather than minutes. When the bells of the nearby churches in Dournazac and Châlus rang to celebrate the birth of a child in long-ago and faraway Bethlehem, Matthew paused to listen to the solemn yet still-exuberant sound.

"What are you thinking?" I asked as the bells died away.

"I was remembering how the village celebrated Saturnalia when I was a child. There were not many Christians, apart from my parents and a few other families. On the last day of the festival—the twenty-third of

December—Philippe went to every house, pagan and Christian, and asked the children what they wished for the New Year." Matthew's smile was wistful. "When we woke up the next morning, we discovered that our wishes had been granted."

"That sounds like your father," I observed. "What did you wish for?"

"More food, usually," Matthew said with a laugh. "My mother said the only way to account for the amount I ate was hollow legs. Once I asked for a sword. Every boy in the village idolized Hugh and Baldwin. We all wanted to be like them. As I recall, the sword I received was made of wood and broke the first time I swung it."

"And now?" I whispered, kissing his eyes, his cheeks, his mouth.

"Now I want nothing more than to grow old with you," Matthew said.

The family came to us on Christmas Day, saving us from having to bundle up Rebecca and Philip yet again. From the changes to their routine, the twins were aware that this was no ordinary day. They demanded to be part of things, and I finally took them to the kitchen with me to keep them quiet. There I constructed a magical mobile out of flying fruit to occupy them while I helped Marthe put the finishing touches on a meal that would make both vampires and warmbloods happy.

Matthew was a nuisance, too, picking at the dish of nuts I'd whipped up from Em's recipe. At this point if any of them lasted till dinner, it was going to be a Christmas miracle.

"Just one more," he wheedled, sliding his hands around my waist.

"You've eaten half a pound of them already. Leave some for Marcus and Jack." I wasn't sure if vampires got sugar highs, but I wasn't eager to find out. "Still liking your Christmas present?"

I'd been trying to figure out what to get the man who had everything ever since the children were born, but when Matthew told me his wish was to grow old with me, I knew exactly what to do for his present.

"I love it." He touched his temples, where a few silver strands showed in the black.

"You always said I was going to give you gray hairs." I grinned.

"And I thought it was impossible. That was before I learned that *impossible n'est pas Diana,*" he said, paraphrasing Ysabeau. Matthew grabbed a handful of nuts and went to the babies before I could react. "Hello, beauty."

Rebecca cooed in response. She and Philip shared a complex vocabulary of coos, grunts, and other soft sounds that Matthew and I were trying to master.

"That's definitely one of her happy noises," I said, putting a pan of cookies in the oven. Rebecca adored her father, especially when he sang. Philip was less sure that singing was a good idea.

"And are you happy, too, little man?" Matthew picked Philip up from his bouncy seat, narrowly missing the flying banana I'd tossed into the mobile at the last minute. It was like a bright yellow comet, streaking through the other orbiting fruit. "What a lucky boy you are to have a mother who will make magic for you."

Philip, like most babies his age, was all eyes as he watched the orange and the lime circle the grapefruit I'd suspended in midair.

"He won't always think that having a witch for a mommy is so wonderful." I went to the fridge and searched for the vegetables I needed for the gratin. When I closed the door, I discovered Matthew waiting for me behind it. I jumped in surprise.

"You have to start making a noise or giving me some other clue to warn me that you're moving," I complained, pressing my hand against my hammering heart.

Matthew's compressed lips told me that he was annoyed.

"Do you see that woman, Philip?" He pointed to me, and Philip directed his wiggling head my way. "She is a brilliant scholar and a powerful witch, though she doesn't like to admit it. And you have the great good fortune to call her *Maman*. That means you are one of the few creatures who will ever learn this family's most cherished secret." Matthew drew Philip close to him and murmured something in his ear.

When Matthew finished and drew away, Philip looked up at his father—and smiled. This was the first time either of the babies had done so, but I had seen this particular expression of happiness before. It was slow and genuine and lit his entire face from within.

Philip might have my hair, but he had Matthew's smile.

"Exactly right." Matthew nodded at his son with approval and returned Philip to his bouncy chair. Rebecca looked at Matthew with a frown, slightly irritated at having been left out of the boys' discussion. Matthew obligingly whispered in her ear as well, then blew a raspberry on her belly.

Rebecca's eyes and mouth were round, as though her father's words had impressed her—though I suspected that the raspberry might have something to do with it, too.

"What nonsense have you told them?" I asked, attacking a potato with a peeler. Matthew removed the two from my fingers.

"It wasn't nonsense," he said calmly. Three seconds later the potato was entirely without skin. He took another from the bowl.

"Tell me."

"Come closer," he said, beckoning to me with the peeler. I took a few steps in his direction. He beckoned again. "Closer."

When I was standing right next to him, Matthew bent his face toward mine.

"The secret is that I may be the head of the Bishop-Clairmont family, but you are its heart," he whispered. "And the three of us are in perfect agreement: The heart is more important."

Matthew had already passed over the box containing letters between Philippe and Godfrey several times.

It was only out of desperation that he riffled through the pages.

"My most reverend sire and father," Godfrey's letter began.

> *The most dangerous among The Sixteen have been executed in Paris, as you ordered. As Matthew was unavailable for the job, Mayenne was happy to oblige, and thanks you for your assistance with the matter of the Gonzaga family. Now that he feels secure, the duke has decided to play both sides, negotiating with Henri of Navarre and Philip of Spain at the same time. But cleverness is not wisdom, as you are wont to say.*

So far the letter contained nothing more than references to Philippe's political machinations.

"As for the other matter," Godfrey continued,

> *I have found Benjamin Ben-Gabriel as the Jews call him, or Benjamin Fuchs as the emperor knows him, or Benjamin the Blessed as he prefers. He is in the east as you feared, moving*

between the emperor's court, the Báthory, the Drăculeşti, and His Imperial Majesty in Constantinople. There are worrying tales of Benjamin's relationship with Countess Erzsébet, which, if circulated more widely, will result in Congregation inquiries detrimental to the family and those we hold dear.

Matthew's term on the Congregation is near an end, as he will have served his half century. If you will not involve him in business that so directly concerns him and his bloodline, then I beg you to see to it yourself or to send some trusted person to Hungary with all speed.

In addition to the tales of excess and murder with Countess Erzsébet, the Jews of Prague similarly speak of the terror Benjamin caused in their district, when he threatened their beloved rabbi and a witch from Chelm. Now there are impossible tales of an enchanted creature made of clay who roams the streets protecting the Jews from those who would feast on their blood. The Jews say Benjamin seeks another witch as well, an Englishwoman who they claim was last seen with Ysabeau's son. But this cannot be true, for Matthew is in England and would never lower himself to associate with a witch.

Matthew's breath hissed from between tight lips.

Perhaps they confuse the English witch with the English daemon Edward Kelley, whom Benjamin visited in the emperor's palace in May. According to your friend Joris Hoefnagel, Kelley was placed in Benjamin's custody a few weeks later after he was accused of murdering one of the emperor's servants. Benjamin took him to a castle in Křivoklát, where Kelley tried to escape and nearly died.

There is one more piece of intelligence I must share with you, Father, though I hesitate to do so, for it may be nothing more than the stuff of fantasy and fear. According to my informants, Gerbert was in Hungary with the countess and Benjamin. The witches of Pozsony have complained formally to the

Congregation about women who have been taken and tortured by these three infamous creatures. One witch escaped and before death took her was able only to say these words: "They search within us for the Book of Life."

Matthew remembered the horrifying image of Diana's parents, split open from throat to groin.

These dark matters put the family in too much danger. Gerbert cannot be allowed to fascinate Benjamin with the power that witches have, as he has been. Matthew's son must be kept away from Erzsébet Báthory, lest your mate's secret be discovered. And we must not let the witches pursue the Book of Life any further. You will know how best to achieve these ends, whether by seeing to them yourself or by summoning the brotherhood.

I remain your humble servant and entrust your soul to God in the hope that He will see us safe together so we might speak more of these matters than present circumstances make wise.

Your loving son, Godfrey

From the Confrérie, Paris, this 20th day of December 1591

Matthew folded the letter carefully.

At last he had some idea where to look. He would go to Central Europe and search for Benjamin himself.

But first he had to tell Diana what he'd learned. He had kept the news of Benjamin from her as long as he could.

The babies' first Christmas was as loving and festive as anyone could wish. With eight vampires, two witches, one human vampire-in-waiting, and three dogs in attendance, it was also lively.

Matthew showed off the half dozen strands of gray hair that had resulted from my Christmas spell and explained happily that every year I'd give him more. I had asked for a six-slice toaster, which I had received, along with a beautiful antique pen inlaid with silver and mother-of-pearl.

Ysabeau criticized these gifts as insufficiently romantic for a couple so recently wed, but I didn't need more jewelry, had no interest in traveling, and wasn't interested in clothes. A toaster suited me to the ground.

Phoebe had encouraged the entire family to think of gifts that were handmade or hand-me-down, which struck us all as both meaningful and practical. Jack modeled the sweater Marthe had knit for him and the cuff links from his grandmother that had once belonged to Philippe. Phoebe wore a pair of glittering emeralds in her ears that I'd assumed had come from Marcus until she blushed furiously and explained that Marcus had given her something handmade, which she had left at Sept-Tours for safety's sake. Given her color, I decided not to inquire further. Sarah and Ysabeau were pleased with the photo albums we'd presented that documented the twins' first month of life.

Then the ponies arrived.

"Philip and Rebecca must ride, of course," Ysabeau said as though this were self-evident. She supervised as her groom, Georges, led two small horses off the trailer. "This way they can grow accustomed to the horses before you put them in the saddle." I suspected she and I might have different ideas on how soon that blessed day might occur.

"They are Paso Finos," Ysabeau continued. "I thought an Andalusian like yours might be too much for a beginner. Phoebe said we are supposed to give hand-it-overs, but I have never been a slave to principle."

Georges led a third animal from the trailer: Rakasa.

"Diana's been asking for a pony since she could talk. Now she's finally got one," Sarah said. When Rakasa decided to investigate her pockets for anything interesting such as apples or peppermints, Sarah jumped away. "Horses have big teeth, don't they?"

"Perhaps Diana will have better luck teaching her manners than I did," Ysabeau said.

"Here, give her to me," Jack said, taking the horse's lead rope. Rakasa followed him, docile as a lamb.

"I thought you were a city boy," Sarah called after him.

"My first job—well, my first honest job—was taking care of gentlemen's horses at the Cardinal's Hat," Jack said. "You forget, Granny Sarah, cities used to be full of horses. Pigs, too. And their sh—"

"Where there's livestock, there's that," Marcus said before Jack could finish. The young Paso Fino he was holding had already proved his point. "You've got the other one, sweetheart?"

Phoebe nodded, completely at ease with her equine charge. She and Marcus followed Jack to the stables.

"The little mare, Rosita, has established herself as head of the herd," Ysabeau said. "I would have brought Balthasar, too, but as Rosita brings out his amorous side I've left him at Sept-Tours—for now." The idea that Matthew's enormous stallion would try to act upon his intentions with a horse as small as Rosita was inconceivable.

We were sitting in the library after dinner, surrounded by the remains of Philippe de Clermont's long life, a fire crackling in the stone fireplace, when Jack stood and went to Matthew's side.

"This is for you. Well, for all of us, really. *Grand-mère* said that all families of worth have them." Jack handed Matthew a piece of paper. "If you like it, Fernando and I will have it made into a standard for the tower here at Les Revenants."

Matthew stared down at the paper.

"If you don't like it—" Jack reached to reclaim his gift.

Matthew's arm shot out and he caught Jack by the wrist.

"I think it's perfect." Matthew looked up at the boy who would always be like our firstborn child, though I had nothing to do with his warmblooded birth and Matthew was not responsible for his rebirth. "Show it to your mother. See what she thinks."

Expecting a monogram or a heraldic shield, I was stunned to see the image Jack had devised to symbolize our family. It was an entirely new orobouros, made not of a single snake with a tail in its mouth but two creatures locked forever in a circle with no beginning and no ending. One was the de Clermont serpent. The other was a firedrake, her two legs tucked against her body and her wings extended. A crown rested on the firedrake's head.

"*Grand-mère* said the firedrake should wear a crown because you're a true de Clermont and outrank the rest of us," Jack explained matter-of-factly. He picked nervously at the pocket of his jeans. "I can take the crown off. And make the wings smaller."

"Matthew's right. It's already perfect." I reached for his hand and pulled him down so I could give him a kiss. "Thank you, Jack."

Everyone admired the official emblem of the Bishop-Clairmont family, and Ysabeau explained that new silver and china would have to be ordered, as well as a flag.

"What a lovely day," I said, one arm around Matthew and the other waving farewell to our family as they departed, my left thumb prickling in sudden warning.

"I don't care how reasonable your plan is. Diana's not going to let you go to Hungary and Poland without her," Fernando said. "Have you forgotten what happened to you when you left her to go to New Orleans?"

Fernando, Marcus, and Matthew had spent most of the hours between midnight and dawn arguing over what to do about Godfrey's letter.

"Diana must go to Oxford. Only she can find the Book of Life," Matthew said. "If something goes wrong and I can't find Benjamin, I'll need that manuscript to lure him into the open."

"And when you do find him?" Marcus said sharply.

"Your job is to take care of Diana and my children," Matthew said, equally sharp. "Leave Benjamin to me."

I watched the heavens for auguries and plucked at every thread that seemed out of place to try to foresee and rectify whatever evil my thumb warned me was abroad.

But the trouble did not gallop over the hill like an apocalyptic horseman, or cruise into the driveway, or even call on the phone.

The trouble was already in the house—and had been for some time.

I found Matthew in the library late one afternoon a few days after Christmas, several folded sheets of paper before him. My hands turned every color in the rainbow, and my heart sank.

"What's that?" I asked.

"A letter from Godfrey." He slid it in my direction. I glanced at it, but it was written in Old French.

"Read it to me," I said, sitting down next to him.

The truth was far worse than I had allowed myself to imagine. Based on the letter Benjamin's killing spree had lasted centuries. He'd preyed on witches, and very probably weavers in particular. Gerbert was almost certainly involved. And that one phrase—*"They search within us for the Book of Life"*—turned my blood to fire and ice.

"We have to stop him, Matthew. If he finds out we've had a daughter . . ." I trailed off. Benjamin's final words to me in the Bodleian haunted me. When I thought of what he might try to do to Rebecca, the power snapped through my veins like the lash of a whip.

"He already knows." Matthew met my eyes, and I gasped at the rage I saw there.

"Since when?"

"Sometime before the christening," Matthew said. "I'm going to look for him, Diana."

"How will you find him?" I asked.

"Not by using computers or by trying to find his IP address. He's too clever for that. I'll find him the way I know best: tracking him, scenting him, cornering him," Matthew said. "Once I do that, I'll tear him limb from limb. If I fail—"

"You can't," I said flatly.

"I may." Matthew's eyes met mine. He needed me to hear him, not reassure him.

"Okay," I said with a calmness I didn't feel, "what happens if you fail?"

"You'll need the Book of Life. It's the only thing that may lure Benjamin out of hiding so he can be destroyed—once and for all."

"The only thing besides me," I said.

Matthew's darkening eyes said that using me as bait to catch Benjamin was not an option.

"I'll leave for Oxford tomorrow. The library is closed for the Christmas vacation. There won't be any staff around except for security," I said.

To my surprise, Matthew nodded. He was going to let me help.

"Will you be all right on your own?" I didn't want to fuss over him, but I needed to know. Matthew had already suffered through one separation. He nodded.

"What shall we do about the children?" Matthew asked.

"They need to stay here, with Sarah and Ysabeau and with enough of my milk and blood to feed them until I return. I'll take Fernando with me—no one else. If someone is watching us and reporting back to Benjamin, then we need to do what we can to make it look as though we're still here and everything is normal."

"Someone is watching us. There's no doubt about it." Matthew pushed his fingers through his hair. "The only question is whether that someone belongs to Benjamin or to Gerbert. That wily bastard's role in this may have been bigger than we thought."

"If he and your son have been in league all this time, there's no telling how much they know," I said.

"Then our only hope is to possess information they don't yet have. Get the book. Bring it back here and see if you can fix it by reinserting the pages Kelley removed," Matthew said. "Meanwhile I'll find Benjamin and do what I should have done long ago."

"When will you leave?" I asked.

"Tomorrow. After you go, so I can make sure that you aren't being followed," he said, rising to his feet.

I watched in silence as the parts of Matthew I knew and loved—the poet and the scientist, the warrior and the spy, the Renaissance prince and the father—fell away until only the darkest, most forbidding part of him remained. He was only the assassin now.

But he was still the man I loved.

Matthew took me by the shoulders and waited until I met his eyes. "Be safe."

His words were emphatic, and I felt the force of them. He cupped my face in his hands, searching every inch as though trying to memorize it.

"I meant what I said on Christmas Day. The family will survive if I don't come back. There are others who can serve as its head. But you are its heart."

I opened my mouth to protest, and Matthew pressed his fingers against my lips, staying my words.

"There is no point in arguing with me. I know this from experience," he said. "Before you I was nothing but dust and shadows. You brought me to life. And I cannot survive without you."

Sol in Capricorn

The tenth house of the zodiack is Capricorn. It signifieth mothers, grandmothers, and ancestors of the female sex. It is the sign of resurrection and rebirth. In this month, plant seedes for the future.

—Anonymous English Commonplace Book, c. 1590, Gonçalves MS 4890, f. 9v

34

Andrew Hubbard and Linda Crosby were waiting for us at the Old Lodge. In spite of my efforts to persuade my aunt to stay at Les Revenants, she insisted on coming with Fernando and me.

"You're not doing this alone, Diana," Sarah said in a tone that didn't invite argument. "I don't care that you're a weaver or that you have Corra for help. Magic on this scale requires three witches. And not just any witches. You need spell casters."

Linda Crosby turned up with the official London grimoire—an ancient tome that smelled darkly of belladonna and wolfsbane. We exchanged hellos while Fernando caught Andrew up on how Jack and Lobero were faring.

"Are you sure you want to get involved with this?" I asked Linda.

"Absolutely. The London coven hasn't been involved in anything half so exciting since we were called in to help foil the 1971 attempt to steal the crown jewels." Linda rubbed her hands together.

Andrew had, through his contacts with the London underworld of grave diggers, tube engineers, and pipe fitters, obtained detailed schematics of the warren of tunnels and shelving that constituted the book-storage facilities for the Bodleian Library. He unrolled these on the long refectory table in the great hall.

"There are no students or library staff on-site at the moment because of the Christmas holiday," Andrew said. "But there are builders everywhere." He pointed to the schematics. "They're converting the former underground book storage into work space for readers."

"First they moved the rare books to the Radcliffe Science Library and now this." I peered at the maps. "When do the work crews finish for the day?"

"They don't," Andrew said. "They've been working around the clock to minimize disruptions during the academic term."

"What if we go to the reading room and you put in a request just as though it were an ordinary day at the Bodleian?" Linda suggested. "You know, fill out the slip, stuff it in the Lamson tube, and hope for the best. We could stand by the conveyor belt and wait for it. Maybe the library knows how to fulfill your request, even without staff." Linda sniffed when she saw my amazed look at her knowledge of the Bodleian's procedures. "I went to St. Hilda's, my girl."

"The pneumatic-tube system was shut down last July. The conveyor belt was dismantled this August." Andrew held up his hands. "Do not harm the messenger, ladies. I am not Bodley's librarian."

"If Stephen's spell is good enough, it won't care about the equipment—just that Diana has requested something she truly needs," Sarah said.

"The only way to know for sure is to go to the Bodleian, avoid the workers, and find a way into the Old Library." I sighed.

Andrew nodded. "My Stan is on the excavation crew. Been digging his whole life. If you can wait until nightfall, he'll let you in. He'll get in trouble, of course, but it won't be the first time, and there's not a prison built that can hold him."

"Good man, Stanley Cripplegate," Linda said with a satisfied nod. "Always such a help in the autumn when you need the daffodil bulbs planted."

Stanley Cripplegate was a tiny whippet of a man with a pronounced underbite and the sinewy outlines of someone who had been malnourished since birth. Vampire blood had given him longevity and strength, but there was only so much it could do to lengthen bones. He distributed bright yellow safety helmets to the four of us.

"Aren't we going to be . . . er, conspicuous in this getup?" Sarah asked.

"Being as you're ladies, you're already conspicuous," Stan said darkly. He whistled. "Oy! Dickie!"

"Quiet," I hissed. This was turning out to be the loudest, most conspicuous book heist in history.

"S'all right. Dickie and me, we go way back." Stan turned to his colleague. "Take these ladies and gents up to the first floor, Dickie."

Dickie deposited us, helmets and all, in the Arts End of Duke Humfrey's Reading Room between the bust of King Charles I and the bust of Sir Thomas Bodley.

"Is it me, or are they watching us?" Linda said, scowling at the unfortunate monarch, hands on her hips.

King Charles blinked.

"Witches have been on the security detail since the middle of the nineteenth century. Stan warned us not to do anything we oughtn't around the pictures, statues, and gargoyles." Dickie shuddered. "I don't mind most of them. They're company on dark nights, but that one's a right creepy old bugger."

"You should have met his father," Fernando commented. He swept his hat off and bowed to the blinking monarch. "Your Majesty."

It was every library patron's nightmare—that you were secretly being observed whenever you took a forbidden cough drop out of your pocket. In the Bodleian's case, it turned out the readers had good reason to worry. The nerve center for a magical security system was hidden behind the eyeballs of Thomas Bodley and King Charles.

"Sorry, Charlie." I tossed my yellow helmet in the air, and it sailed over to land on the king's head. I flicked my fingers, and the brim tilted down over his eyes. "No witnesses for tonight's events." Fernando handed me his helmet.

"Use mine for the founder. Please."

Once I'd obscured Sir Thomas's sight, I began to pluck and tweak the threads that bound the statues to the rest of the library. The spell's knots weren't complicated—just thrice- and four-crossed bindings—but there were so many of them, all piled on top of one another like a severely overtaxed electrical panel. Finally I discovered the main knot through which all the other knots were threaded and carefully untied it. The uncanny feeling of being observed vanished.

"That's better," Linda murmured. "Now what?"

"I promised to call Matthew once we were inside," I said, drawing out my phone. "Give me a minute."

I pushed past the lattice barricade and walked down the silent, echoing main avenue of Duke Humfrey's Library. Matthew picked up on the first ring.

"All right, *mon coeur*?" His voice thrummed with tension, and I briefly filled him in on our progress so far.

"How were Rebecca and Philip after I left?" I asked when my tale was told.

"Fidgety."

"And you?" My voice softened.

"More fidgety."

"Where are you?" I asked. Matthew had waited until after I left for England, then started driving north and east toward Central Europe.

"I just left Germany." He wasn't going to give me any more details in case I encountered an inquisitive witch.

"Be careful. Remember what the goddess said." Her warning that I would have to give something up if I wanted to possess Ashmole 782 still haunted me.

"I will." Matthew paused. "There's something I want you to remember, too."

"What?"

"Hearts cannot be broken, Diana. And only love makes us truly immortal. Don't forget, *ma lionne.* No matter what happens." He disconnected the line.

His words sent a shiver of fear up my spine, setting the goddess's silver arrow rattling. I repeated the words of the charm I'd woven to keep him safe and felt the familiar tug of the chain that bound us together.

"All is well?" Fernando asked quietly.

"As expected." I slipped the phone back into my pocket. "Let's get started."

We had agreed that the first thing we would try was simply to replicate the steps by which Ashmole 782 had come into my hands the first time. With Sarah, Linda, and Fernando looking on, I filled out the boxes on the call slip. I signed it, put my reader's-card number in the appropriate blank, and carried it over to the spot in the Arts End where the pneumatic tube was located.

"The capsule is here," I said, removing the hollow receptacle. "Maybe Andrew was wrong and the delivery system is still working." When I opened it, the capsule was full of dust. I coughed.

"And maybe it doesn't matter one way or the other," Sarah said with a touch of impatience. "Load it up and let her rip."

I put the call slip into the capsule, closed it securely, and placed it back in the compartment.

"What next?" Sarah said a few minutes later.

The capsule was right where I'd left it.

"Let's give it a good whack." Linda slapped the end of the compartment, causing the wooden supports it was attached to—and which held up the gallery above—to shake alarmingly. With an audible whoosh, the capsule disappeared.

"Nice work, Linda," Sarah said with obvious admiration.

"Is that a witch's trick?" Fernando asked, his lips twitching.

"No, but it always improves the Radio 4 signal on my stereo," Linda said brightly.

Two hours later we were all still waiting by the conveyor belt for a manuscript that showed absolutely no sign of arriving.

Sarah sighed. "Plan B."

Without a word Fernando unbuttoned his dark coat and slipped it from his shoulders. A pillowcase was sewn into the back lining. Inside, sandwiched between two pieces of cardboard, were the three pages that Edward Kelley had removed from the Book of Life.

"Here you are," he said, handing over the priceless parcel.

"Where do you want to do it?" Sarah asked.

"The only place that's large enough is there," I said, pointing to the spot between the splendid stained-glass window and the guard's station. "No—don't touch that!" My voice came out in a whispered shriek.

"Why not?" Fernando asked, his hands wrapped around the wooden uprights of a rolling stepladder that blocked our way.

"It's the world's oldest stepladder. It's nearly as ancient as the library." I pressed the manuscript pages to my heart. "Nobody touches it. Ever."

"Move the damn ladder, Fernando," Sarah instructed. "I'm sure Ysabeau has a replacement for it if it gets damaged. Push that chair out of the way while you're at it."

A few nail-biting moments later, I was ripping into a box of salt that Linda had carried up in a Marks & Spencer shopping bag. I whispered prayers to the goddess, asking for her help finding this lost object while I outlined a triangle with the white crystals. When that was done, I doled out the pages from the Book of Life, and Sarah, Linda, and I each stood at one of the points of the triangle. We directed the illustrations into the center, and I repeated the spell I'd written earlier:

Missing pages
Lost then found, show
Me where the book is bound.

"I still think we need a mirror," Sarah whispered after an hour of expectant silence had passed. "How's the library going to show us anything if we don't give her a place to project an apparition?"

"Should Diana have said '*show us* where the book is bound,' not '*show me*'?" Linda looked to Sarah. "There are three of us."

I stepped out of the triangle and put the illustration of the chemical wedding on the guard's desk. "It's not working. I don't feel *anything.* Not the book, not any power, not magic. It's like the whole library has gone dead."

"Well, it's not surprising the library is feeling poorly." Linda clucked in sympathy. "Poor thing. All these people poking at its entrails all day."

"There's nothing for it, honey," Sarah said. "On to Plan C."

"Maybe I should try to revise the spell first." Anything was better than Plan C. It violated the last remaining shreds of the library oath I'd taken when a student, and it posed a very real danger to the building, the books, and the nearby colleges.

But it was more than that. I was hesitating now for some of the same reasons I had hesitated when facing Benjamin in this very place. If I used my full powers here, in the Bodleian, the last remaining links to my life as a scholar would dissolve.

"There's nothing to be afraid of," Sarah said. "Corra will be fine."

"She's a firedrake, Sarah," I retorted. "She can't fly without causing sparks. Look at this place."

"A tinderbox," Linda agreed. "Still, I cannot see another way."

"There has to be one," I said, poking my index finger into my third eye in hopes of waking it up.

"Come on, Diana. Stop thinking about your precious library card. It's time to kick some magical ass."

"I need some air first." I turned and headed downstairs. Fresh air would steady my nerves and help me think. I pounded down the wooden treads that had been laid over the stone and pushed through the glass doors and into the Old Schools Quadrangle, gulping in the cold, dust-free December air, Fernando following at my heels.

"Hello, Auntie."

Gallowglass emerged from the shadows.

His mere presence told me that something terrible had happened.

His next quiet words confirmed it.

"Benjamin has Matthew."

"He can't. I just talked to him." The silver chain within me swayed.

"That was five hours ago," Fernando said, checking his watch. "When you spoke, did Matthew say where he was?"

"Only that he was leaving Germany," I whispered numbly. Stan and Dickie approached, frowns on their faces.

"Gallowglass," Stan said with a nod.

"Stan," Gallowglass replied.

"Problem?" Stan asked.

"Matthew's gone off the grid," Gallowglass explained. "Benjamin's got him."

"Ah." Stan looked worried. "Benjamin always was a bastard. I don't imagine he's improved over the years."

I thought of my Matthew in the hands of that monster.

I remembered what Benjamin had said about his hope that I would bear a girl.

I saw my daughter's tiny, fragile finger touch the tip of Matthew's nose.

"There is no way forward that doesn't have him in it," I said.

Anger burned through my veins, followed by a crashing wave of power—fire, air, earth, and water—that swept everything else before it. I felt a strange absence, a hollowness that told me I had lost something vital.

For a moment I wondered if it were Matthew. But I could still feel the chain that bound us. What was essential to my well-being was still there.

Then I realized it was not something essential I'd lost but something *habitual,* a burden carried so long that I had become inured to its heaviness.

Now that long-cherished thing was gone—just as the goddess had foretold.

I whirled around, blindly seeking the library entrance in the darkness.

"Where are you going, Auntie?" Gallowglass said, holding the door closed so that I couldn't pass. "Did you not hear me? We must go after Matthew. There's no time to lose."

The thick panels of glass turned to glittering sand, and the brass hinges and handles clanged against the stone threshold. I stepped over the debris and half ran, half flew up the stairs to Duke Humfrey's.

"Auntie!" Gallowglass shouted. "Have you lost your mind?"

"No!" I shouted back. "And if I use my magic, I won't lose Matthew either."

"Lose Matthew?" Sarah said as I slid my way into Duke Humfrey's, accompanied by Gallowglass and Fernando.

"The goddess. She told me I would have to give something up if I wanted Ashmole 782," I explained. "But it wasn't Matthew."

The feeling of absence had been replaced by a blooming sensation of released power that banished any remaining worries.

"Corra, fly!" I spread my arms wide, and my firedrake screeched into the room, zooming around the galleries and down the long aisle that connected the Arts End and the Selden End.

"What was it, then?" Linda asked, watching Corra's tail pat Thomas Bodley's helmet.

"Fear."

My mother had warned me of its power, but I had misunderstood, as children often do. I'd thought it was the fear of others that I needed to guard against, but it was my own terror. Because of that misunderstanding, I'd let the fear take root inside me until it clouded my thoughts and affected how I saw the world.

Fear had also choked out any desire to work magic. It had been my crutch and my cloak, keeping me from exercising my power. Fear had sheltered me from the curiosity of others and provided an oubliette where I could forget who I really was: a witch. I'd thought I'd left fear behind me months ago when I learned I was a weaver, but I had been clinging to its last vestiges without knowing it.

No more.

Corra dropped down on a current of air, extending her talons forward and beating her wings to slow herself. I grabbed the pages from the Book of Life and held them up to her nose. She sniffed.

The firedrake's roar of outrage filled the room, rattling the stained glass.

Though she had spoken to me seldom since our first encounter in Goody Alsop's house, preferring to communicate in sounds and gestures, Corra chose to speak now.

"Death lies heavy on those pages. Weaving and bloodcraft, too." She shook her head as if to rid her nostrils of the scent.

"Did she say bloodcraft?" Sarah's curiosity was evident.

"We'll ask the beastie questions later," Gallowglass said, his voice grim.

"These pages come from a book. It's somewhere in this library. I need to find it." I focused on Corra rather than the background chatter. "My only hope of getting Matthew back may be inside it."

"And if I bring you this terrible book, what then?" Corra blinked, her eyes silver and black. I was reminded of the goddess, and of Jack's rage-filled gaze.

"You want to leave me," I said with sudden understanding. Corra was a prisoner just as I had been a prisoner, spellbound with no means to escape.

"Like your fear, I cannot go unless you set me free," Corra said. "I am your familiar. With my help you have learned how to spin what was, weave what is, and knot what must be. You have no more need of me."

But Corra had been with me for months and, like my fear, I had grown used to relying on her. "What if I can't find Matthew without your help?"

"My power will never leave you." Corra's scales were brilliantly iridescent, even in the library's darkness. I thought of the shadow of the firedrake on my lower back and nodded. Like the goddess's arrow and my weaver's cords, Corra's affinity for fire and water would always be within me.

"Where will you go?" I asked.

"To ancient, forgotten places. There I will await those who will come when their weavers release them. You brought the magic back, as it was foretold. Now I will no longer be the last of my kind, but the first." Corra's exhale steamed in the air between us.

"Bring me the book, then go with my blessing." I looked deep into her eyes and saw her yearning to be her own creature. "Thank you, Corra. I may have brought the magic back, but you gave it wings."

"And now it is time for you to use them," Corra said. With three beats of her own spangled, webbed appendages, she climbed to the rafters.

"Why is Corra flying around up here?" Sarah hissed. "Send her down the conveyor-belt shaft and into the library's underground storage rooms. That's where the book is."

"Stop trying to shape the magic, Sarah." Goody Alsop had taught me the dangers of thinking you were smarter than your own power. "Corra knows what she's doing."

"I hope so," Gallowglass said, "for Matthew's sake."

Corra sang out notes of water and fire, and a low, hushed chattering filled the air.

"The Book of Life. Do you hear it?" I asked, looking around for the source of the sound. It wasn't the pages on the guard's desk, though they were starting to murmur, too.

My aunt shook her head.

Corra circled the oldest part of Duke Humfrey's. The murmurs grew louder with every beat of her wings.

"I hear it," Linda said, excited. "A hum of conversation. It's coming from that direction."

Fernando hopped over the lattice barrier into the main aisle of Duke Humfrey's. I followed after him.

"The Book of Life can't be up here," Sarah protested. "Someone would have noticed."

"Not if it's hiding in plain sight," I said, pulling priceless books off a nearby shelf, opening them to examine their contents, then sliding each back into place only to grasp another. The voices still cried out, calling to me, begging me to find them.

"Auntie? I think Corra found your book." Gallowglass pointed.

Corra was perched on the barred cage of the book hold, where the manuscripts were locked away and stored for patrons to use the following day. Her head was inclined as though she were listening to the still-chattering voices. She cooed and clucked in response, her head bobbing up and down.

Fernando had followed the sound to the same place and was standing behind the call desk where Sean spent his days. He was looking up at one of the shelves. There, next to an Oxford University telephone directory, sat a gray cardboard box so ordinary in appearance that it was begging not to be noticed—though it was pretty eye-catching at the moment, with light seeping out from the joins at the corners. Someone had clipped a curling note to it: *"Boxed. Return to stacks after inspection."*

"It can't be." But every instinct told me it was.

I held up my hand, and the box tipped backward and landed in my palm. I lowered it carefully to the desk. When I took my hands from it, the lid blew off, landing several feet away. Inside, the metal clasps were straining to hold the book closed.

Gently, aware of the many creatures within it, I lifted Ashmole 782 out of its protective carton and laid it down on the wooden surface. I rested my hand flat on the cover. The chattering ceased.

Choose, the many voices said as one.

"I choose you," I whispered to the book, releasing the clasps on Ashmole 782. Their metal was warm and comforting to the touch. *My father,* I thought.

Linda thrust the pages that belonged in the Book of Life in my direction.

Slowly, deliberately, I opened the book.

I turned the rough paper that had been inserted into the binding to protect the contents and the parchment page that bore both Elias Ashmole's handwritten title as well as my father's pencil addition. The first of Ashmole 782's alchemical illustrations—a female baby with black hair—stared at me from the next page.

When I first saw this image of the philosophical child, I had been struck by how it deviated from standard alchemical imagery. Now I couldn't help noticing that the baby resembled my own daughter, her tiny hands clutching a silver rose in one hand and a golden rose in the other as though proclaiming to the world that she was the child of a witch and a vampire.

But the alchemical child had never been intended to serve as the first illumination in the Book of Life. She was supposed to follow the chemical wedding. After centuries of separation, it was time to replace the three pages Edward Kelley had removed from this precious book.

The page stubs were just visible in the valley of the Book of Life's spine. I fitted the illustration of the chemical wedding into the gap, pressing the edge to its stub. Page and stub knit themselves together before my eyes, their severed threads joining up once more.

Lines of text raced across the page.

I took up the illumination of the orobouros and the firedrake shedding their blood to create new life and put it in its place.

A strange keening rose from the book. Corra chattered in warning.

Without hesitation and without fear, I slid the final page into Ashmole 782. The Book of Life was once more whole and complete.

A bloodcurdling howl tore what remained of the night in two. A wind rose at my feet, climbing up my body and lifting the hair away from my face and shoulders like strands of fire.

The force of the air turned the pages of the book, flipping them faster and faster. I tried to stop their progress, pressing my fingers against the vellum so that I could read the words that were emerging from the heart of the palimpsest as the alchemical illustrations faded. But there were too many to comprehend. Chris's student was right. The Book of Life wasn't simply a text.

It was a vast repository of knowledge: creature names and their stories, births and deaths, curses and spells, miracles wrought by magic and blood.

It was the story of us—weavers and the vampires who carried blood rage in their veins and the extraordinary children who were born to them.

It told me not only of my predecessors going back countless generations. It told me how such a miraculous creation was possible.

I struggled to absorb the tale the Book of Life told as the pages turned.

> *Here begins the lineage of the ancient tribe known as the Bright Born. Their father was Eternity and their mother Change, and Spirit nurtured them in her womb. . . .*

My mind raced, trying to identify the alchemical text that was so similar.

> *. . . for when the three became one, their power was boundless as the night. . . .*

> *And it came to pass that the absence of children was a burden to the Athanatoi. They sought the daughters. . . .*

Whose daughters? I tried to stop the pages, but it was impossible.

> *. . . discovered that the mystery of bloodcraft was known to the Wise Ones.*

What was bloodcraft?

On and on went the words, racing, twining, twisting. Words split in two, formed other words, mutating and reproducing at a furious pace.

There were names, faces, and places torn from nightmares and woven into the sweetest of dreams.

Their love began with absence and desire, two hearts becoming one. . . .

I heard a whisper of longing, a cry of pleasure, as the pages continued to turn.

. . . when fear overcame them, the city was bathed in the blood of the Bright Born.

A howl of terror rose from the page, followed by a child's frightened whimper.

. . . the witches discovered who among them had lain with the Athanatoi. . . .

I pressed my hands against my ears, wanting to block out the drumbeat litany of names and more names.

Lost . . .
Forgotten . . .
Feared . . .
Outcast . . .
Forbidden . . .

As the pages flew before my eyes, I could see the intricate weaving that had made the book, the ties that bound each page to lineages whose roots lay in the distant past.

When the last page turned, it was blank.

Then new words began to appear there as though an unseen hand were still writing, her job not yet complete.

And thus the Bright Born became the Children of the Night.

Who will end their wandering? the unseen hand wrote.

> *Who will carry the blood of the lion and the wolf?*
>
> *Seek the bearer of the tenth knot, for the last shall once more be the first.*

My mind was dizzy with half-remembered words spoken by Louisa de Clermont and Bridget Bishop, snatches of alchemical poetry from the *Aurora Consurgens,* and the steady flood of information from the Book of Life.

A new page grew out of the spine of the book, extending itself like Corra's wing, unfurling like a leaf on the bough of a tree. Sarah gasped.

An illumination, the colors shining with silver, gold, and precious stones crushed into the pigment, bloomed from the page.

"Jack's emblem!" Sarah cried.

It was the tenth knot, fashioned from a firedrake and an orobouros eternally bound. The landscape that surrounded them was fertile with flowers and greenery so lush that it might have been paradise.

The page turned, and more words flowed forth from their hidden source.

> *Here continues the lineage of the most ancient Bright Born.*

The unseen hand paused, as if dipping a pen in fresh ink.

> *Rebecca Arielle Emily Marthe Bishop-Clairmont, daughter of Diana Bishop, last of her line, and Matthew Gabriel Philippe Bertrand Sébastien de Clermont, first of his line. Born under the rule of the serpent.*
>
> *Philip Michael Addison Sorley Bishop-Clairmont, son of the same Diana and Matthew. Born under the protection of the archer.*

Before the ink could possibly be dry, the pages flipped madly back to the beginning.

While we watched, a new branch sprouted from the trunk of the tree at the center of the first image. Leaves, flowers, and fruit burst forth along its length.

The Book of Life clapped shut, the clasps engaging. The chattering ceased, leaving the library silent. I felt power surge within me, rising to unprecedented levels.

"Wait," I said, scrambling to open the book again so that I could study the new image more closely. The Book of Life resisted me at first, but it sprang open once I wrestled with it.

It was empty. Blank. Panic swept through me.

"Where did it all go?" I turned the pages. "I need the book to get Matthew back!" I looked up at Sarah. "What did I do wrong?"

"Oh, Christ." Gallowglass was white as snow. "Her eyes."

I twisted to glance over my shoulder, expecting to see some spectral librarian glaring at me.

"There's nothing behind you, honey. And the book hasn't gone far." Sarah swallowed hard. "It's inside you."

I was the Book of Life.

"You are so pathetically predictable." Benjamin's voice penetrated the dull fog that had settled over Matthew's brain. "I can only pray that your wife is equally easy to manipulate."

A searing pain shot through his arm, and Matthew cried out, unable to stop himself. The reaction only encouraged Benjamin. Matthew pressed his lips together, determined not to give his son further satisfaction.

A hammer struck iron—a familiar, homely sound he remembered from his childhood. Matthew felt the ring of the metal as a vibration in the marrow of his bones.

"There. That should hold you." Cold fingers gripped his chin. "Open your eyes, Father. If I have to open them for you, I don't think you will like it."

Matthew forced his lids open. Benjamin's inscrutable face was inches away. His son made a soft, regretful sound.

"Too bad. I'd hoped you would resist me. Still, this is only the first act." Benjamin twisted Matthew's head down.

A long, red-hot iron spike was driven through Matthew's right forearm and into the wooden chair beneath him. As it cooled, the stench of burning flesh and bone lessened somewhat. He did not have to see the other arm to know that it had undergone a similar treatment.

"Smile. We don't want the family back home to miss a minute of our reunion." Benjamin grabbed him by the hair and wrenched his head up. Matthew heard the whirring of a camera.

"A few warnings: First, that spike has been positioned carefully between the ulna and the radius. The hot metal will have fused to the surrounding bones just enough that if you struggle, they will splinter. I'm led to believe it's quite painful." Benjamin kicked the chair leg, and Matthew's jaw clamped shut as a terrible pain shot down into his hand. "See? Second, I have no interest in killing you. There is nothing you can do, say, or threaten that will make me deliver you into death's gentler hands. I want to banquet on your agony and savor it."

Matthew knew that Benjamin was expecting him to ask a particular question, but his thick tongue would not obey his brain's commands. Still he persisted. Everything depended on it.

"Where. Is. Diana?"

"Peter tells me she is in Oxford. Knox may not be the most powerful witch to have ever lived, but he has ways of tracking her location. I would let you talk to him directly, but that would spoil the unfolding drama for our viewers back home. By the way, they can't hear you. Yet. I'm saving that for when you break down and beg." Benjamin had carefully positioned himself so his back was to the camera. That way, his lips couldn't be read. But Matthew's face was visible.

"Diana. Not. Here?" Matthew formed each syllable carefully. He needed whoever might be watching to know that his wife was still free.

"The Diana you saw was a mirage, Matthew," Benjamin chortled. "Knox cast a spell, projecting an image of her into that empty room upstairs. Had you watched for a bit longer, you would have seen it loop back to the beginning, like a film."

Matthew had known it was an illusion. The image of Diana was blond, for Knox had not seen his wife since they'd returned from the past. Even had the hair color been right, Matthew would have known that it was not really Diana, for no spark of animation or warmth drew him to her. Matthew had entered Benjamin's compound knowing he would be taken. It was the only way to force Benjamin to make his next move and bring his twisted game to a close.

"If only you had been immune to love, you might have been a great man. Instead you are ruled by that worthless emotion." Benjamin leaned closer, and Matthew could smell the scent of blood on his lips. "It is your great weakness, Father."

Matthew's hand clenched reflexively at the insult, and his forearm paid the price, the ulna cracking like arid clay beneath a baking sun.

"That was foolish, wasn't it? You accomplished nothing. Your body is already suffering enormous stress, your mind filled with anxieties about your wife and children. It will take you twice as long to heal under these conditions." Benjamin forced Matthew's jaws open, studying his gums and tongue. "You're thirsty. Hungry, too. I have a child downstairs—a girl, three or four. When you're ready to feed on her, let me know. I'm trying to determine if the blood of virgins is more restorative than the blood of whores. So far the data is inconclusive." Benjamin made a note on a medical chart attached to a clipboard.

"Never."

"Never is a long time. Philippe taught me that," Benjamin said. "We'll see how you feel later. No matter what you decide, your responses will help me answer another research question: How long does it take to starve the piety out of a vampire so that he stops believing that God will save him?"

A very long time, Matthew thought.

"Your vital signs are still surprisingly strong, considering all the drugs I've pumped into your system. I like the disorientation and sluggishness they provoke. Most prey experience acute anxiety when their reactions and instincts are dulled. I see some evidence of that here, but not enough for my purposes. I'll have to up the dose." Benjamin threw the clipboard onto a small metal cabinet on wheels. It looked to be from World War II. Matthew noticed the metal chair next to the cabinet. The coat on it looked familiar.

His nostrils flared.

Peter Knox. He wasn't in the room now, but he was nearby. Benjamin was not lying about that.

"I'd like to get to know you better, Father. Observation can only help me to discover surface truths. Even ordinary vampires keep so many secrets. And you, my sire, are anything but ordinary." Benjamin advanced on him. He tore open Matthew's shirt, exposing his neck and shoulders. "Over the years I've learned how to maximize the information I glean from a creature's blood. It's all about the pace, you see. One must not rush. Or be too greedy."

"No." Matthew had expected that Benjamin would violate his mind, but it was impossible not to react instinctively against the intrusion. He scrambled against the chair. One forearm snapped. Then the other.

"If you break the same bones over and over, they never heal. Think about that, Matthew, before you try to escape from me again. It's futile. And I can drive spikes between your tibia and fibula to prove it."

Benjamin's sharp nail scored Matthew's skin. The blood welled to the surface, cold and wet.

"Before we are done, Matthew, I will know everything about you and your witch. Given enough time—and vampires have plenty of that—I will be able to witness every touch you've bestowed upon her. I will know what brings her pleasure as well as pain. I will know the power she wields and the secrets of her body. Her vulnerabilities will be as open to me as if her soul were a book." Benjamin stroked Matthew's skin, gradually increasing the circulation to his neck. "I could smell her fear in the Bodleian, of course, but now I want to understand it. So afraid, yet so remarkably brave. It will be thrilling to break her."

Hearts cannot be broken, Matthew reminded himself. He managed to croak out a single word. "Why?"

"Why?" Benjamin's voice crackled with fury. "Because you didn't have the courage to kill me outright. Instead, you destroyed me one day, one drop of blood at a time. Rather than confess to Philippe that you had failed him and revealed the de Clermonts' secret plans for Outremer, you made me a vampire and flung me out into the streets of a city crowded with warmbloods. Do you remember what it's like to feel a hunger for blood that cuts you in two with longing and desire? Do you remember how strong the blood rage is when you are first changed?"

Matthew did remember. And he had hoped—no. God help him, Matthew had *prayed* that Benjamin would be cursed with blood rage.

"You cared more for Philippe's good opinion than you cared for your own child." Benjamin's voice shook with rage, his eyes black as night. "Since the moment I was made a vampire, I have lived to destroy you and Philippe and all of the de Clermonts. My revenge gave me purpose, and time has been my friend. I've waited. I've planned. I've made my own children and taught them how to survive as I learned to survive: by raping and killing. It was the only path you left for me to follow."

Matthew's eyes closed in an attempt to blot out not only Benjamin's face but also the knowledge of his failures as a son and a father. But Benjamin would not allow it.

"Open your eyes," his son snarled. "Soon, you will have no more secrets from me."

Matthew's eyes flew open in alarm.

"As I learn about your mate, I will discover so much about you as well," Benjamin continued. "There is no better way to know a man than to understand his woman. I learned that from Philippe, as well."

The gears in Matthew's brain clinked and clunked. Some awful truth was fighting to make itself known.

"Was Philippe able to tell you about the time he and I spent together during the war? It didn't go according to my plans. Philippe spoiled so many of them when he visited the witch in the camp—an old Gypsy woman," Benjamin explained. "Someone tipped him off to my presence, and as usual Philippe took matters into his own hands. The witch stole most of his thoughts, scrambled the rest like eggs, and then hanged herself. It was a setback, to be sure. He had always had such an orderly mind. I had been looking forward to exploring it, in all its complex beauty."

Matthew's roar of protest came out as a croak, but the screaming in his head went on and on. This he had not expected.

It had been Benjamin—his son—who had tortured Philippe during the war and not some Nazi functionary.

Benjamin struck Matthew across the face, breaking his cheekbone.

"Quiet. I am telling you a bedtime story." Benjamin's fingers pressed into the broken bones of Matthew's face, playing them like an instrument whose only music was pain. "By the time the commander at Auschwitz released Philippe into my custody, it was too late. After the witch there was only one coherent thing left in that once-brilliant mind: Ysabeau. She can be surprisingly sensual, I discovered, for someone so cold."

As much as Matthew wanted to stop his ears against the words, there was no way to do so.

"Philippe hated his own weakness, but he could not let her go," Benjamin continued. "Even in the midst of his madness, weeping like a baby, he thought of Ysabeau—all the while knowing I was sharing in his pleasure." Benjamin smiled, displaying his sharp teeth. "But that's enough family talk for now. Prepare yourself, Matthew. This is going to hurt."

On the plane home, Gallowglass had warned Marcus that something unexpected had happened to me at the Bodleian.

"You will find Diana . . . altered," Gallowglass said carefully into the phone.

Altered. It was an apt description for a creature who was composed of knots, cords, chains, wings, seals, weapons, and now, words and a tree. I didn't know what that made me, but it was a far cry from what I had been before.

Even though he'd been warned of the change, Marcus was visibly shocked when I climbed out of the car at Sept-Tours. Phoebe accepted my metamorphosis with greater equanimity, as she did most things.

"No questions, Marcus," Hamish said, taking my elbow. He'd seen on the plane what questions did to me. No disguising spell could hide the way my eyes went milky white and displayed letters and symbols at even the hint of a query, more letters appearing on my forearms and the backs of my hands.

I expressed silent thanks that my children would never know me any different and would therefore think it normal to have a palimpsest for a mother.

"No questions," Marcus quickly agreed.

"The children are in Matthew's study with Marthe. They have been restless for the past hour, as if they knew you were coming," Phoebe said, following me into the house.

"I'll see Becca and Philip first." In my eagerness I flew up the stairs rather than walking. There seemed little point in doing anything else.

My time with the children was soul shaking. On the one hand, they made me feel closer to Matthew. But with my husband in danger, I couldn't help noticing how much the shape of Philip's blue eyes resembled that of his father's. There was a similarly stubborn cast to his chin, too, young and immature though it was. And Becca's coloring—her hair as dark as a raven's wing, eyes that were not the usual baby blue but already a brilliant gray-green, milky skin—was eerily like Matthew's. I cuddled them close, whispering promises into their ears about what their father would do with them when he returned home.

When I had spent as much time with them as I dared, I returned downstairs, slowly and on foot this time, and demanded to see the video feed from Benjamin.

"Ysabeau is in the family library, watching it now." Miriam's palpable worry made my blood run colder than anything had since Gallowglass materialized at the Bodleian.

I steeled myself for the sight, but Ysabeau slammed the laptop shut as soon as I entered the room.

"I told you not to bring her here, Miriam."

"Diana has a right to know," Miriam said.

"Miriam is right, Granny." Gallowglass gave his grandmother a quick kiss in greeting. "Besides, Auntie won't obey your orders any more than you obeyed Baldwin when he tried to keep you from Philippe until his wounds healed." He pried the laptop from Ysabeau's fingers and opened the lid.

What I saw made me utter a strangled sound of horror. Were it not for Matthew's distinctive gray-green eyes and black hair, I might not have known him.

"Diana." Baldwin strode into the room, his expression carefully schooled to show no reaction to my appearance. But he was a soldier, and he understood that pretending something hadn't happened didn't make it go away. He reached out with surprising gentleness and touched my hairline. "Does it hurt?"

"No." When my body had absorbed the Book of Life, a tree had appeared on it as well. Its trunk covered the back of my neck, perfectly aligned with the column of my spine. Its roots spread across my shoulders. The tree's branches fanned out under my hair, covering my scalp. The tips of the branches peeked out along my hairline, behind my ears, and around the edges of my face. Like the tree on my spell box, the roots and branches were strangely intertwined along the sides of my neck in a pattern resembling Celtic knotwork.

"Why are you here?" I asked. We hadn't heard from Baldwin since the christening.

"Baldwin was the first to see Benjamin's message," Gallowglass explained. "He contacted me straightaway, then shared the news with Marcus."

"Nathaniel had beaten me to it. He traced Matthew's last cell communication—a call made to you—to a location inside Poland," Baldwin said.

"Addie saw Matthew in Dresden, en route to Berlin," Miriam reported. "He asked her for information about Benjamin. While he was with her, Matthew got a text. He left immediately."

"Verin joined Addie there. They've picked up Matthew's trail. One of Marcus's knights spotted him leaving what we used to call Breslau." Baldwin glanced at Ysabeau. "He was traveling southeast. Matthew must have wandered into a trap."

"He was going north until then. Why did he change direction?" Marcus frowned.

"Matthew may have gone to Hungary," I said, trying to envision all this on the map. "We found a letter from Godfrey that mentioned Benjamin's connections there."

Marcus's phone rang.

"What do you have?" Marcus listened for a moment, then went to one of the other laptops dotting the surface of the library table. Once the screen illuminated, he keyed in a Web address. Close-up shots from the video feed appeared, the images enhanced to provide greater clarity. One was of a clipboard. Another, a corner of fabric draped over a chair. The third, a window. Marcus put down his cell phone and turned on the speaker.

"Explain, Nathaniel," he ordered, sounding more like Nathaniel's commanding officer than his friend.

"The room is pretty barren—there's not much in the way of clues that might help us get a better fix on Matthew's location. These items seemed to have the most potential."

"Can you zoom in on the clipboard?"

On the other side of the world, Nathaniel manipulated the image.

"That's the kind we used for medical charts. They were on every hospital ward, hanging on the bed rails." Marcus tilted his head. "It's an intake form. Benjamin's done what any doctor would—taken Matthew's height, weight, blood pressure, pulse." Marcus paused. "And he's indicated the medications Matthew is on."

"Matthew's not on any medications," I said.

"He is now," Marcus said shortly.

"But vampires can only feel the effects of drugs if . . ." I trailed off.

"If they ingest them through a warmblood. Benjamin has been feeding him—or force-feeding him—spiked blood." Marcus braced his arms against the table and swore. "And the drugs in question are not exactly palliative for a vampire."

"What is he on?" My mind felt numb, and the only parts of me that seemed to be alive were the cords running through my body like roots, like branches.

"A cocktail of ketamine, opiates, cocaine, and psilocybin." Marcus's tone was flat and impassive, but his right eyelid twitched.

"Psilocybin?" I asked. The others I was at least familiar with.

"A hallucinogen derived from mushrooms."

"That combination will make Matthew insane," Hamish said.

"Killing Matthew would be too quick for Benjamin's purposes," Ysabeau said. "What about this fabric?" She pointed to the screen.

"I think it's a blanket. It's mostly out of the picture frame, but I included it anyway," Nathaniel said.

"There are no landmarks outside," Baldwin observed. "All you can see is snow and trees. It could be a thousand places in Central Europe at this time of year."

In the central frame, Matthew's head turned slightly.

"Something's happening," I said, pulling the laptop toward me.

Benjamin led a girl into the room. She couldn't have been more than four and had on a long white nightgown with lace at the collar and cuffs. The cloth was stained with blood.

The girl wore a dazed expression, her thumb in her mouth.

"Phoebe, take Diana to the other room." Baldwin's order was immediate.

"No. I'm staying here. Matthew won't feed on her. He won't." I shook my head.

"He's out of his mind with pain, blood loss, and drugs," Marcus said gently. "Matthew's not responsible for his actions."

"My husband will not feed on a child," I said with absolute conviction.

Benjamin arranged the toddler on Matthew's knee and stroked the girl's neck. The skin was torn, and blood had caked around the wound.

Matthew's nostrils flared in instinctive recognition that sustenance was nearby. He turned his head from the girl deliberately.

Baldwin's eyes never left the screen. He watched his brother first warily, then with amazement. As the seconds ticked by, his expression became one of respect.

"Look at that control," Hamish murmured. "Every instinct in him must be screaming for blood and survival."

"Still think Matthew doesn't have what it takes to lead his own family?" I asked Baldwin.

Benjamin's back was turned to us, so we couldn't see his reaction, but the vampire's frustration was evident in the violent blow he slammed across Matthew's face. No wonder my husband's features didn't look familiar. Then Benjamin roughly grabbed the child and held her so that her neck was directly under Matthew's nose. The video feed had no sound, but the child's face twisted as she screamed in terror.

Matthew's lips moved, and the child's head turned, her sobs quieting slightly. Next to me Ysabeau began to sing.

"'*Der Mond ist aufgegangen, / Die goldnen Sternlein prangen / Am Himmel hell und klar.*'" Ysabeau sang the words in time to the movement of Matthew's mouth.

"Don't, Ysabeau," Baldwin bit out.

"What is that song?" I asked, reaching to touch my husband's face. Even in his torment, he remained shockingly expressionless.

"It's a German hymn. Some of the verses have become a popular lullaby. Philippe used to sing it after . . . he came home." Baldwin's face was ravaged for a moment with grief and guilt.

"It is a song about God's final judgment," Ysabeau said.

Benjamin's hands moved. When they stilled, the child's body hung limply, head bent back at an impossible angle. Though he hadn't killed the child, Matthew hadn't been able to save her either. Hers was another death Matthew would carry with him forever. Rage burned in my veins, clear and bright.

"Enough. This ends. Tonight." I grabbed a set of keys that someone had thrown on the table. I didn't care which car they belonged to, though I hoped it was Marcus's—and therefore fast. "Tell Verin I'm on my way."

"No!" Ysabeau's anguished cry stopped me in my tracks. "The window. Can you enlarge that part of the picture for me, Nathaniel?"

"There's nothing out there but snow and trees," Hamish said, frowning.

"The wall next to the window. Focus there." Ysabeau pointed to the grimy wall on the screen as though Nathaniel could somehow see her. Even though he couldn't, Nathaniel obligingly zoomed in.

As a clearer picture emerged, I couldn't imagine what Ysabeau thought she saw. The wall was stained with damp and had not been painted for some time. It might once have been white, like the tiles, but it was grayish now. The image on the screen continued to resolve and sharpen as Nathaniel worked. Some of the grimy smudges turned out to be a series of numbers marching down the wall.

"My clever child," Ysabeau said, her eyes running red with blood and grief. She stood, her limbs trembling. "That monster. I will tear him to pieces."

"What is it, Ysabeau?" I asked.

"The clue was in the song. Matthew knows we are watching him," Ysabeau said.

"What is it, *Grand-mère*?" Marcus repeated, peering at the image. "Is it the numbers?"

"One number. Philippe's number." Ysabeau pointed to the last in the series.

"His number?" Sarah asked.

"It was given to him at Auschwitz-Birkenau. After the Nazis captured Philippe trying to liberate Ravensbrück, they sent him there," Ysabeau said.

These were names out of nightmares, places that would forever be synonymous with the savagery of mankind.

"The Nazis tattooed it on Philippe—over and over again." The fury built in Ysabeau's voice, making it ring like a warning bell. "It is how they discovered he was different."

"What are you saying?" I couldn't believe it, and yet . . .

"It was Benjamin who tortured Philippe," Ysabeau said.

Philippe's image swam before me—the hollow eye socket where Benjamin had blinded him, the horrible scars on his face. I remembered the shaky handwriting on the letter he'd left for me, his body too damaged to control a pen's movement.

And the same creature who had done that to Philippe now had my husband.

"Get out of my way." I tried to push past Baldwin as I raced for the door. But Baldwin held me tight.

"You aren't going to wander into the same trap that he did, Diana," Baldwin said. "That's exactly what Benjamin wants."

"I'm going to Auschwitz. Matthew is not going to die there, where so many died before," I said, twisting in Baldwin's grip.

"Matthew isn't at Auschwitz. Philippe was moved from there to Majdanek on the outskirts of Lublin soon after he was captured. It's where we found my father. I went over every inch of the camp searching for other survivors. There was no room like that in it."

"Then Philippe was taken somewhere else before being sent to Majdanek—to another labor camp. One run by Benjamin. It was he who tortured Philippe. I am certain of it," Ysabeau insisted.

"How could Benjamin be in charge of a camp?" I'd never heard of such a thing. Nazi concentration camps were run by the SS.

"There were tens of thousands of them, all over Germany and Poland—labor camps, brothels, research facilities, farms," Baldwin explained. "If Ysabeau is right, Matthew could be anywhere."

Ysabeau turned on Baldwin. "You are free to stay here and wonder where your brother is, but I am going to Poland with Diana. We will find Matthew ourselves."

"Nobody is going anywhere." Marcus slammed his hand on the table. "Not without a plan. Where exactly was Majdanek?"

"I'll pull up a map." Phoebe reached for the computer.

I stilled her hand. There was something disturbingly familiar about that blanket. . . . It was tweed, a heathery brown with a distinctive weave.

"Is that a button?" I looked more closely. "That's not a blanket. It's a jacket." I stared at it some more. "Peter Knox wore a jacket like that. I remember the fabric from Oxford."

"Vampires won't be able to free Matthew if Benjamin has witches like Knox with him, too!" Sarah exclaimed.

"This is like 1944 all over again," Ysabeau said quietly. "Benjamin is playing with Matthew—and with us."

"If so, then Matthew's capture was not his goal." Baldwin crossed his arms and narrowed his eyes at the screen. "The trap Benjamin set was meant to snare another."

"He wants Auntie," Gallowglass said. "Benjamin wants to know why she can bear a vampire's child."

Benjamin wants me to bear his child, I thought.

"Well, he's not going to experiment on Diana to find out," Marcus said emphatically. "Matthew would rather die where he is than let that happen."

"There's no need for experiments. I already know why weavers can have children with blood-rage vampires." The answer was running up my arms in letters and symbols from languages long dead or never spoken except by witches performing spells. The cords in my body were twisting and turning into brightly hued helices of yellow and white, red and black, green and silver.

"So the answer was in the Book of Life," Sarah said, "just as the vampires thought it would be."

"And it all began with a discovery of witches." I pressed my lips together to avoid revealing any more. "Marcus is right. If we go after Benjamin without a plan and the support of other creatures, he will win. And Matthew will die."

"I'm sending you a road map of southern and eastern Poland now," Nathaniel said over the speaker. Another window opened on the screen. "Here is Auschwitz." A purple flag appeared. "And here is Majdanek." A red flag marked a location on the outskirts of a city so far to the east it was practically in Ukraine. There were miles and miles of Polish ground in between.

"Where do we start?" I asked. "At Auschwitz and move east?"

"No. Benjamin will not be far from Lublin," Ysabeau insisted. "The witches we interrogated when Philippe was found said the creature who tortured him had long-standing ties to that region. We assumed they were talking about a local Nazi recruit."

"What else did the witches say?" I asked.

"Only that Philippe's captor had tortured the witches of Chelm before turning his attentions to my husband," Ysabeau said. "They called him 'the Devil.'"

Chelm. Within seconds I found the city. Chelm was just to the east of Lublin. My witch's sixth sense told me that Benjamin would be there—or very close.

"That's where we should start looking," I said, touching the city on the map as though somehow Matthew could feel my fingers. On the video feed, I saw that he had been left alone with a dead child. His lips were still moving, still singing . . . to a girl who would never hear anything again.

"Why are you so sure?" Hamish asked.

"Because a witch I met in sixteenth-century Prague was born there. The witch was a weaver—like me." As I spoke, names and family lineages emerged on my hands and arms, the marks as black as any tattoo. They appeared for only a moment before fading into invisibility, but I knew what they signaled: Abraham ben Elijah was probably not the first—nor the last—weaver in the city. Chelm was where Benjamin had made his mad attempts to breed a child.

On the screen, Matthew looked down at his right hand. It was spasming, the index finger tapping irregularly on the arm of the chair.

"It looks as though the nerves in his hand have been damaged," Marcus said, watching his father's fingers twitch.

"That's not involuntary movement." Gallowglass bent until his chin practically rested on the keyboard. "That's Morse code."

"What is he saying?" I was frantic at the thought that we might already have missed part of the message.

"D. Four. D. Five. C. Four." Gallowglass spelled out each letter in turn. "Christ. Matthew's making no sense at all. D. X—"

"C4," Hamish said, his voice rising. "DXC4." He whooped in excitement. "Matthew didn't walk into a trap. He sprang it deliberately."

"I don't understand," I said.

"D4 and D5 are the first two moves of the Queen's Gambit—it's one of the classic openings in chess." Hamish went to the fire, where a heavy chess set waited on a table. He moved two pawns, one white and then one black. "White's next move forces Black to either put his key pieces in jeopardy and gain greater freedom or play it safe and limit his maneuverability." Hamish moved another white pawn next to the first.

"But when Matthew is White, he never initiates the Queen's Gambit, and when he's Black, he declines it. Matthew always plays it safe and protects his queen," Baldwin said, crossing his arms over his chest. "He defends her at all costs."

"I know. That's why he loses. But not this time." Hamish picked up the black pawn and knocked over the white pawn that was diagonal to it in the center of the board. "DXC4. Queen's Gambit accepted."

"I thought Diana was the white queen," Sarah said, studying the board. "But you're making it sound like Matthew is playing Black."

"He is," Hamish said. "I think he's telling us the child was Benjamin's white pawn—the player he sacrificed, believing that it would give him an advantage over Matthew. Over us."

"Does it?" I asked.

"That depends on what we do next," Hamish said. "In chess, Black would either continue to attack pawns to gain an advantage in the endgame or get more aggressive and move in his knights."

"Which would Matthew do?" Marcus asked.

"I don't know," Hamish said. "Like Baldwin said, Matthew never accepts the Queen's Gambit."

"It doesn't matter. He wasn't trying to dictate our next move. He was telling us not to protect his queen." Baldwin swung his head around and addressed me directly. "Are you ready for what comes next?"

"Yes."

"You hesitated once before," Baldwin said. "Marcus told me what happened the last time you faced Benjamin in the library. This time, Matthew's life depends on you."

"It won't happen again." I met his gaze, and Baldwin nodded.

"Will you be able to track Matthew, Ysabeau?" Baldwin asked.

"Better than Verin," she replied.

"Then we will leave at once," Baldwin said. "Call your knights to arms, Marcus. Tell them to meet me in Warsaw."

"Kuźma is there," Marcus said. "He will marshal the knights until I arrive."

"You cannot go, Marcus," Gallowglass said. "You must stay here, with the babes."

"No!" Marcus said. "He's my father. I can scent him just as easily as Ysabeau. We'll need every advantage."

"You aren't going, Marcus. Neither is Diana." Baldwin braced his arms on the table and fixed his eyes on Marcus and me. "Everything until now has been a skirmish—a preamble to this moment. Benjamin has had almost a thousand years to plan his revenge. We have hours. We all must be where we are most needed—not where our hearts lead us."

"My *husband* needs me," I said tightly.

"Your husband needs to be found. Others can do that, just as others can fight," Baldwin replied. "Marcus must stay here, because Sept-Tours has the legal status of sanctuary only if the grand master is within its walls."

"And we saw how much good that did us against Gerbert and Knox," Sarah said bitterly.

"One person died." Baldwin's voice was as cold and clear as an icicle. "It was regrettable, and a tragic loss, but if Marcus had not been here, Gerbert and Domenico would have overrun the place with their children and you would all be dead."

"You don't know that," Marcus said.

"I do. Domenico boasted of their plans. You will stay here, Marcus, and protect Sarah and the children so that Diana can do her job."

"My job?" My brows lifted.

"You, sister, are going to Venice."

A heavy iron key flew through the air. I put my hand up, and it landed in my palm. The key was heavy and ornate, with an exquisite bow wrought in the shape of the de Clermont orobouros, a long stem, and a chunky bit with complicated star-shaped wards. I owned a house there, I dimly recalled. Perhaps this was the key to it?

Every vampire in the room was staring at my hand in shock. I turned it this way and that, but there didn't seem to be anything odd about it other than the normal rainbow colors, marked wrist, and odd bits of lettering. It was Gallowglass who regained his tongue first.

"You cannot send Auntie in there," he said, giving Baldwin a combative shove. "What are you thinking, man?"

"That she is a de Clermont—and that I am more useful tracking Matthew with Ysabeau and Verin than I am sitting in a council chamber arguing about the terms of the covenant." Baldwin turned glittering eyes on me. He shrugged. "Maybe Diana can change their mind."

"Wait." Now it was my turn to look amazed. "You can't—"

"Want you to sit in the de Clermont seat at the Congregation's table?" Baldwin's lip curved. "Oh, but I do, sister."

"I'm not a vampire!"

"Nothing says you have to be. The only way that Father would agree to the covenant was if there were always a de Clermont among the Congregation members. The council cannot meet without one of us present. But I've gone over the original treaty. It does not stipulate that the family's representative must be a vampire." Baldwin shook his head. "If I didn't know better, I would think that Philippe foresaw this day and planned it all."

"What do you expect Auntie to do?" Gallowglass demanded. "She may be a weaver, but she's no miracle worker."

"Diana needs to remind the Congregation that this is not the first time complaints have been made about a vampire in Chelm," Baldwin said.

"The Congregation has known about Benjamin and done *nothing*?" I couldn't believe it.

"They didn't know it was Benjamin, but they knew that something was wrong there," Baldwin replied. "Not even the witches cared enough to investigate. Knox may not be the only witch cooperating with Benjamin."

"If so, we'll not get far in Chelm without the Congregation's support," Hamish said.

"And if the witches there have been Benjamin's victims, a group of vampires will need the Chelm coven's blessing if we want to succeed, as well as the Congregation's support," Baldwin added.

"That means persuading Satu Järvinen to side with us," Sarah pointed out, "not to mention Gerbert and Domenico."

"It is impossible, Baldwin. There is too much bad blood between the de Clermonts and the witches," Ysabeau agreed. "They will never help us save Matthew."

"Impossible n'est pas français," I reminded her. "I'll handle Satu. By the time I join you, Baldwin, you'll have the full support of the Congregation's witches. The daemons', too. I make no promises about Gerbert and Domenico."

"That's a tall order," Gallowglass warned.

"I want my husband back." I turned to Baldwin. "What now?"

"We'll go straight to Matthew's house in Venice. The Congregation has demanded that you and Matthew appear before them. If they see the two of us arrive, they'll assume I've done their bidding," Baldwin said.

"Will she be in any danger there?" Marcus asked.

"The Congregation wants a formal proceeding. We will be watched—closely—but no one will want to start a war. Not before the meeting is over, at any rate. I will go with Diana as far as Isola della Stella where the Congregation headquarters, Celestina, is located. After that, she can take two attendants with her into the cloister. Gallowglass? Fernando?" Baldwin turned to his nephew and his brother's mate.

"With pleasure," Fernando replied. "I haven't been to a Congregation meeting since Hugh was alive."

"Of course I'm going to Venice," Gallowglass growled. "If you think Auntie's going without me, you're daft."

"I thought as much. Remember: They can't start the meeting without you, Diana. The council chamber's door won't unlock without the de Clermont key," Baldwin explained.

"Oh. So that's why the key is enchanted," I said.

"Enchanted?" Baldwin asked.

"Yes. A protection spell was forged into the key when it was made." The witches who had done it were skilled, too. Over the centuries the spell's gramarye had hardly weakened at all.

"The Congregation moved into Isola della Stella in 1454. The keys were made then and have been handed down ever since," Baldwin said.

"Ah. That explains it. The spell was cast to ensure that you don't duplicate the key. If you tried, it would destroy itself." I turned the key over in my palm. "Clever."

"Are you sure about this, Diana?" Baldwin studied me closely. "There's no shame in admitting you're not ready to confront Gerbert and Satu again. We can come up with another plan."

I turned and met Baldwin's gaze without flinching.

"I'm sure."

"Good." He reached for a sheet of paper that was waiting on the table. A de Clermont ouroboros was pressed into a disk of black wax at the bottom, next to Baldwin's decisive signature. He handed it to me. "You can present this to the librarian when you arrive."

It was his formal recognition of the Bishop-Clairmont scion.

"I didn't need to see Matthew with that girl to know he was ready to lead his own family," Baldwin said in answer to my amazed expression.

"When?" I asked, unable to say more.

"The moment he let you intervene between us in the church—and didn't succumb to his blood rage," Baldwin replied. "I'll find him, Diana. And I'll bring him home."

"Thank you." I hesitated, then said the word that was not only on my tongue but in my heart. "Brother."

37

The sea and sky were leaden and the wind fierce when the de Clermont plane touched down at the Venice airport.

"Fine Venetian weather, I see." Gallowglass buffered me from the blasts as we descended the airplane stairs behind Baldwin and Fernando.

"At least it's not raining," Baldwin said, scanning the tarmac.

Of the many things I'd been warned about, the fact that the house might have an inch or two of water in the ground floor was the least of my concerns. Vampires could have a maddening sense of what was truly important.

"Can we please go?" I said, marching toward the waiting car.

"It won't make it five o'clock any sooner," Baldwin observed as he followed me. "They refuse to change the meeting time. It's tr—"

"Tradition. I know." I climbed into the waiting car.

The car took us only as far as an airport dock, where Gallowglass helped me into a small, fast boat. It had the de Clermont crest on its gleaming helm and tinted windows on the cabin. Soon we were at another dock, this one floating in front of a fifteenth-century palazzo on the curve of the Grand Canal.

Ca' Chiaromonte was an appropriate dwelling for someone like Matthew who had played a pivotal role in Venetian business and political life for centuries. Its three floors, Gothic façade, and sparkling windows screamed wealth and status. Had I been here for any other reason than to save Matthew, I would have reveled in its beauty, but today the place felt as gloomy as the weather outside. A stout, dark-haired man with a prominent nose, round glasses with thick lenses, and a long-suffering expression was there to greet us.

"Benvegnùa, madame," he said with a bow. "It is an honor to welcome you to your home. And it is always a pleasure to see you again, Ser Baldovino."

"You're a terrible liar, Santoro. We need coffee. And something stronger for Gallowglass." Baldwin handed the man his gloves and coat and guided me toward the palazzo's open door. It was tucked inside a small portico that was, as predicted, a few inches underwater despite the sandbags that had been arranged in piles by the door. Inside, a floor of terra-cotta and white tiles stretched into the distance, with another door at the far end. The dark wood paneling was illuminated by candles set into sconces with mirrored backs to magnify the light. I peeled off the hood on my heavy raincoat, unwound my scarf, and surveyed my surroundings.

"*D'accordo,* Ser Baldovino." Santoro sounded about as sincere as Ysabeau. "And for you, Madame Chiaromonte? Milord Matteo has good taste in wine. A glass of Barolo, perhaps?"

I shook my head.

"It's Ser Matteo now," Baldwin said from the end of the corridor. Santoro's jaw dropped. "Don't tell me you're surprised, you old goat. You've been encouraging Matthew to rebel for centuries." Baldwin stomped up the stairs.

I fumbled with the buttons on my sodden coat. It wasn't raining at the moment, but the air was thick with moisture. Venice, I had discovered, was mostly water, valiantly (if vainly) held together with bricks and mortar. While I did so, I stole a look at the rich furniture in the hall. Fernando saw my wandering attention."

"Venetians understand two languages, Diana: wealth and power. The de Clermonts speak both—fluently," he said. "Besides, the city would have collapsed into the sea long ago if not for Matthew and Baldwin, and the Venetians know it. Neither of them have reason to hide here." Fernando took my coat and handed it to Santoro. "Come, let me show you upstairs."

The bedroom that had been prepared for me was decorated in reds and golds, and the fire in the tiled fireplace was lit, but the flames and bright colors could not warm me. Five minutes after the door closed behind Fernando, I found my way back downstairs.

I sank onto a padded bench in one of the lanternlike bay windows that jutted over the Grand Canal. A fire crackled in one of the house's cavernous fireplaces. A familiar motto—WHAT NOURISHES ME DESTROYS ME—was carved into the wooden mantel. It reminded me of Matthew, of our time in London, of past deeds that even now threatened my family.

"Please, Auntie. You must rest," Gallowglass murmured with concern once he'd discovered me there. "It's hours until the Congregation will hear your case."

But I refused to move. Instead, I sat among the leaded windows, each one capturing a fractured glimpse of the city outside, and listened to the bells mark the slow passing of the hours.

"It's time." Baldwin put his hand on my shoulder.

I stood and turned to face him. I was wearing the brightly embroidered Elizabethan jacket I'd worn home from the past along with a thick black turtleneck and wool trousers. I was dressed for Chelm so I could be ready to leave the moment the proceedings were over.

"You have the key?" Baldwin asked.

I slid it out of my pocket. Fortunately, the coat had been designed to hold an Elizabethan housewife's many accoutrements. Even so, the key to the Congregation chamber was so large it was a tight fit.

"Let's go, then," Baldwin said.

We found Gallowglass downstairs with Fernando. Both were draped in black cloaks, and Gallowglass settled a matching black velvet garment over my shoulders. It was ancient and heavy. My fingers traced Matthew's insignia on the folds of fabric that covered my right arm.

The fierce wind had not abated, and I gripped the bottom of my hood to keep it from blowing open. Fernando and Gallowglass swept into the launch, which lifted and fell with the swell of the waves in the canal.

Baldwin kept a firm grip on my elbow as we walked over the slippery surface. I hopped aboard the launch just as the deck tipped precipitously toward the landing, aided by the sudden application of Gallowglass's boot to a metal cleat on the side of the boat. I ducked into the cabin, and Gallowglass clambered aboard behind me.

We sped through the mouth of the Grand Canal, zipping across the stretch of water in front of San Marco and ducking into a smaller canal that cut through the Castello district and returned us to the lagoon north of the city. We passed by San Michele, with its high walls and cypress trees shielding the gravestones. My fingers twisted, spinning the black and blue cords within me as I murmured a few words to remember the dead.

As we crossed the lagoon, we passed some inhabited islands, like Murano and Burano, and others occupied only by ruins and dormant fruit trees. When the stark walls protecting the Isola della Stella came into view, my flesh tingled. Baldwin explained that the Venetians thought the place was cursed. It was no wonder. There was power here, both elemental magic and the residue left by centuries of spells cast to keep the place secure and turn away curious human eyes.

"The island is going to sense that I shouldn't be entering through a vampire's door," I told Baldwin. I could hear the spirits the witches had bound to the place as they swept around the perimeter making security checks. Whoever warded Isola della Stella and Celestina was far more sophisticated than the witch who had installed the magical surveillance system I'd dismantled at the Bodleian.

"Move quickly, then. Congregation rules forbid expulsion of anyone who reaches the cloister that lies at the center of Celestina. If you have the key, you have the right to enter with two companions. It's always been this way," Baldwin said calmly.

Santoro cut the engines, and the boat moved smoothly into the protected landing. As we passed under the archway, I saw the faint outlines of the de Clermont ouroboros on the keystone. Time and salt air had softened the chiseled insignia, and to a casual viewer it would have looked like nothing more than a shadow.

Inside, the steps that led to the high marble landing were thick with algae. A vampire might risk the climb, but not a witch. Before I could figure out a solution, Gallowglass had sprung from the boat and was on the landing. Santoro tossed a length of rope to him, and Gallowglass tied the boat to a bollard with practiced speed. Baldwin turned to issue his last-minute instructions.

"Once you reach the council chamber, take your seat without engaging in conversation. It's become common practice for the members to chat endlessly before we convene, but this is no ordinary meeting. The de Clermont representative is always the presiding member. Call the creatures to order as quickly as you can."

"Right." This was the part of the day I relished least. "Does it matter where I sit?"

"Your seat is opposite the door—between Gerbert and Domenico." With that, Baldwin gave me a kiss on the cheek. "*Buona fortuna,* Diana."

"Bring him home, Baldwin." I clutched at his sleeve for a moment. It was the last sign of weakness I could afford.

"I will. Benjamin expected his father to look for him, and he believes you will run after him," Baldwin said. "He will not be expecting me."

High above, bells tolled.

"We must go," Fernando said.

"Take care of my sister," Baldwin told him.

"I am taking care of my sire's mate," Fernando replied, "so you need not worry. I will guard her with my life."

Fernando grasped me around the waist and lifted me up, while Gallowglass reached down and snagged me by the arm. In two seconds I was standing on the landing, Fernando beside me. Baldwin hopped from the launch to a smaller speedboat. With a salute he maneuvered his new vessel to the mouth of the slip. He would wait there until the bells rang five o'clock, signaling the beginning of the meeting.

The door that stood between the Congregation and me was heavy and black with age and moisture. The lock was uncannily shiny in comparison and looked as though it had been recently polished. I suspected that magic kept it gleaming, and a brush of my fingers confirmed my suspicion. But this was just a benign protection spell to prevent the elements from damaging the metal. Based on what I'd seen from the windows of Ca' Chiaromonte, an enterprising Venetian witch could make a fortune enchanting the plaster and bricks in the city to stop them from crumbling.

The key felt warm as my hand closed around it. I drew it from my pocket, slipped the end of the stem and the bit into the lock, and turned. The mechanism inside the lock activated quickly and without complaint.

I grasped the heavy ring and pulled the door open. Beyond, there was a dark corridor with a veined-marble floor. I could see no more than a yard ahead of me in the darkness.

"Let me show you the way," Fernando said, taking my arm.

After the gloom of the corridor, I was temporarily blinded when we reached the dim light of the cloister. When my eyes focused, I saw rounded archways that were supported by graceful double columns. In the center of the space was a marble wellhead—a reminder that the cloister had been constructed long before modern conveniences like electricity and running water. In the days when travel was difficult and dangerous, the Congregation had met for months on end, living on the island until their business was finished.

The low murmur of conversation stopped. I pulled the hooded cloak around me, hoping to hide whatever markings of power might be visible on my skin. The thick folds also masked the tote bag slung over my shoulder. Quickly I surveyed the crowd. Satu stood alone. She avoided my eyes, but I was aware of her discomfort at seeing me again. More than that, the witch felt . . . wrong somehow, and my stomach flipped in a minor version of the revulsion I felt when another witch lied to me. Satu was wearing a disguising spell, but it did no good. I knew what she was hiding.

The other creatures present huddled into groups according to species. Agatha Wilson was standing with her two fellow daemons. Domenico and Gerbert were together, exchanging surprised looks. The Congregation's remaining two witches were both women. One was stern-looking, with a tight braided bun woven from brown hair threaded with gray. She wore the ugliest dress I had ever seen, accented by an ornate choker. A small portrait miniature adorned the center of the gold-and-enameled necklace—an ancestor, no doubt. The other witch was pleasantly round-faced, with pink cheeks and white hair. Her skin was remarkably unlined, which made it impossible to determine her age. Something about this witch tugged at me, too, but I couldn't figure out what it was. The flesh on my arms prickled, warning me that the Book of Life held an answer to my unspoken questions, but I couldn't take the time to decipher it now.

"I am pleased to see that the de Clermonts have bowed to the Congregation's request to see this witch." Gerbert appeared before me. I had not seen him since La Pierre. "We meet again, Diana Bishop."

"Gerbert." I met his gaze unflinchingly, though it made my flesh shrink. His lips curled.

"I see you are the same proud creature you were before." Gerbert turned to Gallowglass. "To see such a noble lineage as the de Clermonts brought to confusion and ruin by a girl!"

"They used to say something similar about Granny," Gallowglass shot back. "If we can survive Ysabeau we can survive this 'girl.'"

"You may think differently once you learn the extent of the witch's offenses," Gerbert replied.

"Where is Baldwin?" Domenico joined us, a scowl on his face.

Gears whirred and clanged overhead.

"Saved by the bell," Gallowglass said. "Stand aside, Domenico."

"A change of de Clermont representative at this late hour, and without notification, is most irregular, Gallowglass," Gerbert said.

"What are you waiting for, Gallowglass? Unlock the door," Domenico commanded.

"It's not me who holds the key," Gallowglass said, his voice soft. "Come, Auntie. You have a meeting to attend."

"What do you mean, you don't have the key?" Gerbert asked, his voice so sharp the sound cut through the enchanted carillon playing overhead. "You are the only de Clermont present."

"Not so. Baldwin recognized Diana Bishop as a blood-sworn daughter of Philippe de Clermont weeks ago." Gallowglass gave Gerbert a mocking smile.

Across the cloister, one of the witches gasped and whispered to her neighbor.

"That's impossible," Domenico said. "Philippe de Clermont has been dead for more than half a century. How—"

"Diana Bishop is a timewalker." Gerbert looked at me in loathing. Across the courtyard the white-haired witch's dimples grew deeper. "I should have guessed. This is all part of some vast enchantment she has been working. I warned you that this witch must be stopped. Now we will pay the price for your failure to act appropriately." He pointed an accusing finger at Satu.

The first toll of the hours sounded.

"Time to go," I said briskly. "We wouldn't want to be late and disrupt the Congregation's traditions." Their failure to agree to an earlier meeting time still rankled.

As I approached the door, the weight of the key filled my palm. There were nine locks, and every one had a key in it, save one. I slipped the metal bit into the remaining keyhole and twisted it with a flick of my wrist. The locking mechanisms whirred and clicked. Then the door swung open.

"After you." I stepped aside so the others could file by. My first Congregation meeting was about to begin.

The council chamber was magnificent, decorated with brilliant frescoes and mosaics that were illuminated from the light of torches and hundreds of candles. The vaulted ceiling seemed miles above, and a gallery circled the room three or four stories up. That lofty space was where the Congregation's records were kept. Thousands of years of records, based on a quick visual inventory of the shelves. In addition to books and manuscripts, there were earlier writing technologies, including scrolls and glass frames of the kind that held papyrus fragments. Banks of shallow drawers suggested there might even be clay tablets up there.

My eyes dropped to survey the meeting room, dominated by a large oval table surrounded by high-backed chairs. Like the locks, and the keys that opened them, each chair was inscribed with a symbol. Mine was right where Baldwin had promised it would be: on the far side of the room, opposite the door.

A young human woman stood inside, presenting each Congregation member who entered with a leather folio. At first I thought it must contain the meeting's agenda. Then I noticed that each folio was a different thickness, as though items had been requested from the shelves above according to the members' specific instructions.

I was the last to enter the room, and the door clanged shut behind me.

"Madame de Clermont," the woman said, her dark eyes brimming with intelligence. "I am Rima Jaén, the Congregation's librarian. Here are the documents *Sieur* Baldwin requested for the meeting. If there is anything more you require, you have only to let me know."

"Thank you," I said, taking the materials from her.

She hesitated. "Pardon my presumption, madame, but have we met? You seem so familiar. I know you are a scholar. Have you ever visited the Gonçalves archive in Seville?"

"No, I have never worked there," I said, adding, "but I believe I know the owner."

"Señor Gonçalves nominated me for this job after I was made redundant," Rima said. "The Congregation's former librarian retired quite unexpectedly in July, after suffering a heart attack. The librarians are, by tradition, human. *Sieur* Baldwin took on the task of replacing him."

The librarian's heart attack—and Rima's appointment—had come a few weeks after Baldwin found out about my blood vow. I strongly suspected that my new brother had engineered the whole business. The de Clermonts' king became more interesting by the hour.

"You are keeping us waiting, Professor Bishop," Gerbert said testily, though based on the hum of conversation among the delegates he was the only creature who minded.

"Allow Professor Bishop a chance to get her bearings. It is her first meeting," said the dimpled witch in a broad Scots accent. "Are you able to remember yours, Gerbert, or is that happy day lost in the mists of time?"

"Give that witch a chance and she'll spellbind us all," Gerbert said. "Do not underestimate her, Janet. Knox's assessment of her childhood power and potential was grossly misleading, I fear."

"Thank you kindly, but I don't believe it's I who needs the warning," Janet said with a twinkle in her gray eyes.

I took the folio from Rima and passed her the folded document that gave the Bishop-Clairmont family official standing in the vampire world.

"Can you file that, please?" I asked.

"Happily, Madame de Clermont," Rima said. "The Congregation librarian is also its secretary. I'll take whatever actions the document requires while you are meeting."

Having handed off the papers that formally established the Bishop-Clairmont scion, I circumnavigated the table, the black cloak billowing around my feet.

"Nice tats," Agatha whispered as I walked by, pointing to her own hairline. "Great cape, too."

I smiled at her without comment and kept going. When I reached my chair, I wrestled with the damp cloak, not wanting to relinquish the tote bag while I did so. Finally I managed to get it off and hung it over the back of my chair.

"There are hooks by the door," Gerbert said.

I turned to face him. His eyes widened. My jacket had long sleeves to hide the Book of Life's text, but my eyes were fully on view. And I'd deliberately pulled my hair back into a long red braid that revealed the tips of the branches that covered my scalp.

"My power is unsettled at the moment, and some people are made uncomfortable by my appearance," I said. "I prefer to keep my cloak nearby. Or I can use a disguising spell like Satu. But hiding in plain sight is as much a lie as any spoken form of deceit."

I looked at each creature of the Congregation in turn, daring any of them to react to the letters and symbols that I knew were passing across my eyes.

Satu glanced away, but not quickly enough to mask her frightened look. The sudden movement stretched her poor excuse for a disguising spell. I searched for the spell's signature, but there was none. Satu's disguising spell had not been cast. She herself had woven it—and not very skillfully.

I know your secret, sister, I said silently.

And I have long suspected yours, Satu replied, her voice as bitter as wormwood.

Oh, I've picked up a few more along the way, I said.

After my slow survey of the room, only Agatha risked asking a question. "What happened to you?" she whispered.

"I chose my path." I dropped the tote bag on the table and lowered myself into the chair. The bag was bound to me so tightly that even at this short distance I could feel the tug.

"What's that?" Domenico asked suspiciously.

"A Bodleian Library tote bag." I had taken it from the library shop when we retrieved the Book of Life, making sure to leave a twenty-pound note under the pencil cup near the till. Fittingly, the canvas bag had the library oath emblazoned upon it in red and black letters.

Domenico opened his mouth to ask another question, but I silenced him with a look. I had waited long enough for today's meeting to begin. Domenico could ask me questions after Matthew was free.

"I call this meeting to order. I am Diana Bishop, Philippe de Clermont's blood-sworn daughter, and I represent the de Clermonts." I turned to Domenico. He crossed his arms and refused to speak. I continued.

"This is Domenico Michele, and Gerbert of Aurillac is to my left. I know Agatha Wilson from Oxford, and Satu Järvinen and I spent some time together in France." My back smarted with the memory of her fire. "I'm afraid the rest of you will have to introduce yourselves."

"I am Osamu Watanabe," said the young male daemon sitting next to Agatha. "You look like a manga character. Can I draw you later?"

"Sure," I said, hoping that the character in question didn't turn out to be evil.

"Tatiana Alkaev," said a platinum blond daemon with the dreamy blue eyes. All she needed was a sleigh pulled by white horses and she would be the perfect heroine in a Russian fairy tale. "You're full of answers, but I have no questions at this time."

"Excellent." I turned to the witch with the forbidding expression and the execrable taste in clothing. "And you?"

"I am Sidonie von Borcke," she said, putting on a pair of reading glasses and opening her leather folio with a snap. "And I have no knowledge of this so-called blood vow."

"It's in the librarian's report. Second page, at the bottom, in the addendum, third line," Osamu said helpfully. Sidonie glared at him. "I seem to recall that it begins 'Additions to vampire pedigrees (alphabetical): Almasi, Bettingcourt, de Clermont, Díaz—"

"Yes, I see it now, Mr. Watanabe," Sidonie snapped.

"I believe it's my turn to be introduced, dear Sidonie." The white-haired witch smiled beneficently. "I am Janet Gowdie, and meeting you is a long-awaited pleasure. I knew your father and mother. They were a great credit to our people, and I still feel their loss keenly."

"Thank you," I said, moved by the woman's simple tribute.

"We were told the de Clermonts had a motion for us to consider?" Janet gently steered the meeting back on track.

I gave her a grateful look. "The de Clermonts formally request the assistance of the Congregation in tracking down a member of the Bishop-Clairmont scion, Benjamin Fox or Fuchs. Mr. Fox contracted blood rage from his father, my husband, Matthew Clairmont, and has been kidnapping and raping witches for centuries in an attempt to impregnate them, mostly in the area surrounding the Polish city of Chelm. Some of you may remember complaints made by the Chelm coven, which the Congregation ignored. To date, Benjamin's desire to create a witch-vampire child has been thwarted, in large part because he does not know what the witches discovered long ago—namely, that vampires with blood rage can reproduce biologically, but only with a particular kind of witch called a weaver."

The room was completely quiet. I took a deep breath and continued.

"My husband, in an attempt to draw Benjamin into the open, went into Poland where he disappeared. We believe Benjamin has captured him and is holding him in a facility that served as a Nazi labor camp or research laboratory during the Second World War. The Knights of Lazarus have pledged to get my husband back, but the de Clermonts will need witches and daemons to come to our aid as well. Benjamin must be stopped."

I looked around the room once more. Every person in it save Janet Gowdie was slack-jawed with amazement.

"Discussion? Or should we move straight to the vote?" I asked, eager to forstall a long debate.

After a long silence, the Congregation chamber was filled with an indignant clamor as the representatives began to shout questions at me and accusations at each other.

"Discussion it is," I said.

38

"You must eat something," Gallowglass insisted, pressing a sandwich into my hand.

"I have to go back in there. The second vote will take place soon." I pushed the sandwich away. Baldwin had, among his many other instructions, reminded me about the Congregation's elaborate voting procedures: three votes on any motion, with discussion in between. It was normal for the votes to swing wildly from one position to the other as Congregation members considered—or pretended to consider—opposing views.

I lost the first vote, eight opposed and one—me—in favor. Some voted against me on procedural grounds, since Matthew and I had violated the covenant and the Congregation had already voted to uphold that ancient pact. Others voted it down because the scourge of blood rage threatened the health and safety of all warmbloods—daemon, human, and witch. Newspaper reports of the vampire murders were produced and read aloud. Tatiana objected to rescuing the witches of Chelm, who, she tearfully claimed, had cast a spell on her vacationing grandmother that made her break out in boils. No amount of explaining could convince Tatiana that she was actually thinking of Cheboksary, even though Rima procured aerial photographs to prove that Chelm was not a beachfront spot on the Volga.

"Is there word from Baldwin or Verin?" I asked. Isola della Stella suffered from poor cell-phone reception, and within the walls of Celestina the only way to catch a signal was by standing in the exposed center of the cloister in a steady downpour.

"None." Gallowglass put a mug of tea in my hand and closed my fingers around it. "Drink."

Worry for Matthew and impatience with the Congregation's Byzantine rules and regulations made my stomach flip. I handed the mug back to Gallowglass, untouched.

"Don't take the Congregation's decision to heart, Auntie. My father always said that the first vote was all about posturing and that more often than not the second vote reversed the first."

I picked up the Bodleian tote bag, nodded, and returned to the council chamber. The hostile looks I received from Gerbert and Domenico once I was inside made me wonder if Hugh had been an optimist when it came to Congregation politics.

"Blood rage!" Gerbert hissed, grabbing at my arm. "How did the de Clermonts keep this from us?"

"I don't know, Gerbert," I replied, shaking off his grip. "Ysabeau lived under your roof for weeks and you never discovered it."

"It's half past ten." Sidonie von Borcke strode into the room. "We adjourn at midnight. Let's conclude this sordid business and move on to more important matters—like our investigation of the Bishop family's covenant violations."

There was nothing more pressing than ridding the world of Benjamin but I bit my tongue and took my chair, resting the tote bag on the table in front of me. Domenico reached for it, still curious about its contents.

"Don't." I looked at him. Apparently my eyes spoke volumes, for he withdrew his hand quickly.

"So, Sidonie, am I to understand you're calling the question?" I asked her abruptly. In spite of her calls for a quick resolution, she was proving to be a major impediment to the deliberations, drawing out every exchange with irrelevant detail until I was ready to scream.

"Not at all," she huffed. "I merely wish us to consider the matter with proper efficiency."

"I remain opposed to intervening in what is clearly a family problem," Gerbert said. "Madame de Clermont's proposal seeks to open this unfortunate matter to greater scrutiny. Already the Knights of Lazarus are on the scene and looking for her husband. It is best to let matters take their course."

"And the blood rage?" It was the first time Satu had said anything with the exception of her "no" when called upon in the first vote.

"Blood rage is a matter for the vampires to handle. We will discipline the de Clermont family for their serious lapse in judgment and take appropriate measures to locate and exterminate all who might be infected." Gerbert tented his fingers and looked around the table. "You can all rest easy on that score."

"I agree with Gerbert. Furthermore, no scion can be established under a diseased sire," Domenico said. "It's unthinkable. Matthew Clairmont must be put to death, and all his children with him." The vampire's eyes gleamed.

Osamu raised his hand and waited to be recognized.

"Yes, Mr. Watanabe?" I nodded in his direction.

"What's a weaver?" he asked. "And what do they have in common with vampires who have blood rage?"

"What makes you think they have anything in common?" Sidonie snapped.

"It's only logical that blood-rage vampires and weaving witches have something in common. How could Diana and Matthew have had children otherwise?" Agatha looked at me expectantly. Before I could answer, Gerbert stood and loomed over me.

"Is that what Matthew discovered in the Book of Life?" he demanded. "Did you unearth a spell that joins the two species?"

"Sit down, Gerbert." Janet had been knitting steadily for hours, looking up every now and again to make a judicious comment or smile benignly.

"The witch must answer!" Gerbert exclaimed. "What spell is at work here, and how did you perform it?"

"The answer is in the Book of Life." I dragged the tote bag toward me and drew out the volume that had been hidden for so long in the Bodleian Library.

There were gasps of astonishment around the table.

"This is a trick," Sidonie pronounced. She rose and made her way around the table. "If that is the witches' lost book of spells, I demand to examine it."

"It's the vampire's lost history," Domenico growled as she went past his chair.

"Here." I handed the Book of Life to Sidonie.

The witch tried to spring the clasps, pushing and tugging at the metal fittings, but the book refused to cooperate with her. I held out my hands and the book flew across the space between us, eager to be back where it belonged. Sidonie and Gerbert exchanged a long look.

"You open it, Diana," Agatha said, her eyes round. I thought back to what she'd said in Oxford all those months ago—that Ashmole 782 belonged to the daemons as well as the witches and vampires. Somehow, she had already divined a sense of the contents.

I placed the Book of Life on the table while the Congregation gathered around me. The clasps opened immediately at my touch. Whispers and sighs filled the air, followed by the eldritch traces left by the spirits of the creatures who were bound to the pages.

"Magic isn't permitted on Isola della Stella," Domenico protested, an edge of panic in his voice. "Tell her, Gerbert!"

"If I were working magic, Domenico, you'd know it," I retorted.

Domenico paled as the wraiths grew more coherent, taking on elongated human form with hollow, dark eyes.

I flipped the book open. Everybody bent forward for a closer look.

"There's nothing there," Gerbert said, his face twisted with fury. "The book is blank. What have you done to our book of origins?"

"This book smells . . . odd," Domenico said, giving the air a suspicious sniff. "Like dead animals."

"No, it smells of dead creatures." I ruffled the pages so that the scent rose in the air. "Daemons. Vampires. Witches. They're all in there."

"You mean . . ." Tatiana looked horrified.

"That's right." I nodded. "That's parchment made from creature skin. The leaves are sewn together with creature hair, too."

"But where is the text?" Gerbert asked, his voice rising. "The Book of Life is supposed to hold the key to many mysteries. It's our sacred text—the vampire's history."

"Here is your sacred text." I pushed up my sleeves. Letters and symbols swirled and ran just under my skin, coming to the surface like bubbles on a pond, only to dissolve. I had no idea what my eyes were doing, but I suspected they were full of characters, too. Satu backed away from me.

"You bewitched it," Gerbert snarled.

"The Book of Life was bewitched long ago," I said. "All I did was open it."

"And it chose you." Osamu reached out a finger to touch the letters on my arm. A few of them gathered around the point where his skin met mine before they danced away again.

"Why did the book choose Diana Bishop?" Domenico asked.

"Because I'm a weaver—a maker of spells—and there are precious few of us left." I sought out Satu once more. Her lips were pressed together, and her eyes begged me to remain silent. "We had too much creative power, and our fellow witches killed us."

"The same power that makes it possible for you to create new spells gives you the ability to create new life," Agatha said, her excitement evident.

"It's a special blessing the goddess bestows on female weavers," I replied. "Not all weavers are women, of course. My father was a weaver, too."

"It's impossible," Domenico snarled. "This is more of the witch's treachery. I've never heard of a weaver, and the ancient scourge of blood rage has mutated into an even more dangerous form. As for children born to witches and vampires, we cannot allow such an evil to take root. They would be monsters, beyond reason or control."

"I must take issue with you on that point, Domenico," Janet said.

"On what grounds?" he said with a touch of impatience.

"On the grounds that I am such a creature and am neither evil nor monstrous."

For the first time since my arrival, the attention of the room was directed elsewhere.

"My grandmother was the child of a weaver and a vampire." Janet's gray eyes latched on to mine. "Everyone in the Highlands called him Nickie-Ben."

"Benjamin," I breathed.

"Aye." Janet nodded. "Young witches were told to be careful on moonless nights, lest Nickie-Ben catch them. My great-granny, Isobel Gowdie, didn't listen. They had a mad love affair. The legends say he bit her on the shoulder. When Nickie-Ben went away, he left something behind without knowing it: a daughter. I am named after her."

I looked down at my arms. In a kind of magical Scrabble, letters rose and arranged themselves into a name: *JANET GOWDIE, DAUGHTER OF ISOBEL GOWDIE AND BENJAMIN FOX.* Janet's grandmother had been one of the Bright Born.

"When was your grandmother conceived?" An account of a Bright Born's life might tell me something about my own children's futures.

"In 1662," Janet said. "Granny Janet died in 1912, bless her, at the age of two hundred and fifty. She kept her beauty right until the end, but then, unlike me, Granny Janet was more vampire than witch. She was proud to have inspired the legends of the *baobhan sith,* having lured many a man to her bed only to cause each of them death and ruin. And it was fearful to behold Granny Janet's temper when she was crossed."

"But that would make you . . ." My eyes were round.

"I'll be one hundred and seventy next year," Janet said. She murmured a few words and her white hair was revealed to be a dusky black. Another murmured spell showed her skin was a luminous, pearly white.

Janet Gowdie looked no more than thirty. My children's lives began to take shape in my imagination.

"And your mother?" I asked.

"My mam lived for a full two hundred years. With each passing generation, our lives get shorter."

"How do you hide what you are from the humans?" Osamu asked.

"Same way the vampires do, I suppose. A bit of luck. A bit of help from our fellow witches. A bit of human willingness to turn away from the truth," Janet replied.

"This is utter nonsense," Sidonie said hotly. "You are a famous witch, Janet. Your spell-casting ability is renowned. And you come from a distinguished line of witches. Why you would want to sully your family's reputation with this story is beyond me."

"And there it is," I said, my voice soft.

"There what is?" Sidonie sounded like a testy schoolmarm.

"The disgust. The fear. The dislike of anybody who doesn't conform to your simpleminded expectations of the world and how it should work."

"Listen to me, Diana Bishop—"

But I was through listening to Sidonie or anybody else who used the covenant as a shield to hide their own inner darkness.

"No. You listen to me," I said. "My parents were witches. I'm the bloodsworn daughter of a vampire. My husband, and the father of my children, is a vampire. Janet, too, is descended from a witch and a vampire. When will you stop pretending that there's some pure-blooded witch ideal in the world?"

Sidonie stiffened. "There *is* such an ideal. It is how our power has been maintained."

"No. It's how our power has *died,*" I retorted. "If we keep abiding by the covenant, in a few generations we won't have any power left. The whole purpose of that agreement was to keep the species from mixing and reproducing."

"More nonsense!" Sidonie cried. "The covenant's purpose is first and foremost to keep us safe."

"Wrong. The covenant was drawn up to prevent the birth of children like Janet: powerful, long-lived, neither witch nor vampire nor daemon but something in between," I said. "It's what all creatures have feared. It's what Benjamin wants to control. We cannot let him."

"In between?" Janet arched her brows. They were, now that I was seeing her clearly, as black as night. "Is that the answer, then?"

"Answer to what?" Domenico demanded.

But I was not ready to share that secret from the Book of Life. Not until Miriam and Chris had found the scientific evidence to back up what the manuscript had revealed to me. Once again I was saved from answering by the ringing of Celestina's bells.

"It is nearly midnight. We must adjourn—for now," Agatha Wilson said, her eyes shining. "I call the question. Will the Congregation support the de Clermonts in their efforts to rid the world of Benjamin Fox?"

Everyone returned to their seats and we went around the table one by one, casting our votes.

This time the vote was more encouraging: four in favor and five opposed. I had made progress in the second vote, earning the support of Agatha, Osamu, and Janet, but not enough to guarantee the outcome when the third, and final, vote was taken tomorrow. Especially not when my old enemies, Gerbert, Domenico, and Satu, were among the holdouts.

"The meeting will resume tomorrow afternoon at five o'clock." Aware of every minute that Matthew was spending in Benjamin's custody, I had argued once more for an earlier meeting time. And once more, my request had been denied.

Wearily I gathered up my leather folio—which I'd never opened—and the Book of Life. The past seven hours had been grueling. I couldn't stop thinking about Matthew and what he was enduring while the Congregation hemmed and hawed. And I was worried about the children, too, who were without both of their parents. I waited for the room to empty. Janet Gowdie and Gerbert were the last to leave.

"Gerbert?" I called.

He stopped on his way out the door, his back to me.

"I haven't forgotten what happened in May," I said, the power burning brightly in my hands. "One day you will answer to me for Emily Mather's death."

Gerbert's head swung around. "Peter said you and Matthew were hiding something. I should have listened to him."

"Didn't Benjamin already tip you off about what the witches discovered?" I asked.

But Gerbert hadn't lived so long to be caught so easily. His lip curled.

"Until next evening," he said, giving Janet and me a small, formal bow.

"We should call him Nickie-Bertie," Janet commented. "He and Benjamin would make a right pair of devils."

"They would indeed," I replied uneasily.

"Are you free tomorrow for lunch?" Janet Gowdie asked as we walked out of the meeting chamber and into the cloister, her musical Scots voice reminding me of Gallowglass.

"Me?" Even after all that had happened tonight, I was surprised she would be seen with a de Clermont.

"Neither of us fits into one of the Congregation's tiny boxes, Diana," Janet said, her smooth skin dimpling with amusement.

Gallowglass and Fernando were waiting for me under the cloister's arcade. Gallowglass frowned to see me in a witch's company.

"All right, Auntie?" he asked, worried. "We should go. It's getting late."

"I just want to have a quick word with Janet before we leave." I searched Janet's face, looking for a sign that she might be trying to win my friendship for some nefarious purpose, but all I saw was concern. "Why are you helping me?" I asked bluntly.

"I promised Philippe I would," Janet said. She dropped her knitting bag at her feet and drew up the sleeve of her shirt. "You are not the only one whose skin tells a tale, Diana Bishop."

Tattooed on her arm was a number. Gallowglass swore. I gasped. "Were you at Auschwitz with Philippe?" My heart was in my mouth.

"No. I was at Ravensbrück," she said. "I was working in France for the SOE—the Special Operations Executive—when I was captured. Philippe was trying to liberate the camp. He managed to get a few of us out before the Nazis caught him."

"Do you know where Philippe was held after Auschwitz?" I asked, my tone urgent.

"No, though we did look for him. Was it Nickie-Ben who had him?" Janet's eyes were dark with sympathy.

"Yes," I replied. "We think he was somewhere near Chelm."

"Benjamin had witches working for him then, too. I remember wondering at the time why everything within fifty miles of Chelm was lost in a dense fog. We couldn't find our way through it, no matter how we tried." Janet's eyes filled. "I am sorry we failed Philippe. We will do better this time. 'Tis a matter of Bishop-Clairmont family honor. And I am Matthew de Clermont's kin, after all."

"Tatiana will be the easiest to sway," I said.

"Not Tatiana," Janet said with a shake of her head. "She is infatuated with Domenico. Her sweater does more than enhance her figure. It also hides Domenico's bites. We must persuade Satu instead."

"Satu Järvinen will never help me," I said, thinking of the time we'd spent together at La Pierre.

"Oh, I think she will," Janet said. "Once we explain that we'll offer her up to Benjamin in exchange for Matthew if she doesn't. Satu is a weaver like you, after all. Perhaps Finnish weavers are more fertile than those from Chelm."

Satu was staying at a small establishment on a quiet *campo* on the opposite side of the Grand Canal from Ca' Chiaromonte. It looked perfectly ordinary from the outside, with brightly painted flower boxes and stickers on the windows indicating its rating relative to other area establishments (four stars) and the credit cards it accepted (all of them).

Inside, however, the veneer of normalcy proved thin.

The proprietress, Laura Malipiero, sat behind a desk in the front lobby swathed in purple and black velvet, shuffling a tarot deck. Her hair was wild and curly, with streaks of white through the black. A garland of black paper bats was draped over the mailboxes, and the scent of sage and dragon's-blood incense hung in the air.

"We're full," she said, not looking up from her cards. A cigarette was clasped in the corner of her mouth. It was purple and black, just like her outfit. At first I didn't think it was lit. Signorina Malipiero was sitting under a sign that read VIETATO FUMARE, after all. But then the witch took a deep drag on it. There was indeed no smoke, though the tip glowed.

"They say she's the richest witch in Venice. She made her fortune selling enchanted cigarettes." Janet eyed her with disapproval. She had donned her disguising spell again and to the casual observer looked to be a frail nonagenarian rather than a slender thirty-something.

"I'm sorry, sisters, but the Regata delle Befane is this week, and there isn't a room to be had in this part of Venice." Signorina Malipiero's attention remained on her cards.

I'd seen notices all over town announcing the annual Epiphany gondola race to see who could get from San Tomà to the Rialto the fastest. There were two races, of course: the official regatta in the morning and the far more exciting and dangerous one at midnight that involved not just brute strength but magic, too.

"We aren't interested in a room, Signorina Malipiero. I'm Janet Gowdie, and this is Diana Bishop. We're here to see Satu Järvinen on Congregation business—if she's not practicing for the gondola race, that is."

The Venetian witch looked up in shock, her dark eyes huge and her cigarette dangling.

"Room 17, is it? No need to trouble yourself. We can show ourselves up." Janet beamed at the stunned witch and bundled me off in the direction of the stairs.

"You, Janet Gowdie, are a bulldozer," I said breathlessly as she hustled me down the corridor. "Not to mention a mind reader." It was such a useful magical talent.

"What a lovely thing to say, Diana." Janet knocked on the door. *"Cameriera!"*

There was no answer. And after yesterday's marathon Congregation meeting, I was tired of waiting. I wrapped my fingers around the doorknob and murmured an opening spell. The door swung open. Satu Järvinen was waiting for us inside, both hands up, ready to work magic.

I snared the threads that surrounded her and pulled them tight, binding her arms to her sides. Satu gasped.

"What do you know about weavers?" I demanded.

"Not as much as you do," Satu replied.

"Is this why you treated me so badly at La Pierre?" I asked.

Satu's expression was steely. Her actions then had been taken in the interest of self-preservation. She felt no remorse. "I won't let you expose me. They'll kill us all if they find out what weavers can do," Satu said.

"They'll kill me anyway for loving Matthew. What do I have to lose?"

"Your children," Satu spit.

That, it turned out, was going too far.

"You are unfit to possess a witch's gifts. I bind thee, Satu Järvinen, delivering you into the hands of the goddess without power or craft." With the index finger of my left hand, I pulled the threads one more inch and knotted them tight. My finger flared darkly purple. It was, I had discovered, the color of justice.

Satu's power left her in a *whoosh,* sucking the air out of the room.

"You can't spellbind me!" she cried. "It's forbidden!"

"Report me to the Congregation," I said. "But before you do, know this: Nobody will be able to break the knot that binds you—except me. And what use will you be to the Congregation in this state? If you want to keep your seat, you'll have to keep your silence—and hope that Sidonie von Borcke doesn't notice."

"You will pay for this, Diana Bishop!" Satu promised.

"I already have," I said. "Or have you forgotten what you did to me in the name of sisterly solidarity?"

I advanced on her slowly. "Being spellbound is nothing compared to what Benjamin will do to you if he discovers that you are a weaver. You'll have no way to defend yourself and will be entirely at his mercy. I've seen what Benjamin does to the witches he tries to impregnate. Not even you deserve that."

Satu's eyes flickered with fear.

"Vote for the de Clermont motion this afternoon." I released Satu's arms, but not the binding spell that limited her power. "For your own sake, if not for Matthew."

Satu tried and failed to use her magic against me.

"Your power is gone. I wasn't lying, sister." I turned and stalked away. At the doorway I stopped and turned. "And don't ever threaten my children again. If you do, you'll be begging me to throw you down a hole and forget about you."

Gerbert tried to delay the final vote on procedural grounds, arguing that the current constitution of the governing council did not meet the criteria set out in foundational documents dating from the Crusader period. These stipulated the presence of three vampires, three witches, and three daemons.

Janet stopped me from strangling the creature by quickly explaining that since she and I were both part vampire and part witch, the Congregation was equally balanced. While she argued percentages, I examined Gerbert's so-called foundational documents and discovered words such as "unalienable" that were decidedly eighteenth-century in their tone. Presented with a list of the linguistic anachronisms in this supposedly Crusader document, Gerbert scowled at Domenico and said these were obviously later transcriptions of lost originals.

No one believed him.

Janet and I won the vote: six to three. Satu voted as we told her to do, her attitude subdued and defeated. Even Tatiana joined our ranks thanks to Osamu, who had devoted his morning to mapping the precise location of not only Chelm but every Russian city beginning with *Ch* just to prove that the Polish city's witches had nothing to do with her grandmother's skin affliction. When the two entered the council chamber hand in hand, I figured she might have switched not only sides but boyfriends.

Once the vote was tallied and recorded, we didn't linger to celebrate. Instead Gallowglass, Janet, Fernando, and I took off in the de Clermont launch, headed across the lagoon for the airport.

As planned, I sent a three-letter text to Hamish with the results of the vote: QGA. It stood for Queen's Gambit Accepted, a code to indicate that the Congregation had been persuaded to support Matthew's rescue. We did not know if anyone was monitoring our communications, but we'd decided to be cautious.

His response was immediate.

Well done. Standing by for your arrival.

I checked in with Marcus, who reported that the twins were always hungry and had completely monopolized Phoebe's attention. As for Jack, Marcus said he was as well as could be expected.

After my exchange with Marcus, I sent a text to Ysabeau.

Worried about the bishop pair.

It was another chess reference. We had dubbed Gerbert, onetime bishop of Rome, and his sidekick Domenico the "bishop pair" because they always seemed to be working together. After their latest defeat, they were bound to retaliate. Gerbert might already have warned Knox that I had won the vote and we were on our way.

Ysabeau took longer to reply than Marcus had.

The bishop pair cannot checkmate our king unless the queen and her rook allow it.

There was a long pause, then another message.

And I will die first.

39

The air bit through my thick cloak, making me withdraw from the blast of wind that threatened to split me in two. I had never experienced cold like this and wondered how anyone survived a winter in Chelm.

"There." Baldwin pointed to a low huddle of buildings in the valley below.

"Benjamin has at least a dozen of his children with him." Verin stood at my elbow, a pair of binoculars in her fingers. She offered them to me, in case my warmblooded eyes weren't strong enough to see where my husband was being kept, but I refused them.

I knew exactly where Matthew was. The closer I got to him, the more agitated my power became, leaping to the surface of my skin in an attempt to escape. That, and my witch's third eye, more than made up for any warmblooded deficiencies.

"We'll wait until twilight to strike. That's when a detail of Benjamin's children go out to hunt." Baldwin looked grim. "They've been preying on Chelm and Lublin, bringing back the homeless and the weak for their father to feed on."

"Wait?" I'd done nothing but for three days. "I'm not going to wait another moment!"

"He is still alive, Diana." Ysabeau's response should have brought me comfort, but it only made the ice around my heart thicken at the thought of what Matthew would continue to suffer for the next six hours as we waited for darkness to fall.

"We can't attack the compound when it's at full strength," Baldwin said. "We must be strategic about this, Diana—not emotional."

Think—and stay alive. Reluctantly, I turned away from dreams of Matthew's quick release to focus on the challenges before us. "Janet said Knox put wards around the main building."

Baldwin nodded. "We were waiting for you to disarm them."

"How will the knights get into position without Benjamin knowing?" I asked.

"Tonight the Knights of Lazarus will use the tunnels to enter Benjamin's compound from below." Fernando's expression was calculating. "Twenty, maybe thirty, should be enough."

"Chelm is built on chalk, you see, and the ground beneath it is honeycombed with tunnels," Hamish explained, unrolling a small, crudely drawn map. "The Nazis destroyed some of them, but Benjamin kept these open. They connect his compound and the town and provide a way for him and his children to prey on the city without ever appearing aboveground."

"No wonder Benjamin was so hard to track down," Gallowglass murmured, looking at the underground maze.

"Where are the knights now?" I had yet to see the massing of troops I'd been told were in Chelm.

"Standing by," Hamish replied.

"Fernando will decide when to send them into the tunnels. As Marcus's marshal, the decision is his," Baldwin said, acknowledging Fernando with a nod.

"Actually, it's mine," Marcus said, appearing suddenly against the snow.

"Marcus!" I pushed my hood back, terror gripping me. "What's happened to Rebecca and Philip? Where are they?"

"Nothing has happened. The twins are at Sept-Tours with Sarah, Phoebe, and three dozen knights—all of them handpicked for their loyalty to the de Clermonts and their dislike of Gerbert and the Congregation. Miriam and Chris are there, too." Marcus took my hands in his. "I couldn't sit in France waiting for news. Not when I could be helping to free my father. And Matthew might need my help after that, too."

Marcus was right. Matthew would need a doctor—a doctor who understood vampires and how to heal them.

"And Jack?" It was all I could squeeze out, though Marcus's words had helped my heart rate return to something approaching normal.

"He's fine, too," Marcus said firmly. "Jack had one bad episode last night when I told him he couldn't come along, but Marthe turns out to be something of a hellcat when provoked. She threatened to keep Jack from seeing Philip, and that sobered him right up. He never lets the child out of his sight. Jack says it's his job to protect his godson, no matter what." Marcus turned to Fernando. "Walk me through your plan."

Fernando went over the operation in detail: where the knights would be positioned, when they would move on the compound, the roles that Gallowglass, Baldwin, Hamish, and now Marcus would play.

Even though it all sounded flawless, I was still worried.

"What is it, Diana?" Marcus asked, sensing my concern.

"So much of our strategy relies on the element of surprise," I said. "What if Gerbert has already tipped off Knox and Benjamin? Or Domenico? Even Satu might have decided she was safer from Benjamin if she could gain Knox's trust."

"Don't worry, Auntie," Gallowglass assured me, his blue eyes taking on a stormy cast. "Gerbert, Domenico, and Satu are all sitting on Isola della Stella. The Knights of Lazarus have them surrounded. There's no way for them to get off the island."

Gallowglass's words did little to lessen my concern. The only thing that could help was freeing Matthew and putting an end to Benjamin's machinations—for good.

"Ready to examine the wards?" Baldwin asked, knowing that giving me something to do would help keep my anxiety in check.

After swapping my highly visible black cloak for a pale gray parka that blended into the snow, Baldwin and Gallowglass took me within shouting distance of Benjamin's compound. In silence I took stock of the wards that protected the place. There were a few alarm spells, a trigger spell that I suspected would unleash some kind of elemental conflagration or storm, and a handful of diversions that were designed to do nothing more than delay an attacker until a proper defense could be mounted. Knox had used spells that were complicated, but they were old and worn, too. It wouldn't take much to pick apart the knots and leave the place unguarded.

"I'll need two hours and Janet," I whispered to Baldwin as we withdrew.

Together Janet and I freed the compound from its invisible barbed-wire perimeter. There was one alarm spell we had to leave in place, however. It was linked directly back to Knox, and I feared that even tinkering with the knots would alert him to our presence.

"He's a clever bugger," Janet said, wiping a tired hand across her eyes.

"Too clever for his own good. His spells were lazy," I said. "Too many crossings, not enough threads."

"When this is all over, we are going to have several evenings by the fireside where you explain what you just said," Janet warned.

"When this is over, and Matthew is home, I'll happily sit by the fireside for the rest of my life," I replied.

Gallowglass's hovering presence reminded me that time was passing.

"Time to go," I said briskly, nodding toward the silent Gael.

Gallowglass insisted we eat something and took us to a café in Chelm. There I managed to swallow down some tea and two bites of hot-milk cake while the warmth from the clanging radiator thawed my extremities.

As the minutes ticked by, the regular metallic sounds from the café's heating system began to sound like warning bells. Finally Gallowglass announced that the hour had come when we were to meet up with Marcus's army.

He took us to a prewar house on the outskirts of town. Its owner had been happy to hand over the keys and head to warmer climes in exchange for a hefty cash vacation fund and the promise that he would find his leaking roof fixed when he returned.

The vampire knights who were assembled in the cellar were mostly unfamiliar to me, though I did recognize a few faces from the twins' christening. As I looked at them, rugged of line and quietly ready for whatever awaited them below, I was struck by the fact that these were warriors who had fought in modern world wars and revolutions, as well as medieval Crusades. They were some of the finest soldiers who had ever lived, and like all soldiers they were prepared to sacrifice their lives for something greater than themselves.

Fernando gave his final orders while Gallowglass opened a makeshift door. Beyond it was a small ledge and a rickety ladder that led down into darkness.

"Godspeed," Gallowglass whispered as the first of the vampires dropped out of sight and landed silently on the ground below.

We waited while the knights chosen to destroy Benjamin's hunting party did their work. Still nervous that someone might alert him to our presence and that he might respond by taking Matthew's life, I stared fixedly at the earth between my feet.

It was excruciating. There was no way to receive any progress reports. For all we knew, Marcus's knights could have met with unexpected resistance. Benjamin might have sent out more of his children to hunt. He might have sent out none.

"This is the hell of war," said Gallowglass. "It's not the fighting or even the dying that destroys you. It's the wondering."

No more than an hour later—though it felt like days—Giles pushed open the door. His shirt was stained with gore. There was no way to determine how much of it belonged to him and what might be traces of Benjamin's now-dead children. He beckoned us forward.

"Clear," he told Gallowglass. "But be careful. The tunnels echo, so watch your step."

Gallowglass handed Janet down and then me, making no use of the waiting ladder with its rusted metal treads that might give us away. It was so dark in the tunnel that I couldn't see the faces of the vampires who caught us, but I could smell the battle on them.

We hurried along the tunnel with as much speed as our need for silence allowed. Given the darkness, I was glad to have a vampire on each arm to steer me around the bends and would have fallen several times without the assistance of their keen eyes and quick reflexes.

Baldwin and Fernando were waiting for us at the intersection of three tunnels. Two blood-spattered mounds covered with tarps and a powdery white substance that gave off a faint glow marked where Benjamin's children had met their death.

"We covered the heads and bodies with quicklime to mask the scent," Fernando said. "It won't eliminate it completely, but it should buy us some time."

"How many?" Gallowglass asked.

"Nine," Baldwin replied. One of his hands was completely clean and bore a sword, the other was caked with substances I preferred not to identify. The contrast made my stomach heave.

"How many are still inside?" Janet murmured.

"At least another nine, probably more." Baldwin didn't look worried at the prospect. "If they're anything like this lot, you can expect them to be cocksure and clever."

"Dirty fighters, too," Fernando said.

"As expected," Gallowglass said, his tone easy and relaxed. "We'll be waiting for your signal to move into the compound. Good luck, Auntie."

Baldwin whisked me away before I could say a word of farewell to Gallowglass and Fernando. Perhaps it was better that way, since the single glance I cast over my shoulder captured faces that were etched with exhaustion.

The tunnel that Baldwin took us through led to the gates outside Benjamin's compound where Ysabeau and Hamish were waiting. With all the wards down save the one on the gate that led directly to Knox, the only risk was that a vampire's keen eyes would spot us.

Janet reduced that possibility with an all-encompassing disguising spell that concealed not only me but everybody within twenty feet.

"Where's Marcus?" I had expected to see him here.

Hamish pointed.

Marcus was already inside the perimeter, propped in the crook of a tree, a rifle aimed at a window. He must have breached the compound's stone walls by swinging from tree limb to tree limb. With no wards to worry about, provided he didn't use the gate, Marcus had taken advantage of the pause in the action and would now provide cover for us as we went through the gate and entered the front door.

"Sharpshooter," commented Baldwin.

"Marcus learned to handle a gun as a warmblood. He hunted squirrels when he was a child," added Ysabeau. "Smaller and faster than vampires, I'm told."

Marcus never acknowledged our presence, but he knew we were there. Janet and I set to work on the final knots that bound the alarm spell to Knox. She cast an anchoring spell, the kind witches used to shore up the foundations of their houses and keep their children from wandering away, and as I unbound the ward, I redirected its energy toward her. Our hope was that the spell wouldn't even notice that the heavy object it now guarded was a granite boulder and not a massive iron gate.

It worked.

We would have been inside the house in moments if not for the inconvenient interruption of one of Benjamin's sons, who came out to catch a cigarette only to discover the front gate standing open. His eyes widened.

A small hole appeared in his forehead.

One eye disappeared. Then another.

Benjamin's son clutched at his throat. Blood welled between his fingers, and he emitted a strange whistling sound.

"Hello, *salaud.* I'm your grandmother." Ysabeau thrust a dagger into the man's heart.

The simultaneous loss of blood from so many places made it easy for Baldwin to grab the man's head and twist it, breaking his neck and killing the vampire instantly. With another wrench his head came off his shoulders.

It had taken about forty-five seconds from the time Marcus fired his first shot to the moment Baldwin put the vampire's head facedown in the snow.

Then the dogs started to bark.

"Merde," Ysabeau whispered.

"Now. Go." Baldwin took my arm, and Ysabeau took charge of Janet. Marcus tossed his rifle to Hamish, who caught it easily. He let forth a piercing whistle.

"Shoot anything that comes out of that door," Marcus ordered. "I'm going after the dogs."

Unsure whether the whistle was meant to call the fierce-sounding canines or the waiting Knights of Lazarus, I hurried along into the compound's main building. It was no warmer inside than out. An emaciated rat scurried down the hall, which was lined with identical doors.

"Knox knows we're here," I said. There was no need for quiet or a disguising spell now.

"So does Benjamin," Ysabeau said grimly.

As planned, we parted ways. Ysabeau went in search of Matthew. Baldwin, Janet, and I were after Benjamin and Knox. With luck we would find them all in the same place and converge upon them, supported by the Knights of Lazarus once they breached the lower levels of the compound and made their way upstairs.

A soft cry drew us to one of the closed doors. Baldwin flung it open.

It was the room we'd seen on the video feed: the grimy tiles, drain in the floor, windows overlooking the snow, numbers written with a grease pencil on the walls, even the chair with a tweed coat lying over the back.

Matthew was sitting in another chair, his eyes black and his mouth open in a soundless scream. His ribs had been spread open with a metal device, exposing his slow-beating heart, the regular sound of which had brought me such comfort whenever he drew me close.

Baldwin rushed toward him, cursing Benjamin.

"It's not Matthew," I said.

Ysabeau's shriek in the distance told me she had stumbled onto a similar scene.

"It's not Matthew," I repeated, louder this time. I went to the next door and twisted the knob.

There was Matthew, sitting in the same chair. His hands—his beautiful, strong hands that touched me with such love and tenderness—had been severed at the wrists and were sitting in a surgical basin in his lap.

No matter which door we opened, we found Matthew in some horrific tableau of pain and torment. And every illusory scene had been staged especially for me.

After my hopes had been raised and dashed a dozen times, I blew all the doors in the house off their hinges with a single word. I didn't bother looking inside any of the open rooms. Apparitions could be quite convincing, and Knox's were very good indeed. But they were not flesh and blood. They were not my Matthew, and I was not deceived by them even though those I had seen would remain with me forever.

"Matthew will be with Benjamin. Find him." I walked away without waiting for Baldwin or Janet to agree. "Where are you, Mr. Knox?"

"Dr. Bishop." Knox was waiting for me when I rounded the corner. "Come. Have a drink with me. You won't be leaving this place, and it may be your last chance to enjoy the comforts of a warm room—until you conceive Benjamin's child, that is."

Behind me I slammed down an impenetrable wall of fire and water so that no one could follow.

Then I threw up another behind Knox, boxing us into a small section of the corridor.

"Nicely done. Your spell-casting talents have emerged, I see," said Knox.

"You will find me . . . altered," I said, using Gallowglass's phrase. The magic was waiting inside me, begging to fly. But I kept it under control, and the power obeyed me. I felt it there, still and watchful.

"Where have you been?" Knox asked.

"Lots of places. London. Prague. France." I felt the tingle of magic in my fingertips. "You've been to France, too."

"I went looking for your husband and his son. I found a letter, you see.

In Prague." Knox's eyes gleamed. "Imagine my surprise, stumbling upon Emily Mather—never a terribly impressive witch—binding your mother's spirit inside a stone circle."

Knox was trying to distract me.

"It reminded me of the stone circle I cast in Nigeria to bind your parents. Perhaps that was Emily's intention."

Words crawled beneath my skin, answering the silent questions his words engendered.

"I should never have let Satu do the honors where you were concerned, my dear. I've always suspected that you were different," Knox said. "Had I opened you up last October, as I did your mother and father all those years ago, you could have been spared so much heartache."

But there had been more in the past fourteen months than heartache. There had been unexpected joy, too. I clung to that now, anchoring myself to it as firmly as if Janet were working her magic.

"You're very quiet, Dr. Bishop. Have you nothing to say?"

"Not really. I prefer actions to words these days. They save time."

At last I released the magic spooled tightly within me. The net I'd made to capture Knox was black and purple, woven through with strands of white, silver, and gold. It spread out in wings from my shoulder blades, reminding me of the absent Corra, whose power, as she promised, was still mine.

"With knot of one, the spell's begun." My netlike wings spread wider.

"Very impressive bit of illusory work, Dr. Bishop." Knox's tone was patronizing. "A simple banishing spell will—"

"With knot of two, the spell be true." The silver and gold threads in my net gleamed bright, balancing the dark and light powers that marked the crossroads of the higher magics.

"It's too bad Emily didn't have your skill," Knox said. "She might have gotten more out of your mother's bound spirit than the gibberish I found when I stole her thoughts at Sept-Tours."

"With knot of three, the spell is free." The giant wings beat once, sending a soft eddy of air through the magical box I'd constructed. They gently separated from my body, rising higher until they hovered over Knox. He cast a look upward, then resumed.

"Your mother babbled to Emily about chaos and creativity and repeated the words of that charlatan Ursula Shipton's prophecy: *Old worlds die and new be born.* That's all I got out of Rebecca in Nigeria, too. Being with your father weakened her abilities. She needed a husband who could challenge her."

"With knot of four, the power is stored." A dark, potent spiral slowly unwound at the spot where the two wings were joined.

"Shall we open you up and see if you are more like your mother or your father?" Knox's hand made a lazy gesture, and I felt his magic cut a searing path across my chest.

"With knot of five, this spell will thrive." The purple threads in the net tightened around the spiral. "With knot of six, this spell I fix." The gold threads gleamed. A casual brush of my hand sealed the wound in my chest.

"Benjamin was quite interested in what I told him about your mother and father. He has plans for you, Diana. You will carry Benjamin's children, and they will become like the witches of old: powerful, wise, long-lived. There will be no more hiding in the shadows for us then. We will rule over the other warmbloods, as we should."

"With knot of seven, the spell will waken." A low keening filled the air, reminiscent of the sound the Book of Life made in the Bodleian. Then it had been a cry of terror and pain. Now it sounded like a call for vengeance.

For the first time, Knox looked worried.

"You cannot escape from Benjamin, any more than Emily could escape from me at Sept-Tours. She tried, of course, but I prevailed. All I wanted was the witch's spell book. Benjamin said Matthew once had it." Knox's eyes took on a fevered glint. "When I possess it, I will have the upper hand over the vampires, too. Even Gerbert will bow to me then."

"With knot of eight, the spell will wait." I pulled the net into the twisted shape that signified infinity. As I manipulated the threads, my father's shadowy form appeared.

"Stephen." Knox licked his lips. "This is an illusion, too."

My father ignored him, crossing his arms and looking at me sharply. "You ready to finish this, peanut?"

"I am, Dad."

"You don't have the power to finish me," Knox snarled. "Emily discovered that when she tried to keep me from having knowledge of the lost book of spells. I took her thoughts and stopped her heart. Had she only cooperated—"

"With knot of nine, the spell is mine."

The keening rose into a shriek as all the chaos contained in the Book of Life and all the creative energy that bound the creatures together in one place burst from the web I'd made and engulfed Peter Knox. My father's hands were among those that reached out of the dark void to grasp him while he struggled, keeping him in a whirling vortex of power that would eat him alive.

Knox cried out in terror as the spell drained his life away. He unraveled before my eyes as the spirits of all the weavers who had come before me, including my father, deliberately unpicked the threads that made up this damaged creature, reducing Knox to a lifeless shell.

One day I would pay a price for what I'd done to a fellow witch. But I had avenged Emily, whose life had been taken for no other reason than a dream of power.

I had avenged my mother and father, who loved their daughter enough to die for her.

I drew the goddess's arrow from my spine. A bow crafted from rowan and trimmed with silver and gold appeared in my left hand.

Vengeance had been mine. Now it was time for the goddess's justice.

I turned to my father, a question in my eyes.

"He's upstairs. Third floor. Sixth door on the left." My father smiled. "Whatever price the goddess exacted from you, Matthew is worth it. Just as you were."

"He's worth everything," I said, lowering the magical walls I'd built and leaving the dead behind so I could find the living.

Magic, like any resource, is not infinite in its supply. The spell I'd used to eliminate Knox had drained me of a significant amount of power. But I'd taken the risk knowing that without Knox, Benjamin had only physical strength and cruelty in his arsenal.

I had love and nothing more to lose.

Even without the goddess's arrow, we were evenly matched.

The house had far fewer rooms in it now that Knox's illusions were gone. Instead of an unending array of identical doors, the house now showed its true character: filthy, rife with the scents of death and fear, a place of horror.

My feet raced up the stairs. I couldn't spare an ounce of magic now. I had no idea where any of the others were. But I did know where to find Matthew. I pushed open the door.

"There you are. We've been expecting you." Benjamin was standing behind a chair.

This time the creature in it was undeniably the man I loved. His eyes were black and filled with blood rage and pain, but they flickered in recognition.

"Queen's Gambit complete," I told him.

Relieved, Matthew's eyes drifted closed.

"I hope you know better than to shoot that arrow," Benjamin said. "In case you're not as well versed in anatomy as you are in chemistry, I've made sure that Matthew will die instantly if my hand isn't here to support this."

This was a large iron spike Benjamin had driven into Matthew's neck.

"You remember when Ysabeau poked her finger into me at the Bodleian? It created a seal. That's what I've done here." Benjamin wiggled the spike a bit, and Matthew howled. A few drops of blood appeared. "My father doesn't have much blood left in him. I've fed him nothing but shards of glass for two days and he's been slowly bleeding out internally."

It was then I noticed the pile of dead children in the corner.

"Earlier meals," Benjamin said in response to my glance. "It was a challenge to come up with ways to torment Matthew, since I wanted to make sure he still had eyes to see me take you, and ears to hear your screams. But I found a way."

"You are a monster, Benjamin."

"Matthew made me one. Now, don't waste any more of your energy. Ysabeau and Baldwin are bound to be here soon. This is the very room where I kept Philippe, and I left a trail of bread crumbs to make sure my grandmother finds it. Baldwin will be so surprised to hear who it was that killed his father, don't you think? I saw it all in Matthew's thoughts. As for you . . . well, you cannot imagine the things Matthew would like to do to you in the privacy of his bed. Some of them made me blush, and I'm not exactly prudish."

I felt Ysabeau's presence behind me. A rain of photographs fell upon the floor. Pictures of Philippe. Here. In agony. I shot a look of fury at Benjamin.

"I would like nothing more than to shred you to pieces with my bare hands, but I would not deprive Philippe's daughter of the pleasure." Ysabeau's voice was cold and serrated. It rasped against my ears almost painfully.

"Oh, she'll have pleasure with me, Ysabeau. I assure you of that." Benjamin whispered something in Matthew's ear, and I saw Matthew's hand twitch as if he wanted to strike his son but his broken bones and shredded muscles made that impossible. "Here's Baldwin. It's been a long time, Uncle. I have something to tell you—a secret Matthew has been keeping. He keeps so many, I know, but this is a juicy one, I promise." Benjamin paused for effect. "Philippe did not die because of me. It was Matthew who killed him."

Baldwin stared at him impassively.

"Do you want to take a shot at him before my children send you to hell to see your father?" Benjamin asked.

"Your children won't be sending me anywhere. And if you think I am surprised by this supposed secret, you are even more delusional than I feared," Baldwin said. "I know Matthew's work when I see it. He's almost too good at what he does."

"Drop that." Benjamin's voice cracked like a whip as his cold, unfathomable eyes settled on my left hand.

While the two of them were having their discussion, I'd taken the opportunity to lift the bow.

"Drop it now or he dies." Benjamin withdrew the spike slightly, and the blood flowed.

I dropped the bow with a clatter.

"Smart girl," he said, thrusting the spike home again. Matthew moaned. "I liked you even before I learned you were a weaver. So that's what makes you special? Matthew has been shamefully reluctant to determine the limits of your power, but never fear. I'll make sure we know exactly how far your abilities extend."

Yes, I was a smart girl. Smarter than Benjamin knew. And I understood the limits of my power better than anyone else ever would. As for the goddess's bow, I didn't need it. What I needed in order to destroy Benjamin was still in my other hand.

I lifted my pinkie slightly so that it brushed Ysabeau's thigh in warning. "With knot of ten, it begins again."

My words came out like a breath, insubstantial and easy to ignore, just as the tenth knot was seemingly a simple loop. As they traveled into the room, my spell took on the weight and power of a living thing. I extended my left arm straight as though it still held the goddess's bow. My left index finger burned a bright purple.

My right hand drew back in a lightning-quick move, fingers curled loosely around the white fletchings on the golden arrow's shaft. I stood squarely at the crossroads between life and death.

And I did not hesitate.

"Justice," I said, and unfurled my fingers.

Benjamin's eyes widened.

The arrow sprang from my hand through the center of the spell, picking up momentum as it flew. It hit Benjamin's chest with audible force, cleaving him wide open and bursting his heart. A blinding wave of power engulfed the room. Silver and gold threads shot everywhere, accompanied by strands of purple and green. *The sun king. The moon queen. Justice. The goddess.*

With an otherworldly cry of frustrated anguish, Benjamin loosened his fingers, and the blood-covered spike began to slip.

Working quickly, I twisted the threads surrounding Matthew into a single rope that caught the end of the spike. I pulled it taut, keeping it in place as Benjamin's blood poured forth and he dropped heavily to the floor.

The few bare lightbulbs in the room flickered, then went out. I'd had to draw on every bit of energy in the place to kill Knox and then Benjamin. All that was left now was the power of the goddess: the shimmering rope hanging in the middle of the room, the words moving underneath my skin, the power snapping at the ends of my fingers.

It was over.

Benjamin was dead and could no longer torment anyone.

And Matthew, though broken, was alive.

After Benjamin fell, everything seemed to happen at once. Ysabeau pulled the vampire's dead body away. Baldwin was at Matthew's side, calling for Marcus and checking on his injuries. Verin and Gallowglass and Hamish burst into the room. Fernando followed soon thereafter.

I stood in front of Matthew and cradled his head against my heart, sheltering him from further harm. With one hand I held up the iron implement that was keeping him alive. Matthew let out an exhausted sigh and shifted slightly against me.

"It's all right now. I'm here. You're safe," I murmured, trying to bring him what little comfort I could. "You're alive."

"Couldn't die." Matthew's voice was so faint it didn't even qualify as a whisper. "Not without saying goodbye."

Back in Madison, I'd made Matthew promise not to leave me without a proper farewell. My eyes filled as I thought of all he'd been through to honor his word.

"You kept your promise," I said. "Rest now."

"We need to move him, Diana." Marcus's calm voice couldn't disguise his urgency. He put his hand around the spike, ready to take my place.

"Don't let Diana watch." Matthew's voice was raw and guttural. His skeletal hand twitched on the arm of the chair in protest, but it was not able to do more. "I beg you."

With nearly every inch of Matthew's body injured, there were precious few places I could touch him that wouldn't compound his pain. I located a few centimeters of undamaged flesh gleaming in the glow cast by the Book of Life and dropped a kiss as soft as down on the tip of his nose.

Unsure if he could hear me, and knowing that his eyes were swollen shut, I let my breath wash over him, bathing him in my scent. Matthew's nostrils flared a fraction, signaling that he had registered my proximity. Even that little movement made him wince, and I had to steel myself not to cry out at what Benjamin had done to him.

"You can't hide from me, my love," I said instead. "I see you, Matthew. And you will always be perfect in my eyes."

His breath came out in a ragged gasp, his lungs unable to expand fully because of the pressure from broken ribs. With a herculean effort, Matthew cracked one eye open. It was filmed over with blood, the pupil shot wide and enormous from blood rage and trauma.

"It's dark." Matthew's voice took on a frantic edge, as though he feared that the darkness signaled his death. "Why is it so dark?"

"It's all right. Look." I blew on my fingertip, and a blue-gold star appeared on the tip of my finger. "See. This will light our way."

It was a risk, and I knew it. He might not be able to see the small ball of fire, and then his panic would only increase. Matthew peered at my finger and flinched slightly as the light came into focus. His pupil tightened a tiny amount in response, which I took as a good sign.

His next breath was less ragged as his anxiety subsided.

"He needs blood," Baldwin said, keeping his voice level and low.

I tried to push my sleeve up without lowering my gleaming finger, which Matthew was staring at fixedly.

"Not yours," Ysabeau said, stilling my efforts. "Mine."

Matthew's agitation rose again. It was like watching Jack struggle to rein in his emotions.

"Not here," he said. "Not with Diana watching."

"Not here," Gallowglass agreed, giving my husband back some small measure of control.

"Let his brothers and his son take care of him, Diana." Baldwin lowered my hand.

And so I let Gallowglass, Fernando, Baldwin, and Hamish lace their arms together into a sling while Marcus held the iron spike in place.

"My blood is strong, Diana," Ysabeau promised, gripping my hand tightly. "It will heal him."

I nodded. But I had told Matthew the truth earlier: In my eyes he would always be perfect. His outward wounds didn't matter to me. It was the wounds to his heart, mind, and soul that had me worried, for no amount of vampire blood could heal those.

"Love and time," I murmured, as though trying to figure out the components of a spell, watching from a distance as the men settled an unconscious Matthew into the cargo hold of one of the cars that were waiting for us. "That's what he needs."

Janet came up and put a comforting hand on my shoulder.

"Matthew Clairmont is an ancient vampire," she observed, "and he has you. So I'm thinking love and time will do the trick."

Sol in Aquarius

When the sun passeth through the water-bearer's sign, it betokens great fortune, faithful friends, and the aide of princes. Therefore, do not feare changes that take place when Aquarius ruleth the earth.

—Anonymous English Commonplace Book, c. 1590, Gonçalves MS 4890, f. 10ʳ

Matthew said only one word on the flight: "Home."

We arrived in France six days after the events in Chelm. Matthew still couldn't walk. He wasn't able to use his hands. Nothing remained in his stomach for more than thirty minutes. Ysabeau's blood, as promised, was slowly mending the crushed bones, damaged tissues, and injuries to Matthew's internal organs. After first falling unconscious due to a combination of drugs, pain, and exhaustion, he now refused to close his eyes to rest.

And he hardly ever spoke. When he did, it was usually to refuse something.

"No," he said when we turned toward Sept-Tours. "Our home."

Faced with a range of options, I told Marcus to take us to Les Revenants. It was a strangely fitting name given its present owner, for Matthew had returned home more ghost than man after what Benjamin had done to him.

No one had dreamed that Matthew would prefer Les Revenants to Sept-Tours, and the house was cold and lifeless when we arrived. He sat in the foyer with Marcus while his brother and I raced around lighting fires and making up a bed for him. Baldwin and I were discussing which room would be best for Matthew given his present physical limitations when the convoy of cars from Sept-Tours filled the courtyard. Not even the vampires could beat Sarah to the door, she was so eager to see us. My aunt knelt in front of Matthew. Her face was soft with compassion and concern.

"You look like hell," she said.

"Feel worse." Matthew's once-beautiful voice was harsh and grating, but I treasured every terse word.

"When Marcus says it's okay, I'd like to put a salve on your skin that will help you heal," Sarah said, touching the raw skin on his forearm.

The cry of a furious, hungry baby split the air.

"Becca." My heart leaped at the prospect of seeing the twins again. But Matthew did not seem to share my happiness.

"No." Matthew's eyes were wild, and he shook from head to toe. "No. Not now. Not like this."

Since Benjamin had taken control of Matthew's mind and body, I insisted that now Matthew was free he should be allowed to set the terms of his own daily existence and even his medical treatment. But this I would not allow. I scooped Rebecca out of Ysabeau's arms, kissed her smooth cheek, and dropped the baby into the crook of Matthew's elbow.

The moment Becca saw Matthew's face, she stopped crying.

The moment Matthew had his daughter in his arms, he stopped shaking, just as I had the night she was born. My eyes filled at his terrified, awestruck expression.

"Good thinking," Sarah murmured. She gave me the once-over. "You look like hell, too."

"Mum," Jack said, kissing me on the cheek. He tried to give me Philip, but the baby squirmed away from me, his face twisting and turning.

"What is it, little man?" I touched Philip's face with a fingertip. My hands flashed with power, and the letters that now waited under the surface of my skin rose up, arranging themselves into stories that had yet to be told. I nodded and gave the baby a kiss on the forehead, feeling the tingle on my lips that confirmed what the Book of Life had already revealed to me. My son had power—lots of power. "Take him to Matthew, Jack."

Jack knew full well the horrors Benjamin was capable of committing. He steeled himself to see evidence of them before he turned. I saw Matthew through Jack's eyes: his hero, home from battle, gaunt and wounded. Jack cleared his throat, and the growling sound had me concerned.

"Don't leave Philip out of the reunion, Dad." Jack wedged Philip securely into the crook of Matthew's other arm.

Matthew's eyes flickered with surprise at the greeting. It was such a small word—*Dad*—but Jack had never called Matthew anything except Master Roydon and Matthew. Though Andrew Hubbard had insisted that Matthew was Jack's true father, and Jack had been quick to call me "Mother," he had been strangely reluctant to bestow a similar honor on the man he worshipped.

"Philip gets cross when Becca gets all the attention." Jack's voice was roughened with suppressed rage, and he made his next words deliberately playful and light. "Granny Sarah has all kinds of advice on how to treat younger brothers and sisters. Most of it involves ice cream and trips to the zoo." Jack's banter didn't fool Matthew.

"Look at me." Matthew's voice was weak and raspy, but there was no mistaking that this was an order.

Jack met his eyes.

"Benjamin is dead," Matthew said.

"I know." Jack looked away, shifting restlessly from one foot to the other.

"Benjamin can't hurt you. Not anymore."

"He hurt you. And he would have hurt my mother." Jack looked at me, and his eyes filled with darkness.

Fearing that the blood rage would engulf him, I took a step in Jack's direction. I stopped before taking another, forcing myself to let Matthew handle it.

"Eyes on me, Jack."

Matthew's skin was gray with effort. He had uttered more words since Jack's arrival than he had in a full week, and they were sapping his strength. Jack's wandering attention returned to the head of his clan.

"Take Rebecca. Give her to Diana. Then come back."

Jack did as asked, while the rest of us watched warily in case either he or Matthew lost control.

With Becca safely in my arms, I kissed her and told her in a whisper what a good girl she was not to fuss at being taken from her father.

Becca frowned, indicating she was playing this game under protest.

Back at Matthew's side, Jack reached for Philip.

"No. I'll keep him." Matthew's eyes were getting ominously dark, too. "Take Ysabeau home, Jack. Everybody else go, too."

"But, *Matthieu*," Ysabeau protested. Fernando whispered something in her ear. Reluctantly she nodded. "Come, Jack. On the way to Sept-Tours, I will tell you a story about the time Baldwin attempted to banish me from Jerusalem. Many men died."

After delivering that thinly veiled warning, Ysabeau swept Jack from the room.

"Thank you, *Maman*," Matthew murmured. He was still supporting Philip's weight, and his arms shook alarmingly.

"Call if you need me," Marcus whispered as he headed out the door.

As soon as it was just the four of us in the house, I took Philip from Matthew's lap and plunked both babies in the cradle by the fireplace.

"Too heavy," Matthew said wearily as I tried to lift him from the chair. "Stay here."

"You will not stay here." I studied the situation and decided on a solution. I marshaled the air to support my hastily woven levitation spell. "Stand back, I'm going to try magic." Matthew made a faint sound that might have been an attempt at laughter.

"Don't. The floor's okay," he said, his words slurring with exhaustion.

"The bed's better," I replied firmly as we skimmed over the floor to the elevator.

During our first week at Les Revenants, Matthew permitted Ysabeau to come and feed him. He regained some of his strength and a bit more mobility. He still couldn't walk, but he could stand provided he had assistance, his arms hanging limply at his sides.

"You're making such quick progress," I said brightly, as though everything in the world were rosy.

Inside my head it was very dark indeed. And I was screaming in anger, fear, and frustration as the man I loved struggled to find his way through the shadows of the past that had overtaken him in Chelm.

Sol in Pisces

When the sun is in Pisces, expect weariness and sadness. Those who can banish feare will experience forgiveness and understanding. You will be called to work in faraway places.

—Anonymous English Commonplace Book, c. 1590, Gonçalves MS 4890, f. 10ʳ

"I want some of my books," Matthew said with deceptive casualness. He rattled off a list of titles. "Hamish will know where to find them." His friend had gone back to London briefly, then returned to France. Hamish had been ensconced in Matthew's rooms at Sept-Tours ever since. He spent his days trying to keep clueless bureaucrats from ruining the world economy and his nights depleting Baldwin's wine cellar.

Hamish arrived at Les Revenants with the books, and Matthew asked him to sit and have a glass of Champagne. Hamish seemed to understand that this attempt at normalcy was a turning point in Matthew's recovery.

"Why not? Man cannot live on claret alone." With a subtle glance at me, Hamish indicated that he would take care of Matthew.

Hamish was still there three hours later—and the two of them were playing chess. My knees weakened at the unexpected sight of Matthew sitting on the white side of the board, considering his options. Since Matthew's hands were still useless—the hand was a terribly complicated bit of anatomical engineering, it turned out—Hamish moved the pieces according to Matthew's encoded commands.

"E4," Matthew said.

"The Central Variation? How daring of you." Hamish moved one of the white pawns.

"You accepted the Queen's Gambit," Matthew said mildly. "What did you expect?"

"I expect you to mix things up. Once upon a time, you refused to put your queen at risk. Now you do it every game." Hamish frowned. "It's a poor strategy."

"The queen did just fine last time," I whispered in Matthew's ear, and he smiled.

When Hamish left, Matthew asked me to read to him. It was now a ritual for us to sit in front of the fire, the snow falling past the windows and one of Matthew's beloved books in my hand: Abelard, Marlowe, Darwin, Thoreau, Shelley, Rilke. Often Matthew's lips moved along with the words as I uttered them, proving to me—and, more important, to him—that his mind was as sharp and whole as ever.

"'I am the daughter of Earth and Water, / And the nursling of the Sky,'" I read from his battered copy of *Prometheus Unbound.*

"'I pass through the pores of the ocean and shores,'" Matthew whispered. *"'I change, but I cannot die.'"*

After Hamish's visit our society at Les Revenants gradually expanded. Jack was invited to join Matthew and to bring his cello with him. He played Beethoven for hours on end, and not only did the music have positive effects on my husband, it unfailingly put my daughter to sleep as well.

Matthew was improving, but he still had a long way to go. When he rested fitfully, I dozed at his side and hoped that the babies wouldn't stir. He let me help him bathe and dress, though he hated himself—and me—for it. Whenever I thought I couldn't endure another moment of watching him struggle, I focused on some patch of skin that had knit itself back together. Like the shadows of Chelm, the scars would never fully disappear.

When Sarah came to see him, her worry was palpable. But Matthew was not the cause of her concern.

"How much magic are you using to stay upright?" Accustomed to living with bat-eared vampires, she had waited until I walked her to the car before she asked.

"I'm fine," I said, opening the car door for her.

"That wasn't my question. I can see you're fine. That's what worries me," Sarah said. "Why aren't you at death's door?"

"It doesn't matter," I said, dismissing her question.

"It will when you collapse," Sarah retorted. "You can't possibly keep this up."

"You forget, Sarah: The Bishop-Clairmont family specializes in the impossible." I closed the car door to muffle her ongoing protests.

I should have known that my aunt would not be silenced so easily. Baldwin showed up twenty-four hours after her departure—uninvited and unannounced.

"This is a bad habit of yours," I said, thinking back to the moment he'd returned to Sept-Tours and stripped the sheets from our bed. "Surprise us again and I'll put enough wards on this house to repel the Four Horsemen of the Apocalypse."

"They haven't been spotted in Limousin since Hugh died." Baldwin kissed me on each cheek, taking time in between to make a slow assessment of my scent.

"Matthew isn't receiving visitors today," I said, drawing away. "He had a difficult night."

"I'm not here to see Matthew." Baldwin fixed eagle eyes on me. "I'm here to warn you that if you don't start taking care of yourself, I will put myself in charge here."

"You have no—"

"Oh, but I do. You are my sister. Your husband is not able to look after your welfare at the moment. Look after it yourself or accept the consequences." Baldwin's voice was implacable.

The two of us faced off in silence for a few moments. He sighed when I refused to break my stare.

"It's really quite simple, Diana. If you collapse—and based on your scent, I'd say you have a week at most before that happens—Matthew's instincts will demand that he try to protect his mate. That will distract him from his primary job, which is to heal."

Baldwin had a point.

"The best way to handle a vampire mate—especially one with blood rage like Matthew—is to give him no reason to think you need any protection. Take care of yourself—first and always," Baldwin said. "Seeing you healthy and happy will do Matthew more good, mentally and physically, than his maker's blood or Jack's music. Do we understand each other?"

"Yes."

"I'm so glad." Baldwin's mouth lifted into a smile. "Answer your e-mail while you're at it. I send you messages. You don't answer. It's aggravating."

I nodded, afraid that if I opened my mouth, detailed instructions on just what he could do with his e-mail might pop out.

Baldwin stuck his head into the great hall to check on Matthew. He pronounced him utterly useless because he could not engage in wrestling, warfare, or other brotherly pursuits. Then, mercifully, he left.

Dutifully I opened my laptop.

Hundreds of messages awaited, most from the Congregation demanding explanations and Baldwin giving me orders.

I lowered the lid on my computer and returned to Matthew and my children.

* * *

A few nights after Baldwin's visit, I woke to the sensation of a cold finger jerking against my spine as it traced the trunk of the tree on my neck.

The finger moved in barely controlled fits and starts to my shoulders, where it found the outline left by the goddess's arrow and the star left by Satu Järvinen.

Slowly the finger traveled down to the dragon that encircled my hips.

Matthew's hands were working again.

"I needed the first thing I touched to be you," he said, realizing he'd awakened me.

I was barely able to breathe, and any response on my part was out of the question. But my unspoken words wanted to be set free nevertheless. The magic rose within me, letters forming phrases under my skin.

"The price of power." Matthew's hand circled my forearm, his thumb stroking the words as they appeared. The movement was rough and irregular at first, but it grew smoother and steadier with every pass over my skin. He had observed the changes in me since I'd become the Book of Life but never mentioned them until now.

"So much to say," he murmured, his lips brushing my neck. His fingers delved, parted my flesh, touched my core.

I gasped. It had been so long, but his touch was still familiar. Matthew's fingers went unerringly to the places that brought me the most pleasure.

"But you don't need words to tell me what you feel," Matthew said. "I see you, even when you hide from the rest of the world. I hear you, even when you're silent."

It was a pure definition of love. Like magic, the letters amassing on my forearms disappeared as Matthew stripped my soul bare and guided my body to a place where words were indeed unnecessary. I trembled through my release, and though Matthew's touch became light as a feather, his fingers never stopped moving.

"Again," he said, when my pulse quickened once more.

"It's not possible," I said. Then he did something that made me gasp.

"Impossible n'est pas français," Matthew replied, giving me a nip on the ear. "And next time your brother comes to call, tell him not to worry. I'm perfectly able to take care of my wife."

Sol in Aries

The signe of the ram signifies dominion and wisdom. While the sun resides in Aries, you will see growth in all your works. It is a time for new beginnings.

—Anonymous English Commonplace Book, c. 1590, Gonçalves MS 4890, f. 7v

"Answer your fucking e-mail!"

Apparently Baldwin was having a bad day. Like Matthew, I was beginning to appreciate the ways that modern technology allowed us to keep the other vampires in the family at arm's length.

"I've put them off as long as I can." Baldwin glowered at me from the computer screen, the city of Berlin visible through the huge windows behind him. "You are going to Venice, Diana."

"No I'm not." We had been having some version of this conversation for weeks.

"Yes you are." Matthew leaned over my shoulder. He was walking now, slowly but just as silently as ever. "Diana will meet with the Congregation, Baldwin. But speak to her like that again and I'll cut your tongue out."

"Two weeks," Baldwin said, completely unfazed by his brother's threat. "They've agreed to give her two more weeks."

"It's too soon." The physical effects of Benjamin's torture were fading, but it had left Matthew's control over his blood rage as thin as a knife's edge and his temper just as sharp.

"She'll be there." He closed the lid on the laptop, effectively shutting out his brother and his final demands.

"It's too soon," I repeated.

"Yes, it is—far too soon for me to travel to Venice and face Gerbert and Satu." Matthew's hands were heavy on my shoulders. "If we want the covenant formally set aside—and we do—one of us must make the case to the Congregation."

"What about the children?" I was grasping at straws.

"The three of us will miss you, but we will manage. If I look sufficiently inept in front of Ysabeau and Sarah, I won't have to change a single diaper while you're gone." Matthew's fingers increased in pressure, as did the sense of responsibility resting on my shoulders. "You must do this. For me. For us. For every member of our family who has been harmed because of the covenant: Emily, Rebecca, Stephen, even Philippe. And for our children, so that they can grow up in love instead of fear."

There was no way I could refuse to go to Venice after that.

The Bishop-Clairmont family swung into action, eager to help ready our case for the Congregation. It was a collaborative, multispecies effort that began with honing our argument down to its essential core. Hard as it was to strip away the insults and injuries, large and small, that we had suffered, success depended on being able to make our request not seem like a personal vendetta.

In the end it was breathtakingly simple—at least it was after Hamish took charge. All we needed to do, he said, was establish beyond a doubt that the covenant had been drawn up because of a fear of miscegenation and the desire to keep bloodlines artificially pure to preserve the power balance among creatures.

Like most simple arguments, ours required hours of mind-numbing work. We all contributed our talents to the project. Phoebe, who was a gifted researcher, searched the archives at Sept-Tours for documents that touched on the covenant's inception and the Congregation's first meetings and debates. She called Rima, who was thrilled to be asked to do something other than filing, and had her search for supporting documents in the Congregation library on Isola della Stella.

These documents helped us piece together a coherent picture of what the founders of the Congregation had truly feared: that relationships between creatures would result in children who were neither daemon nor vampire nor witch but some terrifying combination, muddying the ancient, supposedly pure creature bloodlines. Such a concern was warranted given a twelfth-century understanding of biology and the value that was placed on inheritance and lineage at that time. And Philippe de Clermont had had the political acumen to suspect that the children of such unions would be powerful enough to rule the world if they so desired.

What was more difficult, not to mention more dangerous, was demonstrating that this fear had actually contributed to the decline of the otherworldly creatures. Centuries of inbreeding meant that vampires found it difficult to make new vampires, witches were less powerful, and daemons were increasingly prone to madness. To make this part of our case, the Bishop-Clairmonts needed to expose both the blood rage and the weavers in our family.

I wrote up a history of weavers using information from the Book of Life. I explained that the weavers' creative power was difficult to control and made them vulnerable to the animosity of their fellow witches. Over time witches grew complacent and had less use for new spells and charms. The old ones worked fine, and the weavers went from being treasured members of their communities to hunted outcasts. Sarah and I sat down together and drew up an account of my parents' lives in painful detail to drive this point home—my father's desperate attempts to hide his talents, Knox's efforts to discover them, and their terrible deaths.

Matthew and Ysabeau recorded a similarly difficult tale, one of madness and the destructive power of anger. Fernando and Gallowglass scoured Philippe's private papers for evidence of how he had kept his mate safe from extermination and their joint decision to protect Matthew in spite of his showing signs of the illness. Both Philippe and Ysabeau believed that careful upbringing and hard-won control would be a counterweight to whatever illness was present in his blood—a classic example of nurture over nature. And Matthew confessed that his own failures with Benjamin demonstrated just how dangerous blood rage could be if left to develop on its own.

Janet arrived at Les Revenants with the Gowdie grimoire and a copy of her great-grandmother Isobel's trial transcript. The trial records described her amorous relationship with the devil known as Nickie-Ben in great detail, including his nefarious bite. The grimoire proved that Isobel was a weaver of spells, as she proudly identified her unique magical creations and the prices that she'd demanded for sharing them with her sisters in the Highlands. Isobel also identified her lover as Benjamin Fox—Matthew's son. Benjamin had actually signed his name into the family record found in the front of the book.

"It's still not sufficient," Matthew worried, looking over the papers. "We still can't explain *why* weavers and blood-rage vampires like you and I can conceive children."

I could explain it. The Book of Life had shared that secret with me. But I didn't want to say anything until Miriam and Chris delivered the scientific evidence.

I was beginning to think I would have to make our case to the Congregation without their help when a car pulled into the courtyard.

Matthew frowned. "Who could that be?" he asked, putting down his pen and going to the window. "Miriam and Chris are here. Something must be wrong at the Yale lab."

Once the pair were inside and Matthew had received assurances that the research team he'd left in New Haven was thriving, Chris handed me a thick envelope.

"You were right," he said. "Nice work, Professor Bishop."

I hugged the packet to my chest, unspeakably relieved. Then I handed it to Matthew.

He tore into the envelope, his eyes racing over the lines of text and the black-and-white ideograms that accompanied them. He looked up, his lips parted in astonishment.

"I was surprised, too," Miriam admitted. "As long as we approached daemons, vampires, and witches as separate species distantly related to humans but distinct from one another, the truth was going to elude us."

"Then Diana told us the Book of Life was about what joined us together, not what separated us," Chris continued. "She asked us to compare her genome to both the daemon genome and the genomes of other witches."

"It was all there in the creature chromosome," Miriam said, "hiding in plain sight."

"I don't understand," Sarah said, looking blank.

"Diana was able to conceive Matthew's child because they both have daemon blood in them," Chris explained. "It's too early to know for sure, but our hypothesis is that weavers are descended from ancient witch-daemon unions. Blood-rage vampires like Matthew are produced when a vampire with the blood-rage gene creates another vampire from a human with some daemon DNA."

"We didn't find much of a daemonic presence in Ysabeau's genetic sample, or Marcus's either," Miriam added. "That explains why they never manifested the disease like Matthew or Benjamin did."

"But Stephen Proctor's mother was human," Sarah said. "She was a total pain in the ass—sorry, Diana—but definitely not daemonic."

"It doesn't have to be an immediate relationship," Miriam said. "There just has to be enough daemon DNA in the mix to trigger the weaver and blood-rage genes. It could have been one of Stephen's distant ancestors. As Chris said, these findings are pretty raw. We'll need decades to understand them completely."

"One more thing: Baby Margaret is a weaver, too." Chris pointed to the paper in Matthew's hands. "Page thirty. There's no question about it."

"I wonder if that's why Em was so adamant that Margaret shouldn't fall into Knox's hands," Sarah mused. "Maybe she discovered the truth somehow."

"This will shake the Congregation to its foundations," I said.

"It does more than that. The science makes the covenant completely irrelevant," Matthew said. "We're not separate species."

"So we're just different races?" I asked. "That makes our miscegenation argument even stronger."

"You need to catch up on your reading, Professor Bishop," Chris said with a smile. "Racial identity has no biological basis—at least none accepted by most scientists." Matthew had told me something like that long ago in Oxford.

"But that means—" I stopped.

"You aren't monsters after all. There are no such things as daemons, vampires, and witches. Not biologically. You're just humans with a difference." Chris grinned. "Tell the Congregation to stick that in their pipe and smoke it."

I didn't use exactly those words in my cover statement to the enormous dossier that we sent to Venice in advance of the Congregation meeting, but what I did say amounted to the same thing.

The days of the covenant were done.

And if the Congregation wanted to continue to function, it was going to have to find something better to do with its time than police the boundaries between daemon, vampire, witch, and human.

When I went to the library the morning before my departure for Venice, however, I found that something had been left out of the file.

While we were doing our research, it had been impossible to ignore the sticky traces of Gerbert's fingers. He seemed to lurk in the margins of every document and every piece of evidence. It was hard to pin much on him directly, but the circumstantial evidence was clear: Gerbert of Aurillac had known for some time about the special abilities of weavers. He'd even held one in thrall: the witch Meridiana, who had cursed him as she died. And he had been feeding Benjamin Fuchs information about the de Clermonts for centuries. Philippe had found him out and confronted him about it just before he left on his final mission to Nazi Germany.

"Why didn't the information about Gerbert go to Venice?" I demanded of Matthew when at last I found him in the kitchen making my tea. Ysabeau was with him, playing with Philip and Becca.

"Because it's better if the rest of the Congregation doesn't know about Gerbert's involvement," Matthew said.

"Better for whom?" I asked sharply. "I want that creature exposed and punished."

"But the Congregation's punishments are so very unsatisfactory," Ysabeau said, her eyes gleaming. "Too much talking. Not enough pain. If it is punishment you want, let me do it." Her fingernails rapped against the counter, and I shivered.

"You've done enough, *Maman,*" Matthew said, giving her a forbidding glance.

"Oh, that." Ysabeau waved her hand dismissively. "Gerbert has been a very naughty boy. But he will cooperate with Diana tomorrow because of it. You will find Gerbert of Aurillac entirely supportive, daughter."

I sat down on the kitchen stool with a thunk.

"While Ysabeau was being held in Gerbert's house, she and Nathaniel did a bit of snooping," Matthew explained. "They've been monitoring his e-mail and Internet usage ever since."

"Did you know that nothing you see on the Internet ever dies, Diana? It lives on and on, just like a vampire." Ysabeau looked genuinely fascinated by the comparison.

"And?" I still had no idea where this was leading.

"Gerbert isn't just fond of witches," Ysabeau said. "He's had a string of daemon lovers, too. One of them is still living on the Via della Scala in Rome, in a palatial and drafty set of apartments that he bought for her in the seventeenth century."

"Wait. Seventeenth century?" I tried to think straight, though it was difficult with Ysabeau looking like Tabitha after she'd devoured a mouse.

"Not only did Gerbert 'consort' with daemons, he turned one into a vampire. Such a thing is strictly forbidden—not by the covenant but by vampire law. For good reason, it turns out now that we know what triggers blood rage," Matthew said. "Not even Philippe knew about her—though he did know about some of Gerbert's other daemon lovers."

"And we're blackmailing him over it?", I said.

"'Blackmail' is such an ugly word," Ysabeau said. "I prefer to think that Gallowglass was exceptionally persuasive when he dropped by Les Anges Déchus last night to wish Gerbert safe journey."

"I don't want some covert de Clermont operation against Gerbert. I want the world to know what a snake he is," I said. "I want to beat him fair and square in open battle."

"Don't worry. The whole world will know. One day. One war at a time, *ma lionne.*" Matthew softened the commanding edge of his remark with a kiss and a cup of tea.

"Philippe preferred hunting to warfare." Ysabeau dropped her voice, as though she didn't want Becca and Philip to overhear her next words. "You see, when you hunt, you get to play with your prey before you destroy it. That is what we are doing with Gerbert."

"Oh." There was, admittedly, something appealing about that prospect.

"I felt sure you would understand. You are named after the goddess of the chase, after all. Happy hunting in Venice, my dear," Ysabeau said, patting me on the hand.

Sol in Taurus

The Bull governeth money, credit, debts, and gifts. While the sun is in Taurus, deal with unfinished business. Settle your affaires, lest they trouble you later. Should you receive an unexpected reward, invest it for the future.

—*Anonymous English Commonplace Book, c. 1590, Gonçalves Manuscript 4890, f. 7ᵛ*

Venice looked very different to my eyes in May than it had in January, and not solely because the sky was blue and the lagoon tranquil.

When Matthew had been in Benjamin's clutches, the city felt cold and unwelcoming. It was a place I wanted to leave as quickly as possible. When I did, I never expected to return.

But the goddess's justice would not be complete until the covenant was overturned.

And so I found myself back at Ca' Chiaromonte, sitting on a bench in the back garden rather than a bench overlooking the Grand Canal, waiting once more for the Congregation's meeting to begin.

This time Janet Gowdie waited with me. Together we went over our case one last time, imagining what arguments would be made against it while Matthew's precious pet turtles slipped and slid across the gravel paths in pursuit of a mosquito snack.

"Time to go," Marcus announced just before the bells began to ring four o'clock. He and Fernando would accompany us to Isola della Stella. Janet and I had tried to assure the rest of the family that we would be fine on our own, but Matthew wouldn't hear of it.

The Congregation's membership was the same as it had been at the January meeting. Agatha, Tatiana, and Osamu gave me encouraging smiles, though the reception that I received from Sidonie von Borcke and the vampires was decidedly frosty. Satu slipped into the cloister at the last moment as if she hoped not to be noticed. Gone was the self-assured witch who had kidnapped me from the garden at Sept-Tours. Sidonie's appraising stare suggested that Satu's transformation had not gone unnoticed, and I suspected that a change in the witches' representatives would soon be made.

I strolled across the cloister to join the two vampires.

"Domenico. Gerbert," I said, nodding at each in turn.

"Witch," Gerbert sneered.

"And a de Clermont, too." I angled my body so that my lips were close to Gerbert's ear. "Don't get too complacent, Gerbert. The goddess may have saved you for last, but make no mistake: Your day of judgment is coming." I drew away and was gratified to see a spark of fear in his eyes.

When I slid the de Clermont key in the meeting chamber lock, I was overcome by a sense of déjà vu. The doors swung open and the uncanny feeling increased. My eyes locked on the the ouroboros—the tenth knot—carved onto the back of the de Clermont seat and the silver and gold threads in the room snapped with power.

All witches are taught to believe in signs. Happily, the meaning of this one was clear without any need for further magic or complicated interpretation: *This is your seat. Here is where you belong.*

"I call this meeting to order," I said, rapping on the table once I'd reached my assigned place.

My left finger bore a thick ribbon of violet. The goddess's arrow had disappeared after I'd used it to kill Benjamin, but the vivid purple mark—the color of justice—remained.

I studied the room—the wide table, the records of my people and my children's ancestors, the nine creatures gathered to make a decision that would change the lives of thousands like them all around the world. High above I felt the spirits of those who had come before, their glances freezing and nudging and tingling.

"Give us justice," they said with one voice, *"and remember our names."*

"We won," I reported to the members of the de Clermont and Bishop-Clairmont families who had assembled in the salon to greet us when we returned from Venice. "The covenant has been repealed."

There were cheers, and hugs, and congratulations. Baldwin raised his wineglass in my direction, in a less effusive demonstration of approval.

My eyes sought out Matthew.

"No surprise," he said. The silence that followed was heavy with words that, though unspoken, I heard nonetheless. He bent to pick up his daughter. "See, Rebecca? Your mother fixed everything once again."

Becca had discovered the pure pleasure of chewing on her own fingers. I was very glad the vampire equivalent of milk teeth had not come in yet. Matthew removed her hand from her mouth and waved it in my direction, distracting his daughter from the tantrum she was planning. *"Bonjour, Maman."*

Jack was bouncing Philip on his knee. The baby looked both intrigued and concerned. "Nice work, Mum."

"I had plenty of help." My throat thickened as I looked not only at Jack and Philip but at Sarah and Agatha, whose heads were bent close together as they gossiped about the Congregation meeting, Fernando, who was amusing Sophie and Nathaniel with tales of Gerbert's stiff demeanor and Domenico's fury, and Phoebe and Marcus, who were enjoying a lingering reunion kiss. Baldwin stood with Matthew and Becca. I approached them.

"This belongs to you, brother." The de Clermont key rested heavy in the palm of my outstretched hand.

"Keep it." Baldwin closed my fingers around the cool metal.

The conversation in the salon died away.

"What did you say?" I whispered.

"I told you to keep it," Baldwin repeated.

"You can't mean—"

"But I do. Everyone in the de Clermont family has a job. You know that." Baldwin's golden-brown eyes gleamed. "As of today, overseeing the Congregation is yours."

"I can't. I'm a professor!" I protested.

"Set the Congregation's meeting schedule around your classes. As long as you answer your e-mail," Baldwin said with mock severity, "you should have no problem juggling your responsibilities. I've neglected the family's affairs long enough. Besides, I'm a warrior, not a politician."

I looked to Matthew in mute appeal, but he had no intention of rescuing me from this particular plight. His expression was filled with pride, not protectiveness.

"What about your sisters?" I said, my mind racing. "Surely Verin will object."

"It was Verin's suggestion," Baldwin said. "And after all, you are my sister, too."

"That settles it, then. Diana will serve on the Congregation until she tires of the job." Ysabeau kissed me on one cheek, then the other. "Just think of how much it will upset Gerbert when he discovers what Baldwin has done."

Still feeling dazed, I slid the key back into my pocket.

"It has turned into a beautiful day," Ysabeau said, looking out into the spring sunlight. "Let us take a walk in the garden before dinner. Alain and Marthe have prepared a feast—without Fernando's help. Marthe is in an extremely good mood because of it."

Laughter and chatter followed our family out the door. Matthew handed Becca off to Sarah.

"Don't be long, you two," Sarah said.

Once we were alone, Matthew kissed me with a sharp hunger that gradually became something deeper and less desperate. It was a reminder that his blood rage was still not fully in check and my being away had taken a toll.

"Was everything all right in Venice, *mon coeur*?" he inquired when he had regained his equilibrium.

"I'll tell you all about it later," I said. "Though I should warn you: Gerbert is up to no good. He tried to thwart me at every turn."

"What did you expect?" Matthew left my side to join the rest of the family. "Don't worry about Gerbert. We'll figure out what game he's playing, never fear."

Something unexpected caught my eye. I stopped in my tracks.

"Diana?" Matthew looked back at me and frowned. "Are you coming?"

"In a minute," I promised.

He regarded me strangely but stepped outside.

I knew you would be the first to see me. Philippe's voice was a whisper of sound, and I could still see Ysabeau's horrid furniture through him. None of that mattered. He was perfect—whole, smiling, his eyes sparkling with amusement and affection.

"Why me?" I asked.

You have the Book of Life now. You no longer need my help. Philippe's gaze met mine.

"The covenant—" I started.

I heard. I hear most things. Philippe's grin widened. *I am proud that it was one of my children that destroyed it. You have done well.*

"Is seeing you my reward?" I said, fighting back the tears.

One of them, Philippe said. *In time you will have the others.*

"Emily." The moment I said her name, Philippe's form began to fade. "No! Don't go. I won't ask questions. Just tell her I love her."

She knows that. So does your mother. Philippe winked. *I am utterly surrounded by witches. Do not tell Ysabeau. She would not like it.*

I laughed.

And there is my *reward for years of good behavior. Now, I want no more tears, do you understand?* His finger rose. *I am heartily sick of them.*

"What do you want instead?" I wiped at my eyes.

More laughter. More dancing. His expression was mischievous. *And more grandchildren.*

"I had to ask," I said with another laugh.

But the future will not be all laughter, I fear. Philippe's expression sobered. *Your work is not done, daughter. The goddess asked me to give this back to you.* He held out the same gold-and-silver arrow that I had shot into Benjamin's heart.

"I don't want it." I backed away, my hand raised to ward off this unwanted gift.

I didn't want it either, and yet someone must see that justice is done. His arm extended farther.

"Diana?" Matthew called from outside.

I would not be hearing my husband's voice if not for the goddess's arrow.

"Coming!" I called back.

Philippe's eyes filled with sympathy and understanding. I touched the golden point hesitantly. The moment my flesh made contact with it, the arrow vanished and I felt its heavy weight at my back once more.

From the first moment we met, I knew you were the one, Philippe said. His words were a strange echo of what Timothy Weston had told me at the Bodleian last year, and again at his house.

With a final grin, his ghost began to dissipate.

"Wait!" I cried. "The one what?"

The one who could bear my burdens and not break, Philippe's voice whispered in my ear. I felt a subtle press of lips on my cheek. *You will not carry them alone. Remember that, daughter.*

I bit back a sob at his departure.

"Diana?" Matthew called again, this time from the doorway. "What's happened? You look like you've seen a ghost."

I had, but this was not the time to tell Matthew about it. I felt like weeping, but Philippe wanted joy, not sorrow.

"Dance with me," I said, before a single tear could fall.

Matthew folded me into his arms. His feet moved across the floor, sweeping us out of the salon and into the great hall. He asked no questions, even though the answers were in my eyes.

I trod on his toe. "Sorry."

"You're trying to lead again," he murmured. He pressed a kiss to my lips, then whirled me around. "At the moment your job is to follow."

"I forgot," I said with a laugh.

"I'll have to remind you more often, then." Matthew swung me tight to his body. His kiss was rough enough to be a warning and sweet enough to be a promise.

Philippe was right, I thought as we walked out into the garden.

Whether leading or following, I would never be alone in a world that had Matthew in it.

Sol in Gemini

The signe of Gemini dealeth with the partnership between a husband and wife, and all matters that dependeth likewise upon faith. A man born in this sign hath a good and honest heart and a fine wit that will lead him to learn many things. He will be quick to anger, but soon to reconcile. He is bold of speech even before the prince. He is a great dissimulator, a spreader abroad of clever fantasies and lies. He shall be much entangled with troubles by reason of his wife, but he shall prevail against their enemies.

—Anonymous English Commonplace Book, c. 1590,
Gonçalves Manuscript 4890, f. 8r

41

I'm sorry to disturb you, Professor Bishop."

I looked up from my manuscript. The Royal Society's reading room was flooded with summer sunshine. It raked through the tall, multipaned windows and spilled across the generous reading surfaces.

"One of the fellows asked me to give this to you." The librarian handed me an envelope with the Royal Society's insignia on it. Someone had written my name across the front in a dark, distinctive scrawl. I nodded in thanks.

Philippe's ancient silver coin—the one he sent to make sure that someone returned home or obeyed his commands—was inside. I'd found a new use for it, one that was helping Matthew manage his blood rage while I returned to a more active life. My husband's condition was steadily improving after his ordeal with Benjamin but his mood was still volatile and his anger quick to catch. A full recovery would take time. If Matthew felt his need for me rising to dangerous levels, all he had to do was send me this coin, and I would join him right away.

I returned the bound manuscripts I'd been consulting to the attendant on the desk and thanked him for their help. It was the end of my first full week back in the archives—a trial run to see how my magic responded to repeated contact with so many ancient texts and brilliant, though dead, intellects. Matthew was not the only one struggling for control, and I'd had a few tricky moments when it seemed it might be impossible for me to return to the work I loved, but each additional day made that goal more achievable.

Since facing the Congregation in April, I had come to understand myself as a complicated weaving and not just a walking palimpsest. My body was a tapestry of witch, daemon, and vampire. Some of the threads that made me were pure power, as symbolized by Corra's shadowy form. Some were drawn from the skill that my weaver's cords represented. The rest were spun from the knowledge contained in the Book of Life. Every knotted strand gave me the strength to use the goddess's arrow for justice rather than the pursuit of vengeance or power.

Matthew was waiting for me in the foyer when I descended the grand staircase from the library to the main floor. His gaze cooled my skin and heated my blood, just as it always had. I dropped the coin into his waiting palm.

"All right, *mon coeur*?" he asked after kissing me in greeting.

"Perfectly all right." I tugged on the lapel of his black jacket, a small sign of possessiveness. Matthew had dressed the part of the distinguished professor today with his steel gray trousers, crisp white shirt, and fine wool jacket. I'd picked out his tie. Hamish had given it to him this past Christmas, and the green-and-gray Liberty print picked up the changeable colors of his eyes. "How did it go?"

"Interesting discussion. Chris was brilliant, of course," Matthew said, modestly giving my friend center stage.

Chris, Matthew, Miriam, and Marcus had been presenting research findings that expanded the limits of what was considered "human." They showed how the evolution of *Homo sapiens* included DNA from other creatures, like Neanderthals, previously thought to have been a different species. Matthew had been sitting on most of the evidence for years. Chris said Matthew was as bad as Isaac Newton when it came to sharing his research with others.

"Marcus and Miriam performed their usual charmer-and-curmudgeon routine," Matthew said, releasing me at last.

"And what was the fellows' reaction to this bit of news?" I unpinned Matthew's name tag and slipped it into his pocket. PROFESSOR MATTHEW CLAIRMONT, it read, FRS, ALL SOULS (OXON), YALE UNIVERSITY (USA). Matthew had accepted a one-year visiting research appointment in Chris's lab. They'd received a huge grant to study noncoding DNA. It would lay the groundwork for the revelations they would one day make about other hominid creatures who were not extinct like the Neanderthals but were hiding in plain sight among humans. In the fall we would be off to New Haven again.

"They were surprised," Matthew said. "Once they heard Chris's paper, however, their surprise turned to envy. He really was impressive."

"Where is Chris now?" I said, looking over my shoulder for my friend as Matthew steered me toward the exit.

"He and Miriam left for Pickering Place," Matthew said. "Marcus wanted to collect Phoebe before they all go to some oyster bar near Trafalgar Square."

"Do you want to join them?" I asked.

"No." Matthew's hand settled on my waist. "I'm taking you out to dinner, remember?"

Leonard was waiting for us at the curb. "Afternoon, *sieur*. Madame."

"'Professor Clairmont' will do, Leonard," Matthew said mildly as he handed me into the back of the car.

"Righty-ho," Leonard said with a cheerful grin. "Clairmont House?"

"Please," Matthew said, getting into the car with me.

It was a beautiful June day, and it probably would have taken us less time to walk from the Mall to Mayfair than it did to drive, but Matthew insisted we take the car for safety's sake. We had seen no evidence that any of Benjamin's children had survived the battle in Chelm, nor had Gerbert or Domenico given us reason for concern since their stinging defeat in Venice, but Matthew didn't want to take chances.

"Hello, Marthe!" I called into the house as we came in the door. "How is everything?"

"Bien," she said. "*Milord* Philip and *Milady* Rebecca are just waking from their nap."

"I asked Linda Crosby to come over a bit later and lend a hand," Matthew said.

"Already here!" Linda followed us through the door, carrying not one but two Marks & Spencer bags. She handed one to Marthe. "I've brought the next book in the series about that lovely detective and her beau—Gemma and Duncan. And here's the knitting pattern I told you about."

Linda and Marthe had become fast friends, in large part because they had nearly identical interests in murder mysteries, needlecraft, cooking, gardening, and gossip. The two of them had made a compelling and utterly self-serving case that the children should always be attended to by family members or, failing that, both a vampire and a witch working as babysitters. Linda argued that this was a wise precaution because we didn't yet understand the babies' talents and tendencies—though Rebecca's preference for blood and inability to sleep suggested she was more vampire than witch, just as Philip seemed more witch than vampire given the stuffed elephant I sometimes saw swooping over his cradle.

"We can still stay home tonight," I suggested. Matthew's plans involved an evening gown, a tuxedo, and the goddess only knew what else.

"No." Matthew was still overly fond of the word. "I am taking my wife out to dinner." His tone indicated this was no longer a topic for discussion.

Jack pelted down the stairs. "Hi, Mum! I put your mail upstairs. Dad's too. Gotta run. Dinner with Father H tonight."

"Be back by breakfast, please," Matthew said as Jack shot through the open door.

"No worries, Dad. After dinner, I'll be out with Ransome," Jack said as the door banged closed behind him. The New Orleans branch of the Bishop-Clairmont clan had arrived in London two days ago to take in the sights and visit with Marcus.

"Knowing that he's out with Ransome does not alleviate my concerns." Matthew sighed. "I'm going to see the children and get dressed. Are you coming?"

"I'll be right behind you. I just want to stick my head in the ballroom first and see how the caterers are getting along with the preparations for your birthday party."

Matthew groaned.

"Stop being such an old grouch," I said.

Together Matthew and I climbed the stairs. The second floor, which was usually cold and silent, hummed with activity. Matthew followed me to the tall, wide doors. Caterers had set up tables all around the edges of the room, leaving a large space for dancing. In the corner, musicians were practicing tunes for tomorrow night.

"I was born in November, not June," Matthew muttered, his frown deepening. "On All Souls Day. And why did we have to invite so many people?"

"You can grumble and nitpick all you want. It won't change the fact that tomorrow is the anniversary of the day you were reborn a vampire and your family wanted to celebrate it with you." I examined one of the floral arrangements. Matthew had picked the odd selection of plants, which included willow branches and honeysuckle, as well as the wide selection of music from different eras that the band was expected to play during the dancing. "If you don't want so many guests, you should think twice before you make any more children."

"But I like making children with you." Matthew's hand slid around my hip until it came to rest on my abdomen.

"Then you can expect an annual repeat of this event," I said, giving him a kiss. "And more tables with each passing year."

"Speaking of children," Matthew said, cocking his head and listening to some sound inaudible to a warmblood, "your daughter is hungry."

"*Your* daughter is *always* hungry," I said, putting a gentle palm to his cheek.

Matthew's former bedroom had been converted to a nursery and was now the twins' special kingdom—complete with a zoo full of stuffed animals, enough equipment to outfit a baby army, and two tyrants to rule over it.

Philip turned his head to the door when we entered, his look triumphant as he stood and gripped the side of his cradle. He had been peering down into his sister's bed. Rebecca had hauled herself to a seated position and was staring at Philip with interest, as if trying to figure out how he'd managed to grow so quickly.

"Good God. He's standing." Matthew sounded stunned. "But he's not even seven months old."

I glanced at the baby's strong arms and legs and wondered why his father was surprised.

"What have you been up to?" I said, pulling Philip from the cradle and giving him a hug.

A stream of unintelligible sounds came from the baby's mouth, and the letters under my skin surfaced to lend Philip assistance as he answered my question.

"Really? You've had a very lively day, then," I said, handing him to Matthew.

"I believe you are going to be as much of a handful as your namesake," Matthew said fondly, his finger caught in Philip's fierce grip.

We got the children changed and fed, talking more about what I'd discovered in Robert Boyle's papers that day and what new insights the presentations at the Royal Society had afforded Matthew into the problems of understanding the creature genomes.

"Give me a minute. I need to check my e-mail." I received more of it than ever now that Baldwin had appointed me the official de Clermont representative so that he could devote more time to making money and bullying his family.

"Hasn't the Congregation bothered you enough this week?" Matthew asked, his grouchiness returning. I'd spent too many evenings working on policy statements about equality and openness and trying to untangle convoluted daemon logic.

"There is no end in sight, I'm afraid," I said, taking Philip with me into the Chinese Room, which was now my home office. I switched on my computer and held him on my knee while I scrolled through the messages.

"There's a picture from Sarah and Agatha," I called out. The two women were on a beach somewhere in Australia. "Come and see."

"They look happy," Matthew said, looking over my shoulder with Rebecca in his arms. Rebecca made sounds of delight at the sight of her grandmother.

"It's hard to believe it's been more than a year since Em's death," I said. "It's good to see Sarah smiling again."

"Any news from Gallowglass?" Matthew asked. Gallowglass had left for parts unknown and hadn't responded to our invitation to Matthew's party.

"Not so far," I said. "Maybe Fernando knows where he is." I would ask him tomorrow.

"And what does Baldwin allow?" Matthew said, looking at the list of senders and seeing his brother's name.

"He arrives tomorrow." I was pleased that Baldwin was going to be there to wish Matthew well on his birthday. It lent additional weight to the occasion and would quiet any false rumors that Baldwin didn't fully support his brother or the new Bishop-Clairmont scion. "Verin and Ernst will be with him. And I should warn you: Freyja is coming, too."

I hadn't yet met Matthew's middle sister. I was, however, looking forward to it after Janet Gowdie regaled me with tales of her past exploits.

"Christ, not Freyja, too." Matthew groaned. "I need a drink. Do you want anything?"

"I'll have some wine," I said absently, continuing to scroll down through the list of messages from Baldwin, Rima Jaén in Venice, other members of the Congregation, and my department chair at Yale. I was busier than I'd ever been. Happier, too.

When I joined Matthew in his study, he was not fixing our drinks. Instead he was standing in front of the fireplace, Rebecca balanced on his hip, staring up at the wall above the mantel with a curious expression on his face. Following his stare, I could see why.

The portrait of Ysabeau and Philippe that usually hung there was gone. A small tag was pinned to the wall. SIR JOSHUA REYNOLDS'S PORTRAIT OF AN UNKNOWN MARRIED COUPLE TEMPORARILY REMOVED FOR THE EXHIBITION *SIR JOSHUA REYNOLDS AND HIS WORLD* AT THE ROYAL GREENWICH PICTURE GALLERY.

"Phoebe Taylor strikes again," I murmured. She was not yet a vampire but was already well known in vampire circles for her ability to identify the art in their possession that would provide considerable tax relief should they be willing to give the works to the nation. Baldwin adored her.

But the sudden disappearance of his parents was not the real reason Matthew was transfixed.

In place of the Reynolds was another canvas: a portrait of Matthew and me. It was clearly Jack's work, with his trademark combination of seventeenth-century attention to detail and modern sensitivity to color and line. This was confirmed by the small card propped on the mantelpiece with *"Happy birthday, Dad"* scrawled on it.

"I thought he was painting your portrait. It was supposed to be a surprise," I said, thinking of our son's whispered requests that I occupy Matthew's attention while he sketched.

"Jack told me he was painting *your* portrait," Matthew said.

Instead Jack had painted the two of us together, in the formal drawing room by one of the house's grand windows. I was sitting in an Elizabethan chair, a relic from our house in Blackfriars. Matthew stood behind me, his eyes clear and bright as they looked at the viewer. My eyes met the viewer's too, touched by an otherworldliness that suggested I was not an ordinary human.

Matthew reached over my shoulder to clasp my raised left hand, our fingers woven tight. My head was angled slightly toward him, and his was angled slightly down, as though we had been interrupted in midconversation.

The pose exposed my left wrist and the ouroboros that circled my pulse. It sent a message of strength and solidarity, this symbol of the Bishop-Clairmonts. Our family had begun with the surprising love that developed between Matthew and me. It grew because our bond was strong enough to withstand the hatred and fear of others. And it would endure because we had discovered, like the witches so many centuries ago, that a willingness to change was the secret of survival.

More than that, the ouroboros symbolized our partnership. Matthew and I were an alchemical marriage of vampire and witch, death and life, sun and moon. That combination of opposites created something finer and more precious than either of us could ever have been separately.

We were the tenth knot.

Unbreakable.

Without beginning or end.

Acknowledgments

My heartfelt thanks . . .

. . . to my gentle readers for their feedback: Fran, Jill, Karen, Lisa, and Olive.

. . . to Wolf Gruner, Steve Kay, Jake Soll, and Susanna Wang, all of whom were generous with their expertise and kind with their criticisms.

. . . to Lucy Marks, who gathered expert opinions on how much a sheet of vellum might weigh.

. . . to Hedgebrook, for their radical (and much needed) hospitality when I needed it most.

. . . to Sam Stoloff and Rich Green, for championing the All Souls Trilogy from beginning to end.

. . . to Carole DeSanti and the rest of the All Souls team at Viking and Penguin for supporting this book, and the previous two, during every step of the publication process.

. . . to the foreign publishers who brought the story of Diana and Matthew to readers around the world.

. . . to Lisa Halttunen for editing and preparing the manuscript for the publisher.

. . . to my assistants, Jill Hough and Emma Divine, for making my life possible.

. . . to my friends for their steadfastness.

. . . to my family for making life worth living: my parents, Olive and Jack, Karen, John, Lexie, Jake, Lisa.

. . . to my readers for letting the Bishops and de Clermonts into your hearts and lives.

AVAILABLE FROM PENGUIN

A Discovery of Witches

A *New York Times* Bestseller

In book one of the All Souls Trilogy, Diana Bishop, a young scholar and a descendant of witches, discovers a long-lost and enchanted alchemical manuscript, Ashmole 782, deep in Oxford's Bodleian Library. Its reappearance summons a fantastical underworld, which she navigates with vampire geneticist Matthew Clairmont.

Shadow of Night

#1 *New York Times* Bestseller

This #1 *New York Times* bestselling sequel to *A Discovery of Witches* is "as enchanting, engrossing, and impossible to put down as its predecessor" (*Miami Herald*). Diana and Matthew venture through time and plunge into a world of spies, magic, and the School of Night, embarking on a very different—and vastly more dangerous—journey.

PENGUIN BOOKS

PENGUIN BOOKS

SHADOW OF NIGHT

Deborah Harkness is the number one *New York Times* bestselling author of *A Discovery of Witches* and *Shadow of Night*. A professor of history at the University of Southern California, Harkness has received Fulbright, Guggenheim, and National Humanities Center fellowships. Her most recent scholarly work is *The Jewel House: Elizabethan London and the Scientific Revolution*.

Praise for *Shadow of Night*

"Fans of Harkness's 2011 debut *A Discovery of Witches* will be delighted. . . . Harkness delivers enough romance and excitement to keep the pages turning. Readers will devour it."

—*People*

"The joy that Harkness, herself a historian, takes in visiting the past is evident on every page. . . . A great spell, one that can enchant a reader and make a 600-page book fly through her fingertips, is cast. . . . Its enduring rewards are plenty."

—*Entertainment Weekly*

"Deborah Harkness takes us places we've never been before. . . . Readers time travel as precisely and precariously as Diana and Matthew do. . . . *Shadow* ends as *Discovery* did, with promises of more to come. Lucky for us."

—*USA Today*

"A scholar of Elizabethan history, Harkness is an entertaining guide. . . . She weaves a tapestry of sixteenth-century European life that is as densely populated and colorful as a painting by Hieronymus Bosch."

—*The Washington Post*

"Enchanting, engrossing, and as impossible to put down as its predecessor, *Shadow of Night* is a perfect blend of fantasy, history, and romance. . . . If you've already read and enjoyed *A Discovery of Witches*, picking up *Shadow of Night* is an absolute requirement. Otherwise, pick up both and consider your summer reading list complete."

—*The Miami Herald*

"*Shadow of Night* pretty much defines excellence. . . . Adults who've sorely missed the wizardry, romance, and adventure of the Harry Potter books or love *The Hunger Games* will find much to adore here, along with the addition of impeccably researched history." —*The Dallas Morning News*

"Fascinating . . . Harkness immerses the reader in the historical and political milieu of late sixteenth-century London and Prague, where the search for the alchemical philosopher's stone consumes royalty and commoners alike. . . . *Shadow of Night* is compelling as it explores an unconventional couple trying to maintain authentic intimacy despite their opposing natures and other forces attempting to pull them apart. . . . . Also engrossing are descriptions of Diana's training as she learns to release and use her powers, which come in handy against creatures threatening her family."

—*Los Angeles Times*

"This novel is as much a love story about a bygone era as it is about Matthew and Diana. It overflows with a colorful cast of characters, many of whom Harkness has plucked straight from the history books, and Harkness renders the late 1500s in exquisite detail. . . . The writing is so rich, the characters so compelling . . . and best of all, Harkness manages to execute with aplomb the act of answering old questions while posing new ones that will intensify anticipation for the final installment. Readers who have been counting down the days, take heart: The wait was most assuredly worth it." —*BookPage*

DEBORAH HARKNESS

Shadow of Night

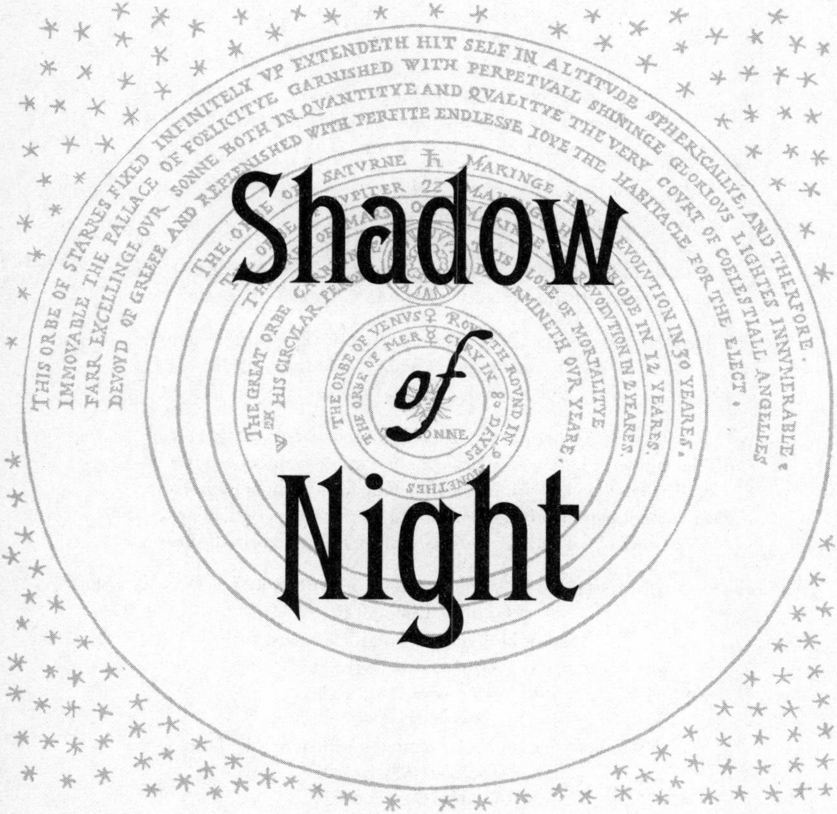

PENGUIN BOOKS

PENGUIN BOOKS
Published by the Penguin Group
Penguin Group (USA) Inc., 375 Hudson Street,
New York, New York 10014, U.S.A.

USA | Canada | UK | Ireland | Australia
New Zealand | India | South Africa | China
Penguin Books Ltd, Registered Offices: 80 Strand, London WC2R 0RL, England
For more information about the Penguin Group visit penguin.com

First published in the United States of America by Viking Penguin,
a member of Penguin Group (USA) Inc. 2012
Published in Penguin Books 2013

THE LIBRARY OF CONGRESS HAS CATALOGED THE HARDCOVER EDITION AS FOLLOWS:
Harkness, Deborah E.
Shadow of night / Deborah Harkness.
p. cm. — (All souls trilogy ; bk. 2)
ISBN 978-0-670-02348-6 (hc.)
ISBN 978-0-14-312362-0 (pbk.)
1. Witches—Fiction. 2. Vampires—Fiction. I. Title.
PS3608.A7436S53 2012
813'.6—dc23 2012005843

Printed in the United States of America
3 5 7 9 10 8 6 4

Set in Adobe Garamond Pro
Designed by Francesca Belanger

PUBLISHER'S NOTE

This is a work of fiction. Names, characters, places, and incidents either are the product of the author's imagination or are used fictitiously, and any resemblance to actual persons, living or dead, business establishments, events, or locales is entirely coincidental.

To Lacey Baldwin Smith, master storyteller and historian,
who suggested some time ago that I should think about writing a novel.

The past cannot be cured.

—Elizabeth I,
Queen of England

Contents

PART I

Woodstock: The Old Lodge

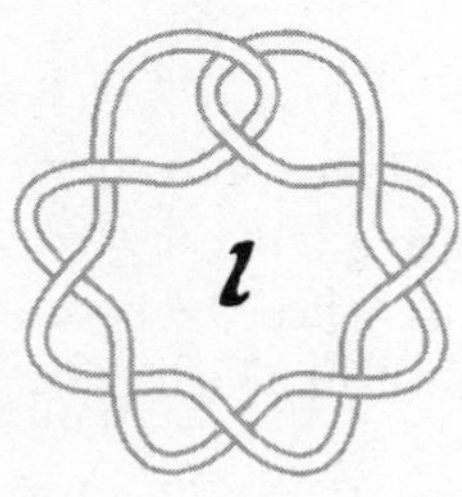

We arrived in an undignified heap of witch and vampire. Matthew was underneath me, his long limbs bent into an uncharacteristically awkward position. A large book was squashed between us, and the force of our landing sent the small silver figurine clutched in my hand sailing across the floor.

"Are we in the right place?" My eyes were screwed shut in case we were still in Sarah's hop barn in twenty-first-century New York, and not in sixteenth-century Oxfordshire. Even so, the unfamiliar scents told me I was not in my own time or place. Among them was something grassy and sweet, along with a waxen smell that reminded me of summer. There was a tang of wood smoke, too, and I heard the crackle of a fire.

"Open your eyes, Diana, and see for yourself." A feather-light touch of cool lips brushed my cheek, followed by a soft chuckle. Eyes the color of a stormy sea looked into mine from a face so pale it could only belong to a vampire. Matthew's hands traveled from neck to shoulders. "Are you all right?"

After journeying so far into Matthew's past, my body felt as though it might come apart with a puff of wind. I hadn't felt anything like it after our brief timewalking sessions at my aunts' house.

"I'm fine. What about you?" I kept my attention fixed on Matthew rather than daring a look around.

"Relieved to be home." Matthew's head fell back on the wooden floorboards with a gentle thunk, releasing more of the summery aroma from the rushes and lavender scattered there. Even in 1590 the Old Lodge was familiar to him.

My eyes adjusted to the dim light. A substantial bed, a small table, narrow benches, and a single chair came into focus. Through the carved uprights supporting the bed's canopy, I spied a doorway that connected this chamber to another room. Light spilled from it onto the coverlet and floor, forming a misshapen golden rectangle. The room's walls had the same fine, linenfold paneling that I remembered from the few times I'd visited Matthew's home in present-day Woodstock. Tipping my head back, I saw the ceiling—thickly plastered, coffered into squares, with a splashy red-and-white Tudor rose picked out in gilt in each recess.

"The roses were obligatory when the house was built," Matthew commented drily. "I can't stand them. We'll paint them all white at the first opportunity."

The gold-and-blue flames in a stand of candles flared in a sudden draft, illuminating the corner of a richly colored tapestry and the dark, glossy stitches that outlined a pattern of leaves and fruit on the pale counterpane. Modern textiles didn't have that luster.

I smiled with sudden excitement. "I really did it. I didn't mess it up or take us somewhere else, like Monticello or—"

"No," he said with an answering smile, "you did beautifully. Welcome to Elizabeth's England."

For the first time in my life, I was absolutely delighted to be a witch. As a historian I studied the past. Because I was a witch, I could actually visit it. We had come to 1590 to school me in the lost arts of magic, yet there was so much more that I could learn here. I bent my head for a celebratory kiss, but the sound of an opening door stopped me.

Matthew pressed a finger to my lips. His head turned slightly, and his nostrils flared. The tension left him when he recognized who was in the next room, where I could hear a faint rustling. Matthew lifted the book and me in one clean move. Taking my hand, he led me to the door.

In the next room, a man with tousled brown hair stood at a table littered with correspondence. He was of average height, with a neat build and expensive, tailored clothes. The tune he hummed was unfamiliar, punctuated now and again with words too low for me to hear.

Shock passed over Matthew's face before his lips curved into an affectionate smile.

"Where are you in truth, my own sweet Matt?" The man held a page up to the light. In a flash, Matthew's eyes narrowed, indulgence replaced by displeasure.

"Looking for something, Kit?" At Matthew's words the young man dropped the paper to the table and pivoted, joy lighting his face. I'd seen that face before, on my paperback copy of Christopher Marlowe's *The Jew of Malta*.

"Matt! Pierre said you were in Chester and might not make it home. But I knew you would not miss our annual gathering." The words were familiar enough but coated in a strange cadence that required me to focus on what he was saying in order to understand them. Elizabethan English was neither as unlike modern English as I had been taught nor as easily understandable as I'd hoped, based on my familiarity with Shakespeare's plays.

"Why no beard? Have you been ill?" Marlowe's eyes flickered when they spotted me, nudging me with the insistent pressure that marked him unmistakably as a daemon.

I suppressed an urge to rush at one of England's greatest playwrights and shake his hand before peppering him with questions. What little information I once knew about him flew from my mind now that he was standing before me. Had any of his plays been performed in 1590? How old was he? Younger than Matthew and I, certainly. Marlowe couldn't yet be thirty. I smiled at him warmly.

"Wherever did you find that?" Marlowe pointed, his voice dripping with contempt. I looked over my shoulder, expecting to see some hideous work of art. There was nothing but empty space.

He meant me. My smile faltered.

"Gently, Kit," Matthew said with a scowl.

Marlowe shrugged off the rebuke. "It is no matter. Take your fill of her before the others arrive, if you must. George has been here for some time, of course, eating your food and reading your books. He is still without a patron and hasn't a farthing to his name."

"George is welcome to whatever I have, Kit." Matthew kept his eyes on the young man, his face expressionless as he drew our intertwined fingers to his mouth. "Diana, this is my dear friend Christopher Marlowe."

Matthew's introduction provided Marlowe with an opportunity to inspect me more openly. His attention crawled from my toes to the top of my head. The young man's scorn was evident, his jealousy better hidden. Marlowe was indeed in love with my husband. I had suspected it back in Madison when my fingers had traveled over his inscription in Matthew's copy of *Doctor Faustus*.

"I had no idea there was a brothel in Woodstock that specialized in overtall women. Most of your whores are more delicate and appealing, Matthew. This one is a positive Amazon," Kit sniffed, looking over his shoulder at the disordered drifts of paper that covered the surface of the table. "According to the Old Fox's latest, it was business rather than lust that took you to the north. Wherever did you find the time to secure her services?"

"It is remarkable, Kit, how easily you squander affection," Matthew drawled, though there was a note of warning in his tone. Marlowe, seemingly intent on the correspondence, failed to recognize it and smirked. Matthew's fingers tightened on mine.

"Is Diana her real name, or was it adopted to enhance her allure among customers? Perhaps a baring of her right breast, or a bow and arrow, is in order," Marlowe suggested, picking up a sheet of paper. "Remember when Blackfriars Bess demanded we call her Aphrodite before she would let us—"

"Diana is my wife." Matthew was gone from my side, his hand no longer wrapped around mine but twisted in Marlowe's collar.

"No." Kit's face registered his shock.

"Yes. That means she is the mistress of this house, bears my name, and is under my protection. Given all that—and our long-standing friendship, of course—no word of criticism or whisper against her virtue will cross your lips in future."

I wiggled my fingers to restore their feeling. The angry pressure from Matthew's grip had driven the ring on the third finger of my left hand into the flesh, leaving a pale red mark. Despite its lack of facets, the diamond in the center captured the warmth of the firelight. The ring had been an unexpected gift from Matthew's mother, Ysabeau. Hours ago—centuries ago? centuries to come?—Matthew had repeated the words of the old marriage ceremony and slid the diamond over my knuckles.

With a clatter of dishes, two vampires appeared in the room. One was a slender man with an expressive face, weather-beaten skin the color of a hazelnut, and black hair and eyes. He was holding a flagon of wine and a goblet whose stem was shaped into a dolphin, the bowl balanced on its tail. The other was a rawboned woman bearing a platter of bread and cheese.

"You are home, *milord*," the man said, obviously confused. Oddly enough, his French accent made him easier to understand. "The messenger on Thursday said—"

"My plans changed, Pierre." Matthew turned to the woman. "My wife's possessions were lost on the journey, Françoise, and the clothes she was wearing were so filthy I burned them." He told the lie with bald confidence. Neither the vampires nor Kit looked convinced by it.

"Your wife?" Françoise repeated, her accent as French as Pierre's. "But she is a w—"

"Warmblood," Matthew finished, plucking the goblet from the tray. "Tell Charles there's another mouth to feed. Diana hasn't been well and must have fresh meat and fish on the advice of her doctor. Someone will need to go to the market, Pierre."

Pierre blinked. "Yes, *milord.*"

"And she will need something to wear," Françoise observed, eyeing me appraisingly. When Matthew nodded, she disappeared, Pierre following in her wake.

"What's happened to your hair?" Matthew held up a strawberry blond curl.

"Oh, no," I murmured. My hands rose. Instead of my usual shoulder-length, straw-colored hair, they found unexpectedly springy reddish-gold locks reaching down to my waist. The last time my hair had developed a mind of its own, I was in college, playing Ophelia in a production of *Hamlet.* Then and now its unnaturally rapid growth and change of hue were not good signs. The witch within me had awakened during our journey to the past. There was no telling what other magic had been unleashed.

Vampires might have smelled the adrenaline and the sudden spike of anxiety that accompanied this realization, or heard the music my blood made. But daemons like Kit could sense the rise in my witch's energy.

"Christ's tomb." Marlowe's smile was full of malice. "You've brought home a witch. What evil has she done?"

"Leave it, Kit. It's not your concern." Matthew's voice took on that note of command again, but his fingers remained gentle on my hair. "Don't worry, *mon coeur.* I'm sure it's nothing but exhaustion."

My sixth sense flared in disagreement. This latest transformation couldn't be explained by simple fatigue. A witch by descent, I was still unsure of the full extent of my inherited powers. Not even my Aunt Sarah and her partner, Emily Mather—witches both—had been able to say for certain what they were or how best to manage them. Matthew's scientific tests had revealed genetic markers for the magical potential in my blood, but there were no guarantees when or if these possibilities would ever be realized.

Before I could worry further, Françoise returned with something that looked like a darning needle, her mouth bristling with pins. An ambulatory mound of velvet, wool, and linen accompanied her. The slender brown legs emerging from the bottom of the pile suggested that Pierre was buried somewhere inside.

"What are they for?" I asked suspiciously, pointing at the pins.

"For getting *madame* into this, of course." Françoise plucked a dull brown garment that looked like a flour sack from the top of the pile of clothes. It didn't seem an obvious choice for entertaining, but with little knowledge of Elizabethan fashion I was at her mercy.

"Go downstairs where you belong, Kit," Matthew told his friend. "We will join you presently. And hold your tongue. This is my tale to tell, not yours."

"As you wish, Matthew." Marlowe pulled at the hem of his mulberry doublet, his nonchalant gesture belied by the trembling of his hands, and made a small, mocking bow. The compact move managed to both acknowledge Matthew's command and undermine it.

With the daemon gone, Françoise draped the sack over a nearby bench and circled me, studying my figure to determine the most favorable line of attack. With an exasperated sigh, she began to dress me. Matthew moved to the table, his attention drawn by the piles of paper strewn over its surface. He opened a neatly folded rectangular packet sealed with a blob of pinkish wax, eyes darting across the tiny handwriting.

"*Dieu*. I forgot about that. Pierre!"

"Milord?" A muffled voice issued from the depths of the fabric.

"Put that down and tell me about Lady Cromwell's latest complaint." Matthew treated Pierre and Françoise with a blend of familiarity and authority. If this was how one dealt with servants, it would take me some time to master the art.

The two muttered by the fire while I was draped, pinned, and trussed into something presentable. Françoise clucked over my single earring, the twisted golden wires hung with jewels that had originally belonged to Ysabeau. Like Matthew's copy of *Doctor Faustus* and the small silver figure of Diana, the earring was one of the three items that had helped us return to this particular past. Françoise rummaged in a nearby chest and found its match easily. My jewelry sorted out, she snaked thick stockings over my knees and secured them with scarlet ribbons.

"I think I'm ready," I said, eager to get downstairs and begin our visit to the sixteenth century. Reading books about the past wasn't the same as experiencing it, as my brief interaction with Françoise and my crash course in the clothing of the period proved.

Matthew surveyed my appearance. "That will do—for now."

"She'll more than do, for she looks modest and forgettable," Françoise said, "which is exactly how a witch should look in this household."

Matthew ignored Françoise's pronouncement and turned to me. "Before we go down, Diana, remember to guard your words. Kit is a daemon, and George knows that I'm a vampire, but even the most open-minded of creatures are leery of someone new and different."

Down in the great hall, I wished George, Matthew's penniless and patronless friend, a formal and, I thought, properly Elizabethan good evening.

"Is that woman speaking *English*?" George gaped, raising a pair of round spectacles that magnified his blue eyes to froglike proportions. His other hand was on his hip in a pose I'd last seen in a painted miniature at the Victoria and Albert Museum.

"She's been living in Chester," Matthew said quickly. George looked skeptical. Apparently not even the wilds of northern England could account for my odd speech patterns. Matthew's accent was softening into something that better matched the cadence and timbre of the time, but mine remained resolutely modern and American.

"She's a witch," corrected Kit, taking a sip of wine.

"Indeed?" George studied me with renewed interest. There were no nudges to indicate that this man was a daemon, no witchy tingles, nor the frosty aftereffects of a vampire's glance. George was just an ordinary, warm-blooded human—one who appeared middle-aged and tired, as though life had already worn him out. "But you do not like witches any more than Kit does, Matthew. You have always discouraged me from attending to the subject. When I set out to write a poem about Hecate, you told me to—"

"I like this one. So much so, I married her," Matthew interrupted, bestowing a firm kiss on my lips to help convince him.

"Married her!" George's eyes shifted to Kit. He cleared his throat. "So there are two unexpected joys to celebrate: You were not delayed on business as Pierre thought, and you have returned to us with a wife. My felicitations." His portentous tone reminded me of a commencement address, and I stifled a smile. George beamed at me in return and bowed. "I am George Chapman, Mistress Roydon."

His name was familiar. I picked through the disorganized knowledge stored in my historian's brain. Chapman was not an alchemist—that was my research specialty, and I did not find his name in the spaces devoted to that arcane subject. He was another writer, like Marlowe, but I couldn't recall any of the titles.

Once we'd dispensed with introductions, Matthew agreed to sit before the fire for a few moments with his guests. There the men talked politics and George made an effort to include me in the conversation by asking about the state of the roads and the weather. I said as little as possible and tried to observe the little tricks of gesture and word choice that would help me pass for an Elizabethan. George was delighted with my attentiveness and rewarded it with a long dissertation on his latest literary efforts. Kit, who didn't enjoy being relegated to a supporting role, brought George's lecture to a halt by offering to read aloud from *Doctor Faustus.*

"It will serve as a rehearsal among friends," the daemon said, eyes gleaming, "before the real performance later."

"Not now, Kit. It's well past midnight, and Diana is tired from her journey," Matthew said, drawing me to my feet.

Kit's eyes remained on us as we left the room. He knew we were hiding something. He had leaped on every strange turn of phrase when I'd ventured into the conversation and grown thoughtful when Matthew couldn't remember where his own lute was kept.

Matthew had warned me before we left Madison that Kit was unusually perceptive, even for a daemon. I wondered how long it would be before Marlowe figured out what that hidden something was. The answer to my question came within hours.

The next morning we talked in the recesses of our warm bed while the household stirred.

At first Matthew was willing to answer my questions about Kit (the son of a shoemaker, it turned out) and George (who was not much older than Marlowe, I learned to my surprise). When I turned to the practical matters of household management and female behavior, however, he was quickly bored.

"What about my clothes?" I asked, trying to focus him on my immediate concerns.

"I don't think married women sleep in these," Matthew said, plucking at my fine linen night rail. He untied its ruffled neckline and was about to plant a kiss underneath my ear to persuade me to his point of view when someone ripped open the bed's curtains. I squinted against the bright sunlight.

"Well?" Marlowe demanded.

A second, dark-complected daemon peered over Marlowe's shoulder. He resembled an energetic leprechaun with his slight build and pointed chin, which was accented by an equally sharp auburn beard. His hair evidently had not seen a comb for weeks. I grabbed at the front of my night rail, keenly aware of its transparency and my lack of underclothes.

"You saw Master White's drawings from Roanoke, Kit. The witch looks nothing at all like the natives of Virginia," the unfamiliar daemon replied, disappointed. Belatedly he noticed Matthew, who was glaring at him. "Oh. Good morning, Matthew. Would you allow me to borrow your sector? I promise not to take it to the river this time."

Matthew lowered his forehead to my shoulder and closed his eyes with a groan.

"She must be from the New World—or Africa," Marlowe insisted, refusing to refer to me by name. "She's not from Chester, nor from Scotland, Ireland, Wales, France, or the Empire. I don't believe she's Dutch or Spanish either."

"Good morning to you, Tom. Is there some reason you and Kit must discuss Diana's birthplace now, and in my bedchamber?" Matthew drew the ties of my night rail together.

"It is too fine to lie abed, even if you have been out of your mind with an ague. Kit says you must have married the witch in the midst of the fever's crisis. Otherwise there is no way to account for your recklessness." Tom rattled on in true daemonic fashion, making no effort to answer Matthew's question. "The roads were dry, and we arrived hours ago."

"And the wine is already gone," Marlowe complained.

"We"? There were more of them? The Old Lodge already felt stuffed to bursting.

"Out! *Madame* must wash before she greets his lordship." Françoise entered the room with a steaming basin of water in her hands. Pierre, as usual, trailed behind.

"Has something of import happened?" George inquired from beyond the curtains. He'd entered the room unannounced, neatly foiling Françoise's efforts to herd the other men from the room. "Lord Northumberland has been left alone in the great hall. If he were my patron, I would not treat him thus!"

"Hal is reading a treatise on the construction of a balance sent to me by a mathematician in Pisa. He's quite content," Tom replied crossly, sitting on the edge of the bed.

He must be talking about Galileo, I realized with excitement. In 1590, Galileo was an entry-level professor at the university in Pisa. His work on the balance wasn't published—yet.

Tom. Lord Northumberland. Someone who corresponded with Galileo.

My lips parted in astonishment. The daemon perched on the quilted coverlet must be Thomas Harriot.

"Françoise is right. Out. All of you," Matthew said, sounding as cross as Tom.

"What should we tell Hal?" Kit asked, sliding a meaningful glance in my direction.

"That I'll be down shortly," Matthew said. He rolled over and pulled me close.

I waited until Matthew's friends streamed out of the room before I thumped his chest.

"What is that for?" He winced in mock pain, but all I'd bruised was my own fist.

"For not telling me who your *friends* are!" I propped up on one elbow and stared down at him. "The great playwright Christopher Marlowe. George Chapman, poet and scholar. Mathematician and astronomer Thomas Harriot, if I'm not mistaken. And the Wizard Earl is waiting downstairs!"

"I can't remember when Henry earned that nickname, but nobody calls him that yet." Matthew looked amused, which only made me more furious.

"All we need is Sir Walter Raleigh and we'll have the entire School of Night in the house." Matthew looked out the window at my mention of this legendary group of radicals, philosophers, and free-thinkers. *Thomas Harriot. Christopher Marlowe. George Chapman. Walter Raleigh. And—*

"Just who *are* you, Matthew?" I hadn't thought to ask him before we departed.

"Matthew Roydon," he said with a tip of his head, as though we were only this moment being introduced. "Friend to poets."

"Historians know almost nothing about you," I said, stunned. Matthew Roydon was the most shadowy figure associated with the mysterious School of Night.

"You aren't surprised, are you, now that you know who Matthew Roydon really is?" His black brow rose.

"Oh, I'm surprised enough to last a lifetime. You might have warned me before dropping me into the middle of all this."

"What would you have done? We barely had time to get dressed before we left, never mind conduct a research project." He sat up and swung his legs onto the floor. Our private time had been lamentably brief. "There's no reason for you to be concerned. They're just ordinary men, Diana."

No matter what Matthew said, there was nothing ordinary about them. The School of Night held heretical opinions, sneered at the corrupt court of Queen Elizabeth, and scoffed at the intellectual pretensions of church and university. "Mad, bad, and dangerous to know" described this group perfectly. We hadn't joined a cozy reunion of friends on Halloween night. We'd fallen into a hornet's nest of Elizabethan intrigue.

"Putting aside how reckless your friends can be, you can't expect me to be blasé when you introduce me to people I've spent my adult life studying," I said. "Thomas Harriot is one of the foremost astronomers of the time. Your friend Henry Percy is an alchemist." Pierre, familiar with the signs of a woman on the edge, hastily thrust a set of black britches at my husband so he wouldn't be bare-legged when my anger erupted.

"So are Walter and Tom." Matthew ignored the proffered clothing and scratched his chin. "Kit dabbles, too, though without any success. Try not to dwell on what you know about them. It's probably wrong anyway. And you should be careful with your modern historical labels, too," he continued, finally snatching at his britches and stepping into them. "Will dreams up the School of Night as a jab at Kit, but not for a few years yet."

"I don't care what William Shakespeare has done, is doing, or will do in the future—provided he isn't at this moment in the great hall with the Earl of Northumberland!" I retorted, sliding out of the high bed.

"Of course Will's not down there." Matthew waved his hand dismissively. "Walter doesn't approve of his command of meter, and Kit thinks he's a hack and a thief."

"Well, that's a relief. What do you plan on telling them about me? Marlowe knows we're hiding something."

Matthew's gray-green eyes met mine. "The truth, I suppose." Pierre handed him a doublet—black, with intricate quilting—and stared fixedly at a point over my shoulder, the very model of a good servant. "That you're a timewalker and a witch from the New World."

"The truth," I said flatly. Pierre could hear every word but showed no reaction, and Matthew ignored him as though he were invisible. I wondered if we would be here long enough for me to become so oblivious to his presence.

"Why not? Tom will write down everything you say and compare it with his notes on the Algonquian language. Otherwise no one will pay much attention." Matthew seemed more concerned with his clothing than with the reactions of his friends.

Françoise returned with two warmblooded young women bearing armfuls of clean clothes. She gestured at my night rail, and I ducked behind the bedpost to disrobe. Grateful that my time in locker rooms had squashed most of my qualms about changing in front of strangers, I drew the linen over my hips and up to my shoulders.

"Kit will. He's been looking for a reason to dislike me, and this will give him several."

"He won't be a problem," Matthew said confidently.

"Is Marlowe your friend or your puppet?" I was still wrestling my head out of the fabric when there was a gasp of horror, a muffled *"Mon Dieu."*

I froze. Françoise had seen my back and the crescent-shaped scar that stretched from one side of my lower rib cage to the other, along with the star that rested between my shoulder blades.

"I will dress *madame,*" Françoise coolly told the maids. "Leave the clothing and return to your work."

The maids departed with nothing more than a curtsy and a look of idle curiosity. They hadn't seen the markings. When they were gone, we all began to speak at once. Françoise's aghast "Who did this?" tumbled over Matthew's "No one must know" and my own, slightly defensive "It's just a scar."

"Someone branded you with a badge of the de Clermont family," Françoise insisted with a shake of her head, "one that is used by *milord.*"

"We broke the covenant." I fought the sick feeling that twisted my stomach whenever I thought about the night another witch had marked me a traitor. "This was the Congregation's punishment."

"So that is why you are both here." Françoise snorted. "The covenant was a foolish idea from the start. Philippe de Clermont should never have gone along with it."

"One that's kept us safe from the humans." I had no great fondness for the agreement, or the nine-member Congregation who enforced it, but its long-term success at hiding otherworldly creatures from unwanted attention was undeniable. The ancient promises made among daemons, vampires, and witches prohibited meddling in human politics or religion and forbade personal alliances among the three different species. Witches were meant to keep to themselves, as were vampires and daemons. They were not supposed to fall in love and intermarry.

"Safe? Do not think you are safe here, *madame.* None of us are. The English are a superstitious people, prone to seeing a ghost in every churchyard and witches around every cauldron. The Congregation is all that is standing between us and utter destruction. You are wise to take refuge here. Come, you must dress and join the others." Françoise helped me out of the night rail and handed me a wet towel and a dish of goop that smelled of rosemary and oranges. I found it odd to be treated like a child but knew that it was customary for people of Matthew's rank to be washed, dressed, and fed like dolls. Pierre handed Matthew a cup of something too dark to be wine.

"She is not only a witch but a *fileuse de temps* as well?" Françoise asked Matthew quietly. The unfamiliar term—*"time spinner"*—conjured up images of the many different-colored threads we'd followed to reach this particular past.

"She is." Matthew nodded, his attention focused on me while he sipped at his cup.

"But if she has come from another time, that means . . ." Françoise began, wide-eyed. Then her expression became thoughtful. Matthew must sound and behave differently.

She suspects that this is not the same Matthew, I realized, alarmed.

"It is enough for us to know that she is under *milord's* protection," Pierre said roughly, a clear warning in his tone. He handed Matthew a dagger. "What it means is not important."

"It means I love her, and she loves me in return." Matthew looked at his servant intently. "No matter what I say to others, that is the truth. Understood?"

"Yes," replied Pierre, though his tone suggested quite the opposite.

Matthew shot an inquiring look at Françoise, who pursed her lips and nodded grudgingly.

She returned her attention to getting me ready, wrapping me in a thick linen towel. Françoise had to have noticed the other marks on my body, those I had received over the course of that one interminable day with the witch Satu, as well as my other, later scars. Françoise asked no further questions, however, but sat me in a chair next to the fire while she ran a comb through my hair.

"And did this insult happen after you declared your love for the witch, *milord*?" Françoise asked.

"Yes." Matthew buckled the dagger around his waist.

"It was not a *manjasang*, then, who marked her," Pierre murmured. He used the old Occitan word for vampire—"*blood eater.*" "None would risk the anger of the de Clermonts."

"No, it was another witch." Even though I was shielded from the cold air, the admission made me shiver.

"Two *manjasang* stood by and let it happen, though," Matthew said grimly. "And they will pay for it."

"What's done is done." I had no wish to start a feud among vampires. We had enough challenges facing us.

"If *milord* had accepted you as his wife when the witch took you, then it is not done." Françoise's swift fingers wove my hair into tight braids. She wound them around my head and pinned them in place. "Your name might be Roydon in this godforsaken country where there is no loyalty to speak of, but we will not forget that you are a de Clermont."

Matthew's mother had warned me that the de Clermonts were a pack. In the twenty-first century, I had chafed under the obligations and restrictions that came with membership. In 1590, however, my magic was unpredictable, my knowledge of witchcraft almost nonexistent, and my earliest known ancestor hadn't yet been born. Here I had nothing to rely on but my own wits and Matthew.

"Our intentions to each other were clear then. But I want no trouble now." I looked down at Ysabeau's ring and felt the band with my thumb. My hope that we could blend seamlessly into the past now seemed unlikely as well as naïve. I looked around me. "And this . . ."

"We're here for only two reasons, Diana: to find you a teacher and to locate that alchemical manuscript if we can." It was the mysterious manuscript called Ashmole 782 that had brought us together in the first place. In the twenty-first century, it had been safely buried among the millions of books in Oxford's Bodleian Library. When I'd filled out the call slip, I'd had no idea that the simple action would unlock an intricate spell that bound the manuscript to the shelves, or that the same spell would reactivate the moment I returned it. I was also ignorant of the many secrets about witches, vampires, and daemons its pages were rumored to reveal. Matthew had thought it would be wiser to locate Ashmole 782 in the past than to try to unlock the spell for a second time in the modern world.

"Until we go back, this will be your home," he continued, trying to reassure me.

The room's solid furnishings were familiar from museums and auction catalogs, but the Old Lodge would never feel like home. I fingered the thick linen of the towel—so different from the faded terry-cloth sets that Sarah and Em owned, all worn thin from too many washes. Voices in another room lilted and swayed in a rhythm that no modern person, historian or not, could have anticipated. But the past was our only option. Other vampires had made that clear during our final days in Madison, when they'd hunted us down and nearly killed Matthew. If the rest of our plan was going to work, passing as a proper Elizabethan woman had to be my first priority.

"'O brave new world.'" It was a gross historical violation to quote from Shakespeare's *Tempest* two decades before it was written, but this had been a difficult morning.

"'Tis new to thee,'" Matthew responded. "Are you ready to meet your trouble, then?"

"Of course. Let's get me dressed." I squared my shoulders and rose from the chair. "How does one say hello to an earl?"

My concern over proper etiquette was unnecessary. Titles and forms of address weren't important when the earl in question was a gentle giant named Henry Percy.

Françoise, to whom propriety mattered, clucked and fussed while she finished dressing me in scavenged apparel: someone else's petticoats; quilted stays to confine my athletic figure into a more traditionally feminine shape; an embroidered smock that smelled of lavender and cedar, with a high, ruffled neck; a black, bell-shaped skirt made of velvet; and Pierre's best jacket, the only tailored article of clothing that was remotely my size. Try though she might, Françoise couldn't button this last item over my breasts. I held my breath, tucked in my stomach, and hoped for a miracle as she pulled the corset's laces tight, but nothing short of divine intervention was going to give me a sylphlike silhouette.

I asked Françoise a number of questions during the complicated process. Portraits of the period had led me to expect an unwieldy birdcage called a farthingale that would hold my skirts out at the hips, but Françoise explained that these were for more formal occasions. Instead she tied a stuffed cloth form shaped like a doughnut around my waist beneath my skirts. The only positive thing to say about it was that it held the layers of fabric away from my legs, enabling me to walk without too much difficulty—provided there was no furniture in the way and my destination could be reached if I moved in a straight line. But I would be expected to curtsy, too. Françoise quickly taught me how to do so while explaining how Henry Percy's various titles worked—he was "Lord Northumberland" even though his last name was Percy and he was an earl.

But I had no chance to use any of this newly acquired knowledge. As soon as Matthew and I entered the great hall, a lanky young man in soft brown leather traveling clothes spattered with mud jumped up to greet us. His broad face was enlivened with an inquisitive look that lifted his heavy, ash-colored eyebrows toward a forehead with a pronounced widow's peak.

"Hal." Matthew smiled with the indulgent familiarity of an older brother. But the earl ignored his old friend and moved in my direction instead.

"M-m-mistress Roydon." The earl's deep bass was toneless, with hardly a trace of inflection or accent. Before coming down, Matthew had explained that Henry was slightly deaf and had stammered since childhood. He was, however, adept at lipreading. Here was someone I could talk to without feeling self-conscious.

"Upstaged by Kit again, I see," Matthew said with a rueful smile. "I had hoped to tell you myself."

"What does it matter who shares such happy news?" Lord Northumberland bowed. "I thank you for your hospitality, mistress, and apologize for greeting you in this state. It is good of you to suffer your husband's friends so soon. We should have left immediately once we learned of your arrival. The inn would be more than adequate."

"You are most welcome here, my lord." This was the moment to curtsy, but my heavy black skirts weren't easy to manage and the corset was laced so tightly I couldn't bend at the waist. I arranged my legs in an appropriately reverential position but teetered as I bent my knees. A large, blunt-fingered hand shot out to steady me.

"Just Henry, mistress. Everyone else calls me Hal, so my given name is considered quite formal." Like many who are hard of hearing, the earl kept his voice deliberately soft. He released me and turned his attention to Matthew. "Why no beard, Matt? Have you been ill?"

"A touch of ague, nothing more. Marriage has cured me. Where are the rest of them?" Matthew glanced around for Kit, George, and Tom.

The Old Lodge's great hall looked very different in daylight. I had seen it only at night, but this morning the heavy paneling turned out to be shutters, all of which were thrown open. It gave the space an airy feeling, despite the monstrous fireplace on the far wall. It was decorated with bits and pieces of medieval stonework, no doubt rescued by Matthew from the rubble of the abbey that once stood here—the haunting face of a saint, a coat of arms, a Gothic quatrefoil.

"Diana?" Matthew's amused voice interrupted my examination of the room and its contents. "Hal says the others are in the parlor, reading and playing cards. He didn't feel it was right to join them until he had been invited to stay by the lady of the house."

"The earl must stay, of course, and we can join your friends immediately." My stomach rumbled.

"Or we could get you something to eat," he suggested, eyes twinkling. Now that I had met Henry Percy without mishap, Matthew was beginning to relax. "Has anyone fed you, Hal?"

"Pierre and Françoise have been attentive as ever," he reassured us. "Of course, if Mistress Roydon will join me . . ." The earl's voice trailed off, and his stomach gurgled with mine. The man was as tall as a giraffe. It must take huge quantities of food to keep his body fueled.

"I, too, am fond of a large breakfast, my lord," I said with a laugh.

"Henry," the earl corrected me gently, his grin showing off the dimple in his chin.

"Then you must call me Diana. I cannot call the Earl of Northumberland by his first name if he keeps referring to me as 'Mistress Roydon.'" Françoise had been insistent on the need to honor the earl's high rank.

"Very well, Diana," Henry said, extending his arm.

He led me across a drafty corridor and into a cozy room with low ceilings. It was snug and inviting, with only a single array of south-facing windows. In spite of its relatively small size, three tables had been wedged into the room, along with stools and benches. A low hum of activity, punctuated by a rattle of pots and pans, told me we were near the kitchens. Someone had tacked a page from an almanac on the wall and a map lay on the central table, one corner held down with a candlestick, the other by a shallow pewter dish filled with fruit. The arrangement looked like a Dutch still life, with its homely detail. I stopped short, dizzied by the scent.

"The quinces." My fingers reached out to touch them. They looked just as they had in my mind's eye back in Madison when Matthew had described the Old Lodge.

Henry seemed puzzled by my reaction to an ordinary dish of fruit but was too well bred to comment. We settled ourselves at the table, and a servant added fresh bread along with a platter of grapes and a bowl of apples to the still life before us. It was comforting to see such familiar fare. Henry helped himself, and I followed his example, carefully noting which foods he selected and how much of them he consumed. It was always the little differences that gave strangers away, and I wanted to appear as ordinary as possible. While we filled our plates, Matthew poured himself a glass of wine.

Throughout our meal Henry behaved with unfailing courtesy. He never asked me anything personal, nor did he pry into Matthew's affairs. Instead he kept us laughing with tales of his dogs, his estates, and his martinet of a mother, all the while providing a steady supply of toasted bread from the fire. He was just beginning an account of moving house in London when a clatter arose in the courtyard. The earl, whose back was to the door, didn't notice.

"She is impossible! You all warned me, but I didn't believe anyone could be so ungrateful. After all the riches I've poured into her coffers, the least she could do was— Oh." Our new guest's broad shoulders filled the doorway, one of them swathed in a cloak as dark as the hair that curled around his splendid feathered hat. "Matthew. Are you ill?"

Henry turned with surprise. "Good day, Walter. Why aren't you at court?"

I tried to swallow a morsel of toast. Our new arrival was almost certainly the missing member of Matthew's School of Night, Sir Walter Raleigh.

"Cast out of paradise for want of a position, Hal. And who is this?" Piercing blue eyes settled on me, and teeth gleamed from his dark beard. "Henry Percy, you sly imp. Kit told me you were intent on bedding the fair Arabella. If I'd known your tastes ran to something more mature than a girl of fifteen, I would have yoked you to a lusty widow long ago."

Mature? *Widow?* I had just turned thirty-three.

"Her charms have induced you to stay home from church this Sunday. We must thank the lady for getting you off your knees and onto a horse, where you belong," Raleigh continued, his accent as thick as Devonshire cream.

The Earl of Northumberland rested his toasting fork on the hearth and considered his friend. He shook his head and returned to his work. "Go out, come in again, and ask Matt for his news. And look contrite when you do it."

"No." Walter stared at Matthew, openmouthed. "She's yours?"

"With the ring to prove it." Matthew kicked a stool from under the table with one long, booted leg. "Sit down, Walter, and have some ale."

"You swore you would never wed," Walter said, clearly confused.

"It took some persuasion."

"I expect it did." Walter Raleigh's appraising glance settled on me once more. "'Tis a pity she is wasted on a cold-blooded creature. I wouldn't have delayed for an instant."

"Diana knows my nature and doesn't mind my 'coldness,' as you put it. Besides, it was she who needed persuading. I fell in love with her at first glance," said Matthew.

Walter snorted in response.

"Don't be so cynical, old friend. Cupid may yet catch you." Matthew's gray eyes lit up with the mischief born from certain knowledge of Raleigh's future.

"Cupid will have to wait to turn his arrows on me. I'm entirely occupied at present fending off the unfriendly advances of the queen and the admiral." Walter tossed his hat onto a nearby table, where it slid over the shiny surface of a backgammon board, disturbing the game in progress. He groaned and sat next to Henry. "Everyone wants a bit of my hide, it seems, but no one will give me a speck of preferment while this business of the colony hangs over my head. The idea for this year's anniversary celebration was mine, yet that woman put Cumberland in charge of the ceremonies." His temper rose again.

"Still no news from Roanoke?" Henry inquired gently, handing Walter a cup of thick, brown ale. My stomach lurched at the mention of Raleigh's doomed venture in the New World. It was the first time anyone had wondered aloud about the outcome of a future event, but it would not be the last.

"White arrived back at Plymouth last week, driven home by foul weather. He had to abandon the search for his daughter and granddaughter." Walter took a long draft of ale and stared into space. "Christ knows what happened to them all."

"Come spring, you will return and find them." Henry sounded sure, but Matthew and I knew that the missing Roanoke colonists would never be found and Raleigh would never again set foot on the soil of North Carolina.

"I pray you are right, Hal. But enough of my troubles. What part of the country are your people from, Mistress Roydon?"

"Cambridge," I said softly, keeping my response brief and as truthful as possible. The town was in Massachusetts, not England, but if I started making things up now, I'd never keep my stories straight.

"So you are a scholar's daughter. Or perhaps your father was a theologian? Matt would be pleased to have someone to talk to about matters of faith. With the exception of Hal, his friends are hopeless when it comes to doctrine." Walter sipped his ale and waited.

"Diana's father died when she was quite young." Matthew took my hand.

"I am sorry for you, Diana. The loss of a f-f-father is a terrible blow," Henry murmured.

"And your first husband, did he leave you with sons and daughters for comfort?" asked Walter, a trace of sympathy creeping into his voice.

Here and now a woman my age would have been married before and have had a brood of three or four children. I shook my head. "No."

Walter frowned, but before he could pursue the matter further, Kit arrived, with George and Tom in tow.

"At last. Talk sense into him, Walter. Matthew cannot keep playing Odysseus to her Circe." Kit grabbed the goblet sitting in front of Henry. "Good day, Hal."

"Talk sense into whom?" Walter asked testily.

"Matt, of course. That woman is a witch. And there's something not quite right about her." Kit's eyes narrowed. "She's hiding something."

"A witch," Walter repeated carefully.

A servant carrying an armful of logs froze in the doorway.

"As I said," Kit affirmed with a nod. "Tom and I recognized the signs straightaway."

The maid dumped the logs in the waiting basket and scurried off.

"For a maker of plays, Kit, you have a lamentable sense of time and place." Walter's blue eyes turned to Matthew. "Shall we go elsewhere to discuss the matter, or is this merely one of Kit's idle fancies? If it is the latter, I would like to stay where it is warm and finish my ale." The two men studied each other. When Matthew's expression didn't waver, Walter cursed under his breath. Pierre appeared, as if on cue.

"There is a fire in the parlor, *milord,*" the vampire told Matthew, "and wine and food are laid out for your guests. You will not be disturbed."

The parlor was neither as cozy as the room where we'd taken our breakfast nor as imposing as the great hall. The abundance of carved armchairs, rich tapestries, and ornately framed paintings suggested that its primary purpose was to entertain the house's most important guests. A splendid rendering of St. Jerome and his lion by Holbein hung by the fireplace. It was unfamiliar to me, as was the Holbein portrait next to it of a piggy-eyed Henry VIII holding a book and a pair of spectacles and looking pensively at the viewer, the table before him strewn with precious objects. Henry's daughter, the first and current Queen Elizabeth, stared at him with hauteur from across the room. Their tense standoff did nothing to lighten the mood as we took our seats. Matthew propped himself up by the fire with his arms crossed over his chest, looking every bit as formidable as the Tudors on the walls.

"Are you still going to tell them the truth?" I whispered to him.

"It is generally easier that way, mistress," Raleigh said sharply, "not to mention more fitting among friends."

"You forget yourself, Walter," Matthew warned, anger flaring.

"Forget myself! This from someone who has taken up with a witch?" Walter had no trouble keeping pace with Matthew when it came to irritation. And there was a note of real fear in his voice as well.

"She is my wife," Matthew retorted. He rubbed his hand over his hair. "As for her being a witch, we are all in this room vilified for something, be it real or imaginary."

"But to wed her—whatever were you thinking?" Walter asked numbly.

"That I loved her," Matthew said. Kit rolled his eyes and poured a fresh cup of wine from a silver pitcher. My dreams of sitting with him by a cozy fire discussing magic and literature faded further in the harsh light of this November morning. I had been in 1590 for less than twenty-four hours, but I was already heartily sick of Christopher Marlowe.

At Matthew's response the room fell silent while he and Walter studied each other. With Kit, Matthew was indulgent and a bit exasperated. George and Tom brought out his patience and Henry his brotherly affection. But Raleigh was Matthew's equal—in intelligence, power, perhaps even in ruthlessness—which meant that Walter's was the only opinion that mattered. They had a wary respect for each other, like two wolves determining who had the strength to lead their pack.

"So it's like that," Walter said slowly, acceding to Matthew's authority.

"It is." Matthew planted his feet more evenly on the hearth.

"You keep too many secrets and have too many enemies to take a wife. And yet you've done so anyway." Walter looked amazed. "Other men have accused you of relying overmuch on your own subtlety, but I never agreed with them until now. Very well, Matthew. If you are so cunning, tell us what to say when questions are raised."

Kit's cup slammed onto the table, red wine sloshing over his hand. "You cannot expect us to—"

"Quiet." Walter shot a furious glance at Marlowe. "Given the lies we tell on your behalf, I'm surprised you would dare to object. Go on, Matthew."

"Thank you, Walter. You are the only five men in the kingdom who might listen to my tale and not think me mad." Matthew raked his hands through his hair. "Do you recall when we spoke last of Giordano Bruno's ideas about an infinite number of worlds, unlimited by time or space?"

The men exchanged glances.

"I am not sure," Henry began delicately, "that we understand your meaning."

"Diana *is* from the New World." Matthew paused, which gave Marlowe the opportunity to look triumphantly about the room. "From the New World to come."

In the silence that followed, all eyes swiveled in my direction.

"She said she was from Cambridge," said Walter blankly.

"Not that Cambridge. My Cambridge is in Massachusetts." My voice creaked from stress and disuse. I cleared my throat. "The colony will exist north of Roanoke in another forty years."

A din of exclamations rose, and questions came at me from all directions. Harriot reached over and hesitantly touched my shoulder. When his finger met solid flesh, he withdrew it in wonder.

"I have heard about creatures who could bend time to their will. This is a marvelous day, is it not, Kit? Did you ever think to know a time spinner? We must be careful around her, of course, or we might get entangled in her web and lose our way." Harriot's face was wistful, as if he might enjoy being caught up in another world.

"And what brings you here, Mistress Roydon?" Walter's deep voice cut through the chatter.

"Diana's father was a scholar," Matthew replied for me. There were murmurs of interest, quelled by Walter's upraised hand. "Her mother, too. Both were witches and died under mysterious circumstances."

"That is something we share, then, D-D-Diana," Henry said with a shudder. Before I could ask the earl what he meant, Walter waved Matthew on.

"As a result her education as a witch was . . . overlooked," Matthew continued.

"It is easy to prey on such a witch." Tom frowned. "Why, in this New World to come, is more care not taken with such a creature?"

"My magic, and my family's long history with it, meant nothing to me. You must understand what it is like to want to go beyond the restrictions of your birth." I looked at Kit, the shoemaker's son, hoping for agreement if not sympathy, but he turned away.

"Ignorance is an unforgivable sin." Kit fussed with a bit of red silk that was peeking out of one of the dozens of jagged slashes cut into his black doublet.

"So is disloyalty," said Walter. "Go on, Matthew."

"Diana may not have been trained in the craft of a witch, but she is far from ignorant. She is a scholar, too," Matthew said proudly, "with a passion for alchemy."

"Lady alchemists are nothing but kitchen philosophers," Kit sniffed, "more interested in improving their complexions than understanding the secrets of nature."

"I study alchemy in the library—not the kitchen," I snapped, forgetting to modulate my tone or accent. Kit's eyes widened. "Then I teach students about the subject at a university."

"They will let *women* teach at the university?" George said, fascinated and repelled in equal measure.

"Matriculate, too," Matthew murmured, pulling on the tip of his nose apologetically. "Diana went to Oxford."

"That must have improved attendance at lectures," Walter commented drily. "Had women been allowed at Oriel, even I might have taken another degree. And are lady scholars under attack in this future colony somewhere north of Roanoke?" It was a reasonable conclusion to have drawn from Matthew's story thus far.

"Not all of them, no. But Diana found a lost book at the university." The members of the School of Night pitched forward in their seats. Lost books were of far more interest to this group than were ignorant witches and lady scholars. "It contains secret information about the world of creatures."

"The Book of Mysteries that is supposed to tell of our creation?" Kit looked amazed. "You've never been interested in those fables before, Matthew. In fact, you've dismissed them as superstition."

"I believe in them now, Kit. Diana's discovery brought enemies to her door."

"And you were with her. So her enemies lifted the latch and entered." Walter shook his head.

"Why did Matthew's regard effect such dire consequences?" George asked. His fingers searched out the black grosgrain ribbon that tied his spectacles to the fastenings on his doublet. The doublet was fashionably puffed out over his stomach and the stuffing rustled like a bag of oatmeal whenever he moved. George lifted the round frames to his face and examined me as if I were an interesting new object of study.

"Because witches and *wearhs* are forbidden to marry," Kit said promptly. I'd never heard the word *wearh* before, with its whistling *w* at the beginning and guttural sound at the end.

"So are daemons and *wearhs.*" Walter clamped a warning hand on Kit's shoulder.

"Really?" George blinked at Matthew, then at me. "Does the queen forbid such a match?"

"It is an ancient covenant between creatures that none dares to disobey." Tom sounded frightened. "Those who do so are called to account by the Congregation and punished."

Only vampires as old as Matthew could remember a time before the covenant had established how creatures were to behave with one another and interact with the humans who surrounded us. "No fraternizing between otherworldly species" was the most important rule, and the Congregation policed the boundaries. Our talents—creativity, strength, supernatural power—were impossible to ignore in mixed groups. It was as if the power of a witch highlighted the creative energy of any nearby daemons, and the genius of a daemon made a vampire's beauty more striking. As for our relationships with humans, we were supposed to keep a low profile and steer clear of politics and religion.

Just this morning Matthew had insisted there were too many other problems facing the Congregation in the sixteenth century—religious war, the burning of heretics, and the popular hunger for the strange and bizarre newly fed by the technology of the printing press—for its members to bother with something so trivial as a witch and a vampire who had fallen in love. Given the bewildering and dangerous events that had taken place since I'd met Matthew in late September, I had found this difficult to believe.

"Which congregation?" George asked with interest. "Is this some new religious sect?"

Walter ignored his friend's question and gave Matthew a piercing look. Then he turned to me. "And do you still have this book?"

"No one has it. It went back into the library. The witches expect me to recall it for them."

"So you are hunted for two reasons. Some want to keep you from a *wearh,* others see you as a necessary means to a desired end." Walter pinched the bridge of his nose and looked at Matthew tiredly. "You are a veritable lodestone when it comes to trouble, my friend. And this couldn't have happened at a more inopportune time. The queen's anniversary celebration is less than three weeks away. You're expected at court."

"Never mind the queen's celebration! We are not safe with a time spinner in our midst. She can see what fate has in store for each of us. The witch will be able to undo our futures, cause ill fortune—even hasten our deaths." Kit rocketed out of his chair to stand before Matthew. "How by all that is holy could you do this?"

"It seems your much-vaunted atheism has failed you, Kit," said Matthew evenly. "Afraid you might have to answer for your sins after all?"

"I may not believe in a beneficent, all-powerful deity as you do, Matthew, but there is more to this world than what's described in your philosophy books. And this woman—this witch—cannot be allowed to meddle in our affairs. *You* may be in her thrall, but I have no intention of putting *my* future in her hands!" Kit retorted.

"A moment." A look of growing astonishment passed over George's face. "Did you come to us from Chester, Matthew, or—"

"No. You must not answer, Matt," Tom said with sudden lucidity. "Janus has come among us to work some purpose, and we must not interfere."

"Talk sense, Tom—if you can," Kit said nastily.

"With one face, Matthew and Diana look to the past. With the other, they consider the future," Tom said, unconcerned with Kit's interruption.

"But if Matt is not . . ." George trailed off into silence.

"Tom is right," Walter said gruffly. "Matthew is our friend and has asked for our help. It is, so far as I can recall, the first time he has done so. That is all we need to know."

"He asks too much," Kit retorted.

"Too much? It's little and late, in my opinion. Matthew paid for one of my ships, saved Henry's estates, and has long kept George and Tom in books and dreams. As for you"—Walter surveyed Marlowe from head to toe—"everything in you and on you—from your ideas to your last cup of wine to the hat on your head—is thanks to Matthew Roydon's good graces. Providing a safe port for his wife during this present tempest is a trifle in comparison."

"Thank you, Walter." Matthew looked relieved, but the smile he turned on me was tentative. Winning over his friends—Walter in particular—had been more difficult than he'd anticipated.

"We will need to devise a story to explain how your wife came to be here," Walter said thoughtfully, "something to divert attention from her strangeness."

"Diana needs a teacher, too," added Matthew.

"She must be taught some manners, certainly," Kit grumbled.

"No, her teacher must be another witch," Matthew corrected him.

Walter made a low sound of amusement. "I doubt there's a witch within twenty miles of Woodstock. Not with you living here."

"And what of this book, Mistress Roydon?" George whipped out a pointed gray stick wrapped in string from a pocket hidden away in the bulbous outlines of his short britches. He licked the tip of his pencil and held it expectantly. "Can you tell me its size and contents? I will look for it in Oxford."

"The book can wait," I said. "First I need proper clothes. I can't go out of the house wearing Pierre's jacket and the skirt that Matthew's sister wore to Jane Seymour's funeral."

"Go out of the house?" Kit scoffed. "Utter lunacy."

"Kit is right," George said apologetically. He made a notation in his book. "Your speech makes it apparent you are a stranger to England. I would be happy to give you elocution lessons, Mistress Roydon." The idea of George Chapman playing Henry Higgins to my Eliza Doolittle was enough to make me look longingly at the exit.

"She shouldn't be allowed to speak at all, Matt. You must keep her quiet," Kit insisted.

"What we need is a woman, someone to advise Diana. Why is there not one daughter, wife, or mistress to be had among the five of you?" Matthew demanded. Deep silence fell.

"Walter?" Kit asked archly, sending the rest of the men into a fit of laughter and lightening the heavy atmosphere as though a summer storm had blown through the room. Even Matthew joined in.

Pierre entered as the laughter faded, kicking up sprigs of rosemary and lavender strewn among the rushes laid down to keep dampness from being tromped through the house. At the same moment, the bells began to toll the hour of twelve. Like the sight of the quinces, the combination of sounds and smells took me straight back to Madison.

Past, present, and future met. Rather than a slow, fluid unspooling, there was a moment of stillness as if time had stopped. My breath hitched.

"Diana?" Matthew said, taking me by the elbows.

Something blue and amber, a weave of light and color, caught my attention. It was tightly meshed in the corner of the room, where nothing could fit but cobwebs and dust. Fascinated, I tried to move toward it.

"Is she having a fit?" Henry asked, his face coming into focus over Matthew's shoulder.

The tolling of the bell stopped, and the scent of lavender faded. Blue and amber flickered to gray and white before disappearing.

"I'm sorry. I thought I saw something in the corner. It must have been a trick of the light," I said, pressing my hand to my cheek.

"Perhaps you are suffering from timelag, *mon coeur,*" Matthew murmured. "I promised you a walk in the park. Will you go outside with me to clear your head?"

Maybe it was the aftereffects of timewalking, and perhaps fresh air would help. But we had just arrived, and Matthew hadn't seen these men for more than four centuries.

"You should be with your friends," I said firmly, though my eyes drifted to the windows.

"They'll still be here, drinking my wine, when we return," Matthew said with a smile. He turned to Walter. "I'm going to show Diana her house and make sure she is able to find her way through the gardens."

"We will need to talk further," Walter warned. "There is business to discuss."

Matthew nodded and tucked his hand around my waist. "It can wait."

We left the School of Night in the warm parlor and headed outdoors. Tom had already lost interest in the problems of vampire and witch and was engrossed in his reading. George was similarly consumed by his own thoughts and busily writing in a notebook. Kit's glance was watchful, Walter's wary, and Henry's eyes were filled with sympathy. The three men looked like an unkindness of ravens with their dark clothes and attentive expressions. It reminded me of what Shakespeare would soon say about this extraordinary group.

"How does it begin?" I murmured softly. "'*Black is the badge of hell*'?"

Matthew looked wistful. "'*Black is the badge of hell / The hue of dungeons, and the school of night.*'"

"The hue of friendship would be more accurate," I said. I'd seen Matthew manage the readers at the Bodleian, but his influence over the likes of Walter Raleigh and Kit Marlowe was still unexpected. "Is there anything they wouldn't do for you, Matthew?"

"Pray God we never find out," he said somberly.

On Monday morning I was tucked into Matthew's office. It was located between Pierre's apartments and a smaller chamber that was used for estate business, and it afforded a view toward the gatehouse and the Woodstock road.

Most of the lads—now that I knew them better, it seemed a far more fitting collective term than the grandiose School of Night—were closeted in what Matthew called the breakfast room, drinking ale and wine and applying their considerable imaginations to my backstory. Walter assured me it would, when complete, explain my sudden appearance at Woodstock to curious residents and alleviate questions about my odd accent and ways.

What they had concocted so far was melodramatic in the extreme. This was not surprising given that our two resident playwrights, Kit and George, came up with the key elements of the plot. The characters included dead French parents, avaricious noblemen who had preyed on a helpless orphan (me), and aged lechers intent on stripping me of my virtue. The tale turned epic with my spiritual trials and conversion from Catholicism to Calvinism. These led to voluntary exile on England's Protestant shores, years of abject poverty, and Matthew's fortuitous rescue and instantaneous regard. George (who really *was* something of a schoolmarm) promised to drill me in the particulars when they had applied the finishing touches to the story.

I was enjoying some quiet, which was a rare commodity in a crowded Elizabethan household of this size. Like a troublesome child, Kit unerringly gauged the worst moment to deliver the mail, announce dinner, or request Matthew's help with some problem. And Matthew was understandably eager to be with friends he had never expected to see again.

At present he was with Walter and I was devoting my attention to a small book while awaiting his return. He'd left his table by the window littered with bags of sharpened quills and glass pots full of ink. Other tools were scattered nearby: a stick of wax to seal his correspondence, a thin knife to open letters, a candle, a silver shaker. This last was full not of salt but sand, as my gritty eggs this morning had proved.

My table held a similar shaker to set the ink on the page and keep it from smudging, a single pot of black ink, and the remains of three pens. I was currently destroying a fourth in an effort to master the complicated swirls of Elizabethan handwriting. Making a to-do list should have been a snap. As a historian I had spent years reading old handwriting and knew exactly how the letters should look, what words were most common, and the erratic spelling choices that were mine to make in a time when there were few dictionaries and grammatical rules.

It turned out that the challenge lay not in knowing what to do but in actually doing it. After working for years to become an expert, I was a student again. Only this time my objective wasn't to understand the past but to live in it. Thus far it had been a humbling experience, and all I'd managed was to make a mess of the first page of the pocket-size blank book Matthew had given me this morning.

"It's the Elizabethan equivalent of a laptop computer," he'd explained, handing me the slim volume. "You're a woman of letters and need somewhere to put them."

I cracked the tight binding, releasing the crisp smell of paper. Most virtuous women of the time used these little books for prayers.

Diana

There was a thick blot where I'd pressed down at the beginning of the D and by the time I reached the last A the pen was out of ink. Still, my effort was a perfectly respectable example of the period's Italic hand. My hand moved far more slowly than Matthew's did when he wrote letters using the squiggly Secretary script. That was the handwriting of lawyers, doctors, and other professionals, but too difficult for me at present.

Bishop

That was even better. But my smile quickly dissolved, and I struck out my last name. I was married now. I dipped the pen in the ink.

de Clermont

Diana de Clermont. That made me sound like a countess, not a historian. A drop of ink fell wetly onto the page below. I stifled a curse at the black splotch. Happily, it hadn't obliterated my name. But that wasn't my name either. I smudged the blob over "de Clermont." You could still read it—barely. I steadied my hand and deliberately formed the correct letters.

Roydon.

That was my name now. Diana Roydon, wife of the most obscure figure associated with the mysterious School of Night. I examined the page critically. My handwriting was a disaster. It looked nothing like what I'd seen of the chemist Robert Boyle's neat, rounded script or that of his brilliant sister, Katherine. I hoped that women's handwriting in the 1590s was far messier than it was in the 1690s. A few more strokes of the pen and a final flourish and I would be done.

Her Booke.

Male voices sounded outside. I put down my pen with a frown and went to the window.

Matthew and Walter were below. The panes of glass muffled their words, but the subject of the conversation was evidently unpleasant, judging from Matthew's harried expression and the bristling line of Raleigh's eyebrows. When Matthew made a dismissive gesture and turned to walk away, Walter stopped him with a firm hand.

Something had been bothering Matthew since he'd received the first batch of mail this morning. A stillness had come over him, and he'd held the pouch without opening it. Though he'd explained that the letters dealt with ordinary estate business, surely there was more there than demands for taxes and bills due.

I pressed my warm palm against the cold pane as if it were only the glass that stood between me and Matthew. The play of temperatures reminded me of the contrast between warmblooded witch and cool-blooded vampire. I returned to my seat and picked up my pen.

"You decided to make your mark on the sixteenth century after all." Matthew was suddenly at my side. The twitch at the corner of his mouth indicated amusement but didn't entirely disguise his tension.

"I'm still not sure that creating a lasting memento of my time here is a good idea," I confessed. "A future scholar might realize there's something odd about it." *Just as Kit had known there was something wrong with me.*

"Don't worry. The book won't leave the house." Matthew reached for his stack of mail.

"You can't be sure of that," I protested.

"Let history take care of itself, Diana," he said decisively, as if the matter were now closed. But I couldn't let go of the future—or my worries about the effects that our presence in the past might have on it.

"I still don't think we should let Kit keep that chess piece." The memory of Marlowe triumphantly brandishing the tiny figure of Diana haunted me. She occupied the role of the white queen in Matthew's costly silver chess set and had been one of the objects I'd used to steer us to the proper place in the past. Two unfamiliar young daemons, Sophie Norman and her husband, Nathaniel Wilson, had unexpectedly delivered it to my aunts' house in Madison just as we were deciding to timewalk.

"Kit won it from me fair and square last night—just as he was supposed to do. At least this time I could see how he managed it. He distracted me with his rook." Matthew dashed off a note with enviable speed before folding the pages into a neat packet. He dropped a molten blob of vermilion across the edges of the letter before pressing his signet ring into it. The golden surface of the ring bore the simple glyph for the planet Jupiter, not the more elaborate emblem that Satu had burned into my flesh. The wax crackled as it cooled. "Somehow my white queen went from Kit to a family of witches in North Carolina. We have to believe that it will do so again, with or without our help."

"Kit didn't know me before. And he doesn't like me."

"All the more reason not to worry. As long as it pains him to look upon the likeness of Diana, he won't be able to part with it. Christopher Marlowe is a masochist of the first order." Matthew took up another letter and sliced it open with his knife.

I surveyed the other items on my table and picked up a pile of coins. A working knowledge of Elizabethan currency had not been covered in my graduate education. Nor had household management, the proper order of donning undergarments, forms of address for servants, or how to make a medicine for Tom's headache. Discussions with Françoise about my wardrobe revealed my ignorance of common names for ordinary colors. "Goose-turd green" was familiar to me, but the peculiar shade of grizzled brown known as "rat hair" was not. My experiences thus far had me planning to throttle the first Tudor historian I met upon my return for gross dereliction of duty.

But there was something compelling about figuring out the details of everyday life, and I quickly forgot my annoyance. I picked through the coins in my palm, looking for a silver penny. It was the cornerstone on which my precarious knowledge was built. The coin was no bigger than my thumbnail, as thin as a wafer, and bore the same profile of Queen Elizabeth as did most of the others. I organized the rest according to relative worth and began an orderly account of them on the next clean page in my book.

"Thank you, Pierre," Matthew murmured, barely glancing up as his servant whisked away the sealed letters and deposited still more correspondence on the surface.

We wrote in companionable silence. Soon finished with my list of coins, I tried to remember what Charles, the household's laconic cook, had taught me about making a caudle—or was it a posset?

> *A Caudle for pains in the head*

Satisfied with the relatively straight line of text, three tiny blots, and the wobbly *C,* I continued.

> *Set your water to boil. Beat two egge yolkes. Add white wine and beat some more. When the water boils, set it to cool, then add the wine and egge. Stirre it as it boils again, adding saffron and honey.*

The resulting mixture had been revolting—violently yellow with the consistency of runny cottage cheese—but Tom had slurped it down without complaint. Later, when I'd asked Charles for the proper proportion of honey to wine, he'd thrown up his hands in disgust at my ignorance and stalked away without a word.

Living in the past had always been my secret desire, but it was far more difficult than I'd ever imagined. I sighed.

"You'll need more than that book to feel at home here." Matthew's eyes didn't leave his correspondence. "You should have a room of your own, too. Why don't you take this one? It's bright enough to serve as a library. Or you could turn it into an alchemical laboratory—although you might want somewhere more private if you're planning to turn lead into gold. There's a room by the kitchen that might do."

"The kitchen may not be ideal. Charles doesn't approve of me," I replied.

"He doesn't approve of anyone. Neither does Françoise—except for Charles, of course, whom she venerates as a misunderstood saint despite his fondness for drink."

Sturdy feet tromped down the hall. The disapproving Françoise appeared at the threshold. "There are men here for Mistress Roydon," she announced, stepping aside to reveal a gray-haired septuagenarian with calloused hands and a much younger man who shifted from one foot to the other. Neither of these men was a creature.

"Somers." Matthew frowned. "And is that young Joseph Bidwell?"

"Aye, Master Roydon." The younger man pulled his cap from his head.

"Mistress Roydon will allow you to take her measurements now," Françoise said.

"Measurements?" The look Matthew directed to me and Françoise demanded an answer—quickly.

"Shoes. Gloves. For *madame*'s wardrobe," Françoise said. Unlike petticoats, shoes were not one-size-fits-most.

"I asked Françoise to send for them," I explained, hoping to gain Matthew's cooperation. Somers's eyes widened at my strange accent before his face returned to an expression of neutral deference.

"My wife's journey was unexpectedly difficult," Matthew said smoothly, coming to stand by my side, "and her belongings were lost. Regrettably, Bidwell, we have no shoes for you to copy." He rested a warning hand on my shoulder, hoping to silence any further commentary.

"May I, Mistress Roydon?" Bidwell asked, lowering himself until his fingers hovered over the ties that secured a pair of ill-fitting shoes to my feet. The borrowed footwear was a giveaway that I wasn't who I was pretending to be.

"Please," Matthew replied before I could respond. Françoise gave me a sympathetic look. She knew what it was like to be silenced by Matthew Roydon.

The young man started when he came into contact with a warm foot and its frequent pulse. Clearly he expected a colder, less lively extremity.

"About your business," Matthew said sharply.

"Sir. My lord. Master Roydon." The young man blurted out most available titles except for "Your Majesty" and "Prince of Darkness." These were implied nonetheless.

"Where's your father, lad?" Matthew's voice softened.

"Sick abed these four days past, Master Roydon." Bidwell drew a piece of felt from a bag tied around his waist and placed each of my feet on it, tracing the outlines with a stick of charcoal. He made some notations on the felt and, quickly finished, released my foot. Bidwell pulled out a curious book made from squares of colored hide sewn together with leather thongs and offered it to me.

"What colors are popular, Master Bidwell?" I asked, waving the leather samples away. I needed advice, not a multiple-choice test.

"Ladies who are going to court are having white stamped with gold or silver."

"We're not going to court," Matthew said swiftly.

"Black then, and a nice tawny." Bidwell held up for approval a patch of leather the color of caramel. Matthew gave it before I could say a word.

Then it was the older man's turn. He, too, was surprised when he took my hand and felt the calluses on my palms. Well-bred ladies who married men such as Matthew didn't row boats. Somers took in the lump on my middle finger. Ladies didn't have bumps from holding pens too tightly either. He slid a buttery-soft glove that was much too large onto my right hand. A needle charged with coarse thread was tucked into the hem.

"Does your father have everything he needs, Bidwell?" Matthew asked the shoemaker.

"Yes, thank you, Master Roydon," Bidwell replied with a bob of his head.

"Charles will send him custard and venison." Matthew's gray eyes flickered over the young man's thin frame. "Some wine, too."

"Master Bidwell will be grateful for your kindness," Somers said, his fingers drawing the thread through the leather so that the glove fit snugly.

"Is anyone else ill?" Matthew asked.

"Rafe Meadows's girl was sick with a terrible fever. We feared for Old Edward, but he is only afflicted with an ague," Somers replied tersely.

"I trust Meadows's daughter has recovered."

"No." Somers snapped the thread. "They buried her three days ago, God rest her soul."

"Amen," said everyone in the room. Françoise lifted her eyebrows and jerked her head in Somers's direction. Belatedly I joined in.

Their business concluded and the shoes and gloves promised for later in the week, both men bowed and departed. Françoise turned to follow them out, but Matthew stopped her.

"No more appointments for Diana." There was no mistaking the seriousness in his tone. "See to it that Edward Camberwell has a nurse to look after him and sufficient food and drink."

Françoise curtsied in acquiescence and departed with another sympathetic glance.

"I'm afraid the men from the village know I don't belong here." I drew a shaking hand across my forehead. "My vowels are a problem. And my sentences go down when they should go up. When are you supposed to say 'amen'? Somebody needs to teach me how to pray, Matthew. I have to start somewhere, and—"

"Slow down," he said, sliding his hands around my corseted waist. Even through several layers of clothing, his touch was soothing. "This isn't an Oxford viva, nor are you making your stage debut. Cramming information and rehearsing your lines isn't going to help. You should have asked me before you summoned Bidwell and Somers."

"How can you pretend to be someone new, someone else, over and over again?" I wondered. Matthew had done this countless times over the centuries as he pretended to die only to reemerge in a different country, speaking a different language, known by a different name.

"The first trick is to stop pretending." My confusion must have been evident, and he continued. "Remember what I told you in Oxford. You can't live a lie, whether it's masquerading as a human when you're really a witch or trying to pass as Elizabethan when you're from the twenty-first century. This is your life for now. Try not to think of it as a role."

"But my accent, the way that I walk . . ." Even I had noticed the length of my steps relative to that of the other women in the house, but Kit's open mockery of my masculine stride had brought the point home.

"You'll adjust. Meanwhile people will talk. But no one's opinion in Woodstock matters. Soon you will be familiar and the gossip will stop."

I looked at him doubtfully. "You don't know much about gossip, do you?"

"Enough to know you are simply this week's curiosity." He glanced at my book, taking in the blotches and indecisive script. "You're holding your pen too tightly. That's why the point keeps breaking and the ink won't flow. You're holding on to your new life too tightly as well."

"I never thought it would be so difficult."

"You're a fast learner, and so long as you're safely at the Old Lodge, you're among friends. But no more visitors for the time being. Now, what have you been writing?"

"My name, mostly."

Matthew flipped a few pages in my book, examining what I'd recorded.

One eyebrow lifted. "You've been preparing for your economics and culinary examinations, too. Why don't you write about what's happening here at the house instead?"

"Because I need to know how to manage in the sixteenth century. Of course, a diary might be useful, too." I considered the possibility. It would certainly help me sort out my still-muddled sense of time. "I shouldn't use full names. People in 1590 use initials to save paper and ink. And nobody reflects on thoughts or emotions. They record the weather and the phases of the moon."

"Top marks on sixteenth-century English record keeping," said Matthew with a laugh.

"Do women write down the same things as men?"

He took my chin in his fingers. "You're impossible. Stop worrying about what other women do. Be your own extraordinary self." When I nodded, he kissed me before returning to his table.

Holding the pen as loosely as possible, I began a fresh page. I decided to use astrological symbols for the days of the week and record the weather as well as a few cryptic notes about life at the Old Lodge. That way no one reading them in a future time would find anything out of the ordinary. Or so I hoped.

> ♄ *31 October 1590 rain, clearing*
> *On this day I was introduced to my husband's good friend CM*
>
> ☉ *1 November 1590 cold and dry*
> *In the early hours of the morning I made the acquaintance of GC. After sunrise, TH, HP, WR arrived, all friends of my husband. The moon was full.*

Some future scholar might suspect that these initials referred to the School of Night, especially given the name Roydon on the first page, but there would be no way to prove it. Besides, these days few scholars were interested in this group of intellectuals. Educated in the finest Renaissance style, the members of the School of Night were able to move between ancient and modern languages with alarming speed. All of them knew Aristotle backward and forward. And when Kit, Walter, and Matthew began talking politics, their encyclopedic command of history and geography made it nearly impossible for anyone else to keep up. Occasionally George and Tom managed to squeak in an opinion, but Henry's stammer and slight deafness made his full participation in the intricate discussions impossible. He spent most of the time quietly observing the others with a shy deference that was endearing, considering that the earl outranked everyone in the room. If there weren't so many of them, I might be able to keep up, too.

As for Matthew, gone was the thoughtful scientist brooding over his test results and worrying about the future of the species. I'd fallen in love with that Matthew but found myself doing so all over again with this sixteenth-century version, charmed by every peal of his laughter and each quick rejoinder he made when battles broke out over some fine point of philosophy. Matthew shared jokes over dinner and hummed songs in the corridors. He wrestled with his dogs by the fire in the bedroom—two enormous, shaggy mastiffs named Anaximander and Pericles. In modern Oxford or France, Matthew had always seemed slightly sad. But he was happy here in Woodstock, even when I caught him looking at his friends as though he couldn't quite believe they were real.

"Did you realize how much you missed them?" I asked, unable to refrain from interrupting his work.

"Vampires can't brood over those we leave behind," he replied. "We'd go mad. I have had more to remember them by than is usually the case: their words, their portraits. You forget the little things, though—a quirk of expression, the sound of their laughter."

"My father kept caramels in his pocket," I whispered. "I had no memory of them, until La Pierre." When I shut my eyes, I could still smell the tiny candies and hear the rustle of the cellophane against the soft broadcloth of his shirts.

"And you wouldn't give up that knowledge now," Matthew said gently, "not even to be rid of the pain."

He took up another letter, his pen scratching against the page. The tight look of concentration returned to his face, along with a small crease over the bridge of his nose. I imitated the angle at which he held the quill, the length of time that elapsed before he dipped it in the ink. It was indeed easier to write when you didn't hold the pen in a death grip. I poised the pen over the paper and prepared to write more.

Today was the feast of All Souls, the traditional day to remember the dead. Everyone in the house was remarking upon the thick frost that iced the leaves in the garden. Tomorrow would be even colder, Pierre promised.

☽ *2 November 1590 frost*
Measured for shoes and gloves. Françoise sewing.

Françoise was making me a cloak to keep the chill away, and a warm suit of clothes for the wintry weather ahead. She had been in the attics all morning, sorting through Louisa de Clermont's abandoned wardrobe. Matthew's sister's gowns were sixty years out of date, with their square necklines and bell-shaped sleeves, but Françoise was altering them to better fit what Walter and George insisted was the current style as well as my less statuesque frame. She wasn't pleased to be ripping apart the seams of one particularly splendid black-and-silver garment, but Matthew had insisted. With the School of Night in residence, I needed formal clothes as well as more practical outfits.

"But Lady Louisa was wed in that gown, my lord," Françoise protested.

"Yes, to an eighty-five-year-old with no living offspring, a bad heart, and numerous profitable estates. I believe the thing has more than repaid the family's investment in it," Matthew replied. "It will do for Diana until you can make her something better."

My book couldn't refer to that conversation, of course. Instead I'd chosen all my words carefully so that they would mean nothing to anyone else even though they conjured vivid images of particular people, sounds, and conversations for me. If this book survived, a future reader would find these tiny snippets of my life sterile and dry. Historians pored over documents like this, hoping in vain to see the rich, complex life hidden behind the simple lines of text.

Matthew swore under his breath. I was not the only one in this house hiding something.

My husband received many letters today and gave me this booke to keep my memories.

As I lifted my pen to replenish its ink, Henry and Tom entered the room looking for Matthew. My third eye blinked open, surprising me with sudden awareness. Since we had arrived, my other nascent powers—witchfire, witchwater, and witchwind—had been oddly absent. With the unexpected extra perception offered by my witch's third eye, I could discern not only the black-red intensity of the atmosphere around Matthew but also Tom's silvery light and Henry's barely perceptible green-black shimmer, each as individual as a fingerprint.

Thinking back on the threads of blue and amber that I'd seen in the corner of the Old Lodge, I wondered what the disappearance of some powers and the emergence of others might signify. There had been the episode this morning, too. . . .

Something in the corner had caught my eye, another glimmer of amber shot through with hints of blue. There was an echo, something so quiet it was more felt than heard. When I'd turned my head to locate its source, the sensation faded. Strands pulsed in my peripheral vision, as if time were beckoning me to return home.

Ever since my first timewalk in Madison, when I'd traveled a brief span of minutes, I'd thought of time as a substance made of threads of light and color. With enough concentration you could focus on a single thread and follow it to its source. Now, after walking through several centuries, I knew that apparent simplicity masked the knots of possibility that tied an unimaginable number of pasts to a million presents and untold potential futures. Isaac Newton had believed that time was an essential force of nature that couldn't be controlled. After fighting our way back to 1590, I was prepared to agree with him.

"Diana? Are you all right?" Matthew's insistent voice broke through my reveries. His friends looked at me with concern.

"Fine," I said automatically.

"You're not fine." He tossed the quill onto the table. "Your scent has changed. I think your magic might be changing, too. Kit is right. We must find you a witch as quickly as possible."

"It's too soon to bring in a witch," I protested. "It's important that I be able to look and sound as if I belong."

"Another witch will know you're a timewalker," he said dismissively. "She'll make allowances. Or is there something else?"

I shook my head, unwilling to meet his eyes.

Matthew hadn't needed to see time unwinding in the corner to sense that something was out of joint. If he already suspected that there was more going on with my magic than I was willing to reveal, there would be no way for me to conceal my secrets from any witch who might soon come to call.

4

The School of Night had been eager to help Matthew find the creature. Their suggestions illuminated a collective disregard for women, witches, and everyone who lacked a university education. Henry thought London might provide the most fertile ground for the search, but Walter assured him that it would be impossible to conceal me from superstitious neighbors in the crowded city. George wondered if the scholars of Oxford might be persuaded to lend their expertise, since they at least had proper intellectual credentials. Tom and Matthew gave a brutal critique of the strengths and weaknesses of the natural philosophers in residence, and that idea was cast aside, too. Kit didn't believe it was wise to trust any woman with the task and drew up a list of local gentlemen who might be willing to establish a training regimen for me. It included the parson of St. Mary's, who was alert to apocalyptic signs in the heavens, a nearby landowner named Smythson, who dabbled in alchemy and had been looking for a witch or daemon to assist him, and a student at Christ Church College who paid his overdue book bills by casting horoscopes.

Matthew vetoed all these suggestions and called on Widow Beaton, Woodstock's cunning woman and midwife. She was poor and female—precisely the sort of creature the School of Night scorned—but this, Matthew argued, would better ensure her cooperation. Besides, Widow Beaton was the only creature for miles with purported magical talents. All others had long since fled, he admitted, rather than live near a *wearh*.

"Summoning Widow Beaton may not be a good idea," I said later when we were getting ready for bed.

"So you've mentioned," Matthew replied with barely concealed impatience. "But if Widow Beaton can't help us, she'll be able to recommend someone who can."

"The late sixteenth century really isn't a good time to openly ask around for a witch, Matthew." I'd been able to do little more than hint at the prospect of witch-hunts when we were with the School of Night, but Matthew knew the horrors to come. Once again he dismissed my concern.

"The Chelmsford witch trials are only memories now, and it will be another twenty years before the Lancashire hunts begin. I wouldn't have brought you here if a witch-hunt were about to break out in England." Matthew picked through a few letters that Pierre had left for him on the table.

"With reasoning like that, it's a good thing you're a scientist and not a historian," I said bluntly. "Chelmsford and Lancashire were extreme outbursts of far more widespread concerns."

"You think a historian can understand the tenor of the present moment better than the men living through it?" Matthew's eyebrow cocked up in open skepticism.

"Yes," I said, bristling. "We often do."

"That's not what you said this morning when you couldn't figure out why there weren't any forks in the house," he observed. It was true that I'd searched high and low for twenty minutes before Pierre gently broke it to me that the utensils were not yet common in England.

"Surely you aren't one of those people who believe that historians do nothing but memorize dates and learn obscure facts," I said. "My job is to understand *why* things happened in the past. When something occurs right in front of you, it's hard to see the reasons for it, but hindsight provides a clearer perspective."

"Then you can relax, because I have both experience *and* hindsight," Matthew said. "I understand your reservations, Diana, but calling on Widow Beaton is the right decision." *Case closed,* his tone made clear.

"In the 1590s there are food shortages, and people are worried about the future," I said, ticking the items off on my fingers. "That means people are looking for scapegoats to take the blame for the bad times. Already, human cunning women and midwives fear being accused of witchcraft, though your male friends may not be aware of it."

"I am the most powerful man in Woodstock," Matthew said, taking me by the shoulders. "No one will accuse you of anything." I was amazed at his hubris.

"I'm a stranger, and Widow Beaton owes me nothing. If I draw curious eyes, I pose a serious threat to her safety," I retorted. "At the very least, I need to pass as an upper-class Elizabethan woman before we ask her for help. Give me a few more weeks."

"This can't wait, Diana," he said brusquely.

"I'm not asking you to be patient so I can learn how to embroider samplers and make jam. There are good reasons for it." I looked at him sourly. "Call in your cunning woman. But don't be surprised when this goes badly."

"Trust me." Matthew lowered his lips toward mine. His eyes were smoky, and his instincts to pursue his prey and push it into submission were sharp. Not only did the sixteenth-century husband want to prevail over his wife, but the vampire wanted to capture the witch.

"I don't find arguments the slightest bit arousing," I said, turning my head. Matthew clearly did, however. I moved a few inches away from him.

"I'm not arguing," Matthew said softly, his mouth close to my ear. "You are. And if you think I would ever touch you in anger, wife, you are very much mistaken." After pinning me to the bedpost with frosty eyes, he turned and snatched up his breeches. "I'm going downstairs. Someone will still be awake to keep me company." He stalked toward the door. Once he'd reached it, he paused.

"And if you really want to behave like an Elizabethan woman, stop questioning me," he said roughly as he departed.

The next day one vampire, two daemons, and three humans examined my appearance in silence across the wide floorboards. The bells of St. Mary's Church sounded the hour, faint echoes of their music lingering long after the peals ceased. Quince, rosemary, and lavender scented the air. I was perched on an uncomfortable wooden chair in a confining array of smocks, petticoats, sleeves, skirts, and a tightly laced bodice. My career-oriented, twenty-first-century life faded further with each restricted breath. I stared out into the murky daylight, where cold rain pinged against the panes of glass in the leaded windows.

"Elle est ici," Pierre announced, his glance flicking in my direction. "The witch is here to see *madame.*"

"At last," Matthew said. The severe lines of his doublet made him look even broader through the shoulders, while the acorns and oak leaves stitched in black around the edges of his white collar accentuated the paleness of his skin. He angled his dark head to gain a fresh perspective on whether I passed muster as a respectable Elizabethan wife.

"Well?" he demanded. "Will that do?"

George lowered his spectacles. "Yes. The russet of this gown suits her far better than the last one did and gives a pleasant cast to her hair."

"Mistress Roydon looks the part, George, it is true. But we cannot explain away her unusual speech simply by saying that she comes from the c-c-country," Henry said in his toneless bass. He stepped forward to twitch the folds of my brocade skirt into place. "And her height. There is no disguising that. She is taller even than the queen."

"Are you sure we can't pass her off as French, Walt, or Dutch?" Tom lifted a clove-studded orange to his nose with ink-stained fingers. "Perhaps Mistress Roydon could survive in London after all. Daemons cannot fail to notice her, of course, but ordinary men may not give her a second glance."

Walter snorted with amusement and unspooled from a low settle. "Mistress Roydon is finely shaped as well as uncommon tall. Ordinary men between the ages of thirteen and sixty will find reason enough to study her. No, Tom, she's better off here, with Widow Beaton."

"Perhaps I could meet Widow Beaton later, in the village, alone?" I suggested, hoping that one of them might see sense and persuade Matthew to let me do this my way.

"No!" cried out six horrified male voices.

Françoise appeared bearing two pieces of starched linen and lace, her bosom swelling like that of an indignant hen facing down a pugnacious rooster. She was as annoyed by Matthew's constant interference as I was.

"Diana's not going to court. That ruff is unnecessary," said Matthew with an impatient gesture. "Besides, it's her hair that's the problem."

"You have no idea what's necessary," Françoise retorted. Though she was a vampire and I was a witch, we had reached unexpected common ground when it came to the idiocy of men. "Which would Madame de Clermont prefer?" She extended a pleated nest of gauzy fabric and something crescent-shaped that resembled snowflakes joined together with invisible stitches.

The snowflakes looked more comfortable. I pointed to them.

While Françoise affixed the collar to the edge of my bodice, Matthew reached up in another attempt to put my hair in a more pleasing arrangement. Françoise slapped his hand away. "Don't touch."

"I'll touch my wife when I like. And stop calling Diana 'Madame de Clermont,'" Matthew rumbled, moving his hands to my shoulders. "I keep expecting my mother to walk through the door." He drew the edges of the collar apart, pulling loose the black velvet cord that hid Françoise's pins.

"*Madame* is a married woman. Her bosom should be covered. There is enough gossip about the new mistress," Françoise protested.

"Gossip? What kind of gossip?" I asked with a frown.

"You were not in church yesterday, so there is talk that you are with child, or afflicted by smallpox. That heretic priest believes you are Catholic. Others say you are Spanish."

"Spanish?"

"*Oui, madame.* Someone heard you in the stables yesterday afternoon."

"But I was practicing my French!" I was a fair mimic and thought that imitating Ysabeau's imperious accent might lend credence to my elaborate cover story.

"The groom's son did not recognize it as such." Françoise's tone suggested that the boy's confusion was warranted. She studied me with satisfaction. "Yes, you look like a respectable woman."

"Fallaces sunt rerum species," said Kit with a touch of acid that brought the scowl back to Matthew's face. "'*Appearances can be deceiving.'* No one will be taken in by her performance."

"It's far too early in the day for Seneca." Walter gave Marlowe a warning look.

"It is never too early for stoicism," Kit replied severely. "You should thank me that it's not Homer. All we've heard lately is inept paraphrases of the *Iliad.* Leave the Greek to someone who understands it, George—someone like Matt."

"My translation of Homer's work is not yet finished!" George retorted, bristling.

His response released a flood of Latin quotations from Walter. One of them made Matthew chuckle, and he said something in what I suspected was Greek. The witch waiting downstairs completely forgotten, the men enthusiastically engaged in their favorite pastime: verbal one-upmanship. I sank back into my chair.

"When they are in a fine humor like this, they are a wonder," Henry whispered. "These are the keenest wits in the kingdom, Mistress Roydon."

Raleigh and Marlowe were now shouting at each other about the merits—or lack thereof—of Her Majesty's policies on colonization and exploration.

"One might as well take fistfuls of gold and dump them into the Thames as give them to an adventurer like you, Walter," Kit chortled.

"Adventurer! You can't step out of your own door in daylight for fear of your creditors." Raleigh's voice shook. "You can be such a fool, Kit."

Matthew had been following the volleys with increasing amusement.

"Who are you in trouble with now?" he asked Marlowe, reaching for his wine. "And how much is it going to cost to get you out of it?"

"My tailor." Kit waved a hand over his expensive suit. "The printer for *Tamburlaine.*" He hesitated, prioritizing the outstanding sums. "Hopkins, that bastard who calls himself my landlord. But I do have this." Kit held up the tiny figure of Diana that he'd won from Matthew when they played chess on Sunday night. Still anxious about letting the statue out of my sight, I inched forward.

"You can't be so hard up as to pawn that bauble for pennies." Matthew's eyes flickered to me, and a small movement of his hand had me sinking back again. "I'll take care of it."

Marlowe bounded to his feet with a grin, pocketing the silver goddess. "You can always be counted on, Matt. I'll pay you back, of course."

"Of course," Matthew, Walter, and George murmured doubtfully.

"Keep enough money to buy yourself a beard, though." Kit stroked his own with satisfaction. "You look dreadful."

"Buy a beard?" I couldn't possibly have understood correctly. Marlowe must be using slang again, even though Matthew had asked him to stop on my account.

"There's a barber in Oxford who is a wizard. Your husband's hair grows slowly, as with all of his kind, and he's clean shaven." When I still looked blank, Kit continued with exaggerated patience. "Matt will be noticed, looking as he does. He needs a beard. Apparently you are not witch enough to provide him with one, so we will have to find someone else to do it."

My eyes strayed to the empty jug on the elm table. Françoise had filled it with clippings from the garden—sprigs of holly oak, branches from a medlar with their brown fruit resembling rose hips, and a few white roses—to bring some color and scent into the room. A few hours ago, I had laced my fingers through the branches to tug the roses and medlars to the forefront of the vase, wondering about the garden all the while. I was pleased with the results for about fifteen seconds, until the flowers and fruit withered before my eyes. The desiccation spread from my fingertips in all directions, and my hands tingled with an influx of information from the plants: the feel of sunlight, the quenching sensation of rain, the strength in the roots that came from resisting the pull of the wind, the taste of the soil.

Matthew was right. Now that we were in 1590, my magic was changing. Gone were the eruptions of witchfire, witchwater, and witchwind that I had experienced after meeting Matthew. Instead I was seeing the bright threads of time and the colorful auras that surrounded living creatures. A white stag stared at me from the shadows under the oaks whenever I walked in the gardens. Now I was making things wither.

"Widow Beaton is waiting," Walter reminded us, ushering Tom toward the door.

"What if she can hear my thoughts?" I worried as we descended the wide oak stairs.

"I'm more worried about what you might say aloud. Do nothing that might stir her jealousy or animosity," Walter advised, following behind with the rest of the School of Night. "If all else fails, lie. Matthew and I do it all the time."

"One witch can't lie to another."

"This will not end well," Kit muttered darkly. "I'd wager money on it."

"Enough." Matthew whirled and grabbed Kit by the collar. The pair of English mastiffs sniffed and growled at Kit's ankles. They were devoted to Matthew—and none too fond of Kit.

"All I said—" Kit began, squirming in an attempt to escape. Matthew gave him no opportunity to finish and jacked him against the wall.

"What you said is of no interest, and what you meant was clear enough." Matthew's grip tightened.

"Put him down." Walter had one hand on Marlowe's shoulder and the other on Matthew. The vampire ignored Raleigh and lifted his friend several more inches. In his red-and-black plumage, Kit looked like an exotic bird that had somehow become trapped in the folds of the carved wooden paneling. Matthew held him there for a few more moments to make his point clear, then let him drop.

"Come, Diana. Everything is going to be fine." Matthew still sounded sure, but an ominous pricking in my thumbs warned me that Kit just might be right.

"God's teeth," Walter muttered in disbelief as we processed into the hall. "Is that Widow Beaton?"

At the far end of the room, standing in the shadows, was the witch from central casting: diminutive, bent, and ancient. As we drew closer, the details of her rusty black dress, stringy white hair, and leathery skin became more apparent. One of her eyes was milky with a cataract, the other a mottled hazel. The eyeball with the cataract had an alarming tendency to swivel in its socket, as though its sight might be improved with a different perspective. Just when I thought it couldn't get worse, I spotted the wart on the bridge of her nose.

Widow Beaton slid a glance in my direction and dipped into a grudging curtsy. The barely perceptible tingle on my skin suggested that she was indeed a witch. Without warning, my third eye fluttered open, looking for further information. Unlike most other creatures, however, Widow Beaton gave off no light at all. She was gray through and through. It was dispiriting to see a witch try so hard to be invisible. Had I been as pallid as that before I touched Ashmole 782? My third eye drooped closed again.

"Thank you for coming to see us, Widow Beaton." Matthew's tone suggested that she should be glad he'd let her into his house.

"Master Roydon." The witch's words rasped like the fallen leaves that swirled on the gravel outside. She turned her one good eye on me.

"Help Widow Beaton to her seat, George."

Chapman leaped forward at Matthew's command, while the rest of us remained at a careful distance. The witch groaned as her rheumatic limbs settled into the chair. Matthew politely waited as she did so, then continued.

"Let us get straight to the heart of the matter. This woman"—he indicated me—"is under my protection and has been having difficulties of late." Matthew made no mention of our marriage.

"You are surrounded by influential friends and loyal servants, Master Roydon. A poor woman can be of little use to a gentleman such as you." Widow Beaton tried to hide the reproach in her words with a false note of courtesy, but my husband had excellent hearing. His eyes narrowed.

"Do not play games with me," he said shortly. "You do not want me as an enemy, Widow Beaton. The woman shows signs of being a witch and needs your help."

"A witch?" Widow Beaton looked politely doubtful. "Was her mother a witch? Or her father a wizard?"

"Both died when she was still a child. We are not certain what powers they possessed," Matthew admitted, telling one of his typically vampiric half-truths. He tossed a small bag of coins into her lap. "I would be grateful if you could examine her."

"Very well." Widow Beaton's gnarled fingers reached for my face. When our flesh touched, an unmistakable surge of energy passed between us. The old woman jumped.

"So?" Matthew demanded.

Widow Beaton's hands dropped to her lap. She clutched at the pouch of money, and for a moment it seemed as though she might hurl it back at him. Then she regained her composure.

"It is as I suspected. This woman is no witch, Master Roydon." Her voice was even, though a bit higher than it had been. A wave of contempt rose from my stomach and filled my mouth with bitterness.

"If you think that, you don't have as much power as the people of Woodstock imagine," I retorted.

Widow Beaton drew herself up indignantly. "I am a respected healer, with a knowledge of herbs to protect men and women from illness. Master Roydon knows my abilities."

"That is the craft of a witch. But our people have other talents as well," I said carefully. Matthew's fingers were painfully tight on my hand, urging me to be silent.

"I know of no such talents," was her quick reply. The old woman was as obstinate as my Aunt Sarah and shared her disdain for witches like me who could draw on the elements without any careful study of the witch's craft tradition. Sarah knew the uses of every herb and plant and could remember hundreds of spells perfectly, but there was more to being a witch. Widow Beaton knew that, even if she wouldn't admit it.

"Surely there is some way to determine the extent of this woman's powers beyond a simple touch. Someone with your abilities must know what they are," Matthew said, his lightly mocking tone a clear challenge. Widow Beaton looked uncertain, weighing the pouch in her hand. In the end its heaviness convinced her to rise to the contest. She slipped the payment into a pocket concealed under her skirts.

"There are tests to determine whether someone is a witch. Some rely on the recitation of a prayer. If a creature stumbles over the words, hesitates even for a moment, then it is a sign that the devil is near," she pronounced, adopting a mysterious tone.

"The devil is not abroad in Woodstock, Widow Beaton," Tom said. He sounded like a parent trying to convince a child there wasn't a monster under the bed.

"The devil is everywhere, sir. Those who believe otherwise fall prey to his wiles."

"These are human fables meant to frighten the superstitious and the weak-minded," said Tom dismissively.

"Not now, Tom," Walter muttered.

"There are other signs, too," George said, eager as ever to share his knowledge. "The devil marks a witch as his own with scars and blemishes."

"Indeed, sir," Widow Beaton said, "and wise men know to look for them."

My blood drained from my head in a rush, leaving me dizzy. If anyone were to do so, such marks would be found on me.

"There must be other methods," Henry said uneasily.

"Yes there are, my lord." Widow Beaton's milky eye swept the room. She pointed at the table with its scientific instruments and piles of books. "Join me there."

Widow Beaton's hand slid through the same gap in her skirts that had provided a hiding place for her coins and drew out a battered brass bell. She set it on the table. "Bring a candle, if you please."

Henry quickly obliged, and the men drew around, intrigued.

"Some say a witch's true power comes from being a creature between life and death, light and darkness. At the crossroads of the world, she can undo the work of nature and unravel the ties that bind the order of things." Widow Beaton pulled one of the books into alignment between the candle in its heavy silver holder and the brass bell. Her voice dropped. "When her neighbors discovered a witch in times past, they cast her out of the church by the ringing of a bell to indicate that she was dead." Widow Beaton lifted the bell and set it tolling with a twist of her wrist. She released it, and the bell remained suspended over the table, still chiming. Tom and Kit edged forward, George gasped, and Henry crossed himself. Widow Beaton looked pleased with their reaction and turned her attention to the English translation of a Greek classic, *Euclid's Elements of Geometrie,* which rested on the table with several mathematical instruments from Matthew's extensive collection.

"Then the priest took up a holy book—a Bible—and closed it to show that the witch was denied access to God." The *Elements of Geometrie* snapped shut. George and Tom jumped. The members of the School of Night were surprisingly susceptible for men who considered themselves immune to superstition.

"Finally the priest snuffed out a candle, to signify that the witch had no soul." Widow Beaton's fingers reached into the flame and pinched the wick. The light went out, and a thin plume of gray smoke rose into the air.

The men were mesmerized. Even Matthew looked unsettled. The only sound in the room was the crackle of the fire and the constant, tinny ringing of the bell.

"A true witch can relight the fire, open the pages of the book, and stop the bell from ringing. She is a wonderful creature in the eyes of God." Widow Beaton paused for dramatic effect, and her milky eye rolled in my direction. "Can you perform these acts, girl?"

When modern witches reached the age of thirteen, they were presented to the local coven in a ceremony eerily reminiscent of Widow Beaton's tests. Witches' altar bells rang to welcome the young witch into the community, though they were typically fashioned from heavy silver, polished and passed down from one generation to the next. Instead of a Bible or a book of mathematics, the young witch's family spell book was brought in to lend the weight of history to the occasion. The only time Sarah had allowed the Bishop grimoire out of the house was on my thirteenth birthday. As for the candle, its placement and purpose were the same. It was why young witches practiced igniting and extinguishing candles from an early age.

My official presentation to the Madison coven had been a disaster, one witnessed by all my relatives. Two decades later I still had the odd nightmare about the candle that would not light, the book that refused to open, the bell that rang for every other witch but not for me. "I'm not sure," I confessed hesitantly.

"Try," Matthew encouraged, his voice confident. "You lit some candles a few days ago."

It was true. I had eventually been able to illuminate the jack-o'-lanterns that lined the driveway of the Bishop house on Halloween. There had been no audience to watch my initial bungled attempts, however. Today Kit's and Tom's eyes nudged me expectantly. I could barely feel the brush of Widow Beaton's glance but was all too aware of Matthew's familiar, cool attention. The blood in my veins turned to ice in response, as if refusing to generate the fire that would be required for this bit of witchcraft. Hoping for the best, I concentrated on the candle's wick and muttered the spell.

Nothing happened.

"Relax," Matthew murmured. "What about the book? Should you start there?"

Putting aside the fact that the proper order of things was important in witchcraft, I didn't know where to begin with *Euclid's Elements.* Was I supposed to focus on the air trapped in the fibers of the paper or summon a breeze to lift the cover? It was impossible to think clearly with the incessant ringing.

"Can you please stop the bell?" I implored as my anxiety rose.

Widow Beaton snapped her fingers, and the brass bell dropped to the table. It gave a final clang that set its misshapen edges vibrating, then fell silent.

"It is as I told you, Master Roydon," Widow Beaton said with a note of triumph. "Whatever magic you think you have witnessed, it was nothing but illusions. This woman has no power. The village has nothing to fear from her."

"Perhaps she is trying to trap you, Matthew," Kit chimed in. "I wouldn't put it past her. Women are duplicitous creatures."

Other witches had made the same proclamation as Widow Beaton, and with similar satisfaction. I had a sudden, intense need to prove her wrong and wipe the knowing look from Kit's face.

"I can't light a candle. And no one has been able to teach me how to open a book or stop a bell from ringing. But if I am powerless, how do you explain this?" A bowl of fruit sat nearby. More quinces, freshly picked from the garden, glowed golden in the bleak light. I selected one and balanced it on my palm where everyone could see it.

The skin on my palm tingled as I focused on the fruit nestled there. Its pulpy flesh was clear to me through the quince's tough skin as though the fruit were made of glass. My eyes drifted closed, while my witch's eye opened and began its search for information. Awareness crept from the center of my forehead, down my arm, and through my fingertips. It extended like the roots of a tree, its fibers snaking into the quince.

One by one I took hold of the fruit's secrets. There was a worm at its core, munching its way through the soft flesh. My attention was caught by the power trapped there, and warmth tingled across my tongue in a taste of sunshine. The skin between my brows fluttered with pleasure as I drank in the light of the invisible sun. *So much power,* I thought. *Life. Death.* My audience faded into insignificance. The only thing that mattered now was the limitless possibility for knowledge resting in my hand.

The sun responded to some silent invitation and left the quince, traveling into my fingers. Instinctively I tried to resist the approaching sunlight and keep it where it belonged—in the fruit—but the quince turned brown, shriveling and sinking into itself.

Widow Beaton gasped, breaking my concentration. Startled, I dropped the misshapen fruit to the floor, where it splattered against the polished wood. When I looked up, Henry was crossing himself again, shock evident in the force of his stare and the slow, automatic movements of his hand. Tom and Walter were focused on my fingers instead, where minuscule strands of sunlight were making a futile attempt to mend the broken connection with the quince. Matthew enfolded my sputtering hands in his, obscuring the signs of my undisciplined power. My hands were still sparking, and I tried to pull away so as not to scorch him. He shook his head, hands steady, and met my eyes as though to say he was strong enough to absorb whatever magic might come his way. After a moment of hesitation, my body relaxed into his.

"It's over. No more," he said emphatically.

"I can *taste* sunlight, Matthew." My voice was sharp with panic. "I can *see* time, waiting in the corners."

"That woman has bewitched a *wearh*. This is the devil's work," Widow Beaton hissed. She was backing carefully away, her fingers forked to ward off danger.

"There is no devil in Woodstock," Tom repeated firmly.

"You have books full of strange sigils and magical incantations," Widow Beaton said, gesturing at *Euclid's Elements*. It was, I thought, a very good thing that she hadn't overheard Kit reading aloud from *Doctor Faustus*.

"That is mathematics, not magic," protested Tom.

"Call it what you will, but I have seen the truth. You are just like them, and called me here to draw me into your dark plans."

"Just like whom?" Matthew asked sharply.

"The scholars from the university. They drove two witches from Duns Tew with their questions. They wanted our knowledge but condemned the women who shared it. And a coven was just beginning to form in Faringdon, but the witches scattered when they caught the attention of men like you." A coven meant safety, protection, community. Without a coven a witch was far more vulnerable to the jealousy and fear of her neighbors.

"No one is trying to force you from Woodstock." I only meant to soothe her, but a single step in her direction sent her retreating further.

"There is evil in this house. Everyone in the village knows it. Yesterday Mr. Danforth preached to the congregation about the danger of letting it take root."

"I am alone, a witch like you, without family to help me," I said, trying to appeal to her sympathy. "Take pity on me before anyone else discovers what I am."

"You are not like me, and I want no trouble. None will give me pity when the village is baying for blood. I have no *wearh* to protect me, and no lords and court gentlemen will step forward to defend my honor."

"Matthew—Master Roydon—will not let any harm come to you." My hand rose in a pledge.

Widow Beaton was incredulous. "*Wearhs* cannot be trusted. What would the village do if they found out what Matthew Roydon really is?"

"This matter is between us, Widow Beaton," I warned.

"Where are you from, girl, that you believe one witch will shelter another? It is a dangerous world. None of us are safe any longer." The old woman looked at Matthew with hatred. "Witches are dying in the thousands, and the cowards of the Congregation do nothing. Why is that, *wearh*?"

"That's enough," Matthew said coldly. "Françoise, please show Widow Beaton out."

"I'll leave, and gladly." The old woman drew herself as straight as her gnarled bones would allow. "But mark my words, Matthew Roydon. Every creature within a day's journey suspects that you are a foul beast who feeds on blood. When they discover you are harboring a witch with these dark powers, God will be merciless on those who have turned against Him."

"Farewell, Widow Beaton." Matthew turned his back on the witch, but Widow Beaton was determined to have the last word.

"Take care, sister," Widow Beaton called as she departed. "You shine too brightly for these times."

Every eye in the room was on me. I shifted, uncomfortable from the attention.

"Explain yourself," Walter said curtly.

"Diana owes you no explanation," Matthew shot back.

Walter raised his hand in silent truce.

"What happened?" Matthew asked in a more measured tone. Apparently I owed *him* one.

"Exactly what I predicted: We've frightened off Widow Beaton. She'll do everything she can to distance herself from me now."

"She should have been biddable. I've done the woman plenty of favors," Matthew muttered.

"Why didn't you tell her who I was to you?" I asked quietly.

"Probably for the same reason you didn't tell me what you could do to ordinary fruit from the garden," he retorted, taking me by the elbow. Matthew turned to his friends. "I need to speak to my wife. Alone." He steered me outside.

"So now I'm your wife again!" I exclaimed, wrenching my elbow from his grip.

"You never stopped being my wife. But not everybody needs to know the details of our private life. Now, what happened in there?" he demanded, standing by one of the neatly clipped knots of boxwood in the garden.

"You were right before: My magic is changing." I looked away. "Something like it happened earlier to the flowers in our bedroom. When I rearranged them, I tasted the soil and air that made them grow. The flowers died at my touch. I tried to make the sunlight return to the fruit. But it wouldn't obey me."

"Widow Beaton's behavior should have unleashed witchwind because you felt trapped, or witchfire because you were in danger. Perhaps timewalking damaged your magic," Matthew suggested with a frown.

I bit my lip. "I should never have lost my temper and shown her what I could do."

"She knew you were powerful. The smell of her fear filled the room." His eyes were grave. "Perhaps it was too soon to put you in front of a stranger."

But it was too late now.

The School of Night appeared at the windows, their pale faces pressing against the glass like stars in a nameless constellation.

"The damp will ruin her gown, Matthew, and it's the only one that looks decent on her," George scolded, sticking his head out of the casement. Tom's elfin face peeked around George's shoulder.

"I enjoyed myself immensely!" Kit shouted, flinging open another window with so much force the panes rattled. "That hag is the perfect witch. I shall put Widow Beaton in one of my plays. Did you ever imagine she could do that with an old bell?"

"Your past history with witches has not been forgotten, Matthew," Walter said, his feet crunching across the gravel as he and Henry joined us outside. "She will talk. Women like Widow Beaton always do."

"If she speaks out against you, Matt, is there a reason for concern?" Henry inquired gently.

"We're creatures, Hal, in a human world. There's always reason for concern," Matthew said grimly.

The School of Night might debate philosophy, but on one point they were agreed: A witch would still have to be found. Matthew dispatched George and Kit to make inquiries in Oxford, as well as to ask after our mysterious alchemical manuscript.

After supper on Thursday evening, we took our places around the hearth in the great hall. Henry and Tom read and argued about astronomy or mathematics. Walter and Kit played dice at a long table, trading ideas about their latest literary projects. I was reading aloud from Walter's copy of *The Faerie Queene* to practice my accent and enjoying it no more than I did most Elizabethan romances.

"The beginning is too abrupt, Kit. You'll frighten the audience so badly they'll leave the playhouse before the second scene," Walter protested. "It needs more adventure." They had been dissecting *Doctor Faustus* for hours. Thanks to Widow Beaton, it had a new opening.

"You are not my Faustus, Walt, for all your intellectual pretentions," Kit said sharply. "Look what your meddling did to Edmund's story. *The Faerie Queene* was a perfectly enjoyable tale about King Arthur. Now it's a calamitous blend of Malory and Virgil, it wends on and on, and Gloriana—please. The queen is nearly as old as Widow Beaton and just as crotchety. It will astonish me if Edmund finishes it, with you telling him what to do all the time. If you want to be immortalized on the boards, talk to Will. He's always hard up for ideas."

"Is that agreeable to you, Matthew?" George prompted. He was updating us on his search for the manuscript that would one day be known as Ashmole 782.

"I'm sorry, George. Did you say something?" There was a flash of guilt in Matthew's distracted gray eyes. I knew the signs of mental multitasking. It had gotten me through many a faculty meeting. His thoughts were probably divided among the conversations in the room, his ongoing review of what went awry with Widow Beaton, and the contents of the mailbags that continued to arrive.

"None of the booksellers have heard of a rare alchemical work circulating in the city. I asked a friend at Christ Church, and he too knows nothing. Shall I keep asking for it?"

Matthew opened his mouth to respond, but a crash sounded in the front hallway as the heavy front door flew open. He was on his feet in an instant. Walter and Henry jumped up and scrabbled for their daggers, which they'd taken to wearing morning, noon, and night.

"Matthew?" boomed an unfamiliar voice with a timbre that instinctively raised the hairs on my arms. It was too clear and musical to be human. "Are you here, man?"

"Of course he's here," someone else replied, his voice lilting in the cadence of a Welsh native. "Use your nose. Who else smells like a grocer's shop the day fresh spices arrive from the docks?"

Moments later two bulky figures swathed in rough brown cloaks appeared at the other end of the room, where Kit and George still sat with their dice and books. In my own time, professional football teams would have recruited the new arrivals. They had overdeveloped arms with prominent tendons, enlarged wrists, thickly muscled legs, and brawny shoulders. As the men drew closer, light from the candles caught their bright eyes and danced off the honed edges of their weapons. One was a blond giant an inch taller than Matthew; the other was a redhead a good six inches shorter with a decided squint to his left eye. Neither could be more than thirty. The blond was relieved, though he hid it quickly. The redhead was furious and didn't care who knew it.

"There you are. You gave us a fright, disappearing without leaving word," the blond man said mildly, drawing to a stop and sheathing his long, exceedingly sharp sword.

Walter and Henry, too, withdrew their weapons. They recognized the men.

"Gallowglass. Why are you here?" Matthew asked the blond warrior with a note of wary confusion.

"We're looking for you, of course. Hancock and I were with you on Saturday." Gallowglass's chilly blue eyes narrowed when he didn't receive a reply. He looked like a Viking on the brink of a killing spree. "In Chester."

"Chester." Matthew's expression turned to dawning horror. "Chester!"

"Aye. Chester," repeated the redheaded Hancock. He glowered and peeled sodden leather gauntlets from his arms, tossing them onto the floor near the fireplace. "When you didn't meet up with us as planned on Sunday, we made inquiries. The innkeeper told us you'd left, which came as something of a surprise, and not only because you hadn't settled the bill."

"He said you were sitting by the fire drinking wine one moment and gone the next," Gallowglass reported. "The maid—the little one with the black hair who couldn't take her eyes off you—caused quite a stir. She insisted you were taken by ghosts."

I closed my eyes in sudden understanding. The Matthew Roydon who had been in sixteenth-century Chester vanished because he was displaced by the Matthew who'd traveled here from modern-day Oxfordshire. When we left, the sixteenth-century Matthew, presumably, would reappear. Time wouldn't allow both Matthews to be in the same place at the same moment. We had already altered history without intending to do so.

"It was All Hallows' Eve, so her story made a certain sort of sense," Hancock conceded, turning his attention to his cloak. He shook the water from its folds and flung it over a nearby chair, releasing the scent of spring grass into the winter air.

"Who are these men, Matthew?" I moved closer to get a better look at the pair. He turned and settled his hands on my upper arms, keeping me where I was.

"They're friends," Matthew said, but his obvious effort to regroup made me wonder if he was telling the truth.

"Well, well. She's no ghost." Hancock peered over Matthew's shoulder, and my flesh turned to ice.

Of course Hancock and Gallowglass were vampires. What other creatures could be that big and bloody-looking?

"Nor is she from Chester," Gallowglass said thoughtfully. "Does she always have such a bright *glaem* about her?"

The word might be unfamiliar, but its meaning was clear enough. I was shimmering again. It sometimes happened when I was angry, or concentrating on a problem. It was another familiar manifestation of a witch's power, and vampires could detect the pale glow with their preternaturally sharp eyes. Feeling conspicuous, I stepped back into Matthew's shadow.

"That's not going to help, lady. Our ears are as sharp as our eyes. Your witch's blood is trilling like a bird." Hancock's bushy red brows rose as he looked sourly at his companion. "Trouble always travels in the company of women."

"Trouble is no fool. Given the choice, I'd rather travel with a woman than with you." The blond warrior addressed Matthew. "It's been a long day, Hancock's arse is sore, and he's hungry. If you don't tell him why there's a witch in your house, and quickly, I don't have high hopes for her continued safety."

"It must have to do with Berwick," Hancock declared. "Bloody witches. Always causing trouble."

"Berwick?" My pulse kicked up a notch. I recognized the name. One of the most notorious witch trials in the British Isles was connected to it. I searched my memory for the dates. Surely it had happened well before or after 1590, or Matthew wouldn't have selected this moment for our timewalk. But Hancock's next words drove all thoughts of chronology and history from my mind.

"That, or some new Congregation business that Matthew will want us to sort out for him."

"The Congregation?" Marlowe's eyes narrowed, and he looked at Matthew appraisingly. "Is this true? Are you one of the mysterious members?"

"Of course it's true! How do you imagine he's kept you from the noose, young Marlowe?" Hancock searched the room. "Is there something to drink other than wine? I hate these French pretensions of yours, de Clermont. What's wrong with ale?"

"Not now, Davy," Gallowglass murmured to his friend, though his eyes were fixed on Matthew.

My eyes were fixed on him, too, as an awful sense of clarity settled over me.

"Tell me you're not," I whispered. "Tell me you didn't keep this from me."

"I can't tell you that," Matthew said flatly. "I promised you secrets but no lies, remember?"

I felt sick. In 1590, Matthew was a member of the Congregation, and the Congregation was our enemy.

"And Berwick? You told me there was no danger of being caught up in a witch-hunt."

"Nothing in Berwick will affect us here," Matthew assured me.

"What has happened in Berwick?" Walter asked, uneasy.

"Before we left Chester, there was news out of Scotland. A great gathering of witches met in a village east of Edinburgh on All Hallows' Eve," Hancock said. "There was talk again of the storm the Danish witches raised this past summer, and the spouts of seawater that foretold the coming of a creature with fearsome powers."

"The authorities have rounded up dozens of the poor wretches," Gallowglass continued, his arctic-blue eyes still on Matthew. "The cunning woman in the town of Keith, Widow Sampson, is awaiting the king's questioning in the dungeons of Holyrood Palace. Who knows how many will join her there before this business is done?"

"The king's torture, you mean," Hancock muttered. "They say the woman has been locked into a witch's bridle so she cannot utter more charms against His Majesty, and chained to the wall without food or drink."

I sat down abruptly.

"Is this one of the accused, then?" Gallowglass asked Matthew. "And I'd like the witch's bargain, too, if I may: secrets, but no lies."

There was a long silence before Matthew answered. "Diana is my wife, Gallowglass."

"You abandoned us in Chester for a *woman*?" Hancock was horrified. "But we had work to do!"

"You have an unerring ability to grab the wrong end of the staff, Davy." Gallowglass's glance shifted to me. "Your *wife*?" he said carefully. "So this is just a legal arrangement to satisfy curious humans and justify her presence here while the Congregation decides her future?"

"Not just my wife," Matthew admitted. "She's my mate, too." A vampire mated for life when compelled to do so by an instinctive combination of affection, affinity, lust, and chemistry. The resulting bond was breakable only by death. Vampires might marry multiple times, but most mated just once.

Gallowglass swore, though the sound of it was almost drowned out by his friend's amusement.

"And His Holiness proclaimed the age of miracles had passed," Hancock crowed. "Matthew de Clermont is mated at last. But no ordinary, placid human or properly schooled female *wearh* who knows her place would do. Not for our Matthew. Now that he's decided at last to settle down with one woman, it had to be a witch. We have more to worry about than the good people of Woodstock, then."

"What's wrong in Woodstock?" I asked Matthew with a frown.

"Nothing," Matthew said breezily. But it was the hulking blond who held my attention.

"Some old besom went into fits on market day. She's blaming it on you." Gallowglass studied me from head to toe as if trying to imagine how someone so unprepossessing had caused so much trouble.

"Widow Beaton," I said breathlessly.

The appearance of Françoise and Charles forestalled further conversation. Françoise had fragrant gingerbread and spiced wine for the warmbloods. Kit (who was never reluctant to sample the contents of Matthew's cellar) and George (who was looking a bit green after the evening's revelations) helped themselves. Both had the air of audience members waiting for the next act to start.

Charles, whose task it was to sustain the vampires, had a delicate pitcher with silver handles and three tall glass beakers. The red liquid within was darker and more opaque than any wine. Hancock stopped Charles on his way to the head of the household.

"I need something to drink more than Matthew does," he said, grabbing a beaker while Charles gasped at the affront. Hancock sniffed the pitcher's contents and took that, too. "I haven't had fresh blood for three days. You have odd taste in women, de Clermont, but no one can criticize your hospitality."

Matthew motioned Charles in the direction of Gallowglass, who also drank thirstily. When Gallowglass took his final draft, he wiped his hand across his mouth.

"Well?" he demanded. "You're tight-lipped, I know, but some explanation as to how you let yourself get into this seems in order."

"This would be better discussed in private," said Walter, eyeing George and the two daemons.

"Why is that, Raleigh?" Hancock's voice took on a pugnacious edge. "De Clermont has a lot to answer for. So does his witch. And those answers had best trip off her tongue. We passed a priest on the way. He was with two gentlemen who had prosperous waistlines. Based on what I heard, de Clermont's mate will have three days—"

"At least five," Gallowglass corrected.

"Maybe five," Hancock said, inclining his head in his companion's direction, "before she's held over for trial, two days to figure out what to say to the magistrates, and less than half an hour to come up with a convincing lie for the good father. You had best start telling us the truth."

All attention settled on Matthew, who stood mute.

"The clock will strike the quarter hour soon," Hancock reminded him after some time had passed.

I took matters into my own hands. "Matthew protected me from my own people."

"Diana," Matthew growled.

"*Matthew* meddled in the affairs of witches?" Gallowglass's eyes widened slightly.

I nodded. "Once the danger passed, we were mated."

"And all this happened between noon and nightfall on Saturday?" Gallowglass shook his head. "You're going to have to do better than that, Auntie."

"'Auntie'?" I turned to Matthew in shock. First Berwick, then the Congregation, and now this. "This . . . berserker is your nephew? Let me guess. He's Baldwin's son!" Gallowglass was almost as muscle-bound as Matthew's copper-headed brother—and as persistent. There were other de Clermonts I knew: Godfrey, Louisa, and Hugh (who received only brief, cryptic mentions). Gallowglass could belong to any of them—or to someone else on Matthew's convoluted family tree.

"Baldwin?" Gallowglass gave a delicate shiver. "Even before I became a *wearh,* I knew better than to let that monster near my neck. Hugh de Clermont was my father. For your information, my people were Úlfhéðnar, not berserkers. And I'm only part Norse—the gentle part, if you must know. The rest is Scots, by way of Ireland."

"Foul-tempered, the Scots," Hancock added.

Gallowglass acknowledged his companion's remark with a gentle tug on his ear. A golden ring glinted in the light, incised with the outlines of a coffin. A man was stepping free of it, and there was a motto around the edges.

"You're knights." I looked for a matching ring on Hancock's finger. There it was, oddly placed on his thumb. Here at last was evidence that Matthew was involved in the business of the Order of Lazarus, too.

"We-elll," Gallowglass drawled, sounding suddenly like the Scot he professed to be, "there's always been a dispute about that. We're not really the shining-armor type, are we, Davy?"

"No. But the de Clermonts have deep pockets. Money like that is hard to refuse," Hancock observed, "especially when they promise you a long life for the enjoying of it."

"They're fierce fighters, too." Gallowglass rubbed the bridge of his nose again. It was flattened, as though it had been broken and never healed properly.

"Oh, aye. The bastards killed me before they saved me. Fixed my bad eye, while they were at it," Hancock said cheerfully, pointing to his gammy lid.

"Then you're loyal to the de Clermonts." Sudden relief washed through me. I would prefer to have Gallowglass and Hancock as allies rather than enemies, given the disaster unfolding.

"Not always," replied Gallowglass darkly.

"Not to Baldwin. He's a sly bugger. And when Matthew behaves like a fool, we pay no attention to him either." Hancock sniffed and pointed to the gingerbread, which lay forgotten on the table. "Is someone going to eat that, or can we pitch it into the fire? Between Matthew's scent and Charles's cooking, I feel ill."

"Given our approaching visitors, our time would be better spent devising a course of action than talking about family history," Walter said impatiently.

"*Jesu,* there's no time to come up with a plan," Hancock said cheerfully. "Matthew and his lordship should say a prayer instead. They're men of God. Maybe He's listening."

"Perhaps the witch could fly away," Gallowglass murmured. He held up both hands in mute surrender when Matthew glared at him.

"Oh, but she can't." All eyes turned to Marlowe. "She can't even conjure Matthew a beard."

"You've taken up with a witch, against all the Congregation's strictures, and she's *worthless*?" It was impossible to tell if Gallowglass was more indignant or incredulous. "A wife who can summon a storm or give your enemy a horrible skin affliction has certain advantages, I grant you. But what good is a witch who can't even serve as her husband's barber?"

"Only Matthew would wed a witch from God-knows-where with no sorcery to speak of," Hancock muttered to Walter.

"Quiet, all of you!" Matthew exploded. "I can't think for all the senseless chatter. It's not Diana's fault that Widow Beaton is a meddling old fool or that she can't perform magic on command. My wife was spellbound. And there's an end to it. If one more person in this room questions me or criticizes Diana, I'll rip your heart out and feed it to you while it still beats."

"There is our lord and master," Hancock said with a mocking salute. "For a minute I was afraid *you* were the one who was bewitched. Hang on, though. If she's spellbound, what's wrong with her? Is she dangerous? Mad? Both?"

Unnerved by the influx of nephews, agitated parsons, and the trouble brewing in Woodstock, I reached behind me for the chair. With my reach restricted by the unfamiliar clothes, I lost my balance and began to fall.

A rough hand shot out and gripped me by the elbow, lowering me to the seat with surprising gentleness.

"It's all right, Auntie." Gallowglass made a soft noise of sympathy. "I'm not sure what's amiss in your head, but Matthew will take care of you. He has a warm spot in his heart for lost souls, bless him."

"I'm dizzy, not deranged," I retorted.

Gallowglass's eyes were flinty as his mouth approached my ear. "Your speech is disordered enough to stand for madness, and I doubt the priest cares one way or the other. Given that you aren't from Chester or anywhere else I've been—and that's a fair number of places, Auntie—you might want to mind your manners unless you want to find yourself locked in the church crypt."

Long fingers clamped around Gallowglass's shoulder and pulled him away. "If you're quite finished trying to frighten my wife—a pointless exercise, I assure you—you might tell me about the men you passed," Matthew said frostily. "Were they armed?"

"No." After a long, interested look at me, Gallowglass turned toward his uncle.

"And who was with the minister?"

"How the hell should we know, Matthew? All three were warmbloods and not worth a second thought. One was fat and gray-haired, the other was medium size and complained about the weather," Gallowglass said impatiently.

"Bidwell," Matthew and Walter said at the same moment.

"It's probably Iffley with him," remarked Walter. "The two of them are always complaining—about the state of the roads, the noise at the inn, the quality of the beer."

"Who's Iffley?" I wondered aloud.

"A man who fancies himself the finest glover in all England. Somers works for him," Walter replied.

"Master Iffley does craft the queen's gloves," George acknowledged.

"He made her a single pair of hunting gauntlets two decades ago. That's hardly enough to make Iffley the most important man for thirty miles, dearly as he might covet the honor." Matthew snorted contemptuously. "Singly none of them are terribly bright. Together they're downright foolish. If that's the best the village can do, we can return to our reading."

"That's it?" Walter's voice was brittle. "We sit and let them come to us?"

"Yes. But Diana doesn't leave my sight—or yours, Gallowglass," Matthew warned.

"You don't have to remind me of my family duty, Uncle. I'll be sure your feisty wife makes it to your bed tonight."

"Feisty, am I? My husband is a member of the Congregation. A posse of men is coming on horseback to accuse me of harming a friendless old woman. I'm in a strange place and keep getting lost on my way to the bedroom. I still have no shoes. And I'm living in a dormitory full of adolescent boys who never stop talking!" I fumed. "But you needn't trouble yourself on my account. I can take care of myself!"

"Take care of yourself?" Gallowglass laughed at me and shook his head. "No you can't. And when the fighting's done, we'll need to see to that accent of yours. I didn't understand half of what you just said."

"She must be Irish," Hancock said, glaring at me. "That would explain the spellbinding and the disordered speech. The whole lot of them are mad."

"She's not Irish," Gallowglass said. "Mad or no, I would have understood her accent if that were the case."

"Quiet!" Matthew bellowed.

"The men from the village are at the gatehouse," Pierre announced in the ensuing silence.

"Go and fetch them," Matthew ordered. He turned his attention to me. "Let me do the talking. Don't answer their questions unless and until I tell you to do so. Now," he continued briskly, "we can't afford to have anything . . . unusual happen tonight as it did when Widow Beaton was here. Are you still dizzy? Do you need to lie down?"

"Curious. I'm curious," I said, hands clenched. "Don't worry about my magic or my health. Worry about how many hours it's going to take you to answer my questions after the minister is gone. And if you try to wiggle out of them with the excuse that 'it's not my tale to tell,' I'll flatten you."

"You are perfectly fine, then." Matthew's mouth twitched. He dropped a kiss on my forehead. "I love you, *ma lionne.*"

"You might reserve your professions of love until later and give Auntie a chance to compose herself," Gallowglass suggested.

"Why does everyone feel compelled to tell me how to manage my own wife?" Matthew shot back. The cracks in his composure were starting to show.

"I really couldn't say," Gallowglass replied serenely. "She reminds me a bit of Granny, though. We give Philippe advice morning, noon, and night about how best to control her. Not that he listens."

The men arranged themselves around the room. The apparent randomness of their positions created a human funnel—wider at the entrance to the room, narrower at the fireside where Matthew and I sat. As George and Kit would be the first to greet the man of God and his companions, Walter whisked away their dice and the manuscript of *Doctor Faustus* in favor of a copy of Herodotus's *Histories.* Though it was not a Bible, Raleigh assured us it would lend proper gravitas to the situation. Kit was still protesting the unfairness of the substitution when footsteps and voices sounded.

Pierre ushered the three men inside. One so strongly resembled the reedy young man who had measured me for shoes that I knew at once he was Joseph Bidwell. He started at the sound of the door closing behind him and looked uneasily over his shoulder. When his bleary eyes faced forward again and he saw the size of the assembly awaiting him, he jumped once more. Walter, who occupied a position of strategic importance in the middle of the room with Hancock and Henry, ignored the nervous shoemaker and cast a look of disdain at a man in a bedraggled religious habit.

"What brings you here on such a night, Mr. Danforth?" Raleigh demanded.

"Sir Walter," Danforth said with a bow, taking a cap from his head and twisting it between his fingers. He spotted the Earl of Northumberland. "My lord! I did not know you were still amongst us."

"Is there something you need?" Matthew asked pleasantly. He remained seated, legs stretched out in apparent relaxation.

"Ah. Master Roydon." Danforth made another bow, this one directed at us. He gave me a curious look before fear overtook him and redirected his eyes to his hat. "We have not seen you in church or in town. Bidwell thought you might be indisposed."

Bidwell shifted on his feet. The leather boots he wore squelched and complained, and the man's lungs joined in the chorus with wheezes and a barking cough. A wilted ruff constricted his windpipe and quivered every time he tried to draw breath. Its pleated linen was distinctly the worse for wear, and a greasy brown spot near his chin suggested he'd had gravy with supper.

"Yes, I was taken sick in Chester, but it has passed with God's grace and thanks to my wife's care." Matthew reached out and clasped my hand with husbandly devotion. "My physician thought it would be best if my hair were shorn to rid me of the fever, but it was Diana's insistence on cool baths that made the difference."

"Wife?" Danforth said faintly. "Widow Beaton did not tell me—"

"I do not share my private affairs with ignorant women," Matthew said sharply.

Bidwell sneezed. Matthew examined him first with concern, then with a carefully managed look of dawning understanding. I was learning a great deal about my husband this evening, including the fact that he could be a surprisingly good actor.

"Oh. But of course you are here to ask Diana to cure Bidwell." Matthew made a sound of regret. "There is so much idle gossip. Has the news of my wife's skill spread already?"

In this period medicinal knowledge was perilously close to a witch's lore. Was Matthew *trying* to get me in trouble?

Bidwell wanted to respond, but all he could manage was a gurgle and a shake of his head.

"If you are not here for physic, then you must be here to deliver Diana's shoes." Matthew looked at me fondly, then to the minister. "As you have no doubt heard, my wife's possessions were lost during our journey, Mr. Danforth." Matthew's attention returned to the shoemaker, and a shade of reproach crept into his tone. "I know you are a busy man, Bidwell, but I hope you've finished the pattens at least. Diana is determined to go to church this week, and the path to the vestry is often flooded. Someone really should see to it."

Iffley's chest had been swelling with indignation since Matthew had started speaking. Finally the man could stand it no more.

"Bidwell brought the shoes you paid for, but we are not here to secure your wife's services or trifle with pattens and puddles!" Iffley drew his cloak around his hips in a gesture that was intended to convey dignity, but the soaked wool only emphasized his resemblance to a drowned rat, with his pointy nose and beady eyes. "Tell her, Mr. Danforth."

The Reverend Danforth looked as though he would rather be roasting in hell than standing in Matthew Roydon's house, confronting his wife.

"Go on. Tell her," urged Iffley.

"Allegations have been made—" That was as far as Danforth got before Walter, Henry, and Hancock closed ranks.

"If you are here to make allegations, sir, you can direct them to me or to his lordship," Walter said sharply.

"Or to me," George piped up. "I am well read in the law."

"Ah . . . Er . . . Yes . . . Well . . ." The cleric subsided into silence.

"Widow Beaton has fallen ill. So has young Bidwell," said Iffley, determined to forge on in spite of Danforth's failing nerve.

"No doubt it is the same ague that afflicted me and now the boy's father," my husband said softly. His fingers tightened on mine. Behind me Gallowglass swore under his breath. "Of what, exactly, are you accusing my wife, Iffley?"

"Widow Beaton refused to join her in some evil business. Mistress Roydon vowed to afflict her joints and head with pains."

"My son has lost his hearing," Bidwell complained, his voice thick with misery and phlegm. "There is a fierce ringing in his ears, like unto the sound of a bell. Widow Beaton says he has been bewitched."

"No," I whispered. The blood left my head in a sudden, startling drop. Gallowglass's hands were on my shoulders in an instant, keeping me upright.

The word "*bewitched*" had me staring into a familiar abyss. My greatest fear had always been that humans would discover I was descended from Bridget Bishop. Then the curious glances would start, and the suspicions. The only possible response was flight. I tried to worm my fingers from Matthew's grasp, but he might have been made of stone for all the good it did me, and Gallowglass still had charge of my shoulders.

"Widow Beaton has long suffered from rheumatism, and Bidwell's son has recurrent putrid throats. They often cause pain and deafness. These illnesses occurred before my wife came to Woodstock." Matthew made a lazy, dismissive gesture with his free hand. "The old woman is jealous of Diana's skill, and young Joseph was taken with her beauty and envious of my married state. These are not allegations, but idle imaginings."

"As a man of God, Master Roydon, it is my responsibility to take them seriously. I have been reading." Mr. Danforth reached into his black robes and pulled out a tattered sheaf of papers. It was no more than a few dozen sheets crudely stitched together with coarse string. Time and heavy use had softened the papers' fibers, fraying the edges and turning the pages gray. I was too far away to make out the title page. All three vampires saw it, though. So did George, who blanched.

"That's part of the *Malleus Maleficarum.* I did not know that your Latin was good enough to comprehend such a difficult work, Mr. Danforth,"

Matthew said. It was the most influential witch-hunting manual ever produced, and a title that struck terror into a witch's heart.

The minister looked affronted. "I attended university, Master Roydon."

"I'm relieved to hear it. That book shouldn't be in the possession of the weak-minded or superstitious."

"You know it?" Danforth asked.

"I, too, attended university," Matthew replied mildly.

"Then you understand why I must question this woman." Danforth attempted to advance into the room. Hancock's low growl brought him to a standstill.

"My wife has no difficulties with her hearing. You needn't come closer."

"I told you Mistress Roydon has unnatural powers!" Iffley said triumphantly.

Danforth gripped his book. "Who taught you these things, Mistress Roydon?" he called down the echoing expanse of the hall. "From whom did you learn your witchcraft?"

This was how the madness began: with questions designed to trap the accused into condemning other creatures. One life at a time, witches were caught up in the web of lies and destroyed. Thousands of my people had been tortured and killed thanks to such tactics. Denials burbled up into my throat.

"Don't." Matthew's single word of warning was uttered in an icy murmur.

"Strange things are happening in Woodstock. A white stag crossed Widow Beaton's path," Danforth continued. "It stopped in the road and stared until her flesh turned cold. Last night a gray wolf was seen outside her house. Its eyes glowed in the darkness, brighter than the lamps that were hung out to help travelers find shelter in the storm. Which of these creatures is your familiar? Who gifted you with it?" Matthew didn't need to tell me to keep silent this time. The priest's questions were following a well-known pattern, one I had studied in graduate school.

"The witch must answer your questions, Mr. Danforth," Iffley insisted, pulling at his companion's sleeve. "Such insolence from a creature of darkness cannot be allowed in a godly community."

"My wife speaks to no one without my consent," said Matthew. "And mind whom you call witch, Iffley." The more the villagers challenged him, the harder it was for Matthew to restrain himself.

The minister's eyes traveled from me to Matthew and back again. I stifled a whimper.

"Her agreement with the devil makes it impossible for her to speak the truth," Bidwell said.

"Hush, Master Bidwell," Danforth chided. "What do you wish to say, my child? Who introduced you to the devil? Was it another woman?"

"Or man," Iffley said under his breath. "Mistress Roydon is not the only child of darkness to be found here. There are strange books and instruments, and midnight gatherings are held to conjure spirits."

Harriot sighed and thrust his book at Danforth. "Mathematics, sir, not magic. Widow Beaton spotted a geometry text."

"It is not your place to determine the extent of the evil here," Iffley sputtered.

"If it's evil you're seeking, look for it at Widow Beaton's." Though he'd done his best to remain calm, Matthew was rapidly losing his temper.

"Do you accuse her of witchcraft, then?" Danforth asked sharply.

"No, Matthew. Not that way," I whispered, tugging on his hand to gain his attention.

Matthew turned to me. His face looked inhuman, his pupils glassy and enormous. I shook my head, and he took a deep breath, trying to calm both his fury at the invasion of his home and his fierce instinct to protect me.

"Stop your ears against his words, Mr. Danforth. Roydon might be an instrument of the devil, too," Iffley warned.

Matthew faced the delegation. "If you have reason to charge my wife with some offense, find a magistrate and do so. Otherwise get out. And before you return, Danforth, consider whether aligning with Iffley and Bidwell is a wise course of action."

The parson gulped.

"You heard him," Hancock barked. "Out!"

"Justice will be served, Master Roydon—God's justice," Danforth proclaimed as he backed out of the room.

"Only if my version doesn't resolve the matter first, Danforth," Walter promised.

Pierre and Charles materialized from the shadows, throwing open the doors to shepherd the wide-eyed warmbloods from the room. Outside, it was blowing a gale. The fierceness of the waiting storm would only confirm their suspicions about my supernatural powers.

Out, out, out! called an insistent voice in my head. Panic flooded my system with adrenaline. I had been reduced to prey once more. Gallowglass and Hancock turned toward me, intrigued by the scent of fear seeping from my pores.

"Stay where you are," Matthew warned the vampires. He crouched before me. "Diana's instincts are telling her to flee. She'll be fine in a moment."

"This is never going to end. We came for help, but even here I'm hunted." I bit my lip.

"There's nothing to fear. Danforth and Iffley will think twice before causing any more trouble," Matthew said firmly, taking my clasped hands in his. "No one wants me for an enemy—not other creatures, not the humans."

"I understand why the creatures might fear you. You're a member of the Congregation and have the power to destroy them. No wonder Widow Beaton came here when you commanded. But that doesn't explain this human reaction to you. Danforth and Iffley must suspect that you're a . . . *wearh.*" I caught myself just before the word "vampire" spilled out.

"Oh, he's in no danger from them," said Hancock dismissively. "These men are nobodies. Unfortunately, they're likely to bring this business to the attention of humans who *do* matter."

"Ignore him," Matthew told me.

"Which humans?" I whispered.

Gallowglass gasped. "By all that is holy, Matthew. I've seen you do terrible things, but how could you keep *this* from your wife, too?"

Matthew looked into the fire. When his eyes finally met mine, they were filled with regret.

"Matthew?" I prompted. The knot that had been forming in my stomach since the arrival of the first bag of mail tightened further.

"They don't think I'm a vampire. They know I'm a spy."

"A spy?" I repeated numbly.

"We prefer to be called intelligencers," Kit said tartly.

"Shut it, Marlowe," Hancock growled, "or I'll stop that mouth for you."

"Spare us, Hancock. No one takes you seriously when you sputter like that." Marlowe's chin jutted into the room. "And if you don't keep a civil tongue with me, there will soon be an end to all these Welsh kings and soldiers on the stage. I'll make you all traitors and servants with low cunning."

"What is a vampire?" George asked, reaching for his notebook with one hand and a piece of gingerbread with the other. As usual, no one was paying much attention to him.

"So you're some kind of Elizabethan James Bond? But . . ." I looked at Marlowe, horrified. He would be murdered in a knife fight in Deptford before he reached the age of thirty, and the crime would be linked to his life as a spy.

"The London hatmaker near St. Dunstan's who turns such a neat brim? That James Bond?" George chuckled. "Whyever would you think Matthew was a hatmaker, Mistress Roydon?"

"No, George, not that James Bond." Matthew remained crouched before me, watching my reactions. "You were better off not knowing about this."

"Bullshit." I neither knew nor cared if this was an appropriately Elizabethan oath. "I deserve the truth."

"Perhaps, Mistress Roydon, but if you truly love him, it is pointless to insist upon it," Marlowe said. "Matthew can no longer distinguish between what is true and what is not. This is why he is invaluable to Her Majesty."

"We're here to find you a teacher," Matthew insisted, his eyes locked on me. "The fact that I am both a member of the Congregation and the queen's agent will keep you from harm. Nothing happens in the country without my being aware of it."

"For someone who claims to know everything, you were blissfully unaware that I've thought for days that something was going on in this house. There is too much mail. And you and Walter have been arguing."

"You see what I want you to see. Nothing more." Even though Matthew's tendency toward imperiousness had grown exponentially since we came to the Old Lodge, my jaw dropped at his tone.

"How dare you," I said slowly. Matthew knew I'd spent my whole life surrounded by secrets. I'd paid a high price for it, too. I stood.

"Sit down," he grated out. "Please." He caught my hand.

Matthew's best friend, Hamish Osborne, had warned me that he wouldn't be the same man here. How could he be, when the world was such a different place? Women were expected to accept without question what a man told them. Among his friends it was all too easy for Matthew to slip back into old behaviors and patterns of thinking.

"Only if you answer me. I want the name of the person you report to and how you got embroiled in this business." I glanced over at his nephew and his friends, worried that these were state secrets.

"They already know about Kit and me," Matthew said, following my eyes. He struggled to find the words. "It all started with Francis Walsingham.

"I'd left England late in Henry's reign. I spent time in Constantinople, went to Cyprus, wandered through Spain, fought at Lepanto—even set up a printing business in Antwerp," Matthew explained. "It's the usual path for a *wearh.* We search for a tragedy, an opportunity to slip into someone else's life. But nothing suited me, so I returned home. France was on the verge of religious and civil war. When you've lived as long as I have, you learn the signs. A Huguenot schoolmaster was happy to take my money and go to Geneva, where he could raise his daughters in safety. I took the identity of his long-dead cousin, moved into his house in Paris, and started over as Matthew de la Forêt."

"'Matthew of the Forest'?" My eyebrows lifted at the irony.

"That *was* the schoolmaster's name," he said wryly. "Paris was dangerous, and Walsingham, as English ambassador, was a magnet for every disenchanted rebel in the country. Late in the summer of 1572, all the simmering anger in France came to a boil. I helped Walsingham survive, along with the English Protestants he was sheltering."

"The massacre on St. Bartholomew's Day." I shivered, thinking of the blood-soaked wedding between a French Catholic princess and her Protestant husband.

"I became the queen's agent later, when she sent Walsingham back to Paris. He was supposed to be brokering Her Majesty's marriage to one of the Valois princes." Matthew snorted. "It was clear the queen had no real interest in the match. It was during that visit that I learned of Walsingham's network of intelligencers."

My husband met my eyes briefly, then looked away. He was still keeping something from me. I reviewed the story, detected the fault lines in his account, and followed them to a single, inescapable conclusion: Matthew was French, Catholic, and he could not possibly have been aligned politically with Elizabeth Tudor in 1572—or in 1590. If he was working for the English Crown, it was for some larger purpose. But the Congregation had vowed to stay out of human politics.

Philippe de Clermont and his Knights of Lazarus had not.

"You're working for your father. And you're not only a vampire but a Catholic in a Protestant country." The fact that Matthew was working for the Knights of Lazarus, not just Elizabeth, exponentially increased the danger. It wasn't just witches who were hunted down and executed in Elizabethan England—so were traitors, creatures with unusual powers, and people of different faiths. "The Congregation is of no help if you get involved with human politics. How could your own family ask you to do something so risky?"

Hancock grinned. "That's why there's always a de Clermont on the Congregation—to make sure lofty ideals don't get in the way of good business."

"This isn't the first time I've worked for Philippe, nor will it be the last. You're good at uncovering secrets. I'm good at keeping them," Matthew said simply.

Scientist. Vampire. Warrior. Spy. Another piece of Matthew fell into place, and with it I better understood his ingrained habit of never sharing anything—major or minor—unless he was forced to do so.

"I don't care how much experience you have! Your safety depends on Walsingham—and you're deceiving him." His words had only made me angrier.

"Walsingham is dead. I report to William Cecil now."

"The canniest man alive," Gallowglass said quietly. "Except for Philippe, of course."

"And Kit? Does he work for Cecil or for you?"

"Tell her nothing, Matthew," Kit said. "The witch cannot be trusted."

"Why, you sly, wee boggart," Hancock said softly. "It's you who's been stirring up the villagers."

Kit's cheeks burned red in twin pronouncements of guilt.

"Christ, Kit. What have you done?" Matthew asked, astonished.

"Nothing," said Marlowe sullenly.

"You've been telling tales again." Hancock waggled his finger in admonishment. "I've warned you before that we won't stand for that, Master Marlowe."

"Woodstock was already buzzing with news of Matthew's wife," Kit protested. "The rumors were bound to bring the Congregation down upon us. How was I supposed to know that the Congregation was already here?"

"Surely you'll let me kill him now, de Clermont. I've wanted to do so for ages," Hancock said, cracking his knuckles.

"No. You can't kill him." Matthew rubbed a hand over his tired face. "There would be too many questions, and I don't have the patience to come up with convincing answers at present. It's just village gossip. I'll handle it."

"This gossip comes at a bad time," Gallowglass reported quietly. "It's not just Berwick. You know how anxious people were about witches in Chester. When we went north into Scotland, the situation was worse."

"If this business spreads south into England, she'll be the death of us," Marlowe promised, pointing at me.

"This trouble will stay confined to Scotland," Matthew retorted. "And there will be no more visits to the village, Kit."

"She appeared on All Hallows' Eve, just when the arrival of a fearsome witch was predicted. Don't you see? Your new wife raised the storms against King James, and now she has turned her attention to England. Cecil must be told. She poses a danger to the queen."

"Quiet, Kit," Henry cautioned, pulling at his arm.

"You cannot silence me. Telling the queen is my duty. Once you would have agreed with me, Henry. But since the witch came, everything's changed! She has enchanted everyone in the house." Kit's eyes were frantic. "You dote on her like a sister. George is half in love. Tom praises her wit, and Walter would have her skirts up and her back against a wall if he weren't afraid of Matt. Return her to where she belongs. We were happy before."

"Matthew wasn't happy." Tom had been drawn to our end of the room by Marlowe's angry energy.

"You say you love him." Kit turned to me, his face full of entreaty. "Do you truly know what he is? Have you seen him feed, felt the hunger in him when a warmblood is near? Can you accept Matthew completely—the blackness in his soul along with the light—as I do? You have your magic for solace, but I am not fully alive without him. All poetry flies from my mind when he is gone, and only Matthew can see what little good I have in me. Leave him to me. Please."

"I can't," I said simply.

Kit wiped his sleeve across his mouth as if the gesture might remove all trace of me. "When the rest of the Congregation discovers your affections for him—"

"If my affection for him is forbidden, so is yours," I interrupted. Marlowe flinched. "But none of us choose whom we love."

"Iffley and his friends won't be the last to accuse you of witchcraft," Kit said with a note of sour triumph. "Mark me well, Mistress Roydon. Daemons often see the future as plainly as witches."

Matthew's hand moved to my waist. The cold, familiar touch of his fingers swept from one side of my rib cage to the other, following the curved path that marked me as belonging to a vampire. For Matthew it was a powerful reminder of his earlier failure to keep me safe. Kit made a horrible, half-swallowed sound of distress at the intimacy of the gesture.

"If you are so prescient, then you should have foreseen what your betrayal would mean to me," Matthew said, gradually unfolding himself. "Get out of my sight, Kit, or so help me God there will be nothing left of you to bury."

"You would have her over me?" Kit sounded dumbfounded.

"In a heartbeat. Get out," repeated Matthew.

Kit's passage out of the room was measured, but once in the corridor his pace quickened. His feet echoed on the wooden stairs, faster and faster, as he climbed to his room.

"We'll have to watch him." Gallowglass's shrewd eyes turned from Kit's departing back to Hancock. "He can't be trusted now."

"Marlowe could never be trusted," Hancock muttered.

Pierre slipped through the open door looking stricken, another piece of mail in his hand.

"Not now, Pierre," Matthew groaned, sitting down and reaching for his wine. His shoulders sagged against the back of his chair. "There simply isn't room in this day for one more crisis—be it queen, country, or Catholics. Whatever it is can wait until morning."

"But . . . *milord,*" Pierre stammered, holding out the letter. Matthew glanced at the decisive writing that marched across the front.

"Christ and all His saints." His fingers rose to touch the paper, then froze. Matthew's throat moved as he struggled for control. Something red and bright appeared in the corner of his eye, then slid down his cheek and splashed onto the folds of his collar. A vampire's blood tear.

"What is it, Matthew?" I looked over his shoulder, wondering what had caused so much grief.

"Ah. The day is not over yet," Hancock said uneasily while he backed away. "There is one small matter that requires your attention. Your father thinks you're dead."

In my own time, it was Matthew's father, Philippe, who was dead—horribly, tragically, irrevocably so. But this was 1590, which meant he was alive. Ever since we'd arrived, I had worried about a chance encounter with Ysabeau or with Matthew's laboratory assistant, Miriam, and the ripples such a meeting might cause in future times. Not once had I considered what seeing Philippe would do to Matthew.

Past, present, and future collided. Had I looked into the corners, I would surely have seen time unspooling in protest at the clash. But my eyes were fixed on Matthew instead, and the blood tear caught in the snowy linen at his throat.

Gallowglass brusquely picked up the tale. "With the news from Scotland and your sudden disappearance, we feared you'd gone north for the queen and been caught up in the madness there. We looked for two days. When we couldn't find a trace of you—hell, Matthew, we had no choice but to tell Philippe you had vanished. It was that or raise the alarm with the Congregation."

"There's more, *milord.*" Pierre flipped the letter over. The seal on it was like the others I associated with the Knights of Lazarus—except that the wax used here was a vivid swirl of black and red and an ancient silver coin had been pushed into its surface, the edges worn and thin, instead of the usual impression of the order's seal. The coin was stamped with a cross and a crescent, two de Clermont family symbols.

"What did you tell him?" Matthew was transfixed by the pale moon of silver floating in its red-black sea.

"Our words are of little consequence now that this has arrived. You must be on French soil within the next week. Otherwise Philippe will set out for England," Hancock mumbled.

"My father cannot come here, Hancock. It is impossible."

"Of course it's impossible. The queen would have his head after all he's done to stir the pot of English politics. You must go to him. So long as you travel night and day, you will have plenty of time," Hancock assured him.

"I can't." Matthew's gaze was fixed on the unopened letter.

"Philippe will have horses waiting. You will be back before long," Gallowglass murmured, resting his hand on his uncle's shoulder. Matthew looked up, eyes suddenly wild.

"It's not the distance. It's—" Matthew stopped abruptly.

"He's your mother's husband, man. Surely you can trust Philippe—unless you've been lying to him as well." Hancock's eyes narrowed.

"Kit's right. No one can trust me." Matthew shot to his feet. "My life is a tissue of lies."

"This isn't the time or place for your philosophical nonsense, Matthew. Even now Philippe wonders if he has lost another son!" Gallowglass exclaimed. "Leave the girl with us, get on your horse, and do what your father commands. If you don't, I'll knock you out and Hancock will carry you there."

"You must be very sure of yourself, Gallowglass, to issue me orders," Matthew said, a dangerous edge to his tone. He braced his hands on the chimneypiece and stared into the fire.

"I'm sure of my grandfather. Ysabeau made you a *wearh,* but it is Philippe's blood that coursed through my father's veins." Gallowglass's words wounded Matthew. His head snapped up when the blow landed, raw emotion overcoming his usual impassiveness.

"George, Tom, go upstairs and see to Kit," Walter murmured, pointing his friends to the door. Raleigh inclined his head in Pierre's direction, and Matthew's servant joined in the efforts to get them out of the room. Calls for more wine and food echoed through the vestibule. Once the two were in Françoise's care, Pierre returned, shut the door firmly, and placed himself before it. With only Walter, Henry, Hancock, and me there to bear witness to the conversation—along with the silent Pierre—Gallowglass continued his efforts with Matthew.

"You must go to Sept-Tours. He won't rest until he claims your body for burial or you are standing before him, alive. Philippe doesn't trust Elizabeth—or the Congregation." Gallowglass intended his words to bring comfort this time, but Matthew's air of remove remained.

Gallowglass made an exasperated sound. "Deceive the others—and yourself, if you must. Discuss alternatives all night if you wish. But Auntie's right: It's all shite." Gallowglass's voice dropped. "Your Diana doesn't smell right. And you smell older than you did last week. I know the secret you're both keeping. He'll know it, too."

Gallowglass had deduced that I was a timewalker. One look at Hancock told me that he had, too.

"Enough!" Walter barked.

Gallowglass and Hancock quieted immediately. The reason blinked on Walter's little finger: a signet bearing the outlines of Lazarus and his coffin.

"So you're a knight, too," I said, stunned.

"Yes," said Walter tersely.

"And you outrank Hancock. What about Gallowglass?" There were too many overlapping layers of loyalty and allegiance in the room. I was desperate to organize them into a navigable structure.

"I outrank everyone in this room, madam, with the exception of your husband," Raleigh cautioned. "And that includes you."

"You have no authority over me," I shot back. "Exactly what is your role in the de Clermont family's business, Walter?"

Over my head, Raleigh's angry blue eyes met Matthew's. "Is she always like this?"

"Usually," Matthew said drily. "It takes some getting used to, but I rather like it. You might, too, given time."

"I already have one demanding woman in my life. I don't need another," Walter snorted. "If you must know, I command the brotherhood in England, Mistress Roydon. Matthew cannot do so, given his position on the Congregation. The other members of the family were otherwise occupied. Or they refused." Walter's eyes flickered to Gallowglass.

"So you're one of the order's eight provincial masters and report directly to Philippe," I said thoughtfully. "I'm surprised you're not the ninth knight." The ninth knight was a mysterious figure in the order, his identity kept secret from all except those at the very highest levels.

Raleigh swore so vehemently that Pierre gasped. "You keep the fact that you're a spy and a member of the Congregation from your wife, yet you tell her the most private business of the brotherhood?"

"She asked," Matthew said simply. "But I think that's enough talk of the Order of Lazarus for tonight."

"Your wife won't be satisfied leaving it there. She will worry at this like a hound with a bone." Raleigh crossed his arms over his chest and scowled. "Very well. If you must know, Henry is the ninth knight. His unwillingness to embrace the Protestant faith makes him vulnerable to allegations of treason here in England, and in Europe he is an easy target for every malcontent who would like to see Her Majesty lose her throne. Philippe offered him the position to shield him from those who would abuse his trusting nature."

"Henry? A rebel?" I looked at the gentle giant, stunned.

"I'm no rebel," Henry said tightly. "But Philippe de Clermont's protection has saved my life on more than one occasion."

"The Earl of Northumberland is a powerful man, Diana," Matthew said quietly, "which makes him a valuable pawn in the hands of an unscrupulous player."

Gallowglass coughed. "Can we leave off talk of the brotherhood and return to more urgent matters? The Congregation will call on Matthew to calm the situation in Berwick. The queen will want him to stir it up further, because so long as the Scots are preoccupied with witches, they won't be able to plan any mischief in England. Matthew's new wife is facing witchcraft accusations at home. And his father has recalled him to France."

"Christ," Matthew said, pinching the bridge of his nose. "What a tangled mess."

"How do you propose we untangle it?" Walter demanded. "You say Philippe cannot come here, Gallowglass, but I fear that Matthew ought not go there either."

"No one ever said that having three masters—and a wife—was going to be easy," Hancock declared sourly.

"So which devil will it be, Matthew?" asked Gallowglass.

"If Philippe doesn't receive the coin embedded in the letter's seal from my own hand, and soon, he'll come looking for me," Matthew said hollowly. "It's a test of loyalty. My father loves tests."

"Your father does not doubt you. This misunderstanding will be set to rights when you see each other," Henry maintained. When Matthew didn't respond, Henry moved to fill the silence. "You are always telling me that I must have a plan, or else be pulled into the designs of other men. Tell us what must be done, and we will see to it."

Without speaking, Matthew picked through options, discarding one after the other. It would have taken any other man days to sift through the possible moves and countermoves. For Matthew it took only minutes. There was little sign of the struggle on his face, but the bunching of his shoulder muscles and the distracted pass of his hand through his hair told another story.

"I'll go," he said at last. "Diana will stay here, with Gallowglass and Hancock. Walter will have to put off the queen with some excuse. And I'll handle the Congregation."

"Diana can't remain in Woodstock," Gallowglass told him firmly. "Not now that Kit's been at work in the village, spreading his lies and asking questions about her. Without your presence neither the queen nor the Congregation will have any incentive to keep your wife from the magistrate."

"We can go to London, Matthew," I urged. "Together. It's a big city. There will be too many witches for anyone to notice me—witches who aren't afraid of power like mine—and messengers to take word to France that you're safe. You don't have to go." *You don't have to see your father again.*

"London!" Hancock scoffed. "You wouldn't last three days there, *madam*. Gallowglass and I will take you into Wales. We'll go to Abergavenny."

"No." My eyes were drawn by the crimson stain at Matthew's neck. "If Matthew is going to France, I'm going with him."

"Absolutely not. I'm not dragging you through a war."

"The war has quieted with the coming of winter," said Walter. "Taking Diana to Sept-Tours may be for the best. Few are brave enough to tangle with you, Matthew. None at all will cross your father."

"You have a choice," I told him fiercely. Matthew's friends and family weren't going to use me to force him to France.

"Yes. And I choose you." He traced my lip with his thumb. My heart sank. He was going to go to Sept-Tours.

"Don't do this," I implored him. I didn't trust myself to say more for fear of betraying the fact that in our own time Philippe was dead, and that it would be torture for Matthew to see him alive again.

"Philippe told me that mating was destiny. Once I found you, there would be nothing to do but accept fate's decision. But that's not how it works at all. In every moment, for the rest of my life, I will be choosing you—over my father, over my own self-interest, even over the de Clermont family." Matthew's lips pressed against mine, silencing my protests. There was no mistaking the conviction in his kiss.

"It's decided, then," Gallowglass said softly.

Matthew's eyes held mine. He nodded. "Yes. Diana and I will go home. Together."

"There's work to do, arrangements to be made," Walter said. "Leave it to us. Your wife looks exhausted, and the journey will be taxing. You both should rest."

Neither of us made any move toward bed once the men had gone off to the parlor.

"Our time in 1590 isn't turning out quite as I hoped," Matthew admitted. "It was supposed to be straightforward."

"How could it possibly be straightforward, with the Congregation, the trials in Berwick, the Elizabethan intelligence service, and the Knights of Lazarus all vying for your attention?"

"Being a member of the Congregation and serving as a spy should be helps—not hindrances." Matthew stared out the window. "I thought we'd come to the Old Lodge, use the services of Widow Beaton, find the manuscript in Oxford, and be gone within a few weeks."

I bit my lip to keep from pointing out the flaws in his strategy—Walter, Henry, and Gallowglass had already done so repeatedly this evening—but my expression gave me away.

"It was shortsighted of me," he said with a sigh. "And it's not just establishing your credibility that's a problem, or avoiding the obvious traps like witch trials and wars. I'm overwhelmed, too. The broad canvas of what I did for Elizabeth and the Congregation—and the countermoves I made on behalf of my father—that's clear, but all the details have faded. I know the date, but not the day of the week. That means I'm not sure which messenger is due to arrive and when the next delivery will be made. I could have sworn I'd parted ways with Gallowglass and Hancock before Halloween."

"The devil is always in the details," I murmured. I brushed at the sooty track of dried blood that marked the passage of his tear. There were specks of it near the corner of his eye, a thin trace down his cheek. "I should have realized your father might contact you."

"It was only a matter of time before his letter came. Whenever Pierre brings the mail, I steel myself. But the courier had already been and gone today. His handwriting took me by surprise, that's all," he explained. "I'd forgotten how strong it once was. When we got him back from the Nazis in 1944, his body was so broken that not even vampire blood could mend it. Philippe couldn't hold a pen. He loved to write, and all he could manage was an illegible scrawl." I knew of Philippe's capture and captivity in World War II, but few details of what he'd suffered at the hands of the Nazis who had wanted to determine how much pain a vampire could endure.

"Maybe the goddess wanted us back in 1590 for more than just my benefit. Seeing Philippe again may reopen these old wounds of yours—and heal them."

"Not before making them worse." Matthew's head dipped.

"But in the end it might make them better." I smoothed his hair over his hard, stubborn skull. "You still haven't opened your father's letter."

"I know what it says."

"Perhaps you should open it anyway."

At last Matthew slid his finger under the seal and broke it. The coin tumbled out of the wax, and he caught it in his palm. When he unfolded the thick paper, it released a faint scent of laurel and rosemary.

"Is that Greek?" I asked, looking over his shoulder at the single line of text and a swirling rendition of the letter *phi* below.

"Yes." Matthew traced the letters, making his first tentative contact with his father. "He commands me to come home. Immediately."

"Can you bear seeing him again?"

"No. Yes." Matthew's fingers crumpled the page into his fist. "I don't know."

I took the page away from him, flattening it back into its rectangle. The coin sparkled in Matthew's palm. It was such a small sliver of metal to have caused so much trouble.

"You won't face him alone." Standing by his side when he saw his dead father wasn't much, but it was all I could do to ease his grief.

"Each of us is alone with Philippe. Some think my father can see into one's very soul," Matthew murmured. "It worries me to take you there. With Ysabeau I could predict how she would react: coldness, anger, then acquiescence. When it comes to Philippe, I have no idea. No one understands the way Philippe's mind works, what information he possesses, what traps he's laid. If I am secretive, then my father is inscrutable. Not even the Congregation knows what he's up to, and God knows they spend enough time trying to figure it out."

"It will be fine," I reassured him. Philippe would have to accept me into the family. Like Matthew's mother and brother, he would have no choice.

"Don't think you can best him," Matthew warned. "You may be like my mother, as Gallowglass said, but even she gets caught in his web from time to time."

"And are you still a member of the Congregation in the present? Is that how you knew that Knox and Domenico were members?" The witch Peter Knox had been stalking me since the moment I called up Ashmole 782 at the Bodleian. As for Domenico Michele, he was a vampire with old animosities when it came to the de Clermonts. He'd been present at La Pierre before yet another member of the Congregation tortured me.

"No," Matthew said shortly, turning away.

"So what Hancock said about a de Clermont always being on the Congregation is no longer true?" I held my breath. *Say yes,* I urged him silently, *even if it's a lie.*

"It's still true," he said evenly, crushing my hope.

"Then who . . . ?" I trailed off. "Ysabeau? Baldwin? Surely not Marcus!" I couldn't believe that Matthew's mother, his brother, or his son could be involved without someone letting it slip.

"There are creatures on my family tree that you don't know, Diana. In any case, I'm not free to divulge the identity of the one who sits at the Congregation's table."

"Do any of the rules that bind the rest of us apply to your family?" I wondered. "You meddle in politics—I've seen the account books that prove it. Are you hoping that when we return to the present, this mysterious family member is going to somehow shield us from the Congregation's wrath?"

"I don't know," Matthew said tightly. "I'm not sure of anything. Not anymore."

Our plans for departure took shape quickly. Walter and Gallowglass argued about the best route, while Matthew set his affairs in order.

Hancock was dispatched to London with Henry and a leather-wrapped packet of correspondence. As a peer of the realm, the earl was required at court for the celebrations of the queen's anniversary on the seventeenth of November. George and Tom were packed off to Oxford with a substantial sum of money and a disgraced Marlowe. Hancock warned them of the dire consequences that would ensue if the daemon caused any more trouble. Matthew might be far away, but Hancock would be within sword's reach and would not hesitate to strike if it was warranted. In addition, Matthew instructed George on exactly what questions about alchemical manuscripts he could ask the scholars of Oxford.

My own affairs were far simpler to arrange. I had few personal items to pack: Ysabeau's earrings, my new shoes, a few items of clothing. Françoise turned all her attention to making me a sturdy, cinnamon-colored gown for the journey. Its high, fur-lined collar was designed to fasten closely and keep out the winds and rain. The silky fox pelts that Françoise stitched into the lining of my cloak would serve the same purpose, as would the bands of fur she inserted into the embroidered edges of my new gloves.

My last act at the Old Lodge was to take the book Matthew had given me to the library. It would be easy to lose such an item on the way to Sept-Tours, and I wanted my diary to be as safe from prying eyes as possible. I stooped to the rushes and picked up sprigs of rosemary and lavender. Then I went to Matthew's desk and selected a quill and a pot of ink and made one final entry.

> *♃ 5 November 1590 cold rain*
> *News from home. We are preparing for a journey.*

After blowing gently on the words to set the ink, I slipped the rosemary and lavender into the crevice between the pages. My aunt used rosemary for memory spells and lavender to breathe a note of caution into love charms—a fitting combination for our present circumstances.

"Wish us luck, Sarah," I whispered as I slid the small volume into the end of the shelf, in hopes that it would still be there should I return.

Rima Jaén hated the month of November. The hours of daylight shrank, giving up their battle against the shadows a few moments earlier with each passing day. And it was a terrible time to be in Seville, with the whole city gearing up for the holiday season and rain just around the corner. The normally erratic driving habits of the city's residents grew worse by the hour.

Rima had been stuck at her desk for weeks. Her boss had decided to clear out the storage rooms in the attic. Last winter the rain had made it through the ancient, cracked roof tiles on top of the decrepit house, and the forecast for the coming months was even worse. There was no money to fix the problem, so the maintenance staff was hauling moldy cardboard boxes down the stairs to make sure that nothing of value was damaged in future storms. Everything else was discreetly gotten rid of in such a way that no potential donors could discover what was afoot.

It was a dirty, deceitful business, but it had to be done, Rima reflected. The library was a small, specialist archive with scant resources. The core of its collections came from a prominent Andalusian family whose members could trace their roots back to the *reconquista,* when the Christians had taken back the peninsula from the Muslim warriors who had claimed it in the eighth century. Few scholars had reason to poke through the bizarre range of books and objects the Gonçalves had collected over the years. Most researchers were down the street at the Archivo General de Indias, arguing about Columbus. Her fellow Sevillanos wanted their libraries to have the latest thriller, not crumbling Jesuit instruction manuals from the 1700s and women's fashion magazines from the 1800s.

Rima picked up the small volume sitting on the corner of her desk and swung a pair of brightly colored glasses down from the top of her head, where they were holding back her black hair. She'd noticed the book a week ago, when one of the maintenance workers had dropped a wooden crate before her with a grunt of displeasure. Since then she'd entered it into the collection as Gonçalve Manuscript 4890 along with the description *"English commonplace book, anonymous, late 16th century."* Like most commonplace books, it was mostly blank. Rima had seen one Spanish example owned by a Gonçalve heir sent to the University of Seville in 1628. It had been finely bound, ruled, and paginated with ornate numbers set in swirls of multicolored ink. There was not a single word in it. Even in the past, people never quite lived up to their aspirations.

Commonplace books like this one were repositories for biblical passages, snatches of poetry, mottoes, and the sayings of classical authors. They typically included doodles and shopping lists as well as lyrics to bawdy songs and accounts of strange and important events. This one was no different, Rima thought. Sadly, someone had ripped out the first page. Once it had probably borne the owner's name. Without it there was virtually no chance of identifying the owner, or any of the other people mentioned only by initials. Historians were far less interested in this sort of nameless, faceless evidence, as though its anonymity somehow made the person behind it less important.

On the remaining pages there was a chart listing all the English coinage in use in the sixteenth century and its relative worth. One page in the back had a hastily scribbled list of clothing: a cloak, two pairs of shoes, a gown trimmed in fur, six smocks, four petticoats, and a pair of gloves. There were a few dated entries that made no sense at all and a headache cure—a caudle, made with milk and wine. Rima smiled and wondered if it would work on her migraines.

She should have returned the little volume to the locked rooms on the third floor where the manuscripts were stored, but something about it made her want to keep it nearby. It was clear that a woman had written it. The round hand was endearingly shaky and uncertain, and the words snaked up and down on pages liberally sprinkled with inkblots. No learned sixteenth-century man wrote like that, unless he was ill or aged. This book's author was neither. There was a curious vibrancy to the entries that was strangely at odds with the tentative handwriting.

She had shown the manuscript to Javier López, the charming yet entirely unqualified person hired by the last of the Gonçalves to transform the family's house and personal effects into a library and museum. His expansive ground-floor office was paneled in fine mahogany and had the only working heaters in the building. During their brief interview, he'd dismissed her suggestion that the book deserved more careful study. He also forbade her to take photographs of it so she could share the images with colleagues in the United Kingdom. As for her belief that the book's owner had been a woman, the director had muttered something about feminists and waved her out of his office.

And so the book remained on her desk. In Seville such a book would always be unwanted and unimportant. Nobody came to Spain to look for English commonplace books. They went to the British Library, or the Folger Shakespeare Library in the United States.

There was that strange man who came by now and again to comb through the collections. He was French, and his appraising stare made Rima uncomfortable. Herbert Cantal—or maybe it was Gerbert Cantal. She couldn't remember. He'd left a card on his last visit and had encouraged her to get in touch if anything interesting turned up. When Rima asked what, exactly, might qualify, the man had said he was interested in everything. It was not the most helpful of responses.

Now something interesting *had* turned up. Unfortunately, the man's business card had not, though she'd cleaned out her desk in an effort to locate it. Rima would have to wait until he appeared again to share this little book with him. Perhaps he would be more interested in it than her boss was.

Rima flipped through the pages. There was a tiny sprig of lavender and a few crumbling rosemary leaves pressed between two of the pages. She hadn't seen them before and picked them carefully from the crevice of the binding. For a moment there was a trace of scent in the faded bloom, forging a connection between herself and a person who had lived hundreds of years ago. Rima smiled wistfully, thinking about the woman she would never know.

"Más basura." Daniel from building maintenance was back, his worn gray overalls grimy from transporting boxes from the attic. He slid several more boxes off the beaten-up dolly and onto the floor. In spite of the cool weather, sweat stood out on his forehead, and he wiped it off with his sleeve, leaving a smudge of black dust. *"Café?"*

It was the third time this week he'd asked her out. Rima knew that he found her attractive. Her mother's Berber ancestry appealed to some men—not surprising, since it had bestowed upon her soft curves, warm skin, and almond-shaped eyes. Daniel had been muttering salacious comments, brushing against her backside when she went to the mail room, and ogling her breasts for years. That he was five inches shorter than she and twice her age didn't seem to deter him.

"Estoy muy ocupada," Rima replied.

Daniel's grunt was infused with deep skepticism. He glanced back at the boxes as he left. The one on top held a moldering fur muff and a stuffed wren attached to a piece of cedar. Daniel shook his head, astonished that she would prefer to spend her time with dead animals than with him.

"Gracias," Rima murmured as he departed. She closed the book gently and returned it to its place on her desk.

While she transferred the box's contents to a nearby table, Rima's eyes strayed back to the little volume in its simple leather cover. In four hundred years, would the only proof of her existence be a page from her calendar, a shopping list, and a scrap of paper with her grandmother's recipe for *alfajores* on it, all placed in a file labeled *"Anonymous, of no importance"* and stored in an archive no one ever visited?

Such dark thoughts were bound to be unlucky. Rima shivered and touched the hand-shaped amulet of the Prophet's daughter, Fatima. It hung around her neck on a leather cord and had been passed down among the women of her family for as long as anyone could remember.

"Khamsa fi ainek," she whispered, hoping her words would ward off any evil spirit she might have unwittingly called.

PART II

Sept-Tours and the Village of Saint-Lucien

"The usual place?" Gallowglass asked quietly as he put down his oars and raised the solitary sail. Though it would be more than four hours before the sun rose, other craft were visible in the darkness. I picked out the shadowed outlines of a sail, a lantern swinging from a post in the stern of a neighboring vessel.

"Walter said we were going to Saint-Malo," I said, my head turning in consternation. Raleigh had accompanied us from the Old Lodge to Portsmouth and had piloted the boat that took us to Guernsey. We'd left him standing on the dock near the village of Saint-Pierre-Port. He could go no farther—not with a price on his head in Catholic Europe.

"I remember well enough where Raleigh told me to go, Auntie, but he's a pirate. And English. And he's not here. I'm asking Matthew."

"'*Immensi tremor oceani,*'" Matthew whispered as he contemplated the heaving seas. Staring out across the black water, he had all the expression of a carved figurehead. And his reply to his nephew's question was odd—*the trembling of the immense ocean.* I wondered if I had somehow misunderstood his Latin.

"The tide will be with us, and it is closer to Fougères by horse than Saint-Malo." Gallowglass continued as though Matthew were making sense. "She'll be no colder on the water than on land in this weather, and still plenty of riding before her."

"And you will be leaving us." It wasn't a question but a pronouncement of fact. Matthew's eyelids dropped. He nodded. "Very well."

Gallowglass drew in the sail, and the boat changed from a southerly to a more easterly course. Matthew sat on the deck, his back against the curved supports of the hull, and drew me into the circle of his arms so that his cloak was wrapped around me.

True sleep was impossible, but I dozed against Matthew's chest. It had been a grueling journey thus far, with horses pushed to the limit and boats commandeered. The temperature was frigid, and a thin layer of frost built up on the nap of our English wool. Gallowglass and Pierre kept up a steady patter of conversation in some French dialect, but Matthew remained quiet. He responded to their questions yet kept his own thoughts hidden behind an eerily composed mask.

The weather changed to a misty snow around dawn. Gallowglass's beard turned white, transforming him into a fair imitation of Santa Claus. Pierre adjusted the sails at his command, and a landscape of grays and whites revealed the coast of France. No more than thirty minutes later, the tide began to race toward the shore. The boat was lifted up on the waves, and through the mist a steeple pierced the clouds. It was surprisingly close, the base of the structure obscured by the weather. I gasped.

"Hold tight," Gallowglass said grimly as Pierre released the sail.

The boat shot through the mist. The call of seagulls and the slap of water against rock told me we were nearing shore, but the boat didn't slow. Gallowglass jammed an oar into the flooding tide, angling us sharply. Someone cried out, in warning or greeting.

"Il est le chevalier de Clermont!" Pierre called back, cupping his hands around his mouth. His words were met with silence before scurrying footfalls sounded through the cold air.

"Gallowglass!" We were heading straight for a wall. I scrabbled for an oar to fend off certain disaster. No sooner had my fingers closed around it than Matthew plucked it from my grasp.

"He's been putting in at this spot for centuries, and his people for longer than that," Matthew said calmly, holding the oar lightly in his hands. Improbably, the boat's bow took another sharp left and the hull was broadside to slabs of rough-hewn granite. High above, four men with hooks and ropes emerged to snare the boat and hold it steady. The water level continued to rise with alarming speed, carrying the boat upward until we were level with a small stone house. A set of stairs climbed into invisibility. Pierre hopped onto the landing, talking fast and low and gesturing at the boat. Two armed soldiers joined us for a moment, then sped off in the direction of the stairs.

"We have arrived at Mont Saint-Michel, *madame.*" Pierre held out his hand. I took it and stepped from the boat. "Here you will rest while *milord* speaks with the abbot."

My knowledge of the island was limited to the stories swapped by friends of mine who sailed every summer around the Isle of Wight: that it was surrounded at low tide by quicksand and at high tide by such dangerous currents that boats were crushed against the rocks. I looked over my shoulder at our tiny boat and shuddered. It was a miracle that we were still alive.

While I tried to get my bearings, Matthew studied his nephew, who remained motionless in the stern. "It would be safer for Diana if you came along."

"When your friends aren't getting her into trouble, your wife seems able to take care of herself." Gallowglass looked up at me with a smile.

"Philippe will ask after you."

"Tell him—" Gallowglass stopped, stared off into the distance. The vampire's blue eyes were deep with longing. "Tell him I have not yet succeeded in forgetting."

"For his sake you must try to forgive," said Matthew quietly.

"I will never forgive," Gallowglass said coldly, "and Philippe would never ask it of me. My father died at the hands of the French, and not a single creature stood up to the king. Until I have made peace with the past, I will not set foot in France."

"Hugh is gone, God rest his soul. Your grandfather is still among us. Don't squander your time with him." Matthew lifted his foot from the boat. Without a word of farewell, he turned and took my elbow, steering me toward a bedraggled huddle of trees with barren branches. Feeling the cold weight of Gallowglass's stare, I turned and locked eyes with the Gael. His hand rose in a silent gesture of leave.

Matthew was quiet as we approached the stairs. I couldn't see where they led and soon lost count of the number of them. I concentrated instead on keeping my footing on the worn, slick treads. Chips of ice fell from the hem of my skirts, and the wind whistled within my wide hood. A sturdy door, ornamented with heavy straps of iron that were rusted and pitted from the salt spray, opened before us.

More steps. I pressed my lips together, lifted my skirts, and kept going.

More soldiers. As we approached, they flattened themselves against the walls to make room for us to pass. Matthew's fingers tightened a fraction on my elbow, but otherwise the men might have been wraiths for all the attention he paid them.

We entered a room with a forest of columns holding up its vaulted roof. Large fireplaces studded the walls, spreading blessed warmth. I sighed with relief and shook out my cloak, shedding water and ice in all directions. A gentle cough directed my attention to a man standing before one of the blazes. He was dressed in the red robes of a cardinal and appeared to be in his late twenties—a terribly young age for someone to have risen so high in the Catholic Church's hierarchy.

"Ah, *Chevalier de Clermont.* Or are we calling you something else these days? You have long been out of France. Perhaps you have taken Walsingham's name along with his position, now that he is gone to hell where he belongs." The cardinal's English was impeccable although heavily accented. "We have, on the *seigneur*'s instructions, been watching for you for three days. There was no mention of a woman."

Matthew dropped my arm so that he could step forward. He genuflected with a smooth bend of his knee and kissed the ring on the man's extended hand. "*Éminence.* I thought you were in Rome, choosing our new pope. Imagine my delight at finding you here." Matthew didn't sound happy. I wondered uneasily what we'd stepped into by coming to Mont Saint-Michel and not Saint-Malo as Walter had planned.

"France needs me more than the conclave does at present. These recent murders of kings and queens do not please God." The cardinal's eyes sparked a warning. "Elizabeth will discover that soon enough, when she meets Him."

"I am not here on English business, Cardinal Joyeuse. This is my wife, Diana." Matthew held his father's thin silver coin between his first and middle fingers. "I am returning home."

"So I am told. Your father sent this to ensure your safe passage." Joyeuse tossed a gleaming object to Matthew, who caught it neatly. "Philippe de Clermont forgets himself and behaves as though he were the king of France."

"My father has no need to rule, for he is the sharp sword that makes and unmakes kings," Matthew said softly. He slid the heavy golden ring over the gloved knuckle of his middle finger. Set within it was a carved red stone. I was sure the pattern incised in the ring was the same as the mark on my back. "Your masters know that if it were not for my father, the Catholic cause would be lost in France. Otherwise you would not be here."

"Perhaps it would be better for all concerned if the *seigneur* really were king, given the throne's present Protestant occupant. But that is a topic for us to discuss in private," Cardinal Joyeuse said tiredly. He gestured to a servant standing in the shadows by the door. "Take the *chevalier*'s wife to her room. We must leave you, *madame.* Your husband has been too long among heretics. An extended period spent kneeling on a cold stone floor will remind him who he truly is."

My face must have shown my dismay at being alone in such a place.

"Pierre will stay with you," Matthew assured me before he bent and pressed his lips to mine. "We ride out when the tide turns."

And that was the last glimpse I had of Matthew Clairmont, scientist. The man who strode toward the door was no longer an Oxford don but a Renaissance prince. It was in his bearing, the set of his shoulders, his aura of banked strength, and the cold look in his eyes. Hamish had been right to warn me that Matthew would not be the same man here. Under Matthew's smooth surface, a profound metamorphosis was taking place.

Somewhere high above, the bells tolled the hours.

Scientist. Vampire. Warrior. Spy. The bells paused before the final knell.

Prince.

I wondered what more our journey would reveal about this complex man I had married.

"Let us not keep God waiting, Cardinal Joyeuse," Matthew said sharply. Joyeuse followed behind, as if Mont Saint-Michel belonged to the de Clermont family and not the church.

Beside me, Pierre let out a gentle exhalation. *"Milord est lui-même,"* he murmured with relief.

Milord is himself. But was he still mine?

Matthew might be a prince, but there was no doubt who was king.

With every strike of our horses' hooves on the frozen roads, the power and influence of Matthew's father grew. As we drew closer to Philippe de Clermont, his son became more remote and imperious—a combination that put my teeth on edge and led to several heated arguments. Matthew always apologized for his high-handed conduct once his temper came off the boil, and, knowing the stress he was under as we approached his reunion with his father, I forgave him.

After braving the exposed sands around Mont Saint-Michel at low tide and traveling inland, de Clermont allies welcomed us into the city of Fougères and lodged us in a comfortably appointed tower on the ramparts overlooking the French countryside. Two nights later, footmen with torches met us on the road outside the city of Baugé. There was a familiar badge on their livery: Philippe's insignia of a cross and crescent moon. I'd seen the symbol before when rooting through Matthew's desk drawer at Sept-Tours.

"What is this place?" I asked after the footmen led us to a deserted château. It was surprisingly warm for an empty residence, and the delicious smell of cooked food floated through the echoing corridors.

"The house of an old friend." Matthew pried the shoes off my frozen feet. His thumbs pressed into my frigid soles, and the blood began to return to my extremities. I groaned. Pierre put a cup of warm, spicy wine in my hands. "This was René's favorite hunting lodge. It was so full of life when he lived here, with artists and scholars in every room. My father manages it now. With the constant wars, there hasn't been an opportunity to give the château the attention it needs."

While we were still at the Old Lodge, Matthew and Walter had lectured me on the ongoing struggles between French Protestants and Catholics over who would control the Crown—and the country. From our windows at Fougères, I'd seen distant plumes of smoke marking the Protestant army's latest encampment, and ruined houses and churches dotted our route. I was shocked by the extent of the devastation.

Because of the conflict, my carefully constructed background story had to change. In England I was supposed to be a Protestant woman of French descent fleeing her native land to save her life and practice her faith. Here it was essential that I be a long-suffering English Catholic. Somehow Matthew managed to remember all the lies and half-truths required to maintain our multiple assumed identities, not to mention the historical details of every place through which we traveled.

"We're in the province of Anjou now." Matthew's deep voice brought my attention back. "The people you meet will suspect you're a Protestant spy because you speak English, no matter what story we tell them. This part of France refuses to acknowledge the king's claim to the throne and would prefer a Catholic ruler."

"As would Philippe," I murmured. It was not just Cardinal Joyeuse who was benefiting from Philippe's influence. Catholic priests with hollow cheeks and haunted eyes had stopped to speak with us along the way, sharing news and sending thanks to Matthew's father for his assistance. None left empty-handed.

"He doesn't care about the subtleties of Christian belief. In other parts of the country, my father supports the Protestants."

"That's a remarkably ecumenical view."

"All Philippe cares about is saving France from itself. This past August our new king, Henri of Navarre, tried to force the city of Paris to his religious and political position. Parisians chose to starve rather than bow to a

Protestant king." Matthew raked his fingers through his hair, a sign of distress. "Thousands died, and now my father does not trust the humans to sort out the mess."

Philippe was not inclined to let his son manage his own affairs either. Pierre woke us before dawn to announce that fresh horses were saddled and ready. He'd received word that we were expected at a town more than a hundred miles away—in two days.

"It's impossible. We can't travel that far so fast!" I was physically fit, but no amount of modern exercise was equivalent to riding more than fifty miles a day across open countryside in November.

"We have little choice," Matthew said grimly. "If we delay, he'll only send more men to hurry us along. Better to do what he asks." Later that day, when I was ready to weep with fatigue, Matthew lifted me into his saddle without asking and rode until the horses ran themselves out. I was too tired to protest.

We reached the stone walls and timbered houses of Saint-Benoît on schedule, just as Philippe had commanded. By that point we were close enough to Sept-Tours that neither Pierre nor Matthew was much concerned with propriety, so I rode astride. In spite of our adherence to his schedule, Philippe continued to increase the number of family retainers accompanying us, as though he feared we might change our minds and return to England. Some dogged our heels on the roads. Others cleared the way, securing food, horses, and places to stay in bustling inns, isolated houses, and barricaded monasteries. Once we climbed into the rocky hills left by the extinct volcanoes of the Auvergne, we often spotted the silhouettes of riders along the forbidding peaks. After they saw us, they whirled away to carry reports of our progress back to Sept-Tours.

Two days later, as twilight fell, Matthew, Pierre, and I stopped on one of these ragged mountaintops, the de Clermont family château barely visible through swirling gusts of snow. The straight lines of the central keep were familiar, but otherwise I might not have recognized the place. Its encircling walls were intact, as were all six of the round towers, each capped by conical copper roofs that had aged to a soft bottle green. Smoke came from chimneys tucked out of sight behind the towers' crenellations, the jagged outlines suggesting that some crazed giant with pinking shears had trimmed every wall. There was a snow-covered garden within the enclosure as well as rectangular beds beyond.

In modern times the fortress was forbidding. Now, with religious and civil war all around, its defensive capabilities were even more obvious. A formidable gatehouse stood vigil between Sept-Tours and the village. Inside, people hurried this way and that, many of them armed. Peering between snowflakes in the dusky light, I spotted wooden structures dotted throughout the enclosed courtyard. The light from their small windows created cubes of warm color in the otherwise unbroken stretches of gray stone and snow-covered ground.

My mare let out a warm, moist exhalation. She was the finest horse I'd ridden since our first day of travel. Matthew's present mount was large, inky-colored, and mean, snapping at everyone who got near him save the creature on his back. Both animals came from the de Clermont stables and knew their way home without any direction, eager to reach their oat buckets and a warm stable.

"*Dieu*. This is the last place on earth I imagined finding myself." Matthew blinked, slowly, as if he expected the château to disappear before his eyes.

I reached over and rested my hand on his forearm. "Even now you have a choice. We can turn back." Pierre looked at me with pity, and Matthew gave me a rueful smile.

"You don't know my father." His gaze returned to the castle.

Torches blazed all along our approach when at last we entered Sept-Tours. The heavy slabs of wood and iron were open in readiness, and a team of four men stood silently by as we passed. The gates slammed shut behind us, and two men drew a long timber from its hiding place in the walls to secure the entrance. Six days spent riding across France had taught me that these were wise precautions. People were suspicious of strangers, fearing the arrival of another marauding band of soldiers, a fresh hell of bloodshed and violence, a new lord to please.

A veritable army—humans and vampires both—awaited us inside. Half a dozen of them took charge of the horses. Pierre handed one a small packet of correspondence, while others asked him questions in low voices while sneaking furtive glances at me. No one came near or offered assistance. I sat atop my horse, shaking with fatigue and cold, and searched the crowd for Philippe. Surely he would order someone to help me down.

Matthew noticed my predicament and swung off his horse with enviably fluid grace. In several long strides, he was at my side, where he gently removed my unfeeling foot from the stirrup and rotated it slightly to restore its mobility. I thanked him, not wanting my first performance at Sept-Tours to involve tumbling into the trampled snow and dirt of the courtyard.

"Which of these men is your father?" I whispered as he crossed under the horse's neck to reach my other foot.

"None of them. He's inside, seemingly unconcerned with seeing us after insisting we ride as though the hounds of hell were in pursuit. You should be inside, too." Matthew began issuing orders in curt French, dispersing the gawking servants in every direction until only one vampire was left standing at the base of a corkscrew of wooden steps that rose to the château's door. I experienced the jarring sense of past and present colliding when I remembered climbing a not-yet-constructed set of stone steps and meeting Ysabeau for the first time.

"Alain." Matthew's face softened with relief.

"Welcome home." The vampire spoke English. As he approached with a slight hitch in his gait, the details of his appearance came into focus: the salt-and-pepper hair, the lines around his kind eyes, his wiry build.

"Thank you, Alain. This is my wife, Diana."

"Madame de Clermont." Alain bowed, keeping a careful, respectful distance.

"It's a pleasure to meet you, Alain." We had never met, but I already associated his name with steadfast loyalty and support. It had been Alain that Matthew called in the middle of the night when he wanted to be sure that there was food waiting for me at Sept-Tours in the twenty-first century.

"Your father is waiting," Alain said, stepping aside to let us pass.

"Have them send food to my rooms—something simple. Diana is tired and hungry." Matthew handed Alain his gloves. "I'll see him momentarily."

"He is expecting both of you now." A carefully neutral expression settled over Alain's face. "Do be careful on the stairs, *madame.* The treads are icy."

"Is he?" Matthew looked up at the square keep, mouth tightening.

With Matthew's hand firmly at my elbow, I had no trouble navigating the stairs. But my legs were shaking so badly after the climb that my feet caught the edge of an uneven flagstone in the entrance. That slip was enough to set Matthew's temper ablaze.

"Philippe is being unreasonable," Matthew snapped as he caught me around the waist. "She's been traveling for days."

"He was most explicit in his orders, sir." Alain's stiff formality was a warning.

"It's all right, Matthew." I pushed my hood from my face to survey the great hall beyond. Gone was the display of armor and pikes I'd seen in the twenty-first century. In their place stood a carved wooden screen that helped deflect the drafts when the door was opened. Gone, too, were the faux-medieval decorations, the round table, the porcelain bowl. Instead tapestries blew gently against stone walls as the warm air from the fireplace mingled with the colder air from outside. Two long tables flanked by low benches filled the remaining space, and men and women shuttled between them laying out plates and cups for supper. There was room for dozens of creatures to gather there. The minstrels' gallery high above wasn't empty now but crowded with musicians readying their instruments.

"Amazing," I breathed from between stiff lips.

Cold fingers grasped my chin and turned it. "You're blue," Matthew said.

"I will bring a brazier for her feet, and warm wine," Alain promised. "And we will build up the fires."

A warmblooded human appeared and took my wet cloak. Matthew turned sharply in the direction of what I knew as the breakfast room. I listened but heard nothing.

Alain shook his head apologetically. "He is not in a good temper."

"Evidently not." Matthew looked down. "Philippe is bellowing for us. Are you sure, Diana? If you don't want to see him tonight, I'll brave his wrath."

But Matthew would not be alone for his first meeting with his father in more than six decades. He had stood by me while I'd faced my ghosts, and I would do the same for him. Then I was going to go to bed, where I planned to remain until Christmas.

"Let's go," I said resolutely, picking up my skirts.

Sept-Tours was too ancient to have modern conveniences like corridors, so we snaked through an arched door to the right of the fireplace and into the corner of a room that would one day be Ysabeau's grand salon. It wasn't overstuffed with fine furniture now but decorated with the same austerity as every other place I'd seen on our journey. The heavy oak furniture resisted casual theft and could sustain the occasional ill effects of battle, as evidenced by the deep slash that cut diagonally across the surface of a chest.

From there Alain led us into the room where Ysabeau and I would one day take our breakfast amid warm terra-cotta walls at a table set with pottery and weighty silver cutlery. It was a far cry from that place in its present state, with only a table and chair. The tabletop was covered with papers and other tools of the secretary. There was no time to see more before we were climbing a worn stone staircase to an unfamiliar part of the château.

The stairs came to an abrupt halt on a wide landing. A long gallery opened up to the left, housing an odd assortment of gadgets, clocks, weaponry, portraits, and furniture. A battered golden crown perched casually on the marble head of some ancient god. A lumpy pigeon's-blood ruby the size of an egg winked malevolently at me from the crown's center.

"This way," Alain said, motioning us forward into the next chamber. Here was another staircase, this one leading up rather than down. A few uncomfortable benches sat on either side of a closed door. Alain waited, patiently and silently, for a response to our presence. When it came, the single Latin word resounded through the thick wood:

"Introite."

Matthew started at the sound. Alain cast a worried look at him and pushed the door. It silently swung open on substantial, well-oiled hinges.

A man sat opposite, his back to us and his hair gleaming. Even seated it was evident that he was quite tall, with the broad shoulders of an athlete. A pen scratched against paper, providing a steady treble note to harmonize with the intermittent pops of wood burning in the fireplace and the gusts of wind howling outside.

A bass note rumbled into the music of the place: *"Sedete."*

Now it was my turn to jump. With no door to muffle its impact, Philippe's voice resonated until my ears tingled. The man was used to being obeyed, at once and without question. My feet moved toward the two awaiting chairs so that I could sit as he'd commanded. I took three steps before realizing that Matthew was still in the doorway. I returned to his side and grasped his hand in mine. Matthew stared down, bewildered, and shook himself free from his memories.

In moments we had crossed the room. I settled into a chair with the promised wine and a pierced-metal foot warmer to prop up my legs. Alain withdrew with a sympathetic glance and a nod. Then we waited. It was difficult for me but impossible for Matthew. His tension increased until he was nearly vibrating with suppressed emotion.

By the time his father acknowledged our presence, my anxiety and temper were both dangerously close to the surface. I was staring down at my hands and wondering if they were strong enough to strangle him when two ferociously cold spots bloomed on my bowed head. Lifting my chin, I found myself gazing into the tawny eyes of a Greek god.

When I had first seen Matthew, my instinctive response had been to run. But Matthew—large and brooding as he'd been that September night in the Bodleian Library—hadn't appeared half so otherworldly. And it wasn't because Philippe de Clermont was a monster. On the contrary. He was, quite simply, the most breathtaking creature I had ever seen—supernatural, preternatural, daemonic, or human.

No one could look at Philippe de Clermont and think he was mortal flesh. The vampire's features were too perfect, and eerily symmetrical. Straight, dark eyebrows settled over eyes that were a pale, mutable golden brown touched with flecks of green. Exposure to sun and elements had touched his brown hair with strands of gleaming gold, silver, and bronze. Philippe's mouth was soft and sensual, though anger had drawn his lips hard and tight tonight.

Pressing my own lips together to keep my jaw from dropping, I met his appraising stare. Once I did, his eyes moved slowly and deliberately to Matthew.

"Explain yourself." The words were quiet, but they didn't conceal Philippe's fury. There was more than one angry vampire in the room, however. Now that the shock of seeing Philippe had passed, Matthew tried to take the upper hand.

"You commanded me to Sept-Tours. Here I am, alive and well, despite your grandson's hysterical reports." Matthew tossed the silver coin onto his father's oak table. It landed on its edge and whirled on an invisible axis before toppling flat.

"Surely it would have been better for your wife to remain at home this time of year." Like Alain, Philippe spoke English as flawlessly as a native.

"Diana is my mate, Father. I could hardly leave her in England with Henry and Walter simply because it might snow."

"Stand down, Matthew," Philippe growled. The sound was as leonine as the rest of him. The de Clermont family was a menagerie of formidable beasts. In Matthew's presence I was always reminded of wolves. With Ysabeau it was falcons. Gallowglass had made me think of a bear. Philippe was akin to yet another deadly predator.

"Gallowglass and Walter tell me the witch requires my protection." The lion reached for a letter. He tapped the edge of it on the table and stared at Matthew. "I thought that protecting weaker creatures was your job now that you occupy the family's seat on the Congregation."

"Diana isn't weak—and she needs more protection than the Congregation can afford, given the fact that she is married to me. Will you bestow it?" The challenge was in Matthew's tone now, as well as his bearing.

"First I need to hear her account," Philippe said. He looked at me and lifted his eyebrows.

"We met by chance. I knew she was a witch, but the bond between us was undeniable," Matthew said. "Her own people have turned on her—"

A hand that might have been mistaken for a paw rose in a gesture commanding quiet. Philippe returned his attention to his son.

"Matthaios." Philippe's lazy drawl had the efficiency of a slow-moving whip, silencing his son immediately. "Am I to understand that *you* need my protection?"

"Of course not," Matthew said indignantly.

"Then hush and let the witch speak."

Intent on giving Matthew's father what he wanted so that we could get out of his unnerving presence as quickly as possible, I considered how best to recount our recent adventures. Rehearsing every detail would take too long, and the chances that Matthew might explode in the meantime were excellent. I took a deep breath and began.

"My name is Diana Bishop, and my parents were both powerful witches. Other witches killed them when they were far from home, while I was still a child. Before they died, they spellbound me. My mother was a seer, and she knew what was to come."

Philippe's eyes narrowed with suspicion. I understood his caution. It was still difficult for me to understand why two people who loved me had broken the witches' ethical code and placed their only daughter in magical shackles.

"Growing up, I was a family disgrace—a witch who couldn't light a candle or perform a spell properly. I turned my back on the Bishops and went to university." With this revelation Matthew began to shift uneasily in his seat. "I studied the history of alchemy."

"Diana studies the *art* of alchemy," Matthew corrected, shooting me a warning glance. But his convoluted half-truths wouldn't satisfy his father.

"I'm a timewalker." The word hung in the air between the three of us. "You call it a *fileuse de temps*."

"Oh, I am well aware of what you are," Philippe said in the same lazy tone. A fleeting look of surprise touched Matthew's face. "I have lived a long time, *madame,* and have known many creatures. You are not from this time, nor the past, so you must be from the future. And *Matthaios* traveled back with you, for he is not the same man he was eight months ago. The Matthew I know would never have looked twice at a witch." The vampire drew in a deep breath. "My grandson warned me that you both smelled very odd."

"Philippe, let me explain—" But Matthew was not destined to finish his sentences this evening.

"As troubling as many aspects of this situation are, I am glad to see that we can look forward to a sensible attitude toward shaving in the years to come." Philippe idly scratched his own neatly clipped beard and mustache. "Beards are a sign of lice, not wisdom, after all."

"I'm told Matthew looks like an invalid." I drew a tired sigh. "But I don't know a spell to fix it."

Philippe waved my words away. "A beard is easy enough to arrange. You were telling me of your interest in alchemy."

"Yes. I found a book—one that many others have sought. I met Matthew when he came to steal it from me, but he couldn't because I'd already let it out of my hands. Every creature for miles was after me then. I had to stop working!"

A sound that might have been suppressed laughter set a muscle in Philippe's jaw throbbing. It was, I discovered, hard to tell with lions whether they were amused or about to pounce.

"We think it's the book of origins," Matthew said. His expression was proud, though my calling of the manuscript had been completely accidental. "It came looking for Diana. By the time the other creatures realized what she'd found, I was already in love."

"So this went on for some time, then." Philippe tented his fingers in front of his chin, resting his elbows on the edges of the table. He was sitting on a simple four-legged stool, even though a splendid, thronelike eyesore sat empty next to him.

"No," I said after doing some calculations, "just a fortnight. Matthew wouldn't admit to his feelings for the longest time, though—not until we were at Sept-Tours. But it wasn't safe here either. One night I left Matthew's bed and went outside. A witch took me from the gardens."

Philippe's eyes darted from me to Matthew. "There was a *witch* inside the walls of Sept-Tours?"

"Yes," said Matthew tersely.

"Down into them," I corrected gently, capturing his father's attention once more. "I don't believe any witch's foot ever touched the ground, if that's important. Well, mine did, of course."

"Of course," Philippe acknowledged with a tip of his head. "Continue."

"She took me to La Pierre. Domenico was there. So was Gerbert." The look on Philippe's face told me that neither the castle nor the two vampires who had met me inside it were unfamiliar.

"Curses, like chickens, come home to roost," Philippe murmured.

"It was the Congregation who ordered my abduction, and a witch named Satu tried to force the magic from me. When she failed, Satu threw me into the oubliette."

Matthew's hand strayed to the small of my back as it always did when that night was mentioned. Philippe watched the movement but said nothing.

"After I escaped, I couldn't stay at Sept-Tours and put Ysabeau in danger. There was all this magic coming out of me, you see, and powers I couldn't control. Matthew and I went home, to my aunts' house." I paused, searching for a way to explain where that house was. "You know the legends told by Gallowglass's people, about lands across the ocean to the west?" Philippe nodded. "That's where my aunts live. More or less."

"And these aunts are both witches?"

"Yes. Then a *manjasang* came to kill Matthew—one of Gerbert's creatures—and she nearly succeeded. There was nowhere we could go that would be beyond the Congregation's reach, except the past." I paused, shocked at the venomous look that Philippe gave Matthew. "But we haven't found a haven here. People in Woodstock know I'm a witch, and the trials in Scotland might affect our lives in Oxfordshire. So we're on the run again." I reviewed the outlines of the story, making sure I hadn't left out anything important. "That's my tale."

"You have a talent for relating complicated information quickly and succinctly, *madame.* If you would be so kind as to share your methods with Matthew, it would be a service to the family. We spend more than we should on paper and quills." Philippe considered his fingertips for a moment, then stood with a vampiric efficiency that turned a simple movement into an explosion. One minute he was seated, and then, the next, his muscles sprang into action so that all six feet of him suddenly, and startlingly, loomed over the table. The vampire fixed his attention on his son.

"This is a dangerous game you are playing, Matthew, one with everything to lose and very little to gain. Gallowglass sent a message after you parted. The rider took a different route and arrived before you did. While you've been taking your time getting here, the king of Scotland has arrested more than a hundred witches and imprisoned them in Edinburgh. The Congregation no doubt thinks you are on your way there to persuade King James to drop this matter."

"All the more reason for you to give Diana your protection," Matthew said tightly.

"Why should I?" Philippe's cold countenance dared him to say it.

"Because I love her. And because you tell me that's what the Order of Lazarus is for: protecting those who cannot protect themselves."

"I protect other *manjasang,* not witches!"

"Maybe you should take a more expansive view," Matthew said stubbornly. "*Manjasang* can normally take care of themselves."

"You know very well that I cannot protect this woman, Matthew. All of Europe is feuding over matters of faith, and warmbloods are seeking scapegoats for their present troubles. Inevitably they turn to the creatures around them. Yet you knowingly brought this woman—a woman you claim is your mate and a witch by blood—into this madness. No." Philippe shook his head vehemently. "You may think you can brazen it out, but I will not put the family at risk by provoking the Congregation and ignoring the terms of the covenant."

"Philippe, you must—"

"Don't use that word with me." A finger jabbed in Matthew's direction. "Set your affairs in order and return whence you came. Ask me for help there—or better yet, ask the witch's aunts. Don't bring your troubles into the past where they don't belong."

But there was no Philippe for Matthew to lean on in the twenty-first century. He was gone—dead and buried.

"I have never asked you for anything, Philippe. Until now." The air in the room dropped several dangerous degrees.

"You should have foreseen my response, *Matthaios*, but as usual you were not thinking. What if your mother were here? What if bad weather hadn't struck Trier? You know she despises witches." Philippe stared at his son. "It would take a small army to keep her from tearing this woman limb from limb, and I don't have one to spare at the moment."

First it had been Ysabeau who'd wished me out of her son's life. Baldwin had made no effort to hide his disdain. Matthew's friend Hamish was wary of me, and Kit openly disliked me. Now it was Philippe's turn. I stood and waited for Matthew's father to look at me. When he did, I met his eyes squarely. His flickered with surprise.

"Matthew couldn't anticipate this, Monsieur de Clermont. He trusted you to stand with him, though his faith was misplaced in this case." I took a steadying breath. "I would be grateful if you would let me stay at Sept-Tours tonight. Matthew hasn't slept for weeks, and he is more likely to do so in a familiar place. Tomorrow I will return to England—without Matthew, if necessary."

One of my new curls tumbled onto my left temple. I reached up to push it away and found my wrist in Philippe de Clermont's grip. By the time I had registered my new position, Matthew was next to his father, palms on his shoulders.

"Where did you get that?" Philippe was gazing at the ring on the third finger of my left hand. *Ysabeau's ring.* Philippe's eyes turned feral, sought out mine. His fingers tightened on my wrist until the bones started to give way. "She would never have given my ring to another, not while we both lived."

"She lives, Philippe." Matthew's words were fast and rough, meant to convey information rather than reassurance.

"But if Ysabeau is alive, then . . ." Philippe trailed off into silence. For a moment he looked dumbfounded before understanding crept over his features. "So I am not immortal after all. And you cannot seek me out when and where these troubles began."

"No." Matthew forced the syllable past his lips.

"Yet you left your mother to face your enemies?" Philippe's expression was savage.

"Marthe is with her. Baldwin and Alain will make certain that she comes to no harm." Matthew's words now came in a soothing stream, but his father still held my fingers. They were growing numb.

"And Ysabeau gave my ring to a witch? How extraordinary. It looks well on her, though," Philippe said absently, turning my hand toward the firelight.

"*Maman* thought it would," said Matthew softly.

"When—" Philippe took a deliberate breath and shook his head. "No. Don't tell me. No creature should know his own death."

My mother had foreseen her gruesome end and my father's, too. Cold, exhausted, and haunted by my own memories, I started to tremble. Matthew's father seemed oblivious to it, staring down at our hands, but his son was not.

"Let her go, Philippe," Matthew commanded.

Philippe looked into my eyes and sighed with disappointment. Despite the ring, I was not his beloved Ysabeau. He withdrew his hand, and I stepped back, well beyond Philippe's long reach.

"Now that you have heard her tale, will you give Diana your protection?" Matthew searched his father's face.

"Is that what you want, *madame?*"

I nodded, my fingers curling around the carved arm of the nearby chair.

"Then yes, the Knights of Lazarus will ensure her well-being."

"Thank you, Father." Matthew's hands tightened on Philippe's shoulder, and then he headed back in my direction. "Diana is tired. We will see you in the morning."

"Absolutely not." Philippe's voice cracked across the room. "Your witch is under my roof and in my care. She will not be sharing a bed with you."

Matthew took my hand in his. "Diana is far from home, Philippe. She's not familiar with this part of the castle."

"She will not be staying in your rooms, Matthew."

"Why not?" I asked, frowning at Matthew and his father in turn.

"Because the two of you are not mated, no matter what pretty lies Matthew told you. And thank the gods for that. Perhaps we can avert disaster after all."

"Not mated?" I asked numbly.

"Exchanging promises and accepting a *manjasang* bond do not make an inviolable agreement, *madame.*"

"He's my husband in every way that matters," I said, color flooding into my cheeks. After I told Matthew I loved him, he had assured me that we were mated.

"You're not properly married either—at least not in a way to stand up to scrutiny," Philippe continued, "and there will be plenty of that if you keep up this pretense. Matthew always did spend more time in Paris brooding over his metaphysics than studying the law. In this case, my son, your instinct should have told you what was necessary even if your intellect did not."

"We swore oaths to each other before we left. Matthew gave me Ysabeau's ring." We'd been through a kind of ceremony during those last minutes in Madison. My mind raced over the sequence of events to find the loophole.

"What constitutes a *manjasang* mating is the same thing that silences all objections to a marriage when priests, lawyers, enemies, and rivals come calling: physical consummation." Philippe's nostrils flared. "And you are not yet joined in that way. Your scents are not only odd but entirely distinct—like two separate creatures instead of one. Any *manjasang* would know you are not fully mated. Gerbert and Domenico certainly knew it as soon as Diana was in their presence. So did Baldwin no doubt."

"We are married and mated. There is no need for any proof other than my assurances. As for the rest, it is none of your affair, Philippe," Matthew said, putting his body firmly between me and his father.

"Oh, *Matthaios,* we are long past that." Philippe sounded tired. "Diana is an unmarried, fatherless woman, and I see no brothers in the room to stand for her. She is entirely my *affair.*"

"We are married in the eyes of God."

"And yet you waited to take her. What are you waiting *for,* Matthew? A sign? She wants you. I can tell by the way she looks at you. For most men that's enough." Philippe's eyes pinned his son and me in turn. Reminded of Matthew's strange reluctance on this score, worry and doubt spread through me like poison.

"We've not known each other long. Even so, I know I will be with her—and only her—for my whole life. She is my mate. You know what the ring says, Philippe: '*a ma vie de coer entier.*'"

"Giving a woman your whole life is meaningless without giving her your whole heart as well. You should pay more attention to the conclusion of that love token, not just the beginning.'"

"She has my heart," Matthew said.

"Not all of it. If she did, every member of the Congregation would be dead, the covenant would be broken forever, and you would be where you belong and not in this room," Philippe said bluntly. "I don't know what constitutes marriage in this future of yours, but in the present moment it is something worth dying for."

"Shedding blood in Diana's name is not the answer to our current difficulties." Despite centuries of experience with his father, Matthew stubbornly refused to admit to what I already knew: There was no way to win an argument with Philippe de Clermont.

"Does a witch's blood not count?" Both men turned to me in surprise. "You've killed a witch, Matthew. And I've killed a vampire—a *manjasang*—rather than lose you. Since we are sharing secrets tonight, your father may as well know the truth." Gillian Chamberlain and Juliette Durand were two casualties in the escalating hostilities caused by our relationship.

"And you think there is time for courtship? For a man who considers himself learned, Matthew, your stupidity is breathtaking," Philippe said, disgusted. Matthew took his father's insult without flinching, then played his trump card.

"Ysabeau accepted Diana as her daughter," he said.

But Philippe would not be so easily swayed.

"Neither your God nor your mother has ever succeeded in making you face the consequences of your actions. Apparently that hasn't changed." Philippe braced his hands on the desk and called for Alain. "Since you are not mated, no permanent damage has been done. This matter can be set to rights before anyone finds out and the family is ruined. I will send to Lyon for a witch to help Diana better understand her power. You can inquire after her book while I do, Matthew. Then you are both going home, where you will forget about this indiscretion and move on with your separate lives."

"Diana and I are going to my rooms. Together. Or so help me—"

"Before you finish delivering that threat, be very sure that you have sufficient might to back it up," Philippe replied dispassionately. "The girl sleeps alone and near me."

A draft told me the door had opened. It carried with it a distinct whiff of wax and cracked pepper. Alain's cold eyes darted around, taking in Matthew's anger and the unrelenting look on Philippe's face.

"You have been outmaneuvered, *Matthaios,*" Philippe said to his son. "I don't know what you've been doing with yourself, but it has made you soft. Come now. Concede the field, kiss your witch, and say your good-nights. Alain, take this woman to Louisa's room. She is in Vienna—or Venice. I cannot keep up with that girl and her endless wanderings.

"As for you," Philippe continued, casting amber eyes over his son, "you will go downstairs and wait for me in the hall until I am finished writing to Gallowglass and Raleigh. It has been some time since you were home, and your friends want to know whether Elizabeth Tudor is a monster with two heads and three breasts as is widely claimed."

Unwilling to relinquish his territory completely, Matthew put his fingers under my chin, looked deep into my eyes, and kissed me rather more thoroughly than his father apparently expected.

"That will be all, Diana," Philippe said, sharply dismissive, when Matthew was finished.

"Come, *madame,*" Alain said, gesturing toward the door.

Awake and alone in another woman's bed, I listened to the crying wind, turning over all that had happened. There was too much subterfuge to sort through, as well as the hurt and sense of betrayal. I knew that Matthew loved me. But he must have known that others would contest our vows.

As the hours passed, I gave up all hope of sleeping. I went to the window and faced the dawn, trying to figure out how our plans had unraveled so much in such a short period of time and wondering what part Philippe de Clermont—and Matthew's secrets—had played in their undoing.

When my door swung open the next morning, Matthew was propped against the stone wall opposite. Judging from his state, he hadn't gotten any sleep either. He sprang to his feet, much to the amusement of the two young servingwomen who stood giggling behind me. They weren't used to seeing him this way, all mussed and tousled. A scowl darkened his face.

"Good morning." I stepped forward, cranberry skirts swinging. Like my bed, my servants, and practically everything else I touched, the outfit belonged to Louisa de Clermont. Her scent of roses and civet had been suffocatingly thick last night, emanating from the embroidered hangings that surrounded the bed. I took a deep breath of cold, clear air and sought out the notes of clove and cinnamon that were essentially and indisputably Matthew. Some of the fatigue left my bones as soon as I detected them, and, comforted by their familiarity, I burrowed into the sleeveless, black wool robe that the maids had lowered over my shoulders. It reminded me of my academic regalia and provided an additional layer of warmth.

Matthew's expression lifted as he drew me close and kissed me with admirable dedication to detail. The maids continued to giggle and make what he took to be encouraging remarks. A sudden gust around my ankles indicated that another witness had arrived. Our lips parted.

"You are too old to moon about in antechambers, *Matthaios*," his father commented, sticking his tawny head out of the next room. "The twelfth century was not good for you, and we allowed you to read entirely too much poetry. Compose yourself before the men see you, please, and bring Diana downstairs. She smells like a beehive at midsummer, and it will take time for the household to grow accustomed to her scent. We don't want any unfortunate bloodshed."

"There would be less chance of that if you would stop interfering. This separation is absurd," Matthew said, grasping my elbow. "We are husband and wife."

"You are not, thank the gods. Go down, and I will join you shortly." He shook his head ruefully and withdrew.

Matthew was tight-lipped as we faced each other across one of the long tables in the chilly great hall. There were few people in the room at this hour, and those who lingered left quickly after getting a good look at his forbidding expression. Bread, hot from the oven, and spiced wine were laid before me on the table. It wasn't tea, but it would do. Matthew waited to speak until I had taken my first long sip.

"I've seen my father. We'll leave at once."

I wrapped my fingers more tightly around the cup without responding. Bits of orange peel floated in the wine, plumped up with the warm liquid. The citrus made it seem slightly more like a breakfast drink.

Matthew looked around the room, his face haunted. "Coming here was unwise."

"Where are we to go instead? It's snowing. Back at Woodstock the village is ready to drag me before a judge on charges of witchcraft. At Sept-Tours we may have to sleep apart and put up with your father, but perhaps he'll be able to find a witch willing to help me." So far Matthew's hasty decisions had not worked out well.

"Philippe is a meddler. As for finding a witch, he's not much fonder of your people than is *Maman*." Matthew studied the scarred wooden table and picked at a bit of candle wax that had trickled down into one of the cracks. "My house in Milan might do. We could spend Christmas there. Italian witches have a considerable reputation for magic and are known for their uncanny foresight."

"Surely not Milan." Philippe appeared before us with the force of a hurricane and slid onto the bench next to me. Matthew carefully moderated his speed and strength in deference to warmblooded nerves. So, too, did Miriam, Marcus, Marthe, and even Ysabeau. His father showed no such consideration.

"I've performed my act of filial piety, Philippe," Matthew said curtly. "There's no reason to tarry, and we will be fine in Milan. Diana knows the Tuscan tongue."

If he meant Italian, I was capable of ordering tagliatelle in restaurants and books at the library. Somehow I doubted that would be sufficient.

"How useful for her. It is regrettable that you are not going to Florence, then. But it will be a long time before you will be welcomed back to that city, after your latest escapades there," Philippe said mildly. *"Parlez-vous français, madame?"*

"Oui," I said warily, certain that this conversation was taking a multilingual turn for the worse.

"Hmm." Philippe frowned. *"Dicunt mihi vos es philologus."*

"She is a scholar," Matthew interjected testily. "If you want a rehearsal of her credentials, I'll be pleased to provide it, in private, after breakfast."

"Loquerisne latine?" Philippe asked me, as if his son hadn't spoken. *"Milás elliniká?"*

"Mea lingua latina est mala," I replied, putting down my wine. Philippe's eyes shot wide at my appallingly schoolgirl response, his expression taking me straight back to the horrors of Latin 101. Put a Latin alchemical text in front of me and I could read it. But I wasn't prepared for a discussion. I soldiered bravely on, hoping I had deduced correctly that his second question probed my grasp of Greek. *"Tamen mea lingua graeca est peior."*

"Then we shall not converse in that language either," murmured Philippe in a pained tone. He turned to Matthew in indignation. *"Den tha ekpaidéfsoun gynaíkes sto méllon?"*

"Women in Diana's time receive considerably more schooling than you would think wise, Father," Matthew answered. "Just not in Greek."

"They have no need for Aristotle in the future? What a strange world it must be. I am glad that I will not encounter it for some time to come." Philippe gave the wine pitcher a suspicious sniff and decided against it. "Diana will have to become more fluent in French and Latin. Only a few of our servants speak English, and none at all belowstairs." He tossed a heavy ring of keys across the table. My fingers opened automatically to catch them.

"Absolutely not," Matthew said, reaching to pluck them from my grasp. "Diana won't be here long enough to trouble herself with the household."

"She is the highest-ranking woman at Sept-Tours, and it is her due. You should begin, I think, with the cook," Philippe said, pointing to the largest of the keys. "That one opens the food stores. The others unlock the bakehouse, the brewhouse, all the sleeping chambers save my own, and the cellars."

"Which one opens the library?" I asked, fingering the worn iron surfaces with interest.

"We don't lock up books in this house," Philippe said, "only food, ale, and wine. Reading Herodotus or Aquinas seldom leads to bad behavior."

"There's a first time for everything," I said under my breath. "And what is the cook's name?"

"Chef."

"No, his given name," I said, confused.

Philippe shrugged. "He is in charge, so he is Chef. I've never called him anything else. Have you, *Matthaios*?" Father and son exchanged a look that had me worried about the future of the trestle table that separated them.

"I thought you were in charge. If I'm to call the cook 'Chef,' what am I to call you?" My sharp tone temporarily distracted Matthew, who was about to toss the table aside and wrap his long fingers around his father's neck.

"Everyone here calls me either 'sire' or 'Father.' Which would you prefer?" Philippe's question was silky and dangerous.

"Just call him Philippe," Matthew rumbled. "He goes by many other titles, but those that fit him best would blister your tongue."

Philippe grinned at his son. "You didn't lose your combativeness when you lost your sense, I see. Leave the household to your woman and join me for a ride. You look puny and need proper exercise." He rubbed his hands together in anticipation.

"I am not leaving Diana," Matthew retorted. He was fiddling nervously with an enormous silver salt, the ancestor of the humble salt crock that sat by my stove in New Haven.

"Why not?" Philippe snorted. "Alain will play nursemaid."

Matthew opened his mouth to reply.

"Father?" I said sweetly, cutting into the exchange. "Might I speak with my husband privately before he meets you in the stables?"

Philippe's eyes narrowed. He stood and bowed slowly in my direction. It was the first time the vampire had moved at anything resembling normal speed. "Of course, *madame.* I will send for Alain to attend upon you. Enjoy your privacy—while you have it."

Matthew waited, his eyes on me, until his father left the room.

"What are you up to, Diana?" he asked quietly as I rose and made a slow progress around the table.

"Why is Ysabeau in Trier?" I asked.

"What does it matter?" he said evasively.

I swore like a sailor, which effectively removed the innocent expression from his face. There had been a lot of time to think last night, lying alone in Louisa's rose-scented room—enough time for me to piece together the events of the past weeks and square them with what I knew about the period.

"It matters because there's nothing much to do in Trier in 1590 but hunt witches!" A servant scuttled through the room, headed for the front door. There were still two men sitting by the fire, so I lowered my voice. "This is neither the time nor the place to discuss your father's current role in early-modern geopolitics, why a Catholic cardinal allowed you to order him around Mont Saint-Michel as if it were your private island, or the tragic death of Gallowglass's father. But you *will* tell me. And we definitely will require further time and privacy for you to explain the more technical aspects of vampire mating."

I whirled around to get away from him. He waited until I was far enough away to think escape was possible before neatly catching my elbow and turning me back. It was the instinctive maneuver of a predator. "No, Diana. We'll talk about our marriage before either of us leaves this room."

Matthew turned in the direction of the last huddle of servants enjoying their morning meal. A jerk of his head sent them scurrying.

"What marriage?" I demanded. Something dangerous sparked in his eyes and was gone.

"Do you love me, Diana?" Matthew's mild question surprised me.

"Yes," I responded instantaneously. "But if loving you were all that mattered, this would be simple and we would still be in Madison."

"It *is* simple." Matthew rose to his feet. "If you love me, my father's words don't have the power to dissolve our promises to each other, any more than the Congregation can make us abide by the covenant."

"If you truly loved me, you would give yourself to me. Body and soul."

"That's not so simple," Matthew said sadly. "From the first I warned you that a relationship with a vampire would be complicated."

"Philippe doesn't seem to think so."

"Then bed him. If it's me you want, you'll wait." Matthew was composed, but it was the calm of a frozen river: hard and smooth on the surface but raging underneath. He'd been using words as weapons since we left the Old Lodge. He'd apologized for the first few cutting remarks, but there would be no apology for this. Now that he was with his father again, Matthew's civilized veneer was too thin for something so modern and human as regret.

"Philippe isn't my type," I said coldly. "You might, however, do me the courtesy of explaining why I should wait for you."

"Because there is no such thing as vampire divorce. There's mating and there's death. Some vampires—my mother and Philippe included—separate for a time if there are"—he paused—"disagreements. They take other lovers. With time and distance, they resolve their differences and come together again. But that isn't going to work for me."

"Good. It wouldn't be my first choice for a marriage either. But I still don't see why that makes you so reluctant to consummate our relationship." He'd already learned my body and its responses with the careful attention of a lover. It wasn't me or the idea of sex that made him hesitate.

"It's too soon to curb your freedom. Once I lose myself inside you, there will be no other lovers and no separations. You need to be sure if being wed to a vampire is what you really want."

"You get to choose me, over and over again, but when I want the same, you think I don't know my own mind?"

"I've had ample opportunity to know what I want. Your fondness for me may be nothing more than a way of alleviating your fear of the unknown, or satisfying your desire to embrace this world of creatures that you've denied for so long."

"Fondness? I love you. It makes no difference whether I have two days or two years. My decision will be the same."

"The difference will be that I will not have done to you what your parents did!" he exploded, pushing past me. "Mating a vampire is no less confining than being spellbound by witches. You're living on your own terms for the first time, yet you're ready to swap one set of restraints for another. But mine aren't the enchanted stuff of fairy tales, and no charm will remove them when they begin to chafe."

"I'm your lover, not your prisoner."

"And I am a vampire, not a warmblood. Mating instincts are primitive and difficult to control. My entire being will be focused on you. No one deserves that kind of ruthless attention, least of all the woman I love."

"So I can either live without you or be locked in a tower by you." I shook my head. "This is fear talking, not reason. You're scared of losing me, and being with Philippe is making it worse. Pushing me away isn't going to ease your pain, but talking about it might."

"Now that I'm with my father again, my wounds open and bleeding, am I not healing as quickly as you hoped?" The cruelty was back in Matthew's tone. I winced. Regret flickered over his features before they hardened again.

"You would rather be anywhere than here. I know that, Matthew. But Hancock was right: I wouldn't last long in a place like London or Paris, where we might be able to find a willing witch. Other women will spot my differences straightaway, and they won't be as forgiving as Walter or Henry. I'd be turned in to the authorities—or the Congregation—in a matter of days."

The acuity of Matthew's gaze gave weight to his warning about what it would feel like to be the object of a vampire's single-minded attention. "Another witch won't care," he said stubbornly, dropping my arms and turning away. "And I can manage the Congregation."

The few feet that separated Matthew and me stretched until we might have been on opposite sides of the world. Solitude, my old companion, no longer felt like a friend.

"We can't go on this way, Matthew. With no family and no property, I'm utterly dependent on you," I continued. Historians had some things right about the past, including the structural weaknesses associated with being female, friendless, and without money. "We need to stay at Sept-Tours until I can walk into a room and not draw every curious eye. I have to be able to manage on my own. Starting with these." I held up the keys to the castle.

"You want to play house?" he said doubtfully.

"I'm not playing house. I'm playing for keeps." Matthew quirked his lips at my words, but it wasn't a real smile. "Go. Spend time with your father. I'll be too busy to miss you."

Matthew left for the stables without a kiss or word of farewell. The absence of his usual reassurances left me feeling strangely unresolved. After his scent had dissipated, I called softly for Alain, who arrived suspiciously quickly, accompanied by Pierre. They must have heard every word of our exchange.

"Staring out the window doesn't hide your thoughts, Pierre. It's one of your master's few tells, and every time he does it, I know he's concealing something."

"Tells?" Pierre looked at me, confused. The game of poker had yet to be invented.

"An outward sign of an inward concern. Matthew looks away when he's anxious or doesn't want to tell me something. And he runs his fingers through his hair when he doesn't know what to do. These are tells."

"So he does, *madame.*" Pierre looked at me, awestruck. "Does *milord* know that you used a witch's powers of divination to see into his soul? Madame de Clermont knows these habits, and *milord*'s brothers and father do as well. But you have known him for such a short time and yet know so much."

Alain coughed.

Pierre looked horrified. "I forget myself, *madame.* Please forgive me."

"Curiosity is a blessing, Pierre. And I used observation, not divination, to know my husband." There was no reason the seeds of the Scientific Revolution shouldn't be planted now, in the Auvergne. "We will, I think, be more comfortable discussing matters in the library." I pointed in what I hoped was the proper direction.

The room where the de Clermonts kept most of their books represented the closest thing to a home-court advantage available to me in sixteenth-century Sept-Tours. Once I was enshrouded in the scent of paper, leather, and stone, some of the loneliness left me. This was a world I knew.

"We have a great deal of work to do," I said quietly, turning to face the family retainers. "First, I would ask both of you to promise me something."

"A vow, *madame*?" Alain looked upon me with suspicion.

I nodded. "If I request something that would require the assistance of *milord* or, more important, his father, please tell me and we will change course immediately. They don't need to worry about my small concerns." The men looked wary but intrigued.

"Òc," Alain agreed with a nod.

Despite such auspicious beginnings, my first team meeting got off to a rocky start. Pierre refused to sit in my presence, and Alain would take a chair only if I did. But remaining motionless wasn't an option, given my rising tide of anxiety about my responsibilities at Sept-Tours, so the three of us completed lap after lap of the library. While we circled, I pointed to books to be brought to Louisa's room, reeled off necessary supplies, and ordered that my traveling clothes be handed to a tailor to serve as a pattern for a basic wardrobe. I was prepared to wear Louisa de Clermont's clothes for two more days. After that I threatened to resort to Pierre's cupboards for breeches and hose. The prospect of such grievous female immodesty clearly struck terror into their hearts.

We spent our second and third hours discussing the inner workings of the château. I had no experience running such a complicated household, but I knew which questions to ask. Alain rehearsed the names and job descriptions of its key officers, provided a brief introduction to leading personalities in the village, accounted for who was staying in the house at present, and speculated about who we could expect to visit over the next few weeks.

Then we decamped to the kitchens, where I had my first encounter with Chef. He was a human, as thin as a reed and no taller than Pierre. Like Popeye, he had all of his bulk concentrated in his forearms, which were the size of hams. The reason for this was apparent when he hefted an enormous lump of dough onto a floury surface and began to work it smooth. Like me, Chef was able to think only when he was in motion.

Word had trickled belowstairs about the warmblooded guest sleeping in a room near the head of the family. So, too, had speculation about my relationship to *milord* and what kind of creature I was, given my scent and eating habits. I caught the words *sorcière* and *masca*—French and Occitan terms for witch—when we entered the inferno of activity and heat. Chef had assembled the kitchen staff, which was vast and Byzantine in its organization. This provided an opportunity for them to study me firsthand. Some were vampires, others were humans. One was a daemon. I made a mental note to ensure that the young woman called Catrine, whose glance nudged against my cheeks with open curiosity, was kindly treated and looked after until her strengths and weaknesses were clearer.

I was resolved to speak English only out of necessity, and even then just to Matthew, his father, Alain, and Pierre. As a result my conversation with Chef and his associates was full of misunderstandings. Fortunately, Alain and Pierre gently untangled the knots when my French and their heavily accented Occitan mingled. Once I had been a decent mimic. It was time to resurrect those talents, and I listened carefully to the dips and sways of the local tongue. I'd already put several language dictionaries on the shopping list for the next time someone went to the nearby city of Lyon.

Chef warmed to me after I complimented his baking skills, praised the order of the kitchens, and requested that he tell me immediately if he needed anything at all to work his culinary magic. Our good relationship was assured, however, when I inquired into Matthew's favorite food and drink. Chef became animated, waving his sticky hands in the air and speaking a mile a minute about *milord*'s skeletal condition, which he blamed entirely on the English and their poor regard for the arts of the kitchen.

"Have I not sent Charles to see to his needs?" Chef demanded in rapid Occitan, picking up his dough and slamming it down. Pierre murmured the translation as quickly as he could. "I lost my best assistant, and it is nothing to the English! *Milord* has a delicate stomach, and he must be tempted to eat or he begins to waste away."

I apologized on behalf of England and asked how he and I might ensure Matthew's return to health, although the thought of my husband being any more robust was alarming. "He enjoys uncooked fish, does he not, as well as venison?"

"*Milord* needs blood. And he will not take it unless it is prepared just so."

Chef led me to the game room, where the carcasses of several beasts were suspended over silver troughs to catch the blood falling from their severed necks.

"Only silver, glass, or pottery should be used to collect blood for *milord,* or he refuses it," Chef instructed with a raised finger.

"Why?" I asked.

"Other vessels taint the blood with bad odors and tastes. This is pure. Smell," Chef instructed, handing me the cup. My stomach heaved at the metallic aroma, and I covered my mouth and nose. Alain motioned the blood away, but I stopped him with a glance.

"Continue, please, Chef."

Chef gave me an approving look and began to describe the other delicacies that made up Matthew's diet. He told me of Matthew's love of beef broth fortified with wine and spices and served cool. Matthew would take partridge blood, provided it was in small quantities and not too early in the day. Madame de Clermont was not so fussy, Chef said with a sorrowful shake of his head, but she had not passed her impressive appetite to her son.

"No," I said tightly, thinking of my hunting trip with Ysabeau.

Chef put the tip of his finger into the silver cup and held it up, shimmering red in the light, before inserting it into his mouth and letting the lifeblood roll over his tongue. "Stag's blood is his favorite, of course. It is not as rich as human blood, but it is similar in taste."

"May I?" I asked hesitantly, extending my little finger toward the cup. Venison turned my stomach. Perhaps the taste of a stag's blood would be different.

"*Milord* would not like it, Madame de Clermont," Alain said, his concern evident.

"But he is not here," I said. I dipped the tip of my little finger into the cup. The blood was thick, and I brought it to my nose and sniffed it as Chef had. What scent did Matthew detect? What flavors did he perceive?

When my finger passed over my lips, my senses were flooded with information: wind on a craggy peak, the comfort of a bed of leaves in a hollow between two trees, the joy of running free. Accompanying it all was a steady, thundering beat. *A pulse, a heart.*

My experience of the deer's life faded all too quickly. I reached out my finger with a fierce desire to know more, but Alain's hand stopped mine. Still the hunger for information gnawed at me, its intensity diminishing as the last traces of blood left my mouth.

"Perhaps *madame* should go back to the library now," Alain suggested, giving Chef a warning look.

On my way out of the kitchens, I told Chef what to do when Matthew and Philippe returned from their ride. We were passing through a long stone corridor when I stopped abruptly at a low, open door. Pierre narrowly avoided plowing into me.

"Whose room is this?" I asked, my throat closing at the scent of the herbs that hung from the rafters.

"It belongs to Madame de Clermont's woman," Alain explained.

"Marthe," I breathed, stepping over the threshold. Earthenware pots stood in neat rows on shelves, and the floor was swept clean. There was something medicinal—mint?—in the tang of the air. It reminded me of the scent that sometimes drifted from the housekeeper's clothes. When I turned, the three of them were blocking the doorway.

"The men are not allowed in here, *madame,*" Pierre confessed, looking over his shoulder as though he feared that Marthe might appear at any moment. "Only Marthe and Mademoiselle Louisa spend time in the stillroom. Not even Madame de Clermont disturbs this place."

Ysabeau didn't approve of Marthe's herbal remedies—this I knew. Marthe was not a witch, but her potions were only a few steps away from Sarah's lore. My eyes swept the room. There was more to be done in a kitchen than cooking, and more to learn from the sixteenth century than the management of household affairs and my own magic.

"I would like to use the stillroom while at Sept-Tours."

Alain looked at me sharply. "Use it?"

I nodded. "For my alchemy. Please have two barrels of wine brought here for my use—as old as possible, but nothing that's turned to vinegar. Give me a few moments alone to take stock of what's here."

Pierre and Alain shifted nervously at the unexpected development. After weighing my resolve against his companions' uncertainty, Chef took charge, pushing the other men in the direction of the kitchens.

As Pierre's grumbling faded, I focused on my surroundings. The wooden table before me was deeply scored from the work of hundreds of knives that had separated leaf from stalk. I ran a finger down one of the grooves and brought it to my nose.

Rosemary. For remembrance.

"Remember?" It was Peter Knox's voice I heard, the modern wizard who had taunted me with memories of my parents' death and wanted Ashmole

782 for himself. Past and present collided once more, and I stole a glance at the corner by the fire. The blue and amber threads were there, just as I expected. I sensed something else as well, some other creature in some other time. My rosemary-scented fingers reached to make contact, but it was too late. Whoever it was had already gone, and the corner had returned to its normal, dusty self.

Remember.

It was Marthe's voice that echoed in my memory now, naming herbs and instructing me to take a pinch of each and make a tea. It would inhibit conception, though I hadn't known it when I'd first tasted the hot brew. The ingredients for it were surely here, in Marthe's stillroom.

The simple wooden box was on the uppermost shelf, safely beyond reach. Rising to my toes, I lifted my arm up and directed my desire toward the box just as I had once called a library book off the Bodleian's shelf. The box slid forward obligingly until my fingers could brush the corners. I snared it and set it down gently on the table.

The lid lifted to reveal twelve equal compartments, each filled with a different substance. *Parsley. Ginger. Feverfew. Rosemary. Sage. Queen Anne's lace seeds. Mugwort. Pennyroyal. Angelica. Rue. Tansy. Juniper root.* Marthe was well equipped to help the women of the village curb their fertility. I touched each in turn, pleased that I remembered their names and scents. My satisfaction turned quickly to shame, however. I knew nothing else—not the proper phase of the moon to gather them or what other magical uses they might have. Sarah would have known. Any sixteenth-century woman would have known, too.

I shook off the regret. For now I knew what these herbs would do if I steeped them in hot water or wine. I tucked the box under my arm and joined the others in the kitchen. Alain stood.

"Are you finished here, *madame*?"

"Yes, Alain. *Mercés,* Chef," I said.

Back in the library, I put the box carefully on the corner of my table and drew a blank sheet of paper toward me. Sitting down, I took a quill from the stand of pens.

"Chef tells me that it will be December on Saturday. I didn't want to mention it in the kitchen, but can someone explain how I misplaced the second half of November?" I dipped my pen in a pot of dark ink and looked at Alain expectantly.

"The English refuse the pope's new calendar," he said slowly, as if talking to a child. "So it is only the seventeenth day of November there, and the twenty-seventh day of November here in France."

I had timewalked more than four centuries and not lost a single hour, yet my trip from Elizabeth's England to war-torn France had cost me nearly three weeks instead of ten days. I smothered a sigh and wrote the correct dates on the top of the page. My pen stilled.

"That means Advent will begin on Sunday."

"*Oui.* The village—and *milord,* of course—will fast until the night before Christmas. The household will break the fast with the *seigneur* on the seventeenth of December." How did a vampire fast? My knowledge of Christian religious ceremonies was of little help.

"What happens on the seventeenth?" I asked, making note of that date, too.

"It is Saturnalia, *madame,*" Pierre said, "the celebration dedicated to the god of the harvest. *Sieur* Philippe still observes the old ways."

"Ancient" would be more accurate. Saturnalia hadn't been practiced since the last days of the Roman Empire. I pinched the bridge of my nose, feeling overwhelmed. "Let's begin at the beginning, Alain. What, exactly, is happening in this house this weekend?"

After thirty minutes of discussion and three more sheets of paper, I was left alone with my books, papers, and a pounding headache. Sometime later I heard a commotion in the great hall, followed by a bellow of laughter. A familiar voice, somehow richer and warmer than I knew it, called out in greeting.

Matthew.

Before I could set my papers aside, he was there.

"Did you notice I was gone after all?" Matthew's face was touched with color. His fingers pulled loose a tendril of hair as he gripped my neck and planted a kiss on my lips. There was no blood on his tongue, only the taste of the wind and the outdoors. Matthew had ridden, but he hadn't fed. "I'm sorry about what happened earlier, *mon coeur,*" he whispered into my ear. "Forgive me for behaving so badly." The ride had lifted his spirits, and his attitude toward his father was natural and unforced for the first time.

"Diana," Philippe said, stepping from behind his son. He reached for the nearest book and took it to the fire, leafing through the pages. "You are reading *The History of the Franks*—not for the first time, I trust. This book would be more enjoyable, of course, if Gregory's mother had overseen the writing of it. Armentaria's Latin was most impressive. It was always a pleasure to receive her letters."

I had never read Gregory of Tours's famous book on French history, but there was no reason for Philippe to know that.

"When he and Matthew attended school in Tours, your famous Gregory was a boy of twelve. Matthew was far older than the teacher, never mind the other pupils, and allowed the boys to ride him like a horse when it was time for their recreation." Philippe scanned the pages. "Where is the part about the giant? It's my favorite."

Alain entered, bearing a tray with two silver cups. He set it on the table by the fire.

"*Merci, Alain.*" I gestured at the tray. "You both must be hungry. Chef sent your meal here. Why don't you tell me about your morning?"

"I don't need—" Matthew began. His father and I both made sounds of exasperation. Philippe deferred to me with a gentle incline of his head.

"Yes you do," I said. "It's partridge blood, which you should be able to stomach at this hour. I hope you will hunt tomorrow, though, and Saturday, too. If you intend to fast for the next four weeks, you have to feed while you can." I thanked Alain, who bowed, shot a veiled glance at his master, and left hastily. "Yours is stag's blood, Philippe. It was drawn only this morning."

"What do you know of partridge blood and fasting?" Matthew's fingers tugged gently on my loose curl. I looked up into my husband's gray-green eyes.

"More than I did yesterday." I freed my hair before handing him his cup.

"I will take my meal elsewhere," Philippe interjected, "and leave you to your argument."

"There's no argument. Matthew must remain healthy. Where did you go on your ride?" I picked up the cup of stag's blood and held it out to Philippe.

Philippe's attention traveled from the silver cup to his son's face and back to me. He gave me a dazzling smile, but there was no mistaking his appraising look. He took the proffered cup and raised it in salute.

"Thank you, Diana," he said, his voice full of friendship.

But those unnatural eyes that missed nothing continued to watch me as Matthew described their morning. A sensation of spring thaw told me when Philippe's attention moved to his son. I couldn't resist glancing in his direction to see if it was possible to tell what he was thinking. Our gazes crossed, clashed. The warning was unmistakable.

Philippe de Clermont was up to something.

"How did you find the kitchens?" Matthew asked, turning the conversation in my direction.

"Fascinating," I said, meeting Philippe's shrewd eyes with a challenging stare. "Absolutely fascinating."

10

Philippe might be fascinating, but he was maddening and inscrutable, too—just as Matthew had promised.

Matthew and I were in the great hall the next morning when my father-in-law seemed to materialize out of thin air. No wonder humans thought vampires could shape-shift into bats. I lifted a spindle of toasted bread from my soft-boiled egg's golden yolk.

"Good morning, Philippe."

"Diana." Philippe nodded. "Come, Matthew. You must feed. Since you will not do so in front of your wife, we will hunt."

Matthew hesitated, restlessly glancing at me and then away. "Perhaps tomorrow."

Philippe muttered something under his breath and shook his head. "You must attend to your own needs, *Matthaios.* A famished, exhausted *manjasang* is not an ideal traveling companion for anyone, least of all a warmblooded witch."

Two men entered the hall, stomping the snow from their boots. Chilly winter air billowed around the wooden screen and through the lacy carvings. Matthew cast a longing look toward the door. Chasing stags across the frozen landscape would not only feed his body—it would clear his mind as well. And if yesterday was any indication, he'd be in a much better mood when he returned.

"Don't worry about me. I have plenty to do," I said, taking his hand in mine to give it a reassuring squeeze.

After breakfast Chef and I discussed the menu for Saturday's pre-Advent feast. This done, I discussed my clothing needs with the village tailor and seamstress. Given my grasp of French, I feared I had ordered a circus tent. By late morning I was desperate for some fresh air, and persuaded Alain to take me on a tour of the courtyard workshops. Almost everything the château residents needed, from candles to drinking water, could be found there. I tried to remember every detail of how the blacksmith smelted his metals, aware that the knowledge would be useful when I returned to my real life as a historian.

With the exception of the hour spent at the forge, my day so far had been typical of a noblewoman's of the time. Feeling that I'd made good progress toward my goal of fitting in, I spent several pleasant hours reading and practicing my handwriting. When I heard the musicians setting up for the last feast before the monthlong fast I asked them to give me a dancing lesson. Later I treated myself to an adventure in the stillroom and was soon happily occupied with a glorified double boiler, a copper still, and a small barrel of old wine. Two young boys borrowed from the kitchens kept the glowing embers of the fire alight with a pair of leather bellows that sighed gently whenever Thomas and Étienne pressed them into action.

Being in the past provided a perfect opportunity for me to practice what I knew only in theory. After poking through Marthe's equipment, I settled on a plan to make spirit of wine, a basic substance used in alchemical procedures. I was soon cursing, however.

"This will never condense properly," I said crossly, looking at the steam escaping from the still. The kitchen boys, who knew no English, made sympathetic noises while I consulted a tome I'd pulled from the de Clermont library. There were all sorts of interesting volumes on the shelves. One of them must explain how to repair leaks.

"Madame?" Alain called softly from the doorway.

"Yes?" I turned and wiped my hands on the bunched-up folds of my linen smock.

Alain surveyed the room, aghast. My dark sleeveless robe was flung over the back of a nearby chair, my heavy velvet sleeves were draped over the edge of a copper pot, and my bodice hung from the ceiling on a convenient pothook. Though relatively unclothed by sixteenth-century standards, I still wore a corset, a high-necked, long-sleeved linen smock, several petticoats, and a voluminous skirt—far more clothing than I normally wore to lecture. Feeling naked nonetheless, I lifted my chin and dared Alain to say a word. Wisely, he looked away.

"Chef does not know what to do about this evening's meal," Alain said.

I frowned. Chef unfailingly knew what to do.

"The household is hungry and thirsty, but they cannot sit down without you. So long as there is a member of the family at Sept-Tours, that person must preside over the evening meal. It is tradition."

Catrine appeared with a towel and a bowl. I dipped my fingers into the warm, lavender-scented water.

"How long have they been waiting?" I took the towel from Catrine's arm. A great hall filled with both hungry warmbloods and equally famished vampires couldn't be wise. My newfound confidence in my ability to manage the de Clermont family home evaporated.

"More than an hour. They will continue to wait until word comes from the village that Roger is closing down for the night. He runs the tavern. It is cold, and many hours until breakfast. *Sieur* Philippe led me to believe . . ." He trailed off into apologetic silence.

"Vite," I said, pointing at my discarded clothing. "You must get me dressed, Catrine."

"Bien sûr." Catrine put down her bowl and headed for my suspended bodice. The large splotch of ink on it put an end to my hope of looking respectable.

When I entered the hall, benches scraped against the stone floor as more than three dozen creatures stood. There was a note of reproach in the sound. Once seated, they ate their delayed meal with gusto, while I picked apart a chicken leg and waved away everything else.

After what seemed an interminable length of time, Matthew and his father returned. "Diana!" Matthew rounded the wooden screen, confused to see me sitting at the head of the family table. "I expected you to be upstairs, or in the library."

"I thought it was more courteous for me to sit here, considering how much work Chef put into preparing the meal." My eyes traveled to Philippe. "How was your hunting, Philippe?"

"Adequate. But animal blood provides only so much nourishment." He beckoned to Alain, and his cold eyes nudged my high collar.

"Enough." Though his voice was low, the warning in Matthew's tone was unmistakable. Heads swiveled in his direction. "You should have instructed them to start without us. Let me take you upstairs, Diana." Heads swiveled back to me, waiting for my reply.

"I have not finished," I said, gesturing at my plate, "nor have the others. Sit by me and take some wine." Matthew might be a Renaissance prince in substance as well as style, but I would not heel when he clicked his fingers.

Matthew sat by my side while I forced myself to swallow some chicken. When the tension was unbearable, I rose. Once more, benches scraped against stone as the household stood.

"Finished so soon?" Philippe asked with surprise. "Good night, then, Diana. Matthew, you will return at once. I have a strange desire to play chess."

Matthew ignored his father and extended his arm. We didn't exchange a word as we passed out of the great hall and climbed to the family rooms. At my door Matthew at last had himself under enough control to risk conversation.

"Philippe is treating you like a glorified housekeeper. It's intolerable."

"Your father is treating me like a woman of the time. I'll manage, Matthew." I paused, gathering my courage. "When did you last feed on a creature that walks on two legs?" I'd forced him to take blood from me before we left Madison, and he'd fed on some nameless warmblood in Canada. Several weeks prior to that, he'd killed Gillian Chamberlain in Oxford. Maybe he had fed on her, too. Otherwise I didn't believe that a drop of anything other than animal blood had crossed his lips in months.

"What makes you ask?" Matthew's tone was sharp.

"Philippe says you aren't as strong as you should be." My hand tightened on his. "If you need to feed and won't take blood from a stranger, then I want you to take mine."

Before Matthew could respond, a chuckle came from the stairs. "Careful, Diana. We *manjasang* have sharp ears. Offer your blood in this house and you'll never keep the wolves at bay." Philippe was standing with arms braced against the sides of the carved stone archway.

Matthew swung his head around, furious. "Go away, Philippe."

"The witch is reckless. It's my responsibility to make sure her impulses don't go unchecked. Otherwise she could destroy us."

"The witch is mine," Matthew said coldly.

"Not yet," Philippe said, descending the stairs with a regretful shake of his head. "Maybe not ever."

After that encounter Matthew was even more guarded and remote. The next day he was angry with his father, but rather than taking his frustration out on its source, Matthew snapped at everyone else: me, Alain, Pierre, Chef, and any other creature unfortunate enough to cross his path. The household was in a state of high anxiety already because of the feast, and after putting up with his bad behavior for several hours, Philippe gave his son a choice. He could sleep off his bad humor or feed. Matthew chose a third option and went off to search the de Clermont archives for some hint as to the present whereabouts of Ashmole 782. Left to my own devices, I returned to the kitchens.

Philippe found me in Marthe's room, crouched over the malfunctioning still with my sleeves rolled up and the room full of steam.

"Has Matthew fed from you?" he asked abruptly, his eyes moving over my forearms.

I lifted my left arm in reply. The soft linen pooled around my shoulder, exposing the pink traces of a jagged scar on my inner elbow. I'd cut into the flesh so that Matthew could drink from me more easily.

"Anywhere else?" Philippe directed his attention to my torso.

With the other hand, I exposed my neck. The wound there was deeper, but it had been made by a vampire and was far neater.

"What a fool you are, to allow a besotted *manjasang* to take the blood from not only your arm but your neck," Philippe said, stunned. "The covenant forbids the *manjasang* to take the blood of witches or daemons. Matthew knows this."

"He was dying, and mine was the only blood available!" I said fiercely. "If it makes you feel better, I had to force him."

"So that's it. My son has no doubt convinced himself that so long as he has taken only your blood and not your body, he will be able to let you go." Philippe shook his head. "He is wrong. I've been watching him. You will never be free of Matthew, whether he beds you or not."

"Matthew knows I'd never leave him."

"Of course you will. One day your life on this earth will draw to a close and you will make your final journey into the underworld. Rather than grieve, Matthew will want to follow you into death." Philippe's words rang with truth.

Matthew's mother had shared with me the story of his making: how he fell from the scaffolding while helping to lay the stones for the village church. Even when I first heard it, I'd wondered if Matthew's despair over losing his wife, Blanca, and his son, Lucas, had driven him to suicide.

"It is too bad that Matthew is a Christian. His God is never satisfied."

"How so?" I asked, perplexed by the sudden change of topic.

"When you or I have done wrong, we settle our accounts with the gods and return to living with the hope of doing better in future. Ysabeau's son confesses his sins and atones again and again—for his life, for who he is, for what he has done. He is always looking backward, and there is no end to it."

"That's because Matthew is a man of great faith, Philippe." There was a spiritual center to Matthew's life that colored his attitudes toward science and death.

"Matthew?" Philippe sounded incredulous. "He has less faith than anyone I have ever known. All he possesses is belief, which is quite different and depends on the head rather than the heart. Matthew has always had a keen mind, one capable of dealing with abstractions like God. It is how he came to accept who he had become after Ysabeau made him one of the family. For every *manjasang* it is different. My sons chose other paths—war, love, mating, conquest, the acquisition of riches. For Matthew it was always ideas."

"It still is," I said softly.

"But ideas are seldom strong enough to provide the basis for courage. Not without hope for the future." His expression turned thoughtful. "You don't know your husband as well as you should."

"Not as well as you do, no. We're a witch and a vampire who love even though we're forbidden to do so. The covenant doesn't permit us lingering public courtship and moonlight strolls." My voice heated as I continued. "I can't hold his hand or touch his face outside of these four walls without fearing that someone will notice and he will be punished for it."

"Matthew goes to the church in the village around midday, when you think he is looking for your book. It's where he went today." Philippe's remark was strangely disconnected from our conversation. "You might follow him one day. Perhaps then you would come to know him better."

I went to the church at eleven on Monday morning, hoping to find it empty. But Matthew was there, just as Philippe had promised.

He couldn't have failed to hear the heavy door close behind me or my steps echoing as I crossed the floor, but he didn't turn around. Instead he remained kneeling just to the right of the altar. In spite of the cold, Matthew was wearing an insubstantial linen shirt, breeches, hose, and shoes. I felt frozen just looking at him and drew my cloak more firmly around me.

"Your father told me I'd find you here," I said, my voice echoing.

It was the first time I'd been in this church, and I looked around with curiosity. Like many religious buildings in this part of France, Saint-Lucien's house of worship was already ancient in 1590. Its simple lines were altogether different from the soaring heights and lacy stonework of a Gothic cathedral. Brightly colored murals surrounded the wide arch separating the apse from the nave and decorated the stone bands that topped the arcades underneath the high clerestory windows. Most of the windows opened to the elements, though someone had made a halfhearted attempt to glaze those closest to the door. The peaked roof above was crisscrossed by stout wooden beams, testifying to the skills of the carpenter as well as the mason.

When I'd first visited the Old Lodge, Matthew's house had reminded me of him. His personality was evident here, too, in the geometric details carved into the beams and in the perfectly spaced arches that spanned the widths between columns.

"You built this."

"Part of it." Matthew's eyes rose to the curved apse with its image of Christ on His throne, one hand raised and ready to mete out justice. "The nave, mostly. The apse was completed while I was . . . away."

The composed face of a male saint stared gravely at me from over Matthew's right shoulder. He held a carpenter's square and a long-stemmed white lily. It was Joseph, the man who asked no questions when he took a pregnant virgin for a wife.

"We have to talk, Matthew." I surveyed the church again. "Maybe we should move this conversation to the château. There's nowhere to sit." I had never thought of wooden pews as inviting until I entered a church without them.

"Churches weren't built for comfort," Matthew said.

"No. But making the faithful miserable couldn't have been their only purpose." I searched the murals. If faith and hope were intertwined as closely as Philippe suggested, then there might be something here to lighten Matthew's mood.

I found Noah and his ark. A global disaster and the narrowly avoided extinction of all life-forms were not auspicious. A saint heroically slew a dragon, but it was too reminiscent of hunting for my comfort. The entrance of the church was dedicated to the Last Judgment. Rows of angels at the top blew golden trumpets as the tips of their wings swept the floor, but the image of hell at the bottom—positioned so that you couldn't leave the church without making eye contact with the damned—was horrifying. The resurrection of Lazarus would be little comfort to a vampire. The Virgin Mary wouldn't help either. She stood across from Joseph at the entrance to the apse, otherworldy and serene, another reminder of all that Matthew had lost.

"At least it's private. Philippe seldom sets foot in here," Matthew said tiredly.

"We'll stay, then." I took a few steps toward him and plunged in. "What's wrong, Matthew? At first I thought it was the shock of being immersed in a former life, then the prospect of seeing your father again while keeping his death a secret." Matthew remained kneeling, head bowed, his back to me. "But your father knows his future now. So there must be another reason for it."

The air in the church was oppressive, as if my words had removed all the oxygen from the place. There wasn't a sound except for the cooing of the birds in the belfry.

"Today is Lucas's birthday," Matthew said at last.

His words hit me with the force of a blow. I sank to my knees behind him, cranberry skirts pooling around me. Philippe was right. I didn't know Matthew as well as I should.

His hand rose and pointed to a spot on the floor between him and Joseph. "He's buried there, with his mother."

No inscription on the stone marked what rested underneath. Instead there were smooth hollows, the kind made by the steady passage of feet on stair treads. Matthew's fingers reached out, fit into the grooves perfectly, stilled, withdrew.

"Part of me died when Lucas did. It was the same for Blanca. Her body followed a few days later, but her eyes were empty and her soul already flown. Philippe chose his name. It's Greek for 'Bright One.' On the night he was born, Lucas was so white and pale. When the midwife held him up in the darkness, his skin caught the light from the fire the way the moon catches her light from the sun. Strange how after so many years my memory of that night is still clear." Matthew paused in his ramblings, wiped at his eye. His fingers came away red.

"When did you and Blanca meet?"

"I threw snowballs at her during her first winter in the village. I'd do anything to get her attention. She was delicate and remote, and many of us sought her company. By the time spring came, Blanca would let me walk her home from the market. She liked berries. Every summer the hedge outside the church was full of them." He examined the red streaks on his hand. "Whenever Philippe saw the stains from their juice on my fingers, he'd laugh and predict a wedding come autumn."

"I take it he was right."

"We wed in October, after the harvest. Blanca was already more than two months pregnant." Matthew could wait to consummate our marriage but hadn't been able to resist Blanca's charms. It was far more than I had wanted to know about their relationship.

"We made love for the first time during the heat of August," he continued. "Blanca was always concerned with pleasing others. When I look back, I wonder if she was abused when she was a child. Not punished—we were all punished, and in ways no modern parent would dream of—but something more. It broke her spirit. My wife had learned to give in to what someone older, stronger, and meaner wanted. I was all of those things, and I wanted her to say yes that summer night, so she did."

"Ysabeau told me the two of you were deeply in love, Matthew. You didn't force her to do anything against her will." I wanted to offer him what comfort I could, in spite of the sting his memories inflicted.

"Blanca didn't possess a will. Not until Lucas. Even then she only exercised it when he was in danger or when I was angry with him. All her life she wanted someone weaker and smaller to protect. Instead Blanca had a succession of what she saw as failures. Lucas wasn't our first child, and with every miscarriage she grew softer and sweeter, more tractable. Less likely to say no."

Except in its general outlines, this was not the tale Ysabeau had told of her son's early life. Hers had been a story of deep love and shared grief. Matthew's version was one of unmitigated sorrow and loss.

I cleared my throat. "And then there was Lucas."

"Yes. After years of filling her with death, I gave her Lucas." He fell silent.

"There was nothing you could do, Matthew. It was the sixth century, and there was an epidemic. You couldn't save either of them."

"I could have stopped myself from having her. Then there would have been no one to lose!" Matthew exclaimed. "She wouldn't say no, but her eyes always held some reluctance when we made love. Each time I promised her that this time the babe would survive. I would have given anything—"

It hurt to know that Matthew was still so deeply attached to his dead wife and son. Their spirits haunted this place, and him, too. But at least now I had an explanation for why he shied away from me: this deep sense of guilt and grief that he'd been carrying for so many centuries. In time, perhaps, I could help loosen Blanca's hold on Matthew. I stood and went to him. He flinched when my fingers came to rest on his shoulder.

"There's more."

I froze.

"I tried to give my own life, too. But God didn't want it." Matthew's head rose. He stared at the worn, grooved stone before him, then at the roof above.

"Oh, Matthew."

"I'd been thinking about joining Lucas and Blanca for weeks, but I was worried that they would be in heaven and God would keep me in hell because of my sins," Matthew said, matter-of-fact. "I asked one of the women in the village for advice. She thought I was being haunted—that Blanca and Lucas were tied to this place because of me. Up on the scaffolding, I looked down and thought their spirits might be trapped under the stone. If I fell on it, God might have no choice but to release them. That or let me join them—wherever they were."

This was the flawed logic of a man in despair, not the lucid scientist I knew.

"I was so tired," he said wearily. "But God wouldn't let me sleep. Not after what I'd done. For my sins He gave me to a creature who transformed me into someone who cannot live, or die, or even find fleeting peace in dreams. All I can do is remember."

Matthew was exhausted again, and so very cold. His skin felt colder than the frigid air that surrounded us. Sarah would have known a spell to ease him, but all I could do was pull his resistant body into mine and lend him what little warmth I could.

"Philippe has despised me ever since. He thinks me weak—far too weak to marry someone like you." Here at last was the key to Matthew's feeling of unworthiness.

"No," I said roughly, "your father loves you." Philippe had exhibited many emotions toward his son in the brief time we'd been at Sept-Tours, but never any hint of disgust.

"Brave men don't commit suicide, except in battle. He said so to Ysabeau when I was newly made. Philippe said I lacked the courage to be a *manjasang.* As soon as my father could, he sent me away to fight. 'If you're determined to end your own life,' he said, 'at least it can be for some greater purpose than self-pity.' I've never forgotten his words."

Hope, faith, courage: the three elements of Philippe's simple creed. Matthew felt he possessed nothing but doubt, belief, and bravado. But I knew different.

"You've been torturing yourself with these memories for so long that you can't see the truth anymore." I moved around to face him and dropped to my knees. "Do you know what I see when I look at you? I see someone very like your father."

"We all want to see Philippe in those we love. But I'm nothing like him. It was Gallowglass's father, Hugh, who if he had lived would have—" Matthew turned away, his hand trembling on his knee. There was something more, a skeleton that he had yet to reveal.

"I've already granted you one secret, Matthew: the name of the de Clermont who is a member of the Congregation in the present. You can't keep two."

"You want me to share my darkest sin?" An interminable time passed before Matthew was willing to reveal it. "I took his life. He begged Ysabeau to do it, but she couldn't." Matthew turned away.

"Hugh?" I whispered, my heart breaking for him and Gallowglass.

"Philippe."

The last barrier between us fell.

"The Nazis drove him insane with pain and deprivation. Had Hugh survived, he might have convinced Philippe that there was still hope for some kind of life in the wreckage that remained. But Philippe said he was too tired to fight. He wanted to sleep, and I . . . I knew what it was to want to close your eyes and forget. God help me, I did what he asked."

Matthew was shaking now. I gathered him in my arms again, not caring that he resisted, knowing only that he needed something—someone—to hold on to while the waves of memory crashed over him.

"After Ysabeau refused his pleas, we found Philippe trying to slit his wrists. He couldn't hold the knife securely enough to do the job. He'd cut himself repeatedly, and there was blood everywhere, but the wounds were shallow and healed quickly." Matthew was speaking rapidly, the words pouring from him at last. "The more blood Philippe shed, the wilder he became. He couldn't stand the sight of it after being in the camp. Ysabeau took the knife from him and said she would help him end his life. But *Maman* would never have forgiven herself."

"So you cut him," I said, meeting his eyes. I had never turned away from the knowledge of what he'd done to survive as a vampire. I couldn't turn away from the sins of the husband, the father, and the son either.

Matthew shook his head. "No. I drank every drop of his blood, so Philippe wouldn't have to watch as his life force was spilled."

"But then you saw . . ." I couldn't keep the horror out of my voice. When a vampire drank from another creature, that creature's memories came along with the fluid in fleeting, teasing glimpses. Matthew had freed his father from torment, but only after first sharing everything Philippe had suffered.

"Most creatures' memories come in a smooth stream, like a ribbon unwinding in the darkness. With Philippe it was like swallowing shards of glass. Even when I got past the recent events, his mind was so badly fractured that I almost couldn't continue." His shaking intensified. "It took forever. Philippe was broken, lost, and frightened, but his heart was still fierce. His last thoughts were of Ysabeau. They were the only memories that were still whole, still his."

"It's all right," I murmured again and again, holding him tightly until finally his limbs began to quiet.

"You asked me who I am at the Old Lodge. I'm a killer, Diana. I've killed thousands," Matthew said eventually, his voice muffled. "But I never had to look any of them in the face again. Ysabeau cannot look at me without remembering my father's death. Now I have to face you, too."

I cradled his head between my hands and drew him away so that our eyes met. Matthew's perfect face usually masked the ravages of time and experience. But all the evidence was on display now, and it only made him more beautiful to me. At last the man I loved made sense: his insistence that I face who and what I was, his reluctance to kill Juliette even to save his own life, his conviction that once I truly knew him, I could never love him.

"I love all of you, Matthew: warrior and scientist, killer and healer, dark and light."

"How can you?" he whispered, disbelieving.

"Philippe couldn't have gone on like that. Your father would have kept trying to take his own life, and from everything you say, he'd suffered enough." I couldn't imagine how much, but my beloved Matthew had witnessed it all. "What you did was an act of mercy."

"I wanted to disappear when it was over, to leave Sept-Tours and never come back," he confessed. "But Philippe made me promise to keep the family and the brotherhood together. I swore that I would take care of Ysabeau, too. So I stayed here, sat in his chair, pulled the political strings he wanted pulled, finished the war he gave his life to win."

"Philippe wouldn't have put Ysabeau's welfare in the hands of someone he despised. Or placed a coward in charge of the Order of Lazarus."

"Baldwin accused me of lying about Philippe's wishes. He thought the brotherhood would go to him. No one could fathom why our father had decided to give the Order of Lazarus to me instead. Perhaps it was his final act of madness."

"It was faith," I said softly, reaching down and lacing my fingers through his. "Philippe believes in you. So do I. These hands built this church. They were strong enough to hold your son and your father during their final moments on this earth. And they still have work to do."

High above there was a beating of wings. A dove had flown through the clerestory windows and lost its way among the exposed roof beams. It struggled, freed itself, and swooped down into the church. The dove landed on the stone that marked the final resting place of Blanca and Lucas and moved its feet in a deliberate circular dance until it faced Matthew and me. Then it cocked its head and studied us with one blue eye.

Matthew shot to his feet at the sudden intrusion, and the startled dove flew toward the other side of the apse. It beat its wings, slowing before the likeness of the Virgin. When I was convinced it was going to crash into the wall, it swiftly reversed direction and flew back out the way it had entered.

A long white feather from the dove's wing drifted and curled on the currents of air, landing on the pavement before us. Matthew bent to pick it up, his expression puzzled as he held it before him.

"I've never seen a white dove in the church before." Matthew looked to the half dome of the apse where the same bird hovered over Christ's head.

"It's a sign of resurrection and hope. Witches believe in signs, you know." I closed his hands around the feather. I kissed him lightly on the forehead and turned to leave. Perhaps now that he had shared his memories, he could find peace.

"Diana?" Matthew called. He was still by his family's grave. "Thank you for hearing my confession."

I nodded. "I'll see you at home. Don't forget your feather."

He watched me as I passed the scenes of torment and redemption on the portal between the world of God and the world of man. Pierre was waiting outside, and he took me back to Sept-Tours without speaking a word. Philippe heard our approach and was waiting for me in the hall.

"Did you find him in the church?" he asked quietly. The sight of him—so hale and hearty—made my heart drop. How had Matthew endured it?

"Yes. You should have told me it was Lucas's birthday." I handed my cloak to Catrine.

"We have all learned to anticipate these black moods when Matthew is reminded of his son. You will, too."

"It's not just Lucas." Fearing I'd said too much, I bit my lip.

"Matthew told you about his own death, too." Philippe tugged his fingers through his hair, a rougher version of his son's habitual gesture. "I understand grief, but not this guilt. When will he put the past behind him?"

"Some things can never be forgotten," I said, looking Philippe squarely in the eye. "No matter what you think you understand, if you love him, you'll let him battle his own demons."

"No. He is my son. I will not fail him." Philippe's mouth tightened. He turned and stalked away. "And I've received word from Lyon, *madame*," he called over his shoulder. "A witch will arrive shortly to help you, just as Matthew wished."

11

"Meet me in the hay barn on your way back from the village." Philippe had resumed his annoying habit of appearing and disappearing in the blink of an eye and was standing before us in the library.

I looked up from my book and frowned. "What's in the hay barn?"

"Hay." Matthew's revelations in the church had only made him more restless and short-tempered. "I'm writing to our new pope, Father. Alain tells me that the conclave will announce today that poor Niccolò has been elected despite begging to be spared the burdens of office. What are the wishes of one man when weighed against the aspirations of Philip of Spain and Philippe de Clermont?"

Philippe reached for his belt. A loud clap exploded from Matthew's direction. Matthew held a dagger between his palms, the point of the blade resting against his breastbone.

"His Holiness can wait." Philippe considered the position of his weapon. "I should have targeted Diana. You would have moved faster."

"You must forgive me for ruining your sport." Matthew was coldly furious. "It's been some time since I've had a knife thrown at me. I fear I am out of practice."

"If you are not at the barn before the clock strikes two, I will come looking for you. And I will be carrying more than this dagger." He plucked it out of Matthew's hands and bellowed for Alain, who was right behind him.

"No one should go to the lower barn until told otherwise," Philippe said as he rammed his weapon back into its leather sheath.

"I had apprehended as much, *sieur.*" It was as close to a reproach as Alain was ever likely to utter.

"I'm tired of living with so much testosterone. No matter what Ysabeau thinks of witches, I wish she were here. And before you ask what testosterone is, it's you," I said, jabbing my finger at Philippe. "And your son is not much better."

"The company of women, eh?" Philippe pulled on his beard and looked at Matthew, openly calculating just how much further he could push his son. "Why did I not think of it before? While we wait for Diana's witch to arrive from Lyon, we should send her to Margot for instruction on how to behave like a proper French lady."

"What Louis and Margot get up to at Usson is worse than anything they did in Paris. That woman isn't a proper role model for anyone, least of all my wife," Matthew told his father with a withering look. "Unless they're more careful, people are going to know that Louis's carefully managed, very expensive assassination was a sham."

"For someone wedded to a witch you are quick to judge the passions of others, *Matthaios*. Louis is your brother."

Goddess bless us, another brother.

"Passions?" Matthew's eyebrow lifted. "Is that what you call taking a string of men and women to bed?"

"There are countless ways to love. What Margot and Louis do is not your concern. Ysabeau's blood runs in Louis's veins, and he will always have my loyalty—as will you, in spite of your own considerable transgressions." Philippe disappeared in a blur of movement.

"Just how many de Clermonts are there? And why do you all have to be men?" I demanded when there was silence once more.

"Because Philippe's daughters were so terrifying we held a family council and begged him to stop making them. Stasia can strip the paint from walls simply by looking at them, and Verin makes her look meek. As for Freyja . . . well, Philippe named her after the Norse goddess of war for a reason."

"They sound wonderful." I gave him a perfunctory peck on the cheek. "You can tell me about them later. I'll be in the kitchen, trying to stop up that leaky cauldron that Marthe calls a still."

"I could take a look at it for you. I'm good with lab equipment," Matthew offered. He was eager to do anything that would keep him from Philippe and the mysterious hay barn. I understood, but there was no way for him to evade his father. Philippe would simply invade my stillroom and harass him there.

"Not necessary," I said over my shoulder as I departed. "Everything is under control."

Everything was *not,* as it turned out. My eight-year-old bellows boys had let the fire go out, but not before the flames had burned too high and produced a thick black residue in the bottom of the distillation apparatus. I made notes in the margins of one of the de Clermonts' alchemical books about what had gone wrong and how it could be fixed, while Thomas, the more trustworthy of my two young assistants, stoked the fire. I was not the first to make use of the book's wide, clean borders, and some of the earlier scribblings had been quite useful. In time maybe mine would be, too.

Étienne, my other errant assistant, ran into the room, whispered in his partner's ear, and received something shiny in exchange.

"Milord encore," the boy whispered back.

"What are you betting on, Thomas?" I demanded. The two of them looked at me blankly and shrugged. Something about their studied innocence made me concerned for Matthew's welfare. "The hay barn. Where is it?" I said, ripping off my apron.

With great reluctance, Thomas and Étienne led me through the castle's front gate and toward a wood-and-stone structure with a steeply pitched roof. A ramp sloped up to the wide, barred entrance doors, but the boys pointed instead to a ladder pushed against the far end. The rungs disappeared into fragrant darkness.

Thomas went up first, making quieting gestures with his hands and imploring me to be silent with facial contortions worthy of an actor in a silent film. Étienne held the ladder while I climbed, and the village blacksmith hauled me into the dusty loft.

My appearance was met with interest, but not surprise, by half of the Sept-Tours staff. I had thought it odd that only one guard was on duty at the front gate. The rest of them were here, along with Catrine, her older sister Jehanne, most of the kitchen crew, the blacksmith, and the grooms.

A softly keening whoosh, unlike anything I'd heard before, captured my attention. The sharp clang and the shriek of metal against metal were more recognizable. Matthew and his father had dispensed with sniping and progressed to armed combat. My hand rose to stifle a gasp when the point of Philippe's sword pierced Matthew's shoulder. Bloody slashes covered their shirts, breeches, and hose. They'd evidently been fighting for some time, and this was no genteel fencing match.

Alain and Pierre stood silently against the opposite wall. The ground around them looked like a pincushion, bristling with a variety of discarded weapons stabbed into the packed soil. Both of the de Clermont servants were acutely aware of what was happening around them, including my arrival. They lifted their eyes a fraction to the loft and slid a worried glance at each other. Matthew was oblivious. His back was to me, and the other strong scents in the barn masked my presence. Philippe, who was facing my way, seemed either not to notice or not to care.

Matthew's blade went straight through Philippe's arm. When Philippe winced, his son gave him a mocking smile. "'Don't consider painful what's good for you,'" Matthew muttered.

"I should never have taught you Greek—or English either. Your knowledge of them has caused me no end of trouble," Philippe replied, unperturbed. He pulled his arm free from the blade.

Swords struck, clashed, and swung. Matthew had a slight height advantage, and his longer arms and legs increased his reach and the span of his lunges. He was fighting with a long, tapering blade, sometimes using one hand, sometimes two. The hilt was constantly shifting in his grip so that he could counter his father's moves. But Philippe had more strength and delivered punishing strikes with a shorter sword that he wielded easily in one hand. Philippe also held a round shield, which he used to deflect Matthew's blows. If Matthew had held such a defensive asset, it was gone now. Though the two men were well matched physically, their styles of fighting were entirely different. Philippe was enjoying himself and kept up a running commentary while he sparred. Matthew, on the other hand, remained largely silent and focused, not betraying by so much as the quirk of an eyebrow that he was listening to what his father was saying.

"I've been thinking of Diana. Neither earth nor ocean produces a creature as savage and monstrous as woman," Philippe said sorrowfully.

Matthew lunged at him, the blade whooshing with amazing speed in a wide arc toward his father's neck. I blinked, during which time Philippe managed to slip beneath the blade. He reappeared on Matthew's other side, slicing at his son's calf.

"Your technique is wild this morning. Is something wrong?" Philippe inquired. This direct question got his son's attention.

"Christ, you are impossible. Yes. Something is wrong," Matthew said between clenched teeth. He swung again, the sword glancing off Philippe's quickly raised shield. "Your constant interference is driving me insane."

"Those whom the gods wish to destroy, they first make mad." Philippe's words caused Matthew to falter. Philippe took advantage of the misstep and slapped him on the backside with the flat of his sword.

Matthew swore. "Did you give away all of your best lines?" he demanded. Then he saw me.

What happened next took place in a heartbeat. Matthew began to straighten from his fighting crouch, his attention fixed on the hayloft where I stood. Philippe's sword plunged, circled, and lifted Matthew's weapon out of his hand. With both swords in his possession, Philippe threw one against the wall and leveled the other at Matthew's jugular.

"I taught you better, *Matthaios.* You do not think. You do not blink. You do not breathe. When you are trying to survive, all you do is react." Philippe raised his voice. "Come down here, Diana."

The blacksmith regretfully helped me to another ladder. *You're in for it now,* promised his expression. I lowered myself onto the floor behind Philippe.

"Is she why you lost?" he demanded, pressing the blade against his son's flesh until a dark ribbon of blood appeared.

"I don't know what you mean. Let me go." Some strange emotion overtook Matthew. His eyes went inky, and he clawed at his father's chest. I took a step toward him.

A shining object flew at me with a whistle, sliding between my left arm and my torso. Philippe had thrown a weapon at me without so much as a backward glance to check his aim, yet it had not even nicked my skin. The dagger pinned my sleeve to a rung of the ladder, and when I wrenched my arm free, the fabric tore across the elbow, exposing my jagged scar.

"That's what I mean. Did you take your eyes off your opponent? Is that how you nearly died, and Diana with you?" Philippe was angrier than I'd ever seen him.

Matthew's concentration flickered to me again. It took no more than a second, but it was long enough for Philippe to find yet another dagger tucked into his boot. He plunged it into the flesh of Matthew's thigh.

"Pay attention to the man with the blade at your throat. If you don't, she's dead." Then Philippe addressed me without turning. "As for you, Diana, stay clear of Matthew when he is fighting."

Matthew looked up at his father, black eyes shining with desperation as the pupils dilated. I'd seen the reaction before, and it usually signaled he was losing his control. "Let me go. I need to be with her. Please."

"You need to stop looking over your shoulder and accept who you are—a *manjasang* warrior with responsibilities to his family. When you put your mother's ring on Diana's finger, did you take time to consider what it promises?" Philippe said, his voice rising.

"My whole life, and the end of it. And a warning to remember the past." Matthew tried to kick his father, but Philippe anticipated the move and reached down to twist the knife still embedded in his son's leg. Matthew hissed with pain.

"It's always the dark things with you, never the light." Philippe swore.

He dropped the sword and kicked it out of Matthew's reach, his fingers tightening on his son's throat. "Do you see his eyes, Diana?"

"Yes," I whispered.

"Take another step toward me."

When I did, Matthew began to thrash, though his father was exerting a crushing pressure on his windpipe. I cried out, and the thrashing worsened.

"Matthew is in a blood rage. We *manjasang* are closer to nature than other creatures—pure predators, no matter how many languages we speak or what fine clothes we wear. This is the wolf in him trying to free himself so that he can kill."

"A blood rage?" My words came out in a whisper.

"Not all of our kind are prone to it. The sickness is in Ysabeau's blood, passed from her maker and on to her children. Ysabeau and Louis were spared, but not Matthew or Louisa. And Matthew's son Benjamin has the affliction, too."

Though I knew nothing of this son, Matthew had told me hair-raising stories about Louisa. The same blood-borne tendency to excess was in Matthew as well—and he could pass it down to any children we might have. Just when I thought I knew all the secrets that kept Matthew from my bed, here was another: the fear of hereditary illness.

"What sets it off?" I forced the words past the tightness in my throat.

"Many things, and it is worse when he is tired or hungry. Matthew does not belong to himself when the rage is upon him, and it can make him act against his true nature."

Eleanor. Could this be how one of Matthew's great loves had died, trapped between an enraged Matthew and Baldwin in Jerusalem? His repeated warnings about his possessiveness, and the danger that would result, didn't seem idle anymore. Like my panic attacks, this was a physiological reaction that Matthew might never be entirely able to control.

"Is this why you ordered him down here today? To force him into showing his vulnerabilities to the world?" I demanded furiously of Philippe. "How could you? You're his father!"

"We are a treacherous breed. I might turn against him one day." Philippe shrugged. "I might turn on you, witch."

At that, Matthew reversed their positions and was pressing Philippe back toward the far wall. Before he could gain the advantage, Philippe grabbed him by the neck. The two of them stood, locked nose to nose.

"Matthew," Philippe said sharply.

His son kept pushing, his humanity gone. Matthew's only desire was to beat his opponent, or kill him if he must. There had been moments in our brief relationship when the frightening human legends about vampires made sense, and this was one of them. But I wanted my Matthew back. I took a step in his direction, but it only made his rage worse.

"Don't come closer, Diana."

"You do not want to do this, *milord,*" Pierre said, going to his master's side. He reached out an arm. I heard a snap, watched the arm drop uselessly to his side thanks to the break at the shoulder and elbow, and saw the blood pouring out of a wound at his neck. Pierre winced, his fingers rising to press against the savage bite.

"Matthew!" I cried.

It was the wrong thing to do. The sound of my distress made him wilder. Pierre was nothing more than an obstacle to him now. Matthew flung him across the room, where he hit the wall of the hay barn, all the while retaining a one-handed grip on his father's throat.

"Silence, Diana. Matthew is beyond reason. *Matthaios!*" Philippe barked out his name. Matthew stopped trying to push his father away from me, though his grip never loosened.

"I know what you have done." Philippe waited while his words penetrated Matthew's awareness. "Do you hear me, Matthew? I know my future. You would have beaten back the rage if you could have."

Philippe had deduced that his son had killed him, but not how or why. The only explanation available to him was Matthew's illness.

"You don't know," Matthew said numbly. "You can't."

"You are behaving as you always do when you regret a kill: guilty, furtive, distracted," Philippe said. *"Te absolvo, Matthaios."*

"I'll take Diana away," Matthew said with sudden lucidity. "Let us both go, Philippe."

"No. We will face it together, the three of us," Philippe said, his face full of compassion. I had been wrong. Philippe had not been trying to break Matthew, but only his guilt. Philippe had not failed his son after all.

"No!" Matthew cried, twisting away. But Philippe was stronger.

"I forgive you," his father repeated, throwing his arms around his son in a fierce embrace. "I forgive you."

Matthew shuddered once, his body shaking from head to foot, then went limp as though some evil spirit had fled. *"Je suis désolé,"* he whispered, the words slurred with emotion. "So sorry."

"And I have forgiven you. Now you must put it behind you." Philippe released his son and looked at me. "Come to him, Diana, but move carefully. He still is not himself."

I ignored Philippe and went to Matthew in a rush. He took me into his arms and breathed in my scent as if it had the power to sustain him. Pierre moved forward, too, his arm already healed. He handed Matthew a cloth for his hands, which were slick with blood. Matthew's ferocious look kept his servant several paces away, the white cloth flapping like a flag of surrender. Philippe retreated a few steps, and Matthew's eyes darted at the sudden movement.

"That's your father and Pierre," I said, taking Matthew's face in my hands. Incrementally, the black in his eyes retreated as a ring of dark green iris appeared first, then a sliver of gray, then the distinctive pale celadon that rimmed the pupil.

"Christ." Matthew sounded disgusted. He reached for my hands and drew them from his face. "I haven't lost control like that for ages."

"You are weak, Matthew, and the blood rage is too close to the surface. If the Congregation were to challenge your right to be with Diana and you responded like this, you would lose. We cannot let there be any question whether she is a de Clermont." Philippe drew his thumb deliberately across his lower teeth. Blood, darkly purple, rose from the wound. "Come here, child."

"Philippe!" Matthew held me back, dumbfounded. "You have never—"

"Never is a very long time. Do not pretend to know more about me than you do, *Matthaios*." Philippe studied me gravely. "There is nothing to fear, Diana." I looked at Matthew, wanting to be sure this wasn't going to cause another outburst of rage.

"Go to him." Matthew released me as the creatures in the loft watched with rapt attention.

"The *manjasang* make families through death and blood," Philippe began when I stood before him. His words sent fear instinctively trilling through my bones. He smudged his thumb in a curve that started in the center of my forehead near my hairline, crept near my temple, and finished at my brow. "With this mark you are dead, a shade among the living without clan or kin." Philippe's thumb returned to the place where he began, and he made a mirror image of the mark on the other side, finishing between my brows. My witch's third eye tingled with the cool sensation of vampire blood. "With this mark you are reborn, my blood-sworn daughter and forever a member of my family."

Hay barns had corners, too. Philippe's words set them alight with shimmering strands of color—not just blue and amber but green and gold. The noise made by the threads rose to a soft keen of protest. Another family awaited me in another time after all. But the murmurs of approval in the barn soon drowned out the sound. Philippe looked up to the loft as if noticing his audience for the first time.

"As for you—*madame* has enemies. Who among you is prepared to stand for her when *milord* cannot?" Those with some grasp of English translated the question for the others.

"Mais il est debout," Thomas protested, pointing at Matthew. Philippe took care of the fact that Matthew was upright by clipping his son's injured leg at the knee, sending him onto his back with a thud.

"Who stands for *madame*?" Philippe repeated, one booted foot placed carefully on Matthew's neck.

"Je vais." It was Catrine, my daemonic assistant and maid, who spoke first.

"Et moi," piped up Jehanne, who, though older, followed wherever her sister led.

Once the girls had declared their allegiance, Thomas and Étienne threw in their lot with me, as did the blacksmith and Chef, who had appeared in the loft carrying a basket of dried beans. After he glared at his staff, they grudgingly acquiesced as well.

"*Madame*'s enemies will come without warning, so you must be ready. Catrine and Jehanne will distract them. Thomas will lie." There were knowing chuckles from the adults. "Étienne, you must run and find help, preferably *milord*. As for you, you know what to do." Philippe regarded Matthew grimly.

"And my job?" I asked.

"To think, as you did today. Think—and stay alive." Philippe clapped his hands. "Enough entertainment. Back to work."

Amid good-natured grumbling, the people in the hayloft scattered to resume their duties. With a cock of his head, Philippe sent Alain and Pierre out after them. Philippe followed, taking off his shirt as he went. Surprisingly, he returned and dropped the wadded-up garment at my feet. Nestled within it was a lump of snow.

"Take care of the wound on his leg, and the one over his kidney that is deeper than I would have wished," Philippe instructed. Then he, too, was gone.

Matthew climbed to his knees and began to tremble. I grabbed him by the waist and lowered him gently to the ground. Matthew tried to pull free and draw me into his arms instead.

"No, you stubborn man," I said. "I don't need comforting. Let me take care of you for once."

I investigated his wounds, beginning with the ones Philippe had flagged. With Matthew's help I cleared the rent hose from the wound on his thigh. The dagger had gone deep, but the gash was already closing thanks to the healing properties of vampire blood. I packed a wad of snow around it anyway—Matthew assured me it would help, though his exhausted flesh was barely warmer. The wound on his kidney was similarly on the mend, but the surrounding bruise made me wince in sympathy.

"I think you're going to live," I said, putting a final ice pack into place over his left flank. I smoothed the hair away from his forehead. A sticky spot of half-dried blood near his eye had captured a few black strands. Gently I freed them.

"Thank you, *mon coeur.* Since you're cleaning me up, would you mind if I returned the favor and removed Philippe's blood from your forehead?" Matthew looked sheepish. "It's the scent, you see. I don't like it on you."

He was afraid of the blood rage's return. I rubbed at the skin myself, and my fingers came away tinged with black and red. "I must look like a pagan priestess."

"More so than usual, yes." Matthew scooped some of the snow from his thigh and used it and the hem of his shirt to remove the remaining evidence of my adoption.

"Tell me about Benjamin," I said while he wiped at my face.

"I made Benjamin a vampire in Jerusalem. I gave him my blood thinking to save his life. But in doing so, I took his reason. I took his soul."

"And he has your tendency toward anger?"

"Tendency! You make it sound like high blood pressure." Matthew shook his head in amazement. "Come. You'll freeze if you stay here any longer."

Slowly we made our way to the château, our hands clasped. For once neither of us cared who might see or what anyone who did see might think.

The snow was falling, making the forbidding, pitted winter landscape appear soft once again. I looked up at Matthew in the fading light and saw his father once more in the strong lines of his face and the way that his shoulders squared under the burdens they bore.

The next day was the Feast of St. Nicholas, and the sun shone on the snow that had fallen earlier in the week. The château perked up considerably with the finer weather, even though it was still Advent, a somber time of reflection and prayer. Humming under my breath, I headed for the library to retrieve my stash of alchemical books. Though I took a few into the stillroom each day, I was careful to return them. Two men were talking inside the book-filled room. Philippe's calm, almost lazy tones I recognized. The other was unfamiliar. I pushed the door open.

"Here she is now," Philippe said as I entered. The man with him turned, and my flesh tingled.

"I am afraid her French is not very good, and her Latin is worse," Philippe said apologetically. "Do you speak English?"

"Enough," the witch replied. His eyes swept my body, making my skin crawl. "The girl seems in good health, but she should not be here among your people, *sieur*."

"I would happily be rid of her, Monsieur Champier, but she has nowhere to go and needs help from a fellow witch. That is why I sent for you. Come, Madame Roydon," Philippe said, beckoning me forward.

The closer I got, the more uncomfortable I became. The air felt full, tingling with an almost electrical current. I half expected to hear a rumble of thunder, the atmosphere was so thick. Peter Knox had been mentally invasive, and Satu had inflicted great pain at La Pierre, but this witch was different and somehow even more dangerous. I walked quickly past the wizard and looked at Philippe in mute appeal for answers.

"This is André Champier," Philippe said. "He is a printer, from Lyon. Perhaps you have heard of his cousin, the esteemed physician, now alas departed from this world and no longer able to share his wisdom on matters philosophical and medical."

"No," I whispered. I watched Philippe, hoping for clues as to what he expected me to do. "I don't believe so."

Champier tilted his head in acknowledgment of Philippe's compliments. "I never knew my cousin, *sieur*, as he was dead before I was born.

But it is a pleasure to hear you speak of him so highly." Since the printer looked at least twenty years older than Philippe, he must know that the de Clermonts were vampires.

"He was a great student of magic, as you are." Philippe's comment was typically matter-of-fact, which kept it from sounding obsequious. To me he explained, "This is the witch I sent for soon after you arrived, thinking he might be able to help solve the mystery of your magic. He says he felt your power while still some distance from Sept-Tours."

"It would seem my instincts have failed me," Champier murmured. "Now that I am with her, she seems to have little power after all. Perhaps she is not the English witch that people were speaking about in Limoges."

"Limoges, eh? How extraordinary for news of her to travel so far so fast. But Madame Roydon is, thankfully, the only wandering Englishwoman we have had to take in, Monsieur Champier." Philippe's dimples flashed as he poured himself some wine. "It is bad enough to be plagued with French vagrants at this time of year, without being overrun with foreigners as well."

"The wars have loosened many from their homes." One of Champier's eyes was blue, the other brown. It was the mark of a powerful seer. The wizard had a wiry energy that fed on the power that pulsed in the atmosphere around him. Instinctively I took a step away. "Is that what happened to you, *madame*?"

"Who can tell what horrors she has seen or been subjected to?" Philippe said with a shrug. "Her husband had been dead ten days when we found her in an isolated farmhouse. Madame Roydon might have fallen victim to all kinds of predators." The elder de Clermont was as talented at fabricating life stories as was his son or Christopher Marlowe.

"I will find out what has happened to her. Give me your hand." When I didn't immediately acquiesce, Champier grew impatient. With a flick of his fingers, my left arm shot toward him. Panic, sharp and bitter, flooded my system as he grasped my hand. He stroked the flesh on my palm, progressing deliberately over each finger in an intimate search for information. My stomach flipped.

"Does her flesh give you knowledge of her secrets?" Philippe sounded only mildly curious, but there was a muscle ticking in his neck.

"A witch's skin can be read, like a book." Champier frowned and brought his fingers to his nose. He sniffed. His face soured. "She has been too long with *manjasang*. Who has been feeding from her?"

"That is forbidden," Philippe said silkily. "No one in my household has shed the girl's blood, for sport or for sustenance."

"The *manjasang* can read a creature's blood as easily as I can read her flesh." Champier yanked at my arm, pushing my sleeve up and ripping the fine cord that held the cuffs snug against my wrist. "You see? Someone has been enjoying her. I am not the only one who wishes to know more about this English witch."

Philippe bent closer to inspect my exposed elbow, his breath a cool puff over my skin. My pulse was beating a tattoo of alarm. What was Philippe after? Why wasn't Matthew's father stopping this?

"That wound is too old for her to have received it here. As I said, she has been in Saint-Lucien for only a week."

Think. Stay alive. I repeated Philippe's instructions from yesterday.

"Who took your blood, sister?" Champier demanded.

"It is a knife wound," I said hesitantly. "I made it myself." It wasn't a lie, but it wasn't the whole truth either. I prayed that the goddess would let it pass. My prayers went unanswered.

"Madame Roydon is keeping something from me—and from you, too, I believe. I must report it to the Congregation. It is my duty, *sieur.*" Champier looked expectantly at Philippe.

"Of course," Philippe murmured. "I would not dream of standing between you and your duty. How might I help?"

"If you would restrain her, I would be grateful. We must delve deeper for the truth," Champier said. "Most creatures find the search painful, and even those with nothing to hide instinctively resist a witch's touch."

Philippe pulled me from Champier's grasp and roughly sat me in his chair. He clamped one hand around my neck, the other at the crown of my head. "Like this?"

"That is ideal, *sieur.*" Champier stood before me, frowning at my forehead. "But what is this?" Fingers stained with ink smoothed over my forehead. His hands felt like scalpels, and I whimpered and twisted.

"Why does your touch cause her such pain?" Philippe wondered.

"It is the act of reading that does it. Think of it as extracting a tooth," Champier explained, his fingers lifting for a brief, blessed moment. "I will take her thoughts and secrets from the root, rather than leaving them to fester. It is more painful but leaves nothing behind and provides a clearer picture of what she is trying to hide. This is the great benefit of magic, you see, and university education. Witchcraft and the traditional arts known to women are crude, even superstitious. My magic is precise."

"A moment, *monsieur.* You must forgive my ignorance. Are you saying this witch will have no memory of what you've done or the pain you've caused?"

"None save a lingering sense that something once had is now lost." Champier's fingers resumed stroking my forehead. He frowned. "But this is very strange. Why did a *manjasang* put his blood here?"

Being adopted into Philippe's clan was a memory of mine that I didn't intend Champier to have. Nor did I want him sifting through my recollections of teaching at Yale, Sarah and Em, or Matthew. *My parents.* My fingers clawed into the arms of the chair while a vampire held my head and a witch prepared to inventory and steal my thoughts. And yet no whisper of witchwind or flicker of witchfire came to my aid. My power had gone entirely quiet.

"It was you who marked this witch," Champier said sharply, his eyes accusing.

"Yes." Philippe offered no explanation.

"That is most irregular, *sieur.*" His fingers kept probing my mind. Champier's eyes opened in wonder. "But this is impossible. How can she be a—" He gasped and looked down at his chest.

A dagger stuck out between two of Champier's ribs, the weapon's blade buried deep within his chest. My fingers were wrapped tightly around the hilt. When he scrabbled to dislodge it, I pushed it in further. The wizard's knees began to crumple.

"Leave it, Diana." Philippe commanded, reaching over to loosen my hand. "He's going to die, and when he does, he will fall. You cannot hold up a dead weight."

But I couldn't let go of the dagger. The man was still alive, and as long as he was breathing, Champier could take what was mine.

A white face with inkblot eyes appeared briefly over Champier's shoulder before a powerful hand wrested his lolling head to the side with a crack of bones and sinew. Matthew battened onto the man's throat, drinking deeply.

"Where have you been, Matthew?" Philippe snapped. "You must move quickly. Diana struck before he could finish his thought."

While Matthew drank, Thomas and Étienne pelted into the room, a dazed Catrine in tow. They stopped, stunned. Alain and Pierre hovered in the hallway with the blacksmith, Chef, and the two soldiers who usually stood by the front gate.

"*Vous avez bien fait,*" Philippe assured them. "It is over now."

"I was supposed to think." My fingers were numb, but I still couldn't seem to unwrap them from the dagger.

"And stay alive. You did that admirably," Philippe replied.

"He's dead?" I croaked.

Matthew removed his mouth from the witch's neck.

"Resolutely so," Philippe said. "Well, I suppose that's one less nosy Calvinist to worry about. Had he told any of his friends he was coming here?"

"Not as far as I could determine," Matthew said. Slowly his eyes turned gray again as he studied me. "Diana. My love. Let me have the dagger." Somewhere in the distance, something metal clattered to the floor, followed by the softer thud of André Champier's mortal remains. Mercifully cool, familiar hands cupped my chin.

"He discovered something in Diana that surprised him," said Philippe.

"I saw as much. But the blade reached his heart before I could find out what." Matthew drew me gently into his arms. My own had gone boneless, and I offered no resistance.

"I didn't—couldn't—think, Matthew. Champier was going to take my memories—extract them from the root. Memories are all I have of my parents. And what if I'd forgotten my historical knowledge? How could I go back home and teach after that?"

"You did the right thing." Matthew had one arm wrapped around my waist. The other circled my shoulders, pressing the side of my face against his chest. "Where did you get the knife?"

"My boot. She must have seen me pull it out yesterday," Philippe replied.

"See. You were thinking, *ma lionne.*" Matthew pressed his lips against my hair. "What the hell drew Champier to Saint-Lucien?"

"I did," replied Philippe.

"You betrayed us to Champier?" Matthew turned on his father. "He's one of the most reprehensible creatures in all of France!"

"I needed to be sure of her, *Matthaios.* Diana knows too many of our secrets. I had to know that she could be trusted with them, even among her own people." Philippe was unapologetic. "I don't take risks with my family."

"And would you have stopped Champier before he stole her thoughts?" Matthew demanded, his eyes blacker by the second.

"That depends."

"On what?" Matthew exploded, his arms tightening around me.

"Had Champier arrived three days ago, I would not have interfered. It would have been a matter between witches, and not worth the trouble to the brotherhood."

"You would have let my mate suffer." Matthew's tone revealed his disbelief.

"As recently as yesterday, it would have been your responsibility to intervene on your mate's behalf. Had you failed to do so, it would have proved that your commitment to the witch was not what it should be."

"And today?" I asked.

Philippe studied me. "Today you are my daughter. So no, I would not have let Champier's attack go much further. But I didn't need to do anything, Diana. You saved yourself."

"Is that why you made me your daughter—because Champier was coming?" I whispered.

"No. You and Matthew survived one test in the church and another in the hay barn. The blood swearing was simply the first step in making you a de Clermont. And now it's time to finish it." Philippe turned toward his second-in-command. "Fetch the priest, Alain, and tell the village to assemble at the church on Saturday. *Milord* is getting married, with book and priest and all of Saint-Lucien to witness the ceremony. There will be nothing hole-in-corner about this wedding."

"I just killed a man! This isn't the moment to discuss our marriage."

"Nonsense. Marrying amid bloodshed is a de Clermont family tradition," Philippe said briskly. "We only seem to mate creatures who are desired by others. It is a messy business."

"I. Killed. Him." Just to be sure my message was clear, I pointed to the body on the floor.

"Alain, Pierre, please remove Monsieur Champier. He is upsetting *madame.* The rest of you have too much to do to remain here gawking." Philippe waited until the three of us were alone before he continued.

"Mark me well, Diana: Lives will be lost because of your love for my son. Some will sacrifice themselves. Others will die because someone must, and it will be for you to decide if it is you or them or someone you love. So you must ask yourself this: What does it matter who deals the deathblow?

If you do not do it, then Matthew will. Would you rather he had Champier's death on his conscience?"

"Of course not," I said quickly.

"Pierre, then? Or Thomas?"

"Thomas? He's just a boy!" I protested.

"That *boy* promised to stand between you and your enemies. Did you see what he clutched in his hands? The bellows from the stillroom. Thomas filed its metal point into a weapon. If you hadn't killed Champier, that *boy* would have shoved it through his guts at the first opportunity."

"We're not animals but civilized creatures," I protested. "We should be able to talk about this and settle our differences without bloodshed."

"Once I sat at a table and talked for three hours with a man—a king. No doubt you and many others would have considered him a civilized creature. At the end of our conversation, he ordered the death of thousands of men, women, and children. Words kill just as swords do."

"She's not accustomed to our ways, Philippe," Matthew warned.

"Then she needs to become so. The time for diplomacy has passed." Philippe's voice never rose, nor did it lose its habitual evenness. Matthew might have tells, but his father had yet to betray his deeper emotions.

"No more discussion. Come Saturday, you and Matthew will be married. Because you are my daughter in blood as well as name, you will be married not only as a good Christian but in a way that will honor my ancestors and their gods. This is your last chance to say no, Diana. If you have reconsidered and no longer want Matthew and the life—and death—that marrying him entails, I will see you safely back to England."

Matthew set me away from him. It was only a matter of inches, but it was symbolic of so much more. Even now he was giving me the choice, though his was long since made. So was mine.

"Will you marry me, Matthew?" Given that I was a murderer, it seemed only right to ask.

Philippe gave a choking cough.

"Yes, Diana. I will marry you. I already have, but I'm happy to do it again to please you."

"I was satisfied the first time. This is for your father." It was impossible to think any more about marriage when my legs were still shaking and there was blood on the floor.

"Then we are all agreed. Take Diana to her room. It would be best if she remained there until we are sure Champier's friends aren't nearby." Philippe paused on his way out the door. "You have found a woman who is worthy of you, with courage and hope to spare, *Matthaios*."

"I know," Matthew said, taking my hand.

"Know this, too: You are equally worthy of her. Stop regretting your life. Start living it."

12

The wedding Philippe planned for us was to span three days. From Friday to Sunday, the château staff, the villagers, and everyone else for miles around would be involved in what he insisted was a small family affair.

"It has been some time since we had a wedding, and winter is a cheerless time of year. We owe it to the village," was how Philippe brushed aside our protests. Chef, too, was irritated when Matthew suggested that it wasn't feasible to produce three last-minute feasts while food stores were running low and Christians practiced abstemiousness. So there was a war on and it was Advent, Chef scoffed. That was no reason to refuse a party.

With the whole house in an uproar and no one interested in our help, Matthew and I were left to our own devices.

"Just what does this marriage ceremony involve?" I wondered as we lay in front of the fire in the library. I was wearing Matthew's wedding gift: one of his shirts, which extended to my knees, and a pair of his old hose. Each leg had been ripped along the top inner seam, and then Matthew had stitched the two legs together into something vaguely approximating leggings—minus the waistband and the spandex. Some gesture toward the former came from a narrow leather belt fashioned from a piece of old tack that Matthew found in the stables. It was the most comfortable clothing I'd worn since Halloween, and Matthew, who had not seen much of my legs lately, was riveted.

"I have no idea, *mon coeur.* I've never attended an ancient Greek wedding before." Matthew's fingers traced the hollow behind my knee.

"Surely the priest won't allow Philippe to do anything overtly pagan. The actual ceremony will have to be Catholic."

"The family never puts 'surely' and 'Philippe' in the same sentence. It always ends badly." Matthew planted a kiss on my hip.

"At least tonight's event is just a feast. I should be able to get through that without too much trouble." Sighing, I rested my head on my hands. "The groom's father usually pays for the rehearsal dinner. I suppose what Philippe is doing is basically the same thing."

Matthew laughed. "Almost indistinguishable—so long as the menu includes grilled eel and a gilded peacock. Besides, Philippe has managed to appoint himself not only the father of the groom, but the father of the bride."

"I still don't see why we have to make such a fuss." Sarah and Em hadn't had a formal ceremony. Instead an elder in the Madison coven performed a handfasting. Looking back, it reminded me of the vows Matthew and I had exchanged before we timewalked: simple, intimate, and quickly over.

"Weddings aren't for the benefit of the bride or the groom. Most couples would be content to go off on their own as we did, say a few words, and then leave for a holiday. Weddings are rites of passage for the community." Matthew rolled over onto his back. I propped myself up on my elbows.

"It's just an empty ritual."

"There's no such thing." Matthew frowned. "If you can't bear it, you must say so."

"No. Let Philippe have his wedding. It's just a bit . . . overwhelming."

"You must wish Sarah and Emily were here to share this with us."

"If they were, they'd be surprised that I'm not eloping. I'm known for being a loner. I used to think you were a loner, too."

"Me?" Matthew laughed. "Except on television or in the movies, vampires are seldom alone. We prefer the company of others. Even witches will do, in a pinch." He kissed me to prove it.

"So if this marriage was taking place in New Haven, who would you invite?" he asked sometime later.

"Sarah and Em, of course. My friend Chris." I bit my lip. "Maybe the chair of my department." Silence fell.

"That's it?" Matthew looked aghast.

"I don't have many friends." Restless, I got to my feet. "I think the fire's going out."

Matthew pulled me back down. "The fire is fine. And you have plenty of kith and kin now."

The mention of family was the opening I'd been waiting for. My eyes strayed to the chest at the end of the bed. Marthe's box was hidden within, tucked into the clean linen.

"There's something we need to discuss." This time he let me go without interfering. I pulled the box free.

"What's that?" Matthew asked, frowning.

"Marthe's herbs—the ones she uses in her tea. I found them in the stillroom."

"I see. And have you been drinking it?" His question was sharp.

"Of course not. Whether we have children or not can't be my decision alone." When I opened the lid, the dusty aroma of dried herbs seeped into the air.

"No matter what Marcus and Miriam said back in New York, there is no evidence whatsoever that you and I can have children. Even herbal contraceptives like these can have unsafe side effects," Matthew said, coolly clinical.

"Let's say, for argument's sake, one of your scientific tests revealed we *could* have children. Would you want me to take the tea then?"

"Marthe's mixture isn't very reliable." Matthew looked away.

"Okay. What are the alternatives?" I asked.

"Abstinence. Withdrawal. And there are condoms, though they're not reliable either. Especially not the kind available to us in this day and age." Matthew was right. Sixteenth-century condoms were made from linen, leather, or animal intestines.

"And if one of these methods were reliable?" My patience was wearing thin.

"If—*if*—we could conceive a child together, it would be a miracle, and therefore no form of contraception would be effective."

"Your time at Paris wasn't a total waste of time, no matter what your father thinks. That was an argument worthy of a medieval theologian." Before I could close the box, Matthew's hands covered mine.

"If we could conceive, and if this tea were effective, I'd still want you to leave the herbs in the stillroom."

"Even though you could pass your blood rage on to another child?" I forced myself to be honest with him, despite the fact that my words would hurt.

"Yes." Matthew considered his words before continuing. "When I study patterns of extinction and see the evidence in the laboratory that we are dying out, the future seems hopeless. But if I detect a single chromosomal shift, or the discovery of an unexpected descendant when I thought a bloodline had died out, the sense of inevitable destruction lifts. I feel the same way now." Usually I had problems when Matthew adopted a position of scientific objectivity, but not this time. He took the box from my hands. "What about you?"

I'd been trying to figure that out for weeks, ever since Miriam and Marcus had appeared at Aunt Sarah's house with my DNA results and first raised the issue of children. I was sure about my future with Matthew but less so about what that future might involve.

"I wish I had more time to decide." It was becoming my common refrain. "If we were still in the twenty-first century, I'd be taking the birth-control pills you prescribed for me." I hesitated. "Even so, I'm not sure the pills would work for us."

Matthew still waited for my answer.

"When I drove Philippe's dagger into Champier, all I could think of was that he was going to take my thoughts and memories and I wouldn't be the same person when I returned to our modern lives. But even if we were to go back right this minute, we would already be different people. All the places we've gone, the people I've met, the secrets we've shared—I'm no longer the same Diana Bishop, and you aren't the same Matthew Clairmont. A baby would change us even more."

"So you want to prevent pregnancy," he said carefully.

"I'm not sure."

"Then the answer is yes. If you're not sure you want to be a parent, we must use whatever birth control is available." Matthew's voice was firm. And so was his chin.

"I do want to be a parent. I'm surprised by how much, if you must know." I pressed my fingers into my temples. "I like the idea of you and me raising a child. It just feels so soon."

"It is soon. So we'll do what we must to limit the possibility until—if—you are ready. But don't get your hopes up. The science is clear, Diana: Vampires reproduce through resurrection, not procreation. Our relationship might be different, but we aren't so special as to overturn thousands of years of biology."

"The picture of the alchemical wedding from Ashmole 782—it is about us. I know it. And Miriam was right: The next step in the process of alchemical transformation after the marriage of gold and silver is conception."

"Conception?" Philippe drawled from the door. His boots creaked as he pushed away from the frame. "No one mentioned that possibility."

"That's because it's impossible. I've had sex with other warmblooded women, and they've never become pregnant. The image of the chemical wedding may have been intended as a message, as Diana says, but the chances of representation becoming reality are slim." Matthew shook his head. "No *manjasang* has ever fathered a child like that before."

"Never is a long time, Matthew, as I told you. As for the impossible, I have walked this earth longer than man's memories and have seen things that later generations discounted as myth. Once there were creatures who swam like fish in the sea and others who wielded lightning bolts instead of spears. They are gone now, replaced with something new. 'Change is the only reliable thing in the world.'"

"Heraclitus," I murmured.

"The wisest of men," said Philippe, pleased that I recognized the quote. "The gods like to surprise us when we grow complacent. It's their favorite form of entertainment." He studied my unusual costume. "Why are you wearing Matthew's shirt and hose?"

"He gave them to me. It's fairly close to what I wear in my own time, and Matthew wanted me to be comfortable. He sewed the legs together himself, I think." I turned to show off the ensemble. "Who knew the de Clermont men could thread a needle, never mind stitch a straight seam?"

Philippe's eyebrows rose. "Did you think Ysabeau mended our torn garments when we came home from battle?"

The idea of Ysabeau sewing quietly while she waited for her men to return made me giggle. "Hardly."

"You know her well, I see. If you are determined to dress like a boy, put breeches on, at the very least. If the priest sees you, his heart will stop and tomorrow's ceremony will have to be delayed."

"But I'm not going outside," I said, frowning.

"I'd like to take you to a place sacred to the old gods before you are wed. It is not far," Philippe said when Matthew drew a breath to complain, "and I'd like us to be alone, *Matthaios.*"

"I'll meet you in the stables," I agreed without hesitation. Some time in the fresh air would provide a welcome opportunity for me to clear my head.

Outside, I enjoyed the sting of the cold air on my cheeks and the wintry peace of the countryside. Soon Philippe and I came to a hilltop that was flatter than most of the rounded ridges around Sept-Tours. The ground was punctuated with protrusions of stone that struck me as oddly symmetrical. Though ancient and overgrown with vegetation, these weren't natural outcroppings. They were man-made.

Philippe swung down from his horse and motioned for me to do the same. Once I dismounted, he took me by the elbow and guided me through two of the strange lumps and into a smooth expanse of snow-covered ground. All that marred the pristine surface were the tracks of wildlife—the heart-shaped outline of a deer's hoof, the five-clawed marks of bear, the combination of triangular and oval pads belonging to a wolf.

"What is this place?" I asked, my voice hushed.

"A temple dedicated to Diana stood here once, overlooking the woods and valleys where the stags liked to run. Those who revered the goddess planted sacred cypress trees to grow alongside the native oak and alder." Philippe pointed to the thin columns of green that stood guard around the area. "I wanted to bring you here because when I was a child, far away and before I became a *manjasang,* brides would go to a temple like this before their wedding and make a sacrifice to the goddess. We called her Artemis then."

"A sacrifice?" My mouth was dry. There had been enough bloodshed.

"No matter how much we change, it is important to remember the past and honor it." Philippe handed me a knife and a bag whose contents shifted and chimed. "It is also wise to set old wrongs to rights. The goddesses have not always been pleased with my actions. I would like to make sure that Artemis receives her due before my son marries you tomorrow. The knife is to take a lock of your hair. It is a symbol of your maidenhood, and the customary gift. The money is a symbol of your worth." Philippe's voice dropped to a conspiratorial whisper. "There would have been more, but I had to save some for Matthew's god, too."

Philippe led me to a small plinth in the center of the ruined structure. An assortment of offerings rested on it—a wooden doll, a child's shoe, a bowl of sodden grain dusted with snow.

"I'm surprised that anyone still comes here," I said.

"All over France women still curtsy to the moon when she is full. Such habits die hard, especially those that sustain people during difficult times." Philippe went forward to the makeshift altar. He didn't bow, or kneel, or make any of the other familiar signs of respect to a deity, but when he began to speak, his voice was so quiet I had to strain to hear him. The strange mixture of Greek and English made little sense. Philippe's solemn intentions were clear, however.

"Artemis Agroterê, renowned huntress, Alcides Leontothymos beseeches you to hold this child Diana in your hand. Artemis Lykeiê, lady of the wolves, protect her in every way. Artemis Patrôia, goddess of my ancestors, bless her with children so that my lineage continues."

Philippe's lineage. I was part of it now, by marriage as well as the swearing of a blood oath.

"Artemis Phôsphoros, bring the light of your wisdom when she is in darkness. Artemis Upis, watch over your namesake during her journey in this world." Philippe finished the invocation and motioned me forward.

After carefully placing the bag of coins next to the child's shoe, I reached up and pulled a strand of hair away from the nape of my neck. The knife was sharp, and it easily removed the curl with a single swipe of the blade.

We stood quietly in the dimming afternoon light. A surge of power washed through the ground underneath my feet. The goddess was here. For a moment I could imagine the temple as it once was—pale, gleaming, whole. I stole a glance at Philippe. With a bear pelt draped over his shoulders, he, too, looked like the savage remainder of a lost world. And he was waiting for something.

A white buck with curved antlers picked its way out of the cypress and stood, breath steaming from its nostrils. With quiet steps the buck picked his way over to me. His huge brown eyes were challenging, and he was close enough for me to see the sharp edges on his horns. The buck looked haughtily at Philippe and bellowed, one beast's greeting to another.

"Sas efharisto," Philippe said gravely, his hand over his heart. He turned to me. "Artemis has accepted your gifts. We can go now."

Matthew had been listening for sounds of our arrival and was waiting, his face uncertain, in the courtyard as we rode up.

"Ready yourself for the banquet," Philippe suggested as I dismounted. "Our guests will be arriving soon."

I gave Matthew what I hoped was a confident smile before I went upstairs. As darkness fell, the hum of activity told me the château was filling up with people. Soon Catrine and Jehanne came to get me dressed. The gown they'd laid out was by far the grandest thing I'd ever worn. The dark green fabric reminded me of the cypress by the temple now, rather than the holly that decorated the château for Advent. And the silver oak leaves embroidered on the bodice caught the light from the candles as the buck's antlers had caught the rays of the setting sun.

The girls' eyes were shining when they finished. I'd been able to get only a glimpse of my hair (swept up into coils and twisted into braids) and my pale face in Louisa's polished silver mirror. But their expressions indicated that my transformation was weddingworthy.

"Bien," Jehanne said softly.

Catrine opened the door with a flourish, and the gown's silver stitches flared to life in the torchlight from the hall. I held my breath while I waited for Matthew's reaction.

"Jesu," he said, stunned. "You are beautiful, *mon coeur.*" Matthew took my hands and lifted my arms to see the full effect. "Good God, are you wearing two sets of sleeves?"

"I think there are three," I said with a laugh. I had on a linen smock with tight lace cuffs, tight green sleeves that matched my bodice and skirts, and voluminous puffs of green silk that fell from my shoulders and were caught up at the elbows and wrists. Jehanne, who had been in Paris last year to attend upon Louisa, assured me the design was *à la mode.*

"But how am I supposed to kiss you with all this in the way?" Matthew drew his finger around my neck. My pleated ruff, which was standing out a good four inches, quivered in response.

"If you squash it, Jehanne will have a stroke," I murmured as he carefully took my face in his hands. She'd employed a contraption resembling a curling iron to bend yards of linen into the crisp figure-eight formations. It had taken her hours.

"Never fear. I'm a doctor." Matthew leaned in and pressed his mouth to mine. "There, not a pleat disturbed."

Alain coughed gently. "They are waiting for you."

"Matthew," I said, catching at his hand, "I need to tell you something."

He motioned to Alain, and we were left alone in the corridor.

"What is it?" he said uneasily.

"I sent Catrine to the stillroom to put away Marthe's herbs." It was a far bigger step into the unknown than the one that I'd taken in Sarah's hop barn to bring us here.

"You're sure?"

"I'm sure," I said, remembering Philippe's words at the temple.

Our entry into the hall was greeted with whispers and sidelong glances. The changes in my appearance had been noted, and the nods told me that at last I looked like someone who was fit to marry *milord.*

"There they are," Philippe boomed from the family's usual table. Someone began to clap, and soon the hall rang with the sound. Matthew's smile was shy at first, but as the noise increased, it broadened into a proud grin.

We were seated in the places of honor on either side of Philippe, who then called for the first course and music to accompany it. I was offered small portions of everything Chef had prepared. There were dozens of dishes: a soup made with chickpeas, grilled eel, a delicious puree of lentils, salt cod in garlic sauce, and an entire fish that swam through a gelatinous sea of aspic, with sprigs of lavender and rosemary impersonating water plants. Philippe explained that the menu had been the subject of heated negotiations between Chef and the village priest. After the exchange of several embassies, the two had finally agreed that tonight's meal would strictly adhere to the Friday dietary prohibitions against meat, milk, and cheese, while tomorrow's banquet would be a no-holds-barred extravaganza.

As befitted the groom, Matthew's portions were somewhat heartier than mine—unnecessarily so, since he ate nothing and drank little. The men at the adjoining tables joked with him about the need to bolster his strength for the ordeals to come.

By the time the hippocras started flowing and a delicious nut brittle made with walnuts and honey was passed along the table, their commentary was downright ribald and Matthew's responses were just as barbed. Happily, most of the insults and advice were delivered in languages I didn't fully understand, but Philippe clapped his hands over my ears occasionally anyway.

My heart lifted as the laughter and music swelled. Tonight Matthew didn't look like a fifteen-hundred-year-old vampire but like every other groom the night before his wedding: sheepish, pleased, a bit anxious. This was the man I loved, and my heart stilled for just a moment whenever his gaze settled on me.

The singing started when Chef served the last selection of wine and the candied fennel and cardamom seeds. A man at the opposite end of the hall sang out in a deep bass, and his neighbors picked up the melody. Soon everybody was joining in, with so much stomping and clapping that you couldn't hear the musicians trying desperately to keep up with them.

While the guests were busily devising new songs, Philippe made the rounds, greeting everyone by name. He threw babies into the air, inquired after animals, and listened attentively while the elderly cataloged their aches and pains.

"Just look at him," Matthew marveled, taking my hand. "How does Philippe manage to make every one of them feel that they're the most important guest in the room?"

"You tell me," I said with a laugh. When Matthew looked confused, I shook my head. "Matthew, you are exactly the same. All you need do to take charge of a roomful of people is to enter it."

"If you want a hero like Philippe, you're going to be disappointed in me," he said.

I took his face in my hands. "For your wedding gift, I wish I had a spell that could make you see yourself as others do."

"Based on what's reflected in your eyes, I look much the same. A little nervous, perhaps, given what Guillaume just shared with me about the carnal appetites of older women," Matthew joked, trying to distract me. But I was having none of it.

"If you aren't seeing a leader of men, then you're not looking carefully." Our faces were so close I could smell the spice on his breath. Without thinking, I drew him to me. Philippe had tried to tell Matthew he was worthy of being loved. Perhaps a kiss would be more convincing.

In the distance I heard shouts and more clapping. Then there was whooping.

"Leave the girl something to look forward to tomorrow, *Matthaios*, or she may not meet you at the church!" Philippe called out, drawing more laughter from the crowd. Matthew and I parted in happy embarrassment. I searched the hall and found Matthew's father by the fireside, tuning an instrument with seven strings. Matthew told me it was a kithara. A hush of anticipation fell over the room.

"When I was a child, there were always stories at the end of a banquet such as this, and tales of heroes and great warriors." Philippe plucked the strings, eliciting a shower of sound. "And just like all men, heroes fall in love." His strumming continued, lulling the audience into the rhythms of his story.

"A hero with dark hair and green eyes named Peleus left his home to seek his fortune. It was a place much like Saint-Lucien, hidden in the mountains, but Peleus had long dreamed of the sea and the adventures he might have in foreign lands. He gathered his friends together, and they voyaged through the oceans of the world. One day they arrived at an island famed for its beautiful women and the powerful magic that they had at their command." Matthew and I exchanged long glances. Philippe's deep voice sang out his next words:

Far happier then were the times for men,
Fondly yearned for now! You heroes, so bred
Of gods in those silver days, favor me
As I call you now with my magic song.

The room was mesmerized by Philippe's otherworldly bass.

"There Peleus first saw Thetis, daughter of Nereus, the god of the sea who told no lies and saw the future. From her father Thetis had the gift of prophecy and could twist her shape from moving water to living fire to the very air itself. Though Thetis was beautiful, no one would take her for a wife, for an oracle foretold that her son would be more powerful than his father.

"Peleus loved Thetis in spite of the prophecy. But to marry such a woman, he had to be brave enough to hold Thetis while she changed from one element into another. Peleus took Thetis from the island and clasped her to his heart while she transformed herself from water to fire to serpent to lioness. When Thetis became a woman once more, he took her to his home and the two were wed."

"And the child? Did Thetis's son destroy Peleus as the omens foretold?" a woman whispered when Philippe fell silent, his fingers still drawing music from the kithara.

"The son of Peleus and Thetis was a great hero, a warrior blessed in both life and death, called Achilles." Philippe gave the woman a smile. "But that is a tale for another night."

I was glad that his father didn't give a full account of the wedding and how the Trojan War got started there. And I was even happier that he didn't go on to tell the tale of Achilles' youth: the horrible spells his mother used to try to make him immortal as she was and the young man's uncontrollable rage—which caused him far more trouble than did his famously unprotected heel.

"It's just a story," Matthew whispered, sensing my unease.

But it was the stories that creatures told, over and over without knowing what they meant, that were often the most important, just as it was these time-worn rituals of honor, marriage, and family that people held most sacred even though they often seemed to ignore them.

"Tomorrow is an important day, one that we have all longed for." Philippe stood, kithara in his hands. "It is customary for the bride and groom to separate until the wedding."

This was another ritual: a final, formal moment of parting to be followed by a lifetime of togetherness.

"The bride may, however, give the groom some token of affection to make sure he does not forget her during the lonely hours of the night," Philippe said, eyes twinkling with mischief.

Matthew and I rose. I smoothed down my skirts, my attention fixed resolutely on his doublet. The stitches on it were very fine, I noticed, tiny and regular. Gentle fingers lifted my chin, and I was lost instead in the play of smooth curves and sharp angles that made up Matthew's face. All sense of performance disappeared as we contemplated each other. We stood in the midst of the hall and the wedding guests, our kiss a spell that carried us to an intimate world of our own.

"I'll see you tomorrow afternoon," Matthew murmured against my lips as we parted.

"I'll be the one in the veil." Most brides didn't wear them in the sixteenth century, but they were an ancient custom, and Philippe said that no daughter of his was going to the church without one.

"I'd know you anywhere," he replied, flashing me a smile, "veil or no veil."

Matthew's eyes never wavered as Alain escorted me from the room. I felt the touch of them, cool and unblinking, long after I left the hall.

The next day Catrine and Jehanne were so quiet that I slumbered through their usual morning chores. The sun was almost fully up when they finally pulled the bed curtains aside and announced it was time for my bath.

A procession of women with pitchers came to my chamber, chattering like magpies and filling an enormous copper tub that I suspected was normally used to make wine or cider. But the water was piping hot and the copper vessel retained the glorious warmth, so I wasn't inclined to quibble. I groaned in ecstasy and sank beneath the water's surface.

The women left me to soak, and I noticed that my few belongings—books, the notes I'd taken on alchemy and Occitan phrases—had disappeared. So, too, had the long, low chest that stored my clothes. When I asked Catrine, she explained that everything had been moved to *milord*'s chambers on the other side of the château.

I was no longer Philippe's putative daughter, but Matthew's wife. My property had been relocated accordingly.

Mindful of their responsibility, Catrine and Jehanne had me out of the tub and dried off by the time the clock struck one. Overseeing their efforts was Marie, Saint-Lucien's best seamstress, who had come to put the finishing touches on her work. The contributions to my wedding gown that had been made by the village's tailor, Monsieur Beaufils, were not acknowledged.

To be fair to Marie, *La Robe* (I thought of my ensemble only in French, and always in capitals) was spectacular. How she had managed to complete it in such a short period of time was a deeply kept secret, though I suspected that every woman in the vicinity had contributed at least a stitch. Before Philippe announced I was getting married, the plan had been for a relatively simple dress of heavy, slate-colored silk. I had insisted on one pair of sleeves, not two, and a high neckline to keep out the winter drafts. There was no need to trouble with embroidery, I told Marie. I had also declined the outrageous birdcagelike supports that would extend the skirt in every direction.

Marie had used her powers of misunderstanding and creativity to modify my initial design long before Philippe told her where and when the gown would be worn. After that there was no holding the woman back.

"Marie, *La Robe est belle,*" I told her, fingering the heavily embroidered silk. Stylized cornucopias, familiar symbols of abundance and fertility, were stitched all over in gold, black, and rose thread. Rosettes and sprigs of leaves accompanied the flower-filled horns, while bands of embroidery edged both pairs of sleeves. The same bands trimmed the edges of the bodice in a sinuous pattern of scrolls, moons, and stars. At the shoulders a row of square flaps called *pickadils* hid the laces that tied sleeve to bodice. Despite the elaborate ornamentation, the bodice's elegant curves fit perfectly, and my wishes on the subject of farthingales had at least been honored. The skirts were full, but that was due to the volume of fabric rather than any wire contraption. The only thing I wore under the petticoats was the stuffed doughnut that rested on my hips, and silk hose.

"It has a strong line. Very simple," Marie assured me, tugging on the bottom of the bodice to help it lie more smoothly.

The women were almost finished with my hair when a knock sounded. Catrine rushed to open the door, turning over a basket of towels on her way.

It was Philippe, looking splendid in a rich brown suit, with Alain standing behind him. Matthew's father stared.

"Diana?" Philippe sounded unsure.

"What? Is something wrong?" I surveyed my gown and anxiously patted at my hair. "We don't have a mirror large enough for me to see—"

"You are beautiful, and the look on Matthew's face when he sees you will tell you this better than any reflection," Philippe said firmly.

"And *you* have a silver tongue, Philippe de Clermont," I said with a laugh. "What do you need?"

"I came to give you your wedding gifts." Philippe held out his hand, and Alain placed a large velvet bag in his palm. "There was no time to have something made, I'm afraid. These are family pieces."

He tipped the bag's contents into his hand. A stream of light and fire poured out: gold, diamonds, sapphires. I gasped. But there were more treasures hidden inside the velvet, including a rope of pearls, several crescent moons encrusted with opals, and an unusually shaped golden arrowhead, its edges softened with age.

"What are they for?" I asked in wonder.

"For you to wear, of course," Philippe said, chuckling. "The chain was mine, but when I saw Marie's gown, I thought the yellow diamonds and the sapphires would not look out of place. The style is old, and some would say it is too masculine for a bride, but the chain will sit on your shoulders and lie flat. Originally a cross hung from the center, but I thought you might prefer to suspend the arrow instead."

"I don't recognize the flowers." The slender yellow buds reminded me of freesia, and they were interspersed with gold fleurs-de-lis rimmed with sapphires.

"*Planta genista.* The English call it broom. The Angevins used it as their emblem."

He meant the Plantagenets: the most powerful royal family in English history. The Plantagenets had expanded Westminster Abbey, given in to the barons and signed the Magna Carta, established Parliament, and supported the foundation of Oxford and Cambridge universities. Plantagenet rulers had fought in the Crusades and through the Hundred Years' War with France. And one of them had given this chain to Philippe as a sign of royal favor. Nothing else could account for its splendor.

"Philippe, I can't possibly—" My protests stopped when he passed the other jewels to Catrine and lowered the chain over my head. The woman who gazed back at me from the murky mirror was no more a modern historian than Matthew was a modern scientist. "Oh," I said in amazement.

"Breathtaking," he agreed. His face softened with regret. "I wish Ysabeau could be here to see you like this, and to witness Matthew's happiness."

"I'll tell her everything one day," I promised softly, holding his reflected gaze as Catrine fastened the arrow to the front of the chain and wound the rope of pearls through my hair. "I'll take good care of the jewels tonight, too, and make sure they're returned to you in the morning."

"These belong to you now, Diana, to do with what you will. As does this." Philippe pulled another bag from his belt, this one made from serviceable leather, and handed it to me.

It was heavy. Very heavy.

"The women in this family manage their own finances. Ysabeau insists upon it. All of the coins in here are English or French. They do not hold their value as well as Venetian ducats, but they will raise fewer questions when you spend them. If you need more, you have only to ask Walter or another member of the brotherhood."

When I'd arrived in France, I was entirely dependent on Matthew. In little more than a week, I had learned how to conduct myself, converse, manage a household, and distill spirit of wine. I now had my own property, and Philippe de Clermont had claimed me publicly as his daughter.

"Thank you, for all of this," I said softly. "I didn't think you wanted me as a daughter-in-law."

"Not at first, perhaps. But even old men can change their minds." Philippe's grin flashed. "And I always get what I want in the end."

The women wrapped me in my cloak. At the very last moment, Catrine and Jehanne dropped a filmy piece of silk over my head and attached it to my hair with the opal crescent moons, which had tiny, tenacious claws on the back.

Thomas and Étienne, who now saw themselves as my personal champions, ran ahead of us through the château and proclaimed our approach at the top of their lungs. Soon we formed a procession, moving through the twilight in the direction of the church. Someone must have been up in the bell tower, and once whoever that was spotted us, the bells began to ring.

I faltered as we came to the church. The entire village had assembled outside its doors, along with the priest. I searched for Matthew and found him standing at the top of the short flight of stairs. Through the transparent veil, I could feel his regard. Like sun and moon, we were unconcerned at this moment with time, distance, and difference. All that mattered was our position relative to each other.

I gathered my skirts and went to him. The brief climb felt endless. Did time misbehave this way for all brides, I wondered, or only for witches?

The priest beamed at me from the door but made no effort to admit us to the church. He was clutching a book in his hands but didn't open it. I frowned in confusion.

"All right, *mon coeur*?" Matthew murmured.

"Aren't we going inside?"

"Marriages take place at the church door to avoid bloody disputes later over whether or not the ceremony took place as reported. We can thank God there isn't a blizzard."

"Commencez!" the priest commanded, nodding at Matthew.

My entire role in the ceremony was to utter eleven words. Matthew was charged with fifteen. Philippe had informed the priest that we would then repeat our vows, in English, because it was important that the bride fully understand what she was promising. This brought the total number of words necessary to make us husband and wife to fifty-two.

"Maintenant!" The priest was shivering and wanted his supper.

"Je, Matthew, donne mon corps à toi, Diana, en loyal mariage." Matthew took my hands in his. "I, Matthew, give my body to you, Diana, in faithful matrimony."

"Et je le reçois," I replied. "And I receive it."

We were halfway through. I took a deep breath and kept going.

"Je, Diana, donne mon corps à toi, Matthew." The hard part over, I quickly said my final line. "I, Diana, give my body to you, Matthew."

"Et je le reçois, avec joie." Matthew drew the veil over my head. "And I receive it, with joy."

"Those aren't the right words," I said fiercely. I had memorized the vows, and there was no *"avec joie"* anywhere in them.

"They are," Matthew insisted, lowering his head.

We'd been married by vampire custom when we mated and again by common law when Matthew had put Ysabeau's ring on my finger in Madison. Now we were married a third time.

What happened afterward was a blur. There were torches and a long walk up the hill surrounded by well-wishers. Chef's feast was already laid out, and people tucked into it with enthusiasm. Matthew and I sat alone at the family table, while Philippe strolled about serving wine and making sure the children got their fair share of spit-roasted hare and cheese fritters. Occasionally he cast a proud look in our direction, as if we'd slain dragons that afternoon.

"I never thought I would see this day," Philippe told Matthew as he placed a slice of custard tart before us.

The feast seemed to be winding down when the men started shoving the tables to the sides of the hall. Pipes and drums sounded from the minstrels' gallery above.

"By tradition the first dance belongs to the bride's father," Philippe said with a bow to me. He led me to the floor. Philippe was a good dancer, but even so I got us tangled.

"May I?" Matthew tapped on his father's shoulder.

"Please. Your wife is trying to break my foot." Philippe's wink took the sting out of his words, and he withdrew, leaving me with my husband.

Others were still dancing, but they drew away and left us in the center of the room. The music deliberately slowed as a musician plucked on the strings of his lute, and the sweet tones of a wind instrument piped an accompaniment. As we parted and came together, once, twice, again, the distractions of the room faded.

"You're a far better dancer than Philippe, no matter what your mother says," I told him, breathless even though the dance was measured.

"That's because you're following my lead," he teased. "You fought Philippe every step of the way."

When the dance brought us together once more, he took me by the elbows, pulled me tight against his body, and kissed me. "Now that we're married, will you keep forgiving my sins?" he asked, swinging back into the regular steps.

"That depends," I said warily. "What have you done now?"

"I've crushed your ruff beyond redemption."

I laughed, and Matthew kissed me again, briefly but emphatically. The drummer took it as a cue, and the music's tempo increased. Other couples whirled and hopped their way across the floor. Matthew drew us into relative safety near the fireplace before we were trampled. Philippe was there a moment later.

"Take your wife to bed and finish this," Philippe murmured.

"But the guests . . ." Matthew protested.

"Take your wife to bed, my son," Philippe repeated. "Steal away now, before the others decide to accompany you upstairs and make sure you do your duty. Leave everything to me." He turned, kissing me formally on both cheeks before murmuring something in Greek and sending us to Matthew's tower.

Though I knew this part of the château in my own time, I had yet to see it in its sixteenth-century splendor. The order of Matthew's apartments had changed. I expected to see books in the room off the first landing, but instead there was a large canopied bed. Catrine and Jehanne brought out a carved box for my new jewels, filled up the basin, and bustled around with fresh linens. Matthew sat before the fire and pulled off his boots, taking up a glass of wine when he was through.

"Your hair, *madame*?" Jehanne asked, eyeing my husband speculatively.

"I'll take care of it," Matthew said gruffly, his eyes on the fire.

"Wait," I said, pulling the moon-shaped jewels free from my hair and putting them in Jehanne's upturned palm. She and Catrine removed the veil and departed, leaving me standing near the bed and Matthew lounging fireside with his feet on one of the clothing chests.

When the door closed, Matthew put down his glass of wine and came to me, twining his fingers in my hair and tugging gently to dislodge in moments what it had taken the girls nearly thirty minutes to achieve. He tossed the rope of pearls aside. My hair tumbled over my shoulders, and Matthew's nostrils flared as he took in my scent. Wordlessly he pulled my body against his and bent to fit his mouth to mine.

But there were questions that needed to be asked and answered first. I drew away.

"Matthew, are you sure . . . ?"

Cool fingers slid underneath my ruff, finding the ties that connected it to my bodice.

Snap. Snap. Snap.

The stiffened linen came free from my neck and fell to the floor. Matthew loosened the buttons that kept my high neckline clasped tight. He bent his head and kissed my throat. I clutched at his doublet.

"Matthew," I repeated. "Is this about—"

He silenced me with another kiss while he lifted the heavy chain from my shoulders. We broke off momentarily so Matthew could get it over my head. Then his hands breached the crenellated line of *pickadils* where sleeves met bodice. His fingers slid among the gaps, searching out a weak point in the garment's defenses.

"There it is," he murmured, hooking his index fingers around the edges and giving a decided yank. One sleeve, then the other, slid down each arm and onto the floor. Matthew seemed entirely unconcerned, but it was my wedding gown and not easily replaced.

"My gown," I said, squirming in his arms.

"Diana." Matthew drew his head back and rested his hands on my waist.

"Yes?" I said breathlessly. I tried to reach the sleeve with the toe of my slipper and push it where it was less likely to be crushed.

"The priest blessed our marriage. The entire village wished us well. There was food, and dancing. I did think we might draw the night to a close by making love. Yet you seem more interested in your wardrobe." He had located still another set of laces that fastened my skirts to the bottom of the pointed bodice, about three inches below my belly button. Lightly, Matthew swept his thumbs between edge of the bodice and my pubic bone.

"I don't want our first time together to be about satisfying your father." In spite of my protests, my hips arched toward him in silent invitation while he kept up that maddening movement of his thumbs, like the beating of an angel's wings. He made a soft sound of satisfaction and untied the bow hidden there.

Tug. Rasp. Tug. Rasp. Tug. Rasp.

Matthew's nimble fingers pulled on each crossing of the laces, drawing them through the concealed holes. There were twelve in all, and my body bowed and straightened with the force of his attentions.

"At last," he said with satisfaction. Then he groaned. "Christ. There are more."

"Oh, you're nowhere near through. I'm trussed up like a Christmas goose," I said as he lifted the bodice away from the skirts, revealing the corset below. "Or, more accurately, an Advent goose."

But Matthew wasn't paying any attention to me. Instead my husband was focused on the place where my nearly transparent high-necked smock disappeared into the heavy reinforced fabric of the corset. He pressed his lips against the swell. Bowing his head in a reverential pose, he took in a jagged breath.

So did I. It was surprisingly erotic, the brush of his lips somehow magnified by the fine lawn boundary. Not knowing what made him stop his previously single-minded efforts to get me unclothed, I cradled his head in my hands and waited for him to make his next move.

At last Matthew took my hands and wrapped them around the carved post that held up the corner of the canopy. "Hold on," he said.

Tug. Rasp. Tug. Rasp. Before he was finished, Matthew took a moment to slide his hands inside the stays. They swooped around my rib cage and found my breasts. I moaned softly as he trapped my smock between the warm, pebbled skin of my nipples and his cool fingers. He pulled me back against him.

"Do I seem like a man interested in pleasing anyone but you?" he murmured into my ear. When I didn't immediately answer, one hand snaked down my stomach to press me closer. The other remained where it was, cupping my breast.

"No." My head tilted back into his shoulder, exposing my neck.

"Then no more talk about my father. And I'll buy you twenty identical gowns tomorrow if you will stop worrying about your sleeves now." Matthew was busily ruching up my smock so that the hem skirted the tops of my legs. I loosed my grip on the bedpost, grabbed at his hand, and placed it at the juncture of my thighs.

"No more talking," I agreed, gasping when his fingers parted my flesh.

Matthew quieted me further with a kiss. The slow movements of his hands were causing an entirely different reaction as the tension in my body rose.

"Too many clothes," I said breathlessly. His agreement was unstated, but evident in the haste with which he slid the corset down my arms. The laces were loose enough now that I could push it over my hips and step out of it. I unfastened his breeches while Matthew unbuttoned his doublet. These two items had been joined at his hips by just as many crossed laces as my bodice and skirt.

When we were both wearing nothing more than hose, I my smock, and Matthew his shirt, we paused, awkwardness returning.

"Will you let me love you, Diana?" Matthew said, sweeping away my anxiety with that simple, courteous question.

"I will," I whispered. He knelt and carefully untied the ribbons that held up my stockings. They were blue, which Catrine said was the color of fidelity. Matthew rolled the hose down my legs, a press of lips on knees and ankles marking their passage. He removed his own hose so quickly that I never had an opportunity to note the color of his garters.

Matthew lifted me slightly so that my toes were barely gripping the floor and he could fit himself into the notch between my legs.

"We may not make it to the bed," I said, grabbing onto his shoulders. I wanted him inside me, quickly.

But we did make it to that soft, shadowed place, ridding ourselves of our linen along the way. Once there, my body welcomed him into the moon of my thighs while my arms reached to draw him down to me. Even so I gasped in surprise when our two bodies became one—warm and cold, light and dark, female and male, witch and vampire, a conjunction of opposites.

Matthew's expression went from reverential to wondering when he began to move within me, and it became intent after he angled his body and I reacted with a pleased cry. He slipped his arm under the small of my back and lifted me into his hips while my hands gripped his shoulders.

We fell into the rhythm unique to lovers, pleasing each other with soft touches of mouth and hands as we rocked together, together until all we had left to give were our hearts and souls. Looking deep into each other's eyes, we exchanged our final vows with flesh and spirit, trembling like newborns.

"Let me love you forever," Matthew murmured against my damp forehead, his lips trailing a cold path across my brow as we lay twined together.

"I will," I promised once more, tucking my body even closer against him.

"I like being married," I said drowsily. Since surviving the day-after feast and the receiving of gifts—most of them mooing or clucking—we'd done nothing for days but make love, talk, sleep, and read. Occasionally Chef sent up a tray of food and drink to sustain us. Otherwise we were left alone. Not even Philippe interrupted our time together.

"You seem to be taking to it well," Matthew said, nuzzling the tip of his cold nose behind my ear. I was lying, facedown and legs sprawled, in a room used to store spare weaponry above the smithy. Matthew was on top of me, shielding me from the draft coming through the gaps in the wooden door. Though I was unsure of how much of my own body would be exposed if someone walked in, Matthew's posterior and bare legs were certainly on view. He moved against me suggestively.

"You can't possibly want to do that again." I laughed happily when he repeated the movement. I wondered if this sexual stamina was a vampire thing or a Matthew thing.

"Are you criticizing my creativity already?" He turned me over and settled between my thighs. "Besides, I was thinking of this instead." He lowered his mouth to mine and slid gently inside me.

"We came out here to work on my shooting," I said sometime later. "Is this what you meant by target practice?"

Matthew rumbled with laughter. "There are hundreds of Auvergnat euphemisms for making love, but I don't believe that's one of them. I'll ask Chef if he's familiar with it."

"You will not."

"Are you being prim, Dr. Bishop?" he asked with mock surprise, picking a piece of straw from the hair tangled at the small of my back. "Don't bother. No one is under any illusions about how we're spending our time."

"I see your point," I said, pulling the hose that were formerly his over my knees. "Now that you've lured me here, you might as well try to figure out what I'm doing wrong."

"You're a novice and can't expect to hit the mark every time," he said, getting to his feet and rummaging for his own hose. One leg was still attached to his breeches, which were lying close by, but the other was nowhere to be seen. I reached underneath my shoulder and handed him the wadded-up ball they'd become.

"With good coaching I could become an expert." I'd now seen Matthew shoot, and he was a born archer with his long arms and fine, strong fingers. I picked up the curved bow, a burnished crescent of horn and wood propped up against a nearby pile of hay. The twisted leather bowstring swung free.

"Then you should be spending time with Philippe, not with me. His handling of the bow is legendary."

"Your father told me Ysabeau is a better shot." I was using her bow, but so far her skills had not rubbed off on me.

"That's because *Maman* is the only creature who has ever landed an arrow in his side." He beckoned at the bow. "Let me string it for you."

There was already a pink stripe across my cheek from the first time I'd tried to attach the bowstring to its ring. It required enormous strength and dexterity to bend back the upper and lower limbs of the bow into proper alignment. Matthew braced the lower limb against his thigh, bent the upper limb back with one hand, and used the other to tie off the bowstring.

"You make that look easy." It had looked easy when he'd twisted the cork from a bottle of champagne back in modern Oxford, too.

"It is—if you're a vampire and have had roughly a thousand years of practice." Matthew handed me the bow with a smile. "Remember, keep your shoulders in a straight line, don't think too long about the shot, and make the release soft and smooth."

He made it *sound* easy, too. I turned to face the target. Matthew had used a few daggers to pin a soft cap, a doublet, and a skirt to a pile of hay. At first I thought the goal was to hit something: the hat, the doublet, the skirt. Matthew explained that the goal was to hit what I was aiming for. He demonstrated his point by shooting a single arrow into a haystack, encircling it clockwise with five other arrows, then splitting the center shaft down the middle with a sixth.

I drew an arrow out of the quiver, nocked it, looked down the line of sight provided by my left arm, and pulled the bowstring back. I hesitated. The bow was already misaligned.

"Shoot," Matthew said sharply.

When I released the string, the arrow whizzed by the hay and fell flat on the ground.

"Let me try again," I said, reaching for the quiver by my feet.

"I've seen you shoot witchfire at a vampire and blow a hole straight through her chest," Matthew said quietly.

"I don't want to talk about Juliette." I tried to set the arrow in place, but my hands shook. I lowered the bow. "Or Champier. Or the fact that my powers seem to have totally disappeared. Or how I can make fruit wither and see colors and lights around people. Can't we just leave it—for one week?" Once again, my magic (or lack thereof) was a regular topic of conversation.

"The archery was supposed to help jostle your witchfire into action," Matthew pointed out. "Talking about Juliette may help."

"Why can't this just be about me getting some exercise?" I asked impatiently.

"Because we need to understand why your power is changing," Matthew said calmly. "Raise the bow, pull the arrow back, and let it fly."

"At least I hit the hay this time," I said after the arrow landed in the upper right corner of the haystack.

"Too bad you were aiming lower."

"You're taking all the fun out of this."

Matthew's expression turned serious. "There's nothing lighthearted about survival. This time nock the arrow but close your eyes before you aim."

"You want me to use my instincts." My laugh was shaky as I placed the arrow in the bow. The target was in front of me, but rather than focus on it I closed my eyes as Matthew suggested. As soon as I did, the weight of the air distracted me. It pressed on my arms, my thighs, and settled like a heavy cloak on my shoulders. The air held the tip of the arrow up, too. I adjusted my stance, shoulders widening as they pushed the air aside. A breeze, a caress of movement, pulled a few strands of hair away from my ear in response.

What do you want? I asked the breeze crossly.

Your trust, it whispered in reply.

My lips parted in astonishment, my mind's eye opened, and I saw the tip of the arrow burning gold with the heat and pressure that had been beaten into it at the forge. The fire that was trapped there wanted to fly free again, but it would stay where it was unless I let go of my fear. I puffed out a soft exhalation, making room for faith. My breath passed along the arrow's shaft, and I released the bowstring. Held aloft on my breath, the arrow flew.

"I hit it." My eyes remained closed, but I didn't need to see to know that my arrow had reached its target.

"You did. The question is how." Matthew took the bow from my fingers before it could fall.

"Fire was trapped in the arrow, and the weight of the air was wrapped around the shaft and the tip." I opened my eyes.

"You felt the elements just as you did the water under Sarah's orchard in Madison and the sunlight in the quince at the Old Lodge." Matthew sounded thoughtful.

"Sometimes it seems like the world is full of invisible potential that is just beyond my grasp. Maybe if I were like Thetis and could shift my shape at will, I would know what to do with it all." I reached for the bow and another arrow. So long as I kept my eyes closed, I hit the target. As soon as I peeked at my surroundings, however, my shots went wide or fell short.

"That's enough for today," Matthew said, working on a knot that was forming next to my right shoulder blade. "Chef expects rain later this week. Maybe we should go riding while we can." Chef was not only a dab hand with pastry but a decent meteorologist, too. He usually sent up a forecast with the breakfast tray.

We rode out into the countryside and spotted several bonfires burning in the fields on our way home, and Sept-Tours blazed with torches. Tonight was Saturnalia, the official beginning of the holiday season at the château. The ecumenical Philippe wanted no one to feel left out and so gave equal time to Roman and Christian traditions. There was even a strand of Norse Yule running through the mix, which I felt sure could be traced to the absent Gallowglass.

"You two can't be tired of each other's company so soon!" Philippe boomed from the minstrels' gallery when we returned. He was wearing a splendid set of antlers atop his head, making him look like a bizarre combination of lion and stag. "We didn't expect to see you for another fortnight. But now that you're here, you can make yourself useful. Take some stars and moons and hang them wherever there is an empty spot."

The great hall was draped in so much greenery that it looked and smelled like the forest. Several wine barrels stood unattended so that revelers could have a cup whenever the spirit moved them. Cheers greeted our return. The decorating crew wanted Matthew to climb up the chimneypiece and affix a large tree limb to one of the beams. He scampered up the stone with an agility that suggested it was not his first time.

It was impossible to resist the holiday spirit, and when supper rolled around, the two of us volunteered to serve the meal to the guests in a ritual of topsy-turvy that made the servants into lords and the lords their servants. My champion Thomas drew the long straw and presided over the celebrations as the Lord of Misrule. He was seated in Philippe's place on a stack of cushions, wearing the priceless gold-and-ruby crown from upstairs as though it were a stage prop. Whatever harebrained request Thomas made was granted by Philippe in his role as court fool. His favors this night included a romantic dance with Alain (Matthew's father opted to take the part of the woman), driving the dogs into a frenzy by playing a whistling flute, and making shadow dragons climb up the wall accompanied by the screams of the children.

Philippe didn't forget the adults, setting up elaborate games of chance to occupy them while he entertained his smallest subjects. He gave each grown-up a bag of beans to make wagers and promised a sack of money to the person with the most at the end of the evening. The enterprising Catrine made a killing by exchanging kisses for beans, and had I been given any tokens, I would have bet them all on her taking the final prize.

Throughout the evening I would look up and see Matthew and Philippe standing side by side, exchanging a few words or sharing a joke. As they bent their heads together, one dark and one bright, the difference in their appearances was striking. But in so many other ways, they were alike. With every passing day, his father's unquenchable high spirits wore down some of Matthew's sharp edges. Hamish had been right: Matthew was not the same man here. He was even finer. And in spite of my fears at Mont Saint-Michel, he was still mine.

Matthew felt my gaze and looked at me quizzically. I smiled and blew him a kiss across the hall. He dipped his head, shyly pleased.

Around five minutes before midnight, Philippe whisked the cover off an item standing by the fireplace.

"Christ. Philippe swore he'd have that clock up and running again, but I didn't believe him." Matthew joined me as the children and adults squealed in delight.

The clock was unlike any I'd ever seen before. A carved and gilded cabinet surrounded a water barrel. A long copper pipe stretched up from the barrel and dropped water into the hull of a splendid model ship suspended by a rope wound around a cylinder. As the ship grew incrementally heavier from the weight of the water, the cylinder turned and moved a single hand around a dial on the face of the clock, indicating the time. The whole structure was nearly as tall as I was.

"What happens at midnight?" I asked.

"No doubt whatever it is involves the gunpowder he asked for yesterday," Matthew said grimly.

Having displayed the clock with suitable ceremony, Philippe began a tribute to friends past and present and family new and old, as befitted a festival honoring the ancient god. He named every creature the community had lost over the past year, including (when prompted by the Lord of Misrule) Thomas's kitten, Prunelle, who had died tragically by misadventure. The hand continued to inch toward twelve.

At midnight precisely, the ship detonated with a deafening explosion. The clock shuddered to a stop in its splintered wooden case.

"Skata." Philippe looked sadly at his ruined clock.

"Monsieur Finé, God rest his soul, would not be pleased with your improvements to his design." Matthew waved the smoke from his eyes as he bent to take a closer look. "Every year Philippe tries something new: jets of water, chiming bells, a mechanical owl to hoot the hours. He's been tinkering with it ever since King François lost it to him in a card game."

"The cannon were supposed to fire little sparks and give a puff of smoke. It would have amused the children," said Philippe indignantly. "Something was amiss with your gunpowder, *Matthaios*."

Matthew laughed. "Evidently not, judging by the wreckage."

"C'est dommage," Thomas said with a sympathetic shake of the head. He was crouched next to Philippe, his crown askew and a look of adult concern on his face.

"Pas de problème. Next year we will do better," Philippe assured Thomas breezily.

Shortly thereafter we left the people of Saint-Lucien to their gambling and revelry. Upstairs, I lingered by the fireside until Matthew doused the candles and got into bed. When I joined him, I hitched up my night rail and straddled his hips.

"What are you doing?" Matthew was surprised to find himself flat on his back in his own bed, his wife looking down at him.

"Misrule wasn't just for men," I said, running my nails down his chest. "I read an article about it in graduate school, called 'Women on Top.'"

"Accustomed as you are to being in charge, I cannot imagine you learned much from it, *mon coeur.*" Matthew's eyes smoldered as I shifted my weight to trap him more securely between my thighs.

"Flatterer." My fingertips traveled from his trim hips up and over the ridges in his abdomen and across the muscles in his shoulders. I leaned over him and pinned his arms to the bed, giving him an excellent view of my body through the night rail's open neckline. He groaned.

"Welcome to the world turned upside down." I released him long enough to remove my night rail, then grasped his hands and lowered myself onto his chest so that the tips of my bare breasts brushed his skin.

"Christ. You're going to kill me."

"Don't you dare die now, vampire," I said, guiding him inside me, rocking gently, holding out the promise of more. Matthew reacted with a low moan. "You like that," I said softly.

He urged me toward a harder, faster rhythm. But I kept my movements slow and steady, reveling in the way our bodies fit. Matthew was a cool presence at my core, a delicious source of friction that heated my blood. I was staring deep into his eyes when he climaxed, and the raw vulnerability there sent me hurtling after him. I collapsed onto his torso, and when I moved to climb off, his arms tightened around me.

"Stay there," he whispered.

I did stay, until Matthew woke me hours later. He made love to me again in the quiet before the dawn and held me as I underwent the metamorphosis from fire to water to air and returned once more to dreams.

Friday marked the shortest day of the year and the celebration of Yule. The village was still recovering from Saturnalia and had Christmas yet before them, but Philippe was undeterred.

"Chef butchered a hog," he said. "How could I disappoint him?"

During a break in the weather, Matthew went to the village to help repair a roof that had collapsed under the weight of the latest snowfall. I left him there, throwing hammers down a ridgepole to another carpenter and delighted at the prospect of a morning of grueling physical labor in freezing temperatures.

I closeted myself in the library with a few of the family's finer alchemical books and some blank sheets of paper. One was partially covered with doodles and diagrams that would have made sense to no one but me. With all that was happening in the château, I'd abandoned my attempts to make spirit of wine. Thomas and Étienne wanted to be running around with their friends and sticking their fingers into Chef's latest cake batter, not helping me with a science experiment.

"Diana." Philippe was moving at great speed and was halfway into the room before he noticed me. "I thought you were with Matthew."

"I couldn't bear to see him up there," I confessed. He nodded in understanding.

"What are you doing?" he asked, looking over my shoulder.

"Trying to figure out what Matthew and I have to do with alchemy." My brain felt fuzzy with disuse and lack of sleep.

Philippe dropped a handful of small paper triangles, scrolls, and squares onto the table and pulled up a chair. He pointed to one of my sketches. "This is Matthew's seal."

"It is. It's also the symbols for silver and gold, the moon and the sun." The hall had been decorated with spangled versions of these heavenly bodies for Saturnalia. "I've been thinking about it since Monday night. I understand why a witch might be symbolized by the crescent moon and silver—they're both linked to the goddess. But why would anyone use a sun or gold to denote a vampire?" It went against every bit of popular lore.

"Because we are unchanging. Our lives do not wax or wane, and, like gold, our bodies resist corruption from death or disease."

"I should have thought of that." I made some notes.

"You have had a few other things on your mind." Philippe smiled. "Matthew is very happy."

"Not only because of me," I said, meeting my father-in-law's gaze. "Matthew is happy to be with you again."

Shadows scudded through Philippe's eyes. "Ysabeau and I like it when our children come home. They have their own lives, but it doesn't make their absence any easier to bear."

"And today you are missing Gallowglass, too," I said. Philippe seemed uncharacteristically subdued.

"I am." He stirred the folded papers with his fingers. "It was Hugh, my eldest, who brought him into the family. Hugh always made wise decisions when it came to sharing his blood, and Gallowglass was no exception. He is a fierce warrior with his father's sense of honor. It comforts me to know that my grandson is in England with Matthew."

"Matthew seldom mentions Hugh."

"He was closer to Hugh than to any of his other brothers. When Hugh died with the last of the Templars at the hands of the church and the king, it shook Matthew's loyalties. It was some time before he was able to free himself of his blood rage and come back to us."

"And Gallowglass?"

"Gallowglass is not yet ready to leave his grief behind, and until he does so, he will not set foot in France. My grandson exacted retribution from the men who betrayed Hugh's trust, as did Matthew, but revenge is never an adequate remedy for loss. One day my grandson will return. I am sure of it." For a moment Philippe looked old, no longer the vigorous ruler of his people but a father who had suffered the misfortune to outlive his sons.

"Thank you, Philippe." I hesitated before covering his hand with mine. He clasped it briefly and stood. Then he took up one of the alchemy books. It was Godfrey's beautifully illustrated copy of the *Aurora Consurgens,* the text that had first lured me to Sept-Tours.

"Such a curious subject, alchemy," Philippe murmured, flipping through the pages. He found the picture of the Sun King and the Moon Queen jousting on the back of a lion and a griffin, and he smiled broadly. "Yes, this will do." He tucked one of his paper shapes between the pages.

"What are you doing?" I was overcome with curiosity.

"It is a game that Ysabeau and I play. When one of us is away, we leave messages hidden in the pages of books. So much happens in a day, it is impossible to remember everything when we see each other again. This way we can come upon little memories like this one when we least expect it, and share them."

Philippe went to the shelves and picked out a volume in a worn leather binding. "This is one of our favorite stories, *The Song of Armouris.* Ysabeau and I have simple tastes and enjoy stories of adventure. We are always hiding messages in this." He stuffed a scroll of paper down the spine between the binding and the gatherings of vellum. A folded rectangle fell out of the bottom as he worked it into the tight space.

"Ysabeau has taken to using a knife so that her messages are harder to find. She is full of tricks, that one. Let's see what she says." Philippe opened up the paper and read it silently. He looked up with a twinkle in his eyes and cheeks that were redder than usual.

I laughed and rose. "I think you might need more privacy to compose your reply!"

"Sieur." Alain shifted in the doorway, his face serious. "Messengers have arrived. One from Scotland. Another from England. A third from Lyon."

Philippe sighed and cursed under his breath. "They might have waited until after the Christian feast."

My mouth soured.

"It cannot be good news," Philippe said, catching my expression. "What did the messenger from Lyon report?"

"Champier took precautions before he left and told others that he had been called here. Now that he has not returned home, his friends are asking questions. A group of witches is preparing to leave the city in search of him, and they are headed in this direction," Alain explained.

"When?" I whispered. It was too soon.

"The snow will slow them, and they will find travel difficult over the holy days. A few more days, perhaps a week."

"And the other messengers?" I asked Alain.

"They are in the village, looking for *milord.*"

"To call him back to England, no doubt," I said.

"If so, Christmas Day will be the best time to set out. Few will be on the roads, and the moon will be dark. These are ideal travel conditions for *manjasang,* but not for warmbloods," Philippe said matter-of-factly. "There are horses and lodgings ready for you as far as Calais. A boat waits to take you to Dover. I sent word to Gallowglass and Raleigh to prepare for your return."

"You've been expecting this," I said, shaken at the prospect of leaving. "But I'm not ready. People still know I'm different."

"You blend in better than you think. You've been conversing with me in perfectly good French and Latin all morning, for instance." My mouth opened in disbelief. Philippe laughed. "It is true. I switched back and forth twice, but you didn't notice." His face grew serious. "Shall I go down and tell Matthew about my arrangements?"

"No," I said, my hand on his arm. "I'll do it."

Matthew was sitting on the ridgepole, a letter in each hand and a frown on his face. When he spotted me, he slid down the slope of an eave and landed on the ground with the grace of a cat. His happiness and lighthearted banter of this morning were nothing more than a memory. Matthew removed his doublet from a rusted torch bracket. Once he'd shrugged it over his shoulders, the carpenter was gone and the prince had returned.

"Agnes Sampson confessed to fifty-three indictments of witchcraft."

Matthew swore. "Scottish officials have yet to learn that heaping on charges makes every single one look less convincing. According to this account, the devil reported to Sampson that King James was his greatest enemy. Elizabeth must be delighted not to find herself in first place."

"Witches don't believe in the devil," I told him. Of all the bizarre things humans said about witches, this was the most incomprehensible.

"Most creatures will believe in anything that promises to bring an end to their immediate misery if they've been starved, tortured, and frightened for weeks on end." Matthew ran his fingers through his hair. "Agnes Sampson's confession—unreliable as it is—provides proof that the witches are meddling in politics, just as King James contends."

"Thereby breaking the covenant," I said, understanding why Agnes had been so vigorously pursued by the Scottish king.

"Yes. Gallowglass wants to know what to do."

"What did you do when you were here . . . before?"

"I let Agnes Sampson's death pass unchallenged, a proper civil punishment for a crime that was outside the bounds of Congregation protection." His eyes met mine. Witch and historian struggled with the impossible choice before me.

"Then you have to keep silent again," I said, the historian winning the contest.

"My silence will mean her death."

"And your speaking out will change the past, perhaps with unimaginable consequences for the present. I don't want the witch to die any more than you do, Matthew. But if we start changing things, where will we stop?" I shook my head.

"So I will watch the whole gruesome business in Scotland unfold, again. This time it looks so different, though," he said reluctantly. "William Cecil has directed me to return home so that I can gather intelligence on the Scottish situation for the queen. I have to obey his orders, Diana. I don't have a choice."

"We'd have to go to England even without Cecil's summons. Champier's friends have noticed he's missing. And we can leave immediately. Philippe's been making arrangements for a speedy departure, just in case."

"That's my father," Matthew said with a humorless laugh.

"I'm sorry we have to leave so soon," I whispered.

Matthew hooked me into his side. "If not for you, my last memories of my father would be of a broken shell of a man. We must take the bitter with the sweet."

Over the next several days, Matthew and his father went through a ritual of farewell that must have been familiar, given all the good-byes the two had exchanged. But this time was unique. It would be a different Matthew who would next come to Sept-Tours, one with no knowledge of me or of Philippe's future.

"The people of Saint-Lucien have long known the company of *manjasang,*" Philippe assured me when I worried how Thomas and Étienne would be able to keep it all secret. "We come, we go. They ask no questions, and we offer no explanations. It has always been this way."

Even so, Matthew made sure his own plans were clear. I overheard him talking with Philippe in the hay barn after a morning of sparring.

"The last thing I will do before we return to our own time is to send you a message. Be ready to order me to Scotland to secure the family's alliance with King James. From there I should go to Amsterdam. The Dutch will be opening up trade routes with the East."

"I can manage, Matthew," Philippe said mildly. "Until then I expect regular updates from England and news of how you and Diana are faring."

"Gallowglass will keep you abreast of our adventures," Matthew promised.

"It is not the same thing as hearing it from you," Philippe said. "It will be very difficult not to gloat over what I know of your future when you get pompous, Matthew. Somehow I will manage that, too."

Time played tricks on us during our last days at Sept-Tours, first dragging, then accelerating without warning. On Christmas Eve, Matthew went down to the church for Mass along with most of the household. I remained in the château and found Philippe in his office on the other side of the great hall. He was, as ever, writing letters.

I knocked on the door. It was a formality, since he had no doubt been tracking my approach since I'd left Matthew's tower, but it didn't seem right to barge in uninvited.

"Introite." It was the same command he'd issued when I'd first arrived, but it sounded so much less forbidding now that I knew him better.

"I'm sorry to disturb you, Philippe."

"Come in, Diana," he said, rubbing his eyes. "Did Catrine find my boxes?"

"Yes, and the cup and pen case, too." He insisted that I take his handsome traveling set on the journey. Each item was made of stiffened leather and could withstand the perils of snow, rain, and rough handling. "I wanted to be sure to thank you before we left—and not just for the wedding. You fixed something in Matthew that was broken."

Philippe pushed his stool back and studied me. "It is I who should be thanking you, Diana. The family has been trying to mend Matthew's spirit for more than a thousand years. If I'm remembering correctly, it took you less than forty days."

"Matthew wasn't like this," I said with a shake of the head, "not until he was here, with you. There was a darkness in him that I couldn't reach."

"A man like Matthew never frees himself of the shadows completely. But perhaps it is necessary to embrace the darkness in order to love him," Philippe continued.

"*'Do not refuse me because I am dark and shadowed,'*" I murmured.

"I do not recognize the verse," Philippe said with a frown.

"It's from that alchemical book I showed you earlier—the *Aurora Consurgens.* The passage reminded me of Matthew, but I still don't understand why. I will, though."

"You are very like that ring, you know," Philippe said, tapping his finger on the table. "It was another of Ysabeau's clever messages."

"She wanted you to know she approved of the marriage," I said, my thumb reaching for the comforting weight.

"No. Ysabeau wanted me to know she approved of *you.* Like the gold from which it is made, you are steadfast. You hide many secrets within you, just as the bands of the ring hide the poesies from view. But it is the stone that best captures who you are: bright on the surface, fiery within, and impossible to break."

"Oh, I'm breakable," I said ruefully. "You can shatter a diamond by hitting it with an ordinary hammer, after all."

"I've seen the scars Matthew left on you. I suspect there are others, too, though less visible. If you did not fall to pieces then, you will not now." Philippe rounded the table. He kissed me tenderly on each cheek, and my eyes filled.

"I should go. We're setting out early tomorrow." I turned to leave, then whirled around and flung my arms around Philippe's massive shoulders. How could such a man ever be broken?

"What is it?" Philippe murmured, taken aback.

"You will not be alone either, Philippe de Clermont," I whispered fiercely. "I'll find a way to be with you in the darkness, I promise. And when you think the whole world has abandoned you, I'll be there, holding your hand."

"How could it be otherwise," Philippe said gently, "when you are in my heart?"

The next morning only a few creatures were gathered in the courtyard to send us on our way. Chef had tucked all sorts of snacks for me into Pierre's saddlebags, and Alain had stuffed the rest of the available space with letters for Gallowglass, Walter, and scores of other recipients. Catrine stood by, eyes puffy with crying. She had wanted to go with us, but Philippe wouldn't allow it.

And there was Philippe, who gathered me up in a bear hug before letting me go. He and Matthew spoke quietly for a few moments. Matthew nodded.

"I am proud of you, *Matthaios,*" said Philippe, clasping him briefly on the shoulder. Matthew moved slightly toward his father when Philippe released him, reluctant to break the connection.

When Matthew turned to me, his face was resolute. He helped me into the saddle before swinging effortlessly onto the back of his horse.

"*Khaire,* Father," Matthew said, eyes gleaming.

"Khairete, Matthaios kai Diana," Philippe replied.

For Matthew there was no turning for a last glimpse of his father and no softening of the stiffness in his back. He kept his eyes on the road ahead, facing the future rather than the past.

I turned once, when a flash of movement caught my eye. It was Philippe, riding along a neighboring ridge, determined not to let go of his son until it was necessary.

"Good-bye, Philippe," I whispered into the wind, hoping that he would hear.

"Ysabeau? Are you all right?"

"Of course." Ysabeau was bending back the covers on a priceless old book and shaking it upside down.

Emily Mather looked at Ysabeau doubtfully. The library was in a state of utter chaos. The rest of the château was neat as a pin, but this room looked as if a tornado had blown through it. Books were strewn everywhere. Someone had pulled them off the shelves and flung them onto every other available surface.

"It must be here. He would have known that the children were together." Ysabeau flung the book aside and reached for another. It pained Emily to her librarian's soul to see books mistreated like this.

"I don't understand. What are you looking for?" She picked up the discarded volume and closed it gently.

"Matthew and Diana were going to 1590. I was not at home then, but in Trier. Philippe would have known about Matthew's new wife. He would have left me word." Ysabeau's hair hung down around her face and flowed nearly to her waist. Impatiently she took it in her hands and twisted it out of her way. After examining the spine and pages of her latest victim, she sliced open the end paper with the sharp nail of her index finger. Finding nothing hidden there, she growled with frustration.

"But these are books, not letters," Emily said carefully. She didn't know Ysabeau well, but Emily was well acquainted with the more gruesome legends about Matthew's mother and what she had done in Trier and other places. The matriarch of the de Clermont family was no friend to witches, and even though Diana trusted the woman, Emily was still not sure.

"I am not looking for a letter. We hid little notes to each other in the pages of books. I searched through every volume in the library when he died, wanting to have every last piece of him. But I must have missed something."

"Maybe it wasn't there to be found—not then." A dry voice spoke from the shadows by the door. Sarah Bishop's red hair was wild and her face white with worry and lack of sleep. "Marthe is going to have a fit when she sees this. And it's a good thing Diana isn't around. She'd give you a lecture on book preservation that would bore you stupid." Tabitha, who accompanied Sarah everywhere, shot from between the witch's legs.

It was Ysabeau's turn to be confused. "What do you mean, Sarah?"

"Time is tricky. Even if everything went according to plan and Diana took Matthew back to the first day of November in 1590, it may still be too soon to look for a message from your husband. And you wouldn't have found a message before, because Philippe hadn't met my niece yet." Sarah paused. "I think Tabitha's eating that book."

Tabitha, delighted to be in a house with an ample supply of mice and plenty of dark corners for hiding, had recently taken to climbing the furniture and the drapes. She was perched on one of the library shelves, gnawing on the corner of a leather-bound volume.

"Kakó gati!" Ysabeau cried, rushing over to the shelves. "That is one of Diana's favorites."

Tabitha, who had never backed down from a confrontation with another predator with the exception of Miriam, swiped at the book so that it fell to the floor. She jumped down after it, hovering over her prize like a lion guarding a particularly desirable treat.

"It's one of those alchemy books with pictures in it," Sarah said, liberating the book from her cat and flipping through the pages. She gave the cover a sniff. "Well, no wonder Tabitha wants to chew on it. It smells of mint and leather, just like her favorite toy."

A square of paper, folded and folded and folded again, fluttered to the floor. Deprived of the book, Tabitha picked up the paper between her sharp teeth and stalked toward the door.

Ysabeau was waiting for her. She picked Tabitha up by the scruff of the neck and pried the paper from the cat's mouth. Then she kissed the surprised feline on the nose. "Clever cat. You will have fish for supper."

"Is that what you were looking for?" Emily eyed the scrap. It didn't seem worth tearing the room apart.

Ysabeau's answer was clear from the way she handled it. She carefully unfolded it to reveal a five-inch square of thick paper, both sides covered in tiny characters.

"That's written in some kind of code," said Sarah. She swung her zebra-striped reading glasses onto her nose from the cord around her neck to get a better look.

"Not a code—Greek." Ysabeau's hands trembled as she smoothed the paper flat.

"What does it say?" Sarah asked.

"Sarah!" Emily scolded. "It's private."

"It's from Philippe. He saw them," Ysabeau breathed, her eyes racing across the text. Her hand went to her mouth, relief vying with disbelief.

Sarah waited for the vampire to finish reading. It took two minutes, which was ninety seconds longer than she would have given anyone else. "Well?"

"They were with him for the holidays. '*On the morning of the Christians' holy celebration, I said farewell to your son. He is happy at last, mated to a woman who walks in the footsteps of the goddess and is worthy of his love,*'" Ysabeau read aloud.

"Are you sure he means Matthew and Diana?" Emily found the phrasing oddly formal and vague for an exchange between husband and wife.

"Yes. Matthew was always the child we worried over, though his brothers and sisters got into far worse predicaments. My one wish was to see Matthew happy."

"And the reference to the 'woman who walks in the footsteps of the goddess' is pretty clear," Sarah agreed. "He couldn't very well give her name and identify Diana as a witch. What if someone else had found it?"

"There is more," Ysabeau continued. "'*Fate still has the power to surprise us, bright one. I fear there are difficult times ahead for all of us. I will do what I can, in what time remains to me, to ensure your safety and that of our children and grandchildren, those whose blessings we already enjoy and those as yet unborn.*'"

Sarah swore. "Unborn, not unmade?"

"Yes," Ysabeau whispered. "Philippe always chose his words carefully."

"So he was trying to tell us something about Diana and Matthew," Sarah said.

Ysabeau sank onto the sofa. "A long, long time ago, there were rumors about creatures who were different—immortal but powerful, too. Around the time the covenant was first signed, some claimed that a witch gave birth to a baby who wept tears of blood like a vampire. Whenever the child did so, fierce winds blew in from the sea."

"I've never heard that before," Emily said, frowning.

"It was dismissed as a myth—a story created to engender fear among creatures. Few among us now would remember, and even fewer would believe it possible." Ysabeau touched the paper in her lap. "But Philippe knew it was true. He held the child, you see, and knew it for what it was."

"Which was what?" Sarah said, stunned.

"A *manjasang* born of a witch. The poor child was starving. The witch's family took the baby boy from her and refused to feed him blood on the grounds that if he was forced to take only milk, it would keep him from turning into one of us."

"Surely Matthew knows this story," Emily said. "You would have told him for his research, if not for Diana's sake."

Ysabeau shook her head. "It was not my tale to tell."

"You and your secrets," Sarah said bitterly.

"And what of *your* secrets, Sarah?" Ysabeau cried. "Do you really believe that the witches—creatures like Satu and Peter Knox—know nothing about this *manjasang* child and its mother?"

"Stop it, both of you," Emily said sharply. "If the story is true, and other creatures know it, then Diana is in grave danger. Sophie too."

"Her parents were both witches, but she is a daemon," Sarah said, thinking of the young couple who had appeared on her doorstep in New York days before Halloween. No one understood how the two daemons fit into this mystery.

"So is Sophie's husband, but their daughter will be a witch. She and Nathaniel are further proof that we don't understand how witches, daemons, and vampires reproduce and pass their abilities on to their children," Emily said, worried.

"Sophie and Nathaniel aren't the only creatures who need to stay clear of the Congregation. It's a good thing Matthew and Diana are safely in 1590 and not here." Sarah was grim.

"But the longer those two stay in the past, the more likely it is they'll change the present," Emily observed. "Sooner or later, Diana and Matthew will give themselves away."

"What do you mean, Emily?" asked Ysabeau.

"Time has to adjust—and not in the melodramatic way people think, with wars averted and presidential elections changed. It will be little things, like this note, that pop up here and there."

"Anomalies," Ysabeau murmured. "Philippe was always looking for anomalies in the world. It is why I still read all the newspapers. It became our habit to look through them each morning." Her eyes closed against the memory. "He loved the sports section, of course, and read the education columns as well. Philippe was worried about what children would learn in the future. He established fellowships for the study of Greek and philosophy, and he endowed colleges for women. I always thought it strange."

"He was looking for Diana," Emily said with the certainty of someone blessed with second sight.

"Perhaps. Once I asked him why he was so preoccupied with current events and what he hoped to discover in the papers. Philippe said he would know it when he saw it," Ysabeau replied. She smiled sadly. "He loved his mysteries and said if it were possible, he would like to be a detective, like Sherlock Holmes."

"We need to make sure we notice any of these little time bumps before the Congregation does," said Sarah.

"I will tell Marcus," Ysabeau agreed with a nod.

"You should have told Matthew about that mixed-species baby." Sarah was unable to keep the note of recrimination from her voice.

"My son loves Diana, and if he had known about that child, Matthew would have turned his back on her rather than put her—and the baby—in danger."

"Bishops aren't so easily cowed, Ysabeau. If Diana wanted your son, she would have found a way to have him."

"Well, Diana did want him, and they have each other now," Emily pointed out. "But we're not going to have to share this news only with Marcus. Sophie and Nathaniel have to know, too."

Sarah and Emily left the library. They were staying in Louisa de Clermont's old room, down the hall from Ysabeau. Sarah thought there were times of day when it smelled a bit like Diana.

Ysabeau remained after they'd gone, gathering up books and reshelving them. When the room was orderly once again, she returned to the sofa and picked up the message from her husband. There was more to it than she had revealed to the witches. She reread the final lines.

"But enough of these dark matters. You must keep yourself safe, too, so that you can enjoy the future with them. It has been two days since I reminded you that you hold my heart. I wish that I could do so every moment, so that you do not forget it, or the name of the man who will cherish yours forevermore. Philipos."

In the last days of his life, there had been moments when Philippe couldn't remember his own name, let alone hers.

"Thank you, Diana," Ysabeau whispered into the night, "for giving him back to me."

Several hours later, Sarah heard a strange sound overhead—like music, but more than music. She stumbled out of the room to find Marthe in the hall, wrapped in an old chenille bathrobe with a frog embroidered on the pocket, a bittersweet expression on her face.

"What is that?" Sarah asked, looking up. Nothing human could hope to produce a sound that beautiful and poignant. There must be an angel on the roof.

"Ysabeau is singing again," Marthe answered. "She has only done so once since Philippe died—when your niece was in danger and needed to be pulled back into this world."

"Is she all right?" There was so much grief and loss in every note that Sarah's heart constricted. There weren't words to describe the sound.

Marthe nodded. "The music is a good thing, a sign that her mourning may at last be coming to an end. Only then will Ysabeau begin to live again."

Two women, vampire and witch, listened until the final notes of Ysabeau's song faded into silence.

PART III

London: The Blackfriars

"It looks like a demented hedgehog," I observed. The London skyline was filled with needlelike spires that stuck up from the huddle of buildings that surrounded them. "What is that?" I gasped, pointing to a vast expanse of stone pierced by tall windows. High above the wooden roof was a charred, stout stump that made the building's proportions look all wrong.

"St. Paul's," Matthew explained. This was not Christopher Wren's graceful white-domed masterpiece, its bulk concealed until the last moment by modern office blocks. Old St. Paul's, perched on London's highest hill, was seen all at once.

"Lightning struck the spire, and the wood of the roof caught fire. The English believe it was a miracle the entire cathedral didn't burn to the ground," he continued.

"The French, not surprisingly, believe that the hand of the Lord was evident somewhat earlier in the event," commented Gallowglass. He had met us at Dover, commandeered a boat in Southwark, and was now rowing us all upstream. "No matter when God showed His true colors, He hasn't provided money for its repair."

"Nor has the queen." Matthew devoted his attention to the wharves on the shoreline, and his right hand rested on the hilt of his sword.

I had never imagined that Old St. Paul's would be so big. I gave myself another pinch. I had been administering them since spotting the Tower (it, too, looked enormous without skyscrapers all around) and London Bridge (which functioned as a suspended shopping mall). Many sights and sounds had impressed me since our arrival in the past, but nothing had taken my breath away like my first glimpses of London.

"Are you sure you don't want to dock in town first?" Gallowglass had been dropping hints about the wisdom of this course of action since we'd climbed into the boat.

"We're going to the Blackfriars," Matthew said firmly. "Everything else can wait."

Gallowglass looked dubious, but he kept rowing until we reached the westernmost reaches of the old, walled city. There we docked at a steep set of stone stairs. The bottom treads were submerged in the river, and from the look of the walls the tide would continue to rise until the rest were underwater, too. Gallowglass tossed a line to a brawny man who thanked him profusely for returning his property in one piece.

"You seem only to travel in other people's boats, Gallowglass. Maybe Matthew should give you your own for Christmas," I said drily. Our return to England—and the old calendar—meant we were celebrating the holiday twice this year.

"And deprive me of one of my few pleasures?" Gallowglass's teeth showed in his beard. Matthew's nephew thanked the boatman and tossed him a coin the size and weight of which reduced the poor fellow's previous anxiety to a hazy glow of appreciation.

We passed from the landing through an archway and onto Water Lane, a narrow, twisting artery crowded with houses and shops. With every rising floor, the houses jutted farther over the street, like a clothes chest with the upper drawers pulled out. This effect was heightened by the linens, carpets, and other items hanging out the windows. Everyone was taking advantage of the unusually fine weather to air out lodgings and garments.

Matthew retained a firm grip on my hand, and Gallowglass walked to my right. Sights and sounds came at us from every direction. Fabrics in saturated red, green, brown, and gray swung from hips and shoulders as skirts and cloaks were twitched away from wagon wheels and caught on the packages and weapons carried by passersby. The ring of hammers, the neighing of horses, the distant lowing of a cow, and the sound of metal rolling on stone competed for attention. Dozens of signs bearing angels, skulls, tools, brightly colored shapes, and mythological figures swayed and squeaked in the wind that blew up from the water. Above my head a wooden sign swung on its metal rod. It was decorated with a white deer, its delicate antlers circled with a golden band.

"Here we are," Matthew said. "The Hart and Crown."

The building was half-timbered, like most on the street. A vaulted passage spanned two arrays of windows. A shoemaker was busy at work on one side of the arch, while the woman opposite kept track of several children, customers, and a large account book. She gave Matthew a brisk nod.

"Robert Hawley's wife rules over his apprentices and customers with an iron fist. Nothing happens in the Hart and Crown without Margaret's knowledge," explained Matthew. I made a mental note to befriend the woman at the earliest opportunity.

The passage emptied out into the building's interior courtyard—a luxury in a city as densely packed as London. The courtyard boasted another rare amenity: a well that provided clean water to the residents of the complex. Someone had taken advantage of the courtyard's southern exposure by tearing up the old paving stones to plant a garden, and now its neat, empty beds patiently awaited spring. A group of washerwomen conducted business out of an old shed next to a shared privy.

To the left, a twisting set of stairs rose to our rooms on the first floor, where Françoise was waiting to welcome us on the wide landing. She'd flung open the stout door into the apartments, crowding a cupboard with pierced sides. A goose, denuded of feathers and with its neck broken, was tied to one of the cupboard's knobs.

"At last." Henry Percy appeared, beaming. "We've been waiting for hours. My good lady mother sent you a goose. She heard reports that no fowl are to be had in the city and became alarmed that you would go hungry."

"It is good to see you, Hal," Matthew said with a laugh and a shake of his head at the goose. "How is your mother?"

"Always a termagant at Christmas, thank you. Most of the family found excuses to be elsewhere, but I am detained here at the queen's pleasure. Her Majesty shouted across the audience chamber that I could not be trusted even so far as P-P-Petworth." Henry stammered and looked ill at the recollection.

"You are more than welcome to spend Christmas with us, Henry," I said, taking off my cloak and stepping inside, where the scent of spices and freshly cut fir filled the air.

"It is good of you to invite me, Diana, but my sister Eleanor and brother George are in town and they shouldn't have to brave her on their own."

"Stay with us this evening at least," Matthew urged, steering him to the right, where warmth and firelight beckoned, "and tell us what has happened while we were away."

"All is quiet here," Henry reported cheerfully.

"Quiet?" Gallowglass stomped up the stairs, looking frostily at the earl. "Marlowe's at the Cardinal's Hat, drunk as a fiddler, trading verses with that impoverished scrivener from Stratford who trails after him in hopes of becoming a playwright. For now Shakespeare seems content with learning how to forge your signature, Matthew. According to the innkeeper's records, you promised to pay Kit's room and board charges last week."

"I left them only an hour ago," Henry protested. "Kit knew that Matthew and Diana were due to arrive this afternoon. He and Will promised to be on their best behavior."

"That explains it, then," Gallowglass muttered sarcastically.

"Is this your doing, Henry?" I looked from the entrance hall into our main living quarters. Someone had tucked holly, ivy, and fir around the fireplace and the window frames and mounded them in the center of an oak table. The fireplace was loaded with logs, and a cheerful fire hissed and crackled.

"Françoise and I wanted your first Christmas to be festive," Henry said, turning pink.

The Hart and Crown represented urban living at its sixteenth-century best. The parlor was a good size but felt snug and comfortable. Its western wall was filled with a multipaned window that overlooked Water Lane. It was perfectly situated for people-watching, with a cushioned seat built into the base. Carved wainscoting warmed the walls, each panel covered with twisting flowers and vines.

The room's furnishings were spare but well made. A wide settle and two deep chairs waited by the fireplace. The oak table in the center of the room was unusually fine, less than three feet across but quite long, its legs decorated with the delicate faces of caryatids and herms. A beam set with candles hung over the table. It could be raised and lowered by use of the smooth rope-and-pulley system suspended from the ceiling. Carved lions' heads snarled from the front band of a monstrous cupboard that held a wide array of beakers, pitchers, cups, and goblets—though very few plates, as befitted a vampire household.

Before we settled down to our dinner of roast goose, Matthew showed me our bedroom and his private office. Both were across the entrance hall opposite the parlor. Gabled windows overlooked the courtyard, making both rooms feel light and surprisingly airy. The bedroom had only three pieces of furniture: a four-poster bed with a carved headboard and heavy wooden tester, a tall linen press with paneled sides and door, and a long, low chest under the windows. The last was locked, and Matthew explained that it held his suit of armor and several spare weapons. Henry and Françoise had been in here, too. Ivy crawled up the bedposts, and they'd tied sprigs of holly to the headboard.

Whereas the bedroom looked barely occupied, Matthew's office was clearly well used. Here there were baskets of paper, bags and tankards full of quills, pots of ink, enough wax to make several dozen candles, balls of twine, and so much waiting mail that my heart sank just thinking about it.

A comfortable-looking chair with a sloping back and curved arms sat before a table with extendable leaves. Except for the heavy table legs with their bulbous, cup-shaped carvings, everything was plain and practical.

Though I had blanched at the piles of work that awaited him, Matthew was unconcerned. "It can all wait. Not even spies conduct business on Christmas Eve," he told me.

Over dinner we talked more about Walter's latest exploits and the shocking state of traffic in London, and we steered clear of more sober subjects, like Kit's latest drinking binge and the enterprising William Shakespeare. After the plates were cleared, Matthew pulled a small game table away from the wall. He removed a deck of cards from the compartment under the tabletop and proceeded to teach me how to gamble, Elizabethan style. Henry had just persuaded Matthew and Gallowglass to play flapdragon—an alarming game that involved setting raisins alight in a dish of brandy and betting on who could swallow the greatest number—when the sound of carolers rose from the street outside the windows. They were not all singing in the same key, and those who didn't know the words were inserting scandalous details about the personal lives of Joseph and Mary.

"Here, *milord,*" Pierre said, thrusting a bag of coins at Matthew.

"Do we have cakes?" Matthew asked Françoise.

She looked at him as if he'd lost his mind. "Of course we have cakes. They are in the new food cupboard on the landing, where the smell will not disturb anyone," Françoise said, pointing in the direction of the stairs. "Last year you gave them wine, but I do not believe they require it tonight."

"I'll go with you, Matt," Henry volunteered. "I like a good song on Christmas Eve."

The appearance of Matthew and Henry downstairs was marked by a definite uptick in the choir's volume. When the carolers came to a rather uneven finish, Matthew thanked them and passed out coins. Henry distributed the cakes, which led to many bows and a hushed "Thank you, my lord" as the news passed that this was the Earl of Northumberland. The carolers moved off to another house, following some mysterious order of precedence that they hoped would ensure them the best refreshments and payments.

Soon I could no longer smother my yawns, and Henry and Gallowglass began to gather up their gloves and cloaks. Both were smiling like satisfied matchmakers when they headed for the door. Matthew joined me in bed, holding me until I fell asleep, humming carols and naming the city's many bells as they sounded the hour.

"There is St. Mary-le-Bow," he said, listening to the sounds of the city. "And St. Katherine Cree."

"Is that St. Paul's?" I asked as a prolonged clarion sounded.

"No. The lightning that took off the steeple destroyed the bells, too," he said. "That's St. Saviour's. We passed it on our way into town." The rest of London's churches caught up with Southwark's cathedral. Finally a straggler finished with a discordant clang, the last sound I heard before sleep overtook me.

In the middle of the night, I was awakened by conversation coming from Matthew's study. I felt the bed, but he was no longer with me. The leather straps that held up the mattress squeaked and stretched as I jumped to the cold floor. I shivered and threw on a shawl before leaving the room.

Judging by the pools of wax in the shallow candlestands, Matthew had been working for hours. Pierre was with him, standing next to the shelves built into a recess by the fireplace. He looked as though he'd been dragged backward through the Thames mud at low tide.

"I've been all over the city with Gallowglass and his Irish friends," Pierre murmured. "If the Scots know anything more about the schoolmaster, they will not divulge it, *milord.*"

"What schoolmaster?" I stepped into the room. It was then I spotted the narrow door hidden in the wooden paneling.

"I am sorry, *madame.* I did not mean to wake you." Pierre's dismay showed through the filth, and the stench that accompanied him made my eyes water.

"It's all right, Pierre. Go. I'll find you later." Matthew waited while his servant fled, shoes squelching. Matthew's eyes drifted to the shadows by the fireplace.

"The room that lies beyond that door wasn't on your welcome tour," I pointed out, going to his side. "What's happened now?"

"More news from Scotland. A jury sentenced a wizard named John Fian—a schoolmaster from Prestonpans—to death. While I was away, Gallowglass tried to find out what truth, if any, lies behind the wild accusations: worshipping Satan, dismembering dead bodies in a graveyard, transforming moles' feet into pieces of silver so he was never without money, going to sea in a ship with the devil and Agnes Sampson to thwart the king's policies." Matthew tossed a paper onto the table in front of him. "So far as I can tell, Fian is one of what we used to call the *tempestarii,* and nothing more."

"A windwitch, or possibly a waterwitch," I said, translating the unfamiliar term.

"Yes," Matthew agreed with a nod. "Fian augmented his teacher's salary by causing thunderstorms during dry spells and early thaws when it looked as if the Scottish winter would never end. His fellow villagers adored him, by all accounts. Even Fian's pupils had nothing but praise. Fian might have been a bit of a seer—he's credited with foretelling people's deaths, but that could have been something Kit cooked up to embellish the story for an English audience. He's obsessed with a witch's second sight, as you'll remember."

"Witches are vulnerable to the shifting moods of our neighbors, Matthew. One minute we're friends, the next we're run out of town—or worse."

"What happened to Fian was definitely worse," Matthew said grimly.

"I can imagine," I said with a shudder. If Fian had been tortured as Agnes Sampson had, he must have welcomed death. "What's in that room?"

Matthew considered telling me that it was a secret but wisely refrained. He stood. "It would be better if I showed you. Stay by me. It's not yet dawn, and we can't take a candle into the room for fear that someone will see it from outside. I don't want you to trip." I nodded mutely and took his hand.

We stepped across the threshold into a long room with a row of windows barely larger than arrow slits tucked under the eaves. After a few moments, my eyes adjusted and gray shapes began to emerge from the gloom. A pair of old garden chairs woven from willow twigs stood across from each other, their backs curved forward. Low, battered benches were set out in two rows down the center of the room. Each bore a strange assortment of objects: books, papers, letters, hats, and clothes. From the right came a gleam of metal: swords, hilts up and points down. A pile of daggers rested on the floor nearby. There was a scratching sound, too, and a scurry of feet.

"Rats." Matthew's voice was matter-of-fact, but I couldn't help drawing my night rail tight against my legs. "Pierre and I do what we can, but it's impossible to get rid of them entirely. They find all this paper irresistible." He gestured up, and I noticed for the first time the bizarre festoons on the walls.

I crept closer and peered at the garlands. Each one hung from a thin, twisted cord affixed to the plaster with a square-headed nail. The cord had then been threaded through the upper-left-hand corner of a series of documents. The knot in the end of the cord was slung back up and looped around the same nail, creating a wreath of paper.

"One of the world's first file cabinets. You say I keep too many secrets," he said softly, reaching out and snagging one of the garlands. "You can add these to your reckoning."

"But there are thousands of them." Surely not even a fifteen-hundred-year-old vampire could possess so many.

"There are," Matthew agreed. He watched as my eyes swept the room, taking in the archive he guarded. "We remember what other creatures want to forget, and that makes it possible for the Knights of Lazarus to protect those in our care. Some of the secrets go back to the reign of the queen's grandfather. Most of the older files have already been moved to Sept-Tours for safekeeping."

"So many trails of paper," I murmured, "and all of them ultimately lead back to you and the de Clermonts." The room faded until I saw only the loops and swirls of the words unwinding into long, intertwined filaments. They formed a map of connections that linked subjects, authors, dates. There was something I needed to understand about these crisscrossing lines. . . .

"I've been going through these papers since you fell asleep, looking for references to Fian. I thought that there might be mention of him here," Matthew said, leading me back into his study, "something that might explain why his neighbors turned on him. There must be a pattern that will tell us why the humans are behaving this way."

"If you find it, my fellow historians will be eager to know. But understanding Fian's case doesn't guarantee you can prevent the same thing from happening to me." The ticking muscle in Matthew's jaw told me that my words found their target. "And I'm quite sure you didn't delve into the matter this closely before."

"I'm no longer that man who turned a blind eye to all this suffering—and I don't want to become him again." Matthew pulled out his chair and dropped heavily into it. "There must be something I can do."

I gathered him in my arms. Even seated, Matthew was so tall that the top of his head hit my rib cage. He burrowed into me. He stilled, then drew slowly away, his eyes fixed on my abdomen.

"Diana. You're—" He stopped.

"Pregnant. I thought so," I said matter-of-factly. "My period's been irregular ever since Juliette, so I wasn't sure. I was sick on the way from Calais to Dover, but the seas were rough and that fish I had before we left was definitely dodgy."

He continued to stare at my belly. I rattled on nervously.

"My high-school health teacher was right: You really can get pregnant the first time you have sex with a guy." I'd done the math and was pretty sure conception had occurred during our wedding weekend.

Still he was silent.

"Say something, Matthew."

"It's impossible." He looked stunned.

"Everything about us is impossible." I lowered a trembling hand to my stomach.

Matthew twined his fingers through mine and finally looked me in the eye. I was surprised by what I saw there: awe, pride, and a hint of panic. Then he smiled. It was an expression of complete joy.

"What if I'm no good at being a parent?" I asked uncertainly. "You've been a father—you know what to do."

"You're going to be a wonderful mother" was his prompt response. "All that children need is love, a grown-up to take responsibility for them, and a soft place to land." Matthew moved our clasped hands over my belly in a gentle caress. "We'll tackle the first two together. The last will be up to you. How are you feeling?"

"A bit tired and queasy, physically. Emotionally, I don't know where to begin." I drew a shaky breath. "Is it normal to be frightened and fierce and tender all at once?"

"Yes—and thrilled and anxious and sick with dread, too," he said softly.

"I know it's ridiculous, but I keep worrying that my magic might hurt the baby, even though thousands of witches give birth every year." *But they aren't married to vampires.*

"This isn't a normal conception," Matthew said, reading my mind. "Still, I don't think you need to concern yourself." A shadow moved through his eyes. I could practically see him adding one more worry to his list.

"I don't want to tell anyone. Not yet." I thought of the room next door. "Can your life include one more secret—at least for a little while?"

"Of course," Matthew said promptly. "Your pregnancy won't show for months. But Françoise and Pierre will know soon from your scent, if they don't already, and so will Hancock and Gallowglass. Happily, vampires don't usually ask personal questions."

I laughed softly. "It figures that I'll be the one to give the secret away. You can't possibly be any more protective, so no one is going to guess what we're hiding based on your behavior."

"Don't be too sure of that," he said, smiling broadly. Matthew flexed his fingers over mine. It was a distinctly protective gesture.

"If you keep touching me that way, people are going to figure it out pretty quickly," I agreed drily, running my fingers along his shoulder. He shivered. "You're not supposed to shiver when you feel something warm."

"That's not why I'm trembling." Matthew stood, blocking out the light from the candles.

My heart caught at the sight of him. He smiled, hearing the slight irregularity, and drew me toward the bed. We shed our clothes, tossing them to the floor, where they lay in two white pools that caught the silvery light from the windows.

Matthew's touches were feather-light while he tracked the minute changes already taking place in my body. He lingered over each centimeter of tender flesh, but his cool attention increased the ache rather than soothing it. Every kiss was as knotted and complex as our feelings about sharing a child. At the same time, the words he whispered in the darkness encouraged me to focus solely on him. When I could bear waiting no longer, Matthew seated himself within me, his movements unhurried and gentle, like his kiss.

I arched my back in an effort to increase the contact between us, and Matthew stilled. With my spine bowed, he was poised at the entrance to my womb. And in that brief, forever moment, father, mother, and child were as close as any three creatures could be.

"My whole heart, my whole life," he promised, moving within me.

I cried out, and Matthew held me close until the trembling stopped. He then kissed his way down the length of my body, starting with my witch's third eye and continuing on to my lips, throat, breastbone, solar plexus, navel, and, at last, my abdomen.

He stared down at me, shook his head, and gave me a boyish grin. "We made a child," he said, dumbfounded.

"We did," I agreed with an answering smile.

Matthew slid his shoulders between my thighs, pushing them wide. With one arm wrapped around my knee, and the other twined around the opposite hip so his hand could rest on the pulse there, he lowered his head onto my belly as though it were a pillow and let out a contented sigh. Utterly quiet, he listened for the soft whooshing of the blood that now sustained our child. When he heard it, he tilted his head so our eyes met. He smiled, bright and true, and returned to his vigil.

In the candlelit darkness of Christmas morning, I felt the quiet power that came from sharing our love with another creature. No longer a solitary meteor moving through space and time, I was now part of a complicated planetary system. I needed to learn how to keep my own center of gravity while being pulled this way and that by bodies larger and more powerful than I was. Otherwise Matthew, the de Clermonts, our child—and the Congregation—might pull me off course.

My time with my mother had been too short, but in seven years she had taught me plenty. I remembered her unconditional love, the hugs that seemed to encompass days, and how she was always right where I needed her to be. It was as Matthew said: Children needed love, a reliable source of comfort, and an adult willing to take responsibility for them.

It was time to stop treating our sojourn here as an advanced seminar in Shakespeare's England and recognize it instead as my last, best chance to figure out who I was, so that I could help my child understand his place in the world.

But first I needed to find a witch.

We passed the weekend quietly, reveling in our secret and indulging in the speculations of all parents-to-be. Would the newest member of the de Clermont clan have black hair like his father but my blue eyes? Would he like science or history? Would he be skilled with his hands like Matthew or all thumbs like me? As for the sex, we had different opinions. I was convinced it was a boy, and Matthew was equally sure it was a girl.

Exhausted and exhilarated, we took a break from thoughts of the future to view sixteenth-century London from the warmth of our rooms. We started at the windows overlooking Water Lane, where I spied the distant towers of Westminster Abbey, and finished in chairs pulled up to the bedroom windows, where we could see the Thames. Neither the cold nor the fact that it was the Christian day of rest kept the watermen from their business making deliveries and ferrying passengers. At the bottom of our street, a group of rowers-for-hire huddled on the stairs that led down to the waterside, their empty boats bobbing up and down on the swells.

Matthew shared his memories of the city during the course of the afternoon as the tide rose and fell. He told me about the time in the fifteenth century when the Thames froze for more than three months—so long that temporary shops were built on the ice to cater to the foot traffic. He also reminisced about his unproductive years at Thavies Inn, where he had gone through the motions of studying the law for the fourth and final time.

"I'm glad you got to see it before we leave," he said, squeezing my hand. One by one, people were illuminating their lamps, hanging them from the prows of boats and setting them in the windows of houses and inns. "We'll even try to fit in a visit to the Royal Exchange."

"We're going back to Woodstock?" I asked, confused.

"For a short time, perhaps. Then we'll be going back to our present."

I stared at him, too startled to speak.

"We don't know what to expect during the gestation period, and for your safety—and the child's—we need to monitor the baby. There are tests to run, and it would be a good idea to have a baseline ultrasound. Besides, you'll want to be with Sarah and Emily."

"But, Matthew," I protested, "we can't go home yet. I don't know how."

His head swung around.

"Em explained it clearly before we left. To travel *back* in time, you need three objects to take you where you want to go. To travel *forward* you need witchcraft, but I can't do spells. It's why we came."

"You can't possibly carry the baby to term here," Matthew said, shooting out of his chair.

"Women do have babies in the sixteenth century," I said mildly. "Besides, I don't feel any different. I can't be more than a few weeks pregnant."

"Will you be powerful enough to carry both her and me back to the future? No, we need to leave as soon as possible, and well before she's born." Matthew drew to a halt. "What if timewalking damages the fetus in some way? Magic is one thing, but this—" He sat down abruptly.

"Nothing has changed," I said soothingly. "The baby can't be much bigger than a grain of rice. Now that we're in London, it shouldn't be difficult to find someone to help me with my magic—not to mention one who understands timewalking better than Sarah and Em."

"She's the size of a lentil." Matthew stopped. He thought for a few moments and came to a decision. "By six weeks all the most critical fetal developments will have taken place. That should give you plenty of time." He sounded like a doctor, not a father. I was beginning to prefer Matthew's premodern rages to his modern objectivity.

"That gives me only a few weeks. What if I need seven?" Had Sarah been in the room, she would have warned him that my reasonableness was not a good sign.

"Seven weeks would be fine," Matthew said, lost in his own thoughts.

"Oh, well, that's good. I'd hate to feel rushed when it comes to something as important as figuring out who I am." I strode toward him.

"Diana, that's not—"

We were standing nose to nose now. "I don't have a chance of being a good mother without knowing more about the power in my blood."

"This isn't good—"

"Don't you dare say this isn't good for the baby. I'm not some *vessel.*" My temper was at full boil now. "First it was my blood you wanted for your scientific experiments, and now it's this baby."

Matthew, damn him, stood quietly by, arms crossed and gray eyes hard.

"Well?" I demanded.

"Well what? Apparently my participation in this conversation isn't required. You're already finishing my sentences. You might as well start them, too."

"This has nothing to do with my hormones," I said. Belatedly it occurred to me that this statement alone was probably evidence to the contrary.

"That hadn't occurred to me until you mentioned it."

"That's not what it sounded like."

His eyebrow rose.

"I'm the same person I was three days ago. Pregnancy isn't a pathological condition, and it doesn't eliminate our reasons for being here. We haven't even had a proper chance to look for Ashmole 782."

"Ashmole 782?" Matthew made an impatient sound. "Everything has changed, and you are *not* the same person. We can't keep this pregnancy a secret indefinitely. In a matter of days, every vampire will be able to smell the changes in your body. Kit will figure it out soon after, and he'll be asking about the father—because it can't be me, can it? A pregnant witch living with a *wearh* will raise the animosity of every creature in this city, even the ones who don't care much for the covenant. Someone could complain to the Congregation. My father will demand we go back to Sept-Tours for your safety, and I can't endure saying good-bye to him one more time." His voice rose steadily with each problem.

"I didn't think—"

"No," Matthew interrupted, "you didn't. You couldn't have. Christ, Diana. Before, you and I were in a forbidden marriage. That's hardly unique. Now you're carrying my child. That's not only unique—other creatures believe it's impossible. Three more weeks, Diana. Not a moment more." He was implacable.

"You might not be able to find a witch willing to help by then," I persisted. "Not with what's happening in Scotland."

"Who said anything about willingness?" Matthew's smile chilled me.

"I'm going to the parlor to read." I turned toward the bedroom, wanting to be as far from him as possible. He was waiting for me in the doorway, his arm barring my passage.

"I will not lose you, Diana," he said, emphatic but quiet. "Not to look for an alchemical manuscript and not for the sake of an unborn child."

"And I will not lose myself," I retorted. "Not to satisfy your need for control. Not before I find out who I am."

* * *

On Monday, I was again sitting in the parlor, picking through *The Faerie Queene* and going out of my mind with boredom when the door opened. *Visitors.* I clapped the book shut eagerly.

"I don't think I'll ever be warm again." Walter stood dripping in the doorway. George and Henry were with him, both looking equally wretched.

"Hello, Diana." Henry sneezed, then greeted me with a formal bow before heading to the fireplace and extending his fingers toward the flames with a groan.

"Where is Matthew?" I asked, motioning George toward a seat.

"With Kit. We left them at a bookseller." Walter gestured in the direction of St. Paul's. "I'm famished. The stew Kit ordered for dinner was inedible. Matt said Françoise should make us something to eat." Raleigh's mischievous grin betrayed his lie.

The lads were on their second plates of food and their third helping of wine when Matthew came home with Kit, an armful of books, and a full complement of facial hair courtesy of one of these wizard barbers I kept hearing about. My husband's trim new mustache suited the width of his mouth, and his beard was fashionably small and well shaped. Pierre followed behind, bearing a linen sack of paper rectangles and squares.

"Thank God," Walter said, nodding approvingly at the beard. "Now you look like yourself."

"Hello, my heart," Matthew said, kissing me on the cheek. "Do you recognize me?"

"Yes—even though you look like a pirate," I said with a laugh.

"It is true, Diana. He and Walter look like brothers now," admitted Henry.

"Why do you persist in calling Matthew's wife by her first name, Henry? Has Mistress Roydon become your ward? Is she your sister now? The only other explanation is that you are planning a seduction," Marlowe grumbled, plunking himself down in a chair.

"Stop poking at the hornet's nest, Kit," Walter chided.

"I have belated Christmas presents," Matthew said, sliding his stack in my direction.

"Books." It was disconcerting to feel their obvious newness—the creak of the tight bindings as they protested being opened for the first time, the smell of paper and the tang of ink. I was used to seeing volumes like these in a worn condition within library reading rooms, not resting on the table where we ate our meals. The top volume was a blank book to replace the one still in Oxford. The next was a book of prayers, beautifully bound. The ornate title page was adorned with a reclining figure of the biblical patriarch Jesse. A sprawling tree emerged from his stomach. My forehead creased. Why had Matthew bought me a prayer book?

"Turn the page," he urged, his hands heavy and quiet against the small of my back.

On the reverse was a woodcut of Queen Elizabeth kneeling in prayer. Skeletons, biblical figures, and classical virtues decorated each page. The book was a combination of text and imagery, just like the alchemical treatises I studied.

"It's exactly the kind of book a respectable married lady would own," Matthew said with a grin. He lowered his voice conspiratorially. "That should satisfy your desire to keep up appearances. But don't worry. The next one isn't respectable at all."

I put the prayer book aside and took the thick volume Matthew offered. Its pages were sewn together and slipped inside a protective wrapper of thick vellum. The treatise promised to explain the symptoms and cures of every disease known to afflict mankind.

"Religious books are popular gifts, and easy to sell. Books about medicine have a smaller audience and are too costly to bind without a commission," Matthew explained as I fingered the limp covering. He handed me yet another volume. "Luckily, I had already ordered a bound copy of this one. It's hot off the presses and destined to be a bestseller."

The item in question was covered in simple black leather, with some silver stamps for ornamentation. Inside was a first edition of Philip Sidney's *Arcadia*. I laughed, remembering how much I'd hated reading it in college.

"A witch cannot live by prayer and physic alone." Matthew's eyes twinkled with mischief. His mustache tickled when he moved to kiss me.

"Your new face is going to take some getting used to," I said, laughing and rubbing my lips at the unexpected sensation.

The Earl of Northumberland eyed me as he would a piece of horseflesh in need of a training regimen. "These few titles will not keep Diana occupied for long. She is used to more varied activity."

"As you say. But she can hardly roam the city and offer classes on alchemy." Matthew's mouth tightened with amusement. Hour by hour, his accent and choice of words molded to the time. He leaned over me, sniffed the wine jug, and grimaced. "Is there something to drink that hasn't been dosed with cloves and pepper? It smells dreadful."

"Diana might enjoy Mary's company," Henry suggested, not having heard Matthew's query.

Matthew stared at Henry. "Mary?"

"They are of a similar age and temperament, I think, and both are paragons of learning."

"The countess is not only learned but also has a propensity for setting things alight," Kit observed, pouring himself another generous beaker of wine. He stuck his nose in it and breathed deeply. It smelled rather like Matthew. "Stay away from her stills and furnaces, Mistress Roydon, unless you want fashionably frizzled hair."

"Furnaces?" I wondered who this could be.

"Ah, yes. The Countess of Pembroke," George said, eyes gleaming at the prospect of patronage.

"Absolutely not." Between Raleigh, Chapman, and Marlowe, I'd met enough literary legends to last me a lifetime. The countess was the foremost woman of letters in the country, and Sir Philip Sidney's sister. "I'm not ready for Mary Sidney."

"Nor is Mary Sidney ready for you, Mistress Roydon, but I suspect that Henry is right. You will soon grow tired of Matthew's friends and need to seek your own. Without them you will be prone to idleness and melancholy." Walter nodded to Matthew. "You should invite Mary here to share supper."

"The Blackfriars would come to a complete standstill if the Countess of Pembroke appeared on Water Lane. It would be far better to send Mistress Roydon to Baynard's Castle. It's just over the wall," Marlowe said, eager to be rid of me.

"Diana would have to walk into the city," Matthew said pointedly.

Marlowe gave a dismissive snort. "It's the week between Christmas and New Year. Nobody will pay attention if two married women share a cup of wine and some gossip."

"I'd be happy to take her," Walter volunteered. "Perhaps Mary will want to know more about my venture in the New World."

"You'll have to ask the countess to invest in Virginia another time. If Diana goes, I'll be with her." Matthew's eyes sharpened. "I wonder if Mary knows any witches?"

"She's a woman, isn't she? Of course she knows witches," Marlowe said.

"Shall I write to her, then, Matt?" Henry inquired.

"Thank you, Hal." Matthew was clearly unconvinced of the merits of the plan. Then he sighed. "It's been too long since I've seen her. Tell Mary we'll call on her tomorrow."

My initial reluctance to meet Mary Sidney faded as our rendezvous approached. The more I remembered—and discovered—about the Countess of Pembroke, the more excited I became.

Françoise was in a state of high anxiety about the visit, and she fussed over my clothes for hours. She fixed a particularly frothy ruff around the high neckline of a black velvet jacket that Maria had fashioned for me in France. She also cleaned and pressed my flattering russet gown with its bands of black velvet. It went well with the jacket and provided a jolt of color. Once I was dressed, Françoise pronounced me passable, though too severe and German-looking for her tastes.

I bolted down some stew filled with chunks of rabbit and barley at midday in an effort to speed our departure. Matthew took an interminable time sipping his wine and questioning me in Latin about my morning. His expression was devilish.

"If you're trying to infuriate me, you're succeeding!" I told him after a particularly convoluted question.

"Refero mihi in latine, quaeso," Matthew said in a professorial tone. When I threw a hunk of bread at him, he laughed and ducked.

Henry Percy arrived just in time to catch the bread neatly with one hand. He returned it to the table without comment, smiled serenely, and asked if we were ready to depart.

Pierre materialized without a sound from the shadows near the entrance to the shoe shop and began walking up the street with a diffident air, his right hand firmly around the hilt of his dagger. When Matthew turned us toward the city, I looked up. There was St. Paul's.

"I'm not likely to get lost with that in the neighborhood," I murmured.

As we made our slow progress toward the cathedral, my senses grew accustomed to the chaos and it was possible to pick out individual sounds, smells, and sights. Bread baking. Coal fires. Wood smoke. Fermentation. Freshly washed garbage, courtesy of yesterday's rains. Wet wool. I breathed deeply, making a mental note to stop telling my students that if you went back in time, you would be knocked over instantly by the foul smell. Apparently that wasn't true, at least not in late December.

Men and women looked up from their work and out their windows with unabashed curiosity as we passed, bobbing their heads respectfully when they recognized Matthew and Henry. We stepped by a printing establishment, passed another where a barber was cutting a man's hair, and skirted a busy workshop where hammers and heat indicated that someone was working in fine metals.

As the strangeness wore off, I was able to focus on what people were saying, the texture of their clothes, the expressions on their faces. Matthew had told me our neighborhood was full of foreigners, but it sounded like Babel. I turned my head. "What language is she speaking?" I whispered with a glance at a plump woman wearing a deep blue-green jacket trimmed with fur. It was, I noted, cut rather like my own.

"Some dialect of German," said Matthew, lowering his head to mine so that I could hear him over the noise in the street.

We passed through the arch of an old gatehouse. The lane widened into a street that had managed against all odds to retain most of its paving. A sprawling, multistoried building to our right buzzed with activity.

"The Dominican priory," Matthew explained. "When King Henry expelled the priests, it became a ruin, then a tenement. There's no telling how many people are crammed in there now." He glanced across the courtyard, where a listing stone-and-timber wall spanned the distance between the tenement and the back of another house. A sorry excuse for a door hung from a single set of hinges.

Matthew looked up at St. Paul's and then down at me. His face softened. "To hell with caution. Come on."

He steered me through an opening between a section of the old city wall and a house that looked as though it were about to tip its third story onto passersby. It was possible to make progress along the slim thoroughfare only because everyone was moving in the same direction: up, north, out. We were carried by the wave of humanity into another street, this one much wider than Water Lane. The noise increased, along with the crowds.

"You said the city was deserted because of the holidays," I remarked.

"It is," Matthew replied. After a few steps, we were pitched into an even greater maelstrom. I stopped in my tracks.

St. Paul's windows glimmered in the pale afternoon light. The churchyard around it was a solid mass of people—men, women, children, apprentices, servants, clergymen, soldiers. Those who weren't shouting were listening to those who were, and everywhere you looked, there was paper. It was hung up on strings outside bookstalls, nailed to any solid surface, made into books, and waved in the faces of onlookers. A group of young men huddled around one post covered with flapping announcements, listening to someone slowly sound out job advertisements. Every now and then, one would break free from the rest, hands slapping him on the back as he pulled his cap down and set off in search of employment.

"Oh, Matthew." It was all I could manage.

People continued to swarm around us, carefully avoiding the tips of the long swords my escorts wore at their waists. A breeze caught at my hood. I felt a tingle, followed by a faint pressure. Somewhere in the busy churchyard, a witch and a daemon had sensed our presence. Three creatures and a nobleman traveling together were hard to ignore.

"We've caught someone's attention," I said. Matthew didn't seem overly concerned as he scanned the nearby faces. "Someone like me. Someone like Kit. No one like you."

"Not yet," he said under his breath. "You aren't to come here by yourself, Diana—ever. Stay in the Blackfriars, with Françoise. If you go any farther than that passageway"—Matthew nodded behind us—"Pierre or I must be with you." When he was satisfied that I had taken his warning seriously, he drew me away. "Let's go see Mary."

We turned south again, toward the river, and the wind flattened my skirts against my legs. Though we were walking downhill, every step was a struggle. A low whistle sounded as we passed by one of London's many churches, and Pierre disappeared into an alley. He popped out of another just as I spotted a familiar-looking building behind a wall.

"That's our house!"

Matthew nodded and directed my attention down the street. "And that is Baynard's Castle."

It was the largest building I had seen yet except for the Tower, St. Paul's, and the distant prospect of Westminster Abbey. Three crenellated towers faced the river, linked by walls that were easily twice the height of any nearby houses.

"Baynard's Castle was built to be approached from the river, Diana," Henry said in an apologetic tone as we traveled down another winding lane. "This is the back entrance, and not how visitors are supposed to arrive—but it is a great deal warmer on a day like this."

We ducked into an imposing gatehouse. Two men wearing charcoal gray uniforms with maroon, black, and gold badges strolled up to identify the visitors. One recognized Henry and grabbed at his companion's sleeve before he could question us.

"Lord Northumberland!"

"We're here to see the countess." Henry swung his cloak in the direction of the guard. "See if you can get that dry. And find Master Roydon's man something hot to drink, if you would." The earl cracked his fingers inside his leather gloves and grimaced.

"Of course, my lord," the gatekeeper said, eyeing Pierre with suspicion.

The castle was arranged around two enormous hollow squares, the central spaces filled with leafless trees and the vestiges of summer flowers. We climbed a wide set of stairs and met up with more liveried servants, one of whom led us to the countess's solar: an inviting room with large, south-facing windows overlooking the river. They provided a view of the same stretch of the Thames that was visible from the Blackfriars.

Despite the similarity of the view, there was no mistaking this lofty, bright space for our house. Though our rooms were large and comfortably furnished, Baynard's Castle was the home of aristocracy, and it showed. Wide, cushioned settles flanked the fireplace, along with chairs so deep that a woman could curl up in one with all her skirts tucked around her. Tapestries enlivened the stone walls with splashes of bright color and scenes from classical mythology. There were signs, too, of a scholar's mind at work. Books, bits of ancient statuary, natural objects, pictures, maps, and other curiosities covered the tables.

"Master Roydon?" A man with a pointed beard and dark hair peppered with gray stood. He held a small board in one hand and a tiny brush in the other.

"Hilliard!" Matthew said, his delight evident. "What brings you here?"

"A commission for Lady Pembroke," the man said, waving his palette. "I must put the finishing touches on this miniature. She wishes to have it for a gift at the New Year." His bright brown eyes studied me.

"I forget, you have not met my wife. Diana, this is Nicholas Hilliard, the limner."

"I am honored," I said, dipping into a curtsy. London had well over a hundred thousand residents. Why did Matthew have to know everyone that historians would one day find significant? "I know and admire your work."

"She has seen the portrait of Sir Walter that you painted for me last year," Matthew said smoothly, covering up my too-effusive greeting.

"One of his best pieces, I agree," Henry said, looking over the artist's shoulder. "This seems destined to rival it, though. What an excellent likeness of Mary, Hilliard. You've captured the intensity of her gaze." Hilliard looked pleased.

A servant appeared with wine, and Henry, Matthew, and Hilliard conversed in low voices while I examined an ostrich egg set in gold and a nautilus shell in a silver stand, both of which sat on a table along with several priceless mathematical instruments that I didn't dare touch.

"Matt!" The Countess of Pembroke stood in the doorway wiping ink-stained fingers on a handkerchief hastily supplied by her maid. I wondered why anyone would bother, since her mistress's dove-gray gown was already splotched and even singed in places. The countess peeled the simple garment from her body, revealing a far more splendid velvet and taffeta outfit in a rich shade of plum. As she passed the early-modern equivalent of a lab coat to her servant, I smelled a distinct whiff of gunpowder. The countess tucked up a tight curl of blond hair that had drifted down by her right ear. She was tall and willowy, with creamy skin and deep-set brown eyes.

She stretched out her hands in welcome. "My dear friend. I have not seen you for years, not since my brother Philip's funeral."

"Mary," Matthew said, bowing over her hand. "You are looking well."

"London does not agree with me, as you know, but it has become a tradition that we travel here for the queen's anniversary celebrations, and I stayed on. I am working on Philip's psalms and a few other fancies and do not mind it so much. And there are consolations, like seeing old friends." Mary's voice was airy, but it still conveyed her sharp intelligence.

"You are indeed flourishing," Henry said, adding his welcome to Matthew's and looking at the countess approvingly.

Mary's brown eyes fixed on me. "And who is this?"

"My happiness at seeing you has pushed my manners aside. Lady Pembroke, this is my wife, Diana. We are recently wed."

"My lady." I dropped the countess a deep curtsy. Mary's shoes were encrusted with fantastic gold and silver embroidery that suggested Eden, covered as they were with snakes, apples, and insects. They must have cost a fortune.

"Mistress Roydon," she said, her eyes snapping with amusement. "Now that that's over with, let us be plain Mary and Diana. Henry tells me that you are a student of alchemy."

"A *reader* of alchemy, my lady," I corrected, "that is all. Lord Northumberland is too generous."

Matthew took my hand in his. "And you are too modest. She knows a vast amount, Mary. As Diana is new to London, Hal thought you might help her find her way in the city."

"With pleasure," the Countess of Pembroke said. "Come, we shall sit by the window. Master Hilliard requires strong light for his work. While he finishes my portrait, you will tell me all the news. Little happens in the kingdom that is beyond Matthew's notice and understanding, Diana, and I have been at home in Wiltshire for months."

Once we were settled, her servant returned with a plate of preserved fruit.

"Ooh," Henry said, happily wiggling his fingers over the yellow, green, and orange confections. "Comfits. You make them like no one else."

"And I shall share my secret with Diana," Mary said, looking pleased. "Of course, once she has the receipt, I may never have the pleasure of Henry's company again."

"Now, Mary, you go too far," he protested around a mouthful of candied orange peel.

"Is your husband with you, Mary, or does the queen's business keep him in Wales?" Matthew inquired.

"The Earl of Pembroke left Milford Haven several days ago but will go to court rather than come here. I have William and Philip with me for company, and we will not linger much longer in the city but go on to Ramsbury. The air is healthier there." A sad look crossed her face.

Mary's words reminded me of the statue of William Herbert in the Bodleian Library quadrangle. The man I passed on the way to Duke Humfrey's every day, and one of the library's greatest benefactors, was this woman's young son. "How old are your children?" I asked, hoping that the question was not too personal.

The countess's face softened. "William is ten, and Philip is just six. My daughter, Anne, is seven but she was ill this past month, and my husband felt she should remain at Wilton."

"Nothing serious?" Matthew frowned.

More shadows scudded across the countess's face. "Any sickness that afflicts my children is serious," she said softly.

"Forgive me, Mary. I spoke without thinking. My intention was only to offer what assistance I can." My husband's voice deepened with regret. The conversation was touching on a shared history unknown to me.

"You have kept those I love from harm on more than one occasion. I haven't forgotten it, Matthew, nor would I fail to call on you again if necessary. But Anne suffered from a child's ague, nothing more. The physicians assure me she will recover." Mary turned to me. "Do you have children, Diana?"

"Not yet," I said, shaking my head. Matthew's gray glance settled on me for a moment, then flitted away. I tugged nervously at the bottom of my jacket.

"Diana has not been married before," Matthew said.

"Never?" The Countess of Pembroke was fascinated by this piece of information and opened her mouth to question me further. Matthew cut her off.

"Her father and mother died when she was young. There was no one to arrange it."

Mary's sympathy increased. "A young girl's life is sadly dependent upon the whims of her guardians."

"Indeed." Matthew arched an eyebrow at me. I could imagine what he was thinking: I was lamentably independent, and Sarah and Em were the least whimsical creatures on earth.

The conversation moved on to politics and current events. I listened attentively for a while, trying to reconcile hazy recollections of a long-ago history class with the complicated gossip that the other three exchanged. There was talk of war, a possible Spanish invasion, Catholic sympathizers, and the religious tension in France, but the names and places were often unfamiliar. As I relaxed into the warmth of Mary's solar, and comforted by the constant chatter, my mind drifted.

"I am done here, Lady Pembroke. My servant Isaac will deliver the miniature by week's end," Hilliard announced, packing up his equipment.

"Thank you, Master Hilliard." The countess extended her hand, sparkling with the jewels from her many rings. He kissed it, nodded to Henry and Matthew, and departed.

"Such a talented man," Mary said, shifting in her chair. "He has grown so popular I was fortunate to secure his services." Her feet twinkled in the firelight, the silver embroidery on her richly colored slippers picking up hints of red, orange, and gold. I wondered idly who had designed the intricate pattern for the embroidery. Had I been closer, I would have asked to touch the stitches. Champier had been able to read my flesh with his fingers. Could an inanimate object provide similar information?

Though my fingers were nowhere near the countess's shoes, I saw the face of a young woman. She was peering at a sheet of paper with the design for Mary's shoes on it. Tiny holes along the lines of the drawing solved the mystery of how its intricacies had been transferred to leather. Focusing on the drawing, my mind's eye took several steps backward in time. Now I saw Mary sitting with a stern, stubborn-jawed man, a table full of insect and plant specimens before them. Both were talking with great animation about a grasshopper, and when the man began to describe it in detail, Mary took up her pen and sketched its outlines.

So Mary is interested in plants and insects, as well as alchemy, I thought, searching her shoes for the grasshopper. There it was, on the heel. So lifelike. And the bee on her right toe looked as though it might fly away at any moment.

A faint buzzing filled my ears as the silver-and-black bee detached itself from the Countess of Pembroke's shoe and took to the air.

"Oh, no," I gasped.

"What a strange bee," Henry commented, swatting at it as it flew past.

But I was looking instead at the snake that was slithering off Mary's foot and into the rushes. "Matthew!"

He shot forward and lifted the snake by the tail. It extended its forked tongue and hissed indignantly at the rough treatment. With a flick of his wrist, he tossed the snake into the fire, where it sizzled for a moment before catching light.

"I didn't mean . . ." I trailed off.

"It's all right, *mon coeur.* You cannot help it." Matthew touched my cheek before he looked at the countess, who was staring down at her mismatching slippers. "We need a witch, Mary. There is some urgency."

"I know no witches," was the Countess of Pembroke's swift reply.

Matthew's eyebrows rose.

"None to whom I would introduce your wife. You know I don't like to speak of such matters, Matthew. When he returned safe from Paris, Philip told me what you were. I was a child then and understood it as a fable. That is how I wish to keep it."

"And yet you practice alchemy," Matthew observed. "Is that a fable, too?"

"I practice alchemy to understand God's miracle of creation!" Mary cried. "There is no . . . witchcraft . . . in alchemy!"

"The word you were searching for is 'evil.'" The vampire's eyes were dark and the set of his mouth forbidding. The countess instinctively recoiled. "You are so sure of yourself and your God that you claim to know His mind?"

Mary felt the rebuke but was not ready to give up the fight. "My God and your God are not the same, Matthew." My husband's eyes narrowed, and Henry picked at his hose nervously. The countess's chin rose. "Philip told me about that, too. You still adhere to the pope and the Mass. He saw past the errors of your faith to the man underneath, and I have done the same in the hope that one day you will perceive the truth and follow it."

"Why, when you see the truth about creatures like Diana and me every day and still deny it?" Matthew sounded weary. He stood. "We will not trouble you again, Mary. Diana will find a witch some other way."

"Why can we not go on as we have before and speak no more about this?" The countess looked at me and bit her lip, uncertainty in her eyes.

"Because I love my wife and want to see her safe."

Mary studied him for a moment, gauging his sincerity. It must have satisfied her. "Diana need not fear me, Matt. But no one else in London should be trusted with the knowledge of her. What is happening in Scotland is making people fearful, and quick to blame others for their misfortunes."

"I'm so sorry about your shoes," I said awkwardly. They would never be the same.

"We will not mention it," Mary said firmly, rising to say her good-byes.

None of us said a word as we left Baynard's Castle. Pierre sauntered out of the gatehouse behind us, jamming his cap on his head.

"That went very well, I think," Henry said, breaking the silence.

We turned on him in disbelief.

"There were a few difficulties, to be sure," he said hastily, "but there was no mistaking Mary's interest in Diana or her continued devotion to you, Matthew. You must give her a chance. She was not raised to trust easily. It's why matters of faith trouble her so." He drew his cloak around him. The wind had not diminished, and it was getting dark. "Alas, I must leave you here. My mother is in Aldersgate and expects me for supper."

"Has she recovered from her indisposition?" Matthew asked. The dowager countess had complained about shortness of breath over Christmas, and Matthew was concerned it might be her heart.

"My mother is a Neville. She will, therefore, live forever and cause trouble at every opportunity!" Henry kissed me on the cheek. "Do not worry about Mary, or about that . . . er, other matter." He wiggled his eyebrows meaningfully and departed.

Matthew and I watched him go before turning toward the Blackfriars. "What happened?" he asked quietly.

"Before, it was my emotions that set off the magic. Now an idle question is enough to make me see beneath the surface of things. But I have no idea how I animated that bee."

"Thank God you were thinking about Mary's shoes. If you'd been examining her tapestries, we would have found ourselves in the midst of a war between the gods on Mount Olympus," he said drily.

We passed quickly through St. Paul's Churchyard and back into the relative quiet of the Blackfriars. The day's earlier frenetic activity had slowed to a more leisurely pace. Craftsmen congregated in doorways to share notes on business, leaving their apprentices to finish up the day's tasks.

"Do you want takeout?" Matthew pointed at a bake shop. "It's not pizza, alas, but Kit and Walter are devoted to Prior's meat pies." My mouth watered at the scent coming from inside, and I nodded.

Master Prior was shocked when Matthew entered his premises and nonplussed when questioned in detail about the sources and relative freshness of his meat. Finally I settled on a savory pie filled with duck. I wasn't having venison, no matter how recently it had been killed.

Matthew paid Prior for the food while the baker's assistants wrapped it. Every few seconds they gave us furtive glances. I was reminded that a witch and a vampire drew human suspicion like a candle drew moths.

Dinner was comfortable and cozy, though Matthew seemed a bit preoccupied. Soon after I'd finished my pie, footsteps sounded on the wooden stairs. *Not Kit,* I thought, crossing my fingers, *not tonight.*

When Françoise opened the door, two men in familiar charcoal livery were waiting. Matthew frowned and stood. "Is the countess unwell? Or one of the boys?"

"All are well, sir." One of them held out a carefully folded piece of paper. On top was an irregular blob of red wax bearing the impression of an arrowhead. "From the Countess of Pembroke," he explained with a bow, "for Mistress Roydon."

It was strange to see the formal address on the reverse: *"Mistress Diana Roydon, at the sign of the Hart and Crown, the Blackfriars."* My wandering fingers easily summoned up an image of Mary Sidney's intelligent face. I carried the letter over to the fire, slid my finger under the seal, and sat down to read. The paper was thick and crackled as I spread it out. A smaller slip of paper fluttered onto my lap.

"What does Mary say?" Matthew asked after dismissing the messengers. He stood behind me and rested his hands on my shoulders.

"She wants me to come to Baynard's Castle on Thursday. Mary has an alchemical experiment under way that she thinks might interest me." I couldn't keep the incredulity out of my voice.

"That's Mary for you. She's cautious but loyal," Matthew said, dropping a kiss on my head. "And she always did have amazing recuperative powers. What's on the other paper?"

I picked it up and read aloud the first lines of the enclosed verses.

"Yea, when all me so misdeemed,
I to most a monster seemed,
Yet in thee my hope was strong."

"Well, well, well," Matthew interrupted with a chuckle. "My wife has arrived." I looked at him in confusion. "Mary's most treasured project is not alchemical but a new rendition of the Psalms for English Protestants. Her brother Philip began it and died before it was complete. Mary's twice the poet he was. Sometimes she suspects as much, though she'll never admit it. That's the beginning of Psalm Seventy-one. She sent it to you to show the world that you're part of her circle—a trusted confidante and friend." His voice dropped to a mischievous whisper. "Even if you did ruin her shoes." With a final chuckle, Matthew withdrew to his study, dogged by Pierre.

I'd taken over one end of the heavy-legged table in the parlor for a desk. Like every work surface I'd ever occupied, it was now littered with both trash and treasures. I rooted around and found my last sheets of blank paper, selected a fresh quill, and swept a spot clear.

It took five minutes to write a brief response to the countess. There were two embarrassing blotches on it, but my Italic hand was reasonably good, and I'd remembered to spell some of the words phonetically so that they wouldn't look too modern. When in doubt I doubled a consonant or added a final *e.* I shook sand on the sheet and waited until it absorbed the excess ink before blowing it into the rushes. Once the letter was folded, I realized that I had no wax or signet to close it. *That will have to be fixed.*

I set my note aside for Pierre and returned to the slip of paper. Mary had sent me all three stanzas of Psalm 71. I took up the new blank book that Matthew had bought for me and opened it to the first page. After dipping the quill into the nearby pot of ink, I moved the sharp point carefully across the sheet.

They by whom my life is hated
With their spies have now debated
Of their talk, and, lo, the sum:
God, they say, hath him forsaken.
Now pursue, he must be taken;
None will to his rescue come.

When the ink was dry, I closed my book and slid it underneath Philip Sidney's *Arcadia.*

There was more to this gift from Mary than a simple offer of friendship, of that I was certain. While the lines I'd read aloud to Matthew were an acknowledgment of his service to her family and a declaration that she would not turn away from him now, the final lines held a message for me: We were being watched. Someone suspected that all was not as it seemed on Water Lane, and Matthew's enemies were betting that even his allies would turn against him once they discovered the truth.

Matthew, a vampire as well as the queen's servant and a member of the Congregation, couldn't be involved with finding a witch to serve as my magical tutor. And with a baby on the way, finding one quickly had taken on a new significance.

I pulled a sheet of paper toward me and began to make a list.

Sealing Waxe
A Signet

London was a big city. And I was going to do some shopping.

17

"I'm going out."

Françoise looked up from her sewing. Thirty seconds later Pierre was climbing the stairs. Had Matthew been at home, he would no doubt have appeared as well, but he was out conducting some mysterious business in the city. I'd woken to the sight of his damp suit still drying by the fireplace. He'd been called away in the night and returned, only to leave once more.

"Indeed?" Françoise's eyes narrowed. She had suspected I was up to no good ever since I'd gotten dressed. Instead of grumbling about the number of petticoats she pulled over my head, today I'd added another made out of warm gray flannel. Then we argued about which gown I should wear. I preferred the comfortable clothes I'd brought from France over Louisa de Clermont's more splendid garments. Matthew's sister, with her dark hair and porcelain skin, could pull off a gown of vivid turquoise velvet ("Verdigris," Françoise had corrected me) or a sickly gray-green taffeta (appropriately called "Dying Spaniard"), but they looked ghastly with my faint freckles and reddish-blond curls, and they were too grand to wear around town.

"Perhaps *madame* should wait until Master Roydon returns," Pierre suggested. He shifted nervously from one foot to the other.

"No, I think not. I've made a list of things I need, and I want to go shopping for them myself." I scooped up the leather bag of coins given to me by Philippe. "Is it all right to carry a bag, or am I supposed to stick the money into my bodice and fish the coins out when necessary?" This aspect of historical fiction had always fascinated me—women stuffing things into their dresses—and I was looking forward to discovering whether the items were as easy to remove in public as the novelists suggested. Sex was certainly not as easy to arrange in the sixteenth century as it was made out to be in some romances. There were too many clothes in the way, for a start.

"*Madame* will not carry money at all!" Françoise pointed to Pierre, who loosened the strings of a bag tied around his waist. It was apparently bottomless and held a considerable stash of pointy implements, including pins, needles, something that looked like a set of picklocks, and a dagger. Once my leather bag was included, it jingled at his slightest movement.

Out on Water Lane, I strode with as much determination as my pattens (those helpful wooden wedges that slipped over my shoes and kept me from the muck) would allow in the direction of St. Paul's. The fur-lined cloak billowed around my feet, its thick fabric a barrier to the clinging fog. We were enjoying a temporary reprieve from the recent downpours, but the weather was by no means dry.

Our first stop was at Master Prior's bakery for some buns studded with currants and candied fruit. I was often hungry in the late afternoons and would want something sweet. My next visit was near the alley that linked the Blackfriars to the rest of London, at a busy printing shop marked with the sign of an anchor.

"Good morning, Mistress Roydon," the proprietor said the moment I crossed the threshold. Apparently my neighbors knew me without introduction. "You are here to pick up your husband's book?"

I nodded confidently in spite of not knowing which book he was talking about, and he pulled at a slim volume that was resting on a high shelf. A flip through the pages revealed that it dealt with military affairs and ballistics.

"I am sorry there was no bound copy of your physic book," he said as he wrapped Matthew's purchase. "When you can part with it, I will have it bound to suit you."

So this was where my compendium of illnesses and cures had come from. "I thank you, Master . . ." I trailed off.

"Field," he supplied.

"Master Field," I repeated. A bright-eyed young woman with a baby on her hip came out of the office at the back of the shop, a toddler clinging to her skirts. Her fingers were rough and ingrained with ink.

"Mistress Roydon, this is my wife, Jacqueline."

"Ah. Madame Roydon." The woman's accent was softly French and reminded me of Ysabeau. "Your husband told us you are a great reader, and Margaret Hawley reports that you study alchemy."

Jacqueline and her husband knew a great deal about my business. No doubt they also were apprised of my shoe size and the type of meat pie I preferred. It struck me as even odder, therefore, that no one in the Blackfriars seemed to have noticed I was a witch.

"Yes," I said, straightening the seams of my gloves. "Do you sell unbound paper, Master Field?"

"Of course," Field said with a confused frown. "Have you filled your book with commonplaces already?" Ah. He was the source of my notebook, too.

"I require paper for correspondence," I explained. "And sealing wax. And a signet. Can I purchase them here?" The Yale bookstore had all kinds of stationery, pens, and sticks of brightly colored, entirely pointless wax along with cheap brass seals made in the shape of letters. Field and his wife exchanged glances.

"I will send more paper this afternoon," he said. "But you'll want a goldsmith for the signet so it can be made into a ring. All I have here are worn letters from the printing press that are waiting to be melted down and recast."

"Or you could see Nicholas Vallin," Jacqueline suggested. "He is expert with metals, Mistress Roydon, and also makes fine clocks."

"Just down the lane?" I said, pointing over my shoulder.

"He is not a goldsmith," Field protested. "We do not want to cause Monsieur Vallin trouble."

Jacqueline was unperturbed. "There are benefits to living in the Blackfriars, Richard. Working outside the regulations of the guilds is one of them. Besides, the Goldsmiths Company will not bother anyone here for something as insignificant as a woman's ring. If you want sealing wax, Mistress Roydon, you will need to go to the apothecary."

Soap was on my list of purchases, too. And apothecaries used distillation apparatus. Even though my focus was necessarily shifting from alchemy to magic, there was no need to forgo an opportunity to learn something more useful.

"Where is the nearest apothecary?"

Pierre coughed. "Perhaps you should consult with Master Roydon."

Matthew would have all sorts of opinions, most of which would involve sending Françoise or Pierre to fetch what I required. The Fields awaited my reply with interest.

"Perhaps," I said, staring at Pierre indignantly. "But I would like Mistress Field's recommendation all the same."

"John Hester is highly regarded," Jacqueline said with a touch of mischief, pulling the toddler free of her skirts. "He provided a tincture for my son's ear that cured its aching." John Hester, if memory served, was interested in alchemy, too. Perhaps he knew a witch. Even better, he might *be* a witch, which would suit my real intentions admirably. I was not simply out shopping today. I was out to be seen. Witches were a curious bunch. If I offered myself up as bait, one would bite.

"It is said that even the Countess of Pembroke seeks his advice for the young lord's *megraines*," her husband added. So the entire neighborhood knew I'd been to Baynard's Castle, too. Mary was right: We were being watched. "Master Hester's shop is near Paul's Wharf, marked with the sign of a still."

"Thank you, Mistress Field." Paul's Wharf must be near St. Paul's Churchyard, and I could go there that afternoon. I redrew my mental map of today's excursion.

After we said our farewells, Françoise and Pierre turned down the lane toward home.

"I'm going on to the cathedral," I said, heading in the other direction.

Impossibly, Pierre was standing before me. "*Milord* will not be pleased."

"*Milord* is not here. Matthew left strict instructions that I wasn't to go there without you. He didn't say I was a prisoner in my own house." I thrust the book and the buns at Françoise. "If Matthew returns before I do, tell him where we are and that I'll be back soon."

Françoise took the parcels, exchanged a long look with Pierre, and proceeded down Water Lane.

"Prenez garde, madame," Pierre murmured as I passed him.

"I'm always careful," I said calmly, stepping straight into a puddle.

Two coaches had collided and were jammed in the street leading to St. Paul's. The lumbering vehicles resembled enclosed wagons and were nothing like the dashing carriages in Jane Austen films. I skirted them with Pierre on my heels, dodging the irritated horses and the no-less-irritated occupants, who stood in the middle of the street and shouted about who was to blame. Only the coachmen seemed unconcerned, chatting to each other quietly from their perches above the fray.

"Does this happen often?" I asked Pierre, pulling back my hood so that I could see him.

"These new conveyances are a nuisance," he said sourly. "It was much better when people walked or rode horses. But it is no matter. They will never catch on."

That's what they told Henry Ford, I thought.

"How far is Paul's Wharf?"

"*Milord* does not like John Hester."

"That's not what I asked, Pierre."

"What does *madame* wish to purchase in the churchyard?" Pierre's distraction technique was familiar to me from years in the classroom. But I had no intention of telling anyone the real reason we were picking our way across London.

"Books," I said shortly.

We entered the precincts of St. Paul's, where every inch not taken up by paper was occupied by someone selling a good or service. A kindly middle-aged man sat on a stool, inside a lean-to affixed to a shed, which was itself built up against one of the cathedral walls. This was by no means an unusual office environment for the place. A huddle of people gathered around his stall. If I were lucky, there would be a witch among them.

I made my way through the crowd. They all seemed to be human. What a disappointment.

The man looked up, startled, from a document he was carefully transcribing for a waiting customer. A scrivener. *Please, let this not be William Shakespeare,* I prayed.

"Can I help you, Mistress Roydon?" he said in a French accent. *Not Shakespeare.* But how did he know my identity?

"Do you have sealing wax? And red ink?"

"I am not an apothecary, Mistress Roydon, but a poor teacher." His customers began to mutter about the scandalous profits enjoyed by grocers, apothecaries, and other extortionists.

"Mistress Field tells me that John Hester makes excellent sealing wax." Heads turned in my direction.

"Rather expensive, though. So is his ink, which he makes from iris flowers." The man's assessment was confirmed by murmurs from the crowd.

"Can you point me in the direction of his shop?"

Pierre grabbed my elbow. *"Non,"* he hissed in my ear. As this only earned us more human attention, he quickly dropped it again.

The scrivener's hand rose and pointed east. "You will find him at Paul's Wharf. Go to the Bishop's Head and then turn south. But Monsieur Cornu knows the way."

I glanced back at Pierre, who was staring fixedly at a spot somewhere above my head. "Does he? Thank you."

"That's Matthew Roydon's *wife*?" someone said with a chuckle as we stepped out of the throng. *"Mon dieu.* No wonder he looks exhausted."

I didn't move immediately in the direction of the apothecary. Instead, with my eyes fixed on the cathedral, I began a slow circumnavigation of its enormous bulk. It was surprisingly graceful given its size, but that unfortunate lightning strike had ruined its appearance forever.

"This is not the fastest way to the Bishop's Head." Pierre was one step behind me instead of his usual three and therefore ran into me when I stopped to look up.

"How tall was the spire?"

"Almost as tall as the building is long. *Milord* was always fascinated by how they managed to build it so high." The missing spire would have made the whole building soar, with the slender pinnacle echoing the delicate lines of the buttresses and the tall Gothic windows.

I felt a surge of energy that reminded me of the temple to the goddess near Sept-Tours. Deep under the cathedral, something sensed my presence. It responded with a whisper, a slight stirring beneath my feet, a sigh of acknowledgment—and then it was gone. There was power here—the kind that was irresistible to witches.

Pushing my hood from my face, I slowly surveyed the buyers and sellers in St. Paul's Churchyard. Daemons, witches, and vampires sent flickers of attention my way, but there was too much activity for me to stand out. I needed a more intimate situation.

I continued past the north side of the cathedral and rounded its eastern end. The noise increased. Here all attention was focused on a man in a raised, open-air pulpit covered by a cross-topped roof. In the absence of an electric public-address system, the man kept his audience engaged by shouting, making dramatic gestures, and conjuring up images of fire and brimstone.

There was no way that one witch could compete with so much hell and damnation. Unless I did something dangerously conspicuous, any witch who spotted me would think I was nothing more than a fellow creature out shopping. I smothered a sigh of frustration. My plan had seemed infallible in its simplicity. In the Blackfriars there were no witches. But here in St. Paul's, there were too many. And Pierre's presence would deter any curious creature who might approach me.

"Stay here and don't move," I ordered, giving him a stern look. My chances of catching the eye of a friendly witch might increase if he weren't standing by radiating vampire disapproval. Pierre leaned against the upright support of a bookstall and fixed his eyes on me without comment.

I waded into the crowd at the foot of Paul's Cross, looking from left to right as if to locate a lost friend. I waited for a witch's tingle. They were here. I could feel them.

"Mistress Roydon?" a familiar voice called. "What brings you here?"

George Chapman's ruddy face poked out between the shoulders of two dour-looking gentlemen who were listening to the preacher blame the ills of the world on an unholy cabal of Catholics and merchant adventurers.

There was no witch to be found, but the members of the School of Night were, as usual, everywhere.

"I'm looking for ink. And sealing wax." The more I repeated this, the more inane it sounded.

"You'll need an apothecary, then. Come, I'll take you to my own man." George held out his elbow. "He is quite reasonable, as well as skilled."

"It is getting late, Master Chapman," Pierre said, materializing from nowhere.

"Mistress Roydon should take the air while she has the opportunity. The watermen say the rain will return soon, and they are seldom wrong. Besides, John Chandler's shop is just outside the walls, on Red Cross Street. It's not half a mile."

Meeting up with George now seemed fortuitous rather than exasperating. Surely we would pass a witch on our stroll.

"Matthew would not object to my walking with Master Chapman—especially not with you accompanying me, too," I told Pierre, taking George's arm. "Is your apothecary anywhere near Paul's Wharf?"

"Quite the opposite," George said. "But you don't want to shop on Paul's Wharf. John Hester is the only apothecary there, and his prices are beyond the bounds of good sense. Master Chandler will do you a better service, at half the cost."

I put John Hester on my to-do list for another day and took George's arm. We strolled out of St. Paul's Churchyard to the north, passing grand houses and gardens.

"That's where Henry's mother lives," George said, gesturing at a particularly imposing set of buildings to our left. "He hates the place and lived around the corner from Matt until Mary convinced him that his lodgings were beneath an earl's dignity. Now he's moved into a house on the Strand.

Mary is pleased, but Henry finds it gloomy, and the damp disagrees with his bones."

The city walls were just beyond the Percy family house. Built by the Romans to defend Londinium from invaders, they still marked its official boundaries. Once we'd passed through Aldersgate and over a low bridge, there were open fields and houses clustered around churches. My gloved hand rose to my nose at the smell that accompanied this pastoral view.

"The city ditch," George said apologetically, gesturing at a river of sludge beneath our feet. "It is, alas, the most direct route. We will be in better air soon." I wiped at my watering eyes and sincerely hoped so.

George steered me along the street, which was broad enough to accommodate passing coaches, wagons full of food, and even a team of oxen. While we walked, he chatted about his visit with his publisher, William Ponsonby. Chapman was crushed that I didn't recognize the name. I knew little about the nuances of the Elizabethan book trade and so drew him out about the subject. George was happy to gossip about the many playwrights Ponsonby snubbed, including Kit. Ponsonby preferred to work with the serious literary set, and his stable of authors was illustrious indeed: Edmund Spenser, the Countess of Pembroke, Philip Sidney.

"Ponsonby would publish Matt's poetry as well, but he has refused." George shook his head, perplexed.

"His poetry?" That brought me to a sudden halt. I knew that Matthew admired poetry, but not that he wrote it.

"Yes. Matt insists his verses are fit only for the eyes of friends. We are all fond of his elegy for Mary's brother, Philip Sidney. *'But eies and eares and ev'ry thought / Were with his sweete perfections caught.'*" George smiled. "It is marvelous work. But Matthew has little use for the press and complains that it has only resulted in discord and ill-considered opinions."

In spite of his modern laboratory, Matthew was an old fuddy-duddy with his fondness for antique watches and vintage automobiles. I pressed my lips together to keep from smiling at this latest evidence of his traditionalism. "What are his poems about?"

"Love and friendship for the most part, though recently he and Walter have been exchanging verses about . . . darker subjects. They seem to think out of a single mind these days."

"Darker?" I frowned.

"He and Walter do not always approve of what happens around them," George said in a low voice, his eyes darting over the faces of passersby.

"They can be prone to impatience—Walter especially—and often give the lie to those in positions of power. It is a dangerous tendency."

"Give the lie," I said slowly. There was a famous poem called "*The Lie.*" It was anonymous, but attributed to Walter Raleigh. "'*Say to the court, it glows / And shines like rotten wood*'?"

"So Matt has shared his verses with you." George sighed once more. "He manages to convey in a few words a full range of feeling and meaning. It is a talent I envy."

Though the poem was familiar, Matthew's relationship to it was not. But there would be plenty of time in the evenings ahead to pursue my husband's literary efforts. I dropped the subject and listened while George offered his opinions on whether writers were now required to publish too much in order to survive, and the need for decent copy editors to keep errors from creeping into printed books.

"There is Chandler's shop," George said, pointing to the intersection where an off-kilter cross sat on a raised platform. A gang of boys was busy chipping one of the rough cobbles out of the base. It didn't take a witch to foresee that the stone might soon be launched through a shop window.

The closer we got to the apothecary's place of business, the colder the air felt. Just as at St. Paul's, there was another surge of power, but an oppressive atmosphere of poverty and desperation hung over the neighborhood. An ancient tower crumbled on the northern side of the street, and the houses around it looked as though a gust of wind might carry them away. Two youths shuffled closer, eyeing us with interest, until a low hiss from Pierre stopped them in their tracks.

John Chandler's shop suited the neighborhood's Gothic atmosphere perfectly. It was dark, pungent, and unsettling. A stuffed owl hung from the ceiling, and the toothy jaws of some unfortunate creature were tacked above a diagram of a body with severed and broken limbs, pierced through with weapons. A carpenter's awl entered the poor fellow's left eye at a jaunty angle.

A stooped man emerged from behind a curtain, wiping his hands on the sleeves of his rusty black bombazine coat. It bore a resemblance to the academic gowns worn by Oxford and Cambridge undergraduates and was just as rumpled. Bright hazel eyes met mine without a trace of hesitation, and my skin tingled with recognition. Chandler was a witch. After crossing most of London, I'd finally located one of my own people.

"The streets around you grow more dangerous with every passing week, Master Chandler." George peered out the door at the gang hovering nearby.

"That pack of boys runs wild," Chandler said. "What can I do for you today, Master Chapman? Are you in need of more tonic? Have your headaches returned?"

George made a detailed accounting of his many aches and pains. Chandler murmured sympathetically every now and then and drew a ledger closer. The men pored over it, giving me a chance to examine my surroundings.

Elizabethan apothecary shops were evidently the general stores of the period, and the small space was stuffed to the rafters with merchandise. There were piles of vividly illustrated broadsides, like the one of the wounded man tacked up on the wall, and jars of candied fruit. Used books sat on one table, along with a few newer titles. A set of pottery crocks offered a splash of brightness in the otherwise dim room, all of them labeled with the names of medicinal spices and herbs. Specimens from the animal kingdom on display included not only the stuffed owl and jawbone but also some wizened rodents tied up by their tails. I spotted pots of ink, quill pens, and spools of string, too.

The shop was organized in loose thematic groupings. The ink was near the quills and the used books, under the wise old owl. The mice hung above a crock labeled *"Ratbane,"* which sat next to a book promising not only to help you catch fish but to build *"sundrie Engines and trappes to take Polcats, Buzzards, rattes, mice, and all other kindes of Vermin and beasts."* I had been wondering how to get rid of the unwanted guests in Matthew's attic. The detailed plans in the pamphlet exceeded my handywoman skills, but I'd find someone who could execute them. If the brace of mice in Chandler's shop was any indication, the traps certainly worked.

"Excuse me, mistress," Chandler murmured, reaching past me. Fascinated, I watched as he took the mice to his workbench and sliced the ears off with delicate precision.

"What are they for?" I asked George.

"Powdered mouse ears are effective against warts," he explained earnestly while Chandler wielded his pestle.

Relieved that I did not suffer from this particular complaint, I drifted over to the owl guarding the stationery department. I found a pot of red ink, deep and rich.

Your wearh *friend will not appreciate having to carry that bottle home, mistress. It is made from hawk's blood and is used for writing out love spells.*

So Chandler had the power of silent speech. I returned the ink to its place and picked up a dog-eared pamphlet. The images on the first sheet showed a wolf attacking a small child and a man being horribly tortured and then executed. It reminded me of the tabloids at the cash registers in modern grocery stores. When I flipped the page over, I was startled to read about someone named Stubbe Peter, who appeared in the shape of a wolf and fed off the blood of men, women, and children until they were dead. It was not only Scottish witches who were in the public eye. So were vampires.

My eyes raced across the page. I noted with relief that Stubbe lived in far-off Germany. The anxiety returned when I saw that the uncle of one of his victims ran the brewery between our house and Baynard's Castle. I was aghast at the gruesome details of the killings, as well as the lengths humans would go to in order to cope with the creatures in their midst. Here Stubbe Peter was depicted as a witch, and his strange behavior was attributed to a pact with the devil that made it possible for him to change shape and satisfy his unnatural taste for blood. But it was far more likely that the man was a vampire. I slid the pamphlet underneath my other book and made my way to the counter.

"Mistress Roydon requires some supplies," George explained to the apothecary as I drew near.

Chandler's mind went carefully blank at the mention of my name.

"Yes," I said slowly. "Red ink, if you have it. And some scented soap, for washing."

"Aye." The wizard searched through some small pewter vessels. When he found the right one, he put it on the counter. "And do you require sealing wax to match the ink?"

"Whatever you have will be fine, Master Chandler."

"I see you have one of Master Hester's books," George said, picking up a nearby volume. "I told Mistress Roydon that your ink is as good as Hester's and half the price."

The apothecary smiled weakly at George's compliment and put several sticks of carnation-colored wax and two balls of sweet-smelling soap on the table next to my ink. I dropped the pest-control manual and the pamphlet about the German vampire onto the surface. Chandler's eyes rose to mine. They were wary.

"Yes," Chandler said, "the printer across the way left a few copies with me, as it dealt with a medical subject."

"That will be of interest to Mistress Roydon, too," George said, plunking it onto my pile. I wondered, not for the first time, how humans could be so oblivious to what happened around them.

"But I am not sure this treatise is appropriate for a lady. . . ." Chandler trailed off, looking meaningfully at my wedding ring.

George's quick response drowned out my own silent retort. "Oh, her husband will not mind. She is a student of alchemy."

"I'll take it," I said decidedly.

As Chandler wrapped our purchases, George asked him if he could recommend a spectacle maker.

"My publisher, Master Ponsonby, is worried my eyes will fail me before my translation of Homer is complete," he explained self-importantly. "I have a receipt from my mother's servant, but it has not resulted in a cure."

The apothecary shrugged. "These old wives' remedies sometimes help, but mine is more reliable. I will send around a poultice made from egg whites and rose water. Soak flax pads in it and apply them to the eyes."

While George and Chandler bargained over the price of the medicine and made arrangements for its delivery, Pierre gathered the packages and stood by the door.

"Farewell, Mistress Roydon," Chandler said with a bow.

"Thank you for your assistance, Master Chandler," I replied. *I am new in town and looking for a witch to help me.*

"You are welcome," he said smoothly, "though there are excellent apothecaries in the Blackfriars." *London is a dangerous place. Have care from whom you request assistance.*

Before I could ask the apothecary how he knew where I lived, George was shepherding me out onto the street with a cheerful good-bye. Pierre was so close behind that I could feel his occasional cool breaths.

The touch of eyes was unmistakable as we made our progress back to town. An alert had been issued while I was in Chandler's shop, and word that a strange witch was near had spread throughout the neighborhood. At last I had achieved my objective for the afternoon. Two witches came out onto their front step, arms linked at the elbows, and scrutinized me with tingling hostility. They were so similar in face and body that I wondered if they were twins.

"Wearh," one mumbled, spitting at Pierre and forking her fingers in a sign against the devil.

"Come, mistress. It is late," Pierre said, his fingers gripping my forearm.

Pierre's desire to get me away from St. Giles as quickly as possible and George's desire for a cup of wine made our return to the Blackfriars far quicker than the journey out. Once we were safely back in the Hart and Crown, there was still no sign of Matthew, and Pierre disappeared in search of him. Soon thereafter Françoise made pointed remarks about the lateness of the hour and my need for rest. Chapman took the hint and said his farewells.

Françoise sat by the fireplace, her sewing at her side, and watched the door. I tried out my new ink by ticking items off my shopping list and adding *"rat trappe."* I turned next to John Hester's book. The blank sheet of paper folded discreetly around it masked the salacious contents. It enumerated cures for venereal diseases, most of them involving toxic concentrations of mercury. No wonder Chandler had objected to selling a copy to a married woman. I had just started the second fascinating chapter when I heard murmurs coming from Matthew's study. Françoise's mouth tightened, and she shook her head.

"He will need more wine tonight than we have in the house," she observed, heading for the stairs with one of the empty jugs that sat by the door.

I followed the sound of my husband's voice. Matthew was still in his study, peeling his clothes off and flinging them into the fire.

"He is an evil man, *milord,*" Pierre said grimly, unbuckling Matthew's sword.

"'Evil' doesn't do that fiend justice. The word that does hasn't been coined yet. After today I'd swear before judges he is the devil himself." Matthew's long fingers loosened the ties of his close-fitting breeches. They dropped to the floor, and he bent to catch them up. They flew through the air and into the fire, but not fast enough to hide the spots of blood. A musty smell of wet stone, age, and filth evoked in me sudden memories of being held captive at La Pierre. The gorge rose in my throat. Matthew spun around.

"Diana." He took in my distress with one deep breath and ripped the shirt above his head before stepping over his discarded boots and coming to my side in nothing but a pair of linen drawers. The firelight played off his shoulders, and one of his many scars—this one long and deep, just over his shoulder joint—winked in and out of sight.

"Are you hurt?" I struggled to get the words out of my constricted throat, and my eyes were glued to the clothes burning in the fireplace. Matthew followed my gaze and swore softly.

"That isn't my blood." That Matthew had someone else's blood on him was not much comfort. "The queen ordered me to be present when a prisoner was . . . questioned." His slight hesitation told me that "tortured" was the word he was avoiding. "Let me wash, and I'll join you for supper." Matthew's words were warm, but he looked tired and angry. And he was careful not to touch me.

"You've been underground." There was no mistaking the smell.

"I've been at the Tower."

"And your prisoner—is he dead?"

"Yes." His hand passed over his face. "I'd hoped to arrive early enough to stop it—this time—but I miscalculated the tides. All I could do, once again, was insist that his suffering end."

Matthew had been through the man's death once before. Today he could have remained at home and not concerned himself with a lost soul in the Tower. A lesser creature would have. I reached out to touch him, but he stepped away.

"The queen will have my hide when she discovers that the man died before revealing his secrets, but I no longer care. Like most humans, Elizabeth finds it easy to turn a blind eye when it suits her," he said.

"Who was he?"

"A witch," Matthew said flatly. "His neighbors reported him for having a poppet with red hair. They feared that it was an image of the queen. And the queen feared that the behavior of the Scottish witches, Agnes Sampson and John Fian, was encouraging English witches to act against her. No, Diana." Matthew gestured for me to stay where I was when I stepped forward to comfort him. "That's as close as you will ever be to the Tower and what happens there. Go to the parlor. I'll join you shortly."

It was difficult to leave him, but honoring his request was all I could do for him now. The wine, bread, and cheese waiting on the table were unappetizing, but I took a piece of one of the buns I'd purchased that morning and slowly reduced it to crumbs.

"Your appetite is off." Matthew slipped into the room, silent as a cat, and poured himself some wine. He drank it down in one long draft and replenished the cup.

"So is yours," I said. "You're not feeding regularly." Gallowglass and

Hancock kept inviting him to join them on their nocturnal hunts, but Matthew always refused.

"I don't want to talk about that. Tell me about your day instead." *Help me to forget.* Matthew's unspoken words whispered around the room.

"We went shopping. I picked up the book you'd ordered from Richard Field and met his wife, Jacqueline."

"Ah." Matthew's smile widened, and a bit of stress lifted from his mouth. "The new Mrs. Field. She outlived her first husband and is now leading her second husband in a merry dance. The two of you will be fast friends by the end of next week. Did you see Shakespeare? He's staying with the Fields."

"No." I added more crumbs to the growing pile on the table. "I went to the cathedral." Matthew pitched slightly forward. "Pierre was with me," I said hastily, dropping the bun on the table. "And I ran into George."

"He was no doubt hanging around the Bishop's Head waiting for William Ponsonby to say something nice to him." Matthew's shoulders lowered as he chuckled.

"I never reached the Bishop's Head," I confessed. "George was at Paul's Cross, listening to a sermon."

"The crowds that gather to hear the preachers can be unpredictable," he said softly. "Pierre knows better than to let you linger there." As if by magic, his servant appeared.

"We didn't stay long. George took me to his apothecary. I bought a few more books and some supplies. Soap. Sealing wax. Red ink." I pressed my lips together.

"George's apothecary lives in Cripplegate." Matthew's voice went flat. He looked up at Pierre. "When Londoners complain about crime, the sheriff goes there and picks up everyone who looks idle or peculiar. He has an easy time of it."

"If the sheriff targets Cripplegate, why are there so many creatures by the Barbican Cross and so few here in the Blackfriars?" The question took Matthew by surprise.

"The Blackfriars was once Christian holy ground. Daemons, witches, and vampires got into the habit of living elsewhere long ago and haven't yet moved back. The Barbican Cross, however, was put up on land where the Jewish cemetery was hundreds of years ago. After the Jews were expelled from England, city officials used the unconsecrated graveyard for criminals, traitors, and excommunicates instead. Humans consider it haunted and avoid the place."

"So it was the unhappiness of the dead I felt, not just the living." The words slipped out before I could stop them. Matthew's eyes narrowed.

Our conversation was not improving his frayed temper, and my uneasiness grew by the minute. "Jacqueline recommended John Hester when I asked after an apothecary, but George said his man was just as good and less expensive. I didn't ask about the neighborhood."

"The fact that John Chandler isn't pushing opiates on his customers like Hester does is rather more important to me than his reasonable rates. Still, I don't want you in Cripplegate. Next time you need writing supplies, send Pierre or Françoise to fetch them. Better yet, visit the apothecary three doors up on the other side of Water Lane."

"Mistress Field did not tell *madame* that there was an apothecary in the Blackfriars. A few months ago, Monsieur de Laune and Jacqueline disagreed about the best treatment for her eldest son's putrid throat," Pierre murmured by way of explanation.

"I don't care if Jacqueline and de Laune pulled swords on each other in the nave of St. Paul's at the stroke of noon. Diana isn't to go traipsing across the city."

"It's not just Cripplegate that's dangerous," I said, pushing the pamphlet about the German vampire across the table. "I bought Hester's treatise on syphilis from Chandler, and a book about trapping animals. This was for sale, too."

"You bought what?" Matthew choked on his wine, his attention fixed on the wrong book.

"Forget about Hester. This pamphlet tells the story of a man in league with the devil who changes into a wolf and drinks blood. One of the men involved in its publication is our neighbor, the brewer by Baynard's Castle." I tapped my finger on the pamphlet for emphasis.

Matthew drew the loosely bound sheets of paper toward him. His breath hitched when he reached the significant part. He handed it to Pierre, who made a similarly quick study of it.

"Stubbe is a vampire, isn't he?"

"Yes. I didn't know that news of his death had traveled this far. Kit is supposed to tell me about the gossip in the broadsides and popular press so we can cover it up if necessary. Somehow he missed this." Matthew shot a grim look at Pierre. "Make sure someone else is assigned to the job, and don't let Kit know." Pierre tilted his head in acknowledgment.

"So these legends about werewolves are just more pitiful human attempts to deny knowledge of vampires." I shook my head.

"Don't be too hard on them, Diana. They're focused on witches at the moment. It will be the daemons' turn in another hundred years or so, thanks to the reform of the asylums. After that, humans will get around to vampires, and witches will be nothing more than a wicked fairy tale to frighten children." Matthew looked worried, in spite of his words.

"Our next-door neighbor is preoccupied with werewolves, not witches. And if you could be mistaken for one, I want you to stop worrying about me and start taking care of yourself. Besides, it shouldn't be long now before a witch knocks on our door." I clung to the certainty that it would be dangerous for Matthew to look any further for a witch. My husband's eyes flashed a warning, but his mouth remained closed until his anger was under control.

"I know you're itching for independence, but the next time you decide to take matters into your own hands, promise you'll discuss it with me first." His response was far milder than I expected.

"Only if you promise to listen. You're being watched, Matthew. I'm sure of it, and so is Mary Sidney. You take care of the queen's business and the problem in Scotland, and let me take care of this."

When he opened his mouth to negotiate further, I shook my head.

"*Listen to me.* A witch will come. I promise."

Matthew was waiting for me in Mary's airy solar at Baynard's Castle the next afternoon, staring out at the Thames with an amused expression. He turned at my approach, grinning at the Elizabethan version of a lab coat that covered my golden brown bodice and skirts. The underlying white sleeves that stuck out from my shoulders were ridiculously padded, but the ruff around my neck was small and unobtrusive, making it one of my more comfortable outfits.

"Mary can't leave her experiment. She said we should come in time for dinner on Monday." I flung my arms around his neck and kissed him soundly. He reared back.

"Why do you smell of vinegar?"

"Mary washes in it. It cleans your hands better than soap."

"You left my house covered with the sweet scent of bread and honey, and the Countess of Pembroke returns you to me smelling like a pickle." Matthew's nose went to the patch of skin behind my ear. He gave a satisfied sigh. "I knew I could find some place the vinegar hadn't reached."

"Matthew," I murmured. The countess's maid, Joan, was standing right behind us.

"You're behaving like a prim Victorian rather than a bawdy Elizabethan," Matthew said, laughing. He straightened with one last caress of my neck. "How was your afternoon?"

"Have you seen Mary's laboratory?" I exchanged the shapeless gray coat for my cloak before sending Joan away to tend to her other duties. "She's taken over one of the castle's towers and painted the walls with images of the philosopher's stone. It's like working inside a Ripley scroll! I've seen the Beinecke's copy at Yale, but it's only twenty feet long. Mary's murals are twice as big. It made it hard to focus on the work."

"What was your experiment?"

"We hunted the green lion," I replied proudly, referring to a stage of the alchemical process that combined two acidic solutions and produced startling color transformations. "We almost caught it, too. But then something went wrong and the flask exploded. It was fantastic!"

"I'm glad you don't work in my lab. Generally speaking, explosions are to be avoided when working with nitric acid. You two might do something a bit less volatile next time, like distilling rose water." Matthew's eyes narrowed. "You weren't working with mercury?"

"Don't worry. I wouldn't do anything that might harm the baby," I said defensively.

"Every time I say something about your well-being, you assume my concern lies elsewhere." His brows drew together in a scowl. Thanks to his dark beard and mustache—which I was still getting used to—Matthew looked even more forbidding. But I didn't want to argue with him.

"Sorry," I said quickly before changing the subject. "Next week we're going to mix up a fresh batch of *prima materia.* That has mercury in it, but I promise not to touch it. Mary wants to see if it will putrefy into the alchemical toad by the end of January."

"That sounds like a festive start to the New Year," Matthew said, settling the cloak over my shoulders.

"What were you looking at?" I peered out the windows.

"Someone's building a bonfire across the river for New Year's Eve. Every time they send the wagon for fresh wood, the local residents filch what's already there. The pile gets smaller by the hour. It's like watching Penelope ply her needle."

"Mary said no one will be working tomorrow. Oh, and to be sure to tell Françoise to buy extra manchet—that's bread, right?—and to soak it in milk and honey to make it soft again for Saturday's breakfast." It was Elizabethan French toast in all but name. "I think Mary's worried I might go hungry in a house run by vampires."

"Lady Pembroke has a don't-ask, don't-tell policy when it comes to creatures and their habits," Matthew observed.

"She certainly never mentioned what happened to her shoes," I said thoughtfully.

"Mary Sidney survives as her mother did: by turning a blind eye to every inconvenient truth. The women in the Dudley family have had to do so."

"Dudley?" I frowned. That was a family of notorious troublemakers—nothing at all like the mild-mannered Mary.

"Lady Pembroke's mother was Mary Dudley, a friend of Her Majesty and sister to the queen's favorite, Robert." Matthew's mouth twisted. "She was brilliant, just like her daughter. Mary Dudley filled her head with ideas so there was no room in it for knowledge of her father's treason, or her brothers' missteps. When she caught smallpox from our blessed sovereign, Mary Dudley never acknowledged that both the queen and her own husband thereafter preferred the company of others rather than face her disfigurement."

I stopped, shocked. "What happened to her?"

"She died alone and embittered, like most Dudley women before her. Her greatest triumph was marrying off her fifteen-year-old namesake to the forty-year-old Earl of Pembroke."

"Mary Sidney was a bride at fifteen?" The shrewd, vibrant woman ran an enormous household, reared a pack of energetic children, and was devoted to her alchemical experiments, all with no apparent effort. Now I understood how. Lady Pembroke was younger than me by a few years, but by the age of thirty she'd been juggling these responsibilities for half her life.

"Yes. But Mary's mother provided her all the tools necessary for her survival: iron discipline, a deep sense of duty, the best schooling money could buy, a love of poetry, and her passion for alchemy."

I touched my bodice, thinking of the life growing within me. What tools would he need to survive in the world?

We talked about chemistry on our way home. Matthew explained that the crystals that Mary brooded over like a hen were oxidized iron ore and that she would later distill them in a flask to make sulfuric acid. I'd always been more interested in the symbolism of alchemy than in its practical aspects, but my afternoon with the Countess of Pembroke had shown me how intriguing the links between the two might be.

Soon we were safely inside the Hart and Crown and I was sipping a warm tisane made from mint and lemon balm. It turned out the Elizabethans did have teas, but they were all herbal. I was chattering on about Mary when I noticed Matthew's smile.

"What's so funny?"

"I haven't seen you like this before," he commented.

"Like what?"

"So animated—full of questions and reports of what you've been doing and all the plans you and Mary have for next week."

"I like being a student again," I confessed. "It was difficult at first, not to have all the answers. Over the years I've forgotten how much fun it is to have nothing but questions."

"And you feel free here, in a way that you didn't in Oxford. Secrets are a lonely business." Matthew's eyes were sympathetic as his fingers moved along my jaw.

"I was never lonely."

"Yes you were. I think you still are," he said softly.

Before I could shape a response, Matthew had me out of my seat and was backing us toward the wall by the fireplace. Pierre, who was nowhere to be seen only moments before, appeared at the threshold.

Then a knock sounded. Matthew's shoulder muscles bunched, and a dagger flashed at his thigh. When he nodded, Pierre stepped out onto the landing and flung open the door.

"We have a message from Father Hubbard." Two male vampires stood there, both dressed in expensive clothes that were beyond the reach of most messengers. Neither was more than fifteen. I'd never seen a teenage vampire and had always imagined there must be prohibitions against it.

"Master Roydon." The taller of the two vampires tugged at the tip of his nose and studied Matthew with eyes the color of indigo. Those eyes moved from Matthew to me, and my skin smarted from the cold. "Mistress." Matthew's hand tightened on his dagger, and Pierre moved to stand more squarely between us and the door.

"Father Hubbard wants to see you," the smaller vampire said, looking with contempt at the weapon in Matthew's hand. "Come when the clocks toll seven."

"Tell Hubbard I'll be there when it's convenient," said Matthew with a touch of venom.

"Not just you," the taller boy said.

"I haven't seen Kit," Matthew said with a touch of impatience. "If he's in trouble, your master has a better idea where to look for him than I do, Corner." It was an apt name for the boy. His adolescent frame was all angles and points.

"Marlowe's been with Father Hubbard all day." Corner's tone dripped with boredom.

"Has he?" Matthew said, eyes sharp.

"Yes. Father Hubbard wants the witch," Corner's companion said.

"I see." Matthew's voice went flat. There was a blur of black and silver, and his polished dagger was quivering, point first, in the doorjamb near Corner's eye. Matthew strolled in their direction. Both vampires took an involuntary step back. "Thank you for the message, Leonard." He nudged the door closed with his foot.

Pierre and Matthew exchanged a long, silent look while adolescent vampire feet racketed down the stairs.

"Hancock and Gallowglass," ordered Matthew.

"At once." Pierre whirled out of the room, narrowly avoiding Françoise. She pulled the dagger from the doorframe.

"We had visitors," Matthew explained before she could complain about the state of the woodwork.

"What is this about, Matthew?" I asked.

"You and I are going to meet an old friend." His voice remained ominously even.

I eyed the dagger, which was now lying on the table. "Is this old friend a vampire?"

"Wine, Françoise." Matthew grabbed at a few sheets of paper, disordering my carefully arranged piles. I muffled a protest as he picked up one of my quills and wrote with furious speed. He hadn't looked at me since the knock on the door.

"There is fresh blood from the butcher. Perhaps you should . . ."

Matthew looked up, his mouth compressed into a thin line. Françoise poured him a large goblet of wine without further protest. When she was finished, he handed her two letters.

"Take this to the Earl of Northumberland at Russell House. The other goes to Raleigh. He'll be at Whitehall." Françoise went immediately, and Matthew strode to the window, staring up the street. His hair was tangled in his high linen collar, and I had a sudden urge to put it to rights for him. But the set of his shoulders warned me that he wouldn't welcome such a proprietary gesture.

"Father Hubbard?" I reminded him. But Matthew's mind was elsewhere.

"You're going to get yourself killed," he said roughly, his back still turned. "Ysabeau warned me you have no instinct for self-preservation. How many times does something like this have to happen before you develop one?"

"What have I done now?"

"You wanted to be seen, Diana," he said harshly. "Well, you were."

"Stop looking out the window. I'm tired of talking to the back of your head." I spoke quietly, though I wanted to throttle him. "Who is Father Hubbard?"

"Andrew Hubbard is a vampire. He rules London."

"What do you mean, he rules London? Do all the vampires in the city obey him?" In the twenty-first century, London's vampires were renowned for their strong allegiance to the pack, their nocturnal habits, and their loyalty—or so I'd heard from other witches. Not as flamboyant as the vampires in Paris, Venice, or Istanbul, nor as bloodthirsty as those in Moscow, New York, and Beijing, London vampires were a well-organized bunch.

"Not just the vampires. Witches and daemons, too." Matthew turned on me, his eyes cold. "Andrew Hubbard is a former priest, one with a poor education and enough grasp of theology to cause trouble. He became a vampire when the plague first came to London. It had killed nearly half the city by 1349. Hubbard survived the first wave of the epidemic, caring for the sick and burying the dead, but in time he succumbed."

"And someone saved him by making him a vampire."

"Yes, though I've never been able to find out who it was. There are plenty of legends, though, most about his supposedly divine resurrection. When he was certain he was going to die, people say he dug a grave for himself in the churchyard and climbed into it to wait for God. Hours later Hubbard rose and walked out among the living." Matthew paused. "I don't believe he's been entirely sane since.

"Hubbard gathers up lost souls," Matthew continued. "There were too many to count in those days. He took them in—orphans, widows, men who had lost entire families in a single week. Those who fell ill he made into vampires, rebaptizing them and ensuring they had homes, food, and jobs. Hubbard considers them his children."

"Even the witches and daemons?"

"Yes," said Matthew tersely. "He takes them through a ritual of adoption, but it's nothing at all like the one Philippe performed. Hubbard tastes their blood. He claims it reveals the content of their souls and provides proof that God has entrusted them to his care."

"It reveals their secrets to him, too," I said slowly.

Matthew nodded. No wonder he wanted me to stay far away from this Father Hubbard. If a vampire tasted my blood, he would know about the baby—and who his father was.

"Philippe and Hubbard reached an agreement that exempted the de Clermonts from his family rituals and obligations. I probably should have told him you were my wife before we entered the city."

"But you chose not to," I said carefully, hands clenching. Now I knew why Gallowglass had requested that we dock somewhere other than at the foot of Water Lane. Philippe was right. There were times when Matthew behaved like an idiot—or the most arrogant man alive.

"Hubbard stays out of my way, and I stay out of his. As soon as he knows you're a de Clermont, he'll leave you alone, too." Matthew spotted something in the street below. "Thank God." Heavy footsteps sounded on the stairs, and a minute later Gallowglass and Hancock stood in our parlor. "It took you two long enough."

"And hello to you, Matthew," Gallowglass said. "So Hubbard's demanded an audience at last. And before you suggest it, don't even think about tweaking his nose by leaving Auntie here. Whatever the plan, she's going, too."

Uncharacteristically, Matthew ran his hand through his hair from back to front.

"Shit," Hancock said, watching the progress of Matthew's fingers. Making his hair stand up like a cockscomb was apparently another of Matthew's tells—one that meant his creative well of evasion and half-truths had run dry. "Your only plan was to avoid Hubbard. You don't have another. We've never been certain if you were a brave man or a fool, de Clermont, but I think this might decide the question—and not in your favor."

"I planned to take Diana to Hubbard on Monday."

"After she'd been in the city for ten days," Gallowglass observed.

"There was no need for haste. Diana is a de Clermont. Besides, we aren't in the city," Matthew said quickly. At my look of confusion, he continued. "The Blackfriars isn't really part of London."

"I'm not going into Hubbard's den and arguing the geography of the city with him again," Gallowglass said, slapping his gloves against his thigh. "He didn't agree when you made this argument so you could station the brotherhood in the Tower after we arrived to help the Lancastrians in 1485, and he's not going to agree to it now."

"Let's not keep him waiting," said Hancock.

"We have plenty of time." Matthew's tone was dismissive.

"You never have understood the tides, Matthew. I assume we're going by water, since you think the Thames isn't really part of the city either. If so, we may already be too late. Let's move." Gallowglass jerked his thumb in the direction of the front door.

Pierre was waiting for us there, tugging black leather over his hands. He'd swapped his usual brown cloak for a black one that was far too long to be fashionable. A silver device covered his right arm: a snake circling a cross with a crescent moon tucked into the upper quadrant. This was Philippe's crest, distinct from Matthew's only by the absence of the star and fleur-de-lis.

Once Gallowglass and Pierre were similarly outfitted, Françoise settled a matching cloak on Matthew's shoulders. Its heavy folds swept the floor, making him look taller and even more imposing. When the four of them stood together, it was an intimidating sight, one that provided a plausible inspiration for every human account of darkly cloaked vampires ever written.

At the bottom of Water Lane, Gallowglass surveyed the available vessels. "That one might hold us all," he said, pointing to a long rowboat and letting out an ear-piercing whistle. When the man standing by it asked where we were headed, the vampire embarked on a complicated set of instructions regarding our route, which of the city's many docks we were going to put in to, and who would be rowing. After Gallowglass growled at him, the poor man huddled near the lamp in the bow of his boat and looked nervously over his shoulder every now and again.

"Frightening every boatman we meet is not going to improve relations with our neighbors," I commented as Matthew boarded, looking pointedly at the brewery next door. Hancock picked me up without ceremony and handed me off to my husband. Matthew's arm tightened around me as the boat shot out into the river. Even the waterman gasped at the speed.

"There's no need to draw attention to ourselves, Gallowglass," Matthew said sharply.

"Do you want to row and I'll keep your wife warm?" When Matthew didn't reply, Gallowglass shook his head. "Thought not."

The soft glow of lamps from London Bridge penetrated the gloom ahead of us, and the crashing sound of fast-moving water became louder with each stroke that Gallowglass took. Matthew eyed the shoreline. "Put in at the Old Swan Stairs. I want to be back in this boat and headed upstream before the tide turns."

"Quiet." Hancock's whisper had a sharp edge. "We're supposed to be sneaking up on Hubbard. We might as well have proceeded down Cheapside with trumpets and banners for all the noise you're making."

Gallowglass turned back toward the stern and gave two powerful pulls with his left hand. A few more pulls put us at the landing—nothing more than a rickety set of steps, really, attached to some listing pylons—where several men waited. The boatman waved them off with a few terse words, hopping out of the boat as soon as he was able.

We climbed to street level and wended through twisting lanes in silence, darting between houses and across small gardens. The vampires moved with the stealth of cats. I moved less surely, stumbling on loose stones and stepping into waterlogged potholes. At last we turned in to a broad street. Laughter came from the far end, and light spilled into the street from wide windows. I rubbed my hands together, drawn to the warmth. Perhaps that was our destination. Perhaps this would be simple, and we could meet Andrew Hubbard, show him my wedding ring, and return home.

Matthew led us across the street instead and into a desolate churchyard whose gravestones tipped toward each other as if the dead sought comfort from one another. Pierre had a solid metal ring full of keys, and Gallowglass fitted one into the lock of the door next to the bell tower. We walked through the ramshackle nave and passed through a wooden door to the left of the altar. Narrow stone stairs plunged down into the darkness. With my limited warm-blooded sight, there was no way to keep my bearings as we twisted and turned through narrow passageways and crossed expanses that smelled of wine, must, and human decay. The experience was straight out of the tales that humans told to discourage people from lingering in church basements and graveyards.

We moved deeper into a warren of tunnels and subterranean rooms and entered a dimly lit crypt. Hollow eyes stared out from the heaped skulls in a small ossuary. A vibration in the stone floor and the muffled sound of bells indicated that somewhere above us the clocks were striking seven. Matthew hurried us along into another tunnel that showed a soft glow in the distance.

At the end we stepped into a cellar used to store wine unloaded from ships on the Thames. A few barrels stood by the walls, and the fresher scent of sawdust competed with the smell of old wine. I spied the source of the former aromas: neatly stacked coffins, arranged by size from long boxes capable of holding Gallowglass to minuscule caskets for infants. Shadows moved and flickered in the deep corners, and in the center of the room a ritual of some kind was taking place amid a throng of creatures.

"My blood is yours, Father Hubbard." The man who spoke was frightened. "I give it willingly, that you might know my heart and number me among your family." There was silence, a cry of pain. Then the air filled with a taut sense of expectation.

"I accept your gift, James, and promise to protect you as my child," a rough voice answered. "In exchange you will honor me as your father. Greet your brothers and sisters."

Amid the hubbub of welcome, my skin registered a sensation of ice.

"You're late." The rumble of sound cut through the chatter and set the hair on my neck prickling. "And traveling with a full retinue, I see."

"That's impossible, since we had no appointment." Matthew gripped my elbow as dozens of glances nudged, tingled, and chilled my skin.

Soft steps approached, circled. A tall, thin man appeared directly before me. I met his stare without flinching, knowing better than to show fear to a vampire. Hubbard's eyes were deep-set under a heavy brow bone with veins of blue, green, and brown radiating through the slate-colored iris.

The vampire's eyes were the only colorful thing about him. Otherwise he was preternaturally pale, with white-blond hair cropped close to his skull, nearly invisible eyebrows and lashes, and a wide horizontal slash of lips set in a clean-shaven face. His long black coat, which looked like a cross between a scholar's gown and a cleric's cassock, accentuated his cadaverous build. There was no mistaking the strength in his broad, slightly stooped shoulders, but the rest of him was practically skeletal.

There was a blur of motion as blunt, powerful fingers took my chin and jerked my head to the side. In the same instant, Matthew's hand wrapped around the vampire's wrist.

Hubbard's cold glance touched my neck, taking in the scar there. For once I wished Françoise had outfitted me with the largest ruff she could find. He exhaled in an icy gust smelling of cinnabar and fir before his wide mouth tightened, the edges of his lips turning from pale peach to white.

"We have a problem, Master Roydon," said Hubbard.

"We have several, Father Hubbard. The first is that you have your hands on something that belongs to me. If you don't remove them, I'll tear this den to pieces before sunrise. What happens afterward will make every creature in the city—daemon, human, *wearh,* and witch—think the end of days is upon us." Matthew's voice vibrated with fury.

Creatures emerged from the shadows. I saw John Chandler, the apothecary from Cripplegate, who met my eyes defiantly. Kit was there, too, standing next to another daemon. When his friend's arm slid through the crook in his elbow, Kit pulled away slightly.

"Hello, Kit," Matthew said, his voice dead. "I thought you would have run off and hidden by now."

Hubbard held my chin for a few moments longer, pulling my head back until I faced him once more. My anger at Kit and the witch who had betrayed us must have shown, and he shook his head in warning.

"'*Thou shalt not hate thy brother in thy heart,*'" he murmured, releasing me. Hubbard's eyes swept the room. "Leave us."

Matthew's hands cupped my face, and his fingers smoothed the skin of my chin to erase Hubbard's scent. "Go with Gallowglass. I'll see you shortly."

"She stays," Hubbard said.

Matthew's muscles twitched. He wasn't used to being countermanded. After a considerable pause, he ordered his friends and family to wait outside. Hancock was the only one not to obey immediately.

"Your father says a wise man can see more from the bottom of a well than a fool can from a mountaintop. Let's hope he's right," Hancock muttered, "because this is one hell of a hole you've put us in tonight." With one last look, he followed Gallowglass and Pierre through a break in the far wall. A heavy door closed, and there was silence.

The three of us stood so close that I could hear the next soft expulsion of air from Matthew's lungs. As for Hubbard, I wondered if the plague had done more than drive him mad. His skin was waxy rather than porcelain, as though he still suffered the lingering effect of illness.

"May I remind you, Monsieur de Clermont, you are here under my sufferance." Hubbard sat in the chamber's grand, solitary chair. "Even though you represent the Congregation, I permit your presence in London because your father demands it. But you have flouted our customs and allowed your wife to enter the city without introducing her to me and to my flock. And then there is the matter of your knights."

"Most of the knights who accompanied me have lived in this city longer than you have, Andrew. When you insisted they join your 'flock' or leave the city boundaries, they resettled outside the walls. You and my father agreed that the de Clermonts would not bring *more* of the brotherhood into the city. I haven't."

"And you think my children care about these subtleties? I saw the rings they wore and the devices on their cloaks." Hubbard leaned forward, his eyes menacing. "I was led to believe you were halfway to Scotland. Why are you still here?"

"Perhaps you don't pay your informants enough," Matthew suggested. "Kit's very short on funds these days."

"I don't buy love and loyalty, nor do I resort to intimidation and torment to have my way. Christopher willingly does what I ask, like all godly children do when they love their father."

"Kit has too many masters to be faithful to any one of them."

"Couldn't the same be said of you?" After delivering his challenge to Matthew, Hubbard turned to me and deliberately drank in my scent. He made a soft, sorrowful sound. "But let us speak of your marriage. Some of my children believe that relationships between a witch and a *wearh* are abhorrent. But the Congregation and its covenant are no more welcome in my city than are your father's vengeful knights. Both interfere with God's wish that we live as one family. Also, your wife is a time spinner," Hubbard said. "I do not approve of time spinners, for they tempt men and women with ideas that do not belong here."

"Ideas like choice and freedom of thought?" I interjected. "What are you afraid—"

"Next," Hubbard interrupted, his focus still on Matthew as though I were invisible, "there is the matter of your feeding on her." His eyes moved to the scar that Matthew had left on my neck. "When the witches discover it, they will demand an inquiry. If your wife is found guilty of willingly offering her blood to a vampire, she will be shunned and cast out of London. If you are found guilty of taking it without her consent, you will be put to death."

"So much for family sentiment," I muttered.

"Diana," Matthew warned.

Hubbard tented his fingers and studied Matthew once more. "And finally, she is breeding. Will the child's father come looking for her?"

That brought my responses to a halt. Hubbard had not yet ferreted out our biggest secret: that Matthew was the father of my child. I fought down the panic. *Think—and stay alive.* Maybe Philippe's advice would get us out of this predicament.

"No," Matthew said shortly.

"So the father is dead—from natural causes or by your hand," Hubbard said, casting a long look at Matthew. "In that case the witch's child will be brought into my flock when it is born. His mother will become one of my children now."

"No," Matthew repeated, "she will not."

"How long do you imagine the two of you will survive outside London when the rest of the Congregation hears of these offenses?" Hubbard shook his head. "Your wife will be safe here so long as she is a member of my family and there is no more sharing of blood between you."

"You will not put Diana through that perverted ceremony. Tell your 'children' that she belongs to you if you must, but you will not take her blood or that of her child."

"I will not lie to the souls in my care. Why is it, my son, that secrets and war are the only responses you have when God puts a challenge before you? They only lead to destruction." Hubbard's throat worked with emotion. "God reserves salvation for those who believe in something greater than themselves."

Before Matthew could shoot back a reply, I put my hand on his arm to quiet him.

"Excuse me, Father Hubbard," I said. "If I understand correctly, the de Clermonts are exempt from your governance?"

"That is correct, Mistress Roydon. But *you* are not a de Clermont. You are merely married to one."

"Wrong," I retorted, keeping my husband's sleeve in a tight grip. "I am Philippe de Clermont's blood-sworn daughter, as well as Matthew's wife. I'm a de Clermont twice over, and neither I nor my child will ever call you father."

Andrew Hubbard looked stunned. As I heaped silent blessings on Philippe for always staying three steps ahead of the rest of us, Matthew's shoulders finally relaxed. Though far away in France, his father had ensured our safety once more.

"Check if you like. Philippe marked my forehead here," I said, touching the spot between my brows where my witch's third eye was located. It was slumbering at the moment, unconcerned with vampires.

"I believe you, Mistress Roydon," Hubbard said finally. "No one would have the temerity to lie about such a thing in a house of God."

"Perhaps you can help me, then. I'm in London to seek help with some finer points of magic and witchcraft. Who among your children would you recommend for the task?" My request erased Matthew's grin.

"Diana," he growled.

"My father would be very pleased if you could assist me," I said, calmly ignoring him.

"And what form would this pleasure take?" Andrew Hubbard was a Renaissance prince, too, and interested in gaining whatever strategic advantage he could.

"First, my father would be pleased to hear about our quiet hours at home on the eve of the New Year," I said, meeting his eyes. "Everything else I tell him in my next letter will depend on the witch you send to the Hart and Crown."

Hubbard considered my request. "I will discuss your needs with my children and decide who might best serve you."

"Whoever he sends will be a spy," Matthew warned.

"You're a spy, too," I pointed out. "I'm tired. I want to go home."

"Our business here is done, Hubbard. I trust that Diana, like all de Clermonts, is in London with your approval." Matthew turned to leave without waiting for an answer.

"Even de Clermonts must be careful in the city," Hubbard called after us. "See that you remember it, Mistress Roydon."

Matthew and Gallowglass spoke in low voices on our row home, but I was silent. I refused help getting out of the boat and began the climb up Water Lane without waiting for them. Even so, Pierre was ahead of me by the time I reached the passage into the Hart and Crown, and Matthew was at my elbow. Inside, Walter and Henry were waiting for us. They shot to their feet.

"Thank God," Walter said.

"We came as soon as we heard that you were in need. George is sick abed, and neither Kit nor Tom could be found," Henry explained, eyes darting anxiously between me and Matthew.

"I'm sorry to have called you. My alarm was premature," Matthew said, his cloak swirling around his feet as he took it from his shoulders.

"If it concerns the order—" Walter began, eyeing the cloak.

"It doesn't," Matthew assured him.

"It concerns *me,*" I said. "And before you come up with some other disastrous scheme, understand this: The witches are my concern. Matthew is being watched, and not just by Andrew Hubbard."

"He's used to it," Gallowglass said gruffly. "Pay the gawpers no mind, Auntie."

"I need to find my own teacher, Matthew," I said. My hand fluttered down to where the point of my bodice covered the top of my belly. "No witch is going to part with her secrets so long as any of you are involved. Everyone who enters this house is either a *wearh,* a philosopher, or a spy. Which means, in the eyes of my people, that any one of you could turn us in to the authorities. Berwick may seem far away, but the panic is spreading."

Matthew's gaze was frosty, but at least he was listening.

"If you order a witch here, one will come. Matthew Roydon always gets his way. But instead of help, I'll get another performance like the one Widow Beaton gave. That's not what I need."

"You need Hubbard's help even less," Hancock said sourly.

"We don't have much time," I reminded Matthew. Hubbard didn't know that the baby was Matthew's, and Hancock and Gallowglass hadn't perceived the changes to my scent—yet. But this evening's events had driven home our precarious position.

"All right, Diana. We'll leave the witches to you. But no lies," Matthew said, "and no secrets either. One of the people in this room has to know where you are at all times."

"Matthew, you cannot—" Walter protested.

"I trust my wife's judgment," Matthew said firmly.

"That's what Philippe says about Granny," Gallowglass muttered under his breath. "Just before all hell breaks loose."

"If this is what hell looks like," Matthew murmured the week after our encounter with Hubbard, "Gallowglass is going to be sadly disappointed."

There was, in truth, very little fire and brimstone about the fourteen-year-old witch standing before us in the parlor.

"Hush," I said, mindful of how sensitive a child that age could be. "Did Father Hubbard explain why you are here, Annie?"

"Yes, mistress," Annie replied miserably. It was difficult to tell if the girl's pallor was due to her natural coloring or some combination of fear and poor nutrition. "I'm to serve you and accompany you about the city on your business."

"No, that wasn't our agreement," Matthew said impatiently, his booted feet landing heavily on the wooden floor. Annie flinched. "Do you have any power or knowledge to speak of, or is Hubbard playing some joke?"

"I have a little skill," Annie stammered, her pale blue eyes contrasting with her white skin. "But I need a place, and Father Hubbard said—"

"Oh, I can imagine what Father Hubbard said," Matthew snorted contemptuously. The look I gave him held sufficient warning that he blinked and was quiet.

"Allow her a chance to explain," I told him sharply before giving the girl an encouraging smile. "Go on, Annie."

"As well as serving you, Father Hubbard said I'm to take you to my aunt when she returns to London. She is at a lying-in at present and refused to leave while the woman still had need of her."

"Your aunt is a midwife as well as a witch?" I asked gently.

"Yes, mistress. A fine midwife and a powerful witch," Annie said proudly, straightening her spine. When she did so, her too-short skirts exposed her skinny ankles to the cold. Andrew Hubbard outfitted his sons in warm, well-fitting clothes, but his daughters received no such consideration. I smothered my irritation. Françoise would have to get her needles out.

"And how did you come to be part of Father Hubbard's family?"

"My mother was not a virtuous woman," Annie murmured, twisting her hands in her thin cloak. "Father Hubbard found me in the undercroft of St. Anne's Church near Aldersgate, my mother dead beside me. My aunt was newly married and soon had babes of her own. I was six years old. Her husband did not want me raised among his sons for fear I would corrupt them with my sinfulness."

So Annie, now a teenager, had been with Hubbard for more than half her life. The thought was chilling, and the idea that a six-year-old could corrupt anyone was beyond comprehension, but this story explained both her abject look and the girl's peculiar name: Annie Undercroft.

"While Françoise gets you something to eat, I can show you where you will sleep." I'd been up to the third floor that morning to inspect the small bed, three-legged stool, and worn chest set aside to hold the witch's belongings. "I'll help carry your things."

"Mistress?" Annie said, confused.

"She brought nothing," Françoise said, casting disapproving looks at the newest member of the household.

"Never mind. She'll have belongings soon enough." I smiled at Annie, who looked uncertain.

Françoise and I spent the weekend making sure that Annie was clean as a whistle, clothed and shod properly, and that she knew enough basic math to make small purchases for me. To test her I sent her to the nearby apothecary for a penny's worth of quill pens and half a pound of sealing wax (Philippe was right: Matthew went through office supplies at an alarming pace), and she came back promptly with change to spare.

"He wanted a shilling!" Annie complained. "That wax isn't even good for candles, is it?"

Pierre took a shine to the girl and made it his business to elicit a rare, sweet smile from Annie whenever he could. He taught her how to play cat's cradle and volunteered to walk with her on Sunday when Matthew dropped broad hints that he would like us to be alone for a few hours.

"He won't . . . take advantage of her?" I asked Matthew as he unbuttoned my favorite item of clothing: a sleeveless boy's jerkin made of fine black wool. I wore it with a set of skirts and a smock when we were at home.

"Pierre? Good Christ no." Matthew looked amused.

"It's a fair question." Mary Sidney had not been much older when she was married off to the highest bidder.

"And I gave you a truthful answer. Pierre doesn't bed young girls." His hands stilled after he freed the last button. "This is a pleasant surprise. You're not wearing a corset."

"It's uncomfortable, and I'm blaming it on the baby."

He lifted the jerkin away from my body with an appreciative sound.

"And he'll keep other men from bothering her?"

"Can this conversation possibly wait until later?" Matthew said, his exasperation showing. "Given the cold, they won't be gone for long."

"You're very impatient in the bedroom," I observed, sliding my hands into the neck of his shirt.

"Really?" Matthew arched his aristocratic brows in mock disbelief. "And here I thought the problem was my admirable restraint."

He spent the next few hours showing me just how limitless his patience could be in an empty house on a Sunday. By the time everybody returned, we were both pleasantly exhausted and in a considerably better frame of mind.

Everything returned to normal on Monday, however. Matthew was distracted and irritable as soon as the first letters arrived at dawn, and he sent his apologies to the Countess of Pembroke when it became clear that the obligations of his many jobs wouldn't allow him to accompany me to our midday meal.

Mary listened without surprise as I explained the reason for Matthew's absence, blinked at Annie like a mildly curious owl, and sent her off to the kitchens in the care of Joan. We shared a delicious lunch, during which Mary offered detailed accounts of the private lives of everyone within shouting distance of the Blackfriars. Afterward, we withdrew to her laboratory with Joan and Annie to assist us.

"And how is your husband, Diana?" the countess asked, rolling up her sleeves, her eyes fixed on the book before her.

"In good health," I said. This, I had learned, was the Elizabethan equivalent of "Fine."

"That is welcome news." Mary turned and stirred something that looked noxious and smelled worse. "Much depends on it, I fear. The queen relies on him more than on any other man in the kingdom except Lord Burghley."

"I wish his good humor was more reliable. Matthew is mercurial these days. He's possessive one moment and ignores me as if I were a piece of furniture the next."

"Men treat their property that way." She picked up a jug of water.

"I am not his property," I said flatly.

"What you and I know, what the law says, and how Matthew himself feels are three entirely separate issues."

"They shouldn't be," I said quickly, ready to argue the point. Mary silenced me with a gentle, resigned smile.

"You and I have an easier time with our husbands than other women do, Diana. We have our books and the leisure to indulge our passions, thank God. Most do not." Mary gave everything in her beaker a final stir and decanted the contents into another glass vessel.

I thought of Annie: a mother who'd died alone in a church cellar, an aunt who couldn't take her in because of her husband's prejudices, a life that promised little in the way of comfort or hope. "Do you teach your female servants how to read?"

"Certainly," Mary responded promptly. "They learn to write and reckon, too. Such skills will make them more valuable to a good husband—one who likes to earn money as well as spend it." She beckoned to Joan, who helped her move the fragile glass bubble full of chemicals to the fire.

"Then Annie shall learn as well," I said, giving the girl a nod. She clung to the shadows, looking ghostly with her pale face and silver-blond hair. Education would increase her confidence. She'd had a definite lilt in her step ever since haggling with Monsieur de Laune over the price of sealing wax.

"She will have reason in future to thank you for it," said Mary. Her face was serious. "We women own nothing absolutely, save what lies between our ears. Our virtue belongs first to our father and then to our husband. We dedicate our duty to our family. As soon as we share our thoughts with another, put pen to paper or thread a needle, all that we do and make belongs to someone else. So long as she has words and ideas, Annie will always possess something that is hers alone."

"If only you were a man, Mary," I said with a shake of my head. The Countess of Pembroke could run rings around most creatures, regardless of their sex.

"Were I a man, I would be on my estates now, or paying court to Her Majesty like Henry, or seeing to matters of state like Matthew. Instead I am here in my laboratory with you. Weighing it all in the balance, I believe we are the better off—even if we are sometimes put on a pedestal or mistaken for a kitchen stool." Mary's round eyes twinkled.

I laughed. "You may be right."

"Had you ever been to court, you would have no doubts on this score. Come," Mary said, turning to her experiment. "Now we wait while the *prima materia* is exposed to the heat. If we have done well, this is what will generate the philosopher's stone. Let us review the next steps of the process in hopes that the experiment will succeed."

I always lost track of time while there were alchemical manuscripts around, and I looked up, dazed, when Matthew and Henry walked in to the laboratory. Mary and I had been deep in conversation about the images in a collection of alchemical texts known as the *Pretiosa Margarita Novella*—the *New Pearl of Great Price.* Was it already late afternoon?

"It can't be time to go. Not yet," I protested. "Mary has this manuscript—"

"Matthew knows the book, for his brother gave it to me. Now that Matthew has a learned wife, he may regret having done so," Mary said with a laugh. "There are refreshments waiting in the solar. I had hoped to see you both today." At this, Henry gave Mary a conspiratorial wink.

"That is kind, Mary," Matthew said, kissing me on the cheek in greeting. "Apparently you two haven't reached the vinegar stage yet. You still smell of vitriol and magnesia."

I put down the book reluctantly and washed while Mary finished making notes of the day's work. Once we were settled in the solar, Henry could no longer curb his excitement.

"Is it time now, Mary?" he asked the countess, shifting in his chair.

"You have the same enthusiasm for giving presents as young William does," she replied with a laugh. "Henry and I have a gift in honor of the New Year and your marriage."

But we had nothing to give them in return. I looked at Matthew, uncomfortable with this one-way exchange.

"I wish you luck, Diana, if you hope to stay ahead of Mary and Henry when it comes to gifts," he said ruefully.

"Nonsense," Mary replied. "Matthew saved my brother Philip's life and Henry's estates. No gifts can repay such debts. Do not ruin our pleasure with such talk. It is a tradition to give gifts to those newly wed, and it is New Year. What did you give the queen, Matthew?"

"After she sent poor King James another clock to remind him to bide his time quietly, I considered giving her a crystal hourglass. I thought it might be a useful reminder of her relative mortality," he said drily.

Henry looked at him with horror. "No. Not really."

"It was an idle thought in a moment of frustration," Matthew reassured him. "I gave her a covered cup, of course, like everyone else."

"Don't forget our gift, Henry," said Mary, now equally impatient.

Henry drew out a velvet pouch and presented it to me. I fumbled with the strings and finally drew out a heavy gold locket on an equally weighty chain. Its face was golden filigree studded with rubies and diamonds, Matthew's moon and star in its center. I flipped the locket over, gasping at the brilliant enamelwork with its flowers and scrolling vines. Carefully I opened the clasp at the bottom, and a miniature rendering of Matthew looked up at me.

"Master Hilliard made the preliminary sketches when he was here. With the holidays he was so busy that his assistant, Isaac, had to help with the painting," Mary explained.

I cupped the miniature in my hand, tilting it this way and that. Matthew was painted as he looked at home when he was working late at night in his study off the bedroom. His shirt open at the neck and trimmed with lace, he met the viewer's gaze with a lift of his right eyebrow in a familiar combination of seriousness and mocking humor. Black hair was swept back from his forehead in its typically disordered fashion, and the long fingers of his left hand held a locket. It was a surprisingly frank and erotic image for the time.

"Is it to your liking?" Henry asked.

"I love it," I said, unable to stop staring at my new treasure.

"Isaac is rather more . . . daring in his composition than his master is, but when I told him it was a wedding gift, he convinced me that such a locket would remain a wife's special secret and could reveal the private man rather than the public." Mary looked over my shoulder. "It is a good likeness, but I do wish Master Hilliard would learn how to better capture a person's chin."

"It's perfect, and I will treasure it always."

"This one is for you," Henry said, handing Matthew an identical bag. "Hilliard felt you might show it to others and wear it at court, so it is somewhat more . . . er, circumspect."

"Is that the locket Matthew is holding in my miniature?" I said, pointing to the distinctive milky stone set in a simple gold frame.

"I believe so," Matthew said softly. "Is it a moonstone, Henry?"

"An ancient specimen," Henry said proudly. "It was among my curiosities, and I wanted you to have it. The intaglio is of the goddess Diana, you see."

The miniature within was more respectable, but startling nonetheless in its informality. I was wearing the russet gown trimmed with black velvet. A delicate ruff framed my face without covering the shining pearls at my throat. But it was the arrangement of my hair that signaled that this was an intimate gift appropriate for a new husband. It flowed freely over my shoulders and down my back in a wild riot of red-gold curls.

"The blue background emphasizes Diana's eyes. And the set of her mouth is so true to life." Matthew, too, was overwhelmed by the gift.

"I had a frame made," Mary said, gesturing at Joan, "to display them when they are not being worn." It was more a shallow box, with two oval niches lined in black velvet. The two miniatures fit perfectly inside and gave the effect of a pair of portraits.

"It was thoughtful of Mary and Henry to give us such a gift," Matthew said later, when we were back at the Hart and Crown. He slid his arms around me from behind and laced his hands over my belly. "I haven't even had time to take your picture. I never imagined my first likeness of you would be by Nicholas Hilliard."

"The portraits are beautiful," I said, covering his hands with mine.

"But . . . ?" Matthew drew back and tilted his head.

"Miniatures by Nicholas Hilliard are sought after, Matthew. These won't disappear when we do. And they're so exquisite I couldn't bear to destroy them before we go." Time was like my ruff: It started out as a smooth, flat, tightly woven fabric. Then it was twisted and cut and made to double back on itself. "We keep touching the past in ways that are bound to leave smudges on the present."

"Maybe that's what we're supposed to be doing," Matthew suggested. "Perhaps the future depends on it."

"I don't see how."

"Not now. But it is possible that we'll look back one day and discover that it was the miniatures that made all the difference." He smiled.

"Imagine what finding Ashmole 782 would do, then." I looked up at him. Seeing Mary's illuminated alchemical books had brought the mysterious volume and our frustrated search for it vividly back to mind. "George had no luck finding it in Oxford, but it must be somewhere in England. Ashmole acquired our manuscript from somebody. Rather than looking for the manuscript, we should look for the person who sold it to him."

"These days there's a steady traffic in manuscripts. Ashmole 782 could be anywhere."

"Or it could be right here," I insisted.

"You may be right," Matthew agreed. But I could tell that his mind was on more immediate concerns than our elusive tome. "I'll send George out to make inquiries among the booksellers."

All thoughts of Ashmole 782 fled the next morning, however, when a note arrived from Annie's aunt, the prosperous midwife. She was back in London.

"The witch will not come to the house of a notorious *wearh* and spy," Matthew reported after he had read its contents. "Her husband objects to the plan, for fear it will ruin his reputation. We are to go to her house near St. James's Church on Garlic Hill." When I didn't react, Matthew scowled and continued. "It's on the other side of town, within spitting distance of Andrew Hubbard's den."

"You are a vampire," I reminded him. "She is a witch. We aren't supposed to mix. This witch's husband is right to be cautious."

Matthew insisted on accompanying Annie and me across town anyway. The area surrounding St. James's Church was far more prosperous than the Blackfriars, with spacious, well-kept streets, large houses, busy shops, and a tidy churchyard. Annie led us into an alley across from the church. Though dark, it was as neat as a pin.

"There, Master Roydon," the girl said. She directed Matthew's attention to the sign with a windmill on it before darting ahead with Pierre to alert the household to our arrival.

"You don't have to stay," I told Matthew. This visit was nerve-racking enough without him hovering and glowering.

"I'm not going anywhere," he replied grimly.

We were met at the door by a round-faced woman with a snub nose, a gentle chin, and rich brown hair and eyes. Her face was serene, although her eyes snapped with irritation. She had stopped Pierre in his tracks. Only Annie had been admitted to the house and stood to one side in the doorway looking dismayed at the impasse.

I also stopped in my tracks, my mouth open in surprise. Annie's aunt was the spitting image of Sophie Norman, the young daemon to whom we'd waved good-bye at the Bishop house in Madison.

"Dieu," Matthew murmured, looking down at me in amazement.

"My aunt, Susanna Norman," Annie whispered. Our reaction had unsettled her. "She says—"

"Susanna *Norman*?" I asked, unable to take my eyes from her face. Her name and strong resemblance to Sophie couldn't be a coincidence.

"As my niece said. You appear to be out of your element, Mistress Roydon," Mistress Norman said. "And you are not welcome here, *wearh*."

"Mistress Norman," Matthew said with a bow.

"Did you not get my letter? My husband wants nothing to do with you." Two boys shot out of the door. "Jeffrey! John!"

"Is this him?" the elder said. He studied Matthew with interest, then turned his attention on me. The child had power. Though he was still on the brink of adolescence, his abilities could already be felt in the crackle of undisciplined magic that surrounded him.

"Use the talents God gave you, Jeffrey, and don't ask idle questions." The witch looked at me appraisingly. "You certainly made Father Hubbard sit up and take notice. Very well, come inside." When we moved to do so, Susanna held up her hand. "Not you, *wearh*. My business is with your wife. The Golden Gosling has decent wine, if you are determined to remain nearby. But it would be better for all concerned if you were to let your man see Mistress Roydon home."

"Thank you for the advice, mistress. I'm sure I'll find something satisfactory at the inn. Pierre will wait in the courtyard. He doesn't mind the cold." Matthew gave her a wolfish smile.

Susanna looked sour and turned smartly. "Come along, Jeffrey," she called over her shoulder. Jeffrey commandeered his younger brother, cast one more interested glance at Matthew, and followed. "When you are ready, Mistress Roydon."

"I can't believe it," I whispered as soon as the Normans were out of sight. "She has to be Sophie's great-grandmother many times over."

"Sophie must be descended through either Jeffrey or John." Matthew pulled thoughtfully on his chin. "One of those boys is the missing link in our chain of circumstances that leads from Kit and the silver chess piece to the Norman family and on to North Carolina."

"The future really is taking care of itself," I said.

"I thought it would. As for the present, Pierre will be right here and I'll be close by." The fine lines around his eyes deepened. He didn't want to be more than six inches away from me at the best of times.

"I'm not sure how long this will take," I said, squeezing his arm.

"It doesn't matter," Matthew assured me, brushing my lips with his. "Stay as long as you need."

Inside, Annie hastily took my cloak and returned to the fire, where she had been stooped over something on the hearth.

"Have a care, Annie," Susanna said, sounding harassed. Annie was carefully lifting a shallow saucepan from a metal stand set over the embers of the fire. "Widow Hackett's daughter requires that draft to help her sleep, and the ingredients are costly."

"I can't figure her out, Mama," Jeffrey said, looking at me. His eyes were disconcertingly wise for one so young.

"Nor I, Jeffrey, nor I. But that's probably why she's here. Take your brother into the other room. And be quiet. Your father is sleeping, and he needs to remain so."

"Yes, Mama." Jeffrey scooped up two wooden soldiers and a ship from the table. "This time I'll let you be Walter Raleigh so you can win the battle," he promised his brother.

Susanna and Annie stared at me in the silence that followed. Annie's faint pulses of power were already familiar. But I was not prepared for the steady current of inquiry that Susanna turned my way. My third eye opened. Finally someone had roused my witch's curiosity.

"That's uncomfortable," I said, turning my head to break the intensity of Susanna's gaze.

"It should be," she said calmly. "Why do you require my help, mistress?"

"I was spellbound. It's not what you think," I said when Annie took an immediate step away from me. "Both of my parents were witches, but neither one understood the nature of my talents. They didn't want me to come to any harm, so they bound me. The bindings have loosened, however, and strange things are happening."

"Such as?" Susanna said, pointing Annie to a chair.

"I've summoned witchwater a few times, though not recently. Sometimes I see colors surrounding people, but not always. And I touched a quince and it shriveled." I was careful not to mention my more spectacular outbreaks of magic. Nor did I mention the odd threads of blue and amber in the corners or the way handwriting had started to escape from Matthew's books and reptiles flee from Mary Sidney's shoes.

"Was your mother or father a waterwitch?" Susanna asked, trying to make sense of my story.

"I don't know," I said honestly. "They died when I was young."

"Perhaps you are better suited to the craft, then. Though many wish to possess the rough magics of water and fire, they are not easy to come by," said Susanna with a touch of pity. My Aunt Sarah thought witches who relied on elemental magic were dilettantes. Susanna, on the other hand, was inclined to see spells as a lesser form of magical knowledge. I smothered a sigh at these bizarre prejudices. Weren't we all witches?

"My aunt was not able to teach me many spells. Sometimes I can light a candle. I have been able to call objects to me."

"But you are a grown woman!" Susanna said, her hands settling on her hips. "Even Annie has more skills than that, and she is but fourteen. Can you concoct philters from plants?"

"No." Sarah had wanted me to learn how to make potions, but I had declined.

"Are you a healer?"

"No." I was beginning to understand Annie's browbeaten expression.

Susanna sighed. "Why Andrew Hubbard requires my assistance, I do not know. I have quite enough to do with my patients, an infirm husband, and two growing sons." She took a chipped bowl from the shelf and a brown egg from a rack by the window. She placed both on the table before me and pulled out a chair. "Sit, and tuck your hands beneath your legs."

Mystified, I did as she requested.

"Annie and I are going to Widow Hackett's house. While we're gone, you are to get the contents of that egg into the bowl without using your hands. It requires two spells: a motion spell and a simple opening charm. My son John is eight, and he can already do it without thinking."

"But—"

"If the egg isn't in the bowl when I return, no one can help you, Mistress Roydon. Your parents may have been right to bind you if your power is so weak that you cannot even crack an egg."

Annie gave me an apologetic look as she lifted the pan into her arms. Susanna clapped a lid on it. "Come, Annie."

Sitting alone in the Normans' gathering room, I considered the egg and the bowl.

"What a nightmare," I whispered, hoping the boys were too far away to hear.

I took a deep breath and gathered my energy. I knew the words to both spells, and I wanted the egg to move—wanted it badly. Magic was nothing more than desire made real, I reminded myself.

I focused my desires on the egg. It hopped on the table, once, then subsided. Silently I repeated the spell. And again. And again.

Minutes later the only result of my efforts was a thin skim of perspiration on my forehead. All I had to do was lift the egg and crack it. And I had failed.

"Sorry," I murmured to my flat stomach. "With any luck you'll take after your father." My stomach flopped over. Nerves and rapidly changing hormones were hell on the digestion.

Did chickens get morning sickness? I tilted my head and looked at the egg. Some poor hen had been robbed of her unhatched chick to feed the Norman family. My nausea increased. Perhaps I should consider vegetarianism, at least during the pregnancy.

But maybe there was no chick at all, I comforted myself. Not every egg was fertilized. My third eye peered under the surface of the shell, through the thickening layers of albumen to the yolk. Traces of life ran in thin streaks of red across the yolk's surface.

"Fertile," I said with a sigh. I shifted on my hands. Em and Sarah had kept hens for a while. It took a hen only three weeks to hatch an egg. Three weeks of warmth and care, and there was a baby chicken. It didn't seem fair that I had to wait months before our child saw the light of day.

Care and warmth. Such simple things, yet they ensured life. What had Matthew said? *All that children need is love, a grown-up to take responsibility for them, and a soft place to land.* The same was true for chicks. I imagined what it would feel like to be surrounded in a mother hen's feathery warmth, safely cocooned from bumps and bruises. Would our child feel like that, floating in the depths of my womb? If not, was there a spell for it? One woven from responsibility, that would wrap the baby in care and warmth and love yet be gentle enough to give him both safety and freedom?

"That's my real desire," I whispered.

Peep.

I looked around. Many households had a few chickens pecking around the hearth.

Peep. It was coming from the egg on the table. There was a crack, then a beak. A bewildered set of black eyes blinked at me from a feathered head slicked down with moisture.

Someone behind me gasped. I turned. Annie's hand was clapped over her mouth, and she was staring at the chick on the table.

"Aunt Susanna," Annie said, dropping her hand. "Is that . . . ?" She trailed off and pointed wordlessly at me.

"Yes. That's the *glaem* left over from Mistress Roydon's new spell. Go. Fetch Goody Alsop." Susanna spun her niece around and sent her back the way she came.

"I didn't get the egg into the bowl, Mistress Norman," I apologized. "The spells didn't work."

The still-wet chick set up a protest, one indignant *peep* after another.

"Didn't work? I am beginning to think you know nothing about being a witch," said Susanna incredulously.

I was beginning to think she was right.

Phoebe found the quiet at Sotheby's Bond Street offices unsettling this Tuesday night. Though she'd been working at the London auction house for two weeks, she was still not accustomed to the building. Every sound—the buzzing of the overhead lights, the security guard pulling on the doors to make sure they were locked, the distant sound of recorded laughter on a television—made her jump.

As the junior person in the department, it had fallen on Phoebe to wait behind a locked door for Dr. Whitmore to arrive. Sylvia, her supervisor, had been adamant that someone needed to see the man after hours. Phoebe suspected that this request was highly irregular but was too new in the job to make more than a weak protest.

"Of course you will stay. He'll be here by seven o'clock," Sylvia had said smoothly, fingering her strand of pearls before picking up her ballet tickets from the desk. "Besides, you don't have anywhere else to be, do you?"

Sylvia was right. Phoebe had nowhere else to be.

"But who is he?" Phoebe asked. It was a perfectly legitimate question, but Sylvia had looked affronted.

"He's from Oxford and an important client of this firm. That's all you need to know," Sylvia replied. "Sotheby's values confidentiality, or did you miss that part of your training?"

And so Phoebe was still at her desk. She waited well beyond the promised hour of seven. To pass the time, she went through the files to find out more about the man. She didn't like meeting people without knowing as much about their background as possible. Sylvia might think all she needed was his name and a vague sense of his credentials, but Phoebe knew different. Her mother had taught her what a valuable weapon such personal information could be when wielded against guests at cocktail parties and formal dinners. Phoebe hadn't been able to find any Whitmores in the Sotheby archives, however, and his customer number led to a simple card in a locked file cabinet that said *"de Clermont Family—inquire with the president."*

At five minutes to nine, she heard someone outside the door. The man's voice was gruff yet strangely musical.

"This is the third wild-goose chase you've sent me on in as many days, Ysabeau. Please try to remember that I have things to do. Send Alain next time. There was a brief pause. "You think I'm not busy? I'll call you after I see them." The man made a muffled oath. "Tell your intuition to take a break, for God's sake."

The man sounded strange: half American and half British, with blurred edges to his accent suggesting that these weren't the only languages he knew. Phoebe's father had been in the queen's diplomatic service, and his voice was similarly ambiguous, as though he hailed from everywhere and nowhere.

The bell rang, another shrill sound that made her flinch, despite the fact that Phoebe was expecting it. She pushed away from her desk and strode across the room. She was wearing her black heels, which had cost a fortune but made her look taller and, Phoebe told herself, more authoritative. It was a trick she'd learned from Sylvia at her first interview, when she had worn flats. Afterward she'd vowed never to appear "adorably petite" again.

She looked through the peephole to see a smooth forehead, scruffy blond hair, and a pair of brilliant blue eyes. Surely this wasn't Dr. Whitmore.

A sudden rap on the door startled her. Whoever this man was, he had no manners. Irritated, Phoebe punched the button on the intercom. "Yes?" she said impatiently.

"Marcus Whitmore here to see Ms. Thorpe."

Phoebe looked through the peephole once more. Impossible. No one this young would warrant Sylvia's attention. "Might I see some identification?" she said crisply.

"Where is Sylvia?" The blue eyes narrowed.

"At the ballet. *Coppélia,* I believe." Sylvia's tickets were the best in the house, the extravagance claimed as a business expense. The man on the other side of the door slapped an identification card flat against the peephole. Phoebe reared back. "If you would be so kind as to step away? I can't see anything at that distance." The card moved a few inches from the door.

"Really, Miss . . . ?"

"Taylor."

"Miss Taylor, I am in a hurry." The card disappeared, replaced by those twin blue beacons. Phoebe drew back again in surprise, but not before she'd made out the name on the card and his affiliation with a scientific research project in Oxford.

It was Dr. Whitmore. What business did a scientist have with Sotheby's? Phoebe pushed the release for the door.

As soon as the click sounded, Whitmore pushed his way through. He was dressed for a club in Soho, with his black jeans, vintage gray U2 T-shirt, and a ridiculous pair of high-top Converse trainers (also gray). A leather cord circled his neck, and a handful of ornaments of dubious provenance and little worth hung down from it. Phoebe straightened the hem of her impeccably clean white blouse and looked at him with annoyance.

"Thank you," Whitmore said, standing far closer to her than was normal in polite society. "Sylvia left a package for me."

"If you would be seated, Dr. Whitmore." She gestured to the chair in front of her desk.

Whitmore's blue eyes moved from the chair to her. "Must I? This won't take long. I'm only here to confirm that my grandmother isn't seeing zebras where there are only horses."

"Excuse me?" Phoebe inched toward her desk. There was a security alarm under the desk's surface, next to the drawer. If the man continued to misbehave, she would use it.

"The package." Whitmore kept his gaze directed at her. There was a spark of interest there. Phoebe recognized it and crossed her arms in an effort to deflect it. He pointed to the padded box on the desk without looking at it. "I'm guessing that's it."

"Please sit down, Dr. Whitmore. It's long past closing time, I'm tired, and there is paperwork to be filled out before I can let you examine whatever it is that Sylvia set aside." Phoebe reached up and rubbed at the back of her neck. It was cricked from looking up at him. Whitmore's nostrils flared, and his eyelids drifted down. Phoebe noticed that his eyelashes were darker than his blond hair, and longer and thicker than hers. Any woman would kill for lashes like those.

"I really think you had better give me the box and let me be on my way, Miss Taylor." The gruff voice smoothed out, deepened into a warning, though Phoebe couldn't understand why. What was he going to do, steal the box? Again she considered sounding the alarm but thought better of it. Sylvia would be furious if she offended a client by calling the guards.

Instead Phoebe stepped to the desk, picked up a paper and a pen, and returned to thrust them at the visitor. "Fine. I'm happy to do this standing up if you prefer, Dr. Whitmore, though it's a great deal less comfortable."

"That's the best offer I've had in some time." Whitmore's mouth twitched. "If we're going to proceed according to Hoyle, though, I think you should call me Marcus."

"Hoyle?" Phoebe flushed and drew herself up to her full height. Whitmore wasn't taking her seriously. "I don't think he works here."

"I certainly hope not." He scrawled a signature. "Edmond Hoyle's been dead since 1769."

"I'm fairly new at Sotheby's. You'll have to forgive me for not understanding the reference." Phoebe sniffed. Once again she was too far from the hidden button underneath her desk to use it. Whitmore might not be a thief, but she was beginning to think he was mad.

"Here's your pen," Marcus said politely, "and your form. See?" He leaned closer. "I did exactly what you asked me to. I'm really very well behaved. My father made sure of it."

Phoebe took the pen and paper from him. As she did, her fingers brushed against the back of Whitmore's hand. Its coldness made her shiver. There was a heavy gold signet on his pinkie finger, she noticed. It looked medieval, but no one walked around London with such a rare and valuable ring on his finger. It must be a fake—though a good one.

She inspected the form as she returned to the desk. It all seemed to be in order, and if this man turned out to be some kind of criminal—which wouldn't surprise her a bit—at least she wouldn't be guilty of breaking the rules. Phoebe lifted the lid of the box, prepared to surrender it to the odd Dr. Whitmore for his examination. She hoped that then she could go home.

"Oh." Her voice caught in surprise. She'd expected to see a fabulous diamond necklace or a Victorian set of emeralds in fussy gold filigree—something her own grandmother would like.

Instead the box contained two oval miniatures, set into niches that had been formed to adhere perfectly to their edges and protect them from damage. One was of a woman with long golden hair tinged with red. An open-necked ruff framed her heart-shaped face. Her pale eyes looked out at the viewer with calm assurance, and her mouth curved in a gentle smile. The background was the vivid blue common to the work of the Elizabethan limner Nicholas Hilliard. The other miniature depicted a man with a shock of black hair brushed back from his forehead. A straggling beard and mustache made him look younger than his black eyes suggested, and his white linen shirt was also open at the neck, showing flesh that was milkier than the cloth. Long fingers held a jewel suspended from a thick chain. Behind the man, golden flames burned and twisted, a symbol of passion.

A soft breath tickled her ear. "Holy Christ." Whitmore looked like he'd seen a ghost.

"They're beautiful, aren't they? This must be the set of miniatures that just arrived. An old couple in Shropshire found them hidden in the back of their silver chest when they were looking for a place to store some new pieces. Sylvia reckons they'll fetch a good price."

"Oh, there's no doubt about that." Marcus pushed a button on his phone.

"Oui?" said an imperious French voice at the other end of the line. This was the problem with cell phones, Phoebe thought. Everybody shouted on them, and you could hear private conversations.

"You were right about the miniatures, *Grand-mère.*"

A self-satisfied sound drifted out of the phone. "Do I have your complete attention now, Marcus?"

"No. And thank God for it. My complete attention isn't good for anybody." Whitmore eyed Phoebe and smiled. The man was charming, Phoebe reluctantly admitted. "But give me a few days before you send me on another errand. Just how much are you willing to pay for them, or shouldn't I ask?"

"N'importe quel prix."

The price doesn't matter. These were words that made auction houses happy. Phoebe stared down at the miniatures. They really were extraordinary.

Whitmore and his grandmother concluded their conversation, and the man's fingers immediately flew across his phone, transmitting another message.

"Hilliard believed that his portrait miniatures were best viewed in private," Phoebe mused aloud. "He felt that the art of limning put too many of his subjects' secrets on display. You can see why. These two look like they kept all kinds of secrets."

"You're right there," Marcus murmured. His face was very close, giving Phoebe an opportunity to examine his eyes more closely. They were bluer than she had first realized, bluer even than the azurite- and ultramarine-enriched pigments Hilliard used.

The phone rang. When Phoebe reached to answer it, she thought his hand drifted down, just for a moment, to her waist.

"Give the man his miniatures, Phoebe." It was Sylvia.

"I don't understand," she said numbly. "I'm not authorized—"

"He's purchased them outright. Our obligation was to get the highest possible price for their pieces. We've done that. The Taverners will be able to spend their autumn years in Monte Carlo if they choose. And you can tell Marcus that if I've missed the *danse de fête,* I'll be enjoying his family's box seats for next season's performances." Sylvia disconnected the line.

The room was silent. Marcus Whitmore's finger rested gently on the gold case that circled the miniature of the man. It looked like a gesture of longing, an attempt to connect to someone long dead and anonymous.

"I almost believe that, were I to speak, he might hear me," Marcus said wistfully.

Something was off. Phoebe couldn't identify what it was, but there was more at stake here than the acquisition of two sixteenth-century miniatures.

"Your grandmother must have a very healthy bank account, Dr. Whitmore, to pay so handsomely for two unidentifiable Elizabethan portraits. As you are also a Sotheby's client, I feel I should tell you that you surely overpaid for them. A portrait of Queen Elizabeth I from this period might go for six figures with the right buyers in the room, but not these." The identity of the sitter was crucial to such valuations. "We'll never know who these two were. Not after so many centuries of obscurity. Names are important."

"That's what my grandmother says."

"Then she is aware that without a definite attribution the value of these miniatures will probably not increase."

"To be honest," Marcus said, "my grandmother doesn't need to make a return on her investment. And Ysabeau would prefer it if no one else knows who they are."

Phoebe frowned at the odd phrasing. Did his grandmother think she *did* know?

"It's a pleasure doing business with you, Phoebe, even if we did do it standing up. This time." Marcus paused, smiled his charming smile. "You don't mind my calling you Phoebe?"

Phoebe *did* mind. She rubbed at her neck in exasperation, pushing aside her black, collar-length hair. Marcus's eyes lingered on the curve of her shoulders. When she made no reply, he closed the box, tucked the miniatures under his arm, and backed away.

"I'd like to take you to dinner," he said mildly, seemingly unaware of Phoebe's clear signals of uninterest. "We can celebrate the Taverners' good fortune, as well as the sizable commission that you will be splitting with Sylvia."

Sylvia? Split a commission? Phoebe's mouth gaped in disbelief. The chances that her boss might do such a thing were less than nil. Marcus's expression darkened.

"It was a condition of the deal. My grandmother wouldn't have it any other way." His voice was gruff. "Dinner?"

"I don't go out with strange men after dark."

"Then I'll ask you out to dinner tomorrow, after we've had lunch. Once you've spent two hours in my company, I won't be 'strange' any longer."

"Oh, you'll still be strange," Phoebe muttered, "and I don't take lunch. I eat at my desk." She looked away in confusion. Had she said the first part aloud?

"I'll pick you up at one," said Marcus, his smile widening. Phoebe's heart sank. She *had* said it aloud. "And don't worry, we won't go far."

"Why not?" Did he think she was afraid of him or couldn't keep up with his strides? God, she hated being short.

"I just wanted you to know that you could wear those shoes again without fearing you'd break your neck," Marcus said innocently. His eyes traveled slowly from her toes over her black leather pumps, lingered on her ankles, and then crawled up the curve of her calf. "I like them."

Who did this man think he was? He was behaving like an eighteenth-century rake. Phoebe took decisive steps toward the door, her heels making satisfyingly sharp clicks. She pushed the button to release the lock and held the door open. Marcus made an appreciative sound as he strolled toward her.

"I shouldn't be so forward. My grandmother disapproves of that almost as much as she disapproves of being cut out of a business deal. But here's the thing, Phoebe." Whitmore lowered his mouth until it was inches from her ear and dropped his voice to a whisper. "Unlike the men who have taken you out to dinner and perhaps gone back to your flat for something afterward, your propriety and fine manners don't frighten me off. Quite the contrary. And I can't help imagining what you're like when that icy control melts."

Phoebe gasped.

Marcus took her hand. His lips pressed against her flesh as he stared into her eyes. "Until tomorrow. And make sure the door locks behind me. You're in enough trouble." Dr. Whitmore walked backward out of the room, gave her another bright smile, turned, and whistled his way out of sight.

Phoebe's hand was trembling. That man—that strange man with no grasp of proper etiquette and startling blue eyes—had kissed her. At her place of work. Without her permission.

And she hadn't slapped him, which is what well-bred daughters of diplomats were taught to do as a last resort against unwanted advances at home and abroad.

She was indeed in trouble.

"Was I right to call you, Goody Alsop?" Susanna twisted her hands in her apron and looked at me anxiously. "I nearly sent her home," she said weakly. "If I had . . ."

"But you didn't, Susanna." Goody Alsop was so old and thin that her skin clung to the bones of her hands and wrists. The witch's voice was strangely hearty for someone so frail, however, and intelligence snapped in her eyes. The woman might be an octogenarian, but no one would dare call her infirm.

Now that Goody Alsop had arrived, the main room in the Norman apartments was full to bursting. With some reluctance Susanna allowed Matthew and Pierre to stand just inside the door, provided they didn't touch anything. Jeffrey and John divided their attention between the vampires and the chick, now safely nestled inside John's cap by the fire. Its feathers were beginning to fluff in the warm air, and it had, mercifully, stopped peeping. I sat on a stool by the fire next to Goody Alsop, who occupied the room's only chair.

"Let me have a look at you, Diana." When Goody Alsop reached her fingers toward my face, just as Widow Beaton and Champier had, I flinched. The witch stopped and frowned. "What is it, child?"

"A witch in France tried to read my skin. It felt like knives," I explained in a whisper.

"It will not be entirely comfortable—what examination is?—but it should not hurt." Her fingers explored my features. Her hands were cool and dry, the veins standing out against mottled skin and crawling over bent joints. I felt a slight digging sensation, but it was nothing like the pain I'd experienced at Champier's hands.

"Ah," she breathed when she reached the smooth skin of my forehead. My witch's eye, which had lapsed into its typical frustrating inactivity the moment Susanna and Annie found me with the chick, opened fully. Goody Alsop was a witch worth knowing.

Looking into Goody Alsop's third eye, I was plunged into a world of color. Try as I might, the brightly woven threads refused to resolve into something recognizable, though I felt once more the tantalizing prospect that they could be put to some use. Goody Alsop's touch tingled as she probed my body and mind with her second sight, energy pulsing around her in a purple-tinged orange. In my limited experience, no one had ever manifested that particular combination of colors. She tutted here and there, made an approving sound or two.

"She's a strange one, isn't she?" Jeffrey whispered, peering over Goody Alsop's shoulder.

"Jeffrey!" Susanna gasped, embarrassed at her son's behavior. "Mistress Roydon, if you please."

"Very well. Mistress Roydon's a strange one," said Jeffrey, unrepentant. He shifted his hands to his knees and bent closer.

"What do you see, young Jeffrey?" Goody Alsop asked.

"She—Mistress Roydon—is all the colors of a rainbow. Her witch's eye is blue, even though the rest of her is green and silver, like the goddess. And why is there a rim of red and black there?" Jeffrey pointed to my forehead.

"That's a *wearh*'s mark," Goody Alsop said, smoothing it with her fingers. "It tells us she belongs to Master Roydon's family. Whenever you see this, Jeffrey—and it is quite rare—you must heed it as a warning. The *wearh* who made it will not take it kindly if you meddle with the warmblood he has claimed."

"Does it hurt?" the child wondered.

"Jeffrey!" Susanna cried again. "You know better than to pester Goody Alsop with questions."

"We face a dark future if children stop asking questions, Susanna," Goody Alsop remarked.

"A *wearh*'s blood can heal, but it doesn't harm," I told the boy before Goody Alsop could answer. There was no need for another witch to grow up fearing what he didn't understand. My eyes shifted to Matthew, whose claim on me went far deeper than his father's blood oath. Matthew was willing to let Goody Alsop's examination continue—for now—but his eyes never left the woman. I mustered a smile, and his mouth tightened a fraction in response.

"Oh." Jeffrey sounded mildly interested at this piece of intelligence. "Can you make the *glaem* again, Mistress Roydon?" To their chagrin, the boys had missed that manifestation of magical energy.

Goody Alsop rested a gnarled finger in the indentation over Jeffrey's lip, effectively silencing the boy. "I need to talk to Annie now. After we're through, Master Roydon's man is going to take all three of you to the river. When you get back, you can ask me whatever you'd like."

Matthew inclined his head toward the door, and Pierre rounded up his two young charges and, after a wary look at the old woman, took them downstairs to wait. Like Jeffrey, Pierre needed to overcome his fear of other creatures.

"Where is the girl?" Goody Alsop asked, turning her head.

Annie crept forward. "Here, Goody."

"Tell us true, Annie," Goody Alsop said in a firm tone. "What have you promised Andrew Hubbard?"

"N-nothing," Annie stammered, her eyes shifting to mine.

"Don't lie, Annie. 'Tis a sin," Goody Alsop chided. "Out with it."

"I'm to send word if Master Roydon plans to leave London again. And Father Hubbard sends one of his men when the mistress and master are still abed to question me about what goes on in the house." Annie's words tumbled out. When through, she clapped her hands over her mouth as though she couldn't believe she'd revealed so much.

"We must abide by the letter of Annie's agreement with Hubbard, if not its spirit." Goody Alsop thought for a moment. "If Mistress Roydon leaves the city for any reason, Annie will send word to me first. Wait an hour before you let Hubbard know, Annie. And if you speak a word to anyone of what happens here, I'll clap a binding spell on your tongue that thirteen witches won't be able to break." Annie looked justifiably terrified at the prospect. "Go and join the boys, but open all the doors and windows before you leave. I will send for you when it is time to return."

Annie's expression while she opened the shutters and doors was full of apology and dread, and I gave her an encouraging nod. The poor child was in no position to stand up to Hubbard and had done what she had to in order to survive. With one more frightened look at Matthew, whose attitude toward her was distinctly chilly, she left.

At last, the house quiet and drafts swirling around my ankles and shoulders, Matthew spoke. He was still propped up against the door, his black clothes absorbing what little light there was in the room.

"Can you help us, Goody Alsop?" His courteous tone bore no resemblance to his high-handed treatment of Widow Beaton.

"I believe so, Master Roydon," Goody Alsop replied.

"Please take your ease," Susanna said, gesturing Matthew toward a nearby stool. There was, alas, little chance of a man of Matthew's size being comfortable on a small three-legged stool, but he straddled it without complaint. "My husband is sleeping in the next room. He mustn't overhear the *wearh,* or our conversation."

Goody Alsop plucked at the gray wool and pearly linen that covered her neck and drew her fingers away, pulling something insubstantial with them. The witch stretched out her hand and flicked her wrist, releasing a shadowy figure into the room. Her exact replica walked off into Susanna's bedchamber.

"What was that?" I asked, hardly daring to breathe.

"My fetch. She will watch over Master Norman and make sure we are not disturbed." Goody Alsop's lips moved, and the drafts stopped. "Now that the doors and windows are sealed, we will not be overheard either. You can rest easy on that score, Susanna."

Here were two spells that might prove useful in a spy's household. I opened my mouth to ask Goody Alsop how she'd managed them, but before I could utter a word, she held up her hand and chuckled.

"You are very curious for a grown woman. I fear you'll try Susanna's patience even more than Jeffrey does." She sat back and regarded me with a pleased expression. "I have waited a long time for you, Diana."

"Me?" I said doubtfully.

"Without question. It has been many years since the first auguries foretold your arrival, and with the passing of time some among us gave up hope. But when our sisters told us of the portents in the north, I knew to expect you." Goody Alsop was referring to Berwick and the strange occurrences in Scotland. I sat forward, ready to question her further, but Matthew shook his head slightly. He still wasn't sure the witch could be trusted. Goody Alsop saw my husband's silent request and chuckled again.

"So I was right, then," Susanna said, relieved.

"Yes, child. Diana is indeed a weaver." Goody Alsop's words reverberated in the room, potent as any spell.

"What's that?" I whispered.

"There is much we don't understand about our present situation, Goody Alsop." Matthew took my hand. "Perhaps you should treat us both like Jeffrey and explain it as you would to a child."

"Diana is a maker of spells," Goody Alsop said. "We weavers are rare creatures. That is why the goddess sent you to me."

"No, Goody Alsop. You're mistaken," I protested with a shake of my head. "I'm terrible with spells. My Aunt Sarah has great skill, but not even she has been able to teach me the craft of the witch."

"Of course you cannot perform the spells of other witches. You must devise your own." Goody Alsop's pronouncement went against everything I'd been taught. I looked at her in amazement.

"Witches learn spells. We don't invent them." Spells were passed from generation to generation, within families and among coven members. We jealously guarded that knowledge, recording words and procedures in grimoires along with the names of the witches who mastered their accompanying magic. More experienced witches trained the younger members of the coven to follow in their footsteps, mindful of the nuances of each spell and every witch's past experience with it.

"Weavers do," Goody Alsop replied.

"I've never heard of a weaver," Matthew said carefully.

"Few have. We are a secret, Master Roydon, one that few witches discover, let alone *wearhs*. You are familiar with secrets and how to keep them, I think." Her eyes twinkled with mischief.

"I've lived many years, Goody Alsop. I find it hard to believe that witches could keep the existence of weavers from other creatures all that time." He scowled. "Is this another of Hubbard's games?"

"I am too old for games, Monsieur de Clermont. Oh, yes, I know who you really are and what position you occupy in our world," Goody Alsop said when Matthew looked surprised. "Perhaps you cannot hide the truth from witches as well as you think."

"Perhaps not," Matthew purred in warning. His growling further amused the old woman.

"That trick might frighten children like Jeffrey and John and moon-touched daemons like your friend Christopher, but it does not scare me." Her voice turned serious. "Weavers hide because once we were sought out and murdered, just like your father's knights. Not everyone approved of our power. As you well know, it can be easier to survive when your enemies think you are already dead."

"But who would do such a thing, and why?" I hoped that the answer wouldn't lead us back to the long-standing enmity between vampires and witches.

"It wasn't the *wearhs* or the daemons who hunted us down, but other witches," Goody Alsop said calmly. "They fear us because we are different. Fear breeds contempt, then hate. It is a familiar story. Once witches destroyed whole families lest the babes grew to be weavers, too. The few weavers who survived sent their own children into hiding. A parent's love for a child is powerful, as you will both soon discover."

"You know about the baby," I said, my hands moving protectively over my belly.

"Yes." Goody Alsop nodded gravely. "You are already making a powerful weaving, Diana. You will not be able to keep it hidden from other witches for long."

"A child?" Susanna's eyes were huge. "Conceived between a witch and a *wearh*?"

"Not just any witch. Only weavers can work such magic. There is a reason the goddess chose you for this task, Susanna, just as there is a reason she called me. You are a midwife, and all your skills will be needed in the days ahead."

"I have no experience that will help Mistress Roydon," Susanna protested.

"You have been assisting women in childbirth for years," Goody Alsop observed.

"Warmblooded women, Goody, with warmblooded babes!" Susanna said indignantly. "Not creatures like—"

"*Wearhs* have arms and legs, just like the rest of us," Goody Alsop interrupted. "I cannot imagine this child will be any different."

"Just because it has ten fingers and ten toes does not mean it has a soul," Susanna said, eyeing Matthew with suspicion.

"I'm surprised at you, Susanna. Master Roydon's soul is as clear to me as your own. Have you been listening to your husband again, and his prattle about the evil in *wearhs* and daemons?"

Susanna's mouth tightened. "What if I have, Goody?"

"Then you are a fool. Witches see the truth plainly—even if their husbands are full of nonsense."

"It is not such an easy matter as you make it out to be," Susanna muttered.

"Nor does it need to be so difficult. The long-awaited weaver is among us, and we must make plans."

"Thank you, Goody Alsop," Matthew said. He was relieved that someone agreed with him at last. "You are right. Diana must learn what she needs to know quickly. She cannot have the child here."

"That isn't entirely your decision, Master Roydon. If the child is meant to be born in London, then that is where it will be born."

"Diana doesn't belong here," Matthew said, adding quickly, "in London."

"Bless us, that is clear enough. But as she is a time spinner, merely moving her to another place will not help. Diana would be no less conspicuous in Canterbury or York."

"So you know another of our secrets." Matthew gave the old woman a cold stare. "As you know so much, you must have also divined that Diana will not be returning to her own time alone. The child and I will be going with her. You will teach her what she needs in order to do it." Matthew was taking charge, which meant that things were about to take their usual turn for the worse.

"Your wife's education is my business now, Master Roydon—unless you think you know more about what it means to be a weaver than I do," Goody Alsop said mildly.

"He knows that this is a matter between witches," I told Goody Alsop, putting a restraining hand on his arm. "Matthew won't interfere."

"Everything about my wife is my business, Goody Alsop," said Matthew. He turned to me. "And this is not a matter solely between witches. Not if the witches here might turn against my mate and my child."

"So it was a witch and not a *wearh* who injured you," Goody Alsop said softly. "I felt the pain and knew that a witch was part of it but hoped that was because the witch was healing the damage done to you rather than causing it. What has the world come to that one witch would do such a thing to another?"

Matthew fixed his attention on Goody Alsop. "Maybe the witch also realized that Diana was a weaver."

It hadn't occurred to me that Satu might have known. Given what Goody Alsop had told me about my fellow witches' attitude toward weavers, the idea that Peter Knox and his cronies in the Congregation might suspect me of harboring such a secret sent my blood racing. Matthew sought my hand, taking it between both of his.

"It is possible, but I cannot say for certain," Goody Alsop told us regretfully. "Nevertheless we must do what we can in the time the goddess provides to prepare Diana for her future."

"Stop," I said, slapping my palm on the table. Ysabeau's ring chimed against the hard wood. "You're all talking as though this weaving business makes sense. But I can't even light a candle. My talents are magical. I have wind, water—even fire—in my blood."

"If I can see your husband's soul, Diana, you will not be surprised that I have also seen your power. But you are not a firewitch or a waterwitch, no matter what you believe. You cannot command these elements. If you were foolish enough to attempt it, you would be destroyed."

"But I nearly drowned in my own tears," I said stubbornly. "And to save Matthew I killed a *wearh* with an arrow of witchfire. My aunt recognized the smell."

"A firewitch has no need of arrows. The fire leaves her and arrives at its target in an instant." Goody Alsop shook her head. "These were but simple weavings, my child, fashioned from grief and love. The goddess has given you her blessing to borrow the powers you need but not to command any of them absolutely."

"Borrow them." I thought over the frustrating events of the past months and the glimmers of magic that would never behave as they were supposed to do. "So that's why these abilities come and go. They were never really mine."

"No witch could hold so much power within her without upsetting the balance of the worlds. A weaver selects carefully from the magic around her and uses it to shape something new."

"But there must be thousands of spells in existence—not to mention charms and potions. Nothing I make could possibly be original." I drew my hand across my forehead, and the spot where Philippe had made his blood oath seemed cold to the touch.

"All spells came from somewhere, Diana: a moment of need, a longing, a challenge that could not be met any other way. And they came from someone, too."

"The first witch," I whispered. Some creatures believed that Ashmole 782 was the first grimoire, a book that contained the original enchantments and charms devised by our people. Here was another connection between me and the mysterious manuscript. I looked at Matthew.

"The first weaver," Goody Alsop corrected gently, "as well as those who followed. Weavers are not simply witches, Diana. Susanna is a great witch, with more knowledge about the magic of the earth and its lore than any of her sisters in London. For all her gifts, though, she cannot weave a new spell. You can."

"I can't even imagine how to begin," I said.

"You hatched that chick," Goody Alsop said, pointing to the sleepy yellow ball of fluff.

"But I was trying to crack an egg!" I protested. Now that I understood marksmanship, I was aware this was a problem. My magic, like my arrows, had missed its target.

"Obviously not. If you were trying simply to crack an egg, we would be enjoying some of Susanna's excellent custard. You had something else in mind." The chick concurred, emitting a particularly loud and clear peep.

She was right. I had indeed had other things on my mind: our child, whether we could nurture him properly, how we might keep him safe.

Goody Alsop nodded. "I thought so."

"I spoke no words, performed no ritual, concocted nothing." I was clinging to what Sarah had taught me about the craft. "All I did was ask some questions. They weren't even particularly good questions."

"Magic begins with desire. The words come much, much later," Goody Alsop explained. "Even then a weaver cannot always reduce a spell to a few lines for another witch to use. Some weavings resist, no matter how hard we try. They are for our use alone. It is why we are feared."

"*'It begins with absence and desire,'*" I murmured. Past and present clashed again as I repeated the first line of the verse that had accompanied the single page of Ashmole 782 someone once sent to my parents. On this occasion, when the corners lit up and illuminated the dust motes in shades of blue and gold, I didn't look away. Neither did Goody Alsop. Matthew's and Susanna's eyes followed ours, but neither saw anything out of the ordinary.

"Exactly. See there, how time feels your absence and wants you back to weave yourself into your former life." She beamed, clapping her hands together as though I'd made her a particularly fine crayon drawing of a house and she planned to display it on her refrigerator door. "Of course, time is not ready for you now. If it were, the blue would be much brighter."

"You make it sound as though it's possible to combine magic and the craft, but they're separate," I said, still confused. "Witchcraft uses spells, and magic is an inherited power over an element, like air or fire."

"Who taught you such nonsense?" Goody Alsop snorted, and Susanna looked appalled. "Magic and witchcraft are but two paths that cross in the wood. A weaver is able to stand at the crossroads with one foot placed on each path. She can occupy the place between, where the powers are the greatest."

Time protested this revelation with a loud cry.

"'A child between, a witch apart,'" I murmured in wonder. The ghost of Bridget Bishop had warned me of the dangers associated with such a vulnerable position. "Before we came here, the ghost of one of my ancestors—Bridget Bishop—told me that was my fate. She must have known I was a weaver."

"So did your parents," Goody Alsop said. "I can see the last remaining threads of their binding. Your father was a weaver, too. He knew you would follow his path."

"Her father?" Matthew asked.

"Weavers are seldom men, Goody Alsop," Susanna cautioned.

"Diana's father was a weaver of great talent but no training. His spell was pieced together rather than properly woven. Still, it was made with love and served its purpose for a time, rather like the chain that binds you to your *wearh,* Diana." The chain was my secret weapon, providing the comforting sensation that I was anchored to Matthew in my darkest moments.

"Bridget told me something else that same night: *'There is no path forward that does not have him in it.'* She must have known about Matthew, too," I confessed.

"You never told me about this conversation, *mon coeur,*" Matthew said, sounding more curious than annoyed.

"Crossroads and paths and vague prophecies didn't seem important then. With everything that happened afterward, I forgot." I looked at Goody Alsop. "Besides, how could I have been making spells without knowing it?"

"Weavers are surrounded by mystery," Goody Alsop told me. "We haven't the time to seek answers to all your questions now but must focus instead on teaching you to manage the magic as it moves through you."

"My powers have been misbehaving," I admitted, thinking of the shriveled quinces and Mary's ruined shoes. "I never know what's going to happen next."

"That's not unusual for a weaver first coming into her power. But your brightness can be seen and felt, even by humans." Goody Alsop sat back in her chair and studied me. "If witches see your *glaem* like young Annie did, they might use the knowledge for their own purposes. We will not let you or the child fall into Hubbard's clutches. I trust you can manage the Congregation?" she said, looking at Matthew. Goody Alsop construed Matthew's silence as consent.

"Very well, then. Come to me on Mondays and Thursdays, Diana. Mistress Norman will see to you on Tuesdays. I shall send for Marjorie Cooper on Wednesdays and Elizabeth Jackson and Catherine Streeter on Fridays. Diana will need their help to reconcile the fire and water in her blood, or she will never produce more than a vapor."

"Perhaps it is not wise to make all those witches privy to this particular secret, Goody," Matthew said.

"Master Roydon is right. There are already too many whispers about the witch. John Chandler has been spreading news of her to ingratiate himself with Father Hubbard. Surely we can teach her ourselves," said Susanna.

"And when did you become a firewitch?" Goody Alsop retorted. "The child's blood is full of flame. My talents are dominated by witchwind, and yours are grounded in the earth's power. We are not sufficient to the task."

"Our gathering will draw too much attention if we proceed with your plan. We are but thirteen witches, yet you propose to involve five of us in this business. Let some other gathering take on the problem of Mistress Roydon—the one in Moorgate, perhaps, or Aldgate."

"The Aldgate gathering has grown too large, Susanna. It cannot govern its own affairs, never mind take on the education of a weaver. Besides, it is too far for me to travel, and the bad air by the city ditch worsens my rheumatism. We will train her in this parish, as the goddess intended."

"I cannot—" Susanna began.

"I am your elder, Susanna. If you wish to protest further, you will need to seek a ruling from the Rede." The air thickened uncomfortably.

"Very well, Goody. I will send my request to Queenhithe." Susanna seemed startled by her own announcement.

"Who is Queen Hithe?" I asked Matthew, my voice low.

"Queenhithe is a place, not a person," he murmured. "But what is this about a reed?"

"I have no idea," I confessed.

"Stop whispering," Goody Alsop said, shaking her head in annoyance. "With the charm on the windows and the doors, your muttering stirs the air and hurts my ears."

Once the air quieted, Goody Alsop continued. "Susanna has challenged my authority in this matter. As I am the leader of the Garlickhythe gathering—and the Vintry's ward elder as well—Mistress Norman must present her case to the other ward elders in London. They will decide on our course of action, as they do whenever there are disagreements between witches. There are twenty-six elders, and together we are known as the Rede."

"So this is just politics?" I said.

"Politics and prudence. Without a way to settle our own disputes, Father Hubbard would have his *wearh* fingers in even more of our affairs," said Goody Alsop. "I am sorry if I offend you, Master Roydon."

"No offense taken, Goody Alsop. But if you take this matter to your elders, Diana's identity will be known across London." Matthew stood. "I can't allow that."

"Every witch in the city has already heard about your wife. News travels quickly here, no small thanks to your friend Christopher Marlowe," Goody Alsop said, craning her neck to meet his eyes. "Sit down, Master Roydon. My old bones no longer bend that way." To my surprise, Matthew sat.

"The witches of London still do not know you are a weaver, Diana, and that is the important thing," Goody Alsop continued. "The Rede will have to be told, of course. When other witches hear that you've been called before the elders, they will assume you are being disciplined for your relationship with Master Roydon, or that you are being bound in some fashion to keep him from gaining access to your blood and power."

"Whatever they decide, will you still be my teacher?" I was used to being the object of other witches' scorn and knew better than to hope that the witches of London would approve of my relationship with Matthew. It mattered little to me whether Marjorie Cooper, Elizabeth Jackson, and Catherine Streeter (whoever they were) participated in Goody Alsop's educational regimen. But Goody Alsop was different. This was one witch whose friendship and help I wanted to have.

"I am the last of our kind in London and one of only three known weavers in this part of the world. The Scottish weaver Agnes Sampson lies in a prison in Edinburgh. No one has seen or heard from the Irish weaver for years. The Rede has no choice but to let me guide you," Goody Alsop assured me.

"When will the witches meet?" I asked.

"As soon as it can be arranged," Goody Alsop promised.

"We will be ready for them," Matthew assured her.

"There are some things that your wife must do for herself, Master Roydon. Carrying the babe and seeing the Rede are among them," Goody Alsop replied. "Trust is not an easy business for a *wearh,* I know, but you must try for her sake."

"I trust my wife. You felt what witches have done to her, so you will not be surprised that I don't trust any of your kind with her," Matthew said.

"You must try," Goody Alsop repeated. "You cannot offend the Rede. If you do, Hubbard will have to intervene. The Rede will not suffer that additional insult and will insist on the Congregation's involvement. No matter our other disagreements, no one in this room wants the Congregation's attention focused on London, Master Roydon."

Matthew took Goody Alsop's measure. Finally he nodded. "Very well, Goody."

I was a weaver.

Soon I would be a mother.

A child between, a witch apart, whispered the ghostly voice of Bridget Bishop.

Matthew's sharp inhalation told me that he had detected some change in my scent. "Diana is tired and needs to go home."

"She is not tired but fearful. The time for that has passed, Diana. You must face who you truly are," Goody Alsop said with mild regret.

But my anxiety continued to rise even after we were safely back in the Hart and Crown. Once there, Matthew took off his quilted jacket. He wrapped it around my shoulders, trying to ward off the chilly air. The fabric retained his smell of cloves and cinnamon, along with traces of smoke from Susanna's fire and the damp air of London.

"I'm a weaver." Perhaps if I kept saying it, this fact would begin to make sense. "But I don't know what that means or who I am anymore."

"You are Diana Bishop—a historian, a witch." He took me by the shoulders. "No matter what else you have been before or might one day be, this is who you are. And you are my life."

"Your wife," I corrected him.

"My life," he repeated. "You are not just my heart but its beating. Before I was only a shadow, like Goody Alsop's fetch." His accent was stronger, his voice rough with emotion.

"I should be relieved to have the truth at last," I said through chattering teeth as I climbed into bed. The cold seemed to have taken root in the marrow of my bones. "All my life I wondered why I was different. Now I know, but it doesn't help."

"One day it will," Matthew promised, joining me under the coverlet. He folded his arms around me. We twined our legs like the roots of a tree, each clinging to the other for support as we worked our bodies closer. Deep within me the chain that I had somehow forged out of love and longing for someone I had yet to meet flexed between us and became fluid. It was thick and unbreakable, filled with a life-giving sap that flowed continuously from witch to vampire and back to witch. Soon I no longer felt between but blissfully, completely centered. I took a deep breath, then another. When I tried to draw away, Matthew refused.

"I'm not ready to let you go yet," he said, pulling me closer.

"You must have work to do—for the Congregation, Philippe, Elizabeth. I'm fine, Matthew," I insisted, though I wanted to stay exactly where I was for as long as possible.

"Vampires reckon time differently than warmbloods do," he said, still unwilling to release me.

"How long is a vampire minute, then?" I asked, snuggling under his chin.

"It's hard to say," Matthew murmured. "Some length of time between an ordinary minute and forever."

Assembling the twenty-six most powerful witches in London was no small feat. The Rede did not take place as I had imagined—in a single, courtroom-style meeting with witches arrayed in neat rows and me standing before them. Instead it unfolded over several days in shops, taverns, and parlors all over the city. There were no formal introductions, and no time was wasted on other social niceties. I saw so many unfamiliar witches that soon they all blurred together.

Some aspects of the experience stood out, however. For the first time I felt the unquestionable power of a firewitch. Goody Alsop hadn't misled me—there was no mistaking the burning intensity of the redheaded witch's gaze or touch. Though the flames in my blood leaped and danced when she was near, I was clearly no firewitch. This was confirmed when I met two more firewitches in a private room at the Mitre, a tavern in Bishopsgate.

"She'll be a challenge," one observed after she'd finished reading my skin.

"A time-spinning weaver with plenty of water and fire in her," the other agreed. "Not a combination I thought to see in my lifetime."

The Rede's windwitches convened at Goody Alsop's house, which was more spacious than its modest exterior suggested. Two ghosts wandered the rooms, as did Goody Alsop's fetch, who met visitors at the door and glided about silently making sure that everyone was comfortable.

The windwitches were a less fearsome lot than the firewitches, their touches light and dry as they quietly assessed my strengths and shortcomings.

"A stormy one," murmured a silver-haired witch of fifty or so. She was petite and lithe and moved with a speed that suggested gravity did not have the same hold on her as on the rest of us.

"Too much direction," another said, frowning. "She needs to let matters take their own course, or every draft she makes is likely to become a full-blown gale."

Goody Alsop accepted their comments with thanks, but when they all left, she seemed relieved.

"I will rest now, child," she said weakly, rising from her chair and moving toward the rear of the house. Her fetch trailed after her like a shadow.

"Are there any men among the Rede, Goody Alsop?" I asked, taking her elbow.

"Only a handful remain. All the young wizards have gone off to university to study natural philosophy," she said with a sigh. "These are strange times, Diana. Everyone is in such a rush for something new, and witches think books will teach them better than experience. I'll take my leave of you now. My ears are ringing from all that talking."

A solitary waterwitch came to the Hart and Crown on Thursday morning. I was lying down, exhausted from traipsing all over town the previous day. Tall and supple, the waterwitch did not so much step as flow into the house. She met a solid obstacle, however, in the wall of vampires in the entrance hall.

"It's all right, Matthew," I said from the door of our bedchamber, beckoning her forward.

When we were alone, the waterwitch surveyed me from head to toe. Her glance tingled like salt water on my skin, as bracing as a dip in the ocean on a summer day.

"Goody Alsop was right," she said in a low, musical voice. "There is too much water in your blood. We cannot meet with you in groups for fear of causing a deluge. You must see us one at a time. It will take all day, I'm afraid."

So instead of my going to the waterwitches, the waterwitches came to me. They trickled in and out of the house, driving Matthew and Françoise mad. But there was no denying my affinity with them, or the undertow that I felt in a waterwitch's presence.

"The water did not lie," one waterwitch murmured after sliding her fingertips over my forehead and shoulders. She turned my hands over to examine the palms. She was scarcely older than me, with striking coloring: white skin, black hair, and eyes the color of the Caribbean.

"What water?" I asked as she traced the tributaries leading away from my lifeline.

"Every waterwitch in London collected rainwater from midsummer to Mabon, then poured it into the Rede's scrying bowl. It revealed that the long-awaited weaver would have water in her veins." The waterwitch let out a sigh of relief and released my hands. "We are in need of new spells after helping turn back the Spanish fleet. Goody Alsop has been able to replenish the windwitches' supply, but the Scottish weaver was gifted with earth, so she could not help us—even if she had wished to. You are a true daughter of the moon, though, and will serve us well."

On Friday morning a messenger came to the house with an address on Bread Street and instructions for me to go there at eleven o'clock to meet the last remaining members of the Rede: the two earthwitches. Most witches had some degree of earth magic within them. It was the foundation for the craft, and in modern covens earthwitches had no special distinction. I was curious to see if the Elizabethan earthwitches were any different.

Matthew and Annie went with me, as Pierre was occupied on an errand for Matthew and Françoise was out shopping. We were just clearing St. Paul's Churchyard when Matthew turned on an urchin with a filthy face and painfully thin legs. Matthew's blade was at the child's ear in a flash.

"Move that finger so much as a hair, lad, and I'll take your ear off," he said softly.

I looked down with surprise to see the child's fingers brushing against the bag I wore at my waist.

There was always a hint of potential violence about Matthew, even in my own time, but in Elizabeth's London it was much closer to the surface. Still, there was no need for him to turn his venom on one so small.

"Matthew," I warned, noting the terror on the child's face, "stop it."

"Another man would have your ear or haul you before the bailiffs." Matthew narrowed his eyes, and the child blanched further.

"Enough," I said shortly. I touched the child's shoulder, and he flinched. In a flash my witch's eye saw a man's heavy hand striking the child and driving him into a wall. Beneath my fingers, concealed by a rough shirt that was all the boy had to keep out the cold, blood suffused his skin in an ugly bruise. "What's your name?"

"Jack, my lady," the boy whispered. Matthew's knife was still pressed to his ear, and we were beginning to attract attention.

"Put the dagger away, Matthew. This child is no danger to either of us."

Matthew withdrew his knife with a hiss.

"Where are your parents?"

Jack shrugged. "Haven't any, my lady."

"Take the boy home, Annie, and have Françoise get him some food and clothes. Introduce him to warm water, if you can, and put him in Pierre's bed. He looks tired."

"You cannot adopt every stray in London, Diana." Matthew drove his dagger into its sheath for emphasis.

"Françoise could use someone to run errands for her." I smoothed the boy's hair back from his forehead. "Will you work for me, Jack?"

"Aye, mistress." Jack's stomach gave an audible gurgle, and his wary eyes held a trace of hope. My witch's third eye opened wide, seeing into his cavernous stomach and hollow, trembling legs. I drew a few coins from my purse.

"Buy him a slice of pie from Master Prior on the way, Annie. He's ready to drop from hunger, but that should hold him until Françoise can make him a proper meal."

"Yes, Mistress," Annie said. She gripped Jack around the arm and towed him in the direction of the Blackfriars.

Matthew frowned at their departing backs and then at me. "You're doing that child no favors. This Jack—if that's his real name, which I sincerely doubt—won't live out the year if he continues to steal."

"The child won't live out the week unless an adult takes responsibility for him. What is that you said? Love, a grown-up to care for them, and a soft place to land?"

"Don't turn my words against me, Diana. That was about our child, not some homeless waif." Matthew, who had met more witches in the past few days than most vampires did in a lifetime, was spoiling for a fight.

"I was a homeless waif once."

My husband drew back as if I'd slapped him.

"Not so easy to turn him away now, is it?" I didn't wait for him to respond. "If Jack doesn't come with us, we might as well take him straight to Andrew Hubbard. There he'll either be fitted for a coffin or had for supper. Either way he'll be looked after better than he would be out here on the streets."

"We have servants enough," Matthew said coolly.

"And you have money to spare. If you can't afford it, I'll pay his wages out of my own funds."

"You'd better come up with a fairy tale to tuck him into bed with while you're at it." Matthew gripped my elbow. "Do you think he won't notice he's living with three *wearhs* and two witches? Human children always see more clearly into the world of creatures than adults do."

"Do you think Jack will care what we are if he has a roof over his head, food in his belly, and a bed where he can sleep the night in safety?" A woman stared at us in confusion from across the street. A vampire and a witch shouldn't be having such a heated discussion in public. I pulled the hood closer around my face.

"The more creatures we let into our lives here, the trickier this all becomes," Matthew said. He noticed the woman watching us and released my arm. "And that goes double for the humans."

After visiting the two solid, grave earthwitches, Matthew and I retreated to opposite ends of the Hart and Crown until our tempers cooled. Matthew attacked his mail, bellowing for Pierre and letting out a voluble stream of curses against Her Majesty's government, his father's whims, and the folly of King James of Scotland. I spent the time talking to Jack about his duties. While the boy had a fine skill set when it came to picking locks, pockets, and country bumpkins who could be fleeced of all their possessions in confidence games, he could not read, write, cook, sew, or do anything else that might assist Françoise and Annie. Pierre, however, took a serious interest in the boy, especially after he recovered his lucky charm from the inner pocket of the boy's secondhand doublet.

"Come with me, Jack," Pierre said, holding open the door and jerking his head toward the stairs. He was on his way out to collect the latest missives from Matthew's informants, and he clearly planned on taking advantage of our young charge's familiarity with London's underworld.

"Yes, sir," Jack said, his voice eager. He already looked better after just one meal.

"Nothing dangerous," I warned Pierre.

"Of course not, *madame,*" the vampire said innocently.

"I mean it," I retorted. "And have him back before dark."

I was sorting through papers on my desk when Matthew came out from his study. Françoise and Annie had gone to Smithfield to see the butchers for meat and blood, and we had the house to ourselves.

"I'm sorry, *mon coeur,*" Matthew said, sliding his hands around my waist from behind. He dropped a kiss on my neck. "Between the Rede and the queen, it's been a long week."

"I'm sorry, too. I understand why you don't want Jack here, Matthew, but I couldn't ignore him. He was hurt and hungry."

"I know," Matthew said, drawing me in tightly so that my back fit against his chest.

"Would your reaction have been different if we'd found the boy in modern Oxford?" I asked, staring into the fire rather than meeting his eyes.

Ever since the incident with Jack, I had been preoccupied with the question of whether Matthew's behavior was rooted in vampire genetics or Elizabethan morals.

"Probably not. It's not easy for vampires to live among warmbloods, Diana. Without an emotional bond, warmbloods are nothing more than a source of nourishment. No vampire, however civilized and well mannered, can remain in close proximity to one without feeling the urge to feed on them." His breath was cool against my neck, tickling the sensitive spot where Miriam had used her blood to heal the wound Matthew had made there.

"You don't seem to want to feed on me." There had been no indication that Matthew wrestled with such an urge, and he had flatly refused his father's suggestions that he take my blood.

"I can manage my cravings far better than when we first met. Now my desire for your blood is not so much about nourishment as control. To feed from you would primarily be an assertion of dominance now that we're mated."

"And we have sex for that," I said matter-of-factly. Matthew was a generous and creative lover, but he definitely considered the bedroom his domain.

"Excuse me?" he said, his eyebrows drawn into a scowl.

"Sex and dominance. It's what modern humans think vampire relationships are all about," I said. "Their stories are full of crazed alpha-male vampires throwing women over their shoulders before dragging them off for dinner and a date."

"Dinner and a date?" Matthew was aghast. "Do you mean . . . ?"

"Uh-huh. You should see what Sarah's friends in the Madison coven read. Vampire meets girl, vampire bites girl, girl is shocked to find out there really are vampires. The sex, blood, and overprotective behavior all come quickly thereafter. Some of it is pretty explicit." I paused. "There's no time for bundling, that's for sure. I don't remember much poetry or dancing either."

Matthew swore. "No wonder your aunt wanted to know if I was hungry."

"You really should read this stuff, if only to see what humans think. It's a public-relations nightmare. Far worse than what witches have to overcome." I turned around to face him. "You'd be surprised how many women seem to want a vampire boyfriend anyway, though."

"What if their vampire boyfriends were to behave like callous bastards in the street and threaten starving orphans?"

"Most fictional vampires have hearts of gold, barring the occasional jealous rage and consequent dismemberment." I smoothed the hair away from his eyes.

"I can't believe we're having this conversation," Matthew said.

"Why? Vampires read books about witches. The fact that Kit's *Doctor Faustus* is pure fantasy doesn't stop you from enjoying a good supernatural yarn."

"Yes, but all that manhandling and then making love . . ." Matthew shook his head.

"You've manhandled me, as you so charmingly put it. I seem to recall being hoisted into your arms at Sept-Tours on more than one occasion," I pointed out.

"Only when you were injured!" Matthew said indignantly. "Or tired."

"Or when you wanted me in one spot and I was in another. Or when the horse was too tall, or the bed was too high, or the seas were too rough. Honestly, Matthew. You have a very selective memory when it suits you. As for making love, it's not always the tender act that you describe. Not in the books I've seen. Sometimes it's just a good, hard—"

Before I could finish my sentence, a tall, handsome vampire flung me over his shoulder.

"We will continue this conversation in private."

"Help! I think my husband is a vampire!" I laughed and pounded on the backs of his thighs.

"Be quiet," he growled. "Or you'll have Mistress Hawley to contend with."

"If I were a human woman and not a witch, that growly sound you just made would make me swoon. I'd be all yours, and you could have your way with me." I giggled.

"You're already all mine," Matthew reminded me, depositing me on the bed. "I'm changing this ridiculous plot, by the way. In the interests of originality—not to mention verisimilitude—we're skipping dinner and moving right on to the date."

"Readers would love a vampire who said that!" I said.

Matthew seemed not to care about my editorial contributions. He was too busy lifting my skirts. We were going to make love fully clothed. How deliciously Elizabethan.

"Wait a minute. At least let me take off my bum roll." Annie had informed me that this was the proper name for the doughnut-shaped thing that kept my skirts respectably full and flouncy.

But Matthew was not inclined to wait.

"To hell with the bum roll." He loosened the front ties on his breeches, grabbed my hands, and pinned them over my head. With one thrust he was inside me.

"I had no idea that talking about popular fiction would have this effect on you," I said breathlessly as he started to move. "Remind me to discuss it with you more often."

We were just sitting down to supper when I was called to Goody Alsop's house.

The Rede had made its ruling.

When Annie and I arrived with our two vampire escorts and Jack trailing behind, we found her in the front parlor with Susanna and three unfamiliar witches. Goody Alsop sent the men to the Golden Gosling and steered me toward the group by the fire.

"Come, Diana, and meet your teachers." Goody Alsop's fetch pointed me to an empty chair and withdrew into her mistress's shadow. All five witches studied me. They looked like a bunch of prosperous city matrons, with their thick woolen gowns in dark, wintry colors. Only their tingling glances gave them away as witches.

"So the Rede agreed with your initial plan," I said slowly, trying to meet their eyes. It was never good to show a teacher fear.

"They did," Susanna said with resignation. "You will forgive me, Mistress Roydon. I have two boys to think of, and a husband too ill to provide for us. A neighbor's goodwill can be lost overnight."

"Let me introduce you to the others," Goody Alsop said, turning slightly toward the woman to her right. She was around sixty, short in stature, round of face, and, if her smile was any indication, generous of spirit. "This is Marjorie Cooper."

"Diana," Marjorie said with a nod that set her small ruff rustling. "Welcome to our gathering."

While meeting the Rede, I'd learned that Elizabethan witches used the term "gathering" much as modern witches used the word "coven" to indicate a recognized community of witches. Like everything else in London, the city's gatherings coincided with parish boundaries. Though it was strange to think of witches' covens and Christian churches fitting so neatly together, it made sound organizational sense and provided an extra measure of safety, since it kept the witches' affairs among close neighbors.

There were, therefore, more than a hundred gatherings in London proper and a further two dozen in the suburbs. Like the parishes, the gatherings were organized into larger districts known as wards. Each ward sent one of its elders to the Rede, which oversaw all of the witches' affairs in the city.

With panics and witch-hunts brewing, the Rede was worried that the old system of governance was breaking down. London was bursting with creatures already, and more poured in every day. I had heard muttering about the size of the Aldgate gathering—which included more than sixty witches instead of the normal thirteen to twenty—as well as the large gatherings in Cripplegate and Southwark. To avoid the notice of humans, some gatherings had started "hiving off" and splitting into different septs. But new gatherings with inexperienced leaders were proving problematic in these difficult times. Witches in the Rede who were gifted with second sight foresaw troubles ahead.

"Marjorie is gifted with the magic of earth, like Susanna. Her specialty is remembering," Goody Alsop explained.

"I have no need of grimoires or these new almanacs all the booksellers are peddling," Marjorie said proudly.

"Marjorie perfectly remembers every spell she has ever mastered and can recall the exact configuration of the stars for every year she has been alive—and for many years when she was not yet born."

"Goody Alsop feared you would not be able to write down all you learn here and take it with you. Not only will I help you find the right words so that another witch might use the spells you devise, but I'll teach you how to be at one with those words so that none can ever take them from you." Marjorie's eyes sparkled, and her voice lowered conspiratorially. "And my husband is a vintner. He can get you much better wine than you are drinking now. I understand wine is important to *wearhs*."

I laughed aloud at this, and the other witches joined in. "Thank you, Mistress Cooper. I will pass your offer on to my husband."

"Marjorie. We are sisters here." For once I didn't cringe at being called another witch's sister.

"I am Elizabeth Jackson," said the elderly woman on the other side of Goody Alsop. She was somewhere between Marjorie and Goody Alsop in age.

"You're a waterwitch." I felt the affinity as soon as she spoke.

"I am." Elizabeth had steely gray hair and eyes and was as tall and straight as Marjorie was short and round. While many of the waterwitches in the Rede had been sinuous and flowing, Elizabeth had the brisk clarity of a mountain stream. I sensed she would always tell me the truth, even when I didn't want to hear it.

"Elizabeth is a gifted seer. She will teach you the art of scrying."

"My mother was known for her second sight," I said hesitantly. "I would like to follow in her footsteps."

"But she had no fire," Elizabeth said decidedly, beginning her truth-telling immediately. "You may not be able to follow your mother in everything, Diana. Fire and water are a potent mix, provided they don't extinguish each other."

"We will see to it that doesn't happen," the last witch promised, turning her eyes to me. Until then she'd been studiously avoiding my gaze. Now I could see why: There were golden sparks in her brown eyes, and my third eye shot open in alarm. With that extra sight, I could see the nimbus of light that surrounded her. This must be Catherine Streeter.

"You're even . . . even more powerful than the firewitches in the Rede," I stammered.

"Catherine is a special witch," Goody Alsop admitted, "a firewitch born of two firewitches. It happens rarely, as though nature herself knows that such a light cannot be hidden."

When my third eye closed, dazzled by the sight of the thrice-blessed firewitch, Catherine seemed to fade. Her brown hair dulled, her eyes dimmed, and her face was handsome but unmemorable. Her magic sprang to life again, however, as soon as she spoke.

"You have more fire than I expected," she said thoughtfully.

"'Tis a pity she was not here when the Armada came," Elizabeth said.

"So it's true? The famous 'English wind' that blew the Spanish ships away from England's shores was raised by witches?" I asked. It was part of witches' lore, but I'd always dismissed it as a myth.

"Goody Alsop was most useful to Her Majesty," Elizabeth said proudly. "Had you been here, I think we might have been able to make burning water—or fiery rain at the very least."

"Let us not get ahead of ourselves," Goody Alsop said, holding up one hand. "Diana has not yet made her weaver's forspell."

"Forspell?" I asked. Like gatherings and the Rede, this was not a term I knew.

"A forspell reveals the shape of a weaver's talents. Together we will form a blessed circle. There we will temporarily turn your powers loose to find their own way, unencumbered by words or desires," Goody Alsop replied. "It will tell us much about your talents and what we must do to train them, as well as reveal your familiar."

"Witches don't have familiars." This was another human conceit, like worshipping the devil.

"Weavers do," Goody Alsop said serenely, motioning toward her fetch. "This is mine. Like all familiars, she is an extension of my talents."

"I'm not sure having a familiar is such a good idea in my case," I said, thinking about the blackened quinces, Mary's shoes, and the chick. "I have enough to worry about."

"That is the reason you cast a forspell—to face your deepest fears so that you can work your magic freely. Still, it can be a harrowing experience. There have been weavers who entered the circle with hair the color of a raven's wing and left it with tresses as white as snow," Goody Alsop admitted.

"But it will not be as heartbreaking as the night the *wearh* left Diana and the waters rose in her," Elizabeth said softly.

"Or as lonely as the night she was closed in the earth," Susanna said with a shiver. Marjorie nodded sympathetically.

"Or as frightening as the time the firewitch tried to open you," Catherine assured me, her fingers turning orange with fury.

"The moon will be full dark on Friday. Candlemas is but a few weeks away. And we are entering a period that is propitious for spells inclining children toward study," Marjorie remarked, her face creased with concentration as she recalled the relevant information from her astonishing memory.

"I thought this was the week for snakebite charms?" Susanna said, drawing a small almanac out of her pocket.

While Marjorie and Susanna discussed the magical intricacies of the schedule, Goody Alsop, Elizabeth, and Catherine stared at me intently.

"I wonder . . ." Goody Alsop looked at me with open speculation and tapped a finger against her lips.

"Surely not," Elizabeth said, voice hushed.

"We are not getting ahead of ourselves, remember?" Catherine said.

"The goddess has blessed us enough." As she said it, her brown eyes sparked green, gold, red, and black in rapid succession. "But perhaps . . ."

"Susanna's almanac is all wrong. But we have decided it will be more auspicious if Diana weaves her forspell next Thursday, under the waxing crescent moon," Marjorie said, clapping her hands with delight.

"Oof," Goody Alsop said, poking her finger in her ear to shield it from the disturbance in the air. "Gently, Marjorie, gently."

With my new obligations to the St. James Garlickhythe gathering and my ongoing interest in Mary's alchemical experiments, I found myself spending more time outside the house while the Hart and Crown continued to serve as a center for the School of Night and the hub for Matthew's work. Messengers came and went with reports and mail, George often stopped by for a free meal and to tell us about his latest futile efforts to find Ashmole 782, and Hancock and Gallowglass dropped off their laundry downstairs and whiled away the hours by my fire, scantily clad, until it was returned to them. Kit and Matthew had reached an uneasy truce after the business with Hubbard and John Chandler, which meant that I often found the playwright in the front parlor, staring moodily into the distance and then writing furiously. The fact that he helped himself to my supply of paper was an additional source of annoyance.

Then there were Annie and Jack. Integrating two children into the household was a full-time business. Jack, whom I supposed to be about seven or eight (he had no idea of his actual age), delighted in deviling the teenage girl. He followed her around and mimicked her speech. Annie would burst into tears and pelt upstairs to fling herself on her bed. When I chastised Jack for his behavior, he sulked. Desperate for a few quiet hours, I found a schoolmaster willing to teach them reading, writing, and reckoning, but the two of them quickly drove the recent Cambridge graduate away with their blank stares and studied innocence. Both preferred shopping with Françoise and running around London with Pierre to sitting quietly and doing their sums.

"If our child behaves like this, I'll drown him," I told Matthew, seeking a moment of respite in his study.

"She *will* behave like this, you can be certain of it. And you won't drown her," Matthew said, putting down his pen. We still disagreed about the baby's sex.

"I've tried everything. I've reasoned, cajoled, pleaded—hell, I even bribed them." Master Prior's buns had only ratcheted up Jack's energy level.

"Every parent makes those mistakes," he said with a laugh. "You're trying to be their friend. Treat Jack and Annie like pups. The occasional sharp nip on the nose will establish your authority better than a mince pie will."

"Are you giving me parenting tips from the animal kingdom?" I was thinking of his early research into wolves.

"As a matter of fact, I am. If this racket continues, they'll have me to contend with, and I don't nip. I bite." Matthew glowered at the door as a particularly loud crash echoed through our rooms, followed by an abject "Sorry, mistress."

"Thanks, but I'm not desperate enough to resort to obedience training. Yet," I said, backing out of the room.

Two days of using my teacher voice and administering time-outs instilled some degree of order, but the children required a great deal of activity to keep their exuberance in check. I abandoned my books and papers and took them on long walks down Cheapside and into the suburbs to the west. We went to the markets with Françoise and watched the boats unloading their cargo at the docks in the Vintry. There we imagined where the goods came from and speculated about the origins of the crews.

Somewhere along the way, I stopped feeling like a tourist and started feeling as though Elizabethan London was my home.

We were shopping Saturday morning at the Leadenhall Market, London's premier emporium for fine groceries, when I saw a one-legged beggar. I was fishing a penny out of my bag for him when the children disappeared into a hatmaker's shop. They could wreak havoc—expensive havoc—in such a place.

"Annie! Jack!" I called, dropping the penny in the man's palm. "Keep your hands to yourselves!"

"You are far from home, Mistress Roydon," a deep voice said. The skin on my back registered an icy stare, and I turned to find Andrew Hubbard.

"Father Hubbard," I said. The beggar inched away.

Hubbard looked around. "Where is your woman?"

"If you are referring to Françoise, she is in the market," I said tartly. "Annie is with me, too. I haven't had a chance to thank you for sending her to us. She is a great help."

"I understand you have met with Goody Alsop."

I made no reply to this blatant fishing expedition.

"Since the Spanish came, she does not stir from her house unless there is good reason."

Still I was silent. Hubbard smiled.

"I am not your enemy, mistress."

"I didn't say you were, Father Hubbard. But who I see and why is not your concern."

"Yes. Your father-in-law—or do you think of him as your father?—made that quite clear in his letter. Philippe thanked me for assisting you, of course. With the head of the de Clermont family, the thanks always precede the threats. It is a refreshing change from your husband's usual behavior."

My eyes narrowed. "What is it that you want, Father Hubbard?"

"I suffer the presence of the de Clermonts because I must. But I am under no obligation to continue doing so if there is trouble." Hubbard leaned toward me, his breath frosty. "And you are causing trouble. I can smell it. Taste it. Since you've come, the witches have been . . . difficult."

"That's an unfortunate coincidence," I said, "but I'm not to blame. I'm so unschooled in the arts of magic that I can't even crack an egg into a bowl." Françoise came out of the market. I dropped Hubbard a curtsy and moved to step past him. His hand shot out and grabbed me around the wrist. I looked down at his cold fingers.

"It's not just creatures who emit a scent, Mistress Roydon. Did you know that secrets have their own distinct odor?"

"No," I said, drawing my wrist from his grasp.

"Witches can tell when someone lies. *Wearhs* can smell a secret like a hound can scent a deer. I will run your secret to ground, Mistress Roydon, no matter how you try to conceal it."

"Are you ready, *madame*?" Françoise asked, frowning as she drew closer. Annie and Jack were with her, and when the girl spotted Hubbard, she blanched.

"Yes, Françoise," I said, finally looking away from Hubbard's uncanny, striated eyes. "Thank you for your counsel, Father Hubbard, and the information."

"If the boy is too much for you, I would be happy to take care of him," Hubbard murmured as I walked by. I turned and strode back to him.

"Keep your hands off what's mine." Our eyes locked, and this time it was Hubbard who looked away first. I returned to my huddle of vampire, witch, and human. Jack looked anxious and was now shifting from one foot to the other as if considering bolting. "Let's go home and have some gingerbread," I said, taking hold of his arm.

"Who is that man?" he whispered.

"That's Father Hubbard" was Annie's hushed reply.

"The one in the songs?" Jack said, looking over his shoulder. Annie nodded.

"Yes, and when he—"

"Enough, Annie. What did you see in the hat shop?" I asked, gripping Jack more tightly. I extended my hand toward the overflowing basket of groceries. "Let me take that, Françoise."

"It will not help, *madame,*" Françoise said, though she handed me the basket. "*Milord* will know you have been with that fiend. Not even the cabbage's scent will hide it." Jack's head turned in interest at this morsel of information, and I gave Françoise a warning look.

"Let's not borrow trouble," I said as we turned toward home.

Back at the Hart and Crown, I divested myself of basket, cloak, gloves, and children and took a cup of wine in to Matthew. He was at his desk, bent over a sheaf of paper. My heart lightened at the now-familiar sight.

"Still at it?" I asked, reaching over his shoulder to put the wine before him. I frowned. His paper was covered with diagrams, X's and O's, and what looked like modern scientific formulas. I doubted that it had anything to do with espionage or the Congregation, unless he was devising a code. "What are you doing?"

"Just trying to figure something out," Matthew said, sliding the paper away.

"Something genetic?" The X's and O's reminded me of biology and Gregor Mendel's peas. I drew the paper back. There weren't just X's and O's on the page. I recognized initials belonging to members of Matthew's family: YC, PC, MC, MW. Others belonged to my own: DB, RB, SB, SP. Matthew had drawn arrows between individuals, and lines crisscrossed from generation to generation.

"Not strictly speaking," Matthew said, interrupting my examination. It was a classic Matthew nonanswer.

"I suppose you'd need equipment for that." At the bottom of the page, a circle surrounded two letters: B and C—*Bishop and Clairmont.* Our child. This had something to do with the baby.

"In order to draw any conclusions, certainly." Matthew picked up the wine and carried it toward his lips.

"What's your hypothesis, then?" I asked. "If it involves the baby, I want to know what it is."

Matthew froze, his nostrils flaring. He put the wine carefully on the table and took my hand, pressing his lips to my wrist in a seeming gesture of affection. His eyes went black.

"You saw Hubbard," he said accusingly.

"Not because I sought him out." I pulled away. That was a mistake.

"Don't," Matthew rasped, his fingers tightening. He drew another shuddering breath. "Hubbard touched you on the wrist. Only the wrist. Do you know why?"

"Because he was trying to get my attention," I said.

"No. He was trying to capture mine. Your pulse is here," Matthew said, his thumb sweeping over the vein. I shivered. "The blood is so close to the surface that I can see it as well as smell it. Its heat magnifies any foreign scent placed there." His fingers circled my wrist like a bracelet. "Where was Françoise?"

"In Leadenhall Market. I had Jack and Annie with me. There was a beggar, and—" I felt a brief, sharp pain. When I looked down, my wrist was torn and blood welled from a set of shallow, curved nicks. *Teeth marks.*

"That's how fast Hubbard could have taken your blood and known everything about you." Matthew's thumb pressed firmly into the wound.

"But I didn't see you move," I said numbly.

His black eyes gleamed. "Nor would you have seen Hubbard, if he'd wanted to strike."

Perhaps Matthew wasn't as overprotective as I thought.

"Don't let him get close enough to touch you again. Are we clear?"

I nodded, and Matthew began the slow business of managing his anger. Only when he was in control of it did he answer my initial question.

"I'm trying to determine the likelihood of passing my blood rage to our child," he said, a tinge of bitterness in his tone. "Benjamin has the affliction. Marcus doesn't. I hate the fact that I could curse an innocent child with it."

"Do you know why Marcus and your brother Louis were resistant, when you, Louisa, and Benjamin were not?" I carefully avoided assuming that this accounted for all his children. Matthew would tell me more when—if—he was able.

His shoulders lost their sharp edge. "Louisa died long before it was possible to run proper tests. I don't have enough data to draw any reliable conclusions."

"You have a theory, though," I said, thinking of his diagrams.

"I've always thought of blood rage as a kind of infection and supposed Marcus and Louis had a natural resistance to it. But when Goody Alsop told us that only a weaver could bear a *wearh* child, it made me wonder if I've been looking at this the wrong way. Perhaps it's not something in Marcus that's resistant but something in me that's receptive, just as a weaver is receptive to a *wearh*'s seed, unlike any other warmblooded woman."

"A genetic predisposition?" I asked, trying to follow his reasoning.

"Perhaps. Possibly something recessive that seldom shows up in the population unless both parents carry the gene. I keep thinking of your friend Catherine Streeter and your description of her as 'thrice-blessed,' as though her genetic whole is somehow greater than the sum of its parts."

Matthew was quickly lost in the intricacies of his intellectual puzzle. "Then I started wondering whether the fact that you are a weaver is sufficient to explain your ability to conceive. What if it's a combination of recessive genetic traits—not only yours but mine as well?" When his hands drove through his hair in frustration, I took it as a sign that the last of the blood rage was gone and heaved a silent sigh of relief.

"When we get back to your lab, you'll be able to test your theory." I dropped my voice. "And once Sarah and Em hear they're going to be aunts, you'll have no problem getting them to give you a blood sample—or to babysit. They both have bad cases of granny lust and have been borrowing the neighbors' children for years to satisfy it."

That conjured a smile at last.

"Granny lust? What a rude expression." Matthew approached me. "Ysabeau's probably developed a dire case of it, too, over the centuries."

"It doesn't bear thinking about," I said with a mock shudder.

It was in these moments—when we talked about the reactions of others to our news rather than analyzing our own responses to it—that I felt truly pregnant. My body had barely registered the new life it was carrying, and in the day-to-day busyness at the Hart and Crown it was easy to forget that we would soon be parents. I could go for days without thinking about it, only to be reminded of my condition when Matthew came to me, deep in the night, to rest his hands on my belly in silent communion while he listened for the signs of new life.

"Nor can I bear to think of you in harm's way." Matthew took me in his arms. "Be careful, *ma lionne,*" he whispered against my hair.

"I will. I promise."

"You wouldn't recognize danger if it came to you with an engraved invitation." He drew away so that he could look into my eyes. "Just remember: Vampires are not like warmbloods. Don't underestimate how lethal we can be."

Matthew's warning echoed long after he delivered it. I found myself watching the other vampires in the household for the small signs that they were thinking of moving or that they were hungry or tired, restless or bored. The signs were subtle and easy to miss. When Annie walked past Gallowglass, his lids dropped to shutter the avid expression in his eyes, but it was over so quickly I might have imagined it, just as I might have imagined the flaring of Hancock's nostrils when a group of warmbloods passed by on the street below.

I was not imagining the extra laundry charges to clean the blood from their linen, however. Gallowglass and Hancock were hunting and feeding in the city, though Matthew did not join them. He confined himself to what Françoise could procure from the butchers.

When Annie and I went to Mary's on Monday afternoon, as was our custom, I remained more alert to my surroundings than I had been since our arrival. This time it wasn't to absorb the details of Elizabethan life but to make sure we weren't being watched or followed. I kept Annie safely within arm's reach, and Pierre retained a firm grip on Jack. We had learned the hard way that it was the only hope we had of keeping the boy from "magpie-ing," as Hancock called it. In spite of our efforts, Jack still managed to commit numerous acts of petty theft. Matthew instituted a new household ritual in an effort to combat it. Jack had to empty his pockets every night and confess how he'd come by his extraordinary assortment of shiny objects. So far it hadn't put a damper on his activities.

Given his light fingers, Jack could not yet be trusted in the Countess of Pembroke's well-appointed home. Annie and I took our leave of Pierre and Jack, and the girl's expression brightened considerably at the prospect of a long gossip with Mary's maid, Joan, and a few hours of freedom from Jack's unwanted attentions.

"Diana!" Mary cried when I crossed the threshold of her laboratory. No matter how many times I entered, it never failed to take my breath away, with its vivid murals illustrating the making of the philosopher's stone. "Come, I have something to show you."

"Is this your surprise?" Mary had been hinting that she would soon delight me with a display of her alchemical proficiency.

"Yes," Mary replied, drawing her notebook from the table. "See here, it is now the eighteenth of January, and I began the work on the ninth of December. It has taken exactly forty days, just as the sages promised."

Forty was a significant number in alchemical work, and Mary could have been conducting any number of experiments. I looked through her laboratory entries in an effort to figure out what she'd been doing. Over the past two weeks, I'd learned Mary's shorthand and the symbols she used for the various metals and substances. If I understood correctly, she began this process with an ounce of silver dissolved in aqua fortis—the "strong water" of the alchemists, known in my own time as nitric acid. To this, Mary added distilled water.

"Is this your mark for mercury?" I asked, pointing to an unfamiliar glyph.

"Yes—but only the mercury I obtain from the finest source in Germany." Mary spared no expense when it came to her laboratory, chemicals, or equipment. She drew me toward another example of her commitment to quality at any price: a large glass flask. It was free of imperfections and clear as crystal, which meant it had come from Venice. The English glass made in Sussex was marred with tiny bubbles and faint shadows. The Countess of Pembroke preferred the Venetian stuff—and could afford it.

When I saw what was inside, a premonitory finger brushed against my shoulders.

A silver tree grew from a small seed in the bottom of the flask. Branches had sprouted from the trunk, forking out and filling the top of the vessel with glittering strands. Tiny beads at the ends of the branches suggested fruit, as though the tree were ripe and ready for harvesting.

"The *arbor Dianæ,*" Mary said proudly. "It is as though God inspired me to make it so that it would be here to welcome you. I have tried to grow the tree before, but it has never taken root. No one could see such a thing and doubt the truth and power of the alchemical art."

Diana's tree was a sight to behold. It gleamed and grew before my eyes, sending out new shoots to fill the remaining space in the vessel. Knowing that it was nothing more than a dendritic amalgam of crystallized silver did little to diminish my wonder at seeing a lump of metal go through what looked like a vegetative process.

On the wall opposite, a dragon sat over a vessel similar to the one Mary had used to house the *arbor Dianæ.* The dragon held his tail in his mouth, and drops of his blood fell into the silvery liquid below. I sought out the next image in the series: the bird of Hermes who flew toward the chemical marriage. The bird reminded me of the illustration of the wedding from Ashmole 782.

"I think it might be possible to devise a quicker method to achieve the same result," Mary said, drawing back my attention. She pulled a quill from her upswept hair, leaving a black smudge over her ear. "What do you imagine would happen if we filed the silver before dissolving it in the aqua fortis?"

We spent a pleasant afternoon discussing new ways to make the *arbor Dianæ,* but it was over all too soon.

"Will I see you Thursday?" Mary asked.

"I'm afraid I have another obligation," I said. I was expected at Goody Alsop's before sunset.

Mary's face fell. "Friday, then?"

"Friday," I agreed.

"Diana," Mary said hesitantly, "are you well?"

"Yes," I said in surprise. "Do I seem ill?"

"You are pale and look tired," she admitted. "Like most mothers I am prone to— Oh." Mary stopped abruptly and turned bright pink. Her eyes dropped to my stomach, then flew back to my face. "You are with child."

"I will have many questions for you in the weeks ahead," I said, taking her hand and giving it a squeeze.

"How far along are you?" she asked.

"Not far," I said, keeping my answer deliberately vague.

"But the child cannot be Matthew's. A *wearh* is not able to father a child," Mary said, her hand rising to her cheek in wonder. "Matthew welcomes the babe, even though it is not his?"

Though Matthew had warned me that everybody would assume the child belonged to another man, we hadn't discussed how to respond. I would have to punt.

"He considers it his own blood," I said firmly. My answer only seemed to increase her concern.

"You are fortunate that Matthew is so selfless when it comes to protecting those who are in need. And you—can *you* love the child, though you were taken against your will?"

Mary thought I'd been raped—and perhaps that Matthew had married me only to shield me from the stigma of being pregnant and single.

"The child is innocent. I cannot refuse it love." I was careful neither to deny nor confirm Mary's suspicions. Happily, she was satisfied with my response, and, characteristically, she probed no further. "As you can imagine," I added, "we are eager to keep this news quiet for as long as possible."

"Of course," Mary agreed. "I will have Joan make you a soft custard that fortifies the blood yet is very soothing to the stomach if taken at night before you sleep. It was a great help to me in my last pregnancy and seemed to lessen my sickness in the morning."

"I have been blessedly free of that complaint so far," I said, drawing on my gloves. "Matthew promises me it will come any day now."

"Hmm," Mary mused, a shadow crossing her face. I frowned, wondering what was worrying her now. She saw my expression and smiled brightly. "You should guard against fatigue. When you are here on Friday, you must not stand so long but take your ease on a stool while we work." Mary fussed over the arrangement of my cloak. "Stay out of drafts. And have Françoise make a poultice for your feet if they start to swell. I will send a receipt for it with the custard. Shall I have my boatman take you to Water Lane?"

"It's only a five-minute walk!" I protested with a laugh. Finally Mary let me leave on foot, but only after I assured her that I would avoid not only drafts but also cold water and loud noises.

That night I dreamed I slept under the limbs of a tree that grew from my womb. Its branches shielded me from the moonlight while, high above, a dragon flew through the night. When it reached the moon, the dragon's tail curled around it and the silver orb turned red.

I awoke to an empty bed and blood-soaked sheets.

"Françoise!" I cried, feeling a sudden, sharp cramp.

Matthew came running instead. The devastated look on his face when he reached my side confirmed my fears.

"We have all lost babes, Diana," Goody Alsop said sadly. "It is a pain most women know."

"All?" I looked around Goody Alsop's keeping room at the witches of the Garlickhythe gathering.

The stories tumbled out, of babies lost in childbirth and others who died at six months or six years. I didn't know any women who had miscarried—or I didn't think I did. Had one of my friends suffered such a loss, without my knowing it?

"You are young and strong," Susanna said. "There is no reason to think you cannot conceive another child."

No reason at all, except for the fact that my husband wouldn't touch me again until we were back in the land of birth control and fetal monitors.

"Maybe," I said with a noncommittal shrug.

"Where is Master Roydon?" Goody Alsop said quietly. Her fetch drifted around the parlor as if she thought she might find him in the window-seat cushions or sitting atop the cupboard.

"Out on business," I said, drawing my borrowed shawl tighter. It was Susanna's, and it smelled like burned sugar and chamomile, just as she did.

"I heard he was at the Middle Temple Hall with Christopher Marlowe last night. Watching a play, by all accounts." Catherine passed the box of comfits she'd brought to Goody Alsop.

"Ordinary men can pine terribly for a lost child. I am not surprised that a *wearh* would find it especially difficult. They are possessive, after all." Goody Alsop reached for something red and gelatinous. "Thank you, Catherine."

The women waited in silence, hoping I'd take Goody Alsop and Catherine up on their circumspect invitation to tell them how Matthew and I were faring.

"He'll be fine," I said tightly.

"He should be here," Elizabeth said sharply. "I can see no reason why his loss should be more painful than yours!"

"Because Matthew has endured a thousand years of heartbreak and I've only endured thirty-three," I said, my tone equally sharp. "He is a *wearh,* Elizabeth. Do I wish he were here rather than out with Kit? Of course. Will I beg him to stay at the Hart and Crown for my sake? Absolutely not." My voice was rising as my hurt and frustration spilled over. Matthew had been unfailingly sweet and tender with me. He'd comforted me as I faced the hundreds of fragile dreams for the future that had been destroyed when I miscarried our child.

It was the hours he was spending elsewhere that had me concerned.

"My head tells me Matthew must have a chance to grieve in his own way," I said. "My heart tells me he loves me even though he prefers to be with his friends now. I just wish he could touch me without regret." I could feel it whenever he looked at me, held me, took my hand. It was unbearable.

"I am sorry, Diana," Elizabeth said, her face contrite.

"It's all right," I assured her.

But it wasn't all right. The whole world felt discordant and wrong, with colors that were too bright and sounds so loud they made me jump. My body felt hollow, and no matter what I tried to read, the words failed to keep my attention.

"We will see you tomorrow, as planned," Goody Alsop said briskly as the witches departed.

"Tomorrow?" I frowned. "I'm in no mood to make magic, Goody Alsop."

"I'm in no mood to go to my grave without seeing you weave your first spell, so I shall expect you when the bells ring six."

That night I stared into the fire as the bells rang six, and seven, and eight, and nine, and ten. When the bells rang three, I heard a sound on the stairs. Thinking it was Matthew, I went to the door. The staircase was empty, but a clutch of objects sat on the stairs: an infant's sock, a sprig of holly, a twist of paper with a man's name written on it. I gathered them all up in my lap as I sank onto one of the worn treads, clutching my shawl tight around me.

I was still trying to figure out what the offerings meant and how they had gotten there when Matthew shot up the stairs in a soundless blur. He stopped abruptly.

"Diana." He drew the back of his hand across his mouth, his eyes green and glassy.

"At least you'll feed when you're with Kit," I said, getting to my feet.

"It's nice to know that your friendship includes more than poetry and chess."

Matthew put his boot on the tread next to my feet. He used his knee to press me toward the wall, effectively trapping me. His breath was sweet and slightly metallic.

"You're going to hate yourself in the morning," I said calmly, turning my head away. I knew better than to run when the tang of blood was still on his lips. "Kit should have kept you with him until the drugs were out of your system. Does all the blood in London have opiates in it?" It was the second night in a row Matthew had gone out with Kit and come home high as a kite.

"Not all," Matthew purred, "but it is the easiest to come by."

"What are these?" I held up the sock, the holly, and the scroll.

"They're for you," Matthew said. "More arrive every night. Pierre and I collect them before you are awake."

"When did this start?" I didn't trust myself to say more.

"The week before— The week you met with the Rede. Most are requests for help. Since you— Since Monday there have been gifts for you, too." Matthew held out his hand. "I'll take care of them."

I drew my hand closer to my heart. "Where are the rest?"

Matthew's mouth tightened, but he showed me where he was keeping them—in a box in the attic, shoved under one of the benches. I picked through the contents, which were somewhat similar to what Jack pulled out of his pockets each night: buttons, bits of ribbon, a piece of broken crockery. There were locks of hair, too, and dozens of pieces of paper inscribed with names. Though they were invisible to most eyes, I could see the jagged threads that hung from every treasure, all waiting to be tied off, joined up, or otherwise mended.

"These are requests for magic." I looked up at Matthew. "You shouldn't have kept this from me."

"I don't want you performing spells for every creature in the city of London," Matthew said, his eyes darkening.

"Well, I don't want you to eat out every night before going drinking with your friends! But you're a vampire, so sometimes that's what you need to do," I retorted. "I'm a witch, Matthew. Requests like this have to be handled carefully. My safety depends on my relations with our neighbors. I can't go stealing boats like Gallowglass or growling at people."

"Milord." Pierre stood at the far end of the attics, where a narrow stair twirled down to a hidden exit behind the laundresses' giant washtubs.

"What?" Matthew said impatiently.

"Agnes Sampson is dead." Pierre looked frightened. "They took her to Castlehill in Edinburgh on Saturday, garroted her, and then burned the body."

"Christ." Matthew paled.

"Hancock said she was fully dead before the wood was lit. She wouldn't have felt anything," Pierre went on. It was a small mercy, one not always afforded to a convicted witch. "They refused to read your letter, *milord.* Hancock was told to leave Scottish politics to the Scottish king or they'd put the screws to him the next time he showed his face in Edinburgh."

"Why can't I fix this?" Matthew exploded.

"So it's not just the loss of the baby that's driven you toward Kit's darkness. You're hiding from the events in Scotland, too."

"No matter how hard I try to set things right, I cannot seem to break this cursed pattern," Matthew said. "Before, as the queen's spy, I delighted in the trouble in Scotland. As a member of the Congregation, I considered Sampson's death an acceptable price to pay to maintain the status quo. But now . . ."

"Now you're married to a witch," I said. "And everything looks different."

"Yes. I'm caught between what I once believed and what I now hold most dear, what I once proudly defended as gospel truth and the magnitude of what I no longer know."

"I will go back into the city," Pierre said, turning toward the door. "There may be more to discover."

I studied Matthew's tired face. "You can't expect to understand all of life's tragedies, Matthew. I wish we still had the baby, too. And I know it seems hopeless right now, but that doesn't mean there isn't a future to look forward to—one in which our children and family are safe."

"A miscarriage this early in pregnancy is almost always a sign of a genetic anomaly that makes the fetus nonviable. If that happened once . . ." His voice trailed off.

"There are genetic anomalies that don't compromise the baby," I pointed out. "Take me, for instance." I was a chimera, with mismatching DNA.

"I can't bear losing another child, Diana. I just . . . can't."

"I know." I was bone weary and wanted the blessed oblivion of sleep as much as he did. I had never known my child as he had known Lucas, and the pain was still unbearable. "I have to be at Goody Alsop's house at six tonight." I looked up at him. "Will you be out with Kit?"

"No," Matthew said softly. He pressed his lips to mine—briefly, regretfully. "I'll be with you."

Matthew was true to his word, and escorted me to Goody Alsop's before going to the Golden Gosling with Pierre. In the most courteous way possible, the witches explained that *wearhs* were not welcome. Taking a weaver safely through her forspell required a considerable mobilization of supernatural and magical energy. *Wearhs* would only get in the way.

My Aunt Sarah would have paid close attention to how Susanna and Marjorie readied the sacred circle. Some of the substances and equipment they used were familiar—like the salt they sprinkled on the floorboards to purify the space—but others were not. Sarah's witch's kit consisted of two knives (one with a black handle and one with a white), the Bishop grimoire, and various herbs and plants. Elizabethan witches required a greater variety of objects to work their magic, including brooms. I'd never seen a witch with a broom except on Halloween when they were de rigueur, along with pointed hats.

Each of the witches of the Garlickhythe gathering brought a unique broom with her to Goody Alsop's house. Marjorie's was fashioned from a cherry branch. At the top of the staff, someone had carved glyphs and symbols. Instead of the usual bristles, Marjorie had tied dried herbs and twigs to the bottom where the central limb forked into thinner branches. She told me that the herbs were important to her magic—agrimony to break enchantments, lacy feverfew with the white-and-yellow flowers still attached for protection, the sturdy stems of rosemary with their glaucous leaves for purification and clarity. Susanna's broom was made from elm, which was symbolic of the phases of life from birth to death and related to her profession as a midwife. So, too, were the plants tied to the staff: the fleshy green leaves of adder's tongue for healing, boneset's frothy white flower heads for protection, the spiky leaves of groundsel for good health.

Marjorie and Susanna carefully swept the salt in a clockwise direction until the fine grains had traveled over every inch of the floor. The salt would not only cleanse the space, Marjorie explained, but also ground it so that my power wouldn't spill over into the world once it was fully unbound.

Goody Alsop stopped up the windows, the doors—even the chimney. The house ghosts were given the option of staying out of the way amid the roof beams or finding temporary refuge with the family who lived downstairs. Not wishing to miss anything, and slightly jealous of the fetch who had no choice but to stay by her mistress, the ghosts flitted among the rafters and gossiped about whether any of the residents of Newgate Street would get a moment's peace now that the specters of medieval Queen Isabella and a murderess named Lady Agnes Hungerford had resumed their squabbling.

Elizabeth and Catherine settled my nerves—and drowned out the gruesome details of Lady Agnes's terrible deeds and death—by sharing some of their early magical adventures and drawing me out about my own. Elizabeth was impressed by how I'd channeled the water from under Sarah's orchard, pulling it into my palms drop by drop. And Catherine crowed with delight when I shared how a bow and arrow rested heavy in my hands just before the witchfire flew.

"The moon has risen," Marjorie said, her round face pink with anticipation. The shutters were closed, but none of the other witches questioned her.

"It is time, then," Elizabeth said briskly, all business.

Each witch went from one corner of the room to the next, breaking off a twig from her broom and placing it there. But these were not random piles. They'd arranged the twigs so as to overlap and form a pentacle, the witch's five-pointed star.

Goody Alsop and I took up our positions at the center of the circle. Though its boundaries were invisible, that would change when the other witches took their appointed places. Once they had, Catherine murmured a spell and a curved line of fire traveled from witch to witch, binding the circle.

Power surged in its center. Goody Alsop had warned me that what we were doing this night invoked ancient magics. Soon the buffeting wave of energy was replaced by something that tingled and snapped like a thousand witchy glances.

"Look around you with your witch's sight," Goody Alsop said, "and tell me what you see."

When my third eye opened, I half expected to find that the air itself had come to life, every particle charged with possibility. Instead the room was filled with filaments of magic.

"Threads," I said, "as though the world is nothing more than a tapestry."

Goody Alsop nodded. "To be a weaver is to be tied to the world around you and see it in strands and hues. While some ties fetter your magic, others yoke the power in your blood to the four elements and the great mysteries that lie beyond them. Weavers learn how to release the ties that bind and use the rest."

"But I don't know how to tell them apart." Hundreds of strands brushed against my skirts and bodice.

"Soon you will test them, like a bird tests its wings, to discover what secrets they hold for you. Now, we will simply cut them all away, so that they can return to you unbound. As I snip the threads, you must resist the temptation to grab at the power around you. Because you are a weaver, you will want to mend what is broken. Leave your thoughts free and your mind empty. Let the power do as it will."

Goody Alsop released my arm and began to weave her spell with sounds that bore no resemblance to speech but were strangely familiar. With each utterance I saw the filaments fall away from me, coiling and twisting. A roaring filled my ears. My arms heeded the sound as if it were a command, rising up and stretching out until I was standing in the same T-shaped position that Matthew had placed me in at the Bishop house when I drew the water from underneath Sarah's old orchard.

The strands of magic—all those threads of power that I could borrow but not hold—crept back toward me as if they were made of iron filings and I were a magnet. As they came to rest in my hands, I struggled against the urge to close my fists around them. The desire to do so was strong, as Goody Alsop predicted it would be, but I let them slide over my skin like the satin ribbons in the stories my mother told me when I was a child.

So far everything had happened as Goody Alsop had told me it would. But no one could predict what might occur when my powers took shape, and the witches around the circle braced themselves to meet the unknown. Goody Alsop had warned me that not all weavers shaped a familiar in their forspell, so I shouldn't expect one to appear. But my life these past months had taught me that the unexpected was more likely than not when I was around.

The roaring intensified, and the air stirred. A swirling ball of energy hung directly over my head. It drew power from the room but kept collapsing into its own center like a black hole. My witch's eye closed tightly against the dizzying, roiling sight.

Something pulsed in the midst of the storm. It pulled free and took on a shadowy form. As soon as it did so, Goody Alsop fell silent. She gave me one final, long look before she left me, alone, in the center of the circle.

There was a beating of wings, the lash of a barbed tail. A hot, moist breath licked across my cheek. A transparent creature with the reptilian head of a dragon hovered in the air, bright wings striking the rafters and sending the ghosts scuttling for cover. It had only two legs, and the curved talons on its feet looked as deadly as the points along its long tail.

"How many legs does it have?" Marjorie called, unable to see clearly from her position. "Is it just a dragon?"

Just a dragon?

"It's a firedrake," Catherine said in wonder. She raised her arms, ready to cast a warding spell if it decided to strike. Elizabeth Jackson's arms moved, too.

"Wait!" Goody Alsop cried, interrupting their magic. "Diana has not yet completed her weaving. Perhaps she will find a way to tame her."

Tame her? I looked at Goody Alsop incredulously. I wasn't even sure if the creature before me was substance or spirit. She seemed real, but I could see right through her.

"I don't know what to do," I said, beginning to panic. Every flap of the creature's wings sent a shower of sparks and drops of fire into the room.

"Some spells begin with an idea, others with a question. There are many ways to think about what comes next: tying a knot, twisting a rope, even forging a chain like the one that you made between you and your *wearh*," Goody Alsop said, her tone low and soothing. "Let the power move through you."

The firedrake roared in impatience, her feet extending toward me. What did she want? A chance to pick me up and carry me from the house? A comfortable place to perch and rest her wings?

The floor underneath me creaked.

"Step aside!" Marjorie cried.

I moved just in time. A moment later a tree sprouted from the place where my feet had recently been planted. The trunk rose up, divided into two stout limbs, and branched out further. Shoots grew into green leaves at the tips, and then came white blossoms, and finally red berries. In a matter of seconds, I was standing beneath a full-grown tree, one that was flowering and fruiting at the same time.

The firedrake's feet gripped at the tree's uppermost branches. For a moment she seemed to rest there. A branch creaked and cracked. The firedrake lifted back into the air, a gnarled piece of the tree clutched in her talons. The firedrake's tongue flicked out in a lash of fire, and the tree burst into flame. There were far too many flammable objects in the room—the wooden floors and furniture, the fabric that clothed the witches. All I could think was that I must stop the fire from spreading. I needed water—and lots of it.

There was a heavy weight in my right hand. I looked down, expecting to see a bucket. Instead I was holding an arrow. Witchfire. But what good was more fire?

"No, Diana! Don't try to shape the spell!" Goody Alsop warned.

I shook myself free of thoughts of rain and rivers. As soon as I did, instinct took over and my two arms rose in front of me, my right hand drew back, and once my fingers unfurled, the arrow flew into the heart of the tree. The flames shot up high and fast, blinding me. The heat died down, and when my sight returned, I found myself atop a mountain under a vast, starry sky. A huge crescent moon hung low in the heavens.

"I've been waiting for you." The goddess's voice was little more than a breath of wind. She was wearing soft robes, her hair cascading down her back. There was no sign of her usual weapons, but a large dog padded along at her side. He was so big and black he might have been a wolf.

"You." A sense of dread squeezed around my heart. I had been expecting to see the goddess since I lost the baby. "Did you take my child in exchange for saving Matthew's life?" My question came out part fury, part despair.

"No. That debt is settled. I have already taken another. A dead child is of no use to me." The huntress's eyes were green as the first shoots of willow in spring.

My blood ran cold. "Whose life have you taken?"

"Yours."

"Mine?" I said numbly. "Am I . . . dead?"

"Of course not. The dead belong to another. It is the living I seek." The huntress's voice was now as piercing and bright as a moonbeam. "You promised I could take anyone—anything—in exchange for the life of the one you love. I chose you. And I am not done with you yet."

The goddess took a step backward. "You gave your life to me, Diana Bishop. It is now time to make use of it."

A cry overhead alerted me to the presence of the firedrake. I looked up, trying to make her out against the moon. When I blinked, her outline was perfectly visible against Goody Alsop's ceiling. I was back in the witch's house, no longer on a barren hilltop with the goddess. The tree was gone, reduced to a heap of ash. I blinked again.

The firedrake blinked back at me. Her eyes were sad and familiar—black, with silver irises rather than white. With another harsh cry, she released her talons. The branch of the tree fell into my arms. It felt like the arrow's shaft, heavier and more substantial than its size would suggest. The firedrake bobbed her head, smoke coming in wisps from her nostrils. I was tempted to reach up and touch her, wondering if her skin would be warm and soft like a snake, but something told me she wouldn't welcome it. And I didn't want to startle her. She might rear back and poke her head through the roof. I was already worried about the condition of Goody Alsop's house after the tree and the fire.

"Thank you," I whispered.

The firedrake replied with a quiet moan of fire and song. Her silver-and-black eyes were ancient and wise as she studied me, her tail flicking back and forth pensively. She stretched her wings to their full extent before tightening them around her body and dematerializing.

All that was left of the firedrake was a tingling sensation in my ribs that told me somehow she was inside me, waiting until I needed her. With the weight of this beast heavily inside me, I fell to my knees, and the branch clattered to the floor. The witches rushed forward.

Goody Alsop reached me first, her thin arms reaching around to gather me close. "You did well, child, you did well," she whispered. Elizabeth cupped her hand and with a few words transformed it into a shallow silver dipper full of water. I drank from it, and when the cup was empty, it went back to being nothing more than a hand.

"This is a great day, Goody Alsop," Catherine said, her face wreathed in smiles.

"Aye, and a hard one for such a young witch," Goody Alsop said. "You do nothing by halves, Diana Roydon. First you are no ordinary witch but a weaver. And then you weave a forspell that called forth a rowan tree simply to tame a firedrake. Had I foreseen this, I would not have believed it."

"I saw the goddess," I explained as they helped me to my feet, "and a dragon."

"That was no dragon," Elizabeth said.

"It had but two legs," Marjorie explained. "That makes her not only a creature of fire but one of water, too, capable of moving between the elements. The firedrake is a union of opposites."

"What is true of the firedrake is true of the rowan tree as well," Goody Alsop said with a proud smile. "It is not every day that a rowan tree pushes its branches into one world while leaving its roots in another."

In spite of the happy chatter of the women who surrounded me, I found myself thinking of Matthew. He was waiting at the Golden Gosling for news. My third eye opened, seeking out a twisted thread of black and red that led from my heart, across the room, through the keyhole, and into the darkness beyond. I gave it a tug, and the chain inside me responded with a sympathetic chime.

"If I'm not very much mistaken, Master Roydon will be around shortly to collect his wife," Goody Alsop said drily. "Let's get you on your feet, or he'll think we cannot be trusted with you."

"Matthew can be protective," I said apologetically. "Even more so since . . ."

"I've never known a *wearh* who wasn't. It's their nature," Goody Alsop said, helping me up. The air had gone particulate again, brushing softly against my skin as I moved.

"Master Roydon need not fear in this case," Elizabeth said. "We will make sure you can find your way back from the darkness, just like your firedrake."

"What darkness?"

The witches went silent.

"What darkness?" I repeated, pushing my fatigue aside.

Goody Alsop sighed. "There are witches—a very few witches—who can move between this world and the next."

"Time spinners," I said with a nod. "Yes, I know. I'm one of them."

"Not between this *time* and the next, Diana, but between this *world* and the next." Marjorie gestured at the branch by my feet. "Life—and death. You can be in both worlds. That is why the rowan chose you, not the alder or the birch."

"We did wonder if this might be the case. You were able to conceive a *wearh*'s child, after all." Goody Alsop looked at me intently. The blood had drained from my face. "What is it, Diana?"

"The quinces. And the flowers." My knees weakened again but I remained standing. "Mary Sidney's shoe. And the oak tree in Madison."

"And the *wearh,*" Goody Alsop said softly, understanding without my telling her. "So many signs pointing to the truth."

A muffled thumping rose from outdoors.

"He mustn't know," I said urgently, grabbing at Goody Alsop's hand. "Not now. It's too soon after the baby, and Matthew doesn't want me meddling with matters of life and death."

"It is a bit late for that," she said sadly.

"Diana!" Matthew's fist pounded on the door.

"The *wearh* will split the wood in two," Marjorie observed. "Master Roydon won't be able to break the binding spell and enter, but the door will make a fearsome crash when it gives way. Think of your neighbors, Goody Alsop."

Goody Alsop gestured with her hand. The air thickened, then relaxed.

Matthew was standing before me in the space of a heartbeat. His gray eyes raked over me. "What happened here?"

"If Diana wants you to know, she will tell you," said Goody Alsop. She turned to me. "In light of what happened tonight, I think you should spend time with Catherine and Elizabeth tomorrow."

"Thank you, Goody," I murmured, grateful that she had not revealed my secrets.

"Wait." Catherine went to the branch from the rowan tree and snapped off a thin twig. "Take this. You should have a piece with you at all times for a talisman." Catherine dropped the bit of wood into my palm.

Not only Pierre but Gallowglass and Hancock were waiting for us in the street. They hustled me into a boat that waited at the bottom of Garlic Hill. After we arrived back at Water Lane Matthew sent everyone away, and we were left in the blissful quiet of our bedchamber.

"I don't need to know what happened," Matthew said roughly, closing the door behind him. "I just need to know that you're truly all right."

"I'm truly fine." I turned my back to him so that he could loosen the laces on my bodice.

"You're afraid of something. I can smell it." Matthew spun me around to face him.

"I'm afraid of what I might find out about myself." I met his eyes squarely.

"You'll find your truth." He sounded so sure, so unconcerned. But he didn't know about the dragon and the rowan and what they meant for a weaver. Matthew didn't know that my life belonged to the goddess either, nor that it was because of the bargain I'd made to save him.

"What if I become someone else and you don't like her?"

"Not possible," he assured me, drawing me closer.

"Even if we find out that the powers of life and death are in my blood?"

Matthew pulled away.

"Saving you in Madison wasn't a fluke, Matthew. I breathed life into Mary's shoes, too—just as I sucked the life out of the oak tree at Sarah's and the quinces here."

"Life and death are big responsibilities." Matthew's gray-green eyes were somber. "But I will love you regardless. You forget, I have power over life and death, too. What is it you told me that night I went hunting in Oxford? You said there was no difference between us. *'Occasionally I eat partridge. Occasionally you feed on deer.'*

"We are more similar, you and I, than either of us imagined," Matthew continued. "But if you can believe good of me, knowing what you do of my past deeds, then you must allow me to believe the same of you."

Suddenly I wanted to share my secrets. "There was a firedrake and a tree—"

"And the only thing that matters is that you are safely home," he said, quieting me with a kiss.

Matthew held me so long and so tightly that for a few blissful moments I—almost—believed him.

The next day I went to Goody Alsop's house to meet with Elizabeth Jackson and Catherine Streeter as promised. Annie accompanied me, but she was sent over to Susanna's house to wait until my lesson was done.

The rowan branch was propped up in the corner. Otherwise the room looked perfectly ordinary and not at all like the kind of place where witches drew sacred circles or summoned firedrakes. Still, I expected some more visible signs that magic was about to be performed—a cauldron, perhaps, or colored candles to signify the elements.

Goody Alsop gestured to the table, where four chairs were arranged.

"Come, Diana, and sit. We thought we might begin at the beginning. Tell us about your family. Much is revealed by following a witch's bloodline."

"But I thought you would teach me how to weave spells with fire and water."

"What is blood, if not fire and water?" Elizabeth said.

Three hours later I was talked out and exhausted from dredging up memories of my childhood—the feeling of being watched, Peter Knox's visit to the house, my parents' death. But the three witches didn't stop there. I relived every moment of high school and college, too: the daemons who followed me, the few spells I could perform without too much trouble, the strange occurrences that began only after I met Matthew. If there was a pattern to any of it, I failed to see it, but Goody Alsop sent me off with assurances that they would soon have a plan.

I dragged myself to Baynard's Castle. Mary tucked me into a chair and refused my help, insisting I rest while she figured out what was wrong with our batch of *prima materia*. It had gone all black and sludgy, with a thin film of greenish goo on top.

My thoughts drifted while Mary worked. The day was sunny, and a beam of light sliced through the smoky air and fell on the mural depicting the alchemical dragon. I sat forward in my chair.

"No," I said. "It can't be."

But it was. The dragon was not a dragon for it had only two legs. It was a firedrake and carried its barbed tail in its mouth, like the ouroboros on the de Clermont banner. The firedrake's head was tilted to the sky, and it held a crescent moon in its jaws. A multipointed star rose above it. *Matthew's emblem.* How had I not noticed before?

"What is it, Diana?" asked a frowning Mary.

"Would you do something for me, Mary, even if the request is strange?" I was already untying the silk cord at my wrists in anticipation of her answer.

"Of course. What is it you need?"

The firedrake dripped squiggly blobs of blood into the alchemical vessel below its wings. There the blood swam in a sea of mercury and silver.

"I want you to take my blood and put it in a solution of aqua fortis, silver, and mercury," I said. Mary's glance moved from me to the firedrake and back. "For what is blood but fire and water, a conjunction of opposites, and a chemical wedding?"

"Very well, Diana," Mary agreed, sounding mystified. But she asked no more questions.

I flicked my finger confidently over the scar on my inner arm. I had no need for a knife this time. The skin parted, as I knew it would, and the blood welled up simply because I had need of it. Joan rushed forward with a small bowl to catch the red liquid. On the wall above, the silver and black eyes of the firedrake followed the drops as they fell.

"'*It begins with absence and desire, it begins with blood and fear,*'" I whispered.

"'*It began with a discovery of witches,*'" time responded, in a primeval echo that set alight the blue and amber threads that flickered against the room's stone walls.

"Is it going to keep doing that?" I stood, frowning, hands on my hips, and stared up at Susanna's ceiling.

"'She,' Diana. Your firedrake is female," Catherine said. She was also looking at the ceiling, her expression bemused.

"She. It. That." I pointed up. I had been trying to weave a spell when my dragon escaped confinement within my rib cage. Again. She was now plastered to the ceiling, breathing out gusts of smoke and chattering her teeth in agitation. "I can't have it—her—flying around the room whenever she feels the urge." The repercussions would be serious should she become loose at Yale among the students.

"That your firedrake broke free is merely a symptom of a much more serious problem." Goody Alsop extended a bunch of brightly colored silken strands, knotted together at the top. The ends flowed free like the ribbons on a maypole and numbered nine in all, in shades of red, white, black, silver, gold, green, brown, blue, and yellow. "You are a weaver and must learn to control your power."

"I am well aware of that, Goody Alsop, but I still don't see how this—embroidery floss—will help," I said stubbornly. The dragon squawked in agreement, waxing more substantial with the sound and then waning into her typical smoky outlines.

"And what do you know about being a weaver?" Goody Alsop asked sharply.

"Not much," I confessed.

"Diana should sip this first." Susanna approached me with a steaming cup. The scents of chamomile and mint filled the air. My dragon cocked her head in interest. "It is a calming draft and may soothe her beast."

"I am not so concerned with the firedrake," Catherine said dismissively. "Getting one to obey is always difficult—like trying to curb a daemon who is intent on making mischief." It was, I thought, easy for her to say. She didn't have to persuade the beast to climb back inside her.

"What plants went into the tisane?" I asked, taking a sip of Susanna's brew. After Marthe's tea I was a bit suspicious of herbal concoctions. No sooner was the question out of my mouth than the cup began to bloom with sprigs of mint, the straw-scented flowers of chamomile, foamy Angelica, and some stiff, glossy leaves that I couldn't identify. I swore.

"You see!" Catherine said, pointing to the cup. "It's as I said. When Diana asks a question, the goddess answers it."

Susanna looked at her beaker with alarm as it cracked under the pressure of the swelling roots. "I think you are right, Catherine. But if she is to weave rather than break things, she will need to ask better questions."

Goody Alsop and Catherine had figured out the secret to my power: It was inconveniently tied to my curiosity. Now certain events made better sense: my white table and its brightly colored puzzle pieces that came to my rescue whenever I faced a problem, the butter flying out of Sarah's refrigerator in Madison when I wondered if there was more. Even the strange appearance of Ashmole 782 at the Bodleian Library could be explained: When I filled out the call slip, I'd wondered what might be in the volume. Earlier today my simple musings about who might have written one of the spells in Susanna's grimoire had caused the ink to unspool from the page and re-form on the table next to it in an exact likeness of her dead grandmother.

I promised Susanna to put the words back as soon as I figured out how.

And so I discovered that the practice of magic was not unlike the practice of history. The trick to both wasn't finding the correct answers but formulating better questions.

"Tell us again about calling witchwater, Diana, and the bow and arrow that appear when someone you love is in trouble," Susanna suggested. "Perhaps that will provide some method we can follow."

I rehearsed the events of the night Matthew had left me at Sept-Tours when the water had come out of me in a flood and the morning in Sarah's orchard when I'd seen the veins of water underground. And I carefully accounted for every time the bow had appeared—even when there was no arrow or when there was but I didn't shoot it. When I finished, Catherine drew a satisfied sigh.

"I see the problem now. Diana is not fully present unless she is protecting someone or when forced to face her fears," Catherine observed. "She is always puzzling over the past or wondering about the future. A witch must be entirely in the here and now to work magic." My firedrake flapped her wings in agreement, sending warm gusts of air around the room.

"Matthew always thought there was a connection between my emotions, my needs, and my magic," I told them.

"Sometimes I wonder if that *wearh* is not part witch," Catherine said. The others laughed at the ridiculous notion of Ysabeau de Clermont's son having even a drop of witch's blood.

"I think it's safe to leave the firedrake to her own devices for the time being and return to the matter of Diana's disguising spell," Goody Alsop said, referring to my need to shield the surfeit of energy that was released whenever I used magic. "Are you making any progress?"

"I felt wisps of smoke form around me," I said hesitantly.

"You need to focus on your knots," Goody Alsop said, looking pointedly at the cords in my lap. Each shade could be found in the threads that bound the worlds, and manipulating the cords—twisting and tying them—worked a sympathetic magic. But first I needed to know which strands to use. I took hold of the colorful cords by the topknot. Goody Alsop had taught me how to blow gently on the strands while focusing my intentions. That was supposed to loosen the appropriate cords for whatever spell I was trying to weave.

I blew into the strands so that they shimmered and danced. The yellow and brown cords worked themselves loose and dropped into my lap, along with the red, blue, silver, and white. I ran my fingers down the nine-inch lengths of twisted silk. Six strands meant six different knots, each one more complex than the last.

My knot-making skills were still clumsy, but I found this part of weaving oddly soothing. When I practiced the elaborate twistings and crossings with ordinary string, the result was something reminiscent of ancient Celtic knotwork. There was a hierarchical order to the knots. The first two were single and double slipknots. Sarah used them sometimes, when she was making a love spell or some other binding. But only weavers could make the intricate knots that involved as many as nine distinct crossings and ended with the two free ends of the cord magically fused to make an unbreakable weaving.

I took a deep breath and refocused my intentions. A disguise was a form of protection, and purple was its color. But there was no purple cord.

Without delay the blue and red cords rose up and spun together so tightly that the final result looked exactly like the mottled purple candles that my mother used to set in the windows on the nights when the moon was dark.

"With knot of one, the spell's begun," I murmured, looping the purple cord into the simple slipknot. The firedrake crooned an imitation of my words.

I looked up at her and was struck once again by the firedrake's changeable appearance. When she breathed out, she faded into a blurred smudge of smoke. When she breathed in, her outlines sharpened. She was a perfect balance of substance and spirit, neither one nor the other. Would I ever feel that coherent?

"With knot of two, the spell be true." I made a double knot along the same purple cord. Wondering if there was a way I could fade into gray obscurity whenever I wished, the way the firedrake did, I ran the yellow cord through my fingers. The third knot was the first true weaver's knot I had to make. Though it involved only three crossings, it was still a challenge.

"With knot of three, the spell is free." I looped and twisted the cord into a trefoil shape, then drew the ends together. They fused to form the weaver's unbreakable knot.

Sighing with relief, I dropped it into my lap, and from my mouth came a gray mist finer than smoke. It hung around me like a shroud. I gasped in surprise, letting out more of the eerie, transparent fog. I looked up. Where had the firedrake gone? The brown cord leaped into my fingers.

"With knot of four, the power is stored." I loved the pretzel-like shape of the fourth knot, with its sinuous bends and twists.

"Very good, Diana," Goody Alsop said. This was the moment in my spells when everything tended to go wrong. "Now, remain in the moment and bid the dragon to stay with you. If she is so inclined, she will hide you from curious eyes."

The firedrake's cooperation seemed too much to hope for, but I made the pentacle-shaped knot anyway, using the white cord. "With knot of five, the spell will thrive."

The firedrake swooped down and nestled her wings against my ribs.

Will you stay with me? I silently asked her.

The firedrake wrapped me in a fine gray cocoon. It dulled the black of my skirts and jacket, turning them a deep charcoal. Ysabeau's ring glittered less brightly, the fire at the heart of the diamond dimmed. Even the silver cord in my lap looked tarnished. I smiled at the firedrake's silent answer.

"With knot of six, this spell I fix," I said. My final knot was not as symmetrical as it should have been, but it held nonetheless.

"You are indeed a weaver, child," Goody Alsop said, letting out her breath.

I felt marvelously inconspicuous on my walk home, wrapped in my firedrake muffler, but came to life again when my feet crossed over the threshold of the Hart and Crown. A package waited for me there, along with Kit. Matthew was still spending too much time with the mercurial daemon. Marlowe and I exchanged cool greetings, and I had started unpicking the package's protective wrappings when Matthew let out a mighty roar.

"Good Christ!" Where moments before there was empty space, there was now Matthew, staring at a piece of paper in disbelief.

"What does the Old Fox want now?" Kit asked sourly, jamming his pen into a pot of ink.

"I just received a bill from Nicholas Vallin, the goldsmith up the lane," Matthew said, scowling. I looked at him innocently. "He charged me fifteen pounds for a mousetrap." Now that I better understood the purchasing power of a pound—and that Mary's servant Joan earned only five pounds a year—I could see why Matthew was shocked.

"Oh. That." I returned my attention to the package. "I asked him to make it."

"You had one of the finest goldsmiths in London make you a mousetrap?" Kit was incredulous. "If you have any more funds to spare, Mistress Roydon, I hope you will allow me to undertake an alchemical experiment for you. I will transmute your silver and gold into wine at the Cardinal's Hat!"

"It's a rat trap, not a mousetrap," I muttered.

"Might I see this rat trap?" Matthew's tone was ominously even.

I removed the last of the wrappings and held out the article in question.

"Silver gilt. And engraved, too," Matthew said, turning it over in his hand. After looking more closely at it, he swore. *"'Ars longa, vita brevis.' Art is long, but life is short.* Indeed."

"It's supposed to be very effective." Monsieur Vallin's cunning design resembled a watchful feline, with a pair of finely worked ears on the hinge, a wide set of eyes carved into the cross brace. The edges of the trap resembled a mouth, complete with lethal teeth. It reminded me a bit of Sarah's cat, Tabitha. Vallin had provided an added bit of whimsy by perching a silver mouse on the cat's nose. The tiny creature bore no resemblance to the long-toothed monsters that prowled around our attics. The mere thought of them munching their way through Matthew's papers while we slept made me shudder.

"Look. He's engraved the bottom of it, too," Kit said, following the romping mice around the base of the trap. "It bears the rest of Hippocrates' aphorism—and in Latin, no less. *'Occasio præceps, experimentum periculosum, iudicium difficile.'*"

"It may be an excessively sentimental inscription, given the instrument's purpose," I admitted.

"Sentimental?" Matthew's eyebrow shot up. "From the viewpoint of the rat, it sounds quite realistic: *Opportunity is fleeting, experiment dangerous, and judgment difficult.*" His mouth twitched.

"Vallin took advantage of you, Mistress Roydon," Kit pronounced. "You should refuse payment, Matt, and send the trap back."

"No!" I protested. "It's not his fault. We were talking about clocks, and Monsieur Vallin showed me some beautiful examples. I shared my pamphlet from John Chandler's shop in Cripplegate—the one with the instructions on how to catch vermin—and told Monsieur Vallin about our rat problem. One thing led to another." I looked down at the trap. It really was an extraordinary piece of craftsmanship, with its tiny gears and springs.

"All of London has a rat problem," Matthew said, struggling for control. "Yet I know of no one who requires a silver-gilt toy to resolve it. A few affordable cats normally suffice."

"I'll pay him, Matthew." Doing so would probably empty out my purse, and I would be forced to ask Walter for more funds, but it couldn't be helped. Experience was always valuable. Sometimes it was costly, too. I held out my hand for the trap.

"Did Vallin design it to strike the hours? If so, and it is the world's only combined timepiece and pest-control device, perhaps the price is fair after all." Matthew was trying to frown, but his face broke into a grin. Instead of giving me the trap, he took my hand, brought it to his mouth, and kissed it. "I'll pay the bill, *mon coeur,* if only to have the right to tease you about it for the next sixty years."

At that moment George hurried into the front hall. A blast of cold air entered with him.

"I have news!" He flung his cloak aside and struck a proud pose.

Kit groaned and put his head in his hands. "Don't tell me. That idiot Ponsonby is pleased with your translation of Homer and wants to publish it without further corrections."

"Not even you will dim my pleasure in today's achievements, Kit." George looked around expectantly. "Well? Are none of you the least bit curious?"

"What is your news, George?" Matthew said absently, tossing the trap into the air and catching it again.

"I found Mistress Roydon's manuscript."

Matthew's grip on the rat trap tightened. The mechanism sprang open. When he released his fingers, it fell to the table with a clatter as it snapped shut again. "Where?"

George took an instinctive step backward. I'd been on the receiving end of my husband's questions and understood how disconcerting a full blast of vampiric attention could be.

"I knew you were the man to find it," I told George warmly, putting my hand on Matthew's sleeve to slow him down. George was predictably mollified by this remark and returned to the table, where he pulled out a chair and sat.

"Your confidence means a great deal to me, Mistress Roydon," George said, taking off his gloves. He sniffed. "Not everyone shares it."

"Where. Is. It?" Matthew asked slowly, his jaw clenched.

"It is in the most obvious place imaginable, hiding in plain sight. I am rather surprised we did not think of it straightaway." He paused once more to make sure he had everyone's full attention. Matthew emitted a barely audible growl of frustration.

"George," Kit warned. "Matthew has been known to bite."

"Dr. Dee has it," George blurted out when Matthew shifted his weight.

"The queen's astrologer," I said. George was right: We should have thought of the man long before this. Dee was an alchemist, too—and had the largest library in England. "But he's in Europe."

"Dr. Dee returned from Europe over a year ago. He's living outside London now."

"Please tell me he isn't a witch, daemon, or vampire," I entreated.

"He's just a human—and an utter fraud," Marlowe said. "I wouldn't trust a thing he says, Matt. He used poor Edward abominably, forcing him to peer into crystal stones and talk to angels about alchemy day and night. Then Dee took all the credit!"

"'Poor Edward'?" Walter scoffed, opening the door without invitation or ceremony and stepping inside. Henry Percy was with him. No member of the School of Night could be within a mile of the Hart and Crown and not be drawn irresistibly to our hearth. "Your daemon friend led him by the nose for years. Dr. Dee is well rid of him, if you ask me." Walter picked up the rat trap. "What's this?"

"The goddess of the hunt has turned her attention to smaller prey," Kit said with a smirk.

"Why, that's a mousetrap. But no one would be foolish enough to make a mousetrap out of silver gilt," Henry said, looking over Walter's shoulder. "It looks like Nicholas Vallin's work. He made Essex a handsome watch when he became a Knight of the Garter. Is it a child's toy of some sort?"

A vampire's fist crashed onto my table, splitting the wood.

"George," Matthew ground out, "do tell us about Dr. Dee."

"Ah. Yes. Of course. There is not much to tell. I did w-what you asked," George stammered. "I visited the bookstalls, but there was no information to be had. There was talk of a volume of Greek poetry for sale that sounded most promising for my translation—but I digress." George stopped and gulped. "Widow Jugge suggested I talk to John Hester, the apothecary at Paul's Wharf. Hester sent me to Hugh Plat—you know, the vintner who lives in St. James Garlickhythe." I followed this complicated intellectual pilgrimage closely, hoping I might reconstruct George's route when I next visited Susanna. Perhaps she and Plat were neighbors.

"Plat is as bad as Will," Walter said under his breath, "forever writing things down that are none of his concern. The fellow asked after my mother's method for making pastry."

"Master Plat said that Dr. Dee has a book from the emperor's library. No man can read it, and there are strange pictures in it, too," George explained. "Plat saw it when he went to Dr. Dee for alchemical guidance."

Matthew and I exchanged looks.

"It's possible, Matthew," I said in a low voice. "Elias Ashmole tracked down what was left of Dee's library after his death, and he was particularly interested in the alchemical books."

"Dee's death. And how did the good doctor meet his end, Mistress Roydon?" Marlowe asked softly, his brown eyes nudging me. Henry, who hadn't heard Kit's question, spoke before I could answer.

"I will ask to see it," Henry said, nodding decidedly. "It will be easy enough to arrange on my way back to Richmond and the queen."

"You might not recognize it, Hal," Matthew said, prepared to ignore Kit as well, even though he had heard him. "I'll go with you."

"You didn't see it either." I shook my head, hoping to loosen Marlowe's prodding stare. "Besides, if there's a visit being paid to John Dee, I'm going."

"You needn't give me that fierce look, *ma lionne.* I know perfectly well that nothing will convince you to leave this to me. Not if there are books and an alchemist involved." Matthew held up an admonishing finger. "But no questions. Understood?" He had seen the magical mayhem that could result.

I nodded, but my fingers were crossed in the fold of my skirt in that age-old charm to ward off the evil consequences that came from knotting up the truth.

"No questions from Mistress Roydon?" Walter muttered. "I wish you luck with that, Matt."

Mortlake was a small hamlet on the Thames located between London and the queen's palace at Richmond. We made the trip in the Earl of Northumberland's barge, a splendid vessel with eight oarsmen, padded seats, and curtains to keep out the drafts. It was a far more comfortable—not to mention more sedate—journey than I was accustomed to when Gallowglass wielded the oars.

We'd sent a letter ahead warning Dee of our intention to visit him. Mrs. Dee, Henry explained with great delicacy, did not appreciate guests who dropped in unannounced. Though I could sympathize, it was unusual at a time when open-door hospitality was the rule.

"The household is somewhat . . . er, irregular because of Dr. Dee's pursuits," Henry explained, turning slightly pink. "And they have a prodigious number of children. It is often rather . . . chaotic."

"So much so that the servants have been known to throw themselves down the well," Matthew observed pointedly.

"Yes. That was unfortunate. I doubt any such thing will happen during our visit," Henry muttered.

I didn't care what state the household was in. We were on the brink of being able to answer so many questions: why this book was so sought after, if it could tell us more about how we creatures had come into being. And of course Matthew believed that it might shed light on why we otherworldly creatures were going extinct in our modern times.

Whether for propriety's sake or to avoid his disorderly brood, Dr. Dee was strolling in his brick-walled garden as if it were high summer and not the end of January. He was wearing the black robes of a scholar, and a tight-fitting hood covered his head and extended down his neck, topped with a flat cap. A long white beard jutted from his chin, and his arms were clasped behind his back as he made his slow progress around the barren garden.

"Dr. Dee?" Henry called over the wall.

"Lord Northumberland! I trust you are in good health?" Dee's voice was quiet and raspy, though he took care (as most did) to alter it slightly for Henry's benefit. He removed his cap and swept a bow.

"Passable for the time of year, Dr. Dee. We are not here about my health, though. I have friends with me, as I explained in my letter. Let me introduce you."

"Dr. Dee and I are already acquainted." Matthew gave Dee a wolfish smile and a low bow. He knew every other strange creature of the time. Why not Dee?

"Master Roydon," Dee said warily.

"This is my wife, Diana," Matthew said, inclining his head in my direction. "She is a friend to the Countess of Pembroke and joins her ladyship in alchemical pursuits."

"The Countess of Pembroke and I have corresponded on alchemical matters." Dee forgot all about me and focused instead on his own close connection to a peer of the realm. "Your message indicated you wanted to see one of my books, Lord Northumberland. Are you here on Lady Pembroke's behalf?"

Before Henry could respond, a sharp-faced, ample-hipped woman came out of the house in a dark brown gown trimmed with fur that had seen better days. She looked irritated, then spotted the Earl of Northumberland and plastered a welcoming look over her face.

"And here is my own dear wife," Dee said uneasily. "The Earl of Northumberland and Master Roydon are arrived, Jane," he called out.

"Why haven't you asked them inside?" Jane scolded, wringing her hands in distress. "They will think we are not prepared to receive guests, which of course we are, at all times. Many seek out my husband's counsel, my lord."

"Yes. That is what brings us here, too. You are in good health I see, Mistress Dee. And I understand from Master Roydon that the queen recently graced your house with a visit."

Jane preened. "Indeed. John has seen Her Majesty three times since November. The last two times she happened upon us at our far gate, as she rode along the Richmond road."

"Her Majesty was generous to us this Christmas," Dee said. He twisted the cap in his hands. Jane looked at him sourly. "We had thought . . . but it is no matter."

"Delightful, delightful," Henry said quickly, rescuing Dee from any potential awkwardness. "But enough small talk. There is a particular book we wished to see—"

"My husband's library is esteemed more than he is!" Jane said sullenly. "Our expenses while visiting the emperor were extreme, and we have many mouths to feed. The queen said she would help us. She did give us a small reward but promised more."

"No doubt the queen was distracted by more pressing concerns." Matthew had a small, heavy pouch in his hands. "I have the balance of her gift here. And I value your husband, Mistress Dee, not just his books. I've added to Her Majesty's purse for his pains on our behalf."

"I . . . I thank you, Master Roydon," Dee stammered, exchanging glances with his wife. "It is kind of you to see to the queen's business. Matters of state must always take precedence over our difficulties, of course."

"Her Majesty does not forget those who have given her good service," Matthew said. It was a blatant untruth, as everyone standing in the snowy garden knew, but it went unchallenged.

"You must all take your ease inside by the fire," Jane said, her interest in hospitality sharply increased. "I will bring wine and see that you are not disturbed." She dropped a curtsy to Henry, an even lower one to Matthew, then bustled back in the direction of the door. "Come, John. They'll turn to ice if you keep them out here any longer."

Twenty minutes spent inside the Dees' house proved that its master and mistress were representatives of that peculiar breed of married people who bickered incessantly over perceived slights and unkindnesses, all the while remaining devoted. They exchanged barbed comments while we admired the new tapestries (a gift from Lady Walsingham), the new wine ewer (a gift from Sir Christopher Hatton), and the new silver salt (a gift from the Marchioness of Northampton). The ostentatious gifts and invective having run their course, we were—at long last—ushered into the library.

"I'm going to have a hell of a time getting you out of here," Matthew whispered, grinning at the expression of wonder on my face.

John Dee's library was nothing like what I had expected. I'd imagined it would look much like a spacious private library belonging to a well-heeled gentleman of the nineteenth century—for reasons that now struck me as completely indefensible. This was no genteel space for smoking pipes and reading by the fire. With only candles for illumination, the room was surprisingly dark on this winter day. A few chairs and a long table awaited readers by a south-facing bay of windows. The walls of the room were hung with maps, celestial charts, anatomical diagrams, and the broadside almanac sheets that could be had at every apothecary and bookshop in London for pennies. Decades of them were on display, presumably maintained as a reference collection for when Dee was drawing up a horoscope or making other heavenly calculations.

Dee owned more books than any of the Oxford or Cambridge colleges, and he required a working library—not one for show. Not surprisingly, the most precious commodity was not light or seating but shelf space. To maximize what was available, Dee's bookshelves were freestanding and set perpendicular to the walls. The simple oak bookshelves were double-faced, with the shelves set at varied heights to hold the different sizes of Elizabethan books. Two sloped reading surfaces topped the shelves, making it possible to study a text and then accurately return it.

"My God," I murmured. Dee turned in consternation at my oath.

"My wife is overwhelmed, Master Dee," Matthew explained. "She has never been in such a grand library."

"There are many libraries that are far more spacious and boast more treasures than mine, Mistress Roydon."

Jane Dee arrived on cue, just when it was possible to divert the conversation to the poverty of the household.

"The Emperor Rudolf's library is very fine," Jane said, heading past us with a tray holding wine and sweetmeats. "Even so, he was not above stealing one of John's best books. The emperor took advantage of my husband's generosity, and we have little hope of compensation."

"Now, Jane," John chided, "His Majesty did give us a book in return."

"Which book was that?" Matthew said carefully.

"A rare text," Dee said unhappily, watching his wife's retreating form as she headed for the table.

"Nothing but gibberish!" Jane retorted.

It was Ashmole 782. It had to be.

"Master Plat told us about just such a book. It is why we are here. Perhaps we might enjoy your wife's hospitality first and then see the emperor's book?" Matthew suggested, smooth as a cat's whisker. He held out his arm to me, and I took it with a squeeze.

While Jane fussed and poured and complained about the cost of nuts over the holiday season and how she had been brought to near bankruptcy by the grocer, Dee went in search of Ashmole 782. He scanned the shelves of one bookcase and pulled a volume free.

"That's not it," I murmured to Matthew. It was too small.

Dee plunked the book on the table in front of Matthew and lifted the limp vellum cover.

"See. There is naught in it but meaningless words and lewd pictures of women in their bath." Jane harrumphed out of the room, muttering and shaking her head.

This was not Ashmole 782, but it was nonetheless a book I knew: the Voynich manuscript, otherwise known as Yale University's Beinecke MS 408. The manuscript's contents were a mystery. No code breaker or linguist had yet figured out what the text said, and botanists hadn't been able to identify the plants. Theories abounded to explain its mysteries, including one suggesting that it had been written by aliens. I let out a disappointed sound.

"No?" Matthew asked. I shook my head and bit my lip in frustration. Dee mistook my expression for annoyance with Jane, and he rushed to explain.

"Please forgive my wife. Jane finds this book most distressing, for it was she who discovered it among our boxes when we returned from the emperor's lands. I had taken another book with me on the journey—a treasured book of alchemy that once belonged to the great English magician Roger Bacon. It was larger than this, and contained many mysteries."

I pitched forward in my seat.

"My assistant, Edward, could understand the text with divine assistance, though I could not," Dee continued. "Before we left Prague, Emperor Rudolf expressed an interest in the work. Edward had told him some of the secrets contained therein—about the generation of metals and a secret method for obtaining immortality."

So Dee had once possessed Ashmole 782 after all. And his daemonic helper, Edward Kelley, could read the text. My hands were shaking with excitement, and I concealed them in the folds of my skirt.

"Edward helped Jane pack up my books when we were ordered home. Jane believes that Edward stole the book away, replacing it with this item from His Majesty's collection." Dee hesitated, looked sorrowful. "I do not like to think ill of Edward, for he was my trusted companion and we spent much time together. He and Jane were never on good terms, and at first I dismissed her theory."

"But now you think it has merit," Matthew observed.

"I go over the events of our last days, Master Roydon, trying to recall a detail that might exonerate my friend. But everything I remember only points the finger of blame more decidedly in his direction." Dee sighed. "Still, this text may yet prove to contain secrets of worth."

Matthew flipped through the pages. "These are chimeras," he said, studying the images of plants. "The leaves and stems and flowers don't match but have been assembled from different plants."

"What do you make of these?" I said, turning to the astrological roundels that followed. I peered at the writing in the center. Funny. I'd seen the manuscript many times before and never paid any attention to the notes.

"These inscriptions are written in the tongue of ancient Occitania," Matthew said quietly. "I knew someone once with handwriting very like this. Did you happen to meet a gentleman from Aurillac while you were at the emperor's court?"

Did he mean *Gerbert*? My excitement turned to anxiety. Had Gerbert mistaken the Voynich manuscript for the mysterious book of origins? At my question the handwriting in the center of the astrological diagram began to quiver. I clapped the book shut to keep it from dancing off the page.

"No, Master Roydon," Dee said with a frown. "Had I done so, I would have asked him about the famed magician from that place who became pope. There are many truths hidden in old tales told around the fire."

"Yes," Matthew agreed, "if only we are wise enough to recognize them."

"That is why I so regret the loss of my book. It was once owned by Roger Bacon, and I was told by the old woman who sold it to me that he prized it for holding divine truths. Bacon called it the *Verum Secretum Secretorum.*" Dee looked wistfully at the Voynich manuscript. "It is my dearest wish to have it returned."

"Perhaps I can be of some use," Matthew said.

"You, Master Roydon?"

"If you would permit me to take this book, I could try to have it put back where it belongs—and have your book restored to its rightful owner." Matthew pulled the manuscript toward him.

"I would be forever in your debt, sir," Dee said, agreeing to the deal without further negotiation.

The minute we pulled away from the public landing in Mortlake, I started peppering Matthew with questions.

"What are you thinking, Matthew? You can't just pack up the Voynich manuscript and send it to Rudolf with a note accusing him of double-dealing. You'll have to find someone crazy enough to risk his life by breaking into Rudolf's library and stealing Ashmole 782."

"If Rudolf has Ashmole 782, it won't be in his library. It will be in his cabinet of curiosities," Matthew said absently, staring at the water.

"So this . . . Voynich was not the book you were seeking?" Henry had been following our exchange with polite interest. "George will be so disappointed not to have solved your mystery."

"George may not have solved it, Hal, but he's shed considerable light on the situation," Matthew said. "Between my father's agents and my own, we'll get Dee's lost book."

We'd caught the tide back to town, which sped our return. The torches were lit on the Water Lane landing in anticipation of our arrival, but two men in the Countess of Pembroke's livery waved us off.

"Baynard's Castle, if you please, Master Roydon!" one called across the water.

"Something must be wrong," Matthew said, standing in the prow of the barge. Henry directed the oarsmen to proceed the extra distance down the river, where the countess's landing was similarly ablaze with beacons and lanterns.

"Is it one of the boys?" I asked Mary when she rushed down the hall to meet us.

"No. They are well. Come to the laboratory. At once," she called over her shoulder, already heading back in the direction of the tower.

The sight that greeted us there was enough to make both Matthew and me gasp.

"It is an altogether unexpected *arbor Dianæ,*" Mary said, crouching down so that she was at eye level with the bulbous chamber at the alembic's base that held the roots of a black tree. It wasn't like the first *arbor Dianæ,* which was entirely silver and far more delicate in its structure. This one, with its stout, dark trunk and bare limbs, reminded me of the oak tree in Madison that had sheltered us after Juliette's attack. I'd pulled the vitality out of that tree to save Matthew's life.

"Why isn't it silver?" Matthew asked, wrapping his hands around the countess's fragile glass alembic.

"I used Diana's blood," Mary replied. Matthew straightened and gave me an incredulous look.

"Look at the wall," I said, pointing at the bleeding firedrake.

"It's the green dragon—the symbol for aqua regia or aqua fortis," he said after giving it a cursory glance.

"No, Matthew. *Look* at it. Forget what you think it depicts and try to see it as if it were the first time."

"Dieu." Matthew sounded shocked. "Is that my insignia?"

"Yes. And did you notice that the dragon has its tail in its mouth? And that it's not a dragon at all? Dragons have four legs. That's a firedrake."

"A firedrake. Like . . ." Matthew swore again.

"There have been dozens of different theories about what ordinary substance was the crucial first ingredient required to make the philosopher's stone. Roger Bacon—who owned Dr. Dee's missing manuscript—believed it was blood." I was confident this piece of information would get Matthew's attention. I crouched down to look at the tree.

"And you saw the mural and followed your instincts." After a momentary pause, Matthew ran his thumb along the vessel's wax seal, cracking the wax. Mary gasped in horror as he ruined her experiment.

"What are you doing?" I asked, shocked.

"Following a hunch of my own and adding something to the alembic." Matthew lifted his wrist to his mouth, bit down on it, and held it over the narrow opening. His dark, thick blood dripped into the solution and fell into the bottom of the vessel. We stared into the depths.

Just when I thought nothing was going to happen, thin streaks of red began to work their way up the tree's skeletal trunk. Then golden leaves sprouted from the branches.

"Look at that," I said, amazed.

Matthew smiled at me. It was a smile still tinged with regret, but there was some hope in it, too.

Red fruits appeared among the leaves, sparkling like tiny rubies. Mary began to murmur a prayer, her eyes wide.

"My blood made the structure of the tree, and your blood made it bear fruit," I said slowly. My hand went to my hollow belly.

"Yes. But why?" Matthew replied.

If anything could tell us about the mysterious transformation that occurred when witch and *wearh* combined their blood, it would be Ashmole 782's strange pictures and mysterious text.

"How long did you say it would take you to get Dee's book back?" I asked Matthew.

"Oh, I don't imagine it will take very long," he murmured. "Not once I put my mind to it."

"The sooner the better," I said mildly, twining my fingers through his as we watched the ongoing miracle that our blood had wrought.

25

The strange tree continued to grow and develop the next day and the next: Its fruit ripened and fell among the tree's roots in the mercury and *prima materia*. New buds formed, blossomed, and flowered. Once a day the leaves turned from gold to green and back to gold. Sometimes the tree put out new branches or a new root stretched out to seek sustenance. "I have yet to find a good explanation for it," Mary said, gesturing at the piles of books that Joan had pulled down from the shelves. "It is as if we have created something entirely new."

In spite of the alchemical distractions, I hadn't forgotten my witchier concerns. I wove and rewove my invisible gray cloak, and each time I did it faster and the results were finer and more effective. Marjorie promised me that I would soon be able to put my weaving to words so other witches could perform the spell.

After walking back home from St. James Garlickhythe a few days later, I climbed the stairs to our rooms at the Hart and Crown, shedding my disguising spell as I did so. Annie was across the courtyard fetching the clean linen from the washerwomen. Jack was with Pierre and Matthew. I wondered what Françoise had procured for dinner. I was famished.

"If someone doesn't feed me in the next five minutes, I'm going to start screaming." My announcement as I crossed the threshold was punctuated by the sound of pins scattering on the wooden floorboards as I pulled free the stiff, embroidered panel on the front of my dress. I tossed the stomacher onto the table. My fingers reached for the laces that held my bodice together.

A gentle cough came from the direction of the fireplace.

I whirled around, my fingers clutching at the fabric covering my breasts.

"Screaming will do little good, I fear." A voice as raspy as sand swirling in a glass came from the depths of the chair that was drawn up to the fireplace. "I sent your servant for wine, and my old limbs do not move fast enough to meet your needs."

Slowly I came around the bulk of the chair. The stranger in my house lifted one gray eyebrow, and his gaze flickered over the site of my immodesty. I frowned at his bold glance.

"Who are you?" The man was not daemon, witch, or vampire but merely a wrinkled human.

"I believe that your husband and his friends call me the Old Fox. I am also, for my sins, the lord high treasurer." The shrewdest man in England, and certainly one of its most ruthless, allowed his words to sink in. His kindly expression did nothing to diminish the sharpness of his gaze.

William Cecil was sitting in my parlor. Too stunned to dip into the appropriately deep curtsy, I gawped at him instead.

"I am somewhat familiar to you, then. I am surprised my reputation has reached so far, for it is clear to me and many others that you are a stranger here." When I opened my mouth to reply, Cecil's hand came up. "It is wise policy, madam, not to share overmuch with me."

"What can I do for you, Sir William?" I felt like a schoolgirl sent to the principal's office.

"My reputation precedes me, but not my title. '*Vanitatis vanitatum, omnis vanitas,*'" Cecil said drily. "I am called Lord Burghley now, Mistress Roydon. The queen is a generous mistress."

I swore silently. I'd never taken any interest in the dates when members of the aristocracy were elevated to even higher levels of rank and privilege. When I needed to know, I looked it up in the *Dictionary of National Biography*. Now I'd insulted Matthew's boss. I would atone by flattering him in Latin.

"'*Honor virtutis praemium,*'" I murmured, gathering my wits about me. *Esteem is the reward of virtue.* One of my neighbors at Oxford was a graduate of the Arnold School. He played rugby and celebrated New College victories by shouting this phrase at the top of his lungs in the Turf, to the delight of his teammates.

"Ah, the Shirley motto. Are you a member of that family?" Lord Burghley tented his fingers before him and looked at me with greater interest. "They are known for their propensity to wander."

"No," I said. "I'm a Bishop . . . not an actual bishop." Lord Burghley inclined his head in silent acknowledgment of my obvious statement. I felt an absurd desire to bare my soul to the man—that or run as far and fast in the opposite direction as possible.

"Her Majesty accepts a married clergy, but female bishops are, thanks be to God, outside the scope of her imagination."

"Yes. No. Is there something I can do for you, my lord?" I repeated, a deplorable note of desperation creeping into my tone. I gritted my teeth.

"I think not, Mistress Roydon. But perhaps I can do something for you. I advise you to return to Woodstock. Without delay."

"Why, my lord?" I felt a flicker of fear.

"Because it is winter and the queen is insufficiently occupied at present." Burghley looked at my left hand. "And you are married to Master Roydon. Her Majesty is generous, but she doesn't approve when one of her favorites marries without her permission."

"Matthew isn't the queen's favorite—he's her spy." I clapped my hand over my mouth, but it was too late to recall the words.

"Favorites and spies are not mutually exclusive—except where Walsingham was concerned. The queen found his strict morality maddening and his sour expression unendurable. But Her Majesty is fond of Matthew Roydon. Some would say dangerously so. And your husband has many secrets." Cecil hauled himself to his feet, using a staff for leverage. He groaned. "Go back to Woodstock, mistress. It is best for all concerned."

"I won't leave my husband." Elizabeth might eat courtiers for breakfast, as Matthew had warned, but she was not going to run me out of town. Not when I was finally getting settled, finding friends, and learning magic. And certainly not when Matthew dragged himself home every day looking as if he'd been pulled backward through a knothole, only to spend all night answering correspondence sent to him by the queen's informants, his father, and the Congregation.

"Tell Matthew that I called." Lord Burghley made his slow way to the door. There he met Françoise, who was carrying a large jug of wine and looking disgruntled. At the sight of me, her eyes widened. She was not pleased to find me home, entertaining, with my bodice undone. "Thank you for the conversation, Mistress Roydon. It was most illuminating."

The lord high treasurer of England crept down the stairs. He was too old to be traveling about in the late afternoon, alone, in January. I followed him to the landing, watching his progress with concern.

"Go with him, Françoise," I urged her, "and make sure Lord Burghley finds his own servants." They were probably at the Cardinal's Hat getting inebriated with Kit and Will, or waiting in the crush of coaches at the top of Water Lane. I didn't want to be the last person to see Queen Elizabeth's chief adviser alive.

"No need, no need," Burghley said over his shoulder. "I am an old man with a stick. The thieves will ignore me in favor of someone with an earring and a slashed doublet. The beggars I can beat off, if need be. And my men are not far from here. Remember my advice, mistress."

With that he disappeared into the dusk.

"Dieu." Françoise crossed herself, then forked her fingers against the evil eye for good measure. "He is an old soul. I do not like the way he looked at you. It is a good thing *milord* is not yet home. He would not have liked it either."

"William Cecil is old enough to be my grandfather, Françoise," I retorted, returning to the warmth of the parlor and, finally, loosening my laces. I groaned as the constriction lessened.

"Lord Burghley did not look at you as though he wanted to bed you." Françoise glanced pointedly at my bodice.

"No? How *did* he look at me, then?" I poured myself some wine and plopped down in my chair. The day was taking a decided turn for the worse.

"Like you were a lamb ready for slaughter and he was weighing the price you would bring."

"Who is threatening to eat Diana for dinner?" Matthew had arrived with the stealth of a cat and was taking off his gloves.

"Your visitor. You just missed him." I took a sip of wine. As soon as I swallowed, Matthew was there to lift it from my hands. I made an exasperated sound. "Can you wave or something to let me know you're about to move? It's disconcerting when you just appear before me like that."

"As you've divined that looking out the window is one of my tells, I feel honor bound to share that changing the subject is one of yours." Matthew took a sip of wine and set the cup on the table. He rubbed tiredly at his face. "What visitor?"

"William Cecil was waiting by the fire when I came home."

Matthew went eerily still.

"He's the scariest grandfatherly person I've ever met," I continued, reaching for the wine again. "Burghley may look like Father Christmas, with his gray hair and beard, but I wouldn't turn my back on him."

"That's very wise," Matthew said quietly. He regarded Françoise. "What did he want?"

She shrugged. "I do not know. He was here when I came home with *madame*'s pork pie. Lord Burghley asked for wine. That daemon drank everything in the house earlier today. I went out for more."

Matthew disappeared. He returned at a more sedate pace, looking relieved. I shot to my feet. *The attics—and all the secrets hidden there.*

"Did he—"

"No," Matthew interrupted. "Everything is exactly as I left it. Did William say why he was here?"

"Lord Burghley told me to tell you he called." I hesitated. "And he told me to leave the city."

Annie entered the room, along with a chattering Jack and a grinning Pierre, but after one look at Matthew's face, Pierre's smile dissolved. I took the linens from Annie.

"Why don't you take the children to the Cardinal's Hat, Françoise?" I said. "Pierre will go, too."

"Huzzah!" Jack shouted, delighted at the prospect of a night out. "Master Shakespeare is teaching me to juggle."

"So long as he doesn't try to improve your penmanship, I have no objection," I said, catching Jack's hat as he tossed it in the air. The last thing we needed was the boy adding forgery to his list of skills. "Go and have your supper. And try to remember what your handkerchief is for."

"I will," Jack said, wiping his nose with his sleeve.

"Why did Lord Burghley come all the way to the Blackfriars to see you?" I asked when we were alone.

"Because I received intelligence from Scotland today."

"What now?" I said, my throat closing. It was not the first time the Berwick witches had been discussed in my presence, but somehow Burghley's presence made it seem as though the evil was creeping over our threshold.

"King James continues to question the witches. William wanted to discuss what—if anything—the queen should do in response." He frowned at the change in my scent as the fear took hold. "You shouldn't trouble yourself with what's happening in Scotland."

"Not knowing doesn't keep it from happening."

"No," Matthew said, his fingers gentle on my neck as he tried to rub the tension away. "Neither does knowing."

The next day I came home from Goody Alsop's carrying a small wooden spell box—a place to let my written spells incubate until they were ready for another witch to use. Finding a way to put my magic to words was the next step in my evolution as a weaver. Right now the box held only my weaver's cords. Marjorie didn't think my disguising spell was quite ready for other witches yet.

A wizard on Thames Street made the box from the limb from the rowan that the firedrake gave me the night I made my forspell. He'd carved a tree on its surface, the roots and branches weirdly intertwined so that you couldn't tell them apart. Not a single nail held the box together. Instead there were nearly invisible joints. The wizard was proud of his work, and I couldn't wait to show it to Matthew.

The Hart and Crown was oddly quiet. Neither the fire nor the candles in the parlor were lit. Matthew was in his study, alone. Three wine jugs stood on the table before him. Two of them were, presumably, empty. Matthew didn't normally drink so heavily.

"What's wrong?"

He picked up a sheet of paper. Thick red wax clung to its folds. The seal was cracked across the middle. "We are called to court."

I sank into the chair opposite. "When?"

"Her Majesty has graciously permitted us to wait until tomorrow." Matthew snorted. "Her father was not half so forgiving. When Henry wanted people to attend him, he sent for them even if they were in their bed and a gale was blowing."

I had been eager to meet the queen of England—when I was back in Madison. After meeting the shrewdest man in the kingdom, I no longer had any desire to meet the canniest woman. "Must we go?" I asked, half hoping Matthew would dismiss the royal command.

"In her letter the queen took pains to remind me of her statute against conjurations, enchantments, and witchcrafts." Matthew tossed the paper onto the table. "It would seem Mr. Danforth wrote a letter to his bishop. Burghley buried the complaint, but it resurfaced." Matthew swore.

"Then why are we going to court?" I clutched at my spell box. The cords inside were slithering around, eager to help answer my question.

"Because if we are not in the audience chamber at Richmond Palace by two in the afternoon tomorrow, Elizabeth will arrest us both." Matthew's eyes looked like chips of sea glass. "It won't take long for the Congregation to learn the truth about us then."

The household was thrown into an uproar at our news. Their anticipation was shared by the neighborhood the next morning when the Countess of Pembroke arrived shortly after dawn with enough garments to outfit the parish. She traveled by river, having taken her barge to the Blackfriars—although the actual distance was no more than a few hundred feet. Her appearance on the Water Lane landing was treated as a public spectacle of enormous importance, and for a few moments a hush fell over our normally raucous street.

Mary looked serene and unperturbed when she finally stepped into the parlor, allowing Joan and a line of lesser servants to file in behind her.

"Henry tells me you are expected at court this afternoon. You have nothing suitable to wear." With an imperious finger, Mary directed still more of her crew in the direction of our bedchamber.

"I was going to wear the gown I was married in," I protested.

"But it is French!" Mary said, aghast. "You cannot wear that!"

Embroidered satins, luscious velvets, sparkling silks interwoven with real gold and silver thread, and piles of diaphanous material of unknown purpose passed by my nose.

"This is too much, Mary. Whatever are you thinking?" I said, narrowly avoiding collision with still one more servant.

"No one goes into battle without proper armor," Mary said with her characteristic blend of airiness and tartness. "And Her Majesty, may God preserve her, is a formidable opponent. You will require all the protection my wardrobe can afford."

Together we picked through the options. How we were going to make the necessary alterations so that Mary's clothes would fit me was a mystery, but I knew better than to inquire. I was Cinderella, and the birds of the forest and the fairies of the wood would be called upon if the Countess of Pembroke felt it necessary.

We finally settled on a black gown thickly embroidered with silver fleurs-de-lis and roses. It was a design from last year, Mary said, and lacked the large cartwheel-shaped skirts now in vogue. Elizabeth would be pleased by my frugal disregard for the whims of fashion.

"And silver and black are the queen's colors. That's why Walter is always wearing them," Mary explained, smoothing the puffed sleeves.

But my favorite garment by far was the white satin petticoat that would be visible at the front of the divided skirts. It was embroidered, too, with mainly flora and fauna, accompanied by bits of classical architecture, scientific instruments, and female personifications of the arts and sciences. I recognized the same hand at work as that of the genius who'd created Mary's shoes. I avoided touching the embroidery to make sure, not wanting Lady Alchemy to walk off the petticoat before I'd had the opportunity to wear it.

It took four women two hours to get me dressed. First I was laced into my clothes, which were padded and puffed to ridiculous proportions, with thick quilting and a wide farthingale that was just as unwieldy as I had imagined. My ruff was suitably large and ostentatious, though not, Mary assured me, as large as the queen's would be. Mary clipped an ostrich fan to my waist. It hung down like a pendulum and swayed when I walked. With its feathery plumes and ruby- and pearl-studded handle, the accessory was easily worth ten times what my mousetrap cost, and I was glad that it was literally attached to me at the hip.

The subject of jewelry proved controversial. Mary had her coffer with her and pulled out one priceless item after another. But I insisted on wearing Ysabeau's earrings rather than the ornate diamond drops that Mary suggested. They went surprisingly well with the rope of pearls Joan slung over my shoulder. To my horror, Mary dismembered the chain of broom blossoms that Philippe had given me for my wedding and pinned one of the floral links to the center of my bodice. She caught the pearls up with a red bow and tied it to the pin. After a long discussion, Mary and Françoise settled on a simple pearl choker to fill my open neckline. Annie affixed my gold arrow to my ruff with another jeweled pin, and Françoise dressed my hair so that it framed my face in a puffed-out heart shape. For the final touch, Mary settled a pearl-studded coif on the back of my head, covering the braided knots that Françoise piled there.

Matthew, who had been in an increasingly foul mood as the hour of doom approached, managed to smile and look suitably impressed.

"I feel like I'm in a stage costume," I said ruefully.

"You look lovely—formidably so," he assured me. He looked splendid, too, in his solid black velvet suit of clothes with tiny touches of white at the wrists and collar. And he was wearing my portrait miniature around his neck. The long chain was looped up on a button so that the moon faced outward and my image was close to his heart.

My first glimpse of Richmond Palace was the top of a creamy stone tower, the royal standard snapping in the breeze. More towers soon appeared, sparkling in the crisp winter air like those of a castle out of a fairy story. Then the vast sprawl of the palace complex came into view: the strange rectangular arcade to the southeast, the three-storied main building to the southwest, surrounded by a wide moat, and the walled orchard beyond.

Behind the main building were still more towers and peaks, including a pair of buildings that reminded me of Eton College. An enormous crane rose up into the air beyond the orchard, and swarms of men unloaded boxes and parcels for the palace's kitchens and storerooms. Baynard's Castle, which had always seemed very grand to me, appeared in retrospect a slightly down-at-the-heels former royal residence.

The oarsmen directed the barge to a landing. Matthew ignored the stares and questions, preferring to let Pierre or Gallowglass respond for him. To the casual observer, Matthew looked slightly bored. But I was close enough to see him scanning the riverbank, alert and on guard.

I looked across the moat to the two-storied arcade. The ground floor's arches were open to the air, but the upper floor was glazed with leaded windows. Eager faces peered out, hoping to catch a glimpse of the new arrivals and obtain a morsel of gossip. Matthew quickly put his bulk between the barge and the curious courtiers, obscuring me from easy view.

Liveried servants, each one bearing a sword or a pike, led us through a simple guard chamber and into the main part of the palace. The warren of ground-floor rooms was as hectic and bustling as any modern office building, with servants and court officers rushing to meet requests and obey orders. Matthew turned to the right; our guards politely blocked his way.

"She'll not see you in private before you've been draped over tenterhooks in public," Gallowglass muttered under his breath. Matthew swore.

We obediently followed our escorts to a grand staircase. It was thronged with people, and the clash of human, floral, and herbal scents was dizzying. Everybody was wearing perfume in an effort to ward off unpleasant odors, but I had to wonder if the result was worse. When the crowd spotted Matthew, there were whispers as the sea of people parted. He was taller than most and gave off the same brutal air as most of the other male aristocrats I'd met. The difference was that Matthew really was lethal—and on some level the warmbloods recognized it.

After passing through a series of three antechambers, each filled to bursting with padded, scented, and jeweled courtiers of both sexes and all ages, we finally arrived at a closed door. There we waited. The whispers around us rose to murmurs. A man shared a joke, and his companions tittered. Matthew's jaw clenched.

"Why are we waiting?" I said, my voice pitched so that only Matthew and Gallowglass could hear.

"To amuse the queen—and to show the court that I am no more than a servant."

When at last we were admitted to the royal presence, I was surprised to find that this room, too, was full of people. "Private" was a relative term in the court of Elizabeth. I searched for the queen, but she was nowhere in sight. Fearing that we were going to have to wait again, my heart sank.

"Why is it that for every year I grow older, Matthew Roydon seems to look two years younger?" said a surprisingly jovial voice from the direction of the fireplace. The most lavishly dressed, heavily scented, and thickly painted creatures in the room turned slightly to study us. Their movement revealed Elizabeth, the queen bee seated at the center of the hive. My heart skipped a beat. Here was a legend brought to life.

"I see no great change in you, Your Majesty," Matthew said, inclining slightly at the waist. "'*Semper eadem,*' as the saying goes." The same words were painted in the banner under the royal crest that ornamented the fireplace. *Always the same.*

"Even my lord treasurer can manage a deeper bow than that, sir, and he suffers from a rheum." Black eyes glittered from a mask of powder and rouge. Beneath her sharply hooked nose, the queen compressed her thin lips into a hard line. "And I prefer a different motto these days: *Video et taceo.*"

I see and am silent. We were in trouble.

Matthew seemed not to notice and straightened as though he were a prince of the realm and not the queen's spy. With his shoulders thrown back and his head erect, he was easily the tallest man in the room. There were only two people remotely close to him in height: Henry Percy, who was standing against the wall looking miserable, and a long-legged man of about the earl's age with a mop of curly hair and an insolent expression, who stood at the queen's elbow.

"Careful," Burghley murmured as he passed by Matthew, camouflaging his admonishment with regular thumps of his staff. "You called for me, Your Majesty?"

"Spirit and Shadow in the same place. Tell me, Raleigh, does that not violate some dark principle of philosophy?" the queen's companion drawled out. His friends pointed at Lord Burghley and Matthew and laughed.

"If you had gone to Oxford and not Cambridge, Essex, you would know the answer and be spared the ignominy of having to ask." Raleigh casually shifted his weight and placed his hand conveniently near the hilt of his sword.

"Now, Robin," the queen said with an indulgent pat on his elbow. "You know that I do not like it when others use my pet names. Lord Burghley and Master Roydon will forgive you for doing so this time."

"I take it the lady is your wife, Roydon." The Earl of Essex turned his brown eyes on me. "We did not know you were wed."

"Who is this *'we'*?" the queen retorted, giving him a smack this time. "It is no business of yours, my Lord Essex."

"At least Matt isn't afraid to be seen around town with her." Walter stroked his chin. "You're recently married, too, my lord. Where is your wife on this fine winter's day?" *Here we go,* I thought as Walter and Essex jockeyed for position.

"Lady Essex is on Hart Street, in her mother's house, with the earl's newborn heir at her side," Matthew replied on Essex's behalf. "Congratulations, my lord. When I called on the countess, she told me he was to be named after you."

"Yes. Robert was baptized yesterday," Essex said stiffly. He looked a bit alarmed at the thought that Matthew had been around his wife and child.

"He was, my lord." Matthew gave the earl a truly terrifying smile. "Strange. I did not see you at the ceremony."

"Enough squabbling!" Elizabeth shouted, angry that the conversation was no longer under her control. She tapped her long fingers on the upholstered arm of her chair. "I gave neither of you permission to wed. You are both ungrateful, grasping wretches. Bring the girl to me."

Nervous, I smoothed my skirts and took Matthew's arm. The dozen steps between the queen and me seemed to stretch on to infinity. When at last I reached her side, Walter looked sharply at the floor. I sank into a curtsy and remained there.

"She has manners at least," Elizabeth conceded. "Raise her up."

When I met her eyes, I learned that the queen was extremely nearsighted. Even though I was no more than three feet from her, she squinted as though she couldn't make out my features.

"Hmph," Elizabeth pronounced when her inspection was through. "Her face is coarse."

"If you think so, then it is fortunate that you are not wed to her," Matthew said shortly.

Elizabeth peered at me some more. "There is ink on her fingers."

I hid the offending digits behind my borrowed fan. The stains from the oak-gall ink were impossible to remove.

"And what fortune am I paying you, Shadow, that your wife can afford such a fan?" Elizabeth's voice had turned petulant.

"If we are going to discuss Crown finances, perhaps the others might take their leave," Lord Burghley suggested.

"Oh, very well," Elizabeth said crossly. "You shall stay, William, and Walter, too."

"And me," Essex said.

"Not you, Robin. You must see to the banquet. I wish to be entertained this evening. I am tired of sermonizing and history lessons, as though I were a schoolgirl. No more tales of King John or adventures of a lovelorn shepherdess pining for her shepherd. I want Symons to tumble. If there must be a play, let it be the one with the necromancer and the brass head that divines the future." Elizabeth rapped her knuckles on the table. "*'Time is, time was, time is past.'* I do love that line."

Matthew and I exchanged looks.

"I believe the play is called *Friar Bacon and Friar Bungay,* Your Majesty," a young woman whispered into her mistress's ear.

"That's the one, Bess. See to it, Robin, and you shall sit by me." The queen was quite an actress herself. She could go from furious to petulant to wheedling without missing a beat.

Somewhat mollified, the Earl of Essex withdrew, but not before shooting Walter a withering stare. Everyone flurried after him. Essex was now the most important person in their proximity, and, like moths to a flame, the other courtiers were eager to share his light. Only Henry seemed reluctant to depart, but he was given no choice. The door closed firmly behind them.

"Did you enjoy your visit to Dr. Dee, Mistress Roydon?" The queen's voice was sharp. There wasn't a cajoling note in it now. She was all business.

"We did, Your Majesty," Matthew replied.

"I know full well your wife can speak for herself, Master Roydon. Let her do so."

Matthew glowered but remained quiet.

"It was most enjoyable, Your Majesty." I had just spoken to Queen Elizabeth I. Pushing aside my disbelief, I continued. "I am a student of alchemy and interested in books and learning."

"I know what you are."

Danger flashed all around me, a firestorm of black threads snapping and crying.

"I am your servant, Your Majesty, like my husband." My eyes remained resolutely focused on the queen of England's slippers. Happily, they weren't particularly interesting and remained inanimate.

"I have courtiers and fools enough, Mistress Roydon. You will not earn a place among them with that remark." Her eyes glittered ominously. "Not all of my intelligencers report to your husband. Tell me, Shadow, what business did you have with Dr. Dee?"

"It was a private matter," Matthew said, keeping his temper with difficulty.

"There is no such thing—not in my kingdom." Elizabeth studied Matthew's face. "You told me not to trust my secrets to those whose allegiance you had not already tested for me," she continued quietly. "Surely my own loyalty is not in question."

"It was a private matter, between Dr. Dee and myself, madam," Matthew said, sticking to his story.

"Very well, Master Roydon. Since you are determined to keep your secret, I will tell you *my* business with Dr. Dee and see if it loosens your tongue. I want Edward Kelley back in England."

"I believe he is Sir Edward now, Your Majesty," Burghley corrected her.

"Where did you hear that?" Elizabeth demanded.

"From me," Matthew said mildly. "It is, after all, my job to know these things. Why do you need Kelley?"

"He knows how to make the philosopher's stone. And I will not have it in Hapsburg hands."

"Is that what you're afraid of?" Matthew sounded relieved.

"I am afraid of dying and leaving my kingdom to be fought over like a scrap of meat between dogs from Spain and France and Scotland," Elizabeth said, rising and advancing on him. The closer she came, the greater their differences in size and strength appeared. She was such a small woman to have survived against impossible odds for so many years. "I am afraid of what will become of my people when I am gone. Every day I pray for God's help in saving England from certain disaster."

"Amen," Burghley intoned.

"Edward Kelley is not God's answer, I promise you that."

"Any ruler who possesses the philosopher's stone will have an inexhaustible supply of riches." Elizabeth's eyes glittered. "Had I more gold at my disposal, I could destroy the Spanish."

"And if wishes were thrushes, beggars would eat birds," Matthew replied.

"Mind your tongue, Roydon," Burghley warned.

"Her Majesty is proposing to paddle in dangerous waters, my lord. It is my job to warn her of that, too." Matthew was carefully formal. "Edward Kelley is a daemon. His alchemical work lies perilously close to magic, as Walter can attest. The Congregation is desperate to keep Rudolf II's fascination for the occult from taking a dangerous turn as it did with King James."

"James had every right to arrest those witches!" Elizabeth said hotly. "Just as I have every right to claim the benefit should one of my subjects make the stone."

"Did you strike such a hard bargain with Walter when he went to the New World?" Matthew inquired. "Had he found gold in Virginia, would you have demanded it all be handed over to you?"

"I believe that's exactly what our arrangement stipulated," Walter said drily, adding a hasty, "though I would, of course, have been delighted for Her Majesty to have it."

"I knew you could not be trusted, Shadow. You are in England to serve me—yet you argue for this Congregation of yours as though their wishes were more important."

"I have the same desire that you do, Your Majesty: to save England from disaster. If you go the way of King James and start persecuting the daemons, witches, and *wearhs* among your subjects, you will suffer for it, and so will the realm."

"What do you propose I do instead?" Elizabeth asked.

"I propose we make an agreement—one not far different from the bargain you struck with Raleigh. I will see to it that Edward Kelley returns to England so that you can lock him in the Tower and force him to deliver up the philosopher's stone—if he can."

"And in return?" Elizabeth was her father's daughter, after all, and understood that nothing in this life was free.

"In return you will harbor as many of the Berwick witches as I can get out of Edinburgh until King James's madness has run its course."

"Absolutely not!" Burghley said. "Think, madam, what might happen to your relationship with our neighbors to the north if you were to invite scores of Scottish witches over the border!"

"There are not so many witches left in Scotland," Matthew said grimly, "since you refused my earlier pleas."

"I did think, Shadow, that one of your occupations while in England was to make sure your people did not meddle in our politics. What if these private machinations are found out? How will you explain your actions?" The queen scrutinized him.

"I will say that misery acquaints every man with strange bedfellows, Your Majesty."

Elizabeth made a soft sound of amusement. "That is doubly true for women," she said drily. "Very well. We are agreed. You will go to Prague and get Kelley. Mistress Roydon may attend upon me, here at court, to ensure your speedy return."

"My wife is not part of our bargain, and there is no need to send me to Bohemia in January. You are determined to have Kelley back. I will see to it that he is delivered."

"You are not king here!" Elizabeth jabbed at his chest with her finger. "You go where I send you, Master Roydon. If you do not, I will have you and your witch of a wife in the Tower for treason. And worse," she said, her eyes sparking.

Someone scratched at the door.

"Enter!" Elizabeth bellowed.

"The Countess of Pembroke requests an audience, Your Majesty," a guard said apologetically.

"God's teeth," the queen swore. "Am I never to know a moment's peace? Show her in."

Mary Sidney sailed into the room, her veils and ruffs billowing as she moved from the chilly antechamber to the overheated room the queen occupied. She dropped a graceful curtsy midway, floated further into the room, and dropped another perfect curtsy. "Your Majesty," she said, head bowed.

"What brings you to court, Lady Pembroke?"

"You once granted me a boon, Your Majesty—a guard against future need."

"Yes, yes," Elizabeth said testily. "What has your husband done now?"

"Nothing at all." Mary got to her feet. "I have come to ask for permission to send Mistress Roydon on an important errand."

"I cannot imagine why," Elizabeth retorted. "She seems neither useful nor resourceful."

"I have need of special glasses for my experiments that can only be acquired from Emperor Rudolf's workshops. My brother's wife—forgive me, for since Philip's death she is now remarried and the Countess of Essex—tells me that Master Roydon is being sent to Prague. Mistress Roydon will go with him, with your blessing, and fetch what I require."

"That vain, foolish boy! The Earl of Essex cannot resist sharing every scrap of intelligence he has with the world." Elizabeth whirled away in a flurry of silver and gold. "I'll have the popinjay's head for this!"

"You did promise me, Your Majesty, when my brother died defending your kingdom, that you would grant me a favor one day." Mary smiled serenely at Matthew and me.

"And you want to waste such a precious gift on these two?" Elizabeth looked skeptical.

"Once Matthew saved Philip's life. He is like a brother to me." Mary blinked at the queen with owlish innocence.

"You can be as smooth as ivory, Lady Pembroke. I wish we saw more of you at court." Elizabeth threw up her hands. "Very well. I will keep my word. But I want Edward Kelley in my presence by midsummer—and I don't want this bungled, or for all of Europe to know my business. Do you understand me, Master Roydon?"

"Yes, Your Majesty," Matthew said through gritted teeth.

"Get yourself to Prague, then. And take your wife with you, to please Lady Pembroke."

"Thank you, Majesty." Matthew looked rather alarmingly as if he wished to rip Elizabeth Tudor's bewigged head from her body.

"Out of my sight, all of you, before I change my mind." Elizabeth returned to her chair and slumped against its carved back.

Lord Burghley indicated with a jerk of his head that we were to follow the queen's instructions. But Matthew couldn't leave matters where they stood.

"A word of caution, Your Majesty. Do not place your trust in the Earl of Essex."

"You do not like him, Master Roydon. Nor does William or Walter. But he makes me feel young again." Elizabeth turned her black eyes on him. "Once you performed that service for me and reminded me of happier times. Now you have found another and I am abandoned."

"'My care is like my shadow in the sun / Follows me flying, flies when I pursue it, / Stands and lies by me, doth what I have done,'" Matthew said softly. "I am your Shadow, Majesty, and have no choice but to go where you lead."

"And I am tired," Elizabeth said, turning her head away, "and have no stomach for poetry. Leave me."

"We're not going to Prague," Matthew said once we were back in Henry's barge and headed toward London. "We must go home."

"The queen will not leave you in peace just because you flee to Woodstock, Matthew," Mary said reasonably, burrowing into a fur blanket.

"He doesn't mean Woodstock, Mary," I explained. "Matthew means somewhere . . . farther."

"Ah." Mary's brow furrowed. "Oh." Her face went carefully blank.

"But we're so close to getting what we wanted," I said. "We know where the manuscript is, and it may answer all our questions."

"And it may be nonsense, just like the manuscript at Dr. Dee's house," Matthew said impatiently. "We'll get it another way."

But later Walter persuaded Matthew that the queen was serious and would have us both in the Tower if we refused her. When I told Goody Alsop, she was as opposed to Prague as Matthew was.

"You should be going to your own time, not traveling to far-off Prague. Even if you were to stay here, it will take weeks to ready a spell that might get you home. Magic has guiding rules and principles that you have yet to master, Diana. All you have now is a wayward firedrake, a *glaem* that is near to blinding, and a tendency to ask questions that have mischievous answers. You do not have enough knowledge of the craft to succeed with your plan."

"I will continue to study in Prague, I promise." I took her hands in mine. "Matthew made a bargain with the queen that might protect dozens of witches. We cannot be separated. It's too dangerous. I won't let him go to the emperor's court without me."

"No," she said with a sad smile. "Not while there is breath in your body. Very well. Go with your *wearh*. But know this, Diana Roydon: You are setting a new course. And I cannot foresee where it might lead."

"The ghost of Bridget Bishop told me *'There is no path forward that does not have him in it.'* When I feel our lives spinning into the unknown, I take comfort from those words," I said, trying to comfort her. "So long as Matthew and I are together, Goody Alsop, our direction does not matter."

Three days later on the feast of St. Brigid, we set sail on our long journey to see the Holy Roman Emperor, find a treacherous English daemon, and, at long last, catch a glimpse of Ashmole 782.

Verin de Clermont sat in her Berlin home and stared down at the newspaper in disbelief.

The Independent
1 February 2010
A Surrey woman has discovered a manuscript belonging to Mary Sidney, famed Elizabethan poetess and sister to Sir Philip Sidney.

"It was in my mother's airing cupboard at the top of the stairs," Henrietta Barber, 62, told the Independent. Mrs. Barber was clearing out her mother's belongings before she went into care. "It looked like a tatty old bunch of paper to me."

The manuscript, experts believe, represents a working alchemical notebook kept by the Countess of Pembroke during the winter of 1590/91. The countess's scientific papers were thought to have been destroyed in a fire at Wilton House in the seventeenth century. It is not clear how the item came to be in the possession of the Barber family.

"We remember Mary Sidney primarily as a poet," commented a representative of Sotheby's Auction House, who will put the item up for bid in May, "but in her own time she was known as a great practitioner of alchemy."

The manuscript is of particular interest as it shows that the countess was assisted in her laboratory. In one experiment, labeled "the making of the arbor Dianæ," she identifies her assistant by the initials DR. "We might never be able to identify the man who helped the Countess of Pembroke," explained historian Nigel Warminster of Cambridge University, "but this manuscript will nevertheless tell us an enormous amount about the growth of experimentation in the Scientific Revolution."

"What is it, *Schatz*?" Ernst Neumann put a glass of wine in front of his wife. She looked far too serious for a Monday night. This was Verin's Friday face.

"Nothing," she murmured, her eyes still fixed on the lines of print before her. "A piece of unfinished family business."

"Is Baldwin involved? Did he lose a million euros today?" His brother-in-law was an acquired taste, and Ernst didn't entirely trust him. Baldwin had trained him in the intricacies of international commerce when Ernst was still a young man. Ernst was nearly sixty now, and the envy of his friends with his young wife. Their wedding photos, which showed Verin looking exactly as she did today and a twenty-five-year-old version of himself, were safely hidden from view.

"Baldwin's never lost a million of anything in his life." Verin hadn't actually answered his question, Ernst noticed.

He pulled the English newspaper toward him and read what was printed there. "Why are you interested in an old book?"

"Let me make a phone call first," she replied cagily. Her hands were steady on the phone, but Ernst recognized the expression in her unusual silver eyes. She was angry, and frightened, and thinking of the past. He'd seen that same look moments before Verin saved his life, wrenching him away from her stepmother.

"Are you calling Mélisande?"

"Ysabeau," Verin said automatically, punching in numbers.

"Ysabeau, yes," Ernst said. Understandably, he found it hard to think of Verin's stepmother by any other name than the one used by the de Clermont family matriarch when she'd killed Ernst's father after the war.

Verin's call took an inordinately long time to connect. Ernst could hear strange clicks, almost as though the call were being forwarded again and again. Finally it went through. The phone rang.

"Who is this?" a young voice asked. He sounded American—or English, maybe, but with his accent nearly gone.

Verin hung up immediately. She dropped the phone to the table and buried her face in her hands. "Oh, God. It's really happening, just as my father said it would."

"You're frightening me, *Schatz,*" Ernst said. He'd seen many horrors in his life, but none so vivid as those that tormented Verin on those rare occasions when she actually slept. The nightmares about Philippe were enough to unravel his normally composed wife. "Who was that on the phone?"

"It wasn't who it was supposed to be," Verin replied, her voice muffled. Gray eyes rose to meet his. "Matthew should have answered, but he can't. Because he's not here. He's there." She looked at the paper.

"Verin, you are not making any sense," Ernst said sternly. He'd never met this troublesome stepbrother, the family intellectual and black sheep.

But she was already dialing the phone again. This time the call went straight through.

"You've read today's papers, Auntie Verin. I've been expecting your call for hours."

"Where are you, Gallowglass?" Her nephew was a drifter. In the past he'd sent postcards with nothing but a phone number on them from whatever stretch of road he was traveling at the moment: the autobahn in Germany, Route 66 in the States, Trollstigen in Norway, the Guoliang Tunnel Road in China. She'd received fewer of these terse announcements since the age of international cell phones. With GPS and the Internet, she could locate Gallowglass anywhere. Verin rather missed the postcards, though.

"Somewhere outside Warrnambool," Gallowglass said vaguely.

"Where the hell is Warrnambool?" Verin demanded.

"Australia," Ernst and Gallowglass said at the same moment.

"Is that a German accent I hear? Have you found a new boyfriend?" Gallowglass teased.

"Watch yourself, pup," Verin snapped. "You may be family, but I can still rip your throat out. That's my husband, Ernst."

Ernst sat forward in his chair and shook his head in warning. He didn't like it when his wife took on a male vampire—even though she was stronger than most. Verin waved off his concern.

Gallowglass chuckled, and Ernst decided that this unfamiliar vampire might be all right. "There's my scary Auntie Verin. It's good to hear your voice after all these years. And don't pretend you're any more surprised to see that story than I was to get your call."

"Part of me hoped he was raving," Verin confessed, remembering the night when she and Gallowglass had sat by Philippe's bed and listened to his ramblings.

"Did you imagine it was contagious and that I was raving, too?" Gallowglass snorted. He sounded very much like Philippe these days, Verin noticed.

"I hoped that was the case, as a matter of fact." It had been easier to believe than the alternative: that her father's impossible tale of a time-spinning witch was true.

"Will you be keeping your promise anyway?" Gallowglass said softly.

Verin hesitated. It was only a moment, but Ernst saw it. Verin always kept her promises. When he'd been a terrified, cowering boy, Verin had promised him that he would grow to be a man. Ernst had clung to that assurance when he was six, just as he clung to the promises Verin had made since.

"You haven't seen Matthew with her. Once you do—"

"I'll think my stepbrother is even more of a problem? Not possible."

"Give her a chance, Verin. She's Philippe's daughter, too. And he had excellent taste in women."

"The witch isn't his real daughter," Verin said quickly.

On a road somewhere near Warrnambool, Gallowglass pressed his lips together and refused to reply. Verin might know more about Diana and Matthew than anyone else in the family, but she didn't know as much as he did. There would be endless opportunities to discuss vampires and children once the couple was back. There was no need to argue about it now.

"Besides, Matthew isn't here," Verin said, looking at the paper. "I called the number. Someone else answered, and it wasn't Baldwin." That's why she had disconnected so quickly. If Matthew wasn't leading the brotherhood, the telephone number should have been passed on to Philippe's only surviving full-blooded son. "The number" had been generated in the earliest years of the telephone. Philippe had picked it: 917, for Ysabeau's birthday in September. With each new technology and every successive change in the national and international telephone system, the number referred seamlessly on to another, more modern iteration.

"You reached Marcus." Gallowglass had called the number, too.

"Marcus?" Verin was aghast. "The future of the de Clermonts depends upon *Marcus*?"

"Give him a chance, too, Auntie Verin. He's a good lad." Gallowglass paused. "As for the family's future, that depends on all of us. Philippe knew that, or he wouldn't have made us promise to return to Sept-Tours."

Philippe de Clermont had been very specific with his daughter and grandson. They were to watch for signs: stories of a young American witch with great power, the name Bishop, alchemy, and then a rash of anomalous historical discoveries.

Then, and only then, were Gallowglass and Verin to return to the de Clermont family seat. Philippe hadn't been willing to divulge why it was so important that the family come together, but Gallowglass knew.

For decades Gallowglass had waited. Then he heard stories of a witch from Massachusetts named Rebecca, one of the last descendants of Salem's Bridget Bishop. Reports of her power spread far and wide, as did news of her tragic death. Gallowglass tracked her surviving daughter to upstate New York. He'd checked on the girl periodically, watching as Diana Bishop played on the monkey bars at the playground, went to birthday parties, and graduated from college. Gallowglass had been as proud as any parent to see her pass her Oxford viva. And he often stood beneath the carillon in Harkness Tower at Yale, the power of the bells' sound reverberating through his body, while the young professor walked across campus. Her clothing was different, but there was no mistaking Diana's determined gait or the set of her shoulders, whether she was wearing a farthingale and ruff or a pair of trousers and an unflattering man's jacket.

Gallowglass tried to keep his distance, but sometimes he had to interfere—like the day her energy drew a daemon to her side and the creature began to follow her. Still, Gallowglass prided himself on the hundreds of other times he'd refrained from rushing down the stairs of Yale's bell tower, throwing his arms around Professor Bishop, and telling her how glad he was to see her after so many years.

When Gallowglass learned that Baldwin had been called to Sept-Tours at Ysabeau's behest for some unspecified emergency involving Matthew, the Gael knew it was only a matter of time before the historical anomalies appeared. Gallowglass had seen the announcement about the discovery of a pair of previously unknown Elizabethan miniatures. By the time he'd managed to reach Sotheby's, they had already been purchased. Gallowglass had panicked, thinking they might have fallen into the wrong hands. But he'd underestimated Ysabeau. When he talked to Marcus this morning, Matthew's son confirmed that they were sitting safely on Ysabeau's desk at Sept-Tours. It had been more than four hundred years since Gallowglass had secreted the pictures away in a house in Shropshire. It would be good to see them—and the two creatures they depicted—once more.

Meanwhile he was preparing for the gathering storm as he always did: by traveling as far and fast as he could. Once it had been the seas and then the rails, but now Gallowglass took to the roads, motorcycling around as many hairpin turns and mountainsides as he could. With the wind streaming through his shaggy hair and his leather jacket fastened tight around his neck to hide the fact that his skin never showed any hint of tan, Gallowglass readied himself for the call of duty to fulfill his long-ago promise to defend the de Clermonts no matter what the cost.

"Gallowglass? Are you still there?" Verin's voice crackled through the phone, pulling her nephew from his reveries.

"Still here, Auntie."

"When are you going?" Verin sighed and rested her head in her hand. She couldn't bring herself to look at Ernst yet. Poor Ernst, who had knowingly married a vampire and, in doing so, had unwittingly involved himself in a tangled tale of blood and desire that looped and swirled through the centuries. But she'd promised her father, and even though Philippe was dead, Verin had no intention of disappointing him now, and for the first time.

"I told Marcus to expect me the day after tomorrow." Gallowglass would no more admit he was relieved by his aunt's decision than Verin would admit that she'd had to consider whether to stand by her oath.

"We'll see you there." That would give Verin some time to break the news to Ernst that he was going to have to share her stepmother's roof. He wasn't going to be pleased.

"Travel safe, Auntie Verin," Gallowglass managed to get out before she hung up.

Gallowglass put the phone in his pocket and stared out to sea. He'd been shipwrecked once on this stretch of Australia's coast. He was fond of the sites where he'd been washed ashore, a merman coming aground in a tempest to find he could live on solid ground after all. He reached for his cigarettes. Like riding a motorcycle without a helmet, smoking was a way of thumbing his nose at the universe that had given him immortality with one hand but with the other taken away everyone he loved.

"And you'll take these from me, too, won't you?" he asked the wind. It sighed out a reply. Matthew and Marcus had very decided opinions about secondhand smoke. Just because it wouldn't kill them, they argued, that didn't mean they should go about exterminating everybody else.

"If we kill them all, what will we eat?" Marcus had pointed out with infallible logic. It was a curious notion for a vampire, but Marcus was known for them, and Matthew wasn't much better. Gallowglass attributed this tendency to too much education.

He finished his cigarette and reached back into his pocket for a small leather pouch. It contained twenty-four disks an inch across and a quarter of an inch thick. They were cut from a branch he'd pulled from an ash tree that grew near his ancestral home. Each one had a mark burned into the surface, an alphabet for a language that no one spoke anymore.

He had always possessed a healthy respect for magic, even before he met Diana Bishop. There were powers abroad on the earth and the seas that no creature understood, and Gallowglass knew well enough to look the other way when they approached. But he couldn't resist the runes. They helped him to navigate the treacherous waters of his fate.

He sifted his fingers through the smooth wooden circles, letting them fall through his hand like water. He wanted to know which way the tide was running—with the de Clermonts or against them?

When his fingers stilled, he drew out the rune that would tell him where matters stood now. *Nyd,* the rune for absence and desire. Gallowglass dipped his hand into the bag again to better understand what he wanted the future to hold. *Odal,* the glyph for home, family, and inheritance. He drew out the final rune, the one that would show him how to fulfill his gnawing wish to belong.

Rad. It was a confusing rune, one that stood for both an arrival and a departure, a journey's beginning and its ending, a first meeting as well as a long-awaited reunion. Gallowglass's hand closed around the bit of wood. This time its meaning was clear.

"You travel safely, too, Auntie Diana. And bring that uncle of mine with you," Gallowglass said to the sea and the sky before he climbed back onto his bike and headed into a future he could no longer imagine nor postpone.

PART IV

The Empire: Prague

"Where are my red hose?" Matthew clomped downstairs and scowled at the boxes scattered all over the ground floor. His mood had taken a decided turn for the worse halfway through our four-week journey when we parted ways with Pierre, the children, and our luggage in Hamburg. We'd lost ten additional days by virtue of traveling from England into a Catholic country that reckoned time by a different calendar. In Prague, it was now the eleventh of March and the children and Pierre had yet to arrive.

"I'll never find them in this mess!" Matthew said, taking out his frustration on one of my petticoats.

After we'd lived out of saddlebags and a single shared trunk for weeks, our belongings had arrived three days after we did at the tall, narrow house perched on the steep avenue leading to Prague Castle known as Sporrengasse. Our German neighbors presumably dubbed it Spur Street because that was the only way you could persuade a horse to make the climb.

"I didn't know you owned red hose," I said, straightening up.

"I do." Matthew started rooting around in a box that contained my linen.

"Well, they won't be in there," I said, pointing out the obvious.

The vampire ground his teeth. "I've looked everywhere else."

"I'll find them." I eyed his perfectly respectable black leggings. "Why red?"

"Because I am trying to catch the Holy Roman Emperor's attention!" Matthew dove into another pile of my clothes.

Bloodred stockings would do more than capture a wandering eye, given that the man who proposed to wear them was a six-foot-three vampire, and most of his height was leg. Matthew's commitment to the plan was unwavering, however. I focused my mind, asked for the hose to show themselves, and followed the red threads. The ability to keep track of people and objects was an unforeseen fringe benefit of being a weaver, and one I'd had several opportunities to use on the trip.

"Has my father's messenger arrived?" Matthew contributed another petticoat to the snowy mountain growing between us and resumed digging.

"Yes. It's over by the door—whatever it is." I fished through contents of an overlooked chest: chain-mail gauntlets, a shield with a double-headed eagle on it, and an elaborately chased cup-and-stick gizmo. Triumphant, I brandished the long red tubes. "Found them!"

Matthew had forgotten the hosiery crisis. His father's package now held his complete attention. I looked to see what had him so amazed.

"Is that . . . a Bosch?" I knew Hieronymus Bosch's work because of his bizarre use of alchemical equipment and symbolism. He covered his panels with flying fish, insects, enormous household implements, and eroticized fruit. Long before psychedelic was stylish, Bosch saw the world in bright colors and unsettling combinations.

Like Matthew's Holbeins at the Old Lodge, however, this work was unfamiliar. It was a triptych, assembled from three hinged wooden panels. Designed to sit on an altar, triptychs were kept closed except for special religious celebrations. In modern museums the exteriors were seldom on display. I wondered what other stunning images I'd been missing.

The artist had covered the outside panels with a velvety black pigment. A wizened tree shimmering in the moonlight spanned the two front panels. A tiny wolf crouched in its roots, and an owl perched in the upper branches. Both animals gazed at the viewer knowingly. A dozen other eyes shone out from the dark ground around the tree, disembodied and staring. Behind the dead oak, a stand of deceptively normal trees with pale trunks and iridescent green branches shed more light on the scene. Only when I took a closer look did I see the ears growing out of them, as though they were listening to the sounds of the night.

"What does it mean?" I asked, staring at Bosch's work in wonder.

Matthew's fingers fiddled with the fastenings on his doublet. "It represents an old Flemish proverb: '*The forest has eyes, and the woods have ears; therefore I will see, be silent, and hear.*'" The words perfectly captured the secretive life Matthew led and reminded me of Elizabeth's current choice of motto.

The triptych's interior showed three interrelated scenes: One panel showed the fallen angels, painted against the same velvety black background. At first glance they looked more like dragonflies with their shimmering double wings, but they had human bodies, with heads and legs that twisted in torment as the angels fell through the heavens. On the opposite panel, the dead rose for the Last Judgment in a scene far more gruesome than the frescoes at Sept-Tours. The gaping jaws of fish and wolves provided entrances to hell, sucking in the damned and consigning them to an eternity of pain and agony.

The center, however, showed a very different image of death: the resurrected Lazarus calmly climbing out of his coffin. With his long legs, dark hair, and serious expression, he looked rather like Matthew. All around the borders of the center panel, lifeless vines produced strange fruits and flowers. Some dripped blood. Others gave birth to people and animals. And no Jesus was in sight.

"Lazarus resembles you. No wonder you don't want Rudolf to have it." I handed Matthew his hose. "Bosch must have known you were a vampire, too."

"Jeroen—or Hieronymus as you know him—saw something he shouldn't have," Matthew said darkly. "I didn't know that Jeroen had witnessed me feeding until I saw the sketches he made of me with a warmblood. From that day on, he believed all creatures had a dual nature, part human and part animal."

"And sometimes part vegetable," I said, studying a naked woman with a strawberry for a head and cherries for hands running away from a pitchfork-wielding devil wearing a stork as a hat. Matthew made a soft sound of amusement. "Does Rudolf know you're a vampire, as Elizabeth does and Bosch did?" I was increasingly concerned by the number of people who were in on the secret.

"Yes. The emperor knows I'm a member of the Congregation, too." He twisted his bright red hose into a knot. "Thank you for finding these."

"Tell me now if you have a habit of losing your car keys, because I'm not putting up with this kind of panic every morning when you get ready for work." I slid my arms around his waist and rested my cheek on his heart. That slow, steady beat always calmed me.

"What are you going to do, divorce me?" Matthew returned the embrace, resting his head on mine so that we fit together perfectly.

"You promised me vampires don't do divorce." I gave him a squeeze. "You're going to look like a cartoon character if you put those red socks on. I'd stick to the black if I were you. You'll stand out regardless."

"Witch," Matthew said, releasing me with a kiss.

He went up the hill to the castle, wearing sober black hose and carrying a long, convoluted message (partially in verse) offering Rudolf a marvelous book for his collections. He came back down four hours later empty-handed, having delivered the note to an imperial flunky. There had been no audience with the emperor. Instead Matthew had been kept waiting along with all the other ambassadors seeking audience.

"It was like being stuck in a cattle truck with all those warm bodies cooped up together. I tried to go somewhere with clear air to breathe, but the nearby rooms were full of witches."

"Witches?" I climbed down from the table I was using to put Matthew's sword safely on top of the linen cupboard in preparation for Jack's arrival.

"Dozens of them," Matthew said. "They were complaining about what's happening in Germany. Where's Gallowglass?"

"Your nephew is buying eggs and securing the services of a housekeeper and a cook." Françoise had flatly refused to join our expedition to Central Europe, which she viewed as a godless land of Lutherans. She was now back at the Old Lodge, spoiling Charles. Gallowglass was serving as my page and general dogsbody until the others arrived. He had excellent German and Spanish, which made him indispensable when it came to provisioning our household. "Tell me more about the witches."

"The city is a safe haven for every creature in Central Europe who fears for his safety—daemon, vampire, or witch. But the witches are especially welcome in Rudolf's court, because he covets their knowledge. And their power."

"Interesting," I said. No sooner had I started wondering about their identities than a series of faces appeared to my third eye. "Who is the wizard with the red beard? And the witch with one blue and one green eye?"

"We aren't going to be here long enough for their identities to matter," Matthew said ominously on his way out the door. Having concluded the day's business for Elizabeth, he was headed across the river to Prague's Old Town on behalf of the Congregation. "I'll see you before dark. Stay here until Gallowglass returns. I don't want you getting lost." More to the point, he didn't want me stumbling upon any witches.

Gallowglass returned to Sporrengasse with two vampires and a pretzel. He handed the latter to me and introduced me to my new servants.

Karolína (the cook) and Tereza (the housekeeper) were members of a sprawling clan of Bohemian vampires dedicated to serving the aristocracy and important foreign visitors. Like the de Clermont retainers, they earned their reputation—and an unusually large salary—because of their preternatural longevity and wolfish loyalty. For the right price, we were also able to buy assurances of secrecy from the clan's elder, who had removed the women from the household of the papal ambassador. The ambassador graciously consented out of deference to the de Clermonts. They had, after all, been instrumental in rigging the last papal election, and he knew who buttered his bread. I cared only that Karolína knew how to make omelets.

Our household established, Matthew loped up the hill each morning to the castle while I unpacked, met my neighbors in the neighborhood below the castle walls called Malá Strana, and watched for the absent members of the household. I missed Annie's cheerfulness and wide-eyed approach to the world, as well as Jack's unfailing ability to get himself into trouble. Our winding street was packed with children of all ages and nationalities, since most of the ambassadors lived there. It turned out that Matthew was not the only foreigner in Prague to be kept at arm's length by the emperor. Every person I met regaled Gallowglass with tales of how Rudolf had snubbed some important personage only to spend hours with a bookish antiquarian from Italy or a humble miner from Saxony.

It was late afternoon on the first day of spring, and the house was filling with the homely scents of pork and dumplings when a scrappy eight-year-old tackled me.

"Mistress Roydon!" Jack crowed, his face buried in my bodice and his arms wrapped tightly around me. "Did you know that Prague is really four towns in one? London is only one town. And there is a castle, too, and a river. Pierre will show me the watermill tomorrow."

"Hello, Jack," I said, stroking his hair. Even on the grueling, freezing journey to Prague, he had managed to shoot up in height. Pierre must have been shoveling food into him. I looked up and smiled at Annie and Pierre. "Matthew will be so glad that you've all arrived. He's missed you."

"We've missed him, too," Jack said, tilting his head back to look at me. He had dark circles under his eyes, and in spite of his growth spurt he looked wan.

"Have you been ill?" I asked, feeling his forehead. Colds could turn deadly in this harsh climate, and there was talk of a nasty epidemic in the Old Town that Matthew thought was a strain of flu.

"He's been having trouble sleeping," Pierre said quietly. I could tell from his serious tone that there was more to the story, but it could wait.

"Well, you'll sleep tonight. There is an enormous featherbed in your room. Go with Tereza, Jack. She'll show you where your things are and get you washed up before supper." In the interests of vampire propriety, the warmbloods would be sleeping with Matthew and me on the second floor, since the house's narrow layout permitted only a keeping room and kitchen on the ground floor. That meant that the first floor was dedicated to formal rooms for receiving guests. The rest of the household's vampires had staked their claim on the lofty third floor, with its expansive views and windows that could be flung open to the elements.

"Master Roydon!" Jack shrieked, hurling himself at the door and flinging it open before Tereza could stop him. How he detected Matthew was a mystery, given the growing darkness and Matthew's head-to-toe adoption of slate-colored wool.

"Easy," Matthew said, catching Jack before he hurt himself running into a pair of solid vampire legs. Gallowglass snatched at Jack's cap as he went by, ruffling the boy's hair.

"We almost froze. In the river. And the sled turned over once, but the dog was not hurt. I ate roasted boar. And Annie caught her skirt in the wagon wheel and almost tumbled out." Jack couldn't get the details of their journey out of his mouth fast enough. "I saw a blazing star. It was not very big, but Pierre told me I must share it with Master Harriot when we return home. I drew a picture of it for him." Jack's hand slid inside his grimy doublet and pulled out an equally grimy slip of paper. He presented this to Matthew with the reverence normally accorded to a holy relic.

"This is quite good," Matthew said, studying the drawing with appropriate care. "I like how you've shown the curve of the tail. And you put the other stars around it. That was wise, Jack. Master Harriot will be pleased at your powers of observation."

Jack flushed. "That was my last piece of paper. Do they sell paper in Prague?" Back in London, Matthew had taken to supplying Jack with a pocketful of paper scraps every morning. How Jack went through them was a matter of some speculation.

"The city is awash in the stuff," Matthew said. "Pierre will take you to the shop in Malá Strana tomorrow."

After that exciting promise, it was hard to get the children upstairs, but Tereza proved to possess the precise mix of gentleness and resolve to accomplish the task. That gave the four grown-ups a chance to talk freely.

"Has Jack been sick?" Matthew asked Pierre with a frown.

"No, *milord.* Since we left you, his sleep has been troubled." Pierre hesitated. "I think the evils in his past haunt him."

Matthew's forehead smoothed out, but he still looked concerned. "And otherwise the journey was as you expected?" This was his cagey way of asking whether they had been set upon by bandits or plagued by supernatural or preternatural beings.

"It was long and cold," Pierre said matter-of-factly, "and the children were always hungry."

Gallowglass bellowed with laughter. "Well, that sounds about right."

"And you, *milord*?" Pierre shot a veiled glance at Matthew. "Is Prague as you expected?"

"Rudolf hasn't seen me. Rumor has it that Kelley is in the uppermost reaches of the Powder Tower blowing up alembics and God-knows-what-else," Matthew reported.

"And the Old Town?" Pierre asked delicately.

"It is much as it ever was." Matthew's tone was breezy and light—a dead giveaway that he was concerned about something.

"So long as you ignore the gossip coming from the Jewish quarter. One of their witches has made a creature from clay who prowls the streets at night." Gallowglass turned innocent eyes on his uncle. "Saving that, it is practically unchanged from the last time we were here to help Emperor Ferdinand secure the city in 1547."

"Thank you, Gallowglass," Matthew said. His tone was as chilly as the wind off the river.

Surely it would require more than an ordinary spell to construct a creature from mud and set it in motion. Such a rumor could mean only one thing: Somewhere in Prague was a weaver like me, one who could move between the world of the living and the world of the dead. But I didn't have to call Matthew on his secret. His nephew beat me to it.

"You didn't think you could keep news of the clay creature from Auntie?" Gallowglass shook his head in amazement. "You don't spend enough time at the market. The women of Malá Strana know everything, including what the emperor is having for breakfast and that he's refused to see you."

Matthew ran his fingers over the painted wooden surface of the triptych and sighed. "You'll have to take this up to the palace, Pierre."

"But that is the altarpiece from Sept-Tours," Pierre protested. "The emperor is known for his caution. Surely it is only a matter of time before he admits you."

"Time is the one commodity we lack—and the de Clermonts have altarpieces aplenty," Matthew said ruefully. "Let me write a note to the emperor, and you can be on your way."

Matthew dispatched Pierre and the painting shortly thereafter. His servant returned just as empty-handed as Matthew had, with no assurances of a future meeting.

All around me the threads that bound the worlds were tightening and shifting in a weaving whose pattern was too large for me to perceive or understand. But something was brewing in Prague. I could feel it.

That night I awoke to the sound of soft voices in the room adjoining our bedchamber. Matthew was not next to me, reading, as he had been when I'd dropped off to sleep. I padded to the door to see who was with him.

"Tell me what happens when I shade the side of the monster's face." Matthew's hand moved swiftly over the large sheet of foolscap before him.

"It makes him seem farther away!" Jack whispered, awestruck by the transformation.

"You try it," Matthew said, handing Jack his pen. Jack gripped it with great concentration, his tongue stuck slightly out. Matthew rubbed the boy's back with his hand, relaxing the taut muscles wrapped around his rangy frame. Jack was not quite sitting on his knee but leaning into the vampire's comforting bulk for support. "So many monsters," Matthew murmured, meeting my eyes.

"Do you want to draw yours?" Jack inched the paper in Matthew's direction. "Then you could sleep, too."

"Your monsters have frightened mine away," Matthew said, returning his attention to Jack, his face grave. My heart hurt for the boy and all he had endured in his brief, hard life.

Matthew met my eyes again and indicated with a slight shift of his head that he had everything under control. I blew him a kiss and returned to the warm, feathery nest of our bed.

The next day we received a note from the emperor. It was sealed with thick wax and ribbons.

"The painting worked, *milord,*" Pierre said apologetically.

"It figures. I loved that altarpiece. Now I'll have a hell of a time getting my hands on it again," Matthew said, sitting back in his chair. The wood creaked in protest. Matthew reached out for the letter. The penmanship was elaborate, with so many swirls and curlicues that the letters were practically unrecognizable.

"Why is the handwriting so ornate?" I wondered.

"The Hoefnagels have arrived from Vienna and have nothing to occupy their time. The fancier the handwriting, the better, as far as His Majesty is concerned," Pierre replied cryptically.

"I'm to go to Rudolf this afternoon," Matthew said with a satisfied smile, folding up the message. "My father will be pleased. He sent some money and jewels, too, but it would appear that the de Clermonts got off lightly this time."

Pierre held out another, smaller letter, addressed in a plainer style. "The emperor added a postscript. In his own hand."

I looked over Matthew's shoulder as he read it.

"Bringen das Buch. Und die Hexe." The emperor's swirling signature, with its elaborate *R,* looping *d* and *l,* and double *f*'s, was at the bottom.

My German was rusty, but the message was clear: *Bring the book. And the witch.*

"I spoke too soon," Matthew muttered.

"I told you to hook him with Titian's great canvas of Venus that Grandfather took off King Philip's hands when his wife objected to it," Gallowglass observed. "Like his uncle, Rudolf has always been unduly fond of redheads. And saucy pictures."

"And witches," my husband said under his breath. He threw the letter on the table. "It wasn't the painting that baited him, but Diana. Maybe I should refuse his invitation."

"That was a command, Uncle." Gallowglass's brow lowered.

"And Rudolf has Ashmole 782," I said. "It's not going to simply appear in front of the Three Ravens on Sporrengasse. We're going to have to find it."

"Are you calling us ravens, Auntie?" Gallowglass said with mock offense.

"I'm talking about the sign on the house, you great oaf." Like every other residence on the street, ours had a symbol over the door rather than a house number. After the neighborhood caught fire in the middle of the century, the emperor's grandfather had insisted on having some way to tell houses apart besides the popular sgraffito decorations scratched into the plaster.

Gallowglass grinned. "I knew very well what you were talking about. But I do love seeing you go all shiny like that when your *glaem*'s raised."

I pulled my disguising spell around me with a harrumph, dimming my shininess to more acceptable, human levels.

"Besides," Gallowglass continued. "Among my people it's a great compliment to be likened to a raven. I'll be Muninn, and Matthew we'll call Huginn. Your name will be Göndul, Auntie. You'll make a fine Valkyrie."

"What is he talking about?" I asked Matthew blankly.

"Odin's ravens. And his daughters."

"Oh. Thank you, Gallowglass," I said awkwardly. It couldn't be a bad thing to be likened to a god's daughter.

"Even if this book of Rudolf's is Ashmole 782, we're not sure it contains answers to our questions." Our experience with the Voynich manuscript still worried Matthew.

"Historians never know if a text will provide answers. If it doesn't, though, we'll still have better questions as a result," I replied.

"Point taken." Matthew's lips quirked. "As I can't get in to see the emperor or his library without you, and you won't leave Prague without the book, there is nothing for it. We'll both go to the palace."

"You've been hoist by your own petard, Uncle," Gallowglass said cheerfully. He gave me a broad wink.

When compared to our visit to Richmond, the trip up the street to see the emperor seemed almost like popping next door to borrow a cup of sugar from a neighbor—though it required a more formal costume. The papal ambassador's mistress was much my size, and her wardrobe had provided me with a suitably luxurious and circumspect garment for the wife of an English dignitary—or a de Clermont, she quickly added. I loved the style of clothing worn by well-heeled women in Prague: simple gowns with high necks, bell-shaped skirts, embroidered coats with hanging sleeves trimmed in fur. The small ruffs they wore served as another welcome barrier between the elements and me.

Matthew had happily abandoned his dreams of red hose in favor of his usual gray and black, accented with a deep green that was the most attractive color I had ever seen him wear. This afternoon it provided flashes of color peeking through the slashes on his bulbous britches and the lining peeking around the open collar of his jacket.

"You look splendid," I said after inspecting him.

"And you look like a proper Bohemian aristocrat," he replied, kissing me on the cheek.

"Can we go now?" Jack said, dancing with impatience. Someone had found him a suit of black-and-silver livery and put a cross and crescent moon on the sleeve.

"So we are going as de Clermonts, not as Roydons," I said slowly.

"No. We are Matthew and Diana Roydon," Matthew replied. "We're just traveling with the de Clermont family servants."

"That should confuse everybody," I commented as we left the house.

"Exactly," Matthew said with a smile.

Had we been going as ordinary citizens, we would have climbed the new palace steps, which clung to the ramparts and provided a safe way for pedestrians. Instead we wended our way up Sporrengasse on horseback as befitted a representative of the queen of England, which gave me a chance to fully take in the houses with their canted foundations, colorful sgraffito, and painted signs. We passed the house of the Red Lion, the Golden Star, the Swan, and the Two Suns. At the top of the hill, we took a sharp turn into a neighborhood filled with the mansions of aristocrats and court appointees, called Hradčany.

It was not my first glimpse of the castle, for I'd seen it looming over its surroundings when we came into Prague and could look up to its ramparts from our windows. But this was the closest I'd yet been to it. The castle was even larger and more sprawling at close range than it had appeared at a distance, like an entirely separate city full of trade and industry. Ahead were the Gothic pinnacles of St. Vitus Cathedral, with round towers punctuating the walls. Though built for defense, the towers now housed workshops for the hundreds of artisans who made their home at Rudolf's court.

The palace guard admitted us through the west gate and into an enclosed courtyard. After Pierre and Jack took charge of the horses, our armed escorts headed for a range of buildings tucked against the castle walls. They had been built relatively recently, and the stone was crisp-edged and gleaming. These looked like office buildings, but beyond them I could see high roofs and medieval stonework.

"What's happened now?" I whispered to Matthew. "Why aren't we going to the palace?"

"Because there's nobody there of any importance," said Gallowglass. He held the Voynich manuscript in his arms, safely wrapped in leather and bound with straps to keep the pages from warping in the damp weather.

"Rudolf found the old Royal Palace drafty and dark," Matthew explained, helping me over the slick cobbles. "His new palace faces south and overlooks a private garden. Here he's farther away from the cathedral—and the priests."

The halls of the residence were busy, with people rushing to and fro shouting in German, Czech, Spanish, and Latin depending on which part of Rudolf's empire they came from. The closer we got to the emperor, the more frenetic the activity became. We passed a room filled with people arguing over architectural drawings. Another room housed a lively debate about the merits of an elaborate gold-and-stone bowl fashioned to look like a seashell. Finally the guards left us in a comfortable salon with heavy chairs, a tiled stove that pumped out a significant amount of heat, and two men in deep conversation. They turned toward us.

"Good day, old friend," a kindly man of around sixty said in English. He beamed at Matthew.

"Tadeáš." Matthew gripped his arm warmly. "You are looking well."

"And you are looking young." The man's eyes twinkled. His glance caused no tell-tale reaction on my skin. "And here is the woman everyone is talking about. I am Tadeáš Hájek." The human bowed, and I curtsied in response.

A slender gentleman with an olive complexion and hair nearly as dark as Matthew's strolled over to us. "Master Strada," Matthew said with a bow. He was not as pleased to see this man as he was the first.

"Is she truly a witch?" Strada surveyed me with interest. "If so, my sister Katharina would like to meet her. She is with child, and the pregnancy troubles her."

"Surely Tadeáš—the royal physician—is better suited to seeing after the birth of the emperor's child," Matthew said, "or have matters with your sister changed?"

"The emperor still treasures my sister," Strada said frostily. "For that reason alone, her whims should be indulged."

"Have you seen Joris? He has been talking about nothing but your altarpiece since His Majesty opened it," Tadeáš asked, changing the subject.

"Not yet, no." Matthew's eyes went to the door. "Is the emperor in?"

"Yes. He is looking at a new painting by Master Spranger. It is very large and . . . ah, detailed."

"Another picture of Venus," Strada said with a sniff.

"This Venus looks rather like your sister, sir." Hájek smiled.

"Ist das Matthäus höre ich?" said a nasal voice from the far end of the room. Everyone turned and swept into deep bows. I curtsied automatically. It was going to be a challenge to follow the conversation. I had expected Rudolf to speak Latin, not German. *"Und Sie das Buch und die Hexe gebracht, ich verstehe. Und die norwegische Wolf."*

Rudolf was a small man with a disproportionately long chin and a pronounced underbite. The full, fleshy lips of the Hapsburg family exaggerated the prominence of the lower half of his face, although this was somewhat balanced by his pale, protruding eyes and thick, flattened nose. Years of good living and fine drink had given him a portly profile, but his legs remained thin and spindly. He tottered toward us on high-heeled red shoes ornamented with gold stamps.

"I brought my wife, Your Majesty, as you commanded," Matthew said, placing a slight emphasis on the word "wife." Gallowglass translated Matthew's English into flawless German, as if my husband didn't know the language—which I knew he did, after traveling with him from Hamburg to Wittenberg to Prague by sled.

"Y su talento para los juegos también," Rudolf said, switching effortlessly into Spanish as though that might convince Matthew to converse with him directly. He studied me slowly, lingering over the curves of my body with a thoroughness that made me long for a shower. *"Es una lástima que se casó en absoluto, pero aún más lamentable que ella está casada con usted."*

"Very regrettable, Majesty," Matthew said sharply, sticking resolutely to English. "But I assure you we are thoroughly wed. My father insisted upon it. So did the lady." This remark only made Rudolf scrutinize me with greater interest.

Gallowglass took mercy on me and thumped the book onto the table. *"Das Buch."*

That got their attention. Strada unwrapped it while Hájek and Rudolf speculated on just how wonderful this new addition to the imperial library might prove to be. When it was exposed to view, however, the air in the room thickened with disappointment.

"What joke is this?" Rudolf snapped in German.

"I am not sure I take Your Majesty's meaning," Matthew replied. He waited for Gallowglass to translate.

"I mean that I already know this book," Rudolf sputtered.

"That doesn't surprise me, Your Majesty, since you gave it to John Dee—by mistake, I am told." Matthew bowed.

"The emperor does not make mistakes!" Strada said, pushing the book away in disgust.

"We all make mistakes, Signor Strada," Hájek said gently. "I am sure, though, that there is some other explanation as to why this book has been returned to the emperor. Perhaps Dr. Dee uncovered its secrets."

"It is nothing but childish pictures," retorted Strada.

"Is that why this picture book found its way into Dr. Dee's baggage? Did you hope he would be able to understand what you could not?" Matthew's words were having an adverse effect on Strada, who turned purple. "Perhaps you borrowed Dee's book, Signor Strada, the one with alchemical pictures from Roger Bacon's library, in hope that it would help you decipher this one. That is a far more pleasant prospect than imagining you would have tricked poor Dr. Dee out of his treasure. Of course His Majesty could not have known of such an evil business." Matthew's smile was chilling.

"And is this book that you say I have the only treasure of mine you wish to take back to England?" Rudolf asked sharply. "Or does your avarice extend to my laboratories?"

"If you mean Edward Kelley, the queen needs some assurance that he is here of his own free will. Nothing more," Matthew lied. He then took the conversation in a less trying direction. "Do you like your new altarpiece, Your Majesty?"

Matthew had provided the emperor just enough room to regroup—and save face. "The Bosch is exceptional. My uncle will be most aggrieved to learn that I have acquired it." Rudolf looked around. "Alas, this room is not suitable for its display. I wanted to show it to the Spanish ambassador, but here you cannot get far enough from the painting to view it properly. It is a work that you must come upon slowly, allowing the details to emerge naturally. Come. See where I have put it."

Matthew and Gallowglass arranged themselves so that Rudolf couldn't get too close to me as we trooped through the door and into a room that looked like the storeroom for an overstuffed and understaffed museum. Shelves and cabinets held so many shells, books, and fossils that they threatened to topple over. Huge canvases—including the new painting of Venus, which was not simply detailed but openly erotic—were propped up against bronze statues. This must be Rudolf's famed curiosity cabinet, his room of wonders and marvels.

"Your Majesty needs more space—or fewer specimens," Matthew commented, grabbing a piece of porcelain to keep it from smashing to the floor.

"I will always find a place for new treasures." The emperor's gaze settled on me once more. "I am building four new rooms to hold them all. You can see them working." He pointed out the window to two towers and the long building that was beginning to connect them to the emperor's apartments and another new piece of construction opposite. "Until then Ottavio and Tadeáš are cataloging my collection and instructing the architects on what I require. I do not want to move everything into the new *Kunstkammer* only to outgrow it again."

Rudolf led us through a warren of additional storerooms until we finally arrived at a long gallery with windows on both sides. It was full of light, and after the gloom and dust of the preceding chambers, entering it felt like taking in a lungful of clean air.

The sight in the center of the room brought me up short. Matthew's altarpiece sat open on a long table covered with thick green felt. The emperor was right: You couldn't fully appreciate the colors when you stood close to the work.

"It is beautiful, Dona Diana." Rudolf took advantage of my surprise to grasp my hand. "Notice how what you perceive changes with each step. Only vulgar objects can be seen at once, for they have no mysteries to reveal."

Strada looked at me with open animosity, Hájek with pity. Matthew was not looking at me at all, but at the emperor.

"Speaking of which, Majesty, might I see Dee's book?" Matthew's expression was guileless, but no one in the room was fooled for an instant. The wolf was on the prowl.

"Who knows where it is?" Rudolf had to drop my hand in order to wave vaguely at the rooms we had just left.

"Signor Strada must be neglecting his duties, if such a precious manuscript cannot be found when the emperor requires it," Matthew said softly.

"Ottavio is very busy at present, with matters of importance!" Rudolf glared at Matthew. "And I do not trust Dr. Dee. Your queen should beware his false promises."

"But you trust Kelley. Perhaps he knows its whereabouts?"

At this the emperor looked distinctly uneasy. "I do not want Edward disturbed. He is at a very delicate stage in the alchemical work."

"Prague has many charms, and Diana has been commissioned to purchase some alchemical glassware for the Countess of Pembroke. We will occupy ourselves with that task until Sir Edward is able to receive visitors. Perhaps Signor Strada will be able to find your missing book by then."

"This Countess of Pembroke is the sister of the queen's hero, Sir Philip Sidney?" Rudolf asked, his interest caught. When Matthew opened his mouth to answer, Rudolf stopped him with a raised hand. "It is Dona Diana's business. We will let her answer."

"Yes, Your Majesty," I responded in Spanish. My pronunciation was atrocious. I hoped that would diminish his interest.

"Charming," Rudolf murmured. *Damn.* "Very well then, Dona Diana must visit my workshops. I enjoy fulfilling a lady's wishes."

It was not clear which lady he meant.

"As for Kelley and the book, we shall see. We shall see." Rudolf turned back to the triptych. "*'I will see, be silent, and hear.'* Isn't that the proverb?"

"Did you see the werewolf, Frau Roydon? He is the emperor's gamekeeper, and my neighbor Frau Habermel has heard him howling at night. They say he feeds on the imperial deer running in the Stag Moat." Frau Huber picked up a cabbage in her gloved hand and gave it a suspicious sniff. Herr Huber had been a merchant at London's Steelyard, and though she bore no love for the city, she spoke English fluently.

"Pah. There is no werewolf," Signorina Rossi said, turning her long neck and tutting over the price of the onions. "My Stefano tells me there are many daemons in the palace, however. The bishops at the cathedral wish to exorcise them, but the emperor refuses." Like Frau Huber, Rossi had spent time in London. Then she had been mistress to an Italian artist who wanted to bring mannerism to the English. Now she was mistress to another Italian artist who wanted to introduce the art of glass cutting to Prague.

"I saw no werewolves or daemons," I confessed. The women's faces fell. "But I did see one of the emperor's new paintings." I dropped my voice. "It showed Venus. Rising from her bath." I gave them both significant looks.

In the absence of otherworldly gossip, the perversions of royalty would suffice. Frau Huber drew herself straight.

"Emperor Rudolf needs a wife. A good Austrian woman, who will cook for him." She condescended to buy a cabbage from the grateful vegetable seller, who had been putting up with her criticisms of his produce for nearly thirty minutes. "Tell us again about the unicorn's horn. It is supposed to have miraculous curative powers."

It was the fourth time in two days I'd been asked to account for the marvels among the emperor's curiosities. News of our admittance to Rudolf's private apartments preceded our return to the Three Ravens, and the ladies of Malá Strana were lying in wait the next morning, eager for my impressions.

Since then the appearance of imperial messengers at the house, as well as the liveried servants of dozens of Bohemian aristocrats and foreign dignitaries, had roused their curiosity further. Now that Matthew had been received at court, his star was sufficiently secure in the imperial heavens that his old friends were willing to acknowledge his arrival—and ask for his help. Pierre pulled out the ledgers, and soon the Prague branch of the de Clermont bank was open for business, though I saw precious little money received and a steady stream of funds flow out to settle overdue accounts with the merchants of Prague's Old Town.

"You received a package from the emperor," Matthew told me when I returned from the market. He pointed with his quill at a lumpy sack. "If you open it, Rudolf will expect you to express your thanks personally."

"What could it be?" I felt the outlines of the object inside. It wasn't a book.

"Something we'll regret receiving, I warrant." Matthew jammed the quill in the inkpot, causing a minor eruption of thick black liquid onto the surface of the desk. "Rudolf is a collector, Diana. And he's not simply interested in narwhal horns and bezoar stones. He covets people as well as objects and is just as unlikely to part with them once they're in his possession."

"Like Kelley," I said, loosening the parcel's strings. "But I'm not for sale."

"We are all for sale." Matthew's eyes widened. "Good Christ."

A two-foot-tall, gold-and-silver statue of the goddess Diana sat between us, naked except for her quiver, riding sidesaddle on the back of a stag with her ankles demurely crossed. A pair of hunting dogs sat at her feet.

Gallowglass whistled. "Well, I'd say the emperor has made his desires known in this case."

But I was too busy studying the statue to pay much attention. A small key was embedded in the base. I gave it a turn, and the stag took off across the floor. "Look, Matthew. Did you see that?"

"You're in no danger of losing Uncle's attention," Gallowglass assured me.

It was true: Matthew was staring angrily at the statue.

"Whoa, young Jack." Gallowglass caught Jack by the collar as the boy sped into the room. But Jack was a professional thief, and such delaying tactics were of little use when he smelled something of value. He slid to the floor in a boneless heap, leaving Gallowglass holding the jacket, and sprang after the deer.

"Is it a toy? Is it for me? Why is that lady not wearing any clothes? Isn't she cold?" The questions poured out of Jack in an unbroken torrent. Tereza, who was as interested in spectacle as any of the other women in Malá

Strana, came to see what the fuss was about. She gasped at the naked woman in her employer's office and clapped her hand over Jack's eyes.

Gallowglass peered at the statue's breasts. "Aye, Jack. I'd say she's cold." This earned him a cuff on the head from Tereza, who still retained a firm grip on the squirming child.

"It's an automaton, Jack," Matthew said, picking the thing up. When he did, the stag's head sprang open, revealing the hollow chamber within. "This one is meant to run down the emperor's dinner table. When it stops, the person closest must drink from the stag's neck. Why don't you go show Annie what it does?" He snapped the head back in place and handed the priceless object to Gallowglass. Then he gave me a serious look. "We need to talk."

Gallowglass propelled Jack and Tereza out of the room with promises of pretzels and skating.

"You're in dangerous territory, my love." Matthew ran his fingers through his hair, which never failed to make him look more handsome. "I've told the Congregation that your status as my wife is a convenient fiction to protect you from charges of witchcraft and to keep the Berwick witch-hunts confined to Scotland."

"But our friends and your fellow vampires know it's more than that," I said. A vampire's sense of smell didn't lie, and Matthew's unique scent covered me. "And the witches know there's something more to our relationship than meets even their third eye."

"Perhaps, but Rudolf is neither a vampire nor a witch. The emperor will have been assured by his own contacts within the Congregation that there is no relationship between us. Therefore there is nothing to preclude his chasing after you." Matthew's fingers found my cheek. "I don't share, Diana. And if Rudolf were to go too far . . ."

"You'd keep your temper in check." I covered his hand with mine. "You know that I'm not going to let the Holy Roman Emperor—or anybody else, for that matter—seduce me. We need Ashmole 782. Who cares if Rudolf stares at my breasts?"

"Staring I can handle." Matthew kissed me. "There's something else you should know before you go off to thank the emperor. The Congregation has fed Rudolf's appetites for women and curiosities for some time as a way to win his cooperation. If the emperor wishes to have you and takes the matter to the other eight members, their judgment won't be in our favor. The Congregation will turn you over to him because they cannot afford to have Prague fall into the hands of men like the archbishop of Trier and his Jesuit friends. And they don't want Rudolf to become another King James, out for creatures' blood. Prague may appear to be an oasis for the otherworldly. But like all oases, its refuge is a mirage."

"I understand," I said. Why did everything touching Matthew have to be so snarled? Our lives reminded me of the knotted cords in my spell box. No matter how many times I picked them apart, they soon tangled again.

Matthew released me. "When you go to the palace, take Gallowglass with you."

"You're not coming?" Given his concerns, I was shocked that Matthew was going to let me out of his sight.

"No. The more Rudolf sees us together, the more active his imagination and his acquisitiveness will become. And Gallowglass just may be able to wheedle his way in to Kelley's laboratory. My nephew is far more charming than I am." Matthew grinned, but the expression did nothing to alleviate the darkness in his eyes.

Gallowglass insisted he had a plan, one that would keep me from having to speak to Rudolf privately yet would display my gratitude publicly. It wasn't until I heard the bells ringing the hour of three that I caught my first glimmer of what his plan might entail. The crush of people trying to enter St. Vitus Cathedral through the pointed arches of the side entrance confirmed it.

"There goes Sigismund," Gallowglass said, bending close to my ear. The noise from the bells was deafening, and I could barely hear him. When I looked at him in confusion, he pointed up, to a golden grille on the adjacent steeple. "Sigismund. The big bell. That's how you know you're in Prague."

St. Vitus Cathedral was textbook Gothic with its flying buttresses and needlelike pinnacles. On a dark winter afternoon, it was even more so. The candles inside were blazing, but in the vast expanse of the cathedral they provided nothing more than pinpricks of yellow in the gloom. Outside, the light had faded so much that the colorful stained glass and vivid frescoes were of minimal help in lifting the oppressively heavy atmosphere. Gallowglass carefully stationed us under a brace of torches.

"Give your disguising spell a good shake," he suggested. "It's so dark in here that Rudolf might miss you."

"Are you telling me to get shiny?" I gave him my most repressive schoolmarm expression. His only reply was a grin.

We waited for Mass to begin with an interesting assortment of humble palace staff, royal officials, and aristocrats. Some of the artisans still bore the stains and singes associated with their work, and most of them looked exhausted. Once I'd surveyed the crowd, I looked up to take in the size and style of the cathedral.

"That's a whole lot of vaulting," I murmured. The ribbing was far more complicated than in most Gothic churches in England.

"That's what happens when Matthew gets an idea in his head," Gallowglass commented.

"Matthew?" I gaped.

"He was passing through Prague long ago, and Peter Parler, the new architect, was too green for such an important commission. The first outbreak of the plague had killed most of the master masons, however, so Parler was left in charge. Matthew took him under his wing, and the two of them went a bit mad. Can't say I ever understood what he and young Peter were trying to accomplish, but it's eye-catching. Wait until you see what they did to the Great Hall."

I had my mouth open to ask another question when a hush fell over the assembled crowd. Rudolf had arrived. I craned my neck in an effort to see.

"There he is," Gallowglass murmured, jerking his head up and to the right. Rudolf had entered St. Vitus on the second floor, from the enclosed walkway that I'd spotted spanning the courtyard between the palace and the cathedral. He was standing on a balcony decorated with colorful heraldic shields celebrating his many titles and honors. Like the ceiling, the balcony was held up by unusually ornate vaulting, though in this case it resembled the gnarled branches of a tree. Based on the breathtaking purity of the cathedral's other architectural supports, I didn't think this was Matthew's work.

Rudolf took his seat overlooking the central nave while the crowd bowed and curtsied in the direction of the royal box. For his part, Rudolf looked uncomfortable at having been noticed. In his private chambers, he was at ease with his courtiers, but here he seemed shy and reserved. He turned to listen to a whispering attendant and caught sight of me. He inclined his head graciously and smiled. The crowd swung around to see whom the emperor had singled out for his benediction.

"Curtsy," Gallowglass hissed. I dropped down again.

We managed to get through the actual Mass without incident. I was relieved to find that no one, not even the emperor, was expected to take the sacrament, and the whole ceremony was over quickly. At some point Rudolf quietly slipped away to his private apartments, no doubt to pore over his treasures.

With the emperor and priests gone, the nave turned into a cheerful gathering place as friends exchanged news and gossip. I spotted Ottavio Strada in the distance, deep in conversation with a florid gentleman in expensive woolen robes. Dr. Hájek was here, too, laughing and talking to a young couple who were obviously in love. I smiled at him, and he made a small bow in my direction. Strada I could do without, but I liked the emperor's physician.

"Gallowglass? Shouldn't you be hibernating, like the rest of the bears?" A slight man with deep-set eyes approached, his mouth twisted into a wry smile. He was wearing simple, expensive clothes, and the gold ring on his fingers spoke of his prosperity.

"We should all be hibernating in this weather. It is good to see you in such health, Joris." Gallowglass clasped his hand and struck him on the back. The man's eyes popped at the force of the blow.

"I would say the same about you, but since you are always healthy, I will spare us both the empty courtesy." The man turned to me. "And here is La Diosa."

"Diana," I said, bobbing a greeting.

"That is not your name here. Rudolf calls you 'La Diosa de la Caza.' It is Spanish for the goddess of the chase. The emperor has commanded poor Master Spranger to abandon his latest sketches of Venus in her bath in favor of a new subject: Diana interrupted at her toilette. We all wait eagerly to see if Spranger is capable of making such an enormous change on such short notice." The man bowed. "Joris Hoefnagel."

"The calligrapher," I said, thinking back to Pierre's remark about the ornate penmanship on Matthew's official summons to Rudolf's court. But that name was familiar. . . .

"The artist," Gallowglass corrected gently.

"La Diosa." A gaunt man swept his hat off with scarred hands. "I am Erasmus Habermel. Would you be so kind as to visit my workshop as soon as you are able? His Majesty would like you to have an astronomical compendium so as to better note the changes in the fickle moon, but it must be exactly to your liking."

Habermel was a familiar name, too. . . .

"She is coming to me tomorrow." A portly man in his thirties pushed his way through the growing crowd. His accent was distinctly Italian. "La Diosa is to sit for a portrait. His Majesty wishes to have her likeness engraved in stone as a symbol of her permanence in his affections." Perspiration broke out on his upper lip.

"Signor Miseroni!" another Italian said, clasping his hands melodramatically to his heaving chest. "I thought we understood each other. La Diosa must practice her dance if she is to take part in the entertainment next week as the emperor wishes." He bowed in my direction. "I am Alfonso Pasetti, La Diosa, His Majesty's dancing master."

"But my wife does not like to dance," said a cool voice behind me. A long arm snaked around and took my hand, which was fiddling with the edge of my bodice. "Do you, *mon coeur*?" This last endearment was accompanied by a kiss on the knuckles and a warning nip of teeth.

"Matthew is right on cue, as always," Joris said with a hearty laugh. "How are you?"

"Disappointed not to find Diana at home," Matthew said in a slightly aggrieved tone. "But even a devoted husband must yield to God in his wife's affections."

Hoefnagel watched Matthew closely, gauging every change of expression. I suddenly realized who this was: the great artist who was such an acute observer of nature that his illustrations of flora and fauna seemed as though they, like the creatures on Mary's shoes, could come to life.

"Well, God is done with her for today. I think you are free to take your wife home," Hoefnagel said mildly. "You promise to enliven what would otherwise be a very dull spring, La Diosa. For that we are all grateful."

The men dispersed after getting assurances from Gallowglass that he would keep track of my varied, conflicting appointments. Hoefnagel was the last to leave.

"I will keep an eye out for your wife, *Schaduw*. Perhaps you should, too."

"My attention is always on my wife, where it belongs. How else did I know to be here?"

"Of course. Forgive my meddling. *The forest has ears, and the fields have eyes.*" Hoefnagel bowed. "I will see you at court, La Diosa."

"Her name is Diana," Matthew said tightly. "Madame de Clermont will also serve."

"And here I was led to understand it was Roydon. My mistake." Hoefnagel took a few steps backward. "Good evening, Matthew." His footsteps echoed on the stone floors and faded into silence.

"Schaduw?" I asked. "Does that mean what it sounds like?"

"It's Dutch for 'Shadow.' Elizabeth isn't the only person to call me by that name." Matthew looked to Gallowglass. "What is this entertainment Signor Pasetti mentioned?"

"Oh, nothing out of the ordinary. It will no doubt be mythological in theme, with terrible music and even worse dancing. Having had too much to drink, the courtiers will all stumble into the wrong bedchambers at the end of the night. Nine months later there will be a flock of noble babes of uncertain parentage. The usual."

"'*Sic transit gloria mundi,*'" Matthew murmured. He bowed to me. "Shall we go home, La Diosa?" The nickname made me uncomfortable when strangers used it, but when it came out of Matthew's mouth, it was almost unbearable. "Jack tells me that tonight's stew is particularly appetizing."

Matthew was distant all evening, watching me with heavy eyes as I heard about the children's day and Pierre brought him up to date on various happenings in Prague. The names were unfamiliar and the narrative so confusing that I gave up trying to follow it and went to bed.

Jack's cries woke me, and I rushed to him only to discover that Matthew had already reached the boy. He was wild, thrashing and crying out for help.

"My bones are flying apart!" he kept saying. "It hurts! It hurts!"

Matthew bundled him up tight against his chest so that he couldn't move. "Shh. I've got you now." He continued to hold Jack until only faint tremors radiated through the child's slender limbs.

"All the monsters looked like ordinary men tonight, Master Roydon," Jack told him, snuggling deeper into my husband's arms. He sounded exhausted, and there were blue smudges under his eyes that made him look far older than his years.

"They often do, Jack," Matthew said. "They often do."

The next few weeks were a whirlwind of appointments—with the emperor's jeweler, the emperor's instrument maker, and the emperor's dancing master. Each encounter took me deeper into the heart of the huddle of buildings that composed the imperial palace, to workshops and residences that were reserved for Rudolf's prize artists and intellectuals.

Between engagements Gallowglass took me to parts of the palace that I had not yet seen. To the menagerie, where Rudolf kept his leopards and lions much as he kept his limners and musicians on the narrow streets east of the cathedral. To the Stag Moat, which had been altered so that Rudolf could enjoy better sport. To the sgraffito-covered games hall, where courtiers could take their exercise. To the new greenhouses built to protect the emperor's precious fig trees from the harsh Bohemian winter.

But there was one place where not even Gallowglass could gain admission: the Powder Tower, where Edward Kelley worked over his alembics and crucibles in an attempt to make the philosopher's stone. We stood outside it and tried to talk our way past the guards stationed at the entrance. Gallowglass even resorted to bellowing a hearty greeting. It brought the neighbors running to see if there was a fire but didn't elicit a reaction from Dr. Dee's erstwhile assistant.

"It's as if he's a prisoner," I told Matthew after the supper dishes were cleared and Jack and Annie were safely tucked into their beds. They'd enjoyed another exhausting round of skating, sledding, and pretzels. We'd given up the pretense that they were our servants. I hoped the opportunity to behave like a normal eight-year-old boy would help to end Jack's nightmares. But the palace was no place for them. I was terrified they might wander off and get lost forever, unable to speak the language or tell people to whom they belonged.

"Kelley *is* a prisoner," Matthew said, toying with the stem of his goblet. It was heavy silver and glinted in the firelight.

"They say he goes home occasionally, usually in the middle of the night when there is no one around to see. At least he gets some relief from the emperor's constant demands."

"You haven't met Mistress Kelley," Matthew said drily.

I hadn't, which struck me as odd the more I considered it. Perhaps I was taking the wrong route to meet the alchemist. I'd allowed myself to be swept into court life with the hope of knocking on Kelley's laboratory door and walking straight in to demand Ashmole 782. But given my new familiarity with courtly life, such a direct approach was unlikely to succeed.

The next morning I made it a point to go with Tereza to do the shopping. It was absolutely frigid outside, and the wind was fierce, but we trudged to the market nonetheless.

"Do you know my countrywoman Mistress Kelley?" I asked Frau Huber as we waited for the baker to wrap our purchases. The housewives of

Malá Strana collected the bizarre and unusual as avidly as Rudolf did. "Her husband is one of the emperor's servants."

"One of the emperor's caged alchemists, you mean," Frau Huber said with a snort. "There are always odd things happening in that household. And it was worse when the Dees were here. Herr Kelley was always looking at Frau Dee with lust."

"And Mistress Kelley?" I prompted her.

"She does not go out much. Her cook does the shopping." Frau Huber did not approve of this delegation of housewifely responsibility. It opened the door to all sorts of disorder, including (she contended) Anabaptism and a thriving black market in purloined kitchen staples. She had made her feelings on this point clear at our first meeting, and it was one of the chief reasons I went out in all weathers to buy cabbage.

"Are we discussing the alchemist's wife?" Signorina Rossi said, tripping across the frozen stones and narrowly avoiding a wheelbarrow full of coal. "She is English and therefore very strange. And her wine bills are much larger than they should be."

"How do you two know so much?" I asked when I'd finished laughing.

"We share the same laundress," Frau Huber said, surprised.

"None of us have any secrets from our laundresses," Signorina Rossi agreed. "She did the washing for the Dees, too. Until Signora Dee fired her for charging so much to clean the napkins."

"A difficult woman, Jane Dee, but you could not fault her thrift," Frau Huber admitted with a sigh.

"Why do you need to see Mistress Kelley?" Signorina Rossi inquired, stowing a braided loaf of bread in her basket.

"I want to meet her husband. I am interested in alchemy and have some questions."

"Will you pay?" Frau Huber asked, rubbing her fingers together in a universal and apparently timeless gesture.

"For what?" I said, confused.

"His answers, of course."

"Yes," I agreed, wondering what devious plan she was concocting.

"Leave it to me," Frau Huber said. "I am hungry for schnitzel, and the Austrian who owns the tavern near your house, Frau Roydon, knows what schnitzel should be."

The Austrian schnitzel wizard's teenage daughter, it turned out, shared a tutor with Kelley's ten-year-old stepdaughter, Elisabeth. And his cook was married to the laundress's aunt, whose sister-in-law helped out around the Kelleys' house.

It was thanks to this occult chain of relationships forged by women, and not Gallowglass's court connections, that Matthew and I found ourselves in the Kelleys' second-floor parlor at midnight, waiting for the great man to arrive.

"He should be here at any moment," Joanna Kelley assured us. Her eyes were red-rimmed and bleary, though whether this resulted from too much wine or from the cold that seemed to afflict the entire household was not clear.

"Do not trouble yourself on our account, Mistress Kelley. We keep late hours," Matthew said smoothly, giving her a dazzling smile. "And how do you like your new house?"

After much espionage and investigation among the Austrian and Italian communities, we discovered that the Kelleys had recently purchased a house around the corner from the Three Ravens in a complex known for its inventive street sign. Someone had taken a few leftover wooden figures from a nativity scene, sawed them in half, and arranged them on a board. They had, in the process, removed the infant Jesus from his crèche and replaced it with the head of Mary's donkey.

"The Donkey and Cradle meets our needs at present, Master Roydon." Mistress Kelley issued forth an awe-inspiring sneeze and took a swig of wine. "We had thought the emperor would set aside a house for us in the palace itself, given Edward's work, but this will do." A regular thumping sounded on the winding stairs. "Here is Edward."

A walking staff appeared first, then a stained hand, followed by an equally stained sleeve. The rest of Edward Kelley looked just as disreputable. His long beard was unkempt and stuck out from a dark skullcap that hid his ears. If he'd had a hat, it was gone now. And he was fond of his dinners, gauging by his Falstaffian proportions. Kelley limped into the room whistling, then froze at the sight of Matthew.

"Edward." Matthew rewarded the man with another of those dazzling smiles, but Kelley didn't seem nearly as pleased to receive it as his wife had. "Imagine us meeting again so far from home."

"How did you . . . ?" Edward said hoarsely. He looked around the room, and his eyes fell on me with a nudging glance that was as insidious as any I'd felt from a daemon. But there was more: disturbances in the threads that surrounded him, irregularities in the weaving that suggested he was not just daemonic—he was unstable. His lips curled. "The witch."

"The emperor has elevated her rank, just as he did yours. She is La Diosa—the goddess—now," Matthew said. "Do sit down and rest your leg. It troubles you in the cold, as I remember."

"What business do you have with me, Roydon?" Edward Kelley gripped his staff tighter.

"He is here on behalf of the queen, Edward. I was in my bed," Joanna said plaintively. "I get so little rest. And because of this dreadful ague, I have not yet met our neighbors. You did not tell me there were English people living so close. Why, I can see Mistress Roydon's house from the tower window. You are at the castle. I am alone, longing to speak my native tongue, and yet—"

"Go back to bed, my dear," Kelley said, dismissing Joanna. "Take your wine with you."

Mrs. Kelley sniffled off obligingly, her expression miserable. To be an Englishwoman in Prague without friends or family was difficult, but to have your husband welcomed in places where you were forbidden to go must make it doubly so. When she was gone, Kelley clumped over to the table and sat down in his wife's chair. With a grimace he lifted his leg into place. Then he pinned his dark, hostile eyes on Matthew.

"Tell me what I must do to get rid of you," he said bluntly. Kelley might have Kit's cunning, but he had none of his charm.

"The queen wants you," Matthew said, equally blunt. "We want Dee's book."

"Which book?" Edward's reply was quick—too quick.

"For a charlatan you are an abominable liar, Kelley. How do you manage to take them all in?" Matthew swung his long, booted legs onto the table. Kelley cringed when the heels struck the surface.

"If Dr. Dee is accusing me of theft," Kelley blustered, "then I must insist on discussing this matter in the emperor's presence. He would not want me treated thus, my honor impugned in my own house."

"Where is it, Kelley? In your laboratory? In Rudolf's bedchamber? I will find it with or without your help. But if you were to tell me your secret, I might be inclined to let the other matter rest." Matthew picked at a speck on his britches. "The Congregation is not pleased with your recent behavior." Kelley's staff clattered to the floor. Matthew obligingly picked it up. He touched the worn end to Kelley's neck. "Is this where you touched the tapster at the inn, when you threatened his life? That was careless, Edward.

All this pomp and privilege has gone to your head." The staff dropped down to Kelley's considerable belly and rested there.

"I cannot help you." Kelley winced as Matthew increased the pressure on the stick. "It is the truth! The emperor took the book from me when . . ." Kelley trailed off, rubbing his hand across his face as if to erase the vampire sitting across from him.

"When what?" I said, leaning forward. When I touched Ashmole 782 in the Bodleian, I'd immediately known it was different.

"You must know more about this book than I do," Kelley spit at me, his eyes blazing. "You witches were not surprised to hear of its existence, though it took a daemon to recognize it!"

"I am losing my patience, Edward." The wooden staff cracked in Matthew's hands. "My wife asked you a question. Answer it."

Kelley gave Matthew a slow, triumphant look and pushed at the end of the staff, dislodging it from his abdomen. "You hate witches—or so everyone believes. But I see now that you share Gerbert's weakness for the creatures. You are in love with this one, just as I told Rudolf."

"Gerbert." Matthew's tone was flat.

Kelley nodded. "He came when Dee was still in Prague, asking questions about the book and nosing about in my business. Rudolf let him enjoy one of the witches from the Old Town—a seventeen-year-old girl and very pretty, with rosy hair and blue eyes just like your wife. No one has seen her since. But there was a very fine fire that Walpurgis Night. Gerbert was given the honor of lighting it." Kelley shifted his eyes to me. "I wonder if we will have a fire again this year?"

The mention of the ancient tradition of burning a witch to celebrate spring was the final straw for Matthew. He had Kelley half out the window by the time I realized what was happening.

"Look down, Edward. It is not a steep fall. You would survive it, I fear, though you might break a bone or two. I would collect you and take you up to your bedchamber. That has a window, too, no doubt. Eventually I will find a place that is high enough to snap your sorry carcass in two. By then every bone in your body will be in pieces and you will have told me what I want to know." Matthew turned black eyes on me when I rose. "Sit. Down." He took a deep breath. "Please." I did.

"Dee's book shimmered with power. I could smell it the moment he pulled it off the shelf at Mortlake. He was oblivious to its significance, but

I knew." Kelley couldn't talk fast enough now. When he paused to take a breath, Matthew shook him. "The witch Roger Bacon owned it and valued it for a great treasure. His name is on the title page, along with the inscription *'Verum Secretum Secretorum.'*"

"But it's nothing like the *Secretum,*" I said, thinking of the popular medieval work. "That's an encyclopedia. This has alchemical illustrations."

"The illustrations are nothing but a screen against the truth," Kelley said, wheezing. "That is why Bacon called it *The True Secret of Secrets.*"

"What does it say?" I asked, rising with excitement. This time Matthew didn't warn me off. He also dragged Kelley back inside. "Were you able to read the words?"

"Perhaps," Kelley said, straightening his robe.

"He couldn't read the book either." Matthew released Kelley with disgust. "I can smell the duplicity through his fear."

"It's written in a foreign tongue. Not even Rabbi Loew could decipher it."

"The Maharal has seen the book?" Matthew had that still, alert look that he got just before he pounced.

"Apparently you didn't ask Rabbi Loew about it when you were in the Jewish Town to seek out the witch who made this clay creature they call the golem. Nor could you find the culprit and his creation." Kelley looked contemptuous. "So much for your famous power and influence. You couldn't even frighten the Jews."

"I don't think the words are Hebrew," I said, remembering the fast-moving symbols I'd glimpsed in the palimpsest.

"They aren't. The emperor had Rabbi Loew come to the palace just to be sure." Kelley had revealed more than he'd intended. His eyes shifted to his staff, and the threads around him warped and twisted. An image came to me of Kelley lifting his staff to strike someone. What was he up to?

Then I realized: He was planning on striking *me.* An unintelligible sound broke free from my mouth, and when I held out my hand, Kelley's staff flew straight into it. My arm transformed into a branch for a moment before returning to its normal outlines. I prayed that it had all happened too fast for Kelley to perceive the change. The look on his face told me my hopes were in vain.

"Don't let the emperor see you do that," Kelley smirked, "or he'll have you locked away, yet another curiosity for him to savor. I've told you what you wanted to know, Roydon. Call off the Congregation's dogs."

"I don't think I can," Matthew said, taking the staff from me. "You are not harmless, no matter what Gerbert thinks. But I'll leave you alone—for now. Don't do anything more to warrant my attention and you just may see the summer." He tossed the staff into the corner.

"Good night, Master Kelley." I gathered up my cloak, wanting to be as far away from the daemon as fast as possible.

"Enjoy your moment in the sun, witch. They pass quickly in Prague." Kelley remained where he was while Matthew and I started to descend the stairs.

I could still feel his nudging glances in the street. And when I looked back toward the Donkey and Cradle, the crooked and broken threads that bound Kelley to the world shimmered with malevolence.

29

After days of careful negotiation, Matthew was able to arrange a visit to Rabbi Judah Loew. To make room for it, Gallowglass had to cancel my upcoming appointments at court, citing illness.

Unfortunately, this announcement caught the emperor's attention, and the house was flooded with medicines: terra sigillata, the clay with marvelous healing properties; bezoar stones harvested from the gallbladders of goats to ward off poison; a cup made of unicorn horn with one of the emperor's family recipes for an electuary. The latter involved roasting an egg with saffron before beating it into a powder with mustard seed, angelica, juniper berries, camphor, and several other mysterious substances, then turning it into a paste with treacle and lemon syrup. Rudolf sent Dr. Hájek along to administer it. But I had no intention of swallowing this unappetizing concoction, as I informed the imperial physician.

"I will assure the emperor that you will recover," he said drily. "Happily, His Majesty is too concerned with his own health to risk traveling down Sporrengasse to confirm my prognosis."

We thanked him profusely for his discretion and sent him home with one of the roasted chickens that had been delivered from the royal kitchens to tempt my appetite. I threw the note that accompanied it into the fire—"*Ich verspreche Sie werden nicht hungern. Ich halte euch zufrieden. Rudolff*"—after Matthew explained that the wording left some doubt as to whether Rudolf was referring to the chicken when he promised to satisfy my hunger.

On our way across the Moldau River to Prague's Old Town, I had my first opportunity to experience the hustle and bustle of the city center. There, affluent merchants conducted business in arcades nestled beneath the three- and four-story houses that lined the twisting streets. When we turned north, the city's character changed: The houses were smaller, the residents more shabbily dressed, the businesses less prosperous. Then we crossed over a wide street and passed through a gate into the Jewish Town. More than five thousand Jews lived in this small enclave smashed between the industrial riverbank, the Old Town's main square, and a convent. The

Jewish quarter was crowded—inconceivably so, even by London standards—with houses that were not so much constructed as grown, each structure evolving organically from the walls of another like the chambers in a snail's shell.

We found Rabbi Loew via a serpentine route that made me long for a bag of bread crumbs to be sure we could find our way back. The residents slid cautious glances in our direction, but few dared to greet us. Those who did called Matthew "Gabriel." It was one of his many names, and the use of it here signaled that I'd slipped down one of Matthew's rabbit holes and was about to meet another of his past selves.

When I stood before the kindly gentleman known as the Maharal, I understood why Matthew spoke of him in hushed tones. Rabbi Loew radiated the same quiet sense of power that I'd seen in Philippe. His dignity made Rudolf's grandiose gestures and Elizabeth's petulance seem laughable in comparison. And it was all the more striking in this age, when brute force was the usual method of imposing one's will on others. The Maharal's reputation was based on scholarship and learning, not physical prowess.

"The Maharal is one of the finest men who has ever lived," Matthew said simply when I asked him to tell me more about Judah Loew. Considering how long Matthew had roamed the earth, this was a considerable accolade.

"I did think, Gabriel, that we had concluded our business," Rabbi Loew said sternly in Latin. He looked and sounded very much like a headmaster. "I would not share the name of the witch who made the golem before, and I will not do so now." Rabbi Loew turned to me. "I am sorry, Frau Roydon. My impatience with your husband made me forget my manners. It is a pleasure to meet you."

"I haven't come about the golem," Matthew replied. "My business today is private. It concerns a book."

"What book is that?" Though the Maharal did not blink, a disturbance in the air around me suggested some subtle reaction on his part. Since meeting Kelley, I realized that my magic had been tingling as though plugged into an invisible current. My firedrake was stirring. And the threads surrounding me kept bursting into color, highlighting an object, a person, a path through the streets as if trying to tell me something.

"It is a volume my wife found at a university far away from here," Matthew said. I was surprised that he was being this truthful. So was Rabbi Loew.

"Ah. I see we are to be honest with each other this afternoon. We should do so where it is quiet enough for me to enjoy the experience. Come into my study."

He led us into one of the small rooms tucked into the warren of a ground floor. It was comfortingly familiar, with its scarred desk and piles of books. I recognized the smell of ink and something that reminded me of the rosin box in my childhood dance studio. An iron pot by the door held what looked like small brown apples, bobbing up and down in an equally brown liquid. Its appearance was witchworthy, conjuring up concerns about what else might be lurking in the cauldron's unsavory depths.

"Is this batch of ink more satisfactory?" Matthew said, poking at one of the floating balls.

"It is. You have done me a service by telling me to add those nails to the pot. It does not require so much soot to make it black, and the consistency is better." Rabbi Loew gestured toward a chair. "Please sit." He waited until I was settled and then took the only other seat: a three-legged stool. "Gabriel will stand. He is not young, but his legs are strong."

"I'm young enough to sit at your feet like one of your pupils, Maharal." Matthew grinned and folded himself gracefully into a cross-legged position.

"My students have better sense than to take to the floor in this weather." Rabbi Loew studied me. "Now. To business. Why has the wife of Gabriel ben Ariel come so far to look for a book?" I had a disconcerting sense that he wasn't talking about my trip across the river, or even across Europe. How could he possibly know that I wasn't from this time?

As soon as my mind formed the question, a man's face swam in the air over Rabbi Loew's shoulder. The face, though young, already showed worry creases around deep-set gray eyes, and the dark brown beard was graying in the center of his chin.

"Another witch told you about me," I said softly.

Rabbi Loew nodded. "Prague is a wonderful city for news. Alas, half of what is said is untrue." He waited for a moment. "The book?" Rabbi Loew reminded me.

"We think it might tell us about how creatures like Matthew and me came to be," I explained.

"This is not a mystery. God made you, just as he made me and Emperor Rudolf," the Maharal replied, settling more deeply into his chair. It was a typical posture for a teacher, one that developed naturally after years spent giving students the space to wrestle with new ideas. I felt a familiar sense of anticipation and dread as I prepared my response. I didn't want to disappoint Rabbi Loew.

"Perhaps, but God has given some of us additional talents. You cannot make the dead live again, Rabbi Loew," I said, responding to him as if he were a tutor at Oxford. "Nor do strange faces appear before you when you pose a simple question."

"True. But you do not rule Bohemia, and your husband's German is better than mine even though I have conversed in the language since a child. Each of us is uniquely gifted, Frau Roydon. In the world's apparent chaos, there is still evidence of God's plan."

"You speak of God's plan with such confidence because you know your origins from the Torah," I replied. "*Bereishit*—'In the beginning'—is what you call the book the Christians know as Genesis. Isn't that right, Rabbi Loew?"

"It seems I have been discussing theology with the wrong member of Ariel's family," Rabbi Loew said drily, though his eyes twinkled with mischief.

"Who is Ariel?" I asked.

"My father is known as Ariel among Rabbi Loew's people," Matthew explained.

"The angel of wrath?" I frowned. That didn't sound like the Philippe I knew.

"The lord with dominion over the earth. Some call him the Lion of Jerusalem. Recently my people have had reason to be grateful to the Lion, though the Jews have not—and will never—forget his many past wrongs. But Ariel makes an effort to atone. And judgment belongs to God." Rabbi Loew considered his options and came to a decision. "The emperor did show me such a book. Alas, His Majesty did not give me much time to study it."

"Anything you could tell us about it would be useful," Matthew said, his excitement visible. He leaned forward and hugged his knees to his chest, just as Jack did when he was listening intently to one of Pierre's stories. For a few moments, I was able to see my husband as he must have looked as a child learning the carpenter's craft.

"Emperor Rudolf called me to his palace in hope that I would be able to read the text. The alchemist, the one they call Meshuggener Edward, had it from the library of his master, the Englishman John Dee." Rabbi Loew sighed and shook his head. "It is difficult to understand why God chose to make Dee learned but foolish and Edward ignorant yet cunning.

"Meshuggener Edward told the emperor that this ancient book contained the secrets of immortality," Loew continued. "To live forever is every powerful man's dream. But the text was written in a language no one understood, except for the alchemist."

"Rudolf called upon you, thinking it was an ancient form of Hebrew," I said, nodding.

"It may well be ancient, but it is not Hebrew. There were pictures, too. I did not understand the meaning, but Edward said they were alchemical in nature. Perhaps the words explain those images."

"When you saw it, Rabbi Loew, were the words moving?" I asked, thinking back to the lines I'd seen lurking under the alchemical illustrations.

"How could they be moving?" Loew frowned. "They were just symbols, written in ink on the page."

"Then it isn't broken—not yet," I said, relieved. "Someone removed several pages from it before I saw it in Oxford. It was impossible to figure out the text's meaning because the words were racing around looking for their lost brothers and sisters."

"You make it sound as though this book is alive," Rabbi Loew said.

"I think it is," I confessed. Matthew looked surprised. "It sounds unbelievable, I know. But when I think back to that night, and what happened when I touched the book, that's the only way to describe it. The book recognized me. It was . . . hurting somehow, as though it had lost something essential."

"There are stories among my people of books written in living flame, with words that move and twist so that only those chosen by God can read them." Rabbi Loew was testing me again. I recognized the signs of a teacher quizzing his students.

"I've heard those stories," I replied slowly. "And the stories about other lost books, too—the tablets Moses destroyed, Adam's book in which he recorded the true names of every part of creation."

"If your book is as significant as they are, perhaps it is God's will that it remain hidden." Rabbi Loew sat back once more and waited.

"But it's not hidden," I said. "Rudolf knows where it is, even if he cannot read it. Who would you rather had the custody of such a powerful object: Matthew or the emperor?"

"I know many wise men who would say that to choose between Gabriel ben Ariel and His Majesty would only determine the lesser of two evils." Rabbi Loew's attention shifted to Matthew. "Happily, I do not count myself among them. Still, I cannot help you further. I have seen this book—but I do not know its present location."

"The book is in Rudolf's possession—or at least it was. Until you confirmed that, we only had Dr. Dee's suspicions and the assurances of the aptly named Crazy Edward," Matthew said grimly.

"Madmen can be dangerous," observed Rabbi Loew. "You should be more careful who you hang out of windows, Gabriel."

"You heard about that?" Matthew looked sheepish.

"The town is buzzing with reports that Meshuggener Edward was flying around Malá Strana with the devil. Naturally, I assumed you were involved." This time Rabbi Loew's tone held a note of gentle reproof. "Gabriel, Gabriel. What will your father say?"

"That I should have dropped him, no doubt. My father has little patience with creatures like Edward Kelley."

"You mean madmen."

"I meant what I said, Maharal," Matthew said evenly.

"The man you talk so easily about killing is, alas, the only person who can help you find your wife's book." Rabbi Loew stopped, considered his words. "But do you truly want to know its secrets? Life and death are great responsibilities."

"Given what I am, you will not be surprised that I am familiar with their particular burdens." Matthew's smile was humorless.

"Perhaps. But can your wife also carry them? You may not always be with her, Gabriel. Some who would share their knowledge with a witch will not do so with you."

"So there *is* a maker of spells in the Jewish Town," I said. "I wondered when I heard about the golem."

"He has been waiting for you to seek him out. Alas, he will see only a fellow witch. My friend fears Gabriel's Congregation, and with good reason," Rabbi Loew explained.

"I would like to meet him, Rabbi Loew." There were precious few weavers in the world. I couldn't miss the opportunity to know this one.

Matthew stirred, a protest rising to his lips.

"This is important, Matthew." I rested my hand on his arm. "I promised Goody Alsop not to ignore this part of me while we are here."

"One should find wholeness in marriage, Gabriel, but it should not be a prison for either party," said Rabbi Loew.

"This isn't about our marriage or the fact that you're a witch." Matthew rose, his large frame filling the room. "It can be dangerous for a Christian woman to be seen with a Jewish man." When I opened my mouth to protest, Matthew shook his head. "Not for you. For him. You must do what Rabbi Loew tells you to do. I don't want him or anyone else in the Jewish Town to come to harm—not on our account."

"I won't do anything to bring attention to myself—or to Rabbi Loew," I promised.

"Then go and see this weaver. I'll be in the Ungelt, waiting." Matthew brushed his lips against my cheek and was gone before he could have second thoughts. Rabbi Loew blinked.

"Gabriel is remarkably quick for one so large," the rabbi said, getting to his feet. "He reminds me of the emperor's tiger."

"Cats do recognize Matthew as one of their kind," I said, thinking of Sarah's cat, Tabitha.

"The notion that you have married an animal does not distress you. Gabriel is fortunate in his choice of wife." Rabbi Loew picked up a dark robe and called to his servant that we were leaving.

We departed in what I supposed was a different direction, but I couldn't be sure, since all my attention was focused on the freshly paved streets, the first I'd seen since arriving in the past. I asked Rabbi Loew who had provided such an unusual convenience.

"Herr Maisel paid for them, along with a bathhouse for the women. He helps the emperor with small financial matters—like his holy war against the Turks." Rabbi Loew picked his way around a puddle. It was then that I saw the golden ring stitched onto the fabric over his heart.

"What is that?" I said, nodding at the badge.

"It warns unsuspecting Christians that I am a Jew." Rabbi Loew's expression was wry. "I have long believed that even the dullest would eventually discover it, with or without the badge. But the authorities insist that there can be no doubt." Rabbi Loew's voice dropped. "And it is far preferable to the hat the Jews were once required to wear. Bright yellow and shaped like a chess piece. Just try to ignore *that* in the market."

"That's what humans would do to me and Matthew if they knew we were living among them." I shivered. "Sometimes it's better to hide."

"Is that what Gabriel's Congregation does? It keeps you hidden?"

"If so, then they're doing a poor job of it," I said with a laugh. "Frau Huber thinks there's a werewolf prowling around the Stag Moat. Your neighbors in Prague believe that Edward Kelley can fly. Humans are hunting for witches in Germany and Scotland. And Elizabeth of England and Rudolf of Austria know all about us. I suppose we should be thankful that some kings and queens tolerate us."

"Toleration is not always enough. The Jews are tolerated in Prague—for the moment—but the situation can change in a heartbeat. Then we would find ourselves out in the countryside, starving in the snow." Rabbi Loew turned in to a narrow alley and entered a house identical to most other houses in most of the other alleys we passed through. Inside, two men sat at a table covered with mathematical instruments, books, candles, and paper.

"Astronomy will provide a common ground with Christians!" one of the men exclaimed in German, pushing a piece of paper toward his companion. He was around fifty, with a thick gray beard and heavy brow bones that shielded his eyes. His shoulders had the chronic stoop of most scholars.

"Enough, David!" the other exploded. "Maybe common ground is not the promised land we hope for."

"Abraham, this lady wishes to speak with you," Rabbi Loew said, interrupting their debate.

"All the women in Prague are eager to meet Abraham." David, the scholar, stood. "Whose daughter wants a love spell this time?"

"It is not her father that should interest you but her husband. This is Frau Roydon, the Englishman's wife."

"The one the emperor calls La Diosa?" David laughed and clasped Abraham's shoulder. "Your luck has turned, my friend. You are caught between a king, a goddess, and a *nachzehrer*." My limited German suggested this unfamiliar word meant "devourer of the dead."

Abraham said something rude in Hebrew, if Rabbi Loew's disapproving expression was any indication, and turned to face me at last. He and I looked at each other, witch to witch, but neither of us could bear it for long. I twisted away with a gasp, and he winced and pressed his eyelids with his fingers. My skin was tingling all over, not just where his eyes had fallen. And the air between us was a mass of different, bright hues.

"Is she the one you were waiting for, Abraham ben Elijah?" Rabbi Loew asked.

"She is," Abraham said. He turned away from me and rested his fists on the table. "My dreams did not tell me that she was the wife of an *alukah,* however."

"Alukah?" I looked to Rabbi Loew for an explanation. If the word was German, I couldn't decipher it.

"A leech. It is what we Jews call creatures like your husband," he replied. "For what it is worth, Abraham, Gabriel consented to the meeting."

"You think I trust the word of the monster who judges my people from his seat on the Qahal while turning a blind eye to those who murder them?" Abraham cried.

I wanted to protest that this was not the same Gabriel—the same Matthew—but stopped. Something I said might get everyone in this room killed in another six months when the sixteenth-century Matthew was back in his rightful place.

"I am not here for my husband or the Congregation," I said, stepping forward. "I am here for myself."

"Why?" Abraham demanded.

"Because I, too, am a maker of spells. And there aren't many of us left."

"There were more, before the Qahal—the Congregation—set up their rules," Abraham said, a challenge in his tone. "God willing, we will live to see children born with these gifts."

"Speaking of children, where is your golem?" I asked.

David guffawed. "Mother Abraham. What would your family in Chelm say?"

"They would say I had befriended an ass with nothing in his head but stars and idle fancies, David Gans!" Abraham said, turning red.

My firedrake, which had been restive for days, roared to life with all this merriment. Before I could stop her, she was free. Rabbi Loew and his friends gaped at the sight.

"She does this sometimes. It's nothing to worry about." My tone went from apologetic to brisk as I reprimanded my unruly familiar. "Come down from there!"

My firedrake tightened her grip on the wall and shrieked at me. The old plaster was not up to the task of supporting a creature with a ten-foot wingspan. A large chunk fell free, and she chattered in alarm. Her tail lashed out to the side and anchored itself into the adjacent wall for added security. The firedrake hooted triumphantly.

"If you don't stop that, I'm going to have Gallowglass give you a really evil name," I muttered. "Does anyone see her leash? It looks like a gauzy chain." I searched along the skirting boards and found it behind the kindling basket, still connected to me. "Can one of you hold the slack for a minute while I rein her in?" I turned, my hands full of translucent links.

The men were gone.

"Typical," I muttered. "Three grown men and a woman, and guess who gets stuck with the dragon?"

Heavy feet clomped across the wooden floors. I angled my body so that I could see around the door. A small, reddish gray creature wearing dark clothes and a black cap on his bald head was staring at my firedrake.

"No, Yosef." Abraham stood between me and the creature, his hands raised as if he were trying to reason with it. But the golem—for this must be the legendary creature fashioned from the mud of the Moldau and animated with a spell—kept moving his feet in the firedrake's direction.

"Yosef is fascinated by the witch's dragon," said David.

"I believe the golem shares his maker's fondness for pretty girls," Rabbi Loew said. "My reading suggests that a witch's familiar often has some of his maker's characteristics."

"The golem is Abraham's familiar?" I was shocked.

"Yes. He didn't appear when I made my first spell. I was beginning to think I didn't have a familiar." Abraham waved his hands at Yosef, but the golem stared unblinking at the firedrake sprawled against the wall. As if she knew she had an admirer, the firedrake stretched her wings so that the webbing caught the light.

I held up my chain. "Didn't he come with something like this?"

"That chain doesn't seem to be helping *you* much," Abraham observed.

"I have a lot to learn!" I said indignantly. "The firedrake appeared when I wove my first spell. How did you make Yosef?"

Abraham pulled a rough set of cords from his pocket. "With ropes like these."

"I have cords, too." I reached into the purse hidden in my skirt pocket for my silks.

"Do the colors help you to separate out the world's threads and use them more effectively?" Abraham stepped toward me, interested in this variation of weaving.

"Yes. Each color has a meaning, and to make a new spell I use the cords to focus on a particular question." I looked at the golem in confusion. He was still staring at the firedrake. "But how did you go from cords to a creature?"

"A woman came to me to ask for a new spell to help her conceive. I started making knots in the rope while I considered her request and ended up with something that looked like the skeleton of a man." Abraham went to the desk, took up a piece of David's paper, and, in spite of his friend's protests, sketched out what he meant.

"It's like a poppet," I said, looking at his drawing. Nine knots were connected by straight lines of rope: a knot for its head, one for its heart, two knots for hands, another knot for the pelvis, two more for knees, and a final two for the feet.

"I mixed clay with some of my own blood and put it on the rope like flesh. The next morning Yosef was sitting by the fireplace."

"You brought the clay to life," I said, looking at the enraptured golem.

Abraham nodded. "A spell with the secret name of God is in his mouth. So long as it remains there, Yosef walks and obeys my instructions. Most of the time."

"Yosef is incapable of making his own decisions," Rabbi Loew explained. "Breathing life into clay and blood does not give a creature a soul, after all. So Abraham cannot let the golem out of his sight for fear Yosef will make mischief."

"I forgot to take the spell out of his mouth one Friday when it was time for prayers," Abraham admitted sheepishly. "Without someone to tell him what to do, Yosef wandered out of the Jewish Town and frightened our Christian neighbors. Now the Jews think Yosef's purpose is to protect us."

"A mother's work is never done," I murmured with a smile. "Speaking of which . . ." My firedrake had fallen asleep and was gently snoring, her cheek pillowed against the plaster. Gently, so as not to irritate her, I drew on the chain until she released her grip on the wall. She flapped her wings sleepily, became as transparent as smoke, and slowly dissolved into nothingness as she was absorbed back into my body.

"I wish Yosef could do that," Abraham said enviously.

"And I wish I could keep her quiet by removing a piece of paper from under her tongue!" I retorted.

Seconds later I felt the sense of ice on my back.

"Who is this?" said a low voice.

The new arrival was not large or physically intimidating—but he was a vampire, one with dark blue eyes set into a long, pale face under dusky hair. There was something commanding about the look he gave me, and I took an instinctive step away from him.

"It is nothing that concerns you, Herr Fuchs," Abraham said curtly.

"There is no need for bad manners, Abraham." Rabbi Loew's attention turned to the vampire. "This is Frau Roydon, Herr Fuchs. She has come from Malá Strana to visit the Jewish Town."

The vampire fixed his eyes on me, and his nostrils flared just as Matthew's did when he was picking up a new scent. His eyelids drifted closed. I took another step away.

"Why are you here, Herr Fuchs? I told you I would meet you outside the synagogue," Abraham said, clearly rattled.

"You were late." Herr Fuchs's blue eyes snapped open, and he smiled at me. "But now that I know why you were detained, I no longer mind."

"Herr Fuchs is visiting from Poland, where he and Abraham knew each other," Rabbi Loew said, finishing his introductions.

Someone on the street called out in greeting. "Here is Herr Maisel," Abraham said. He sounded as relieved as I felt.

Herr Maisel, provider of paved streets and fulfiller of imperial defense budgets, broadcast his prosperity from his immaculately cut woolen suit, his fur-lined cape, and the bright yellow circle that proclaimed him a Jew. This last was affixed to the cape with golden thread, which made it look like a nobleman's insignia rather than a mark of difference.

"There you are, Herr Fuchs." Herr Maisel handed a pouch to the vampire. "I have your jewel." Maisel bowed to Rabbi Loew and to me. "Frau Roydon."

The vampire took the pouch and removed a heavy chain and pendant. I couldn't see the design clearly, though the red and green enamel were plain. The vampire bared his teeth.

"Thank you, Herr Maisel." Fuchs held up the jewel, and the colors caught the light. "The chain signifies my oath to slay dragons, no matter where they are found. I have missed wearing it. The city is full of dangerous creatures these days."

Herr Maisel snorted. "No more than usual. And leave the city's politics alone, Herr Fuchs. It will be better for all of us if you do so. Are you ready to meet your husband, Frau Roydon? He is not the most patient of men."

"Herr Maisel will see you safely to the Ungelt," Rabbi Loew promised. He leveled a long look at Herr Fuchs. "See Diana to the street, Abraham. You will stay with me, Herr Fuchs, and tell me about Poland."

"Thank you, Rabbi Loew." I curtsied in farewell.

"It was a pleasure, Frau Roydon." Rabbi Loew paused. "And if you have time, you might reflect on what I said earlier. None of us can hide forever."

"No." Given the horrors the Jews of Prague would see over the next centuries, I wished he were wrong. With a final nod to Herr Fuchs, I left the house with Herr Maisel and Abraham.

"A moment, Herr Maisel," Abraham said when we were out of earshot of the house.

"Make it quick, Abraham," Herr Maisel said, withdrawing a few feet.

"I understand you are looking for something in Prague, Frau Roydon. A book."

"How do you know that?" I felt a whisper of alarm.

"Most of the witches in the city know it, but I can see how you are connected to it. The book is closely guarded, and force will not work to free it." Abraham's face was serious. "The book must come to you, or you will lose it forever."

"It's a book, Abraham. Unless it sprouts legs, we are going to have to go into Rudolf's palace and fetch it."

"I know what I see," Abraham said stubbornly. "The book will come to you, if only you ask for it. Don't forget."

"I won't," I promised. Herr Maisel looked pointedly in our direction. "I have to go. Thank you for meeting me and introducing me to Yosef."

"May God keep you safe, Diana Roydon," Abraham said solemnly, his face grave.

Herr Maisel escorted me the short distance from the Jewish Town to the Old Town. Its spacious square was thronged with people. The twin towers of Our Lady of Tyn rose to our left, while the stolid outlines of the Town Hall crouched to our right.

"If we didn't have to meet Herr Roydon, we would stop and see the clock strike the hours," Herr Maisel said apologetically. "You must ask him to take you past it on your way to the bridge. Every visitor to Prague should see it."

At the Ungelt, where the foreign merchants traded under the watchful eyes of the customs officer, the merchants looked at Maisel with open hostility.

"Here is your wife, Herr Roydon. I made sure she noticed all the best shops on her way to meet you. She will have no problem finding the finest craftsmen in Prague to see to her needs and those of your household." Maisel beamed at Matthew.

"Thank you, Herr Maisel. I am grateful for your assistance and will be sure to let His Majesty know of your kindness."

"It is my job, Herr Roydon, to see to the prosperity of His Majesty's people. And it was a pleasure, too, of course," he said. "I took the liberty of hiring horses for your journey back. They are waiting for you near the town clock." Maisel touched the side of his nose and winked conspiratorially.

"You think of everything, Herr Maisel," Matthew murmured.

"Someone has to, Herr Roydon," responded Maisel.

Back at the Three Ravens, I was still taking my cloak off when an eight-year-old boy and a flying mop practically knocked me off my feet. The mop was attached to a lively pink tongue and a cold black nose.

"What is this?" Matthew bellowed, steadying me so that I could locate the mop's handle.

"His name is Lobero. Gallowglass says he will grow into a great beast and that he might as well have a saddle fitted for him as a leash. Annie loves him, too. She says he will sleep with her, but I think we should share. What do you think?" Jack said, dancing with excitement.

"The wee mop came with a note," Gallowglass said. He pushed himself away from the doorframe and strolled over to Matthew to deliver it.

"Need I ask who sent the creature?" Matthew said, snatching at the paper.

"Oh, I don't think so," Gallowglass said. His eyes narrowed. "Did something happen while you were out, Auntie? You look done in."

"Just tired," I said with a breezy wave of my hand. The mop had teeth as well as a tongue, and he bit down on my fingers as they passed by his as-yet-undiscovered mouth. "Ouch!"

"This has to stop." Matthew crushed the note in his fingers and flung it to the floor. The mop pounced on it with a delighted bark.

"What did the note say?" I was pretty sure I knew who had sent the puppy.

"'Ich bin Lobero. Ich will euch aus den Schatten der Nacht zu schützen,'" Matthew said flatly.

I made an impatient sound. "Why does he keep writing to me in German? Rudolf knows I have a hard time understanding it."

"His Majesty delights in knowing I will have to translate his professions of love."

"Oh." I paused. "What did this note say?"

"'I am Lobero. I will protect you from the shadow of night.'"

"And what does 'Lobero' mean?" Once, many moons ago, Ysabeau had taught me that names were important.

"It means 'Wolf Hunter' in Spanish, Auntie." Gallowglass picked up the mop. "This bit of fluff is a Hungarian guard dog. Lobero will grow so big he'll be able to take down a bear. They're fiercely protective—and nocturnal."

"A bear! When we bring him back to London, I will tie a ribbon around his neck and take him to the bearbaitings so that he can learn how to fight," Jack said with the gruesome delight of a child. "Lobero is a brave name, don't you think? Master Shakespeare will want to use it in his next play." Jack wriggled his fingers in the puppy's direction, and Gallowglass obligingly deposited the squirming mass of white fur in the boy's arms. "Annie! I will feed Lobero next!" Jack pelted up the stairs, holding the dog in a death grip.

"Shall I take them away for a few hours?" Gallowglass asked after getting a good look at Matthew's stormy face.

"Is Baldwin's house empty?"

"There are no tenants in it, if that's what you mean."

"Take everybody." Matthew lifted my cloak from my shoulders.

"Even Lobero?"

"Especially Lobero."

Jack chattered like a magpie throughout supper, picking fights with Annie and managing to send a fair bit of food Lobero's way through a variety of occult methods. Between the children and the dog, it was almost possible to ignore the fact that Matthew was reconsidering his plans for the evening. On the one hand, he was a pack animal and something in him enjoyed having so many lives to take care of. On the other hand, he was a predator and I had an uneasy feeling that I was tonight's prey. The predator won. Not even Tereza and Karolína were allowed to stay.

"Why did you send them all away?" We were still by the fire in the house's main, first-floor room, where the comforting smells of dinner still filled the air.

"What happened this afternoon?" he asked.

"Answer my question first."

"Don't push me. Not tonight," Matthew warned.

"You think *my* day has been easy?" The air between us was crackling with blue and black threads. It looked ominous and felt worse.

"No." Matthew slid his chair back. "But you're keeping something from me, Diana. What happened with the witch?"

I stared at him.

"I'm waiting."

"You can wait until hell freezes over, Matthew, because I'm not your servant. I asked you a question." The threads went purple, beginning to twist and distort.

"I sent them away so that they wouldn't witness this conversation. Now, what happened?" The smell of cloves was choking.

"I met the golem. And his maker, a Jewish weaver named Abraham. He has the power of animation, too."

"I've told you I don't like it when you play with life and death." Matthew poured himself more wine.

"You play with them all the time, and I accept that as part of who you are. You're going to have to accept it's part of me, too."

"And this Abraham. Who is he?" Matthew demanded.

"God, Matthew. You cannot be jealous because I met another weaver."

"Jealous? I am long past that warmblooded emotion." He took a mouthful of wine.

"Why was this afternoon different from every other day we spend apart while you're out working for the Congregation and your father?"

"It's different because I can smell every single person you've been in contact with today. It's bad enough that you always carry the scent of Annie and Jack. Gallowglass and Pierre try not to touch you, but they can't help it—they're around you too much. Then we add the scents of the Maharal, and Herr Maisel, and at least two other men. The only scent I can bear to have mixed with yours is my own, but I cannot keep you in a cage, and so I endure it the best I can." Matthew put down his cup and shot to his feet in an attempt to put some distance between us.

"That sounds like jealousy to me."

"It's not. I could manage jealousy," he said, furious. "What I am feeling now—this terrible gnawing sense of loss and rage because I cannot get a clear impression of *you* in the chaos of our life—is beyond my control." His pupils were large and getting larger.

"That's because you are a vampire. You're possessive. It's who you are," I said flatly, approaching him in spite of his anger. "And I am a witch. You promised to accept me as I am—light and dark, woman and witch, my own person as well as your wife." What if he had changed his mind? What if he wasn't willing to have this kind of unpredictability in his life?

"I do accept you." Matthew reached out a gentle finger and touched my cheek.

"No, Matthew. You tolerate me, because you think that one day I'll beat my magic into submission. Rabbi Loew warned me that tolerance can be withdrawn, and then you're out in the cold. My magic isn't something to manage. It's *me.* And I'm not going to hide myself from you. That's not what love is."

"All right. No more hiding."

"Good." I sighed with relief, but it was short-lived.

Matthew had me out of the chair and up against the wall in one clean move, his thigh pressed between mine. He pulled a curl free so that it trailed down my neck and onto my breast. Without releasing me, he bent his head and pressed his lips to the edge of my bodice. I shivered. It had been some time since he'd kissed me there, and our sex life had been practically nonexistent since the miscarriage. Matthew's lips brushed along my jaw and over the veins of my neck.

I grabbed his hair and pulled his head away. "Don't. Not unless you plan on finishing what you start. I've had enough bundling and regretful kisses to last a lifetime."

With a few blindingly fast vampire moves, Matthew had loosened the fastenings on his britches, rucked my skirts around my waist, and plunged inside me. It wasn't the first time I'd been taken against the wall by someone trying to forget his troubles for a few precious moments. On several occasions I'd even been the aggressor.

"This is about you and me—nothing else. Not the children. Not the damn book. Not the emperor and his gifts. Tonight the only scents in this house will be ours."

Matthew's hands gripped my buttocks, and his fingers were all that was saving me from being bruised as his thrusts carried my body toward the wall. I wrapped my hands in the collar of his shirt and pulled his face toward mine, ravenous for the taste of him. But Matthew was no more willing to let me control the kiss than he was our lovemaking. His lips were hard and demanding, and when I persisted in my attempts to get the upper hand, he gave me a warning nip on the lower lip.

"Oh, God," I said breathlessly as his steady rhythm set my nerves rushing toward a release. "Oh—"

"Tonight I won't even share you with Him." Matthew kissed the rest of my exclamation away. One hand retained its grip on my buttock, the other dipped between my legs.

"Who has your heart, Diana?" Matthew asked, a stroke of his thumb threatening to take me over the edge of sanity. He moved, moved again. Waited for my answer. "Say it," he growled.

"You know the answer," I said. "You have my heart."

"Only me," he said, moving once more so that the coiled tension in both of us finally found release.

"Only . . . forever . . . you," I gasped, my legs shaking around his hips. I slid my feet to the floor.

Matthew was breathing heavily, his forehead pressed to mine. His eyes showed a flash of regret as he lowered my skirts. He kissed me gently, almost chastely.

Our lovemaking, no matter how intense, had not satisfied whatever was driving Matthew to keep pursuing me in spite of the fact that I was indisputably his. I was beginning to worry that nothing could.

My frustration burbled over, taking shape in a concussive wave of air that carried him away from me and into the opposite wall. Matthew's eyes went black at his change of position.

"And how was that for you, my heart?" I asked softly. His face registered surprise. I snapped my fingers, releasing the air's hold on him. His muscles flexed as he regained his mobility. He opened his mouth to speak. "Don't you dare apologize," I said fiercely. "If you'd touched me in a way I didn't like, I would have said no."

Matthew's mouth tightened.

"I can't help thinking about your friend Giordano Bruno: *'Desire urges me on, as fear bridles me.'* I'm not afraid of your power, or your strength, or anything else about you," I said. "What are *you* afraid of, Matthew?"

Regretful lips brushed over mine. That, and a whisper of breeze against my skirts, told me he had fled rather than answer.

30

"Master Habermel stopped by. Your compendium is on the table." Matthew didn't look up from the plans to Prague Castle that he'd somehow procured from the emperor's architects. In the past few days, he'd given me wide berth and taken to channeling his energy into unearthing the secrets of the palace guard so that he could breach Rudolf's security. In spite of Abraham's advice, which I'd duly conveyed, Matthew preferred a proactive strategy. He wanted us out of Prague. Now.

I approached his side, and he looked up with restless, hungry eyes.

"It's just a gift." I put down my gloves and kissed him deeply. "My heart is yours, remember?"

"It isn't just a gift. It came with an invitation to go hunting tomorrow." Matthew wrapped his hands around my hips. "Gallowglass informed me that we will be accepting it. He's found a way into the emperor's apartments by seducing some poor maid into showing him Rudolf's erotic-picture collection. The palace guard will either be hunting with us or napping. Gallowglass figures it's as good a chance as we're going to get to look for the book."

I glanced over at Matthew's desk, where another small parcel lay. "Do you know what that is, too?"

He nodded and reached over and picked it up. "You're always receiving gifts from other men. This one is from me. Hold out your hand." Intrigued, I did what he asked.

He pressed something round and smooth into my palm. It was the size of a small egg.

A stream of cool, heavy metal flowed around the mysterious egg as tiny salamanders filled my hand. They were made of silver and gold, with diamonds set into their backs. I lifted one of the creatures, and up came a chain made entirely of paired salamanders, their heads joined at the mouth and their tails entwined. Still nestled in my palm was a ruby. A very large, very red ruby.

"It's beautiful!" I looked up at Matthew. "When did you have time to buy this?" It wasn't the kind of chain that goldsmiths stocked for drop-in customers.

"I've had it for a while," Matthew confessed. "My father sent it with the altarpiece. I wasn't sure you'd like it."

"Of course I like it. Salamanders are alchemical, you know," I said, giving him another kiss. "Besides, what woman would object to two feet of silver, gold, and diamond salamanders and a ruby big enough to fill an eggcup?"

"These particular salamanders were a gift from the king when I returned to France late in 1541. King Francis chose the salamander in flames for his emblem, and his motto was *'I nourish and extinguish.'*" Matthew laughed. "Kit enjoyed the conceit so much he adapted it for his own use: *'What nourishes me destroys me.'*"

"Kit is definitely a glass-half-empty daemon," I said, joining in his laughter. I poked at one of the salamanders, and it caught the light from the candles. I started to speak, then stopped.

"What?" Matthew said.

"Have you given this to someone . . . before?" After the other night, my own sudden insecurity was embarrassing.

"No," Matthew said, taking my hand and its treasure between his.

"I'm sorry. It's ridiculous, I know, especially considering Rudolf's behavior. I'd rather not wonder, that's all. If you give me something you once gave to a former lover, just tell me."

"I wouldn't give you something I'd first given to someone else, *mon coeur.*" Matthew waited until I met his eyes. "Your firedrake reminded me of Francis's gift, so I asked my father to fish it out of its hidey-hole. I wore it once. Since then it's been sitting in a box."

"It's not exactly everyday wear," I said, trying to laugh. But it didn't quite work. "I don't know what's wrong with me."

Matthew pulled me down into a kiss. "My heart belongs to you no less than yours belongs to me. Never doubt it."

"I won't."

"Good. Because Rudolf is doing everything he can to wear us both down. We need to keep our heads. And then we need to get the hell out of Prague."

Matthew's words came back to haunt me the next afternoon, when we joined Rudolf's closest companions at court for an afternoon of sport. The plan had been to ride out to the emperor's hunting lodge at White Mountain to shoot deer, but the heavy gray skies kept us closer to the palace. It was the second week of April, but spring came slowly to Prague, and snow was still possible.

Rudolf called Matthew over to his side, leaving me to the mercy of the women of the court. They were openly curious and entirely at a loss about what to do with me.

The emperor and his companions drank freely from the wine that the servants passed. Given the high speeds of the impending chase, I wished there were regulations about drinking and riding. Not that I had much to worry about in Matthew's case. For one thing, he was being rather abstemious. And there was little chance of him dying, even if his horse did crash into a tree.

Two men arrived, a long pole resting on their shoulders to provide a perch for the splendid assortment of falcons that would be bringing down the birds this afternoon. Two more men followed bearing a single, hooded bird with a lethal curved beak and brown feathered legs that gave the effect of boots. It was huge.

"Ah!" Rudolf said, rubbing his hands together with delight. "Here is my eagle, Augusta. I wanted La Diosa to see her, even though we cannot fly her here. She requires more room to hunt than the Stag Moat provides."

Augusta was a fitting name for such a proud creature. The eagle was nearly three feet tall and, though hooded, held her head at a haughty angle.

"She can sense that we are watching her," I murmured.

Someone translated this for the emperor, and he smiled at me approvingly. "One huntress understands another. Take her hood off. Let Augusta and La Diosa get acquainted."

A wizened old man with bowed legs and a cautious expression approached the eagle. He pulled on the leather strings that tightened the hood around Augusta's head and gently drew it away from the bird. The golden feathers around her neck and head ruffled in the breeze, highlighting their texture. Augusta, sensing freedom and danger both, spread her wings in a gesture that could be read either as the promise of imminent flight or as a warning.

But I was not the one Augusta wanted to meet. With unerring instinct her head turned to the only predator in the company more dangerous than she was. Matthew stared back at her gravely, his eyes sad. Augusta cried out in acknowledgment of his sympathy.

"I did not bring Augusta out to amuse Herr Roydon but to meet La Diosa," Rudolf grumbled.

"And I thank you for the introduction, Your Majesty," I said, wanting to capture the moody monarch's attention.

"Augusta has taken down two wolves, you know," Rudolf said with a pointed look at Matthew. The emperor's feathers were far more ruffled than those of his prize bird. "They were both bloody struggles."

"Were I the wolf, I would simply lie down and let the lady have her way," Matthew said lazily. He was every inch the courtier this afternoon in a green-and-gray ensemble, his black hair pushed under a rakish cap that provided little protection from the elements but did provide an opportunity to display a silver badge on its crown—the de Clermont family's ouroboros—lest Rudolf forgot with whom he was dealing.

The other courtiers smirked and tittered at his daring remark. Rudolf, once he had made sure the laughter was not directed at him, joined in. "It is another thing we have in common, Herr Roydon," he said, pounding on Matthew's shoulder. He surveyed me. "Neither of us fears a strong woman."

The tension broken, the falconer returned Augusta to her perch with some relief and asked the emperor which bird he wished to use this afternoon to take down the royal grouse. Rudolf fussed over his selection. Once the emperor chose a large gyrfalcon, the Austrian archdukes and German princes fought over the remaining birds until only a single animal was left. It was small and shivering in the cold. Matthew reached for it.

"That is a woman's bird," Rudolf said with a snort, settling into his saddle. "I had it sent for La Diosa."

"In spite of her name, Diana doesn't like hunting. But it's no matter. I will fly the merlin," Matthew said. He ran the jesses through his fingers, put out his hand, and the bird stepped onto his gloved wrist. "Hello, beauty," he murmured while the bird adjusted her feet. With every small step, her bells jingled.

"Her name is Šárka," the gamekeeper whispered with a smile.

"Is she as clever as her namesake?" Matthew asked him.

"More so," the old man answered with a grin.

Matthew leaned toward the bird and took one of the strings that held her hood in his teeth. His mouth was so close to Šárka, and the gesture so intimate, that it could have been mistaken for a kiss. Matthew drew the string back. Once that was done, it was easy for him to remove the hood with his other hand and slip the decorated leather blindfold into a pocket.

Šárka blinked as the world came into view. She blinked again, studying me and then the man who held her.

"Can I touch her?" There was something irresistible about the soft layers of brown-and-white feathers.

"I wouldn't. She's hungry. I don't think she gets her fair share of kills," Matthew said. He looked sad again, even wistful. Šárka made low, chortling sounds and kept her eyes on Matthew.

"She likes you." It was no wonder. They were both hunters by instinct, both fettered so that they couldn't give in to the urge to track and kill.

We rode on a twisting path down into the river gorge that had once served as the palace moat. The river was gone and the gorge fenced in to keep the emperor's game from roaming the city. Red deer, roe deer, and boar all prowled the grounds. So, too, did the lions and other big cats from the menagerie on those days when Rudolf decided to hunt down his prey with them rather than birds.

I expected utter chaos, but hunting was as precisely choreographed as any ballet. As soon as Rudolf released his gyrfalcon into the air, the birds resting in the trees rose up in a cloud, taking flight to avoid becoming a snack. The gyrfalcon swooped down and flew over the brush, the wind whistling through the bells on his feet. Startled grouse erupted from cover, running and flapping in all directions before taking to the air. The gyrfalcon banked, selected a target, harried it into position, and shot forward to hit it with talons and beak. The grouse fell from the sky, the falcon pursuing it relentlessly to the ground, where the grouse, startled and injured, was finally killed. The gamekeepers released the dogs and ran with them across the snowy ground. The horses thundered after, the men's cries of triumph drowned out by the baying of the hounds.

When the horses and riders caught up, we found the falcon standing by its prey, its wings curved to shield the grouse from rival claimants. Matthew had adopted a similar stance at the Bodleian Library, and I felt his eyes fall on me to make sure that I was nearby.

Now that the emperor had the first kill, the others were free to join in the hunt. Together they caught more than a hundred birds, enough to feed a fair number of courtiers. There was only one altercation. Not surprisingly, it occurred between Rudolf's magnificent silver gyrfalcon and Matthew's small brown-and-white merlin.

Matthew had been hanging back from the rest of the male pack. He released his bird well after the others and was unhurried in claiming the grouse that she brought down. Though none of the other men got off their mounts, Matthew did, coaxing Šárka away from her prey with a murmured word and a bit of meat that he'd pulled off a previous kill.

Once, however, Šárka failed to connect with the grouse she was pursuing. It eluded her, flying straight into the path of Rudolf's gyrfalcon. But Šárka refused to yield. Though the gyrfalcon was larger, Šárka was scrappier and more agile. To reach her grouse, the merlin flew past my head so closely that I felt the changing pressure in the air. She was such a little thing—smaller even than the grouse, and definitely outsized by the emperor's bird. The grouse flew higher, but there was no escape. Šárka quickly reversed direction and sank her curved talons into her prey, her weight carrying them both down. The indignant gyrfalcon screamed in frustration, and Rudolf added his own loud protest.

"Your bird interfered with mine," Rudolf said furiously as Matthew kicked his horse forward to fetch the merlin.

"She isn't my bird, Your Majesty," Matthew said. Šárka, who had puffed herself up and stretched out her wings to look as large and menacing as possible, let out a shrill peep as he approached. Matthew murmured something that sounded vaguely familiar and more than a little amorous, and the bird's feathers smoothed. "Šárka belongs to you. And today she has proved to be a worthy namesake of a great Bohemian warrior."

Matthew picked up the merlin, grouse and all, and held it up for the court to see. Šárka's jesses swung freely, and her bells tinkled with sound as he circled her around. Unsure what their response should be, the courtiers waited for Rudolf to do something. I intervened instead.

"Was this a female warrior, husband?"

Matthew stopped in his rotation and grinned. "Why, yes, wife. The real Šárka was small and feisty, just like the emperor's bird, and knew that a warrior's greatest weapon lies between the ears." He tapped his head to make sure everyone received the message. Rudolf not only received it, he looked nonplussed.

"She sounds rather like the ladies of Malá Strana," I said drily. "And what did Šárka do with her intelligence?" Before Matthew could answer, an unfamiliar young woman spoke.

"Šárka took down a troop of soldiers," she explained in fluid Latin with a heavy Czech accent. A white-bearded man I took to be her father looked at her approvingly, and she blushed.

"Really?" I said, interested. "How?"

"By pretending she needed rescuing and then inviting the soldiers to celebrate her freedom with too much wine." Another woman, this one elderly with a beak of a nose to rival Augusta's, snorted in disgust. "Men fall for that every time."

I burst out laughing. To her evident surprise, so did the beaky, aristocratic old lady.

"I fear, Emperor, that the ladies will not have their heroine blamed for the faults of others." Matthew reached into his pocket for the hood and gently set it over the crown of Šárka's proud head. He leaned in and tightened the cord with his teeth. The gamekeeper took the merlin to a smattering of approving applause.

We adjourned to a red-and-white-roofed Italianate house set at the edge of the palace grounds for wine and refreshments, though I would have preferred to linger in the gardens where the emperor's narcissi and tulips were blooming. Other members of the court joined us, including the sour-faced Strada, Master Hoefnagel, and the instrument maker Erasmus Habermel, whom I thanked for my compendium.

"What we need to lift our boredom is a spring feast now that Lent is almost over," said one young male courtier in a loud voice. "Don't you think so, Your Majesty?"

"A masque?" Rudolf took a sip of his wine and stared at me. "If so, the theme should be Diana and Actaeon."

"That theme is so common, Your Majesty, and rather English," Matthew said sadly. Rudolf flushed. "Perhaps we might do Demeter and Persephone instead. It is more fitting for the season."

"Or the story of Odysseus," Strada suggested, shooting me a nasty look. "Frau Roydon could play Circe and turn us into piglets."

"Interesting, Ottavio," Rudolf said, tapping his full lower lip with his index finger. "I might enjoy playing Odysseus."

Not on your life, I thought. Not with the requisite bedroom scene and Odysseus making Circe promise not to forcibly take his manhood.

"If I might offer a suggestion," I said, eager to stave off disaster.

"Of course, of course," Rudolf said earnestly, taking my hand and giving it a solicitous pat.

"The story I have in mind requires someone to take the role of Zeus, the king of the gods," I told the emperor, drawing my hand gently away.

"I would be a convincing Zeus," he said eagerly, a smile lighting his face. "And you will play Callisto?" *Absolutely not.* I was not going to let Rudolf pretend to ravage and impregnate me.

"No, Your Majesty. If you insist that I take part in the entertainment, I will play the goddess of the moon." I slid my hand into the bend of Matthew's arm. "And to atone for his earlier remark, Matthew will play Endymion."

"Endymion?" Rudolf's smile wavered.

"Poor Rudolf. Outfoxed again," Matthew murmured for only me to hear. "Endymion, Your Majesty," he said, this time in a voice pitched to carry, "the beautiful youth who is cast into enchanted sleep so as to preserve his immortality and Diana's chastity."

"I know the legend, Herr Roydon!" Rudolf warned.

"Apologies, Your Majesty," Matthew said with a graceful, albeit shallow, bow. "Diana will look splendid, arriving in her chariot so that she can gaze wistfully upon the man she loves."

Rudolf was imperial purple by this point. We were waved out of the royal presence and left the palace to make the brief, downhill trip to the Three Ravens.

"I have only one request," Matthew said as we entered our front door. "I may be a vampire, but April is a cold month in Prague. In deference to the temperature, the costumes you design for Diana and Endymion should be more substantial than a lunar crescent for your hair and a dishcloth to drape around my hips."

"I've only just cast you in this role and you're already making artistic demands!" I flung up one hand in mock indignation. "Actors!"

"That's what you deserve for working with amateurs," Matthew said with a smile. "I know just how the masque should begin: '*And lo! from opening clouds, I saw emerge / The loveliest moon, that ever silver'd o'er / A shell for Neptune's goblet.*'"

"You cannot use Keats!" I laughed. "He's a Romantic poet—it's three hundred years too soon."

"'*She did soar / So passionately bright, my dazzled soul / Commingling with her argent spheres did roll / Through clear and cloudy, even when she went / At last into a dark and vapoury tent,*'" he exclaimed dramatically, pulling me into his arms.

"And I suppose you'll want *me* to find you a tent," Gallowglass said, thundering down the stairs.

"And some sheep. Or maybe an astrolabe. Endymion can be either a shepherd or an astronomer," Matthew said, weighing his options.

"Rudolf's gamekeeper will never part with one of his strange sheep," Gallowglass said dourly.

"Matthew is welcome to use my compendium." I looked around. It was supposed to be on the mantelpiece, out of Jack's reach. "Where has it gone?"

"Annie and Jack are showing it to Mop. They think it's enchanted."

Until then I hadn't noticed the threads running straight up the stairs from the fireplace—silver, gold, and gray. In my rush to reach the children and find out what was going on with the compendium, I stepped on the hem of my skirt. By the time I reached Annie and Jack, I'd managed to give the bottom a new, scalloped edge.

Annie and Jack had the little brass-and-silver compendium opened up like a book, its inner wings folded out to their full extent. Rudolf's desire had been to give me something to track the movements of the heavens, and Habermel had outdone himself. The compendium contained a sundial, a compass, a device to compute the length of the hours at different seasons of the year, an intricate lunar volvelle—whose gears could be set to tell the date, time, ruling sign of the zodiac, and phase of the moon—and a latitude chart that included (at my request) the cities of Roanoke, London, Lyon, Prague, and Jerusalem. One of the wings had a spine into which I could fit one of the hottest new technologies: the erasable tablet, which was made of specially treated paper that one could write on and then carefully wipe off to make fresh notes.

"Look, Jack, it's doing it again," Annie said, peering down at the instrument. Mop (no one in the house called him Lobero anymore, except for Jack) started barking, wagging his tail with excitement as the lunar volvelle began to spin of its own accord.

"I bet you a penny that the full moon will be in the window when the spinning stops," Jack said, spitting in his hand and holding it out to Annie.

"No betting," I said automatically, crouching down next to Jack.

"When did this start, Jack?" Matthew asked, fending off Mop.

Jack shrugged.

"It's been happening since Herr Habermel sent it," Annie confessed.

"Does it spin like this all day or only at certain times?" I asked.

"Only once or twice. And the compass just spins once." Annie looked miserable. "I should have told you. I knew it was magical from the way it feels."

"It's all right." I smiled at her. "No harm done." With that I put my finger in the center of the volvelle and commanded the thing to stop. It did. As soon as the revolutions ceased, the silver and gold threads around the compendium slowly dissolved, leaving only the gray thread behind. It was quickly lost among the many colorful strands that filled our house.

"What does it mean?" Matthew asked later, when the house was quiet and I had my first opportunity to put the compendium out of the children's reach. I'd decided to leave it atop the flat canopy over our bed. "By the way, everybody hides things on top of the tester. It will be the first place Jack searches for it."

"Somebody is looking for us." I pulled the compendium back down and sought out a new place to conceal it.

"In Prague?" Matthew held out his hand for the small instrument, and when I handed it to him, he slipped it into his doublet.

"No. In time."

Matthew sat down on the bed with a thunk and swore.

"It's my fault." I looked at him sheepishly. "I tried to weave a spell so that the compendium would warn me if somebody was thinking of stealing it. The spell was supposed to keep Jack out of trouble. I guess I need to go back to the drawing board."

"What makes you think it's someone in another time?" Matthew asked.

"Because the lunar volvelle is a perpetual calendar. The gears were spinning as though it were trying to input information beyond its technical specifications. It reminds me of the words racing around in Ashmole 782."

"Maybe the whirring of the compass indicates that whoever is looking for us is in a different place, too. Like the lunar volvelle, the compass can't find true north because it's being asked to compute two sets of directions: one for us in Prague and one for someone else."

"Do you think it's Ysabeau or Sarah, and they need our help?" It was Ysabeau who had sent Matthew the copy of *Doctor Faustus* to help us reach 1590. She knew where we were headed.

"No," Matthew said, his voice sure. "They wouldn't give us away. It's someone else." His gray-green eyes settled on me. The restless, regretful look was back.

"You're looking at me as though I've betrayed you somehow." I sat next to him on the bed. "If you don't want me to do the masque, I won't."

"It's not that." Matthew got up and walked away. "You're still keeping something from me."

"We all keep things to ourselves, Matthew," I said. "Little things that don't matter. Sometimes big things, say, like being on the Congregation." His accusations rankled, given all that I still did not know about him.

Matthew's hands were suddenly on my shoulders, lifting me up. "You will never forgive me for that." His eyes looked black, and his fingers dug into my arms.

"You promised me you would tolerate my secrets," I said. "Rabbi Loew is right. Tolerance isn't enough."

Matthew released me with a curse. I heard Gallowglass on the steps, Jack's sleepy murmurs down the hall.

"I'm taking Jack and Annie to Baldwin's house," Gallowglass said from the door. "Tereza and Karolína have already gone. Pierre will come with me, and so will the dog." His voice dropped. "You frighten the boy when you argue, and he's known enough fear in his short life. Sort yourselves out or I'll take them back to London and leave the two of you here to shift for yourselves." Gallowglass's blue eyes were fierce.

Matthew sat silently by the fire, a cup of wine in his hands and a dark expression on his face as he stared into the flames. As soon as the group departed, he was on his feet and headed to the door.

Without thinking or planning, I released my firedrake. *Stop him,* I commanded. She covered him in a gray mist as she flew over and around him, took solid form by the door, and dug the spiked edges of her wings onto either side of its frame. When Matthew got too close, a tongue of fire shot out of her mouth in warning.

"You're not going anywhere," I said. It took enormous effort to keep my voice from rising. Matthew might be able to overpower me, but I doubted he could successfully wrestle with my familiar. "My firedrake is a bit like Šárka: small but scrappy. I wouldn't piss her off."

Matthew turned, his eyes cold.

"If you're angry with me, say it. If I've done something you don't like, tell me. If you want to end this marriage, have the courage to end it cleanly so that I might—might—be able to recover from it. Because if you keep looking at me as though you wish we weren't married, you're going to destroy me."

"I have no desire to end this marriage," he said tightly.

"Then be my husband." I advanced on him. "Do you know what I thought watching those beautiful birds fly today? 'That's what Matthew would look like, if only he were free to be himself.' And when I saw you put on Šárka's hood, blinding her so that she couldn't hunt as her instincts tell her to do, I saw the same look of regret in her eyes that I have seen in yours every day since I lost the baby."

"This isn't about the baby." His eyes held a warning now.

"No. It's about me. And you. And something so terrifying you can't acknowledge it: that in spite of your so-called powers over life and death, you don't control everything and can't keep me, or anyone else you love, from harm."

"And you think it's losing the baby that brought that fact home?"

"What else could it be? Your guilt over Blanca and Lucas nearly destroyed you."

"You're wrong." Matthew's hands were wrapped in my hair, pulling down the knot of braids and releasing the scent of chamomile and mint from the soap I used. His pupils looked inky and huge. He drank in the scent of me, and some of the green returned.

"Tell me what it is, then."

"This." He reached for the edge of my bodice and rent it in two. Then he loosened the cord that kept the wide neckline of my smock from sliding off my shoulders so that it exposed the tops of my breasts. His finger traced the blue vein that surfaced there and continued beneath the folds of linen.

"Every day of my life is a battle for control. I fight my anger and the sickness that follows in its wake. I struggle with hunger and thirst, because I don't believe it is right for me to take blood from other creatures—not even the animals, though I can bear that better than taking it from someone I might see again on the street." His eyes rose to mine. "And I am at war with myself over this unspeakable urge to possess you body and soul in ways that no warmblood can fathom."

"You want my blood," I whispered in sudden understanding. "You lied to me."

"I lied to myself."

"I told you—repeatedly—that you can have it," I said. I grabbed at the smock and tore it further, bending my head to the side and exposing my jugular. "Take it. I don't care. I just want you back." I bit back a sob.

"You're my mate. I would never voluntarily take blood from your neck." Matthew's fingers were cool on my flesh as he drew the smock back into place. "When I did so in Madison, it was because I was too weak to stop myself."

"What's wrong with my neck?" I said, confused.

"Vampires only bite strangers and subordinates on the neck. Not lovers. Certainly not mates."

"Dominance," I said, thinking back to our previous conversations about vampires, blood, and sex, "and feeding. So it's mostly humans who get bitten there. There's the kernel of truth in that vampire legend."

"Vampires bite their mates here," Matthew said, "near the heart." His lips pressed against the bare flesh above the edge of my smock. It was where he had kissed me on our wedding night, when his emotions had overwhelmed him.

"I thought your wanting to kiss me there was just ordinary lust," I said.

"There is nothing ordinary about a vampire's desire to take blood from this vein." He moved his mouth a centimeter lower along the blue line and pressed his lips again.

"But if it's not about feeding or dominance, what is it about?"

"Honesty." When Matthew met my eyes, they were still more black than green. "Vampires keep too many secrets to ever be completely honest. We could never share them all verbally, and most are too complex to make sense, even when you try. And there are prohibitions against sharing secrets in my world."

"'It's not your tale to tell,'" I said. "I've heard that a few times."

"To drink from your lover is to know that nothing is hidden." Matthew stared down at my breast, touched the vein again with his fingertip. "We call this the heart vein. The blood tastes sweeter here. There is a sense of complete possession and belonging—but it requires complete control, too, not to be swept up in the strong emotions that result." His voice was sad.

"And you don't trust your control because of the blood rage."

"You've seen me in its grip. It's sparked by protectiveness. And who poses a greater danger to you than I do?"

I shrugged the smock off my shoulders, pulling my arms out of the sleeves until I was bare from the waist up. I felt for the lacings on my skirt and yanked them free.

"Don't." Matthew's eyes had blackened further. "There is no one here in case—"

"You drain me?" I stepped out of my skirt. "If you couldn't trust yourself to do this when Philippe was within earshot, you're not likely to do it with Gallowglass and Pierre standing by to help."

"This isn't a matter for jokes."

"No." I took his hands in mine. "It's a matter for husbands and wives.

It's a matter of honesty and trust. I have nothing to hide from you. If taking blood from my vein is going to put an end to your incessant need to hunt down what you imagine to be my secrets, then that is what you're going to do."

"It isn't something a vampire does just once," Matthew warned, trying to pull away.

"I didn't think it was." I threaded my fingers into the hair at the nape of his neck. "Take my blood. Take my secrets. Do what your instincts are screaming for you to do. There are no hoods or jesses here. In my arms you should be free, even if nowhere else."

I drew his mouth to mine. He responded tentatively at first, his fingers wrapped around my wrists as if he hoped to break away at the earliest opportunity. But his instincts were strong and his yearning palpable. The threads that bound the world shifted and adjusted around me as if to make room for such powerful feelings. I drew gently away, my breasts lifting with each breath.

He looked so frightened that it hurt my heart. But there was desire, too. *Fear and desire.* No wonder they'd featured in his All Souls essay back when he'd won his fellowship. Who could understand the war between them better than a vampire?

"I love you," I whispered, dropping my hands so that they hung by my sides. He had to do this himself. I couldn't play any role in bringing his mouth to my vein.

The wait was excruciating, but at last he lowered his head. My heart was beating fast, and I heard him draw in a deep, long breath.

"Honey. You always smell like honey," he murmured in amazement, just before his sharp teeth broke the skin.

When he'd taken my blood before, Matthew had been careful to anesthetize the site with a touch of his own blood so that I felt no pain. Not so this time, but soon the skin went numb from the pressure of Matthew's mouth on my flesh. His hands cradled me as he angled me back toward the surface of the bed. I hung in midair waiting for him to be satisfied that there was nothing between us but love.

About thirty seconds after he started, Matthew stopped. He looked up at me in surprise, as if he'd discovered something unexpected. His eyes went full black, and for one fleeting moment I thought that the blood rage was surfacing.

"It's all right, my love," I whispered.

Matthew lowered his head, drinking in more until he discovered what he needed. It took little more than a minute. He kissed the place over my heart with the same expression of gentle reverence he had worn on our wedding night at Sept-Tours and looked up at me shyly.

"And what did you find?" I asked.

"You. Only you," Matthew murmured.

His shyness quickly turned to hunger as he kissed me, and before long we were twined together. Except for our brief encounter standing against the wall, we had not made love for weeks, and our rhythm was awkward at first as we remembered how to move together. My body coiled tighter and tighter. Another fast glide, a deep kiss, was all it would take to set me flying.

Matthew slowed instead. Our eyes met and locked. I had never seen him look the way he did at that moment—vulnerable, hopeful, beautiful, free. There were no secrets between us now, no emotions guarded in case disaster struck and we were swept along into the dark places where hope couldn't survive.

"Can you feel me?" Matthew was now a point of stillness at my core. I nodded again. He smiled and moved with deliberate care. "I'm inside you, Diana, giving you life."

I'd said the same words to him as he drank my blood and pulled himself from the edge of death back into the world. I didn't think he'd been aware of them at the time.

He moved within me again, repeating the words like an incantation. It was the simplest, purest form of magic in the world. Matthew was already woven into my soul. He was now woven into my body, just as I was woven into his. My heart, which had broken and broken again in the past months with every sad touch and regretful look, began to knit together once more.

When the sun crept over the horizon, I reached up and touched him between the eyes.

"I wonder if I could read your thoughts, too."

"You already have," Matthew said, lowering my fingers and kissing their tips. "Back in Oxford, when you received the picture of your parents. You weren't conscious of what you were doing. But you kept answering questions I wasn't able to ask aloud."

"Can I try again?" I asked, half expecting him to say no.

"Of course. If you were a vampire I would already have offered my blood." He lay back on the pillow.

I hesitated for a moment, stilled my thoughts, and focused on a simple question. *How can I know Matthew's heart?*

A single silver thread shimmered between my own heart and the spot on his forehead where his third eye would be if he were a witch. The thread shortened, drawing me closer until my lips pressed against his skin.

An explosion of sights and sounds burst in my head like fireworks. I saw Jack and Annie, Philippe and Ysabeau. I saw Gallowglass and men I didn't recognize who occupied important places in Matthew's memories. I saw Eleanor and Lucas. There was a feeling of triumph as he conquered some scientific mystery, a shout of joy as he rode out in the forest to hunt and kill as he was made to do. I saw myself, smiling up at him.

Then I saw the face of Herr Fuchs, the vampire I'd met in the Jewish Town, and heard quite distinctly the words *My son, Benjamin*.

I sat back on my heels abruptly, my fingers touching my trembling lips.

"What is it?" Matthew said, sitting up and frowning.

"Herr Fuchs!" I looked at him in horror, afraid he had thought the worst. "I didn't realize he was your son, that he was Benjamin." There hadn't been a hint of blood rage about the creature.

"It's not your fault. You're not a vampire, and Benjamin only reveals what he chooses." Matthew's voice was soothing. "I must have sensed his presence around you—a trace of scent, some inkling that he was near. That's what made me think you were keeping something from me. I was wrong. I'm sorry for doubting you, *mon coeur*."

"But Benjamin must have known who I was. Your scent would have been all over me."

"Of course he knew," Matthew said dispassionately. "I will look for him tomorrow, but if Benjamin doesn't want to be found, there will be nothing to do but warn Gallowglass and Philippe. They'll let the rest of the family know that Benjamin has reappeared."

"Warn them?" My skin pricked with fear at his nod.

"The only thing more frightening than Benjamin in the grip of blood rage is Benjamin when he is lucid, as he was when you were with Rabbi Loew. It is as Jack said," Matthew replied. "The most terrifying monsters always look just like ordinary men."

31

That night marked the true beginning of our marriage. Matthew was more centered than I had ever seen him. Gone were the sharp retorts, abrupt changes of direction, and impulsive decisions that had characterized our time together thus far. Instead Matthew was methodical, measured—but no less deadly. He fed more regularly, hunting in the city and the villages nearby. As his muscles gained in weight and strength, I came to see what Philippe had already observed: Unlikely though it might seem given his size, his son had been wasting away for want of proper nourishment.

I was left with a silvery moon on my breast marking the place where he drank. It was unlike any other scar on my body, lacking the tough buildup of protective tissue that formed over most wounds. Matthew told me that this was due to a property in his saliva, which sealed the bite without letting it heal completely.

Matthew's ritual taking of his mate's blood from a vein near the heart and my new ritual of the witch's kiss that gave me access to his thoughts provided us with a deeper intimacy. We didn't make love every time he joined me in bed, but when we did, it was always preceded and followed by those two searing moments of absolute honesty that removed not only Matthew's greatest worry but mine: that our secrets would somehow destroy us. And even when we didn't make love, we talked in the open, easy way that lovers dream of doing.

The next morning, Matthew told Gallowglass and Pierre about Benjamin. Gallowglass's fury was shorter-lived than Pierre's fear, which rose to the surface whenever someone knocked on the door or approached me in the market. The vampires searched for him day and night, with Matthew planning the expeditions.

But Benjamin could not be found. He had simply vanished.

Easter came and went, and our plans for Rudolf's spring festival the following Saturday reached their final stages. Master Hoefnagel and I transformed the palace's Great Hall into a blooming garden with pots of tulips.

I was in awe of the place, with its graceful curved vaults supporting the arched roof like the branches of a willow tree.

"We'll move the emperor's orange trees here as well," Hoefnagel said, his eyes gleaming with possibilities. "And the peacocks."

On the day of the performance, servants dragged every spare candelabrum in the palace and cathedral into the echoing expanse of stone to provide the illusion of a starry night sky and spread fresh rushes on the floor. For the stage we used the base of the stairs leading up to the royal chapel. It was Master Hoefnagel's idea, since then I could appear at the top of the staircase, like the moon, while Matthew charted my changing position with one of Master Habermel's astrolabes.

"You don't think we're being too philosophical?" I wondered aloud, worrying at my lip with my fingers.

"This is the court of Rudolf II," Hoefnagel said drily. "There is no such thing as too philosophical."

When the court filed in for the banquet, they gasped in amazement at the scene we'd set.

"They like it," I whispered to Matthew from behind the curtain that concealed us from the crowd. Our grand entrance was scheduled for the dessert course, and we were holed up in the Knights' Staircase off the hall until then. Matthew had been keeping me occupied with tales of olden times, when he had ridden his horse up the wide stone steps for a joust. When I'd questioned the room's suitability for this particular purpose, he quirked an eyebrow at me.

"Why do you think we made the room so big and the ceiling so high? Prague winters can be damn long, and bored young men with weapons are dangerous. Far better to have them run at each other at high speed than start wars with neighboring kingdoms."

With the free pouring of wine and the liberal serving of food, the din in the room was soon deafening. When the desserts went by, Matthew and I slipped into our places. Master Hoefnagel had painted some lovely pastoral scenery for Matthew and grudgingly allotted him one of the orange trees to sit beneath on his felt-covered stool meant to look like a rock. I would wait for my cue and then come out of the chapel and stand behind an old wooden door turned on its side and painted to resemble a chariot.

"Don't you dare make me laugh," I warned Matthew when he kissed me on the cheek for luck.

"I do love a challenge," he whispered back.

As strains of music filled through the room, the courtiers gradually hushed. When the room was fully quiet, Matthew lifted his astrolabe to the heavens and the masque began.

I had decided that our best approach to the production involved minimal dialogue and maximum dancing. For one thing, who wanted to sit around after a big dinner and listen to speeches? I'd been to enough academic events to know that wasn't a good idea. Signor Pasetti was delighted to teach some of the court ladies a "dance of the wandering stars," which would provide Matthew something heavenly to observe while he waited for his beloved moon to appear. With famous court beauties given a role in the entertainment and wearing fabulously spangled and jeweled costumes, the masque quickly took on the tone of a school play, complete with admiring parents. Matthew made agonized faces as though he weren't sure he could endure the spectacle for one more moment.

When the dance ended, the musicians cued my entrance with a crash of drums and blare of trumpets. Master Hoefnagel had rigged up a curtain over the chapel doors, so that all I had to do was push my way through them with a goddess's éclat (and without spearing my moon headdress on the fabric as I had done in rehearsal) and stare wistfully down at Matthew. He, goddess willing, would stare raptly at me without crossing his eyes or looking suggestively at my breasts.

I took a moment to get in character, drew in a deep breath, and pushed confidently through the curtains, trying to glide and float like the moon.

The court gasped in wonder.

Pleased that I had made such a convincing entrance, I looked down at Matthew. His eyes were round as saucers.

Oh, no. I felt with my toe for the floor, but as I suspected, I was already a few inches above it—and rising. I reached out a hand to anchor myself to the edge of my chariot and saw that a distinctively pearly gleam was emanating from my skin. Matthew jerked his head up in the direction of my tiara and its little silver crescent moon. Without a mirror I had no idea what it was doing, but I feared the worst.

"La Diosa!" Rudolf said, standing up and applauding. "Wonderful! A wonderful effect!"

Uncertainly, the court joined in. A few of them crossed themselves first.

Holding the room's complete attention, I clasped my hands to my bosom and batted my eyes at Matthew, who returned my admiring looks with a grim smile. I concentrated on lowering myself to the floor so that I could make my way to Rudolf's throne. As Zeus, he occupied the most splendid carved piece of furniture we could find in the palace attics. It was unbelievably ugly, but it suited the occasion.

Happily, I was not glowing so much anymore as I approached the emperor, and the audience had stopped looking at my head as if it were a Roman candle. I sank into a curtsy.

"Greetings, La Diosa," Rudolf boomed in what was meant to be a godlike tone but was only a classic example of overacting.

"I am in love with the beautiful Endymion," I said, rising and gesturing back to the staircase, where Matthew had sunk into a downy nest of feather beds and was feigning sleep. I had written the lines myself. (Matthew suggested I say, "If you do not agree to leave me in peace, Endymion will tear your throat out." I vetoed that, along with the Keats.) "He looks so peaceful. And though I am a goddess and will never age, fair Endymion will soon grow old and die. I beg of you, make him immortal so that he can stay with me always."

"On one condition!" Rudolf shouted, abandoning all pretense of godlike sonorousness in favor of simple volume. "He must sleep for the rest of time, never waking. Only then will he remain young."

"Thank you, mighty Zeus," I said, trying not to sound too much like a member of a British comedy troupe. "Now I can gaze upon my beloved forevermore."

Rudolf scowled. It was a good thing he hadn't been granted script approval.

I withdrew to my chariot and walked slowly backward through the curtains while the court ladies performed their final dance. When it was over, Rudolf led the court in a round of loud stomping and clapping that almost brought the roof down. What it did not do was rouse Endymion.

"Get up!" I hissed as I went past to thank the emperor for providing us an opportunity to entertain his royal self. All I got in response was a theatrical snore.

And so I curtsied alone in front of Rudolf and made speeches in praise of Master Habermel's astrolabe, Master Hoefnagel's sets and special effects, and the quality of the music.

"I was greatly entertained, La Diosa—much more than I expected to be. You may ask Zeus for a reward," Rudolf said, his eyes drifting over my shoulder and down to the swell of my breasts. "Whatever you wish. Name it and it shall be yours."

The room's idle chatter stopped. In the silence I heard Abraham's words: *The book will come to you, if only you ask for it.* Could it really be that simple?

Endymion stirred in his downy bed. Not wanting him to interfere, I flapped my hands behind my back to encourage him to return to his dreams. The court held its breath, waiting for me to name a prestigious title, a piece of land, a fortune in gold.

"I would like to see Roger Bacon's alchemical book, Your Majesty."

"You have balls of iron, Auntie," Gallowglass said in a tone of hushed admiration on the way home. "Not to mention a way with words."

"Why, thank you," I said, pleased. "By the way, what was my head doing during the masque? People were staring at it."

"Wee stars rose out of the moon and then faded away. I wouldn't worry. It looked so real that everybody will assume it was an illusion. Most of Rudolf's aristocrats are human, after all."

Matthew's response was more guarded. "Don't be too pleased yet, *mon coeur.* Rudolf may have had no other choice than to agree, given the situation, but he hasn't produced the manuscript. This is a very complicated dance you're doing. And you can be sure the emperor will want something from you in return for a glimpse of his book."

"Then we will have to be long gone before he can insist upon it," I said.

But it turned out that Matthew was right to be cautious. I had imagined that he and I would be invited to view the treasure the next day, in private. Yet no such invitation arrived. Days passed before we received a formal summons to dine at the palace with some up-and-coming Catholic theologians. Afterward, the note promised, a select group would be invited back to Rudolf's rooms to see items of particular mystical and religious import from the emperor's collections. Among the visitors was one Johannes Pistorius, who had grown up Lutheran, converted to Calvinism, and was about to become a Catholic priest.

"We're being set up," Matthew said, fingers running back and forth through his hair. "Pistorius is a dangerous man, a ruthless adversary, and a witch. He will be back here in ten years to serve as Rudolf's confessor."

"Is it true he's being groomed for the Congregation?" Gallowglass asked quietly.

"Yes. He's just the kind of intellectual thug that the witches want representing them. No offense meant, Diana. It is a difficult time for witches," he conceded.

"None taken," I said mildly. "But he's not a member of the Congregation yet. You are. What are the chances he'll want to cause trouble with you watching him, if he has those aspirations?"

"Excellent—or Rudolf wouldn't have asked him to dine with us. The emperor is drawing his battle lines and rallying his troops."

"What, exactly, is he planning to fight over?"

"The manuscript—and you. He won't give up either."

"I told you before that I wasn't for sale. I'm not war booty either."

"No, but you're unclaimed territory so far as Rudolf's concerned. Rudolf is an Austrian archduke, king of Hungary, Croatia, and Bohemia, margrave of Moravia, and Holy Roman Emperor. He is also Philip of Spain's nephew. The Hapsburgs are an acquisitive and competitive family and will stop at nothing to get what they want."

"Matthew's not coddling you, Auntie," Gallowglass said somberly when I started to protest. "If you were my wife, you'd have been out of Prague the day the first gift arrived."

Because of the delicacy of the situation, Pierre and Gallowglass accompanied us to the palace. Three vampires and a witch caused the expected ripples of interest as we went toward the Great Hall, which, once upon a time, Matthew had helped to design.

Rudolf seated me near him, and Gallowglass took up a position behind my chair like a well-mannered servant. Matthew was placed at the opposite end of the banqueting table with an attentive Pierre. To a casual observer, Matthew was having a grand time among a raucous group of ladies and young men who were eager to find a role model with more dash than the emperor. Gales of laughter occasionally drifted in our direction from Matthew's rival court, which did nothing to brighten His Majesty's dour mood.

"But why does there have to be so much bloodshed, Father Johannes?" Rudolf complained to the fleshy, middle-aged physician sitting to his left. Pistorius's ordination was still several months away, but, with the zeal typical of the convert, he made no objection to his premature elevation to the priesthood.

"Because heresy and unorthodoxies must be rooted out completely, Your Majesty. Otherwise they find fresh soil in which to grow." Pistorius's heavy-lidded eyes fell on me, his glance probing. My witch's third eye opened, indignant at his rude attempts to capture my attention, which was strikingly similar to Champier's method for ferreting out my secrets. I was beginning to dislike university-educated wizards. I put down my knife and returned his stare. He was the first to break it.

"My father believed that tolerance was a wiser policy," Rudolf replied. "And you have studied the Jewish wisdom of the kabbalah. There are men of God who would call that heresy."

Matthew's keen hearing allowed him to zero in on my conversation as intensely as Šárka had pursued her grouse. He frowned.

"My husband tells me you are a physician, Herr Pistorius." It was not a smooth conversational segue, but it did the job.

"I am, Frau Roydon. Or I was, before I turned my attention from the preservation of bodies to the salvation of souls."

"Father Johannes's reputation is based on his cures for the plague," Rudolf said.

"I was merely a vehicle for God's will. He is the only true healer," Pistorius said modestly. "Out of love for us, He created many natural remedies that can effect miraculous results in our imperfect bodies."

"Ah, yes. I remember your advocacy of bezoars as panaceas against illness. I sent La Diosa one of my stones when she was lately ill." Rudolf smiled at him approvingly.

Pistorius studied me. "Your cure evidently worked, Your Majesty."

"Yes. La Diosa is fully recovered. She looks very well," Rudolf said, his lower lip jutting out even further as he examined me. I wore a simple black gown embroidered in white covered with a black velvet robe. A gauzy ruff winged away from my face, and the red ruby of Matthew's salamander necklace was arranged to hang in the notch of my throat, providing the only splash of color in my otherwise somber outfit. Rudolf's attention fixed on the beautiful piece of jewelry. He frowned and motioned to a servant.

"It's hard to say whether the bezoar stone or Emperor Maximilian's electuary was the more beneficial," I said, looking to Dr. Hájek for assistance while Rudolf held his whispered conversation. He was tucking into the third game course, and after a startled cough to free the bit of venison he had just swallowed, Hájek rose to the occasion.

"I believe it was the electuary, Dr. Pistorius," Hájek admitted. "I prepared it in a cup made from the unicorn's horn. Emperor Rudolf believed this would increase its efficacy."

"La Diosa took the electuary from a horn spoon, too," Rudolf said, his eyes lingering on my lips now, "for additional surety."

"Will this cup and spoon be among the specimens we see tonight in your cabinet of wonders, Your Majesty?" Pistorius asked. The air between me and the other witch came to sudden, crackling life. Threads surrounding the physician-priest exploded in violent red and orange hues, warning me of the danger. Then he smiled. *I do not trust you, witch,* he whispered into my mind. *Nor does your would-be lover, Emperor Rudolf.*

The wild boar that I was chewing—a delicious dish flavored with rosemary and black pepper that, according to the emperor, was supposed to heat the blood—turned to dust in my mouth. Instead of its achieving its desired effect, my blood ran cold.

"Is something wrong?" Gallowglass murmured, bending low over my shoulder. He handed me a shawl, which I hadn't asked for and didn't know he was carrying.

"Pistorius has been invited upstairs to see the book," I said, turning my head toward him and speaking in rapid English to reduce the risk of being understood. Gallowglass smelled of sea salt and mint, a bracing and reassuring combination. My nerves steadied.

"Leave it to me," he replied, giving my shoulder a squeeze. "By the way, you're a bit shiny, Auntie. It would be best if no one saw stars tonight."

Having delivered his warning shot across the bow, Pistorius turned the conversation to other topics and engaged Dr. Hájek in a lively debate about the medical benefits of theriac. Rudolf divided his time between sneaking melancholic looks at me and glaring at Matthew. The closer we got to seeing Ashmole 782, the less appetite I had, so I made small talk with the noblewoman next to me. It was only after five more courses—including a parade of gilded peacocks and a tableau of roast pork and suckling pigs—that the banquet finally concluded.

"You look pale," Matthew said, whisking me away from the table.

"Pistorius suspects me." The man reminded me of Peter Knox and Champier, and for similar reasons. "Intellectual thug" was the perfect description for both of them. "Gallowglass said he would take care of it."

"No wonder Pierre followed on his heels, then."

"What is Pierre going to do?"

"Make sure Pistorius gets out of here alive," Matthew said cheerfully. "Left to his own devices, Gallowglass would strangle the man and throw him into the Stag's Moat for the lions' midnight snack. My nephew is almost as protective of you as I am."

Rudolf's invited guests accompanied him to his inner sanctum: the private gallery where Matthew and I viewed the Bosch altarpiece. Ottavio Strada met us there to guide us through the collection and answer our questions.

When we entered the room, Matthew's altarpiece still sat in the center of the green-covered table. Rudolf had scattered other objects around it for our viewing pleasure. While the guests oohed and aahed over Bosch's work, I scanned the room. There were some stunning cups made out of semiprecious stones, an enameled chain of office, a long horn reputedly from a unicorn, some statuary, and a carved Seychelles nut—a nice mix of the expensive, the medicinal, and the exotic. But no alchemical manuscript.

"Where is it?" I hissed to Matthew. Before he could respond, I felt the touch of a warm hand on my arm. Matthew stiffened.

"I have a gift for you, *querida diosa*." Rudolf's breath smelled of onions and red wine, and my stomach flopped over in protest. I turned, expecting to see Ashmole 782. Instead the emperor was holding up the enameled chain. Before I could protest, he draped it over my head and settled it on my shoulders. I looked down and saw a green ouroboros hanging from a circle of red crosses, thickly encrusted with emeralds, rubies, diamonds, and pearls. The color scheme reminded me of the jewel Herr Maisel gave to Benjamin.

"That is a strange gift to give my wife, Your Majesty," Matthew said softly. He was standing right behind the emperor and looking at the necklace with distaste. This was my third such chain, and I knew there must be a meaning behind the symbolism. I lifted the ouroboros so that I could study the enameling. It wasn't an ouroboros, exactly, because it had feet. It looked more like a lizard or a salamander than a snake. A bloody red cross emerged from the lizard's flayed back. Most important, the tail was not held in the creature's mouth but wrapped around the lizard's throat, strangling it.

"It is a mark of respect, Herr Roydon." Rudolf placed a subtle emphasis on the name. "This once belonged to King Vladislaus and was passed on to my grandmother. The insignia belongs to a brave company of Hungarian knights known as the Order of the Defeated Dragon."

"Dragon?" I said faintly, looking at Matthew. With its stumpy legs, this might well be a dragon. But it was otherwise strikingly similar to the de

Clermont family's emblem—except this ouroboros was dying a slow, painful death. I remembered Herr Fuchs's oath—Benjamin's oath—to slay dragons wherever he found them.

"The dragon symbolizes our enemies, especially those who might wish to interfere with our royal prerogatives." Rudolf said it in a civilized tone, but it was a virtual declaration of war on the whole de Clermont clan. "It would please me if you would wear it next time you come to court." Rudolf's finger touched the dragon at my breast lightly and lingered there. "Then you can leave your little French salamanders at home."

Matthew's eyes, which were glued to the dragon and the imperial finger, went black when Rudolf made his insulting remark about French salamanders. I tried to think like Mary Sidney and come up with a response that was appropriate for the period and likely to calm the vampire. I'd deal with my outraged sense of feminism later.

"Whether or not I wear your gift will be up to my husband, Your Majesty," I said coolly, forcing myself not to step away from Rudolf's finger. I heard gasps, a few hushed whispers. But the only reaction I cared about was Matthew's.

"I see no reason you should not wear it for the rest of the evening, *mon coeur,*" Matthew said agreeably. He was no longer concerned that the queen of England's ambassador sounded like a French aristocrat. "Salamanders and dragons are kin, after all. Both will endure the flames to protect those they love. And the emperor is being kind enough to show you his book." Matthew looked around. "Though it seems Signor Strada's incompetency continues, for the book is not here." Another bridge burned behind us.

"Not yet, not yet," Rudolf said testily. "I have something else to present to La Diosa first. Go see my carved nut from the Maldives. It is the only one of its kind." Everybody but Matthew trooped off obediently in the direction of Strada's pointing finger. "You, too, Herr Roydon."

"Of course," Matthew murmured, imitating his mother's tone perfectly. He slowly trailed after the crowd.

"Here is something I requested especially. Father Johannes helped to procure the treasure." Rudolf looked around the room but failed to locate Pistorius. He frowned. "Where has he gone, Signor Strada?"

"I have not seen him since we left the Great Hall, Your Majesty," Strada replied.

"You!" Rudolf pointed to a servant. "Go and find him!" The man left immediately, and at a run. The emperor gathered his composure and returned his attention to the strange object in front of us. It looked like a crude carving of a naked man. "This, La Diosa, is a fabled root from Eppendorf. A century ago a woman stole a consecrated host from the church and planted it by the light of the full moon to increase her garden's fertility. The next morning they discovered an enormous cabbage."

"Growing out of the host?" Surely something was being lost in translation, unless I very much misunderstood the nature of the Christian Eucharist. An *arbor Dianæ* was one thing. An *arbor brassicæ* was quite another.

"Yes. It was a miracle. And when the cabbage was dug up, its root resembled the body of Christ." Rudolf held out the item to me. It was crowned with a golden diadem studded with pearls. Presumably that had been added later.

"Fascinating," I said, trying to look and sound interested.

"I wanted you to see it in part because it resembles a picture in the book you requested. Fetch Edward, Ottavio."

Edward Kelley entered, clutching a leather-bound volume to his chest.

As soon as I saw it, I knew. My entire body was tingling while the book was still across the room. Its power was palpable—far more so than it had been at the Bodleian on that September night when my whole life changed.

Here was the missing Ashmole manuscript—before it belonged to Elias Ashmole and before it went missing.

"You will sit here, with me, and we will look at the book together." Rudolf gestured toward a table and two chairs that were set up in an intimate tête-à-tête. "Give me the book, Edward." Rudolf held out his hand, and Kelley reluctantly placed the book in it.

I shot Matthew a questioning look. What if the manuscript started to glow as it had in the Bodleian or behaved strangely in some other way? And what if I weren't able to stop my mind from wondering about the book or its secrets? An eruption of magic at this point would be disastrous.

This is why we're here, said his confident nod.

I sat down next to the emperor, and Strada ushered the courtiers around the room to the unicorn's horn. Matthew drifted still closer. I stared at the book in front of me, hardly daring to believe that the moment had come when I would at last see Ashmole 782 whole and complete.

"Well?" Rudolf demanded. "Are you going to open it?"

"Of course," I said, pulling the book closer. No iridescence escaped from the pages. For purposes of comparison, I rested my hand on the cover for just a moment, as I had when I'd retrieved Ashmole 782 from the stacks.

Then it had sighed in recognition, as though it had been waiting for me to show up. This time the book lay still.

I flipped open the hide-bound wooden board of the front cover, revealing a blank sheet of parchment. My mind raced back over what I'd seen months ago. This was the sheet on which Ashmole and my father would one day write the book's title.

I turned the page and felt the same sense of uncanny heaviness. When the page fell open, I gasped.

The first, missing page of Ashmole 782 was a glorious illumination of a tree. The tree's trunk was knotted and gnarled, thick and yet sinuous. Branches sprang from the top, twisting and turning their way across the page and ending in a defiant combination of leaves, bright red fruit, and flowers. It was like the *arbor Dianæ* that Mary had made using blood drawn from Matthew and me.

When I bent closer, my breath caught in my throat. The tree's trunk was not made of wood, sap, and bark. It was made of hundreds of bodies—some writhing and thrashing in pain, some serenely entwined, others alone and frightened.

At the bottom of the page, written in a late-thirteenth-century hand, was the title Roger Bacon had given it: *The True Secret of Secrets.*

Matthew's nostrils flared, as though he were trying to identify a scent. The book did have a strange odor—the same musty smell that I had noticed at Oxford.

I turned the page. Here was the image sent to my parents, the one the Bishop house had saved for so many years: the phoenix enfolding the chemical wedding in her wings, while mythical and alchemical beasts witnessed the union of Sol and Luna.

Matthew looked shocked, and he was now staring at the book. I frowned. He was still too far away to see it clearly. What had surprised him?

Quickly, I flipped over the image of the alchemical wedding. The third missing page turned out to be two alchemical dragons, their tails intertwined and their bodies locked in either a battle or an embrace—it was impossible to tell which. A rain of blood fell from their wounds, pooling in a basin from which sprang dozens of naked, pale figures. I'd never seen an alchemical image like it.

Matthew stood over the emperor's shoulder, and I expected his shock to turn to excitement at seeing these new images and getting closer to solving the book's mysteries. But he looked as if he'd seen a ghost. A white hand covered his mouth and nose. When I frowned with concern, Matthew nodded to me, a sign that I should keep going.

I took a deep breath and turned to what should be the first of the strange alchemical images I'd seen in Oxford. Here, as expected, was the baby girl with the two roses. What was unexpected was that every inch of space around her was covered in text. It was an odd mix of symbols and a few scattered letters. In the Bodleian this text had been hidden by a spell that transformed the book into a magical palimpsest. Now, with the book intact, the secret text was on full view. Though I could see it, I still couldn't read it.

My fingers traced the lines of text. My touch unmade the words, transforming them into a face, a silhouette, a name. It was as though the text were trying to tell a story involving thousands of creatures.

"I would have given you anything you asked for," Rudolf said, his breath hot against my cheek. Once again I smelled onions and wine. It was so unlike Matthew's clean, spicy scent. And Rudolf's warmth was off-putting now that I was used to a vampire's cool temperature. "Why did you choose this? It cannot be understood, though Edward believes it contains a great secret."

A long arm reached between us and gently touched the page. "Why, this is as meaningless as the manuscript you foisted off on poor Dr. Dee." Matthew's face belied his words. Rudolf might not have seen the muscle ticking in Matthew's jaw or known how the fine lines around his eyes deepened when he concentrated.

"Not necessarily," I said hastily. "Alchemical texts require study and contemplation if you wish to understand them fully. Perhaps if I spent more time with it . . ."

"Even then one must have God's special blessing," Rudolf said, scowling at Matthew. "Edward is touched by God in ways you are not, Herr Roydon."

"Oh, he's touched all right," Matthew said, looking over at Kelley. The English alchemist was acting strange now that the book was not in his possession. There were threads connecting him and the book. But why was Kelley bound to Ashmole 782?

As the question went through my mind, the fine yellow and white threads tying Kelley to Ashmole 782 took on a new appearance. Instead of the normal tight twist of two colors or a weave of horizontal and vertical threads, these spooled loosely around an invisible center, like the curling ribbons on a birthday present. Short, horizontal threads kept the curls from touching. It looked like—

A double helix. My hand rose to my mouth, and I stared down at the manuscript. Now that I'd touched the book, its musty smell was on my fingers. It was strong, gamy, like—

Flesh and blood. I looked to Matthew, knowing that the expression on my face mirrored the shocked look I had seen on his.

"You don't look well, *mon coeur,*" he said solicitously, helping me to my feet. "Let me take you home." Edward Kelley chose this moment to lose control.

"I hear their voices. They speak in tongues I cannot understand. Can you hear them?"

He moaned in distress, his hands clapped over his ears.

"What are you chattering about?" Rudolf said. "Dr. Hájek, something is wrong with Edward."

"You will find your name in it, too," Edward told me, his voice getting louder, as if he were trying to drown out some other sound. "I knew it the moment I saw you."

I looked down. Curling threads bound me to the book, too—only mine were white and lavender. Matthew was bound to it by curling strands of red and white.

Gallowglass appeared, unannounced and uninvited. A burly guard followed him, clutching at his own limp arm.

"The horses are ready," Gallowglass informed us, gesturing toward the exit.

"You do not have permission to be here!" Rudolf shouted, his fury mounting as his careful arrangements disintegrated. "And you, La Diosa, do not have permission to leave."

Matthew paid absolutely no attention to Rudolf. He simply took my arm and strode in the direction of the door. I could feel the manuscript pulling on me, the threads stretching to bring me back to its side.

"We can't leave the book. It's—"

"I know what it is," Matthew said grimly.

"Stop them!" Rudolf screamed.

But the guard with the broken arm had already tangled with one angry vampire tonight. He wasn't going to tempt fate by interfering with Matthew. Instead his eyes rolled up into his head and he dropped to the floor in a faint.

Gallowglass threw my cloak over my shoulders as we pelted down the stairs. Two more guards—both unconscious—lay at the bottom.

"Go back and get the book!" I ordered Gallowglass, breathless from my constrictive corset and the speed at which we were moving across the courtyard. "We can't let Rudolf have it now that we know what it is."

Matthew stopped, his fingers digging into my arm. "We won't leave Prague without the manuscript. I'll go back and get it, I promise. But first we are going home. You must have the children ready to leave the moment I get back."

"We've burned our bridges, Auntie," Gallowglass said grimly. "Pistorius is locked up in the White Tower. I killed one guard and injured three more. Rudolf touched you most improperly, and I have a strong desire to see him dead, too."

"You don't understand, Gallowglass. That book may be the answer to *everything,*" I managed to squeak out before Matthew had me in motion again.

"Oh, I understand more than you think I do." Gallowglass's voice floated in the breeze next to me. "I picked up the scent of it downstairs when I knocked out the guards. There are dead *wearhs* in that book. Witches and daemons, too, I warrant. Whoever could have imagined that the lost Book of Life would stink to high heaven of death?"

32

"Who would make such a thing?" Twenty minutes later I was shivering by the fireplace in our main first-floor room, clutching a beaker of herbal tea. "It's gruesome."

Like most manuscripts, Ashmole 782 was made of vellum—specially prepared skin that had been soaked in lime to remove the hair, scraped to take away the subcutaneous layers of flesh and fat, then soaked again before being stretched on a frame and scraped some more.

The difference here was that the creatures used to make the vellum were not sheep, calves, or goats but daemons, vampires, and witches.

"It must have been kept as a record." Matthew was still trying to come to terms with what we had seen.

"But it has hundreds of pages," I said in disbelief. The thought of someone flaying so many daemons, vampires, and witches and making vellum from their skins was incomprehensible. I wasn't sure I would ever sleep through the night again.

"Which means the book contains hundreds of distinct pieces of DNA." Matthew had run his fingers through his hair so many times he was starting to resemble a porcupine.

"The threads twisting between us and Ashmole 782 looked like double helices," I said. We'd had to explain modern genetics to Gallowglass, who, without the intervening four and a half centuries of biology and chemistry, was doing his best to follow it.

"So D-N-A is like a family tree, but its branches cover more than just one family?" Gallowglass sounded out "DNA" slowly, with a break between each letter.

"Yes," Matthew said. "That's about it."

"Did you see the tree on the first page?" I asked Matthew. "The trunk was made of bodies, and the tree was flowering, fruiting, and leafing out just like the *arbor Dianæ* we made in Mary's laboratory."

"No, but I saw the creature with its tail in its mouth," Matthew said.

I tried feverishly to recall what I'd seen, but my photographic memory failed me when I needed it most. There was too much new information to absorb.

"The picture showed two creatures fighting—or embracing, I couldn't tell which. I didn't have a chance to count their legs. Their falling blood was generating hundreds of creatures. Although if one of them was not a four-legged dragon but a snake . . ."

"And one was a two-legged firedrake, then those alchemical dragons could symbolize you and me." Matthew swore, briefly but with feeling.

Gallowglass listened patiently until we were through, then went back to his original topic. "And this D-N-A, it lives in our skin?"

"Not just your skin, but your blood, bones, hair, nails—it's throughout your entire body," Matthew explained.

"Huh." Gallowglass rubbed his chin. "And what question is it you have in mind, exactly, when you say this book might have all the answers?"

"Why we're different from the humans," Matthew said simply. "And why a witch like Diana might carry a *wearh*'s child."

Gallowglass gave us a radiant smile. "You mean your child, Matthew. I knew full well Auntie was capable of that back in London. She never smelled like anyone but herself—and you. Did Philippe know?"

"Few people knew," I said quickly.

"Hancock did. So did Françoise and Pierre. My guess is Philippe was told all about it." Gallowglass stood. "I'll just go fetch Auntie's book, then. If it has to do with de Clermont babes, we must have it."

"Rudolf will have locked it up tight or tucked it into bed with him," Matthew predicted. "It's not going to be easy to take it from the palace, especially not if they've found Pistorius and he's out casting spells and making mischief."

"Speaking of Emperor Rudolf, can we get that necklace off Auntie's shoulders? I hate that bloody insignia."

"Gladly," I said, plucking at the chain and tossing the garish object onto the table. "What, exactly, does the Order of the Defeated Dragon have to do with the de Clermonts? I assume that they must not be friends with the Knights of Lazarus, given the fact that the poor ouroboros has been partially skinned and is strangling itself."

"They hate us and wish us dead," Matthew said flatly. "The Drăculeşti disapprove of my father's broad-minded views on Islam and the Ottomans and have vowed to bring us all down. That way they can fulfill their political aspirations unchecked."

"And they want the de Clermont money," Gallowglass observed.

"The Drăculeşti?" My voice was faint. "But Dracula is a human myth—one meant to spread fear about vampires." It was *the* human myth about vampires.

"That would come as some surprise to the patriarch of the clan, Vlad the Dragon," Gallowglass commented, "though he would be pleased to know he will go on terrifying people."

"The humans' Dracula—the Dragon's son known as the Impaler—was only one of Vlad's brood," Matthew explained.

"The Impaler was a nasty bastard. Happily, he's dead now, and all we have to worry about are his father, his brothers, and their Báthory allies." Gallowglass looked somewhat cheered.

"According to human accounts, Dracula lived on for centuries—he may still be living. Are you sure he's really dead?" I asked.

"I watched Baldwin rip his head off and bury it thirty miles away from the rest of his body. He was really dead then, and he's really dead now." Gallowglass looked at me reprovingly. "You should know better than to believe these human stories, Auntie. They've never got more than a speck of truth in them."

"I think Benjamin had one of these dragon emblems. Herr Maisel gave it to him. I noticed the similarity in colors when the emperor first held it out."

"You told me Benjamin left Hungary," Matthew said accusingly to his nephew.

"He did. I swear it. Baldwin ordered him to leave or face the same fate as the Impaler. You should have seen Baldwin's face. The devil himself wouldn't have disobeyed your brother."

"I want us all as far from Prague as possible by the time the sun rises," Matthew said grimly. "Something is very wrong. I can smell it."

"That may not be such a good idea. Do you not know what night it is?" Gallowglass asked. Matthew shook his head. "Walpurgisnacht. They are lighting bonfires all around the city and burning effigies of witches—unless they can find a real one, of course."

"Christ." Matthew drove his fingers through his hair, giving it a good shake as he did. "At least the fires will provide some distraction. We have to figure out how to circumvent Rudolf's guards, get into his private chambers, and find the book. Then, fires or no fires, we are getting out of the city."

"We're *wearhs,* Matthew. If anyone can steal it, we can," Gallowglass said confidently.

"It's not going to be as easy as you think. We may get in, but will we get out?"

"I can help, Master Roydon." Jack's voice sounded like a flute compared to Gallowglass's rumbling bass and Matthew's baritone. Matthew turned and scowled at him.

"No, Jack," he said firmly. "You aren't to steal anything, remember? Besides, you've only been to the palace stables. You wouldn't have any idea where to look."

"Er . . . that's not strictly true." Gallowglass looked uncomfortable. "I took him to the cathedral. And the Great Hall to see the cartoons you once drew on the walls of the Knights' Staircase. And he's been to the kitchens. Oh," Gallowglass said as an afterthought, "Jack went to the menagerie, too, of course. It would have been cruel not to let him see the animals."

"He has been to the castle with me as well," Pierre said from the doorway. "I didn't want him to go adventuring one day and get lost."

"And where did *you* take him, Pierre?" Matthew's tone was icy. "The throne room, so he could jump up and down on the royal seat?"

"No, *milord.* I took him to the blacksmith's shop and to meet Master Hoefnagel." Pierre drew himself up to his full, relatively diminutive height and stared his employer down. "I thought he should show his drawings to someone with real skill in these matters. Master Hoefnagel was most impressed and drew a pen-and-ink portrait of him on the spot for a reward."

"Pierre also took me to the guards' chamber," Jack said in a small voice. "That's where I got these." He held up a ring of keys. "I only wanted to see the unicorn, for I couldn't imagine how a unicorn climbed the stairs and thought they must have wings. Then Master Gallowglass showed me the Knights' Staircase—I like your drawing of the running deer very much, Master Roydon. The guards were talking. I couldn't understand everything, but the word *einhorn* stuck out, and I thought maybe they knew where it was, and—"

Matthew took Jack by the shoulders and crouched down so that their eyes met. "Do you know what they would have done if they'd caught you?" My husband looked as fearful as the child did.

Jack nodded.

"And seeing a unicorn was worth being beaten?"

"I've been beaten before. But I've never seen a magical beast. Except for the lion in the emperor's menagerie. And Mistress Roydon's dragon." Jack looked horrified and clapped his hand over his mouth.

"So you've seen that, too? Prague has been an eye-opening experience for all concerned, then." Matthew stood and held out his hand. "Give me the keys." Jack did so, reluctantly. Matthew bowed to the boy. "I am in your debt, Jack."

"But I was bad," Jack whispered. He rubbed his backside, as if he had already felt the punishment Matthew was bound to dole out.

"I'm bad all the time," Matthew confessed. "Sometimes good comes of it."

"Yes, but nobody beats *you,*" Jack said, still trying to understand this strange world where grown men were in debt to little boys and his hero was not perfect after all.

"Matthew's father beat him with a sword once. I saw it." The firedrake's wings fluttered softly within my rib cage in silent agreement. "Then he knocked him over and stood on him."

"He must be as big as the emperor's bear Sixtus," Jack said, awed at the thought of anyone conquering Matthew.

"He is," Matthew said, growling like the bear in question. "Back to bed. Now."

"But I'm nimble—and quick," Jack protested. "I can get Mistress Roydon's book without anyone seeing me."

"So can I, Jack," Matthew promised.

Matthew and Gallowglass returned from the palace covered with blood, dirt, and soot—and bearing Ashmole 782.

"You got it!" I cried. Annie and I were waiting on the first floor. We had small bags packed with traveling essentials.

Matthew opened the cover. "The first three pages are gone."

The book that had been whole just hours before was now broken, the text racing across the page. I'd planned on running my fingers over the letters and symbols once it was in our possession to determine its meaning. Now that was impossible. As soon as my fingertips touched the page, the words skittered in every direction.

"We found Kelley with the book. He was bent over it and crooning like a madman." Matthew paused. "The book was talking back."

"He tells you true, Auntie. I heard the words, though I couldn't make them out."

"Then the book really is alive," I murmured.

"And really dead, too," Gallowglass said, touching the binding. "It's an evil thing as well as a powerful one."

"When Kelley spotted us, he screamed at the top of his lungs and started ripping pages from the book. Before I could reach him, the guards were there. I had to choose between the book and Kelley." Matthew hesitated. "Did I do the right thing?"

"I think so," I said. "When I found the book in England, it was broken. And it may be easier to find the fugitive pages in the future than it would be now." Modern search engines and library catalogs would be enormously helpful since I knew what I was seeking.

"Provided the pages weren't destroyed," Matthew said. "If that's the case . . ."

"Then we'll never know all of the book's secrets. Even so, your modern laboratory might reveal more about what's left than we imagined when we set out on this quest."

"So you're ready to go back?" Matthew asked. There was a spark of something in his eye. He smothered it quickly. Was it excitement? Dread?

I nodded. "It's time."

We fled Prague by the light of the bonfires. Our fellow creatures were in hiding on Walpurgisnacht, not wanting to be seen by the revelers in case they found themselves flung onto the pyre.

The frigid waters of the North Sea were just navigable, and the spring thaw had broken up the ice in the harbors. Boats were leaving the ports for England, and we were able to catch one without delay. Even so, the weather was stormy when we pulled away from the European shore.

In our cabin belowdecks, I found Matthew studying the book. He had discovered that it was sewn together with long strands of hair.

"Dieu," he murmured, "how much more genetic information might this thing contain?" Before I could stop him, he touched the tip of his pinkie to his tongue and then to the drops of blood showering down from the baby's hair on the first extant page.

"Matthew!" I said, horrified.

"Just as I thought. The inks contain blood. And if that's the case, my guess is that the gold and silver leaf on these illustrations is applied to a glue base made from bones. Creature bones."

The boat lurched leeward, and my stomach went along with it. When I was through being sick, Matthew held me in his arms. The book lay between us, slightly open, the lines of text searching to find their place in the order of things.

"What have we done?" I whispered.

"We've found the Tree of Life and the Book of Life, all wrapped up in one." Matthew rested his cheek on my hair.

"When Peter Knox told me the book held all the witches' original spells, I told him he was mad. I couldn't imagine anyone being so foolish as to put so much knowledge in one place." I touched the book. "But this book contains so much more—and we still don't know what the words say. If this were to fall into the wrong hands in our own time—"

"It could be used to destroy us all," Matthew finished.

I craned my head to look at him. "What are we going to do with it, then? Take it back with us to the future or leave it here?"

"I don't know, *mon coeur*." He gathered me closer, muffling the sound of the storm as it lashed against the hull.

"But this book may well hold the key to all your questions." I was surprised that Matthew could part with it now that he knew what it contained.

"Not all," he said. "There's one only you can answer."

"What's that?" I asked with a frown.

"Are you seasick or are you with child?" Matthew's eyes were as heavy and stormy as the sky, with glints of bright lightning.

"You would know better than I." We had made love only a few days ago, soon after I realized that my period was late.

"I didn't see the child in your blood or hear its heart—not yet. It's the change in your scent that I noticed. I remember it from last time. You can't be more than a few weeks pregnant."

"I would have thought my being pregnant would make you more eager than ever to keep the book with you."

"Maybe my questions don't need answers as urgently as I thought they did." To prove his point, Matthew put the book on the floor, out of sight. "I thought it would tell me who I am and why I'm here. Perhaps I already know."

I waited for him to explain.

"After all my searching, I discover that I am who I always was: Matthew de Clermont. Husband. Father. Vampire. And I am here for only one reason: To make a difference."

33

Peter Knox dodged the puddles in the courtyard of the Strahov Monastery in Prague. He was on his annual spring circuit of libraries in central and Eastern Europe. When the tourists and scholars were at their lowest ebb, Knox went from one old repository to another, making sure that nothing untoward had turned up in the past twelve months that might cause the Congregation—or him—trouble. In each library he had a trusted informant, a member of staff who was of sufficiently high standing to have free access to the books and manuscripts, but not so elevated that he might later be required to take a principled stand against library treasures simply . . . disappearing.

Knox had been making regular visits like this since he'd finished his doctorate and begun working for the Congregation. Much had changed since World War II, and the Congregation's administrative structure had adjusted to the times. With the transportation revolution of the nineteenth century, trains and roads allowed a new style of governance, with each species policing its own kind rather than overseeing a geographic location. It meant a lot of traveling and letter writing, both possible in the Age of Steam. Philippe de Clermont had been instrumental in modernizing the Congregation's operations, though Knox had long suspected he did it more to protect vampire secrets than to promote progress.

Then the world wars disrupted communications and transportation networks, and the Congregation reverted to its old ways. It was more sensible to break up the globe into slices than to crisscross it tracking down a specific individual accused of wrongdoing. No one would have dared to suggest such a radical change when Philippe was alive. Happily, the former head of the de Clermont family was no longer around to resist. The Internet and e-mail threatened to make such trips unnecessary, but Knox liked tradition.

Knox's mole at the Strahov Library was a middle-aged man named Pavel Skovajsa. He was brown all over, like foxed paper, and wore a pair of Communist-era glasses that he refused to replace, though it was unclear whether his reluctance was for historical or sentimental reasons. Usually the two men met in the monastery brewery, which had gleaming copper tanks and served an excellent amber beer named after St. Norbert, whose earthly remains rested nearby.

But this year Skovajsa had actually found something.

"It is a letter. In Hebrew," Skovajsa had whispered down the phone line. He was suspicious of new technology, didn't have a cell phone, and detested e-mail. That's why he was employed in the conservation department, where his idiosyncratic approach to knowledge wouldn't slow the library's steady march toward modernity.

"Why are you whispering, Pavel?" Knox had asked in irritation. The only problem with Skovajsa was that he liked to think of himself as a spy hewn from the ice of the Cold War. As a result he was a tad paranoid.

"Because I took a book apart to get at it. Someone hid it underneath the endpapers of a copy of Johannes Reuchlin's *De Arte Cabalistica*," Skovajsa explained, his excitement mounting. Knox looked at his watch. It was so early that he hadn't had his coffee yet. "You must come, at once. It mentions alchemy and that Englishman who worked for Rudolf II. It may be important."

Knox was on the next flight out of Berlin. And now Skovajsa had spirited him away to a dingy room in the basement of the library illuminated by a single bare lightbulb.

"Isn't there somewhere more comfortable for us to conduct business?" Knox said, eyeing the metal table (also Communist-era) with suspicion. "Is that goulash?" He pointed to a sticky spot on its surface.

"The walls have ears, and the floors have eyes." Skovajsa wiped at the spot with the hem of his brown sweater. "We are safer here. Sit. Let me bring you the letter."

"And the book," Knox said sharply. Skovajsa turned, surprised at his tone.

"Yes, of course. The book, too."

"That isn't *On the Art of Kabbalah*," Knox said when Skovajsa returned, growing more irritated with each passing moment. Johannes Reuchlin's book was slim and elegant. This monstrosity had to be nearly eight hundred pages long. When it hit the table, the impact reverberated across the top and down the metal legs.

"Not exactly," Skovajsa said defensively. "It's Galatino's *De Arcanis Catholicae Veritatis*. But the Reuchlin is in it." A cavalier approach to precise bibliographic details was one of Knox's bêtes noires.

"The title page has inscriptions in Hebrew, Latin, and French." Skovajsa flung open the cover. Since there was nothing to support the spine of the large tome, Knox was not surprised to hear an ominous crack. He looked at Skovajsa in alarm. "Don't worry," the conservationist reassured him, "it isn't cataloged. I only discovered it because it was shelved next to our other copy, which was due to go out for rebinding. It probably came here by mistake when our books were returned in 1989."

Knox dutifully examined the title page and its inscriptions.

> בנימין זאב יטרף בבקר יאכל עד ולערב יחלק שלל Genesis 49:27
>
> *Beniamin lupus rapax mane comedet praedam et vespere dividet spolia.*
>
> *Benjamin est un loup qui déchire; au matin il dévore la proie, et sur le soir il partage le butin.*

"It is an old hand, is it not? And the owner was clearly well educated," Skovajsa said.

"*'Benjamin shall raven as a wolf: in the morning he shall devour the prey, and at night he shall divide the spoil,'*" Knox mused. He couldn't imagine what these verses had to do with *De Arcanis.* Galatino's work contributed a single shot in the Catholic Church's war against Jewish mysticism—the same war that had led to book burnings, inquisitorial proceedings, and witch-hunts in the sixteenth century. Galatino's position on these matters was given away by his title: *Concerning Secrets of the Universal Truth.* In a nifty bit of intellectual acrobatics, Galatino argued that the Jews had anticipated Christian doctrines and that the study of kabbalah could help Catholic efforts to convert the Jews to the true faith.

"Perhaps the owner's name was Benjamin?" Skovajsa looked over his shoulder and passed Knox a file. Knox was happy to see that it was not stamped TOP SECRET in red letters. "And here is the letter. I do not know Hebrew, but the name Edwardus Kellaeus and alchemy—*alchymia*—are in Latin."

Knox turned the page. He was dreaming. He had to be. The letter was dated from the second day of Elul 5369—1 September 1609 in the Christian calendar. And it was signed Yehuda ben Bezalel, a man most knew as Rabbi Judah Loew.

"You know Hebrew, yes?" Skovajsa said.

"Yes." This time it was Knox who was whispering. "Yes," he said more strongly. He stared at the letter.

"Well?" Skovajsa said after nearly a minute of silence had passed. "What does it say?"

"It seems that a Jew from Prague met Edward Kelley and was writing to a friend to tell him so." It was true—in a way.

"Long life and peace to you, Benjamin, son of Gabriel, cherished friend," Rabbi Loew wrote.

> *I received your letter from my birth city with great joy. Poznań is a better place for you than Hungary, where nothing awaits you but misery. Though I am an old man, your letter brought back clearly the strange events that occurred in the spring of 5351 when Edwardus Kellaeus, student of alchymia and beloved of the emperor, came to me. He raved about a man he had killed and that the emperor's guards would soon arrest him for murder and treason. He foresaw his own death, crying out, "I will fall like the angels into hell." He also spoke of this book you seek, which was stolen from Emperor Rudolf, as you know. Kellaeus sometimes called it the Book of Creation and sometimes the Book of Life. Kellaeus wept, saying that the end of the world was upon us. He kept repeating omens, such as "It begins with absence and desire," "It begins with blood and fear," "It begins with a discovery of witches," and so forth.*
>
> *In his madness Kellaeus had removed three pages from this Book of Life even before it was taken from the emperor. He gave one leaf to me. Kellaeus would not tell me to whom he had given the other pages, speaking in riddles about the angel of death and the angel of life. Alas, I do not know the book's present whereabouts. I no longer have my leaf from it, having given it to Abraham ben Elijah for safekeeping. He died of the pestilence, and the page may be forever lost. The only one who might be able to shed light on the mystery is your maker. May your interest in healing this broken book extend to healing your broken lineage so that you might find peace with the Father who gave you life and breath. The Lord guard your spirit, from your loving friend Yehuda of the holy city of Prague, son of Bezalel, 2nd of the month Elul 5369*

"That's all?" Skovajsa said after another long pause. "It's just about a meeting?"

"In essence." Knox made rapid calculations on the back of the folder. Loew died in 1609. Kelley visited him eighteen years before that. *Spring 1591.* He dug in his pocket for his phone and looked at the display in disgust. "Don't you get a signal up here?"

"We're underground," Skovajsa said, shrugging as he pointed to the thick walls. "So was I right to tell you about this?" He licked his lips in anticipation.

"You did well, Pavel. I'm taking the letter. And the book." They were the only items Knox had ever removed from the Strahov Library.

"Good. I thought it was worth your time, what with the mention of alchemy." Pavel grinned.

What happened next was regrettable. Skovajsa had the misfortune, after years of rooting about without success, of finding something precious to Knox. With a few words and a small gesture, Knox made sure Pavel would never be able to share what he had seen with another creature. For sentimental and ethical reasons, Knox didn't kill him. That would have been a vampire's response, as he knew from finding Gillian Chamberlain propped up against his door at the Randolph Hotel last autumn. Being a witch, he simply freed the clot already lurking in Skovajsa's thigh so it could travel up to his brain. Once there, it caused a massive stroke. It would be hours before someone found him, and too late for any good to come of it.

Knox found his way back to his rental car with the biblically proportioned book and the letter safely tucked under his arm. Once he was far enough from the Strahov complex, he pulled over to the side of the road and took out the letter, his hands shaking.

Everything the Congregation knew about the mysterious book of origins—Ashmole 782—was based on fragments such as this. Any new discovery dramatically increased their knowledge. And this letter contained more than just a brief description of the book and some veiled hints as to its significance. There were names and dates and the startling revelation that the book Diana Bishop had seen in Oxford was missing three pages.

Knox looked over the letter again. He wanted to know more—to squeeze every potentially useful bit of information from it. This time certain words and phrases stood out: *your broken lineage; the Father who gave you life and breath; your maker.* On the first reading, Knox assumed that

Loew was talking about God. Upon the second he came to a very different conclusion. Knox picked up his phone and punched in a single number.

"Oui."

"Who is Benjamin ben Gabriel?" Knox demanded.

There was a moment of complete silence.

"Hello, Peter," said Gerbert of Aurillac. Knox's free hand curled into a fist at the bland response. This was so typical of the vampires on the Congregation. They talked about honesty and cooperation, but they had lived too long and knew too much. And, like all predators, they weren't eager to share their spoils.

"*'Benjamin shall raven like a wolf.'* I know Benjamin ben Gabriel is a vampire. Who is he?"

"No one of importance."

"Do you know what happened in Prague in 1591?" Knox asked tightly.

"A great many things. You cannot expect me to rehearse every event for you, like a grammar-school history teacher."

Knox heard a faint tremble in Gerbert's voice, something that only someone who knew the man well would catch. Gerbert, the venerable vampire who was never at a loss for words, was nervous.

"Dr. Dee's assistant, Edward Kelley, was in the city in 1591."

"We've been over this before. It's true, the Congregation once believed that Ashmole 782 might have been in Dee's library. But I met with Edward Kelley in Prague when those suspicions first surfaced in the spring of 1586. Dr. Dee had a book full of pictures. It wasn't ours. Since then we've tracked down every item from Dee's library just to be sure. Elias Ashmole didn't come into possession of the manuscript through Dee or Kelley."

"You're wrong. Kelley had the book in May 1591." Knox paused. "And he took it apart. The book Diana Bishop saw in Oxford was missing three pages."

"What do you know, Peter?" Gerbert said sharply.

"What do *you* know, Gerbert?" Knox didn't like the vampire, but they had been allies for years. Both men understood that cataclysmic change was coming to their world. In the aftermath there would be winners and losers. Neither man had any intention of being on the losing side.

"Benjamin ben Gabriel is Matthew Clairmont's son," Gerbert said reluctantly.

"His son?" Knox repeated numbly. Benjamin de Clermont was on none of the elaborate vampire genealogies the Congregation kept.

"Yes. But Benjamin disowned his bloodline. It is not something that a vampire does lightly, for the rest of the family is likely to kill him to protect their secrets. Matthew forbade any de Clermont to take his son's life. And no one has caught a glimpse of Benjamin since the nineteenth century, when he disappeared in Jerusalem."

The bottom dropped out of Knox's world. Matthew Clairmont couldn't be allowed to have Ashmole 782. Not if it held the witches' most cherished lore.

"Well, we're going to have to find him," Knox said grimly, "because according to this letter Edward Kelley scattered the three pages. One he gave to Rabbi Loew, who passed it on to someone called Abraham ben Elijah of Chelm."

"Abraham ben Elijah was once known as a very powerful witch. Do you creatures know anything about your own history?"

"We know not to trust vampires. I'd always dismissed that prejudice as histrionics, not history, but now I'm not so sure." Knox paused. "Loew told Benjamin to ask his father for help. I knew that de Clermont was hiding something. We have to find Benjamin de Clermont and make him tell us what he—and his father—know about Ashmole 782."

"Benjamin de Clermont is a volatile young man. He was afflicted with the same illness that plagued Matthew's sister Louisa." The vampires called it blood rage, and the Congregation wondered if the disease was not somehow related to the new illness afflicting vampires—the one that was resulting in so many warmblooded deaths after failed attempts to make new vampires. "If there really are three lost sheets from Ashmole 782, we will find them without his help. It will be better that way."

"No. It's time for the vampires to yield their secrets." Knox knew that the success or failure of their plans might well depend on this unstable branch of the de Clermont family tree. He looked at the letter once more. Loew was clear that he had wanted Benjamin to heal not only the book but his relationship with his family. Matthew Clairmont might know more about this business than any of them suspected.

"I suppose you'll be wanting to timewalk to Rudolphine Prague now to look for Edward Kelley," Gerbert grumbled, trying to stifle an impatient sigh. Witches could be so impulsive.

"On the contrary. I'm going to Sept-Tours."

Gerbert snorted. Storming the de Clermont family château was an even more ridiculous idea than going back to the past.

"Tempting though that might be, it isn't wise. Baldwin turns a blind eye only because of the rift between him and Matthew." It was Philippe's only strategic failure, so far as Gerbert could remember, to hand over the Knights of Lazarus to Matthew rather than to the elder son who had always thought he was entitled to the position. "Besides, Benjamin no longer considers himself a de Clermont—and the de Clermonts certainly don't believe he's one of theirs. The last place we would find him is Sept-Tours."

"For all we know, Matthew de Clermont has had one of the missing pages in his possession for centuries. The book is of no use to us if it's incomplete. Besides, it's time that vampire pays for his sins—and those of his mother and father, too." Together they had been responsible for the deaths of thousands of witches. Let the vampires worry about placating Baldwin. Knox had justice on his side.

"Don't forget the sins of his lover," Gerbert said, his voice vicious. "I miss my Juliette. Diana Bishop owes me a life for the one she took."

"I have your support, then?" Knox didn't care one way or the other. He'd be leading a raiding party of witches against the de Clermont stronghold before the week's end, with or without Gerbert's help.

"You do," Gerbert agreed reluctantly. "They are all gathering there, you know. The witches. The vampires. There are even a few daemons inside. They are calling themselves the Conventicle. Marcus sent a message to the vampires on the Congregation demanding that the covenant be repealed."

"But that would mean—"

"The end of our world," Gerbert finished.

PART V

London: The Blackfriars

"You failed me!"

A red damask shoe sailed through the air. Matthew tilted his head just before it struck. The shoe continued past his ear, knocked a bejeweled armillary sphere off the table, and came to rest on the floor. The interlocking rings of the sphere spun around in their fixed orbits in impotent frustration.

"I wanted Kelley, you fool. Instead I got the emperor's ambassador, who told me of your many indiscretions. When he demanded to see me, it was not yet eight o'clock and the sun had barely risen." Elizabeth Tudor was afflicted with a toothache, which didn't improve her disposition. She sucked in one cheek to cushion the infected molar and grimaced. "And where were you? Creeping back into my presence with no concern for my suffering."

A blue-eyed beauty stepped forward and handed Her Majesty a cloth saturated with clove oil. With Matthew seething next to me, the spiciness in the room was already overpowering. Elizabeth placed the cloth delicately between her cheek and gums, and the woman stepped away, her green gown swishing around her ankles. It was an optimistic hue for this cloudy day in May, as if she hoped to speed summer's arrival. The fourth-floor tower room in Greenwich Palace afforded a sweeping view of the gray river, muddy ground, and England's stormy skies. In spite of the many windows, the silvery morning light did little to dispel the heaviness of the room, which was resolutely masculine and early Tudor in its furnishings. The carved initials on the ceiling—an intertwined *H* and *A* for Henry VIII and Anne Boleyn—indicated that the room had been decorated around the time of Elizabeth's birth and seldom used since.

"Perhaps we should hear Master Roydon out before you throw the inkwell," William Cecil suggested mildly. Elizabeth's arm stopped, but she didn't put down the weighty metal object.

"We do have news of Kelley," I began, hoping to help.

"We did not seek your opinion, Mistress Roydon," the queen of England said sharply. "Like too many women at my court, you are utterly without governance or decorum. If you wish to remain at Greenwich with your husband rather than being sent back to Woodstock where you belong, you would be wise to take Mistress Throckmorton as your model. She does not speak unless directed to do so."

Mistress Throckmorton glanced at Walter, who was standing next to Matthew. We had met him on the back stairs to the queen's private chambers, and though Matthew dismissed it as unnecessary, Walter had insisted on accompanying us into the lion's den.

Bess's lips compressed as she held back her amusement, but her eyes danced. The fact that the queen's attractive young ward and her dashing, saturnine pirate were intimate was apparent to everyone save Elizabeth. Cupid had managed to ensnare Sir Walter Raleigh, just as Matthew promised. The man was utterly besotted.

Walter's mouth softened at his lover's challenging stare, and the frank appraisal he gave her in return promised that the subject of her decorum would be addressed in a more private venue.

"As you do not require Diana's presence, perhaps you will let my wife go home and take her rest as I requested," Matthew said evenly, though his eyes were as black and angry as the queen's. "She has been traveling for some weeks." The royal barge had intercepted us before we'd even set foot at the Blackfriars.

"Rest! I have had nothing but sleepless nights since hearing of your adventures in Prague. She will rest when I am through with you!" Elizabeth shrieked, the inkwell following in the path of the royal footwear. When it veered toward me like a late-breaking curveball, Matthew reached out and caught it. Wordlessly he passed it to Raleigh, who tossed it to the groom already in possession of the queen's shoe.

"Master Roydon would be far more difficult to replace than that astronomical toy, Majesty." Cecil held out an embroidered cushion. "Perhaps you would consider this if you are in need of further ammunition."

"Do not think to direct me, Lord Burghley!" the queen fumed. She turned with fury on Matthew. "Sebastian St. Clair did not treat my father thus. He would not have dared to provoke the Tudor lion."

Bess Throckmorton blinked at the unfamiliar name. Her golden head turned from Walter to the queen like a spring daffodil seeking out the sun. Cecil coughed gently at the young woman's evident confusion.

"Let us reminisce about your blessed father at some other time, when we can devote proper attention to his memory. Did you not have questions for Master Roydon?" The queen's secretary looked at Matthew apologetically. *Which devil would you prefer?* his expression seemed to say.

"You are right, William. It is not in the nature of lions to dally with mice and other insignificant creatures." The queen's disdain somehow managed to diminish Matthew to the size of a small boy. Once he looked suitably contrite—though the muscle ticking in his jaw made me wonder how sincere his remorse really was—she took a moment to steady herself, her hands retaining a white-knuckled grip on the chair's arms.

"I wish to know how my Shadow bungled matters so badly." Her voice turned plaintive. "The emperor has alchemists aplenty. He does not need mine."

Walter's shoulders lowered a fraction, and Cecil smothered a sigh of relief. If the queen was calling Matthew by his nickname, then her anger was already softening.

"Edward Kelley cannot be plucked from the emperor's court like a stray weed, no matter how many roses grow there," Matthew said. "Rudolf values him too highly."

"So Kelley has succeeded at last. The philosopher's stone *is* in his possession," Elizabeth said with a sharp intake of breath. She clutched at the side of her face as the air hit her sore tooth.

"No, he hasn't succeeded—and that's the heart of the matter. So long as Kelley promises more than he is able to produce, Rudolf will never part with him. The emperor behaves like an inexperienced youth rather than a seasoned monarch, fascinated by what he cannot have. His Majesty loves the chase. It fills his days and occupies his dreams," Matthew said impassively.

The sodden fields and swollen rivers of Europe had put us at a considerable distance from Rudolf II, but there were moments when I could still feel his unwelcome touch and acquisitive glances. In spite of the May warmth and the fire blazing in the hearth, I shivered.

"The new French ambassador writes to me that Kelley has turned copper into gold."

"Philippe de Mornay is no more trustworthy than your former ambassador—who, as I recall, attempted to assassinate you." Matthew's tone was perfectly poised between obsequiousness and irritation. Elizabeth did a double take.

"Are you baiting me, Master Roydon?"

"I would never bait a lion—or even the lion's cub," Matthew drawled.

Walter closed his eyes as if he couldn't bear to witness the inevitable devastation Matthew's words would cause. "I was badly scarred after one such encounter and have no desire to mar my beauty further for fear that you could no longer abide the sight of me."

There was a shocked silence, broken at last by an unladylike bellow of laughter. Walter's eyes popped open.

"You got what you deserved, sneaking up on a young maid when she was sewing," Elizabeth said with something that sounded very much like indulgence. I shook my head slightly, sure I was hearing things.

"I shall keep that in mind, Majesty, should I happen upon another young lioness with a sharp pair of shears."

Walter and I were now as confused as Bess. Only Matthew, Elizabeth, and Cecil seemed to understand what was being said—and what was not.

"Even then you were my Shadow." The look Elizabeth gave Matthew made her appear to be a girl again and not a woman fast approaching sixty. Then I blinked, and she was an aging, tired monarch once more. "Leave us."

"Your . . . M-majesty?" Bess stammered.

"I wish to speak to Master Roydon privately. I don't suppose he will permit his loose-tongued wife out of his sight, so she may stay, too. Wait for me in my privy chamber, Walter. Take Bess with you. We shall join you presently."

"But—" Bess protested. She looked about nervously. Staying near the queen was her job, and without protocol to guide her she was at sea.

"You shall have to help me instead, Mistress Throckmorton." Cecil took several painful steps away from the queen, aided by his heavy stick. As he passed by Matthew, Cecil gave him a hard look. "We will leave Master Roydon to see to Her Majesty's welfare."

When the queen waved the grooms out of the room, the three of us were left alone.

"Jesu," Elizabeth said with a groan. "My head feels like a rotten apple about to split. Could you not have chosen a more opportune time to cause a diplomatic incident?"

"Let me examine you," Matthew requested.

"You think to provide me care that my surgeon cannot, Master Roydon?" said the queen with wary hope.

"I believe I can spare you some pain, if God wills it."

"Even unto his death, my father spoke of you with longing." Elizabeth's hands twitched against the folds of her skirt. "He likened you to a tonic, whose benefits he had failed to appreciate."

"How so?" Matthew made no effort to hide his curiosity. This was not a story he had heard before.

"He said you could rid him of an evil humor faster than any man he had ever known—though, like most physic, you could be difficult to swallow." Elizabeth smiled at Matthew's booming laughter, and then her smile faltered. "He was a great and terrible man—and a fool."

"All men are fools, Your Majesty," Matthew said swiftly.

"No. Let us speak plainly to each other again, as though I were not queen of England and you were not a *wearh.*"

"Only if you let me look at your tooth," Matthew said, crossing his arms over his chest.

"Once an invitation to share intimacies with me would have been sufficient inducement, and you would not have attached further conditions to my proposal." Elizabeth sighed. "I am losing more than my teeth. Very well, Master Roydon." She opened her mouth obediently. Even though I was a few feet away, I could smell the decay. Matthew took her head in his hands so that he could see the problem more clearly.

"It is a miracle you have any teeth at all," he said sternly. Elizabeth turned pink with irritation and struggled to reply. "You may shout at me when I am done. By then you will have good reason to do so, as I will have confiscated your candied violets and sweet wine. That will leave you with nothing more damaging to drink than peppermint water and nothing to suck on but a clove rub for your gums. They are badly abscessed."

Matthew drew his finger along her teeth. Several of them wiggled alarmingly, and Elizabeth's eyes bulged. He made a sound of displeasure.

"You may be queen of England, Lizzie, but that doesn't give you a knowledge of physic and surgery. It would have been wiser to heed the surgeon's advice. Now, hold still."

While I tried to regain my composure after hearing my husband call the queen of England "Lizzie," Matthew withdrew his index finger, rubbed it against his own sharp eyetooth so that it drew a bead of blood, and returned it to Elizabeth's mouth. Though he was careful, the queen winced. Then her shoulders lowered in relief.

"'Ank 'ewe," she mumbled around his fingers.

"Don't thank me yet. There won't be a comfit or sweetmeat for five miles when I'm through. And the pain will return, I'm afraid." Matthew drew his fingers away, and the queen felt around her mouth with her tongue.

"Aye, but for now it is gone," she said gratefully. Elizabeth gestured at the nearby chairs. "I fear there is nothing left but to settle accounts. Sit down and tell me about Prague."

After spending weeks at the emperor's court, I knew it was an extraordinary privilege to be invited to sit in the presence of any ruler, but I was doubly grateful for the chance to do so now. The voyage had exacerbated the normal fatigue of the first weeks of pregnancy. Matthew pulled out one of the chairs for me, and I lowered myself into it. I pressed the small of my back against the carving, using its knobs and bumps to give the aching joints a massage. Matthew's hand automatically reached for the same area, pushing and kneading to relieve the soreness. Envy flashed across the queen's features.

"You are in pain, too, Mistress Roydon?" the queen inquired solicitously. She was being too nice. When Rudolf treated a courtier like this, something sinister was usually afoot.

"Yes, Your Majesty. Alas, it is nothing peppermint water will solve," I said ruefully.

"Nor will it smooth the emperor's ruffled feathers. His ambassador tells me that you have stolen one of Rudolf's books."

"Which book?" Matthew asked. "Rudolf has so many." As most vampires had not been acquainted with the state of innocence for some time, his performance of it rang hollow.

"We are not playing games, Sebastian," the queen said quietly, confirming my suspicion that Matthew had gone by the name of Sebastian St. Clair when he was at Henry's court.

"You are always playing games," he shot back. "In this you are no different from the emperor, or Henry of France."

"Mistress Throckmorton told me that you and Walter have been exchanging verses about the fickleness of power. But I am not one of those vain potentates, fit for nothing save scorn and ridicule. I was raised by hard schoolmasters," the queen retorted. "Those around me—mother, aunts, stepmothers, uncles, cousins—are gone. I survived. So do not give me the lie and think to get away with it. I ask you again, what of the book?"

"We don't have it," I interjected.

Matthew looked at me in shock.

"The book is not in our possession. At present." It was doubtless already at the Hart and Crown, safely tucked into Matthew's attic archive. I'd passed the book to Gallowglass, wrapped in protective oilskin and leather, when the royal barge had pulled alongside us on our way up the Thames.

"Well, well." Elizabeth's mouth slowly widened, showing her blackened teeth. "You surprise me. And your husband too, it seems."

"I am nothing but surprises, Your Majesty. Or so I am told." No matter how many times Matthew referred to her as Lizzie or she called him Sebastian, I was careful to address her formally.

"The emperor seems to be in the grip of some illusion, then. How do you account for it?"

"There is nothing remarkable about that," Matthew said with a snort. "I fear the madness that has afflicted his family is now touching Rudolf. Even now his brother Matthias plots his downfall and positions himself to seize power when the emperor can no longer rule."

"No wonder the emperor is so eager to keep Kelley. The philosopher's stone will cure him and make the issue of his successor moot." The queen's expression soured. "He will live on forever, without fear."

"Come, Lizzie. You know better than that. Kelley cannot make the stone. He cannot save you or anyone else. Even queens and emperors must one day die."

"We are friends, Sebastian, but do not forget yourself." Elizabeth's eyes glittered.

"When you were seven and asked me if your father planned to kill his new wife, I told you the truth. I was honest with you then, and I will be honest with you now, however much it angers you. Nothing will bring your youth back, Lizzie, or resurrect those you have lost," Matthew said implacably.

"Nothing?" Elizabeth slowly studied him. "I see no lines or gray hairs on you. You look exactly as you did fifty years ago at Hampton Court when I took my shears to you."

"If you are asking me to use my blood to make you a *wearh,* Your Majesty, the answer must be no. The covenant forbids meddling in human politics—and that certainly includes altering the English succession by placing a creature on the throne." Matthew's expression was forbidding.

"And would that be your answer if Rudolf made this request?" Elizabeth asked, black eyes glittering.

"Yes. It would lead to chaos—and worse." The prospect was chilling.

"Your realm is safe," Matthew assured her. "The emperor is behaving like a spoiled child denied a treat. That is all."

"Even now his uncle, Philip of Spain, is building ships. He plans another invasion!"

"And it will come to nothing," Matthew promised.

"You sound very sure."

"I am."

Lion and wolf regarded each other across the table. When at last Elizabeth was satisfied, she looked away with a sigh.

"Very well. You don't have the emperor's book, and I do not have Kelley or the stone. We must all learn to live with disappointment. Still, I must give the emperor's ambassador something to sweeten his mood."

"What about this?" I drew my purse from my skirts. Apart from Ashmole 782 and the ring on my finger, it contained my most treasured possessions—the silken cords that Goody Alsop had given me to weave my spells, a smooth pebble of glass Jack had found in the sands of the Elbe and taken for a jewel, a fragment of precious bezoar stone for Susanna to use in her medicines, Matthew's salamanders. And one hideously ornate collar with a dying dragon hanging from it that had been given to me by the Holy Roman Emperor. I placed the last on the table between the queen and me.

"That is a bauble for a queen, not a gentleman's wife." Elizabeth reached out to touch the sparkling dragon. "What did you give to Rudolf that he would bestow this upon you?"

"It is as Matthew said, Your Majesty. The emperor covets what he can never have. He thought this might win my affections. It did not," I said with a shake of my head.

"Perhaps Rudolf cannot bear to have others know that he let something so valuable slip away," Matthew suggested.

"Do you mean your wife or this jewel?"

"My wife," Matthew said shortly.

"The jewel might be useful anyway. Perhaps he meant to give the necklace to me," Elizabeth mused, "but you took it upon yourself to carry it here for its greater safety."

"Diana's German is not very good," Matthew agreed with a wry smile. "When Rudolf put it over her shoulders, he might have been doing so only to better imagine how it would look on you."

"Oh, I doubt that," Elizabeth said drily.

"If the emperor intended this necklace for the queen of England, he would have wished to give it to her with appropriate ceremony. If we give the ambassador the credit he is due . . ." I suggested.

"There's a pretty solution. It will satisfy no one, of course, but it will give my courtiers something to cut their teeth on until some new curiosity emerges." Elizabeth tapped the table pensively. "But there's still the matter of this book."

"Would you believe me if I told you it wasn't important?" Matthew asked.

Elizabeth shook her head. "No."

"I thought not. What of the opposite—that the future may depend upon it?" Matthew asked.

"That is even more far-fetched. But since I have no desire for Rudolf or any of his kin to hold the future in their grasp, I will leave the matter of returning it to you—should it ever come into your possession again, of course."

"Thank you, Your Majesty," I said, relieved that the matter had been resolved with relatively few lies.

"I did not do it for you," Elizabeth reminded me sharply. "Come, Sebastian. Hang the jewel around my neck. Then you can transform yourself back into Master Roydon and we will go down to the presence chamber and put on a show of gratitude to amaze them all."

Matthew did as he was bid, his fingers lingering on the queen's shoulders longer than was necessary. She patted his hand.

"Is my wig straight?" Elizabeth asked me as she rose to her feet.

"Yes, Your Majesty." In truth it was slightly askew after Matthew's ministrations.

Elizabeth reached up and gave her wig a tug. "Teach your wife how to tell a convincing lie, Master Roydon. She will need to be better schooled in the arts of deceit, or she will not survive long at court."

"The world needs honesty more than it needs another courtier," commented Matthew, taking her elbow. "Diana will remain as she is."

"A husband who values honesty in his own wife." Elizabeth shook her head. "This is the best evidence I have yet seen that the world is coming to an end as Dr. Dee foretold."

When Matthew and the queen appeared in the doorway to the privy chamber, a hush fell over the crowd. The room was packed to the rafters, and wary glances darted from the queen to a youth the age of an undergraduate I took to be the imperial ambassador, to William Cecil and back.

Matthew released the queen's hand, which was held aloft on his bent arm. My firedrake's wings beat with alarm inside my ribs.

I put my hand on my diaphragm to soothe the beast. *Here be the real dragons,* I silently warned.

"I thank the emperor for his gift, Your Excellency," Elizabeth said, walking straight toward the teenager with her hand extended for him to kiss. The young man stared at her blankly. *"Gratias tibi ago."*

"They get younger all the time," Matthew murmured as he drew me next to him.

"That's what I say about my students," I whispered back. "Who is he?"

"Vilém Slavata. You must have seen his father in Prague."

I studied young Vilém and tried to imagine what he might look like in twenty years. "Was his father the round one with the dimpled chin?"

"One of them. You've described most of Rudolf's officials," Matthew pointed out when I shot him an exasperated glance.

"Stop whispering, Master Roydon!" Elizabeth turned a withering glance on my husband, who bowed apologetically. Her Majesty continued, rattling on in Latin. *"'Decet eum qui dat, non meminisse beneficii: eum vero, qui accipit, intueri non tam munus quam dantis animum.'"* The queen of England had set the ambassador a language examination to see if he was worthy of her.

Slavata blanched. The poor boy was going to fail it.

It becomes him who gives not to remember the favor: but it becomes she who receives not to look upon the gift as much as the soul of the giver. I coughed to hide my chortle once I'd sorted out the translation.

"Your Majesty?" Vilém stammered in heavily accented English.

"Gift. From the emperor." Elizabeth pointed imperiously at the collar of enameled crosses draped over her slim shoulders. The dragon hung down further on Her Majesty than it had on me. She sighed with exaggerated exasperation. "Tell him what I said in his own language, Master Roydon. I do not have the patience for Latin lessons. Does the emperor not educate his servants?"

"His Excellency knows Latin, Your Majesty. Ambassador Slavata attended university at Wittenberg and went on to study law at Basel, if my memory serves. It is not the language that confuses him but your message."

"Then let us be right clear so that he—and his master—receive it. And not for my sake," Elizabeth said darkly. "Proceed." With a shrug, Matthew repeated Her Majesty's message in Slavata's native tongue.

"I understood what she said," young Slavata responded, dazed. "But what does she mean?"

"You are confused," Matthew continued sympathetically in Czech. "It is common among new ambassadors. Don't worry about it. Tell the queen that Rudolf is delighted to give her this jewel. Then we can have dinner."

"Will you tell her for me?" Slavata was completely out of his depth.

"I do hope you have not caused another misunderstanding between Emperor Rudolf and me, Master Roydon," Elizabeth said, plainly irritated that her command of seven languages did not extend to Czech.

"His Excellency reports that the emperor wishes Your Majesty health and happiness. And Ambassador Slavata is delighted that the necklace is where it belongs and not missing, as the emperor feared." Matthew looked at his mistress benignly. She started to say something, closed her mouth with a snap, and glared at him. Slavata, eager to learn, wanted to know how Matthew had managed to silence the queen of England. When the ambassador made a gesture to encourage Matthew to translate, Cecil took the young man in hand.

"Delightful news, Excellency. I think you've had lessons enough for one day. Come, dine with me," Cecil said, steering him to a nearby table. The queen, upstaged now by both her spy and her chief adviser, harrumphed as she climbed the dais, helped up the three low stairs by Bess Throckmorton and Raleigh.

"What happens now?" I whispered. The show was over, and the room's occupants were displaying signs of restlessness.

"I will wish to talk further, Master Roydon," Elizabeth called while her cushions were being arranged to her satisfaction. "Do not go far."

"Pierre will be in the presence chamber next door. He'll show you to my room, where there's a bed and some peace and quiet. You can rest until Her Majesty frees me. It shouldn't take long. She only wants a full report on Kelley." Matthew brought my hand to his lips and gave it a formal kiss.

Knowing Elizabeth's fondness for her male attendants, it could well take hours.

Even though I was braced for the clamor of the presence chamber, it knocked me back a step. Courtiers not sufficiently important to warrant dining in the privy chamber jostled me as they passed, eager to get to their own dinner before the food was gone. My stomach flipped over at the scent of roasted venison. I would never get used to it, and the baby didn't like it either.

Pierre and Annie were standing by the wall with the other servants. They both looked relieved as I came into view.

"Where is *milord*?" Pierre asked, pulling me out of the crush of bodies.

"Waiting on the queen," I said. "I'm too tired to stand up—or eat. Can you take me to Matthew's room?"

Pierre cast a worried look at the entrance to the privy chamber. "Of course."

"I know the way, Mistress Roydon," Annie said. Newly returned from Prague and well into her second visit to the court of Elizabeth, Annie was affecting an attitude of studied nonchalance.

"I showed her *milord*'s room when you were led away to see Her Majesty," Pierre assured me. "It is just downstairs, below the apartments once used by the king's wife."

"And now used by the queen's favorites, I suppose," I said under my breath. No doubt that's where Walter was sleeping—or not sleeping, as the case may be. "Wait here for Matthew, Pierre. Annie and I can find our way."

"Thank you, *madame*." Pierre looked at me gratefully. "I do not like to leave him too long with the queen."

The members of the queen's staff were tucking into their dinner in the far-less-splendid surrounds of the guard chamber. They regarded Annie and me with idle curiosity as we walked through.

"There must be a more direct route," I said, biting my lip and looking down the long flight of stairs. The Great Hall would be even more crowded.

"I'm sorry, mistress, but there isn't," Annie said apologetically.

"Let's face the mob, then," I said with a sigh.

The Great Hall was thronged with petitioners for the queen's attention. A rustle of excitement greeted my appearance from the direction of the royal apartments, followed by murmurs of disappointment when I proved to be no one of consequence. After Rudolf's court I was more accustomed to being an object of attention, but it was still uncomfortable to feel the heavy gaze of the humans, the few nudges from daemons, the tingling glance of a solitary witch. When the cold stare of a vampire settled on my back, though, I looked around in alarm.

"Mistress?" Annie inquired.

My eyes scanned the crowd, but I was unable to locate the source.

"Nothing, Annie," I murmured, uneasy. "It's just my imagination playing tricks."

"You are in need of rest," she chided, sounding very like Susanna.

But no rest awaited me in Matthew's spacious ground-floor rooms overlooking the queen's private gardens. Instead I found England's premier playwright. I sent Annie to extract Jack from whatever mess he'd gotten himself into and steeled myself to face Christopher Marlowe.

"Hello, Kit," I said. The daemon looked up from Matthew's desk, pages of verse scattered around him. "All alone?"

"Walter and Henry are dining with the queen. Why are you not with them?" Kit looked pale, thin, and distracted. He rose and began to gather his papers, glancing anxiously at the door as though he expected someone to walk in and interrupt us.

"Too tired." I yawned. "But there's no need for you to go. Stay and wait for Matthew. He will be glad to see you. What are you writing?"

"A poem." After this abrupt reply, Kit sat. Something was off. The daemon seemed positively twitchy.

The tapestry on the wall behind him showed a golden-haired maiden standing in a tower overlooking the sea. She held up a lantern and peered into the distance. *That explains it.*

"You're writing about Hero and Leander." It was not phrased as a question. Kit had probably been pining for Matthew and working on the epic love poem since we'd boarded ship at Gravesend back in January. He didn't respond.

After a few moments I recited the relevant lines.

"Some swore he was a maid in mans attire,
For in his lookes were all that men desire,
A pleasant smiling cheeke, a speaking eye,
A brow for Love to banquet roiallye,
And such as knew he was a man would say,
Leander, thou art made for amorous play:
Why art thou not in love and lov'd of all?"

Kit exploded from his seat. "What witch's mischief is this? You know what I am doing as soon as I do it."

"No mischief, Kit. Who would understand how you feel better than I?" I said carefully.

Kit seemed to gather his control, though his hands were shaking as he stood. "I must go. I am to meet someone in the tiltyard. There is talk of a special pageant next month before the queen sets off for her summer travels. I've been asked to assist." Every year Elizabeth progressed around the country with a wagon train of attendants and courtiers, sponging off her nobles and leaving behind enormous debts and empty larders.

"I'll be sure to tell Matthew you were here. He'll be sorry he missed you."

A bright gleam entered Marlowe's eyes. "Perhaps you would like to come with me, Mistress Roydon. It is a fine day, and you have not seen Greenwich."

"Thank you, Kit." I was puzzled by his rapid change of mood, but he was, after all, a daemon. And he was mooning over Matthew. Though I'd hoped to rest, and Kit's overtures were stilted, I should make an effort in the interests of harmony. "Is it far? I'm somewhat tired after the journey."

"Not far at all." Kit bowed. "After you."

The tiltyard at Greenwich resembled a grand track-and-field stadium, with roped-off areas for athletes, stands for spectators, and scattered equipment. Two sets of barricades stretched down the center of the compacted surface.

"Is that where the jousting takes place?" I could imagine the sound of hooves pounding the earth as knights sped toward each other, their lances angled across the necks of their mounts so they could strike their opponent's shield and unseat him.

"Yes. Would you like to take a closer look?" Kit asked.

The place was deserted. Lances were stuck in the ground here and there. I saw something that looked alarmingly similar to a gibbet, with its upright pole and long arm. Rather than a body, however, a bag of sand swung at the end. It had been run through, and sand trickled out in a thin stream.

"A quintain," Marlowe explained, gesturing at the device. "Riders aim their lances at the sandbag." He reached up and gave the arm a push to show me. It swung around, providing a moving target to hone the knight's skill. Marlowe's eyes scanned the tiltyard.

"Is the man you're meeting here?" I looked around, too. But the only person I could see was a tall, dark-haired woman wearing a lavish red dress. She was far in the distance, no doubt having some romantic assignation before dinner.

"Have you seen the other quintain?" Kit pointed in the opposite direction, where a mannequin made of straw and rough burlap was tied to a post. This, too, looked more like a form of execution than a piece of sporting equipment.

I felt a cold, focused glance. Before I could turn around, a vampire caught me with arms that had the familiar sense of being more steel than flesh. But these arms did not belong to Matthew.

"Why, she is even more delicious than I'd hoped," a woman said, her cold breath snaking around my throat.

Roses. Civet. I registered the scents, tried to remember where I'd smelled the combination before.

Sept-Tours. Louisa de Clermont's room.

"Something in her blood is irresistible to *wearhs,*" Kit said roughly. "I do not understand what it is, but even Father Hubbard seems to be in her thrall."

Sharp teeth rasped against my neck, though they did not break the skin. "It will be amusing to play with her."

"Our plan was to kill her," Kit complained. He was even twitchier and more restless now that Louisa was here. I remained silent, trying desperately to figure out what game they were playing. "Then everything will be as it was before."

"Patience." Louisa drank in my scent. "Can you smell her fear? It always sharpens my appetite."

Kit inched closer, fascinated.

"But you are pale, Christopher. Do you need more physic?" Louisa modified her grasp on me so that she could reach into her purse. She handed Kit a sticky brown lozenge. He took it from her eagerly, thrusting the ball into his mouth. "They are miraculous, are they not? The warmbloods in Germany call them 'Stones of Immortality,' for the ingredients somehow make even pitiful humans feel that they are divine. And they have made you feel strong again."

"It is the witch who weakens me, just as she weakened your brother." Kit's eyes turned glassy, and there was a sickeningly sweet tang to his breath. *Opiates.* No wonder he was behaving so strangely.

"Is that true, witch? Kit says you bound my brother against his will." Louisa swung me around. Her beautiful face embodied every warmblood's nightmare of a vampire: porcelain-pale skin, dusky black hair, and dark eyes that were as fogged with opium as Kit's. Malevolence rolled off her, and her perfectly bowed red lips were not only sensual but cruel. This was a creature who would hunt and kill without a hint of remorse.

"I did not bind your brother. I chose him—and he chose me, Louisa."

"You know who I am?" Louisa's dark eyebrows rose.

"Matthew doesn't keep secrets from me. We are mates. Husband and wife, too. Your father presided over our marriage." *Thank you, Philippe.*

"Liar!" Louisa screamed. Her pupils engulfed the iris as her control snapped. It was not just drugs that I would have to contend with but blood rage, too.

"Trust nothing she says," Kit warned. He pulled a dagger from his doublet and grabbed my hair. I cried out at the pain as he wrenched my head back. Kit's dagger orbited my right eye. "I am going to pluck out her eyes so that she can no longer use them for enchantments or to see my fate. She knows my death. I am sure of it. Without her witch's sight, she will have no hold on us—or on Matthew."

"The witch does not deserve such a swift death," Louisa said bitterly.

Kit pressed the point into my flesh just under the brow bone, and a drop of blood rolled down my cheek. "That wasn't our agreement, Louisa. To break her spell, I must have her eyes. Then I want her dead and gone. So long as the witch lives, Matthew will not forget her."

"Shh, Christopher. Do I not love you? Are we not allies?" Louisa reached for Kit and kissed him deeply. She moved her mouth along his jaw and down to where the blood pounded in his veins. Her lips brushed against the skin, and I saw the smear of blood that accompanied her movement. Kit drew a shuddering breath and closed his eyes.

Louisa drank hungrily from the daemon's neck. While she did, we stood in a tight knot, locked together in the vampire's strong arms. I tried to squirm away, but her grip on me only tightened as her teeth and lips battened on Kit.

"Sweet Christopher," she murmured when she had drunk her fill, licking at the wound. The mark on Kit's neck was silvery and soft, just like the scar on my breast. Louisa must have fed from him before. "I can taste the immortality in your blood and see the beautiful words that dance through your thoughts. Matthew is a fool not to want to share them with you."

"He wants only the witch." Kit touched his neck, imagining that it was Matthew, and not his sister, who had drunk from his veins. "I want her dead."

"As do I." Louisa turned her bottomless black eyes on me. "And so we will compete for her. Whoever wins may do with her as she—or he—will to make her atone for the wrongs she has done my brother. Do you agree, my darling boy?"

The two of them were high as kites now that Louisa had shared Kit's opiate-laden blood. I started to panic, then recalled Philippe's instructions at Sept-Tours.

Think. Stay alive.

Then I remembered the baby, and my panic returned. I couldn't endanger our child.

Kit nodded. "I will do anything to have Matthew's regard once more."

"I thought so." Louisa smiled and kissed him deeply again. "Shall we choose our colors?"

"You are making a terrible mistake, Louisa," I warned, struggling against my bonds. She and Kit had removed the shapeless straw-and-burlap mannequin and tied me to the post in its place. Then Kit had blindfolded me with a strip of dark blue silk taken from the tip of one of the waiting lances, so that I could not enchant them with my gaze. The two stood nearby, arguing over who would use the black-and-silver lance and who the green-and-gold.

"You'll find Matthew with the queen. He'll explain everything." I tried to keep my voice steady, but it trembled. Matthew had told me about his sister in modern Oxford, while we drank tea by his fireplace at the Old Lodge. She was as vicious as she was beautiful.

"You dare to utter his name?" Kit was wild with anger.

"Do not speak again, witch, or I will let Christopher remove your tongue after all." Louisa's voice was venomous, and I didn't need to see her eyes to know that poppy and blood rage were not a good mix. The point of Ysabeau's diamond scratched lightly against my cheek, drawing blood. Louisa had broken my finger wrenching it off and was now wearing it herself.

"I am Matthew's wife, his mate. What do you imagine his reaction will be when he finds out what you've done?"

"You are a monster—a beast. If I win the challenge, I will strip you of your false humanity and expose what lies underneath." Louisa's words trickled into my ears like poison. "Once I have, Matthew will see what you truly are, and he will share in our pleasure at your death."

When their conversation faded into the distance, I had no way of knowing where they were or from which direction they might return. I was utterly alone.

Think. Stay alive.

Something fluttered in my chest. But it wasn't panic. It was my firedrake. I wasn't alone. And I was a witch. I didn't need my eyes to see the world around me.

What do you see? I asked the earth and the air.

It was my firedrake who answered. She chirped and chattered, her wings stirring in the space between my belly and lungs as she assessed the situation.

Where are they? I wondered.

My third eye opened wide, revealing the shimmering colors of late spring in all their blue and green glory. One darker green thread was twisted with white and tangled with something black. I followed it to Louisa, who was climbing onto the back of an agitated horse. It wouldn't stand still for the vampire and kept shying away. Louisa bit it on the neck, which made the horse stand stock-still but did nothing to alleviate its terror.

I followed another set of threads, these crimson and white, thinking they might lead to Matthew. Instead I saw a bewildering whirl of shapes and colors. I fell—far, far until I landed on a cold pillow. *Snow.* I drew the cold winter air into my lungs. I was no longer tied to a stake on a late-May afternoon at Greenwich Palace. I was four or five, lying on my back in the small yard behind our house in Cambridge.

And I remembered.

My father and I had been playing after a heavy snowfall. My mittens were Harvard crimson against the white. We were making angels, our arms and legs sweeping up and down. I was fascinated by how, if I moved my arms quickly enough, the white wings seemed to take on a red tinge.

"It's like the dragon with the fiery wings," I whispered to my father. His arms stilled.

"When did you see a dragon, Diana?" His voice was serious. I knew the difference between that tone and his usual teasing one. It meant he expected an answer—and a truthful one.

"Lots of times. Mostly at night." My arms beat faster and faster. The snow underneath their span was changing color, shimmering with green and gold, red and black, silver and blue.

"And where was it?" he whispered, staring at the snowdrifts. They were mounting up around me, heaving and rumbling as though alive. One grew tall and stretched itself into a slender dragon's head. The drift stretched wide into a pair of wings. The dragon shook flakes of snow from its white scales. When it turned and looked at my father, he murmured something and patted its nose as though he and the dragon had already met. The dragon breathed warm vapor into the frigid air.

"Mostly it's inside me—here." I sat up to show my father what I meant. My

mittened hands went to the curved bones of my ribs. They were warm through the skin, through my jacket, through the chunky knit of the mittens. "But when she needs to fly, I have to let her out. There's not enough room for her wings otherwise."

A pair of shining wings rested on the snow behind me.

"You left your own wings behind," my father said gravely.

The dragon wormed her way out of the snowdrift. Her silver-and-black eyes blinked as she pulled free, rose into the air, and disappeared over the apple tree, becoming more insubstantial with every flap of her wings. Mine were already fading on the snow behind me.

"The dragon won't take me with her. And she never stays around for very long," I said with a sigh. "Why is that, Daddy?"

"Maybe she has somewhere else to be."

I considered this possibility. "Like when you and Mommy go to school?" It was perplexing to think of parents going to school. All the children on the block thought so, even though most of their parents spent all day at school, too.

"Just like that." My father was still sitting in the snow, his arms wrapped around his knees. He smiled. "I love the witch in you, Diana."

"She scares Mommy."

"Nah." My father shook his head. "Mommy is just scared of change."

"I tried to keep the dragon a secret, but I think she knows anyway," I said glumly.

"Mommies usually do," my father said. He looked down at the snow. My wings were entirely gone now. "But she knows when you want hot chocolate, too. If we go inside, my guess is she'll have it ready." My father got to his feet and held out his hand.

I slipped mine, still wearing crimson mittens, into his warm grip.

"Will you always be here to hold my hand when it gets dark?" I asked. Night was falling, and I was suddenly afraid of the shadows. Monsters lurked in the gloom, strange creatures who watched me as I played.

"Nope," my father said with a shake of his head. My lip trembled. That wasn't the answer I wanted. "But don't worry." His voice dropped to a whisper. "You'll always have your dragon."

A drop of blood fell from the pierced skin around my eye to the ground by my feet. Even though I was blindfolded, I could see its leisurely movement and the way it landed with a wet splat. A black shoot emerged from the spot.

Hooves thundered toward me. Someone gave a high, keening cry that conjured up images of ancient battles. The sound made the firedrake even more restless. I needed to free myself. Fast.

Instead of trying to see the threads that led to Kit and Louisa, I focused on the ones wrapped in the fibers that bound my wrists and ankles. I was starting to make progress loosening them when something sharp and heavy splintered against my ribs. The impact knocked the breath from my body.

"A hit!" Kit cried. "The witch is mine!"

"A glancing blow," Louisa corrected. "You must seat the lance in her body to claim her as your prize."

Sadly, I didn't know the rules—neither of jousting nor of magic, either. Goody Alsop had made that plain before we left for Prague. *All you have now is a wayward firedrake, a glaem that is near to blinding, and a tendency to ask questions that have mischievous answers,* she'd said. I'd been neglecting my weaving in favor of court intrigue and stopped pursuing my magic to hunt for Ashmole 782. Perhaps if I'd stayed in London, I would have known how to get myself out of this mess. Instead I was bound to a thick log like a witch about to be set alight.

Think. Stay alive.

"We must try again," Louisa said. Her words faded as she wheeled her horse around and rode away.

"Don't do this, Kit," I said. "Think what it will do to Matthew. If you want me gone, I'll go. I promise."

"Your promises are nothing, witch. You will cross your fingers and find a way to wriggle out of your assurances. I can see the *glaem* about you even now as you try to work your magic against me."

A glaem near to blinding. Questions that elicit mischievous answers. And a wayward firedrake.

Everything went still.

What should we do? I asked the firedrake.

Her response was to snap her wings, extending them fully. They slid between my ribs, through the flesh, and emerged on either side of my spine. The firedrake stayed where she was, her tail wrapped protectively around my womb. She peeked out from behind my sternum, her silver-and-black eyes bright, and flapped her wings again.

Stay alive, she whispered in reply, her words sending a pall of gray mist into the air around me.

The force of her wings snapped the thick wooden pole at my back, and the barbs on their scalloped edges sliced through the rope that bound my wrists. Something sharp and clawlike cut through the bindings around my ankles, too. I rose twenty feet up into the air as Kit and Louisa entered the firedrake's disorienting gray cloud. They were moving too quickly to stop or change direction. Their lances crossed, tangled, and the force of the clash sent them both flying from their saddles onto the hard earth below.

I ripped the blindfold from my eyes with my undamaged hand just as Annie appeared at the edge of the tiltyard.

"Mistress!" she cried. But I didn't want her here, not around Louisa de Clermont.

"Go!" I hissed. My words emerged in fire and smoke as I circled above Kit and Louisa.

Blood trickled from my wrists and feet. Wherever the red beads fell, a black shoot grew. Soon a palisade of slender black trunks surrounded the dazed daemon and vampire. Louisa tried to pull them from the ground, but my magic held.

"Shall I tell you your futures?" I asked harshly. Both stared up at me from their pen with avid, fearful eyes. "You will never get your heart's desire, Kit, because sometimes what we want most, we cannot have. And you will never fill the hollow places inside you, Louisa—neither with blood nor with anger. And both of you will die, because death comes for all of us sooner or later. But your deaths will not be gentle. I promise you that."

A whirlwind approached. It stilled, became recognizable as Hancock.

"Davy!" Louisa's pearly fingers gripped the black stakes that surrounded her. "Help us. The witch used her magic to bring us down. Take her eyes and you will take her power, too."

"Matthew is already on his way, Louisa," Hancock answered. "You are safer in that stockade under Diana's protection than you would be running from his anger."

"None of us is safe. She will fulfill the ancient prophecy, the one that Gerbert shared with *Maman* all those years ago. She will bring down the de Clermonts!"

"There's no truth in it," Hancock said with pity.

"There is!" Louisa insisted. "'*Beware the witch with the blood of the lion and the wolf, for with it she shall destroy the children of night.*' This is the witch of the prophecy! Don't you see?"

"You're not well, Louisa. I can see that plainly."

Louisa drew herself up, indignant. "I am a *manjasang* and in perfect health, Hancock."

Henry and Jack arrived next, their sides heaving with exertion. Henry scanned the tiltyard.

"Where is she?" he shouted at Hancock, spinning around.

"Up there," Hancock said, jerking his thumb in the air. "Just like Annie said."

"Diana." Henry sighed with relief.

A dark cyclone of gray and black whipped across the tiltyard and came to rest at a broken stake that marked the spot where I had been bound. Matthew needed no one to tell him where I was now. His eyes unerringly found me.

Walter and Pierre were the last to arrive. Pierre was carrying Annie piggyback, her thin arms wrapped tight around his neck. When he stopped, she slid from his back.

"Walter!" Kit cried, joining Louisa at the barrier. "She must be stopped. Let us out. I know what to do now. I spoke with a witch in Newgate, and—"

An arm punched through the black railings, and long, white fingers grabbed Kit around the throat. Marlowe gurgled to silence.

"Not. One. Word." Matthew's eyes swept over Louisa.

"*Matthieu.*" Blood and drugs further slurred Louisa's French pronunciation of his name. "Thank God you are here. I am glad to see you."

"You shouldn't be." Matthew flung Kit away.

I lowered down behind him, the newly sprouted wings withdrawing back inside my ribs. My firedrake remained alert, however, her tail tightly coiled. Matthew sensed me there and hooked me into his arm, though he never took his eyes off my captives. His fingers brushed against the spot where the lance had gone through bodice, corset, and skin only to be stopped by the bony cage of my ribs. It was damp where the blood had soaked through.

Matthew spun me around and fell to his knees, tearing the fabric from the wound. He swore. One hand settled on my abdomen, and his eyes searched mine.

"I'm fine. We're fine," I assured him.

He stood, his eyes black and the vein in his temple throbbing.

"Master Roydon?" Jack sidled closer to Matthew. His chin was trembling. Matthew's hand shot out and grabbed him by the collar, stopping him before he could get too close to me. Jack didn't flinch. "Are you having a nightmare?"

Matthew's hand dropped, releasing the boy. "Yes, Jack. A terrible nightmare."

Jack slid his hand into Matthew's. "I will wait by your side until it passes." My eyes pricked with tears. It was what Matthew said to him deep in the night, when Jack's terrors threatened to engulf him.

Matthew's hand tightened on Jack's in silent acknowledgment. The two of them stood—one tall and broad and filled with preternatural health, the other slight and awkward and only now shedding the shadows of neglect. Matthew's rage began to ebb.

"When Annie told me a female *wearh* had you, I never imagined—" He couldn't continue.

"It was Christopher!" Louisa cried, distancing herself from the wild daemon at her side. "He said you were enchanted. But I can smell her blood on you. You are not under her spell, but feeding from her."

"She is my mate," Matthew explained, his tone deadly. "And she is with child."

Marlowe's breath came out in a hiss. His eyes nudged my belly. My broken hand moved to protect our child from the daemon's gaze.

"'Tis impossible. Matthew cannot . . ." Kit's confusion turned to fury. "Even now she has bewitched him. How could you betray him thus? Who fathered your child, Mistress Roydon?"

Mary Sidney had assumed I had been raped. Gallowglass had first attributed the baby to a deceased lover or husband, either of which would have roused Matthew's protective instincts and explained our swift romance. For Kit the only possible answer was that I had cuckolded the man he loved.

"Take her, Hancock!" Louisa begged. "We cannot allow a witch to introduce her bastard into the de Clermont family."

Hancock shook his head at Louisa and crossed his arms.

"You tried to run my mate down. You drew her blood," Matthew said. "And the child is no bastard. It's mine."

"It is not possible," Louisa said, but she sounded uncertain.

"The child is *mine,*" her brother repeated fiercely. "My flesh. My blood."

"She carries the blood of the wolf," Louisa whispered. "The witch *is* the one the prophecy foretold. If the baby lives, it will destroy us all!"

"Get them out of my sight." Matthew's voice was dead with rage. "Before I tear them into pieces and feed them to the dogs." He kicked down the palisade and grabbed his friend and his sister.

"I'm not going—" Louisa began. She looked down to find Hancock's hand wrapped around her arm.

"Oh, you'll go where I take you," he said softly. Hancock worked Ysabeau's ring from her finger and tossed it to Matthew. "I believe that belongs to your wife."

"And Kit?" Walter asked, eyeing Matthew warily.

"As they're so fond of each other, lock him up with Louisa." Matthew thrust the daemon at Raleigh.

"But she'll—" Walter began.

"Feed on him?" Matthew looked sour. "She has already. The only way a vampire feels the effects of wine or physic is from a warmblood's vein."

Walter gauged Matthew's mood and nodded. "Very well, Matthew. We will follow your wishes. Take Diana and the children to the Blackfriars. Leave everything else to Hancock and me."

"I told him there was nothing to worry about. The baby is fine." I lowered my smock. We'd come straight home, but Matthew had sent Pierre to fetch Susanna and Goody Alsop anyway. Now the house was full to bursting with angry vampires and witches. "Maybe you can convince him of it."

Susanna rinsed her hands in the basin of hot, soapy water. "If your husband will not believe his own eyes, nothing I can do or say will persuade him." She called for Matthew. Gallowglass came with him, the two of them filling the doorway.

"Are you all right, in truth?" Gallowglass's face was ashen.

"I had a broken finger and a cracked rib. I could have gotten them falling on the stairs. Thanks to Susanna, my finger is completely healed." I stretched my hand. It was still swollen, and I had to wear Ysabeau's ring on my other hand, but I could move the fingers without pain. The gash in my side would take more time. Matthew had refused to use vampire blood to heal it, so Susanna had resorted to a few magical stitches and a poultice instead.

"There are many good reasons to hate Louisa at this moment," Matthew said grimly, "but here is something to be thankful for: She did not wish to kill you. Louisa's aim is impeccable. Had she wanted to put her lance through your heart, you would be dead."

"Louisa was too preoccupied with the prophecy that Gerbert shared with Ysabeau."

Gallowglass and Matthew exchanged looks.

"It's nothing," Matthew said dismissively, "just some idiotic thing he dreamed up to excite *Maman.*"

"It was Meridiana's prophecy, wasn't it?" I had known it in my bones ever since Louisa mentioned it. The words brought back memories of Gerbert's touch at La Pierre. And they had made the air around Louisa snap with electricity, as though she were Pandora and had taken the lid off a trove of long-forgotten magic.

"Meridiana wanted to frighten Gerbert about the future. She did." Matthew shook his head. "It's got nothing to do with you."

"Your father is the lion. You are the wolf." Ice pooled in the pit of my stomach. It told me something was wrong with me, inside where the light could never quite reach. I looked at my husband, one of the children of the night mentioned in the prophecy. Our first child had already died. I shuttered my thoughts, not wanting to hold them in my heart or my head long enough to make an impression. But it did no good. There was too much honesty between us now to hide from Matthew—or myself.

"You have nothing to fear," Matthew said, brushing his lips over mine. "You are too full of life to be a harbinger of destruction."

I let him reassure me, but my sixth sense ignored him. Somehow, somewhere, a dangerous and deadly force had been unleashed. Even now I could feel its threads tightening, drawing me toward the darkness.

36

I was waiting under the sign of the Golden Gosling for Annie to pick up some stew for tonight's supper when the steady regard of a vampire drove the hint of summer from the air.

"Father Hubbard," I said, turning in the direction of the coldness.

The vampire's eyes flickered over my rib cage. "I am surprised your husband allows you to walk about the city unaccompanied, given what happened at Greenwich—and that you are carrying his child."

My firedrake, who had become fiercely protective since the incident in the tiltyard, coiled her tail around my hips.

"Everybody knows that *wearhs* can't father children on warmblooded women," I said dismissively.

"It seems that the impossible holds little sway with a witch such as you." Hubbard's grim countenance tightened further. "Most creatures believe that Matthew's contempt for witches is unchangeable, for example. Few would entertain the notion that it was he who made it possible for Barbara Napier to escape the pyre in Scotland." The events in Berwick continued to occupy Matthew's time as well as creature and human gossip in London.

"Matthew was nowhere near Scotland at the time."

"He didn't need to be. Hancock was in Edinburgh, posing as one of Napier's 'friends.' It was he who brought the matter of her pregnancy to the court's attention." Hubbard's breath was cold and smelled of the forest.

"The witch was innocent of the charges against her," I said brusquely, drawing my shawl around my shoulders. "The jury acquitted her."

"Of a single charge." Hubbard held my gaze. "She was found guilty of many more. And, given your recent return, perhaps you have not heard: King James found a way to reverse the jury's decision in Napier's case."

"Reverse it? How?"

"The king of Scots is not greatly enamored of the Congregation these days, no small thanks to your husband. Matthew's slippery sense of the covenant and his interference in Scottish politics have inspired His Majesty to find his own legal loopholes. James is putting the jurors who acquitted the witch on trial. They are charged with miscarrying the king's justice. Intimidating the jurors will better ensure the outcome of future trials."

"That wasn't Matthew's plan," I said, my mind reeling.

"It sounds sufficiently devious for Matthew de Clermont. Napier and her babe may live, but dozens more innocent creatures will die because of it." Hubbard's expression was deadly. "Isn't that what the de Clermonts want?"

"How dare you!"

"I have the—" Annie stepped out onto the street and nearly dropped her pot. I reached out and hooked her into my arm.

"Thank you, Annie."

"Do you know where your husband is this fine May morning, Mistress Roydon?"

"He is out on business." Matthew had made sure I ate my breakfast, kissed me, and left the house with Pierre. Jack had been inconsolable when Matthew told him he must stay behind with Harriot. I felt a flicker of unease. It wasn't like Matthew to refuse Jack a trip into town.

"No," Hubbard said softly, "he is in Bedlam with his sister and Christopher Marlowe."

Bedlam was an oubliette in all but name—a place for forgetting, where the insane were locked up with those interred by their own families on some trumped-up charge simply to be rid of them. With nothing but straw for bedding, no regular supply of food, not a shred of kindness from the jailers, and no treatment of any sort, most inmates never escaped. If they did, they rarely recovered from the experience.

"Not content with altering the judgment in Scotland, Matthew now seeks to mete out his own justice here in London," Hubbard continued. "He went to question them this morning. I understand he is still there."

It was past noon.

"I have seen Matthew de Clermont kill quickly, when he is enraged. It is terrible to behold. To see him do so slowly, painstakingly, would make the most resolute atheist believe in the devil."

Kit. Louisa was a vampire and shared Ysabeau's blood. She could fend for herself. But a daemon . . .

"Go to Goody Alsop, Annie. Tell her I've gone to Bedlam to look after Master Marlowe and Master Roydon's sister." I turned the girl in the proper direction and released her, putting my own body squarely between her and the vampire.

"I must stay with you," Annie said, her eyes huge. "Master Roydon made me promise!"

"Someone must know where I've gone, Annie. Tell Goody Alsop what you heard here. I can find my way to Bedlam." In truth I had only a vague notion of the notorious asylum's location, but I had other means of discovering Matthew's whereabouts. I wrapped imaginary fingers around the chain within me and got ready to pull it.

"Wait." Hubbard's hand closed around my wrist. I jumped. He called to someone in the shadows. It was the angular young man Matthew referred to by the strangely fitting name Amen Corner. "My son will take you."

"Matthew will know I've been with you now." I looked down at Hubbard's hand. It was still wrapped around my wrist, transferring his telltale scent to my warm skin. "He'll take it out on the boy."

Hubbard's grip tightened, and I let out a soft sound of understanding.

"If you wanted to accompany me to Bedlam as well, Father Hubbard, all you needed to do was ask."

Hubbard knew every shortcut and back alley between St. James Garlickhythe and Bishopsgate. We passed beyond the city limits and into one of London's squalid suburbs. Like Cripplegate, the area around Bedlam was poverty-stricken and desperately crowded. But the true horrors were yet to come.

The keeper met us at the gate and led us into what had once been known as the Hospital of St. Mary of Bethlehem. Master Sleford was well acquainted with Father Hubbard and could not bow and scrape enough as he led us to one of the stout doors across the pitted courtyard. Even with the thick wood and stone of the old medieval priory between us, the inmates' screams were piercing. Most of the windows were unglazed and open to the elements. The stench of rot, filth, and age was overwhelming.

"Don't," I said, refusing Hubbard's proffered hand as we entered the dank, close confines. There was something obscene about taking his help when I was free and the inmates were offered no assistance at all.

Inside, I was bombarded by the ghosts of past inmates and the jagged threads that twisted around the hospital's current tormented inhabitants. I dealt with the horror by engaging in macabre mathematical exercises, dividing the men and women I saw into smaller groups only to lump them together in a new way.

I counted twenty inmates during our walk down the corridor. Fourteen were daemons. A half dozen of the twenty were completely unclothed, and ten more were dressed only in rags. A woman wearing a filthy though expensive man's suit stared at us with open hostility. She was one of the three humans in the place. There were two witches and one vampire as well. Fifteen of the poor souls were manacled to the wall, chained to the floor, or both. Four of the other five were unable to stand and crouched by the walls chattering and scraping at the stone. One of the patients was free. He danced, naked, down the corridor ahead of us.

One room had a door. Something told me that Louisa and Kit were behind it.

The keeper unlocked the door and knocked sharply. When he didn't get an immediate response, he pounded.

"I heard you the first time, Master Sleford." Gallowglass looked decidedly the worse for wear, with fresh scratches down his cheek and blood on his doublet. When he saw me standing behind Sleford, he did a double take. "Auntie."

"Let me in."

"That's not such a good—" Gallowglass took another look at my expression and stepped aside. "Louisa's lost a fair bit of blood. She's hungry. Stay away from her, unless you're of a mind to be bitten or clawed. I've trimmed her nails, but there's not much I can do about her teeth."

Although nothing stood in my way, I remained rooted to the threshold. The beautiful, cruel Louisa was chained to an iron ring set into the stone floor. Her dress was in tatters, and blood from deep gashes in her neck covered her. Someone had been asserting his dominance over Louisa—someone stronger and angrier than she was.

I searched the shadows until I found a dark figure crouched over a lump on the floor. Matthew's head swung up, his face ghostly pale and his eyes black as night. Not a speck of blood was on him. Like Hubbard's offer of help, his cleanliness was somehow obscene.

"You should be at home, Diana." Matthew stood.

"I am exactly where I need to be, thank you." I moved in my husband's direction. "Blood rage and poppy don't mix, Matthew. How much of their blood have you taken?" The lump on the floor stirred.

"I am here, Christopher," Hubbard called. "You will come to no more harm."

Marlowe wept with relief, his body racked with sobs.

"Bedlam isn't in London, Hubbard," Matthew said coldly. "You're out of your bailiwick, and Kit is beyond your protection."

"Christ, here we go again." Gallowglass closed the door in Sleford's stunned face. "Lock it!" he barked through the wood, punctuating his command with a thud of his fist.

Louisa sprang to her feet when the metal mechanism ground shut, the chains rattling around her ankles and wrists. One of them snapped, and I jumped as the broken links chimed against the floor. A sympathetic banging of chains sounded along the corridor.

"Notmybloodnotmybloodnotmyblood," Louisa chanted. She was as flat as possible against the far wall. When I met her eyes, she whimpered and turned away. "Begone, *fantôme.* I have already died once and have nothing to fear from ghosts like you."

"Be quiet." Matthew's voice was low, but it cracked through the room with enough force that we all jumped.

"Thirsty," Louisa croaked. "Please, Matthew."

There was a regular splat of wetness against stone. With each splash Louisa's body jerked. Someone had suspended a stag's head by the antlers, its eyes empty and staring. Blood fell, one drop at a time, from its severed neck and onto the floor just beyond the reach of Louisa's chains.

"Stop torturing her!" I stepped forward, but Gallowglass's hand held me back.

"I can't let you interfere, Auntie," he said firmly. "Matthew's right: You don't belong in the middle of this."

"Gallowglass." Matthew shook his head in warning. Gallowglass released my arm and watched his uncle warily.

"Very well, then. Let me answer your earlier question, Auntie. Matthew has had just enough of Kit's blood to keep his blood rage burning. You may need this if you want to talk to him." Gallowglass tossed me a knife. I made no move to catch it, and the blade clattered to the stones.

"You are more than this disease, Matthew." I stepped over the blade and made my way to his side. We stood so close that my skirts brushed against his boots. "Let Father Hubbard see to Kit."

"No." Matthew's expression was unyielding.

"What would Jack think if he saw you this way?" I was willing to use guilt rather than steel to bring Matthew to his senses. "You're his hero. Heroes do not torment their friends or family."

"They tried to kill you!" Matthew's roar reverberated through the small room.

"They were out of their minds with opiates and alcohol. Neither of them knew what they were doing," I retorted. "Nor, may I add, do you in your present state."

"Don't fool yourself. Both of them knew exactly what they were doing. Kit was ridding himself of an obstacle to his happiness without a care for anyone else. Louisa was succumbing to the same cruel urges she's indulged since the day she was made." Matthew ran his fingers through his hair. "I know what I'm doing, too."

"Yes—you're punishing yourself. You are convinced that biology is destiny, at least so far as your own blood rage is concerned. As a result you think you're just like Louisa and Kit. Just another madman. I asked you to stop denying your instincts, Matthew, not to become a slave to them."

This time, when I took a step toward Matthew's sister, she sprang at me, spitting and snarling.

"And there's your greatest fear for the future: that you will be reduced to an animal, chained up and waiting for the next punishment because it's what you deserve." I went back to him, gripping his shoulders. "You are not this man, Matthew. You never were."

"I've told you before not to romanticize me," he said shortly. He dragged his eyes away from mine, but not before I'd seen the desperation there.

"So this is for my benefit, too? You're still trying to prove that you're not worth loving?" His hands were clenched at his sides. I reached for them and forced them open, pulling them flat against my belly. "Hold our child, look me in the eye, and tell us that there's no hope for a different ending to this story."

As on the night I'd waited for him to take my vein, time stretched out to infinity while Matthew wrestled with himself. Now, as then, I could do nothing to speed the process or help him choose life over death. He had to grab hope's fragile thread without any help from me.

"I don't know," he finally admitted. "Once I knew that love between a vampire and a witch was wrong. I was sure the four species were distinct. I accepted the deaths of witches if it meant that vampires and daemons survived." Though his pupils still eclipsed his eyes, a bright sliver of green appeared. "I told myself that the madness among daemons and the weaknesses among vampires were relatively recent developments, but now that I see Louisa and Kit . . ."

"You don't know." I lowered my voice. "None of us do. It's a frightening prospect. But we have to hope in the future, Matthew. I don't want our children to be born under this same shadow, hating and fearing who they are."

I waited for him to fight me further, but he remained silent.

"Let Gallowglass take responsibility for your sister. Allow Hubbard to tend to Kit. And try to forgive them."

"*Wearhs* do not forgive as easily as warmbloods do," Gallowglass said gruffly. "You cannot ask that of him."

"Matthew asked it of you," I pointed out.

"Aye, and I told him the best he could hope for was that I might, in time, forget. Don't demand more from Matthew than he can give, Auntie. He is his own worst rack master, and he needs no assistance from you." Gallowglass's voice held a warning.

"I would like to forget, witch," Louisa said primly, as if she were making a simple choice of fabric for a new gown. She waved her hand in the air. "All of this. Use your magic and make these horrible dreams go away."

It was in my power to do it. I could see the threads binding her to Bedlam, to Matthew, and to me. But though I didn't want to torture Louisa, I was not so forgiving as to grant her peace.

"No, Louisa," I said. "You will remember Greenwich for the rest of your days, and me, and even how you hurt Matthew. Let that be your prison, and not this place." I turned to Gallowglass. "Make sure she isn't a danger to herself or anyone else, before you set her free."

"Oh, she won't enjoy any freedom," Gallowglass promised. "She'll go from here to wherever Philippe sends her. After what she's done, my grandfather will never let her roam again."

"Tell them, Matthew!" Louisa pleaded. "You understand what it is to have these . . . things crawling in your skull. I cannot bear them!" She pulled at her hair with a manacled hand.

"And Kit?" Gallowglass asked. "You are sure you want him in Hubbard's custody, Matthew? I know that Hancock would be delighted to dispatch him."

"He is Hubbard's creature, not mine." Matthew's tone was absolute. "I care not what happens to him."

"What I did was out of love—" Kit began.

"You did it out of spite," Matthew said, turning his back on his best friend.

"Father Hubbard," I called as he rushed to collect his charge. "Kit's actions at Greenwich will be forgotten, provided that what happened here stays within these walls."

"You promise this, on behalf of all the de Clermonts?" Hubbard's pale eyebrows lifted. "Your husband must give me this assurance, not you."

"My word is going to have to be enough," I said, standing my ground.

"Very well, Madame de Clermont." It was the first time that Hubbard had used the title. "You are indeed Philippe's daughter. I accept your family's terms."

Even after we left Bedlam, I could feel its darkness clinging to us. Matthew did, too. It followed us everywhere we went in London, accompanied us to dinner, visited with our friends. There was only one way to rid ourselves of it.

We had to return to our present.

Without discussion or conscious plans, we both began putting our affairs in order, snipping the threads that bound us to the past we now shared. Françoise had been planning to rejoin us in London, but we sent word for her to remain at the Old Lodge. Matthew had long and complicated conversations with Gallowglass about the lies his nephew would have to tell so as not to reveal to the sixteenth-century Matthew that he'd been temporarily replaced by his future self. The sixteenth-century Matthew could not be allowed to see Kit or Louisa, for neither could be trusted. Walter and Henry would make up some story to explain any discontinuities in behavior. Matthew sent Hancock to Scotland to prepare for a new life there. I worked with Goody Alsop, perfecting the knots I would use to weave the spell that would carry us into the future.

Matthew met me in St. James Garlickhythe after one of my lessons and suggested we stroll through St. Paul's Churchyard on our way home. It was two weeks from midsummer, and the days were sunny and bright in spite of Bedlam's persistent pall.

Though Matthew still looked drawn after his experience with Louisa and Kit, it felt almost like old times when we stopped at the booksellers to see the latest titles and news. I was reading a fresh volley in the war of words between two spatting Cambridge graduates when Matthew stiffened.

"Chamomile. Oak leaves. And coffee." His head swung around at the unfamiliar scent.

"Coffee?" I asked, wondering how something that had not yet come to England could possibly be scenting the air around St. Paul's. But Matthew was no longer beside me to answer. Instead he was pushing his way through the crowd, his sword in one hand.

I sighed. Matthew couldn't stop himself from going after every thief in the market. At times I wished his eyesight were not so keen, his moral compass less absolute.

This time he was pursuing a man about five inches shorter than he was, with thick brown curls peppered with gray. The man was slender and slightly stooped at the shoulders, as though he spent too much time hunched over books. Something about the combination tugged at my memory.

The man sensed the danger approaching and turned. Alas, he carried a pitifully small dagger no bigger than a penknife. That wasn't going to be much use against Matthew. Hoping to avoid a bloodbath, I hurried after my husband.

Matthew grabbed the poor man's hand so tightly that his inadequate weapon fell to the ground. With one knee the vampire pressed his prey against the bookstall, the flat of his sword against the man's neck. I did a double take.

"Daddy?" I whispered. It couldn't be. I stared at him incredulously, my heart hammering with excitement and shock.

"Hello, Miss Bishop," my father replied, glancing up from Matthew's sharp-edged blade. "Fancy meeting you here."

My father looked calm as he faced an unfamiliar, armed vampire and his own grown daughter. Only the slight tremor in his voice and his white-knuckled grip on the stall gave him away.

"Dr. Proctor, I presume." Matthew stepped away and sheathed his weapon.

My father straightened his serviceable brown jacket. It was all wrong. Someone—probably my mother—had tried to modify a Nehru jacket into something resembling a cleric's cassock. And his britches were too long, more like something Ben Franklin would wear than Walter Raleigh. But his familiar voice, which I hadn't heard for twenty-six years, was exactly right.

"You've grown in the past three days," he said shakily.

"You look just as I remember," I said numbly, still stunned by the fact that he was standing before me. Mindful that two witches and a *wearh* might be too much for the St. Paul's Churchyard crowd, and unsure what to do in this novel situation, I fell back on social convention. "Do you want to come back to our house for a drink?" I suggested awkwardly.

"Sure, honey. That would be great," he said with a tentative nod.

My father and I couldn't stop looking at each other—not on our way home nor when we reached the safety of the Hart and Crown, which was, miraculously, empty. There he caught me up in a fierce hug.

"It's really you. You sound just like your mom," he said, holding me at arm's length to study my features. "You look like her, too."

"People tell me I have your eyes," I said, studying him in turn. When you're seven, you don't notice such things. You only think to look for them afterward, when it's too late.

"So you do." Stephen laughed.

"Diana has your ears, too. And your scents are somewhat similar. It's how I recognized you at St. Paul's." Matthew ran his hand nervously over his cropped hair, then stuck it out to my father. "I'm Matthew."

My father eyed the offered hand. "No last name? Are you some sort of celebrity, like Halston or Cher?" I had a sudden, vivid image of what I'd missed by not having my father around when I was a teenager, making an ass out of himself when he met the boys I dated. My eyes filled.

"Matthew has plenty of last names. It's just . . . complicated," I said, sniffing back the tears. My father looked alarmed at the sudden welling up of emotion.

"Matthew Roydon will do for now," Matthew said, capturing my father's attention. He and my father shook hands.

"So you're the vampire," my father said. "Rebecca is worried sick about the practicalities of your relationship with my daughter, and Diana can't even ride a bicycle yet."

"Oh, Dad." The minute the words were out of my mouth I blushed. I sounded as if I were twelve. Matthew smiled as he moved to the table.

"Won't you sit down and have some wine, Stephen?" Matthew handed him a cup and then pulled out a chair for me. "Seeing Diana must be something of a shock."

"You could say so. I'd love some." My father sat, took a sip of wine, and nodded approvingly before making a visible effort to take charge. "So," he said briskly, "we've said hello, you've invited me back to your house, and now I've had a drink. These are the essential Western greeting rituals. Now we can get down to it. What are you doing here, Diana?"

"Me? What are *you* doing here? And where is Mom?" I pushed away the wine that Matthew poured for me.

"Your mother is at home taking care of you." My father shook his head, amazed. "I can't believe it. You can't be more than ten years younger than I am."

"I always forget you're so much older than Mom."

"You're with a vampire and you have something against our May-December romance?" My father's whimsical expression invited me to laugh.

I did, while quickly doing the math. "So you've come from around 1980?"

"Yep. I finally got my grades turned in and headed out to do some exploring." Stephen studied us. "Is this when and where you two met?"

"No. We met in September 2009 at Oxford. In the Bodleian Library." I looked at Matthew, who gave me an encouraging smile. I turned back to my father and took a deep breath. "I can timewalk like you. I brought Matthew with me."

"I know you can timewalk, peanut. You scared the hell out of your mother last August when you disappeared on your third birthday. A time-walking toddler is a mother's worst nightmare." He looked at me shrewdly. "So you've got my eyes, ears, scent, and timewalking ability. Anything else?"

I nodded. "I can make up spells."

"Oh. We hoped you would be inclined toward fire like your mom, but no such luck." My father looked uncomfortable and dropped his voice. "You probably shouldn't mention your talent in the company of other witches. And when they try to teach you their spells, just let them go in one ear and out the other. Don't even attempt to learn them."

"I wish you'd told me that before. It would have helped me with Sarah," I said.

"Good old Sarah." My father's laugh was warm and infectious.

There was a thunder of feet on the stairs, and then a four-legged mop and a boy hurtled across the threshold, banging the door into the wall with the force of their enthusiastic entrance.

"Master Harriot said I may go out with him again and look at the stars, and he promises not to forget me this time. Master Shakespeare gave me this." Jack waved a slip of paper in the air. "He says it is a letter of credit. And Annie kept staring at a boy in the Cardinal's Hat while she ate her pie. Who is that?" The last was said with one grimy finger pointed in my father's direction.

"That's Master Proctor," Matthew said, catching Jack around the waist. "Did you feed Mop on your way in?" There had been no way to separate boy and dog in Prague, so Mop had come to London, where his strange appearance made him something of a local curiosity.

"Of course I fed Mop. He eats my shoes if I forget, and Pierre said he would pay for one new pair without telling you about it, but not a second." Jack clapped his hand over his mouth.

"I am sorry, Mistress Roydon. He ran down the street and I couldn't catch him." A frowning Annie rushed into the room, then stopped short, the color draining from her face as she stared at my father.

"It's all right, Annie," I said gently. She had been afraid of unfamiliar creatures ever since Greenwich. "This is Master Proctor. He's a friend."

"I have marbles. Do you know how to play ring taw?" Jack was eyeing my father with open speculation as he tried to determine whether the new arrival would be a useful person to have around.

"Master Proctor is here to speak with Mistress Roydon, Jack." Matthew spun him around. "We need water, wine, and bread. You and Annie divide up the chores, and when Pierre gets back, he'll take you to Moorfields."

With some grumbling Jack accompanied Annie back out into the street. I met my father's eyes at last. He had been watching Matthew and me without speaking, and the air was thick with his questions.

"Why are you here, honey?" my father repeated quietly when the children were gone.

"We thought we might find someone to help me out with some questions about magic and alchemy." For some reason I didn't want my father to know the details. "My teacher is called Goody Alsop. She and her coven have taken me in."

"Nice try, Diana. I'm a witch, too, so I know when you're skirting the truth." My father sat back in his chair. "You'll have to tell me eventually. I just thought this would save some time."

"Why are *you* here, Stephen?" Matthew asked.

"Just hanging out. I'm an anthropologist. It's what I do. What do you do?"

"I'm a scientist—a biochemist, based in Oxford."

"You're not just 'hanging out' in Elizabethan London, Dad. You have the page from Ashmole 782 already." I suddenly understood why he was here. "You're looking for the rest of the manuscript." I lowered the wooden candle beam. Master Habermel's astronomical compendium was nestled between two candles. We had to move it every day, because Jack found it every day.

"What page?" my father asked, sounding suspiciously innocent.

"The page with the picture of the alchemical wedding on it. It came from a Bodleian Library manuscript." I opened the compendium. It was completely still, just as I expected. "Look, Matthew."

"Cool," my father said with a whistle.

"You should see her mousetrap," Matthew said under his breath.

"What does it do?" My father reached for the compendium to take a closer look.

"It's a mathematical instrument for telling time and tracking astronomical events like the phases of the moon. It started to move on its own when we were in Prague. I thought it meant someone was looking for Matthew and me, but now I wonder if it wasn't picking up on you, looking for the manuscript." It still acted up periodically, its wheels spinning without warning. Everybody in the house called it the "witch clock."

"Maybe I should go get the book," Matthew said, rising.

"It's all right," my father replied, motioning for him to sit. "There's no rush. Rebecca isn't expecting me for a few days."

"So you'll be here—in London?"

My father's face softened. He nodded.

"Where are you staying?" Matthew asked.

"Here!" I said indignantly. "He's staying here." After so many years without him, letting him out of my sight was unthinkable.

"Your daughter has very definite opinions about her family checking into hotels," Matthew told my father with a wry smile, remembering how I'd reacted when he'd tried to put Marcus and Miriam up in an inn in Cazenovia. "You're welcome to stay with us, of course."

"I've got rooms on the other side of town," my father said hesitantly.

"Stay." I pressed my lips together and blinked to keep back the tears. "Please." I had so much I wanted to ask him, so many questions only he could answer. My father and husband exchanged a long look.

"All right," my father said finally. "It would be great to hang out with you for a little while."

I tried to give him our room, since Matthew wouldn't be able to sleep with a strange person in the house and I could easily fit on the window seat, but my father refused. Pierre gave up his bed instead. I stood on the landing and listened enviously while Jack and my father chattered away like old friends.

"I think Stephen has everything he needs," Matthew said, sliding his arms around me.

"Is he disappointed in me?" I wondered aloud.

"Your father?" Matthew sounded incredulous. "Of course not!"

"He seems a little uncomfortable."

"When Stephen kissed you good-bye a few days ago, you were a toddler. He's overwhelmed, that's all."

"Does he know what's going to happen to him and Mom?" I whispered.

"I don't know, *mon coeur,* but I think so." Matthew drew me toward our bedchamber. "Come to bed. Everything will look different in the morning."

Matthew was right: My father was a bit more relaxed the next day, though he didn't look as if he'd slept much. Neither did Jack.

"Does the kid always have such bad nightmares?" my father asked.

"I'm sorry he kept you up," I apologized. "Change makes him anxious. Matthew usually takes care of him."

"I know. I saw him," my father said, sipping at the herbal tisane that Annie prepared.

That was the problem with my father: He saw everything. His watchfulness put vampires to shame. Though I had hundreds of questions—about my mother and her magic, about the page from Ashmole 782—they all seemed to dry up under his quiet regard. Occasionally he asked me about something trivial. Could I throw a baseball? Did I think Bob Dylan was a genius? Had I been taught how to pitch a tent? He asked no questions about Matthew and me, or where I went to school, or even what I did for a living. Without any expression of interest on his part, I felt awkward volunteering the information. By the end of our first day together, I was practically in tears.

"Why won't he talk to me?" I demanded as Matthew unlaced my corset.

"Because he's too busy listening. He's an anthropologist—a professional watcher. You're the historian in the family. Questions are your forte, not his."

"I get tongue-tied around him and don't know where to start. And when he does talk to me, it's always about strange topics, like whether allowing designated hitters has ruined baseball."

"That's what a father would talk to his daughter about when he started taking her to baseball games. So Stephen does know he won't see you grow up. He just doesn't know how much time he has left with you."

I sank onto the edge of the bed. "He was a huge Red Sox fan. I remember Mom saying that between getting her pregnant and Carlton Fisk hitting a home run in the sixth game of the World Series, 1975 was the best fall semester of his life, even if Cincinnati did beat Boston in the end."

Matthew laughed softly. "I'm sure the fall semester of 1976 topped it."

"Did the Sox actually win that year?"

"No. Your father did." Matthew kissed me and blew out the candle.

When I came home from running errands the next day, I found my father sitting in the parlor of our empty apartments with Ashmole 782 open in front of him.

"Where did you find that?" I asked, putting my parcels on the table. "Matthew was supposed to hide it." I had a hard enough time keeping the children away from that blasted compendium.

"Jack gave it to me. He calls it 'Mistress Roydon's book of monsters.'

I was understandably eager to see it once I heard that." My father turned the page. His fingers were shorter than Matthew's, and blunt and forceful rather than tapered and dexterous. "Is this the book the picture of the wedding came from?"

"Yes. There were two other pictures in it as well: one of a tree, another of two dragons shedding their blood." I stopped. "I'm not sure how much more I should tell you, Dad. I know things about your relationship to this book that you don't know—things that haven't even happened yet."

"Then tell me what happened to you after you discovered it in Oxford. And I want the truth, Diana. I can see the damaged threads between you and the book, all twisted and snarled. And someone harmed you physically."

Silence lay heavily in the room, and there was nowhere to hide from my father's scrutiny. When I couldn't stand it any longer, I met his eyes.

"It was witches. Matthew fell asleep, and I went outside to get some air. It was supposed to be safe. A witch captured me." I shifted in my seat. "End of story. Let's talk about something else. Don't you want to know where I went to school? I'm a historian. I have tenure. At Yale." I would talk about anything with my father—except the chain of events that started with the delivery of an old photo to my rooms at New College and ended with the death of Juliette.

"Later. Now I need to know why another witch wanted this book so badly she was willing to kill you for it. Oh, yes," he said at my incredulous look, "I figured that out on my own. A witch used an opening spell on your back and left a terrible scar. I can feel the wound. Matthew's eyes linger there, and your dragon—I know about her, too—shields it with her wings."

"Satu—the witch who captured me—isn't the only creature who wants the book. So does Peter Knox. He's a member of the Congregation."

"Peter Knox," my father said softly. "Well, well, well."

"Have you two met?"

"Unfortunately, yes. He's always had a thing for your mother. Happily, she loathes him." My father looked grim and turned another page. "I sure as hell hope Peter doesn't know about the dead witches in this. There's some dark magic hanging around this book, and Peter has always been interested in that aspect of the craft. I know why he might want it, but why do you and Matthew need it so badly?"

"Creatures are disappearing, Dad. The daemons are getting wilder. Vampire blood is sometimes incapable of transforming a human. And witches aren't producing as many offspring. We're dying out. Matthew believes that this book might help us understand why," I explained. "There's a lot of genetic information in the book—skin, hair, even blood and bones."

"You've married the creature equivalent of Charles Darwin. And is he interested in origins as well as extinction?"

"Yes. He's been trying for a long time to figure out how daemons, witches, and vampires are related to one another and to humans. This manuscript—if we could put it back together and understand its contents—might provide important clues."

My father's hazel eyes met mine. "And these are simply theoretical concerns for your vampire?"

"Not anymore. I'm pregnant, Dad." My hand settled lightly on my abdomen. It had been doing so a lot lately, without my thinking about it.

"I know." He smiled. "I figured that out, too, but it's good to hear you say it."

"You've only been here for forty-eight hours. I don't like to rush things any more than you do," I said, feeling shy. My father got up and took me in his arms. He held me tight. "Besides, you should be surprised. Witches and vampires aren't supposed to fall in love. And they're definitely not supposed to have babies together."

"Your mother warned me about it—she's seen it all with that uncanny sight of hers." He laughed. "What a worrywart. If it's not you she's fussing over, it's the vampire. Congratulations, honey. A child is a wonderful gift."

"I just hope we can handle it. Who knows what our child will be like?"

"You can handle more than you think." My father kissed me on the cheek. "Come on, let's take a walk. You can show me your favorite places in the city. I'd love to meet Shakespeare. One of my idiot colleagues actually thinks Queen Elizabeth wrote *Hamlet*. And speaking of colleagues: How, after years of buying you Harvard bibs and mittens, did I end up with a daughter who teaches at Yale?"

"I'm curious about something," my father said, staring into his wine.

The two of us had enjoyed a lovely walk, we'd all finished a leisurely supper, the children had been sent to bed, and Mop was snoring by the fireplace. Thus far, it had been a perfect day.

"What's that, Stephen?" Matthew asked, looking up from his own cup with a smile.

"How long do you two think you can keep this crazy life you're leading under control?"

Matthew's smile dissolved. "I'm not sure I understand your question," he said stiffly.

"The two of you hold on to everything so damn tightly." My father took a sip of his wine and stared pointedly at Matthew's clenched fist over the rim of his cup. "You might inadvertently destroy what you most love with that grip, Matthew."

"I'll keep that in mind." Matthew was controlling his temper—barely. I opened my mouth to smooth things over.

"Stop trying to fix things, honey," my father said before I could utter a word.

"I'm not," I protested.

"Yes, you are," Stephen said. "Your mother does it all the time, and I recognize the signs. This is my one chance to talk to you as an adult, Diana, and I'm not going to mince words because they make you—or him—uncomfortable."

My father stuck his hand in his jacket and drew out a pamphlet. "You've been trying to fix things, too, Matthew."

"Newes from Scotland," read the small print above the larger type of the headline: DECLARING THE DAMNABLE LIFE OF DOCTOR FIAN A NOTABLE SORCERER, WHO WAS BURNED IN EDENBROUGH IN JANUARIE LAST.

"The whole town is talking about the witches in Scotland," my father said, pushing the pages toward Matthew. "But the creatures are telling a different tale than the warmbloods are. They say that the great and terrible Matthew Roydon, enemy to witches, has been defying the Congregation's wishes and saving the accused."

Matthew's fingers stopped the pages' progress. "You shouldn't believe everything you hear, Stephen. Londoners are fond of idle gossip."

"For two control freaks, you certainly are stirring up a world of trouble. And the trouble won't end here. It will follow you home, too."

"The only thing that is going to follow us home from 1591 is Ashmole 782," I said.

"You can't take the book." My father was emphatic. "It belongs here. You've twisted time enough, staying as long as you have."

"We've been very careful, Dad." I was stung by his criticism.

"Careful? You've been here for seven months. You've conceived a child. The longest I've ever spent in the past is two weeks. You aren't timewalkers anymore. You've succumbed to one of the most basic transgressions of anthropological fieldwork: You've gone native."

"I was here before, Stephen," Matthew said mildly, though his fingers drummed on his thigh. That was never a good sign.

"I'm aware of that, Matthew," my father shot back. "But you've introduced far too many variables for the past to remain as it was."

"The past has changed us," I said, facing down my father's angry stare. "It stands to reason that *we've* changed *it,* too."

"And that's okay? Timewalking is a serious business, Diana. Even for a brief visit, you need a plan—one that includes leaving everything behind as you found it."

I shifted in my seat. "We weren't supposed to be here this long. One thing led to another, and now—"

"Now you're going to leave a mess. You'll probably find one when you get home, too." My father looked at us somberly.

"I get it, Dad. We screwed up."

"You did," he said gently. "You two might want to think about that while I go to the Cardinal's Hat. Someone named Gallowglass introduced himself in the courtyard. He says he's Matthew's relative and promised to help me meet Shakespeare, since my own daughter refused." My father gave me a peck on the cheek. There was disappointment in it, as well as forgiveness. "Don't wait up for me."

Matthew and I sat in silence while the sound of my father's footsteps faded. I took a shaky breath.

"Did we screw up, Matthew?" I reviewed the past months: meeting Philippe, breaking through Matthew's defenses, getting to know Goody Alsop and the other witches, finding out I was a weaver, befriending Mary and the ladies of Malá Strana, taking Jack and Annie into our home and our hearts, recovering Ashmole 782, and, yes, conceiving a child. My hand dropped to my belly in a protective gesture. There wasn't a single thing I would change, if given the choice.

"It's hard to know, *mon coeur,*" Matthew said somberly. "Time will tell."

"I thought we could go see Goody Alsop. She's helping me with my spell to return to the future." I stood before my father, my spell box clutched in my hands. I was still uneasy around him after the lecture he'd given Matthew and me last night.

"It's about time," my father said, reaching for his jacket. He still wore it like a modern man, taking it off the minute he was indoors and rolling up his shirtsleeves. "I didn't think any of my hints were getting through to you. I can't wait to meet an experienced weaver. And are you finally going to show me what's in the box?"

"If you were curious about it, why didn't you ask?"

"You'd covered it so carefully with that wispy thing of yours that I figured you didn't want anybody to mention it," he said as we descended the stairs.

When we arrived in the parish of St. James Garlickhythe, Goody Alsop's fetch opened the door.

"Come in, come in," the witch said, beckoning us toward her seat by the fire. Her eyes were bright and snapping with excitement. "We've been waiting for you."

The whole coven was there, sitting on the edge of their seats.

"Goody Alsop, this is my father, Stephen Proctor."

"The weaver." Goody Alsop beamed with satisfaction. "You're a watery one, like your daughter." My father hung back as he always did, watching everybody and saying as little as possible while I made the introductions. All the women smiled and nodded, though Catherine had to repeat everything to Elizabeth Jackson because my father's accent was so strange.

"But we are being rude. Would you care to share your creature's name?" Goody Alsop peered at my father's shoulders, where the faint outlines of a heron could be seen. I'd never noticed it before.

"You can see Bennu?" my father said, surprised.

"Of course. He perches, open-winged, across your shoulders. My familiar spirit does not have wings, even though I am strongly tied to the air. She was easier to tame for that reason, I suspect. When I was a girl, a weaver came to London with a harpy for a familiar. Ella was her name, and she was very difficult to train."

Goody Alsop's fetch wafted around my father, crooning softly to the bird as it became more visible.

"Perhaps your Bennu can coax Diana's firedrake to give up her name. It would make it much easier for your daughter to return to her own time, I think. We don't want any trace of her familiar left here, dragging Diana back to London."

"Wow." My father was struggling to take it all in—the gathering of witches, Goody Alsop's fetch, the fact that his secrets were on display.

"Who?" Elizabeth Jackson asked politely, assuming she'd misunderstood.

My father drew back and studied Elizabeth carefully. "Have we met?"

"No. It is the water in my veins that you recognize. We are happy to have you among us, Master Proctor. London has not had three weavers within her walls in some time. The city is abuzz."

Goody Alsop motioned to the chair beside her. "Do sit."

My father took the place of honor. "Nobody at home knows about this weaving business."

"Not even Mom?" I was aghast. "Dad, you've got to tell her."

"Oh, she knows. But I didn't have to tell her. I showed her." My father's fingers curled and released in an instinctive gesture of command.

The world lit up in shades of blue, gray, lavender, and green as he plucked at all the hidden watery threads in the room: the willow branches in a jug by the window, the silver candlestick that Goody Alsop used for her spells, the fish that was waiting to be roasted for supper. Everyone and everything in the room was cast into those same watery hues. Bennu took flight, his silver-tipped wings stirring the air into waves. Goody Alsop's fetch was blown this way and that in the currents, her shape shifting into a long-stemmed lily, then returning to human form and sprouting wings. It was as if the two familiars were playing. At the prospect of recreation, my firedrake flicked her tail and beat her own wings against my ribs.

"Not now," I told her tightly, gripping at my bodice. The last thing we needed was a cavorting firedrake. My control over the past might have slipped, but I knew better than to let go of a dragon in Elizabethan London.

"Let her out, Diana," my father urged. "Ben will take care of her."

But I couldn't bring myself to do it. My father called to Bennu, who faded into his shoulders. The watery magic around me faded, too.

"Why are you so afraid?" my father asked quietly.

"I'm afraid because of this!" I waved my cords in the air. "And this!" I hit my ribs, jostling my firedrake. She belched in response. My hand slid down to where our child was growing. "And this. It's too much. I don't need to use showy elemental magic the way you just did. I'm happy as I am."

"You can weave spells, command a firedrake, and bend the rules that govern life and death. You're as volatile as creation itself, Diana. These are powers any self-respecting witch would kill for."

I looked at him in horror. He'd brought the one thing I couldn't face into the room: Witches had already killed for these powers. They'd killed my father, and my mother, too.

"Putting your magic into neat little boxes and keeping it separate from your craft isn't going to keep Mom and me from our fates," my father continued sadly.

"That's not what I'm trying to do."

"Really?" His eyebrows lifted. "You want to try that again, Diana?"

"Sarah says elemental magic and the craft are separate. She says—"

"Forget what Sarah says!" My father took me by the shoulders. "You aren't Sarah. You aren't like any other witch who has ever lived. And you don't have to choose between spells and the power that's right at your fingertips. We're weavers, right?"

I nodded.

"Then think of elemental magic as the warp—the strong fibers that make up the world—and spells as the weft. They're both part of a single tapestry. It's all one big system, honey. And you can master it, if you set aside your fear."

I could see the possibilities shimmering around me in webs of color and shadow, yet the fear remained.

"Wait. I have a connection to fire, like Mom does. We don't know how the water and fire will react. I haven't had those lessons yet." *Because of Prague,* I thought. *Because we got distracted by the hunt for Ashmole 782 and forgot to focus on the future and getting back to it.*

"So you're a switch-hitter—a witchy secret weapon." He laughed. He *laughed.*

"This is serious, Dad."

"It doesn't have to be." My father let that sink in, then crooked his finger, catching a single gray-green thread on the end of it.

"What are you doing?" I asked suspiciously.

"Watch," he said in a whisper like waves against the shore. He drew his finger toward him and pursed his lips as if he were holding an invisible bubble wand. When he blew out, a ball of water formed. He flicked his fingers in the direction of the water bucket near the hearth, and the ball turned to ice, floated over, and dropped into it with a splash. "Bull's-eye."

Elizabeth giggled, releasing a stream of water bubbles that popped in the air, each one sending out a tiny shower of water.

"You don't like the unknown, Diana, but sometimes you've got to embrace it. You were terrified when I put you on a tricycle the first time. And you threw your blocks at the wall when you couldn't get them all to fit back in their box. We made it through those crises. I'm sure we can handle this." My father held his hand out.

"But it's so . . ."

"Messy? So is life. Stop trying to be perfect. Try being real for a change." My father's arm swept through the air, revealing all the threads that were normally hidden from view. "The whole world is in this room. Take your time and get to know it."

I studied the patterns, saw the clumps of color around the witches that indicated their particular strengths. Threads of fire and water surrounded me in a mess of conflicting shades. My panic returned.

"Call the fire," my father said, as if it were as simple as ordering a pizza.

After a moment of hesitation, I crooked my finger and wished for the fire to come to me. An orange-red thread caught on the tip, and when I let my breath out through pursed lips, dozens of tiny bubbles of light and heat flew into the air like fireflies.

"Lovely, Diana!" Catherine cried out, clapping her hands.

Between the clapping and the fire, my firedrake wanted to be released. Bennu cried out from my father's shoulders, and the firedrake answered. "No," I said, gritting my teeth.

"Don't be such a spoilsport. She's a dragon—not a goldfish. Why are you always trying to pretend that the magical is ordinary? Let her fly!"

I relaxed just a fraction, and my ribs softened, opening away from my spine like the leaves of a book. My firedrake escaped the bony confines at the first opportunity, flapping her wings as they metamorphosed from gray and insubstantial to iridescent and gleaming. Her tail curled up in a loose knot, and she soared around the room. The firedrake caught the tiny balls of light in her teeth, swallowing them down like candy. She then turned her attention to my father's water bubbles as if they were fine champagne. When she was through with her treats, the firedrake hovered in the air before me, her tail flicking at the floor. She cocked her head and waited.

"What are you?" I asked, wondering how she managed to absorb all the conflicting powers of water and fire.

"You, but not you." The firedrake blinked, her glassy eyes studying me. A swirling ball of energy balanced at the end of her spade-shaped tail. The firedrake gave her tail a flick, tipping the ball into my cupped hands. It looked just like the one I had given Matthew back in Madison.

"What is your name?" I whispered.

"You may call me Corra," she said in a language of smoke and mist. Corra bobbed her head in farewell, melted into a gray shadow, and disappeared.

Her weight thudded into my center, her wings curved around my back, and there was stillness. I took a deep breath.

"That was great, honey." My father squeezed me tight. "You were thinking like fire. Empathy is the secret to most things in life—including magic. Look how bright the threads are now!"

All around us the world gleamed with possibility. And, in the corners, the steadily brightening indigo and amber weave warned that time was growing impatient.

"My two weeks are up. It's time for me to go."

My father's words weren't unexpected, but they felt like a blow nevertheless. My eyelids dropped to cover my reaction.

"Your mother will think I've taken up with an orange seller if I don't show up soon."

"Orange sellers are more of a seventeenth-century thing," I said absently, picking at the cords in my lap. I was now making steady progress with everything from simple charms against headaches to the more complicated weavings that could make waves ruffle on the Thames. I twined the gold and blue strands around my fingers. *Strength and understanding.*

"Wow. Nice recovery, Diana." My father turned to Matthew. "She bounces back fast."

"Tell me about it," was my husband's equally dry reply. They both relied on humor to smooth over the rough edges of their interactions, which sometimes made them unbearable.

"I'm glad I got to know you, Matthew—despite that scary look you get when you think I'm bossing Diana around," my father said with a laugh.

Ignoring their banter, I twisted the yellow cord in with the gold and blue. *Persuasion.*

"Can you stay until tomorrow? It would be a shame to miss the celebrations." It was Midsummer Eve, and the city was in a holiday mood. Worried that a final evening with his daughter would not be sufficient inducement, I shamelessly appealed to my father's academic interests. "There will be so many folk customs for you to observe."

"Folk customs?" My father laughed. "Very slick. Of course I'm staying until tomorrow. Annie made a wreath of flowers for my hair, and Will and I are going to share some tobacco with Walter. Then I'm going to visit with Father Hubbard."

Matthew frowned. "You know Hubbard?"

"Oh, sure. I introduced myself to him when I arrived. I had to, since he was the man in charge. Father Hubbard figured out I was Diana's father pretty quickly. You all have an amazing sense of smell." My father looked at

Matthew benignly. "An interesting man, with his ideas about creatures all living as one big, happy family."

"It would be utter chaos," I pointed out.

"We all made it through last night with three vampires, two witches, a daemon, two humans, and a dog sharing one roof. Don't be so quick to dismiss new ideas, Diana." My father looked at me disapprovingly. "Then I suppose I'll hang out with Catherine and Marjorie. Lots of witches will be on the prowl tonight. Those two will definitely know where the most fun can be found." Apparently he was on a first-name basis with half the town.

"And you'll be careful. Especially around Will, Daddy. No 'Wow' or 'Well played, Shakespeare.'" My father was fond of slang. It was, he said, the hallmark of the anthropologist.

"If only I could take Will home with me, he'd make a cool—sorry, honey—colleague. He has a sense of humor. Our department could do with someone like him. Put a bit of leavening in the lump, if you know what I mean." My father rubbed his hands together. "What are your plans?"

"We don't have any." I looked at Matthew blankly, and he shrugged.

"I thought I would answer some letters," he said hesitantly. The mail had piled up to alarming levels.

"Oh, no." My father sat back in his chair, looking horrified.

"What?" I turned my head to see who or what had entered the room.

"Don't tell me you're the kind of academics who can't tell the difference between their life and their job." He flung up his hands as if warding off the plague. "I refuse to believe that my daughter could be one of them."

"That's a bit melodramatic, Daddy," I said stiffly. "We could spend the evening with you. I've never smoked. It will be historic to do it with Walter for the first time, since he introduced tobacco into England."

My father looked even more horrified. "Absolutely not. We'll be bonding as fellow men. Lionel Tiger argues—"

"I'm not a big fan of Tiger," Matthew interjected. "The social carnivore never made sense to me."

"Can we put the topic of eating people aside for a moment and discuss why you don't want to spend your last night with Matthew and me?" I was hurt.

"It's not that, honey. Help me out here, Matthew. Take Diana out on a date. You must be able to think of something to do."

"Like roller-skating?" Matthew's brows shot up. "There aren't any skating rinks in sixteenth-century London—and precious few of them left in the twenty-first century, I might add."

"Damn." My father and Matthew had been playing "fad versus trend" for days, and while my father was delighted to know that the popularity of disco and the Pet Rock would fade, he was shocked to hear that other things—like the leisure suit—were now the butt of jokes. "I love roller-skating. Rebecca and I go to a place in Dorchester when we want to get away from Diana for a few hours, and—"

"We'll go for a walk," I said hastily. My father could be unnecessarily frank when it came to discussing how he and my mother spent their free time. He seemed to think it might shock Matthew's sense of propriety. When that failed, he took to calling Matthew "Sir Lancelot" for an added measure of annoyance.

"A walk. You'll take a walk." My father paused. "You mean that literally, don't you?"

He pushed away from the table. "No wonder creatures are going the way of the dodo. Go out. Both of you. Now. And I'm ordering you to have fun." He ushered us toward the door.

"How?" I asked, utterly mystified.

"That is not a question a daughter should ask her father. It's Midsummer Eve. Go out and ask the first person you meet what you should do. Better yet, follow someone else's example. Howl at the moon. Make magic. Make out, at the very least. Surely even Sir Lancelot makes out." He waggled his eyebrows. "Get the picture, Miss Bishop?"

"I think so." My tone reflected my doubts about my father's notion of fun.

"Good. I won't be back until sunrise, so don't wait up. Better yet, stay out all night yourselves. Jack is with Tommy Harriot. Annie is with her aunt. Pierre is— I don't know where Pierre is, but he doesn't need a babysitter. I'll see you at breakfast."

"When did you start calling Thomas Harriot 'Tommy'?" I asked. My father pretended not to hear me.

"Give me a hug before you go. And don't forget to have fun, okay?" He enveloped me in his arms. "Catch you on the flip side, baby."

Stephen pushed us out the door and shut it in our faces. I extended my hand to the latch and found it taken into a vampire's cool grip.

"He'll be leaving in a few hours, Matthew." I reached for the door with the other hand. Matthew took that one, too.

"I know. So does he," Matthew explained.

"Then he should understand that I want to spend more time with him." I stared at the door, willing my father to open it. I could see the threads leading from me, through the grain in the wood, to the wizard on the other side. One of the threads snapped and struck the back of my hand like a rubber band. I gasped. "Daddy!"

"Get moving, Diana!" he shouted.

Matthew and I wandered around town, watching the shops close early and noting the revelers already filling the pubs. More than one butcher was casually stacking bones by the front door. They were white and clean, as though they had been boiled.

"What's going on with the bones?" I asked Matthew after we saw the third such display.

"They're for the bone fires."

"Bonfires?"

"No," Matthew said, "the bone fires. Traditionally, people celebrate Midsummer Eve by lighting fires: bone fires, wood fires, and mixed fires. The mayor's warnings to cease and desist all such superstitious celebrations go up every year, and people light them anyway."

Matthew treated me to dinner at the famous Belle Savage Inn just outside the Blackfriars on Ludgate Hill. More than a simple eatery, the Belle Savage was an entertainment complex where customers could see plays and fencing matches—not to mention Marocco, the famous horse who could pick virgins out of the crowd. It wasn't roller-skating in Dorchester, but it was close.

The city's teenagers were out in force, shouting insults and innuendos at one another as they went from one watering hole to another. During the day most were hard at work as servants or apprentices. Even in the evenings their time was not their own, since their masters expected them to watch over the shops and houses, tend children, fetch food and water, and do the hundred other small chores that were required to keep an early-modern household going. Tonight London belonged to them, and they were making the most of it.

We passed back through Ludgate and approached the entrance to the Blackfriars as the bells tolled nine o'clock. It was the time the members of the Watch started to make their rounds, and people were expected to head for home, but no one seemed to be enforcing the rules tonight. Though the sun had set an hour earlier, the moon was only one day away from full, and the city streets were still bright with moonlight.

"Can we keep walking?" I asked. We were always going somewhere specific—to Baynard's Castle to see Mary, to St. James Garlickhythe to visit with the gathering, to St. Paul's Churchyard for books. Matthew and I had never taken a walk through the city without a destination in mind.

"I don't see why not, since we were ordered to stay out and have fun," Matthew said. He dipped his head and stole a kiss.

We walked around the western door of St. Paul's, which was bustling in spite of the hour, and out of the churchyard to the north. This put us on Cheapside, London's most spacious and prosperous street, where the goldsmiths plied their trade. We rounded the fountain at Cheapside Cross, which was being used as a paddling pool by a group of roaring boys, and headed east. Matthew traced the route of Anne Boleyn's coronation procession for me and pointed out the house where Geoffrey Chaucer had lived as a child. Some merchants invited Matthew to join them in a game of bowls. They booed him out of the competition after his third strike in a row, however.

"Happy now that you've proven you're top dog?" I teased as he put his arm around me and pulled me close.

"Very," he said. He pointed to a fork in the road. "Look."

"The Royal Exchange." I turned to him in excitement. "At night! You remembered."

"A gentleman never forgets," he murmured with a low bow. "I'm not sure if any shops are still open, but the lamps will be lit. Will you join me in a promenade across the courtyard?"

We entered through the wide arches next to the bell tower topped with a golden grasshopper. Inside, I turned around slowly to get the full experience of the four-storied building with its hundred shops selling everything from suits of armor to shoehorns. Statues of English monarchs looked down on the customers and merchants, and a further plague of grasshoppers ornamented the peak of each dormer window.

"The grasshopper was Gresham's emblem, and he wasn't shy about self-promotion," Matthew said with a laugh, following my eyes.

Some shops were indeed open, the lamps in the arcades around the central courtyard were lit, and we were not the only ones enjoying the evening.

"Where is the music coming from?" I asked, looking around for the minstrels.

"The tower," Matthew said, pointing in the direction we had entered. "The merchants chip in and sponsor concerts in the warm weather. It's good for business."

Matthew was good for business, too, based on the number of shopkeepers who greeted him by name. He joked with them and asked after their wives and children.

"I'll be right back," he said, darting into a nearby store. Mystified, I stood listening to the music and watching an authoritative young woman organize an impromptu ball. People formed circles, holding hands and jumping up and down like popcorn in a hot skillet.

When he came back, Matthew presented to me—with all due ceremony—

"A mousetrap," I said, giggling at the little wooden box with its sliding door.

"*That* is a proper mousetrap," he said, taking my hand. He started walking backward, pulling me into the center of the merriment. "Dance with me."

"I definitely don't know that dance." It was nothing like the sedate dances at Sept-Tours or at Rudolf's court.

"Well, I do," Matthew said, not bothering to look at the whirling couples behind him. "It's an old dance—the Black Nag—with easy steps." He pulled me into place at one end of the line, plucking my mousetrap out of my hand and giving it into the safekeeping of an urchin. He promised the boy a penny if he returned it to us at the end of the song.

Matthew took my hand, stepped into the line of dancers, and when the others moved, we followed. Three steps and a little kick forward, three steps and a little dip back. After a few repetitions, we came to the more intricate steps when the line of twelve dancers divided into two lines of six and started changing places, crossing in diagonal paths from one line to the other, weaving back and forth.

When the dance finished, there were calls for more music and requests for specific tunes, but we left the Royal Exchange before the dances became any more energetic. Matthew retrieved my mousetrap and, instead of taking me straight home, wended his way south toward the river. We turned down so many alleys and cut across so many churchyards that I was hopelessly disoriented by the time we reached All Hallows the Great, with its tall, square tower and abandoned cloister where the monks had once walked. Like most of London's churches, All Hallows was on its way to becoming a ruin, its medieval stonework crumbling.

"Are you up for a climb?" Matthew asked, ducking into the cloister and through a low wooden door.

I nodded, and we began our ascent. We passed by the bells, which were happily not clanging at the moment, and Matthew pushed open a trapdoor in the roof. He scampered through the hole, then reached down and lifted me up to join him. Suddenly we were standing behind the tower's crenellations, with all of London spread at our feet.

The bonfires on the hills outside the city already burned bright, and lanterns bobbed up and down on the bows of boats and barges crossing the Thames. At this distance, with the darkness of the river as a backdrop, they looked like fireflies. I heard laughter, music, all the ordinary sounds of life I'd grown so accustomed to during the months we'd been here.

"So you've met the queen, seen the Royal Exchange at night, and actually *been* in a play instead of just watching one," Matthew said, ticking items off on his fingers.

"We found Ashmole 782, too. And I discovered I'm a weaver and that magic isn't as disciplined as I'd hoped." I surveyed the city, remembering when we'd first arrived and Matthew had to point out the landmarks for fear I'd get lost. Now I could name them myself. "There's Bridewell." I pointed. "And St. Paul's. And the bearbaiting arenas." I turned toward the quiet vampire standing beside me. "Thank you for tonight, Matthew. We've never been on a date-date—out in public like this. It was magical."

"I didn't do a very good job courting you, did I? We should have had more nights like this one, with dancing and looking at the stars." He tilted his face up, and the moon glanced off his pale skin.

"You're practically glowing," I said softly, reaching up to touch his chin.

"So are you." Matthew's hands slid to my waist, his gesture bringing the baby into our embrace. "That reminds me. Your father gave us a list, too."

"We've had fun. You made magic by taking me to the exchange and then surprising me with this view."

"That leaves only two more items. Lady's choice: I can howl at the moon or we can make out."

I smiled and looked away, strangely shy. Matthew tilted his head up to the moon again, readying himself.

"No howling. You'll bring out the Watch," I protested with a laugh.

"Kissing it is," he said softly, fitting his mouth to mine.

* * *

The next morning the entire household was yawning its way through breakfast after staying out until the early hours. Tom and Jack had just risen and were wolfing down bowls of porridge when Gallowglass came in and whispered something to Matthew. My mouth went dry at Matthew's sad look.

"Where's my dad?" I shot to my feet.

"He's gone home," Gallowglass said gruffly.

"Why didn't you stop him?" I asked Gallowglass, tears threatening. "He can't be gone. I just needed a few more hours with him."

"All the time in the world wouldn't have been enough, Auntie," Gallowglass said with a sad expression.

"But he didn't say good-bye," I whispered numbly.

"A parent should never have to say a final good-bye to his child," Matthew said.

"Stephen asked me to give you this," Gallowglass said. It was a piece of paper, folded up into an origami sailboat.

"Daddy sucked at swans," I said, wiping my eyes, "but he was really good at making boats." Carefully, I unfolded the note.

Diana:

You are everything we dreamed you would one day become.
Life is the strong warp of time. Death is only the weft.
It will be because of your children, and your children's children,
that I will live forever.

Dad

P.S. Every time you read "something is rotten in the state of Denmark" in Hamlet, *think of me.*

"You tell me that magic is just desire made real. Maybe spells are nothing more than words that you believe with all your heart," Matthew said, coming to rest his hands on my shoulders. "He loves you. Forever. So do I."

His words wove through the threads that connected us, witch and vampire. They carried the conviction of his feelings with them: tenderness, reverence, constancy, hope.

"I love you, too," I whispered, reinforcing his spell with mine.

39

My father had left London without saying a proper good-bye. I was determined to take my own leave differently. As a result my final days in the city were a complex weaving of words and desires, spells and magic.

Goody Alsop's fetch was waiting sadly for me at the end of the lane when I made my last visit to my teacher's house. She trailed listlessly behind me as I climbed the stairs to the witch's rooms.

"So you are leaving us," Goody Alsop said from her chair by the fire. She was wearing wool and a shawl, and a fire was blazing as well.

"We must." I bent down and kissed her papery cheek. "How are you today?"

"Somewhat better, thanks to Susanna's remedies." Goody Alsop coughed, and the force of it bent her frail frame in two. When she was recovered, she studied me with bright eyes and nodded. "This time the babe has taken root."

"It has," I said with a smile. "I have the sickness to prove it. Would you like me to tell the others?" I didn't want Goody Alsop to shoulder any extra burdens, emotional or physical. Susanna was worried about her frailty, and Elizabeth Jackson was already taking on some of the duties usually performed by the gathering's elder.

"No need. Catherine was the one to tell me. She said Corra was flying about a few days ago, chortling and chattering as she does when she has a secret."

We had come to an agreement, my firedrake and I, that she would limit her open-air flying to once a week, and only at night. I'd reluctantly agreed to a second night out during the dark of the moon, when the risk of anyone's seeing her and mistaking her for a fiery portent of doom was at its lowest.

"So that's where she went," I said with a laugh. Corra found the witch's company soothing, and Catherine enjoyed challenging her to fire-breathing contests.

"We are all glad that Corra has found something to do with herself besides clinging to the chimneypieces and shrieking at the ghosts." Goody

Alsop pointed to the chair opposite. "Will you not sit with me? The goddess may not afford us another chance."

"Did you hear the news from Scotland?" I asked as I took my seat.

"I have heard nothing since you told me that pleading her belly did not save Euphemia MacLean from the pyre." Goody Alsop's decline began the night I'd told her that a young witch from Berwick had been burned, in spite of Matthew's efforts.

"Matthew finally convinced the rest of the Congregation that the spiral of accusations and executions had to stop. Two of the accused witches have overturned their testimony and said their confessions were the result of torture."

"It must have given the Congregation pause to have a *wearh* speak out on behalf of a witch." Goody Alsop looked at me sharply. "He would give himself away if you were to stay. Matthew Roydon lives in a world of half-truths, but no one can avoid detection forever. Because of the babe, you must take greater care."

"We will," I assured her. "Meanwhile I'm still not absolutely sure my eighth knot is strong enough for the timewalking. Not with Matthew and the baby."

"Let me see it," Goody Alsop said, stretching out her hand. I leaned forward and put the cords into her palm. I would use all nine cords when we timewalked and make a total of nine different knots. No spell used more.

With practiced hands Goody Alsop made eight crossings in the red cord and then bound the ends together so that the knot was unbreakable. "That is how I do it." It was beautifully simple, with open loops and swirls like the stone traceries in a cathedral window.

"Mine did not look like that." My laugh was rueful. "It wiggled and squiggled around."

"Every weaving is as unique as the weaver who makes it. The goddess does not want us to imitate some ideal of perfection, but to be our true selves."

"Well, I must be all wiggle, then." I reached for the cords to study the design.

"There is another knot I would show you," Goody Alsop said.

"Another?" I frowned.

"A tenth knot. It is impossible for me to make it, though it should be the simplest." Goody Alsop smiled, but her chin trembled. "My own teacher could not make the knot either, but still we passed it on, in hope that a weaver such as you might come along."

Goody Alsop released the just-tied knot with a flick of her gnarled index finger. I handed the red silk back to her, and she made a simple loop. For a moment the cord fused in an unbroken ring. As soon as she took her fingers from it, however, the loop released.

"But you drew the ends together just a minute ago, and with a far more complicated weaving," I said, confused.

"As long as there is a crossing in the cord, I can bind the ends and complete the spell. But only a weaver who stands between worlds can make the tenth knot," she replied. "Try it. Use the silver silk."

Mystified, I joined the ends of the cord into a circlet. The fibers snapped together to form a loop with no beginning and no ending. I lifted my fingers from the silk, but the circle held.

"A fine weaving," Goody Alsop said with satisfaction. "The tenth knot captures the power of eternity, a weaving of life and death. It is rather like your husband's snake, or the way Corra carries her tail in her mouth sometimes when it gets in her way." She held up the tenth knot. It was another ouroboros. The sense of the uncanny built in the room, lifting the hairs on my arm. "Creation and destruction are the simplest magics, and the most powerful, just as the simplest knot is the most difficult to make."

"I don't want to use magic to destroy anything," I said. The Bishops had a strong tradition of not doing harm. My Aunt Sarah believed that any witch who strayed away from this fundamental tenet would find the evil coming back to her in the end."

"No one wants to use the goddess's gifts as a weapon, but sometimes it is necessary. Your *wearh* knows that. After what happened here and in Scotland, you know it, too."

"Perhaps. But my world is different," I said. "There's less call for magical weapons."

"Worlds change, Diana." Goody Alsop fixed her attention on some distant memory. "My teacher, Mother Ursula, was a great weaver. I was reminded of one of her prophecies on All Hallows' Eve, when the terrible events in Scotland began—and when you came to change our world."

Her voice took on the singsong quality of an incantation.

"For storms will rage and oceans roar
When Gabriel stands on sea and shore.

And as he blows his wondrous horn,
Old worlds die, and new be born."

Not a breeze or a crackle of flame disturbed the room when Goody Alsop finished. She took a deep breath.

"It is all one, you see. Death and birth. The tenth knot with no beginning and no ending, and the *wearh*'s snake. The full moon that shone earlier this week and the shadow Corra cast upon the Thames in a portent of your leaving. The old world and the new." Goody Alsop's smile wavered. "I was glad when you came to me, Diana Roydon. And when you go, as you must, my heart will be heavy."

"Usually Matthew tells me when he is leaving my city." Andrew Hubbard's white hands rested on the carved arms of his chair in the church crypt. High above us someone prepared for an upcoming church service. "What brings you here, Mistress Roydon?"

"I came to talk to you about Annie and Jack."

Hubbard's strange eyes studied me as I pulled a small leather purse from my pocket. It contained five years of wages for each of them.

"I'm leaving London. I would like you to have this, for their care." I thrust the money in Hubbard's direction. He made no move to take it.

"That isn't necessary, mistress."

"Please. I would take them with me if I could. Since they cannot go, I need to know that someone will be watching out for them."

"And what will you give me in return?"

"Why . . . the money, of course." I held the pouch out once more.

"I don't want or need the money, Mistress Roydon." Hubbard settled back in his chair, his eyes drifting closed.

"What do you—" I stopped. "No."

"God does nothing in vain. There are no accidents in His plans. He wanted you to come here today, because He wants to be sure that no one of your blood will have anything to fear from me or mine."

"I have protectors enough," I protested.

"And can the same be said for your husband?" Hubbard glanced at my breast. "Your blood is stronger in his veins now than when you arrived. And there is the child to consider."

My heart stuttered. When I took my Matthew back to our present,

Andrew Hubbard would be one of the few people who would know his future—and that there was a witch in it.

"You wouldn't use the knowledge of me against Matthew. Not after what he's done—how he's changed."

"Wouldn't I?" Hubbard's tight smile told me he would do whatever it took to protect his flock. "There is a great deal of bad blood between us."

"I'll find another way to see them safe," I said, deciding to go.

"Annie is my child already. She is a witch, and part of my family. I will see to her welfare. Jack Blackfriars is another matter. He is not a creature and will have to fend for himself."

"He's a child—a boy!"

"But not my child. Nor are you. I do not owe either of you anything. Good day, Mistress Roydon." Hubbard turned away.

"And if I were one of your family, what then? Would you honor my request about Jack? Would you recognize Matthew as one of my blood and therefore under your protection?" It was the sixteenth-century Matthew that I was thinking of now. When we returned to the present, that other Matthew would still be here in the past.

"If you offer me your blood, neither Matthew nor Jack nor your unborn child has anything to fear from me or mine." Hubbard imparted the information dispassionately, but his glance was touched with the avarice I'd seen in Rudolf's eyes.

"And how much blood would you need?" *Think. Stay alive.*

"Very little. No more than a drop." Hubbard's attention was unwavering.

"I couldn't let you take it directly from my body. Matthew would know—we are mates, after all," I said. Hubbard's eyes flickered to my breast.

"I always take my tribute directly from my children's neck."

"I'm sure you do, Father Hubbard. But you can understand why that isn't possible, or even desirable, in this case." I fell silent, hoping that Hubbard's hunger—for power, for knowledge of Matthew and me, for something to hold over the de Clermonts if he ever needed it—would win. "I could use a cup."

"No," Hubbard said with a shake of his head. "Your blood would be tainted. It must be pure."

"A silver cup, then," I said, thinking of Chef's lectures at Sept-Tours.

"You will open the vein in your wrist over my mouth and let the blood fall into it. We will not touch." Hubbard scowled at me. "Otherwise I will doubt the sincerity of your offer."

"Very well, Father Hubbard. I accept your terms." I loosened the tie at my right cuff and pushed up the sleeve. While I did so, I whispered a silent request to Corra. "Where do you wish to do this? From what I saw before, your children kneel before you, but that will not work if I'm to drip the blood into your mouth."

"It is a sacrament. It does not matter to God who kneels." To my surprise, Hubbard dropped to the floor before me. He handed me a knife.

"I don't need that." I flicked my finger at the blue traceries on my wrist and murmured a simple unbinding charm. A line of crimson appeared. The blood welled.

Hubbard opened his mouth, his eyes on my face. He was waiting for me to renege, or cheat him somehow. But I would obey the letter of this agreement, though not its spirit. *Thank you, Goody Alsop,* I said, sending her a silent blessing for showing me how to handle the man.

I held my wrist over his mouth and clenched my fist. A drop of blood rolled over the edge of my arm and began to fall. Hubbard's eyes flickered closed, as if he wanted to concentrate on what my blood would tell him.

"What is blood, if not fire and water?" I murmured. I called on the wind to slow the droplet's fall. As the power of the air increased, it froze the falling bead of blood so that it was crystalline and sharp when it landed on Hubbard's tongue. The vampire's eyes shot open in confusion.

"No more than a drop." The wind had dried the remaining blood against my skin in a maze of red streaks over the blue veins. "You are a man of God, a man of your word, are you not, Father Hubbard?"

Corra's tail loosened from around my waist. She'd used it to block our baby from having any knowledge of this sordid transaction, but now she seemed to want to use it to beat Hubbard senseless.

Slowly I withdrew my arm. Hubbard thought about grabbing it back to his mouth. I saw the idea cross his mind as clearly as I had seen Edward Kelley contemplate clubbing me with his walking stick. But he thought better of it. I whispered another simple spell to close the wound, and turned wordlessly to leave.

"When you are next in London," Hubbard said softly, "God will whisper it to me. And if He wills it, we shall meet again. But remember this. No matter where you go from now, even unto death, some small piece of you will live within me."

I stopped and looked back at him. His words were menacing, but the expression on his face was thoughtful, even sad. My pace quickened as I left the church crypt, wanting to put as much distance as I could between me and Andrew Hubbard.

"Farewell, Diana Bishop," he called after me.

I was halfway across town before I realized that no matter how little that single drop of blood might have revealed, Father Hubbard now knew my real name.

Walter and Matthew were shouting at each other when I returned to the Hart and Crown. Raleigh's groom could hear them, too. He was in the courtyard, holding the reins of Walter's black beast of a horse and listening to their argument through the open windows.

"It will mean my death—and hers, too! No one must know she is with child!" Oddly enough, it was Walter speaking.

"You cannot abandon the woman you love and your own child in an attempt to stay true to the queen, Walter. Elizabeth will find out that you have betrayed her, and Bess will be ruined forever."

"What do you expect me to do? Marry her? If I do so without the queen's permission, I'll be arrested."

"You'll survive no matter what happens," Matthew said flatly. "If you leave Bess without your protection, she will not."

"How can you pretend concern for marital honesty after all the lies you've told about Diana? Some days you insisted you were married but made us swear to deny it should any strange witches or *wearhs* come sniffing around asking questions." Walter's voice dropped, but the ferocity remained. "Do you expect me to believe you're going to return whence you came and acknowledge her as your wife?"

I slipped into the room unnoticed.

Matthew hesitated.

"I thought not," Walter said. He was pulling on his gloves.

"Is this how you two want to say your farewells?" I asked.

"Diana," Walter said warily.

"Hello, Walter. Your groom is downstairs with the horse."

He started toward the door, stopped. "Be sensible, Matthew. I cannot lose all credit at court. Bess understands the dangers of the queen's anger better than anyone. At the court of Elizabeth, fortune is fleeting, but disgrace endures forever."

Matthew watched his friend thud down the stairs. "God forgive me. The first time I heard this plan, I told him it was wise. Poor Bess."

"What will happen to her when we are gone?" I asked.

"Come autumn, Bess's pregnancy will begin to show. They will marry in secret. When the queen questions their relationship, Walter will deny it. Repeatedly. Bess's reputation will be ruined, her husband will be found out to be a liar, and they will both be arrested."

"And the child?" I whispered.

"Will be born in March and dead the following autumn." Matthew sat down at the table, his head in his hands. "I will write to my father and make sure that Bess receives his protection. Perhaps Susanna Norman will see to her during the pregnancy."

"Neither your father nor Susanna can shield her from the blow of Raleigh's denial." I rested my hands on his sleeve. "And will you deny that we are married when we return?"

"It's not that simple," Matthew said, looking at me with haunted eyes.

"That's what Walter said. You told him he was wrong." I remembered Goody Alsop's prophecy. "'*Old worlds die, and new be born.*' The time is coming when you will have to choose between the safety of the past and the promise of the future, Matthew."

"And the past cannot be cured, no matter how hard I try," he said. "It's something I'm always telling the queen when she agonizes over a bad decision. Hoist by my own petard again, as Gallowglass would be quick to point out."

"You beat me to it, Uncle." Gallowglass had soundlessly entered the room and was unloading parcels. "I've got your paper. And your pens. And some tonic for Jack's throat."

"That's what he gets for spending all his time up towers with Tom, talking about the stars." Matthew rubbed his face. "We will have to make sure Tom is provided for, Gallowglass. Walter won't be able to keep him in service much longer. Henry Percy will need to step into the breach—again—but I should contribute something to his upkeep, too."

"Speaking of Tom, have you seen his plans for a one-eyed spectacle to view the heavens? He and Jack are calling it a star glass."

My scalp tingled as the threads of the room snapped with energy. Time sounded a low protest in the corners.

"A star glass." I kept my voice even. "What does it look like?"

"Ask him yourself," Gallowglass said, turning his head toward the stairs. Jack and Mop careened into the room. Tom followed absently behind, a pair of broken spectacles in his hand.

"You will certainly leave a mark on the future if you meddle with this, Diana," Matthew warned.

"Look, look, look." Jack brandished a thick piece of wood. Mop followed its movements and snapped his jaws at the stick as it went by. "Master Harriot said if we hollowed this out and put a spectacle lens in the end, it would make faraway things seem near. Do you know how to carve, Master Roydon? If not, do you think the joiner in St. Dunstan's might teach me? Are there any more buns? Master Harriot's stomach has been growling all afternoon."

"Let me see that," I said, holding out my hand for the wooden tube. "The buns are in the cupboard on the landing, Jack, where they always are. Give one to Master Harriot, and take one for yourself. And no," I said, cutting the child off when he opened his mouth, "Mop doesn't get to share yours."

"Good day, Mistress Roydon," Tom said dreamily. "If such a simple pair of spectacles can make a man see God's words in the Bible, surely they could be made more complex to help him see God's works in the Book of Nature. Thank you, Jack." Tom absently bit into the bun.

"And how would you make them more complex?" I wondered aloud, hardly daring to breathe.

"I would combine convex and concave lenses, as the Neapolitan gentleman Signor della Porta suggested in a book I read last year. My arm cannot hold them apart at the proper distance. So we are trying to extend our arm's reach with that piece of wood."

With those words Thomas Harriot changed the history of science. And I didn't have to meddle with the past—I only had to see to it that the past was not forgotten.

"But these are just idle imaginings. I will put these ideas down on paper and think about them later." Tom sighed.

This was the problem with early-modern scientists: They didn't understand the necessity of publishing. In the case of Thomas Harriot, his ideas had definitely perished for want of a publisher.

"I think you're right, Tom. But this wooden tube is not long enough." I smiled at him brightly. "As for the joiner in St. Dunstan's, Monsieur Vallin might be of more help if a long, hollow tube is what you need. Shall we go and see him?"

"Yes!" Jack shouted, jumping into the air. "Monsieur Vallin has all sorts of gears and springs, Master Harriot. He gave me one, and it is in my treasure box. Mine is not as big as Mistress Roydon's, but it holds enough. Can we go now?"

"What is Auntie up to?" Gallowglass asked Matthew, both mystified and wary.

"I think she's getting back at Walter for not paying sufficient attention to the future," Matthew said mildly.

"Oh. That's all right, then. And here I thought I smelled trouble."

"There's always trouble," Matthew said. "Are you sure you know what you're doing, *ma lionne*?"

So much had happened that I could not fix. I couldn't bring my first child back or save the witches in Scotland. We'd brought Ashmole 782 all the way from Prague, only to discover that it could not be taken safely into the future. We had said good-bye to our fathers and were about to leave our friends. Most of these experiences would vanish without a trace. But I knew exactly how to ensure that Tom's telescope survived.

I nodded. "The past has changed us, Matthew. Why should we not change it, too?"

Matthew caught my hand in his and kissed it. "Go to Monsieur Vallin, then. Have him send me the bill."

"Thank you." I bent and whispered in his ear. "Don't worry. I'll take Annie with me. She'll wear him down on the price. Besides, who knows what to charge for a telescope in 1591?"

And so a witch, a daemon, two children, and a dog paid a short visit to Monsieur Vallin that afternoon. That evening I sent out invitations to our friends to join us the next night. It would be the last time we saw them. While I dealt with telescopes and supper plans, Matthew delivered Roger Bacon's *Verum Secretum Secretorum* to Mortlake. I did not want to see Ashmole 782 pass to Dr. Dee. I knew it had to go back into the alchemist's enormous library so that Elias Ashmole could acquire it in the seventeenth century. But it was not easy to give the book into someone else's keeping, any more than it had been to surrender the small figurine of the goddess Diana to Kit when we arrived. The practical details surrounding our departure we left to Gallowglass and Pierre. They packed trunks, emptied coffers, redistributed funds, and sent personal belongings to the Old Lodge with a practiced efficiency that showed how many times they had done this before.

Our departure was only hours away. I was returning from Monsieur Vallin's with an awkward package wrapped in soft leather when I was brought up short by the sight of a ten-year-old girl standing on the street outside the pie shop, staring with fascination at the wares in the window. She reminded me of myself at that age, from the unruly straw-blond hair to the arms that were too long for the rest of her frame. The girl stiffened as if she knew she was being watched. When our eyes met, I knew why: She was a witch.

"Rebecca!" a woman called as she came from inside the shop. My heart leaped at the sight, for she looked like a combination of my mother and Sarah.

Rebecca said nothing but continued to stare at me as though she had seen a ghost. Her mother looked to see what had captured the girl's attention and gasped. Her glance tingled over my skin as she took in my face and form. She was a witch, too.

I forced my feet toward the pie shop. Every step took me closer to the two witches. The mother gathered the child to her skirts, and Rebecca squirmed in protest.

"She looks like Grand-dame," Rebecca whispered, trying to get a closer look at me.

"Hush," her mother told her. She looked at me apologetically. "You know that your grand-dame is dead, Rebecca."

"I am Diana Roydon." I nodded to the sign over their shoulders. "I live here at the Hart and Crown."

"But then you are—" The woman's eyes widened as she drew Rebecca closer.

"I am Rebecca White," the girl said, unconcerned with her mother's reaction. She bobbed a shallow, teetering curtsy. That looked familiar, too.

"It is a pleasure to meet you. Are you new to the Blackfriars?" I wanted to make small talk for as long as possible, if only to stare at their familiar-yet-strange faces.

"No. We live by the hospital near Smithfield Market," Rebecca explained.

"I take in patients when their wards are full." The woman hesitated. "I am Bridget White, and Rebecca is my daughter."

Even without the familiar names of Rebecca and Bridget, I recognized these two creatures in the marrow of my bones. Bridget Bishop had been born around 1632, and the first name in the Bishop grimoire was Bridget's grandmother, Rebecca Davies. Would this ten-year-old girl one day marry and bear that name?

Rebecca's attention was caught by something at my neck. I reached up. *Ysabeau's earrings.*

I had used three objects to bring Matthew and me to the past: a manuscript copy of *Doctor Faustus,* a silver chess piece, and an earring hidden in Bridget Bishop's poppet. This earring. I reached up and took the fine golden wire out of my ear. Knowing from my experience with Jack that it was wise to make direct eye contact with children if you wanted to leave a lasting impression, I crouched down until we were at an equal level.

"I need someone to keep this safe for me." I held out the earring. "One day I will have need of it. Would you keep it close?"

Rebecca looked at me solemnly and nodded. I took her hand, feeling a current of awareness pass between us, and put the jeweled wires into her palm. She wrapped her fingers tightly around them. "Can I, Mama?" she whispered belatedly to Bridget.

"I think that would be all right," her mother replied warily. "Come, Rebecca. We must go."

"Thank you," I said, rising and patting Rebecca on the shoulder while looking Bridget in the eye. "Thank you."

I felt a nudging glance. I waited until Rebecca and Bridget were out of sight before I turned to face Christopher Marlowe.

"Mistress Roydon." Kit's voice was hoarse, and he looked like death. "Walter told me you were leaving tonight."

"I asked him to tell you." I forced Kit to meet my eyes through an act of sheer will. This was another thing I could fix: I could make sure that Matthew said a proper good-bye to a man who had once been his closest friend.

Kit looked down at his feet, hiding his face. "I should never have come."

"I forgive you, Kit."

Marlowe's head swung up in surprise at my words. "Why?" he asked, dumbstruck.

"Because you love him. And because as long as Matthew blames you for what happened to me, a part of him remains with you. Forever," I said simply. "Come upstairs and say your farewells."

Matthew was waiting for us on the landing, having divined that I was bringing someone home. I kissed him softly on the mouth as I went past on the way to our bedroom.

"Your father forgave you," I murmured. "Give Kit the same gift in return."

Then I left them to patch up what they could in what little time remained.

A few hours later, I handed Thomas Harriot a steel tube. "Here is your star glass, Tom."

"I fashioned it from a gun barrel—with adjustments, of course," explained Monsieur Vallin, famous maker of mousetraps and clocks. "And it is engraved, as Mistress Roydon requested."

There on the side, set in a lovely little silver banner, was the legend N. VALLIN ME FECIT, T. HARRIOT ME INVENIT, 1591.

"N. Vallin made me, T. Harriot invented me, 1591." I smiled warmly at Monsieur Vallin. "It's perfect."

"Can we look at the moon now?" Jack cried, racing for the door. "It already looks bigger than St. Mildred's clock!"

And so Thomas Harriot, mathematician and linguist, made scientific history in the courtyard of the Hart and Crown while sitting in a battered wicker garden chair pulled down from our attics. He trained the long metal tube fitted with two spectacle lenses at the full moon and sighed with pleasure.

"Look, Jack. It is just as Signor della Porta said." Tom invited the boy into his lap and positioned one end of the tube at his enthusiastic assistant's eye. "Two lenses, one convex and one concave, are indeed the solution if held at the right distance."

After Jack we all took a turn.

"Well, that is not at all what I expected," George Chapman said, disappointed. "Did you not think the moon would be more dramatic? I believe I prefer the poet's mysterious moon to this one, Tom."

"Why, it is not perfect at all," Henry Percy complained, rubbing his eyes and then peering through the tube again.

"Of course it isn't perfect. Nothing is," Kit said. "You cannot believe everything philosophers tell you, Hal. It is a sure way to ruin. You see how little philosophy has done for Tom."

I glanced at Matthew and grinned. It had been some time since we'd enjoyed the School of Night's verbal ripostes.

"At least Tom can feed himself, which is more than I can say for any of the playwrights of my acquaintance." Walter peered through the tube and whistled. "I wish you had come up with this notion before we went to Virginia, Tom. It would have been useful for surveying the shore while we were safely aboard ship. Look through this, Gallowglass, and tell me I am wrong."

"You're never wrong, Walter," Gallowglass said with a wink at Jack. "Mind me well, young Jack. The one who pays your wages is correct in all things."

I'd invited Goody Alsop and Susanna to join us, too, and even they took a peek through Tom's star glass. Neither woman seemed overly impressed with the invention, although they both made enthusiastic noises when prompted.

"Why do men bother with these trifles?" Susanna whispered to me. "I could have told them the moon is not perfectly smooth, even without this new instrument. Do they not have eyes?"

After the pleasure of viewing the heavens, only the painful farewells remained. We sent Annie off with Goody Alsop, using the excuse that Susanna needed another set of hands to help the old woman across town. My good-bye was brisk, and Annie looked at me uncertainly.

"Are you all right, mistress? Shall I stay here instead?"

"No, Annie. Go with your aunt and Goody Alsop." I blinked back the tears. How did Matthew bear these repeated farewells?

Kit, George, and Walter left next, with gruff good-byes and hands clamped on Matthew's arm to wish him well.

"Come, Jack. You and Tom will go home with me," Henry Percy said. "The night is still young."

"I don't want to go," Jack said. He swung around to Matthew, eyes huge. The boy sensed the impending change.

Matthew knelt before him. "There's nothing to be afraid of, Jack. You know Master Harriot and Lord Northumberland. They won't let you come to harm."

"What if I have a nightmare?" Jack whispered.

"Nightmares are like Master Harriot's star glass. They are a trick of the light, one that makes something distant seem closer and larger than it really is."

"Oh." Jack considered Matthew's response. "So even if I see a monster in my dreams, it cannot reach me?"

Matthew nodded. "But I will tell you a secret. A dream is a nightmare in reverse. If you dream of someone you love, that person will seem closer, even if far away." He stood and put his hand on Jack's head for a moment in a silent blessing.

Once Jack and his guardians had departed, only Gallowglass remained. I took the cords from my spell box, leaving a few items within: a pebble, a white feather, a bit of the rowan tree, my jewelry, and the note my father had left.

"I'll take care of it," he promised, taking the box from me. It looked oddly small in his huge hand. He wrapped me up in a bear hug.

"Keep the other Matthew safe, so he can find me one day," I whispered in his ear, my eyes scrunched tight.

I released him and stepped aside. The two de Clermonts said their goodbyes as all de Clermonts did—briefly but with feeling.

Pierre was waiting with the horses outside the Cardinal's Hat. Matthew handed me up into the saddle and climbed into his own.

"Farewell, *madame,*" Pierre said, letting go of the reins.

"Thank you, friend," I said, my eyes filling once more.

Pierre handed Matthew a letter. I recognized Philippe's seal. "Your father's instructions, *milord.*"

"If I don't turn up in Edinburgh in two days, come looking for me."

"I will," Pierre promised as Matthew clucked to his horse and we turned toward Oxford.

We changed horses three times and were at the Old Lodge before sunrise. Françoise and Charles had been sent away. We were alone.

Matthew left the letter from Philippe propped up on his desk, where the sixteenth-century Matthew could not fail to see it. It would send him to Scotland on urgent business. Once there, Matthew Roydon would stay at the court of King James for a time before disappearing to start a new life in Amsterdam.

"The king of Scots will be pleased to have me back to my former self," Matthew commented, touching the letter with his fingertip. "I won't be making any more attempts to save witches, certainly."

"You made a difference here, Matthew," I said, sliding my arm around his waist. "Now we need to sort things out in our present."

We stepped into the bedroom where we'd arrived all those months before.

"You know I can't be sure that we'll slip through the centuries and land in exactly the right time and place," I warned.

"You've explained it to me, *mon coeur.* I have faith in you." Matthew hooked his arm through mine to anchor me. "Let's go meet our future. Again."

"Good-bye, house." I looked around our first home one last time. Even though I would see it again, it would not be the same as it was on this June morning.

The blue and amber threads in the corners snapped and keened impatiently, filling the room with light and sound. I took a deep breath and knotted my brown cord, leaving the end hanging free. Apart from Matthew and the clothes on our backs, my weaver's cords were the only objects we were taking back with us.

"With knot of one, the spell's begun," I whispered. Time's volume increased with every knot I made until the shrieking and keening was nearly deafening.

As the ends of the ninth cord fused together, we picked up our feet and our surroundings slowly dissolved.

All the English papers had some variation of the same headline, but Ysabeau thought the one in the *Times* was the cleverest.

English Man Wins Race to See into Space

30 June 2010

THE WORLD's leading expert on early scientific instruments at Oxford University's Museum of the History of Science, Anthony Carter, confirmed today that a refracting telescope bearing the names of Elizabethan mathematician and astronomer Thomas Harriot and Nicholas Vallin, a Huguenot clockmaker who fled France for religious reasons, is indeed genuine. In addition to the names, the telescope is engraved with the date 1591.

The discovery has electrified the scientific and historical communities. For centuries, Italian mathematician Galileo Galilei had been credited with borrowing rudimentary telescope technology from the Dutch in order to view the moon in 1609.

"The history books will have to be rewritten," said Carter. "Thomas Harriot had read Giambattista della Porta's *Natural Magic* and become intrigued with how convex and concave lenses could be used to 'see both things afar off, and things near hand, both greater and clearly.'"

Thomas Harriot's contributions to the field of astronomy were overlooked in part because he did not publish them, preferring to share his discoveries with a close group of friends some call "The School of Night." Under the patronage of Walter Raleigh and Henry Percy, the "Wizard Earl" of Northumberland, Harriot was financially free to explore his interests.

Mr I. P. Riddell discovered the telescope, along with a

> box of assorted mathematical papers in Thomas Harriot's hand and an elaborate silver mousetrap also signed by Vallin. He was repairing the bells of St. Michael's Church, near the Percy family's seat in Alnwick, when a particularly strong gust of wind brought down a faded tapestry of St. Margaret slaying the dragon, revealing the box that had been secreted there.
>
> "It is rare for instruments of this period to have so many identifying marks," Dr Carter explained to reporters, revealing the date mark stamped into the telescope, which confirms the item was made in 1591–92. "We owe a great debt to Nicholas Vallin, who knew that this was an important development in the history of scientific instrumentation and took unusual measures to record its genealogy and provenance."

"They refuse to sell it," Marcus said, leaning against the doorframe. With his arms and legs crossed, he looked very much like Matthew. "I've spoken with everyone from the Alnwick church officials to the Duke of Northumberland to the Bishop of Newcastle. They're not going to give up the telescope, not even for the small fortune you've offered. I think I've convinced them to let me buy the mousetrap, though."

"The whole world knows about it," Ysabeau said. "Even *Le Monde* has reported the story."

"We should have tried harder to squash the story. This could give the witches and their allies vital information," Marcus said. The growing number of people living inside the walls of Sept-Tours had been worrying for weeks about what the Congregation might do if the exact whereabouts of Diana and Matthew were discovered.

"What does Phoebe think?" Ysabeau asked. She had taken an instant liking to the observant young human with her firm chin and gentle ways.

Marcus's face softened. It made him look as he had before Matthew left, when he was carefree and joyful. "She thinks it's too soon to tell what damage has been done by the telescope's discovery."

"Smart girl," Ysabeau said with a smile.

"I don't know what I'd do—" Marcus began. His expression turned fierce. "I love her, *Grand-mère*."

"Of course you do. And she loves you, too." After the events of May, Marcus had wanted her with the rest of the family and had brought her to

Sept-Tours to stay. The two of them were inseparable. And Phoebe had shown remarkable savoir faire as she met the assembly of daemons, witches, and vampires currently in residence. If she had been surprised to learn there were other creatures sharing the world with humans, she had not revealed it.

Membership in Marcus's Conventicle had swelled considerably over the past months. Matthew's assistant, Miriam, was now a permanent resident at the château, as were Philippe's daughter Verin and her husband Ernst. Gallowglass, Ysabeau's restless grandson, had shocked them all by staying put there for six whole weeks. Even now he showed no signs of leaving. Sophie Norman and Nathaniel Wilson welcomed their new baby, Margaret, into the world under Ysabeau's roof, and now the baby's authority in the château was second only to the de Clermont matriarch's. With her grandchild living at Sept-Tours, Nathaniel's mother Agatha appeared and reappeared without warning, as did Matthew's best friend, Hamish. Even Baldwin flitted through occasionally.

Never in her long life had Ysabeau expected to be chatelaine of such a household.

"Where is Sarah?" Marcus asked, tuning in to the hum of activity all around. "I don't hear her."

"In the Round Tower." Ysabeau ran her sharp nail around the edge of the newspaper story and neatly lifted the clipped columns from their printed surround. "Sophie and Margaret sat with her for a while. Sophie says Sarah is keeping watch."

"For what? What's happened now?" Marcus said, snatching at the newspaper. He'd read them all that morning, tracking the subtle shifts in money and influence that Nathaniel had found a way to analyze and isolate so that they could be better prepared for the Congregation's next move. A world without Phoebe was inconceivable, but Nathaniel had become nearly as indispensable. "That damn telescope is going to be a problem. I just know it. All the Congregation needs is a timewalking witch and this story and they'll have everything they need to go back into the past and find my father."

"Your father won't be there for much longer, if he's still there at all."

"Really, *Grand-mère,*" Marcus said with a note of exasperation, his attention still glued to the text surrounding the hole that Ysabeau had left in the *Times.* "How can you possibly know that?"

"First there were the miniatures, then the laboratory records, and now this telescope. I know my daughter-in-law. This telescope is exactly the kind of gesture Diana would make if she had nothing left to lose." Ysabeau brushed past her grandson. "Diana and Matthew are coming home."

Marcus's expression was unreadable.

"I expected you to be happier about your father's return," Ysabeau said quietly, stopping by the door.

"It's been a difficult few months," Marcus said somberly. "The Congregation made it clear they want the book and Nathaniel's daughter. Once Diana is here . . ."

"They will stop at nothing." Ysabeau took in a slow breath. "At least we will no longer have to worry about something happening to Diana and Matthew in the past. We will be together, at Sept-Tours, fighting side by side." *Dying side by side.*

"So much has changed since last November." Marcus stared into the shining surface of the table as though he were a witch and it might show him the future.

"In their lives, too, I suspect. But your father's love for you is a constant. Sarah needs Diana now. You need Matthew, too."

Ysabeau took her clipping and headed for the Round Tower, leaving Marcus to his thoughts. Once it had been Philippe's favorite jail. Now it was used to store old family papers. Though the door to the room on the third floor was ajar, Ysabeau rapped on it smartly.

"You don't have to knock. This is your house." The rasp in Sarah's voice indicated how many cigarettes she'd been smoking and how much whiskey she'd been drinking.

"If that's how you behave, I am glad not to be your guest," Ysabeau said sharply.

"My guest?" Sarah laughed softly. "I would never have let you into my house."

"Vampires don't usually require an invitation." Ysabeau and Sarah had perfected the art of acerbic banter. Marcus and Em had tried without success to persuade them to obey the rules of courteous communication, but the two clan matriarchs knew that their sharp exchanges helped maintain their fragile balance of power. "You should not be up here, Sarah."

"Why not? Afraid I'll catch my death of cold?" Sarah's voice hitched with sudden pain, and she doubled over as if she'd been struck. "Goddess help me, I miss her. Tell me this is a dream, Ysabeau. Tell me that Emily is still alive."

"It's not a dream," Ysabeau said as gently as she could. "We all miss her. I know that you are empty and aching inside, Sarah."

"And it will pass," Sarah said dully.

"No. It won't."

Sarah looked up, surprised at Ysabeau's vehemence.

"Every day of my life, I yearn for Philippe. The sun rises and my heart cries out for him. I listen for his voice, but there is silence. I crave his touch. When the sun sets, I retire in the knowledge that my mate is gone from this world and I will never see his face again."

"If you're trying to make me feel better, it's not working," Sarah said, the tears streaming.

"Emily died so that Sophie and Nathaniel's child might live. Those who played a part in killing her will pay for it, I promise you. The de Clermonts are very good at revenge, Sarah."

"And revenge will make me feel better?" Sarah squinted up through her tears.

"No. Seeing Margaret grow to womanhood will help. So will this." Ysabeau dropped the cutting into the witch's lap. "Diana and Matthew are coming home."

PART VI

New World, Old World

41

My attempts to reach the Old Lodge's future from its past were unsuccessful. I focused on the look and smell of the place and saw the threads that bound Matthew and me to the house—brown and green and gold. But they slipped out of my fingers repeatedly.

I tried for Sept-Tours instead. The threads that linked us there were tinged with Matthew's idiosyncratic blend of red and black shot through with silver. I imagined the house full of familiar faces—Sarah and Em, Ysabeau and Marthe, Marcus and Miriam, Sophie and Nathaniel. But I couldn't reach that safe port either.

Resolutely ignoring the rising panic, I searched among hundreds of options for an alternative destination. Oxford? The Blackfriars underground station in modern London? St. Paul's Cathedral?

My fingers kept returning to the same strand in the warp and weft of time that was not silky and smooth but hard and rough. I inched along its twisting length and discovered that it was not a thread but a root connected to some unseen tree. With that realization I tripped, as over an invisible threshold, and fell into the keeping room of the Bishop House.

Home. I landed on my hands and knees, the knotted cords flattened between my palms and the floor. Centuries of polish and the passage of hundreds of ancestral feet had long since smoothed out its wide pine boards. They felt familiar under my hands, a token of permanence in a world of change. I looked up, half expecting to see my aunts waiting in the front hall. It had been so easy to find my way back to Madison that I assumed they were guiding us. But the air in the Bishop House was still and lifeless, as though not a soul had disturbed it since Halloween. Not even the ghosts seemed to be in residence.

Matthew was kneeling next to me, his arm still linked to mine and his muscles trembling from the stress of moving through time.

"Are we alone?" I asked.

He took in the house's scents. "Yes."

With his quiet response, the house wakened and the atmosphere went from flat and lifeless to thick and uneasy in a blink. Matthew looked at me and smiled. "Your hair. It's changed again."

I glanced down to find not the strawberry blond curls I'd grown accustomed to but straight, silky strands that were a brighter reddish gold—just like my mother's hair.

"It must be the timewalking."

The house creaked and moaned. I felt it gathering its energy for an outburst.

"It's only me and Matthew."

My words were soothing, but my voice was oddly accented and harsh. The house recognized it nonetheless, and a sigh of relief filled the room. A breeze came down the chimney, carrying an unfamiliar aroma of chamomile mixed with cinnamon. I looked over my shoulder to the fireplace and the cracked wooden panels that surrounded it and scrambled to my feet.

"What the hell is that?"

A tree had erupted from under the grate. Its black trunk filled the chimney, and its limbs had pushed through the stone and the surrounding wood paneling.

"It's like the tree from Mary's alembic." Matthew crouched down by the hearth in his black velvet breeches and embroidered linen shirt. His finger touched a small lump of silver embedded in the bark. Like mine, his voice sounded out of time and place.

"That looks like your pilgrim's badge." The outline of Lazarus's coffin was barely recognizable. I joined him, my full black skirts belling out over the floor.

"I think it is. The ampulla had two gilded hollows inside to hold holy water. Before I left Oxford, I'd filled one with my blood and the other with yours." Matthew's eyes met mine. "Having our blood so close made me feel as though we could never be separated."

"It looks as though the ampulla was exposed to heat and partially melted. If the inside of the ampulla was gilded, traces of mercury would have been released along with the blood."

"So this tree was made with some of the same ingredients as Mary's *arbor Dianæ*." Matthew looked up into the bare branches.

The scent of chamomile and cinnamon intensified. The tree began to bloom—but not the usual fruit or flowers. Instead a key and a single sheet of vellum sprouted from the branches.

"It's the page from the manuscript," said Matthew, pulling it free.

"That means the book is still broken and incomplete in the twenty-first century. Nothing we did in the past altered that fact." I took a steadying breath.

"Then the likelihood is that Ashmole 782 is safely hidden in the Bodleian Library," Matthew said quietly. "This is the key to a car." He snagged it off the branches. For months I hadn't thought about any form of transportation besides a horse or a ship. I looked out the front window, but no vehicle awaited us there. Matthew's eyes followed mine.

"Marcus and Hamish would have made sure we had a way to get to Sept-Tours as planned without calling them for help. They probably have cars waiting all over Europe and America just in case. But they wouldn't have left one visible," Matthew continued.

"There's no garage."

"The hop barn." Matthew's hand automatically moved to slide the key into the pocket at his hip, but his clothing had no such modern conveniences.

"Would they have thought to leave clothes for us, too?" I gestured down at my embroidered jacket and full skirts. They were still dusty from the unpaved, sixteenth-century Oxford road.

"Let's find out." Matthew carried the key and the page from Ashmole 782 into the family room and kitchen.

"Still brown," I commented, looking at the checked wallpaper and ancient refrigerator.

"Still home," Matthew said, drawing me into the crook of his arm.

"Not without Em and Sarah." In contrast with the overstuffed household that had surrounded us for so many months, our modern family seemed fragile and its membership small. Here there was no Mary Sidney to discuss my troubles with in the course of a stormy evening. Neither Susanna nor Goody Alsop would drop by the house in the afternoon for a cup of wine and to help me perfect my latest spell. I wouldn't have Annie's cheerful assistance to get me out of my corset and skirts. Mop wasn't underfoot, or Jack. And if we needed help, there was no Henry Percy to rush to our aid without question or hesitation. I slid my hand around Matthew's waist, needing a reminder of his solid indestructibility.

"You will always miss them," he said softly, gauging my mood, "but the pain will fade in time."

"I'm beginning to feel more like a vampire than a witch," I said ruefully. "Too many good-byes, too many missing loved ones." I spotted the calendar on the wall. It showed the month of November. I pointed it out to Matthew.

"Is it possible that no one has been here since last year?" he wondered, worried.

"Something must be wrong," I said, reaching for the phone.

"No," said Matthew. "The Congregation could be tracing the calls or watching the house. We're expected at Sept-Tours. Whether our time away can be measured in an hour or a year, that's where we need to go."

We found our modern clothes on top of the dryer, slipped into a pillowcase to keep them from getting dusty. Matthew's briefcase sat neatly beside them. Em at least had been here since we left. No one else would have thought of such practicalities. I wrapped our Elizabethan clothes in the linens, reluctant to let go of these tangible remnants of our former lives, and tucked them under my arms like two lumpy footballs. Matthew slid the page from Ashmole 782 into his leather bag, closing it securely.

Matthew scanned the orchard and the fields before we left the house, his keen eyes alert to possible danger. I made my own sweep of the place with my witch's third eye, but no one seemed to be out there. I could see the water under the orchard, hear the owls in the trees, taste the summer sweetness in the dusk air, but that was all.

"Come on," Matthew said, grabbing one of the bundles and taking my hand. We ran across the open space to the hop barn. Matthew put all his weight against the sliding door and pushed, but it wouldn't budge.

"Sarah put a spell on it." I could see it, twisted around the handle and through the grain of the wood. "A good one, too."

"Too good to break?" Matthew's mouth was tight with worry. It wasn't surprising that he was concerned. Last time we were here, I hadn't been able to light the Halloween pumpkins. I located the loose ends of the bindings and grinned.

"No knots. Sarah's good, but she's not a weaver." I'd tucked my Elizabethan silks into the waistband of my leggings. When I pulled them free, the green and brown cords in my hand reached out and latched onto Sarah's spell, loosening the restrictions my aunt had placed on the door faster than even our master thief Jack could have managed it.

Sarah's Honda was parked inside the barn.

"How the hell are we going to fit you into that?" I wondered.

"I'll manage," Matthew said, tossing our clothes into the back. He handed me the briefcase, folded himself into the front seat, and after a few false starts the car sputtered to life.

"Where next?" I asked, fastening my seat belt.

"Syracuse. Then Montreal. Then Amsterdam, where I have a house." Matthew put the car into drive and quietly rolled it into the field. "If anyone is watching for us, they'll be looking in New York, London, and Paris."

"We don't have passports," I observed.

"Look under the mat. Marcus would have told Sarah to leave them there," he said. I peeled up the filthy mats and found Matthew's French passport and my American one.

"Why isn't your passport burgundy?" I asked, taking them out of the sealed plastic bag (another Em touch, I thought).

"Because it's a diplomatic passport." He steered out onto the road and switched on the headlights. "There should be one for you."

My French diplomatic passport, inscribed with the name Diana de Clermont and noting my marital status relative to Matthew, was folded inside the ordinary U.S. version. How Marcus had managed to duplicate my photograph without damaging the original was anyone's guess.

"Are you a spy now, too?" I asked faintly.

"No. It's like the helicopters," he replied with a smile, "just another perk associated with being a de Clermont."

I left Syracuse as Diana Bishop and entered Europe the next day as Diana de Clermont. Matthew's house in Amsterdam turned out to be a seventeenth-century mansion on the most beautiful stretch of the Herengracht. He had, Matthew explained, bought it right after he left Scotland in 1605.

We lingered there only long enough to shower and change clothes. I kept on the same leggings that I'd worn since Madison, and swapped out my shirt for one of Matthew's. He donned his habitual gray and black cashmere and wool, even though it was late June according to the newspapers. It was odd not to see his legs. I'd grown accustomed to their being on display.

"It seems a fair trade," Matthew commented. "I haven't seen your legs for months, except in the privacy of our bedchamber."

Matthew nearly had a heart attack when he discovered that his beloved Range Rover was not waiting for him in the underground garage. Instead we found a navy sports car with a soft top.

"I'm going to kill him," Matthew said when he saw the low-slung vehicle. He used his house key to unlock a metal box bolted to the wall. Inside were another key and a note: *"Welcome home. No one will expect you to be driving this. It's safe. And fast. Hi, Diana. M."*

"What is it?" I said, looking at the airplane-style dials set into a flashy chrome dashboard.

"A Spyker Spyder. Marcus collects cars named after arachnids." Matthew activated the car doors, and they scissored up like the wings on a jet fighter. He swore. "It's the most conspicuous car imaginable."

We only made it as far as Belgium before Matthew pulled in to a car dealership, handed over the keys to Marcus's car, and pulled off the lot in something bigger and far less fun to drive. Safe in its heavy, boxy confines, we entered into France and some hours later began our slow ascent through the mountains of the Auvergne to Sept-Tours.

Glimpses of the fortress flickered between the trees—the pinkish gray stone, a dark tower window. I couldn't help drawing comparisons between the castle and its adjacent town now and how it had looked when last I saw it in 1590. This time no smoke hung over Saint-Lucien in a gray pall. A sound of distant bells made me turn my head, thinking to spot the descendants of the goats I had known coming home for their evening meal. Pierre wouldn't rush out with torches to meet us, though. Chef wasn't in the kitchen decapitating pheasants with a cleaver as the freshly killed game was efficiently prepared to feed both warmbloods and vampires.

And there would be no Philippe, and therefore no shouts of laughter, shrewd observations on human frailty lifted from Euripides, or acute insights into the problems that would face us now that we had returned to the present. How long would it take to stop bracing myself for the rush of motion and bellow of sound that heralded Philippe's arrival in a room? My heart hurt at the thought of my father-in-law. This harshly lit, fast-paced modern world had no place for heroes such as he.

"You're thinking of my father," Matthew murmured. Our silent rituals of a vampire's blood-taking and a witch's kiss had strengthened our ability to gauge each other's thoughts.

"So are you," I observed. He had been since we'd crossed over the border into France.

"The château has felt empty to me since the day he died. It has provided refuge, but little comfort." Matthew's eyes lifted to the castle, then settled back on the road before us. The air was heavy with responsibility and a son's need to live up to his father's legacy.

"Maybe it will be different this time. Sarah and Em are there. Marcus, too. Not to mention Sophie and Nathaniel. And Philippe is still here, if only we can learn to focus on his presence rather than his absence." He would be in the shadows of every room, every stone in the walls. I studied my husband's beautifully austere face, understanding better how experience and pain had shaped it. One hand curved around my belly, while the other sought him out to offer the comfort he so desperately needed.

His fingers clasped mine, squeezed. Then Matthew released me, and we didn't speak for a time. My fingers soon beat an impatient tattoo on my thigh in the quiet, however, and I was tempted several times to open the car's moonroof and fly to the château's front door.

"Don't you dare." Matthew's wide grin softened the warning note in his voice. I returned his smile as he downshifted around a deep curve.

"Hurry, then," I said, scarcely able to control myself. Despite my entreaties the speedometer stayed exactly where it was. I groaned with impatience. "We should have stuck with Marcus's car."

"Patience. We're almost there." *And there's no chance of my going any faster,* Matthew thought as he downshifted again.

"What did Sophie say about Nathaniel's driving when she was pregnant? 'He drives like an old lady.'"

"Imagine how Nathaniel might drive if he actually *was* an old lady—a centuries-old old lady, like me. That's how I will drive for the rest of my days, so long as you are in the car." He reached for my hand again, bringing it to his lips.

"Both hands on the wheel, old lady," I joked as we rounded the last bend, putting a straight stretch of road and walnut trees between us and the château's courtyard.

Hurry, I begged him silently. My eyes fixed on the roof of Matthew's tower as it came into view. When the car slowed, I looked at him in confusion.

"They've been expecting us," he explained, angling his head toward the windshield.

Sophie, Ysabeau, and Sarah were waiting, motionless, in the middle of the road.

Daemon, vampire, witch—and one more. Ysabeau held a baby in her arms. I could see its rich brown thatch of hair and chubby, long legs. One of the baby's hands was wrapped firmly around a strand of the vampire's honeyed locks, while her other hand stretched imperiously in our direction. There was a tiny, undeniable tingle when the baby's eyes focused on me. Sophie and Nathaniel's child was a witch, just as she had foretold.

I unbuckled the seat belt, flung the door open, and sped up the road before Matthew could bring the car to a complete stop. Tears streamed down my face, and Sarah ran to enfold me in familiar textures of fleece and flannel, surrounding me with the scents of henbane and vanilla.

Home, I thought.

"I'm so glad you're back safely," she said fiercely.

Over Sarah's shoulder I watched while Sophie gently took the baby from Ysabeau's grasp. Matthew's mother's face was as inscrutable and lovely as ever, but the tightness around her mouth suggested strong emotions as she gave up the child. That tightness was one of Matthew's tells, too. They were so much more similar in flesh and blood than the method of Matthew's making would suggest was possible.

Pulling myself loose from Sarah's embrace, I turned to Ysabeau.

"I was not sure you would come back. You were gone so long. Then Margaret began to demand that we take her to the road, and it was possible for me to believe that you might return to us safely after all." Ysabeau searched my face for some piece of information that I had not yet given her.

"We're back now. To stay." There had been enough loss in her long life. I kissed her softly on one cheek, then the other.

"Bien," she murmured with relief. "It will please us all to have you here—not just Margaret." The baby heard her name and began to chant "D-d-d-d" while her arms and legs moved like eggbeaters in an attempt to get to me. "Clever girl," Ysabeau said approvingly, giving Margaret and then Sophie a pat on the head.

"Do you want to hold your goddaughter?" Sophie asked. Her smile was wide, though there were tears in her eyes. She looked so much like Susanna.

"Please," I said, taking the baby into my arms in exchange for a kiss on Sophie's cheek.

"Hello, Margaret," I whispered, breathing in her baby smell.

"D-d-d-d." Margaret grabbed a hank of my hair and began to wave it around in her fist.

"You are a troublemaker," I said with a laugh. She dug her feet into my ribs and grunted in protest.

"She's as stubborn as her father, even though she's a Pisces," Sophie said serenely. "Sarah went through the ceremony in your place. Agatha was here. She's gone at the moment, but I suspect she'll be back soon. She and Marthe made a special cake wrapped up in strands of sugar. It was amazing. And Margaret's dress was beautiful. You sound different—as if you spent a lot of time in a foreign country. And I like your hair. It's different, too. Are you hungry?" Sophie's words came out of her mouth in a disorganized tumble, just like Tom or Jack. I felt the loss of our friends, even here in the midst of our family.

After kissing Margaret on the forehead, I handed her back to her mother. Matthew was still standing behind the Range Rover's open door, one foot in the car and the other resting on the ground of the Auvergne, as though he were unsure if we should be there.

"Where's Em?" I asked. Sarah and Ysabeau exchanged a look.

"Everybody is waiting for you in the château. Why don't we walk back?" Ysabeau suggested. "Just leave the car. Someone will get it. You must want to stretch your legs."

I put my arm around Sarah and took a few steps. Where was Matthew? I turned and held out my free hand. *Come to your family,* I said silently as our eyes connected. *Come be with the people who love you.*

He smiled, and my heart leaped in response.

Ysabeau hissed in surprise, a sibilant noise that carried in the summer air more surely than a whisper. "Heartbeats. Yours. And . . . two more?" Her beautiful green eyes darted to my abdomen and a tiny red drop welled up and threatened to fall. Ysabeau looked to Matthew in wonder. He nodded, and his mother's blood tear fully formed and slid down her cheek.

"Twins run in my family," I said by way of explanation. Matthew had detected the second heartbeat in Amsterdam, just before we'd climbed into Marcus's Spyder.

"Mine, too," Ysabeau whispered. "Then it is true, what Sophie has seen in her dreams? You are with child—Matthew's child?"

"Children," I said, watching the blood tear's slow progress.

"It's a new beginning, then," Sarah said, wiping a tear from her own eye. Ysabeau gave my aunt a bittersweet smile.

"Philippe had a favorite saying about beginnings. Something ancient. What was it, Matthew?" Ysabeau asked her son.

Matthew stepped fully out of the car at last, as if some spell had been holding him back and its conditions had finally been met. He walked the few steps to my side, then kissed his mother softly on the cheek before reaching out and clasping my hand.

"'*Omni fine initium novum,*'" Matthew said, gazing upon the land of his father as though he had, at last, come home.

"'*In every ending there is a new beginning.*'"

30 May 1593

Annie brought the small statue of Diana to Father Hubbard, just as Master Marlowe had made her promise to do. Her heart tightened to see it in the *wearh*'s palm. The tiny figure always reminded her of Diana Roydon. Even now, nearly two years after her mistress's sudden departure, Annie missed her.

"And he said nothing else?" Hubbard demanded, turning the figurine this way and that. The huntress's arrow caught the light and sparked as though it were about to fly.

"Nothing, Father. Before he left for Deptford this morning, he bade me bring this to you. Master Marlowe said you would know what must be done."

Hubbard noticed a slip of paper inserted into the slim quiver, rolled up and tucked alongside the goddess's waiting arrows. "Give me one of your pins, Annie."

Annie removed a pin from her bodice and handed it to him with a mystified look. Hubbard poked the sharp end at the paper and caught it on the point. Carefully he slid it out.

Hubbard read the lines, frowned, and shook his head. "Poor Christopher. He was ever one of God's lost children."

"Master Marlowe is not coming back?" Annie smothered a small sigh of relief. She had never liked the playwright, and her regard for him had not recovered after the dreadful events in the tiltyard at Greenwich Palace. Since her mistress and master had departed, leaving no clues to their whereabouts, Marlowe had gone from melancholy to despair to something darker. Some days Annie was sure that the blackness would swallow him whole. She wanted to be sure it didn't catch her, too.

"No, Annie. God tells me Master Marlowe is gone from this world and on to the next. I pray he finds peace there, for it was denied him in this life." Hubbard considered the girl for a moment. She had grown into a striking young woman. Maybe she would cure Will Shakespeare of his love for that other man's wife. "But you are not to worry. Mistress Roydon bade me treat you like my own. I take care of my children, and you will have a new master."

"Who, Father?" She would have to take whatever position Hubbard offered her. Mistress Roydon had been clear how much money she would require to set herself up as an independent seamstress in Islington. It was going to take time and considerable thrift to gather such a sum.

"Master Shakespeare. Now that you can read and write, you are a woman of value, Annie. You can be of help to him in his work." Hubbard considered the slip of paper in his hand. He was tempted to keep it with the parcel that had arrived from Prague, sent to him through the formidable network of mail carriers and merchants established by the Dutch vampires.

Hubbard still wasn't sure why Edward Kelley had sent him the strange picture of the dragons. Edward was a dark and slippery creature, and Hubbard had not approved of his moral code that saw nothing wrong with open adultery or theft. Taking his blood in the ritual of family and sacrifice had been a chore, not the pleasure it usually was. In the exchange, Hubbard had seen enough of Kelley's soul to know he didn't want him in London. So he sent him to Mortlake instead. It had stopped Dee's incessant pestering for lessons in magic.

But Marlowe had meant this statue to go to Annie, and Hubbard would not alter a dying man's wish. He handed the small figurine and slip of paper to Annie. "You must give this to your aunt, Mistress Norman. She will keep it safe for you. The paper can be another remembrance of Master Marlowe."

"Yes, Father Hubbard," Annie said, though she would have liked to sell the silver object and put the proceeds in her stocking.

Annie left the church where Andrew Hubbard held court and trudged the streets to Will Shakespeare's house. He was less mercurial than Marlowe, and Mistress Roydon had always spoken of him with respect even though the master's friends were quick to mock him.

She settled quickly into the player's household, her spirits lifting with each passing day. When news reached them of Marlowe's gruesome death, it only confirmed how fortunate she was to be free of him. Master Shakespeare was shaken, too, and drank too much one night, which brought him to the attention of the master of the revels. Shakespeare had explained himself satisfactorily, though, and all was returned to normal now.

Annie was cleaning grime from the windowpane to provide better light for her employer to read by. She dipped her cloth into fresh water, and a small curl of paper drifted down from her pocket, carried on a breeze from the open casement.

"What is that, Annie?" Shakespeare asked suspiciously, pointing with the feathered end of his quill. The girl had worked for Kit Marlowe. She could be passing information to his rivals. He couldn't afford to have anyone know about his latest bids for patronage. With all the playhouses closed on account of the plague, it would be a challenge to keep body and soul together. *Venus and Adonis* could do it—provided nobody stole the idea out from under him.

"Nothing, M-M-Master Shakespeare," Annie stammered, bending to retrieve the paper.

"Bring it here, since it is nothing," he commanded.

As soon as it was in his possession, Shakespeare recognized the distinctive penmanship. The hair on the back of his neck prickled. It was a message from a dead man.

"When did Marlowe give this to you?" Shakespeare's voice was sharp.

"He didn't, Master Shakespeare." As ever, Annie couldn't bring herself to lie. She had few other witchy traits, but Annie possessed honesty in abundance. "It was hidden. Father Hubbard found it and gave it to me. For a remembrance, he said."

"Did you find this after Marlowe died?" The prickling sensation at the back of Shakespeare's neck was quieted by the rush of interest.

"Yes," Annie whispered.

"I will hold on to it for you then. For safekeeping."

"Of course." Annie's eyes flickered with concern as she watched the last words of Christopher Marlowe disappear into her new master's closed fist.

"Be about your business, Annie." Shakespeare waited until his maid had gone to fetch more rags and water. Then he scanned the lines.

Black is the badge of true love lost.
The hue of daemons,
And the Shadow of Night.

Shakespeare sighed. Kit's choice of meter never made any sense to him. And his melancholy humor and morbid fascinations were too dark for these sad times. They made audiences uncomfortable, and there was sufficient death in London. He twirled the quill.

True love lost. Indeed. Shakespeare snorted. He'd had quite enough of true love, though the paying customers never seemed to tire of it. He struck out the words and replaced them with a single syllable, one that more accurately captured what he felt.

Daemons. The success of Kit's *Faustus* still rankled him. Shakespeare had no talent for writing about creatures beyond the limits of nature. He was far better with ordinary, flawed mortals caught in the snares of fate. Sometimes he thought he might have a good ghost story in him. Perhaps a wronged father who haunted his son. Shakespeare shuddered. His own father would make a terrifying specter, should the Lord tire of his company after John Shakespeare's final accounts were settled. He struck out that offending word and chose a different one.

Shadow of Night. It was a limp, predictable ending to the verses—the kind that George Chapman would fall upon for lack of something more original. But what would better serve the purpose? He obliterated another word and wrote *"scowl"* above it. *Scowl of Night.* That wasn't quite right either. He crossed it out and wrote *"sleeve."* That was just as bad.

Shakespeare wondered idly about the fate of Marlowe and his friends, all of them as insubstantial as shadows now. Henry Percy was enjoying a rare period of royal benevolence and was forever at court. Raleigh had married in secret and fallen from the queen's favor. He was now rusticated to Dorset, where the queen hoped he would be forgotten. Harriot was in seclusion somewhere, no doubt bent over a mathematical puzzle or staring at the heavens like a moonstruck Robin Goodfellow. Rumor had it that Chapman was on some mission for Cecil in the Low Countries and penning long poems about witches. And Marlowe was recently murdered in Deptford, though there was talk that it had been an assassination. Perhaps that strange Welshman would know more about it, for he'd been at the tavern with Marlowe. Roydon—who was the only truly powerful man Shakespeare had ever met—and his mysterious wife had both utterly vanished in the summer of 1591 and had not been seen since.

The only one of Marlowe's circle that Shakespeare still heard from regularly was the big Scot named Gallowglass, who was more princely than a servant ought to be and told such wonderful tales of fairies and sprites. It was thanks to Gallowglass's steady employment that Shakespeare had a roof over his head. Gallowglass always seemed to have a job that required Shakespeare's talents as a forger. He paid well, too—especially when he wanted Shakespeare to imitate Roydon's hand in the margins of some book or pen a letter with his signature.

What a crew, Shakespeare thought. *Traitors, atheists, and criminals, the lot of them.* His pen hesitated over the page. After writing another word, this one decisively thick and black, Shakespeare sat back and studied his new verses.

Black is the badge of hell
The hue of dungeons and the school of night.

It was no longer recognizable as Marlowe's work. Through the alchemy of his talent, Shakespeare had transformed a dead man's ideas into something suitable for ordinary Londoners rather than dangerous men like Roydon. And it had taken him only a few moments.

Shakespeare felt not a single pang of regret as he altered the past, thereby changing the future. Marlowe's turn on the world's stage had ended, but Shakespeare's was just beginning. Memories were short and history unkind. It was the way of the world.

Pleased, Shakespeare put the bit of paper into a stack of similar scraps weighted down with a dog's skull on the corner of his desk. He'd find a use for the snippet of verse one day. Then he had second thoughts.

Perhaps he'd been too hasty to dismiss *"true love lost."* There was potential there—unrealized, waiting for someone to unlock it. Shakespeare reached for a scrap he'd cut off a partially filled sheet of paper in a half-hearted attempt at economy after Annie had shown him the last butcher's bill.

"Love's Labour's Lost," he wrote in large letters.

Yes, Shakespeare mused, he'd definitely use that one day.

Libri Personæ: The People of the Book

*Those noted thus * acknowledged by historians.*

Part I: Woodstock: The Old Lodge

Diana Bishop, a witch
Matthew de Clermont, known as *Roydon, a vampire
* Christopher Marlowe, a daemon and maker of plays
Françoise and Pierre, both vampires and servants
* George Chapman, a writer of some reputation and little patronage
* Thomas Harriot, a daemon and astronomer
* Henry Percy, the Earl of Northumberland
* Sir Walter Raleigh, an adventurer
Joseph Bidwell, senior and junior, shoemakers
Master Somers, a glover
Widow Beaton, a cunning woman
Mister Danforth, a clergyman
Master Iffley, another glover
Gallowglass, a vampire and soldier of fortune
* Davy Gam, known as Hancock, a vampire, his Welsh companion

Part II: Sept-Tours and the Village of Saint-Lucien

* Cardinal Joyeuse, a visitor to Mont Saint-Michel
Alain, a vampire and servant to the Sieur de Clermont
Philippe de Clermont, a vampire and lord of Sept-Tours
Chef, a cook
Catrine, Jehanne, Thomas, and Étienne, servants
Marie, who makes gowns
André Champier, a wizard of Lyon

Part III: London: The Blackfriars

* Robert Hawley, a shoemaker
* Margaret Hawley, his wife
* Mary Sidney, the Countess of Pembroke
Joan, her maid

* Nicholas Hilliard, a limner
Master Prior, a maker of pies
* Richard Field, a printer
* Jacqueline Vautrollier Field, his wife
* John Chandler, an apothecary near the Barbican Cross
Amen Corner and Leonard Shoreditch, vampires
Father Hubbard, the vampire king of London
Annie Undercroft, a young witch with some skill and little power
* Susanna Norman, a midwife and witch
* John and Jeffrey Norman, her sons
Goody Alsop, a windwitch of St. James Garlickhythe
Catherine Streeter, a firewitch
Elizabeth Jackson, a waterwitch
Marjorie Cooper, an earthwitch
Jack Blackfriars, a nimble orphan
* Doctor John Dee, a learned man with a library
* Jane Dee, his disgruntled wife
* William Cecil, Lord Burghley, the lord high treasurer of England
* Robert Devereux, the Earl of Essex
* Elizabeth I, queen of England
* Elizabeth (Bess) Throckmorton, maid of honor to the queen

Part IV: The Empire: Prague

Karolína and Tereza, vampires and servants
* Tadeáš Hájek, physician to His Majesty
* Ottavio Strada, Imperial librarian and historian
* Rudolf II, Holy Roman Emperor and King of Bohemia
Frau Huber, an Austrian, and Signorina Rossi, an Italian, women of Malá Strana
* Joris Hoefnagel, an artist
* Erasmus Habermel, maker of mathematical instruments
* Signor Miseroni, a carver of precious stones
* Signor Pasetti, His Majesty's dancing master
* Joanna Kelley, a woman far from home
* Edward Kelley, a daemon and alchemist
* Rabbi Judah Loew, a wise man
Abraham ben Elijah of Chelm, a wizard with a problem
* David Gans, an astronomer

Herr Fuchs, a vampire
* Mordechai Maisel, a prosperous merchant of the Jewish Town
Lobero, a Hungarian dog sometimes mistaken for a mop, probably just a Komondor
* Johannes Pistorius, a wizard and theologian

Part V: London: The Blackfriars

* Vilém Slavata, a very young ambassador
Louisa de Clermont, a vampire and sister to Matthew de Clermont
* Master Sleford, keeper of the poor souls of Bedlam
Stephen Proctor, a wizard
Rebecca White, a witch
Bridget White, her daughter

Part VI: New World, Old World

Sarah Bishop, a witch and aunt to Diana Bishop
Ysabeau de Clermont, a vampire and mother to Matthew de Clermont
Sophie Norman, a daemon
Margaret Wilson, her daughter, a witch

Other Characters in Other Times

Rima Jaén, a librarian of Seville
Emily Mather, a witch and partner to Sarah Bishop
Marthe, housekeeper to Ysabeau de Clermont
Phoebe Taylor, very proper, who knows something about art
Marcus Whitmore, Matthew de Clermont's son, a vampire
Verin de Clermont, a vampire
Ernst Neumann, her husband
Peter Knox, a witch and member of the Congregation
Pavel Skovajsa, who works in a library
* Gerbert of Aurillac in the Cantal, a vampire and ally of Peter Knox
* William Shakespeare, a scrivener and forger who also makes plays

Acknowledgments

So many people helped bring this book into the world.

First, thanks to my always gentle, always candid first readers: Cara, Fran, Jill, Karen, Lisa, and Olive. And a special thanks to Margie for claiming she was bored just as I was struggling with the last edit and offering to read the manuscript with her discerning writer's eye.

Carole DeSanti, my editor, served as midwife during the writing process and knows (literally) where all the bodies are buried. Thank you, Carole, for always being ready to lend assistance with a sharp pencil and a sympathetic ear.

The extraordinary team at Viking, who alchemically transforms stacks of typescript into beautiful books, continues to astonish me with their enthusiasm and professionalism. Special thanks go to my copy editor, Maureen Sugden, whose eagle eye rivals that of Augusta. And to my publishers around the world, thank you for all you have done (and continue to do) to introduce Diana and Matthew to new readers.

My literary agent, Sam Stoloff, of the Frances Goldin Agency, remains my most steadfast supporter. Thanks, Sam, for providing perspective and doing the behind-the-scenes work that makes it possible for me to write. Thanks are also due to my film agent, Rich Green, of the Creative Artists Agency, who has become an indispensable resource for advice and good humor even in the most challenging of circumstances.

My assistant, Jill Hough, defended my time and my sanity during the past year with the fierceness of a firedrake. I literally could not have completed the book without her.

Lisa Halttunen once again readied the manuscript for submission. Though I fear I will never master more than a few of the grammatical rules at her command, I am eternally grateful that she continues to be willing to straighten out my prose and punctuation.

Patrick Wyman provided insights into the twists and turns of medieval and military history that took the characters—and the story—in surprising directions. Though Carole knows where the bodies are buried, Patrick understands how they got there. Thank you, Patrick, for helping me to see

Gallowglass, Matthew, and above all Philippe in a new light. Thanks also to Cleopatra Comnenos, for answering my queries about the Greek language.

I would also like to express my appreciation to the Pasadena Roving Archers, who helped me understand just how difficult it is to shoot an arrow at a target. Scott Timmons of Aerial Solutions introduced me to Fokker and his other beautiful raptors at the Terranea Resort in California. And Andrew at the Apple Store in Thousand Oaks saved the author, her computer—and the book itself—from a potentially terminal meltdown at a crucial point in the writing process.

This book is dedicated to historian Lacey Baldwin Smith, who took me on as a graduate student and has inspired thousands of students with his passion for Tudor England. Whenever he spoke about Henry VIII or his daughter Elizabeth I, it always seemed as if they had just had lunch together. Once, he gave me a brief list of facts and told me to imagine how I would handle them if I was writing a chronicle, or a saint's life, or a medieval romance. At the end of one of my exceedingly short stories, he wrote "*What happens next? You should think about writing a novel.*" Perhaps that is when the seeds of the All Souls trilogy were first planted.

And last, but not least, I am sincerely grateful to my long-suffering family and friends (you know who you are!) who saw very little of me during my sojourn in 1590 and welcomed me back when I returned to the present.

AVAILABLE FROM PENGUIN BOOKS

A Discovery of Witches

In book one of the #1 *New York Times* bestselling All Souls Trilogy, Diana Bishop, a young scholar and descendant of witches, discovers a long-lost and enchanted alchemical manuscript, Ashmole 782, deep in Oxford's Bodleian Library. Its reappearance summons a fantastical underworld, which she navigates with vampire geneticist Matthew Clairmont.

"A wonderfully imaginative grown-up fantasy with all the magic of Harry Potter *or* Twilight *. . . An irresistible tale of wizardry, science, and forbidden love,* A Discovery of Witches *will leave you longing for the sequel."* —People

The Book of Life

In this gripping, action-packed finale to the All Souls Trilogy, the search for Ashmole 782 and its missing pages takes on even more urgency. Diana and Matthew finally learn what the witches discovered centuries ago, bringing this superb series to a satisfying close.

"Weaving an extraordinarily rich story of magic and science, history and fiction, passion and power, secrets and truths, Harkness delivers an unforgettable and spellbinding finale that's not to be missed." —USA Today

PENGUIN
BOOKS

Praise for *A Discovery of Witches*

"A wonderfully imaginative grown-up fantasy with all the magic of *Harry Potter* or *Twilight* . . . An irresistible tale of wizardry, science, and forbidden love, *A Discovery of Witches* will leave you longing for the sequel." —*People*

"A thoroughly grown-up novel packed with gorgeous historical detail and a gutsy, brainy heroine to match: Diana Bishop, a renowned scholar of seventeenth-century chemistry and a descendant of accomplished witches. . . . Harkness writes with thrilling gusto about the magical world."

—Karen Valby, *Entertainment Weekly*

"Harkness conjures up a scintillating paranormal story. . . . Discover why everyone's talking about this magical book." —*USA Today*

"Delightfully well-crafted and enchantingly imaginative . . . An enthralling and deeply enjoyable read, *A Discovery of Witches* is to be the first in a trilogy and will likely draw considerable cross-genre interest. Its fantasy, historical, and romance genre appeal is clear, but it also has some of the same ineluctable atmosphere that made Anne Rice's vampire books such a popular success." —*The Miami Herald*

"A debut novel with a big supernatural canvas . . . Its ambitions are world-sized, ranging across history and zeroing in on DNA, human and otherworldly. Age-old tensions between science and magic and between evolution and alchemy erupt as Diana seeks to unlock the secrets of Ashmole 782."

—*Los Angeles Times*

"Harkness, an eloquent writer, conjures this world of witches with Ivy League degrees and supernatural creatures completely—and believably—while maintaining a sense of wonder. Her large cast of characters is vivid and real. . . . *A Discovery of Witches* is that rare historical novel that manages to be as intelligent as it is romantic. And it is supernatural fiction that those of us who usually prefer to stay grounded in reality can get caught up in. Pardon the pun, but *Witches* is truly spellbinding." —*San Antonio Express-News*

"A scintillating debut . . . Harkness imbues Bishop and Clairmont's romantic adventure with an odd charm, a sweet joy in the life of the mind."

—*The Seattle Times*

"Readers who thrilled to Elizabeth Kostova's 2005 blockbuster, *The Historian*, will note the parallels, but *A Discovery of Witches* is a modern Romeo and Juliet story, with older, wiser lovers. Blood will flow when a witch and a vampire fallfor each other. Author Deborah Harkness, a UCLA history professor, brings vast knowledge and research to the page."

—*The Cleveland Plain Dealer*

"Enthralling . . . A rollicking mystery." —*Pittsburgh Post-Gazette*

"Fascinating and delightful . . . Harkness introduces elements of mystery, subtly builds up a romance, interjects some breathtaking action scenes, and brings it all to a cliff-hanger of an ending, all the while weaving strong threads of historical fact into the fabric of her fiction." —*The Tulsa World*

"Harkness works her own form of literary alchemy by deftly blending fantasy, romance, history, and horror into one completely bewitching book."
—*Chicago Tribune*

"A shrewdly written romp and a satisfying snow-day read for those of us who heartily enjoyed the likes of Anne Rice and Marion Zimmer Bradley. By the book's rousing end . . . I was impatient for the sequel." —NPR

"Five hundred and eighty pages of sheer pleasure. Harkness's sure hand when it comes to star-crossed love and chilling action sequences in striking locales makes for an enchanting debut." —*Parade*

"Fans of historical fiction will be mesmerized. . . . Harkness's attention to historical detail [and] the rich fantasy world she creates . . . hold us thoroughly."
—*Paste*

"A riveting tale full of romance and danger that will have you on the edge of your seat, yet its chief strength lies in the wonderfully rich and ingenious mythology underlying the story. *A Discovery of Witches* is a captivating tale that will ensnare the heart and imagination of even the most skeptical reader. . . . Literary magic at its most potent." —Stephanie Harrison, *BookPage*

"Deborah Harkness is a creative genius. She has taken a genre that is saturated with vampires, witches, and daemons, and has created something unique, with its own rich history and mythology, that draws you into her world with captivating storytelling. . . . Hands down the best book I have read in a very long time." —Molly Seddon, *Words and Pieces*

"Harkness creates a spectacular fusion of historical and scientific facts, fantastical elements and creatures, fantasy, romance, and highly intellectual characters and dialogue." —*Among the Muses*

"Pure literary brain candy, but unlike many works of its type, it's very well written and chock-full of fascinating bits from Harkness's research. . . . One of those books that I wanted to rip through quickly so I could find out what happens, but also wanted to read very slowly so that I didn't have to be done too fast. I'll be waiting—impatiently—to find out what comes next."
—Jeremy Dibbell, *PhiloBiblos*

"We cannot give Harkness's debut enough praise. It is quite simply stunning. Blending fact and fiction, history and present, delicate courtship and tempestuous tantrums, understanding your identity and losing yourself: it is a beautiful work of fiction that fastens onto your heart and feeds your mind. In other words: probably perfection." —*The Truth About Books*

"*A Discovery of Witches* actually made me excited for vampires again. Deborah Harkness has written one of the most fantastic books I've read in ages. A flawless mixture of well-researched history and magic." —Vampires.com

"A masterpiece of literary fiction, filled with factional and fantastical beings brought to us by the lyrical narrative of a most talented storyteller . . . An epic tale that will alter your ideas of good versus evil, it's a mystery of historic proportion and is filled with the fantasy that readers today can't seem to get enough of."

—*The Reading Frenzy*

"Set in our contemporary world with a magical twist, this sparkling debut by a history professor features a large cast of fascinating characters, and readers will find themselves invested in Diana's success at unlocking the secrets of the manuscript. Although not a nail-biting cliff-hanger, the finale skillfully provides a sense of completion while leaving doors open for the possibility of wonderful sequel adventures. This reviewer, for one, hopes they come soon! Destined to be popular . . . this enchanting novel is an essential purchase. Harkness is an author to watch." —*Library Journal* (starred review)

"Harkness creates a compelling and sweeping tale that moves from Oxford to Paris to upstate New York and into both Diana's and Matthew's complex families and histories. All her characters are fully fleshed and unique, which, when combined with the complex and engaging plot, results in . . . essential reading."

—*Booklist* (starred review)

"Harkness's lively debut . . . imagines a crowded universe where normal and paranormal creatures observe a tenuous peace. . . . She brings this world to vibrant life and makes the most of the growing popularity of gothic adventure with an ending that keeps the Old Lodge door wide open."

—*Publishers Weekly*

"A strange and wonderful novel of forbidden love and ancient spells that turns every preconception about magic on its head . . . I fell in love with it from the very first page." —Danielle Trussoni, author of *Angelology*

"Deborah Harkness's novel is a brilliant synthesis of magic and history. A gripping story of dangerous passion, intellectual intrigue, and fantastical beings." —Ivy Pochoda, author of *The Art of Disappearing*

"A fleet-footed novel set in a vivid otherworld, richly peppered with scholarly tidbits. Huge fun—with serious underpinnings of history."

—Jane Borodale, author of *The Book of Fires*

ABOUT THE AUTHOR

Deborah Harkness is a professor of history at the University of Southern California. She has received Fulbright, Guggenheim, and National Humanities Center fellowships, and her most recent scholarly work is *The Jewel House: Elizabethan London and the Scientific Revolution*. She also writes an award-winning wine blog.

DEBORAH HARKNESS

A Discovery of Witches

PENGUIN BOOKS

PENGUIN BOOKS
Published by the Penguin Group
Penguin Group (USA) Inc., 375 Hudson Street, New York, New York 10014, U.S.A.
Penguin Group (Canada), 90 Eglinton Avenue East, Suite 700, Toronto,
Ontario, Canada M4P 2Y3 (a division of Pearson Penguin Canada Inc.)
Penguin Books Ltd, 80 Strand, London WC2R 0RL, England
Penguin Ireland, 25 St. Stephen's Green, Dublin 2, Ireland (a division of Penguin Books Ltd)
Penguin Books Australia Ltd, 250 Camberwell Road, Camberwell,
Victoria 3124, Australia (a division of Pearson Australia Group Pty Ltd)
Penguin Books India Pvt Ltd, 11 Community Centre, Panchsheel Park, New Delhi–110 017, India
Penguin Group (NZ), 67 Apollo Drive, Auckland, North Shore 0632,
New Zealand (a division of Pearson New Zealand Ltd)
Penguin Books (South Africa) (Pty) Ltd, 24 Sturdee Avenue,
Rosebank, Johannesburg 2196, South Africa

Penguin Books Ltd, Registered Offices: 80 Strand, Lonon WC2R 0RL, England

First published in the United States of America by Viking Penguin,
a member of Penguin Group (USA) Inc. 2011
Published in Penguin Books 2011

3 5 7 9 10 8 6 4

Publisher's Note: This is a work of fiction. Names, characters, places, and incidents either are the product of the author's imagination or are used fictitiously, and any resemblance to actual persons, living or dead, business establishments, events, or locales is entirely coincidental.

THE LIBRARY OF CONGRESS HAS CATALOGED THE HARDCOVER EDITION AS FOLLOWS:
Harkness, Deborah E., 1965–
A discovery of witches : a novel / Deborah Harkness
p. cm.
ISBN 978-0-670-02241-0 (hc.)
ISBN 978-0-670-02261-8 (hc. export edition)
ISBN 978-0-14-311968-5 (pbk.)
1. Vampires—Fiction. 2. Witches—Fiction. 3. Alchemy—Manuscripts—Fiction.
4. Science and magic—Fiction.
I. Title
PS3608.A7436D57 2011
813'.6—dc22 2010030425

Printed in the United States of America
Set in Adobe Garamond Pro
Designed by Francesca Belanger

For Lexie and Jake, and their bright futures

It begins with absence and desire.

It begins with blood and fear.

It begins with a discovery of witches.

Chapter 1

The leather-bound volume was nothing remarkable. To an ordinary historian, it would have looked no different from hundreds of other manuscripts in Oxford's Bodleian Library, ancient and worn. But I knew there was something odd about it from the moment I collected it.

Duke Humfrey's Reading Room was deserted on this late-September afternoon, and requests for library materials were filled quickly now that the summer crush of visiting scholars was over and the madness of the fall term had not yet begun. Even so, I was surprised when Sean stopped me at the call desk.

"Dr. Bishop, your manuscripts are up," he whispered, voice tinged with a touch of mischief. The front of his argyle sweater was streaked with the rusty traces of old leather bindings, and he brushed at it self-consciously. A lock of sandy hair tumbled over his forehead when he did.

"Thanks," I said, flashing him a grateful smile. I was flagrantly disregarding the rules limiting the number of books a scholar could call in a single day. Sean, who'd shared many a drink with me in the pink-stuccoed pub across the street in our graduate-student days, had been filling my requests without complaint for more than a week. "And stop calling me Dr. Bishop. I always think you're talking to someone else."

He grinned back and slid the manuscripts—all containing fine examples of alchemical illustrations from the Bodleian's collections—over his battered oak desk, each one tucked into a protective gray cardboard box. "Oh, there's one more." Sean disappeared into the cage for a moment and returned with a thick, quarto-size manuscript bound simply in mottled calfskin. He laid it on top of the pile and stooped to inspect it. The thin gold rims of his glasses sparked in the dim light provided by the old bronze reading lamp that was attached to a shelf. "This one's not been called up for a while. I'll make a note that it needs to be boxed after you return it."

"Do you want me to remind you?"

"No. Already made a note here." Sean tapped his head with his fingertips.

"Your mind must be better organized than mine." My smile widened.

Sean looked at me shyly and tugged on the call slip, but it remained where it was, lodged between the cover and the first pages. "This one doesn't want to let go," he commented.

Muffled voices chattered in my ear, intruding on the familiar hush of the room.

"Did you hear that?" I looked around, puzzled by the strange sounds.

"What?" Sean replied, looking up from the manuscript.

Traces of gilt shone along its edges and caught my eye. But those faded touches of gold could not account for a faint, iridescent shimmer that seemed to be escaping from between the pages. I blinked.

"Nothing." I hastily drew the manuscript toward me, my skin prickling when it made contact with the leather. Sean's fingers were still holding the call slip, and now it slid easily out of the binding's grasp. I hoisted the volumes into my arms and tucked them under my chin, assailed by a whiff of the uncanny that drove away the library's familiar smell of pencil shavings and floor wax.

"Diana? Are you okay?" Sean asked with a concerned frown.

"Fine. Just a bit tired," I replied, lowering the books away from my nose.

I walked quickly through the original, fifteenth-century part of the library, past the rows of Elizabethan reading desks with their three ascending bookshelves and scarred writing surfaces. Between them, Gothic windows directed the reader's attention up to the coffered ceilings, where bright paint and gilding picked out the details of the university's crest of three crowns and open book and where its motto, "God is my illumination," was proclaimed repeatedly from on high.

Another American academic, Gillian Chamberlain, was my sole companion in the library on this Friday night. A classicist who taught at Bryn Mawr, Gillian spent her time poring over scraps of papyrus sandwiched between sheets of glass. I sped past her, trying to avoid eye contact, but the creaking of the old floor gave me away.

My skin tingled as it always did when another witch looked at me.

"Diana?" she called from the gloom. I smothered a sigh and stopped.

"Hi, Gillian." Unaccountably possessive of my hoard of manuscripts, I remained as far from the witch as possible and angled my body so they weren't in her line of sight.

"What are you doing for Mabon?" Gillian was always stopping by my desk to ask me to spend time with my "sisters" while I was in town. With the Wiccan celebrations of the autumn equinox just days away, she was redoubling her efforts to bring me into the Oxford coven.

"Working," I said promptly.

"There are some very nice witches here, you know," Gillian said with prim disapproval. "You really should join us on Monday."

"Thanks. I'll think about it," I said, already moving in the direction of the Selden End, the airy seventeenth-century addition that ran perpendicular to the main axis of Duke Humfrey's. "I'm working on a conference paper, though, so don't count on it." My aunt Sarah had always warned me it wasn't possible for one witch to lie to another, but that hadn't stopped me from trying.

Gillian made a sympathetic noise, but her eyes followed me.

Back at my familiar seat facing the arched, leaded windows, I resisted the temptation to dump the manuscripts on the table and wipe my hands. Instead, mindful of their age, I lowered the stack carefully.

The manuscript that had appeared to tug on its call slip lay on top of the pile. Stamped in gilt on the spine was a coat of arms belonging to Elias Ashmole, a seventeenth-century book collector and alchemist whose books and papers had come to the Bodleian from the Ashmolean Museum in the nineteenth century, along with the number 782. I reached out, touching the brown leather.

A mild shock made me withdraw my fingers quickly, but not quickly enough. The tingling traveled up my arms, lifting my skin into tiny goose pimples, then spread across my shoulders, tensing the muscles in my back and neck. These sensations quickly receded, but they left behind a hollow feeling of unmet desire. Shaken by my response, I stepped away from the library table.

Even at a safe distance, this manuscript was challenging me—threatening the walls I'd erected to separate my career as a scholar from my birthright as the last of the Bishop witches. Here, with my hard-earned doctorate, tenure, and promotions in hand and my career beginning to blossom, I'd renounced my family's heritage and created a life that depended on reason and scholarly abilities, not inexplicable hunches and spells. I was in Oxford to complete a research project. Upon its conclusion, my findings would be published, substantiated with extensive analysis and footnotes, and presented to human colleagues, leaving no room for mysteries and no place in my work for what could be known only through a witch's sixth sense.

But—albeit unwittingly—I had called up an alchemical manuscript that I needed for my research and that also seemed to possess an otherworldly power that was impossible to ignore. My fingers itched to open it and learn more. Yet an even stronger impulse held me back: Was my curiosity intellectual, related to my scholarship? Or did it have to do with my family's connection to witchcraft?

I drew the library's familiar air into my lungs and shut my eyes, hoping that would bring clarity. The Bodleian had always been a sanctuary to me, a place unassociated with the Bishops. Tucking my shaking hands under my elbows, I stared at Ashmole 782 in the growing twilight and wondered what to do.

My mother would instinctively have known the answer, had she been standing in my place. Most members of the Bishop family were talented witches, but my mother, Rebecca, was special. Everyone said so. Her supernatural abilities had manifested early, and by the time she was in grade school, she could outmagic most of the senior witches in the local coven with her intuitive understanding of spells, startling foresight, and uncanny knack for seeing beneath the surface of people and events. My mother's younger sister, my Aunt Sarah, was a skilled witch, too, but her talents were more mainstream: a deft hand with potions and a perfect command of witchcraft's traditional lore of spells and charms.

My fellow historians didn't know about the family, of course, but everyone in Madison, the remote town in upstate New York where I'd lived with Sarah since the age of seven, knew all about the Bishops. My ancestors had moved from Massachusetts after the Revolutionary War. By then more than a century had passed since Bridget Bishop was executed at Salem. Even so, rumors and gossip followed them to their new home. After pulling up stakes and resettling in Madison, the Bishops worked hard to demonstrate how useful it could be to have witchy neighbors for healing the sick and predicting the weather. In time the family set down roots in the community deep enough to withstand the inevitable outbreaks of superstition and human fear.

But my mother had a curiosity about the world that led her beyond the safety of Madison. She went first to Harvard, where she met a young wizard named Stephen Proctor. He also had a long magical lineage and a desire to experience life outside the scope of his family's New England history and influence. Rebecca Bishop and Stephen Proctor were a charming couple, my mother's all-American frankness a counterpoint to my father's more formal, old-fashioned ways. They became anthropologists, immersing themselves in foreign cultures and beliefs, sharing their intellectual passions along with their deep devotion to each other. After securing positions on the faculty in area schools—my mother at her alma mater, my father at Wellesley—they made research trips abroad and made a home for their new family in Cambridge.

I have few memories of my childhood, but each one is vivid and surprisingly clear. All feature my parents: the feel of corduroy on my father's elbows, the lily of the valley that scented my mother's perfume, the clink of their wineglasses on Friday nights when they'd put me to bed and dine together by candlelight. My mother told me bedtime stories, and my father's brown briefcase clattered when he dropped it by the front door. These memories would strike a familiar chord with most people.

Other recollections of my parents would not. My mother never seemed to do laundry, but my clothes were always clean and neatly folded. Forgotten permission slips for field trips to the zoo appeared in my desk when the teacher came to collect them. And no matter what condition my father's study was in when I went in for a good-night kiss (and it usually looked as if something had exploded), it was always perfectly orderly the next morning. In kindergarten I'd asked my friend Amanda's mother why she bothered washing the dishes with soap and water when all you needed to do was stack them in the sink, snap your fingers, and whisper a few words. Mrs. Schmidt laughed at my strange idea of housework, but confusion had clouded her eyes.

That night my parents told me we had to be careful about how we spoke about magic and with whom we discussed it. Humans outnumbered us and found our power frightening, my mother explained, and fear was the strongest force on earth. I hadn't confessed at the time that magic—my mother's especially—frightened me, too.

By day my mother looked like every other kid's mother in Cambridge: slightly unkempt, a bit disorganized, and perpetually harassed by the pressures of home and office. Her blond hair was fashionably tousled even though the clothes she wore remained stuck in 1977—long billowy skirts, oversize pants and shirts, and men's vests and blazers she picked up in thrift stores the length and breadth of Boston in imitation of Annie Hall. Nothing would have made you look twice if you passed her in the street or stood behind her in the supermarket.

In the privacy of our home, with the curtains drawn and the door locked, my mother became someone else. Her movements were confident and sure, not rushed and hectic. Sometimes she even seemed to float. As she went around the house, singing and picking up stuffed animals and books, her face slowly transformed into something otherworldly and beautiful.

When my mother was lit up with magic, you couldn't tear your eyes away from her.

"Mommy's got a firecracker inside her," was the way my father explained it with his wide, indulgent grin. But firecrackers, I learned, were not simply bright and lively. They were unpredictable, and they could startle and frighten you, too.

My father was at a lecture one night when my mother decided to clean the silver and became mesmerized by a bowl of water she'd set on the dining-room table. As she stared at the glassy surface, it became covered with a fog that twisted itself into tiny, ghostly shapes. I gasped with delight as they grew, filling the room with fantastic beings. Soon they were crawling up the drapes and clinging to the ceiling. I cried out for my mother's help, but she remained intent on the water. Her concentration didn't waver until something half human and half animal crept near and pinched my arm. That brought her out of her reveries, and she exploded into a shower of angry red light that beat back the wraiths and left an odor of singed feathers in the house. My father noticed the strange smell the moment he returned, his alarm evident. He found us huddled in bed together. At the sight of him, my mother burst into apologetic tears. I never felt entirely safe in the dining room again.

Any remaining sense of security evaporated after I turned seven, when my mother and father went to Africa and didn't come back alive.

I shook myself and focused again on the dilemma that faced me. The manuscript sat on the library table in a pool of lamplight. Its magic pulled on something dark and knotted inside me. My fingers returned to the smooth leather. This time the prickling sensation felt familiar. I vaguely remembered experiencing something like it once before, looking through some papers on the desk in my father's study.

Turning resolutely away from the leather-bound volume, I occupied myself with something more rational: searching for the list of alchemical texts I'd generated before leaving New Haven. It was on my desk, hidden among the loose papers, book call slips, receipts, pencils, pens, and library maps, neatly arranged by collection and then by the number assigned to each text by a library clerk when it had entered into the Bodleian. Since arriving a few weeks ago, I had been working through the list methodically. The copied-out catalog description for Ashmole 782 read, "*Anthropologia, or a treatis containing a short description of Man in two parts: the first Anatomical, the second Psychological*." As with most of the works I studied, there was no telling what the contents were from the title.

My fingers might be able to tell me about the book without even cracking open the covers. Aunt Sarah always used her fingers to figure out what was in the mail before she opened it, in case the envelope contained a bill she didn't want to pay. That way she could plead ignorance when it turned out she owed the electric company money.

The gilt numbers on the spine winked.

I sat down and considered the options.

Ignore the magic, open the manuscript, and try to read it like a human scholar?

Push the bewitched volume aside and walk away?

Sarah would chortle with delight if she knew my predicament. She had always maintained that my efforts to keep magic at arm's length were futile. But I'd been doing so ever since my parents' funeral. There the witches among the guests had scrutinized me for signs that the Bishop and Proctor blood was in my veins, all the while patting me encouragingly and predicting it was only a matter of time before I took my mother's place in the local coven. Some had whispered their doubts about the wisdom of my parents' decision to marry.

"Too much power," they muttered when they thought I wasn't listening. "They were bound to attract attention—even without studying ancient ceremonial religion."

This was enough to make me blame my parents' death on the supernatural power they wielded and to search for a different way of life. Turning my back on anything to do with magic, I buried myself in the stuff of human adolescence—horses and boys and romantic novels—and tried to disappear among the town's ordinary residents. At puberty I had problems with depression and anxiety. It was all very normal, the kindly human doctor assured my aunt.

Sarah didn't tell him about the voices, about my habit of picking up the phone a good minute before it rang, or that she had to enchant the doors and windows when there was a full moon to keep me from wandering into the woods in my sleep. Nor did she mention that when I was angry the chairs in the house rearranged themselves into a precarious pyramid before crashing to the floor once my mood lifted.

When I turned thirteen, my aunt decided it was time for me to channel some of my power into learning the basics of witchcraft. Lighting candles with a few whispered words or hiding pimples with a time-tested potion—these were a teenage witch's habitual first steps. But I was unable to master even the simplest spell, burned every potion my aunt taught me, and stubbornly refused to submit to her tests to see if I'd inherited my mother's uncannily accurate second sight.

The voices, the fires, and other unexpected eruptions lessened as my hormones quieted, but my unwillingness to learn the family business remained. It made my aunt anxious to have an untrained witch in the house, and it was with some relief that Sarah sent me off to a college in Maine. Except for the magic, it was a typical coming-of-age story.

What got me away from Madison was my intellect. It had always been precocious, leading me to talk and read before other children my age. Aided by a prodigious, photographic memory—which made it easy for me to recall the layouts of textbooks and spit out the required information on tests—my schoolwork was soon established as a place where my family's magical legacy was irrelevant. I'd skipped my final years of high school and started college at sixteen.

There I'd first tried to carve out a place for myself in the theater department, my imagination drawn to the spectacle and the costumes—and my mind fascinated by how completely a playwright's words could conjure up other places and times. My first few performances were heralded by my professors as extraordinary examples of the way good acting could transform an ordinary college student into someone else. The first indication that these metamorphoses might not have been the result of theatrical talent came while I was playing Ophelia in *Hamlet.* As soon as I was cast in the role, my hair started growing at an unnatural rate, tumbling down from shoulders to waist. I sat for hours beside the college's lake, irresistibly drawn to its shining surface, with my new hair streaming all around me. The boy playing Hamlet became caught up in the illusion, and we had a passionate though dangerously volatile affair. Slowly I was dissolving into Ophelia's madness, taking the rest of the cast with me.

The result might have been a riveting performance, but each new role brought fresh challenges. In my sophomore year, the situation became impossible when I was cast as Annabella in John Ford's *'Tis Pity She's a Whore.* Like the character, I attracted a string of devoted suitors—not all of them human—who followed me around campus. When they refused to leave me alone after the final curtain fell, it was clear that whatever had been unleashed couldn't be controlled. I wasn't sure how magic had crept into my acting, and I didn't want to find out. I cut my hair short. I stopped wearing flowing skirts and layered tops in favor of the black turtlenecks, khaki trousers, and loafers that the solid, ambitious prelaw students were wearing. My excess energy went into athletics.

After leaving the theater department, I attempted several more majors, looking for a field so rational that it would never yield a square inch to magic. I lacked the precision and patience for mathematics, and my efforts at biology were a disaster of failed quizzes and unfinished laboratory experiments.

At the end of my sophomore year, the registrar demanded I choose a major or face a fifth year in college. A summer study program in England offered me the opportunity to get even farther from all things Bishop. I fell in love with Oxford, the quiet glow of its morning streets. My history courses covered the exploits of kings and queens, and the only voices in my head were those that whispered from books penned in the sixteenth and seventeenth centuries. This was entirely attributable to great literature. Best of all, no one in this university town knew me, and if there were witches in the city that summer, they stayed well away. I returned home, declared a major in history, took all the required courses in record time, and graduated with honors before I turned twenty.

When I decided to pursue my doctorate, Oxford was my first choice among the possible programs. My specialty was the history of science, and my research focused on the period when science supplanted magic—the age when astrology and witch-hunts yielded to Newton and universal laws. The search for a rational order in nature, rather than a supernatural one, mirrored my own efforts to stay away from what was hidden. The lines I'd already drawn between what went on in my mind and what I carried in my blood grew more distinct.

My Aunt Sarah had snorted when she heard of my decision to specialize in seventeenth-century chemistry. Her bright red hair was an outward sign of her quick temper and sharp tongue. She was a plain-speaking, no-nonsense witch who commanded a room as soon as she entered it. A pillar of the Madison community, Sarah was often called in to manage things when there was a crisis, large or small, in town. We were on much better terms now that I wasn't subjected to a daily dose of her keen observations on human frailty and inconsistency.

Though we were separated by hundreds of miles, Sarah thought my latest attempts to avoid magic were laughable—and told me so. "We used to call that alchemy," she said. "There's a lot of magic in it."

"No, there's not," I protested hotly. The whole point of my work was to show how scientific this pursuit really was. "Alchemy tells us about the growth of experimentation, not the search for a magical elixir that turns lead into gold and makes people immortal."

"If you say so," Sarah said doubtfully. "But it's a pretty strange subject to choose if you're trying to pass as human."

After earning my degree, I fought fiercely for a spot on the faculty at Yale, the only place that was more English than England. Colleagues warned that I had little chance of being granted tenure. I churned out two books, won a handful of prizes, and collected some research grants. Then I received tenure and proved everyone wrong.

More important, my life was now my own. No one in my department, not even the historians of early America, connected my last name with that of the first Salem woman executed for witchcraft in 1692. To preserve my hard-won autonomy, I continued to keep any hint of magic or witchcraft out of my life. Of course there were exceptions, like the time I'd drawn on one of Sarah's spells when the washing machine wouldn't stop filling with water and threatened to flood my small apartment on Wooster Square. Nobody's perfect.

Now, taking note of this current lapse, I held my breath, grasped the manuscript with both hands, and placed it in one of the wedge-shaped cradles the library provided to protect its rare books. I had made my decision: to behave as a serious scholar and treat Ashmole 782 like an ordinary manuscript. I'd ignore my burning fingertips, the book's strange smell, and simply describe its contents. Then I'd decide—with professional detachment—whether it was promising enough for a longer look. My fingers trembled when I loosened the small brass clasps nevertheless.

The manuscript let out a soft sigh.

A quick glance over my shoulder assured me that the room was still empty. The only other sound was the loud ticking of the reading room's clock.

Deciding not to record "Book sighed," I turned to my laptop and opened up a new file. This familiar task—one that I'd done hundreds if not thousands of times before—was as comforting as my list's neat checkmarks. I typed the manuscript name and number and copied the title from the catalog description. I eyed its size and binding, describing both in detail.

The only thing left to do was open the manuscript.

It was difficult to lift the cover, despite the loosened clasps, as if it were stuck to the pages below. I swore under my breath and rested my hand flat on the leather for a moment, hoping that Ashmole 782 simply needed a chance to know me. It wasn't magic, exactly, to put your hand on top of a book. My palm tingled, much as my skin tingled when a witch looked at me, and the tension left the manuscript. After that, it was easy to lift the cover.

The first page was rough paper. On the second sheet, which was parchment, were the words "*Anthropologia, or a treatis containing a short description of Man*," in Ashmole's handwriting. The neat, round curves were almost as familiar to me as my own cursive script. The second part of the title—"*in two parts: the first Anatomical, the second Psychological*"—was written in a later hand, in pencil. It was familiar, too, but I couldn't place it. Touching the writing might give me some clue, but it was against the library's rules and it would be impossible to document the information that my fingers might gather. Instead I made notes in the computer file regarding the use of ink and pencil, the two different hands, and the possible dates of the inscriptions.

As I turned the first page, the parchment felt abnormally heavy and revealed itself as the source of the manuscript's strange smell. It wasn't simply ancient. It was something more—a combination of must and musk that had no name. And I noticed immediately that three leaves had been cut neatly out of the binding.

Here, at last, was something easy to describe. My fingers flew over the keys: "*At least three folios removed, by straightedge or razor.*" I peered into the valley of the manuscript's spine but couldn't tell whether any other pages were missing. The closer the parchment to my nose, the more the manuscript's power and odd smell distracted me.

I turned my attention to the illustration that faced the gap where the missing pages should be. It showed a tiny baby girl floating in a clear glass vessel. The baby held a silver rose in one hand, a golden rose in the other. On its feet were tiny wings, and drops of red liquid showered down on the baby's long black hair. Underneath the image was a label written in thick black ink indicating that it was a depiction of the philosophical child—an allegorical representation of a crucial step in creating the philosopher's stone, the chemical substance that promised to make its owner healthy, wealthy, and wise.

The colors were luminous and strikingly well preserved. Artists had once mixed crushed stone and gems into their paints to produce such powerful colors. And the image itself had been drawn by someone with real artistic skill. I had to sit on my hands to keep them from trying to learn more from a touch here and there.

But the illuminator, for all his obvious talent, had the details all wrong. The glass vessel was supposed to point up, not down. The baby was supposed to be half black and half white, to show that it was a hermaphrodite. It should have had male genitalia and female breasts—or two heads, at the very least.

Alchemical imagery was allegorical, and notoriously tricky. That's why I was studying it, searching for patterns that would reveal a systematic, logical approach to chemical transformation in the days before the periodic table of the elements. Images of the moon were almost always representations of silver, for example, while images of the sun referred to gold. When the two were combined chemically, the process was represented as a wedding. In time the pictures had been replaced by words. Those words, in turn, became the grammar of chemistry.

But this manuscript put my belief in the alchemists' logic to the test. Each illustration had at least one fundamental flaw, and there was no accompanying text to help make sense of it.

I searched for something—anything—that would agree with my knowledge of alchemy. In the softening light, faint traces of handwriting appeared on one of the pages. I slanted the desk lamp so that it shone more brightly.

There was nothing there.

Slowly I turned the page as if it were a fragile leaf.

Words shimmered and moved across its surface—hundreds of words—invisible unless the angle of light and the viewer's perspective were just right.

I stifled a cry of surprise.

Ashmole 782 was a palimpsest—a manuscript within a manuscript. When parchment was scarce, scribes carefully washed the ink from old books and then wrote new text on the blank sheets. Over time the former writing often reappeared underneath as a textual ghost, discernible with the help of ultraviolet light, which could see under ink stains and bring faded text back to life.

There was no ultraviolet light strong enough to reveal these traces, though. This was not an ordinary palimpsest. The writing hadn't been washed away—it had been hidden with some sort of spell. But why would anyone go to the trouble of bewitching the text in an alchemical book? Even experts had trouble puzzling out the obscure language and fanciful imagery the authors used.

Dragging my attention from the faint letters that were moving too quickly for me to read, I focused instead on writing a synopsis of the manuscript's contents. *"Puzzling,"* I typed. *"Textual captions from the fifteenth to seventeenth centuries, images mainly fifteenth century. Image sources possibly older? Mixture of paper and vellum. Colored and black inks, the former of unusually high quality. Illustrations are well executed, but details are incorrect, missing. Depicts the creation of the philosopher's stone, alchemical birth/creation, death, resurrection, and transformation. A confused copy of an earlier manuscript? A strange book, full of anomalies."*

My fingers hesitated above the keys.

Scholars do one of two things when they discover information that doesn't fit what they already know. Either they sweep it aside so it doesn't bring their cherished theories into question or they focus on it with laserlike intensity and try to get to the bottom of the mystery. If this book hadn't been under a spell, I might have been tempted to do the latter. Because it was bewitched, I was strongly inclined toward the former.

And when in doubt, scholars usually postpone a decision.

I typed an ambivalent final line: *"Needs more time? Possibly recall later?"*

Holding my breath, I fastened the cover with a gentle tug. Currents of magic still thrummed through the manuscript, especially fierce around the clasps.

Relieved that it was closed, I stared at Ashmole 782 for a few more moments. My fingers wanted to stray back and touch the brown leather. But this time I resisted, just as I had resisted touching the inscriptions and illustrations to learn more than a human historian could legitimately claim to know.

Aunt Sarah had always told me that magic was a gift. If it was, it had strings attached that bound me to all the Bishop witches who had come before me. There was a price to be paid for using this inherited magical power and for working the spells and charms that made up the witches' carefully guarded craft. By opening Ashmole 782, I'd breached the wall that divided my magic from my scholarship. But back on the right side of it again, I was more determined than ever to remain there.

I packed up my computer and notes and picked up the stack of manuscripts, carefully putting Ashmole 782 on the bottom. Mercifully, Gillian wasn't at her desk, though her papers were still strewn around. She must be planning on working late and was off for a cup of coffee.

"Finished?" Sean asked when I reached the call desk.

"Not quite. I'd like to reserve the top three for Monday."

"And the fourth?"

"I'm done with it," I blurted, pushing the manuscripts toward him. "You can send it back to the stacks."

Sean put it on top of a pile of returns he had already gathered. He walked with me as far as the staircase, said good-bye, and disappeared behind a swinging door. The conveyor belt that would whisk Ashmole 782 back into the bowels of the library clanged into action.

I almost turned and stopped him but let it go.

My hand was raised to push open the door on the ground floor when the air around me constricted, as if the library were squeezing me tight. The air shimmered for a split second, just as the pages of the manuscript had shimmered on Sean's desk, causing me to shiver involuntarily and raising the tiny hairs on my arms.

Something had just happened. Something magical.

My face turned back toward Duke Humfrey's, and my feet threatened to follow.

It's nothing, I thought, resolutely walking out of the library.

Are you sure? whispered a long-ignored voice.

Chapter 2

Oxford's bells chimed seven times. Night didn't follow twilight as slowly as it would have a few months ago, but the transformation was still lingering. The library staff had turned on the lamps only thirty minutes before, casting small pools of gold in the gray light.

It was the twenty-first day of September. All over the world, witches were sharing a meal on the eve of the autumn equinox to celebrate Mabon and greet the impending darkness of winter. But the witches of Oxford would have to do without me. I was slated to give the keynote address at an important conference next month. My ideas were still unformed, and I was getting anxious.

At the thought of what my fellow witches might be eating somewhere in Oxford, my stomach rumbled. I'd been in the library since half past nine that morning, with only a short break for lunch.

Sean had taken the day off, and the person working at the call desk was new. She'd given me some trouble when I requested one crumbling item and tried to persuade me to use microfilm instead. The reading room's supervisor, Mr. Johnson, overheard and came out of his office to intervene.

"My apologies, Dr. Bishop," he'd said hurriedly, pushing his heavy, dark-rimmed glasses over the bridge of his nose. "If you need to consult this manuscript for your research, we will be happy to oblige." He disappeared to fetch the restricted item and delivered it with more apologies about the inconvenience and the new staff. Gratified that my scholarly credentials had done the trick, I spent the afternoon happily reading.

I pulled two coiled weights from the upper corners of the manuscript and closed it carefully, pleased at the amount of work I'd completed. After encountering the bewitched manuscript on Friday, I'd devoted the weekend to routine tasks rather than alchemy in order to restore a sense of normalcy. I filled out financial-reimbursement forms, paid bills, wrote letters of recommendation, and even finished a book review. These chores were interspersed with more homey rituals like doing laundry, drinking copious amounts of tea, and trying recipes from the BBC's cooking programs.

After an early start this morning, I'd spent the day trying to focus on the work at hand, rather than dwelling on my recollections of Ashmole 782's strange illustrations and mysterious palimpsest. I eyed the short list of to-dos jotted down over the course of the day. Of the four questions on my follow-up list, the third was easiest to resolve. The answer was in an arcane periodical, *Notes and Queries,* which was shelved on one of the bookcases that stretched up toward the room's high ceilings. I pushed back my chair and decided to tick one item off my list before leaving.

The upper shelves of the section of Duke Humfrey's known as the Selden End were reachable by means of a worn set of stairs to a gallery that looked over the reading desks. I climbed the twisting treads to where the old buckram-covered books sat in neat chronological rows on wooden shelves. No one but me and an ancient literature don from Magdalen College seemed to use them. I located the volume and swore softly under my breath. It was on the top shelf, just out of reach.

A low chuckle startled me. I turned my head to see who was sitting at the desk at the far end of the gallery, but no one was there. I was hearing things again. Oxford was still a ghost town, and anyone who belonged to the university had left over an hour earlier to down a glass of free sherry in their college's senior common room before dinner. Given the Wiccan holiday, even Gillian had left in the late afternoon, after extending one final invitation and glancing at my pile of reading material with narrowed eyes.

I searched for the gallery's stepstool, which was missing. The Bodleian was notoriously short on such items, and it would easily take fifteen minutes to locate one in the library and haul it upstairs so that I could retrieve the volume. I hesitated. Even though I'd held a bewitched book, I'd resisted considerable temptations to work further magic on Friday. Besides, no one would see.

Despite my rationalizations, my skin prickled with anxiety. I didn't break my rules very often, and I kept mental accounts of the situations that had spurred me to turn to my magic for assistance. This was the fifth time this year, including putting the spell on the malfunctioning washing machine and touching Ashmole 782. Not too bad for the end of September, but not a personal best either.

I took a deep breath, held up my hand, and imagined the book in it.

Volume 19 of *Notes and Queries* slid backward four inches, tipped at an angle as if an invisible hand were pulling it down, and fell into my open palm with a soft thwack. Once there, it flopped open to the page I needed.

It had taken all of three seconds. I let out another breath to exhale some of my guilt. Suddenly two icy patches bloomed between my shoulder blades.

I had been seen, and not by an ordinary human observer.

When one witch studies another, the touch of their eyes tingles. Witches aren't the only creatures sharing the world with humans, however. There are also daemons—creative, artistic creatures who walk a tightrope between madness and genius. "Rock stars and serial killers" was how my aunt described these strange, perplexing beings. And there are vampires, ancient and beautiful, who feed on blood and will charm you utterly if they don't kill you first.

When a daemon takes a look, I feel the slight, unnerving pressure of a kiss.

But when a vampire stares, it feels cold, focused, and dangerous.

I mentally shuffled through the readers in Duke Humfrey's. There had been one vampire, a cherubic monk who pored over medieval missals and prayer books like a lover. But vampires aren't often found in rare-book rooms. Occasionally one succumbed to vanity and nostalgia and came in to reminisce, but it wasn't common.

Witches and daemons were far more typical in libraries. Gillian Chamberlain had been in today, studying her papyri with a magnifying glass. And there were definitely two daemons in the music reference room. They'd looked up, dazed, as I walked by on the way to Blackwell's for tea. One told me to bring him back a latte, which was some indication of how immersed he was in whatever madness gripped him at the moment.

No, it was a vampire who watched me now.

I'd happened upon a few vampires, since I worked in a field that put me in touch with scientists, and there were vampires aplenty in laboratories around the world. Science rewards long study and patience. And thanks to their solitary work habits, scientists were unlikely to be recognized by anyone except their closest co-workers. It made a life that spanned centuries rather than decades much easier to negotiate.

These days vampires gravitated toward particle accelerators, projects to decode the genome, and molecular biology. Once they had flocked to alchemy, anatomy, and electricity. If it went bang, involved blood, or promised to unlock the secrets of the universe, there was sure to be a vampire around.

I clutched my ill-gotten copy of *Notes and Queries* and turned to face the witness. He was in the shadows on the opposite side of the room in front of the paleography reference books, lounging against one of the graceful wooden pillars that held up the gallery. An open copy of Jane Roberts's *Guide to Scripts Used in English Handwriting Up to 1500* was balanced in his hands.

I had never seen this vampire before—but I was fairly certain he didn't need pointers on how to decipher old penmanship.

Anyone who has read paperback bestsellers or even watched television knows that vampires are breathtaking, but nothing prepares you to actually see one. Their bone structures are so well honed that they seem chiseled by an expert sculptor. Then they move, or speak, and your mind can't begin to absorb what you're seeing. Every movement is graceful; every word is musical. And their eyes are arresting, which is precisely how they catch their prey. One long look, a few quiet words, a touch: once you're caught in a vampire's snare you don't stand a chance.

Staring down at this vampire, I realized with a sinking feeling that my knowledge on the subject was, alas, largely theoretical. Little of it seemed useful now that I was facing one in the Bodleian Library.

The only vampire with whom I had more than a passing acquaintance worked at the nuclear particle accelerator in Switzerland. Jeremy was slight and gorgeous, with bright blond hair, blue eyes, and an infectious laugh. He'd slept with most of the women in the canton of Geneva and was now working his way through the city of Lausanne. What he did after he seduced them I had never wanted to inquire into too closely, and I'd turned down his persistent invitations to go out for a drink. I'd always figured that Jeremy was representative of the breed. But in comparison to the one who stood before me now, he seemed raw-boned, gawky, and very, very young.

This one was tall—well over six feet even accounting for the problems of perspective associated with looking down on him from the gallery. And he definitely was not slight. Broad shoulders narrowed into slender hips, which flowed into lean, muscular legs. His hands were strikingly long and agile, a mark of physiological delicacy that made your eyes drift back to them to figure out how they could belong to such a large man.

As my eyes swept over him, his own were fixed on me. From across the room, they seemed black as night, staring up under thick, equally black eyebrows, one of them lifted in a curve that suggested a question mark. His face was indeed striking—all distinct planes and surfaces, with high-angled cheekbones meeting brows that shielded and shadowed his eyes. Above his chin was one of the few places where there was room for softness—his wide mouth, which, like his long hands, didn't seem to make sense.

But the most unnerving thing about him was not his physical perfection. It was his feral combination of strength, agility, and keen intelligence that was palpable across the room. In his black trousers and soft gray sweater, with a shock of black hair swept back from his forehead and cropped close to the nape of his neck, he looked like a panther that could strike at any moment but was in no rush to do so.

He smiled. It was a small, polite smile that didn't reveal his teeth. I was intensely aware of them anyway, sitting in perfectly straight, sharp rows behind his pale lips.

The mere thought of *teeth* sent an instinctive rush of adrenaline through my body, setting my fingers tingling. Suddenly all I could think was, *Get out of this room NOW.*

The staircase seemed farther away than the four steps it took to reach it. I raced down to the floor below, stumbled on the last step, and pitched straight into the vampire's waiting arms.

Of course he had beaten me to the bottom of the stairs.

His fingers were cool, and his arms felt steelier than flesh and bone. The scent of clove, cinnamon, and something that reminded me of incense filled the air. He set me on my feet, picked *Notes and Queries* off the floor, and handed it to me with a small bow. "Dr. Bishop, I presume?"

Shaking from head to toe, I nodded.

The long, pale fingers of his right hand dipped into a pocket and pulled out a blue-and-white business card. He extended it. "Matthew Clairmont."

I gripped the edge of the card, careful not to touch his fingers in the process. Oxford University's familiar logo, with the three crowns and open book, was perched next to Clairmont's name, followed by a string of initials indicating he had already been made a member of the Royal Society.

Not bad for someone who appeared to be in his mid- to late thirties, though I imagined that his actual age was at least ten times that.

As for his research specialty, it came as no surprise that the vampire was a professor of biochemistry and affiliated with Oxford Neuroscience at the John Radcliffe Hospital. Blood and anatomy—two vampire favorites. The card bore three different laboratory numbers in addition to an office number and an e-mail address. I might not have seen him before, but he was certainly not unreachable.

"Professor Clairmont." I squeaked it out before the words caught in the back of my throat, and I quieted the urge to run screaming toward the exit.

"We've not met," he continued in an oddly accented voice. It was mostly Oxbridge but had a touch of softness that I couldn't place. His eyes, which never left my face, were not actually dark at all, I discovered, but dominated by dilated pupils bordered with a gray-green sliver of iris. Their pull was insistent, and I found myself unable to look away.

The vampire's mouth was moving again. "I'm a great admirer of your work."

My eyes widened. It was not impossible that a professor of biochemistry would be interested in seventeenth-century alchemy, but it seemed highly unlikely. I picked at the collar of my white shirt and scanned the room. We were the only two in it. There was no one at the old oak card file or at the nearby banks of computers. Whoever was at the collection desk was too far away to come to my aid.

"I found your article on the color symbolism of alchemical transformation fascinating, and your work on Robert Boyle's approach to the problems of expansion and contraction was quite persuasive," Clairmont continued smoothly, as if he were used to being the only active participant in a conversation. "I've not yet finished your latest book on alchemical apprenticeship and education, but I'm enjoying it a great deal."

"Thank you," I whispered. His gaze shifted from my eyes to my throat. I stopped picking at the buttons around my neck.

His unnatural eyes floated back to mine. "You have a marvelous way of evoking the past for your readers." I took that as a compliment, since a vampire would know if it was wrong. Clairmont paused for a moment. "Might I buy you dinner?"

My mouth dropped open. Dinner? I might not be able to escape from him in the library, but there was no reason to linger over a meal—especially one he would not be sharing, given his dietary preferences.

"I have plans," I said abruptly, unable to formulate a reasonable explanation of what those plans might involve. Matthew Clairmont must know I was a witch, and I was clearly not celebrating Mabon.

"That's too bad," he murmured, a touch of a smile on his lips. "Another time, perhaps. You are in Oxford for the year, aren't you?"

Being around a vampire was always unnerving, and Clairmont's clove scent brought back the strange smell of Ashmole 782. Unable to think straight, I resorted to nodding. It was safer.

"I thought so," said Clairmont. "I'm sure our paths will cross again. Oxford is such a small town."

"Very small," I agreed, wishing I had taken leave in London instead.

"Until then, Dr. Bishop. It has been a pleasure." Clairmont extended his hand. With the exception of their brief excursion to my collar, his eyes had not drifted once from mine. I didn't think he had blinked either. I steeled myself not to be the first to look away.

My hand went forward, hesitating for a moment before clasping his. There was a fleeting pressure before he withdrew. He stepped backward, smiled, then disappeared into the darkness of the oldest part of the library.

I stood still until my chilled hands could move freely again, then walked back to my desk and switched off my computer. *Notes and Queries* asked me accusingly why I had bothered to go and get it if I wasn't even going to look at it; my to-do list was equally full of reproach. I ripped it off the top of the pad, crumpled it up, and tossed it into the wicker basket under the desk.

"'Sufficient unto the day is the evil thereof,'" I muttered under my breath.

The reading room's night proctor glanced down at his watch when I returned my manuscripts. "Leaving early, Dr. Bishop?"

I nodded, my lips closed tightly to keep myself from asking whether he knew there had been a vampire in the paleography reference section.

He picked up the stack of gray cardboard boxes that held the manuscripts. "Will you need these tomorrow?"

"Yes," I whispered. "Tomorrow."

Having observed the last scholarly propriety of exiting the library, I was free. My feet clattered against the linoleum floors and echoed against the stone walls as I sped through the reading room's lattice gate, past the books guarded with velvet ropes to keep them from curious fingers, down the worn wooden stairs, and into the enclosed quadrangle on the ground floor. I leaned against the iron railings surrounding the bronze statue of William Herbert and sucked the chilly air into my lungs, struggling to get the vestiges of clove and cinnamon out of my nostrils.

There were always things that went bump in the night in Oxford, I told myself sternly. So there was one more vampire in town.

No matter what I told myself in the quadrangle, my walk home was faster than usual. The gloom of New College Lane was a spooky proposition at the best of times. I ran my card through the reader at New College's back gate and felt some of the tension leave my body when the gate clicked shut behind me, as if every door and wall I put between me and the library somehow kept me safe. I skirted under the chapel windows and through the narrow passage into the quad that had views of Oxford's only surviving medieval garden, complete with the traditional mound that had once offered a green prospect for students to look upon and contemplate the mysteries of God and nature. Tonight the college's spires and archways seemed especially Gothic, and I was eager to get inside.

When the door of my apartment closed behind me, I let out a sigh of relief. I was living at the top of one of the college's faculty staircases, in lodgings reserved for visiting former members. My rooms, which included a bedroom, a sitting room with a round table for dining, and a decent if small kitchen, were decorated with old prints and warm wainscoting. All the furniture looked as if it had been culled from previous incarnations of the senior common room and the master's house, with down-at-the-heels late-nineteenth-century design predominant.

In the kitchen I put two slices of bread in the toaster and poured myself a cold glass of water. Gulping it down, I opened the window to let cool air into the stuffy rooms.

Carrying my snack back into the sitting room, I kicked off my shoes and turned on the small stereo. The pure tones of Mozart filled the air. When I sat on one of the maroon upholstered sofas, it was with the intention to rest for a few moments, then take a bath and go over my notes from the day.

At half past three in the morning, I woke with a pounding heart, a stiff neck, and the strong taste of cloves in my mouth.

I got a fresh glass of water and closed the kitchen window. It was chilly, and I shivered at the touch of the damp air.

After a glance at my watch and some quick calculations, I decided to call home. It was only ten-thirty there, and Sarah and Em were as nocturnal as bats. Slipping around the rooms, I turned off all the lights except the one in my bedroom and picked up my mobile. I was out of my grimy clothes in a matter of minutes—how do you get so filthy in a library?—and into a pair of old yoga pants and a black sweater with a stretched-out neck. They were more comfortable than any pajamas.

The bed felt welcoming and firm underneath me, comforting me enough that I almost convinced myself a phone call home was unnecessary. But the water had not been able to remove the vestiges of cloves from my tongue, and I dialed the number.

"We've been waiting for your call" were the first words I heard.

Witches.

I sighed. "Sarah, I'm fine."

"All signs to the contrary." As usual, my mother's younger sister was not going to pull any punches. "Tabitha has been skittish all evening, Em got a very clear picture of you lost in the woods at night, and I haven't been able to eat anything since breakfast."

The real problem was that damn cat. Tabitha was Sarah's baby and picked up any tension within the family with uncanny precision. "I'm *fine.* I had an unexpected encounter in the library tonight, that's all."

A click told me that Em had picked up the extension. "Why aren't you celebrating Mabon?" she asked.

Emily Mather had been a fixture in my life for as long as I could remember. She and Rebecca Bishop had met as high-school students working in the summer at Plimoth Plantation, where they dug holes and pushed wheelbarrows for the archaeologists. They became best friends, then devoted pen pals when Emily went to Vassar and my mother to Harvard. Later the two reconnected in Cambridge when Em became a children's librarian. After my parents' death, Em's long weekends in Madison soon led to a new job in the local elementary school. She and Sarah became inseparable partners, even though Em had maintained her own apartment in town and the two of them had made a big deal of never being seen heading into a bedroom together while I was growing up. This didn't fool me, the neighbors, or anyone else living in town. Everybody treated them like the couple they were, regardless of where they slept. When I moved out of the Bishop house, Em moved in and had been there ever since. Like my mother and my aunt, Em came from a long line of witches.

"I was invited to the coven's party but worked instead."

"Did the witch from Bryn Mawr ask you to go?" Em was interested in the classicist, mostly (it had turned out over a fair amount of wine one summer night) because she'd once dated Gillian's mother. "It was the sixties" was all Em would say.

"Yes." I sounded harassed. The two of them were convinced I was going to see the light and begin taking my magic seriously now that I was safely tenured. Nothing cast any doubt on this wishful prognostication, and they were always thrilled when I had any contact with a witch. "But I spent the evening with Elias Ashmole instead."

"Who's he?" Em asked Sarah.

"You know, that dead guy who collected alchemy books" was Sarah's muffled reply.

"Still here, you two," I called into the phone.

"So who rattled your cage?" Sarah asked.

Given that both were witches, there was no point in trying to hide anything. "I met a vampire in the library. One I've never seen before, named Matthew Clairmont."

There was silence on Em's end as she flipped through her mental card file of notable creatures. Sarah was quiet for a moment, too, deciding whether or not to explode.

"I hope he's easier to get rid of than the daemons you have a habit of attracting," she said sharply.

"Daemons haven't bothered me since I stopped acting."

"No, there was that daemon who followed you into the Beinecke Library when you first started working at Yale, too," Em corrected me. "He was just wandering down the street and came looking for you."

"He was mentally unstable," I protested. Like using witchcraft on the washing machine, the fact that I'd somehow caught the attention of a single, curious daemon shouldn't count against me.

"You draw creatures like flowers draw bees, Diana. But daemons aren't half as dangerous as vampires. Stay away from him," Sarah said tightly.

"I have no reason to seek him out." My hands traveled to my neck again. "We have nothing in common."

"That's not the point," Sarah said, voice rising. "Witches, vampires, and daemons aren't supposed to mix. You know that. Humans are more likely to notice us when we do. No daemon or vampire is worth the risk." The only creatures in the world that Sarah took seriously were other witches. Humans struck her as unfortunate little beings blind to the world around them. Daemons were perpetual teenagers who couldn't be trusted. Vampires were well below cats and at least one step below mutts within her hierarchy of creatures.

"You've told me the rules before, Sarah."

"Not everyone obeys the rules, honey," Em observed. "What did he want?"

"He said he was interested in my work. But he's a scientist, so that's hard to believe." My fingers fiddled with the duvet cover on the bed. "He invited me to dinner."

"To *dinner*?" Sarah was incredulous.

Em just laughed. "There's not much on a restaurant menu that would appeal to a vampire."

"I'm sure I won't see him again. He's running three labs from the look of his business card, and he holds two faculty positions."

"Typical," Sarah muttered. "That's what happens when you have too much time on your hands. And stop picking at that quilt—you'll put a hole in it." She'd switched on her witch's radar full blast and was now seeing as well as hearing me.

"It's not as if he's stealing money from old ladies and squandering other people's fortunes on the stock market," I countered. The fact that vampires were reputed to be fabulously wealthy was a sore spot with Sarah. "He's a biochemist and a physician of some sort, interested in the brain."

"I'm sure that's fascinating, Diana, but what did he *want*?" Sarah matched my irritation with impatience—the one-two punch mastered by all Bishop women.

"Not dinner," Em said with certainty.

Sarah snorted. "He wanted something. Vampires and witches don't go on dates. Unless he was planning to dine on you, of course. They love nothing more than the taste of a witch's blood."

"Maybe he was just curious. Or maybe he does like your work." Em said it with such doubt that I had to laugh.

"We wouldn't be having this conversation at all if you'd just take some elementary precautions," Sarah said tartly. "A protection spell, some use of your abilities as a seer, and—"

"I'm not using magic or witchcraft to figure out why a vampire asked me to dinner," I said firmly. "Not negotiable, Sarah."

"Then don't call us looking for answers when you don't want to hear them," Sarah said, her notoriously short temper flaring. She hung up before I could think of a response.

"Sarah does worry about you, you know," Em said apologetically. "And she doesn't understand why you won't use your gifts, not even to protect yourself."

Because the gifts had strings attached, as I'd explained before. I tried again.

"It's a slippery slope, Em. I protect myself from a vampire in the library today, and tomorrow I protect myself from a hard question at a lecture. Soon I'll be picking research topics based on knowing how they'll turn out and applying for grants that I'm sure to win. It's important to me that I've made my reputation on my own. If I start using magic, nothing would belong entirely to me. I don't want to be the next Bishop witch." I opened my mouth to tell Em about Ashmole 782, but something made me close it again.

"I know, I know, honey." Em's voice was soothing. "I do understand. But Sarah can't help worrying about your safety. You're all the family she has now."

My fingers slid through my hair and came to rest at my temples. Conversations like this always led back to my mother and father. I hesitated, reluctant to mention my one lingering concern.

"What is it?" Em asked, her sixth sense picking up on my discomfort.

"He knew my name. I've never seen him before, but he knew who I was."

Em considered the possibilities. "Your picture's on the inside of your latest book cover, isn't it?"

My breath, which I hadn't been aware I was holding, came out with a soft whoosh. "Yes. That must be it. I'm just being silly. Can you give Sarah a kiss from me?"

"You bet. And, Diana? Be careful. English vampires may not be as well behaved around witches as the American ones are."

I smiled, thinking of Matthew Clairmont's formal bow. "I will. But don't worry. I probably won't see him again."

Em was quiet.

"Em?" I prompted.

"Time will tell."

Em wasn't as good at seeing the future as my mother was reputed to have been, but something was niggling at her. Convincing a witch to share a vague premonition was almost impossible. She wasn't going to tell me what worried her about Matthew Clairmont. Not yet.

Chapter 3

The vampire sat in the shadows on the curved expanse of the bridge that spanned New College Lane and connected two parts of Hertford College, his back resting against the worn stone of one of the college's newer buildings and his feet propped up on the bridge's roof.

The witch appeared, moving surprisingly surely across the uneven stones of the sidewalk outside the Bodleian. She passed underneath him, her pace quickening. Her nervousness made her look younger than she was and accentuated her vulnerability.

So that's the formidable historian, he thought wryly, mentally going over her vita. Even after looking at her picture, Matthew expected Bishop to be older, given her professional accomplishments.

Diana Bishop's back was straight and her shoulders square, in spite of her apparent agitation. Perhaps she would not be as easy to intimidate as he had hoped. Her behavior in the library had suggested as much. She'd met his eyes without a trace of the fear that Matthew had grown to rely upon from those who weren't vampires—and many of those who were.

When Bishop rounded the corner, Matthew crept along the rooflines until he reached the New College wall. He slipped silently down into its boundaries. The vampire knew the college's layout and had anticipated where her rooms would be. He was already tucked into a doorway opposite her staircase when she began her climb.

Matthew's eyes followed her around the apartment as she moved from room to room, turning on the lights. She pushed the kitchen window open, left it ajar, disappeared.

That will save me from me breaking the window or picking her lock, he thought.

Matthew darted across the open space and scaled her building, his feet and hands finding sure holds in the old mortar with the help of a copper downspout and some robust vines. From his new vantage point, he could detect the witch's distinctive scent and a rustle of turning pages. He craned his neck to peer into the window.

Bishop was reading. In repose her face looked different, he reflected. It was as if her skin fit the underlying bones properly. Her head bobbed slowly, and she slid against the cushions with a soft sigh of exhaustion. Soon the sound of regular breathing told Matthew she was asleep.

He swung out from the wall and kicked his feet up and through the witch's kitchen window. It had been a very long time since the vampire had climbed into a woman's rooms. Even then the occasions were rare and usually linked to moments when he was in the grip of infatuation. This time there was a far different reason. Nonetheless, if someone caught him, he'd have a hell of a time explaining what it was.

Matthew had to know if Ashmole 782 was still in Bishop's possession. He hadn't been able to search her desk at the library, but a quick glance had suggested that it wasn't among the manuscripts she'd been consulting today. Still, there was no chance that a witch—a Bishop—would have let the volume slip through her fingers. With inaudible steps he traveled through the small set of rooms. The manuscript wasn't in the witch's bathroom or her bedroom. He crept quietly past the couch where she lay sleeping.

The witch's eyelids were twitching as if she were watching a movie only she could see. One of her hands was drawn into a fist, and every now and then her legs danced. Bishop's face was serene, however, unperturbed by whatever the rest of her body thought it was doing.

Something wasn't right. He'd sensed it from the first moment he saw Bishop in the library. Matthew crossed his arms and studied her, but he still couldn't figure out what it was. This witch didn't give off the usual scents—henbane, sulfur, and sage. *She's hiding something,* the vampire thought, *something more than the lost manuscript.*

Matthew turned away, seeking out the table she was using as a desk. It was easy to spot, littered with books and papers. That was the likeliest place for her to have put the smuggled volume. As he took a step toward it, he smelled electricity and froze.

Light was seeping from Diana Bishop's body—all around the edges, escaping from her pores. The light was a blue so pale it was almost white, and at first it formed a cloudlike shroud that clung to her for a few seconds. For a moment she seemed to shimmer. Matthew shook his head in disbelief. It was impossible. It had been centuries since he'd seen such a luminous outpouring from a witch.

But other, more urgent matters beckoned, and Matthew resumed the hunt for the manuscript, hurriedly searching through the items on her desk. He ran his fingers through his hair in frustration. The witch's scent was everywhere, distracting him. Matthew's eyes returned to the couch. Bishop was stirring and shifting again, her knees creeping toward her chest. Once more, luminosity pulsed to the surface, shimmered for a moment, retreated.

Matthew frowned, puzzled at the discrepancy between what he'd overheard last night and what he was witnessing with his own eyes. Two witches had been gossiping about Ashmole 782 and the witch who'd called it. One had suggested that the American historian didn't use her magical power. But Matthew had seen it in the Bodleian—and now watched it wash through her with evident intensity. He suspected she used magic in her scholarship, too. Many of the men she wrote about had been friends of his—Cornelius Drebbel, Andreas Libavius, Isaac Newton. She'd captured their quirks and obsessions perfectly. Without magic how could a modern woman understand men who had lived so long ago? Fleetingly, Matthew wondered if Bishop would be able to understand him with the same uncanny accuracy.

The clocks struck three, startling him. His throat felt parched. He realized he'd been standing for several hours, motionless, watching the witch dream while her power rose and fell in waves. He briefly considered slaking his thirst with this witch's blood. A taste of it might reveal the location of the missing volume and indicate what secrets the witch was keeping. But he restrained himself. It was only his desire to find Ashmole 782 that made him linger with the enigmatic Diana Bishop.

If the manuscript wasn't in the witch's rooms, then it was still in the library.

He padded to the kitchen, slid out the window, and melted into the night.

Chapter 4

Four hours later I woke up on top of the duvet, clutching the phone. At some point I'd kicked off my right slipper, leaving my foot trailing over the edge of the bed. I looked at the clock and groaned. There was no time for my usual trip to the river, or even for a run.

Cutting my morning ritual short, I showered and then drank a scalding cup of tea while drying my hair. It was straw blond and unruly, despite the ministrations of a hairbrush. Like most witches, I had a problem getting the shoulder-length strands to stay put. Sarah blamed it on pent-up magic and promised that the regular use of my power would keep the static electricity from building and make my hair more obedient.

After brushing my teeth, I slipped on a pair of jeans, a fresh white blouse, and a black jacket. It was a familiar routine, and this was my habitual outfit, but neither proved comforting today. My clothes seemed confining, and I felt self-conscious in them. I jerked on the jacket to see if that would make it fit any better, but it was too much to expect from inferior tailoring.

When I looked into the mirror, my mother's face stared back. I could no longer remember when I'd developed this strong resemblance to her. Sometime in college, perhaps? No one had commented on it until I came home for Thanksgiving break during freshman year. Since then it was the first thing I heard from those who had known Rebecca Bishop.

Today's check in the mirror also revealed that my skin was pale from lack of sleep. This made my freckles, which I'd inherited from my father, stand out in apparent alarm, and the dark blue circles under my eyes made them appear lighter than usual. Fatigue also managed to lengthen my nose and render my chin more pronounced. I thought of the immaculate Professor Clairmont and wondered what *he* looked like first thing in the morning. Probably just as pristine as he had last night, I decided—the beast. I grimaced at my reflection.

On my way out the door, I stopped and surveyed my rooms. Something niggled at me—a forgotten appointment, a deadline. There was something I was missing that was important. The sense of unease wrapped around my stomach, squeezed, then let go. After checking my datebook and the stacks of mail on my desk, I wrote it off as hunger and went downstairs. The obliging ladies in the kitchen offered me toast when I passed by. They remembered me as a graduate student and still tried to force-feed me custard and apple pie when I looked stressed.

Munching on toast and slipping along the cobblestones of New College Lane was enough to convince me that last night had been a dream. My hair swung against my collar, and my breath showed in the crisp air. Oxford is quintessentially normal in the morning, with the delivery vans pulled up to college kitchens, the aromas of burned coffee and damp pavement, and fresh rays of sunlight slanting through the mist. It was not a place that seemed likely to harbor vampires.

The Bodleian's blue-jacketed attendant went through his usual routine of scrutinizing my reader's card as if he had never seen me before and suspected I might be a master book thief. Finally he waved me through. I deposited my bag in the cubbyholes by the door after first removing my wallet, computer, and notes, and then I headed up to the twisting wooden stairs to the third floor.

The smell of the library always lifted my spirits—that peculiar combination of old stone, dust, woodworm, and paper made properly from rags. Sun streamed through the windows on the staircase landings, illuminating the dust motes flying through the air and shining bars of light on the ancient walls. There the sun highlighted the curling announcements for last term's lecture series. New posters had yet to go up, but it would only be a matter of days before the floodgates opened and a wave of undergraduates arrived to disrupt the city's tranquillity.

Humming quietly to myself, I nodded to the busts of Thomas Bodley and King Charles I that flanked the arched entrance to Duke Humfrey's and pushed through the swinging gate by the call desk.

"We'll have to set him up in the Selden End today," the supervisor was saying with a touch of exasperation.

The library had been open for just a few minutes, but Mr. Johnson and his staff were already in a flap. I'd seen this kind of behavior before, but only when the most distinguished scholars were expected.

"He's already put in his requests, and he's waiting down there." The unfamiliar female attendant from yesterday scowled at me and shifted the stack of books in her arms. "These are his, too. He had them sent up from the New Bodleian Reading Room."

That's where they kept the East Asia books. It wasn't my field, and I quickly lost interest.

"Get those to him now, and tell him we'll bring the manuscripts down within the hour." The supervisor sounded harassed as he returned to his office.

Sean rolled his eyes heavenward as I approached the collection desk. "Hi, Diana. Do you want the manuscripts you put on reserve?"

"Thanks," I whispered, thinking of my waiting stack with relish. "Big day, huh?"

"Apparently," he said drily, before disappearing into the locked cage that held the manuscripts overnight. He returned with my stack of treasures. "Here you go. Seat number?"

"A4." It's where I always sat, in the far southeastern corner of the Selden End, where the natural light was best.

Mr. Johnson came scurrying toward me. "Ah, Dr. Bishop, we've put Professor Clairmont in A3. You might prefer to sit in A1 or A6." He shifted nervously from one foot to the other and pushed his glasses up, blinking at me through the thick glass.

I stared at him. "Professor *Clairmont*?"

"Yes. He's working on the Needham papers and requested good light and room to spread out."

"Joseph Needham, the historian of Chinese science?" Somewhere around my solar plexus, my blood started to seethe.

"Yes. He was a biochemist, too, of course—hence Professor Clairmont's interest," Mr. Johnson explained, looking more flustered by the moment. "Would you like to sit in A1?"

"I'll take A6." The thought of sitting next to a vampire, even with an empty seat between us, was deeply unsettling. Sitting across from one in A4 was unthinkable, however. How could I concentrate, wondering what those strange eyes were seeing? Had the desks in the medieval wing been more comfortable, I would have parked myself under one of the gargoyles that guarded the narrow windows and braved Gillian Chamberlain's prim disapproval instead.

"Oh, that's splendid. Thank you for understanding." Mr. Johnson sighed with relief.

As I came into the light of the Selden End, my eyes narrowed. Clairmont looked immaculate and rested, his pale skin startling against his dark hair. This time his open-necked gray sweater had flecks of green, and his collar stood up slightly in the back. A peek under the table revealed charcoal gray trousers, matching socks, and black shoes that surely cost more than the average academic's entire wardrobe.

The unsettled feeling returned. What was Clairmont doing in the library? Why wasn't he in his lab?

Making no effort to muffle my footsteps, I strode in the vampire's direction. Clairmont, seated diagonally across from me at the far end of the cluster of desks and seemingly oblivious to my approach, continued reading. I dumped my plastic bag and manuscripts onto the space marked A5, staking out the outer edges of my territory.

He looked up, brows arching in apparent surprise. "Dr. Bishop. Good morning."

"Professor Clairmont." It occurred to me that he'd overheard everything said about him at the reading room's entrance, given that he had the hearing of a bat. I refused to meet his eyes and started pulling individual items out of my bag, building a small fortification of desk supplies between me and the vampire. Clairmont watched until I ran out of equipment, then lowered his eyebrows in concentration and returned to his reading.

I took out the cord for my computer and disappeared under the desk to shove it into the power strip. When I righted myself, he was still reading but was also trying not to smile.

"Surely you'd be more comfortable in the northern end," I grumbled under my breath, rooting around for my list of manuscripts.

Clairmont looked up, dilating pupils making his eyes suddenly dark. "Am I bothering you, Dr. Bishop?"

"Of course not," I said hastily, my throat closing at the sudden, sharp aroma of cloves that accompanied his words, "but I'm surprised you find a southern exposure comfortable."

"You don't believe everything you read, do you?" One of his thick, black eyebrows rose into the shape of a question mark.

"If you're asking whether I think you're going to burst into flames the moment the sunlight hits you, the answer is no." Vampires didn't burn at the touch of sunlight, nor did they have fangs. These were human myths. "But I've never met . . . *someone like you* who liked to bask in its glow either."

Clairmont's body remained still, but I could have sworn he was repressing a laugh. "How much direct experience have you had, Dr. Bishop, with 'someone like me'?"

How did he know I hadn't had much experience with vampires? Vampires had preternatural senses and abilities—but no supernatural ones, like mind reading or precognition. Those belonged to witches and, on rare occasions, could sometimes crop up in daemons, too. This was the natural order, or so my aunt had explained when I was a child and couldn't sleep for fear that a vampire would steal my thoughts and fly out the window with them.

I studied him closely. "Somehow, Professor Clairmont, I don't think years of experience would tell me what I need to know right now."

"I'd be happy to answer your question, if I can," he said, closing his book and placing it on the desk. He waited with the patience of a teacher listening to a belligerent and not very bright student.

"What is it that *you* want?"

Clairmont sat back in his chair, his hands resting easily on the arms. "I want to examine Dr. Needham's papers and study the evolution of his ideas on morphogenesis."

"Morphogenesis?"

"The changes to embryonic cells that result in differentiation—"

"I know what morphogenesis is, Professor Clairmont. That's not what I'm asking."

His mouth twitched. I crossed my arms protectively across my chest.

"I see." He tented his long fingers, resting his elbows on the chair. "I came into Bodley's Library last night to request some manuscripts. Once inside, I decided to look around a bit—I like to know my environment, you understand, and don't often spend time here. There you were in the gallery. And of course what I saw after that was quite unexpected." His mouth twitched again.

I flushed at the memory of how I'd used magic just to get a book. And I tried not to be disarmed by his old-fashioned use of "Bodley's Library" but was not entirely successful.

Careful, Diana, I warned myself. *He's trying to charm you.*

"So your story is that this has just been a set of odd coincidences, culminating in a vampire and a witch sitting across from each other and examining manuscripts like two ordinary readers?"

"I don't think anyone who took the time to examine me carefully would think I was ordinary, do you?" Clairmont's already quiet voice dropped to a mocking whisper, and he tilted forward in his chair. His pale skin caught the light and seemed to glow. "But otherwise, yes. It's just a series of coincidences, easily explained."

"I thought scientists didn't believe in coincidences anymore."

He laughed softly. "Some have to believe in them."

Clairmont kept staring at me, which was unnerving in the extreme. The female attendant rolled the reading room's ancient wooden cart up to the vampire's elbow, boxes of manuscripts neatly arrayed on the trolley's shelves.

The vampire dragged his eyes from my face. "Thank you, Valerie. I appreciate your assistance."

"Of course, Professor Clairmont," Valerie said, gazing at him raptly and turning pink. The vampire had charmed her with no more than a thank-you. I snorted. "Do let us know if you need anything else," she said, returning to her bolt-hole by the entrance.

Clairmont picked up the first box, undid the string with his long fingers, and glanced across the table. "I don't want to keep you from your work."

Matthew Clairmont had taken the upper hand. I'd had enough dealings with senior colleagues to recognize the signs and to know that any response would only make the situation worse. I opened my computer, punched the power button with more force than necessary, and picked up the first of my manuscripts. Once the box was unfastened, I placed its leather-bound contents on the cradle in front of me.

Over the next hour and a half, I read the first pages at least thirty times. I started at the beginning, reading familiar lines of poetry attributed to George Ripley that promised to reveal the secrets of the philosopher's stone. Given the surprises of the morning, the poem's descriptions of how to make the Green Lion, create the Black Dragon, and concoct a mystical blood from chemical ingredients were even more opaque than usual.

Clairmont, however, got a prodigious amount done, covering pages of creamy paper with rapid strokes of his Montblanc Meisterstück mechanical pencil. Every now and again, he'd turn over a sheet with a rustle that set my teeth on edge and begin once more.

Occasionally Mr. Johnson drifted through the room, making sure no one was defacing the books. The vampire kept writing. I glared at both of them.

At 10:45, there was a familiar tingle when Gillian Chamberlain bustled into the Selden End. She started toward me—no doubt to tell me what a splendid time she'd had at the Mabon dinner. Then she saw the vampire and dropped her plastic bag full of pencils and paper. He looked up and stared until she scampered back to the medieval wing.

At 11:10, I felt the insidious pressure of a kiss on my neck. It was the confused, caffeine-addicted daemon from the music reference room. He was repeatedly twirling a set of white plastic headphones around his fingers, then unwinding them to send them spinning through the air. The daemon saw me, nodded at Matthew, and sat at one of the computers in the center of the room. A sign was taped to the screen: OUT OF ORDER. TECHNICIAN CALLED. He remained there for the next several hours, glancing over his shoulder and then at the ceiling periodically as if trying to figure out where he was and how he'd gotten there.

I returned my attention to George Ripley, Clairmont's eyes cold on the top of my head.

At 11:40, icy patches bloomed between my shoulder blades.

This was the last straw. Sarah always said that one in ten beings was a creature, but in Duke Humfrey's this morning the creatures outnumbered humans five to one. Where had they all come from?

I stood abruptly and whirled around, frightening a cherubic, tonsured vampire with an armful of medieval missals just as he was lowering himself into a chair that was much too small for him. He let out a squeak at the sudden, unwanted attention. At the sight of Clairmont, he turned a whiter shade than I thought was possible, even for a vampire. With an apologetic bow, he scuttled off to the library's dimmer recesses.

Over the course of the afternoon, a few humans and three more creatures entered the Selden End.

Two unfamiliar female vampires who appeared to be sisters glided past Clairmont and came to a stop among the local-history shelves under the window, picking up volumes about the early settlement of Bedfordshire and Dorset and writing notes back and forth on a single pad of paper. One of them whispered something, and Clairmont's head swiveled so fast it would have snapped the neck of a lesser being. He made a soft hissing sound that ruffled the hair on my own neck. The two exchanged looks and departed as quietly as they had appeared.

The third creature was an elderly man who stood in a full beam of sunlight and stared raptly at the leaded windows before turning his eyes to me. He was dressed in familiar academic garb—brown tweed jacket with suede elbow patches, corduroy pants in a slightly jarring tone of green, and a cotton shirt with a button-down collar and ink stains on the pocket—and I was ready to dismiss him as just another Oxford scholar before my skin tingled to tell me that he was a witch. Still, he was a stranger, and I returned my attention to my manuscript.

A gentle sensation of pressure on the back of my skull made it impossible to keep reading, however. The pressure flitted to my ears, growing in intensity as it wrapped around my forehead, and my stomach clenched in panic. This was no longer a silent greeting, but a threat. Why, though, would he be threatening me?

The wizard strolled toward my desk with apparent casualness. As he approached, a voice whispered in my now-throbbing head. It was too faint to distinguish the words. I was sure it was coming from this male witch, but who on earth was he?

My breath became shallow. *Get the hell out of my head,* I said fiercely if silently, touching my forehead.

Clairmont moved so quickly I didn't see him round the desks. In an instant he was standing with one hand on the back of my chair and the other resting on the surface in front of me. His broad shoulders were curved around me like the wings of a falcon shielding his prey.

"Are you all right?" he asked.

"I'm fine," I replied with a shaking voice, utterly confused as to why a vampire would need to protect me from another witch.

In the gallery above us, a reader craned her neck to see what all the fuss was about. She stood, her brow creased. Two witches and a vampire were impossible for a human to ignore.

"Leave me alone. The humans have noticed us," I said between clenched teeth.

Clairmont straightened to his full height but kept his back to the witch and his body angled between us like an avenging angel.

"Ah, my mistake," the witch murmured from behind Clairmont. "I thought this seat was available. Excuse me." Soft steps retreated into the distance, and the pressure on my head gradually subsided.

A slight breeze stirred as the vampire's cold hand reached toward my shoulder, stopped, and returned to the back of the chair. Clairmont leaned over. "You look quite pale," he said in his soft, low voice. "Would you like me to take you home?"

"No." I shook my head, hoping he would go sit down and let me gather my composure. In the gallery the human reader kept a wary eye on us.

"Dr. Bishop, I really think you should let me take you home."

"No!" My voice was louder than I intended. It dropped to a whisper. "I am not being driven out of this library—not by you, not by anyone."

Clairmont's face was disconcertingly close. He took a slow breath in, and once again there was a powerful aroma of cinnamon and cloves. Something in my eyes convinced him I was serious, and he drew away. His mouth flattened into a severe line, and he returned to his seat.

We spent the remainder of the afternoon in a state of détente. I tried to read beyond the second folio of my first manuscript, and Clairmont leafed through scraps of paper and closely written notebooks with the attention of a judge deciding on a capital case.

By three o'clock my nerves were so frayed that I could no longer concentrate. The day was lost.

I gathered my scattered belongings and returned the manuscript to its box.

Clairmont looked up. "Going home, Dr. Bishop?" His tone was mild, but his eyes glittered.

"Yes," I snapped.

The vampire's face went carefully blank.

Every creature in the library watched me on my way out—the threatening wizard, Gillian, the vampire monk, even the daemon. The afternoon attendant at the collection desk was a stranger to me, because I never left at this time of day. Mr. Johnson pushed his chair back slightly, saw it was me, and looked at his watch in surprise.

In the quadrangle I pushed the glass doors of the library open and drank in the fresh air. It would take more than fresh air, though, to turn the day around.

Fifteen minutes later I was in a pair of fitted, calf-length pants that stretched in six different directions, a faded New College Boat Club tank, and a fleece pullover. After tying on my sneakers I set off for the river at a run.

When I reached it, some of my tension had already abated. "Adrenaline poisoning," one of my doctors had called these surges of anxiety that had troubled me since childhood. The doctors explained that, for reasons they could not understand, my body seemed to think it was in a constant state of danger. One of the specialists my aunt consulted explained earnestly that it was a biochemical leftover from hunter-gatherer days. I'd be all right so long as I rid my bloodstream of the adrenaline load by running, just as a frightened ibex would run from a lion.

Unfortunately for that doctor, I'd gone to the Serengeti with my parents as a child and had witnessed such a pursuit. The ibex lost. It had made quite an impression on me.

Since then I'd tried medication and meditation, but nothing was better for keeping panic at bay than physical activity. In Oxford it was rowing each morning before the college crews turned the narrow river into a thoroughfare. But the university was not yet in session, and the river would be clear this afternoon.

My feet crunched against the crushed gravel paths that led to the boathouses. I waved at Pete, the boatman who prowled around with wrenches and tubs of grease, trying to put right what the undergraduates mangled in the course of their training. I stopped at the seventh boathouse and bent over to ease the stitch in my side before retrieving the key from the top of the light outside the boathouse doors.

Racks of white and yellow boats greeted me inside. There were big, eight-seated boats for the first men's crew, slightly leaner boats for the women, and other boats of decreasing quality and size. A sign hung from the bow of one shiny new boat that hadn't been rigged yet, instructing visitors that NO ONE MAY TAKE THE FRENCH LIEUTENANT'S WOMAN OUT OF THIS HOUSE WITHOUT THE PERMISSION OF THE NCBC PRESIDENT. The boat's name was freshly stenciled on its side in a Victorian-style script, in homage to the New College graduate who had created the character.

At the back of the boathouse, a whisper of a boat under twelve inches wide and more than twenty-five feet long rested in a set of slings positioned at hip level. *God bless Pete,* I thought. He'd taken to leaving the scull on the floor of the boathouse. A note resting on the seat read, "College training next Monday. Boat will be back in racks."

I kicked off my sneakers, picked two oars with curving blades from the stash near the doors, and carried them down to the dock. Then I went back for the boat.

I plopped the scull gently into the water and put one foot on the seat to keep it from floating away while I threaded the oars into the oarlocks. Holding both oars in one hand like a pair of oversize chopsticks, I carefully stepped into the boat and pushed the dock with my left hand. The scull floated out onto the river.

Rowing was a religion for me, composed of a set of rituals and movements repeated until they became a meditation. The rituals began the moment I touched the equipment, but its real magic came from the combination of precision, rhythm, and strength that rowing required. Since my undergraduate days, rowing had instilled a sense of tranquillity in me like nothing else.

My oars dipped into the water and skimmed along the surface. I picked up the pace, powering through each stroke with my legs and feeling the water when my blade swept back and slipped under the waves. The wind was cold and sharp, cutting through my clothes with every stroke.

As my movements flowed into a seamless cadence, it felt as though I were flying. During these blissful moments, I was suspended in time and space, nothing but a weightless body on a moving river. My swift little boat darted along, and I swung in perfect unison with the boat and its oars. I closed my eyes and smiled, the events of the day fading in significance.

The sky darkened behind my closed lids, and the booming sound of traffic overhead indicated that I'd passed underneath the Donnington Bridge. Coming through into the sunlight on the other side, I opened my eyes—and felt the cold touch of a vampire's gaze on my sternum.

A figure stood on the bridge, his long coat flapping around his knees. Though I couldn't see his face clearly, the vampire's considerable height and bulk suggested that it was Matthew Clairmont. Again.

I swore and nearly dropped one oar. The City of Oxford dock was nearby. The notion of pulling an illegal maneuver and crossing the river so that I could smack the vampire upside his beautiful head with whatever piece of boat equipment was handy was very tempting. While formulating my plan, I spotted a slight woman standing on the dock wearing paint-stained overalls. She was smoking a cigarette and talking into a mobile phone.

This was not a typical sight for the City of Oxford boathouse.

She looked up, her eyes nudging my skin. A daemon. She twisted her mouth into a wolfish smile and said something into the phone.

This was just too weird. First Clairmont and now a host of creatures appearing whenever he did? Abandoning my plan, I poured my unease into my rowing.

I managed to get down the river, but the serenity of the outing had evaporated. Turning the boat in front of the Isis Tavern, I spotted Clairmont standing beside one of the pub's tables. He'd managed to get there from the Donnington Bridge—on foot—in less time than I'd done it in a racing scull.

Pulling hard on both oars, I lifted them two feet off the water like the wings of an enormous bird and glided straight into the tavern's rickety wooden dock. By the time I'd climbed out, Clairmont had crossed the twenty-odd feet of grass lying between us. His weight pushed the floating platform down slightly in the water, and the boat wiggled in adjustment.

"What the hell do you think you're doing?" I demanded, stepping clear of the blade and across the rough planks to where the vampire now stood. My breath was ragged from exertion, my cheeks flushed. "Are you and your friends *stalking* me?"

Clairmont frowned. "They aren't my friends, Dr. Bishop."

"No? I haven't seen so many vampires, witches, and daemons in one place since my aunts dragged me to a pagan summer festival when I was thirteen. If they're not your friends, why are they always hanging around you?" I wiped the back of my hand across my forehead and pushed the damp hair away from my face.

"Good God," the vampire murmured incredulously. "The rumors are true."

"What rumors?" I said impatiently.

"You think these . . . *things* want to spend time with me?" Clairmont's voice dripped with contempt and something that sounded like surprise. "Unbelievable."

I worked my fleece pullover up above my shoulders and yanked it off. Clairmont's eyes flickered to my collarbones, over my bare arms, and down to my fingertips. I felt uncharacteristically naked in my familiar rowing clothes.

"Yes," I snapped. "I've lived in Oxford. I visit every year. The only thing that's been different this time is *you.* Since you showed up last night, I've been pushed out of my seat in the library, stared at by strange vampires and daemons, and threatened by unfamiliar witches."

Clairmont's arms rose slightly, as if he were going to take me by the shoulders and shake me. Though I was by no means short at just under five-seven, he was so tall that my neck had to bend sharply so I could make eye contact. Acutely aware of his size and strength relative to my own, I stepped back and crossed my arms, calling upon my professional persona to steel my nerves.

"They're not interested in me, Dr. Bishop. They're interested in *you.*"

"Why? What could they possibly want from me?"

"Do you really not know why every daemon, witch, and vampire south of the Midlands is following you?" There was a note of disbelief in his voice, and the vampire's expression suggested he was seeing me for the first time.

"No," I said, my eyes on two men enjoying their afternoon pint at a nearby table. Thankfully, they were absorbed in their own conversation. "I've done nothing in Oxford except read old manuscripts, row on the river, prepare for my conference, and keep to myself. It's all I've ever done here. There's no reason for any creature to pay this kind of attention to me."

"Think, Diana." Clairmont's voice was intense. A ripple of something that wasn't fear passed across my skin when he said my first name. "What have you been reading?"

His eyelids dropped over his strange eyes, but not before I'd seen their avid expression.

My aunts had warned me that Matthew Clairmont wanted something. They were right.

He fixed his odd, gray-rimmed black eyes on me once more. "They're following you because they believe you've found something lost many years ago," he said reluctantly. "They want it back, and they think you can get it for them."

I thought about the manuscripts I'd consulted over the past few days. My heart sank. There was only one likely candidate for all this attention.

"If they're not your friends, how do you know what they want?"

"I hear things, Dr. Bishop. I have very good hearing," he said patiently, reverting to his characteristic formality. "I'm also fairly observant. At a concert on Sunday evening, two witches were talking about an American—a fellow witch—who found a book in Bodley's Library that had been given up for lost. Since then I've noticed many new faces in Oxford, and they make me uneasy."

"It's Mabon. That explains why the witches are in Oxford." I was trying to match his patient tone, though he hadn't answered my last question.

Smiling sardonically, Clairmont shook his head. "No, it's not the equinox. It's the manuscript."

"What do you know about Ashmole 782?" I asked quietly.

"Less than you do," said Clairmont, his eyes narrowing to slits. It made him look even more like a large, lethal beast. "I've never seen it. You've held it in your hands. Where is it now, Dr. Bishop? You weren't so foolish as to leave it in your room?"

I was aghast. "You think I *stole* it? From the Bodleian? How dare you suggest such a thing!"

"You didn't have it Monday night," he said. "And it wasn't on your desk today either."

"You *are* observant," I said sharply, "if you could see all that from where you were sitting. I returned it Friday, if you must know." It occurred to me, belatedly, that he might have riffled through the things on my desk. "What's so special about the manuscript that you'd snoop through a colleague's work?"

He winced slightly, but my triumph at catching him doing something so inappropriate was blunted by a twinge of fear that this vampire was following me as closely as he obviously was.

"Simple curiosity," he said, baring his teeth. Sarah had not misled me—vampires don't have fangs.

"I hope you don't expect me to believe that."

"I don't care what you believe, Dr. Bishop. But you should be on your guard. These creatures are serious. And when they come to understand what an unusual witch you are?" Clairmont shook his head.

"What do you mean?" All the blood drained from my head, leaving me dizzy.

"It's uncommon these days for a witch to have so much . . . potential." Clairmont's voice dropped to a purr that vibrated in the back of his throat. "Not everyone can see it—yet—but I can. You shimmer with it when you concentrate. When you're angry, too. Surely the daemons in the library will sense it soon, if they haven't already."

"I appreciate the warning. But I don't need your help." I prepared to stalk away, but his hand shot out and gripped my upper arm, stopping me in my tracks.

"Don't be too sure of that. Be careful. Please." Clairmont hesitated, his face shaken out of its perfect lines as he wrestled with something. "Especially if you see that wizard again."

I stared fixedly at the hand on my arm. Clairmont released me. His lids dropped, shuttering his eyes.

My row back to the boathouse was slow and steady, but the repetitive movements weren't able to carry away my lingering confusion and unease. Every now and again, there was a gray blur on the towpath, but nothing else caught my attention except for people bicycling home from work and a very ordinary human walking her dog.

After returning the equipment and locking the boathouse, I set off down the towpath at a measured jog.

Matthew Clairmont was standing across the river in front of the University Boat House.

I began to run, and when I looked back over my shoulder, he was gone.

Chapter 5

After dinner I sat down on the sofa by the sitting room's dormant fireplace and switched on my laptop. Why would a scientist of Clairmont's caliber want to see an alchemical manuscript—even one under a spell—so much that he'd sit at the Bodleian all day, across from a witch, and read through old notes on morphogenesis? His business card was tucked into one of the pockets of my bag. I fished it out, propping it up against the screen.

On the Internet, below an unrelated link to a murder mystery and the unavoidable hits from social-networking sites, a string of biographical listings looked promising: his faculty Web page, a Wikipedia article, and links to the current fellows of the Royal Society.

I clicked on the faculty Web page and snorted. Matthew Clairmont was one of those faculty members who didn't like to post any information—even academic information—on the Net. On Yale's Web site, a visitor could get contact information and a complete vita for practically every member of the faculty. Oxford clearly had a different attitude toward privacy. No wonder a vampire taught here.

There hadn't been a hit for Clairmont at the hospital, though the affiliation was on his card. I typed *"John Radcliffe Neurosciences"* into the search box and was led to an overview of the department's services. There wasn't a single reference to a physician, however, only a lengthy list of research interests. Clicking systematically through the terms, I finally found him on a page dedicated to the "frontal lobe," though there was no additional information.

The Wikipedia article was no help at all, and the Royal Society's site was no better. Anything useful hinted at on the main pages was hidden behind passwords. I had no luck imagining what Clairmont's user name and password might be and was refused access to anything at all after my sixth incorrect guess.

Frustrated, I entered the vampire's name into the search engines for scientific journals.

"Yes." I sat back in satisfaction.

Matthew Clairmont might not have much of a presence on the Internet, but he was certainly active in the scholarly literature. After clicking a box to sort the results by date, I was provided with a snapshot of his intellectual history.

My initial sense of triumph faded. He didn't have one intellectual history. He had four.

The first began with the brain. Much of it was beyond me, but Clairmont seemed to have made a scientific and medical reputation at the same time by studying how the brain's frontal lobe processes urges and cravings. He'd made several major breakthroughs related to the role that neural mechanisms play in delayed-gratification responses, all of which involved the prefrontal cortex. I opened a new browser window to view an anatomical diagram and locate which bit of the brain was at issue.

Some argued that all scholarship is thinly veiled autobiography. My pulse jumped. Given that Clairmont was a vampire, I sincerely hoped delayed gratification was something he was good at.

My next few clicks showed that Clairmont's work took a surprising turn away from the brain and toward wolves—Norwegian wolves, to be precise. He must have spent a considerable amount of time in the Scandinavian nights in the course of his research—which posed no problem for a vampire, considering their body temperature and ability to see in the dark. I tried to imagine him in a parka and grubby clothes with a notepad in the snow—and failed.

After that, the first references to blood appeared.

While the vampire was with the wolves in Norway, he'd started analyzing their blood to determine family groups and inheritance patterns. Clairmont had isolated four clans among the Norwegian wolves, three of which were indigenous. The fourth he traced back to a wolf that had arrived in Norway from Sweden or Finland. There was, he concluded, a surprising amount of mating across packs, leading to an exchange of genetic material that influenced species evolution.

Now he was tracing inherited traits among other animal species as well as in humans. Many of his most recent publications were technical—methods for staining tissue samples and processes for handling particularly old and fragile DNA.

I grabbed a fistful of my hair and held tight, hoping the pressure would increase blood circulation and get my tired synapses firing again. This made no sense. No scientist could produce this much work in so many different subdisciplines. Acquiring the skills alone would take more than a lifetime—*a human lifetime, that is.*

A vampire might well pull it off, if he had been working on problems like this over the span of decades. Just how old was Matthew Clairmont behind that thirty-something face?

I got up and made a fresh cup of tea. With the mug steaming in one hand, I rooted through my bag until I found my mobile and punched in a number with my thumb.

One of the best things about scientists was that they always had their phones. They answered them on the second ring, too.

"Christopher Roberts."

"Chris, it's Diana Bishop."

"Diana!" Chris's voice was warm, and there was music blaring in the background. "I heard you won another prize for your book. Congratulations!"

"Thanks," I said, shifting in my seat. "It was quite unexpected."

"Not to me. Speaking of which, how's the research going? Have you finished writing your keynote?"

"Nowhere near," I said. That's what I *should* be doing, not tracking down vampires on the Internet. "Listen, I'm sorry to bother you in the lab. Do you have a minute?"

"Sure." He shouted for someone to turn down the noise. It remained at the same volume. "Hold on." There were muffled sounds, then quiet. "That's better," he said sheepishly. "The new kids are pretty high energy at the beginning of the semester."

"Grad students are always high energy, Chris." I felt a tiny pang at missing the rush of new classes and new students.

"You know it. But what about you? What do you need?"

Chris and I had taken up our faculty positions at Yale in the same year, and he wasn't supposed to get tenure either. He'd beaten me to it by a year, picking up a MacArthur Fellowship along the way for his brilliant work as a molecular biologist.

He didn't behave like an aloof genius when I cold-called him to ask why an alchemist might describe two substances heated in an alembic as growing branches like a tree. Nobody else in the chemistry department had been interested in helping me, but Chris sent two Ph.D. students to get the materials necessary to re-create the experiment, then insisted I come straight to the lab. We'd watched through the walls of a glass beaker while a lump of gray sludge underwent a glorious evolution into a red tree with hundreds of branches. We'd been friends ever since.

I took a deep breath. "I met someone the other day."

Chris whooped. He'd been introducing me to men he'd met at the gym for years.

"There's no romance," I said hastily. "He's a scientist."

"A gorgeous scientist is exactly what you need. You need a challenge—and a life."

"Look who's talking. What time did you leave the lab yesterday? Besides, there's already one gorgeous scientist in my life," I teased.

"No changing the subject."

"Oxford is such a small town, I'm bound to keep running into him. And he seems to be a big deal around here." Not strictly true, I thought, crossing my fingers, but close enough. "I've looked up his work and can understand some of it, but I must be missing something, because it doesn't seem to fit together."

"Tell me he's not an astrophysicist," Chris said. "You know I'm weak on physics."

"You're supposed to be a genius."

"I am," he said promptly. "But my genius doesn't extend to card games or physics. Name, please." Chris tried to be patient, but no one's brain moved fast enough for him.

"Matthew Clairmont." His name caught in the back of my throat, just as the scent of cloves had the night before.

Chris whistled. "The elusive, reclusive Professor Clairmont." Gooseflesh rose on my arms. "What did you do, put him under a spell with those eyes of yours?"

Since Chris didn't know I was a witch, his use of the word "spell" was entirely accidental. "He admires my work on Boyle."

"Right," Chris scoffed. "You turned those crazy blue-and-gold starbursts on him and he was thinking about Boyle's law? He's a scientist, Diana, not a monk. And he is a big deal, incidentally."

"Really?" I said faintly.

"Really. He was a phenom, just like you, and started publishing while he was still a grad student. Good stuff, not crap—work you'd be happy to have your name on if you managed to produce it over the course of a career."

I scanned my notes, scratched out on a yellow legal pad. "This was his study of neural mechanisms and the prefrontal cortex?"

"You've done your homework," he said approvingly. "I didn't follow much of Clairmont's early work—his chemistry is what interests me—but his publications on wolves caused a lot of excitement."

"How come?"

"He had amazing instincts—why the wolves picked certain places to live, how they formed social groups, how they mated. It was almost like he was a wolf, too."

"Maybe he is." I tried to keep my voice light, but something bitter and envious bloomed in my mouth and it came out harshly instead.

Matthew Clairmont didn't have a problem using his preternatural abilities and thirst for blood to advance his career. If the vampire had been making the decisions about Ashmole 782 on Friday night, he would have touched the manuscript's illustrations. I was sure of it.

"It would have been easier to explain the quality of his work if he *were* a wolf," Chris said patiently, ignoring my tone. "Since he isn't, you just have to admit he's very good. He was elected to the Royal Society on the basis of it, after they published his findings. People were calling him the next Attenborough. After that, he dropped out of sight for a while."

I'll bet he did. "Then he popped up again, doing evolution and chemistry?"

"Yeah, but his interest in evolution was a natural progression from the wolves."

"So what is it about his chemistry that interests you?"

Chris's voice got tentative. "Well, he's behaving like a scientist does when he's discovered something big."

"I don't understand." I frowned.

"We get jumpy and weird. We hide in our labs and don't go to conferences for fear we might say something and help someone else have a breakthrough."

"You behave like wolves." I now knew a great deal about wolves. The possessive, guarded behaviors Chris described fit the Norwegian wolf nicely.

"Exactly." Chris laughed. "He hasn't bitten anyone or been caught howling at the moon?"

"Not that I'm aware of," I murmured. "Has Clairmont always been so reclusive?"

"I'm the wrong person to ask," Chris admitted. "He does have a medical degree, and must have seen patients, although he never had any reputation as a clinician. And the wolves liked him. But he hasn't been at any of the obvious conferences in the past three years." He paused. "Wait a minute, though, there was something a few years back."

"What?"

"He gave a paper—I can't remember the particulars—and a woman asked him a question. It was a smart question, but he was dismissive. She was persistent. He got irritated and then mad. A friend who was there said he'd never seen anybody go from courteous to furious so fast."

I was already typing, trying to find information about the controversy. "Dr. Jekyll and Mr. Hyde, huh? There's no sign of the ruckus online."

"I'm not surprised. Chemists don't air their dirty laundry in public. It hurts all of us at grant time. We don't want the bureaucrats thinking we're high-strung megalomaniacs. We leave that to the physicists."

"Does Clairmont get grants?"

"Oho. Yes. He's funded up to his eyeballs. Don't you worry about Professor Clairmont's career. He may have a reputation for being contemptuous of women, but it hasn't dried up the money. His work is too good for that."

"Have you ever met him?" I asked, hoping to get Chris's judgment of Clairmont's character.

"No. You probably couldn't find more than a few dozen people who could claim they had. He doesn't teach. There are lots of stories, though—he doesn't like women, he's an intellectual snob, he doesn't answer his mail, he doesn't take on research students."

"Sounds like you think that's all nonsense."

"Not nonsense," Chris said thoughtfully. "I'm just not sure it matters, given that he might be the one to unlock the secrets of evolution or cure Parkinson's disease."

"You make him sound like a cross between Salk and Darwin."

"Not a bad analogy, actually."

"He's that good?" I thought of Clairmont studying the Needham papers with ferocious concentration and suspected he was better than good.

"Yes." Chris dropped his voice. "If I were a betting man, I'd put down a hundred dollars that he'll win a Nobel before he dies."

Chris was a genius, but he didn't know that Matthew Clairmont was a vampire. There would be no Nobel—the vampire would see to that, to preserve his anonymity. Nobel Prize winners have their photos taken.

"It's a bet," I said with a laugh.

"You should start saving up, Diana, because you're going to lose this one." Chris chuckled.

He'd lost our last wager. I'd bet him fifty dollars that he'd be tenured before I was. His money was stuck inside the same frame that held his picture, taken the morning the MacArthur Foundation had called. In it, Chris was dragging his hands over his tight black curls, a sheepish smile lighting his dark face. His tenure had followed nine months later.

"Thanks, Chris. You've been a big help," I said sincerely. "You should get back to the kids. They've probably blown something up by now."

"Yeah, I should check on them. The fire alarms haven't gone off, which is a good sign." He hesitated. "'Fess up, Diana. You're not worried about saying the wrong thing if you see Matthew Clairmont at a cocktail party. This is how you behave when you're working on a research problem. What is it about him that's hooked your imagination?"

Sometimes Chris seemed to suspect I was different. But there was no way to tell him the truth.

"I have a weakness for smart men."

He sighed. "Okay, don't tell me. You're a terrible liar, you know. But be careful. If he breaks your heart, I'll have to kick his ass, and this is a busy semester for me."

"Matthew Clairmont isn't going to break my heart," I insisted. "He's a colleague—one with broad reading interests, that's all."

"For someone so smart, you really are clueless. I bet you ten dollars he asks you out before the week is over."

I laughed. "Are you ever going to learn? Ten dollars, then—or the equivalent in British sterling—when I win."

We said our good-byes. I still didn't know much about Matthew Clairmont—but I had a better sense of the questions that remained, most important among them being why someone working on a breakthrough in evolution would be interested in seventeenth-century alchemy.

I surfed the Internet until my eyes were too tired to continue. When the clocks struck midnight, I was surrounded by notes on wolves and genetics but was no closer to unraveling the mystery of Matthew Clairmont's interest in Ashmole 782.

Chapter 6

The next morning was gray and much more typical of early autumn. All I wanted to do was cocoon myself in layers of sweaters and stay in my rooms.

One glance at the heavy weather convinced me not to return to the river. I set out for a run instead, waving at the night porter in the lodge, who gave me an incredulous look followed by an encouraging thumbs-up.

With each slap of my feet on the sidewalk, some stiffness left my body. By the time they reached the gravel paths of the University Parks, I was breathing deeply and felt relaxed and ready for a long day in the library—no matter how many creatures were gathered there.

When I got back, the porter stopped me. "Dr. Bishop?"

"Yes?"

"I'm sorry about turning your friend away last night, but it's college policy. Next time you're having guests, let us know and we'll send them straight up."

The clearheadedness from my run evaporated.

"Was it a man or a woman?" I asked sharply.

"A woman."

My shoulders floated down from around my ears.

"She seemed perfectly nice, and I always like Australians. They're friendly without being, you know . . ." The porter trailed off, but his meaning was clear. Australians were like Americans—but not so pushy. "We did call up to your rooms."

I frowned. I'd switched off the phone's ringer, because Sarah never calculated the time difference between Madison and Oxford correctly and was always calling in the middle of the night. That explained it.

"Thank you for letting me know. I'll be sure to tell you about any future visitors," I promised.

Back in my rooms, I flipped on the bathroom light and saw that the past two days had taken a toll. The circles that had appeared under my eyes yesterday had now blossomed into something resembling bruises. I checked my arm for bruises, too, and was surprised not to find any. The vampire's grip had been so strong that I was sure Clairmont had broken the blood vessels under the skin.

I showered and dressed in loose trousers and a turtleneck. Their unalleviated black accentuated my height and minimized my athletic build, but it also made me resemble a corpse, so I tied a soft periwinkle sweater around my shoulders. That made the circles under my eyes look bluer, but at least I no longer looked dead. My hair threatened to stand straight up from my head and crackled every time I moved. The only solution for it was to scrape it back into a messy knot at the nape of my neck.

Clairmont's trolley had been stuffed with manuscripts, and I was resigned to seeing him in Duke Humfrey's Reading Room. I approached the call desk with shoulders squared.

Once again the supervisor and both attendants were flapping around like nervous birds. This time their activity was focused on the triangle between the call desk, the manuscript card catalogs, and the supervisor's office. They carried stacks of boxes and pushed carts loaded with manuscripts under the watchful eyes of the gargoyles and into the first three bays of ancient desks.

"Thank you, Sean." Clairmont's deep, courteous voice floated from their depths.

The good news was that I would no longer have to share a desk with a vampire.

The bad news was that I couldn't enter or leave the library—or call a book or manuscript—without Clairmont's tracking my every move. And today he had backup.

A diminutive girl was stacking up papers and file folders in the second alcove. She was dressed in a long, baggy brown sweater that reached almost to her knees. When she turned, I was startled to see a full-grown adult. Her eyes were amber and black, and as cold as frostbite.

Even without their touch, her luminous, pale skin and unnaturally thick, glossy hair gave her away as a vampire. Snaky waves of it undulated around her face and over her shoulders. She took a step toward me, making no effort to disguise the swift, sure movements, and gave me a withering glance. This was clearly not where she wanted to be, and she blamed me.

"Miriam," Clairmont called softly, walking out into the center aisle. He stopped short, and a polite smile shaped his lips. "Dr. Bishop. Good morning." He raked his fingers through his hair, which only made it look more artfully tousled. I patted my own hair self-consciously and tucked a stray strand behind my ear.

"Good morning, Professor Clairmont. Back again, I see."

"Yes. But today I won't be joining you in the Selden End. They've been able to accommodate us here, where we won't disturb anyone."

The female vampire rapped a stack of papers sharply against the top of the desk.

Clairmont smiled. "May I introduce my research colleague, Dr. Miriam Shephard. Miriam, this is Dr. Diana Bishop."

"Dr. Bishop," Miriam said coolly, extending her hand in my direction. I took it and felt a shock at the contrast between her tiny, cold hand and my own larger, warmer one. I began to draw back, but her grip grew firmer, crushing the bones together. When she finally let go, I had to resist the urge to shake out my hand.

"Dr. Shephard." The three of us stood awkwardly. What were you supposed to ask a vampire first thing in the morning? I fell back on human platitudes. "I should really get to work."

"Have a productive day," Clairmont said, his nod as cool as Miriam's greeting.

Mr. Johnson appeared at my elbow, my small stack of gray boxes waiting in his arms.

"We've got you in A4 today, Dr. Bishop," he said with a pleased puff of his cheeks. "I'll just carry these back for you." Clairmont's shoulders were so broad that I couldn't see around him to tell if there were bound manuscripts on his desk. I stifled my curiosity and followed the reading-room supervisor to my familiar seat in the Selden End.

Even without Clairmont sitting across from me, I was acutely aware of him as I took out my pencils and turned on my computer. My back to the empty room, I picked up the first box, pulled out the leather-bound manuscript, and placed it in the cradle.

The familiar task of reading and taking notes soon absorbed my attention, and I finished with the first manuscript in less than two hours. My watch revealed that it was not yet eleven. There was still time for another before lunch.

The manuscript inside the next box was smaller than the last, but it contained interesting sketches of alchemical apparatus and snippets of chemical procedures that read like some unholy combination of *Joy of Cooking* and a poisoner's notebook. *"Take your pot of mercury and seethe it over a flame for three hours,"* began one set of instructions, *"and when it has joined with the Philosophical Child take it and let it putrefy until the Black Crow carries it away to its death."* My fingers flew over the keyboard, picking up momentum as the minutes ticked by.

I had prepared myself to be stared at today by every creature imaginable. But when the clocks chimed one, I was still virtually alone in the Selden End. The only other reader was a graduate student wearing a red-, white-, and blue-striped Keble College scarf. He stared morosely at a stack of rare books without reading them and bit his nails with occasional loud clicks.

After filling out two new request slips and packing up my manuscripts, I left my seat for lunch, satisfied with the morning's accomplishments. Gillian Chamberlain stared at me malevolently from an uncomfortable-looking seat near the ancient clock as I passed by, the two female vampires from yesterday drove icicles into my skin, and the daemon from the music reference room had picked up two other daemons. The three of them were dismantling a microfilm reader, the parts scattered all around them and a roll of film unspooling, unnoticed, on the floor at their feet.

Clairmont and his vampire assistant were still stationed near the reading room's call desk. The vampire claimed that the creatures were flocking to me, not to him. But their behavior today suggested otherwise, I thought with triumph.

While I was returning my manuscripts, Matthew Clairmont eyed me coldly. It took a considerable effort, but I refrained from acknowledging him.

"All done with these?" Sean asked.

"Yes. There are still two more at my desk. If I could have these as well, that would be great." I handed over the slips. "Do you want to join me for lunch?"

"Valerie just stepped out. I'm stuck here for a while, I'm afraid," he said with regret.

"Next time." Gripping my wallet, I turned to leave.

Clairmont's low voice stopped me in my tracks. "Miriam, it's lunchtime."

"I'm not hungry," she said in a clear, melodic soprano that contained a rumble of anger.

"The fresh air will improve your concentration." The note of command in Clairmont's voice was indisputable. Miriam sighed loudly, snapped her pencil onto her desk, and emerged from the shadows to follow me.

My usual meal consisted of a twenty-minute break in the nearby bookstore's second-floor café. I smiled at the thought of Miriam occupying herself during that time, trapped in Blackwell's where the tourists congregated to look at postcards, smack between the Oxford guidebooks and the true-crime section.

I secured a sandwich and some tea and squeezed into the farthest corner of the crowded room between a vaguely familiar member of the history faculty who was reading the paper and an undergraduate dividing his attention between a music player, a mobile phone, and a computer.

After finishing my sandwich, I cupped the tea in my hands and glanced out the windows. I frowned. One of the unfamiliar daemons from Duke Humfrey's was lounging against the library gates and looking up at Blackwell's windows.

Two nudges pressed against my cheekbones, as gentle and fleeting as a kiss. I looked up into the face of another daemon. She was beautiful, with arresting, contradictory features—her mouth too wide for her delicate face, her chocolate brown eyes too close together given their enormous size, her hair too fair for skin the color of honey.

"Dr. Bishop?" The woman's Australian accent sent cold fingers moving around the base of my spine.

"Yes," I whispered, glancing at the stairs. Miriam's dark head failed to emerge from below. "I'm Diana Bishop."

She smiled. "I'm Agatha Wilson. And your friend downstairs doesn't know I'm here."

It was an incongruously old-fashioned name for someone who was only about ten years older than I was, and far more stylish. Her name was familiar, though, and I dimly remembered seeing it in a fashion magazine.

"May I sit down?" she asked, gesturing at the seat just vacated by the historian.

"Of course," I murmured.

On Monday I'd met a vampire. On Tuesday a witch tried to worm his way into my head. Wednesday, it would appear, was daemon day.

Even though they'd followed me around college, I knew even less about daemons than I did about vampires. Few seemed to understand the creatures, and Sarah had never been able to answer my questions about them. Based on her accounts, daemons constituted a criminal underclass. Their superabundance of cleverness and creativity led them to lie, steal, cheat, and even kill, because they felt they could get away with it. Even more troublesome, as far as Sarah was concerned, were the conditions of their birth. There was no telling where or when a daemon would crop up, since they were typically born to human parents. To my aunt this only compounded their already marginal position in the hierarchy of beings. She valued a witch's family traditions and bloodlines, and she didn't approve of daemonic unpredictability.

Agatha Wilson was content to sit next to me quietly at first, watching me hold my tea. Then she started to talk in a bewildering swirl of words. Sarah always said that conversations with daemons were impossible, because they began in the middle.

"So much energy is bound to attract us," she said matter-of-factly, as if I'd asked her a question. "The witches were in Oxford for Mabon, and chattering as if the world weren't full of vampires who hear *everything*." She fell silent. "We weren't sure we'd ever see it again."

"See what?" I said softly.

"The book," she confided in a low voice.

"The book," I repeated, my voice flat.

"Yes. After what the witches did to it, we didn't think we'd catch a glimpse of it again."

The daemon's eyes were focused on a spot in the middle of the room. "Of course, you're a witch, too. Perhaps it's wrong to talk to you. I would have thought you of all witches would be able to figure out how they did it, though. And now there's this," she said sadly, picking up the abandoned newspaper and handing it to me.

The sensational headline immediately caught my attention: VAMPIRE ON THE LOOSE IN LONDON. I hurriedly read the story.

> Metropolitan Police have no new leads in the puzzling murder of two men in Westminster. The bodies of Daniel Bennett, 22, and Jason Enright, 26, were found in an alley behind the White Hart pub on St Alban's Street early Sunday morning by the pub's owner, Reg Scott. Both men had severed carotid arteries and multiple lacerations on the neck, arms, and torso. Forensic tests revealed that massive loss of blood was the cause of death, although no blood evidence was found at the scene.
>
> Authorities investigating the "vampire murders," as they were dubbed by local residents, sought the advice of Peter Knox. The author of bestselling books on modern occultism, including Dark Matters: The Devil in Modern Times and

> Magic Rising: The Need for Mystery in the Age of Science, Knox has been consulted by agencies around the world in cases of suspected satanic and serial killings.
>
> "There is no evidence that these are ritual murders," Knox told reporters at a news conference. "Nor does it seem that this is the work of a serial killer," he concluded, in spite of the similar murders of Christiana Nilsson in Copenhagen last summer and Sergei Morozov in St Petersburg in the fall of 2007. When pressed, Knox conceded that the London case may involve a copycat killer or killers.
>
> Concerned residents have instituted a public watch, and local police have launched a door-to-door safety campaign to answer questions and provide support and guidance. Officials urge London residents to take extra precautions for their safety, especially at night.

"That's just the work of a newspaper editor in search of a story," I said, handing the paper back to the daemon. "The press is preying on human fears."

"Are they?" she asked, glancing around the room. "I'm not so sure. I think it's much more than that. One never knows with vampires. They're only a step away from animals." Agatha Wilson's mouth drew tight in a sour expression. "And you think *we're* the unstable ones. Still, it's dangerous for any of us to catch human attention."

This was too much talk of witches and vampires for a public place. The undergraduate still had his earphones in, however, and all the other patrons were deep into their own thoughts or had their heads close to their lunch companions'.

"I don't know anything about the manuscript or what the witches did to it, Ms. Wilson. I don't have it either," I said hastily, in case she, too, thought I might have stolen it.

"You must call me Agatha." She focused on the pattern of the carpet. "The library has it now. Did they tell you to send it back?"

Did she mean witches? Vampires? The librarians? I picked the likeliest culprits.

"Witches?" I whispered.

Agatha nodded, her eyes drifting around the room.

"No. When I was done with it, I simply returned it to the stacks."

"Ah, the stacks," Agatha said knowingly. "Everybody thinks the library is just a building, but it isn't."

Once again I remembered the eerie constriction I'd felt after Sean had put the manuscript on the conveyor belt.

"The library is whatever the witches want it to be," she went on. "But the book doesn't belong to you. Witches shouldn't get to decide where it's kept and who sees it."

"What's so special about this manuscript?"

"The book explains why we're here," she said, her voice betraying a hint of desperation. "It tells our story—beginning, middle, even the end. We daemons need to understand our place in the world. Our need is greater than that of the witches or vampires." There was nothing addled about her now. She was like a camera that had been chronically out of focus until someone came by and twisted the lenses into alignment.

"You know your place in the world," I began. "There are four kinds of creatures—humans, daemons, vampires, and witches."

"And where do daemons come from? How are we made? Why are we here?" Her brown eyes snapped. "Do you know where *your* power comes from? Do you?"

"No," I whispered, shaking my head.

"Nobody knows," she said wistfully. "Every day we wonder. Humans thought daemons were guardian angels at first. Then they believed we were gods, bound to the earth and victims of our own passions. Humans hated us because we were different and abandoned their children if they turned out to be daemons. They accused us of possessing their souls and making them insane. Daemons are brilliant, but we're not vicious—not like the vampires." Her voice was clearly angry now, though it never lifted above a murmur. "We would never make someone insane. Even more than witches, we're victims of human fear and envy."

"Witches have their share of nasty legends to contend with," I said, thinking of the witch-hunts and the executions that followed.

"Witches are born to witches. Vampires make other vampires. You have family stories and memories to comfort you when you're lonely or confused. We have nothing but tales told to us by humans. It's no wonder so many daemons are broken in spirit. Our only hope lies in brushing against other daemons one day and knowing we're like them. My son was one of the lucky ones. Nathaniel had a daemon for a mother, someone who saw the signs and could help him understand." She looked away for a moment, regaining her composure. When her eyes again met mine, they were sad. "Maybe the humans are right. Maybe we are possessed. I see things, Diana. Things I shouldn't."

Daemons could be visionaries. No one knew if their visions were reliable, like the visions that witches had.

"I see blood and fear. I see you," she said, her eyes losing focus again. "Sometimes I see the vampire. He's wanted this book for a very long time. Instead he's found you. Curious."

"Why does Matthew Clairmont want the book?"

Agatha shrugged. "Vampires and witches don't share their thoughts with us. Not even your vampire tells us what he knows, though he's fonder of daemons than most of his kind. So many secrets, and so many clever humans these days. They'll figure it out if we're not careful. Humans like power—secrets, too."

"He's not *my* vampire." I flushed.

"Are you sure?" she asked, staring into the chrome on the espresso machine as if it were a magic mirror.

"Yes," I said tightly.

"A little book can hold a big secret—one that might change the world. You're a witch. You know words have power. And if your vampire knew the secret, he wouldn't need you." Agatha's brown eyes were now melting and warm.

"Matthew Clairmont can call the manuscript himself if he wants it so badly." The idea that he might be doing so now was unaccountably chilling.

"When you get it back," she said urgently, grabbing my arm, "promise me you'll remember that you aren't the only ones who need to know its secrets. Daemons are part of the story, too. Promise me."

I felt a flicker of panic at her touch, felt suddenly aware of the heat of the room and the press of people in it. Instinctively I searched for the nearest exit while focusing on my breathing, trying to curb the beginnings of a fight-or-flight response.

"I promise," I murmured hesitantly, not sure what it was I was agreeing to.

"Good," she said absently, dropping my arm. Her eyes drifted away. "It was good of you to speak with me." Agatha was staring at the carpet once more. "We'll see each other again. Remember, some promises matter more than others."

I dropped my teapot and cup into the gray plastic tub on top of the trash and threw away the bag from my sandwich. When I glanced over my shoulder, Agatha was reading the sports section of the historian's discarded London daily.

On my way out of Blackwell's, I didn't see Miriam, but I could feel her eyes.

The Selden End had filled with ordinary human beings while I was gone, all of them busy with their own work and completely oblivious to the creature convention around them. Envious of their ignorance, I took up a manuscript, determined to concentrate, but instead found myself reviewing my conversation in Blackwell's and the events of the past few days. On an immediate level, the illustrations in Ashmole 782 didn't seem related to what Agatha Wilson had said the book was about. And if Matthew Clairmont and the daemon were so interested in the manuscript, why didn't they request it?

I closed my eyes, recalling the details of my encounter with the manuscript and trying to make some pattern of the events of the past few days by emptying my mind and imagining the problem as a jigsaw puzzle sitting on a white table, then rearranging the colorful shapes. But no matter where they were placed, no clear picture emerged. Frustrated, I pushed my chair away from my desk and walked toward the exit.

"Any requests?" Sean asked as he took the manuscripts from my arms. I handed him a bunch of freshly filled-out call slips. He smiled at the stack's thickness but didn't say a word.

Before leaving, I needed to do two things. The first was a matter of simple courtesy. I wasn't sure how they'd done it, but the vampires had kept me from being distracted by an endless stream of creatures in the Selden End. Witches and vampires didn't often have occasion to thank one another, but Clairmont had protected me twice in two days. I was determined not to be ungrateful, or bigoted like Sarah and her friends in the Madison coven.

"Professor Clairmont?"

The vampire looked up.

"Thank you," I said simply, meeting his gaze and holding it until he looked away.

"You're welcome," he murmured, a note of surprise in his voice.

The second was more calculated. If Matthew Clairmont needed me, I needed him, too. I wanted him to tell me why Ashmole 782 was attracting so much attention.

"Perhaps you should call me Diana," I said quickly, before I lost my nerve.

Matthew Clairmont smiled.

My heart stopped beating for a fraction of a second. This was not the small, polite smile with which I was now familiar. His lips curved toward his eyes, making his whole face sparkle. God, he was beautiful, I thought again, slightly dazzled.

"All right," he said softly, "but then you must call me Matthew."

I nodded in agreement, my heart still beating in erratic syncopation. Something spread through my body, loosening the vestiges of anxiety that remained after the unexpected meeting with Agatha Wilson.

Matthew's nose flared delicately. His smile grew a bit wider. Whatever my body was doing, he had smelled it. What's more, he seemed to have identified it.

I flushed.

"Have a pleasant evening, Diana." His voice lingered on my name, making it sound exotic and strange.

"Good night, Matthew," I replied, beating a hasty retreat.

That evening, rowing on the quiet river as sunset turned to dusk, I saw an occasional smoky smudge on the towpath, always slightly ahead of me, like a dark star guiding me home.

Chapter 7

At two-fifteen I was ripped from sleep by a terrible sensation of drowning. Flailing my way out from under the covers, transformed into heavy, wet seaweed by the power of the dream, I moved toward the lighter water above me. Just when I was making progress, something grabbed me by the ankle and pulled me down deeper.

As usual with nightmares, I awoke with a start before finding out who had caught me. For several minutes I lay disoriented, my body drenched with sweat and my heart sounding a staccato beat that reverberated through my rib cage. Gingerly, I sat up.

A white face stared at me from the window with dark, hollow eyes.

Too late I realized that it was just my reflection in the glass. I barely made it to the bathroom before being sick. Then I spent the next thirty minutes curled into a ball on the cold tile floor, blaming Matthew Clairmont and the other, gathering creatures for my unease. Finally I crawled back into bed and slept for a few hours. At dawn I dragged myself into rowing gear.

When I got to the lodge, the porter gave me an amazed look. "You're not going out at this hour in the fog, Dr. Bishop? You look like you've been burning the candle at both ends, if you don't mind me saying so. Wouldn't a nice lie-in be a better idea? The river will still be there tomorrow."

After considering Fred's advice, I shook my head. "No, I'll feel better for it." He looked doubtful. "And the students are back this weekend."

The pavement was slick with moisture, so I ran more slowly than usual to make allowances for the weather as well as my fatigue. My familiar route took me past Oriel College and to the tall, black iron gates between Merton and Corpus Christi. They were locked from dusk until dawn to keep people out of the meadows that bordered the river, but the first thing you learned when you rowed at Oxford was how to scale them. I climbed them with ease.

The familiar ritual of putting the boat in the water did its work. By the time it slipped away from the dock and into the fog, I felt almost normal.

When it's foggy, rowing feels even more like flying. The air muffles the normal sounds of birds and automobiles and amplifies the soft thwack of oars in the water and the swoosh of the boat seats. With no shorelines and familiar landmarks to orient you, there's nothing to steer by but your instincts.

I fell into an easy, swinging rhythm in the scull, my ears and eyes tuned to the slightest change in the sound of my oars that would tell me I was getting too close to the banks or a shadow that would indicate the approach of another boat. The fog was so thick that I considered turning back, but the prospect of a long, straight stretch of river was too enticing.

Just shy of the tavern, I carefully turned the boat. Two rowers were downstream, engaged in a heated discussion about competing strategies for winning the idiosyncratic Oxbridge style of racing known as "bumps."

"Do you want to go ahead of me?" I called.

"Sure!" came the quick response. The pair shot past, never breaking their stroke.

The sound of their oars faded. I decided to row back to the boathouse and call it quits. It was a short workout, but the stiffness from my third consecutive night of little sleep had lessened.

The equipment put away, I locked the boathouse and walked slowly along the path toward town. It was so quiet in the early-morning mist that time and place receded. I closed my eyes, imagining that I was nowhere—not in Oxford, nor anywhere that had a name.

When I opened them, a dark outline had risen up in front of me. I gasped in fear. The shape shot toward me, and my hands instinctively warded off the danger.

"Diana, I'm so sorry. I thought you had seen me." It was Matthew Clairmont, his face creased with concern.

"I was walking with my eyes closed." I grabbed at the neck of my fleece, and he backed away slightly. I propped myself against a tree until my breathing slowed.

"Can you tell me something?" Clairmont asked once my heart stopped pounding.

"Not if you plan to ask why I'm out on the river in the fog when there are vampires and daemons and witches following me." I wasn't up for a lecture—not this morning.

"No"—his voice held a touch of acid—"although that's an excellent question. I was going to ask why you walk with your eyes closed."

I laughed. "What—you don't?"

Matthew shook his head. "Vampires have only five senses. We find it best to use all of them," he said sardonically.

"There's nothing magical about it, Matthew. It's a game I've played since I was a child. It made my aunt crazy. I was always coming home with bruised legs and scratches from running into bushes and trees."

The vampire looked thoughtful. He shoved his hands into his slate gray trouser pockets and gazed off into the fog. Today he was wearing a blue-gray sweater that made his hair appear darker, but no coat. It was a striking omission, given the weather. Suddenly feeling unkempt, I wished my rowing tights didn't have a hole in the back of the left thigh from catching on the boat's rigging.

"How was your row this morning?" Clairmont asked finally, as if he didn't already know. He wasn't out for a morning stroll.

"Good," I said shortly.

"There aren't many people here this early."

"No, but I like it when the river isn't crowded."

"Isn't it risky to row in this kind of weather, when so few people are out?" His tone was mild, and had he not been a vampire watching my every move, I might have taken his inquiry for an awkward attempt at conversation.

"Risky how?"

"If something were to happen, it's possible nobody would see it."

I'd never been afraid before on the river, but he had a point. Nevertheless, I shrugged it off. "The students will be here on Monday. I'm enjoying the peace while it lasts."

"Does term really start next week?" Clairmont sounded genuinely surprised.

"You *are* on the faculty, aren't you?" I laughed.

"Technically, but I don't really see students. I'm here in more of a research capacity." His mouth tightened. He didn't like being laughed at.

"Must be nice." I thought of my three-hundred-seat introductory lecture class and all those anxious freshmen.

"It's quiet. My laboratory equipment doesn't ask questions about my long hours. And I have Dr. Shephard and another assistant, Dr. Whitmore, so I'm not entirely alone."

It was damp, and I was cold. Besides, there was something unnatural about exchanging pleasantries with a vampire in the pea-soup gloom. "I really should go home."

"Would you like a ride?"

Four days ago I wouldn't have accepted a ride home from a vampire, but this morning it seemed like an excellent idea. Besides, it gave me an opportunity to ask why a biochemist might be interested in a seventeenth-century alchemical manuscript.

"Sure," I said.

Clairmont's shy, pleased look was utterly disarming. "My car's parked nearby," he said, gesturing in the direction of Christ Church College. We walked in silence for a few minutes, wrapped up in the gray fog and the strangeness of being alone, witch and vampire. He deliberately shortened his stride to keep in step with me, and he seemed more relaxed outdoors than he had in the library.

"Is this your college?"

"No, I've never been a member here." The way he phrased it made me wonder what colleges he *had* been a member of. Then I began to consider how long his life had been. Sometimes he seemed as old as Oxford itself.

"Diana?" Clairmont had stopped.

"Hmm?" I'd started to wander off toward the college's parking area.

"It's this way," he said, pointing in the opposite direction.

Matthew led me to a tiny walled enclave. A low-slung black Jaguar was parked under a bright yellow sign that proclaimed POSITIVELY NO PARKING HERE. The car had a John Radcliffe Hospital permit hanging from the rear-view mirror.

"I see," I said, putting my hands on my hips. "You park pretty much wherever you want."

"Normally I'm a good citizen when it comes to parking, but this morning's weather suggested that an exception might be made," Matthew said defensively. He reached a long arm around me to unlock the door. The Jaguar was an older model, without the latest technology of keyless entries and navigation systems, but it looked as if it had just rolled off the showroom floor. He pulled the door open, and I climbed in, the caramel-colored leather upholstery fitting itself to my body.

I'd never been in a car so luxurious. Sarah's worst suspicions about vampires would be confirmed if she knew they drove Jaguars while she drove a broken-down purple Honda Civic that had oxidized to the brownish lavender of roasted eggplant.

Clairmont rolled along the drive to the gates of Christ Church, where he waited for an opening in the early-morning traffic dominated by delivery trucks, buses, and bicycles. "Would you like some breakfast before I take you home?" he asked casually, gripping the polished steering wheel. "You must be hungry after all that exercise."

This was the second meal Clairmont had invited me to (not) share with him. Was this a vampire thing? Did they like to watch other people eat?

The combination of vampires and eating turned my mind to the vampire's dietary habits. Everyone on the planet knew that vampires fed on human blood. But was that all they ate? No longer sure that driving around in a car with a vampire was a good idea, I zipped up the neck of my fleece pullover and moved an inch closer to the door.

"Diana?" he prompted.

"I could eat," I admitted hesitantly, "and I'd kill for some tea."

He nodded, his eyes back on the traffic. "I know just the place."

Clairmont steered up the hill and took a right down the High Street. We passed the statue of George II's wife standing under the cupola at The Queen's College, then headed toward Oxford's botanical gardens. The hushed confines of the car made Oxford seem even more otherworldly than usual, its spires and towers appearing suddenly out of the quiet and fog.

We didn't talk, and his stillness made me realize how much I moved, constantly blinking, breathing, and rearranging myself. Not Clairmont. He never blinked and seldom breathed, and his every turn of the steering wheel or push of the pedals was as small and efficient as possible, as if his long life required him to conserve energy. I wondered again how old Matthew Clairmont was.

The vampire darted down a side street, pulling up in front of a tiny café that was packed with locals bolting down plates of food. Some were reading the newspaper; others were chatting with their neighbors at adjoining tables. All of them, I noted with pleasure, were drinking huge mugs of tea.

"I didn't know about this place," I said.

"It's a well-kept secret," he said mischievously. "They don't want university dons ruining the atmosphere."

I automatically turned to open my car door, but before I could touch the handle, Clairmont was there, opening it for me.

"How did you get here so fast?" I grumbled.

"Magic," he replied through pursed lips. Apparently Clairmont did not approve of women who opened their own car doors any more than he reportedly approved of women who argued with him.

"I am capable of opening my own door," I said, getting out of the car.

"Why do today's women think it's important to open a door themselves?" he said sharply. "Do you believe it's a testament to your physical power?"

"No, but it is a sign of our independence." I stood with my arms crossed, daring him to contradict me and remembering what Chris had said about

Clairmont's behavior toward a woman who'd asked too many questions at a conference.

Wordlessly he closed the car's door behind me and opened the café door. I stood resolutely in place, waiting for him to enter. A gust of warm, humid air carried the smell of bacon fat and toasted bread. My mouth started to water.

"You're impossibly old-fashioned," I said with a sigh, deciding not to fight it. He could open doors for me this morning so long as he was prepared to buy me a hot breakfast.

"After you," he murmured.

Once inside, we wended our way through the crowded tables. Clairmont's skin, which had looked almost normal in the fog, was conspicuously pale under the café's stark overhead lighting. A couple of humans stared as we passed. The vampire stiffened.

This wasn't a good idea, I thought uneasily as more human eyes studied us.

"Hiya, Matthew," a cheerful female voice called from behind the counter. "Two for breakfast?"

His face lightened. "Two, Mary. How's Dan?"

"Well enough to complain that he's fed up being in bed. I'd say he's definitely on the mend."

"That's wonderful news," Clairmont said. "Can you get this lady some tea when you have a chance? She's threatened to kill for it."

"Won't be necessary, dearie," Mary told me with a smile. "We serve tea without bloodshed." She eased her ample body out from behind the Formica counter and led us to a table tucked into the far corner next to the kitchen door. Two plastic-covered menus hit the table with a slap. "You'll be out of the way here, Matthew. I'll send Steph around with the tea. Stay as long as you like."

Clairmont made a point of settling me with my back to the wall. He sat opposite, between me and the rest of the room, curling the laminated menu into a tube and letting it gently unfurl in his fingers, visibly bristling. In the presence of others, the vampire was restless and prickly, just as he had been in the library. He was much more comfortable when the two of us were alone.

I recognized the significance of this behavior thanks to my new knowledge of the Norwegian wolf. He was protecting me.

"Just who do you think poses a threat, Matthew? I told you I could take care of myself." My voice came out a little more tartly than I had intended.

"Yes, I'm sure you can," he said doubtfully.

"Look," I said, trying to keep my tone even, "you've managed to keep . . . them away from me so I could get some work done." The tables were too close together for me to include any more details. "I'm grateful for that. But this café is full of humans. The only danger now would come from your drawing their attention. You're officially off duty."

Clairmont cocked his head in the direction of the cash register. "That man over there told his friend that you looked 'tasty.'" He was trying to make light of it, but his face darkened. I smothered a laugh.

"I don't think he's going to bite me," I said.

The vampire's skin took on a grayish hue.

"From what I understand of modern British slang, 'tasty' is a compliment, not a threat."

Clairmont continued to glower.

"If you don't like what you're hearing, stop listening in on other people's conversations," I offered, impatient with his male posturing.

"That's easier said than done," he pronounced, picking up a jar of Marmite.

A younger, slightly svelter version of Mary came up with an enormous brown stoneware teapot and two mugs. "Milk and sugar are on the table, Matthew," she said, eyeing me with curiosity.

Matthew made the necessary introductions. "Steph, this is Diana. She's visiting from America."

"Really? Do you live in California? I'm dying to get to California."

"No, I live in Connecticut," I said regretfully.

"That's one of the little states, isn't it?" Steph was clearly disappointed.

"Yes. And it snows."

"I fancy palm trees and sunshine, myself." At the mention of snow, she'd lost interest in me entirely. "What'll it be?"

"I'm really hungry," I said apologetically, ordering two scrambled eggs, four pieces of toast, and several rashers of bacon.

Steph, who had clearly heard far worse, wrote down the order without comment and picked up our menus. "Just tea for you, Matthew?"

He nodded.

Once Steph was out of earshot, I leaned across the table. "Do they know about you?"

Clairmont tilted forward, his face a foot away from mine. This morning he smelled sweeter, like a freshly picked carnation. I inhaled deeply.

"They know I'm a little different. Mary may suspect I'm more than a little different, but she's convinced that I saved Dan's life, so she's decided it doesn't matter."

"How did you save her husband?" Vampires were supposed to take human lives, not save them.

"I saw him on a rotation at the Radcliffe when they were short staffed. Mary had seen a program that described the symptoms of stroke, and she recognized them when her husband began to struggle. Without her he'd be dead or seriously incapacitated."

"But she thinks you saved Dan?" The vampire's spiciness was making me dizzy. I lifted the lid from the teapot, replacing the aroma of carnations with the tannic smell of black tea.

"Mary saved him the first time, but after he was admitted into hospital he had a terrible reaction to his medication. I told you she's observant. When she took her concerns to one of the physicians, he brushed them aside. I . . . overheard—and intervened."

"Do you often see patients?" I poured each of us a steaming mug of tea so strong you could stand a spoon up in it. My hands trembled slightly at the idea of a vampire prowling the wards at the John Radcliffe among the sick and injured.

"No," he said, toying with the sugar jar, "only when they have an emergency."

Pushing one of the mugs toward him, I fixed my eyes on the sugar. He handed it to me. I put precisely half a teaspoon of sugar and half a cup of milk into my tea. This was just how I liked it—black as tar, a hint of sugar to cut the edge off the bitterness, then enough milk to make it look less like stew. This done, I stirred the concoction clockwise. As soon as experience told me it wouldn't burn my tongue, I took a sip. Perfect.

The vampire was smiling.

"What?" I asked.

"I've never seen anyone approach tea with that much attentiveness to detail."

"You must not spend much time with serious tea drinkers. It's all about being able to gauge the strength before you put the sugar and milk in it." His steaming mug sat untouched in front of him. "You like yours black, I see."

"Tea's not really my drink," he said, his voicing dropping slightly.

"What *is* your drink?" The minute the question was out of my mouth, I wished I could call it back. His mood went from amusement to tight-lipped fury.

"You have to ask?" he said scathingly. "Even humans know the answer to that question."

"I'm sorry. I shouldn't have." I gripped the mug, trying to steady myself.

"No, you shouldn't."

I drank my tea in silence. We both looked up when Steph approached with a toast rack full of grilled bread and a plate heaped high with eggs and bacon.

"Mum thought you needed veg," Steph explained when my eyes widened at the mound of fried mushrooms and tomatoes that accompanied the breakfast. "She said you looked like death."

"Thank you!" I said. Mary's critique of my appearance did nothing to diminish my appreciation for the extra food.

Steph grinned and Clairmont offered me a small smile when I picked up the fork and applied myself to the plate.

Everything was piping hot and fragrant, with the perfect ratio of fried surface to melting, tender insides. My hunger appeased, I started a methodical attack on the toast rack, taking up the first triangle of cold toast and scraping butter over its surface. The vampire watched me eat with the same acute attention he'd devoted to watching me make my tea.

"So why science?" I ventured, tucking the toast into my mouth so he'd have to answer.

"Why history?" His voice was dismissive, but he wasn't going to fend me off that easily.

"You first."

"I suppose I need to know why I'm here," he said, looking fixedly at the table. He was building a moated castle from the sugar jar and a ring of blue artificial-sweetener packets.

I froze at the similarity between his explanation and what Agatha had told me the day before about Ashmole 782. "That's a question for philosophers, not scientists." I sucked a drop of butter off my finger to hide my confusion.

His eyes glittered with another wave of sudden anger. "You don't really believe that—that scientists don't care about why."

"They used to be interested in the whys," I conceded, keeping a wary eye on him. His sudden shifts in mood were downright frightening. "Now it seems all they're concerned with is the question of how—how does the body work, how do the planets move?"

Clairmont snorted. "Not the good scientists." The people behind him got up to leave, and he tensed, ready if they decided to rush the table.

"And you're a good scientist."

He let my assessment pass without comment.

"Someday you'll have to explain to me the relationship between neuroscience, DNA research, animal behavior, and evolution. They don't obviously fit together." I took another bite of toast.

Clairmont's left eyebrow rose toward his hairline. "You've been catching up on your scientific journals," he said sharply.

I shrugged. "You had an unfair advantage. You knew all about my work. I was just leveling the playing field."

He mumbled something under his breath that sounded French. "I've had a lot of time to think," he replied flatly in English, enlarging the moat around his castle with another ring of sweetener packets. "There's no connection between them."

"Liar," I said softly.

Not surprisingly, my accusation made Clairmont furious, but the speed of the transformation still took me aback. It was a reminder that I was having breakfast with a creature who could be lethal.

"Tell me what the connection is, then," he said through clenched teeth.

"I'm not sure," I said truthfully. "Something's holding them all together, a question that links your research interests and gives meaning to them. The only other explanation is that you're an intellectual magpie—which is ridiculous, given how highly regarded your work is—or maybe you get bored easily. You don't seem the type to be prone to intellectual ennui. Quite the opposite, in fact."

Clairmont studied me until the silence grew uncomfortable. My stomach was starting to complain at the amount of food I'd expected it to absorb. I poured fresh tea and doctored it while waiting for him to speak.

"For a witch you're observant, too." The vampire's eyes showed grudging admiration.

"Vampires aren't the only creatures who can hunt, Matthew."

"No. We all hunt something, don't we, Diana?" He lingered over my name. "Now it's my turn. Why history?"

"You haven't answered all my questions." And I hadn't yet asked him my most important question.

He shook his head firmly, and I redirected my energy from ferreting out information to protecting myself from Clairmont's attempts to obtain it.

"At first it was the neatness of it, I suppose." My voice sounded surprisingly tentative. "The past seemed so predictable, as if nothing that happened there was surprising."

"Spoken like someone who wasn't there," the vampire said drily.

I gave a short laugh. "I found that out soon enough. But in the beginning that's how it seemed. At Oxford the professors made the past a tidy story with a beginning, a middle, and an end. Everything seemed logical, inevitable. Their stories hooked me, and that was it. No other subject interested me. I became a historian and have never looked back."

"Even though you discovered that human beings—past or present—aren't logical?"

"History only became more challenging when it became less neat. Every time I pick up a book or a document from the past, I'm in a battle with people who lived hundreds of years ago. They have their secrets and obsessions—all the things they won't or can't reveal. It's my job to discover and explain them."

"What if you can't? What if they defy explanation?"

"That's never happened," I said after considering his question. "At least I don't think it has. All you have to do is be a good listener. Nobody really wants to keep secrets, not even the dead. People leave clues everywhere, and if you pay attention, you can piece them together."

"So you're the historian as detective," he observed.

"Yes. With far lower stakes." I sat back in my chair, thinking the interview was over.

"Why the history of science, then?" he continued.

"The challenge of great minds, I suppose?" I tried not to sound glib, nor to let my voice rise up at the end of the sentence into a question, and failed on both counts.

Clairmont bowed his head and slowly began to take apart his moated castle.

Common sense told me to remain silent, but the knotted threads of my own secrets began to loosen. "I wanted to know how humans came up with a view of the world that had so little magic in it," I added abruptly. "I needed to understand how they convinced themselves that magic wasn't important."

The vampire's cool gray eyes lifted to mine. "Have you found out?"

"Yes and no." I hesitated. "I saw the logic that they used, and the death of a thousand cuts as experimental scientists slowly chipped away at the belief that the world was an inexplicably powerful, magical place. Ultimately they failed, though. The magic never really went away. It waited, quietly, for people to return to it when they found the science wanting."

"So alchemy," he said.

"No," I protested. "Alchemy is one of the earliest forms of experimental science."

"Perhaps. But you don't believe that alchemy is devoid of magic." Matthew's voice was certain. "I've read your work. Not even you can keep it away entirely."

"Then it's science with magic. Or magic with science, if you prefer."

"Which do you prefer?"

"I'm not sure," I said defensively.

"Thank you." Clairmont's look suggested he knew how difficult it was for me to talk about this.

"You're welcome. I think." I pushed my hair back from my eyes, feeling a little shaky. "Can I ask you something else?" His eyes were wary, but he nodded. "Why are you interested in my work—in alchemy?"

He almost didn't answer, ready to brush the question aside, then reconsidered. I'd given him a secret. Now it was his turn.

"The alchemists wanted to know why we're here, too." Clairmont was telling the truth—I could see that—but it got me no closer to understanding his interest in Ashmole 782. He glanced at his watch. "If you're finished, I should get you back to college. You must want to get into warm clothes before you go to the library."

"What I need is a shower." I stood and stretched, twisting my neck in an effort to ease its chronic tightness. "And I *have* to go to yoga tonight. I'm spending too much time sitting at a desk."

The vampire's eyes glinted. "You practice yoga?"

"Couldn't live without it," I replied. "I love the movement, and the meditation."

"I'm not surprised," he said. "That's the way you row—a combination of movement and meditation."

My cheeks colored. He was watching me as closely on the river as he had in the library.

Clairmont put a twenty-pound note on the table and waved at Mary. She waved back, and he touched my elbow lightly, steering me between the tables and the few remaining customers.

"Whom do you take class with?" he asked after he opened the car door and settled me inside.

"I go to that studio on the High Street. I haven't found a teacher I like yet, but it's close, and beggars can't be choosers." New Haven had several yoga studios, but Oxford was lagging behind.

The vampire settled himself in the car, turned the key, and neatly reversed in a nearby driveway before heading back to town.

"You won't find the class you need there," he said confidently.

"You do yoga, too?" I was fascinated by the image of his massive body twisting itself through a practice.

"Some," he said. "If you want to go to yoga with me tomorrow, I could pick you up outside Hertford at six. This evening you'd have to brave the studio in town, but tomorrow you'd have a good practice."

"Where's your studio? I'll call and see if they have a class tonight."

Clairmont shook his head. "They aren't open tonight. Monday, Wednesday, Friday, and Sunday evenings only."

"Oh," I said, disappointed. "What's the class like?"

"You'll see. It's hard to describe." He was trying not to smile.

To my surprise, we'd arrived at the lodge. Fred craned his neck to see who was idling inside the gates, saw the Radcliffe tag, and strolled over to see what was going on.

Clairmont let me out of the car. Outside, I gave Fred a wave, and extended my hand. "I enjoyed breakfast. Thanks for the tea and company."

"Anytime," he said. "I'll see you in the library."

Fred whistled as Clairmont pulled away. "Nice car, Dr. Bishop. Friend of yours?" It was his job to know as much as possible about what happened in the college for safety's sake as well as to satisfy the unabashed curiosity that was part of a porter's job description.

"I suppose so," I said thoughtfully.

In my rooms I pulled out my passport case and removed a ten-dollar bill from my stash of American currency. It took me a few minutes to find an envelope. After slipping the bill inside without a note, I addressed it to Chris, wrote *"AIR MAIL"* on the front in capital letters, and stuck the required postage in the upper corner.

Chris was never going to let me forget he'd won this bet. Never.

Chapter 8

Honestly, that car is such a cliché." The hair clung to my fingers, crackling and snapping as I tried to push it from my face.

Clairmont was lounging against the side of his Jaguar looking unrumpled and at ease. Even his yoga clothes, characteristically gray and black, looked bandbox fresh, though considerably less tailored than what he wore to the library.

Contemplating the sleek black car and the elegant vampire, I felt unaccountably cross. It had not been a good day. The conveyor belt broke in the library, and it took forever for them to fetch my manuscripts. My keynote address remained elusive, and I was beginning to look at the calendar with alarm, imagining a roomful of colleagues peppering me with difficult questions. It was nearly October, and the conference was in November.

"You think a subcompact would be better subterfuge?" he asked, holding out his hand for my yoga mat.

"Not really, no." Standing in the fall twilight, he positively screamed vampire, yet the rising tide of undergraduates and dons passed him without a second glance. If they couldn't sense what he was—*see* what he was, standing in the open air—the car was immaterial. The irritation built under my skin.

"Have I done something wrong?" His gray-green eyes were wide and guileless. He opened the car door, taking a deep breath as I slid past.

My temper flared. "Are you smelling me?" After yesterday I suspected that my body was giving him all kinds of information I didn't want him to have.

"Don't tempt me," he murmured, shutting me inside. The hair on my neck rose slightly as the implication of his words sank in. He popped open the trunk and put my mat inside.

Night air filled the car as the vampire climbed in without any visible effort or moment of limb-bent awkwardness. His face creased into the semblance of a sympathetic frown. "Bad day?"

I gave him a withering glance. Clairmont knew exactly how my day had been. He and Miriam had been in Duke Humfrey's again, keeping the other creatures out of my immediate environment. When we left to change for yoga, Miriam had remained to make sure we weren't followed by a train of daemons—or worse.

Clairmont started the car and headed down the Woodstock Road without further attempts at small talk. There was nothing on it but houses.

"Where are we going?" I asked suspiciously.

"To yoga," he replied calmly. "Based on your mood, I'd say you need it."

"And where is yoga?" I demanded. We were headed out to the countryside in the direction of Blenheim.

"Have you changed your mind?" Matthew's voice was touched with exasperation. "Should I take you back to the studio on the High Street?"

I shuddered at the memory of last night's uninspiring class. "No."

"Then relax. I'm not kidnapping you. It can be pleasant to let someone else take charge. Besides, it's a surprise."

"Hmph," I said. He switched on the stereo system, and classical music poured from the speakers.

"Stop thinking and listen," he commanded. "It's impossible to be tense around Mozart."

Hardly recognizing myself, I settled in the seat with a sigh and shut my eyes. The Jaguar's motion was so subtle and the sounds from outside so muffled that I felt suspended above the ground, held up by invisible, musical hands.

The car slowed, and we pulled up to a set of high iron gates that even I, though practiced, couldn't have scaled. The walls on either side were warm red brick, with irregular forms and intricate woven patterns. I sat up a little straighter.

"You can't see it from here," Clairmont said, laughing. He rolled down his window and punched a series of numbers into a polished keypad. A tone sounded, and the gates swung open.

Gravel crunched under the tires as we passed through another set of gates even older than the first. There was no scrolled ironwork here, just an archway spanning brick walls that were much lower than the ones facing the Woodstock Road. The archway had a tiny room on top, with windows on all sides like a lantern. To the left of the gate was a splendid brick gatehouse, with twisted chimneys and leaded windows. A small brass plaque with weathered edges read THE OLD LODGE.

"Beautiful," I breathed.

"I thought you'd like it." The vampire looked pleased.

Through the growing darkness, we passed into a park. A small herd of deer skittered off at the sound of the car, jumping into the protective shadows as the Jaguar's headlights swept the grounds. We climbed a slight hill and rounded a curve in the drive. The car slowed to a crawl as we reached the top of the rise and the headlights dipped over into blackness.

"There," Clairmont said, pointing with his left hand.

A two-story Tudor manor house was arranged around a central courtyard. Its bricks glowed in the illumination of powerful spotlights that shone up through the branches of gnarled oak trees to light the face of the building.

I was so dumbfounded that I swore. Clairmont looked at me in shock, then chuckled.

He pulled the car in to the circular drive in front and parked behind a late-model Audi sports car. A dozen more cars were already parked there, and headlights continued to sweep down over the hill.

"Are you sure I'm going to be all right?" I'd been doing yoga for more than a decade, but that didn't mean I was any good at it. It had never occurred to me to ask whether this might be the kind of class where people balanced on one forearm with their feet suspended in midair.

"It's a mixed class," he assured me.

"Okay." My anxiety went up a notch in spite of his easy answer.

Clairmont took our yoga mats out of the trunk. Moving slowly as the last of the arrivals headed for the wide entry, he finally reached my door and put out his hand. *This is new,* I noted before putting my hand in his. I was still not entirely comfortable when our bodies came into contact. He was shockingly cold, and the contrast between our body temperatures took me aback.

The vampire held my hand lightly and tugged on it gently to help me out of the car. Before releasing me, he gave a soft encouraging squeeze. Surprised, I glanced at him and caught him doing the same thing. Both of us looked away in confusion.

We entered the house through another arched gate and a central courtyard. The manor was in an astonishing state of preservation. No later architects had been allowed to cut out symmetrical Georgian windows or affix fussy Victorian conservatories to it. We might have been stepping back in time.

"Unbelievable," I murmured.

Clairmont grinned and steered me through a big wooden door propped open with an iron doorstop. I gasped. The outside was remarkable, but the inside was stunning. Miles of linenfold paneling extended in every direction, all burnished and glowing. Someone had lit a fire in the room's enormous fireplace. A single trestle table and some benches looked about as old as the house, and electric lights were the only evidence that we were in the twenty-first century.

Rows of shoes sat in front of the benches, and mounds of sweaters and coats covered their dark oak surfaces. Clairmont laid his keys on the table and removed his shoes. I kicked off my own and followed him.

"Remember I said this was a mixed class?" the vampire asked when we reached a door set into the paneling. I looked up, nodded. "It is. But there's only one way to get into this room—you have to be one of us."

He pulled open the door. Dozens of curious eyes nudged, tingled, and froze in my direction. The room was full of daemons, witches, and vampires. They sat on brightly colored mats—some with crossed legs, others kneeling—waiting for class to begin. Some of the daemons had headphones jammed into their ears. The witches were gossiping in a steady hum. The vampires sat quietly, their faces displaying little emotion.

My jaw dropped.

"Sorry," Clairmont said. "I was afraid you wouldn't come if I told you—and it really is the best class in Oxford."

A tall witch who had short, jet-black hair and skin the color of coffee with cream walked toward us, and the rest of the room turned away, resuming their silent meditations. Clairmont, who'd tensed slightly when we entered, visibly relaxed as the witch approached us.

"Matthew." Her husky voice was brushed with an Indian accent. "Welcome."

"Amira." He nodded in greeting. "This is the woman I told you about, Diana Bishop."

The witch looked at me closely, her eyes taking in every detail of my face. She smiled. "Diana. Nice to meet you. Are you new to yoga?"

"No." My heart pounded with a fresh wave of anxiety. "But this is my first time here."

Her smile widened. "Welcome to the Old Lodge."

I wondered if anyone here knew about Ashmole 782, but there wasn't a single familiar face and the atmosphere in the room was open and easy, with none of the usual tension between creatures.

A warm, firm hand closed around my wrist, and my heart slowed immediately. I looked at Amira in astonishment. How had she done that?

She let loose my wrist, and my pulse remained steady. "I think that you and Diana will be most comfortable here," she told Clairmont. "Get settled and we'll begin."

We unrolled our mats in the back of the room, close to the door. There was no one to my immediate right, but across a small expanse of open floor two daemons sat in lotus position with their eyes closed. My shoulder tingled. I started, wondering who was looking at me. The feeling quickly disappeared.

Sorry, a guilty voice said quite distinctly within my skull.

The voice came from the front of the room, from the same direction as the tingle. Amira frowned slightly at someone in the first row before bringing the class to attention.

Out of sheer habit, my body folded obediently into a cross-legged position when she began to speak, and after a few seconds Clairmont followed suit.

"It's time to close your eyes." Amira picked up a tiny remote control, and the soft strains of a meditative chant came out of the walls and ceiling. It sounded medieval, and one of the vampires sighed happily.

My eyes wandered, distracted by the ornate plasterwork of what must once have been the house's great hall.

"Close your eyes," Amira suggested again gently. "It can be hard to let go of our worries, our preoccupations, our egos. That's why we're here tonight."

The words were familiar—I'd heard variations on this theme before, in other yoga classes—but they took on new meaning in this room.

"We're here tonight to learn to manage our energy. We spend our time striving and straining to be something that we're not. Let those desires go. Honor who you are."

Amira took us through some gentle stretches and got us onto our knees to warm up our spines before we pushed back into downward dog. We held the posture for a few breaths before walking our hands to our feet and standing up.

"Root your feet into the earth," she instructed, "and take mountain pose."

I concentrated on my feet and felt an unexpected jolt from the floor. My eyes widened.

We followed Amira as she began her *vinyasas.* We swung our arms up toward the ceiling before diving down to place our hands next to our feet. We rose halfway, spines parallel to the floor, before folding over and shooting our legs back into a pushup position. Dozens of daemons, vampires, and witches dipped and swooped their bodies into graceful, upward curves. We continued to fold and lift, sweeping our arms overhead once more before touching palms lightly together. Then Amira freed us to move at our own pace. She pushed a button on the stereo's remote, and a slow, melodic cover of Elton John's "Rocket Man" filled the room.

The music was oddly appropriate, and I repeated the familiar movements in time to it, breathing into my tight muscles and letting the flow of the class push all thoughts from my head. After we'd started the series of poses for a third time, the energy in the room shifted.

Three witches were floating about a foot off the wooden floorboards.

"Stay grounded," Amira said in a neutral voice.

Two quietly returned to the floor. The third had to swan-dive to get back down, and even then his hands reached the floor before his feet.

Both the daemons and the vampires were having trouble with the pacing. Some of the daemons were moving so slowly that I wondered if they were stuck. The vampires were having the opposite problem, their powerful muscles coiling and then springing with sudden intensity.

"Gently," Amira murmured. "There's no need to push, no need to strain."

Gradually the room's energy settled again. Amira moved us through a series of standing poses. Here the vampires were clearly at their best, able to sustain them for minutes without effort. Soon I was no longer concerned with who was in the room with me or whether I could keep up with the class. There was only the moment and the movement.

By the time we took to the floor for back bends and inversions, everyone in the room was dripping wet—except for the vampires, who didn't even look dewy. Some performed death-defying arm balances and handstands, but I wasn't among them. Clairmont was, however. At one point he looked to be attached to the ground by nothing more than his ear, his entire body in perfect alignment above him.

The hardest part of any practice for me was the final corpse pose—*savasana*. I found it nearly impossible to lie flat on my back without moving. The fact that everyone else seemed to find it relaxing only added to my anxiety. I lay as quietly as possible, eyes closed, trying not to twitch. A swoosh of feet moved between me and the vampire.

"Diana," Amira whispered, "this pose is not for you. Roll over onto your side."

My eyes popped open. I stared into the witch's wide black eyes, mortified that she had somehow uncovered my secret.

"Curl into a ball." Mystified, I did what she said. My body instantly relaxed. She patted me lightly on the shoulder. "Keep your eyes open, too."

I had turned toward Clairmont. Amira lowered the lights, but the glow of his luminous skin allowed me to see his features clearly.

In profile he looked like a medieval knight lying atop a tomb in Westminster Abbey: long legs, long torso, long arms, and a remarkably strong face. There was something ancient about his looks, even though he appeared to be only a few years older than I was. I mentally traced the line of his forehead with an imaginary finger, from where it started at his uneven hairline up slightly over his prominent brow bone with its thick, black brows. My imaginary finger crested the tip of his nose and the bowing of his lips.

I counted as he breathed. At two hundred his chest lifted. He didn't exhale for a long, long time afterward.

Finally Amira told the class it was time to rejoin the world outside. Matthew turned toward me and opened his eyes. His face softened, and my own did the same. There was movement all around us, but the socially correct had no pull on me. I stayed where I was, staring into a vampire's eyes. Matthew waited, utterly still, watching me watch him. When I sat up, the room spun at the sudden movement of blood through my body.

At last the room stopped its dizzying revolutions. Amira closed the practice with chant and rang some tiny silver bells that were attached to her fingers. Class was over.

There were gentle murmurs throughout the room as vampire greeted vampire and witch greeted witch. The daemons were more ebullient, arranging for midnight meetings at clubs around Oxford, asking where the best jazz could be found. They were following the energy, I realized with a smile, thinking back to Agatha's description of what tugged at a daemon's soul. Two investment bankers from London—both vampires—were talking about a spate of unsolved London murders. I thought of Westminster and felt a flicker of unease. Matthew scowled at them, and they began arranging lunch tomorrow instead.

Everyone had to file by us as they left. The witches nodded at us curiously. Even the daemons made eye contact, grinning and exchanging meaningful glances. The vampires studiously avoided me, but every one of them said hello to Clairmont.

Finally only Amira, Matthew, and I remained. She gathered up her mat and padded toward us. "Good practice, Diana," she said.

"Thank you, Amira. This was a class I'll never forget."

"You're welcome anytime. With or without Matthew," she added, tapping him lightly on the shoulder. "You should have warned her."

"I was afraid Diana wouldn't come. And I thought she'd like it, if she gave it a chance." He looked at me shyly.

"Turn out the lights, will you, when you leave?" Amira called over her shoulder, already halfway out of the room.

My eyes traveled around the perfect jewel of a great hall. "This was certainly a surprise," I said drily, not yet ready to let him off the hook.

He came up behind me, swift and soundless. "A pleasant one, I hope. You did like the class?"

I nodded slowly and turned to reply. He was disconcertingly close, and the difference in our heights meant that I had to lift my eyes so as not to be staring straight into his sternum. "I did."

Matthew's face split into his heart-stopping smile. "I'm glad." It was difficult to pull free from the undertow of his eyes. To break their spell, I bent down and began rolling up my mat. Matthew turned off the lights and grabbed his own gear. We slid our shoes on in the gallery, where the fire had burned down to embers.

He picked up his keys. "Can I interest you in some tea before we head back to Oxford?"

"Where?"

"We'll go to the gatehouse," Matthew said matter-of-factly.

"There's a café there?"

"No, but there's a kitchen. A place to sit down, too. I can make tea," he teased.

"Matthew," I said, shocked, "is this your house?"

By that time we were standing in the doorway, looking out into the courtyard. I saw the keystone over the house's gate: 1536.

"I built it," he said, watching me closely.

Matthew Clairmont was at least five hundred years old.

"The spoils of the Reformation," he continued. "Henry gave me the land, on the condition that I tear down the abbey that was here and start over. I saved what I could, but it was difficult to get away with much. The king was in a foul mood that year. There's an angel here and there, and some stonework I couldn't bear to destroy. Other than that, it's all new construction."

"I've never heard anyone describe a house built in the early sixteenth century as 'new construction' before." I tried to see the house not only through Matthew's eyes but as a part of him. This was the house he had wanted to live in nearly five hundred years ago. In seeing it I knew him better. It was quiet and still, just as he was. More than that, it was solid and true. There was nothing unnecessary—no extra ornamentation, no distractions.

"It's beautiful," I said simply.

"It's too big to live in now," he replied, "not to mention too fragile. Every time I open a window, something seems to fall off it, despite careful maintenance. I let Amira live in some of the rooms and open the house to her students a few times a week."

"You live in the gatehouse?" I asked as we walked across the open expanse of cobbles and brick to the car.

"Part of the time. I live in Oxford during the week but come here on the weekends. It's quieter."

I thought that it must be challenging for a vampire to live surrounded by noisy undergraduates whose conversations he couldn't help overhearing.

We got back into the car and drove the short distance to the gatehouse. As the manor's onetime public face, it had slightly more frills and embellishments than the main house. I studied the twisted chimneys and the elaborate patterns in the brick.

Matthew groaned. "I know. The chimneys were a mistake. The stonemason was dying to try his hand at them. His cousin worked for Wolsey at Hampton Court, and the man simply wouldn't take no for an answer."

He flipped a light switch near the door, and the gatehouse's main room was bathed in a golden glow. It had serviceable flagstone floors and a big stone fireplace suitable for roasting an ox.

"Are you cold?" Matthew asked as he went to the part of the space that had been turned into a sleek, modern kitchen. It was dominated by a refrigerator rather than a stove. I tried not to think about what he might keep in it.

"A little bit." I drew my sweater closer. It was still relatively warm in Oxford, but my drying perspiration made the night air feel chilly.

"Light the fire, then," Matthew suggested. It was already laid, and I set it alight with a long match drawn from an antique pewter tankard.

Matthew put the kettle on, and I walked around the room, taking in the elements of his taste. It ran heavily toward brown leather and dark polished wood, which stood out handsomely against the flagstones. An old carpet in warm shades of red, blue, and ocher provided jolts of color. Over the mantel there was an enormous portrait of a dark-haired, late-seventeenth-century beauty in a yellow gown. It had certainly been painted by Sir Peter Lely.

Matthew noticed my interest. "My sister Louisa," he said, coming around the counter with a fully outfitted tea tray. He looked up at the canvas, his face touched with sadness. "*Dieu,* she was beautiful."

"What happened to her?"

"She went to Barbados, intent on making herself queen of the Indies. We tried to tell her that her taste for young gentlemen was not likely to go unnoticed on a small island, but she wouldn't listen. Louisa loved plantation life. She invested in sugar—and slaves." A shadow flitted across his face. "During one of the island's rebellions, her fellow plantation owners, who had figured out what she was, decided to get rid of her. They sliced off Louisa's head and cut her body into pieces. Then they burned her and blamed it on the slaves."

"I'm so sorry," I said, knowing that words were inadequate in the face of such a loss.

He mustered a small smile. "The death was only as terrible as the woman who suffered it. I loved my sister, but she didn't make that easy. She absorbed every vice of every age she lived through. If there was excess to be had, Louisa found it." Matthew shook himself free from his sister's cold, beautiful face with difficulty. "Will you pour?" he asked. He put the tray on a low, polished oak table in front of the fireplace between two overstuffed leather sofas.

I agreed, happy to lighten the mood even though I had enough questions to fill more than one evening of conversation. Louisa's huge black eyes watched me, and I made sure not to spill a drop of liquid on the shining wooden surface of the table just in case it had once been hers. Matthew had remembered the big jug of milk and the sugar, and I doctored my tea until it was precisely the right color before sinking back into the cushions with a sigh.

Matthew held his mug politely without once lifting it to his lips.

"You don't have to for my sake, you know," I said, glancing at the cup.

"I know." He shrugged. "It's a habit, and comforting to go through the motions."

"When did you start practicing yoga?" I asked, changing the subject.

"The same time that Louisa went to Barbados. I went to the other Indies—the East Indies—and found myself in Goa during the monsoons.

There wasn't a lot to do but drink too much and learn about India. The yogis were different then, more spiritual than most teachers today. I met Amira a few years ago when I was speaking at a conference in Mumbai. As soon as I heard her lead a class, it was clear to me that she had the gifts of the old yogis, and she didn't share the concerns some witches have about fraternizing with vampires." There was a touch of bitterness in his voice.

"You invited her to come to England?"

"I explained what might be possible here, and she agreed to give it a try. It's been almost ten years now, and the class is full to capacity every week. Of course, Amira teaches private classes, too, mainly to humans."

"I'm not used to seeing witches, vampires, and daemons sharing anything—never mind a yoga class," I confessed. The taboos against mixing with other creatures were strong. "If you'd told me it was possible, I wouldn't have believed you."

"Amira is an optimist, and she loves a challenge. It wasn't easy at first. The vampires refused to be in the same room with the daemons during the early days, and of course no one trusted the witches when they started showing up." His voice betrayed his own ingrained prejudices. "Now most in the room accept we're more similar than different and treat one another with courtesy."

"We may look similar," I said, taking a gulp of tea and drawing my knees toward my chest, "but we certainly don't feel similar."

"What do you mean?" Matthew said, looking at me attentively.

"The way we know that someone is one of us—a creature," I replied, confused. "The nudges, the tingles, the cold."

Matthew shook his head. "No, I don't know. I'm not a witch."

"You can't feel it when I look at you?" I asked.

"No. Can you?" His eyes were guileless and caused the familiar reaction on my skin.

I nodded.

"Tell me what it feels like." He leaned forward. Everything seemed perfectly ordinary, but I felt that a trap was being set.

"It feels . . . cold," I said slowly, unsure how much to divulge, "like ice growing under my skin."

"That sounds unpleasant." His forehead creased slightly.

"It's not," I replied truthfully. "Just a little strange. The daemons are the worst—when they stare at me, it's like being kissed." I made a face.

Matthew laughed and put his tea down on the table. He rested his elbows on his knees and kept his body angled toward mine. "So you do use some of your witch's power."

The trap snapped shut.

I looked at the floor, furious, my cheeks flushing. "I wish I'd never opened Ashmole 782 or taken that damn journal off the shelf! That was only the fifth time I've used magic this year, and the washing machine shouldn't count, because if I hadn't used a spell the water would have caused a flood and wrecked the apartment downstairs."

Both his hands came up in a gesture of surrender. "Diana, I don't care if you use magic or not. But I'm surprised at how much you do."

"I don't use magic or power or witchcraft or whatever you want to call it. It's not who I am." Two red patches burned on my cheeks.

"It is who you are. It's in your blood. It's in your bones. You were born a witch, just as you were born to have blond hair and blue eyes."

I'd never been able to explain to anyone my reasons for avoiding magic. Sarah and Em had never understood. Matthew wouldn't either. My tea grew cold, and my body remained in a tight ball as I struggled to avoid his scrutiny.

"I don't want it," I finally said through gritted teeth, "and never asked for it."

"What's wrong with it? You were glad of Amira's power of empathy tonight. That's a large part of her magic. It's no better or worse to have the talents of a witch than it is to have the talent to make music or to write poetry—it's just different."

"I don't want to be different," I said fiercely. "I want a simple, ordinary life . . . like humans enjoy." *One that doesn't involve death and danger and the fear of being discovered,* I thought, my mouth closed tight against the words. "You must wish you were normal."

"I can tell you as a scientist, Diana, that there's no such thing as 'normal.'" His voice was losing its careful softness. "'Normal' is a bedtime story—a fable—that humans tell themselves to feel better when faced with overwhelming evidence that most of what's happening around them is not 'normal' at all."

Nothing he said would shake my conviction that it was dangerous to be a creature in a world dominated by humans.

"Diana, look at me."

Against my instincts I did.

"You're trying to push your magic aside, just as you believe your scientists did hundreds of years ago. The problem is," he continued quietly, "it didn't work. Not even the humans among them could push the magic out of their world entirely. You said so yourself. It kept returning."

"This is different," I whispered. "This is my life. I can control my life."

"It isn't different." His voice was calm and sure. "You can try to keep the magic away, but it won't work, any more than it worked for Robert Hooke or Isaac Newton. They both knew there was no such thing as a world without magic. Hooke was brilliant, with his ability to think through scientific problems in three dimensions and construct instruments and experiments. But he never reached his full potential because he was so fearful of the mysteries of nature. Newton? He had the most fearless intellect I've ever known. Newton wasn't afraid of what couldn't be seen and easily explained—he embraced it all. As a historian you know that it was alchemy and his belief in invisible, powerful forces of growth and change that led him to the theory of gravity."

"Then I'm Robert Hooke in this story," I said. "I don't need to be a legend like Newton." *Like my mother.*

"Hooke's fears made him bitter and envious," Matthew warned. "He spent his life looking over his shoulder and designing other people's experiments. It's no way to live."

"I'm not having magic involved in my work," I said stubbornly.

"You're no Hooke, Diana," Matthew said roughly. "He was only a human, and he ruined his life trying to resist the lure of magic. You're a witch. If you do the same, it will destroy you."

Fear began to worm its way into my thoughts, pulling me away from Matthew Clairmont. He was alluring, and he made it seem as if you could be a creature without any worries or repercussions. But he was a vampire and couldn't be trusted. And he was wrong about the magic. He had to be. If not, then my whole life had been a fruitless struggle against an imaginary enemy.

And it was my own fault I was afraid. I'd let magic into my life—against my own rules—and a vampire had crept in with it. Dozens of creatures had followed. Remembering the way that magic had contributed to the loss of my parents, I felt the beginnings of panic in shallow breath and prickling skin.

"Living without magic is the only way I know to survive, Matthew." I breathed slowly so that the feelings wouldn't take root, but it was difficult with the ghosts of my mother and father in the room.

"You're living a lie—and an unconvincing one at that. You think you pass as a human." Matthew's tone was matter-of-fact, almost clinical. "You don't fool anyone except yourself. I've seen them watching you. They know you're different."

"That's nonsense."

"Every time you look at Sean, you reduce him to speechlessness."

"He had a crush on me when I was a graduate student," I said dismissively.

"Sean still has a crush on you—that's not the point. Is Mr. Johnson one of your admirers, too? He's nearly as bad as Sean, trembling at your slightest change of mood and worrying because you might have to sit in a different seat. And it's not just the humans. You frightened Dom Berno nearly to death when you turned and glared at him."

"That monk in the library?" My tone was disbelieving. "*You* frightened him, not *me*!"

"I've known Dom Berno since 1718," Matthew said drily. "He knows me far too well to fear me. We met at the Duke of Chandos's house party, where he was singing the role of Damon in Handel's *Acis and Galatea*. I assure you, it was your power and not mine that startled him."

"This is a human world, Matthew, not a fairy tale. Humans outnumber and fear us. And there's nothing more powerful than human fear—not magic, not vampire strength. Nothing."

"Fear and denial are what humans do best, Diana, but it's not a way that's open to a witch."

"I'm not afraid."

"Yes you are," he said softly, rising to his feet. "And I think it's time I took you home."

"Look," I said, my need for information about the manuscript pushing all other thoughts aside, "we're both interested in Ashmole 782. A vampire and a witch can't be friends, but we should be able to work together."

"I'm not so sure," Matthew said impassively.

The ride back to Oxford was quiet. Humans had it all wrong when it came to vampires, I reflected. To make them frightening, humans imagined vampires as bloodthirsty. But it was Matthew's remoteness, combined with his flashes of anger and abrupt mood swings, that scared me.

When we arrived at the New College lodge, Matthew retrieved my mat from the trunk.

"Have a good weekend," he said without emotion.

"Good night, Matthew. Thank you for taking me to yoga." My voice was as devoid of expression as his, and I resolutely refused to look back, even though his cold eyes watched me walk away.

Chapter 9

Matthew crossed the river Avon, driving over the bridge's high, arched spans. He found the familiar Lanarkshire landscape of craggy hills, dark sky, and stark contrasts soothing. Little about this part of Scotland was soft or inviting, and its forbidding beauty suited his present mood. He downshifted through the lime alley that had once led to a palace and now led nowhere, an odd remnant of a grand life no one wanted to live anymore. Pulling up to what had been the back entrance of an old hunting lodge, where rough brown stone stood in sharp contrast to the creamy stuccoed front, he climbed out of his Jaguar and lifted his bags from the trunk.

The lodge's welcoming white door opened. "You look like hell." A wiry daemon with dark hair, twinkling brown eyes, and a hooked nose stood with his hand on the latch and inspected his best friend from head to foot.

Hamish Osborne had met Matthew Clairmont at Oxford nearly twenty years ago. Like most creatures, they'd been taught to fear each other and were uncertain how to behave. The two became inseparable once they'd realized they shared a similar sense of humor and the same passion for ideas.

Matthew's face registered anger and resignation in quick succession. "Nice to see you, too," he said gruffly, dropping his bags by the door. He drank in the house's cold, clear smell, with its nuances of old plaster and aging wood, and Hamish's unique aroma of lavender and peppermint. The vampire was desperate to get the smell of witch out of his nose.

Jordan, Hamish's human butler, appeared silently and brought with him the scent of lemon furniture polish and starch. It didn't drive Diana's honeysuckle and horehound entirely from Matthew's nostrils, but it helped.

"Good to see you, sir," he said before heading for the stairs with Matthew's bags. Jordan was a butler of the old school. Even had he not been paid handsomely to keep his employer's secrets, he would never divulge to a soul that Osborne was a daemon or that he sometimes entertained vampires. It would be as unthinkable as letting slip that he was occasionally asked to serve peanut butter and banana sandwiches at breakfast.

"Thank you, Jordan." Matthew surveyed the downstairs hall so that he wouldn't have to meet Hamish's eyes. "You've picked up a new Hamilton, I see." He stared raptly at the unfamiliar landscape on the far wall.

"You don't usually notice my new acquisitions." Like Matthew's, Hamish's accent was mostly Oxbridge with a touch of something else. In his case it was the burr of Glasgow's streets.

"Speaking of new acquisitions, how is Sweet William?" William was Hamish's new lover, a human so adorable and easygoing that Matthew had nicknamed him after a spring flower. It stuck. Now Hamish used it as an endearment, and William had started bothering florists in the city for pots of it to give to friends.

"Grumpy," Hamish said with a chuckle. "I'd promised him a quiet weekend at home."

"You didn't have to come, you know. I didn't expect it." Matthew sounded grumpy, too.

"Yes, I know. But it's been awhile since we've seen each other, and Cadzow is beautiful this time of year."

Matthew glowered at Hamish, disbelief evident on his face.

"Christ, you do need to go hunting, don't you?" was all Hamish could say.

"Badly," the vampire replied, his voice clipped.

"Do we have time for a drink first, or do you need to get straight to it?"

"I believe I can manage a drink," Matthew said in a withering tone.

"Excellent. I've got a bottle of wine for you and some whiskey for me." Hamish had asked Jordan to pull some of the good wine out of the cellar shortly after he'd received Matthew's dawn call. He hated to drink alone, and Matthew refused to touch whiskey. "Then you can tell me why you have such an urgent need to go hunting this fine September weekend."

Hamish led the way across the gleaming floors and upstairs to his library. The warm brown paneling had been added in the nineteenth century, ruining the architect's original intention to provide an airy, spacious place for eighteenth-century ladies to wait while their husbands busied themselves with sport. The original white ceiling remained, festooned with plaster garlands and busy angels, a constant reproach to modernity.

The two men settled into the leather chairs that flanked the fireplace, where a cheerful blaze was already taking the edge off the autumn chill. Hamish showed Matthew the bottle of wine, and the vampire made an appreciative sound. "That will do nicely."

"I should think so. The gentlemen at Berry Brothers and Rudd assured me it was excellent." Hamish poured the wine and pulled the stopper from his decanter. Glasses in hand, the two men sat in companionable silence.

"I'm sorry to drag you into all this," Matthew began. "I'm in a difficult situation. It's . . . complicated."

Hamish chuckled. "It always is, with you."

Matthew had been drawn to Hamish Osborne in part because of his directness and in part because, unlike most daemons, he was levelheaded and difficult to unsettle. Over the years a number of the vampire's friends had been daemons, gifted and cursed in equal measure. Hamish was far more comfortable to be around. There were no blazing arguments, bursts of wild activity, or dangerous depressions. Time with Hamish consisted of long stretches of silence, followed by blindingly sharp conversation, all colored by his serene approach to life.

Hamish's differences extended to his work, which was not in the usual daemonic pursuits of art or music. Instead he had a gift for money—for making it and for spotting fatal weaknesses in international financial instruments and markets. He took a daemon's characteristic creativity and applied it to spreadsheets rather than sonatas, understanding the intricacies of currency exchange with such remarkable precision that he was consulted by presidents, monarchs, and prime ministers.

The daemon's uncommon predilection for the economy fascinated Matthew, as did his ease among humans. Hamish loved being around them and found their faults stimulating rather than aggravating. It was a legacy of his childhood, with an insurance broker for a father and a housewife as a mother. Having met the unflappable Osbornes, Matthew could understand Hamish's fondness.

The crackling of the fire and the smooth smell of whiskey in the air began to do their work, and the vampire found himself relaxing. Matthew sat forward, holding his wineglass lightly between his fingers, the red liquid winking in the firelight.

"I don't know where to begin," he said shakily.

"At the end, of course. Why did you pick up the phone and call me?"

"I needed to get away from a witch."

Hamish watched his friend for a moment, noting Matthew's obvious agitation. Somehow Hamish was certain the witch wasn't male.

"What makes this witch so special?" he asked quietly.

Matthew looked up from under his heavy brows. "Everything."

"Oh. You are in trouble, aren't you?" Hamish's burr deepened in sympathy and amusement.

Matthew laughed unpleasantly. "You could say that, yes."

"Does this witch have a name?"

"Diana. She's a historian. And American."

"The goddess of the hunt," Hamish said slowly. "Apart from her ancient name, is she an ordinary witch?"

"No," Matthew said abruptly. "She is far from ordinary."

"Ah. The complications." Hamish studied his friend's face for signs that he was calming down but saw that Matthew was spoiling for a fight instead.

"She's a Bishop." Matthew waited. He'd learned it was never a good idea to anticipate that the daemon wouldn't grasp the significance of a reference, no matter how obscure.

Hamish sifted and sorted through his mind and found what he was seeking. "As in Salem, Massachusetts?"

Matthew nodded grimly. "She's the last of the Bishop witches. Her father is a Proctor."

The daemon whistled softly. "A witch twice over, with a distinguished magical lineage. You never do things by half, do you? She must be powerful."

"Her mother is. I don't know much about her father. Rebecca Bishop, though—that's a different story. She was doing spells at thirteen that most witches can't manage after a lifetime of study and experience. And her childhood abilities as a seer were astonishing."

"Do you know her, Matt?" Hamish had to ask. Matthew had lived many lives and crossed paths with too many people for his friend to keep track of them all.

Matthew shook his head. "No. There's always talk about her, though—and plenty of envy. You know how witches are," he said, his voice taking on the slightly unpleasant tone it did whenever he referred to the species.

Hamish let the remark about witches pass and eyed Matthew over the rim of his glass.

"And Diana?"

"She claims she doesn't use magic."

There were two threads in that brief sentence that needed pulling. Hamish tugged on the easier one first. "What, not for anything? Finding a lost earring? Coloring her hair?" Hamish sounded doubtful.

"She's not the earrings and colored hair type. She's more the three-mile run followed by an hour on the river in a dangerously tiny boat type."

"With her background I find it difficult to believe she never uses her power." Hamish was a pragmatist as well as a dreamer. It was why he was so good with other people's money. "And you don't believe it either, or you wouldn't suggest that she's lying." There was the second thread pulled.

"She says she uses magic only occasionally—for little things." Matthew hesitated, raked his fingers through his hair so half of it stood on end, and took a gulp of wine. "I've been watching her, though, and she's using it more than that. I can smell it," he said, his voice frank and open for the first time since his arrival. "The scent is like an electrical storm about to break, or summer lightning. There are times when I can see it, too. Diana shimmers when she's angry or lost in her work." *And when she's asleep,* he thought, frowning. "Christ, there are times when I think I can even taste it."

"She shimmers?"

"It's nothing you would see, though you might sense the energy some other way. The *chatoiement*—her witch's shimmer—is very faint. Even when I was a young vampire, only the most powerful witches emitted these tiny pulses of light. It's rare to see it today. Diana's unaware she's doing it, and she's oblivious to its significance." Matthew shuddered and balled up his fist.

The daemon glanced at his watch. The day was young, but he already knew why his friend was in Scotland.

Matthew Clairmont was falling in love.

Jordan came in, his timing impeccable. "The gillie dropped off the Jeep, sir. I told him you wouldn't need his services today." The butler knew there was little need for a guide to track down deer when you had a vampire in the house.

"Excellent," Hamish said, rising to his feet and draining his glass. He sorely wanted more whiskey, but it was better to keep his wits about him.

Matthew looked up. "I'll go out by myself, Hamish. I'd rather hunt alone." The vampire didn't like hunting with warmbloods, a category that included humans, daemons, and witches. He usually made an exception for Hamish, but today he wanted to be on his own while he got his craving for Diana Bishop under control.

"Oh, we're not going hunting," Hamish said with a wicked glint in his eye. "We're going stalking." The daemon had a plan. It involved occupying his friend's mind until he let down his guard and willingly shared what was going on in Oxford rather than requiring Hamish to drag it out of him. "Come on, it's a beautiful day. You'll have fun."

Outside, Matthew grimly climbed into Hamish's beat-up Jeep. It was what the two of them preferred to roam around in when they were at Cadzow, even though a Land Rover was the vehicle of choice in grand Scottish hunting lodges. Matthew didn't mind that it was freezing to drive in, and Hamish found its hypermasculinity amusing.

In the hills Hamish ground the Jeep's gears—the vampire cringed at the sound each time—as he climbed to where the deer grazed. Matthew spotted a pair of stags on the next crag and told Hamish to stop. He got out of the Jeep quietly and crouched by the front tire, already mesmerized.

Hamish smiled and joined him.

The daemon had stalked deer with Matthew before and understood what he needed. The vampire did not always feed, though today Hamish was certain that, left to his own devices, Matthew would have come home sated after dark—and there would be two fewer stags on the estate. His friend was as much predator as carnivore. It was the hunt that defined vampires' identity, not their feeding or what they fed upon. Sometimes, when Matthew was restless, he just went out and tracked whatever he could chase without making a kill.

While the vampire watched the deer, the daemon watched Matthew. There was trouble in Oxford. He could feel it.

Matthew sat patiently for the next several hours, considering whether the stags were worth pursuing. Through his extraordinary senses of smell, sight, and hearing, he tracked their movements, figured out their habits, and gauged their every response to a cracking twig or a bird in flight. The vampire's attention was avid, but he never showed impatience. For Matthew the crucial moment came when his prey acknowledged that it was beaten and surrendered.

The light was dimming when he finally rose and nodded to Hamish. It was enough for the first day, and though he didn't need the light to see the deer, he knew that Hamish needed it to get back down the mountain.

By the time they reached the lodge, it was pitch black, and Jordan had turned on every lamp, which made the building look even more ridiculous, sitting on a rise in the middle of nowhere.

"This lodge never did make any sense," Matthew said in a conversational tone that was nevertheless intended to sting. "Robert Adam was insane to take the commission."

"You've shared your thoughts on my little extravagance many times, Matthew," Hamish said serenely, "and I don't care if you understand the principles of architectural design better than I do or whether you believe that Adam was a madman to construct—what do you always call it?—an 'ill-conceived folly' in the Lanarkshire wilderness. I love it, and nothing you say is going to change that." They'd had versions of this conversation regularly since Hamish's announcement he'd purchased the lodge—complete with all its furnishings, the gillie, and Jordan—from an aristocrat who had no use for the building and no money to repair it. Matthew had been horrified. To Hamish, however, Cadzow Lodge was a sign he had risen so far above his Glasgow roots that he could spend money on something impractical that he could love for its own sake.

"Hmph," Matthew said with a scowl.

Grumpiness was preferable to agitation, Hamish thought. He moved on to the next step of his plan.

"Dinner's at eight," he said, "in the dining room."

Matthew hated the dining room, which was grand, high-ceilinged, and drafty. More important, it upset the vampire because it was gaudy and feminine. It was Hamish's favorite room.

Matthew groaned. "I'm not hungry."

"You're famished," Hamish said sharply, taking in the color and texture of Matthew's skin. "When was your last real meal?"

"Weeks ago." Matthew shrugged with his usual disregard for the passage of time. "I can't remember."

"Tonight you're having wine and soup. Tomorrow—it's up to you what you eat. Do you want some time alone before dinner, or will you risk playing billiards with me?" Hamish was extremely good at billiards and even better at snooker, which he had learned to play as a teenager. He'd made his first money in Glasgow's billiards halls and could beat almost anyone. Matthew refused to play snooker with him anymore on the grounds that it was no fun to lose every time, even to a friend. The vampire had tried to teach him carambole instead, the old French game involving balls and cues, but Matthew always won those games. Billiards was the sensible compromise.

Unable to resist a battle of any sort, Matthew agreed. "I'll change and join you."

Hamish's felt-covered billiards table was in a room opposite the library. He was there in a sweater and trousers when Matthew arrived in a white shirt and jeans. The vampire avoided wearing white, which made him look startling and ghostly, but it was the only decent shirt he had with him. He'd packed for a hunting trip, not a dinner party.

He picked up his cue and stood at the end of the table. "Ready?"

Hamish nodded. "Let's say an hour of play, shall we? Then we'll go down for a drink."

The two men bent over their cues. "Be gentle with me, Matthew," Hamish murmured just before they struck the balls. The vampire snorted as they shot to the far end, hit the cushion, and rebounded.

"I'll take the white," said Matthew when the balls stopped rolling and his was closest. He palmed the other and tossed it to Hamish. The daemon put a red ball on its mark and stood back.

As in hunting, Matthew was in no rush to score points. He shot fifteen hazards in a row, putting the red ball in a different pocket each time. "If you don't mind," he drawled, pointing to the table. The daemon put his yellow ball on it without comment.

Matthew mixed up simple shots that took the red ball into the pockets with trickier shots known as cannons that were not his forte. Cannons involved hitting both Hamish's yellow ball and the red ball with one strike of the cue, and they required not only strength but finesse.

"Where did you find the witch?" Hamish asked casually after Matthew cannoned the yellow and red balls.

Matthew retrieved the white ball and prepared for his next shot. "The Bodleian."

The daemon's eyebrows rose in surprise. "The Bodleian? Since when have you been a regular at the library?"

Matthew fouled, his white ball hopping over the cushion and onto the floor. "Since I was at a concert and overheard two witches talking about an American who'd got her hands on a long-lost manuscript," he said. "I couldn't figure out why the witches would give a damn." He stepped back from the table, annoyed at his error.

Hamish quickly played his fifteen hazards. Matthew placed his ball on the table and picked up the chalk to mark down Hamish's score.

"So you just strolled in there and struck up a conversation with her to find out?" The daemon pocketed all three balls with a single shot.

"I went looking for her, yes." Matthew watched while Hamish moved around the table. "I was curious."

"Was she happy to see you?" Hamish asked mildly, making another tricky shot. He knew that vampires, witches, and daemons seldom mixed. They preferred to spend time within close-knit circles of similar creatures. His friendship with Matthew was a relative rarity, and Hamish's daemonic friends thought it was madness to let a vampire get so close. On a night like this one, he thought they might have a point.

"Not exactly. Diana was frightened at first, even though she met my eyes without flinching. Her eyes are extraordinary—blue and gold and green and gray," Matthew mused. "Later she wanted to hit me. She smelled so angry."

Hamish bit back a laugh. "Sounds like a reasonable response to being ambushed by a vampire in the Bodleian." He decided to be kind to Matthew and save him from a reply. The daemon shot his yellow ball over the red, deliberately nicking it just enough that the red ball drifted forward and collided with it. "Damn," he groaned. "A foul."

Matthew returned to the table, shot a few hazards, and tried a cannon or two.

"Have you seen each other outside the library?" Hamish asked when the vampire had regained some of his composure.

"I don't see her much, actually, even in the library. I sit in one part and she sits in another. I've taken her to breakfast, though. And to the Old Lodge, to meet Amira."

Hamish kept his jaw closed with difficulty. Matthew had known women for years without taking them to the Old Lodge. And what was this about sitting at opposite ends of the library?

"Wouldn't it be easier to sit next to her in the library, if you're interested in her?"

"I'm not interested in *her*!" Matthew's cue exploded into the white ball. "I want the manuscript. I've been trying to get my hands on it for more than a hundred years. She just put in the slip and up it came from the stacks." His voice was envious.

"What manuscript, Matt?" Hamish was doing his best to be patient, but the exchange was rapidly becoming unendurable. Matthew was giving out information like a miser parting with pennies. It was intensely aggravating for quick-minded daemons to deal with creatures who didn't consider any division of time smaller than a decade particularly important.

"An alchemical book that belonged to Elias Ashmole. Diana Bishop is a highly respected historian of alchemy."

Matthew fouled again by striking the balls too hard. Hamish respotted the balls and continued to rack up points while his friend simmered down. Finally Jordan came to tell them that drinks were available downstairs.

"What's the score?" Hamish peered at the chalk marks. He knew he'd won, but the gentlemanly thing was to ask—or so Matthew had told him.

"You won, of course."

Matthew stalked out of the room and pounded down the stairs at considerably more than a human pace. Jordan eyed the polished treads with concern.

"Professor Clairmont is having a difficult day, Jordan."

"So it would seem," the butler murmured.

"Better bring up another bottle of red. It's going to be a long night."

They had their drinks in what had once been the lodge's reception area. Its windows looked out on the gardens, which were still kept in orderly, classical parterres despite the fact that their proportions were all wrong for a hunting lodge. They were too grand—they belonged to a palace, not a folly.

In front of the fireplace, drinks in hand, Hamish could at last press his way into the heart of the mystery. "Tell me about this manuscript of Diana's, Matthew. It contains what, exactly? The recipe for the philosopher's stone that turns lead into gold?" Hamish's voice was lightly mocking. "Instructions on how to concoct the elixir of life so you can transform mortal into immortal flesh?"

The daemon stopped his teasing the instant Matthew's eyes rose to meet his.

"You aren't serious," Hamish whispered, his voice shocked. The philosopher's stone was just a legend, like the Holy Grail or Atlantis. It couldn't possibly be real. Belatedly, he realized that vampires, daemons, and witches weren't supposed to be real either.

"Do I look like I'm joking?" Matthew asked.

"No." The daemon shuddered. Matthew had always been convinced that he could use his scientific skills to figure out what made vampires resistant to death and decay. The philosopher's stone fit neatly into those dreams.

"It's the lost book," Matthew said grimly. "I know it."

Like most creatures, Hamish had heard the stories. One version suggested the witches had stolen a precious book from the vampires, a book that held the secret of immortality. Another claimed the vampires had snatched an ancient spell book from the witches and then lost it. Some whispered that it was not a spell book at all, but a primer covering the basic traits of all four humanoid species on earth.

Matthew had his own theories about what the book might contain. An explanation of why vampires were so difficult to kill and accounts of early human and creature history were only a small part of it.

"You really think this alchemical manuscript is your book?" he asked. When Matthew nodded, Hamish let out his breath with a sigh. "No wonder the witches were gossiping. How did they discover Diana had found it?"

Matthew turned, ferocious. "Who knows or cares? The problems began when they couldn't keep their mouths shut."

Hamish was reminded once again that Matthew and his family really didn't like witches.

"I wasn't the only one to overhear them on Sunday. Other vampires did, too. And then the daemons sensed that something interesting was happening, and—"

"Now Oxford is crawling with creatures," the daemon finished. "What a mess. Isn't term about to start? The humans will be next. They're about to return in droves."

"It gets worse." Matthew's expression was grim. "The manuscript wasn't simply lost. It was under a spell, and Diana broke it. Then she sent it back to the stacks and shows no interest in recalling it. And I'm not the only one waiting for her to do so."

"Matthew," Hamish said, voice tense, "are you protecting her from other witches?"

"She doesn't seem to recognize her own power. It puts her at risk. I couldn't let them get to her first." Matthew seemed suddenly, disconcertingly, vulnerable.

"Oh, Matt," Hamish said, shaking his head. "You shouldn't interfere between Diana and her own people. You'll only cause more trouble. Besides," he continued, "no witch will be openly hostile to a Bishop. Her family's too old and distinguished."

Nowadays creatures no longer killed one another except in self-defense. Aggression was frowned on in their world. Matthew had told Hamish what it was like in the old days, when blood feuds and vendettas had raged and creatures were constantly catching human attention.

"The daemons are disorganized, and the vampires won't dare to cross me. But the witches can't be trusted." Matthew rose, taking his wine to the fireplace.

"Let Diana Bishop be," Hamish advised. "Besides, if this manuscript is bewitched, you're not going to be able to examine it."

"I will if she helps me," Matthew said in a deceptively easy tone, staring into the fire.

"Matthew," the daemon said in the same voice he used to let his junior partners know when they were on thin ice, "leave the witch and the manuscript alone."

The vampire placed his wineglass carefully on the mantel and turned away. "I don't think I can, Hamish. I'm . . . craving her." Even saying the word made the hunger spread. When his hunger focused, grew insistent like this, not just any blood would do. His body demanded something more specific. If only he could taste it—taste Diana—he would be satisfied and the painful longing would subside.

Hamish studied Matthew's tense shoulders. He wasn't surprised that his friend craved Diana Bishop. A vampire had to desire another creature more than anyone or anything else in order to mate, and cravings were rooted in desire. Hamish strongly suspected that Matthew—despite his previous fervent declarations that he was incapable of finding anyone who would stir that kind of feeling—was mating.

"Then the real problem you're facing at the moment is not the witches, nor Diana. And it's certainly not some ancient manuscript that may or may not hold the answers to your questions." Hamish let his words sink in before continuing. "You do realize you're hunting her?"

The vampire exhaled, relieved that it had been said aloud. "I know. I climbed into her window when she was sleeping. I follow her when she's running. She resists my attempts to help her, and the more she does, the hungrier I feel." He looked so perplexed that Hamish had to bite the inside of his lip to keep from smiling. Matthew's women didn't usually resist him. They did what he told them to do, dazzled by his good looks and charm. No wonder he was fascinated.

"But I don't need Diana's blood—not physically. I won't give in to this craving. Being around her needn't be a problem." Matthew's face crumpled unexpectedly. "What am I saying? We can't be near each other. We'll attract attention."

"Not necessarily. *We've* spent a fair bit of time together, and no one has been bothered," Hamish pointed out. In the early years of their friendship, the two had struggled to mask their differences from curious eyes. They were brilliant enough separately to attract human interest. When they were together—their dark heads bent to share a joke at dinner or sitting in the quadrangle in the early hours of the morning with empty champagne bottles at their feet—they were impossible to ignore.

"It's not the same thing, and you know it," Matthew said impatiently.

"Oh, yes, I forgot." Hamish's temper snapped. "Nobody cares what daemons do. But a vampire and a witch? That's important. *You're* the creatures who really matter in this world."

"Hamish!" Matthew protested. "You know that's not how I feel."

"You have the characteristic vampire contempt for daemons, Matthew. Witches, too, I might add. Think long and hard how you feel about other creatures before you take this witch to bed."

"I have no intention of taking Diana to bed," Matthew said, his voice acid.

"Dinner is served, sir." Jordan had been standing in the doorway, unobserved, for some time.

"Thank God," Hamish said with relief, getting up from his chair. The vampire was easier to manage if he was dividing his attention between the conversation and something—anything—else.

Seated in the dining room at one end of a vast table designed to feed a house party's worth of guests, Hamish tucked into the first of several courses while Matthew toyed with a soup spoon until his meal cooled. The vampire leaned over the bowl and sniffed.

"Mushrooms and sherry?" he asked.

"Yes. Jordan wanted to try something new, and since it didn't contain anything you find objectionable, I let him."

Matthew didn't ordinarily require much in the way of supplemental sustenance at Cadzow Lodge, but Jordan was a wizard with soup, and Hamish didn't like to eat alone any more than he liked drinking alone.

"I'm sorry, Hamish," Matthew said, watching his friend eat.

"I accept your apology, Matt," Hamish said, the soup spoon hovering near his mouth. "But you cannot imagine how difficult it is to accept being a daemon or a witch. With vampires it's definite and incontrovertible. You're not a vampire, and then you are. No question, no room for doubt. The rest of us have to wait, watch, and wonder. It makes your vampire superiority doubly hard to take."

Matthew was twirling the spoon's handle in his fingers like a baton. "Witches know they're witches. They're not like daemons at all," he said with a frown.

Hamish put his spoon down with a clatter and topped off his wineglass. "You know full well that having a witch for a parent is no guarantee. You can turn out perfectly ordinary. Or you can set your crib on fire. There's no telling if, when, or how your powers are going to manifest." Unlike Matthew, Hamish had a friend who was a witch. Janine did his hair, which had never looked better, and made her own skin lotion, which was nothing short of miraculous. He suspected that witchcraft was involved.

"It's not a total surprise, though," Matthew persisted, scooping some soup into his spoon and waving it slightly to cool it further. "Diana has centuries of family history to rely upon. It's nothing like what you went through as a teenager."

"I had a breeze of a time," Hamish said, recalling some of the daemonic coming-of-age stories he'd been privy to over the years.

When Hamish was twelve, his life had gone topsy-turvy in the space of one afternoon. He had come to realize, over the long Scottish autumn, that he was far smarter than his teachers. Most children who reach twelve suspect this, but Hamish knew it with deeply upsetting certainty. He responded by feigning sickness so he could skip school and, when that no longer worked, by doing his schoolwork as rapidly as he could and abandoning all pretense of normalcy. In desperation his schoolmaster sent for someone from the university mathematics department to evaluate Hamish's troublesome ability to solve in minutes problems that occupied his schoolmates for a week or more.

Jack Watson, a young daemon from the University of Glasgow with red hair and brilliant blue eyes, took one look at elfin Hamish Osborne and suspected that he, too, was a daemon. After going through the motions of a formal evaluation, which produced the expected documentary proof that Hamish was a mathematical prodigy whose mind did not fit within normal parameters, Watson invited him to attend lectures at the university. He also explained to the headmaster that the child could not be accommodated within a normal classroom without becoming a pyromaniac or something equally destructive.

After that, Watson made a visit to the Osbornes' modest home and told an astonished family how the world worked and exactly what kinds of creatures were in it. Percy Osborne, who came from a staunch Presbyterian background, resisted the notion of multiple supernatural and preternatural creatures until his wife pointed out that he had been raised to believe in witches—why not daemons and vampires, too? Hamish wept with relief, no longer feeling utterly alone. His mother hugged him fiercely and told him that she had always known he was special.

While Watson was still sitting in front of their electric fire drinking tea with her husband and son, Jessica Osborne thought she might as well take the opportunity to broach other aspects of Hamish's life that might make him feel different. She informed her son over chocolate biscuits that she also knew he was unlikely to marry the girl next door, who was infatuated with him. Instead Hamish was drawn to the girl's elder brother, a strapping lad of fifteen who could kick a football farther than anyone else in the neighborhood. Neither Percy nor Jack seemed remotely surprised or distressed by the revelation.

"Still," Matthew said now, after his first sip of tepid soup, "Diana's whole family must have expected her to be a witch—and she is, whether she uses her magic or not."

"I should think that would be every bit as bad as being among a bunch of clueless humans. Can you imagine the pressure? Not to mention the awful sense that your life didn't belong to you?" Hamish shuddered. "I'd prefer blind ignorance."

"What did it feel like," Matthew asked hesitantly, "the first day you woke up knowing you were a daemon?" The vampire didn't normally ask such personal questions.

"Like being reborn," Hamish said. "It was every bit as powerful and confusing as when you woke up craving blood and hearing the grass grow, blade by blade. Everything looked different. Everything felt different. Most of the time I smiled like a fool who'd won the lottery, and the rest of the time I cried in my room. But I don't think I believed it—you know, *really* believed it—until you smuggled me into the hospital."

Matthew's first birthday present to Hamish, after they became friends, had involved a bottle of Krug and a trip to the John Radcliffe. There Matthew sent Hamish through the MRI while the vampire asked him a series of questions. Afterward they compared Hamish's scans with those of an eminent brain surgeon on the staff, both of them drinking champagne and the daemon still in a surgical gown. Hamish made Matthew play the scans back repeatedly, fascinated by the way his brain lit up like a pinball machine even when he was replying to basic questions. It remained the best birthday present he'd ever received.

"From what you've told me, Diana is where I was before that MRI," Hamish said. "She knows she's a witch. But she still feels she's living a lie."

"She *is* living a lie," Matthew growled, taking another sip of soup. "Diana's pretending she's human."

"Wouldn't it be interesting to know why that's the case? More important, can you be around someone like that? You don't like lies."

Matthew looked thoughtful but didn't respond.

"There's something else," Hamish continued. "For someone who dislikes lies as much as you do, you keep a lot of secrets. If you need this witch, for whatever reason, you're going to have to win her trust. And the only way to do that is by telling her things you don't want her to know. She's roused your protective instincts, and you're going to have to fight them."

While Matthew mulled the situation over, Hamish turned the conversation to the latest catastrophes in the City and the government. The vampire calmed further, caught up in the intricacies of finance and policy.

"You've heard about the murders in Westminster, I presume," Hamish said when Matthew was completely at ease.

"I have. Somebody needs to put a stop to it."

"You?" Hamish asked.

"It's not my job—yet."

Hamish knew that Matthew had a theory about the murders, one that was linked to his scientific research. "You still think the murders are a sign that vampires are dying out?"

"Yes," Matthew said.

Matthew was convinced that creatures were slowly becoming extinct. Hamish had dismissed his friend's hypotheses at first, but he was beginning to think Matthew might be right.

They returned to less disturbing topics of conversation and, after dinner, retreated upstairs. The daemon had divided one of the lodge's redundant reception rooms into a sitting room and a bedroom. The sitting room was dominated by a large, ancient chessboard with carved ivory and ebony pieces that by all rights should be in a museum under protective glass rather than in a drafty hunting lodge. Like the MRI, the chess set had been a present from Matthew.

Their friendship had deepened over long evenings like this one, spent playing chess and discussing their work. One night Matthew began to tell Hamish stories of his past exploits. Now there was little about Matthew

Clairmont that the daemon did not know, and the vampire was the only creature Hamish had ever met who wasn't frightened of his powerful intellect.

Hamish, as was his custom, sat down behind the black pieces.

"Did we finish our last game?" Matthew asked, feigning surprise at the neatly arranged board.

"Yes. You won," Hamish said curtly, earning one of his friend's rare, broad smiles.

The two began to move their pieces, Matthew taking his time and Hamish moving swiftly and decisively when it was his turn. There was no sound except for the crackle of the fire and the ticking of the clock.

After an hour of play, Hamish moved to the final stage of his plan.

"I have a question." His voice was careful as he waited for his friend to make his next move. "Do you want the witch for herself—or for her power over that manuscript?"

"I don't want her power!" Matthew exploded, making a bad decision with his rook, which Hamish quickly captured. He bowed his head, looking more than ever like a Renaissance angel focused on some celestial mystery. "Christ, I don't know what I want."

Hamish sat as still as possible. "I think you do, Matt."

Matthew moved a pawn and made no reply.

"The other creatures in Oxford," Hamish continued, "they'll know soon, if they don't know already, that you're interested in more than this old book. What's your endgame?"

"I don't know," the vampire whispered.

"Love? Tasting her? Making her like you?"

Matthew snarled.

"Very impressive," Hamish said in a bored tone.

"There's a lot I don't understand about all this, Hamish, but there are three things I do know," Matthew said emphatically, picking up his wine-glass from the floor by his feet. "I will not give in to this craving for her blood. I do not want to control her power. And I certainly have no wish to make her a vampire." He shuddered at the thought.

"That leaves love. You have your answer, then. You do know what you want."

Matthew swallowed a gulp of wine. "I want what I shouldn't want, and I crave someone I can never have."

"You're not afraid you'd hurt her?" Hamish asked gently. "You've had relationships with warm-blooded women before, and you've never harmed any of them."

Matthew's heavy crystal wine goblet snapped in two. The bowl toppled to the floor, red wine spreading on the carpet. Hamish saw the glint of powdered glass between the vampire's index finger and thumb.

"Oh, Matt. Why didn't you tell me?" Hamish governed his features, making sure that not a particle of his shock was evident.

"How could I?" Matthew stared at his hands and ground the shards between his fingertips until they sparkled reddish black from the mixture of glass and blood. "You always had too much faith in me, you know."

"Who was she?"

"Her name was Eleanor." Matthew stumbled over the name. He dashed the back of his hand across his eyes, a fruitless attempt to wipe the image of her face from his mind. "My brother and I were fighting. Now I can't even remember what the argument was about. Back then I wanted to destroy him with my bare hands. Eleanor tried to make me see reason. She got between us and—" The vampire's voice broke. He cradled his head without bothering to clean the bloody residue from his already healed fingers. "I loved her so much, and I killed her."

"When was this?" Hamish whispered.

Matthew lowered his hands, turning them over to study his long, strong fingers. "Ages ago. Yesterday. What does it matter?" he asked with a vampire's disregard for time.

"It matters enormously if you made this mistake when you were a newly minted vampire and not in control of your instincts and your hunger."

"Ah. Then it will also matter that I killed another woman, Cecilia Martin, just over a century ago. I wasn't 'a newly minted vampire' then." Matthew got up from his chair and walked to the windows. He wanted to run into the night's blackness and disappear so he wouldn't have to see the horror in Hamish's eyes.

"Are there more?" Hamish asked sharply.

Matthew shook his head. "Two is enough. There can't be a third. Not ever."

"Tell me about Cecilia," Hamish commanded, leaning forward in his chair.

"She was a banker's wife," Matthew said reluctantly. "I saw her at the opera and became infatuated. Everyone in Paris was infatuated with someone else's wife at the time." His finger traced the outline of a woman's face on the pane of glass before him. "It didn't strike me as a challenge. I only wanted a taste of her, that night I went to her house. But once I started, I couldn't stop. And yet I couldn't let her die either—she was mine, and I wouldn't give her up. I barely stopped feeding in time. *Dieu,* she hated being a vampire. Cecilia walked into a burning house before I could stop her."

Hamish frowned. "Then you didn't kill her, Matt. She killed herself."

"I fed on her until she was at the brink of death, forced her to drink my blood, and turned her into a creature without her permission because I was selfish and scared," he said furiously. "In what way did I not kill her? I took her life, her identity, her vitality—that's death, Hamish."

"Why did you keep this from me?" Hamish tried not to care that his best friend had done so, but it was difficult.

"Even vampires feel shame," Matthew said tightly. "I hate myself—and I should—for what I did to those women."

"This is why you have to stop keeping secrets, Matt. They're going to destroy you from the inside." Hamish thought about what he wanted to say before he continued. "You didn't set out to kill Eleanor and Cecilia. You're not a murderer."

Matthew rested his fingertips on the white-painted window frame and pressed his forehead against the cold panes of glass. When he spoke, his voice was flat and dead. "No, I'm a monster. Eleanor forgave me for it. Cecilia never did."

"You're not a monster," Hamish said, worried by Matthew's tone.

"Maybe not, but I am dangerous." He turned and faced Hamish. "Especially around Diana. Not even Eleanor made me feel this way." The mere thought of Diana brought the craving back, the tightness spreading from his heart to his abdomen. His face darkened with the effort to bring it under control.

"Come back here and finish this game," Hamish said, his voice rough.

"I could go, Hamish," Matthew said uncertainly. "You don't have to share your roof with me."

"Don't be an idiot," Hamish replied as quick as a whip. "You're not going anywhere."

Matthew sat. "I don't understand how you can know about Eleanor and Cecilia and not hate me, too," he said after a few minutes.

"I can't conceive of what you would have to do to make me hate you, Matthew. I love you like a brother, and I will until I draw my last breath."

"Thank you," Matthew said, his face somber. "I'll try to deserve it."

"Don't try. Do it," Hamish said gruffly. "You're about to lose your bishop, by the way."

The two creatures dragged their attention back to the game with difficulty, and they were still playing in the early morning when Jordan brought up coffee for Hamish and a bottle of port for Matthew. The butler picked up the ruined wineglass without comment, and Hamish sent him off to bed.

When Jordan was gone, Hamish surveyed the board and made his final move. "Checkmate."

Matthew let out his breath and sat back in his chair, staring at the chessboard. His queen stood encircled by his own pieces—pawns, a knight, and a rook. Across the board his king was checked by a lowly black pawn. The game was over, and he had lost.

"There's more to the game than protecting your queen," Hamish said. "Why do you find it so difficult to remember that it's the king who's not expendable?"

"The king just sits there, moving one square at a time. The queen can move so freely. I suppose I'd rather lose the game than forfeit her freedom."

Hamish wondered if he was talking about chess or Diana. "Is she worth the cost, Matt?" he asked softly.

"Yes," Matthew said without a moment of hesitation, lifting the white queen from the board and holding it between his fingers.

"I thought so," Hamish said. "You don't feel this way now, but you're lucky to have found her at last."

The vampire's eyes glittered, and his mouth twisted into a crooked smile. "But is she lucky, Hamish? Is she fortunate to have a creature like me in pursuit?"

"That's entirely up to you. Just remember—no secrets. Not if you love her."

Matthew looked into his queen's serene face, his fingers closing protectively around the small carved figure.

He was still holding it when the sun rose, long after Hamish had gone to sleep.

Chapter 10

Still trying to shake the ice from my shoulders left by Matthew's stare, I opened the door to my rooms. Inside, the answering machine greeted me with a flashing red "13." There were nine additional voice-mail messages on my mobile. All of them were from Sarah and reflected an escalating concern about what her sixth sense told her was happening in Oxford.

Unable to face my all-too-prescient aunts, I turned down the volume on the answering machine, turned off the ringers on both phones, and climbed wearily into bed.

Next morning, when I passed through the porter's lodge for a run, Fred waved a stack of message slips at me.

"I'll pick them up later," I called, and he flashed his thumb in acknowledgment.

My feet pounded on familiar dirt paths through the fields and marshes north of the city, the exercise helping to keep at bay both my guilt over not calling my aunts and the memory of Matthew's cold face.

Back in college I collected the messages and threw them into the trash. Then I staved off the inevitable call home with cherished weekend rituals: boiling an egg, brewing tea, gathering laundry, piling up the drifts of papers that littered every surface. After I'd wasted most of the morning, there was nothing left to do but call New York. It was early there, but there was no chance that anyone was still in bed.

"What do you think you're up to, Diana?" Sarah demanded in lieu of hello.

"Good morning, Sarah." I sank into the armchair by the defunct fireplace and crossed my feet on a nearby bookshelf. This was going to take awhile.

"It is not a good morning," Sarah said tartly. "We've been beside ourselves. What's going on?"

Em picked up the extension.

"Hi, Em," I said, recrossing my legs. This was going to take a *long* while.

"Is that vampire bothering you?" Em asked anxiously.

"Not exactly."

"We know you've been spending time with vampires and daemons," my aunt broke in impatiently. "Have you lost your mind, or is something seriously wrong?"

"I haven't lost my mind, and nothing's wrong." The last bit was a lie, but I crossed my fingers and hoped for the best.

"Do you really think you're going to fool us? You cannot lie to a fellow witch!" Sarah exclaimed. "Out with it, Diana."

So much for that plan.

"Let her speak, Sarah," Em said. "We trust Diana to make the right decisions, remember?"

The ensuing silence led me to believe that this had been a matter of some controversy.

Sarah drew in her breath, but Em cut her off. "Where were you last night?"

"Yoga." There was no way of squirming out of this inquisition, but it was to my advantage to keep all responses brief and to the point.

"Yoga?" Sarah asked, incredulous. "Why are you doing yoga with those creatures? You know it's dangerous to mix with daemons and vampires."

"The class was led by a witch!" I became indignant, seeing Amira's serene, lovely face before me.

"This yoga class, was it his idea?" Em asked.

"Yes. It was at Clairmont's house."

Sarah made a disgusted sound.

"Told you it was him," Em muttered to my aunt. She directed her next words to me. "I see a vampire standing between you and . . . something. I'm not sure what, exactly."

"And I keep telling you, Emily Mather, that's nonsense. Vampires don't protect witches." Sarah's voice was crisp with certainty.

"This one does," I said.

"What?" Em asked and Sarah shouted.

"He has been for days." I bit my lip, unsure how to tell the story, then plunged in. "Something happened at the library. I called up a manuscript, and it was bewitched."

There was silence.

"A bewitched book." Sarah's voice was keen with interest. "Was it a grimoire?" She was an expert on grimoires, and her most cherished possession was the ancient volume of spells that had been passed down in the Bishop family.

"I don't think so," I said. "All that was visible were alchemical illustrations."

"What else?" My aunt knew that the visible was only the beginning when it came to bewitched books.

"Someone's put a spell on the manuscript's text. There were faint lines of writing—layers upon layers of them—moving underneath the surface of the pages."

In New York, Sarah put down her coffee mug with a sharp sound. "Was this before or after Matthew Clairmont appeared?"

"Before," I whispered.

"You didn't think this was worth mentioning when you told us you'd met a vampire?" Sarah did nothing to disguise her anger. "By the goddess, Diana, you can be so reckless. How was this book bewitched? And don't tell me you don't know."

"It smelled funny. It felt . . . wrong. At first I couldn't lift the book's cover. I put my palm on it." I turned my hand over on my lap, recalling the sense of instant recognition between me and the manuscript, half expecting to see the shimmer that Matthew had mentioned.

"And?" Sarah asked.

"It tingled against my hand, then sighed and . . . relaxed. I could feel it, through the leather and the wooden boards."

"How did you manage to unravel this spell? Did you say any words? What were you thinking?" Sarah's curiosity was now thoroughly roused.

"There was no witchcraft involved, Sarah. I needed to look at the book for my research, and I laid my palm flat on it, that's all." I took a deep breath. "Once it was open, I took some notes, closed it, and returned the manuscript."

"You *returned it*?" There was a loud clatter as Sarah's phone hit the floor. I winced and held the receiver away from my head, but her colorful language was still audible.

"Diana?" Em said faintly. "Are you there?"

"I'm here," I said sharply.

"Diana Bishop, you know better." Sarah's voice was reproachful. "How could you send back a magical object you didn't fully understand?"

My aunt had taught me how to recognize enchanted and bewitched objects—and what to do with them. You were to avoid touching or moving them until you knew how their magic worked. Spells could be delicate, and many had protective mechanisms built into them.

"What was I supposed to do, Sarah?" I could hear my defensiveness. "Refuse to leave the library until you could examine it? It was a Friday night. I wanted to go home."

"What happened when you returned it?" Sarah said tightly.

"The air might have been a little funny," I admitted. "And the library might have given the impression it shrank for just a moment."

"You sent the manuscript back and the spell reactivated," Sarah said. She swore again. "Few witches are adept enough to set up a spell that automatically resets when it's broken. You're not dealing with an amateur."

"That's the energy that drew them to Oxford," I said, suddenly understanding. "It wasn't my opening the manuscript. It was the resetting of the spell. The creatures aren't just at yoga, Sarah. I'm surrounded by vampires and daemons in the Bodleian. Clairmont came to the library on Monday night, hoping to catch a glimpse of the manuscript after he heard two witches talking about it. By Tuesday the library was crawling with them."

"Here we go again," Sarah said with a sigh. "Before the month's out, daemons will be showing up in Madison looking for you."

"There must be witches you can rely on for help." Em was making an effort to keep her voice level, but I could hear the concern in it.

"There are witches," I said haltingly, "but they're not helpful. A wizard in a brown tweed coat tried to force his way into my head. He would have succeeded, too, if not for Matthew."

"The vampire put himself between you and another witch?" Em was horrified. "That's not done. You never interfere in business between witches if you're not one of us."

"You should be grateful!" I might not want to be lectured by Clairmont or have breakfast with him again, but the vampire deserved some credit. "If he hadn't been there, I don't know what would have happened. No witch has ever been so . . . invasive with me before."

"Maybe you should get out of Oxford for a while," Em suggested.

"I'm not going to leave because there's a witch with no manners in town."

Em and Sarah whispered to each other, their hands over the receivers.

"I don't like this one bit," my aunt finally said in a tone that suggested that the world was falling apart. "Bewitched books? Daemons following you? Vampires taking you to yoga? Witches threatening a Bishop? Witches are supposed to avoid notice, Diana. Even the humans are going to know something's going on."

"If you stay in Oxford, you'll have to be more inconspicuous," Em agreed. "There's nothing wrong with coming home for a while and letting the situation cool off, if that becomes impossible. You don't have the manuscript anymore. Maybe they'll lose interest."

None of us believed that was likely.

"I'm not running away."

"You wouldn't be," Em protested.

"I would." And I wasn't going to display a shred of cowardice so long as Matthew Clairmont was around.

"He can't be with you every minute of every day, honey," Em said sadly, hearing my unspoken thoughts.

"I should think not," Sarah said darkly.

"I don't need Matthew Clairmont's help. I can take care of myself," I retorted.

"Diana, that vampire isn't protecting you out of the goodness of his heart," Em said. "You represent something he wants. You have to figure out what it is."

"Maybe he *is* interested in alchemy. Maybe he's just bored."

"Vampires do not get bored," Sarah said crisply, "not when there's a witch's blood around."

There was nothing to be done about my aunt's prejudices. I was tempted to tell her about yoga class, where for over an hour I'd been gloriously free from fear of other creatures. But there was no point.

"Enough." I was firm. "Matthew Clairmont won't get any closer, and you needn't worry about my fiddling with more bewitched manuscripts. But I'm not leaving Oxford, and that's final."

"All right," Sarah said. "But there's not much we can do from here if things go wrong."

"I know, Sarah."

"And the next time you get handed something magical—whether you expected it or not—behave like the witch you are, not some silly human. Don't ignore it or tell yourself you're imagining things." Willful ignorance and dismissing the supernatural were at the top of Sarah's list of human pet peeves. "Treat it with respect, and if you don't know what to do, ask for help."

"Promise," I said quickly, wanting to get off the phone. But Sarah wasn't through yet.

"I never thought I'd see the day when a Bishop relied on a vampire for protection, rather than her own power," she said. "My mother must be turning in her grave. This is what comes from avoiding who you are, Diana. You've got a mess on your hands, and it's all because you thought you could ignore your heritage. It doesn't work that way."

Sarah's bitterness soured the atmosphere in my room long after I'd hung up the phone.

The next morning I stretched my way through some yoga poses for half an hour and then made a pot of tea. Its vanilla and floral aromas were comforting, and it had just enough caffeine to keep me from dozing in the afternoon without keeping me awake at night. After the leaves steeped, I wrapped the white porcelain pot in a towel to hold in the heat and carried it to the chair by the fireplace reserved for my deep thinking.

Calmed by the tea's familiar scent, I pulled my knees up to my chin and reviewed my week. No matter where I started, I found myself returning to my last conversation with Matthew Clairmont. Had my efforts to prevent magic from seeping into my life and work meant nothing?

Whenever I was stuck with my research, I imagined a white table, gleaming and empty, and the evidence as a jigsaw puzzle that needed to be pieced together. It took the pressure off and felt like a game.

Now I tumbled everything from the past week onto that table—Ashmole 782, Matthew Clairmont, Agatha Wilson's wandering attention, the tweedy wizard, my tendency to walk with my eyes closed, the creatures in the Bodleian, how I'd fetched *Notes and Queries* from the shelf, Amira's yoga class. I swirled the bright pieces around, putting some together and trying to form a picture, but there were too many gaps, and no clear image emerged.

Sometimes picking up a random piece of evidence helped me figure out what was most important. Putting my imaginary fingers on the table, I drew out a shape, expecting to see Ashmole 782.

Matthew Clairmont's dark eyes looked back at me.

Why was this vampire so important?

The pieces of my puzzle started to move of their own volition, swirling in patterns that were too fast to follow. I slapped my imaginary hands on the table, and the pieces stopped their dance. My palms tingled with recognition.

This didn't seem like a game anymore. It seemed like magic. And if it was, then I'd been using it in my schoolwork, in my college courses, and now in my scholarship. But there was no room in my life for magic, and my mind closed resolutely against the possibility that I'd been violating my own rules without knowing it.

The next day I arrived in the library's cloakroom at my normal time, went up the stairs, rounded the corner near the collection desk, and braced myself to see him.

Clairmont wasn't there.

"Do you need something?" Miriam said in an irritable voice, scraping her chair against the floor as she stood.

"Where is Professor Clairmont?"

"He's hunting," Miriam said, eyes snapping with dislike, "in Scotland."

Hunting. I swallowed hard. "Oh. When will he be back?"

"I honestly don't know, Dr. Bishop." Miriam crossed her arms and put out a tiny foot.

"I was hoping he'd take me to yoga at the Old Lodge tonight," I said faintly, trying to come up with a reasonable excuse for stopping.

Miriam turned and picked up a ball of black fluff. She tossed it at me, and I grabbed it as it flew by my hip. "You left that in his car on Friday."

"Thank you." My sweater smelled of carnations and cinnamon.

"You should be more careful with your things," Miriam muttered. "You're a witch, Dr. Bishop. Take care of *yourself* and stop putting Matthew in this impossible situation."

I turned on my heel without comment and went to pick up my manuscripts from Sean.

"Everything all right?" he asked, eyeing Miriam with a frown.

"Perfectly." I gave him my usual seat number and, when he still looked concerned, a warm smile.

How dare Miriam speak to me like that? I fumed while settling into my workspace.

My fingers itched as if hundreds of insects were crawling under the skin. Tiny sparks of blue-green were arcing between my fingertips, leaving traces of energy as they erupted from the edges of my body. I clenched my hands and quickly sat on top of them.

This was *not* good. Like all members of the university, I'd sworn an oath not to bring fire or flame into Bodley's Library. The last time my fingers had behaved like this, I was thirteen and the fire department had to be called to extinguish the blaze in the kitchen.

When the burning sensation abated, I looked around carefully and sighed with relief. I was alone in the Selden End. No one had witnessed my fireworks display. Pulling my hands from underneath my thighs, I scrutinized them for further signs of supernatural activity. The blue was already diminishing to a silvery gray as the power retreated from my fingertips.

I opened the first box only after ascertaining I wouldn't set fire to it and pretended that nothing unusual had happened. Still, I hesitated to touch my computer for fear that my fingers would fuse to the plastic keys.

Not surprisingly, it was difficult to concentrate, and that same manuscript was still before me at lunchtime. Maybe some tea would calm me down.

At the beginning of term, one would expect to see a handful of human readers in Duke Humfrey's medieval wing. Today there was only one: an elderly human woman examining an illuminated manuscript with a magnifying glass. She was squashed between an unfamiliar daemon and one of the female vampires from last week. Gillian Chamberlain was there, too, glowering at me along with four other witches as if I'd let down our entire species.

Hurrying past, I stopped at Miriam's desk. "I presume you have instructions to follow me to lunch. Are you coming?"

She put down her pencil with exaggerated care. "After you."

Miriam was in front of me by the time I reached the back staircase. She pointed to the steps on the other side. "Go down that way."

"Why? What difference does it make?"

"Suit yourself." She shrugged.

One flight down I glanced through the small window stuck into the swinging door that led to the Lower Reading Room, and I gasped.

The room was full to bursting with creatures. They had segregated themselves. One long table held nothing but daemons, conspicuous because not a single book—open or closed—sat in front of them. Vampires sat at another table, their bodies perfectly still and their eyes never blinking. The witches appeared studious, but their frowns were signs of irritation rather than concentration, since the daemons and vampires had staked out the tables closest to the staircase.

"No wonder we're not supposed to mix. No human could ignore this," Miriam observed.

"What have I done now?" I asked in a whisper.

"Nothing. Matthew's not here," she said matter-of-factly.

"Why are they so afraid of Matthew?"

"You'll have to ask him. Vampires don't tell tales. But don't worry," she continued, baring her sharp, white teeth, "these work perfectly, so you've got nothing to fear."

Shoving my hands into my pockets, I clattered down the stairs, pushing through the tourists in the quadrangle. At Blackwell's, I swallowed a sandwich and a bottle of water. Miriam caught my eye as I passed by her on the way to the exit. She put aside a murder mystery and followed me.

"Diana," she said quietly as we passed through the library's gates, "what are you up to?"

"None of your business," I snapped.

Miriam sighed.

Back in Duke Humfrey's, I located the wizard in brown tweed. Miriam watched intently from the center aisle, still as a statue.

"Are you in charge?"

He tipped his head to the side in acknowledgment.

"I'm Diana Bishop," I said, sticking out my hand.

"Peter Knox. And I know very well who you are. You're Rebecca and Stephen's child." He touched my fingertips lightly with his own. There was a nineteenth-century grimoire sitting in front of him, a stack of reference books at his side.

The name was familiar, though I couldn't place it, and hearing my parents' names come out of this wizard's mouth was disquieting. I swallowed, hard. "Please clear your . . . friends out of the library. The new students arrive today, and we wouldn't want to frighten them."

"If we could have a quiet word, Dr. Bishop, I'm sure we could come to some arrangement." He pushed his glasses up over the bridge of his nose. The closer I was to Knox, the more danger I felt. The skin under my fingernails started to prickle ominously.

"You have nothing to fear from me," he said sorrowfully. "That vampire, on the other hand—"

"You think I found something that belongs to the witches," I interrupted. "I no longer have it. If you want Ashmole 782, there are request slips on the desk in front of you."

"You don't understand the complexity of the situation."

"No, and I don't *want* to know. Please, leave me alone."

"Physically you are very like your mother." Knox's eyes swept over my face. "But you have some of Stephen's stubbornness as well, I see."

I felt the usual combination of envy and irritation that accompanied a witch's references to my parents or family history—as if they had an equal claim to mine.

"I'll try," he continued, "but I don't control those animals." He waved across the aisle, where one of the Scary Sisters was watching Knox and me with interest. I hesitated, then crossed over to her seat.

"I'm sure you heard our conversation, and you must know I'm under the direct supervision of two vampires already," I said. "You're welcome to stay, if you don't trust Matthew and Miriam. But clear the others out of the Lower Reading room."

"Witches are hardly ever worth a moment of a vampire's time, but you are full of surprises today, Diana Bishop. Wait until I tell my sister Clarissa what she's missed." The female vampire's words came out in a lush, unhurried drawl redolent of impeccable breeding and a fine education. She smiled, teeth gleaming in the low light of the medieval wing. "Challenging Knox—a child like you? What a tale I'll have to tell."

I dragged my eyes away from her flawless features and went off in search of a familiar daemonic face.

The latte-loving daemon was drifting around the computer terminals wearing headphones and humming under his breath to some unheard music as the end of the cord was swinging freely around the tops of his thighs. Once he pulled the white plastic disks from his ears, I tried to impress upon him the seriousness of the situation.

"Listen, you're welcome to keep surfing the Net up here. But we've got a problem downstairs. It's not necessary for two dozen daemons to be watching me."

The daemon made an indulgent sound. "You'll know soon enough."

"Could they watch me from farther away? The Sheldonian? The White Horse?" I was trying to be helpful. "If not, the human readers will start asking questions."

"We're not like you," he said dreamily.

"Does that mean you can't help or you won't?" I tried not to sound impatient.

"It's all the same thing. We need to know, too."

This was impossible. "Whatever you can do to take some of the pressure off the seats would be greatly appreciated."

Miriam was still watching me. Ignoring her, I returned to my desk.

At the end of the completely unproductive day, I pinched the bridge of my nose, swore under my breath, and packed up my things.

The next morning the Bodleian was far less crowded. Miriam was scribbling furiously and didn't look up when I passed. There was still no sign of Clairmont. Even so, everybody was observing the rules that he had clearly, if silently, laid down, and they stayed out of the Selden End. Gillian was in the medieval wing, crouched over her papyri, as were both Scary Sisters and a few daemons. With the exception of Gillian, who was doing real work, the rest went through the motions with perfect respectability. And when I stuck my head around the swinging door into the Lower Reading Room after a hot cup of tea at midmorning, only a few creatures looked up. The musical, coffee-loving daemon was among them. He tipped his fingers and winked at me knowingly.

I got a reasonable amount of work done, although not enough to make up for yesterday. I began by reading alchemical poems—the trickiest of texts—that were attributed to Mary, the sister of Moses. "*Three things if you three hours attend,*" read one part of the poem, "*Are chained together in the End.*" The meaning of the verses remained a mystery, although the most likely subject was the chemical combination of silver, gold, and mercury. Could Chris produce an experiment from this poem? I wondered, noting the possible chemical processes involved.

When I turned to another, anonymous poem, entitled "Verse on the Threefold Sophic Fire," the similarities between its imagery and an illumination I'd seen yesterday of an alchemical mountain, riddled with mines and miners digging in the ground for precious metals and stones, were unmistakable.

Within this Mine two Stones of old were found,
Whence this the Ancients called Holy Ground;
Who knew their Value, Power and Extent,
And Nature how with Nature to Ferment
For these if you Ferment with Natural Gold
Or Silver, their hid Treasures they unfold.

I stifled a groan. My research would become exponentially more complicated if I had to connect not only art and science but art and poetry.

"It must be hard to concentrate on your research with vampires watching you."

Gillian Chamberlain was standing next to me, her hazel eyes sparking with suppressed malevolence.

"What do you want, Gillian?"

"I'm just being friendly, Diana. We're sisters, remember?" Gillian's shiny black hair swung above her collar. Its smoothness suggested that she was not troubled by surges of static electricity. Her power must be regularly released. I shivered.

"I have no sisters, Gillian. I'm an only child."

"It's a good thing, too. Your family has caused more than enough trouble. Look at what happened at Salem. It was all Bridget Bishop's fault." Gillian's tone was vicious.

Here we go again, I thought, closing the volume before me. As usual, the Bishops were proving to be an irresistible topic of conversation.

"What are you talking about, Gillian?" My voice was sharp. "Bridget Bishop was found guilty of witchcraft and executed. She didn't instigate the witch-hunt—she was a victim of it, just like the others. You know that, as does every other witch in this library."

"Bridget Bishop drew human attention, first with those poppets of hers and then with her provocative clothes and immorality. The human hysteria would have passed if not for her."

"She was found innocent of practicing witchcraft," I retorted, bristling.

"In 1680—but no one believed it. Not after they found the poppets in her cellar wall, pins stuck through them and the heads ripped off. Afterward Bridget did nothing to protect her fellow witches from falling under suspicion. She was so independent." Gillian's voice dropped. "That was your mother's fatal flaw, too."

"Stop it, Gillian." The air around us seemed unnaturally cold and clear.

"Your mother and father were standoffish, just like you, thinking they didn't need the Cambridge coven's support after they got married. They learned, didn't they?"

I shut my eyes, but it was impossible to block out the image I'd spent most of my life trying to forget: my mother and father lying dead in the middle of a chalk-marked circle somewhere in Nigeria, their bodies broken and bloody. My aunt wouldn't share the details of their death at the time, so I'd slipped into the public library to look them up. That's where I'd first seen the picture and the lurid headline that accompanied it. The nightmares had gone on for years afterward.

"There was nothing the Cambridge coven could do to prevent my parents' murder. They were killed on another continent by fearful humans." I gripped the arms of my chair, hoping that she wouldn't see my white knuckles.

Gillian gave an unpleasant laugh. "It wasn't humans, Diana. If it had been, their killers would have been caught and dealt with." She crouched down, her face close to mine. "Rebecca Bishop and Stephen Proctor were keeping secrets from other witches. We needed to discover them. Their deaths were unfortunate, but necessary. Your father had more power than we ever dreamed."

"Stop talking about *my* family and *my* parents as though they belong to you," I warned. "They were killed by humans." There was a roaring in my ears, and the coldness that surrounded us was intensifying.

"Are you sure?" Gillian whispered, sending a fresh chill into my bones. "As a witch, you'd know if I was lying to you."

I governed my features, determined not to show my confusion. What Gillian said about my parents couldn't be true, and yet there were none of the subtle alarms that typically accompanied untruths between witches—the spark of anger, an overwhelming feeling of contempt.

"Think about what happened to Bridget Bishop and your parents the next time you turn down an invitation to a coven gathering," Gillian murmured, her lips so close to my ear that her breath swept against my skin. "A witch shouldn't keep secrets from other witches. Bad things happen when she does."

Gillian straightened and stared at me for a few seconds, the tingle of her glance growing uncomfortable the longer it lasted. Staring fixedly at the closed manuscript before me, I refused to meet her eyes.

After she left, the air's temperature returned to normal. When my heart stopped pounding and the roaring in my ears abated, I packed my belongings with shaking hands, badly wanting to be back in my rooms. Adrenaline was coursing through my body, and I wasn't sure how long it would be possible to fend off my panic.

I managed to get out of the library without incident, avoiding Miriam's sharp glance. If Gillian was right, it was the jealousy of fellow witches that I needed to be wary of, not human fear. And the mention of my father's hidden powers made something half remembered flit at the edges of my mind, but it eluded me when I tried to fix it in place long enough to see it clearly.

At New College, Fred hailed me from the porter's lodge with a fistful of mail. A creamy envelope, thick with a distinctive woven feeling, lay on top.

It was a note from the warden, summoning me for a drink before dinner.

In my rooms I considered calling his secretary and feigning illness to get out of the invitation. My head was reeling, and there was little chance I could keep down even a drop of sherry in my present state.

But the college had behaved handsomely when I'd requested a place to stay. The least I could do was express my thanks personally. My sense of professional obligation began to supplant the anxiety stirred up by Gillian. Holding on to my identity as a scholar like a lifeline, I resolved to make my appreciation known.

After changing, I made my way to the warden's lodgings and rang the bell. A member of the college staff opened the door and ushered me inside, leading me to the parlor.

"Hello, Dr. Bishop." Nicholas Marsh's blue eyes crinkled at the corners, and his snowy white hair and round red cheeks made him look like Santa Claus. Soothed by his warmth and armored with a sense of professional duty, I smiled.

"Professor Marsh." I took his outstretched hand. "Thank you for inviting me."

"It's overdue, I'm afraid. I was in Italy, you know."

"Yes, the bursar told me."

"Then you have forgiven me for neglecting you for so long," he said. "I hope to make it up to you by introducing you to an old friend of mine who is in Oxford for a few days. He's a well-known author and writes about subjects that might interest you."

Marsh stood aside, giving me a glimpse of a thick head of brown hair peppered with gray and the sleeve of a brown tweed jacket. I froze in confusion.

"Come and meet Peter Knox," the warden said, taking my elbow gently. "He's acquainted with your work."

The wizard stood. Finally I recognized what had been eluding me. Knox's name had been in the newspaper story about vampire murders. He was the expert the police called in to examine deaths that had an occult twist. My fingers started to itch.

"Dr. Bishop," Knox said, holding out his hand. "I've seen you in the Bodleian."

"Yes, I believe you have." I extended my own and was relieved to see that it was not emitting sparks. We clasped hands as briefly as possible.

His right fingertips flickered slightly, a tiny furl and a release of bones and skin that no human would have noticed. It reminded me of my childhood, when my mother's hands had flickered and furled to produce pancakes and fold laundry. Shutting my eyes, I braced for an outpouring of magic.

The phone rang.

"I must get that, I'm afraid," Marsh apologized. "Do sit down."

I sat as far from Knox as possible, perched on a straight-backed wooden chair usually reserved for disgraced junior members of the college.

Knox and I remained silent while Marsh murmured and tutted into the phone. He punched a button on the console and approached me, a glass of sherry in his hand. "That's the vice-chancellor. Two freshers have gone missing," he said, using the university's slang term for new students. "You two chat while I deal with this in my study. Please excuse me."

Distant doors opened and closed, and muffled voices conferred in the hall before there was silence.

"Missing students?" I said blandly. Surely Knox had magically engineered both the crisis and the phone call that had drawn Marsh away.

"I don't understand, Dr. Bishop," Knox murmured. "It seems unfortunate for the university to misplace two children. Besides, this gives us a chance to talk privately."

"What do we have to talk about?" I sniffed my sherry and prayed for the warden's return.

"A great many things."

I glanced at the door.

"Nicholas will be quite busy until we're through."

"Let's get this over with, then, so that the warden can return to his drink."

"As you wish," Knox said. "Tell me what brought you to Oxford, Dr. Bishop."

"Alchemy." I would answer the man's questions, if only to get Marsh back into the room, but wasn't going to tell him more than was necessary.

"You must have known that Ashmole 782 was bewitched. No one with even a drop of Bishop blood in her veins could have failed to notice. Why did you send it back?" Knox's brown eyes were sharp. He wanted the manuscript as much as Matthew Clairmont did—if not more.

"I was done with it." It was difficult to keep my voice even.

"Was there nothing about the manuscript that piqued your interest?"

"Nothing."

Peter Knox's mouth twisted into an ugly expression. He knew I was lying. "Have you shared your observations with the vampire?"

"I take it you mean Professor Clairmont." When creatures refused to use proper names, it was a way of denying that those who were not like you were your equals.

Knox's fingers unwound once more. When I thought he might point them at me, he curled them around the arms of his chair instead. "We all respect your family and what you've endured. Nevertheless, questions have been raised about your unorthodox relationship with this creature. You are betraying your ancestral lineage with this self-indulgent behavior. It must stop."

"Professor Clairmont is a professional colleague," I said, steering the conversation away from my family, "and I know nothing about the manuscript. It was in my possession for a matter of minutes. Yes, I knew it was under a spell. But that was immaterial to me, since I'd requested it to study the contents."

"The vampire has wanted that book for more than a century," Knox said, his voice vicious. "He mustn't be allowed to have it."

"Why?" My voice crackled with suppressed anger. "Because it belongs to the witches? Vampires and daemons can't enchant objects. A witch put that book under a spell, and now it's back under the same spell. What are you worried about?"

"More than you could possibly comprehend, Dr. Bishop."

"I'm confident I can keep up, *Mr.* Knox," I replied. Knox's mouth tightened with displeasure when I emphasized his position outside the academy. Every time the wizard used my title, his formality sounded like a taunt, as if he were trying to make a point that he, not I, was the real expert. I might not use my power, and I couldn't have conjured up my own lost keys, but being patronized by this wizard was intolerable.

"I am disturbed that you—a Bishop—are associating with a vampire." He held up his hand as a protest bubbled to my lips. "Let's not insult each other with further untruths. Instead of the natural revulsion you should feel for that animal, you feel gratitude."

I remained silent, seething.

"And I'm concerned because we are perilously close to catching human attention," he continued.

"I tried to get the creatures out of the library."

"Ah, but it's not just the library, is it? A vampire is leaving drained, bloodless corpses around Westminster. The daemons are unusually restless, vulnerable as ever to their own madness and the swings of energy in the world. We can't afford to be noticed."

"You told the reporters that there was nothing supernatural about those deaths."

Knox looked incredulous. "You don't expect me to tell *humans* everything?"

"I do, actually, when they're paying you."

"You're not only self-indulgent, you're foolish. That surprises me, Dr. Bishop. Your father was known for his good sense."

"I've had a long day. Is that all?" Standing abruptly, I moved toward the door. Even in normal circumstances, it was difficult to listen to anyone but Sarah and Em talking about my parents. Now—after Gillian's revelations—there was something almost obscene about it.

"No, it is not," said Knox unpleasantly. "What I am most intrigued by, at present, is the question of how an ignorant witch with no training of any sort managed to break a spell that has defied the efforts of those far more adept than you will ever be."

"So that's why you're all watching me." I sat down, my back pressing against the chair's slats.

"Don't look so pleased with yourself," he said curtly. "Your success may have been a fluke—an anniversary reaction related to when the spell was first cast. The passage of time can interfere with witchcraft, and anniversaries are particularly volatile moments. You haven't tried to recall it yet, but when you do, it may not come as easily as it did the first time."

"And what anniversary would we be celebrating?"

"The sesquicentennial."

I had wondered why a witch would put a spell on the manuscript in the first place. Someone must have been looking for it all those years ago, too. I blanched.

We were back to Matthew Clairmont and his interest in Ashmole 782.

"You *are* managing to keep up, aren't you? The next time you see your vampire, ask him what he was doing in the autumn of 1859. I doubt he'll tell you the truth, but he might reveal enough for you to figure it out on your own."

"I'm tired. Why don't you tell me, witch to witch, what *your* interest is in Ashmole 782?" I'd heard why the daemons wanted the manuscript. Even Matthew had given me some explanation. Knox's fascination with it was a missing piece of the puzzle.

"That manuscript belongs to us," Knox said fiercely. "We're the only creatures who can understand its secrets and the only creatures who can be trusted to keep them."

"*What is in the manuscript?*" I said, temper flaring at last.

"The first spells ever constructed. Descriptions of the enchantments that bind the world together." Knox's face grew dreamy. "The secret of immortality. How witches made the first daemon. How vampires can be destroyed, once and for all." His eyes pierced mine. "It's the source of all our power, past and present. It cannot be allowed to fall into the hands of daemons or vampires—or humans."

The events of the afternoon were catching up with me, and I had to press my knees together to keep them from shaking. "Nobody would put all that information in a single book."

"The first witch did," Knox said. "And her sons and daughters, too, down through time. It's our history, Diana. Surely you want to protect it from prying eyes."

The warden entered the room as if he'd been waiting by the door. The tension was suffocating, but he seemed blissfully unaware of it.

"What a palaver over nothing." Marsh shook his white head. "The freshers illegally obtained a punt. They were located, stuck under a bridge and a little worse for wine, utterly content with their situation. A romance may result."

"I'm so glad," I murmured. The clocks struck forty-five minutes past the hour, and I stood. "Is that the time? I have a dinner engagement."

"You won't be joining us for dinner?" the warden asked with a frown. "Peter has been looking forward to talking to you about alchemy."

"Our paths will cross again. Soon," Knox said smoothly. "My visit was such a surprise, and of course the lady has better things to do than have dinner with two men our age."

Be careful with Matthew Clairmont. Knox's voice rang in my head. *He's a killer.*

Marsh smiled. "Yes, of course. I do hope to see you again—when the freshers have settled down."

Ask him about 1859. See if he'll share his secrets with a witch.

It's hardly a secret if you know it. Surprise registered on Knox's face when I replied to his mental warning in kind. It was the sixth time I'd used magic this year, but these were surely extenuating circumstances.

"It would be a pleasure, Warden. And thank you again for letting me stay in college this year." I nodded to the wizard. "Mr. Knox."

Fleeing from the warden's lodgings, I turned toward my old refuge in the cloisters and walked among the pillars until my pulse stopped racing. My mind was occupied with only one question: what to do now that two witches—my own people—had threatened me in the space of a single afternoon. With sudden clarity I knew the answer.

In my rooms I searched my bag until my fingers found Clairmont's crumpled business card, and then I dialed the first number.

He didn't answer.

After a robotic voice indicated that it was ready to receive my message, I spoke.

"Matthew, it's Diana. I'm sorry to bother you when you're out of town." I took a deep breath, trying to dispel some of the guilt associated with my decision not to tell Clairmont about Gillian and my parents, but only about Knox. "We need to talk. Something has happened. It's that wizard from the library. His name is Peter Knox. If you get this message, please call me."

I'd assured Sarah and Em that no vampire would meddle in my life. Gillian Chamberlain and Peter Knox had changed my mind. With shaking hands I lowered the shades and locked the door, wishing I'd never heard of Ashmole 782.

Chapter 11

That night, sleep was impossible. I sat on the sofa, then on the bed, the phone at my side. Not even a pot of tea and a raft of e-mail took my mind off the day's events. The notion that witches might have murdered my parents was beyond my comprehension. Pushing back those thoughts, I instead puzzled over the spell on Ashmole 782 and Knox's interest in it.

Still awake at dawn, I showered and changed. The idea of breakfast was uncharacteristically unappetizing. Rather than eat, I perched by the door until the Bodleian opened, then walked the short distance to the library and took my regular seat. My phone was in my pocket, set to vibrate, even though I hated it when other people's phones started buzzing and hopping in the quiet.

At half past ten, Peter Knox strolled in and sat at the opposite end of the room. On the premise of returning a manuscript, I walked back to the call desk to make sure that Miriam was still in the library. She was—and she was angry.

"Tell me that witch didn't take a seat down there."

"He did. He keeps staring at my back while I work."

"I wish I were larger," Miriam said with a frown.

"Somehow I think it would take more than size to deter that creature." I gave her a lopsided smile.

When Matthew came into the Selden End, without warning or sound, no icy patches announced his arrival. Instead there were touches of snowflakes all along my hair, shoulders, and back, as if he were checking quickly to make sure I was all in one piece.

My fingers gripped the table in front of me. For a few moments, I didn't dare turn in case it was simply Miriam. When I saw it was indeed Matthew, my heart gave a single loud thump.

But the vampire was no longer looking in my direction. He was staring at Peter Knox, his face ferocious.

"Matthew," I called softly, rising to my feet.

He dragged his eyes from the witch and strode to my side. When I frowned uncertainly at his fierce expression, he gave me a reassuring smile. "I understand there's been some excitement." He was so close that the coolness of his body felt as refreshing as a breeze on a summer day.

"Nothing we couldn't handle," I said evenly, conscious of Peter Knox.

"Can our conversation wait—just until the end of the day?" he asked. Matthew's fingers strayed up to touch a bump on his sternum that was visible under the soft fibers of his sweater. I wondered what he was wearing, close to his heart. "We could go to yoga."

Though I'd had no sleep, a drive to Woodstock in a moving vehicle with very good sound insulation, followed by an hour and a half of meditative movement, sounded perfect.

"That would be wonderful," I said sincerely.

"Would you like me to work here, with you?" he asked, leaning toward me. His scent was so powerful it was dizzying.

"That's not necessary," I said firmly.

"Let me know if you change your mind. Otherwise I'll see you outside Hertford at six." Matthew held my eyes a few moments longer. Then he sent a look of loathing in Peter Knox's direction and returned to his seat.

When I passed his desk on the way to lunch, Matthew coughed. Miriam slammed her pencil down in irritation and joined me. Knox would not be following me to Blackwell's. Matthew would see to that.

The afternoon dragged on interminably, and it was almost impossible to stay awake. By five o'clock, I was more than ready to leave the library. Knox remained in the Selden End, along with a motley assortment of humans. Matthew walked me downstairs, and my spirits lightened as I raced back to college, changed, and picked up my yoga mat. When his car pulled up to Hertford's metal railings, I was waiting for him.

"You're early," he observed with a smile, taking my mat and putting it into the trunk. Matthew breathed in sharply as he helped me into the car, and I wondered what messages my body had passed on to him.

"We need to talk."

"There's no rush. Let's get out of Oxford first." He closed the car door behind me and climbed into the driver's seat.

The traffic on the Woodstock Road was heavier due to the influx of students and dons. Matthew maneuvered deftly around the slow spots.

"How was Scotland?" I asked as we cleared the city limits, not caring what he talked about so long as he talked.

Matthew glanced at me and returned his eyes to the road. "Fine."

"Miriam said you were hunting."

He exhaled softly, his fingers rising to the bump under his sweater. "She shouldn't have."

"Why?"

"Because some things shouldn't be discussed in mixed company," he said with a touch of impatience. "Do witches tell creatures who aren't witches that they've just returned from four days of casting spells and boiling bats?"

"Witches don't boil bats!" I said indignantly.

"The point remains."

"Were you alone?" I asked.

Matthew waited a long time before answering. "No."

"I wasn't alone in Oxford either," I began. "The creatures—"

"Miriam told me." His hands tightened on the wheel. "If I'd known that the witch bothering you was Peter Knox, I'd never have left Oxford."

"You were right," I blurted, needing to make my own confession before tackling the subject of Knox. "I've never kept the magic out of my life. I've been using it in my work, without realizing it. It's in everything. I've been fooling myself for years." The words tumbled from my mouth. Matthew remained focused on the traffic. "I'm frightened."

His cold hand touched my knee. "I know."

"What am I going to do?" I whispered.

"We'll figure it out," he said calmly, turning in to the Old Lodge's gates. He scrutinized my face as we crested the rise and pulled in to the circular drive. "You're tired. Can you manage yoga?"

I nodded.

Matthew got out of the car and opened the door for me. This time he didn't help me out. Instead he fished around in the trunk, pulled out our mats, and shouldered both of them himself. Other members of the class filtered by, casting curious looks in our direction.

He waited until we were the only ones on the drive. Matthew looked down at me, wrestling with himself over something. I frowned, my head tilted back to meet his eyes. I'd just confessed to engaging in magic without realizing it. What was so awful that he couldn't tell me?

"I was in Scotland with an old friend, Hamish Osborne," he finally said.

"The man the newspapers want to run for Parliament so he can be chancellor of the exchequer?" I said in amazement.

"Hamish will not be running for Parliament," Matthew said drily, adjusting the strap of his yoga bag with a twitch.

"So he *is* gay!" I said, thinking back to a recent late-night news program.

Matthew gave me a withering glance. "Yes. More important, he's a daemon." I didn't know much about the world of creatures, but participating in human politics or religion was also forbidden.

"Oh. Finance is an odd career choice for a daemon." I thought for a moment. "It explains why he's so good at figuring out what to do with all that money, though."

"He is good at figuring things out." The silence stretched on, and Matthew made no move for the door. "I needed to get away and hunt."

I gave him a confused look.

"You left your sweater in my car," he said, as if that were an explanation.

"Miriam gave it back to me already."

"I know. I couldn't hold on to it. Do you understand why?"

When I shook my head, he sighed and then swore in French.

"My car was full of your scent, Diana. I needed to leave Oxford."

"I still don't understand," I admitted.

"I couldn't stop thinking about you." He raked his hand through his hair and looked down the drive.

My heart was beating irregularly, and the reduced blood flow slowed my mental processes. Finally, though, I understood.

"You're not afraid you would hurt me?" I had a healthy fear of vampires, but Matthew seemed different.

"I can't be sure." His eyes were wary, and his voice held a warning.

"So you didn't go because of what happened Friday night." My breath released in sudden relief.

"No," he said gently, "it had nothing to do with that."

"Are you two coming in, or are you going to practice out here on the drive?" Amira called from the doorway.

We went in to class, occasionally glancing at each other when one of us thought the other wasn't looking. Our first honest exchange of information had altered things. We were both trying to figure out what was going to happen next.

After class ended, when Matthew swung his sweater over his head, something shining and silver caught my eye. The object was tied around his neck on a thin leather cord. It was what he kept touching through his sweater, over and over, like a talisman.

"What's that?" I pointed.

"A reminder," Matthew said shortly.

"Of what?"

"The destructive power of anger."

Peter Knox had warned me to be careful around Matthew.

"Is it a pilgrim's badge?" The shape reminded me of one in the British Museum. It looked ancient.

He nodded and pulled the badge out by the cord. It swung freely, glinting as the light struck it. "It's an ampulla from Bethany." It was shaped like a coffin and just big enough to hold a few drops of holy water.

"Lazarus," I said faintly, eyeing the coffin. Bethany was where Christ had resurrected Lazarus from the dead. And though raised a pagan, I knew why Christians went on pilgrimage. They did it to atone for their sins.

Matthew slid the ampulla back into his sweater, concealing it from the eyes of the creatures who were still filing out of the room.

We said good-bye to Amira and stood outside the Old Lodge in the crisp autumn air. It was dark, despite the floodlights that bathed the bricks of the house.

"Do you feel better?" Matthew asked, breaking into my thoughts. I nodded. "Then tell me what's happened."

"It's the manuscript. Knox wants it. Agatha Wilson—the creature I met in Blackwell's—said the daemons want it. You want it, too. But Ashmole 782 is under a spell."

"I know," he said again.

A white owl swooped down in front of us, its wings beating the air. I flinched and lifted my arms to protect myself, convinced it was going to strike me with its beak and talons. But then the owl lost interest and soared up into the oak trees along the drive.

My heart was pounding, and a sudden rush of panic swept up from my feet. Without any warning, Matthew pulled open the back door of the Jaguar and pushed me into the seat. "Keep your head down and breathe," he said, crouching on the gravel with his fingers resting on my knees. The bile rose—there was nothing in my stomach but water—and crawled up my throat, choking me. I covered my mouth with my hand and retched convulsively. He reached over and tucked a wayward piece of hair behind my ear, his fingers cool and soothing.

"You're safe," he said.

"I'm so sorry." My shaking hand passed across my mouth as the nausea subsided. "The panic started last night after I saw Knox."

"Do you want to walk a bit?"

"No," I said hastily. The park seemed overly large and very black, and my legs felt like they were made of rubber bands.

Matthew inspected me with his keen eyes. "I'm taking you home. The rest of this conversation can wait."

He pulled me up from the backseat and held my hand loosely until he had me settled in the front of the car. I closed my eyes while he climbed in. We sat for a moment in silence, and then Matthew turned the key in the ignition. The Jaguar quickly sprang to life.

"Does this happen often?" he asked, his voice neutral.

"No, thank God," I said. "It happened a lot when I was a child, but it's much better now. It's just an excess of adrenaline." Matthew's glance settled on my hands as I pushed my hair from my face.

"I know," he said yet again, disengaging the parking brake and pulling out onto the drive.

"Can you smell it?"

He nodded. "It's been building up in you since you told me you were using magic. Is this why you exercise so much—the running, the rowing, the yoga?"

"I don't like taking drugs. They make me feel fuzzy."

"The exercise is probably more effective anyway."

"It hasn't done the trick this time," I murmured, thinking of my recently electrified hands.

Matthew pulled out of the Old Lodge's grounds and onto the road. He concentrated on his driving while the car's smooth movements rocked me gently.

"Why did you call me?" Matthew asked abruptly, interrupting my reveries.

"Because of Knox and Ashmole 782," I said, flickers of panic returning at his sudden shift in mood.

"I know that. What I'm asking is why you called *me*. Surely you have friends—witches, humans—who could help you."

"Not really. None of my human friends know I'm a witch. It would take days just to explain what's really happening in this world—if they stuck around long enough for me to finish, that is. I don't have friends who are witches, and I can't drag my aunts into this. It's not their fault I did something stupid and sent the manuscript back when I didn't understand it." I bit my lip. "Should I not have called you?"

"I don't know, Diana. On Friday you said witches and vampires couldn't be friends."

"On Friday I told you lots of things."

Matthew was quiet, giving his full attention to the curves in the road.

"I don't know what to think anymore." I paused, considering my next words carefully. "But there is one thing I know for sure. I'd rather share the library with you than with Knox."

"Vampires are never completely trustworthy—not when they're around warmbloods." Matthew's eyes focused on me for a single, cold moment.

"Warmbloods?" I asked with a frown.

"Humans, witches, daemons—everyone who's not a vampire."

"I'll risk your bite before I let Knox slither into my brain to fish for information."

"Has he tried to do that?" Matthew's voice was quiet, but there was a promise of violence in it.

"It was nothing," I said hastily. "He was just warning me about you."

"So he should. Nobody can be what he's not, no matter how hard he tries. You mustn't romanticize vampires. Knox may not have your best interests at heart, but he was right about me."

"Other people don't pick my friends—certainly not bigots like Knox." My fingers began to prickle as my anger mounted, and I shoved them under my thighs.

"Is that what we are, then? Friends?" Matthew asked.

"I think so. Friends tell each other the truth, even when it's difficult." Disconcerted by the seriousness of the conversation, I toyed with the ties on my sweater.

"Vampires aren't particularly good at friendship." He sounded angry again.

"Look, if you want me to leave you alone—"

"Of course not," Matthew interrupted. "It's just that vampire relationships are . . . complicated. We can be protective—possessive, even. You might not like it."

"A little protectiveness sounds pretty good to me about now."

My answer brought a look of raw vulnerability to Matthew's eyes. "I'll remind you of that when you start complaining," he said, the rawness quickly replaced with wry amusement.

He pulled off Holywell Street into the arched gates of the lodge. Fred glanced at the car and grinned before looking discreetly away. I waited for Matthew to open the door, checking the car carefully to make sure that nothing of mine was left there—not even a hair elastic—so as not to drive him back to Scotland.

"But there's more to all this than Knox and the manuscript," I said urgently when he handed me the mat. From his behavior you would think there weren't creatures closing in on me from every direction.

"It can wait, Diana. And don't worry. Peter Knox won't get within fifty feet of you again." His voice was grim, and he touched the ampulla under his sweater.

We needed time together—not in the library, but alone.

"Would you like to come to dinner tomorrow?" I asked him, my voice low. "We could talk about what happened then."

Matthew froze, confusion flitting over his face along with something I couldn't name. His fingers flexed slightly around the pilgrim's badge before he released it.

"I'd like that," he said slowly.

"Good." I smiled. "How's half past seven?"

He nodded and gave me a shy grin. I managed to walk two steps before realizing there was one matter that needed to be resolved before tomorrow night.

"What do you eat?" I whispered, my face flushing.

"I'm omnivorous," Matthew said, his face brightening further into a smile that made my heart skip a beat.

"Half past seven, then." I turned away, laughing and shaking my head at his unhelpful answer. "Oh, one more thing," I said, turning back. "Let Miriam do her own work. I really can take care of myself."

"So she tells me," Matthew said, walking around to the driver's side of the car. "I'll consider it. But you'll find me in Duke Humfrey's tomorrow, as usual." He got into the car, and when I showed no sign of moving, he rolled down his window.

"I'm not leaving until you're out of my sight," he said, looking at me in disapproval.

"Vampires," I muttered, shaking my head at his old-fashioned ways.

Chapter 12

Nothing in my culinary experience had taught me what to feed a vampire when he came for dinner.

In the library I spent most of the day on the Internet looking for recipes that involved raw foods, my manuscripts forgotten on the desk. Matthew said he was omnivorous, but that couldn't be true. A vampire must be more likely to tolerate uncooked food if he was used to a diet of blood. But he was so civilized he would no doubt eat whatever I put in front of him.

After undertaking extensive gastronomical research, I left the library at midafternoon. Matthew had held down Fortress Bishop by himself today, which must have pleased Miriam. There was no sign of Peter Knox or Gillian Chamberlain anywhere in Duke Humfrey's, which made me happy. Even Matthew looked in good humor when I trotted down the aisle to return my manuscripts.

Passing by the dome of the Radcliffe Camera, where the undergraduates read their assigned books, and the medieval walls of Jesus College, I went shopping along the aisles of Oxford's Covered Market. List in hand, I made my first stop at the butcher for fresh venison and rabbit, and then to the fishmonger for Scottish salmon.

Did vampires eat greens?

Thanks to my mobile, I was able to reach the zoology department and inquire about the feeding habits of wolves. They asked me what kind of wolves. I'd seen gray wolves on a long-ago field trip to the Boston zoo, and it was Matthew's favorite color, so that was my answer. After rattling off a long list of tasty mammals and explaining that they were "preferred foods," the bored voice on the other end told me that gray wolves also ate nuts, seeds, and berries. "But you shouldn't feed them!" the voice warned. "They're not house pets!"

"Thanks for the advice," I said, trying not to giggle.

The grocer apologetically sold me the last of the summer's black currants and some fragrant wild strawberries. A bag of chestnuts found its way into my expanding shopping bag, too.

Then it was off to the wine store, where I found myself at the mercy of a viticultural evangelist who asked if "the gentleman knew wine." That was enough to send me into a tailspin. The clerk seized upon my confusion to sell me what ended up being a remarkably few French and German bottles of wine for a king's ransom. He then tucked me into a cab to recover from the sticker shock during the drive back to college.

In my rooms I swept all the papers off a battered eighteenth-century table that served as both desk and dining room and moved it closer to the fireplace. I set the table carefully, using the old porcelain and silver that was in my cupboards, along with heavy crystal glasses that had to be the final remainders of an Edwardian set once used in the senior common room. My loyal kitchen ladies had supplied me with stacks of crisp white linen, which were now draped over the table, folded next to the silver, and spread on the chipped wooden tray that would help me carry things the short distance from the kitchen.

Once I started making dinner, it became clear that cooking for a vampire doesn't take much time. You don't actually *cook* much of anything.

By seven o'clock the candles were lit, the food was ready except for what could be done only at the last minute, and all that was left to get ready was me.

My wardrobe contained precious little that said "dinner with a vampire." There was no way I was dining with Matthew in a suit or in the outfit I'd worn to meet the warden. The number of black trousers and leggings I owned was mind-boggling, all with different degrees of spandex, but most were splotched with tea, boat grease, or both. Finally I found a pair of swishy black trousers that looked a bit like pajama bottoms but with slightly more style. They'd do.

Wearing nothing but a bra and the trousers, I ran into the bathroom and dragged a comb through my shoulder-length, straw-colored hair. Not only was it tied in knots at the end, it was daring me to make it behave by lifting up from my scalp with every touch of the comb. I briefly considered resorting to the curling iron, but chances were excellent I'd get only half my head done by the time Matthew arrived. He was going to be on time. I just knew it.

While brushing my teeth, I decided the only thing to do about my hair was to pull it away from my face and twist it into a knot. This made my chin and nose look more pointed but created the illusion of cheekbones and got my hair out of my eyes, which is where it gravitated these days. I pinned it back, and one piece immediately flopped forward. I sighed.

My mother's face stared back at me from the mirror. I thought of how beautiful she'd looked when she sat down to dinner, and I wondered what she'd done to make her pale eyebrows and lashes stand out the way they did and why her wide mouth looked so different when she smiled at me or my father. The clock ruled out any idea of achieving a similar transformation cosmetically. I had only three minutes to find a shirt, or I was going to be greeting Matthew Clairmont, distinguished professor of biochemistry and neuroscience, in my underwear.

The wardrobe contained two possibilities, one black and one midnight blue. The midnight blue had the virtue of being clean, which was the determining factor in its favor. It also had a funny collar that stood up in the back and winged toward my face before descending into a V-shaped neckline. The arms were relatively snug and ended in long, stiff cuffs that flared out slightly and ended up somewhere around the middle of the back of my hand. I was sticking a pair of silver earrings through my ears when there was a knock at the door.

My chest fluttered at the sound, as if this were a date. I squashed the thought immediately.

When I pulled the door open, Matthew stood outside looking like the prince in a fairy tale, tall and straight. In a break with his usual habits, he wore unadulterated black, which only made him look more striking—and more a vampire.

He waited patiently on the landing while I examined him.

"Where are my manners? Please come in, Matthew. Will that do as a formal invitation to enter my house?" I had seen that on TV or read it in a book.

His lips curved into a smile. "Forget most of what you think you know about vampires, Diana. This is just normal politeness. I'm not being held back by a mystical barrier standing between me and a fair maiden." Matthew had to stoop slightly to make it through the doorframe. He cradled a bottle of wine and carried some white roses.

"For you," he said, giving me an approving look and handing me the flowers. "Is there somewhere I can put this until dessert?" He glanced down at the bottle.

"Thank you, I love roses. How about the windowsill?" I suggested, before heading to the kitchen to look for a vase. My other vase had turned out to be a decanter, according to the senior common room's wine steward, who had come to my rooms a few hours earlier to point it out to me when I expressed doubt that I had such an item.

"Perfect," Matthew replied.

When I returned with the flowers, he was drifting around the room looking at the engravings.

"You know, these really aren't too bad," he said as I set the vase on a scarred Napoleonic-era chest of drawers.

"Mostly hunting scenes, I'm afraid."

"That had not escaped my attention," Matthew said, his mouth curved in amusement. I flushed with embarrassment.

"Are you hungry?" I had completely forgotten the obligatory nibbles and drinks you were supposed to serve before dinner.

"I could eat," the vampire said with a grin.

Safely back in the kitchen, I pulled two plates out of the refrigerator. The first course was smoked salmon with fresh dill sprinkled on top and a small pile of capers and gherkins arranged artistically on the side, where they could be construed as garnish if vampires didn't eat greens.

When I returned with the food, Matthew was waiting by the chair that was farthest from the kitchen. The wine was waiting in a high-sided silver coaster I'd been using to hold change but which the same helpful member of the senior common room's staff had explained was actually intended to hold wine. Matthew sat down while I extracted the cork from a bottle of German Riesling. I poured two glasses without spilling a drop and joined him.

My dinner guest was lost in concentration, holding the Riesling in front of his long, aquiline nose. I waited for him to finish whatever he was doing, wondering how many sensory receptors vampires had in their noses, as opposed to dogs.

I really didn't know the first thing about vampires.

"Very nice," he finally said, opening his eyes and smiling at me.

"I'm not responsible for the wine," I said quickly, snapping my napkin onto my lap. "The man at the wine store picked everything out, so if it's no good, it's not my fault."

"Very nice," he said again, "and the salmon looks wonderful."

Matthew picked up his knife and fork and speared a piece of fish. Watching him from under my lashes to see if he could actually eat it, I piled a bit of pickle, a caper, and some salmon on the back of my own fork.

"You don't eat like an American," he commented after he'd taken a sip of wine.

"No," I said, looking at the fork in my left hand and the knife in my right. "I expect I've spent too much time in England. Can you really eat this?" I blurted, unable to stand it anymore.

He laughed. "Yes, I happen to like smoked salmon."

"But you don't eat everything," I insisted, turning my attention back to my plate.

"No," he admitted, "but I can manage a few bites of most food. It doesn't taste like much to me, though, unless it's raw."

"That's odd, considering that vampires have such perfect senses. I'd think that all food would taste wonderful." My salmon tasted as clean as fresh, cold water.

He picked up his wineglass and looked into the pale, golden liquid. "Wine tastes wonderful. Food tastes wrong to a vampire once it's been cooked to death."

I reviewed the menu with enormous relief.

"If food doesn't taste good, why do you keep inviting me out to eat?" I asked.

Matthew's eyes flicked over my cheeks, my eyes, and lingered on my mouth. "It's easier to be around you when you're eating. The smell of cooked food nauseates me."

I blinked at him, still confused.

"As long as I'm nauseated, I'm not hungry," Matthew said, his voice exasperated.

"Oh!" The pieces clicked together. I already knew he liked the way I smelled. Apparently that made him hungry.

Oh. I flushed.

"I thought you knew that about vampires," he said more gently, "and that's why you invited me for dinner."

I shook my head, tucking another bundle of salmon together. "I probably know less about vampires than most humans do. And the little my Aunt Sarah taught me has to be treated as highly suspect, given her prejudices. She was quite clear, for instance, on your diet. She said vampires will consume only blood, because it's all you need to survive. But that isn't true, is it?"

Matthew's eyes narrowed, and his tone was suddenly frosty. "No. You need water to survive. Is that all you drink?"

"Should I not be talking about this?" My questions were making him angry. Nervously I wrapped my legs around the base of the chair and realized I'd never put on any shoes. I was entertaining in bare feet.

"You can't help being curious, I suppose," Matthew replied after considering my question for a long moment. "I drink wine and can eat food—preferably uncooked food, or food that's cold, so that it doesn't smell."

"But the food and wine don't nourish you," I guessed. "You feed on blood—all kinds of blood." He flinched. "And you don't have to wait outside until I invite you into my house. What else do I have wrong about vampires?"

Matthew's face adopted an expression of long-suffering patience. He sat back in his chair, taking the wineglass with him. I stood up slightly and reached across the table to pour him some more. If I was going to ply him with questions, I could at least ply him with wine, too. Leaning over the candles, I almost set my shirt on fire. Matthew grabbed the wine bottle.

"Why don't I do that?" he suggested. He poured himself some more and topped up my glass as well before he answered. "Most of what you know about me—about vampires—was dreamed up by humans. These legends made it possible for humans to live around us. Creatures frighten them. And I'm not talking solely about vampires."

"Black hats, bats, brooms." It was the unholy trinity of witchcraft lore, which burst into spectacular, ridiculous life every year on Halloween.

"Exactly." Matthew nodded. "Somewhere in each of these stories, there's a nugget of truth, something that frightened humans and helped them deny we were real. The strongest distinguishing characteristic of humans is their power of denial. I have strength and long life, you have supernatural abilities, daemons have awe-inspiring creativity. Humans can convince themselves up is down and black is white. It's their special gift."

"What's the truth in the story about vampires not being allowed inside without an invitation?" Having pressed him on his diet, I focused on the entrance protocols.

"Humans are with us all the time. They just refuse to acknowledge our existence because we don't make sense in their limited world. Once they allow us in—see us for who we really are—then we're in to stay, just as someone you've invited into your home can be hard to get rid of. They can't ignore us anymore."

"So it's like the stories of sunlight," I said slowly. "It's not that you can't be in sunlight, but when you are, it's harder for humans to ignore you. Rather than admit that you're walking among them, humans tell themselves you can't survive the light."

Matthew nodded again. "They manage to ignore us anyway, of course.

We can't stay indoors until it's dark. But we make more sense to humans after twilight—and that goes for you, too. You should see the looks when you walk into a room or down the street."

I thought about my ordinary appearance and glanced at him doubtfully. Matthew chuckled.

"You don't believe me, I know. But it's true. When humans see a creature in broad daylight, it makes them uneasy. We're too much for them—too tall, too strong, too confident, too creative, too powerful, too different. They try very hard to push our square pegs into their round holes all day long. At night it's a bit easier to dismiss us as merely odd."

I stood up and removed the fish plates, happy to see that Matthew had eaten everything but the garnish. He poured a bit more of the German wine into his glass while I pulled two more plates out of the refrigerator. Each held neatly arranged slices of raw venison so thin that the butcher insisted you could read the *Oxford Mail* through them. Vampires didn't like greens. We'd see about root vegetables and cheese. I heaped beets in the center of each plate and shaved Parmesan on top.

A broad-bottomed decanter full of red wine went into the center of the table, where it quickly caught Matthew's attention.

"May I?" he asked, no doubt worried about my burning down the college. He reached for the plain glass container, poured a bit of wine into our glasses, then held it up to his nose.

"Côte-Rôtie," he said with satisfaction. "One of my favorites."

I eyed the plain glass container. "You can tell that just from smelling it?"

He laughed. "Some vampire stories are true. I have an exceptional sense of smell—and excellent sight and hearing, too. But even a human could tell that this was Côte-Rôtie." He closed his eyes again. "Is it 2003?"

My mouth gaped open. "Yes!" This was better than watching a game show. There had been a little crown on the label. "Does your nose tell you who made it?"

"Yes, but that's because I've walked the fields where the grapes were grown," he confessed sheepishly, as if he'd been caught pulling a trick on me.

"You can smell the fields in this?" I stuck my nose in the glass, relieved that the odor of horse manure was no longer there.

"Sometimes I believe I can remember everything I've ever smelled. It's probably vanity," he said ruefully, "but scents bring back powerful memories. I remember the first time I smelled chocolate as if it were yesterday."

"Really?" I pitched forward in my chair.

"It was 1615. War hadn't broken out yet, and the French king had married a Spanish princess that no one liked—especially not the king." When I smiled, he smiled back, though his eyes were fixed on some distant image. "She brought chocolate to Paris. It was as bitter as sin and as decadent, too. We drank the cacao straight, mixed with water and no sugar."

I laughed. "It sounds awful. Thank goodness someone figured out that chocolate deserved to be sweet."

"That was a human, I'm afraid. The vampires liked it bitter and thick."

We picked up our forks and started in on the venison. "More Scottish food," I said, gesturing at the meat with my knife.

Matthew chewed a piece. "Red deer. A young Highlands stag from the taste of it."

I shook my head in amazement.

"As I said," he continued, "some of the stories are true."

"Can you fly?" I asked, already knowing the answer.

He snorted. "Of course not. We leave that to the witches, since you can control the elements. But we're strong and fast. Vampires can run and jump, which makes humans think we can fly. We're efficient, too."

"Efficient?" I put my fork down, unsure whether raw venison was to my liking.

"Our bodies don't waste much energy. We have a lot of it to spend on moving when we need to."

"You don't breathe much," I said, thinking back to yoga and taking a sip of wine.

"No," Matthew said. "Our hearts don't beat very often. We don't need to eat very often. We run cold, which slows down most bodily processes and helps explain why we live so long."

"The coffin story! You don't sleep much, but when you do, you sleep like the dead."

He grinned. "You're getting the hang of this, I see."

Matthew's plate was empty of everything except for the beets, and mine was empty except for the venison. I cleared away the second course and invited him to pour more wine.

The main dish was the only part of the meal that required heat, and not much of it. I had already made a bizarre biscuitlike thing from ground chestnuts. All that was left for me to do was sear some rabbit. The list of ingredients included rosemary, garlic, and celery. I decided to forgo the garlic. With his sense of smell, garlic must overpower everything else—there was the nugget of truth in *that* vampire legend. The celery was also ruled out. Vampires categorically did not like vegetables. Spices didn't seem to pose a problem, so I kept the rosemary and ground some pepper over the rabbit while it seared in the pan.

Leaving Matthew's rabbit a little underdone, I cooked mine a bit more than was required, in the hope that it would get the taste of raw venison out of my mouth. After assembling everything in an artistic pile, I delivered it to the table. "This is cooked, I'm afraid—but barely."

"You don't think this is a test of some sort, do you?" Matthew's face creased into a frown.

"No, no," I said hurriedly. "But I'm not used to entertaining vampires."

"I'm relieved to hear it," he murmured. He gave the rabbit a sniff. "It smells delicious." While he was bent over his plate, the heat from the rabbit amplified his distinctive scent of cinnamon and clove. Matthew forked up a bit of the chestnut biscuit. As it traveled to his mouth, his eyes widened. "Chestnuts?"

"Nothing but chestnuts, olive oil, and a bit of baking powder."

"And salt. And water, rosemary, and pepper," he commented calmly, taking another bite of the biscuit.

"Given your dietary restrictions, it's a good thing you can figure out exactly what you're putting in your mouth," I grumbled jokingly.

With most of the meal behind us, I began to relax. We chatted about Oxford while I cleared the plates and brought cheese, berries, and roasted chestnuts to the table.

"Help yourself," I said, putting an empty plate in front of him. Matthew savored the aroma of the tiny strawberries and sighed happily as he picked up a chestnut.

"These really are better warm," he observed. He cracked the hard nut easily in his fingers and popped the meat out of the shell. The nutcracker hanging off the edge of the bowl was clearly optional equipment with a vampire at the table.

"What do I smell like?" I asked, toying with the stem of my wineglass.

For a few moments, it seemed as though he wasn't going to answer. The silence stretched thin before he turned wistful eyes on me. His lids fell, and he inhaled deeply.

"You smell of willow sap. And chamomile that's been crushed underfoot." He sniffed again and smiled a small, sad smile. "There's honeysuckle and fallen oak leaves, too," he said softly, breathing out, "along with witch hazel blooming and the first narcissus of spring. And ancient things—horehound, frankincense, lady's mantle. Scents I thought I'd forgotten."

His eyes opened slowly, and I looked into their gray depths, afraid to breathe and break the spell his words had cast.

"What about me?" he asked, his eyes holding on to mine.

"Cinnamon." My voice was hesitant. "And cloves. Sometimes I think you smell of carnations—not the kind in the florist shops but the old-fashioned ones that grow in English cottage gardens."

"Clove pinks," Matthew said, his eyes crinkling at the corners in amusement. "Not bad for a witch."

I reached for a chestnut. Cupping the nut in my palms, I rolled it from one hand to the other, the warmth traveling up my suddenly chilly arms.

Matthew sat back in his chair again, surveying my face with little flicks of his eyes. "How did you decide what to serve for dinner tonight?" He gestured at the berries and nuts that were left from the meal.

"Well, it wasn't magic. The zoology department helped a lot," I explained.

He looked startled, then roared with laughter. "You asked the zoology department what to make me for dinner?"

"Not exactly," I said defensively. "There were raw-food recipes on the Net, but I got stuck after I bought the meat. They told me what gray wolves ate."

Matthew shook his head, but he was still smiling, and my irritation dissolved. "Thank you," he said simply. "It's been a very long time since someone made me a meal."

"You're welcome. The wine was the worst part."

Matthew's eyes brightened. "Speaking of wine," he said, standing up and folding his napkin, "I brought us something to have after dinner."

He asked me to fetch two fresh glasses from the kitchen. An old, slightly lopsided bottle was sitting on the table when I returned. It had a faded cream label with simple lettering and a coronet. Matthew was working the corkscrew carefully into a cork that was crumbly and black with age.

His nostrils flared when he pulled it free, his face taking on the look of a cat in secure possession of a delectable canary. The wine that came out of the bottle was syrupy, its golden color glinting in the light of the candles.

"Smell it," he commanded, handing me one of the glasses, "and tell me what you think."

I took a sniff and gasped. "It smells like caramels and berries," I said, wondering how something so yellow could smell of something red.

Matthew was watching me closely, interested in my reactions. "Take a sip," he suggested.

The wine's sweet flavors exploded in my mouth. Apricots and vanilla custard from the kitchen ladies tumbled across my tongue, and my mouth tingled with them long after I'd swallowed. It was like drinking magic.

"What is this?" I finally said, after the taste of the wine had faded.

"It was made from grapes picked a long, long time ago. That summer had been hot and sunny, and the farmers worried that the rains were going to come and ruin the crop. But the weather held, and they got the grapes in just before the weather changed."

"You can taste the sunshine," I said, earning myself another beautiful smile.

"During the harvest a comet blazed over the vineyards. It had been visible through astronomers' telescopes for months, but in October it was so bright you could almost read by its light. The workers saw it as a sign that the grapes were blessed."

"Was this in 1986? Was it Halley's comet?"

Matthew shook his head. "No. It was 1811." I stared in astonishment at the almost two-hundred-year-old wine in my glass, fearing it might evaporate before my eyes. "Halley's comet came in 1759 and 1835." He pronounced the name "Hawley."

"Where did you get it?" The wine store by the train station did not have wine like this.

"I bought it from Antoine-Marie as soon as he told me it was going to be extraordinary," he said with amusement.

Turning the bottle, I looked at the label. Château Yquem. Even I had heard of that.

"And you've had it ever since," I said. He'd drunk chocolate in Paris in 1615 and received a building permit from Henry VIII in 1536—of course he was buying wine in 1811. And there was the ancient-looking ampulla he was wearing around his neck, the cord visible at his throat.

"Matthew," I said slowly, watching him for any early warning signs of anger. "How old are you?"

His mouth hardened, but he kept his voice light. "I'm older than I look."

"I know that," I said, unable to curb my impatience.

"Why is my age important?"

"I'm a historian. If somebody tells me he remembers when chocolate was introduced into France or a comet passing overhead in 1811, it's difficult not to be curious about the other events he might have lived through. You were alive in 1536—I've been to the house you had built. Did you know Machiavelli? Live through the Black Death? Attend the University of Paris when Abelard was teaching there?"

He remained silent. The hair on the back of my neck started to prickle.

"Your pilgrim's badge tells me you were once in the Holy Land. Did you go on crusade? See Halley's comet pass over Normandy in 1066?"

Still nothing.

"Watch Charlemagne's coronation? Survive the fall of Carthage? Help keep Attila from reaching Rome?"

Matthew held up his right index finger. "Which fall of Carthage?"

"You tell me!"

"Damn you, Hamish Osborne," he muttered, his hand flexing on the tablecloth. For the second time in two days, Matthew struggled over what to say. He stared into the candle, drawing his finger slowly through the flame. His flesh erupted into angry red blisters, then smoothed itself out into white, cold perfection an instant later without a flicker of pain evident on his face.

"I believe that my body is nearly thirty-seven years of age. I was born around the time Clovis converted to Christianity. My parents remembered that, or I'd have no idea. We didn't keep track of birthdays back then. It's tidier to pick the date of five hundred and be done with it." He looked up at me, briefly, and returned his attention to the candles. "I was reborn a vampire in 537, and with the exception of Attila—who was before my time—you've touched on most of the high and low points in the millennium between then and the year I put the keystone into my house in Woodstock. Because you're a historian, I feel obligated to tell you that Machiavelli was not nearly as impressive as you all seem to think he was. He was just a Florentine politician—and not a terribly good one at that." A note of weariness had crept into his voice.

Matthew Clairmont was more than fifteen hundred years old.

"I shouldn't pry," I said by way of apology, unsure of where to look and mystified as to what had led me to think that knowing the historical events this vampire had lived through would help me know him better. A line from Ben Jonson floated into my mind. It seemed to explain Matthew in a way that the coronation of Charlemagne could not. "'*He was not of an age, but for all time,*'" I murmured.

"'*With thee conversing I forget all time,*'" he responded, traveling further into seventeenth-century literature and offering up a line from Milton.

We looked at each other for as long as we could stand it, working another fragile spell between us. I broke it.

"What were you doing in the fall of 1859?"

His face darkened. "What has Peter Knox been telling you?"

"That you were unlikely to share your secrets with a witch." My voice sounded calmer than I felt.

"Did he?" Matthew said softly, sounding less angry than he clearly was. I could see it in the set of his jaw and shoulders. "In September 1859 I was looking through the manuscripts in the Ashmolean Museum."

"Why, Matthew?" *Please tell me,* I urged silently, crossing my fingers in my lap. I'd provoked him into revealing the first part of his secret but wanted him to freely give me the rest. *No games, no riddles. Just tell me.*

"I'd recently finished reading a book manuscript that was soon going to press. It was written by a Cambridge naturalist." Matthew put down his glass.

My hand flew to my mouth as the significance of the date registered. "*Origin.*" Like Newton's great work of physics, the *Principia,* this was a book that did not require a full citation. Anyone who'd passed high-school biology knew Darwin's *On the Origin of Species.*

"Darwin's article the previous summer laid out his theory of natural selection, but the book was quite different. It was marvelous, the way he established easily observable changes in nature and inched you toward accepting something so revolutionary."

"But alchemy has nothing to do with evolution." Grabbing the bottle, I poured myself more of the precious wine, less concerned that it might vanish than that I might come unglued.

"Lamarck believed that each species descended from different ancestors and progressed independently toward higher forms of being. It's remarkably similar to what your alchemists believed—that the philosopher's stone was the elusive end product of a natural transmutation of base metals into more exalted metals like copper, silver, and gold." Matthew reached for the wine, and I pushed it toward him.

"But Darwin disagreed with Lamarck, even if he did use the same word—'transmutation'—in his initial discussions of evolution."

"He disagreed with linear transmutation, it's true. But Darwin's theory of natural selection can still be seen as a series of linked transmutations."

Maybe Matthew was right and magic really was in everything. It was in Newton's theory of gravity, and it might be in Darwin's theory of evolution, too.

"There are alchemical manuscripts all over the world." I was trying to remain moored to the details while coming to terms with the bigger picture. "Why the Ashmole manuscripts?"

"When I read Darwin and saw how he seemed to explore the alchemical theory of transmutation through biology, I remembered stories about a mysterious book that explained the origin of our three species—daemons, witches, and vampires. I'd always dismissed them as fantastic." He took a sip of wine. "Most suggested that the story was concealed from human eyes in a book of alchemy. The publication of *Origin* prompted me to look for it, and if such a book existed, Elias Ashmole would have bought it. He had an uncanny ability to find bizarre manuscripts."

"You were looking for it here in Oxford, one hundred and fifty years ago?"

"Yes," Matthew said. "And one hundred and fifty years before you received Ashmole 782, I was told that it was missing."

My heart sped up, and he looked at me in concern. "Keep going," I said, waving him on.

"I've been trying to get my hands on it ever since. Every other Ashmole manuscript was there, and none seemed promising. I've looked at manuscripts in other libraries—at the Herzog August Bibliothek in Germany, the Bibliothèque Nationale in France, the Medici Library in Florence, the Vatican, the Library of Congress."

I blinked, thinking of a vampire wandering the hallways of the Vatican.

"The only manuscript I haven't seen is Ashmole 782. By simple process of elimination, it must be the manuscript that contains our story—if it still survives."

"You've looked at more alchemical manuscripts than I have."

"Perhaps," Matthew admitted, "but it doesn't mean I understand them as well as you do. What all the manuscripts I've seen have in common, though, is an absolute confidence that the alchemist can help one substance change into another, creating new forms of life."

"That sounds like evolution," I said flatly.

"Yes," Matthew said gently, "it does."

We moved to the sofas, and I curled up into a ball at the end of one while Matthew sprawled in the corner of the other, his long legs stretched out in front of him. Happily, he'd brought the wine. Once we were settled, it was time for more honesty between us.

"I met a daemon, Agatha Wilson, at Blackwell's last week. According to the Internet, she's a famous designer. Agatha told me the daemons believe that Ashmole 782 is the story of all origins—even human origins. Peter Knox told me a different story. He said it was the first grimoire, the source of all witches' power. Knox believes that the manuscript contains the secret of immortality," I said, glancing at Matthew, "and how to destroy vampires. I've heard the daemon and witch versions of the story—now I want yours."

"Vampires believe the lost manuscript explains our longevity and our strength," he said. "In the past, our fear was that this secret—if it fell into witches' hands—would lead to our extermination. Some fear that magic was involved in our making and that the witches might find a way to reverse the magic and destroy us. It seems that that part of the legend might be true." He exhaled softly, looking worried.

"I still don't understand why you're so certain that this book of origins—whatever it may contain—is hidden inside an alchemy book."

"An alchemy book could hide these secrets in plain sight—just like Peter Knox hides his identity as a witch under the veneer that he's an expert in the occult. I think it was vampires who learned that the book was alchemical. It's too perfect a fit to be coincidence. The human alchemists seemed to capture what it is to be a vampire when they wrote about the philosopher's stone. Becoming a vampire makes us nearly immortal, it makes most of us rich, and it gives us the chance to accrue unimaginable knowledge and learning."

"That's the philosopher's stone, all right." The parallels between this mythic substance and the creature sitting opposite me were striking—and chilling. "But it's still hard to imagine such a book really exists. For one thing, all the stories contradict one another. And who would be so foolish as to put so much information in one place?"

"As with the legends about vampires and witches, there's at least a nugget of truth in all the stories about the manuscript. We just have to figure out what that nugget is and strip away the rest. Then we'll begin to understand."

Matthew's face bore no trace of deceit or evasion. Encouraged by his use of "we," I decided he'd earned more information.

"You're right about Ashmole 782. The book you've been seeking is inside it."

"Go on," Matthew said softly, trying to control his curiosity.

"It's an alchemy book on the surface. The images contain errors, or deliberate mistakes—I still can't decide which." I bit my lip in concentration, and his eyes fixed on the place where my teeth had drawn a tiny bead of blood to the surface.

"What do you mean 'it's an alchemy book on the surface'?" Matthew held his glass closer to his nose.

"It's a palimpsest. But the ink hasn't been washed away. Magic is hiding the text. I almost missed the words, they're hidden so well. But when I turned one of the pages, the light was at just the right angle and I could see lines of writing moving underneath."

"Could you read it?"

"No." I shook my head. "If Ashmole 782 contains information about who we are, how we came to be, and how we might be destroyed, it's deeply buried."

"It's fine if it remains buried," Matthew said grimly, "at least for now. But the time is quickly coming when we will need that book."

"Why? What makes it so urgent?"

"I'd rather show you than tell you. Can you come to my lab tomorrow?"

I nodded, mystified.

"We can walk there after lunch," he said, standing up and stretching. We had emptied the bottle of wine amid all this talk of secrets and origins. "It's late. I should go."

Matthew reached for the doorknob and gave it a twist. It rattled, and the catch sprang open easily.

He frowned. "Have you had trouble with your lock?"

"No," I said, pushing the mechanism in and out, "not that I'm aware of."

"You should have them look at that," he said, still jiggling the door's hardware. "It might not close properly until you do."

When I looked up from the door, an emotion I couldn't name flitted across his face.

"I'm sorry the evening ended on such a serious note," he said softly. "I did have a lovely time."

"Was the dinner really all right?" I asked. We'd talked about the secrets of the universe, but I was more worried about how his stomach was faring.

"It was more than all right," he assured me.

My face softened at his beautiful, ancient features. How could people walk by him on the street and not gasp? Before I could stop myself, my toes were gripping the old rug and I was stretching up to kiss him quickly on the cheek. His skin felt smooth and cold like satin, and my lips felt unusually warm against his flesh.

Why did you do that? I asked myself, coming down off my toes and gazing at the questionable doorknob to hide my confusion.

It was over in a matter of seconds, but as I knew from using magic to get *Notes and Queries* off the Bodleian's shelf, a few seconds was all it took to change your life.

Matthew studied me. When I showed no sign of hysteria or an inclination to make a run for it, he leaned toward me and kissed me slowly once, twice in the French manner. His face skimmed over mine, and he drank in my scent of willow sap and honeysuckle. When he straightened, Matthew's eyes looked smokier than usual.

"Good night, Diana," he said with a smile.

Moments later, leaning against the closed door, I spied the blinking number one on my answering machine. Mercifully, the machine's volume was turned down.

Aunt Sarah wanted to ask the same question I'd asked myself.

I just didn't want to answer.

Chapter 13

Matthew came to collect me after lunch—the only creature among the human readers in the Selden End. While he walked me under the ornately painted exposed beams, he kept up a steady patter of questions about my work and what I'd been reading.

Oxford had turned resolutely cold and gray, and I pulled my collar up around my neck, shivering in the damp air. Matthew seemed not to mind and wasn't wearing a coat. The gloomy weather made him look a little less startling, but it wasn't enough to make him blend in entirely. People turned and stared in the Bodleian's central courtyard, then shook their heads.

"You've been noticed," I told him.

"I forgot my coat. Besides, they're looking at you, not me." He gave me a dazzling smile. A woman's jaw dropped, and she poked her friend, inclining her head in Matthew's direction.

I laughed. "You are so wrong."

We headed toward Keble College and the University Parks, making a right turn at Rhodes House before entering the labyrinth of modern buildings devoted to laboratory and computer space. Built in the shadow of the Museum of Natural History, the enormous redbrick Victorian cathedral to science, these were monuments of unimaginative, functional contemporary architecture.

Matthew pointed to our destination—a nondescript, low-slung building—and fished in his pocket for a plastic identity card. He swiped it through the reader at the door handle and punched in a set of codes in two different sequences. Once the door unlocked, he ushered me to the guard's station, where he signed me in as a guest and handed me a pass to clip to my sweater.

"That's a lot of security for a university laboratory," I commented, fiddling with the badge.

The security only increased as we walked down the miles of corridors that somehow managed to fit behind the modest façade. At the end of one hallway, Matthew took a different card out of his pocket, swiped it, and put his index finger on a glass panel next to a door. The glass panel chimed, and a touch pad appeared on its surface. Matthew's fingers raced over the numbered keys. The door clicked softly open, and there was a clean, slightly antiseptic smell reminiscent of hospitals and empty professional kitchens.

It derived from unbroken expanses of tile, stainless steel, and electronic equipment.

A series of glass-enclosed rooms stretched ahead of us. One held a round table for meetings, a black monolith of a monitor, and several computers. Another held an old wooden desk, a leather chair, an enormous Persian rug that must have been worth a fortune, telephones, fax machines, and still more computers and monitors. Beyond were other enclosures that held banks of file cabinets, microscopes, refrigerators, autoclaves, racks upon racks of test tubes, centrifuges, and dozens of unrecognizable devices and instruments.

The whole area seemed unoccupied, although from somewhere there came faint strains of a Bach cello concerto and something that sounded an awful lot like the latest hit recorded by the Eurovision song-contest winners.

As we passed by the two office spaces, Matthew gestured at the one with the rug. "My office," he explained. He then steered me into the first laboratory on the left. Every surface held some combination of computers, microscopes, and specimen containers arranged neatly in racks. File cabinets ringed the walls. One of their drawers had a label that read "<o."

"Welcome to the history lab." The blue light made his face look whiter, his hair blacker. "This is where we're studying evolution. We take in physical specimens from old burial sites, excavations, fossilized remains, and living beings, and extract DNA from the samples." Matthew opened a different drawer and pulled out a handful of files. "We're just one laboratory among hundreds all over the world using genetics to study problems of species origin and extinction. The difference between our lab and the rest is that humans aren't the only species we're studying."

His words dropped, cold and clear, around me.

"You're studying vampire genetics?"

"Witches and daemons, too." Matthew hooked a wheeled stool with his foot and gently sat me on top of it.

A vampire wearing black Converse high-tops came rocketing around the corner and squeaked to a halt, pulling on a pair of latex gloves. He was in his late twenties, with the blond hair and blue eyes of a California surfer. Standing next to Matthew, his average height and build made him look slight, but his body was wiry and energetic.

"AB-positive," he said, studying me admiringly. "Wow, terrific find." He closed his eyes and inhaled deeply. "And a witch, too!"

"Marcus Whitmore, meet Diana Bishop. She's a professor of history from Yale"—Matthew frowned at the younger vampire—"and is here as a guest, not a pincushion."

"Oh." Marcus looked disappointed, then brightened. "Would you mind if I took some of your blood anyway?"

"Yes, as a matter of fact." I had no wish to be poked and prodded by a vampire phlebotomist.

Marcus whistled. "That's some fight-or-flight response you have there, Dr. Bishop. Smell that adrenaline."

"What's going on?" a familiar soprano voice called out. Miriam's diminutive frame was visible a few seconds later.

"Dr. Bishop is a bit overwhelmed by the laboratory, Miriam."

"Sorry. I didn't realize it was her," Miriam said. "She smells different. Is it adrenaline?"

Marcus nodded. "Yep. Are you always like this? All dressed up in adrenaline and no place to go?"

"Marcus." Matthew could issue a bone-chilling warning in remarkably few syllables.

"Since I was seven," I said, meeting his startling blue eyes.

Marcus whistled again. "That explains a lot. No vampire could turn his back on that." Marcus wasn't referring to my physical features, even though he gestured in my direction.

"What are you talking about?" I asked, curiosity overcoming my nerves.

Matthew pulled on the hair at his temples and gave Marcus a glare that would curdle milk. The younger vampire looked blasé and cracked his knuckles. I jumped at the sharp sound.

"Vampires are predators, Diana," Matthew explained. "We're attracted to the fight-or-flight response. When people or animals become agitated, we can smell it."

"We can taste it, too. Adrenaline makes blood even more delicious," Marcus said. "Spicy, silky, and then it turns sweet. Really good stuff."

A low rumble started in Matthew's throat. His lips curled away from his teeth, and Marcus stepped backward. Miriam placed her hand firmly on the blond vampire's forearm.

"What? I'm not hungry!" Marcus protested, shaking off Miriam's hand.

"Dr. Bishop may not know that vampires don't have to be physically hungry to be sensitive to adrenaline, Marcus." Matthew controlled himself with visible effort. "Vampires don't always need to feed, but we always crave the hunt and the adrenaline reaction of prey to predator."

Given my struggle to control anxiety, it was no wonder Matthew was always asking me out for a meal. It wasn't my honeysuckle scent that made him hungry—it was my excess adrenaline.

"Thank you for explaining, Matthew." Even after last night, I was still relatively ignorant about vampires. "I'll try to calm down."

"There's no need," Matthew said shortly. "It's not your job to calm down. It's our job to exercise a modicum of courtesy and control." He glowered at Marcus and pulled one of the files forward.

Miriam shot a worried glance in my direction. "Maybe we should start at the beginning."

"No. I think it's better to start at the end," he replied, opening the file.

"Do they know about Ashmole 782?" I asked Matthew when Miriam and Marcus showed no sign of leaving. He nodded. "And you told them what I saw?" He nodded again.

"Did you tell anyone else?" Miriam's question to me reflected centuries of suspicion.

"If you mean Peter Knox, no. Only my aunt and her partner, Emily, know."

"Three witches and three vampires sharing a secret," Marcus said thoughtfully, glancing at Matthew. "Interesting."

"Let's hope we can do a better job keeping it than we have done at hiding this." Matthew slid the file toward me.

Three sets of vampire eyes watched me attentively as I opened it. VAMPIRE ON THE LOOSE IN LONDON, the headline screamed. My stomach flopped over, and I moved the newspaper clipping aside. Underneath was the report of another mysterious death involving a bloodless corpse. Below that was a magazine story accompanied by a picture that made its contents clear despite my inability to read Russian. The victim's throat had been ripped open from jaw to carotid artery.

There were dozens more murders, and reports in every language imaginable. Some of the deaths involved beheadings. Some involved corpses drained of blood, without a speck of blood evidence found at the scene. Others suggested an animal attack, due to the ferocity of the injuries to the neck and torso.

"We're dying," Matthew said when I pushed the last of the stories aside.

"Humans are dying, that's for sure." My voice was harsh.

"Not just the humans," he said. "Based on this evidence, vampires are exhibiting signs of species deterioration."

"This is what you wanted to show me?" My voice shook. "What do these have to do with the origin of creatures or Ashmole 782?" Gillian's recent warnings had stirred painful memories, and these pictures only brought them into sharper focus.

"Hear me out," Matthew said quietly. "Please."

He might not be making sense, but he wasn't deliberately frightening me either. Matthew must have had a good reason for sharing this. Hugging the file folder, I sat down on my stool.

"These deaths," he began, drawing the folder gently away from me, "result from botched attempts to transform humans into vampires. What was once second nature to us has become difficult. Our blood is increasingly incapable of making new life out of death."

Failure to reproduce would make any species extinct. Based on the pictures I'd just seen, however, the world didn't need more vampires.

"It's easier for those who are older—vampires such as myself who fed predominantly on human blood when we were young," Matthew continued. "As a vampire ages, however, we feel less compulsion to make new vampires. Younger vampires, though, are a different story. They want to start families to dispel the loneliness of their new lives. When they find a human they want to mate with, or try to make children, some discover that their blood isn't powerful enough."

"You said we're all going extinct," I reminded him evenly, my anger still simmering.

"Modern witches aren't as powerful as their ancestors were." Miriam's voice was matter-of-fact. "And you don't produce as many children as in times past."

"That doesn't sound like evidence—it sounds like a subjective assessment," I said.

"You want to see the evidence?" Miriam picked up two more file folders and tossed them across the gleaming surface so that they slid into my arms. "There it is—though I doubt you'll understand much of it."

One had a purple-edged label with "Benvenguda" typed neatly on it. The other had a red-edged label, bearing the name "Good, Beatrice." The folders contained nothing but graphs. Those on top were hoop-shaped and brilliantly colored. Underneath, more graphs showed black and gray bars marching across white paper.

"That's not fair," Marcus protested. "No historian could read those."

"These are DNA sequences," I said, pointing to the black-and-white images. "But what are the colored graphs?"

Matthew rested his elbows on the table next to me. "They're also genetic test results," he said, drawing the hoop-covered page closer. "These tell us about the mitochondrial DNA of a woman named Benvenguda, which she inherited from her mother, and her mother's mother, and every female ancestor before her. They tell us the story of her matrilineage."

"What about her father's genetic legacy?"

Matthew picked up the black-and-white DNA results. "Benvenguda's human father is here, in her nuclear DNA—her genome—along with her mother, who was a witch." He returned to the multicolored hoops. "But the mitochondrial DNA, outside the cell's nucleus, records only her maternal ancestry."

"Why are you studying both her genome and her mitochondrial DNA?" I had heard of the genome, but mitochondrial DNA was new territory for me.

"Your nuclear DNA tells us about you as a unique individual—how the genetic legacy of your mother and father recombined to create you. It's the mixture of your father's genes and your mother's genes that gave you blue eyes, blond hair, and freckles. Mitochondrial DNA can help us to understand the history of a whole species."

"That means the origin and evolution of the species is recorded in every one of us," I said slowly. "It's in our blood and every cell in our body."

Matthew nodded. "But every origin story tells another tale—not of beginnings but of endings."

"We're back to Darwin," I said, frowning. "*Origin* wasn't entirely about where different species came from. It was about natural selection and species extinction, too."

"Some would say *Origin* was mostly about extinction," Marcus agreed, rolling up to the other side of the lab bench.

I looked at Benvenguda's brilliant hoops. "Who was she?"

"A very powerful witch," Miriam said, "who lived in Brittany in the seventh century. She was a marvel in an age that produced many marvels. Beatrice Good is one of her last-known direct descendants."

"Did Beatrice Good's family come from Salem?" I whispered, touching her folder. There had been Goods living there alongside the Bishops and Proctors.

"Beatrice's lineage includes Sarah and Dorothy Good of Salem," Matthew said, confirming my hunch. He opened Beatrice's file folder and put her mitochondrial test results next to those of Benvenguda.

"But they're different," I said. You could see it in the colors and the way they were arranged.

"Not so different," Matthew corrected me. "Beatrice's nuclear DNA has fewer markers common among witches. This indicates that her ancestors, as the centuries passed, relied less and less on magic and witchcraft as they struggled to survive. Those changing needs began to force mutations in her DNA—mutations that pushed the magic aside." His message sounded perfectly scientific, but it was meant for me.

"Beatrice's ancestors pushed their magic aside, and that will eventually destroy the family?"

"It's not entirely the witches' fault. Nature is to blame, too." Matthew's eyes were sad. "It seems that witches, like vampires, have also felt the pressures of surviving in a world that is increasingly human. Daemons, too. They exhibit less genius—which was how we used to distinguish them from the human population—and more madness."

"The humans aren't dying out?" I asked.

"Yes and no," Matthew said. "We think that the humans have—until now—proved better at adapting. Their immune systems are more responsive, and they have a stronger urge to reproduce than either vampires or witches. Once the world was divided more evenly between humans and creatures. Now humans are in the majority and creatures make up only ten percent of the world's population."

"The world was a different place when there were as many creatures as humans." Miriam sounded regretful that the genetic deck was no longer stacked in our favor. "But their sensitive immune systems are going to get humans in the end."

"How different are we—the creatures—from humans?"

"Considerably, at least on the genetic level. We appear similar, but under the surface our chromosomal makeup is distinctive." Matthew sketched a diagram on the outside of Beatrice Good's folder. "Humans have twenty-three chromosomal pairs in every cell nucleus, each arranged in long code sequences. Vampires and witches have twenty-four chromosome pairs."

"More than humans, pinot noir grapes, or pigs." Marcus winked.

"What about daemons?"

"They have the same number of chromosome pairs as humans—but they also have a single extra chromosome. As far as we can tell, it's their extra chromosome that makes them daemonic," Matthew replied, "and prone to instability."

While I was studying his pencil sketch, a piece of hair fell into my eyes. I pushed at it impatiently. "What's in the extra chromosomes?" It was as hard for me to keep up with Matthew now as it had been managing to pass college biology.

"Genetic material that distinguishes us from humans," Matthew said, "as well as material that regulates cell function or is what scientists call 'junk DNA.'"

"It's not junk, though," Marcus said. "All that genetic material has to be left over from previous selection, or it's waiting to be used in the next evolutionary change. We just don't know what its purpose is—yet."

"Wait a minute," I interjected. "Witches and daemons are born. I was born with an extra pair of chromosomes, and your friend Hamish was born with a single extra chromosome. But vampires aren't born—you're made, from human DNA. Where do you acquire an extra chromosome pair?"

"When a human is reborn a vampire, the maker first removes all the human's blood, which causes organ failure. Before death can occur, the maker gives his or her blood to the one being reborn," replied Matthew. "As far as we can tell, the influx of a vampire's blood forces spontaneous genetic mutations in every cell of the body."

Matthew had used the term "reborn" last night, but I'd never heard the word "maker" in connection with vampires before.

"The maker's blood floods the reborn's system, carrying new genetic information with it," Miriam said. "Something similar happens with human blood transfusions. But a vampire's blood causes hundreds of modifications in the DNA."

"We started looking in the genome for evidence of such explosive change," Matthew explained. "We found it—mutations proving that all new vampires went through a spontaneous adaptation to survive when they absorbed their makers' blood. That's what prompts the development of an extra chromosome pair."

"A genetic big bang. You're like a galaxy born from a dying star. In a few moments, your genes transform you into something else—something inhuman." I looked at Matthew in wonder.

"Are you all right?" he asked. "We can take a break."

"Could I have some water?"

"I'll get it." Marcus hopped up from his stool. "There's some in the specimen fridge."

"Humans provided the first clue that acute cellular stress from bacteria and other forms of genetic bombardment could trigger quick mutations, rather than the slower changes of natural selection." Miriam pulled a folder out of a file drawer. Opening it, she pointed to a section of a black-and-white graph. "This man died in 1375. He survived smallpox, but the disease forced a mutation on the third chromosome as his body quickly coped with the influx of bacteria."

Marcus returned with my water. I took the cap off and drank thirstily.

"Vampire DNA is full of similar mutations resulting from disease resistance. Those changes might be slowly leading to our extinction." Matthew looked worried. "Now we're trying to focus on what it is about vampire blood that triggers the generation of new chromosomes. The answer may lie in the mitochondria."

Miriam shook her head. "No way. The answer's in the nuclear DNA. When a body is assaulted by vampire blood, it must trigger a reaction that makes it possible for the body to capture and assimilate the changes."

"Maybe, but if so, we need to look more closely at the junk DNA, too. Everything must be there to generate new chromosomes," Marcus insisted.

While the three of them argued, I was rolling up my sleeve. When the fabric cleared my elbow and the veins in my arm were exposed to the cool air of the laboratory, they directed their freezing attention at my skin.

"Diana," Matthew said coldly, touching his Lazarus badge, "what are you doing?"

"Do you still have your gloves handy, Marcus?" I asked, continuing to inch my sleeve up.

Marcus grinned. "Yeah." He stood and pulled a pair of latex gloves out of a nearby box.

"You don't have to do this." Matthew's voice caught in his throat.

"I know that. I want to." My veins looked even bluer in the lab's light.

"Good veins," Miriam said with a nod of approval, eliciting a warning purr from the tall vampire standing next to me.

"If this is going to be a problem for you, Matthew, wait outside," I said calmly.

"Before you do this, I want you to think about it," Matthew said, bending over me protectively as he had when Peter Knox had approached me at the Bodleian. "We have no way of predicting what the tests will reveal. It's your whole life, and your family's history, all laid out in black and white. Are you absolutely sure you want that scrutinized?"

"What do you mean, my whole life?" The intensity of his stare made me squirm.

"These tests tell us about a lot more than the color of your eyes and your hair. They'll indicate what other traits your mother and father passed down to you. Not to mention traits from all your female ancestors." We exchanged a long look.

"That's why I want you to take a sample from me," I said patiently. Confusion passed over his face. "I've wondered my whole life what the Bishop blood was doing as it pumped through my veins. Everyone who knew about my family wondered. Now we'll know."

It seemed very simple to me. My blood could tell Matthew things I didn't want to risk discovering haphazardly. I didn't want to set fire to the furniture, or fly through the trees, or think a bad thought about someone only to have that person fall deathly ill two days later. Matthew might think giving blood was risky. To me it seemed safe as houses, all things considered.

"Besides, you told me witches are dying out. I'm the last Bishop. Maybe my blood will help you figure out why."

We stared at each other, vampire and witch, while Miriam and Marcus waited patiently. Finally Matthew made a sound of exasperation. "Bring me a specimen kit," he told Marcus.

"I can do it," Marcus said defensively, snapping the wrist on his latex gloves. Miriam tried to hold him back, but Marcus kept coming at me with a box of vials and sharps.

"Marcus," Miriam warned.

Matthew grabbed the equipment from Marcus and stopped the younger vampire with a startling, deadly look. "I'm sorry, Marcus. But if anyone is going to take Diana's blood, it's going to be me."

Holding my wrist in his cold fingers, he bent my arm up and down a few times before extending it fully and resting my hand gently on the stainless surface. There was something undeniably creepy about having a vampire stick a needle into your vein. Matthew tied a piece of rubber tubing above my elbow.

"Make a fist," he said quietly, pulling on his gloves and preparing the hollow needle and the first vial.

I did as he asked, clenching my hand and watching the veins bulge.

Matthew didn't bother with the usual announcement that I would feel a prick or a sting. He just leaned down without ceremony and slid the sharp metal instrument into my arm.

"Nicely done." I loosened my fist to get the blood flowing freely.

Matthew's wide mouth tightened while he changed vials. When he was finished, he withdrew the needle and tossed it into a sealed biohazard container. Marcus collected the vials and handed them to Miriam, who labeled them in a tiny, precise script. Matthew put a square of gauze over the stick site and held it there with strong, cold fingers. With his other hand, he picked up a roll of adhesive tape and attached it securely across the pad.

"Date of birth?" Miriam asked crisply, pen poised above the test tube.

"August thirteenth, 1976."

Miriam stared. "August thirteenth?"

"Yes. Why?"

"Just being sure," she murmured.

"In most cases we like to take a cheek swab, too." Matthew opened a package and removed two white pieces of plastic. They were shaped like miniature paddles, the wide ends slightly rough.

Wordlessly I opened my mouth and let Matthew twirl first one swab, then the other, against the inside of my cheek. Each swab went into a different sealed plastic tube. "All done."

Looking around the lab, at the quiet serenity of stainless steel and blue lights, I was reminded of my alchemists, toiling away over charcoal fires in dim light with improvised equipment and broken clay crucibles. What they would have given for the chance to work in a place like this—with tools that might have helped them understand the mysteries of creation.

"Are you looking for the first vampire?" I asked, gesturing at the file drawers.

"Sometimes," Matthew said slowly. "Mostly we're tracking how food and disease affect the species, and how and when certain family lines go extinct."

"And is it really true we're four distinct species, or do daemons, humans, vampires, and witches share a common ancestor?" I'd always wondered if Sarah's insistence that witches shared little of consequence with humans or other creatures was based on anything more than tradition and wishful thinking. In Darwin's time many thought that it was impossible for a pair of common human ancestors to have produced so many different racial types. When some white Europeans looked at black Africans, they embraced the theory of polygenism instead, which argued that the races had descended from different, unrelated ancestors.

"Daemons, humans, vampires, and witches vary considerably at the genetic level." Matthew's eyes were piercing. He understood why I was asking, even though he refused to give me a straight answer.

"If you prove we aren't different species, but only different lineages within the same species, it will change everything," I warned.

"In time we'll be able to figure out how—if—the four groups are related. We're still a long way from that point, though." He stood. "I think that's enough science for today."

After saying good-bye to Miriam and Marcus, Matthew drove me to New College. He went to change and returned to pick me up for yoga. We rode to Woodstock in near silence, both lost in our own thoughts.

At the Old Lodge, Matthew let me out as usual, unloaded the mats from the trunk, and slung them over his shoulder.

A pair of vampires brushed by. One touched me briefly, and Matthew's hand was lightning fast as he laced his fingers through mine. The contrast between us was so striking, his skin so pale and cold, and mine so alive and warm in comparison.

Matthew held on to me until we got inside. After class we drove back to Oxford, talking first about something Amira had said, then about something one of the daemons had inadvertently done or not done that seemed to perfectly capture what it was to be a daemon. Once inside the New College gates, Matthew uncharacteristically turned off the car before he let me out.

Fred looked up from his security monitors when the vampire went to the lodge's glass partition. The porter slid it open. "Yes?"

"I'd like to walk Dr. Bishop to her rooms. Is it all right if I leave the car here, and the keys, too, in case you need to shift it?"

Fred eyed the John Radcliffe tag and nodded. Matthew tossed the keys through the window.

"Matthew," I said urgently, "it's just across the way. You don't have to walk me home."

"I am, though," he said, in a tone that inhibited further discussion. Beyond the lodge's archways and out of Fred's sight, he caught my hand again. This time the shock of his cold skin was accompanied by a disturbing lick of warmth in the pit of my stomach.

At the bottom of my staircase, I faced Matthew, still holding his hand. "Thanks for taking me to yoga—again."

"You're welcome." He tucked my impossible piece of hair back behind my ear, fingers lingering on my cheek. "Come to dinner tomorrow," he said softly. "My turn to cook. Can I pick you up here at half past seven?"

My heart leaped. *Say no,* I told myself sternly in spite of its sudden jump.

"I'd love to" came out instead.

The vampire pressed his cold lips first to one cheek, then the other. *"Ma vaillante fille,"* he whispered into my ear. The dizzying, alluring smell of him filled my nose.

Upstairs, someone had tightened the doorknob as requested, and it was a struggle to turn the key in the lock. The blinking light on the answering machine greeted me, indicating there was another message from Sarah. I crossed to the window and looked down, only to see Matthew looking up. I waved. He smiled, put his hands in his pockets, and turned back to the lodge, slipping into the night's darkness as if it belonged to him.

Chapter 14

Matthew was waiting for me in the lodge at half past seven, immaculate as always in a monochromatic combination of dove and charcoal, his dark hair swept back from his uneven hairline. He patiently withstood the inspection of the weekend porter, who sent me off with a nod and a deliberate, "We'll see you later, Dr. Bishop."

"You do bring out people's protective instincts," Matthew murmured as we passed through the gates.

"Where are we going?" There was no sign of his car in the street.

"We're dining in college tonight," he answered, gesturing down toward the Bodleian. I had fully anticipated he would take me to Woodstock, or an apartment in some Victorian pile in North Oxford. It had never occurred to me that he might live in a college.

"In hall, at high table?" I felt terribly underdressed and pulled at the hem of my silky black top.

Matthew tilted his head back and laughed. "I avoid hall whenever possible. And I'm certainly not taking you in there, to sit in the Siege Perilous and be inspected by the fellows."

We rounded the corner and turned toward the Radcliffe Camera. When we passed by the entrance to Hertford College without stopping, I put my hand on his arm. There was one college in Oxford notorious for its exclusivity and rigid attention to protocol.

It was the same college famous for its brilliant fellows.

"You aren't."

Matthew stopped. "Why does it matter what college I belong to?" He looked away. "If you'd rather be around other people, of course, I understand."

"I'm not worried you're going to eat *me* for dinner, Matthew. I've just never been inside." A pair of ornate, scrolled gates guarded his college as if it were Wonderland. Matthew made an impatient noise and caught my hand to prevent me from peering through them.

"It's just a collection of people in a set of old buildings." His gruffness did nothing to detract from the fact that he was one of six dozen or so fellows in a college with no students. "Besides, we're going to my rooms."

We walked the remaining distance, Matthew relaxing into the darkness with every step as if in the company of an old friend. We passed through a low wooden door that kept the public out of his college's quiet confines. There was no one in the lodge except the porter, no undergraduates or graduates on the benches in the front quad. It was as quiet and hushed as if its members truly were the "souls of all the faithful people deceased in the university of Oxford."

Matthew looked down with a shy smile. "Welcome to All Souls."

All Souls College was a masterpiece of late Gothic architecture, resembling the love child of a wedding cake and a cathedral, with its airy spires and delicate stonework. I sighed with pleasure, unable to say much—at least not yet. But Matthew was going to have a lot of explaining to do later.

"Evening, James," he said to the porter, who looked over his bifocals and nodded in welcome. Matthew held up his hand. An ancient key dangled off his index finger from a leather loop. "I'll be just a moment."

"Right, Professor Clairmont."

Matthew took my hand again. "Let's go. We need to continue your education."

He was like a mischievous boy on a treasure hunt, pulling me along. We ducked through a cracked door black with age, and Matthew switched on a light. His white skin leaped out of the dark, and he looked every inch a vampire.

"It's a good thing I'm a witch," I teased. "The sight of you here would be enough to scare a human to death."

At the bottom of a flight of stairs, Matthew entered a long string of numbers at a security keypad, then hit the star key. I heard a soft click, and he pulled another door open. The smell of must and age and something else that I couldn't name hit me in a wave. Blackness extended away from the stairway lights.

"This is straight out of a Gothic novel. Where are you taking me?"

"Patience, Diana. It's not much farther." Patience, alas, was not the strong suit of Bishop women.

Matthew reached past my shoulder and flipped another switch. Suspended on wires like trapeze artists, a string of old bulbs cast pools of light over what looked like horse stalls for miniature Shetland ponies.

I stared at Matthew, a hundred questions in my eyes.

"After you," he said with a bow.

Stepping forward, I recognized the strange smell. It was stale alcohol—like the pub on Sunday morning. "Wine?"

"Wine."

We passed dozens of small enclosures that contained bottles in racks, piles, and crates. Each had a small slate tag, a year scrawled on it in chalk. We wandered past bins that held wine from the First World War and the Second, as well as bottles that Florence Nightingale might have packed in her trunks for the Crimea. There were wines from the year the Berlin Wall was built and the year it came down. Deeper into the cellar, the years scrawled on the slates gave way to broad categories like "Old Claret" and "Vintage Port."

Finally we reached the end of the room. A dozen small doors stood locked and silent, and Matthew opened one of them. There was no electricity here, but he picked up a candle and wedged it securely into a brass holder before lighting it.

Inside, everything was as neat and orderly as Matthew himself, but for a layer of dust. Tightly spaced wooden racks held the wine off the floor and made it possible to remove a single bottle without making the whole arrangement tumble down. There were red stains next to the jamb where wine had been spit, year after year. The smell of old grapes, corks, and a trace of mildew filled the air.

"Is this yours?" I was incredulous.

"Yes, it's mine. A few of the fellows have private cellars."

"What can you possibly have in here that isn't already out there?" The room behind me must contain a bottle of every wine ever produced. Oxford's finest wine emporium now seemed barren and oddly sterile in comparison.

Matthew smiled mysteriously. "All sorts of things."

He moved quickly around the small, windowless room, happily pulling out wines here and there. He handed me a heavy, dark bottle with a gold shield for a label and a wire basket over the cork. Champagne—Dom Perignon.

The next bottle was made from dark green glass, with a simple cream label and black script. He presented it to me with a little flourish, and I saw the date: 1976.

"The year I was born!" I said.

Matthew emerged with two more bottles: one with a long, octagonal label bearing a picture of a château on it and thick red wax around the top; the other lopsided and black, bearing no label and sealed with something that looked like tar. An old manila tag was tied around the neck of the second bottle with a dirty piece of string.

"Shall we?" Matthew asked, blowing out the candle. He locked the door carefully behind him, balancing the two bottles in his other hand, and slipped the key into his pocket. We left behind the smell of wine and climbed back to ground level.

In the dusky air, Matthew seemed to shine with pleasure, his arms full of wine. "What a wonderful night," he said happily.

We went up to his rooms, which were grander than I had imagined in some ways and much less grand in others. They were smaller than my rooms at New College, located at the very top of one of the oldest blocks in All Souls, full of funny angles and odd slopes. Though the ceilings were tall enough to accommodate Matthew's height, the rooms still seemed too small to contain him. He had to stoop through every door, and the windowsills reached down to somewhere near his thighs.

What the rooms lacked in size they more than made up for in furnishings. A faded Aubusson rug stretched across the floors, anchored with a collection of original William Morris furniture. Somehow the fifteenth-century architecture, the eighteenth-century rug, and the nineteenth-century roughhewn oak looked splendid together and gave the rooms the atmosphere of a select Edwardian gentlemen's club.

A vast refectory table stood at the far side of the main room, with newspapers, books, and the assorted detritus of academic life neatly arranged at one end—memos about new policies, scholarly journals, requests for letters and peer reviews. Each pile was weighted down with a different object. Matthew's paperweights included the genuine article in heavy blown glass, an old brick, a bronze medal that was no doubt some award he'd won, and a small fire poker. At the other end of the table, a soft linen cloth had been thrown over the wood, held down by the most gorgeous Georgian silver candlesticks I'd ever seen outside a museum. A full array of different-shaped wineglasses stood guard over simple white plates and more Georgian silver.

"I love it." I looked around with delight. Not a stick of furniture or a single ornament in this room belonged to the college. It was all perfectly, quintessentially Matthew.

"Have a seat." He rescued the two wine bottles from my slack fingers and whisked them off to what looked like a glorified closet. "All Souls doesn't believe that fellows should eat in their rooms," he said by way of explanation as I eyed the meager kitchen facilities, "so we'll get by as best we can."

What I was about to eat would equal the finest dinner in town, no doubt.

Matthew plunked the champagne into a silver bucket full of ice and joined me in one of the cozy chairs flanking his nonfunctional fireplace. "Nobody lets you build fires in Oxford fireplaces anymore." He motioned ruefully at the empty stone enclosure. "When every fireplace was lit, the city smelled like a bonfire."

"When did you first come to Oxford?" I hoped the openness of my question would assure him I wasn't prying into his past lives.

"This time it was 1989." He stretched his long legs out with a sigh of relaxation. "I came to Oriel as a science student and stayed on for a doctorate. When I won an All Souls Prize Fellowship, I switched over here for a few years. When my degree was completed, the university offered me a place and the members elected me a fellow." Every time he opened his mouth, something amazing popped out. A Prize Fellow? There were only two of those a year.

"And this is your first time at All Souls?" I bit my lip, and he laughed.

"Let's get this over with," he said, holding up his hands and beginning to tick off colleges. "I've been a member—once—of Merton, Magdalen, and University colleges. I've been a member of New College and Oriel twice each. And this is the first time All Souls has paid any attention to me."

Multiplying this answer by a factor of Cambridge, Paris, Padua, and Montpellier—all of which, I was sure, had once had a student on their books named Matthew Clairmont, or some variation thereof—sent a dizzying set of degrees dancing through my head. What must he have studied, all those many years, and whom had he studied with?

"Diana?" Matthew's amused voice penetrated my thoughts. "Did you hear me?"

"I'm sorry." I closed my eyes and tightened my hands on my thighs in an effort to keep my mind from wandering. "It's like a disease. I can't keep the curiosity at bay when you start reminiscing."

"I know. It's one of the difficulties a vampire faces when he spends time with a witch who's a historian." Matthew's mouth was bent in a mock frown, but his eyes twinkled like black stars.

"If you want to avoid these difficulties in future, I suggest you avoid the Bodleian's paleography reference section," I said tartly.

"One historian is all I can manage at the moment." Matthew rose smoothly to his feet. "I asked if you were hungry."

Why he continued to do so was a mystery—when was I not hungry?

"Yes," I said, trying to extract myself from a deep Morris chair. Matthew stuck out his hand. I grasped it, and he lifted me easily.

We stood facing each other, our bodies nearly touching. I fixed my attention on the bump of his Bethany ampulla under his sweater.

His eyes flickered over me, leaving their trail of snowflakes. "You look lovely." I ducked my head, and the usual piece of hair fell over my face. He reached up as he had several times recently and tucked it behind my ear. This time his fingers continued to the base of my skull. He lifted my hair away from my neck and let it fall through his fingers as if it were water. I shivered at the touch of cool air on my skin.

"I love your hair," he murmured. "It has every color imaginable—even strands of red and black." I heard the sharp intake of breath that meant he had picked up a new scent.

"What do you smell?" My voice was thick, and I still hadn't dared to meet his eyes.

"You," he breathed.

My eyes floated up to his.

"Shall we have dinner?"

After that, it was hard to concentrate on the food, but I did my best. Matthew pulled out my rush-seated chair, which had a full view of the warm, beautiful room. From a minuscule refrigerator, he removed two plates, each with six fresh oysters nestled on top of a bed of crushed ice like the rays of a star.

"Lecture One of your continuing education consists of oysters and champagne." Matthew sat down and held up a finger like a don about to embark on a favorite subject. He reached for the wine, which was within the wingspan of his long arm, and pulled it from the bucket. With one turn he popped the cork free of the neck of the bottle.

"I usually find that more difficult," I commented drily, looking at his strong, elegant fingers.

"I can teach you to knock the cork off with a sword if you want." Matthew grinned. "Of course, a knife works, too, if you don't have a sword lying around." He poured some of the liquid into our glasses, where it fizzed and danced in the candlelight.

He raised his glass to me. *"À la tienne."*

"À la tienne." I lifted my own flute and watched the bubbles break on the surface. "Why are the bubbles so tiny?"

"Because the wine is so old. Most champagne is drunk long before this. But I like the old wine—it reminds me of the way champagne used to taste."

"How old is it?"

"Older than you are," Matthew replied. He was pulling the oyster shells apart with his bare hands—something that usually required a very sharp knife and a lot of skill—and chucking the shells into a glass bowl in the center of the table. He handed one plate over to me. "It's from 1961."

"Please tell me this is the oldest thing we're drinking tonight," I said, thinking back to the wine he'd brought to dinner on Thursday, the bottle from which was now holding the last of his white roses on my bedside table.

"Not by a long shot," he said with a grin.

I tipped the contents of the first shell into my mouth. My eyes popped open as my mouth filled with the taste of the Atlantic.

"Now drink." He picked up his own glass and watched me take a sip of the golden liquid. "What do you taste?"

The creaminess of the wine and the oysters collided with the taste of sea salt in ways that were utterly bewitching. "It's as if the whole ocean is in my mouth," I answered, taking another sip.

We finished the oysters and moved on to an enormous salad. It had every expensive green known to mankind, nuts, berries, and a delicious dressing made with champagne vinegar and olive oil that Matthew whisked together at the table. The tiny slices of meat that adorned it were partridge from the Old Lodge's grounds. We sipped at what Matthew called my "birthday wine," which smelled like lemon floor polish and smoke and tasted like chalk and butterscotch.

The next course was a stew, with chunks of meat in a fragrant sauce. My first bite told me it was veal, fixed with apples and a bit of cream, served atop rice. Matthew watched me eat, and he smiled as I tasted the tartness of the apple for the first time. "It's an old recipe from Normandy," he said. "Do you like it?"

"It's wonderful. Did you make it?"

"No," he said. "The chef from the Old Parsonage's restaurant made it—and provided precise instructions on how not to burn it to a crisp when I reheated it."

"You can reheat my dinner anytime." I let the warmth of the stew soak into my body. "You aren't eating, though."

"No, but I'm not hungry." He continued to watch me eat for a few moments, then returned to the kitchen to fetch another wine. It was the bottle sealed with red wax. He sliced through the wax and pulled the cork out of the bottle. "Perfect," he pronounced, pouring the scarlet liquid carefully into a nearby decanter.

"Can you already smell it?" I was still unsure of the range of his olfactory powers.

"Oh, yes. This wine in particular." Matthew poured me a bit and splashed some into his own glass. "Are you ready to taste something miraculous?" he asked. I nodded. "This is Château Margaux from a very great vintage. Some people consider it the finest red wine ever made."

We picked up our glasses, and I mimicked each of Matthew's movements. He put his nose in his glass, and I in mine. The smell of violets washed over me. My first taste was like drinking velvet. Then there was milk chocolate, cherries, and a flood of flavors that made no sense and brought back memories of the long-ago smell of my father's study after he'd been smoking and of emptying the shavings from the pencil sharpener in second grade. The very last thing I noted was a spicy taste that reminded me of Matthew.

"This tastes like you!" I said.

"How so?" he asked.

"Spicy," I said, flushing suddenly from my cheeks to my hairline.

"Just spicy?"

"No. First I thought it would taste like flowers—violets—because that's how it smelled. But then I tasted all kinds of things. What do you taste?"

This was going to be far more interesting and less embarrassing than my reaction. He sniffed, swirled, and tasted. "Violets—I agree with you there. Those purple violets covered with sugar. Elizabeth Tudor loved candied violets, and they ruined her teeth." He sipped again. "Cigar smoke from good cigars, like they used to have at the Marlborough Club when the Prince of Wales stopped in. Blackberries picked wild in the hedgerows outside the Old Lodge's stables and red currants macerated in brandy."

Watching a vampire use his sensory powers had to be one of the most surreal experiences anyone could have. It was not just that Matthew could see and hear things I could not—it was that when he did sense something, the perception was so acute and precise. It wasn't any blackberry—it was a particular blackberry, from a particular place or a particular time.

Matthew kept drinking his wine, and I finished my stew. I took up my wineglass with a contented sigh, toying with the stem so that it caught the light from the candles.

"What do you think I would taste like?" I wondered aloud, my tone playful.

Matthew shot to his feet, his face white and furious. His napkin fell, unnoticed, to the floor. A vein in his forehead pulsed once before subsiding. I had said something wrong.

He was at my side in the time it took me to blink, pulling me up from my chair. His fingers dug into my elbows.

"There's one legend about vampires we haven't discussed, isn't there?" His eyes were strange, his face frightening. I tried to squirm out of his reach, but his fingers dug deeper. "The one about a vampire who finds himself so bewitched by a woman that he cannot help himself."

My mind sped over what had happened. He'd asked me what I tasted. I'd tasted him. Then he told me what he tasted and I said—"Oh, Matthew," I whispered.

"Do you wonder what it would be like for me to taste you?" Matthew's voice dropped from a purr toward something deeper and more dangerous. For a moment I felt revulsion.

Before that feeling could grow, he released my arms. There was no time to react or draw away. Matthew had woven his fingers through my hair, his thumbs pressing against the base of my skull. I was caught again, and a feeling of stillness came over me, spreading out from his cold touch. Was I drunk from two glasses of wine? Drugged? What else would explain the feeling that I couldn't break free?

"It's not only your scent that pleases me. I can *hear* your witch's blood as it moves through your veins." Matthew's cold lips were against my ear, and his breath was sweet. "Did you know that a witch's blood makes music? Like a siren who sings to the sailor, asking him to steer his ship into the rocks, the call of your blood could be my undoing—and yours." His words were so quiet and intimate he seemed to be talking directly into my mind.

The vampire's lips began to move incrementally along my jawbone. Each place his mouth touched froze, then burned as my blood rushed back to the skin's surface.

"Matthew," I breathed around the catch in my throat. I closed my eyes, expecting to feel teeth against my neck yet unable—unwilling—to move.

Instead Matthew's hungry lips met mine. His arms locked around me, and his fingertips cradled my head. My lips parted under his, my hands trapped between his chest and mine. Underneath my palms his heart beat, once.

With the thump of his heart, the kiss changed. Matthew was no less demanding, but the hunger in his touch turned to something bittersweet. His hands moved forward smoothly until he was cupping my face, and he pulled away reluctantly. For the first time, I heard a soft, ragged sound. It was not like human breathing. It was the sound of minute amounts of oxygen passing through a vampire's powerful lungs.

"I took advantage of your fear. I shouldn't have," he whispered.

My eyes were closed, and I still felt intoxicated, his cinnamon and clove scent driving off the scent of violets from the wine. Restless, I stirred in his grip.

"Be still," he said, voice harsh. "I might not be able to control myself if you step away."

He'd warned me in the lab about the relationship between predator and prey. Now he was trying to get me to play dead so the predator in him would lose interest in me.

But I wasn't dead.

My eyes flew open. There was no mistaking the sharp look on his face. It was avid, hungry. Matthew was a creature of instinct now. But I had instincts, too.

"I'm safe with you." I formed the words with lips that were freezing and burning at the same time, unused to the feeling of a vampire's kiss.

"A witch—safe with a vampire? Never be sure of that. It would only take a moment. You wouldn't be able to stop me if I struck, and I wouldn't be able to stop myself." Our eyes met and locked, neither of us blinking. Matthew made a low sound of surprise. "How brave you are."

"I've never been brave."

"When you gave blood in the lab, the way you meet a vampire's eyes, how you ordered the creatures out of the library, even the fact that you go back there day after day, refusing to let people keep you from what you want to do—it's all bravery."

"That's stubbornness." Sarah had explained the difference a long time ago.

"I've seen courage like yours before—from women, mostly." Matthew continued as if I hadn't spoken. "Men don't have it. Our resolve is born out of fear. It's merely bravado."

His glance flickered over me in snowflakes that melted into mere coolness the moment they touched me. One cold finger reached out and captured a tear from the tips of my eyelashes. His face was sad as he lowered me gently into the chair and crouched next to me, resting one hand on my knee and the other on the arm of the rush-seated chair in a protective circle. "Promise me that you will never joke with a vampire—not even me—about blood or how you might taste."

"I'm sorry," I whispered, forcing myself not to look away.

He shook his head. "You told me before that you don't know much about vampires. What you need to understand is that no vampire is immune to this temptation. Vampires with a conscience spend most of their time trying *not* to imagine how people would taste. If you were to meet one without a conscience—and there are plenty who fit that category—then God help you."

"I didn't think." I still couldn't. My mind was whirling with the memory of his kiss, his fury, and his palpable hunger.

He bowed his head, resting the crown against my shoulder. The ampulla from Bethany tumbled out of the neck of his sweater and swung like a pendulum, its tiny coffin glinting in the light from the candles.

He spoke so softly that I had to strain to hear. "Witches and vampires aren't meant to feel this way. I'm experiencing emotions I've never—" He broke off.

"I know." Carefully I leaned my cheek against his hair. It felt as satiny as it looked. "I feel them, too."

Matthew's arms had remained where he left them, one hand on my knee and the other on the arm of the chair. At my words he moved them slowly and clasped my waist. The coldness of his flesh cut through my clothing, but I didn't shiver. Instead I moved closer so that I could rest my arms on his shoulders.

A vampire evidently could have remained comfortable in that position for days. For a mere witch, however, it wasn't an option. When I shifted slightly, he looked at me in confusion, and then his face lightened in recognition.

"I forgot," he said, rising with his swift smoothness and stepping away from me. I moved first one leg and then the other, restoring the circulation to my feet.

Matthew handed me my wine and returned to his own seat. Once he was settled, I tried to give him something to think about other than how I might taste.

"What was the fifth question you had to answer for the Prize Fellowship?" Candidates were invited to sit an exam that involved four questions combining thought-provoking breadth and depth with devilish complexity. If you survived the first four questions, you were asked the famous "fifth question." It was not a question at all, but a single word like "water," or "absence." It was up to the candidate to decide how to respond, and only the most brilliant answer won you a place at All Souls.

He reached across the table—without setting himself on fire—and poured some more wine into my glass. "Desire," he said, studiously avoiding my eyes.

So much for that diversionary plan.

"Desire? What did you write?"

"As far as I can tell, there are only two emotions that keep the world spinning, year after year." He hesitated, then continued. "One is fear. The other is desire. That's what I wrote about."

Love hadn't factored into his response, I noticed. It was a brutal picture, a tug-of-war between two equal but opposing impulses. It had the ring of truth, however, which was more than could be said of the glib "love makes the world go round." Matthew kept hinting that his desire—for blood, chiefly—was so strong that it put everything else at risk.

But vampires weren't the only creatures who had to manage such strong impulses. Much of what qualified as magic was simply desire in action. Witchcraft was different—that took spells and rituals. But magic? A wish, a need, a hunger too strong to be denied—these could turn into deeds when they crossed a witch's mind.

And if Matthew was going to tell me his secrets, it didn't seem fair to keep mine so close.

"Magic is desire made real. It's how I pulled down *Notes and Queries* the night we met," I said slowly. "When a witch concentrates on something she wants, and then imagines how she might get it, she can make it happen. That's why I have to be so careful about my work." I took a sip of wine, my hand trembling on the glass.

"Then you spend most of your time trying not to want things, just like me. For some of the same reasons, too." Matthew's snowflake glances flickered across my cheeks.

"If you mean the fear that if I started, there would be no stopping me—yes. I don't want to look back on a life where I took everything rather than earned it."

"So you earn everything twice over. First you earn it by not simply taking it, and then you earn it again through work and effort." He laughed bitterly. "The advantages of being an otherworldly creature don't amount to much, do they?"

Matthew suggested we sit by his fireless fireplace. I lounged on the sofa, and he carried some nutty biscuits over to the table by me, before disappearing into the kitchen once more. When he returned, he was carrying a small tray with the ancient black bottle on it—the cork now pulled—and two glasses of amber-colored liquid. He handed one to me.

"Close your eyes and tell me what you smell," he instructed in his Oxford don's voice. My lids dropped obediently. The wine seemed at once old and vibrant. It smelled of flowers and nuts and candied lemons and of some other, long-past world that I had—until now—been able only to read about and imagine.

"It smells like the past. But not the dead past. It's so alive."

"Open your eyes and take a sip."

As the sweet, bright liquid went down my throat, something ancient and powerful entered my bloodstream. *This must be what vampire blood tastes like.* I kept my thoughts to myself.

"Are you going to tell me what it is?" I asked around the flavors in my mouth.

"Malmsey," he replied with a grin. "Old, old malmsey."

"How old?" I said suspiciously. "As old as you are?"

He laughed. "No. You don't want to drink anything as old as I am. It's from 1795, from grapes grown on the island of Madeira. It was quite popular once, but nobody pays much attention to it now."

"Good," I said with greedy satisfaction. "All the more for me." He laughed again and sat easily in one of his Morris chairs.

We talked about his time at All Souls, about Hamish—the other Prize Fellow, it turned out—and their adventures in Oxford. I laughed at his stories of dining in hall and how he'd bolted to Woodstock after every meal to clean the taste of overcooked beef from his mouth.

"You look tired," he finally said, standing after another glass of malmsey and another hour of conversation.

"I am tired." Despite my fatigue, there was something I needed to tell him before he took me home. I put my glass down carefully. "I've made a decision, Matthew. On Monday I'll be recalling Ashmole 782."

The vampire sat down abruptly.

"I don't know how I broke the spell the first time, but I'll try to do it again. Knox doesn't have much faith that I'll succeed." My mouth tightened. "What does he know? He hasn't been able to break the spell once. And you might be able to see the words in the magical palimpsest that lie under the images."

"What do you mean, you don't know what you did to break the spell?" Matthew's forehead creased with confusion. "What words did you use? What powers did you call upon?"

"I broke the spell without realizing it," I explained.

"Christ, Diana." He shot to his feet again. "Does Knox know that you didn't use witchcraft?"

"If he knows, I didn't tell him." I shrugged. "Besides, what does it matter?"

"It matters because if you didn't break the enchantment, then you met its conditions. Right now the creatures are waiting to observe whatever counterspell you used, copy it if they can, and get Ashmole 782 themselves. When your fellow witches discover that the spell opened for you of its own accord, they won't be so patient and well behaved."

Gillian's angry face swam before my eyes, accompanied by a vivid recollection of the lengths she reported witches had gone to in order to pry secrets from my parents. I brushed the thoughts aside, my stomach rolling, and focused on the flaws in Matthew's argument.

"The spell was constructed more than a century before I was born. That's impossible."

"Just because something seems impossible doesn't make it untrue," he said grimly. "Newton knew that. There's no telling what Knox will do when he understands your relationship to the spell."

"I'm in danger whether I recall the manuscript or not," I pointed out. "Knox isn't going to let this go, is he?"

"No," he agreed reluctantly. "And he wouldn't hesitate to use magic against you even if every human in the Bodleian saw him do it. I might not be able to reach you in time."

Vampires were fast, but magic was faster.

"I'll sit near the desk with you, then. We'll know as soon as the manuscript's delivered."

"I don't like this," Matthew said, clearly worried. "There's a fine line between bravery and recklessness, Diana."

"It's not reckless—I just want my life back."

"What if this is your life?" he asked. "What if you can't keep the magic away after all?"

"I'll keep parts of it." Remembering his kiss, and the sudden, intense feeling of vitality that had accompanied it, I looked straight into his eyes so

I'm not going to be bullied."

an as he walked me home. When

back entrance, he caught my

he look that porter gave me? I

ywell Street, past the entrance

ege gates. We strolled by the

w asked at the bottom of my

of recommendation to write.

lesk."

he said casually.

ually.

be out culling my own deer?"

sionally you feed on deer." I

."

s fingers slightly but didn't let

ps and put a slow kiss on the

gers. His eyes left trails of ice and

er my face but my body, too.

stonished that a kiss on the palm

cou

"G ng with my next exhale. "I'll see you Monday."

I climbed the narrow steps to my rooms. Whoever tightened the doorknob had made a mess of the lock, and the metal hardware and the wood were covered in fresh scratches. Inside, I switched on the lights. The answering machine was blinking, of course. At the window I raised my hand to show that I was safely inside.

When I peeked out a few seconds later, Matthew was already gone.

Chapter 15

On Monday morning the air had that magically still quality common in autumn. The whole world felt crisp and bright, and time seemed suspended. I shot out of bed at dawn and pulled on my waiting rowing gear, eager to be outdoors.

The river was empty for the first hour. As the sun broke over the horizon, the fog burned off toward the waterline so that I was slipping through alternate bands of mist and rosy sunshine.

When I pulled up to the dock, Matthew was waiting for me on the curving steps that led to the boathouse's balcony, an ancient brown-and-bone-striped New College scarf hanging around his neck. I climbed out of the boat, put my hands on my hips, and stared at him in disbelief.

"Where did you get that thing?" I pointed at the scarf.

"You should have more respect for the old members," he said with his mischievous grin, tossing one end of it over his shoulder. "I think I bought it in 1920, but I can't honestly remember. After the Great War ended, certainly."

Shaking my head, I took the oars into the boathouse. Two crews glided by the dock in perfect, powerful unison just as I was lifting my boat out of the water. My knees dipped slightly and the boat swung up and over until its weight rested on my head.

"Why don't you let me help you with that?" Matthew said, rising from his perch.

"No chance." My steps were steady as I walked the boat inside. He grumbled something under his breath.

With the boat safely in its rack, Matthew easily talked me into breakfast at Mary and Dan's café. He was going to have to sit next to me much of the day, and I was hungry after the morning's exertions. He steered me by the elbow around the other diners, his hand firmer on my back than before. Mary greeted me like an old friend, and Steph didn't bother with a menu, just announced "the usual" when she came by the table. There wasn't a hint of a question in her voice, and when the plate came—laden with eggs, bacon, mushrooms, and tomatoes—I was glad I hadn't insisted on something more ladylike.

After breakfast I trotted through the lodge and up to my rooms for a shower and a change of clothes. Fred peered around his window to see if it was indeed Matthew's Jaguar pulled up outside the gates. The porters were no doubt laying wagers on competing predictions regarding our oddly formal relationship. This morning was the first time I'd managed to convince my escort to simply drop me off.

"It's broad daylight, and Fred will have kittens if you clog up his gate during delivery hours," I protested when Matthew started to get out of the car. He'd glowered but agreed that merely pulling straight across the entrance to bar possible vehicular attack was sufficient.

This morning every step of my routine needed to be slow and deliberate. My shower was long and leisurely, the hot water slipping against my tired muscles. Still in no rush, I put on comfortable black trousers, a turtleneck to keep my shoulders from seizing up in the increasingly chilly library, and a reasonably presentable midnight blue cardigan to break up the unalleviated black. My hair was caught in a low ponytail. The short piece in the front fell forward as it always did, and I grumbled and shoved it behind my ear.

In spite of my efforts, my anxiety rose as I pushed open the library's glass doors. The guard's eyes narrowed at my uncharacteristically warm smile, and he took an inordinate amount of time checking my face against the picture on my reader's card. Finally he admitted me, and I pelted up the stairs to Duke Humfrey's.

It had been no more than an hour since I'd been with Matthew, but the sight of him stretched out among the first bay of Elizabethan desks in one of the medieval wing's purgatorial chairs was welcome. He looked up when my laptop dropped on the scarred wooden surface.

"Is he here?" I whispered, reluctant to say Knox's name.

Matthew nodded grimly. "In the Selden End."

"Well, he can wait down there all day as far as I'm concerned," I said under my breath, picking up a blank request slip from the shallow rectangular tray on the desk. On it I wrote *"Ashmole MS 782,"* my name, and my reader number.

Sean was at the collection desk. "I've got two items on reserve," I told him with a smile. He went into the cage and returned with my manuscripts, then held out his hand for my new request. He put the slip into the worn, gray cardboard envelope that would be sent to the stacks.

"May I talk to you a minute?" Sean asked.

"Sure." I gestured to indicate that Matthew should stay where he was and followed Sean through the swinging gate into the Arts End, which, like the Selden End, ran perpendicular to the length of the old library. We stood beneath a bank of leaded windows that let in the weak morning sunshine.

"Is he bothering you?"

"Professor Clairmont? No."

"It's none of my business, but I don't like him." Sean looked down the central aisle as if he expected Matthew to pop out and glare at him. "The whole place has been full of strange ducks over the last week or so."

Unable to disagree, I resorted to muffled noises of sympathy.

"You'd let me know if there was something wrong, wouldn't you?"

"Of course, Sean. But Professor Clairmont's okay. You don't have to worry about him."

My old friend looked unconvinced.

"Sean may know I'm different—but it seems I'm not as different as you," I told Matthew after returning to my seat.

"Few are," he said darkly, picking up his reading.

I turned on my computer and tried to concentrate on my work. It would take hours for the manuscript to appear. But thinking about alchemy was harder than ever, caught as I was between a vampire and the call desk. Every time new books emerged from the stacks, I looked up.

After several false alarms, soft steps approached from the Selden End. Matthew tensed in his chair.

Peter Knox strolled up and stopped. "Dr. Bishop," he said coolly.

"Mr. Knox." My voice was equally chilly, and I returned my attention to the open volume before me. Knox took a step in my direction.

Matthew spoke quietly, without raising his eyes from the Needham papers. "I'd stop there unless Dr. Bishop wishes to speak with you."

"I'm very busy." A sense of pressure wound around my forehead, and a voice whispered in my skull. Every ounce of my energy was devoted to keeping the witch out of my thoughts. "I said I'm busy," I repeated stonily.

Matthew put his pencil down and pushed away from the desk.

"Mr. Knox was just leaving, Matthew." Turning to my laptop, I typed a few sentences of utter nonsense.

"I hope you understand what you're doing," Knox spit.

Matthew growled, and I laid a hand lightly on his arm. Knox's eyes fixed on the spot where the bodies of a witch and a vampire touched.

Until that moment Knox had only suspected that Matthew and I were too close for the comfort of witches. Now he was sure.

You've told him what you know about our book. Knox's vicious voice sounded through my head, and though I tried to push against his intrusion, the wizard was too strong. When he resisted my efforts, I gasped in surprise.

Sean looked up from the call desk in alarm. Matthew's arm was vibrating, his growl subsiding into a somehow more menacing purr.

"Who's caught human attention now?" I hissed at the witch, squeezing Matthew's arm to let him know I didn't need his help.

Knox smiled unpleasantly. "You've caught the attention of more than humans this morning, Dr. Bishop. Before nightfall every witch in Oxford will know you're a traitor."

Matthew's muscles coiled, and he reached up to the coffin he wore around his neck.

Oh, God, I thought, *he's going to kill a witch in the Bodleian.* I placed myself squarely between the two of them.

"Enough," I told Knox quietly. "If you don't leave, I'm going to tell Sean you're harassing me and have him call security."

"The light in the Selden End is rather glaring today," Knox said at last, breaking the standoff. "I believe I'll move to this part of the library." He strolled away.

Matthew lifted my hand from his arm and began to pack up his belongings. "We're leaving."

"No we're not. We are not leaving until we get that manuscript."

"Were you listening?" Matthew said hotly. "He threatened you! I don't need this manuscript, but I do need—" He stopped abruptly.

I pushed Matthew into his seat. Sean was still staring in our direction, his hand hovering above the phone. Smiling, I shook my head at him before returning my attention to the vampire.

"It's my fault. I shouldn't have touched you while he was standing there," I murmured, looking down at his shoulder, where my hand still rested.

Matthew's cool fingers lifted my chin. "Do you regret the touch—or the fact that the witch saw you?"

"Neither," I whispered. His gray eyes went from sad to surprised in an instant. "But you don't want me to be reckless."

As Knox approached again, Matthew's grip on my chin tightened, his senses tuned into the witch. When Knox remained a few desks away, the vampire returned his attention to me. "One more word from him and we're leaving—manuscript or no manuscript. I mean it, Diana."

Thinking about alchemical illustrations proved impossible after that.

Gillian's warning about what happened to witches who kept secrets from other witches, and Knox's firm pronouncement that I was a traitor, resounded through my head. When Matthew tried to get me to stop for lunch, I refused. The manuscript had still not appeared, and we couldn't be at Blackwell's when it arrived—not with Knox so close.

"Did you see what I had for breakfast?" I asked when Matthew insisted. "I'm not hungry."

My coffee-loving daemon drifted by shortly afterward, swinging his headset by the cord. "Hey," he said with a wave at Matthew and me.

Matthew looked up sharply.

"Good to see you two again. Is it okay if I check my e-mail down there since the witch is here with you?"

"What's your name?" I asked, smothering a smile.

"Timothy," he answered, rocking back on his heels. He was wearing mismatched cowboy boots, one red and one black. His eyes were mismatched, too—one was blue and one was green.

"You're more than welcome to check your e-mail, Timothy."

"You're the one." He tipped his fingers at me, pivoted on the heel of the red boot, and walked away.

An hour later I stood, unable to control my impatience. "The manuscript should have arrived by now."

The vampire's eyes followed me across the six feet of open space to the call desk. They felt hard and crisp like ice, rather than soft as snowfall, and they clung to my shoulder blades.

"Hi, Sean. Will you check to see if the manuscript I requested this morning has been delivered?"

"Someone else must have it," Sean said. "Nothing's come up for you."

"Are you sure?" Nobody else had it.

Sean riffled through the slips and found my request. Paper-clipped to it was a note. "It's missing."

"It's not missing. I saw it a few weeks ago."

"Let's see." He rounded the desk, headed for the supervisor's office. Matthew looked up from his papers and watched as Sean rapped against the open doorframe.

"Dr. Bishop wants this manuscript, and it's been noted as missing," Sean explained. He held out the slip.

Mr. Johnson consulted a book on his desk, running his finger over lines scrawled by generations of reading-room supervisors. "Ah, yes. Ashmole

782. That's been missing since 1859. We don't have a microfilm." Matthew's chair scraped away from his desk.

"But I saw it a few *weeks* ago."

"That's not possible, Dr. Bishop. No one has seen this manuscript for one hundred and fifty years." Mr. Johnson blinked behind his thick-rimmed glasses.

"Dr. Bishop, could I show you something when you have a moment?" Matthew's voice made me jump.

"Yes, of course." I turned blindly toward him. "Thank you," I whispered to Mr. Johnson.

"We're leaving. Now," Matthew hissed. In the aisle an assortment of creatures was focused intently on us. I saw Knox, Timothy, the Scary Sisters, Gillian—and a few more unfamiliar faces. Above the tall bookcases, the old portraits of kings, queens, and other illustrious persons that decorated the walls of Duke Humfrey's Reading Room stared at us, too, with every bit as much sour disapproval.

"It can't be missing. I just saw it," I repeated numbly. "We should have them check."

"Don't talk about it now—don't even think about it." He gathered up my things with lightning speed, his hands a blur as he saved my work and shut down the computer.

I obediently started reciting English monarchs in my head, beginning with William the Conqueror, to rid my mind of thoughts of the missing manuscript.

Knox passed by, busily texting on his mobile. He was followed by the Scary Sisters, who looked grimmer than usual.

"Why are they all leaving?" I asked Matthew.

"You didn't recall Ashmole 782. They're regrouping." He thrust my bag and computer at me and picked up my two manuscripts. With his free hand, he snared my elbow and moved us toward the call desk. Timothy waved sadly from the Selden End before making a peace sign and turning away.

"Sean, Dr. Bishop is going back to college with me to help solve a problem I've found in the Needham papers. She won't require these for the rest of the day. And I won't be returning either." Matthew handed Sean the boxed manuscripts. Sean gave the vampire a dark look before thumping them into a neater pile and heading for the locked manuscript hold.

We didn't exchange a word on the way down the stairs, and by the time we pushed through the glass doors into the courtyard, I was ready to explode with questions.

Peter Knox was lounging against the iron railings surrounding the bronze statue of William Herbert. Matthew stopped abruptly and, with a fast step in front of me and a flick of his shoulder, placed me behind his considerable bulk.

"So, Dr. Bishop, you didn't get it back," Knox said maliciously. "I told you it was a fluke. Not even a Bishop could break that spell without proper training in witchcraft. Your mother might have managed it, but you don't appear to share her talents."

Matthew curled his lip but said nothing. He was trying not to interfere between witches, yet he wouldn't be able to resist throttling Knox indefinitely.

"It's missing. My mother was gifted, but she wasn't a bloodhound." I bristled, and Matthew's hand rose slightly to quiet me.

"It's been missing," Knox said. "You found it anyway. It's a good thing you didn't manage to break the spell a second time, though."

"Why is that?" I asked impatiently.

"Because we cannot let our history fall into the hands of animals like him. Witches and vampires don't mix, Dr. Bishop. There are excellent reasons for it. Remember who you are. If you don't, you *will* regret it."

A witch shouldn't keep secrets from other witches. Bad things happen when she does. Gillian's voice echoed in my head, and the walls of the Bodleian drew closer. I fought down the panic that was burbling to the surface.

"Threaten her again and I'll kill you on the spot." Matthew's voice was calm, but a passing tourist's frozen look suggested that his face betrayed stronger emotions.

"Matthew," I said quietly. "Not here."

"Killing witches now, Clairmont?" Knox sneered. "Have you run out of vampires and humans to harm?"

"Leave her alone." Matthew's voice remained even, but his body was poised to strike if Knox moved a muscle in my direction.

The witch's face twisted. "There's no chance of that. She belongs to us, not you. So does the manuscript."

"Matthew," I repeated more urgently. A human boy of thirteen with a nose ring and a troubled complexion was now studying him with interest. "The humans are staring."

He reached back and grabbed my hand in his. The shock of cold skin against warm and the sensation that I was tethered to him were simultaneous. He pulled me forward, tucking me under his shoulder.

Knox laughed scornfully. "It will take more than that to keep her safe, Clairmont. She'll get the manuscript back for us. We'll make sure of it."

Without another word, Matthew propelled me through the quadrangle and onto the wide cobblestone path surrounding the Radcliffe Camera. He eyed All Souls' closed iron gates, swore quickly and enthusiastically, and kept me going toward the High Street.

"Not much farther," he said, his hand gripping mine a bit more tightly.

Matthew didn't let go of me in the lodge, and he gave a curt nod to the porter on the way to his rooms. Up we climbed to his garret, which was just as warm and comfortable as it had been Saturday evening.

Matthew threw his keys onto the sideboard and deposited me unceremoniously on the sofa. He disappeared into the kitchen and returned with a glass of water. He handed it to me, and I held it without drinking until he scowled so darkly that I took a sip and almost choked.

"Why couldn't I get the manuscript a second time?" I was rattled that Knox had been proved right.

"I should have followed my instincts." Matthew was standing by the window, clenching and unclenching his right hand and paying absolutely no attention to me. "We don't understand your connection to the spell. You've been in grave danger since you saw Ashmole 782."

"Knox may threaten, Matthew, but he's not going to do something stupid in front of so many witnesses."

"You're staying at Woodstock for a few days. I want you away from Knox—no more chance meetings in college, no passing by him in the Bodleian."

"Knox was right: I can't get the manuscript back. He won't pay any more attention to me."

"That's wishful thinking, Diana. Knox wants to understand the secrets of Ashmole 782 as much as you or I do." Matthew's normally impeccable appearance was suffering. He'd run his fingers through his hair until it stood up like a scarecrow's in places.

"How can you both be so certain there are secrets in the hidden text?" I wondered, moving toward the fireplace. "It's an alchemy book. Maybe that's all it is."

"Alchemy is the story of creation, told chemically. Creatures are chemistry, mapped onto biology."

"But when Ashmole 782 was written, they didn't know about biology or share your sense of chemistry."

Matthew's eyes collapsed into slits. "Diana Bishop, I'm shocked at your narrow-mindedness." He meant it, too. "The creatures who made the manuscript might not have known about DNA, but what proof do you have that they weren't asking the same questions about creation as a modern scientist?"

"Alchemical texts are allegories, not instruction manuals." I redirected the fear and frustration of the past several days at him. "They may hint at larger truths, but you can't build a reliable experiment from them."

"I never said you could," he replied, his eyes still dark with suppressed anger. "But we're talking about potential readers who are witches, daemons, and vampires. A little supernatural reading, a bit of otherworldly creativity, and some long memories to fill in the blanks may give creatures information we don't want them to have."

"Information *you* don't want them to have!" I remembered my promise to Agatha Wilson, and my voice rose. "You're as bad as Knox. You want Ashmole 782 to satisfy your own curiosity." My hands itched as I grabbed at my things.

"Calm down." There was an edge to his voice that I didn't like.

"Stop telling me what to do." The itching sensation intensified.

My fingers were brilliant blue and shooting out little arcs of fire that sputtered at the edges like the sparklers on birthday cakes. I dropped my computer and held them up.

Matthew should have been horrified. Instead he looked intrigued.

"Does that happen often?" His voice was carefully neutral.

"Oh, *no*." I ran for the kitchen, trailing sparks.

Matthew beat me to the door. "Not water," he said sharply. "They smell electrical."

Ah. That explained the last time I set fire to the kitchen.

I stood mutely, holding my hands up between us. We watched for a few minutes while the blue left my fingertips and the sparks went out entirely, leaving behind a definite smell of bad electrical wiring.

When the fireworks ended, Matthew was lounging against the kitchen doorframe with the nonchalant air of a Renaissance aristocrat waiting to have his portrait painted.

"Well," he said, watching me with the stillness of an eagle ready to pounce on his prey, "*that* was interesting. Are you always like that when you get angry?"

"I don't do angry," I said, turning away from him. His hand shot out and whirled me back around to face him.

"You're not getting off that easy." Matthew's voice was soft, but the sharp edge was back. "You do angry. I just saw it. And you left at least one hole in my carpet to prove it."

"Let me go!" My mouth contorted into what Sarah called my "sour-puss." It was enough to make my students quake. Right now I hoped it would make Matthew curl up into a ball and roll away. At the very least, I wanted him to take his hand off my arm so I could get out of there.

"I warned you. Friendships with vampires are complicated. I couldn't let you go now—even if I wanted to."

My eyes lowered deliberately to his hand. Matthew removed it with a snort of impatience, and I turned to pick up my bag.

You really shouldn't turn your back on a vampire if you've been arguing.

Matthew's arms shot around me from behind, pressing my back against his chest so hard that I could feel every flexed muscle. "Now," he said directly into my ear, "we're going to talk like civilized creatures about what happened. You are not running away from this—or from me."

"Let me go, Matthew." I struggled in his arms.

"No."

No man had ever refused when I asked him to stop doing something—whether it was blowing his nose in the library or trying to slip a hand up my shirt after a movie. I struggled again. Matthew's arms got tighter.

"Stop fighting me." He sounded amused. "You'll get tired long before I do, I assure you."

In my women's self-defense class, they'd taught me what to do if grabbed from behind. I lifted my foot to stomp on his. Matthew moved out of the way, and it smashed into the floor instead.

"We can do this all afternoon if you want," he murmured. "But I honestly can't recommend it. My reflexes are much faster than yours."

"Let me go and we can talk," I said through clenched teeth.

He laughed softly, his spicy breath tickling the exposed skin at the base of my skull. "That wasn't a worthy attempt at negotiation, Diana. No, we're going to talk like this. I want to know how often your fingers have turned blue."

"Not often." My instructor had recommended I relax if grabbed from behind and slip out of an assailant's arms. Matthew's grip on me only tightened. "A few times, when I was a child, I set fire to things—the kitchen cabinets, but that may have been because I tried to put my hands out in the sink and the fire got worse. My bedroom curtains, once or twice. A tree outside the house—but it was just a small tree."

"Since then?"

"It happened last week, when Miriam made me angry."

"How did she do that?" he asked, resting his cheek against the side of my head. It was comforting, if I overlooked the fact that he was holding me against my wishes.

"She told me I needed to learn how to take care of myself and stop relying on you to protect me. She basically accused me of playing the damsel in distress." Just the thought made my blood simmer and my fingers itch all over again.

"You are many things, Diana, but a damsel in distress is not one of them. You've had this reaction twice in less than a week." Matthew's voice was thoughtful. "Interesting."

"I don't think so."

"No, I don't imagine you do," he said, "but it is interesting just the same. Now let's turn to another topic." His mouth drifted toward my ear, and I tried—unsuccessfully—to pull it away. "What is this nonsense about my not being interested in anything but an old manuscript?"

I flushed. This was mortifying. "Sarah and Em said you were only spending time with me because you wanted something. I assume it's Ashmole 782."

"But that's not true, is it?" he said, running his lips and cheek gently against my hair. My blood started to sing in response. Even I could hear it. He laughed again, this time with satisfaction. "I didn't think you believed it. I just wanted to be sure."

My body relaxed into his. "Matthew—" I began.

"I'm letting you go," he said, cutting me off. "But don't bolt for the door, understand?"

We were prey and predator once more. If I ran, his instincts would tell him to give chase. I nodded, and he slipped his arms from me, leaving me oddly unsteady.

"What am I going to do with you?" He was standing with his hands on his hips, a lopsided smile on his face. "You are the most exasperating creature I've ever met."

"No one has ever known what to do with me."

"That I believe." He surveyed me for a moment. "We're going to Woodstock."

"No! I'm perfectly safe in college." He'd warned me about vampires and protectiveness. He was right—I didn't like it.

"You are not," he said with an angry glint in his eyes. "Someone's tried to break in to your rooms."

"What?" I was aghast.

"The loose lock, remember?"

In fact, there were fresh scratches on the hardware. But Matthew did not need to know about that.

"You'll stay at Woodstock until Peter Knox leaves Oxford."

My face must have betrayed my dismay.

"It won't be so bad," he said gently. "You'll have all the yoga you want."

With Matthew in bodyguard mode, I didn't have much choice. And if he was right—which I suspected he was—someone had already gotten past Fred and into my rooms.

"Come," he said, picking up my computer bag. "I'll take you to New College and wait while you get your things. But this conversation about the connection between Ashmole 782 and your blue fingers is not over," he continued, forcing me to meet his eyes. "It's just beginning."

We went down to the fellows' car park, and Matthew retrieved the Jaguar from between a modest blue Vauxhall and an old Peugeot. Given the city's restrictive traffic patterns, it took twice as long to drive as it would have to walk.

Matthew pulled in to the lodge gates. "I'll be right back," I said, slinging my computer bag over my shoulder as he let me out of the car.

"Dr. Bishop, you have mail," Fred called from the lodge.

I collected the contents of my pigeonhole, my head pounding with stress and anxiety, and waved my mail at Matthew before heading toward my rooms.

Inside, I kicked off my shoes, rubbed my temples, and glanced at the message machine. Mercifully, it wasn't blinking. The mail contained nothing but bills and a large brown envelope with my name typed on it. There was no stamp, indicating it came from someone within the university. I slid my finger under the flap and pulled out the contents.

A piece of ordinary paper was clipped to something smooth and shiny. Typed on the paper was a single line of text.

"Remember?"

Hands shaking, I pulled off the slip. The paper fluttered to the floor, revealing a familiar glossy photograph. I'd only seen it reproduced in black and white, though, in the newspapers. This was in color, and as bright and vivid as the day it had been taken, in 1983.

My mother's body lay facedown in a chalk circle, her left leg at an impossible angle. Her right arm reached toward my father, who was lying faceup, his head caved in on one side and a gash splitting his torso from throat to groin. Some of his entrails had been pulled out and were lying next to him on the ground.

A sound between a moan and a scream slipped from my mouth. I dropped to the floor, trembling but unable to tear my eyes from the image.

"Diana!" Matthew's voice sounded frantic, but he was too far away for me to care. In the distance someone jiggled the doorknob. Feet clattered up the stairs, a key scraped in the lock.

The door burst open, and I looked up into Matthew's ashen face, along with Fred's concerned one.

"Dr. Bishop?" Fred asked.

Matthew moved so quickly that Fred had to know he was a vampire. He crouched in front of me. My teeth chattered with shock.

"If I give you my keys, can you move the car to All Souls for me?" Matthew asked over his shoulder. "Dr. Bishop isn't well, and she shouldn't be alone."

"No worries, Professor Clairmont. We'll keep it here in the warden's lot," replied Fred. Matthew threw his keys at the porter, who caught them neatly. Flashing me a worried look, Fred closed the door.

"I'm going to be sick," I whispered.

Matthew pulled me to my feet and led me to the bathroom. Sinking next to the toilet, I threw up, dropping the picture on the floor to grip the sides of the bowl. Once my stomach was empty, the worst of the shaking subsided, but every few seconds a tremble radiated through me.

I closed the lid and reached up to flush, pushing down on the toilet for leverage. My head spun. Matthew caught me before I hit the bathroom wall.

Suddenly my feet were not on the ground. Matthew's chest was against my right shoulder and his arms underneath my knees. Moments later he laid me gently on my bed and turned the light on, angling the shade away. My wrist was in his cool fingers, and with his touch my pulse began to slow. That made it possible for me to focus on his face. It looked as calm as ever, except that the tiny dark vein in his forehead throbbed slightly every minute or so.

"I'm going to get you something to drink." He let go of my wrist and stood.

Another wave of panic washed over me. I bolted to my feet, all my instincts telling me to run as far and as fast as possible.

Matthew grabbed me by the shoulders, trying to make eye contact. "Stop, Diana."

My stomach had invaded my lungs, pressing out all the air, and I struggled against his grasp, not knowing or caring what he was saying. "Let me go," I pleaded, pushing against his chest with both hands.

"Diana, look at me." There was no ignoring Matthew's voice, or the moonlike pull of his eyes. "What's wrong?"

"My parents. Gillian told me witches killed my parents." My voice was high and tight.

Matthew said something in a language I didn't understand. "When did this happen? Where were they? Did the witch leave a message on your phone? Did she threaten you?" His hold on me strengthened.

"Nigeria. She said the Bishops have always been trouble."

"I'll go with you. Let me make a few phone calls first." Matthew took in a deep, shuddering breath. "I'm so sorry, Diana."

"Go where?" Nothing was making any sense.

"To Africa." Matthew sounded confused. "Someone will have to identify the bodies."

"My parents were killed when I was seven."

His eyes widened with shock.

"Even though it happened so long ago, they're all the witches want to talk about these days—Gillian, Peter Knox." Shivering as the panic escalated, I felt a scream rise up in my throat. Matthew pressed me to him before it could erupt, holding me so tightly that the outlines of his muscles and bones were sharp against my skin. The scream turned into a sob. "Bad things happen to witches who keep secrets. Gillian said so."

"No matter what she said, I will not let Knox or any other witch harm you. I've got you now." Matthew's voice was fierce, and he bowed his head and rested his cheek on my hair while I cried. "Oh, Diana. Why didn't you tell me?"

Somewhere in the center of my soul, a rusty chain began to unwind. It freed itself, link by link, from where it had rested unobserved, waiting for him. My hands, which had been balled up and pressed against his chest, unfurled with it. The chain continued to drop, to an unfathomable depth where there was nothing but darkness and Matthew. At last it snapped to its full length, anchoring me to a vampire. Despite the manuscript, despite the fact that my hands contained enough voltage to run a microwave, and despite the photograph, as long as I was connected to him, I was safe.

When my sobs quieted, Matthew drew away. "I'm going to get you some water, and then you're going to rest." His tone did not invite discussion, and he was back in a matter of seconds carrying a glass of water and two tiny pills.

"Take these," he said, handing them to me along with the water.

"What are they?"

"A sedative." His stern look encouraged me to pop both pills into my mouth, immediately, along with a gulp of water. "I've been carrying one since you told me you suffered from panic attacks."

"I hate taking tranquilizers."

"You've had a shock, and you've got too much adrenaline in your system. You need to rest." Matthew dragged the duvet around me until I was encased in a lumpy cocoon. He sat on the bed, and his shoes thumped against the floor before he stretched out, his back propped up against the pillows. When he gathered my duvet-wrapped body against him, I sighed. Matthew reached across with his left arm and held me securely. My body, for all its wrappings, fit against him perfectly.

The drug worked its way through my bloodstream. As I was drifting off to sleep, Matthew's phone shook in his pocket, startling me into wakefulness.

"It's nothing, probably Marcus," he said, brushing his lips against my forehead. My heartbeat settled. "Try to rest. You aren't alone anymore."

I could still feel the chain that anchored me to Matthew, witch to vampire.

With the links of that chain tight and shining, I slept.

Chapter 16

The sky was dark outside Diana's windows before Matthew could leave her side. Restless at first, she had at last fallen into deep sleep. He noted the subtle changes of scent as her shock subsided, a cold fierceness sweeping over him every time he thought of Peter Knox and Gillian Chamberlain.

Matthew couldn't remember when he'd felt so protective of another being. He felt other emotions as well, that he was reluctant to acknowledge or name.

She's a witch, he reminded himself as he watched her sleep. *She's not for you.*

The more he said it, the less it seemed to matter.

At last he gently extracted himself and crept from the room, leaving the door open a crack in case she stirred.

Alone in the hall, the vampire let surface the cold anger that had been seething inside for hours. The intensity of it almost choked him. He drew the leather cord from the neck of his sweater and touched the worn, smooth surfaces of Lazarus's silver coffin. The sound of Diana's breathing was all that kept him from leaping through the night to hunt down two witches.

The clocks of Oxford struck eight, their familiar, weary tolling reminding Matthew of the call he'd missed. He pulled his phone out of his pocket and checked the messages, quickly thumbing through the automatic notifications from the security systems at the labs and the Old Lodge. There were several messages from Marcus.

Matthew frowned and punched the number to retrieve them. Marcus was not prone to alarm. What could be so urgent?

"Matthew." The familiar voice held none of its usual playful charm. *"I have Diana's DNA test results. They're . . . surprising. Call me."*

The recorded voice was still speaking when the vampire's finger punched another single key on the phone. He raked his hair with his free hand while he waited for Marcus to pick up. It took only one ring.

"Matthew." There was no warmth in Marcus's response, only relief. It had been hours since he'd left the messages. Marcus had even checked Matthew's favorite Oxford haunt, the Pitt Rivers Museum, where the vampire could often be found dividing his attention between the skeleton of an iguanodon and a likeness of Darwin. Miriam had finally banished him from the lab, irritated by his constant questions about where Matthew might be and with whom.

"He's with her, of course," Miriam had said in the late afternoon, her voice full of disapproval. "Where else? And if you're not going to do any work, go home and wait for his call there. You're in my way."

"What did the tests show?" Matthew's voice was low, but his rage was audible.

"What's happened?" Marcus asked quickly.

A picture lying faceup on the floor of the bathroom caught Matthew's attention. Diana had been clutching it that afternoon. His eyes narrowed to slits as he took in the image. "Where are you?" he rasped.

"Home," Marcus answered uneasily.

Matthew picked the photo off the floor and traced its scent to where a piece of paper had slid half under the couch. He read the single word of the message, took a sharp breath. "Bring the reports and my passport to New College. Diana's rooms are in the garden quadrangle at the top of staircase seven."

Twenty minutes later Matthew opened the door, his hair standing on end and a ferocious look on his face. The younger vampire had to school himself not to take a step backward.

Marcus held out a manila folder with a maroon passport folded around it, every move deliberate, and patiently waited. He wasn't about to enter the witch's rooms without Matthew's permission, not when the vampire was in this state.

Permission was slow in coming, but at last Matthew took the folder and stepped aside to let Marcus enter.

While Matthew scrutinized Diana's test results, Marcus studied him. His keen nose took in the old wood and well-worn textiles, along with the smell of the witch's fear and the vampire's barely controlled emotions. His own hackles rose at the volatile combination, and a reflexive growl caught in his throat.

Over the years Marcus had come to appreciate Matthew's finer qualities—his compassion, his conscience, his patience with those he loved. He also knew his faults, anger chief among them. Typically, Matthew's rage was so destructive that once the poison was out of his system, he disappeared for months or even years to come to terms with what he'd done.

And Marcus had never seen his father so coldly furious as he was now.

Matthew Clairmont had entered Marcus's life in 1777 and changed it—forever. He had appeared in the Bennett farmhouse at the side of an improvised sling that carried the wounded Marquis de Lafayette from the killing fields at the Battle of Brandywine. Matthew towered over the other men, barking orders at everyone regardless of rank.

No one disputed his commands—not even Lafayette, who joked with his friend despite his injuries. The marquis's good humor couldn't stave off a tongue-lashing from Matthew, however. When Lafayette protested that he could manage while soldiers with more serious injuries were tended to, Clairmont released a volley of French so laced with expletives and ultimatums that his own men looked at him with awe and the marquis subsided into silence.

Marcus had listened, wide-eyed, when the French soldier railed at the head of the army's medical corps, the esteemed Dr. Shippen, rejecting his treatment plan as "barbaric." Clairmont demanded that the doctor's second in command, John Cochran, treat Lafayette instead. Two days later Clairmont and Shippen could be heard arguing the finer points of anatomy and physiology in fluent Latin—to the delight of the medical staff and General Washington.

Matthew had killed more than his share of British soldiers before the Continental Army was defeated at Brandywine. Men brought into the hospital spun impossible tales of his fearlessness in battle. Some claimed he walked straight into enemy lines, unfazed by bullets and bayonets. When the guns stopped, Clairmont insisted that Marcus remain with the marquis as his nurse.

In the autumn, once Lafayette was able to ride again, the two of them disappeared into the forests of Pennsylvania and New York. They returned with an army of Oneida warriors. The Oneida called Lafayette "Kayewla" for his skill with the horse. Matthew they referred to as "atlutanu'n," the warrior chief, because of his ability to lead men into battle.

Matthew remained with the army long after Lafayette returned to France. Marcus continued to serve, too, as a lowly surgeon's assistant. Day after day he tried to stanch the wounds of soldiers injured by musket, cannon, and sword. Clairmont always sought him out whenever one of his own men was injured. Marcus, he said, had a gift for healing.

Shortly after the Continental Army arrived in Yorktown in 1781, Marcus caught a fever. His gift for healing meant nothing then. He lay cold and shivering, tended to only when someone had the time. After four days of suffering, Marcus knew he was dying. When Clairmont came to visit some of his own stricken men, accompanied once again by Lafayette, he saw Marcus on a broken cot in the corner and smelled the scent of death.

The French officer sat at the young man's side as night turned toward day and shared his story. Marcus thought he was dreaming. A man who drank blood and found it impossible to die? After hearing that, Marcus became convinced that he was already dead and being tormented by one of the devils his father had warned him would prey on his sinful nature.

The vampire explained that Marcus could survive the fever, but there would be a price. First he would have to be reborn. Then he would have to hunt, and kill, and drink blood—even human blood. For a time his need for it would make working among the injured and sick impossible. Matthew promised to send Marcus to university while he got used to his new life.

Sometime before dawn, when the pain became excruciating, Marcus decided he wanted to live more than he feared the new life the vampire had laid out for him. Matthew carried him, limp and burning with fever, out of the hospital and into the woods, where the Oneida waited to lead them into the mountains. Matthew drained him of his blood in a remote hollow, where no one could hear his screams. Even now Marcus remembered the powerful thirst that had followed. He'd been mad with it, desperate to swallow anything cold and liquid.

Finally Matthew had slashed his own wrist with his teeth and let Marcus drink. The vampire's powerful blood brought him back to startling life.

The Oneida waited impassively at the mouth of the cave and prevented him from wreaking havoc on the nearby farms when his hunger for blood surfaced. They had recognized what Matthew was the moment he appeared in their village. He was like Dagwanoenyent, the witch who lived in the whirlwind and could not die. Why the gods had decided to give the French warrior these gifts was a mystery to the Oneida, but the gods were known for their puzzling decisions. All they could do was make sure their children knew Dagwanoenyent's legend, carefully instructing them how to kill such a creature by burning him, grinding his bones into powder, and dispersing it to the four winds so that he could not be reborn.

Thwarted, Marcus had behaved like the child he was, howling with frustration and shaking with need. When Matthew hunted down a deer to feed the young man who had been reborn as his son, Marcus quickly sucked it dry. It sated his hunger but didn't dull the thrumming in his veins as Matthew's ancient blood suffused his body.

After a week of bringing fresh kills back to their den, Matthew decided Marcus was ready to hunt for himself. Father and son tracked deer and bear through deep forests and along moonlit mountain ridges. Matthew trained him to smell the air, to watch in the shadows for the smallest hint of movement, and to feel changes in the wind that would bring fresh scents their way. And he taught the healer how to kill.

In those early days, Marcus wanted richer blood. He needed it, too, to quench his deep thirst and feed his ravenous body. But Matthew waited until Marcus could track a deer quickly, bring it down, and drain its blood without making a mess before he let him hunt humans. Women were off-limits. Too confusing for newly reborn vampires, Matthew explained, as the lines between sex and death, courtship and hunting, were too finely drawn.

First father and son fed on sick British soldiers. Some begged Marcus to spare their life, and Matthew taught him how to feed on warmbloods without killing them. Then they hunted criminals, who cried for mercy and didn't deserve it. In every case Matthew made Marcus explain why he'd picked a particular man as his prey. Marcus's ethics developed, in the halting, deliberate way that they must when a vampire comes to terms with what he needs to do in order to survive.

Matthew was widely known for his finely developed sense of right and wrong. All his mistakes in judgment could be traced back to decisions made in anger. Marcus had been told that his father was not as prone to that dangerous emotion as he'd been in the past. Perhaps so, but tonight in Oxford, Matthew's face wore the same murderous expression it had at Brandywine—and there was no battlefield to vent his rage.

"You've made a mistake." Matthew's eyes were wild when he finished poring over the witch's DNA tests.

Marcus shook his head. "I analyzed her blood twice. Miriam confirmed my findings with the DNA from the swab. I admit the results are surprising."

Matthew drew in a shaky breath. "They're preposterous."

"Diana possesses nearly every genetic marker we've ever seen in a witch." His mouth tightened into a grim line as he flipped to the final pages. "But these sequences have us concerned."

Matthew leafed quickly through the data. There were more than two dozen sequences of DNA, some short and some long, with Miriam's tiny red question marks next to them.

"Christ," he said, tossing them back at his son. "We already have enough to worry about. That bastard Peter Knox has threatened her. He wants the manuscript. Diana tried to recall it, but Ashmole 782 has gone back into the library and won't come out again. Happily, Knox is convinced—for now—that she first obtained it by deliberately breaking its spell."

"She didn't?"

"No. Diana doesn't have the knowledge or control to do anything that intricate. Her power is completely undisciplined. She put a hole in my rug." Matthew looked sour, and his son struggled not to smile. His father did love his antiques.

"Then we'll keep Knox away and give Diana a chance to come to terms with her abilities. That doesn't sound too difficult."

"Knox is not my only concern. Diana received these in the mail today." Matthew picked up the photograph and its accompanying slip of paper and handed them to his son. When he continued, his voice had a dangerous, flat tone. "Her parents. I remember hearing about two American witches killed in Nigeria, but it was so long ago. I never connected them to Diana."

"Holy God," Marcus said softly. Staring at the picture, he tried to imagine what it would be like to receive a photo of his own father ripped to pieces and tossed into the dirt to die.

"There's more. From what I can piece together, Diana has long believed that her parents were killed by humans. That's the chief reason she's tried to keep magic from her life."

"That won't work, will it?" muttered Marcus, thinking of the witch's DNA.

"No," Matthew agreed, grim-faced. "While I was in Scotland, another American witch, Gillian Chamberlain, informed her that it wasn't humans at all—but fellow witches—who murdered her parents."

"Did they?"

"I'm not sure. But there's clearly more to this situation than a witch's discovery of Ashmole 782." Matthew's tone turned deadly. "I intend to find out what it is."

Something silver glinted against his father's dusky sweater. *He's wearing Lazarus's coffin,* Marcus realized.

No one in the family talked openly about Eleanor St. Leger or the events surrounding her death, for fear of driving Matthew into one of his rages. Marcus understood that his father hadn't wanted to leave Paris in 1140, where he was happily studying philosophy. But when the head of the family, Matthew's own father, Philippe, called him back to Jerusalem to help resolve the conflicts that continued to plague the Holy Land long after the conclusion of Urban II's Crusade, Matthew obeyed without question. He had met Eleanor, befriended her sprawling English family, and fallen resolutely in love.

But the St. Legers and the de Clermonts were often on opposite sides in the disputes, and Matthew's older brothers—Hugh, Godfrey, and Baldwin—urged him to put the woman aside, leaving a clear path for them to destroy her family. Matthew refused. One day a squabble between Baldwin and Matthew over some petty political crisis involving the St. Legers spiraled out of control. Before Philippe could be found and made to stop it, Eleanor intervened. By the time Matthew and Baldwin came to their senses, she'd lost too much blood to recover.

Marcus still didn't understand why Matthew had let Eleanor die if he'd loved her so much.

Now Matthew wore his pilgrim's badge only when he was afraid he was going to kill someone or when he was thinking of Eleanor St. Leger—or both.

"That picture is a threat—and not an idle one. Hamish thought the Bishop name would make the witches more cautious, but I fear the opposite is true. No matter how great her innate talents might be, Diana can't protect herself, and she's too damn self-reliant to ask for help. I need you to stay with her for a few hours." Matthew dragged his eyes from the picture of Rebecca Bishop and Stephen Proctor. "I'm going to find Gillian Chamberlain."

"You can't be sure it was Gillian who delivered that picture," Marcus pointed out. "There are two different scents on it."

"The other belongs to Peter Knox."

"But Peter Knox is a member of the Congregation!" Marcus knew that a nine-member council of daemons, witches, and vampires had been formed during the Crusades—three representatives from each species. The Congregation's job was to ensure every creature's safety by seeing to it that no one caught the attention of humans. "If you make a move in his direction, it will be seen as a challenge to their authority. The whole family will be implicated. You aren't seriously considering endangering us just to avenge a witch?"

"You aren't questioning my loyalty, are you?" Matthew purred.

"No, I'm questioning your judgment," Marcus said hotly, facing his father without fear. "This ridiculous romance is bad enough. The Congregation already has one reason to take steps against you. Don't give them another."

During Marcus's first visit to France, his vampire grandmother had explained that he was now bound by a covenant that prohibited close relationships between different orders of creatures, as well as any meddling in human religion and politics. All other interactions with humans—including affairs of the heart—were to be avoided but were permitted as long as they didn't lead to trouble. Marcus preferred spending time with vampires and always had, so the covenant's terms had mattered little to him—until now.

"Nobody cares anymore," Matthew said defensively, his gray eyes drifting in the direction of Diana's bedroom door.

"My God, she doesn't understand about the covenant," Marcus said contemptuously, "and you have no intention of telling her. You damn well know you can't keep this secret from her indefinitely."

"The Congregation isn't going to enforce a promise made nearly a thousand years ago in a very different world." Matthew's eyes were now fixed on an antique print of the goddess Diana aiming her bow at a hunter fleeing through the forest. He remembered a passage from a book written long ago by a friend—"*for they are no longer hunters, but the hunted*"—and shivered.

"Think before you do this, Matthew."

"I've made my decision." He avoided his son's eyes. "Will you check on her while I'm gone, make sure she's all right?"

Marcus nodded, unable to deny the raw appeal in his father's voice.

After the door closed behind his father, Marcus went to Diana. He lifted one of her eyelids, then the other, and picked up her wrist. He sniffed, noting the fear and shock that surrounded her. He also detected the drug that was still circulating through her veins. *Good,* he thought. At least his father had had the presence of mind to give her a sedative.

Marcus continued to probe Diana's condition, looking minutely at her skin and listening to the sound of her breath. When he was finished, he stood quietly at the witch's bedside, watching her dream. Her forehead was creased into a frown, as if she were arguing with someone.

After his examination Marcus knew two things. First, Diana would be fine. She'd had a serious shock and needed rest, but no permanent damage had been done. Second, his father's scent was all over her. He'd done it deliberately, to mark Diana so that every vampire would know to whom she belonged. That meant the situation had gone further than Marcus had believed possible. It was going to be difficult for his father to detach himself from this witch. And he would have to, if the stories that Marcus's grandmother had told him were true.

It was after midnight when Matthew reappeared. He looked even angrier than when he'd left, but he was spotless and impeccable as always. He ran his fingers through his hair and strode straight into Diana's room without a word to his son.

Marcus knew better than to question Matthew then. After he emerged from the witch's room, Marcus asked only, "Will you discuss the DNA findings with Diana?"

"No," Matthew said shortly, without a hint of guilt over keeping information of this magnitude from her. "Nor am I going to share what the witches of the Congregation might do to her. She's been through enough."

"Diana Bishop is less fragile than you think. You have no right to keep that information to yourself, if you are going to continue to spend time with her." Marcus knew that a vampire's life was measured not in hours or years but in secrets revealed and kept. Vampires guarded their personal relationships, the names they'd adopted, and the details of the many lives they'd led. Nonetheless, his father kept more secrets than most, and his urge to hide things from his own family was intensely aggravating.

"Stay out of this, Marcus," his father snarled. "It's not your business."

Marcus swore. "Your damned secrets are going to be the family's undoing."

Matthew had his son by the scruff of the neck before he'd finished speaking. "My secrets have kept this family safe for many centuries, my son. Where would you be today if not for my secrets?"

"Food for worms in an unmarked Yorktown grave, I expect," Marcus said breathlessly, his vocal cords constricted.

Over the years Marcus had tried with little success to uncover some of his father's secrets. He'd never been able to discover who tipped Matthew off that Marcus was raising hell in New Orleans after Jefferson made the Louisiana Purchase, for example. There he'd created a vampire family as boisterous and charming as himself from the city's youngest, least responsible citizens. Marcus's brood—which included an alarming number of gamblers and ne'er-do-wells—risked human discovery every time they went out after dark. The witches of New Orleans, Marcus remembered, had made it clear they wanted them to leave town.

Then Matthew had shown up, uninvited and unannounced, with a gorgeous mixed-race vampire: Juliette Durand. Matthew and Juliette had waged a campaign to bring Marcus's family to heel. Within days they'd formed an unholy alliance with a foppish young French vampire in the Garden District who had implausibly golden hair and a streak of ruthlessness as wide as the Mississippi. That was when the real trouble began.

By the end of the first fortnight, Marcus's new family was considerably, and mysteriously, smaller. As the number of deaths and disappearances mounted, Matthew threw up his hands and murmured about the dangers of New Orleans. Juliette, whom Marcus had grown to detest in the few days he'd known her, smiled secretively and cooed encouraging words in his father's ears. She was the most manipulative creature Marcus had ever met, and he was thrilled when she and his father parted ways.

Under pressure from his remaining children, Marcus made devout assurances to behave if only Matthew and Juliette would leave.

Matthew agreed, after setting out what was expected of members of the de Clermont family in exacting detail. "If you are determined to make me a grandfather," his father instructed during an extremely unpleasant interview held in the presence of several of the city's oldest and most powerful vampires, "take more care." The memory still made Marcus blanch.

Who or what gave Matthew and Juliette the authority to act as they did remained a mystery. His father's strength, Juliette's cunning, and the luster of the de Clermont name may have helped them gain the support of the vampires. But there was more to it than that. Every creature in New Orleans—even the witches—had treated his father like royalty.

Marcus wondered if his father had been a member of the Congregation, all those years ago. It would explain a great deal.

Matthew's voice sent his son's memories flying. "Diana may be brave, Marcus, but she doesn't need to know everything now." He released Marcus and stepped away.

"Does she know about our family, then? Your other children?" *Does she know about your father?* Marcus didn't say the last aloud.

Matthew knew what he was thinking anyway. "I don't tell other vampires' tales."

"You're making a mistake," said Marcus, shaking his head. "Diana won't thank you for keeping things from her."

"So you and Hamish say. When she's ready, I'll tell her everything—but not before." His father's voice was firm. "My only concern right now is getting Diana out of Oxford."

"Will you drop her off in Scotland? Surely she'll be beyond anyone's reach there." Marcus thought at once of Hamish's remote estate. "Or will you leave her at Woodstock before you go?"

"Before I go where?" Matthew's face was puzzled.

"You had me bring your passport." Now it was Marcus who was puzzled. That's what his father did—he got angry and went away by himself until he was under better control.

"I have no intention of leaving Diana," Matthew said icily. "I'm taking her to Sept-Tours."

"You can't possibly put her under the same roof as Ysabeau!" Marcus's shocked voice rang in the small room.

"It's my home, too," Matthew said, jaw set in a stubborn line.

"Your mother openly boasts about the witches she's killed and blames every witch she meets for what happened to Louisa and your father."

Matthew's face crumpled, and Marcus at last understood. The photograph had reminded Matthew of Philippe's death and Ysabeau's battle with madness in the years that followed.

Matthew pressed the palms of his hands against his temples, as if desperately trying to shape a better plan from the outside in. "Diana had nothing to do with either tragedy. Ysabeau will understand."

"She won't—you know she won't," Marcus said obstinately. He loved his grandmother and didn't want her hurt. And if Matthew—her favorite—brought a witch home, it was going to hurt her. Badly.

"There's nowhere as safe as Sept-Tours. The witches will think twice before tangling with Ysabeau—especially at her own home."

"For God's sake, don't leave the two of them alone together."

"I won't," Matthew promised. "I'll need you and Miriam to move into the gatehouse in hopes that will convince everyone Diana is there. They'll figure out the truth eventually, but it may win us a few days. My keys are with the porter. Come back in a few hours, when we've gone. Take the duvet from her bed—it will have her scent on it—and drive to Woodstock. Stay there until you hear from me."

"Can you protect yourself and that witch at the same time?" Marcus asked quietly.

"I can handle it," Matthew said with certainty.

Marcus nodded, and the two vampires gripped forearms, exchanging a meaningful look. Anything they needed to say to each other at moments like these had long since been said.

When Matthew was alone again, he sank into the sofa and cradled his head in his hands. Marcus's vehement opposition had shaken him.

He looked up and stared again at the print of the goddess of the hunt stalking her prey. Another line from the same old poem came into his mind. "'*I saw her coming from the forest,*'" he whispered, "'*Huntress of myself, beloved Diana.*'"

In the bedroom, too far away for a warmblood to have heard, Diana stirred and cried out. Matthew sped to her side and gathered her into his arms. The protectiveness returned, and with it a renewed sense of purpose.

"I'm here," he murmured against the rainbow strands of her hair. He looked down at Diana's sleeping face, her mouth puckered and a fierce frown between her eyes. It was a face he'd studied for hours and knew well, but its contradictions still fascinated him. "Have you bewitched me?" he wondered aloud.

After tonight Matthew knew his need for her was greater than anything else. Neither his family nor his next taste of blood mattered as much as knowing that she was safe and within arm's reach. If that was what it meant to be bewitched, he was a lost man.

His arms tightened, holding Diana in sleep as he would not allow himself to do when she was awake. She sighed, nestling closer.

Were he not a vampire he wouldn't have caught her faint, murmured words as she clutched both his ampulla and the fabric of his sweater, her fist resting firmly against his heart.

"You're not lost. I found you."

Matthew wondered fleetingly if he'd imagined it but knew that he hadn't.

She could hear his thoughts.

Not all the time, not when she was conscious—not yet. But it was only a matter of time before Diana knew everything there was to know about him. She would know his secrets, the dark and terrible things he wasn't brave enough to face.

She answered with another faint murmur. "I'm brave enough for both of us."

Matthew bent his head toward hers. "You'll have to be."

Chapter 17

There was a powerful taste of cloves in my mouth, and I'd been mummified in my own duvet. When I stirred in my wrappings, the bed's old springs gave slightly.

"Shh." Matthew's lips were at my ear, and his body formed a shell against my back. We lay there like spoons in a drawer, tight against each other.

"What time is it?" My voice was hoarse.

Matthew pulled away slightly and looked at his watch. "It's after one."

"How long have I been asleep?"

"Since around six last night."

Last night.

My mind shattered into words and images: the alchemical manuscript, Peter Knox's threat, my fingers turning blue with electricity, the photograph of my parents, my mother's hand frozen in a never-ending reach.

"You gave me drugs." I pushed against the duvet, trying to work my hands free. "I don't like taking drugs, Matthew."

"Next time you go into shock, I'll let you suffer needlessly." He gave a single twitch to the bed covering that was more effective than all my previous wrestling with it.

Matthew's sharp tone shook the shards of memory, and new images rose to the surface. Gillian Chamberlain's twisted face warned me about keeping secrets, and the piece of paper commanded me to remember. For a few moments, I was seven again, trying to understand how my bright, vital parents could be gone from my life.

In my rooms I reached toward Matthew, while in my mind's eye my mother's hand reached for my father across a chalk-inscribed circle. The lingering childhood desolation of their death collided with a new, adult empathy for my mother's desperate attempt to touch my father. Abruptly pulling from Matthew's arms, I lifted my knees to my chest in a tight, protective ball.

Matthew wanted to help—I could see that—but he was unsure of me, and the shadow of my own conflicted emotions fell over his face.

Knox's voice sounded again in my mind, full of poison. *Remember who you are.*

"Remember?" the note asked.

Without warning, I turned back toward the vampire, closing the distance between me and him in a rush. My parents were gone, but Matthew was here. Tucking my head under his chin, I listened for several minutes for the next pump of blood through his system. The leisurely rhythms of his vampire heart soon put me to sleep.

My own heart was pounding when I awoke again in the dark, kicking at the loosened duvet and swimming to a seated position. Behind me, Matthew turned on the lamp, its shade still angled away from the bed.

"What is it?" he asked.

"The magic found me. The witches did, too. I'll be killed for my magic, like my parents were killed." The words rushed from my mouth, panic speeding their passage, and I stumbled to my feet.

"No." Matthew rose and stood between me and the door. "We're going to face this, Diana, whatever it is. Otherwise you'll never stop running."

Part of me knew that what he said was true. The rest wanted to flee into the darkness. But how could I, with a vampire standing in the way?

The air began to stir around me as if trying to drive off the feeling of being trapped. Chilly wisps edged up the legs of my trousers. The air crept up my body, lifting the hair around my face in a gentle breeze. Matthew swore and stepped toward me, his arm outstretched. The breeze increased into gusts of wind that ruffled the bedclothes and the curtains.

"It's all right." His voice was pitched deliberately to be heard above the whirlwind and to calm me at the same time.

But it wasn't enough.

The force of the wind kept rising, and with it my arms rose, too, shaping the air into a column that enclosed me as protectively as the duvet. On the other side of the disturbance, Matthew stood, one hand still extended, eyes fixed on mine. When I opened my mouth to warn him to stay away, nothing came out but frigid air.

"It's all right," he said again, not breaking his gaze. "I won't move."

I hadn't realized that was the problem until he said the words.

"I promise," he said firmly.

The wind faltered. The cyclone surrounding me became a whirlwind, then a breeze, then disappeared entirely. I gasped and dropped to my knees.

"What is happening to me?" Every day I ran and rowed and did yoga, and my body did what I told it to. Now it was doing unimaginable things. I looked down to make sure my hands weren't sparkling with electricity and my feet weren't still being buffeted by winds.

"That was a witchwind," Matthew explained, not moving. "Do you know what that is?"

I'd heard of a witch in Albany who could summon storms, but no one had ever called it a "witchwind."

"Not really," I confessed, still sneaking glances at my hands and feet.

"Some witches have inherited the ability to control the element of air. You're one of them," he said.

"That wasn't control."

"It was your first time." Matthew was matter-of-fact. He gestured around the small bedroom: the intact curtains and sheets, all the clothing strewn on the chest of drawers and floor exactly where they'd been left that morning. "We're both still standing, and the room doesn't look like a tornado went through it. That's control—for now."

"But I didn't ask for it. Do these things just happen to witches—electrical fires and winds they didn't summon?" I pushed the hair out of my eyes and swayed, exhausted. Too much had happened in the past twenty-four hours. Matthew's body inclined toward me as if to catch me should I fall.

"Witchwinds and blue fingers are rare these days. There's magic inside you, Diana, and it wants to get out, whether you ask for it or not."

"I felt trapped."

"I shouldn't have cornered you last night." Matthew looked ashamed. "Sometimes I don't know what to do with you. You're like a perpetual-motion machine. All I wanted was for you to stand still for a moment and listen."

It must be even harder to cope with my incessant need to move if you were a vampire who seldom needed to breathe. Once again the space between Matthew and me was suddenly too large. I started to rise.

"Am I forgiven?" he asked sincerely. I nodded. "May I?" he asked, gesturing at his feet. I nodded again.

He took three fast steps in the time it took me to stand up. My body pitched into him just as it had in the Bodleian the first night I saw him, standing aristocratic and serene in Duke Humfrey's Reading Room. This time, however, I didn't pull away so quickly. Instead I rested against him willingly, his skin soothingly cool rather than frightening and cold.

We stood silent for a few moments, holding each other. My heart quieted, and his arms remained loose, although his shuddering breath suggested that this was not easy.

"I'm sorry, too." My body softened into him, his sweater scratchy on my cheek. "I'll try to keep my energy under control."

"There's nothing to be sorry about. And you shouldn't try so hard to be something you're not. Would you drink tea if I made you some?" he asked, his lips moving against the top of my head.

Outside, the night was unalleviated by any hint of sunrise. "What time is it now?"

Matthew's hand swiveled between my shoulder blades so that he could see the face of his watch. "Just after three."

I groaned. "I'm so tired, but tea sounds wonderful."

"I'll make it, then." He gently loosened my arms from around his waist. "Be right back."

Not wanting to let him out of my sight, I drifted along. He rummaged through the tins and bags of available teas.

"I told you I liked tea," I said apologetically as he found yet another brown bag in the cupboard, tucked behind a coffee press I seldom used.

"Do you have a preference?" He gestured at the crowded shelf.

"The one in the black bag with the gold label, please." Green tea seemed the most soothing option.

He busied himself with the kettle and pot. He poured hot water over the fragrant leaves and thrust a chipped old mug in my direction once it was ready. The aromas of green tea, vanilla, and citrus were so very different from Matthew, but comforting nevertheless.

He made himself a mug, too, his nostrils flaring in appreciation. "That actually doesn't smell too bad," he acknowledged, taking a small sip. It was the only time I'd seen him drink anything other than wine.

"Where shall we sit?" I asked, cradling the warm mug in my hands.

Matthew inclined his head toward the living room. "In there. We need to talk."

He sat in one corner of the comfortable old sofa, and I arranged myself opposite. The steam from the tea rose around my face, a gentle reminder of the witchwind.

"I need to understand why Knox thinks you've broken the spell on Ashmole 782," Matthew said when we were settled.

I replayed the conversation in the warden's rooms. "He said that spells become volatile around the anniversaries of their casting. Other witches—ones who know witchcraft—have tried to break it, and they've failed. He figured I was just in the right place at the right time."

"A talented witch bound Ashmole 782, and I suspect this spell is nearly impossible to break. No one who's tried to get the manuscript before met its conditions, no matter how much witchcraft they knew or what time of year they tried." He stared into the depths of his tea. "You did. The question is how, and why."

"The idea that I could fulfill the conditions of a spell cast before I was born is harder to believe than that it was just an anniversary aberration. And if I fulfilled the conditions once, why not again?" Matthew opened his mouth, and I shook my head. "No, it's not because of you."

"Knox knows witchcraft, and spells are complicated. I suppose it's possible that time pulls them out of shape every now and again." He looked unconvinced.

"I wish I could see the pattern in all this." My white table rose into view, with pieces of the puzzle laid on it. Though I moved a few pieces around—Knox, the manuscript, my parents—they refused to form an image. Matthew's voice broke through my reveries.

"Diana?"

"Hmm?"

"What are you doing?"

"Nothing," I said, too quickly.

"You're using magic," he said, putting his tea down. "I can smell it. See it, too. You're shimmering."

"It's what I do when I can't solve a puzzle—like now." My head was bowed to hide how difficult it was to talk about this. "I see a white table and imagine all the different pieces. They have shapes and colors, and they move around until they form a pattern. When the pattern forms, they stop moving to show I'm on the right track."

Matthew waited a long time before he responded. "How often do you play this game?"

"All the time," I said reluctantly. "While you were in Scotland, I realized that it was yet more magic, like knowing who's looking at me without turning my head."

"There is a pattern, you know," he said. "You use your magic when you're not thinking."

"What do you mean?" The puzzle pieces started dancing on the white table.

"When you're moving, you don't think—not with the rational part of your mind, at least. You're somewhere else entirely when you row, or run, or do yoga. Without your mind keeping your gifts in check, out they come."

"But I was thinking before," I said, "and the witchwind came anyway."

"Ah, but then you were feeling a powerful emotion," he explained, leaning forward and resting his elbows on his knees. "That always keeps the intellect at bay. It's the same thing that happened when your fingers turned blue with Miriam and then with me. This white table of yours is an exception to the general rule."

"Moods and movement are enough to trigger these forces? Who would want to be a witch if something so simple can make all hell break loose?"

"A great many people, I would imagine." Matthew glanced away. "I want to ask you to do something for me," he said. The sofa creaked as he faced me once more. "And I want you to think about it before you answer. Will you do that?"

"Of course." I nodded.

"I want to take you home."

"I'm not going back to America." It had taken me five seconds to do exactly what he'd asked me not to.

Matthew shook his head. "Not your home. My home. You need to get out of Oxford."

"I already told you I'd go to Woodstock."

"The Old Lodge is my *house*, Diana," Matthew explained patiently. "I want to take you to my *home*—to France."

"France?" I pushed the hair out of my face to get a clearer view of him.

"The witches are intent on getting Ashmole 782 and keeping it from the other creatures. Their theory that you broke the spell and the prominence of your family are all that's kept them at arm's length. When Knox and the others find out that you used no witchcraft to obtain the manuscript—that the spell was set to open for you—they'll want to know how and why."

My eyes closed against the sudden, sharp image of my father and mother. "And they won't ask nicely."

"Probably not." Matthew took a deep breath, and the vein in his forehead throbbed. "I saw the photo, Diana. I want you away from Peter Knox and the library. I want you under *my* roof for a while."

"Gillian said it was witches." When my eyes met his, I was struck by how tiny the pupils were. Usually they were black and enormous, but something was different about Matthew tonight. His skin was less ghostly, and there was a touch more color in his normally pale lips. "Was she right?"

"I can't know for sure, Diana. The Nigerian Hausa believe that the source of a witch's power is contained in stones in the stomach. Someone went looking for them in your father," he said regretfully. "Another witch is the most likely scenario."

There was a soft click, and the light on the answering machine began to blink. I groaned.

"That's the fifth time your aunts have called," Matthew observed.

No matter how low the volume, the vampire was going to be able to hear the message. I walked to the table near him and picked up the receiver.

"I'm here, I'm here," I began, talking over my aunt's agitated voice.

"We thought you were dead," Sarah said. The realization that she and I were the last remaining Bishops struck me forcefully. I could picture her sitting in the kitchen, phone to her ear and hair wild around her face. She was getting older, and despite her feistiness, the fact that I was far away and in danger had rocked her.

"I'm not dead. I'm in my rooms, and Matthew is with me." I smiled at him weakly. He didn't smile back.

"What's going on?" Em asked from another extension. After my parents died, Em's hair had turned silver in the space of a few months. At the time she was still a young woman—not yet thirty—but Em had always seemed more fragile after that, as if she might blow away in the next puff of wind. Like my aunt, she was clearly upset at what her sixth sense told her was happening in Oxford.

"I tried to recall the manuscript, that's all," I said lightly, making an effort not to worry them further. Matthew stared at me disapprovingly, and I turned away. It didn't help. His glacial eyes bored into my shoulder instead. "But this time it didn't come up from the stacks."

"You think we're calling because of that *book*?" demanded Sarah.

Long, cold fingers grasped the phone and drew it away from my ear.

"Ms. Bishop, this is Matthew Clairmont," he said crisply. When I reached to take the receiver from him, Matthew gripped my wrist and shook his head, once, in warning. "Diana's been threatened. By other witches. One of them is Peter Knox."

I didn't need to be a vampire to hear the outburst on the other end of the line. He dropped my wrist and handed me the phone.

"Peter Knox!" Sarah cried. Matthew's eyes closed as if the sound hurt his eardrums. "How long has he been hanging around?"

"Since the beginning," I said, my voice wavering. "He was the brown wizard who tried to push his way into my head."

"You didn't let him get very far, did you?" Sarah sounded frightened.

"I did what I could, Sarah. I don't exactly know what I'm doing, magic-wise."

Em intervened. "Honey, a lot of us have problems with Peter Knox. More important, your father didn't trust him—not at all."

"My *father*?" The floor shifted under my feet, and Matthew's arm circled my waist, keeping me steady. I wiped at my eyes but couldn't remove the sight of my father's misshapen head and gashed torso.

"Diana, what else happened?" Sarah said softly. "Peter Knox should scare the socks off you, but there's more to it than that."

My free hand clutched at Matthew's arm. "Somebody sent me a picture of Mom and Dad."

The silence stretched on the other end of the line. "Oh, Diana," Em murmured.

"*That* picture?" Sarah asked grimly.

"Yes," I whispered.

Sarah swore. "Put him back on the phone."

"He can hear you perfectly from where he's standing," I remarked. "Besides, anything you have to say to him you can say to me, too."

Matthew's hand moved from my waist to the small of my back. He began to rub it with the heel of his hand, pressing into the rigid muscles until they started to relax.

"Both of you listen to me, then. Get far, far away from Peter Knox. And that vampire had better see that you do, or I'm holding him responsible. Stephen Proctor was the most easygoing man alive. It took a lot to make him dislike someone—and he detested that wizard. Diana, you will come home *immediately*."

"I will not, Sarah! I'm going to France with Matthew." Sarah's far less attractive option had just convinced me.

There was silence.

"France?" Em said faintly.

Matthew held out his hand.

"Matthew would like to speak to you." I handed him the phone before Sarah could protest.

"Ms. Bishop? Do you have caller ID?"

I snorted. The brown phone hanging on the kitchen wall in Madison had a rotary dial and a cord a mile long so that Sarah could wander around while she talked. It took forever to simply dial a local number. Caller ID? Not likely.

"No? Take down these numbers, then." Matthew slowly doled out the number to his mobile and another that presumably belonged to the house, along with detailed instructions on international dialing codes. "Call at any time."

Sarah then said something pointed, based on Matthew's startled expression.

"I'll make sure she's safe." He handed me the phone.

"I'm getting off now. I love you both. Don't worry."

"Stop telling us not to worry," Sarah scolded. "You're our niece. We're good and worried, Diana, and likely to stay that way."

I sighed. "What can I do to convince you that I'm all right?"

"Pick up the phone more often, for starters," she said grimly.

When we'd said our good-byes, I stood next to Matthew, unwilling to meet his eyes. "All this is my fault, just like Sarah said. I've been behaving like a clueless human."

He turned away and walked to the end of the sofa, as far from me as he could get in the small room, and sank into the cushions. "This bargain you made about magic and its place in your life—you made it when you were a lonely, frightened child. Now, every time you take a step, it's as though your future hinges on whether you manage to put your foot down in the right place."

Matthew looked startled when I sat next to him and silently took his hands in mine, resisting the urge to tell him it was going to be all right.

"In France maybe you can just *be* for a few days—not trying, not worrying about making a mistake," he continued. "Maybe you could rest—although I've never seen you stop moving long enough. You even move in your sleep, you know."

"I don't have time to rest, Matthew." I was already having second thoughts about leaving Oxford. "The alchemy conference is less than six weeks away. They're expecting me to deliver the opening lecture. I've barely started it, and without access to the Bodleian there's no chance of finishing it in time."

Matthew's eyes narrowed speculatively. "Your paper is on alchemical illustrations, I assume?"

"Yes, on the allegorical image tradition in England."

"Then I don't suppose you would be interested in seeing my fourteenth-century copy of *Aurora Consurgens.* It's French, regrettably."

My eyes widened. *Aurora Consurgens* was a baffling manuscript about the opposing forces of alchemical transformation—silver and gold, female and male, dark and light. Its illustrations were equally complex and puzzling.

"The earliest known copy of the *Aurora* is from the 1420s."

"Mine is from 1356."

"But a manuscript from such an early date won't be illustrated," I pointed out. Finding an illuminated alchemical manuscript from before 1400 was as unlikely as discovering a Model-T Ford parked on the battlefield at Gettysburg.

"This one is."

"Does it contain all thirty-eight images?"

"No. It has forty." He smiled. "It would seem that previous historians have been wrong about several particulars."

Discoveries on this scale were rare. To get first crack at an unknown, fourteenth-century illustrated copy of *Aurora Consurgens* represented the opportunity of a lifetime for a historian of alchemy.

"What do the extra illustrations show? Is the text the same?"

"You'll have to come to France to find out."

"Let's go, then," I said promptly. After weeks of frustration, writing my keynote address suddenly seemed possible.

"You won't go for your own safety, but if there's a manuscript involved?" He shook his head ruefully. "So much for common sense."

"I've never been known for my common sense," I confessed. "When do we leave?"

"An hour?"

"An hour." This was no spur-of-the-moment decision. He'd been planning it since I'd fallen asleep the night before.

He nodded. "There's a plane waiting at the airstrip by the old American air force base. How long will it take you to get your things together?"

"That depends on what I need to bring with me," I said, my head spinning.

"Nothing much. We won't be going anywhere. Pack warm clothes, and I don't imagine you'll consider leaving without your running shoes. It will be just the two of us, along with my mother and her housekeeper."

His. Mother.

"Matthew," I said faintly, "I didn't know you had a mother."

"Everybody has a mother, Diana," he said, turning his clear gray eyes to mine. "I've had two. The woman who gave birth to me and Ysabeau—the woman who made me a vampire."

Matthew was one thing. A houseful of unfamiliar vampires was quite another. Caution about taking such a dangerous step pushed aside some of my eagerness to see the manuscript. My hesitation must have shown.

"I hadn't thought," he said, his voice tinged with hurt. "Of course you have no reason to trust Ysabeau. But she did assure me that you would be safe with her and Marthe."

"If you trust them, then I do, too." To my surprise, I meant it—in spite of the niggling worry that he'd had to ask them if they planned on taking a piece out of my neck.

"Thank you," he said simply. Matthew's eyes drifted to my mouth, and my blood tingled in response. "You pack, and I'll wash up and make a few phone calls."

When I passed by his end of the sofa, he caught my hand in his. Once again the shock of his cold skin was counteracted by an answering warmth in my own.

"You're doing the right thing," he murmured before he released me.

It was almost laundry day, and my bedroom was draped with dirty clothes. A rummage through the wardrobe yielded several nearly identical pairs of black pants that were clean, a few pairs of leggings, and half a dozen long-sleeved T-shirts and turtlenecks. There was a beat-up Yale duffel bag on top of it, and I jumped up and snagged the strap with one hand. The clothes all went into the old blue-and-white canvas bag, along with a few sweaters and a fleece pullover. I also chucked in sneakers, socks, and underwear, along with some old yoga clothes. I didn't own decent pajamas and could sleep in those. Remembering Matthew's French mother, I slipped in one presentable shirt and pair of trousers.

Matthew's low voice floated down the hall. He talked first to Fred, then to Marcus, and then to a cab company. With the bag's strap over my shoulder, I maneuvered myself awkwardly into the bathroom. Toothbrush, soap, shampoo, and a hairbrush all went inside, along with a hair dryer and a tube of mascara. I hardly ever wore the stuff, but on this occasion a cosmetic aid seemed a good idea.

When I was finished, I rejoined Matthew in the living room. He was thumbing through the messages on his phone, my computer case at his feet. "Is that it?" he asked, eyeing the duffel bag with surprise.

"You told me I didn't need much."

"Yes, but I'm not used to women listening to me when it comes to luggage. When Miriam goes away for the weekend, she packs enough to outfit the French Foreign Legion, and my mother requires multiple steamer trunks. Louisa wouldn't have crossed the street with what you're carrying, never mind leave the country."

"Along with having no common sense, I'm not known for being high maintenance either."

Matthew nodded appreciatively. "Do you have your passport?"

I pointed. "It's in my computer bag."

"We can go, then," Matthew said, his eyes sweeping the rooms one last time.

"Where's the photo?" It seemed wrong to just leave it.

"Marcus has it," he said quickly.

"When was Marcus here?" I asked with a frown.

"While you were sleeping. Do you want me to get it back for you?" His finger hovered over a key on his phone.

"No." I shook my head. There was no reason for me to look at it again.

Matthew took my bags and managed to get them and me down the stairs with no mishaps. A cab was waiting outside the college gates. Matthew stopped for a brief conversation with Fred. The vampire handed the porter a card, and the two men shook hands. Some deal had been struck, the particulars of which would never be disclosed to me. Matthew tucked me into the cab, and we drove for about thirty minutes, leaving the lights of Oxford behind us.

"Why didn't we take your car?" I asked as we headed into the countryside.

"This is better," he explained. "There's no need to have Marcus fetch it later."

The sway of the cab was rocking me to sleep. Leaning against Matthew's shoulder, I dozed.

At the airport we were airborne soon after we'd had our passports checked and the pilot filed the paperwork. We sat opposite each other on couches arranged around a low table during the takeoff. I yawned every few moments, ears popping as we climbed. Once we reached cruising altitude,

Matthew unsnapped his seat belt and gathered up some pillows and a blanket from a cabinet under the windows.

"We'll be in France soon." He propped the pillows at the end of my sofa, which was about as deep as a twin bed, and held the blanket open to cover me. "Meanwhile you should get some sleep."

I didn't want to sleep. The truth was, I was afraid to. That photograph was etched on the inside of my eyelids.

He crouched next to me, the blanket hanging lightly from his fingers. "What is it?"

"I don't want to close my eyes."

Matthew tossed all the pillows except one onto the floor. "Come here," he said, sitting beside me and patting the fluffy white rectangle invitingly. I swung around, shimmied down the leather-covered surface, and put my head on his lap, stretching out my legs. He tossed the edge of the blanket from his right hand to his left so that it covered me in soft folds.

"Thank you," I whispered.

"You're welcome." He took his fingers and touched them to his lips, then to mine. I tasted salt. "Sleep. I'll be right here."

I did sleep, heavy and deep with no dreams, waking only when Matthew's cool fingers touched my face and he told me we were about to land.

"What time is it?" I asked, now thoroughly disoriented.

"It's about eight," he said, looking at his watch.

"Where are we?" I swung to a seated position and rooted for my seat belt.

"Outside Lyon, in the Auvergne."

"In the center of the country?" I asked, imagining the map of France. He nodded. "Is that where you're from?"

"I was born and reborn nearby. My home—my family's home—is an hour or two away. We should arrive by midmorning."

We landed in the private area of the busy regional airport and had our passports and travel documents checked by a bored-looking civil servant who snapped to attention the moment he saw Matthew's name.

"Do you always travel this way?" It was far easier than flying a commercial airline through London's Heathrow or Paris's Charles de Gaulle airport.

"Yes," he said without apology or self-consciousness. "The one time I'm entirely glad that I'm a vampire and have money to burn is when I travel."

Matthew stopped behind a Range Rover the size of Connecticut and fished a set of keys out of his pocket. He opened the back door, stowing my bags inside. The Range Rover was slightly less deluxe than his Jaguar, but what it lacked in elegance it more than made up for in heft. It was like traveling in an armored personnel carrier.

"Do you really need this much car to drive in France?" I eyed the smooth roads.

Matthew laughed. "You haven't seen my mother's house yet."

We drove west through beautiful countryside, studded here and there with grand châteaus and steep mountains. Fields and vineyards stretched in all directions, and even under the steely sky the land seemed to blaze with the color of turning leaves. A sign indicated the direction of Clermont-Ferrand. That couldn't be a coincidence, in spite of the different spelling.

Matthew kept heading west. He slowed, turned down a narrow road, and pulled to the side. He pointed off to the distance. "There," he said. "Sept-Tours."

In the center of rolling hills was a flattened peak dominated by a crenellated hulk of buff and rose stone. Seven smaller towers surrounded it, and a turreted gatehouse stood guard in front. This was not a pretty, fairy-tale castle made for moonlit balls. Sept-Tours was a fortress.

"That's home?" I gasped.

"That's home." Matthew took his phone out of his pocket and dialed a number. "*Maman?* We're almost there."

Something was said on the other end, and the line went dead. Matthew smiled tightly and pulled back onto the road.

"She's expecting us?" I asked, just managing to keep the tremor out of my voice.

"She is."

"And this is all right with her?" I didn't ask the real question—*Are you sure it's okay that you're bringing a witch home?*—but didn't need to.

Matthew's eyes remained fixed on the road. "Ysabeau doesn't like surprises as much as I do," he said lightly, turning on to something that looked like a goat track.

We drove between rows of chestnut trees, climbing until we reached Sept-Tours. Matthew steered the car between two of the seven towers and through to a paved courtyard in front of the entrance to the central structure. Parterres and gardens peeked out to the right and left, before the forest took over. The vampire parked the car.

"Ready?" he asked with a bright smile.

"As I'll ever be," I replied warily.

Matthew opened my car door and helped me down. Pulling at my black jacket, I looked up at the château's imposing stone façade. The forbidding lines of the castle were nothing compared to what awaited me inside. The door swung open.

"*Courage*," Matthew said, kissing me gently on the cheek.

Chapter 18

Ysabeau stood in the doorway of her enormous château, regal and icy, and glared at her vampire son as we climbed the stone stairs.

Matthew stooped a full foot to kiss her softly on both cheeks. "Shall we come inside, or do you wish to continue our greetings out here?"

His mother stepped back to let us pass. I felt her furious gaze and smelled something reminiscent of sarsaparilla soda and caramel. We walked through a short, dark hallway, lined in a none-too-welcoming fashion with pikes that pointed directly at the visitor's head, and into a room with high ceilings and wall paintings that had clearly been done by some imaginative nineteenth-century artist to reflect a medieval past that never was. Lions, fleurs-de-lis, a snake with his tail in his mouth, and scallop shells were painted on white walls. At one end a circular set of stairs climbed to the top of one of the towers.

Indoors I faced the full force of Ysabeau's stare. Matthew's mother personified the terrifying elegance that seemed bred to the bone in Frenchwomen. Like her son—who disconcertingly appeared to be slightly older than she was—she was dressed in a monochromatic palette that minimized her uncanny paleness. Ysabeau's preferred colors ranged from cream to soft brown. Every inch of her ensemble was expensive and simple, from the tips of her soft, buff-colored leather shoes to the topazes that fluttered from her ears. Slivers of startling, cold emerald surrounded dark pupils, and the high slashes of her cheekbones kept her perfect features and dazzling white skin from sliding into mere prettiness. Her hair had the color and texture of honey, a golden pour of silk caught at the base of her skull in a heavy, low knot.

"You might have shown some consideration, Matthew." Her accent softened his name, making it sound ancient. Like all vampires she had a seductive and melodic voice. In Ysabeau's case it sounded of distant bells, pure and deep.

"Afraid of the gossip, *Maman*? I thought you prided yourself on being a radical." Matthew sounded both indulgent and impatient. He tossed the keys onto a nearby table. They slid across the perfect finish and landed with a clatter at the base of a Chinese porcelain bowl.

"I have never been a radical!" Ysabeau was horrified. "Change is very much overrated."

She turned and surveyed me from head to toe. Her perfectly formed mouth tightened.

She did not like what she saw—and it was no wonder. I tried to see myself through her eyes—the sandy hair that was neither thick nor well behaved, the dusting of freckles from being outdoors too much, the nose that was too long for the rest of my face. My eyes were my best feature, but they were unlikely to make up for my fashion sense. Next to her elegance and Matthew's perpetually unruffled self, I felt—and looked—like a gauche country mouse. I pulled at the hem of my jacket with my free hand, glad to see that there was no sign of magic at the fingertips, and hoped that there was also no sign of that phantom "shimmering" that Matthew had mentioned.

"*Maman,* this is Diana Bishop. Diana, my mother, Ysabeau de Clermont." The syllables rolled off his tongue.

Ysabeau's nostrils flared delicately. "I do not like the way witches smell." Her English was flawless, her glittering eyes fixed on mine. "She is sweet and repulsively green, like spring."

Matthew launched into a volley of something unintelligible that sounded like a cross between French, Spanish, and Latin. He kept his voice low, but there was no disguising the anger in it.

"*Ça suffit,*" Ysabeau retorted in recognizable French, drawing her hand across her throat. I swallowed hard and reflexively reached for the collar of my jacket.

"Diana." Ysabeau said it with a long *e* rather than an *i* and an emphasis on the first rather than the second syllable. She extended one white, cold hand, and I took her fingers lightly in mine. Matthew grabbed my left hand in his, and for a moment we made an odd chain of vampires and a witch. "*Encantada.*"

"She's pleased to meet you," Matthew said, translating for me and shooting a warning glance at his mother.

"Yes, yes," Ysabeau said impatiently, turning back to her son. "Of course she speaks only English and new French. Modern warmbloods are so poorly educated."

A stout old woman with skin like snow and a mass of incongruously dark hair wrapped around her head in intricate braids stepped into the front hall, her arms outstretched. "Matthew!" she cried. "*Cossí anatz?*"

"*Va plan, mercés. E tu?*" Matthew caught her in a hug, and kissed her on both cheeks.

"*Aital aital*," she replied, grabbing her elbow and grimacing.

Matthew murmured in sympathy, and Ysabeau appealed to the ceiling for deliverance from the emotional spectacle.

"Marthe, this is my friend Diana," he said, drawing me forward.

Marthe, too, was a vampire, one of the oldest I'd ever seen. She had to have been in her sixties when she was reborn, and though her hair was dark, there was no mistaking her age. Lines crisscrossed her face, and the joints of her hands were so gnarled that apparently not even vampiric blood could straighten them.

"Welcome, Diana," she said in a husky voice of sand and treacle, looking deep into my eyes. She nodded at Matthew and reached for my hand. Her nostrils flared. *"Elle est une puissante sorcière,"* she said to Matthew, her voice appreciative.

"She says you're a powerful witch," Matthew explained. His closeness somewhat diminished my instinctive concern with having a vampire sniff me.

Having no idea what the proper French response was to such a comment, I smiled weakly at Marthe and hoped that would do.

"You're exhausted," Matthew said, his eyes flicking over my face. He began rapidly questioning the two vampires in the unfamiliar language. This led to a great deal of pointing, eye rolling, emphatic gestures, and sighs. When Ysabeau mentioned the name Louisa, Matthew looked at his mother with renewed fury. His voice took on a flat, abrupt finality when he answered her.

Ysabeau shrugged. "Of course, Matthew," she murmured with patent insincerity.

"Let's get you settled." Matthew's voice warmed as he spoke to me.

"I will bring food and wine," Marthe said in halting English.

"Thank you," I said. "And thank you, Ysabeau, for having me in your home." She sniffed and bared her teeth. I hoped it was a smile but feared it was not.

"And water, Marthe," Matthew added. "Oh, and food is coming this morning."

"Some of it has already arrived," his mother said tartly. "Leaves. Sacks of vegetables and eggs. You were very bad to ask them to drive it down."

"Diana needs to eat, *Maman*. I didn't imagine you had a great deal of proper food in the house." Matthew's long ribbon of patience was fraying from the events of last evening and now his lukewarm homecoming.

"*I* need fresh blood, but I don't expect Victoire and Alain to fetch it from Paris in the middle of the night." Ysabeau looked vastly pleased with herself as my knees swayed.

Matthew exhaled sharply, his hand under my elbow to steady me. "Marthe," he asked, pointedly ignoring Ysabeau, "can you bring up eggs and toast and some tea for Diana?"

Marthe eyed Ysabeau and then Matthew as if she were at center court at Wimbledon. She cackled with laughter. "*Òc,*" she replied, with a cheerful nod.

"We'll see you two at dinner," Matthew said calmly. I felt four icy patches on my shoulders as the women watched us depart. Marthe said something to Ysabeau that made her snort and Matthew smile broadly.

"What did Marthe say?" I whispered, remembering too late that there were few conversations, whispered or shouted, that would not be overheard by everyone in the house.

"She said we looked good together."

"I don't want Ysabeau to be furious with me the whole time we're here."

"Pay no attention to her," he said serenely. "Her bark is worse than her bite."

We passed through a doorway into a long room with a wide assortment of chairs and tables of many different styles and periods. There were two fireplaces, and two knights in glistening armor jousted over one of them, their bright lances crossing neatly without a drop of bloodshed. The fresco had clearly been painted by the same dewy-eyed chivalric enthusiast who'd decorated the hall. A pair of doors led to another room, this one lined with bookcases.

"Is that a library?" I asked, Ysabeau's hostility momentarily forgotten. "Can I see your copy of *Aurora Consurgens* now?"

"Later," Matthew said firmly. "You're going to eat something and then sleep."

He led the way to another curving staircase, navigating through the labyrinth of ancient furniture with the ease of long experience. My own passage was more tentative, and my thighs grazed a bow-fronted chest of drawers, setting a tall porcelain vase swaying. When we finally reached the bottom of the staircase, Matthew paused.

"It's a long climb, and you're tired. Do you need me to carry you?"

"No," I said indignantly. "You are not going to sling me over your shoulder like a victorious medieval knight making off with the spoils of battle."

Matthew pressed his lips together, eyes dancing.

"Don't you dare laugh at me."

He did laugh, the sound bouncing off the stone walls as if a pack of amused vampires were standing in the stairwell. This was, after all, precisely the kind of place where knights would have carried women upstairs. But I didn't plan on being counted among them.

By the fifteenth tread, my sides were heaving with effort. The tower's worn stone steps were not made for ordinary feet and legs—they had clearly been designed for vampires like Matthew who were either over six feet tall, extremely agile, or both. I gritted my teeth and kept climbing. Around a final bend in the stairs, a room opened up suddenly.

"Oh." My hand traveled to my mouth in amazement.

I didn't have to be told whose room this was. It was Matthew's, through and through.

We were in the château's graceful round tower—the one that still had its smooth, conical copper roof and was set on the back of the massive main building. Tall, narrow windows punctuated the walls, their leaded panes letting in slashes of light and autumn colors from the fields and trees outside.

The room was circular, and high bookcases smoothed its graceful curves into occasional straight lines. A large fireplace was set squarely into the walls that butted up against the château's central structure. This fireplace had miraculously escaped the attention of the nineteenth-century fresco painter. There were armchairs and couches, tables and hassocks, most in shades of green, brown, and gold. Despite the size of the room and the expanses of gray stone, the overall effect was of cozy warmth.

The room's most intriguing objects were those Matthew had chosen to keep from one of his many lives. A painting by Vermeer was propped up on a bookshelf next to a shell. It was unfamiliar—not one of the artist's few known canvases. The subject looked an awful lot like Matthew. A broadsword so long and heavy that no one but a vampire could have wielded it hung over the fireplace, and a Matthew-size suit of armor stood in one corner. Opposite, there was an ancient-looking human skeleton hanging from a wooden stand, the bones tied together with something resembling piano wire. On the table next to it were two microscopes, both made in the seventeenth century unless I was very much mistaken. An ornate crucifix studded with large red, green, and blue stones was tucked into a niche in the wall along with a stunning ivory carving of the Virgin.

Matthew's snowflakes drifted across my face as he watched me survey his belongings.

"It's a Matthew museum," I said softly, knowing that every object there told a story.

"It's just my study."

"Where did you—" I began, pointing at the microscopes.

"Later," he said again. "You have thirty more steps to climb."

Matthew led me to the other side of the room and a second staircase. This one, too, curved up toward the heavens. Thirty slow steps later, I stood on the edge of another round room dominated by an enormous walnut four-poster bed complete with tester and heavy hangings. High above it were the exposed beams and supports that held the copper roof in place. A table was pushed against one wall, a fireplace was tucked into another, and a few comfortable chairs were arranged before it. Opposite, a door stood ajar, revealing an enormous bathtub.

"It's like a falcon's lair," I said, peering out the window. Matthew had been looking at this landscape from these windows since the Middle Ages. I wondered, briefly, about the other women he'd brought here before me. I was sure I wasn't the first, but I didn't think there had been many. There was something intensely private about the château.

Matthew came up behind me and looked over my shoulder. "Do you approve?" His breath was soft against my ear. I nodded.

"How long?" I asked, unable to help myself.

"This tower?" he asked. "About seven hundred years."

"And the village? Do they know about you?"

"Yes. Like witches, vampires are safer when they're part of a community who knows what they are but doesn't ask too many questions."

Generations of Bishops had lived in Madison without anyone's making a fuss. Like Peter Knox, we were hiding in plain sight.

"Thank you for bringing me to Sept-Tours," I said. "It does feel safer than Oxford." *In spite of Ysabeau.*

"Thank you for braving my mother." Matthew chuckled as if he'd heard my unspoken words. The distinctive scent of carnations accompanied the sound. "She's overprotective, like most parents."

"I felt like an idiot—and underdressed, too. I didn't bring a single thing to wear that will meet with her approval." I bit my lip, my forehead creased.

"Coco Chanel didn't meet with Ysabeau's approval. You may be aiming a bit high."

I laughed and turned, my eyes seeking his. When they met, my breath caught. Matthew's gaze lingered on my eyes, cheeks, and finally my mouth. His hand rose to my face.

"You're so alive," he said gruffly. "You should be with a man much, much younger."

I lifted to my toes. He bent his head. Before our lips touched, a tray clattered on the table.

"'*Vos etz arbres e branca*,'" Marthe sang, giving Matthew a wicked look.

He laughed and sang back in a clear baritone, "'*On fruitz de gaug s'asazona.*'"

"What language is that?" I asked, getting down off my tiptoes and following Matthew to the fireplace.

"The old tongue," Marthe replied.

"Occitan." Matthew removed the silver cover from a plate of eggs. The aroma of hot food filled the room. "Marthe decided to recite poetry before you sat down to eat."

Marthe giggled and swatted at Matthew's wrist with a towel that she pulled from her waist. He dropped the cover and took a seat.

"Come here, come here," she said, gesturing at the chair across from him. "Sit, eat." I did as I was told. Marthe poured Matthew a goblet of wine from a tall, silver-handled glass pitcher.

"Mercés," he murmured, his nose going immediately to the glass in anticipation.

A similar pitcher held icy-cold water, and Marthe put this in another goblet, which she handed to me. She poured a steaming cup of tea, which I recognized immediately as coming from Mariage Frères in Paris. Apparently Matthew had raided my cupboards while I slept last night and been quite specific with his shopping lists. Marthe poured thick cream into the cup before he could stop her, and I shot him a warning glance. At this point I needed allies. Besides, I was too thirsty to care. He leaned back in his chair meekly, sipping his wine.

Marthe pulled more items from her tray—a silver place setting, salt, pepper, butter, jam, toast, and a golden omelet flecked with fresh herbs.

"Merci, Marthe," I said with heartfelt gratitude.

"Eat!" she commanded, aiming her towel at me this time.

Marthe looked satisfied with the enthusiasm of my first few bites. Then she sniffed the air. She frowned and directed an exclamation of disgust at Matthew before striding to the fireplace. A match snapped, and the dry wood began to crackle.

"Marthe," Matthew protested, standing up with his wineglass, "I can do that."

"She is cold," Marthe grumbled, clearly aggravated that he hadn't anticipated this before he sat down, "and you are thirsty. I will make the fire."

Within minutes there was a blaze. Though no fire would make the enormous room toasty, it took the chill from the air. Marthe brushed her hands together and stood. "She must sleep. I can smell she has been afraid."

"She'll sleep when she's through eating," Matthew said, holding up his right hand in a pledge. Marthe looked at him for a long moment and shook her finger at him as though he were fifteen, and not fifteen hundred, years old. Finally his innocent expression convinced her. She left the room, her ancient feet moving surely down the challenging stairs.

"Occitan is the language of the troubadours, isn't it?" I asked, after Marthe had departed. The vampire nodded. "I didn't realize it was spoken this far north."

"We're not that far north," Matthew said with a smile. "Once, Paris was nothing more than an insignificant borderlands town. Most people spoke Occitan then. The hills kept the northerners—and their language—at a distance. Even now people here are wary of outsiders."

"What do the words mean?" I asked.

"'You are the tree and branch,'" he said, fixing his eyes on the slashes of countryside visible through the nearest window, "'where delight's fruit ripens.'" Matthew shook his head ruefully. "Marthe will hum the song all afternoon and make Ysabeau crazy."

The fire continued to spread its warmth through the room, and the heat made me drowsy. By the time the eggs were gone, it was difficult to keep my eyes open.

I was in the middle of a jaw-splitting yawn when Matthew drew me from the chair. He scooped me into his arms, my feet swinging in midair. I started to protest.

"Enough," he said. "You can barely sit up straight, never mind walk."

He put me gently on the end of the bed and pulled the coverlet back.

The snowy-white sheets looked so crisp and inviting. I dropped my head onto the mountain of down pillows arranged against the bed's intricate walnut carvings.

"Sleep." Matthew took the bed's curtains in both hands and gave them a yank.

"I'm not sure I'll be able to," I said, stifling another yawn. "I'm not good at napping."

"All appearances to the contrary," he said drily. "You're in France now. You're not supposed to try. I'll be downstairs. Call if you need anything."

With one staircase leading from the hall up to his study and the other staircase leading to the bedroom from the opposite side, no one could reach this room without going past—and through—Matthew. The rooms had been designed as if he needed to protect himself from his own family.

A question rose to my lips, but he gave the curtains a final tug until they were closed, effectively silencing me. The heavy bed hangings didn't allow the light to penetrate, and they shut out the worst of the drafts as well. Relaxing into the firm mattress, my body's warmth magnified by the layers of bedding, I quickly fell asleep.

I woke up to the rustle of turning pages and sat bolt upright, trying to imagine why someone had shut me into a box made of fabric. Then I remembered.

France. Matthew. At his home.

"Matthew?" I called softly.

He parted the curtains and looked down with a smile. Behind him, candles were lit—dozens and dozens of them. Some were set into the sconces around the room, and others stood in ornate candelabras on the floor and tables.

"For someone who doesn't nap, you slept quite soundly," he said with satisfaction. As far as he was concerned, the trip to France had already proved a success.

"What time is it?"

"I'm going to get you a watch if you don't stop asking me that." Matthew glanced at his old Cartier. "It's nearly two in the afternoon. Marthe will probably be here any minute with some tea. Do you want to shower and change?"

The thought of a hot shower had me eagerly pushing back the covers. "Yes, please!"

Matthew dodged my flying limbs and helped me to the floor, which was farther away than I had expected. It was cold, too, the stone flagstones stinging against my bare feet.

"Your bag is in the bathroom, the computer is downstairs in my study, and there are fresh towels. Take your time." He watched as I skittered into the bathroom.

"This is a palace!" I exclaimed. An enormous white, freestanding tub was tucked between two of the windows, and a long wooden bench held my dilapidated Yale duffel. In the far corner, a showerhead was set into the wall.

I started running the water, expecting to wait a long time for it to heat up. Miraculously, steam enveloped me immediately, and the honey-and-nectarine scent of my soap helped to lift the tension of the past twenty-four hours.

Once my muscles were unkinked, I slipped on jeans and a turtleneck, along with a pair of socks. There was no outlet for my blow dryer, so I settled instead for roughly toweling my hair and dragging a comb through it before tying it back in a ponytail.

"Marthe brought up tea," he said when I walked into the bedroom, glancing at a teapot and cup sitting on the table. "Do you want me to pour you some?"

I sighed with pleasure as the soothing liquid went down my throat. "When can I see the *Aurora* manuscript?"

"When I'm sure you won't get lost on your way to the library. Ready for the grand tour?"

"Yes, please." I slid loafers on over my socks and ran back into the bathroom to get a sweater. As I raced around, Matthew waited patiently, standing near the top of the stairs.

"Should we take the teapot down?" I asked, skidding to a halt.

"No, she'd be furious if I let a guest touch a dish. Wait twenty-four hours before helping Marthe."

Matthew slipped down the stairs as if he could handle the uneven, smooth treads blindfolded. I crept along, guiding my fingers against the stone wall.

When we reached his study, he pointed to my computer, already plugged in and resting on a table by the window, before we descended to the salon. Marthe had been there, and a warm fire was crackling in the fireplace, sending the smell of wood smoke through the room. I grabbed Matthew.

"The library," I said. "The tour needs to start there."

It was another room that had been filled over the years with bric-a-brac and furniture. An Italian Savonarola folding chair was pulled up to a French Directory secretary, while a vast oak table circa 1700 held display cabinets that looked as if they'd been plucked from a Victorian museum. Despite the mismatches, the room was held together by miles of leather-bound books on walnut shelving and by an enormous Aubusson carpet in soft golds, blues, and browns.

As in most old libraries, the books were shelved by size. There were thick manuscripts in leather bindings, shelved with spines in and ornamental clasps out, the titles inked onto the fore edges of the vellum. There were tiny incunabula and pocket-size books in neat rows on one bookcase, spanning the history of print from the 1450s to the present. A number of rare modern first editions, including a run of Arthur Conan Doyle's Sherlock Holmes stories and T. H. White's *The Sword in the Stone,* were there, too. One case held nothing but large folios—botanical books, atlases, medical books. If all this was downstairs, what treasures lived in Matthew's tower study?

He let me circle the room, peering at the titles and gasping. When I returned to his side, all I could do was shake my head in disbelief.

"Imagine what you'd have if you'd been buying books for centuries," Matthew said with a shrug that reminded me of Ysabeau. "Things pile up. We've gotten rid of a lot over the years. We had to. Otherwise this room would be the size of the Bibliothèque Nationale."

"So where is it?"

"You're already out of patience, I see." He went to a shelf, his eyes darting among the volumes. He pulled out a small book with black tooled covers and presented it to me.

When I looked for a velveteen cradle to put it on, he laughed.

"Just open it, Diana. It's not going to disintegrate."

It felt strange to hold such a manuscript in my hands, trained as I was to think of them as rare, precious objects rather than reading material. Trying not to open the covers too wide and crack the binding, I peeked inside. An explosion of bright colors, gold, and silver leaped out.

"Oh," I breathed. The other copies I'd seen of *Aurora Consurgens* were not nearly so fine. "It's beautiful. Do you know who did the illuminations?"

"A woman named Bourgot Le Noir. She was quite popular in Paris in the middle of the fourteenth century." Matthew took the book from me and opened it fully. "There. Now you can see it properly."

The first illumination showed a queen standing on a small hill, sheltering seven small creatures inside her outspread cloak. Delicate vines framed the image, twisting and turning their way across the vellum. Here and there, buds burst into flowers, and birds sat on the branches. In the afternoon light, the queen's embroidered golden dress glowed against a brilliant vermilion background. At the bottom of the page, a man in a black robe sat atop a shield that bore a coat of arms in black and silver. The man's attention was directed at the queen, a rapt expression on his face and his hands raised in supplication.

"Nobody is going to believe this. An unknown copy of *Aurora Consurgens*—with illuminations by a *woman*?" I shook my head in amazement. "How will I cite it?"

"I'll loan the manuscript to the Beinecke Library for a year, if that helps. Anonymously, of course. As for Bourgot, the experts will say it's her father's work. But it's all hers. We probably have the receipt for it somewhere," Matthew said vaguely, looking around. "I'll ask Ysabeau where Godfrey's things are."

"Godfrey?" The unfamiliar coat of arms featured a fleur-de-lis, surrounded by a snake with its tail in its mouth.

"My brother." The vagueness left his voice, and his face darkened. "He died in 1668, fighting in one of Louis XIV's infernal wars." Closing the manuscript gently, he put it on a nearby table. "I'll take this up to my study later so you can look at it more closely. In the morning Ysabeau reads her newspapers here, but otherwise it sits empty. You're welcome to browse the shelves whenever you like."

With that promise he moved me through the salon and into the great hall. We stood by the table with the Chinese bowl, and he pointed out features of the room, including the old minstrels' gallery, the trapdoor in the roof that had let the smoke out before the fireplaces and chimneys were constructed, and the entrance to the square watchtower overlooking the main approach to the château. That climb could wait until another day.

Matthew led me down to the lower ground floor, with its maze of storerooms, wine cellars, kitchens, servants' rooms, larders, and pantries. Marthe stepped out of one of the kitchens, flour covering her arms up to the elbows, and handed me a warm roll fresh from the oven. I munched on it as Matthew walked the corridors, pointing out the old purposes of every room—where the grain was stored, the venison hung, the cheese made.

"Vampires don't eat anything," I said, confused.

"No, but our tenants did. Marthe loves to cook."

I promised to keep her busy. The roll was delicious, and the eggs had been perfect.

Our next stop was the gardens. Though we had descended a flight of stairs to get to the kitchens, we left the château at ground level. The gardens were straight out of the sixteenth century, with divided beds full of herbs and autumn vegetables. Rosebushes, some with a few lonely blooms remaining, filled the borders.

But the aroma that intrigued me wasn't floral. I made a beeline for a low-slung building.

"Be careful, Diana," he called, striding across the gravel, "Balthasar bites."

"Which one is Balthasar?"

He rounded the stable entrance, an anxious look on his face. "The stallion using your spine as a scratching post," Matthew replied tightly. I was standing with my back to a large, heavy-footed horse while a mastiff and a wolfhound circled my feet, sniffing me with interest.

"Oh, he won't bite me." The enormous Percheron maneuvered his head so he could rub his ears on my hip. "And who are these gentlemen?" I asked, ruffling the fur on the wolfhound's neck while the mastiff tried to put my hand in his mouth.

"The hound is Fallon, and the mastiff is Hector." Matthew snapped his fingers, and both dogs came running to his side, where they sat obediently and watched his face for further instructions. "Please step away from that horse."

"Why? He's fine." Balthasar stamped the ground in agreement and pitched an ear back to look haughtily at Matthew.

"'*If the butterfly wings its way to the sweet light that attracts it, it's only because it doesn't know that the fire can consume it,*'" Matthew murmured under his breath. "Balthasar is only fine until he gets bored. I'd like you to move away *before* he kicks the stall door down."

"We're making your master nervous, and he's started reciting obscure bits of poetry written by mad Italian clerics. I'll be back tomorrow with something sweet." I turned and kissed Balthasar on the nose. He nickered, his hooves dancing with impatience.

Matthew tried to cover his surprise. "You recognized that?"

"Giordano Bruno. '*If the thirsty stag runs to the brook, it's only because he isn't aware of the cruel bow,*'" I continued. "'*If the unicorn runs to its chaste nest, it's only because he doesn't see the noose prepared for him.*'"

"You know the work of the Nolan?" Matthew used the sixteenth-century mystic's own way of referring to himself.

My eyes narrowed. Good God, had he known Bruno as well as Machiavelli? Matthew seemed to have been attracted to every strange character who'd ever lived. "He was an early supporter of Copernicus, and I'm a historian of science. How do you know Bruno's work?"

"I'm a great reader," he said evasively.

"You knew him!" My tone was accusing. "Was he a daemon?"

"One who crossed the madness-genius divide rather too frequently, I'm afraid."

"I should have known. He believed in extraterrestrial life and cursed his inquisitors on the way to the stake," I said, shaking my head.

"Nevertheless, he understood the power of desire."

I looked sharply at the vampire. "'*Desire urges me on, as fear bridles me.*' Did Bruno feature in your essay for All Souls?"

"A bit." Matthew's mouth flattened into a hard line. "Will you please come away from there? We can talk about philosophy another time."

Other passages drifted through my mind. There was something else about Bruno's work that might make Matthew think of him. He wrote about the goddess Diana.

I stepped away from the stall.

"Balthasar isn't a pony," Matthew warned, pulling my elbow.

"I can see that. But I could handle that horse." Both the alchemical manuscript and the Italian philosopher vanished from my mind at the thought of such a challenge.

"You don't ride as well?" Matthew asked in disbelief.

"I grew up in the country and have ridden since I was a child—dressage, jumping, everything." Being on a horse was even more like flying than rowing was.

"We have other horses. Balthasar stays where he is," he said firmly.

Riding was an unforeseen bonus of coming to France, one that almost made Ysabeau's cold presence bearable. Matthew led me to the other end of the stables, where six more fine animals waited. Two of them were big and black—although not as large as Balthasar—one a fairly round chestnut mare, another a bay gelding. There were two gray Andalusians as well, with large feet and curved necks. One came to the door to see what was going on in her domain.

"This is Nar Rakasa," he said, gently rubbing her muzzle. "Her name means 'fire dancer.' We usually just call her Rakasa. She moves beautifully, but she's willful. You two should get along famously."

I refused to take the bait, though it was charmingly offered, and let Rakasa sniff at my hair and face. "What's her sister's name?"

"Fiddat—'silver.'" Fiddat came forward when Matthew said her name, her dark eyes affectionate. "Fiddat is Ysabeau's horse, and Rakasa is her sister." Matthew pointed to the two blacks. "Those are mine. Dahr and Sayad."

"What do their names mean?" I asked, walking to their stalls.

"Dahr is Arabic for 'time,' and Sayad means 'hunter,'" Matthew explained, joining me. "Sayad loves riding across the fields chasing game and jumping hedges. Dahr is patient and steady."

We continued the tour, Matthew pointing out features of the mountains and orienting me to the town. He showed me where the château had been modified and how restorers had used a different kind of stone because the original was no longer available. By the time we were finished, I wasn't likely to get lost—in part due to the central keep, which was hard to misplace.

"Why am I so tired?" I yawned as we returned to the château.

"You're hopeless," Matthew said in exasperation. "Do you really need me to recount the events of the past thirty-six hours?"

At his urging I agreed to another nap. Leaving him in the study, I climbed the stairs and flung myself into bed, too tired to even blow out the candles.

Moments later I was dreaming of riding through a dark forest, a loose green tunic belted around my waist. There were sandals tied onto my feet, their leather fastenings crossed around my ankles and calves. Dogs bayed and hooves crashed in the underbrush behind me. A quiver of arrows nestled against my shoulder, and in one fist I held a bow. Despite the ominous sounds of my pursuers, I felt no fear.

In my dream I smiled with the knowledge I could outrun those who hunted me.

"Fly," I commanded—and the horse did.

Chapter 19

The next morning my first thoughts were also of riding.

I ran a brush through my hair, rinsed my mouth out, and threw on a close-fitting pair of black leggings. They were the nearest thing to riding breeches that I had with me. Running shoes would make it impossible to keep my heels down in the stirrups, so on went my loafers instead. Not exactly proper footwear, but they'd do. A long-sleeved T-shirt and a fleece pullover completed my ensemble. Dragging my hair back into a ponytail, I returned to the bedroom.

Matthew lifted his eyebrow as I rocketed into the room, his arm barring me from going any farther. He was leaning against the wide archway that led to the stairs, well groomed as always, wearing dark gray breeches and a black sweater. "Let's ride in the afternoon."

I'd been expecting this. Dinner with Ysabeau had been tense at best, and afterward my sleep had been punctuated with nightmares. Matthew had climbed the stairs to check on me several times.

"I'm fine. Exercise and fresh air will be the best thing in the world for me." When I tried to get past him again, he stopped me with only a dark look.

"If you so much as sway in the saddle, I'm bringing you home. Understood?"

"Understood."

Downstairs, I headed for the dining room, but Matthew pulled me in the other direction. "Let's eat in the kitchens," he said quietly. No formal breakfast with Ysabeau staring at me over *Le Monde.* That was welcome news.

We ate in what were ostensibly the housekeeper's rooms, in front of a blazing fire at a table set for two—though I would be the only one eating Marthe's excellent, abundant food. A huge pot of tea sat on the scarred, round wooden table, wrapped in a linen towel to keep it hot. Marthe glanced at me with concern, tutting at my dark circles and pale skin.

When my fork slowed, Matthew reached for a pyramid of boxes crowned with a black-velvet-covered helmet. "For you," he said, putting them on the table.

The helmet was self-explanatory. It was shaped like a high-crowned baseball hat, with a fold of black grosgrain ribbon at the nape. Despite its velvet covering and ribbon, the helmet was sturdy and made expressly to keep soft human skulls from cracking if they met with the ground. I hated them, but it was a wise precaution.

"Thank you," I said. "What's in the boxes?"

"Open them and see."

The first box held a pair of black breeches with suede patches inside the knees to grip the saddle. They would be far more pleasant to ride in than my thin, slippery leggings and looked like they would fit, too. Matthew must have been making more phone calls and relaying approximate measurements while I napped. I smiled at him in gratitude.

The box also held a black padded vest with a long tail and stiff metal supports sewn into the seams. It looked and would no doubt feel like a turtle's shell—uncomfortable and unwieldy.

"This isn't necessary." I held it up, frowning.

"It is if you're going riding." His voice didn't show the slightest hint of emotion. "You tell me you're experienced. If so, you won't have a problem adjusting to its weight."

My color rose and my fingertips gave a warning tingle. Matthew watched me with interest, and Marthe came to the door and gave a sniff. I breathed in and out until the tingling stopped.

"You wear a seat belt in my car," Matthew said evenly. "You'll wear a vest on my horse."

We stared at each other in a standoff of wills. The thought of the fresh air defeated me, and Marthe's eyes glittered with amusement. No doubt our negotiations were as much fun to watch as were the volleys between Matthew and Ysabeau.

I pulled the final box toward me in silent concession. It was long and heavy, and there was a sharp tang of leather when the lid lifted.

Boots. Knee-length, black boots. I'd never shown horses and had limited resources, so I had never owned a proper pair of riding boots. These were beautiful, with their curved calves and supple leather. My fingers touched their shining surfaces.

"Thank you," I breathed, delighted with his surprise.

"I'm pretty sure they'll fit," Matthew said, his eyes soft.

"Come, girl," Marthe said cheerfully from the door. "You change."

She barely got me into the laundry room before I'd kicked off my loafers and peeled the leggings from my body. She took the worn Lycra and cotton from me while I wriggled into the breeches.

"There was a time when women didn't ride like men," Marthe said, looking at the muscles in my legs and shaking her head.

Matthew was on his phone when I returned, sending out instructions to all the other people in his world who required his management. He looked up with approval.

"Those will be more comfortable." He stood and picked up the boots. "There's no jack in here. You'll have to wear your other shoes to the stables."

"No, I want to put them on now," I said, fingers outstretched.

"Sit down, then." He shook his head at my impatience. "You'll never get them on the first time without help." Matthew picked up my chair with me in it and turned it so he had more room to maneuver. He held out the right boot, and I stuck my foot in as far as the ankle. He was right. No amount of tugging was going to get my foot around the stiff bend. He stood over my foot, grasping the heel and toe of the boot and wriggling it gently as I pulled the leather in the other direction. After several minutes of struggle, my foot worked its way into the shank. Matthew gave the sole a final, firm push, and the boot snuggled against my bones.

Once both boots were on, I held my legs out to admire. Matthew tugged and patted, sliding his cold fingers around the top rim to make sure my blood could circulate. I stood, my legs feeling unusually long, took a few stiff-ankled steps, and did a little twirl.

"Thank you." I threw my arms around his neck, the toes of my boots grazing the floor. "I love them."

Matthew carried my vest and hat to the stables, much as he had carried my computer and yoga mat in Oxford. The stable doors were flung open, and there were sounds of activity.

"Georges?" Matthew called. A small, wiry man of indeterminate age—though not a vampire—came around the corner, carrying a bridle and a curry comb. When we passed Balthasar's stall, the stallion stomped angrily and tossed his head. *You promised,* he seemed to say. Inside my pocket was a tiny apple that I'd wheedled from Marthe.

"Here you go, baby," I said, holding it out on a flat palm. Matthew watched warily as Balthasar extended his neck and reached with delicate lips to pick the fruit from my hand. Once it was in his mouth, he looked at his owner triumphantly.

"Yes, I see that you are behaving like a prince," Matthew said drily, "but that doesn't mean you won't behave like a devil at the first opportunity." Balthasar's hooves struck the ground in annoyance.

We passed by the tack room. In addition to the regular saddles, bridles, and reins, there were freestanding wooden frames that held something like a small armchair with odd supports on one side.

"What are they?"

"Sidesaddles," Matthew said, kicking off his shoes and stepping into a tall pair of well-worn boots. His foot slid down easily with a simple stamp on the heel and a tug at the top. "Ysabeau prefers them."

In the paddock Dahr and Rakasa turned their heads and looked with interest while Georges and Matthew began a detailed discussion of all the natural obstacles we might encounter. I held my palm out to Dahr, sorry that there were no more apples in my pocket. The gelding looked disappointed, too, once he picked up the sweet scent.

"Next time," I promised. Ducking under his neck, I arrived at Rakasa's side. "Hello, beauty."

Rakasa picked up her right front foot and cocked her head toward me. I ran my hands over her neck and shoulders, getting her used to my scent and touch, and gave the saddle a tug, checking the tightness of the girth strap and making sure the blanket underneath was smooth. She reached around and gave me an inquiring smell and a snuffle, nosing at my pullover where the apple had been. She tossed her head in indignation.

"You, too," I promised her with a laugh, placing my left hand firmly on her rump. "Let's have a look."

Horses like having their feet touched about as much as most witches like being dunked in water—which is to say not much. But, out of habit and superstition, I'd never ridden a horse without first checking to make sure that nothing was lodged in their soft hooves.

When I straightened, the two men were watching me closely. Georges said something that indicated I would do. Matthew nodded thoughtfully, holding out my vest and hat. The vest was snug and hard—but it wasn't as bad as I'd expected. The hat interfered with my ponytail, and I slid the elastic band lower to accommodate it before snapping the chin band together. Matthew was at my back in the time it took me to grab the reins and lift my foot to Rakasa's stirrup.

"Will you never wait until I help you?" he growled into my ear.

"I can get onto a horse myself," I said hotly.

"But you don't need to." Matthew's hands cupped my shin, lifting me effortlessly into the saddle. After that, he checked my stirrup length, rechecked the girth strap, and finally went to his own horse. He swung into the saddle with a practiced air that suggested he'd been on horseback for hundreds of years. Once there, he looked like a king.

Rakasa started to dance in impatience, and I pushed my heels down. She stopped, looking puzzled. "Quiet," I whispered. She nodded her head and stared forward, her ears working back and forth.

"Take her around the paddock while I check my saddle," Matthew said casually, swinging his left knee onto Dahr's shoulder and fiddling with his stirrup leather. My eyes narrowed. His stirrups needed no adjustment. He was checking out my riding skills.

I walked Rakasa halfway around the paddock, to feel her gait. The Andalusian really did dance, delicately picking up her feet and putting them down firmly in a beautiful, rocking movement. When I pressed both heels into her sides, Rakasa's dancing walk turned into an equally rollicking, smooth trot. We passed Matthew, who had given up all pretense of adjusting his saddle. Georges leaned against the fence, smiling broadly.

Beautiful girl, I breathed silently. Her left ear shot back, and she picked up the pace slightly. My calf pressed into her flank, just behind the stirrup, and she broke into a canter, her feet reaching out into the air and her neck arched. How angry would Matthew be if we jumped the paddock fence?

Angry, I was sure.

Rakasa rounded the corner, and I slowed her to a trot. "Well?" I demanded.

Georges nodded and opened the paddock gate.

"You have a good seat," Matthew said, eyeing my backside. "Good hands, too. You'll be all right. By the way," he continued in a conversational tone, leaning toward me and dropping his voice, "if you'd jumped the fence back there, today's outing would have been over."

Once we'd cleared the gardens and passed through the old gate, the trees thickened, and Matthew scanned the forest. A few feet into the woods, he began to relax, having accounted for every creature within and discovered that none of them were of the two-legged variety.

Matthew kicked Dahr into a trot, and Rakasa obediently waited for me to kick her as well. I did, amazed all over again at how smoothly she moved.

"What kind of horse is Dahr?" I asked, noticing his equally smooth gait.

"I suppose you'd call him a destrier," Matthew explained. That was the mount that carried knights to the Crusades. "He was bred for speed and agility."

"I thought destriers were enormous warhorses." Dahr was bigger than Rakasa, but not much.

"They were large for the time. But they weren't big enough to carry any of the men in this family into battle, not once we had armor on our backs, and weapons. We trained on horses like Dahr and rode them for pleasure, but we fought on Percherons like Balthasar."

I stared between Rakasa's ears, working up the courage to broach another subject. "May I ask you something about your mother?"

"Of course," Matthew said, twisting in his saddle. He put one fist on his hip and held his horse's reins lightly in the other hand. I now knew with absolute certainty how a medieval knight looked on horseback.

"Why does she hate witches so much? Vampires and witches are traditional enemies, but Ysabeau's dislike of me goes beyond that. It seems personal."

"I suppose you want a better answer than that you smell like spring."

"Yes, I want the real reason."

"She's jealous." Matthew patted Dahr's shoulder.

"What on earth is she jealous of?"

"Let's see. Your power—especially a witch's ability to see the future. Your ability to bear children and pass that power to a new generation. And the ease with which you die, I suppose," he said, his voice reflective.

"Ysabeau had you and Louisa for children."

"Yes, Ysabeau made both of us. But it's not quite the same as bearing a child, I think."

"Why does she envy a witch's second sight?"

"That has to do with how Ysabeau was made. Her maker didn't ask permission first." Matthew's face darkened. "He wanted her for a wife, and he just took her and turned her into a vampire. She had a reputation as a seer and was young enough to still hope for children. When she became a vampire, both of those abilities were gone. She's never quite gotten over it, and witches are a constant reminder of the life she lost."

"Why does she envy that witches die so easily?"

"Because she misses my father." He abruptly stopped talking, and it was clear I'd pressed him enough.

The trees thinned, and Rakasa's ears shot back and forth impatiently.

"Go ahead," he said with resignation, gesturing at the open field before us.

Rakasa leaped forward at the touch of my heels, catching the bit in her teeth. She slowed climbing the hill, and once on the crest she pranced and tossed her head, clearly enjoying the fact that Dahr was standing at the bottom while she was on top. I circled her into a fast figure eight, changing her leads on the fly to keep her from stumbling as she went around corners.

Dahr took off—not at a canter but a gallop—his black tail streaming out behind him and his hooves striking the earth with unbelievable speed. I gasped and pulled lightly on Rakasa's reins to make her stop. So that was the point of destriers. They could go from zero to sixty like a finely tuned sports car. Matthew made no effort to slow his horse as he approached, but Dahr stopped on a dime about six feet away from us, his sides bowed out slightly with the exertion.

"Show-off! You won't let me jump a fence and you put on that display?" I teased.

"Dahr doesn't get enough exercise either. This is exactly what he needs." Matthew grinned and patted his horse on the shoulder. "Are you interested in a race? We'll give you a head start, of course," he said with a courtly bow.

"You're on. Where to?"

Matthew pointed to a solitary tree on the top of the ridge and watched me, alert for the first indication of movement. He'd picked something that you could shoot past without running into anything. Maybe Rakasa wasn't as good at abrupt stops as Dahr was.

There was no way I was going to surprise a vampire and no way my horse—for all her smooth gait—was going to beat Dahr up the ridge. Still, I was eager to see how well she would perform. I leaned forward and patted Rakasa on the neck, resting my chin for just a moment on her warm flesh and closing my eyes.

Fly, I encouraged her silently.

Rakasa shot forward as if she'd been slapped on the rump, and my instincts took over.

I lifted myself out of the saddle to make it easier for her to carry my weight, tying a loose knot in the reins. When her speed stabilized, I lowered myself into the saddle, clutching her warm body between my legs. My feet kicked free from the unnecessary stirrups, and my fingers wove through her mane. Matthew and Dahr thundered behind us. It was like my dream, the one where dogs and horses were chasing me. My left hand curled as if holding something, and I bent low along Rakasa's neck, eyes closed.

Fly, I repeated, but the voice in my head no longer sounded like my own. Rakasa responded with still more speed.

I felt the tree grow closer. Matthew swore in Occitan, and Rakasa swerved to the left at the last minute, slowing to a canter and then a trot. There was a tug on her reins. My eyes shot open in alarm.

"Do you always ride unfamiliar horses at top speed, with your eyes closed, no reins, and no stirrups?" Matthew's voice was coldly furious. "You row with your eyes closed—I've seen you. And you walk with them closed, too. I always suspected that magic was involved. You must use your power to ride as well. Otherwise you'd be dead. And for what it's worth, I believe you're telling Rakasa what to do with your mind and not with your hands and legs."

I wondered if what he said was true. Matthew made an impatient sound and dismounted by swinging his right leg high over Dahr's head, kicking his left foot out of the stirrup, and sliding down the horse's side facing front.

"Get down from there," he said roughly, grabbing Rakasa's loose reins.

Dismounting the traditional way, I swung my right leg over Rakasa's rump. When my back was to him, Matthew reached up and scooped me off the horse. Now I knew why he preferred to face front. It kept you from being grabbed from behind and hauled off your mount. He turned me around and crushed me to his chest.

"*Dieu,*" he whispered into my hair. "Don't do anything like that again, please."

"You told me not to worry about what I was doing. It's why you brought me to France," I said, confused by his reaction.

"I'm sorry," he said earnestly. "I'm trying not to interfere. But it's difficult to watch you using powers you don't understand—especially when you're not aware you're doing it."

Matthew left me to tend to the horses, tying their reins so that they wouldn't step on them but giving them the freedom to nibble the sparse fall grass. When he returned, his face was somber.

"There's something I need to show you." He led me to the tree, and we sat underneath it. I folded my legs carefully to the side so that my boots didn't cut into my legs. Matthew simply dropped, his knees on the ground and his feet curled under his thighs.

He reached into the pocket of his breeches and drew out a piece of paper with black and gray bars on a white background. It had been folded and refolded several times.

It was a DNA report. "Mine?"

"Yours."

"When?" My fingers traced the bars along the page.

"Marcus brought the results to New College. I didn't want to share them with you so soon after you were reminded of your parents' death." He hesitated. "Was I right to wait?"

When I nodded, Matthew looked relieved. "What does it say?" I asked.

"We don't understand everything," he replied slowly. "But Marcus and Miriam did identify markers in your DNA that we've seen before."

Miriam's tiny, precise handwriting marched down the left side of the page, and the bars, some circled with red pen, marched down the right. "This is the genetic marker for precognition," Matthew continued, pointing to the first circled smudge. His finger began slowly moving down the page. "This one is for flight. This helps witches find things that are lost."

Matthew kept reeling off powers and abilities one at a time until my head spun.

"This one is for talking with the dead, this is transmogrification, this is telekinesis, this is spell casting, this one is charms, this one is curses. And you've got mind reading, telepathy, and empathy—they're next to one another."

"This can't be right." I'd never heard of a witch with more than one or two powers. Matthew had already reached a dozen.

"I think the findings are right, Diana. These powers may never manifest, but you've inherited the genetic predisposition for them." He flipped the page. There were more red circles and more careful annotations by Miriam. "Here are the elemental markers. Earth is present in almost all witches, and some have either earth and air or earth and water. You've got all three, which we've never seen before. And you've also got fire. Fire is very, very rare." Matthew pointed to the four smudges.

"What are elemental markers?" My feet were feeling uncomfortably breezy, and my fingers were tingling.

"Indications that you have the genetic predisposition to control one or more of the elements. They explain why you could raise a witchwind. Based on this, you could command witchfire and what's called witchwater as well."

"What does earth do?"

"Herbal magic, the power to affect growing things—the basics. Combined with spell casting, cursing, and charms—or any one of them, really—it means you have not only powerful magical abilities but an innate talent for witchcraft."

My aunt was good with spells. Emily wasn't but could fly for short distances and see the future. These were classic differences among witches—dividing those who used witchcraft, like Sarah, from those who used magic. It all boiled down to whether words shaped your power or whether you just had it and could wield it as you liked. I buried my face in my hands. The prospect of seeing the future as my mother could had been scary enough. Control of the elements? Talking with the dead?

"There is a long list of powers on that sheet. We've only seen—what?—four or five of them?" It was terrifying.

"I suspect we've seen more than that—like the way you move with your eyes closed, your ability to communicate with Rakasa, and your sparkly fingers. We just don't have names for them yet."

"Please tell me that's all."

Matthew hesitated. "Not quite." He flipped to another page. "We can't yet identify these markers. In most cases we have to correlate accounts of a witch's activities—some of them centuries old—with DNA evidence. It can be hard to match them up."

"Do the tests explain why my magic is emerging now?"

"We don't need a test for that. Your magic is behaving as if it's waking after a long sleep. All that inactivity has made it restless, and now it wants to have its way. Blood will out," Matthew said lightly. He rocked gracefully to his feet and lifted me up. "You'll catch cold sitting on the ground, and I'll have a hell of a time explaining myself to Marthe if you get sick." He whistled to the horses. They strolled in our direction, still munching on their unexpected treat.

We rode for another hour, exploring the woods and fields around Sept-Tours. Matthew pointed out the best place to hunt rabbits and where his father had taught him to shoot a crossbow without taking out his own eye. When we turned back to the stables, my worries over the test results had been replaced with a pleasant feeling of exhaustion.

"My muscles will be sore tomorrow," I said, groaning. "I haven't been on a horse for years."

"Nobody would have guessed that from the way that you rode today," he said. We passed out of the forest and entered the château's stone gate. "You're a good rider, Diana, but you mustn't go out by yourself. It's too easy to lose your way."

Matthew wasn't worried I'd get lost. He was worried I'd be found.

"I won't."

His long fingers relaxed on the reins. He'd been clutching them for the past five minutes. This vampire was used to giving orders that were obeyed instantly. He wasn't accustomed to making requests and negotiating agreements. And his usual quick temper was nowhere in evidence.

Sidling Rakasa closer to Dahr, I reached over and raised Matthew's palm to my mouth. My lips were warm against his hard, cold flesh.

His pupils dilated in surprise.

I let go and, clucking Rakasa forward, headed into the stables.

Chapter 20

Ysabeau was mercifully absent at lunch. Afterward I wanted to go straight to Matthew's study and start examining *Aurora Consurgens,* but he convinced me to take a bath first. It would, he promised, make the inevitable muscle stiffness more bearable. Halfway upstairs, I had to stop and rub a cramp in my leg. I was going to pay for the morning's enthusiasm.

The bath was heavenly—long, hot, and relaxing. I put on loose black trousers, a sweater, and a pair of socks and padded downstairs, where a fire was blazing. My flesh turned orange and red as I held my hands out to the flames. What would it be like to control fire? My fingers tingled in response to the question, and I slid them safely into my pockets.

Matthew looked up from his desk. "Your manuscript is next to your computer."

Its black covers drew me as surely as a magnet. I sat down at the table and opened them, holding the book carefully. The colors were even brighter than I remembered. After staring at the queen for several minutes, I turned the first page.

"Incipit tractatus Aurora Consurgens intitulatus." The words were familiar—"Here begins the treatise called the Rising of the Dawn"—but I still felt the shiver of pleasure associated with seeing a manuscript for the first time. *"Everything good comes to me along with her. She is known as the Wisdom of the South, who calls out in the streets, and to the multitudes,"* I read silently, translating from the Latin. It was a beautiful work, full of paraphrases from Scripture as well as other texts.

"Do you have a Bible up here?" It would be wise for me to have one handy as I made my way through the manuscript.

"Yes—but I'm not sure where it is. Do you want me to look for it?" Matthew rose slightly from his chair, but his eyes were still glued to his computer screen.

"No, I'll find it." I got up and ran my finger down the edge of the nearest shelf. Matthew's books were arranged not by size but in a running time line. Those on the first bookshelf were so ancient that I couldn't bear to think about what they contained—the lost works of Aristotle, perhaps? Anything was possible.

Roughly half of Matthew's books were shelved spine in to protect the books' fragile edges. Many of these had identifying marks written along the edges of the pages, and thick black letters spelled out a title here, an author's name there. Halfway around the room, the books began to appear spine out, their titles and authors embossed in gold and silver.

I slid past the manuscripts with their thick and bumpy pages, some with small Greek letters on the front edge. I kept going, looking for a large, fat, printed book. My index finger froze in front of one bound in brown leather and covered with gilding.

"Matthew, please tell me 'Biblia Sacra 1450' is not what I think it is."

"Okay, it's not what you think it is," he said automatically, fingers racing over the keys with more than human speed. He was paying little attention to what I was doing and none at all to what I was saying.

Leaving Gutenberg's Bible where it was, I continued along the shelves, hoping that it wasn't the only one available to me. My finger froze again at a book labeled *Will's Playes*. "Were these books given to you by friends?"

"Most of them." Matthew didn't even look up.

Like German printing, the early days of English drama were a subject for later discussion.

For the most part, Matthew's books were in pristine condition. This was not entirely surprising, given their owner. Some, though, were well worn. A slender, tall book on the bottom shelf, for instance, had corners so torn and thin you could see the wooden boards peeking through the leather. Curious to see what had made this book a favorite, I pulled it out and opened the pages. It was Vesalius's anatomy book from 1543, the first to depict dissected human bodies in exacting detail.

Now hunting for fresh insights into Matthew, I sought out the next book to show signs of heavy use. This time it was a smaller, thicker volume. Inked onto the fore edge was the title *De motu*. William Harvey's study of the circulation of the blood and his explanation of how the heart pumped must have been interesting reading for vampires when it was first published in the 1620s, though they must already have had some notion that this might be the case.

Matthew's well-worn books included works on electricity, microscopy, and physiology. But the most battered book I'd seen yet was resting on the nineteenth-century shelves: a first edition of Darwin's *On the Origin of Species*.

Sneaking a glance at Matthew, I pulled the book off the shelf with the stealth of a shoplifter. Its green cloth binding, with the title and author stamped in gold, was frayed with wear. Matthew had written his name in a beautiful copperplate script on the flyleaf.

There was a letter folded inside.

"Dear Sir," it began. *"Your letter of 15 October has reached me at last. I am mortified at my slow reply. I have for many years been collecting all the facts which I could in regard to the variation and origin of species, and your approval of my reasonings comes as welcome news as my book will soon pass into the publisher's hands."* It was signed "*C. Darwin,*" and the date was 1859.

The two men had been exchanging letters just weeks prior to *Origin*'s publication in November.

The book's pages were covered with the vampire's notes in pencil and ink, leaving hardly an inch of blank paper. Three chapters were annotated even more heavily than the rest. They were the chapters on instinct, hybridism, and the affinities between the species.

Like Harvey's treatise on the circulation of blood, Darwin's seventh chapter, on natural instincts, must have been page-turning reading for vampires. Matthew had underlined specific passages and written above and below the lines as well as in the margins as he grew more excited by Darwin's ideas. *"Hence, we may conclude, that domestic instincts have been acquired and natural instincts have been lost partly by habit, and partly by man selecting and accumulating during successive generations, peculiar mental habits and actions, which at first appeared from what we must in our ignorance call an accident.*" Matthew's scribbled remarks included questions about which instincts might have been acquired and whether accidents were possible in nature. "*Can it be that we have maintained as instincts what humans have given up through accident and habit?"* he asked across the bottom margin. There was no need for me to ask who was included in "we." He meant creatures—not just vampires, but witches and daemons, too.

In the chapter on hybridism, Matthew's interest had been caught by the problems of crossbreeding and sterility. "*First crosses between forms sufficiently distinct to be ranked as species, and their hybrids,*" Darwin wrote, "*are very generally, but not universally, sterile.*" A sketch of a family tree crowded the margins next to the underlined passage. There was a question mark where the roots belonged and four branches. *"Why has inbreeding not led to sterility or madness?"* Matthew wondered in the tree's trunk. At the top of the page, he had written, *"1 species or 4?"* and *"comment sont faites les dāēōs?"*

I traced the writing with my finger. This was my specialty—turning the scribbles of scientists into something sensible to everyone else. In his last note, Matthew had used a familiar technique to hide his thoughts. He'd written in a combination of French and Latin—and used an archaic abbreviation for daemons for good measure in which the consonants save the first and last had been replaced with lines over the vowels. That way no one paging through his book would see the word "daemons" and stop for a closer look.

"How are daemons made?" Matthew had wondered in 1859. He was still looking for the answer a century and a half later.

When Darwin began discussing the affinities between species, Matthew's pen had been unable to stop racing across the page, making it nearly impossible to read the printed text. Against a passage explaining, *"From the first dawn of life, all organic beings are found to resemble each other in descending degrees, so that they can be classed in groups under groups,"* Matthew had written *"ORIGINS"* in large black letters. A few lines down, another passage had been underlined twice: *"The existence of groups would have been of simple signification, if one group had been exclusively fitted to inhabit the land, and another the water; one to feed on flesh, another on vegetable matter, and so on; but the case is widely different in nature; for it is notorious how commonly members of even the same subgroup have different habits."*

Did Matthew believe that the vampire diet was a habit rather than a defining characteristic of the species? Reading on, I found the next clue. *"Finally, the several classes of facts which have been considered in this chapter, seem to me to proclaim so plainly, that the innumerable species, genera, and families of organic beings, with which this world is peopled, have all descended, each within its own class or group, from common parents, and have all been modified in the course of descent."* In the margins Matthew had written *"COMMON PARENTS"* and *"ce qui explique tout."*

The vampire believed that monogenesis explained everything—or at least he had in 1859. Matthew thought it was possible that daemons, humans, vampires, and witches shared common ancestors. Our considerable differences were matters of descent, habit, and selection. He had evaded me in his laboratory when I asked whether we were one species or four, but he couldn't do so in his library.

Matthew remained fixated on his computer. Closing the covers of *Aurora Consurgens* to protect its pages and abandoning my search for a more ordinary Bible, I carried his copy of Darwin to the fire and curled up on the sofa. I opened it, intending to try to make sense of the vampire based on the notes he'd made in his book.

He was still a mystery to me—perhaps even more so here at Sept-Tours. Matthew in France was different from Matthew in England. He'd never lost himself in his work this way. Here his shoulders weren't fiercely squared but relaxed, and he'd caught his lower lip in his slightly elongated, sharp cuspid as he typed. It was a sign of concentration, as was the crease between his eyes. Matthew was oblivious to my attention, his fingers flying over the keys, clattering on the computer with a considerable amount of force. He must go through laptops at quite a rate, given their delicate plastic parts. He reached the end of a sentence, leaned back in his chair, and stretched. Then he yawned.

I'd never seen him yawn before. Was his yawn, like his lowered shoulders, a sign of relaxation? The day after we'd first met, Matthew had told me that he liked to know his environment. Here he knew every inch of the place—every smell was familiar, as was every creature who roamed nearby. And then there was his relationship with his mother and Marthe. They were a family, this odd assortment of vampires, and they had taken me in for Matthew's sake.

I turned back to Darwin. But the bath, the warm fire, and the constant background noise of his clacking fingers lulled me to sleep. I woke up covered with a blanket, *On the Origin of Species* lying on the floor nearby, neatly closed with a slip of paper marking my place.

I flushed.

I'd been caught snooping.

"Good evening," Matthew said from the sofa opposite. He slid a piece of paper into the book that he was reading and rested it on his knee. "Can I interest you in some wine?"

Wine sounded very, very good. "Yes, please."

Matthew went to a small eighteenth-century table near the landing. There was a bottle with no label, the cork pulled and lying at its side. He poured two glasses and carried one to me before he sat down. I sniffed, anticipating his first question.

"Raspberries and rocks."

"For a witch you're really quite good at this." Matthew nodded in approval.

"What is it that I'm drinking?" I asked, taking a sip. "Is it ancient? Rare?"

Matthew put his head back and laughed. "Neither. It was probably put in the bottle about five months ago. It's local wine, from vineyards down the road. Nothing fancy, nothing special."

It may not have been fancy or special, but it was fresh and tasted woody and earthy like the air around Sept-Tours.

"I see that you gave up your search for a Bible in favor of something more scientific. Were you enjoying Darwin?" he asked mildly after watching me drink for a few moments.

"Do you still believe that creatures and humans are descended from common parents? Is it really possible that the differences between us are merely racial?"

He made a small sound of impatience. "I told you in the lab that I didn't know."

"You were sure in 1859. And you thought that drinking blood might be simply a dietary habit, not a mark of differentiation."

"Do you know how many scientific advances have taken place between Darwin's time and today? It's a scientist's prerogative to change his mind as new information comes to light." He drank some wine and rested the glass against his knee, turning it this way and that so the firelight played on the liquid inside. "Besides, there's no longer much scientific evidence for human notions of racial distinctions. Modern research suggests that most ideas about race are nothing more than an outmoded human method for explaining easily observable differences between themselves and someone else."

"The question of why you're here—how we're all here—really does consume you," I said slowly. "I could see it on every page of Darwin's book."

Matthew studied his wine. "It's the only question worth asking."

His voice was soft, but his profile was stern, with its sharp lines and heavy brow. I wanted to smooth the lines and lift his features into a smile but remained seated while the firelight danced over his white skin and dark hair. Matthew picked up his book again, cradling it in one set of long fingers while his wineglass rested in the other.

I stared at the fire as the light dimmed. When a clock on the desk struck seven, Matthew put down his book. "Should we join Ysabeau in the salon before dinner?"

"Yes," I replied, squaring my shoulders slightly. "But let me change first." My wardrobe couldn't hold a candle to Ysabeau's, but I didn't want Matthew to be completely ashamed of me. As ever, he looked ready for a boardroom or a Milan catwalk in a simple pair of black wool trousers and a fresh selection from his endless supply of sweaters. My recent close encounters with them had convinced me they were all cashmere—thick and luscious.

Upstairs, I rooted through the items in my duffel bag and selected a gray pair of trousers and a sapphire blue sweater made out of finely spun wool with a tight, funnel-shaped neck and bell-shaped sleeves. My hair had a wave in it thanks to my earlier bath and the fact that it had finished drying scrunched under my head on the sofa.

With the minimum conditions of presentability met, I slid on my loafers and started down the stairs. Matthew's keen ears had picked up the sound of my movements, and he met me on the landing. When he saw me, his eyes lit up and his smile was wide and slow.

"I like you in blue as much as I like you in black. You look beautiful," he murmured, kissing me formally on both cheeks. The blood moved toward them as Matthew lifted my hair around my shoulders, the strands falling through his long white fingers. "Now, don't let Ysabeau get under your skin no matter what she says."

"I'll try," I said with a little laugh, looking up at him uncertainly.

When we reached the salon, Marthe and Ysabeau were already there. His mother was surrounded by newspapers written in every major European language, as well as one in Hebrew and another in Arabic. Marthe, on the other hand, was reading a paperback murder mystery with a lurid cover, her black eyes darting over the lines of print with enviable speed.

"Good evening, *Maman,*" Matthew said, moving to give Ysabeau a kiss on each cold cheek. Her nostrils flared as he moved his body from one side to the other, and her cold eyes fixed on mine angrily.

I knew what had earned me such a black look.

Matthew smelled like me.

"Come, girl," Marthe said, patting the cushion next to her and shooting Matthew's mother a warning glance. Ysabeau closed her eyes. When they opened again, the anger was gone, replaced by something like resignation.

"*Gab es einen anderen Tod,*" Ysabeau murmured to her son as Matthew picked up *Die Welt* and began scanning the headlines with a sound of disgust.

"Where?" I asked. Another bloodless corpse had been found. If Ysabeau thought she was going to shut me out of the conversation with German, she'd better think again.

"Munich," Matthew said, his face buried in the pages. "Christ, why doesn't someone *do* something about this?"

"We must be careful what we wish for, Matthew," Ysabeau said. She changed the subject abruptly. "How was your ride, Diana?"

Matthew peered warily at his mother over *Die Welt*'s headlines.

"It was wonderful. Thank you for letting me ride Rakasa," I replied, sitting back next to Marthe and forcing myself to meet Ysabeau's eyes without blinking.

"She is too willful for my liking," she said, shifting her attention to her son, who had the good sense to put his nose back in his paper. "Fiddat is much more biddable. As I get older, I find that quality admirable in horses."

In sons, too, I thought.

Marthe smiled encouragingly at me and got up to fuss at a sideboard. She carried a large goblet of wine to Ysabeau and a much smaller one to me. Marthe returned to the table and came back with another glass for Matthew. He sniffed it appreciatively.

"Thank you, *Maman,*" he said, raising his glass in tribute.

"*Hein*, it's not much," Ysabeau said, taking a sip of the same wine.

"No, not much. Just one of my favorites. Thank you for remembering." Matthew savored the wine's flavors before swallowing the liquid down.

"Are all vampires as fond of wine as you are?" I asked Matthew, smelling the peppery wine. "You drink it all the time, and you never get the slightest bit tipsy."

Matthew grinned. "Most vampires are much fonder of it. As for getting drunk, our family has always been known for its admirable restraint, hasn't it, *Maman*?"

Ysabeau gave a most unladylike snort. "Occasionally. With respect to wine, perhaps."

"You should be a diplomat, Ysabeau. You're very good with a quick non-answer," I said.

Matthew shouted with laughter. "*Dieu,* I never thought the day would come when my mother would be thought diplomatic. Especially not with her tongue. Ysabeau's always been much better with the diplomacy of the sword."

Marthe snickered in agreement.

Ysabeau and I both looked indignant, which only made him shout again.

The atmosphere at dinner was considerably warmer than it had been last night. Matthew sat at the head of the table, with Ysabeau to his left and me at his right. Marthe traveled incessantly from kitchen to fireside to table, sitting now and again to take a sip of wine and make small contributions to the conversation.

Plates full of food came and went—everything from wild mushroom soup to quail to delicate slices of beef. I marveled aloud that someone who no longer ate cooked food could have such a deft hand with spices. Marthe blushed and dimpled, swatting at Matthew when he tried to tell stories of her more spectacular culinary disasters.

"Do you remember the live pigeon pie?" He chortled. "No one ever explained that you had to keep the birds from eating for twenty-four hours before you baked it or the inside would resemble a birdbath." That earned him a sharp tap on the back of his skull.

"Matthew," Ysabeau warned, wiping the tears from her eyes after a prolonged bout of laughter, "you shouldn't bait Marthe. You have had your share of disasters over the years, too."

"And I have seen them all," Marthe pronounced, carrying over a salad. Her English got stronger by the hour, as she switched into the language whenever she talked in front of me. She returned to the sideboard and fetched a bowl of nuts, which she put between Matthew and Ysabeau. "When you flooded the castle with your idea for capturing water on the roof, for one," she said, ticking it off on her fingers. "When you forgot to collect the taxes, two. It was spring, you were bored, and so you got up one morning and went to Italy to make war. Your father had to beg forgiveness from the king on his knees. And then there was New York!" she shouted triumphantly.

The three vampires continued to swap reminiscences. None of them talked about Ysabeau's past, though. When something came up that touched on her, or Matthew's father, or his sister, the conversation slid gracefully away. I noticed the pattern and wondered about the reasons for it but said nothing, content to let the evening develop as they wished it to and strangely comforted to be part of a family again—even a family of vampires.

After dinner we returned to the salon, where the fire was larger and more impressive than before. The castle's chimneys were heating up with each log thrown into the grate. The fires burned hotter, and the room almost felt warm as a result. Matthew made sure that Ysabeau was comfortable, getting her yet another glass of wine, and fiddled with a nearby stereo. Marthe made me tea instead, thrusting the cup and saucer into my hands.

"Drink," she instructed, her eyes attentive. Ysabeau watched me drink, too, and gave Marthe a long look. "It will help you sleep."

"Did you make this?" It tasted of herbs and flowers. Normally I didn't like herbal tea, but this one was fresh and slightly bitter.

"Yes," she answered, turning up her chin at Ysabeau's stare. "I have made it for a long time. My mother taught me. I will teach you as well."

The sound of dance music filled the room, lively and rhythmic. Matthew adjusted the position of the chairs by the fireplace, clearing a spot on the floor.

"Vòles dançar amb ieu?" Matthew asked his mother, holding out both hands.

Ysabeau's smile was radiant, transforming her lovely, cold features into something indescribably beautiful. *"Òc,"* she said, putting her tiny hands into his. The two of them took their places in front of the fire, waiting for the next song to start.

When Matthew and his mother began to dance, they made Astaire and Rogers look clumsy. Their bodies came together and drew apart, turned in circles away from each other and then dipped and turned. The slightest touch from Matthew sent Ysabeau reeling, and the merest hint of an undulation or a hesitation from Ysabeau caused a corresponding response in him.

Ysabeau dipped into a graceful curtsy, and Matthew swept into a bow at the precise moment the music drew to its close.

"What was that?" I asked.

"It started out as a tarantella," Matthew said, escorting his mother back to her chair, "but *Maman* never can stick to one dance. So there were elements of the volta in the middle, and we finished with a minuet, didn't we?" Ysabeau nodded and reached up to pat him on the cheek.

"You always were a good dancer," she said proudly.

"Ah, but not as good as you—and certainly not as good as Father was," Matthew said, settling her in her chair. Ysabeau's eyes darkened, and a heartbreaking look of sadness crossed her face. Matthew picked up her hand and brushed his lips across her knuckles. Ysabeau managed a small smile in return.

"Now it's your turn," he said, coming to me.

"I don't like to dance, Matthew," I protested, holding up my hands to fend him off.

"I find that hard to believe," he said, taking my right hand in his left and drawing me close. "You contort your body into improbable shapes, skim across the water in a boat the width of a feather, and ride like the wind. Dancing should be second nature."

The next song sounded like something that might have been popular in Parisian dance halls in the 1920s. Notes of trumpet and drum filled the room.

"Matthew, be careful with her," Ysabeau warned as he moved me across the floor.

"She won't break, *Maman.*" Matthew proceeded to dance, despite my best efforts to put my feet in his way at every opportunity. With his right hand at my waist, he gently steered me into the proper steps.

I started to think about where my legs were in an effort to help the process along, but this only made things worse. My back stiffened, and Matthew clasped me tighter.

"Relax," he murmured into my ear. "You're trying to lead. Your job is to follow."

"I can't," I whispered back, gripping his shoulder as if he were a life preserver.

Matthew spun us around again. "Yes you can. Close your eyes, stop thinking about it, and let me do the rest."

Inside the circle of his arms, it was easy to do what he instructed. Without the whirling shapes and colors of the room coming at me from all directions, I could relax and stop worrying that we were about to crash. Gradually the movement of our bodies in the darkness became enjoyable. Soon it was possible for me to concentrate not on what *I* was doing but on what his legs and arms were telling me *he* was about to do. It felt like floating.

"Matthew." Ysabeau's voice held a note of caution. *"Le chatoiement."*

"I know," he murmured. The muscles in my shoulders tensed with concern. "Trust me," he said quietly into my ear. "I've got you."

My eyes remained tightly closed, and I sighed happily. We continued to swirl together. Matthew gently released me, spinning me out to the end of his fingers, then rolled me back along his arm until I came to rest, my back tight against his chest. The music stopped.

"Open your eyes," he said softly.

My eyelids slowly lifted. The feeling of floating remained. Dancing was better than I had expected it to be—at least it was with a partner who'd been dancing for more than a millennium and never stepped on your toes.

I tilted my face up to thank him, but his was much closer than expected.

"Look down," Matthew said.

Turning my head in the other direction revealed that my toes were dangling several inches above the floor. Matthew released me. He wasn't holding me up.

I was holding me up.

The air was holding me up.

With that realization the weight returned to the lower half of my body. Matthew gripped both elbows to keep my feet from smashing into the floor.

From her seat by the fire, Marthe hummed a tune under her breath. Ysabeau's head whipped around, eyes narrowed. Matthew smiled at me reassuringly, while I concentrated on the uncanny feeling of the earth under my feet. Had the ground always seemed so alive? It was as if a thousand tiny hands were waiting under the soles of my shoes to catch me or give me a push.

"Was it fun?" Matthew asked as the last notes of Marthe's song faded, eyes gleaming.

"It was," I answered, laughing, after considering his question.

"I hoped it would be. You've been practicing for years. Now maybe you'll ride with your eyes open for a change." He caught me up in an embrace full of happiness and possibility.

Ysabeau began to sing the same song Marthe had been humming.

"Whoever sees her dance,
And her body move so gracefully,
Could say, in truth,
That in all the world she has no equal,
our joyful queen.
Go away, go away, jealous ones,
Let us, let us,
Dance together, together."

"*Go away, go away, jealous ones,*" Matthew repeated as the final echo of his mother's voice faded, "*let us dance together.*"

I laughed again. "With you I'll dance. But until I figure out how this flying business works, there will be no other partners."

"Properly speaking, you were floating, not flying," Matthew corrected me.

"Floating, flying—whatever you call it, it would be best not to do it with strangers."

"Agreed," he said.

Marthe had vacated the sofa for a chair near Ysabeau. Matthew and I sat together, our hands still entwined.

"This was her first time?" Ysabeau asked him, her voice genuinely puzzled.

"Diana doesn't use magic, *Maman,* except for little things," he explained.

"She is full of power, Matthew. Her witch's blood sings in her veins. She should be able to use it for big things, too."

He frowned. "It's hers to use or not."

"Enough of such childishness," she said, turning her attention to me. "It is time for you to grow up, Diana, and accept responsibility for who you are."

Matthew growled softly.

"Do not growl at me, Matthew de Clermont! I am saying what needs to be said."

"You're telling her what to do. It's not your job."

"Nor yours, my son!" Ysabeau retorted.

"Excuse me!" My sharp tone caught their attention, and the de Clermonts, mother and son, stared at me. "It's my decision whether—and how—to use my magic. But," I said, turning to Ysabeau, "it can't be ignored any longer. It seems to be bubbling out of me. I need to learn how to control my power, at the very least."

Ysabeau and Matthew continued to stare. Finally Ysabeau nodded. Matthew did, too.

We continued to sit by the fire until the logs burned down. Matthew danced with Marthe, and each of them broke into song occasionally when a piece of music reminded them of another night, by another fire. But I didn't dance again, and Matthew didn't press me.

Finally he stood. "I am taking the only one of us who needs her sleep up to bed."

I stood as well, smoothing my trousers against my thighs. "Good night,

Ysabeau. Good night, Marthe. Thank you both for a lovely dinner and a surprising evening."

Marthe gave me a smile in return. Ysabeau did her best but managed only a tight grimace.

Matthew let me lead the way and put his hand gently against the small of my back as we climbed the stairs.

"I might read for a bit," I said, turning to face him when we reached his study.

He was directly behind me, so close that the faint, ragged sound of his breath was audible. He took my face in his hands.

"What spell have you put on me?" He searched my face. "It's not simply your eyes—though they do make it impossible for me to think straight—or the fact you smell like honey." He buried his face in my neck, the fingers of one hand sliding into my hair while the other drifted down my back, pulling my hips toward him.

My body softened into his, as if it were meant to fit there.

"It's your fearlessness," he murmured against my skin, "and the way you move without thinking, and the shimmer you give off when you concentrate—or when you fly."

My neck arched, exposing more flesh to his touch. Matthew slowly turned my face toward him, his thumb seeking out the warmth of my lips.

"Did you know that your mouth puckers when you sleep? You look as though you might be displeased with your dreams, but I prefer to think you wish to be kissed." He sounded more French with each word that he spoke.

Aware of Ysabeau's disapproving presence downstairs, as well as her acute, vampiric hearing, I tried to pull away. It wasn't convincing, and Matthew's arms tightened.

"Matthew, your mother—"

He gave me no chance to complete my sentence. With a soft, satisfied sound, he deliberately fitted his lips to mine and kissed me, gently but thoroughly, until my entire body—not just my hands—was tingling. I kissed him back, feeling a simultaneous sense of floating and falling until I had no clear awareness of where my body ended and his began. His mouth drifted to my cheeks and eyelids. When it brushed against my ear, I gasped. Matthew's lips curved into a smile, and he pressed them once more against my own.

"Your lips are as red as poppies, and your hair is so alive," he said when he was quite finished kissing me with an intensity that left me breathless.

"What is it with you and my hair? Why anyone with a head of hair like yours would be impressed with this," I said, grabbing a fistful of it and pulling, "is beyond me. Ysabeau's hair looks like satin, so does Marthe's. Mine is a mess—every color of the rainbow and badly behaved as well."

"That's why I love it," Matthew said, gently freeing the strands. "It's imperfect, just like life. It's not vampire hair, all polished and flawless. I like that you're not a vampire, Diana."

"And I like that you *are* a vampire, Matthew."

A shadow flitted across his eyes, gone in a moment.

"I like your strength," I said, kissing him with the same enthusiasm as he had kissed me. "I like your intelligence. Sometimes I even like your bossiness. But most of all"—I rubbed the tip of my nose gently against his—"I like the way you smell."

"You do?"

"I do." My nose went into the hollow between his collarbones, which I was fast learning was the spiciest, sweetest part of him.

"It's late. You need your rest." He released me reluctantly.

"Come to bed with me."

His eyes widened with surprise at the invitation, and the blood coursed to my face.

Matthew brought my hand to his heart. It beat once, powerfully. "I will come up," he said, "but not to stay. We have time, Diana. You've known me for only a few weeks. There's no need to rush."

Spoken like a vampire.

He saw my dejection and drew me closer for another lingering kiss. "A promise," he said, when he was finished, "of what's to come. In time."

It *was* time. But my lips were alternately freezing and burning, making me wonder for a fleeting second if I was as ready as I thought.

Upstairs, the room was ablaze with candles and warm from the fire. How Marthe had managed to get up here, change dozens of candles, and light them so that they would still be burning at bedtime was a mystery, but the room didn't have a single electrical outlet, so I was doubly grateful for her efforts.

Changing in the bathroom behind a partially closed door, I listened to Matthew's plans for the next day. These involved a long walk, another long ride, and more work in the study.

I agreed to all of it—provided that the work came first. The alchemical manuscript was calling to me, and I was eager to get a closer look at it.

I got into Matthew's vast four-poster, and he tightened the sheets around my body before pinching out the candles.

"Sing to me," I said, watching his long fingers fearlessly move through the flames. "An old song—one Marthe likes." Her wicked fondness for love songs had not gone unnoticed.

He was quiet for a few moments while he walked through the room, snuffing the candles and trailing shadows behind him as the room fell into darkness. He began to sing in his rich baritone.

"Ni muer ni viu ni no guaris,
Ni mal no·m sent e si l'ai gran,
Quar de s'amor no suy devis,
Ni no sai si ja n'aurai ni quan,
Qu'en lieys es tota le mercés
Que·m pot sorzer o decazer."

The song was full of yearning, and teetered on the edge of sadness. By the time he returned to my side, the song was finished. Matthew left one candle burning next to the bed.

"What do the words mean?" I reached for his hand.

"'*Not dying nor living nor healing, there is no pain in my sickness, for I am not kept from her love.*'" He leaned down and kissed me on the forehead. "'*I don't know if I will ever have it, for all the mercy that makes me flourish or decay is in her power.*'"

"Who wrote that?" I asked, struck by the aptness of the words when sung by a vampire.

"My father wrote it for Ysabeau. Someone else took the credit, though," Matthew said, his eyes gleaming and his smile bright and content. He hummed the song under his breath as he went downstairs. I lay in his bed, alone, and watched the last candle burn until it guttered out.

Chapter 21

A vampire holding a breakfast tray greeted me the next morning after my shower.

"I told Marthe you wanted to work this morning," Matthew explained, lifting the cover that was keeping the food warm.

"You two are spoiling me." I unfolded the napkin waiting on a nearby chair.

"I don't think your character is in any real danger." Matthew stooped and gave me a lingering kiss, his eyes smoky. "Good morning. Did you sleep well?"

"Very well." I took the plate from his hands, my cheeks reddening at the memory of the invitation I'd extended to him last night. There was still a twinge of hurt when I recalled his gentle rebuff, but this morning's kiss confirmed that we had slipped past the limits of friendship and were moving in a new direction.

After my breakfast we headed downstairs, turned on our computers, and got to work. Matthew had left a perfectly ordinary nineteenth-century copy of an early English translation of the Vulgate Bible on the table next to his manuscript.

"Thank you," I called over my shoulder, holding it up.

"I found it downstairs. Apparently the one I have isn't good enough for you." He grinned.

"I absolutely refuse to treat a Gutenberg Bible as a reference book, Matthew." My voice came out more sternly than anticipated, making me sound like a schoolmarm.

"I know the Bible backwards and forwards. If you have a question, you could just ask me," he suggested.

"I'm not using you as a reference book either."

"Suit yourself," he said with a shrug and another smile.

With my computer at my side and an alchemical manuscript before me, I was soon absorbed in reading, analyzing, and recording my ideas. There was one distracting incident when I asked Matthew for something to weight down the book's pages while I typed. He rummaged around and found a bronze medal with the likeness of Louis XIV on it and a small wooden foot that he claimed came from a German angel. He wouldn't surrender the two objects without sureties for their return. Finally he was satisfied by several more kisses.

Aurora Consurgens was one of the most beautiful texts in the alchemical tradition, a meditation on the female figure of Wisdom as well as an exploration of the chemical reconciliation of opposing natural forces. The text in Matthew's copy was nearly identical to the copies I'd consulted in Zurich, Glasgow, and London. But the illustrations were quite different.

The artist, Bourgot Le Noir, had been a true master of her craft. Each illumination was precise and beautifully executed. But her talent did not lie simply in technical mastery. Her depictions of the female characters showed a different sensibility. Bourgot's Wisdom was full of strength, but there was a softness to her as well. In the first illumination, where Wisdom shielded the personification of the seven metals in her cloak, she bore an expression of fierce, maternal pride.

There were two illuminations—just as Matthew had promised—that weren't included in any known copy of *Aurora Consurgens.* Both appeared in the final parable, devoted to the chemical wedding of gold and silver. The first accompanied words spoken by the female principle in alchemical change. Often represented as a queen dressed in white with emblems of the moon to show her association with silver, she had been transformed by Bourgot into a beautiful, terrifying creature with silvery snakes instead of hair, her face shadowed like a moon eclipsed by the sun. Silently I read the accompanying text, translating the Latin into English: *"Turn to me with all your heart. Do not refuse me because I am dark and shadowed. The fire of the sun has altered me. The seas have encompassed me. The earth has been corrupted because of my work. Night fell over the earth when I sank into the miry deep, and my substance was hidden."*

The Moon Queen held a star in one outstretched palm. *"From the depths of the water I cried out to you, and from the depths of the earth I will call to those who pass by me,"* I continued. *"Watch for me. See me. And if you find another who is like me, I will give him the morning star."* My lips formed the words, and Bourgot's illumination brought the text to life in the Moon Queen's expression that showed both her fear of rejection and her shy pride.

The second unique illumination came on the next page and accompanied the words spoken by the male principal, the golden Sun King. The hair on my neck rose at Bourgot's depiction of a heavy stone sarcophagus, its lid open just enough to reveal a golden body lying within. The king's eyes were closed peacefully, and there was a look of hope on his face as if he were dreaming of his release. *"I will rise now and go about the city. In its streets I will seek out a pure woman to marry,"* I read, *"her face beautiful, her body more beautiful, her raiment most beautiful. She will roll away the stone from the entrance of my tomb and give me the wings of a dove so that I might fly with her to the heavens to live forever and be at rest."* The passage reminded me of Matthew's badge from Bethany and Lazarus's tiny silver coffin. I reached for the Bible.

"Mark 16, Psalms 55, and Deuteronomy 32, verse 40." Matthew's voice cut through the quiet, spouting references like an automated biblical concordance.

"How did you know what I was reading?" I twisted in my chair to get a better view of him.

"Your lips were moving," he replied, staring fixedly at his computer screen, his fingers clattering on the keys.

Pressing my lips together I returned to the text. The author had drawn on every biblical passage that fit the alchemical story of death and creation, paraphrasing and cobbling them together. I pulled the Bible across the desk. It was bound in black leather and a gold cross adorned the cover. Opening it to the Gospel of Mark, I scanned chapter 16. There it was, Mark 16:3, *"And they said one to another: Who shall roll us back the stone from the door of the sepulchre?"*

"Find it?" Matthew inquired mildly.

"Yes."

"Good."

The room grew silent once more.

"Where's the verse about the morning star?" Sometimes my pagan background was a serious professional liability.

"Revelation 2, verse 28."

"Thank you."

"My pleasure." A smothered laugh came from the other desk. I bent my head to the manuscript and ignored it.

After two hours of reading tiny, Gothic handwriting and searching for corresponding biblical references, I was more than ready to go riding when Matthew suggested it was time for a break. As an added bonus, he promised to tell me over lunch how he knew the seventeenth-century physiologist William Harvey.

"It's not a very interesting story," Matthew had protested.

"Maybe not to you. But to a historian of science? It's the closest thing I'll get to meeting the man who figured out that the heart is a pump."

We hadn't seen the sun since we'd arrived at Sept-Tours, but neither of us minded. Matthew seemed more relaxed, and I was surprisingly happy to be out of Oxford. Gillian's threats, the picture of my parents, even Peter Knox—they all receded with each hour that passed.

As we walked out into the gardens, Matthew chatted animatedly about a problem at work that involved a missing strand of something that should have been present in a blood sample but wasn't. He sketched out a chromosome in the air in an effort to explain, pointing to the offending area, and I nodded even though what was at stake remained mysterious. The words continued to roll out of his mouth, and he put an arm around my shoulder, drawing me close.

We rounded a line of hedges. A man in black stood outside the gate we'd passed through yesterday on our ride. The way he leaned against a chestnut tree, with the elegance of a leopard on the prowl, suggested he was a vampire.

Matthew scooped me behind him.

The man pulled himself gracefully away from the tree's rough trunk and strolled toward us. The fact that he was a vampire was now confirmed by his unnaturally white skin and huge, dark eyes, emphasized by his black leather jacket, jeans, and boots. This vampire didn't care who knew he was different. His wolfish expression was the only imperfection in an otherwise angelic face, with symmetrical features and dark hair worn curling low onto his collar. He was smaller and slighter than Matthew, but the power he exuded was undeniable. His eyes sent coldness deep under my skin, where it spread like a stain.

"Domenico," Matthew said calmly, though his voice was louder than usual.

"Matthew." The glance the vampire turned on Matthew was full of hate.

"It's been years." Matthew's casual tone suggested that the vampire's sudden appearance was an everyday occurrence.

Domenico looked thoughtful. "When was that? In Ferrara? We were both fighting the pope—though for different reasons, as I remember. I was trying to save Venice. You were trying to save the Templars."

Matthew nodded slowly, his eyes fixed on the other vampire. "I think you must be right."

"After that, my friend, you seemed to disappear. We shared so many adventures in our youth: on the seas, in the Holy Land. Venice was always full of amusements for a vampire such as you, Matthew." Domenico shook his head in apparent sorrow. The vampire inside the château gate did look Venetian—or like some unholy cross between an angel and a devil. "Why did you not come and visit me when you passed between France and one of your other haunts?"

"If I caused offense, Domenico, it was surely too long ago to be of any concern to us now."

"Perhaps, but one thing hasn't changed in all these years. Whenever there's a crisis, there's a de Clermont nearby." He turned to me, and something avaricious bloomed on his face. "This must be the witch I've heard so much about."

"Diana, go back to the house," Matthew said sharply.

The sense of danger was palpable, and I hesitated, not wanting to leave him alone.

"Go," he said again, his voice as keen edged as a sword.

Our vampire visitor spotted something over my shoulder and smiled. An icy breeze brushed past me and a cold, hard arm linked through mine.

"Domenico," chimed Ysabeau's musical voice. "What an unexpected visit."

He bowed formally. "My lady, it is a pleasure to see you in such good health. How did you know I was here?"

"I smelled you," Ysabeau said contemptuously. "You come here, to my house, uninvited. What would your mother say if she knew you behaved in such a fashion?"

"If my mother was still alive, we could ask her," Domenico said with barely concealed savagery.

"*Maman,* take Diana back to the house."

"Of course, Matthew. We will leave the two of you to talk." Ysabeau turned, tugging me along with her.

"I'll be gone more quickly if you let me deliver my message," Domenico warned. "If I have to come back, I won't be alone. Today's visit was a courtesy to you, Ysabeau."

"She doesn't have the book," Matthew said sharply.

"I'm not here about the witches' damned book, Matthew. Let them keep it. I've come from the Congregation."

Ysabeau exhaled, soft and long, as if she'd been holding her breath for days. A question burbled to my lips, but she silenced it with a warning look.

"Well done, Domenico. I'm surprised you have the time to call on old friends, with all your new responsibilities." Matthew's voice was scornful. "Why is the Congregation wasting time paying official visits on the de Clermont family when there are vampires leaving bloodless corpses all over Europe for humans to find?"

"It's not forbidden for vampires to feed on humans—though the carelessness is regrettable. As you know, death follows vampires wherever we go." Domenico shrugged off the brutality, and I shivered at his casual disregard for frail, warmblooded life. "But the covenant clearly forbids any liaison between a vampire and a witch."

I turned and stared at Domenico. "*What* did you say?"

"She can speak!" Domenico clasped his hands in mock delight. "Why not let the witch take part in this conversation?"

Matthew reached around and drew me forward. Ysabeau remained entwined through my other arm. We stood in a short, tight line of vampire, witch, and vampire.

"Diana Bishop." Domenico bowed low. "It's an honor to meet a witch of such ancient, distinguished lineage. So few of the old families are still with us." Every word he uttered—no matter how formally phrased—sounded like a threat.

"Who are you?" I asked. "And why are you concerned with whom I spend time?"

The Venetian looked at me with interest before his head fell back and he howled with laughter. "They said you were argumentative like your father, but I didn't believe them."

My fingers tingled slightly, and Ysabeau's arm grew fractionally tighter.

"Have I made your witch angry?" Domenico's eyes were fixed on Ysabeau's arm.

"Say what you came to say and get off our land." Matthew's voice was entirely conversational.

"My name is Domenico Michele. I have known Matthew since I was reborn, and Ysabeau nearly as long. I know neither of them so well as I knew the lovely Louisa, of course. But we should not speak lightly of the dead." The Venetian crossed himself piously.

"You should try not to speak of my sister at all." Matthew sounded calm, but Ysabeau looked murderous, her lips white.

"You still haven't answered my question," I said, drawing Domenico's attention once more.

The Venetian's eyes glittered with frank appraisal.

"Diana," Matthew said, unable to stop the rumble in his throat. It was as close as he'd ever been to growling at me. Marthe came out of the kitchens, a look of alarm on her face.

"She is more fiery than most of her kind, I see. Is that why you're risking everything to keep her with you? Does she amuse you? Or do you intend to feed on her until you get bored and then discard her, as you have with other warmbloods?"

Matthew's hands strayed to Lazarus's coffin, evident only as a bump under his sweater. He hadn't touched it since we'd arrived in Sept-Tours.

Domenico's keen eyes noticed the gesture, too, and his answering smile was vindictive. "Feeling guilty?"

Furious at the way Domenico was baiting Matthew, I opened my mouth to speak.

"Diana, go back to the house immediately." Matthew's tone suggested that we would have a serious, unpleasant talk later. He pushed me slightly in Ysabeau's direction and put himself even more squarely between his mother, me, and the dark Venetian. By that time Marthe was nearby, her arms crossed over her sturdy body in a striking imitation of Matthew.

"Not before the witch hears what I have to say. I have come to serve you with a warning, Diana Bishop. Relationships between witches and vampires are forbidden. You must leave this house and no longer associate with Matthew de Clermont or any of his family. If you don't, the Congregation will take whatever steps are necessary to preserve the covenant."

"I don't know your Congregation, and I agreed to no such covenant," I said, still furious. "Besides, covenants aren't enforceable. They're voluntary."

"Are you a lawyer as well as a historian? You modern women with your fine educations are so fascinating. But women are no good at theology," Domenico continued sorrowfully, "which is why we never thought it worth educating you in the first place. Do you think we adhered to the ideas of that heretic Calvin when we made these promises to one another? When the covenant was sworn, it bound all vampires, daemons, and witches—past, present, and future. This is not a path you can follow or not as you please."

"You've delivered your warning, Domenico," Matthew said in a voice like silk.

"That's all I have to say to the witch," the Venetian replied. "I have more to say to you."

"Then Diana will return to the house. Get her out of here, *Maman,*" he said tersely.

This time his mother did what he asked immediately, and Marthe followed. "Don't," Ysabeau hissed when I turned to look back at Matthew.

"Where did that thing come from?" Marthe asked once we were safely inside.

"From hell, presumably," said Ysabeau. She touched my face briefly with her fingertips, drawing them back hastily when they met the warmth of my angry cheeks. "You are brave, girl, but what you did was reckless. You are not a vampire. Do not put yourself at risk by arguing with Domenico or any of his allies. Stay away from them."

Ysabeau gave me no time to respond, speeding me through the kitchens, the dining room, the salon, and into the great hall. Finally she towed me toward the arch that led to the keep's most formidable tower. My calves seized up at the thought of the climb.

"We must," she insisted. "Matthew will be looking for us there."

Fear and anger propelled me halfway up the stairs. The second half I conquered through sheer determination. Lifting my feet from the final tread, I found myself on a flat roof with a view for miles in every direction. A faint breeze blew, loosening my braided hair and coaxing the mist around me.

Ysabeau moved swiftly to a pole that extended another dozen feet into the sky. She raised a forked black banner adorned with a silver ouroboros. It unfurled in the gloomy light, the snake holding its shimmering tail in its mouth. I ran to the far side of the crenellated walls, and Domenico looked up.

Moments later a similar banner rose over the top of a building in the village and a bell began to toll. Men and women slowly came out of houses, bars, shops, and offices, their faces turned toward Sept-Tours, where the ancient symbol of eternity and rebirth snapped in the wind. I looked at Ysabeau, my question evident on my face.

"Our family's emblem, and a warning to the village to be on their guard," she explained. "We fly the banner only when others are with us. The villagers have grown too accustomed to living among vampires, and though they have nothing to fear from us, we have kept it for times such as this. The world is full of vampires who cannot be trusted, Diana. Domenico Michele is one of them."

"You didn't need to tell me that. Who the hell is he?"

"One of Matthew's oldest friends," Ysabeau murmured, eyes on her son, "which makes him a very dangerous enemy."

My attention turned to Matthew, who continued to exchange words with Domenico across a precisely drawn zone of engagement. There was a blur of black and gray movement, and the Venetian hurtled backward toward the chestnut tree he'd been leaning against when we first spotted him. A loud crack carried across the grounds.

"Well done," Ysabeau muttered.

"Where's Marthe?" I looked over my shoulder toward the stairs.

"In the hall. Just in case." Ysabeau's keen eyes remained fixed on her son.

"Would Domenico really come in here and rip my throat open?"

Ysabeau turned her black, glittering gaze on me. "That would be all too easy, my dear. He would play with you first. He always plays with his prey. And Domenico loves an audience."

I swallowed hard. "I'm capable of taking care of myself."

"You are, if you have as much power as Matthew believes. Witches are very good at protecting themselves, I've found, with a little effort and a drop of courage," Ysabeau said.

"What is this Congregation that Domenico mentioned?" I asked.

"A council of nine—three from each order of daemons, witches, and vampires. It was established during the Crusades to keep us from being exposed to the humans. We were careless and became too involved in their politics and other forms of insanity." Ysabeau's voice was bitter. "Ambition, pride, and grasping creatures like Michele who were never content with their lot in life and always wanted more—they drove us to the covenant."

"And you agreed to certain conditions?" It was ludicrous to think that promises made by creatures in the Middle Ages could affect Matthew and me.

Ysabeau nodded, the breeze catching a few strands of her heavy, honeyed hair and moving them around her face. "When we mixed with one another, we were too conspicuous. When we became involved in human affairs, they grew suspicious of our cleverness. They are not quick, the poor creatures, but they are not entirely stupid either."

"By 'mixing,' you don't mean dinners and dancing."

"No dinners, no dancing—and no kissing and singing songs to each other," Ysabeau said pointedly. "And what comes after the dancing and the kissing was forbidden as well. We were full of arrogance before we agreed to the covenant. There were more of us, and we'd become accustomed to taking whatever we wanted, no matter the cost."

"What else does this promise cover?"

"No politics or religion. Too many princes and popes were otherworldly creatures. It became more difficult to pass from one life to the next once humans started writing their chronicles." Ysabeau shuddered. "Vampires found it difficult to feign a good death and move on to a new life with humans nosing around."

I glanced quickly at Matthew and Domenico, but they were still talking outside the château's walls. "So," I repeated, ticking items off my fingers. "No mixing between different types of creatures. No careers in human politics or religion. Anything else?" Apparently my aunt's xenophobia and fierce opposition to my studying the law derived from her imperfect understanding of this long-ago agreement.

"Yes. If any creature breaks the covenant, it is the responsibility of the Congregation to see that the misconduct is stopped and the oath is upheld."

"And if *two* creatures break the covenant?"

The silence stretched taut between us.

"To my knowledge it has never happened," she said grimly. "It is a very good thing, therefore, that the two of you have not done so."

Last night I'd made a simple request that Matthew join me in my bed. But he'd known it wasn't a simple request. It wasn't me he was unsure of, or his feelings. Matthew wanted to know how far he could go before the Congregation would intervene.

The answer had come quickly. They weren't going to let us get very far at all.

My relief was quickly replaced by anger. Had no one complained, as our relationship developed, he might never have told me about the Congregation or the covenant. And his silence would have had implications for my relationship with my own family, and with his. I might have gone to my grave believing that my aunt and Ysabeau were bigots. Instead they were living up to a promise made long ago—which was less understandable but somehow more excusable.

"Your son needs to stop keeping things from me." My temper rose, the tingling mounting in my fingertips. "And you should worry less about the Congregation and more about what I'm going to do when I see him again."

She snorted. "You won't get the chance to do much before he takes you to task for questioning his authority in front of Domenico."

"I'm not under Matthew's authority."

"You, my dear, have a great deal to learn about vampires," she said with a note of satisfaction.

"And you have a great deal to learn about me. So does the Congregation."

Ysabeau took me by the shoulders, her fingers digging into the flesh of my arms. "This is not a game, Diana! Matthew would willingly turn his back on creatures he has known for centuries to protect your right to be whatever you imagine you want to be in your fleeting life. I'm begging you not to let him do it. They will kill him if he persists."

"He's his own man, Ysabeau," I said coldly. "I don't tell Matthew what to do."

"No, but you have the power to send him away. Tell him you refuse to break the covenant for him, for his sake—or that you feel nothing more for him than curiosity—witches are famous for it." She flung me away. "If you love him, you'll know what to say."

"It is over," Marthe called from the top of the stairs.

We both rushed to the edge of the tower. A black horse and rider streaked out of the stables and cleared the paddock fence before thundering into the forest.

Chapter 22

We'd been waiting in the salon, the three of us, since he'd ridden off on Balthasar in the late morning. Now the shadows were lengthening toward twilight. A human would be half dead from the prolonged effort needed to control that enormous horse in the open countryside. However, the events of the morning had reminded me that Matthew wasn't human, but a vampire—with many secrets, a complicated past, and frightening enemies.

Overhead, a door closed.

"He's back. He will go to his father's room, as he always does when he is troubled," Ysabeau explained.

Matthew's beautiful young mother sat and stared at the fire, while I wrung my hands in my lap, refusing everything Marthe put in front of me. I hadn't eaten since breakfast, but my hollowness had nothing to do with hunger.

I felt shattered, surrounded by the broken pieces of my formerly ordered life. My degree from Oxford, my position at Yale, and my carefully researched and written books had long provided meaning and structure to my life. But none of them were of comfort to me in this strange new world of menacing vampires and threatening witches. My exposure to it had left me raw, with a new fragility linked to a vampire and the invisible, undeniable movement of a witch's blood in my veins.

At last Matthew entered the salon, clean and dressed in fresh clothes. His eyes sought me out immediately, their cold touch fluttering over me as he checked that I was unharmed. His mouth softened in relief.

It was the last hint of comforting familiarity that I detected in him.

The vampire who entered the salon was not the Matthew that I knew. He was not the elegant, charming creature who had slipped into my life with a mocking smile and invitations to breakfast. Nor was he the scientist, absorbed in his work and preoccupied with the question of why he was here. And there was no sign of the Matthew who had swung me into his arms and kissed me with such passionate intensity only the night before.

This Matthew was cold and impassive. The few soft edges he'd once possessed—around his mouth, in the delicacy of his hands, the stillness of his eyes—had been replaced by hard lines and angles. He seemed older than

I remembered, a combination of weariness and careful remove reflecting every moment of his nearly fifteen hundred years of age.

A log broke in the fireplace. The sparks caught my eye, burning blood orange as they fell in the grate.

Nothing but the color red appeared at first. Then the red took on a texture, strands of red burnished here and there with gold and silver. The texture became a thing—hair, Sarah's hair. My fingers caught the strap of a backpack from my shoulder, and I dropped my lunch box on the floor of the family room with the same officious clatter as my father when he dropped his briefcase by the door.

"I'm home." My child's voice was high and bright. "Are there cookies?"

Sarah's head turned, red and orange, catching sparks in the late-afternoon light.

But her face was pure white.

The white overwhelmed the other colors, became silver, and assumed a texture like the scales of a fish. Chain mail clung to a familiar, muscular body. Matthew.

"I'm through." His white hands tore at a black tunic with a silver cross on the front, rending it at the shoulders. He flung it at someone's feet, turned, and strode away.

With a single blink of my eyes, the vision was gone, replaced by the warm tones of the salon at Sept-Tours, but the startling knowledge of what had happened lingered. As with the witchwind, there had been no warning when this hidden talent of mine was released. Had my mother's visions come on so suddenly and had such clarity? I glanced around the room, but the only creature who seemed to have noticed something was odd was Marthe, who looked at me with concern.

Matthew went to Ysabeau and kissed her lightly on both of her flawless white cheeks. "I'm so sorry, *Maman,*" he murmured.

"*Hein,* he was always a pig. It's not your fault." Ysabeau gave her son's hand a gentle squeeze. "I am glad you are home."

"He's gone. There's nothing to worry about tonight," Matthew said, his mouth tight. He drew his fingers through his hair.

"Drink." Marthe belonged to the sustenance school of crisis management. She handed a glass of wine to Matthew and plunked yet another cup of tea next to me. It sat on the table, untouched, sending tendrils of steam into the room.

"Thank you, Marthe." Matthew drank deeply. As he did, his eyes returned to mine, but he deliberately looked away as he swallowed. "My phone," he said, turning toward his study.

He descended the stairs a few moments later. "For you." He gave me the phone in such a way that our hands didn't need to touch.

I knew who was on the line. "Hello, Sarah."

"I've been calling for more than eight hours. What on earth is wrong?" Sarah knew something bad was happening—she wouldn't have called a vampire otherwise. Her tense voice conjured up the image of her white face from my vision. She'd been frightened in it, not just sad.

"There's nothing wrong," I said, not wanting her to be scared anymore. "I'm with Matthew."

"Being with Matthew is what got you into this trouble in the first place."

"Sarah, I can't talk now." The last thing I needed was to argue with my aunt.

She drew in her breath. "Diana, there are a few things you need to know before you decide to throw in your lot with a vampire."

"Really?" I asked, my temper flaring. "Do you think now is the time to tell me about the covenant? You don't by any chance know the witches who are among the current members of the Congregation, do you? I have a few things I'd like to say to them." My fingers were burning, and the skin under my nails was becoming a vivid sky blue.

"You turned your back on your power, Diana, and refused to talk about magic. The covenant wasn't relevant to your life, nor was the Congregation." Sarah sounded defensive.

My bitter laugh helped the blue tinge fade from my fingers. "Justify it any way you want, Sarah. After Mom and Dad were killed, you and Em should have told me, and not just hinted at something in mysterious half-truths. But it's too late now. I need to talk to Matthew. I'll call you tomorrow." After severing the connection and flinging the phone onto the ottoman at my feet, I closed my eyes and waited for the tingling in my fingers to subside.

All three vampires were staring at me—I could feel it.

"So," I said into the silence, "are we to expect more visitors from this Congregation?"

Matthew's mouth tightened. "No."

It was a one-word answer, but at least it was the word I wanted to hear. Over the past few days, I'd had a respite from Matthew's mood changes and had almost forgotten how alarming they could be. His next words wiped away my hope that this latest outburst would soon pass.

"There will be no visits from the Congregation because we aren't going to break the covenant. We'll stay here for a few more days, then return to Oxford. Is that all right with you, *Maman*?"

"Of course," Ysabeau replied promptly. She sighed with relief.

"We should keep the standard flying," Matthew continued, his voice businesslike. "The village should know to be on its guard."

Ysabeau nodded, and her son took a sip of his wine. I stared, first at one and then the other. Neither responded to my silent demand for more information.

"It's only been a few days since you took me *out* of Oxford," I said after no one rose to my wordless challenge.

Matthew's eyes lifted to mine in forbidding response. "Now you're going back," he said evenly. "Meanwhile there will be no walks outside the grounds. No riding on your own." His present coldness was more frightening than anything Domenico had said.

"And?" I pressed him.

"No more dancing," Matthew said, his abruptness suggesting that a host of other activities were included in this category. "We're going to abide by the Congregation's rules. If we stop aggravating them, they'll turn their attention to more important matters."

"I see. You want me to play dead. And you'll give up your work and Ashmole 782? I don't believe that." I stood and moved toward the door.

Matthew's hand was rough on my arm. It violated all the laws of physics that he could have reached my side so quickly.

"Sit down, Diana." His voice was as rough as his touch, but it was oddly gratifying that he was showing any emotion at all.

"Why are you giving in?" I whispered.

"To avoid exposing us all to the humans—and to keep you alive." He pulled me back to the sofa and pushed me onto the cushions. "This family is not a democracy, especially not at a time like this. When I tell you to do something, you do it, without hesitation or question. Understood?" Matthew's tone indicated that the discussion was over.

"Or what?" I was deliberately provoking him, but his aloofness frightened me.

He put down his wine, and the crystal captured the light from the candles.

I felt myself falling, this time into a pool of water.

The pool became a drop, the drop a tear glistening on a white cheek.

Sarah's cheeks were covered in tears, her eyes red and swollen. Em was in the kitchen. When she joined us, it was evident that she'd been crying, too. She looked devastated.

"What?" I said, fear gripping my stomach. "What's happened?"

Sarah wiped at her eyes, her fingers stained with the herbs and spices she used in her spell casting.

Her fingers grew longer, the stains dissolving.

"What?" Matthew said, his eyes wild, white fingers brushing a tiny, blood-stained tear from an equally white cheek. "What's happened?"

"Witches. They have your father," Ysabeau said, her voice breaking.

As the vision faded, I searched for Matthew, hoping his eyes would exert their usual pull and relieve my lingering disorientation. As soon as our glances met, he came and hovered over me. But there was none of the usual comfort associated with his presence.

"I will kill you myself before I let anyone hurt you." The words caught in his throat. "And I don't want to kill you. So please do what I tell you."

"So that's it?" I asked when I could manage it. "We're going to abide by an ancient, narrow-minded agreement made almost a thousand years ago. Case closed."

"You mustn't be under the Congregation's scrutiny. You have no control over your magic and no understanding of your relationship to Ashmole 782. At Sept-Tours you may be protected from Peter Knox, Diana, but I've told you before that you aren't safe around vampires. No warmblood is. Ever."

"You won't hurt me." In spite of what had happened over the past several days, on this point I was absolutely certain.

"You persist in this romantic vision of what it is to be a vampire, but despite my best efforts to curb it I have a taste for blood."

I made a dismissive gesture. "You've killed humans. I know this, Matthew. You're a vampire, and you've lived for hundreds of years. Do you think I imagined you survived on nothing but animals?"

Ysabeau was watching her son closely.

"Saying you know I've killed humans and understanding what that means are two different things, Diana. You have no idea what I'm capable of." He touched his talisman from Bethany and moved away from me with swift, impatient steps.

"I know who you are." Here was another point of absolute certainty. I wondered what made me so instinctively sure of Matthew as the evidence about the brutality of vampires—even witches—mounted.

"You don't know yourself. And three weeks ago you'd never heard of me." Matthew's gaze was restless and his hands, like mine, were shaking. This worried me less than the fact that Ysabeau had pitched farther forward in her seat. He picked up a poker and gave the fire a vicious thrust before throwing it aside. The metal rang against the stone, gouging the hard surface as if it were butter.

"We will figure this out. Give us some time." I tried to make my voice low and soothing.

"There's nothing to figure out." Matthew was pacing now. "You have too much undisciplined power. It's like a drug—a highly addictive, dangerous drug that other creatures are desperate to share. You'll never be safe so long as a witch or vampire is near you."

My mouth opened to respond, but the place where he'd been standing was empty. Matthew's icy fingers were on my chin, lifting me to my feet.

"I'm a predator, Diana." He said it with the seductiveness of a lover. The dark aroma of cloves made me dizzy. "I have to hunt and kill to survive." He turned my face away from him with a savage twist, exposing my neck. His restless eyes raked over my throat.

"Matthew, put Diana down." Ysabeau sounded unconcerned, and my own faith in him remained unshaken. He wanted to frighten me off for some reason, but I was in no real danger—not as I had been with Domenico.

"She thinks she knows me, *Maman,*" he purred. "But Diana doesn't know what it's like when the craving for a warmblood tightens your stomach so much that you're mad with need. She doesn't know how much we want to feel the blood of another heart pulsing through our veins. Or how difficult it is for me to stand here, so close, and not taste her."

Ysabeau rose but remained where she was. "Now is not the time to teach her, Matthew."

"You see, it's not just that I could kill you outright," he continued, ignoring his mother. His black eyes were mesmerizing. "I could feed on you slowly, taking your blood and letting it replenish, only to begin again the next day." His grip moved from my chin to circle my neck, and his thumb stroked the pulse at my throat as if he were gauging just where to sink his teeth into my flesh.

"Stop it," I said sharply. His scare tactics had gone on long enough.

Matthew dropped me abruptly on the soft carpet. By the time I felt the impact, the vampire was across the room, his back to me and his head bowed.

I stared at the pattern on the rug beneath my hands and knees.

A swirl of colors, too many to distinguish, moved before my eyes.

They were leaves dancing against the sky—green, brown, blue, gold.

"It's your mom and dad," Sarah was explaining, her voice tight. "They've been killed. They're gone, honey."

I dragged my eyes from the carpet to the vampire standing with his back to me.

"No." I shook my head.

"What is it, Diana?" Matthew turned, concern momentarily pushing the predator away.

The swirl of colors captured my attention again—green, brown, blue, gold. They were leaves, caught in an eddy on a pool of water, falling onto the ground around my hands. A bow, curved and polished, rested next to a scattering of arrows and a half-empty quiver.

I reached for the bow and felt the taut string cut into my flesh.

"Matthew," Ysabeau warned, sniffing the air delicately.

"I know, I can smell it, too," he said grimly.

He's yours, a strange voice whispered. *You mustn't let him go.*

"I know," I murmured impatiently.

"What do you know, Diana?" Matthew took a step toward me.

Marthe shot to my side. "Leave her," she hissed. "The child is not in this world."

I was nowhere, caught between the terrible ache of losing my parents and the certain knowledge that soon Matthew, too, would be gone.

Be careful, the strange voice warned.

"It's too late for that." I raised my hand from the floor and smashed it into the bow, snapping it in two. "Much too late."

"What's too late?" Matthew asked.

"I've fallen in love with you."

"You can't have," he said numbly. The room was utterly silent, except for the crackling of the fire. "It's too soon."

"Why do vampires have such a strange attitude toward time?" I mused aloud, still caught in a bewildering mix of past and present. The word "love" had sent feelings of possessiveness through me, however, drawing me to the here and now. "Witches don't have centuries to fall in love. We do it quickly. Sarah says my mother fell in love with my father the moment she saw him. I've loved you since I decided not to hit you with an oar on the City of Oxford's dock." The blood in my veins began to hum. Marthe looked startled, suggesting she could hear it, too.

"You don't understand." It sounded as if Matthew, like the bow, might snap in two.

"I do. The Congregation will try to stop me, but they won't tell me who to love." When my parents were taken from me, I was a child with no options and did what people told me. I was an adult now, and I was going to fight for Matthew.

"Domenico's overtures are nothing compared to what you can expect from Peter Knox. What happened today was an attempt at rapprochement, a diplomatic mission. You aren't ready to face the Congregation, Diana, no matter what you think. And if you did stand up to them, what then? Bringing these old animosities to the surface could spin out of control, expose us to humans. Your family might suffer." Matthew's words were brutal, meant to make me stop and reconsider. But nothing he said outweighed what I felt for him.

"I love you, and I'm not going to stop." Of this, too, I was certain.

"You are not in love with me."

"I decide who I love, and how, and when. Stop telling me what to do, Matthew. My ideas about vampires may be romantic, but your attitudes toward women need a major overhaul."

Before he could respond, his phone began to hop across the ottoman. He swore an oath in Occitan that must have been truly awe-inspiring, because even Marthe looked shocked. He reached down and snagged the phone before it could skitter onto the floor.

"What is it?" he said, his eyes fixed on me.

There were faint murmurs on the other end of the line. Marthe and Ysabeau exchanged worried glances.

"When?" Matthew's voice sounded like a gunshot. "Did they take anything?" My forehead creased at the anger in his voice. "Thank God. Was there damage?"

Something had happened in Oxford while we were gone, and it sounded like a robbery. I hoped it wasn't the Old Lodge.

The voice on the other end of the phone continued. Matthew passed a hand over his eyes.

"What else?" he asked, his voice rising.

There was another long silence. He turned away and walked to the fireplace, his right hand splayed flat against the mantel.

"So much for diplomacy." Matthew swore under his breath. "I'll be there in a few hours. Can you pick me up?"

We were going back to Oxford. I stood.

"Fine. I'll call before I land. And, Marcus? Find out who else besides Peter Knox and Domenico Michele are members of the Congregation."

Peter Knox? The pieces of the puzzle began to click into place. No wonder Matthew had come back to Oxford so quickly when I'd told him who the brown wizard was. It explained why he was so eager to push me away now, too. We were breaking the covenant, and it was Knox's job to enforce it.

Matthew stood silently for a few moments after the line went dead, one hand clenched as if he were resisting the urge to beat the stone mantel into submission.

"That was Marcus. Someone tried to break in to the lab. I need to go back to Oxford." He turned, his eyes dead.

"Is everything all right?" Ysabeau shot a worried look in my direction.

"They didn't make it through the security controls. Still, I need to talk to the university officials and make sure whoever it was doesn't succeed the next time." Nothing that Matthew was saying made sense. If the burglars had failed, why wasn't he relieved? And why was he shaking his head at his mother?

"Who were they?" I asked warily.

"Marcus isn't sure."

That was odd, given a vampire's preternaturally sharp sense of smell. "Was it humans?"

"No." We were back to the monosyllabic answers.

"I'll get my things." I turned toward the stairs.

"You aren't coming. You're staying here." Matthew's words brought me to a standstill.

"I'd rather be in Oxford," I protested, "with you."

"Oxford's not safe at the moment. I'll be back when it is."

"You just told me we should return there! Make up your mind, Matthew. Where is the danger? The manuscript and the witches? Peter Knox and the Congregation? Or Domenico Michele and the vampires?"

"Were you listening? *I* am the danger." Matthew's voice was sharp.

"Oh, I heard you. But you're keeping something from me. It's a historian's job to uncover secrets," I promised him softly. "And I'm very good at it." He opened his mouth to speak, but I stopped him. "No more excuses or false explanations. Go to Oxford. I'll stay here."

"Do you need anything from upstairs?" Ysabeau asked. "You should take a coat. Humans will notice if you're wearing only a sweater."

"Just my computer. My passport's in the bag."

"I'll get them." Wanting a respite from all the de Clermonts for a moment, I pelted up the stairs. In Matthew's study I looked around the room that held so much of him.

The armor's silvery surfaces winked in the firelight, holding my attention while a jumble of faces flashed through my mind, the visions as swift as comets through the sky. There was a pale woman with enormous blue eyes and a sweet smile, another woman whose firm chin and square shoulders exuded determination, a man with a hawkish nose in terrible pain. There were other faces, too, but the only one I recognized was Louisa de Clermont, holding dripping, bloody fingers in front of her face.

Resisting the vision's pull helped the faces fade, but it left my body shaking and my mind bewildered. The DNA report had indicated that visions were likely to come. But there'd been no more warning of their arrival than there had been last night when I floated in Matthew's arms. It was as if someone had pulled the stopper on a bottle and my magic—released at last—was rushing to get out.

Once I was able to jerk the cord from the socket I slid it into Matthew's bag, along with the computer. His passport was in the front pocket, as he'd said it would be.

When I returned to the salon, Matthew was alone, his keys in his hands and a suede barn jacket draped across his shoulders. Marthe muttered and paced in the great hall.

I handed him his computer and stood far away to better resist the urge to touch him once more. Matthew pocketed his keys and took the bag.

"I know this is hard." His voice was hushed and strange. "But you need to let me take care of it. And I need to know that you're safe while I'm doing that."

"I'm safe with you, wherever we are."

He shook his head. "My name should have been enough to protect you. It wasn't."

"Leaving me isn't the answer. I don't understand all of what's happened today, but Domenico's hatred goes beyond me. He wants to destroy your family and everything else you care about. Domenico might decide this isn't the right time to pursue his vendetta. But Peter Knox? He wants Ashmole 782, and he thinks I can get it for him. He won't be put off so easily." I shivered.

"He'll make a deal if I offer him one."

"A deal? What do you have to trade?"

The vampire fell silent.

"Matthew?" I insisted.

"The manuscript," he said flatly. "I'll leave it—and you—alone if he promises the same. Ashmole 782 has been undisturbed for a century and a half. We'll let it remain that way."

"You can't make a deal with Knox. He can't be trusted." I was horrified. "Besides, you have all the time you need to wait for the manuscript. Knox doesn't. Your deal won't appeal to him."

"Just leave Knox to me," he said gruffly.

My eyes snapped with anger. "Leave Domenico to you. Leave Knox to you. What do you imagine *I'm* going to do? You said I'm not a damsel in distress. So stop treating me like one."

"I suppose I deserved that," he said slowly, his eyes black, "but you have a lot to learn about vampires."

"So your mother tells me. But you may have a few things to learn about witches, too." I pushed the hair out of my eyes and crossed my arms over my chest. "Go to Oxford. Sort out what happened there." *Whatever happened that you won't share with me.* "But for God's sake, Matthew, don't negotiate with Peter Knox. Decide how *you* feel about *me*—not because of what the covenant forbids, or the Congregation wants, or even what Peter Knox and Domenico Michele make you afraid of."

My beloved vampire, with a face that would make an angel envious, looked at me with sorrow. "You know how I feel about you."

I shook my head. "No, I don't. When you're ready, you'll tell me."

Matthew struggled with something and left it unsaid. Wordlessly he walked toward the door into the hall. When he reached it, he gave me a long look of snowflakes and frost before walking through.

Marthe met him in the hall. He kissed her softly on both cheeks and said something in rapid Occitan.

"*Compreni, compreni,*" she said, nodding vehemently and looking past him at me.

"*Mercés amb tot meu còr,*" he said quietly.

"*Al rebèire. Mèfi.*"

"*T'afortissi.*" Matthew turned to me. "And you'll promise me the same thing—that you'll be careful. Listen to Ysabeau."

He left without a glance or a final, reassuring touch.

I bit my lip and tried to swallow the tears, but they spilled out. After three slow steps toward the watchtower stairs, my feet began to run, tears streaming down my face. With a look of understanding, Marthe let me go.

When I came out into the cold, damp air, the de Clermont standard was snapping gently to and fro and the clouds continued to obscure the moon. Darkness pressed on me from every direction, and the one creature who kept it at bay was leaving, taking the light with him.

Peering down over the tower's ramparts, I saw Matthew standing by the Range Rover, talking furiously to Ysabeau. She looked shocked and grabbed the sleeve of his jacket as if to stop him from getting in the car.

His hand was a white blur as he pulled his arm free. His fist pounded, once, into the car's roof. I jumped. Matthew had never used his strength on anything bigger than a walnut or an oyster shell when he was around me, and the dent he'd left in the metal was alarmingly deep.

He hung his head. Ysabeau touched him lightly on the cheek, his sad features gleaming in the dim light. He climbed into the car and said a few more words. His mother nodded and looked briefly at the watchtower. I stepped back, hoping neither of them had seen me. The car turned over, and its heavy tires crunched across the gravel as Matthew pulled away.

The Range Rover's lights disappeared below the hill. With Matthew gone, I slid down the stone wall of the keep and gave in to the tears.

It was then that I discovered what witchwater was all about.

Chapter 23

Before I met Matthew, there didn't seem to be room in my life for a single additional element—especially not something as significant as a fifteen-hundred-year-old vampire. But he'd slipped into unexplored, empty places when I wasn't looking.

Now that he'd left, I was terribly aware of his absence. As I sat on the roof of the watchtower, my tears softened my determination to fight for him. Soon there was water everywhere. I was sitting in a puddle of it, and the level just kept rising.

It wasn't raining, despite the cloudy skies.

The water was coming out of me.

My tears fell normally but swelled as they dropped into globules the size of snowballs that hit the stone roof of the watchtower with a splash. My hair snaked over my shoulders in sheets of water that poured over the curves of my body. I opened my mouth to take a breath because the water streaming down my face was blocking my nose, and water gushed out in a torrent that tasted of the sea.

Through a film of moisture, Marthe and Ysabeau watched me. Marthe's face was grim. Ysabeau's lips were moving, but the roar of a thousand seashells made it impossible to hear her.

I stood, hoping the water would stop. It didn't. I tried to tell the two women to let the water carry me away along with my grief and the memory of Matthew—but all that produced was another gush of ocean. I reached out, thinking that would help the water drain from me. Even more water cascaded from my fingertips. The gesture reminded me of my mother's arm reaching toward my father, and the waves increased.

As the water poured forth, my control slipped further. Domenico's sudden appearance had frightened me more than I'd been willing to admit. Matthew was gone. And I had vowed to fight for him against enemies I couldn't identify and didn't understand. It was now clear that Matthew's past was not composed simply of homely elements of firelight, wine, and books. Nor had it unfolded solely within the limits of a loyal family. Domenico had alluded to something darker that was full of enmity, danger, and death.

Exhaustion overtook me, and the water pulled me under. A strange sense of exhilaration accompanied the fatigue. I was poised between mortality and something elemental that held within it the promise of a vast, incomprehensible power. If I surrendered to the undertow, there would be no more Diana Bishop. Instead I would become water—nowhere, everywhere, free of my body and the pain.

"I'm sorry, Matthew." My words were nothing more than a burble as the water began its inexorable work.

Ysabeau stepped toward me, and a sharp crack sounded in my brain. My warning to her was lost in a roar like a tidal wave coming ashore. The winds rose around my feet, whipping the water into a hurricane. I raised my arms to the sky, water and wind shaping themselves into a funnel that encircled my body.

Marthe grabbed Ysabeau's arm, her mouth moving rapidly. Matthew's mother tried to pull away, her own mouth shaping the word "no," but Marthe held on, staring at her fixedly. After a few moments, Ysabeau's shoulders slumped. She turned toward me and started to sing. Haunting and yearning, her voice penetrated the water and called me back to the world.

The winds began to die down. The de Clermont standard, which had been whipping around, resumed its gentle swaying. The cascade of water from my fingertips slowed to a river, then to a trickle, and stopped entirely. The waves flowing from my hair subsided into swells, and then they, too, disappeared. At last nothing came out of my mouth but a gasp of surprise. The balls of water falling from my eyes were the last vestige of the witchwater to disappear, just as they had been the first sign of its power moving through me. The remains of my deluge sluiced toward small holes at the base of the crenellated walls. Far, far below, water splashed onto the courtyard's thick bed of gravel.

When the last of the water left me, I felt scooped out like a pumpkin, and freezing cold, too. My knees buckled, banging painfully on the stone.

"Thank God," Ysabeau murmured. "We almost lost her."

I was shaking violently from exhaustion and cold. Both women flew at me and lifted me to my feet. They each gripped an elbow and supported me down the curving flight of stairs with a speed that made me shiver. Once in the hall, Marthe headed toward Matthew's rooms and Ysabeau pulled in the opposite direction.

"Mine are closer," Matthew's mother said sharply.

"She will feel safer closer to him," Marthe said.

With a sound of exasperation, Ysabeau conceded.

At the bottom of Matthew's staircase, Ysabeau blurted out a string of colorful phrases that sounded totally incongruous coming from her delicate mouth. "I'll carry her," she said when she was finished cursing her son, the forces of nature, the powers of the universe, and many other unspecified individuals of questionable parentage who'd taken part in building the tower. Ysabeau lifted my much larger body easily. "Why he had to make these stairs so twisting—and in two separate flights—is beyond my understanding."

Marthe tucked my wet hair into the crook of Ysabeau's elbow and shrugged. "To make it harder, of course. He has always made things harder. For him. For everyone else, too."

No one had thought to come up in the late afternoon to light the candles, but the fire still smoldered and the room retained some of its warmth. Marthe disappeared into the bathroom, and the sound of running water made me examine my fingers with alarm. Ysabeau threw two enormous logs onto the grate as if they were kindling, snapping a long splinter off one before it caught. She stirred the coals into flames with it and then used it to light a dozen candles in the space of a few seconds. In their warm glow, she surveyed me anxiously from head to foot.

"He will never forgive me if you become ill," she said, picking up my hands and examining my nails. They were bluish again, but not from electricity. Now they were blue with cold and wrinkled from witchwater. She rubbed them vigorously between her palms.

Still shaking so much that my teeth were chattering, I withdrew my hands to hug myself in an attempt to conserve what little warmth was left in my body. Ysabeau picked me up again without ceremony and swept me into the bathroom.

"She needs to be in there now," Ysabeau said brusquely. The room was full of steam, and Marthe turned from the bath to help strip off my clothes. Soon I was naked and the two of them were lifting me into the hot water, one cold, vampiric hand in each armpit. The shock of the water's heat on my frigid skin was extreme. Crying out, I struggled to pull myself from Matthew's deep bathtub.

"Shh," Ysabeau said, holding my hair away from my face while Marthe pushed me back into the water. "It will warm you. We must get you warm."

Marthe stood sentinel at one end of the tub, and Ysabeau remained at the other, whispering soothing sounds and humming softly under her breath. It was a long time before the shaking stopped.

At one point Marthe murmured something in Occitan that included the name Marcus.

Ysabeau and I said no at the same moment.

"I'll be fine. Don't tell Marcus what happened. Matthew mustn't know about the magic. Not now," I said through chattering teeth.

"We just need some time to warm you." Ysabeau sounded calm, but she looked concerned.

Slowly the heat began to reverse the changes the witchwater had worked on my body. Marthe kept adding fresh hot water to the tub as my body cooled it down. Ysabeau grabbed a beat-up tin pitcher from under the window and dipped it into the bath, pouring hot water over my head and shoulders. Once my head was warm, she wrapped it in a towel and pushed me slightly lower in the water.

"Soak," she commanded.

Marthe bustled between the bathroom and the bedroom, carrying clothes and towels. She tutted over my lack of pajamas and the old yoga clothes I'd brought to sleep in. None of them met her requirements for warmth.

Ysabeau felt my cheeks and the top of my head with the back of her hand. She nodded.

They let me get myself out of the tub. The water falling off my body reminded me of the watchtower roof, and I dug my toes into the floor to resist the element's insidious pull.

Marthe and Ysabeau bundled me into towels fresh from the fireside that smelled faintly of wood smoke. In the bedroom they somehow managed to dry me without ever exposing an inch of my flesh to the air, rolling me this way and that inside the towels until I could feel heat radiating from my body. Rough strokes of another towel scratched against my hair before Marthe's fingers raked through the strands and twisted them into a tight braid against my scalp. Ysabeau tossed the damp towels onto a chair near the fire as I shed them to dress, seemingly unconcerned by their contact with antique wood and fine upholstery.

Now fully clothed, I sat down and stared mindlessly at the fire. Marthe disappeared without a word into the lower regions of the château and returned with a tray of tiny sandwiches and a steaming pot of her herbal tea.

"You will eat. Now." It was not a request but a command.

I brought one of the sandwiches to my mouth and nibbled around the edges.

Marthe's eyes narrowed at this sudden change in my eating habits. "Eat."

The food tasted like sawdust, but my stomach rumbled nonetheless.

After I'd swallowed two of the tiny sandwiches, Marthe thrust a mug into my hands. She didn't need to tell me to drink. The hot liquid slid down my throat, carrying away the water's salty vestiges.

"Was that witchwater?" I shivered at the memory of all that water coming out of me.

Ysabeau, who had been standing by the window looking out into the darkness, walked toward the opposite sofa. "Yes," she said. "It has been a long time, though, since we have seen it come forth like that."

"Thank God that wasn't the usual way," I said faintly, swallowing another sip of tea.

"Most witches today are not powerful enough to draw on the witchwater as you did. They can make waves on ponds and cause rain when there are clouds. They do not become the water." Ysabeau sat across from me, studying me with evident curiosity.

I had become the water. Knowing that this was no longer common made me feel vulnerable—and even more alone.

A phone rang.

Ysabeau reached into her pocket and pulled out a small red phone that seemed uncharacteristically bright and high-tech against her pale skin and classic, buff-colored clothes.

"*Oui?* Ah, good. I am glad that you are there and safe." She spoke English out of courtesy to me and nodded in my direction. "Yes, she is fine. She is eating." She stood and handed me the phone. "Matthew would like to speak with you."

"Diana?" Matthew was barely audible.

"Yes?" I didn't trust myself to say much for fear that more than words would tumble out.

He made a soft sound of relief. "I just wanted to make sure you were all right."

"Your mother and Marthe are taking good care of me." *And I didn't flood the castle,* I thought.

"You're tired." The distance between us was making him anxious, and he was tuned into every nuance of our exchange.

"I am. It's been a long day."

"Sleep, then," he said, his tone unexpectedly gentle. My eyes closed against the sudden sting of tears. There would be little sleep for me tonight. I was too worried about what he might do in some half-baked, heroic attempt to protect me.

"Have you been to the lab?"

"I'm headed there now. Marcus wants me to go over everything carefully and make sure we've taken all the necessary precautions. Miriam's checked the security at the house as well." He told the half-truth with smooth conviction, but I knew it for what it was. The silence stretched out until it became uncomfortable.

"Don't do it, Matthew. Please don't try to negotiate with Knox."

"I'll make sure you're safe before you return to Oxford."

"Then there's nothing more to say. You've decided. So have I." I returned the phone to Ysabeau.

She frowned, her cold fingers pulling it from my grip. Ysabeau said good-bye to her son, his reply audible only as a staccato burst of unintelligible sound.

"Thank you for not telling him about the witchwater," I said quietly after she'd disconnected the line.

"That is your tale to tell, not mine." Ysabeau drifted toward the fireplace.

"It's no good trying to tell a story you don't understand. Why is the power coming out now? First it was the wind, then the visions, and now the water, too." I shuddered.

"What kinds of visions?" Ysabeau asked, her curiosity evident.

"Didn't Matthew tell you? My DNA has all this . . . *magic,*" I said, stumbling over the word, "in it. The tests warned there might be visions, and they've begun."

"Matthew would never tell me what your blood revealed—certainly not without your permission, and probably not with your permission either."

"I've seen them here in the château." I hesitated. "How did you learn to control them?"

"Matthew told you that I had visions before I became a vampire." Ysabeau shook her head. "He should not have."

"Were you a witch?" That might explain why she disliked me so much.

"A witch? No. Matthew wonders if I was a daemon, but I'm sure I was an ordinary human. They have their visionaries, too. It's not only creatures who are blessed and cursed in this way."

"Did you ever manage to control your second sight and anticipate it?"

"It gets easier. There are warning signs. They can be subtle, but you will learn. Marthe helped me as well."

It was the only piece of information I had about Marthe's past. Not for the first time, I wondered how old these two women were and what workings of fate had brought them together.

Marthe stood with her arms crossed. "*Òc,*" she said, giving Ysabeau a tender, protective look. "It is easier if you let the visions move through you without fighting."

"I'm too shocked to fight," I said, thinking back to the salon and the library.

"Shock is your body's way of resisting," Ysabeau said. "You must try to relax."

"It's difficult to let go when you see knights in armor and the faces of women you've never met mixed up with scenes from your own past." My jaw cracked with a yawn.

"You are too exhausted to think about this now." Ysabeau rose to her feet.

"I'm not ready to sleep." I smothered another yawn with the back of my hand.

She eyed me speculatively, like a beautiful falcon scrutinizing a field mouse. Ysabeau's glance turned mischievous. "Get into bed, and I will tell you how I made Matthew."

Her offer was too tempting to resist. I did as she told me while she pulled up a chair and Marthe busied herself with dishes and towels.

"So where do I begin?" She drew herself straighter in the chair and stared into the candles' flames. "I cannot begin simply with my part of the story but must start with his birth, here in the village. I remember him as a baby, you know. His father and mother came when Philippe decided to build on this land back when Clovis was king. That's the only reason the village is here—it was where the farmers and craftsmen who built the church and castle lived."

"Why did your husband pick this spot?" I leaned against the pillows, my knees folded close to my chest under the bedclothes.

"Clovis promised him the land in hopes it would encourage Philippe to fight against the king's rivals. My husband was always playing both sides against the middle." Ysabeau smiled wistfully. "Very few people caught him at it, though."

"Was Matthew's father a farmer?"

"A farmer?" Ysabeau looked surprised. "No, he was a carpenter, as was Matthew—before he became a stonemason."

A mason. The tower's stones all fit together so smoothly they didn't seem to require mortar. And there were the oddly ornate chimneys at the Old Lodge gatehouse that Matthew just had to let some craftsman try his hand at constructing. His long, slender fingers were strong enough to twist open an oyster shell or crack a chestnut. Another piece of Matthew fell into place, fitting perfectly next to the warrior, the scientist, and the courtier.

"And they both worked on the château?"

"Not this château," Ysabeau said, looking around her. "This was a present from Matthew, when I was sad over being forced to leave a place that I loved. He tore down the fortress his father had built and replaced it with a new one." Her green-and-black eyes glittered with amusement. "Philippe was furious. But it was time for a change. The first château was made of wood, and even though there had been stone additions over the years, it was a bit ramshackle."

My mind tried to take in the time line of events, from the construction of the first fortress and its village in the sixth century to Matthew's tower in the thirteenth century.

Ysabeau's nose crinkled in distaste. "Then he stuck this tower onto the back when he returned home and didn't want to live so close to the family. I never liked it—it seemed a romantic trifle—but it was his wish, and I let him." She shrugged. "Such a funny tower. It didn't help defend the castle. He had already built far more towers here than we needed."

Ysabeau continued to spin her tale, seeming only partially in the twenty-first century.

"Matthew was born in the village. He was always such a bright child, so curious. He drove his father mad, following him to the château and picking up tools and sticks and stones. Children learned their trades early then, but Matthew was precocious. By the time he could hold a hatchet without injuring himself, he was put to work."

An eight-year-old Matthew with gangly legs and gray-green eyes ran around the hills in my imagination.

"Yes." She smiled, agreeing with my unspoken thoughts. "He was indeed a beautiful child. A beautiful young man as well. Matthew was unusually tall for the time, though not as tall as he became once he was a vampire.

"And he had a wicked sense of humor. He was always pretending that something had gone wrong or that instructions had not been given to him regarding this roof beam or that foundation. Philippe never failed to believe the tall tales Matthew told him." Ysabeau's voice was indulgent. "Matthew's first father died when he was in his late teens, and his first mother had been dead for years by then. He was alone, and we worried about him finding a woman to settle down with and start a family.

"And then he met Blanca." Ysabeau paused, her look level and without malice. "You cannot have imagined that he was without the love of women." It was a statement, not a question. Marthe shot Ysabeau an evil look but kept quiet.

"Of course not," I said calmly, though my heart felt heavy.

"Blanca was new to the village, a servant to one of the master masons Philippe had brought in from Ravenna to construct the first church. She was as pale as her name suggested, with white skin, eyes the color of a spring sky, and hair that looked like spun gold."

A pale, beautiful woman had appeared in my visions when I went to fetch Matthew's computer. Ysabeau's description of Blanca fit her perfectly.

"She had a sweet smile, didn't she?" I whispered.

Ysabeau's eyes widened. "Yes, she did."

"I know. I saw her when Matthew's armor caught the light in his study."

Marthe made a warning sound, but Ysabeau continued.

"Sometimes Blanca seemed so delicate that I feared she would break when drawing water from the well or picking vegetables. My Matthew was drawn to that delicacy, I suppose. He has always liked fragile things." Ysabeau's eyes flicked over my far-from-fragile form. "They were married when Matthew turned twenty-five and could support a family. Blanca was just nineteen.

"They were a beautiful couple, of course. There was such a strong contrast between Matthew's darkness and Blanca's pale prettiness. They were very much in love, and the marriage was a happy one. But they could not seem to have children. Blanca had miscarriage after miscarriage. I cannot imagine what it was like inside their house, to see so many children of your body die before they drew breath." I wasn't sure if vampires could cry, though I remembered the bloodstained tear on Ysabeau's cheek from my earlier visions in the salon. Even without the tears, however, she looked now as though she were weeping, her face a mask of regret.

"Finally, after so many years of trying and failing, Blanca was with child. It was 531. Such a year. There was a new king to the south, and the battles had started all over again. Matthew began to look happy, as if he dared to hope this baby would survive. And it did. Lucas was born in the autumn and was baptized in the unfinished church that Matthew was helping to build. It was a hard birth for Blanca. The midwife said that he would be the last child she bore. For Matthew, though, Lucas was enough. And he was so like his father, with his black curls and pointed chin—and those long legs."

"What happened to Blanca and Lucas?" I asked softly. We were only six years from Matthew's transformation into a vampire. Something must have happened, or he would never have let Ysabeau exchange his life for a new one.

"Matthew and Blanca watched their son grow and thrive. Matthew had learned to work in stone rather than wood, and he was in high demand among the lords from here to Paris. Then fever came to the village. Everyone fell ill. Matthew survived. Blanca and Lucas did not. That was in 536. The year before had been strange, with very little sunshine, and the winter was cold. When spring came, the sickness came, too, and carried Blanca and Lucas away."

"Didn't the villagers wonder why you and Philippe remained healthy?"

"Of course. But there were more explanations then than there would be today. It was easier to think God was angry with the village or that the castle was cursed than to think that the *manjasang* were living among them."

"*Manjasang*?" I tried to roll the syllables around my mouth as Ysabeau had.

"It is the old tongue's word for vampire—'blood eater.' There were those who suspected the truth and whispered by the fireside. But in those days the return of the Ostrogoth warriors was a far more frightening prospect than a *manjasang* overlord. Philippe promised the village his protection if the raiders came back. Besides, we made it a point never to feed close to home," she explained primly.

"What did Matthew do after Blanca and Lucas were gone?"

"He grieved. Matthew was inconsolable. He stopped eating. He looked like a skeleton, and the village came to us for help. I took him food"—Ysabeau smiled at Marthe—"and made him eat and walked with him until he wasn't so restless. When he could not sleep, we went to church and prayed for the souls of Blanca and Lucas. Matthew was very religious in those days. We talked about heaven and hell, and he worried about where their souls were and if he would be able to find them again."

Matthew was so gentle with me when I woke up in terror. Had the nights before he'd become a vampire been as sleepless as those that came after?

"By autumn he seemed more hopeful. But the winter was difficult. People were hungry, and the sickness continued. Death was everywhere. The spring could not lift the gloom. Philippe was anxious about the church's progress, and Matthew worked harder than ever. At the beginning of the second week in June, he was found on the floor beneath its vaulted ceiling, his legs and back broken."

I gasped at the thought of Matthew's soft, human body plummeting to the hard stones.

"There was no way he could survive the fall, of course," Ysabeau said softly. "He was a dying man. Some of the masons said he'd slipped. Others said he was standing on the scaffolding one moment and gone the next. They thought Matthew had jumped and were already talking about how he could not be buried in the church because he was a suicide. I could not let him die fearing he might not be saved from hell. He was so worried about being with Blanca and Lucas—how could he go to his death wondering if he would be separated from them for all eternity?"

"You did the right thing." It would have been impossible for me to walk away from him no matter what the state of his soul. Leaving his body broken and hurting was unthinkable. If my blood would have saved him, I would have used it.

"Did I?" Ysabeau shook her head. "I have never been sure. Philippe told me it was my decision whether to make Matthew one of our family. I had made other vampires with my blood, and I would make others after him. But Matthew was different. I was fond of him, and I knew that the gods were giving me a chance to make him my child. It would be my responsibility to teach him how a vampire must be in the world."

"Did Matthew resist you?" I asked, unable to stop myself.

"No," she replied. "He was out of his mind with pain. We told everyone to leave, saying we would fetch a priest. We didn't, of course. Philippe and I went to Matthew and explained we could make him live forever, without pain, without suffering. Much later Matthew told us that he thought we were John the Baptist and the Blessed Mother come to take him to heaven to be with his wife and child. When I offered him my blood, he thought I was the priest offering him last rites."

The only sounds in the room were my quiet breathing and the crackle of logs in the fireplace. I wanted Ysabeau to tell me the particulars of how she had made Matthew, but I was afraid to ask in case it was something that vampires didn't talk about. Perhaps it was too private, or too painful. Ysabeau soon told me without prompting.

"He took my blood so easily, like he was born to it," she said with a rustling sigh. "Matthew was not one of those humans who turn their face from the scent or sight. I opened my wrist with my own teeth and told him my blood would heal him. He drank his salvation without fear."

"And afterward?" I whispered.

"Afterward he was . . . difficult," Ysabeau said carefully. "All new vampires are strong and full of hunger, but Matthew was almost impossible to control. He was in a rage at being a vampire, and his need to feed was endless. Philippe and I had to hunt all day for weeks to satisfy him. And his body changed more than we expected. We all get taller, finer, stronger. I was much smaller before I became a vampire. But Matthew developed from a reed-thin human into a formidable creature. My husband was larger than my new son, but in the first flush of my blood Matthew was a handful even for Philippe."

I forced myself not to shrink from Matthew's hunger and rage. Instead my eyes remained fixed on his mother, not closing my eyes for an instant against the knowledge of him. This was what Matthew feared, that I would come to understand who he had been—who he still was—and feel revulsion.

"What calmed him?" I asked.

"Philippe took him hunting," Ysabeau explained, "once he thought that Matthew would no longer kill everything in his path. The hunt engaged his mind, and the chase engaged his body. He soon craved the hunt more than the blood, which is a good sign in young vampires. It meant he was no longer a creature of pure appetite but was once again rational. After that, it was only a matter of time before his conscience returned and he began to think before he killed. Then all we had to fear were his black periods, when he felt the loss of Blanca and Lucas again and turned to humans to dull his hunger."

"Did anything help Matthew then?"

"Sometimes I sang to him—the same song I sang to you tonight, and others as well. That often broke the spell of his grief. Other times Matthew would go away. Philippe forbade me to follow or to ask questions when he returned." Ysabeau's eyes were black as she looked at me. Our glances confirmed what we both suspected: that Matthew had been lost with other women, seeking solace in their blood and the touch of hands that belonged to neither his mother nor his wife.

"He's so controlled," I mused aloud, "it's hard to imagine him like that."

"Matthew feels deeply. It is a blessing as well as a burden to love so much that you can hurt so badly when love is gone."

There was a threat in Ysabeau's voice. My chin went up in defiance, my fingers tingling. "Then I'll have to make sure my love never leaves him," I said tightly.

"And how will you do that?" Ysabeau taunted. "Would you become a vampire, then, and join us in our hunting?" She laughed, but there was neither joy nor mirth in the sound. "No doubt that's what Domenico suggested. One simple bite, the draining of your veins, the exchange of our blood for yours. The Congregation would have no grounds to intrude on your business then."

"What do you mean?" I asked numbly.

"Don't you see?" Ysabeau snarled. "If you must be with Matthew, then become one of us and put him—and yourself—out of danger. The witches may want to keep you as their own, but they cannot object to your relationship if you are a vampire, too."

A low rumble started in Marthe's throat.

"Is that why Matthew went away? Did the Congregation order him to make me a vampire?"

"Matthew would never make you a *manjasang,*" Marthe said scornfully, her eyes snapping with fury.

"No." Ysabeau's voice was softly malicious. "He has always loved fragile things, as I told you."

This was one of the secrets that Matthew was keeping. If I were a vampire, there would be no prohibitions looming over us and thus no reason to fear the Congregation. All I had to do was become something else.

I contemplated the prospect with surprisingly little panic or fear. I could be with Matthew, and I might even be taller. Ysabeau would do it. Her eyes glittered as she took in the way my hand moved to my neck.

But there were my visions to consider, not to mention the power of the wind and the water. I didn't yet understand the magical potential in my blood. And as a vampire I might never solve the mystery of Ashmole 782.

"I promised him," Marthe said, her voice rough. "Diana must stay as she is—a witch."

Ysabeau bared her teeth slightly, unpleasantly, and nodded.

"Did you also promise not to tell me what really happened in Oxford?"

Matthew's mother scrutinized me closely. "You must ask Matthew when he returns. It is not my tale to tell."

I had other questions as well—questions that Matthew might have been too distracted to mark as off-limits.

"Can you tell me why it matters that it was a creature who tried to break in to the lab, rather than a human?"

There was silence while Ysabeau considered my words. Finally, she replied.

"Clever girl. I did not promise Matthew to remain silent about appropriate rules of conduct, after all." She looked at me with a touch of approval. "Such behavior is not acceptable among creatures. We must hope it was a mischievous daemon who does not realize the seriousness of what he has done. Matthew might forgive that."

"He has always forgiven daemons," Marthe muttered darkly.

"What if it wasn't a daemon?"

"If it was a vampire, it represents a terrible insult. We are territorial creatures. A vampire does not cross into another vampire's house or land without permission."

"Would Matthew forgive such an insult?" Given the look on Matthew's face when he'd thrown a punch at the car, I suspected that the answer was no.

"Perhaps," Ysabeau said doubtfully. "Nothing was taken, nothing was harmed. But it is more likely Matthew would demand some form of retribution."

Once more I'd been dropped into the Middle Ages, with the maintenance of honor and reputation the primary concern.

"And if it was a witch?" I asked softly.

Matthew's mother turned her face away. "For a witch to do such a thing would be an act of aggression. No apology would be adequate."

Alarm bells sounded.

I flung the covers aside and swung my legs out of bed. "The break-in was meant to provoke Matthew. He went to Oxford thinking he could make a good-faith deal with Knox. We have to warn him."

Ysabeau's hands were firm on my knees and shoulder, stopping my motion.

"He already knows, Diana."

That information settled in my mind. "Is that why he wouldn't take me to Oxford with him? Is *he* in danger?"

"Of course he is in danger," Ysabeau said sharply. "But he will do what he can to put an end to this." She lifted my legs back onto the bed and tucked the covers tightly around me.

"I should be there," I protested.

"You would be nothing but a distraction. You will stay here, as he told you."

"Don't I get a say in this?" I asked for what seemed like the hundredth time since I came to Sept-Tours.

"No," both women said at the same moment.

"You really do have a lot to learn about vampires," Ysabeau said once again, but this time she sounded mildly regretful.

I had a lot to learn about vampires. This I knew.

But who was going to teach me? And when?

Chapter 24

"From afar I beheld a black cloud covering the earth. It absorbed the earth and covered my soul as the seas entered, becoming putrid and corrupted at the prospect of hell and the shadow of death. A tempest had overwhelmed me,'" I read aloud from Matthew's copy of *Aurora Consurgens.*

Turning to my computer, I typed notes about the imagery my anonymous author had used to describe *nigredo,* one of the dangerous steps in alchemical transformation. During this part of the process, the combination of substances like mercury and lead gave off fumes that endangered the alchemist's health. Appropriately, one of Bourgot Le Noir's gargoylelike faces pinched his nose tight shut, avoiding the cloud mentioned in the text.

"Get your riding clothes on."

My head lifted from the pages of the manuscript.

"Matthew made me promise to take you outdoors. He said it would keep you from getting sick," Ysabeau explained.

"You don't have to, Ysabeau. Domenico and the witchwater have depleted my adrenaline supply, if that's your concern."

"Matthew must have told you how alluring the smell of panic is to a vampire."

"Marcus told me," I corrected her. "Actually, he told me what it tastes like. What does it smell like?"

Ysabeau shrugged. "Like it tastes. Maybe a bit more exotic—a touch of muskiness, perhaps. I was never much drawn to it. I prefer the kill to the hunt. But to each her own."

"I'm not having as many panic attacks these days. There's no need for you to take me riding." I turned back to my work.

"Why do you think they have gone away?" Ysabeau asked.

"I honestly don't know," I said with a sigh, looking at Matthew's mother.

"You have been like this for a long time?"

"Since I was seven."

"What happened then?"

"My parents were killed in Nigeria," I replied shortly.

"This was the picture you received—the one that caused Matthew to bring you to Sept-Tours."

When I nodded in response, Ysabeau's mouth flattened into a familiar, hard line. "Pigs."

There were worse things to call them, but "pigs" did the job pretty well. And if it grouped whoever had sent me the photograph with Domenico Michele, then it was the right category.

"Panic or no panic," Ysabeau said briskly, "we are going to exercise as Matthew wanted."

I powered off the computer and went upstairs to change. My riding clothes were folded neatly in the bathroom, courtesy of Marthe, though my boots were in the stables, along with my helmet and vest. I slithered into the black breeches, added a turtleneck, and slipped on loafers over a pair of warm socks, then went downstairs in search of Matthew's mother.

"I'm in here," she called. I followed the sound to a small room painted warm terra-cotta. It was ornamented with old plates, animal horns, and an ancient dresser large enough to store an entire inn's worth of plates, cups, and cutlery. Ysabeau peered over the pages of *Le Monde,* her eyes covering every inch of me. "Marthe tells me you slept."

"Yes, thank you," I shifted from one foot to the other as if waiting to see the school principal to explain my misbehavior.

Marthe saved me from further discomfort by arriving with a pot of tea. She, too, surveyed me from head to foot.

"You are better today," she finally announced, handing me a mug. She stood there frowning until Matthew's mother put down her paper, and then she departed.

When I was finished with my tea, we went to the stables. Ysabeau had to help with my boots, since they were still too stiff to slide on and off easily, and she watched carefully while I put on my turtle shell of a vest and the helmet. Clearly safety equipment had been part of Matthew's instructions. Ysabeau, of course, wore nothing more protective than a brown quilted jacket. The relative indestructibility of vampire flesh was a boon if you were a rider.

In the paddock Fiddat and Rakasa stood side by side, mirror images right down to the armchair-style saddles on their backs.

"Ysabeau," I protested, "Georges put the wrong tack on Rakasa. I don't ride sidesaddle."

"Are you afraid to try?" Matthew's mother looked at me appraisingly.

"No!" I said, tamping down my temper. "I just prefer to ride astride."

"How do you know?" Her emerald eyes flickered with a touch of malice.

We stood for a few moments, staring at each other. Rakasa stamped her hoof and looked over her shoulder.

Are you going to ride or talk? she seemed to be asking.

Behave, I replied brusquely, walking over and putting her fetlock against my knee.

"Georges has seen to this," Ysabeau said in a bored tone.

"I don't ride horses I haven't checked myself." I examined Rakasa's hooves, ran my hands over her reins, and slid my fingers under the saddle.

"Philippe never did either." Ysabeau's voice held a note of grudging respect. With poorly concealed impatience, she watched me finish. When I was done, she led Fiddat over to a set of steps and waited for me to follow. After she'd helped me get into the strange contraption of a saddle, she hopped onto her own horse. I took one look at her and knew I was in for quite a morning. Judging from her seat, Ysabeau was a better rider than Matthew—and he was the best I'd ever seen.

"Walk around," Ysabeau said. "I need to make sure you won't fall off and kill yourself."

"Show a little faith, Ysabeau." *Don't let me fall,* I bargained with Rakasa, *and I'll make sure you get an apple a day for the rest of your life.* My mount's ears shot forward, then back, and she nickered gently. We circled the paddock twice before I drew to a gentle stop in front of Matthew's mother. "Satisfied?"

"You're a better rider than I expected," she admitted. "You could probably jump, but I promised Matthew we would not."

"He managed to wheedle a fair number of promises out of you before he left," I muttered, hoping she wouldn't hear me.

"Indeed," she said crisply, "some of them harder to keep than others."

We passed through the open paddock gate. Georges touched his cap to Ysabeau and shut the gate behind us, grinning and shaking his head.

Matthew's mother kept us on relatively flat ground while I got used to the strange saddle. The trick was to keep your body square despite how off-kilter you felt.

"This isn't too bad," I said after about twenty minutes.

"It is better now that the saddles have two pommels," Ysabeau said. "Before, all sidesaddles were good for was being led around by a man." Her disgust was audible. "It was not until the Italian queen put a pommel and stirrup on her saddle that we could control our own horses. Her husband's mistress rode astride so she could go with him when he exercised. Catherine was always being left at home, which is most unpleasant for a wife." She shot me a withering glance. "Henry's whore was named after the goddess of the hunt, like you."

"I wouldn't have crossed Catherine de' Medici." I shook my head.

"The king's mistress, Diane de Poitiers, was the dangerous one," Ysabeau said darkly. "She was a witch."

"Actually or metaphorically?" I asked with interest.

"Both," Matthew's mother said in a tone that could strip paint. I laughed. Ysabeau looked surprised, then joined in.

We rode a bit farther. Ysabeau sniffed the air and sat taller in the saddle, her face alert.

"What is it?" I asked anxiously, keeping Rakasa under a tight rein.

"Rabbit." She kicked Fiddat into a canter. I followed closely, reluctant to see if it was as difficult to track a witch in the forest as Matthew had suggested.

We streaked through the trees and out into the open field. Ysabeau held Fiddat back, and I pulled alongside her.

"Have you ever seen a vampire kill?" Ysabeau asked, watching my reaction carefully.

"No," I said calmly.

"Rabbits are small. That's where we will begin. Wait here." She swung out of the saddle and dropped lightly to the ground. Fiddat stood obediently, watching her mistress. "Diana," she said sharply, never taking her eyes off her prey, "do not come near me while I'm hunting or feeding. Do you understand?"

"Yes." My mind raced at the implications. Ysabeau was going to chase down a rabbit, kill it, and drink its blood in front of me? Staying far away seemed an excellent suggestion.

Matthew's mother darted across the grassy field, moving so fast it was impossible to keep her in focus. She slowed just as a falcon does in midair before it swoops in for the kill, then bent and grabbed a frightened rabbit by the ears. Ysabeau held it up triumphantly before sinking her teeth directly into its heart.

Rabbits may be small, but they are surprisingly bloody if you bite into them while they're still alive. It was horrifying. Ysabeau sucked the blood out of the animal, which quickly ceased struggling, then wiped her mouth clean on its fur and tossed its carcass into the grass. Three seconds later she was swinging herself back into the saddle. Her cheeks were slightly flushed, and her eyes sparkled more than usual. Once mounted, she looked at me.

"Well?" she asked. "Shall we look for something more filling, or do you need to return to the house?"

Ysabeau de Clermont was testing me.

"After you," I said grimly, touching Rakasa's flank with my heel.

The remainder of our ride was measured not by the movement of the sun, which was still hidden behind clouds, but by the increasing amounts of blood Ysabeau's hungry mouth drew from her kills. She was a relatively neat eater. Still, it would be some time before I was happy at the prospect of a large steak.

I was numb to the sight of blood after the rabbit, the enormous squirrel-like creature that Ysabeau told me was a marmot, the fox, and the wild goat—or so I thought. When Ysabeau gave chase to a young doe, however, something prickled inside me.

"Ysabeau," I protested. "You can't still be hungry. Leave it."

"What? The goddess of the hunt objects to my pursuit of her deer?" Her voice mocked, but her eyes were curious.

"Yes," I said promptly.

"I object to your hunting of my son. See what good that has done." Ysabeau swung down from her horse.

My fingers itched to intervene, and it was all I could do to stay out of Ysabeau's way while she stalked her prey. After each kill, her eyes revealed that she wasn't completely in command of her emotions—or her actions.

The doe tried to escape. It almost succeeded by darting into some underbrush, but Ysabeau frightened the animal back into the open. After that, fatigue put the doe at a disadvantage. The chase touched off something visceral within me. Ysabeau killed swiftly, and the doe didn't suffer, but I had to bite my lip to keep from shouting.

"There," she said with satisfaction, returning to Fiddat. "We can go back to Sept-Tours."

Wordlessly I turned Rakasa's head in the direction of the château.

Ysabeau grabbed my horse's reins. There were tiny drops of blood on her cream shirt. "Do you think vampires are beautiful now? Do you still think it would be easy to live with my son, knowing that he must kill to survive?"

It was difficult for me to put "Matthew" and "killing" in the same sentence. Were I to kiss him one day, when he was just returned from hunting, there might still be the taste of blood on his lips. And days like the one I was now spending with Ysabeau would be regular occurrences.

"If you're trying to frighten me away from your son, Ysabeau, you failed," I said resolutely. "You're going to have to do better than this."

"Marthe said this would not be enough to make you reconsider," she confessed.

"She was right." My voice was curt. "Is the trial over? Can we go home now?"

We rode toward the trees in silence. Once we were within the forest's leafy green confines, Ysabeau turned to me. "Do you understand why you must not question Matthew when he tells you to do something?"

I sighed. "School is over for the day."

"Do you think our dining habits are the only obstacle standing between you and my son?"

"Spit it out, Ysabeau. Why must I do what Matthew says?"

"Because he is the strongest vampire in the château. He is the head of the house."

I stared at her in astonishment. "Are you saying I have to listen to him because he's the alpha dog?"

"You think *you* are?" Ysabeau chortled.

"No," I conceded. Ysabeau wasn't the alpha dog either. She did what Matthew told her to do. So did Marcus, Miriam, and every vampire at the Bodleian Library. Even Domenico had ultimately backed down. "Are these the de Clermont pack rules?"

Ysabeau nodded, her green eyes glittering. "It is for your safety—and his, and everyone else's—that you must obey. This is not a game."

"I understand, Ysabeau." I was losing my patience.

"No, you don't," she said softly. "You won't either, until you are forced to see, just as I made you see what it is for a vampire to kill. Until then these are only words. One day your willfulness will cost your life, or someone else's. Then you will know why I told you this."

We returned to the château without further conversation. When we passed through Marthe's ground-floor domain, she came out of the kitchen, a small chicken in her hands. I blanched. Marthe took in the tiny spots of blood on Ysabeau's cuffs and gasped.

"She needs to know," Ysabeau hissed.

Marthe said something low and foul-sounding in Occitan, then nodded at me. "Here, girl, come with me and I will teach you to make my tea."

Now it was Ysabeau's turn to look furious. Marthe made me something to drink and handed me a plate with a few crumbly biscuits studded with nuts. Eating chicken was out of the question.

Marthe kept me busy for hours, sorting dried herbs and spices into tiny piles and teaching me their names. By midafternoon I could identify them by smell with my eyes closed as well as by appearance.

"Parsley. Ginger. Feverfew. Rosemary. Sage. Queen Anne's lace seeds. Mugwort. Pennyroyal. Angelica. Rue. Tansy. Juniper root." I pointed to each in turn.

"Again," Marthe said serenely, handing me a bunch of muslin bags.

I picked the strings apart, laying them individually on the table just as she did, reciting the names back to her one more time.

"Good. Now fill the bags with a pinch of each."

"Why don't we just mix it all together and spoon it into the bags?" I asked, taking a bit of pennyroyal between my fingers and wrinkling my nose at its minty smell.

"We might miss something. Each bag must have every single herb—all twelve."

"Would missing a tiny seed like this really make a difference to the taste?" I held a tiny Queen Anne's lace seed between my index finger and thumb.

"One pinch of each," Marthe repeated. "Again."

The vampire's experienced hands moved surely from pile to pile, neatly filling the bags and tightening their strings. After we finished, Marthe brewed me a cup of tea using a bag I'd filled myself.

"It's delicious," I said, happily sipping my very own herbal tea.

"You will take it back to Oxford with you. One cup a day. It will keep you healthy." She started putting bags into a tin. "When you need more, you will know how to make it."

"Marthe, you don't have to give me all of it," I protested.

"You will drink this for Marthe, one cup a day. Yes?"

"Of course." It seemed the least I could do for my sole remaining ally in the house—not to mention the person who fed me.

After my tea I went upstairs to Matthew's study and switched on my computer. All that riding had made my forearms ache, so I moved the computer and manuscript to his desk, hoping that it might be more comfortable to work there rather than at my table by the window. Unfortunately, the leather chair was made for someone Matthew's height, not mine, and my feet swung freely.

Sitting in Matthew's chair made him seem closer, however, so I remained there while waiting for my computer to boot up. My eyes fell on a dark object tucked into the tallest shelf. It blended into the wood and the books' leather bindings, which hid it from casual view. From Matthew's desk, however, you could see its outlines.

It wasn't a book but an ancient block of wood, octagonal in shape. Tiny arched windows were carved into each side. The thing was black, cracked, and misshapen with age.

With a pang of sadness, I realized it was a child's toy.

Matthew had made it for Lucas before Matthew became a vampire, while he was building the first church. He'd tucked it into the corner of a shelf where no one would notice it—except him. He couldn't fail to see it, every time he sat at his desk.

With Matthew at my side, it was all too easy to think we were the only two in the world. Not even Domenico's warnings or Ysabeau's tests had shaken my sense that our growing closeness was a matter solely between him and me.

But this little wooden tower, made with love an unimaginably long time ago, brought my illusions to an end. There were children to consider, both living and dead. There were families involved, including my own, with long and complicated genealogies and deeply ingrained prejudices, including my own. And Sarah and Em still didn't know that I was in love with a vampire. It was time to share that news.

Ysabeau was in the salon, arranging flowers in a tall vase on top of a priceless Louis XIV escritoire with impeccable provenance—and a single owner.

"Ysabeau?" My voice sounded hesitant. "Is there a phone I could use?"

"He will call you when he wants to talk to you." She took great care placing a twig with turning leaves still attached to it among the white and gold flowers.

"I'm not calling Matthew, Ysabeau. I need to speak to my aunt."

"The witch who called the other night?" she asked. "What is her name?"

"Sarah," I said with a frown.

"And she lives with a woman—another witch, yes?" Ysabeau kept putting white roses into the vase.

"Yes. Emily. Is that a problem?"

"No," Ysabeau said, eyeing me over the blooms. "They are both witches. That's all that matters."

"That and they love each other."

"Sarah is a good name," Ysabeau continued, as if I hadn't spoken. "You know the legend, of course."

I shook my head. Ysabeau's changes in conversation were almost as dizzying as her son's mood swings.

"The mother of Isaac was called Sarai—'quarrelsome'—but when God told her she would have a child, He changed it to Sarah, which means 'princess.'"

"In my aunt's case, Sarai is much more appropriate." I waited for Ysabeau to tell me where the phone was.

"Emily is also a good name, a strong, Roman name." Ysabeau clipped a rose stem between her sharp fingernails.

"What does Emily mean, Ysabeau?" Happily I was running out of family members.

"It means 'industrious.' Of course, the most interesting name belonged to your mother. Rebecca means 'captivated,' or 'bound,'" Ysabeau said, a frown of concentration on her face as she studied the vase from one side and then the other. "An interesting name for a witch."

"And what does your name mean?" I said impatiently.

"I was not always Ysabeau, but it was the name Philippe liked for me. It means 'God's promise.'" Ysabeau hesitated, searching my face, and made a decision. "My full name is Geneviève Mélisande Hélène Ysabeau Aude de Clermont."

"It's beautiful." My patience returned as I speculated about the history behind the names.

Ysabeau gave me a small smile. "Names are important."

"Does Matthew have other names?" I took a white rose from the basket and handed it to her. She murmured her thanks.

"Of course. We give all of our children many names when they are reborn to us. But Matthew was the name he came to us with, and he wanted to keep it. Christianity was very new then, and Philippe thought it might be useful if our son were named after an evangelist."

"What are his other names?"

"His full name is Matthew Gabriel Philippe Bertrand Sébastien de Clermont. He was also a very good Sébastien, and a passable Gabriel. He hates Bertrand and will not answer to Philippe."

"What is it about Philippe that bothers him?"

"It was his father's favorite name." Ysabeau's hands stilled for a moment. "You must know he is dead. The Nazis caught him fighting for the Resistance."

In the vision I'd had of Ysabeau, she'd said Matthew's father was captured by witches.

"Nazis, Ysabeau, or witches?" I asked quietly, fearing the worst.

"Did Matthew tell you?" Ysabeau looked shocked.

"No. I saw you in one of my visions yesterday. You were crying."

"Witches and Nazis both killed Philippe," she said after a long pause. "The pain is recent, and sharp, but it will fade in time. For years after he was gone I hunted only in Argentina and Germany. It kept me sane."

"Ysabeau, I'm so sorry." The words were inadequate, but they were heartfelt. Matthew's mother must have heard my sincerity, and she gave me a hesitant smile.

"It is not your fault. You were not there."

"What names would you give me if you had to choose?" I asked softly, handing another stem to Ysabeau.

"Matthew is right. You are only Diana," she said, pronouncing it in the French style as she always did, with the emphasis on the first syllable. "There are no other names for you. It is who you are." Ysabeau pointed her white finger at the door to the library. "The phone is inside."

Seated at the desk in the library, I switched on the lamp and dialed New York, hoping that both Sarah and Em were home.

"Diana." Sarah sounded relieved. "Em said it was you."

"I'm sorry I couldn't call back last night. A lot happened." I picked up a pencil and began to twirl it through my fingers.

"Would you like to talk about it?" Sarah asked. I almost dropped the phone. My aunt demanded we talk about things—she never *requested*.

"Is Em there? I'd rather tell the story once."

Em picked up the extension, her voice warm and comforting. "Hi, Diana. Where are you?"

"With Matthew's mother near Lyon."

"Matthew's mother?" Em was curious about genealogy. Not just her own, which was long and complicated, but everyone else's, too.

"Ysabeau de Clermont." I did my best to pronounce it as Ysabeau did, with its long vowels and swallowed consonants. "She's something, Em. Sometimes I think she's the reason humans are so afraid of vampires. Ysabeau's straight out of a fairy tale."

There was a pause. "Do you mean you're with *Mélisande* de Clermont?" Em's voice was intense. "I didn't even think of the de Clermonts when you told me about Matthew. You're sure her name is Ysabeau?"

I frowned. "Actually, her name is Geneviève. I think there's a Mélisande in there, too. She just prefers Ysabeau."

"Be careful, Diana," Em warned. "Mélisande de Clermont is notorious. She hates witches, and she ate her way through most of Berlin after World War II."

"She has good reason to hate witches," I said, rubbing my temples. "I'm surprised she let me into her house." If the situation was reversed, and vampires were involved in my parents' death, I wouldn't be so forgiving.

"What about the water?" Sarah interjected. "I'm more worried about the vision Em had of a tempest."

"Oh. I started raining last night after Matthew left." The soggy memory made me shiver.

"Witchwater," Sarah breathed, now understanding. "What brought it on?"

"I don't know, Sarah. I felt . . . empty. When Matthew pulled out of the driveway, the tears I'd been fighting since Domenico showed up all just poured out of me."

"Domenico who?" Emily flipped through her mental roster of legendary creatures again.

"Michele—a Venetian vampire." My voice filled with anger. "And if he bothers me again, I'm going to rip his head off, vampire or not."

"He's dangerous!" Em cried. "That creature doesn't play by the rules."

"I've been told that many times over, and you can rest easy knowing I'm under guard twenty-four hours a day. Don't worry."

"We'll worry until you're no longer hanging around with vampires," Sarah observed.

"You'll be worrying for a good long time, then," I said stubbornly. "I love Matthew, Sarah."

"That's impossible, Diana. Vampires and witches—" Sarah began.

"Domenico told me about the covenant," I interjected. "I'm not asking anyone else to break it, and I understand that this might mean you can't or won't have anything to do with me. For me there's no choice."

"But the Congregation will do what they must to end this relationship," Em said urgently.

"I've been told that, too. They'll have to kill me to do it." Until this moment I hadn't said the words out loud, but I'd been thinking them since last night. "Matthew's harder to get rid of, but I'm a pretty easy target."

"You can't just walk into danger that way." Em was fighting back tears.

"Her mother did," Sarah said quietly.

"What about my mother?" My voice broke at the mention of her, along with my composure.

"Rebecca walked straight into Stephen's arms even though people said it was a bad idea for two witches with their talents to be together. And she refused to listen when people told her to stay out of Nigeria."

"All the more reason that Diana should listen now," Em said. "You've only known him for a few weeks. Come back home and see if you can forget about him."

"*Forget* about him?" It was ridiculous. "This isn't a crush. I've never felt this way about anyone."

"Leave her alone, Em. We've had enough of that kind of talk in this family. I didn't forget about you, and she's not going to forget about him." Sarah let out her breath with a sigh that carried all the way to the Auvergne. "This may not be the life I would have chosen for you, but we all have to decide for ourselves. Your mother did. I did—and your grandmother did not have an easy time with it, by the way. Now it's your turn. But no Bishop ever turns her back on another Bishop."

Tears stung my eyes. "Thank you, Sarah."

"Besides," Sarah continued, working herself into a state, "if the Congregation is made up of *things* like Domenico Michele, then they can all go to hell."

"What does Matthew say about this?" Em asked. "I'm surprised he would leave you once you two had decided to break with a thousand years of tradition."

"Matthew hasn't told me how he feels yet." I methodically unbent a paper clip.

There was dead silence on the line.

Finally Sarah spoke. "What is he waiting for?"

I laughed out loud. "You've done nothing but warn me to stay away from Matthew. Now you're upset because he refuses to put me in greater danger than I'm already in?"

"You want to be with him. That should be enough."

"This isn't some kind of magical arranged marriage, Sarah. I get to make my decision. So does he." The tiny clock with the porcelain face that was sitting on the desk indicated it had been twenty-four hours since he left.

"If you're determined to stay there, with those creatures, then be careful," Sarah warned as we said good-bye. "And if you need to come home, come home."

After I hung up, the clock struck the half hour. It was already dark in Oxford.

To hell with waiting. I lifted the receiver again and dialed his number.

"Diana?" He was clearly anxious.

I laughed. "Did you know it was me, or was it caller ID?"

"You're all right." The anxiety was replaced with relief.

"Yes, your mother is keeping me vastly entertained."

"I was afraid of that. What lies has she been telling you?"

The more trying parts of the day could wait. "Only the truth," I said. "That her son is some diabolical combination of Lancelot and Superman."

"That sounds like Ysabeau," he said with a hint of laughter. "What a relief to know that she hasn't been irreversibly changed by sleeping under the same roof as a witch."

Distance no doubt helped me evade him with my half-truths. Distance couldn't diminish my vivid picture of his sitting in his Morris chair at All Souls, however. The room would be glowing from the lamps, and his skin would look like polished pearl. I imagined him reading, the deep crease of concentration between his brows.

"What are you drinking?" It was the only detail my imagination couldn't supply.

"Since when have you cared about wine?" He sounded genuinely surprised.

"Since I found out how much there was to know." *Since I found out that you cared about wine, you idiot.*

"Something Spanish tonight—Vega Sicilia."

"From when?"

"Do you mean which vintage?" Matthew teased. "It's 1964."

"A relative baby, then?" I teased back, relieved at the change in his mood.

"An infant," he agreed. I didn't need a sixth sense to know that he was smiling.

"How did everything go today?"

"Fine. We've increased our security, though nothing was missing. Someone tried to hack into the computers, but Miriam assures me there's no way anyone could break into her system."

"Are you coming back soon?" The words escaped before I could stop them, and the ensuing silence stretched longer than was comfortable. I told myself it was the connection.

"I don't know," he said coolly. "I'll be back when I can."

"Do you want to talk to your mother? I could find her for you." His sudden aloofness hurt, and it was a struggle to keep my voice even.

"No, you can tell her the labs are fine. The house, too."

We said good-bye. My chest was tight, and it was difficult to inhale. When I managed to stand and turn around, Matthew's mother was waiting in the doorway.

"That was Matthew. Nothing at the lab or the house was damaged. I'm tired, Ysabeau, and not very hungry. I think I'll go to bed." It was nearly eight, a perfectly respectable time to turn in.

"Of course." Ysabeau stepped out of my way with glittering eyes. "Sleep well, Diana."

Chapter 25

Marthe had been up to Matthew's study while I was on the phone, and sandwiches, tea, and water were waiting for me. She'd loaded the fireplace with logs to burn through the night, and a handful of candles shed their golden glow. The same inviting light and warmth upstairs would be in the bedroom, too, but my mind would not shut off, and trying to sleep would be futile. The *Aurora* manuscript was waiting for me on Matthew's desk. Sitting down at my computer, I avoided the sight of his winking armor and switched on his space-age, minimalist desk light to read.

"I spoke aloud: Give me knowledge of my end and the measure of my days, so I may know my frailty. My lifetime is no longer than the width of my hand. It is only a moment, compared to yours."

The passage only made me think of Matthew.

Trying to concentrate on alchemy was pointless, so I decided to make a list of queries regarding what I'd already read. All that was needed was a pen and a piece of paper.

Matthew's massive mahogany desk was as dark and solid as its owner, and it exuded the same gravitas. It had drawers extending down both sides of the space left for his knees, the drawers resting on round, bun-shaped feet. Just below the writing surface, running all around the perimeter, was a thick band of carving. Acanthus leaves, tulips, scrolls, and geometrical shapes invited you to trace their outlines. Unlike the surface of my desk—which was always piled so high with papers, books, and half-drunk cups of tea that you risked disaster whenever you tried to work on it—this desk held only an Edwardian desk pad, a sword-shaped letter opener, and the lamp. Like Matthew, it was a bizarrely harmonious blend of ancient and modern.

There were, however, no office supplies in sight. I grasped the round brass pull on the top right-hand drawer. Inside, everything was neat and precisely arranged. The Montblanc pens were segregated from the Montblanc pencils, and the paper clips were arranged by size. After selecting a pen and putting it on the desk, I attempted to open the remaining drawers. They were locked. The key wasn't underneath the paper clips—I dumped them on the desk, just to be sure.

An unmarked sheet of pale green blotting paper stretched between the desk pad's leather bumpers. In lieu of a legal pad, that would have to do. Picking up my computer to clear the desk, I knocked the pen to the floor.

It had fallen under the drawers and was just out of reach. I crawled into the desk's kneehole to retrieve it. Worming my hand under the drawers, my fingers found the thick barrel just as my eyes spotted the outline of a drawer in the dark wood above.

Frowning, I wriggled out from under the desk. There was nothing in the deep carving circling the desktop that released the catch on the concealed drawer. Leave it to Matthew to stash basic supplies in a drawer that was difficult to open. It would serve him right if every inch of his blotter was covered with graffiti when he returned home.

I wrote the number 1 in thick black ink on the green paper. Then I froze.

A desk drawer that was difficult to find was designed to hide something.

Matthew kept secrets—this I knew. But we had known each other only a few weeks, and even the closest of lovers deserved privacy. Still, Matthew's tight-lipped manner was infuriating, and his secrets surrounded him like a fortress devised to keep other people—me—out.

Besides, I only needed a piece of paper. Hadn't he riffled through my belongings at the Bodleian when he was looking for Ashmole 782? We'd barely met when he pulled that stunt. And he had left me to shift for myself in France.

As I carefully recapped the pen, my conscience nevertheless prickled. But my sense of injury helped me to cast that warning aside.

Pushing and pulling at every bump and bulge, my fingers searched the carvings on the desk's front edge once more without success. Matthew's letter opener rested invitingly near my right hand. It might be possible to wedge it into the seam underneath and pry the drawer open. Given the age of the desk, the historian in me squawked—much louder than my conscience had. Violating Matthew's privacy and engaging in ethically questionable behavior might be permissible, but I wasn't going to deface an antique.

Under the desk once more, I found it was too dark to see the underside of the drawer clearly, but my fingers located something cold and hard embedded in the wood. To the left of the drawer's nearly imperceptible join was a small metal bump approximately one long vampire reach from the front of the desk. It was round and had cross-hatching in the center—to make it look like a screw or an old nail head.

There was a soft click overhead when I pushed it.

Standing, I stared into a tray about four inches deep. It was lined with black velvet, and there were three depressions in the thick padding. Each held a bronze coin or medal.

The largest one had a building's outline cut into its surface and rested in the midst of a hollow nearly four inches across. The image was surprisingly detailed and showed four steps leading up to a door flanked by two columns. Between them was a shrouded figure. The building's crisp outlines were marred by fragments of black wax. Around the edge of the coin were the words "*militie Lazari a Bethania.*"

The knights of Lazarus of Bethany.

Gripping the tray's edges to steady myself, I abruptly sat down.

The metal disks weren't coins or medals. They were seals—the kind used to close official correspondence and certify property transactions. A wax impression attached to an ordinary piece of paper could once have commanded armies to leave the field or auctioned off great estates.

Based on the residue, at least one seal had been used recently.

Fingers shaking, I pried one of the smaller disks from the tray. Its surface bore a copy of the same building. The columns and the shrouded figure of Lazarus—the man from Bethany whom Christ raised from the dead after he'd been entombed for four days—were unmistakable. Here Lazarus was depicted stepping out of a shallow coffin. But no words encircled this seal. Instead the building was surrounded by a snake, its tail in its mouth.

I couldn't close my eyes quickly enough to banish the sight of the de Clermont family standard and its silver ouroboros snapping in the breeze above Sept-Tours.

The seal lay in my palm, its bronze surfaces gleaming. I focused on the shiny metal, willing my new visionary power to shed light on the mystery. But I'd spent more than two decades ignoring the magic in my blood, and it felt no compunction to come to my aid now.

Without a vision, my mundane historical skills would have to be put to work. I examined the back of the small seal closely, taking in its details. A cross with flared edges divided the seal into quarters, similar to the one Matthew had worn on his tunic in my vision. In the upper right quadrant of the seal was a crescent moon, its horns curved upward and a six-pointed star nestled in its belly. In the lower left quadrant was a fleur-de-lis, the traditional symbol of France.

Inscribed around the edge of the seal was the date MDCI—1601 in

Roman numerals—along with the words *"secretum Lazari"*—"the secret of Lazarus."

It couldn't be a coincidence that Lazarus, like a vampire, had made the journey from life to death and back again. Moreover, the cross, combined with a legendary figure from the Holy Land and the mention of knights, strongly suggested that the seals in Matthew's desk drawer belonged to one of the orders of Crusader knights established in the Middle Ages. The best known were the Templars, who had mysteriously disappeared in the early fourteenth century after being accused of heresy and worse. But I'd never heard of the Knights of Lazarus.

Turning the seal this way and that to catch the light, I focused on the date 1601. It was late for a medieval chivalric order. I searched my memory for important events of that year that might shed light on the mystery. Queen Elizabeth I beheaded the Earl of Essex, and the Danish astronomer Tycho Brahe died under far less colorful circumstances. Neither of these events seemed remotely relevant.

My fingers moved lightly over the carving. The meaning of MDCI washed over me.

Matthew de Clermont.

These were letters, not Roman numerals. It was an abbreviation of Matthew's name: MDCl. I was misreading the final letter.

The two-inch disk sat in my palm, and my fingers closed firmly around it, pressing the incised surface deep into the skin.

This smaller disk must have been Matthew's private seal. The power of such seals was so great that they were usually destroyed when someone died or left office so that no one else could use them to commit fraud.

And only one knight would have both the great seal and a personal seal in his possession: the order's leader.

Why Matthew kept the seals hidden puzzled me. Who cared about or even remembered the Knights of Lazarus, never mind his onetime role in the order? My attention was captured by the black wax on the great seal.

"It's not possible," I whispered numbly, shaking my head. Knights in shining armor belonged to the past. They weren't active today.

The Matthew-size suit of armor gleamed in the candlelight.

I dropped the metal disk into the drawer with a clatter. The flesh of my palm had poured into the impressions and now carried its image, right down to its flared cross, crescent moon and star, and fleur-de-lis.

The reason Matthew had the seals, and the reason fresh wax clung to one of them, was that they were still in use. The Knights of Lazarus were still in existence.

"Diana? Are you all right?" Ysabeau's voice echoed up from the foot of the stairs.

"Yes, Ysabeau!" I called, staring at the seal's image on my hand. "I'm reading my e-mail and got some unexpected news, that's all!"

"Shall I send Marthe up for the tray?"

"No!" I blurted. "I'm still eating."

Her footsteps receded toward the salon. When there was complete silence, I let out my breath.

Moving as quickly and quietly as possible, I flipped the other seal over in its velvet-lined niche. It was nearly identical to Matthew's, except that the upper right quadrant held only the crescent moon and *"Philippus"* was inscribed around the border.

This seal had belonged to Matthew's father, which meant that the Knights of Lazarus were a de Clermont family affair.

Certain there would be no more clues about the order in the desk, I turned the seals so that Lazarus's tomb was facing me once more. The drawer made a hushed click as it slid invisibly into position underneath the desk.

I picked up the table that Matthew used to hold his afternoon wine and carried it over to the bookcases. He wouldn't mind me looking through his library—or so I told myself, kicking off my loafers. The table's burnished surface gave a warning creak when I swung my feet onto it and stood, but the wood held fast.

The wooden toy at the far right of the top shelf was at eye level now. I sucked in a deep breath and pulled out the first item from the opposite end. It was ancient—the oldest manuscript I'd ever handled. The leather cover complained when it opened, and the smell of old sheepskin rose from the pages.

"Carmina qui quondam studio florente peregi, / Flebilis heu maestos cogor inire modos" read the first lines. My eyes pricked with tears. It was Boethius's sixth-century work, *The Consolation of Philosophy,* written in prison while he was awaiting death. *"To pleasant songs my work was once given, and bright were all my labors then; / But now in tears to sad refrains I must return."* I imagined Matthew, bereft of Blanca and Lucas and bewildered by his new identity as a vampire, reading words written by a condemned man. Giving

silent thanks to whoever had offered him this in hope of lessening his grief, I slid the book back into place.

The next volume was a beautifully illustrated manuscript of Genesis, the biblical story of creation. Its strong blues and reds looked as fresh as the day they had been painted. Another illustrated manuscript, this one a copy of Dioscorides' book of plants, was also on the top shelf, along with more than a dozen other biblical books, several law books, and a book in Greek.

The shelf below held more of the same—books of the Bible mostly, along with a medical book and a very early copy of a seventh-century encyclopedia. It represented Isidore of Seville's attempt to capture all of human knowledge, and it would have appealed to Matthew's endless curiosity. At the bottom of the first folio was the name "*MATHIEU,*" along with the phrase "*meus liber*"—"my book."

Feeling the same urge to trace the letters as when I faced Ashmole 782 in the Bodleian, my fingers faltered on their way to the surface of the vellum. Then I'd been too afraid of the reading-room supervisors and my own magic to risk it. Now it was fear of learning something unexpected about Matthew that held me back. But there was no supervisor here, and my fears became insignificant when weighed against my desire to understand the vampire's past. I traced Matthew's name. An image of him, sharp and clear, came to me without the use of stern commands or shining surfaces.

He was seated at a plain table by a window, looking just as he did now, biting his lip with concentration as he practiced his writing. Matthew's long fingers gripped a reed pen, and he was surrounded by sheets of vellum, all of which bore repeated blotchy attempts to write his own name and copy out biblical passages. Following Marthe's advice, I didn't fight the vision's arrival or departure, and the experience was not as disorienting as it had been last night.

Once my fingers had revealed all they could, I replaced the encyclopedia and continued working my way through the remaining volumes in the case. There were history books, more law books, books on medicine and optics, Greek philosophy, books of accounts, the collected works of early church notables like Bernard of Clairvaux, and chivalric romances—one involving a knight who changed into a wolf once a week. But none revealed fresh information about the Knights of Lazarus. I bit back a sound of frustration and climbed down from the table.

My knowledge of Crusader orders was sketchy. Most of them started out as military units that were renowned for bravery and discipline. The Templars were famous for being the first to enter the field of battle and the last to leave. But the orders' military efforts were not limited to the area around Jerusalem. The knights fought in Europe, too, and many answered only to the pope rather than to kings or other secular authorities.

Nor was the power of the chivalric orders solely military. They'd built churches, schools, and leper hospitals. The military orders safeguarded Crusader interests, whether spiritual, financial, or physical. Vampires like Matthew were territorial and possessive to the last, and therefore ideally suited to the role of guardians.

But the power of the military orders led ultimately to their downfall. Monarchs and popes were jealous of their wealth and influence. In 1312 the pope and the French king saw to it that the Templars were disbanded, ridding themselves of the threat posed by the largest, most prestigious brotherhood. Most of the other orders gradually petered out due to lack of support and interest.

There were all those conspiracy theories, of course. A vast, complex international institution is hard to dismantle overnight, and the sudden dissolution of the Knights Templar had led to all sorts of fantastic tales about rogue Crusaders and underground operations. People still searched for traces of the Templars' fabulous wealth. The fact that no one had ever found evidence of how it was disbursed only added to the intrigue.

The money. It was one of the first lessons historians learned: follow the money. I refocused my search.

The sturdy outlines of the first ledger were visible on the third shelf, tucked between Al-Hazen's *Optics* and a romantic French chanson de geste. A small Greek letter was inked on the manuscript's fore edge: α. Figuring it must be an indexing mark of some sort, I scanned the shelves and located the second account book. It, too, had a small Greek letter, β. My eyes lit on γ, δ, and ε, scattered among the shelves, too. A more careful search would locate the rest, I was sure.

Feeling like Eliot Ness waving a fistful of tax receipts in pursuit of Al Capone, I held up my hand. There was no time to waste on climbing to retrieve it. The first account book slid from its resting place and fell into my waiting palm.

Its entries were dated 1117 and were made by a number of different hands. Names and numbers danced across the pages. My fingers were busy, taking in all the information they could from the writing. A few faces bloomed out of the vellum repeatedly—Matthew, the dark man with the hawkish nose, a man with bright hair the color of burnished copper, another with warm brown eyes and a serious face.

My hands stilled over an entry for money received in 1149. "*Eleanor Regina, 40,000 marks.*" It was a staggering sum—more than half the yearly income of the kingdom of England. Why was the queen of England giving so much to a military order led by vampires? But the Middle Ages were too far outside my expertise for me to be able to answer that question or to know much about the people engaging in the transfers. I shut the book with a snap and went to the sixteenth- and seventeenth-century bookcases.

Nestled among the other books was a volume bearing the identifying mark of a Greek lambda. My eyes widened once it was open.

Based on this ledger, the Knights of Lazarus had paid—somewhat unbelievably—for a wide range of wars, goods, services, and diplomatic feats, including providing Mary Tudor's dowry when she married Philip of Spain, buying the cannon for the Battle of Lepanto, bribing the French so they'd attend the Council of Trent, and financing most of the military actions of the Lutheran Schmalkaldic League. Apparently the brotherhood didn't allow politics or religion to get in the way of their investment decisions. In a single year, they'd bankrolled Mary Stuart's return to the Scottish throne and paid off Elizabeth I's sizable debts to the Antwerp Bourse.

I walked along the shelves looking for more books marked with Greek letters. On the nineteenth-century shelves, there was one with the forked letter psi on its faded blue buckram spine. Inside, vast sums of money were meticulously accounted for, along with property sales that made my head spin—how did one secretly purchase most of the factories in Manchester?—and familiar names belonging to royalty, aristocrats, presidents, and Civil War generals. There were also smaller payouts for school fees, clothing allowances, and books, along with entries concerning dowries paid, hospital bills settled, and past-due rents brought up to date. Next to all the unfamiliar names was the abbreviation "MLB" or "FMLB."

My Latin was not as good as it should be, but I was sure the abbreviations stood for the Knights of Lazarus of Bethany—*militie Lazari a Bethania*—or for *filia militie* or *filius militie,* the daughters and sons of the knights. And if the order was still disbursing funds in the middle of the nineteenth century, the same was probably true today. Somewhere in the world, a piece of paper—a real-estate transaction, a legal agreement—bore an impression of the order's great seal in thick, black wax.

And Matthew had applied it.

Hours later I was back in the medieval section of Matthew's library and opened my last account book. This volume spanned the period from the late thirteenth century to the first half of the fourteenth century. The staggering sums were now expected, but around 1310 the number of entries increased dramatically. So, too, did the flow of money. A new annotation accompanied some of the names: a tiny red cross. In 1313, next to one of these marks, was a name I recognized: Jacques de Molay, the last grand master of the Knights Templar.

He'd been burned at the stake for heresy in 1314. A year before he was executed, he'd turned over everything he owned to the Knights of Lazarus.

There were hundreds of names marked with red crosses. Were they all Templars? If so, then the mystery of the Templars was solved. The knights and their money hadn't disappeared. Both had simply been absorbed into the order of Lazarus.

It couldn't be true. Such a thing would have taken too much planning and coordination. And no one could have kept such a grand scheme secret. The idea was as implausible as stories about—

Witches and vampires.

The Knights of Lazarus were no more or less believable than I was.

As for conspiracy theories, their chief weakness was that they were so complex. No lifetime was sufficient to gather the necessary information, build the links between all the required elements, and then set the plans in motion. Unless, of course, the conspirators were vampires. If you were a vampire—or, better yet, a family of vampires—then the passage of time would matter little. As I knew from Matthew's scholarly career, vampires had all the time they needed.

The enormity of what it meant to love a vampire struck home as I slid the account book back onto the shelf. It was not just his age that posed the difficulties, or his dining habits, or the fact that he had killed humans and would do so again. It was the secrets.

Matthew had been accumulating secrets—large ones like the Knights of Lazarus and his son Lucas, small ones like his relationships with William Harvey and Charles Darwin—for well over a millennium. My life might be too brief to hear them all, never mind understand them.

But it was not only vampires who kept secrets. All creatures learned to do so out of fear of discovery and to preserve something—anything—just for ourselves within our clannish, almost tribal, world. Matthew was not simply a hunter, a killer, a scientist, or a vampire, but a web of secrets, just as I was. For us to be together, we needed to decide which secrets to share and then let the others go.

The computer chimed in the quiet room when my finger pressed the power button. Marthe's sandwiches were dry and the tea was cold, but I nibbled so that she wouldn't think her efforts had gone unappreciated.

Finished, I sat back and stared into the fire. The Knights of Lazarus roused me as a historian, and my witch's instincts told me the brotherhood was important to understanding Matthew. But their existence was not his most important secret. Matthew was guarding himself—his innermost nature.

What a complicated, delicate business it was going to be to love him. We were the stuff of fairy tales—vampires, witches, knights in shining armor. But there was a troubling reality to face. I had been threatened, and creatures watched me in the Bodleian in hopes I'd recall a book that everyone wanted but no one understood. Matthew's laboratory had been targeted. And our relationship was destabilizing the fragile détente that had long existed among daemons, humans, vampires, and witches. This was a new world, in which creatures were pitted against creatures and a silent, secret army could be called into action by a stamp in a pool of black wax. It was no wonder that Matthew might prefer to put me aside.

I snuffed the candles and climbed the stairs to bed. Exhausted, I quickly drifted off, my dreams filled with knights, bronze seals, and endless books of accounts.

A cold, slender hand touched my shoulder, waking me instantly.

"Matthew?" I sat bolt upright.

Ysabeau's white face glimmered in the darkness. "It's for you." She handed me her red mobile and left the room.

"Sarah?" I was terrified that something had happened to my aunts.

"It's all right, Diana."

Matthew.

"What's happened?" My voice shook. "Did you make a deal with Knox?"

"No. I can't make any progress there. There's nothing left for me in Oxford. I want to be home, with you. I should be there in a few hours." He sounded strange, his voice thick.

"Am I dreaming?"

"You're not dreaming," Matthew said. "And, Diana?" He hesitated. "I love you."

It was what I most wanted to hear. The forgotten chain inside me started to sing, quietly, in the dark.

"Come here and tell me that," I said softly, my eyes filling with tears of relief.

"You haven't changed your mind?"

"Never," I said fiercely.

"You'll be in danger, and your family, too. Are you willing to risk that, for my sake?"

"I made my choice."

We said good-bye and hung up reluctantly, afraid of the silence that would follow after so much had been said.

While he was gone, I had stood at a crossroads, unable to see a way forward.

My mother had been known for her uncanny visionary abilities. Would she have been powerful enough to see what awaited us as we took our first steps, together?

Chapter 26

I'd been waiting for the crunch of tires on gravel since pushing the disconnect button on Ysabeau's tiny mobile phone—and since then it hadn't been out of my sight.

A fresh pot of tea and breakfast rolls were waiting for me when I emerged from the bathroom, phone in hand. I bolted the food, flung on the first clothes that my fingers touched, and flew down the stairs with wet hair. Matthew wouldn't reach Sept-Tours for hours, but I was determined to be waiting when he pulled up.

First I waited in the salon on a sofa by the fire, wondering what had happened in Oxford to make Matthew change his mind. Marthe brought me a towel and roughly dried my hair with it when I showed no inclination to use it myself.

As the time of his arrival grew nearer, pacing in the hall was preferable to sitting in the salon. Ysabeau appeared and stood with her hands on her hips. I continued, despite her forbidding presence, until Marthe brought a wooden chair to the front door. She convinced me to sit, though the chair's carving had clearly been designed to acquaint its occupants with the discomforts of hell, and Matthew's mother retreated to the library.

When the Range Rover entered the courtyard, I flew outside. For the first time in our relationship, Matthew didn't beat me to the door. He was still straightening his long legs when my arms locked around his neck, my toes barely touching the ground.

"Don't do that again," I whispered, my eyes shut against sudden tears. "Don't ever do that again."

Matthew's arms went around me, and he buried his face in my neck. We held each other without speaking. Matthew reached up and loosened my grip, gently setting me back on my feet. He cupped my face, and familiar touches of snow and frost melted on my skin. I committed new details of his features to memory, such as the tiny creases at the corners of his eyes and the precise curve of the hollow under his full lower lip.

"*Dieu,*" he whispered in wonder, "I was wrong."

"Wrong?" My voice was panicky.

"I thought I knew how much I missed you. But I had no idea."

"Tell me." I wanted to hear again the words he'd said on the phone last night.

"I love you, Diana. God help me, I tried not to."

My face softened into his hands. "I love you, too, Matthew, with all my heart."

Something in his body altered subtly at my response. It wasn't his pulse, since he didn't have much of a pulse, nor his skin, which remained deliciously cool. Instead there was a sound—a catch in his throat, a murmur of longing that sent a shock of desire through me. Matthew detected it, and his face grew fierce. He bent his head, fitting his cold lips to mine.

The resulting changes in my body were neither slight nor subtle. My bones turned to fire, and my hands crept around his back and slid down. When he tried to draw away, I pulled his hips back toward me.

Not so fast, I thought.

His mouth hovered above mine in surprise. My hands slid lower, holding on to his backside possessively, and his breath caught again until it purred in his throat.

"Diana," he began, a note of caution in his voice.

My kiss demanded he tell me what the problem was.

Matthew's only answer was to move his mouth against mine. He stroked the pulse in my neck, then floated his hand down to cup my left breast, now stroking the fabric over the sensitive skin between my arm and my heart. With his other hand at my waist, he pulled me more tightly against him.

After a long while, Matthew loosened his hold enough that he could speak. "You are *mine* now."

My lips were too numb to reply, so I nodded and kept a firm grip on his backside.

He stared down at me. "Still no doubts?"

"None."

"We are one, from this moment forward. Do you understand?"

"I think so." I understood, at the very least, that no one and nothing was going to keep me from Matthew.

"She has no idea." Ysabeau's voice rang through the courtyard. Matthew stiffened, his arms circling me protectively. "With that kiss you have broken every rule that holds our world together and keeps us safe. Matthew, you have marked that witch as your own. And, Diana, you have offered your witch's blood—your power—to a vampire. You have turned your back on your own kind and pledged yourself to a creature who is your enemy."

"It was a kiss," I said, shaken.

"It was an oath. And having made this promise to each other, you are outlaws. May the gods help you both."

"Then we are outlaws," Matthew said quietly. "Should we leave, Ysabeau?" There was a vulnerable child's voice behind the man's, and something inside me broke for making him choose between us.

His mother strode forward and slapped him, hard, across the face. "How dare you ask that question?"

Mother and son both looked shocked. The mark of Ysabeau's slender hand stood out against Matthew's cheek for a split second—red, then blue—before it faded.

"You are my most beloved son," she continued, her voice as strong as iron. "And Diana is now my daughter—my responsibility as well as yours. Your fight is my fight, your enemies are my enemies."

"You don't have to shelter us, *Maman*." Matthew's voice was taut as a bowstring.

"Enough of that nonsense. You are going to be hounded to the ends of the earth because of this love you share. We fight as a family." Ysabeau turned to me. "As for you, daughter—you *will* fight, as you promised. You are reckless—the truly brave always are—but I cannot fault your courage. Still, you need him as much as you need the air you breathe, and he wants you as he's wanted nothing and no one since I made him. So it is done, and we will make the best of it." Ysabeau unexpectedly pulled me toward her and pressed her cold lips to my right cheek, then my left. I'd been living under the woman's roof for days, but this was my official welcome. She looked coolly at Matthew and made her real point.

"The way we will make the best of it begins with Diana behaving like a witch and not some pathetic human. The women of the de Clermont family defend themselves."

Matthew bristled. "I'll see that she's safe."

"This is why you are always losing at chess, Matthew." Ysabeau shook her finger at him. "Like Diana, the queen has almost unlimited power. Yet you insist on surrounding her and leaving yourself vulnerable. This is not a game, however, and her weakness puts us all at risk."

"Stay out of this, Ysabeau," Matthew warned. "Nobody is going to force Diana to be something she isn't."

His mother gave an elegant, expressive snort.

"Exactly. We are no longer going to let Diana force herself to be a human, which she is not. She is a witch. You are a vampire. If this was not true, we would not be in such a mess. Matthew, *mon cher*, if the witch is brave enough to want you, she has no reason to fear her own power. You could rip her apart if you wanted to. And so can the ones who will come for you when they realize what you have done."

"She's right, Matthew," I said.

"Come, we should go inside." He kept a wary eye on his mother. "You're cold, and we need to talk about Oxford. Then we'll tackle the subject of magic."

"I need to tell you what happened here, too." If this was going to work, we would have to reveal some of our secrets—such as the possibility that I might turn into running water at any moment.

"There's plenty of time for you to tell me everything," said Matthew, leading me toward the château.

Marthe was waiting for him when he walked through the door. She gave him a fierce hug, as if he'd returned in triumph from battle, and settled us all in front of the salon's blazing fire.

Matthew positioned himself next to me and watched me drink some tea. Every few moments he put his hand on my knee, or smoothed the sweater across my shoulders, or tucked a bit of hair back into place, as if trying to make up for his brief absence. Once he'd begun to relax, the questions began. They were innocently ordinary in the beginning. Soon the conversation turned to Oxford.

"Were Marcus and Miriam in the lab when the break-in was attempted?" I asked.

"They were," he said, taking a sip from the glass of wine Marthe had put beside him, "but the thieves didn't get far. The two of them weren't in any real danger."

"Thank God," Ysabeau murmured, staring at the fire.

"What were they looking for?"

"Information. About you," he said reluctantly. "Someone broke in to your rooms at New College as well."

There was one secret out in the open.

"Fred was horrified," Matthew continued. "He assured me they'll put new locks on your doors and a camera in your stairwell."

"It's not Fred's fault. With the new students, all you need to get past the porters is a confident step and a university scarf. But there was nothing for them to take! Were they after my research?" The mere thought of such a thing was ridiculous. Who cared enough about the history of alchemy to engineer a break-in?

"You have your computer, with your research notes on it." Matthew gripped my hands tighter. "But it wasn't your work they were after. They tore apart your bedroom and the bathroom. We think they were looking for a sample of your DNA—hair, skin, fingernail clippings. When they couldn't get into the lab, they went looking in your rooms."

My hand was shaking slightly. I tried to pull it from his grip, not wanting him to know how badly this news had jangled me. Matthew held on.

"You're not alone in this, remember?" He fixed his gaze on me.

"So it wasn't an ordinary burglar. It was a creature, someone who knows about us and about Ashmole 782."

He nodded.

"Well, they won't find much. Not in my rooms." When Matthew looked puzzled, I explained. "My mother insisted that I clean my hairbrush before leaving for school each morning. It's an ingrained habit. She made me flush the hair down the toilet—my nail clippings, too."

Matthew now appeared stunned. Ysabeau didn't look surprised at all.

"Your mother sounds more and more like someone I would have been eager to know," Ysabeau said quietly.

"Do you remember what she told you?" Matthew asked.

"Not really." There were faint memories of sitting on the edge of the bathtub while my mother demonstrated her morning and evening routine, but little more. I frowned with concentration, the flickering recollections growing brighter. "I remember counting to twenty. Somewhere along the way, I twirled around and said something."

"What could she have been thinking?" Matthew mused out loud. "Hair and fingernails carry a lot of genetic information."

"Who knows? My mother was famous for her premonitions. Then again, she could just have been thinking like a Bishop. We're not the sanest bunch."

"Your mother was not mad, Diana, and not everything can be explained by your modern science, Matthew. Witches have believed for centuries that hair and fingernails had power," said Ysabeau.

Marthe muttered in agreement and rolled her eyes at the ignorance of youth.

"Witches use them to work spells," Ysabeau continued. "Binding spells, love magic—they depend on such things."

"You told me you weren't a witch, Ysabeau," I said, astonished.

"I have known many witches over the years. Not one of them would leave a strand of her hair or scrap of her nails for fear that another witch would find them."

"My mother never told me." I wondered what other secrets my mother had kept.

"Sometimes it is best for a mother to reveal things slowly to her children." Ysabeau's glance flicked from me to her son.

"Who broke in?" I remembered Ysabeau's list of possibilities.

"Vampires tried to get into the lab, but we're less sure about your rooms. Marcus thinks it was vampires and witches working together, but I think it was just witches."

"Is this why you were so angry? Because those creatures violated my territory?"

"Yes."

We were back to monosyllables. I waited for the rest of the answer.

"I might overlook a trespasser on my land or in my lab, Diana, but I cannot stand by while someone does it to you. It feels like a threat, and I simply . . . can't. Keeping you safe is instinctive now." Matthew ran his white fingers through his hair, and a patch stuck out over his ear.

"I'm not a vampire, and I don't know the rules. You have to explain how this works," I said, smoothing his hair into place. "So it was the break-in at New College that convinced you to be with me?"

Matthew's hands moved in a flash to rest on either side of my face. "I needed no encouragement to be with you. You say you've loved me since you resisted hitting me with an oar at the river." His eyes were unguarded. "I've loved you longer than that—since the moment you used magic to take a book from its shelf at the Bodleian. You looked so relieved, and then so terribly guilty."

Ysabeau stood, uncomfortable with her son's open affection. "We will leave you."

Marthe started rustling at the table, preparing to depart for the kitchens, where she would doubtless begin whipping up a ten-course feast.

"No, *Maman*. You should hear the rest."

"So you are not merely outlaws." Ysabeau's voice was heavy. She sank back onto her chair.

"There's always been animosity between creatures—vampires and witches especially. But Diana and I have brought those tensions into the open. It's just an excuse, though. The Congregation isn't really bothered by our decision to break the covenant."

"Stop speaking in riddles, Matthew," Ysabeau said sharply. "I'm out of patience with them."

Matthew looked at me regretfully before he responded. "The Congregation has become interested in Ashmole 782 and the mystery of how Diana acquired it. Witches have been watching the manuscript for at least as long as I have. They never foresaw that you would be the one to reclaim it. And no one imagined that I would reach you first."

Old fears wriggled to the surface, telling me there was something wrong deep inside me.

"If not for Mabon," Matthew continued, "powerful witches would have been in the Bodleian, witches who knew the manuscript's importance. But they were busy with the festival and let their guard down. They left the task to that young witch, and she let you—and the manuscript—slip through her fingers."

"Poor Gillian," I whispered. Peter Knox must be furious with her.

"Indeed." Matthew's mouth tightened. "But the Congregation has been watching you, too—for reasons that go well beyond the book and have to do with your power."

"How long?" I wasn't able to finish my sentence.

"Probably your whole life."

"Since my parents died." Unsettling memories from childhood floated back to me, of feeling the tingles of a witch's attention while on the swings at school and a vampire's cold stare at a friend's birthday party. "They've been watching me since my parents died."

Ysabeau opened her mouth to speak, saw her son's face, and thought better of it.

"If they have you, they'll have the book, too, or so they think. You're connected to Ashmole 782 in some powerful way I don't yet understand. I don't believe they do either."

"Not even Peter Knox?"

"Marcus asked around. He's good at wheedling information out of people. As far as we can tell, Knox is still mystified."

"I don't want Marcus to put himself at risk—not for me. He needs to stay out of this, Matthew."

"Marcus knows how to take care of himself."

"I have things to tell you, too." I'd lose my nerve entirely if given a chance to reconsider.

Matthew took both my hands, and his nostrils flared slightly. "You're tired," he said, "and hungry. Maybe we should wait until after lunch."

"You can smell when I'm *hungry*?" I asked incredulously. "That's not fair."

Matthew's head tipped back, and he laughed. He kept my hands in his, pulling them behind me so that my arms were shaped like wings.

"This from a witch, who could, if she felt like it, read my thoughts as if they were written on ticker tape. Diana, my darling, I know when you change your mind. I know when you're thinking bad thoughts, like how much fun it would be to jump the paddock fence. And I most definitely know when you're hungry," he said, kissing me to make his point clear.

"Speaking of my being a witch," I said, slightly breathless when he was finished, "we've confirmed witchwater on the list of genetic possibilities."

"What?" Matthew looked at me with concern. "When did that happen?"

"The moment you pulled away from Sept-Tours. I wouldn't let myself cry while you were here. Once you were gone, I cried—a lot."

"You've cried before," he said thoughtfully, bringing my hands forward again. He turned them over and examined my palms and fingers. "The water came out of your hands?"

"It came out of everywhere." I said. His eyebrows rose in alarm. "My hands, my hair, my eyes, my feet—even my mouth. It was like there was no me left, or if there was, I was nothing but water. I thought I'd never taste anything except salt again."

"Were you alone?" Matthew's voice turned sharp.

"No, no, of course not," I said hurriedly. "Marthe and your mother were there. They just couldn't get near me. There was a lot of water, Matthew. Wind, too."

"What made it stop?" he asked.

"Ysabeau."

Matthew gave his mother a long look.

"She sang to me."

The vampire's heavy lids dropped, shielding his eyes. "Once she sang all the time. Thank you, *Maman*."

I waited for him to tell me that she used to sing to him and that Ysabeau hadn't been the same since Philippe died. But he told me none of those things. Instead he wrapped me up in a fierce hug, and I tried not to mind that he wouldn't trust me with these parts of himself.

As the day unfolded, Matthew's happiness at being home was infectious. We moved from lunch to his study. On the floor in front of the fireplace, he discovered most of the places that I was ticklish. Throughout, he never let me behind the walls he'd so carefully constructed to keep creatures away from his secrets.

Once I reached out with invisible fingers to locate a chink in Matthew's defenses. He looked up at me in surprise.

"Did you say something?" he asked.

"No," I said, drawing hastily away.

We enjoyed a quiet dinner with Ysabeau, who followed along in Matthew's lighthearted wake. But she watched him closely, a look of sadness on her face.

Putting on my sorry excuse for pajamas after dinner, I worried about the desk drawer and whether my scent would be on the velvet that cushioned the seals, and I steeled myself to say good night before Matthew retreated, alone, to his study.

He appeared shortly afterward wearing a pair of loose, striped pajama bottoms and a faded black T-shirt, with no shoes on his long, slender feet. "Do you want the left side or the right?" he asked casually, waiting by the bedpost with his arms crossed.

I wasn't a vampire, but I could turn my head fast enough when it was warranted.

"If it doesn't matter to you, I'd prefer the left," he said gravely. "It will be easier for me to relax if I'm between you and the door."

"I . . . I don't care," I stammered.

"Then get in and slide over." Matthew took the bedding out of my hand, and I did as he asked. He slid under the sheets behind me with a groan of satisfaction.

"This is the most comfortable bed in the house. My mother doesn't believe we need to bother with good mattresses since we spend so little time sleeping. Her beds are purgatorial."

"Are you going to sleep with me?" I squeaked, trying and failing to sound as nonchalant as he did.

Matthew put his right arm out and hooked me into it until my head was resting on his shoulder. "I thought I might," he said. "I won't actually sleep, though."

Snuggled against him, I placed my palm flat on his heart so that I would know every time it beat. "What will you do?"

"Watch you, of course." His eyes were bright. "And when I get tired of doing that—*if* I get tired of doing that"—he dropped a kiss on each eyelid—"I'll read. Will the candles bother you?"

"No," I responded. "I'm a sound sleeper. Nothing wakes me up."

"I like a challenge," he said softly. "If I'm bored, I'll figure out something that will wake you up."

"Do you bore easily?" I teased, reaching up and threading my fingers through the hair at the base of his skull.

"You'll have to wait and see," he said with a wicked grin.

His arms were cool and soothing, and the feeling of safety in his presence was more restful than any lullaby.

"Will this ever stop?" I asked quietly.

"The Congregation?" Matthew's voice was worried. "I don't know."

"No." My head rose in surprise. "I don't care about that."

"What do you mean, then?"

I kissed him on his quizzical mouth. "This feeling when I'm with you—as if I'm fully alive for the first time."

Matthew smiled, his expression uncharacteristically sweet and shy. "I hope not."

Sighing with contentment, I lowered my head onto his chest and fell into dreamless sleep.

Chapter 27

It occurred to me the next morning that my days with Matthew, thus far, had fallen into one of two categories. Either he steered the day along, keeping me safe and making sure nothing upset his careful arrangements, or the day unfolded without rhyme or reason. Not long ago what happened in my day had been determined by carefully drawn-up lists and schedules.

Today I was going to take charge. Today Matthew was going to let me into his life as a vampire.

Unfortunately my decision was bound to ruin what promised to be a wonderful day.

It started at dawn with Matthew's physical proximity, which sent the same shock of desire through me that I'd felt yesterday in the courtyard. It was more effective than any alarm clock. His response was gratifyingly immediate as well, and he kissed me with enthusiasm.

"I thought you'd never wake up," he grumbled between kisses. "I feared I would have to send to the village for the town band, and the only trumpeter who knew how to sound reveille died last year."

Lying at his side, I noticed he was not wearing the ampulla from Bethany.

"Where did your pilgrim's badge go?" It was the perfect opportunity for him to tell me about the Knights of Lazarus, but he didn't take it.

"I don't need it anymore," he'd said, distracting me by winding a lock of my hair around his finger and then pulling it to the side so he could kiss the sensitive flesh behind my ear. "Tell me," I'd insisted, squirming away slightly.

"Later," he said, lips drifting down to the place where neck met shoulder.

My body foiled any further attempts at rational conversation. We both behaved instinctually, touching through the barriers of thin clothing and noting the small changes—a shiver, an eruption of gooseflesh, a soft moan—that promised greater pleasure to come. When I became insistent, reaching to seize bare flesh, Matthew stopped me.

"No rushing. We have time."

"Vampires" was all I managed to say before he stopped my words with his mouth.

We were still behind the bed curtains when Marthe entered the room. She left the breakfast tray on the table with an officious clatter and threw two logs on the fire with the enthusiasm of a Scot tossing the caber. Matthew peered out, proclaimed it a perfect morning, and declared that I was ravenous.

Marthe erupted into a string of Occitan and departed, humming a song under her breath. He refused to translate on the grounds that the lyrics were too bawdy for my delicate ears.

This morning, instead of quietly watching me eat, Matthew complained that he was bored. He did it with a wicked gleam in his eyes, his fingers restless on his thighs.

"We'll go riding after breakfast," I promised, forking some eggs into my mouth and taking a scalding sip of tea. "My work can wait until later."

"Riding won't fix it," Matthew purred.

Kissing worked to drive away his ennui. My lips felt bruised, and I had a much finer understanding of the interconnectedness of my own nervous system when Matthew finally conceded it was time to go riding.

He went downstairs to change while I showered. Marthe came upstairs to retrieve the tray, and I told her my plans while braiding my hair into a thick rope. Her eyes widened at the important part, but she agreed to send a small pack of sandwiches and a bottle of water out to Georges for Rakasa's saddlebag.

After that, there was nothing left but to inform Matthew.

He was humming and sitting at his desk, clattering on his computer and occasionally reaching over to thumb through messages on his phone. He looked up and grinned.

"There you are," he said. "I thought I was going to have to fish you out of the water."

Desire shot through me, and my knees went weak. The feelings were exacerbated by the knowledge that what I was about to say would wipe the smile clean off his face.

Please let this be right, I whispered to myself, resting my hands on his shoulders. Matthew tilted his head back against my chest and smiled up at me.

"Kiss me," he commanded.

I complied without a second thought, amazed at the comfort between us. This was so different from books and movies, where love was made into something tense and difficult. Loving Matthew was much more like coming into port than heading out into a storm.

"How do you manage it?" I asked him, holding his face in my hands. "I feel like I've known you forever."

Matthew smiled happily and returned his attention to his computer, shutting down his various programs. While he did, I drank in his spicy scent and smoothed his hair along the curve of his skull.

"That feels wonderful," he said, leaning back into my hand.

It was time to ruin his day. Crouching down, I rested my chin on his shoulder.

"Take me hunting."

Every muscle in his body stiffened.

"That's not funny, Diana," he said icily.

"I'm not trying to be." My chin and hands remained where they were. He tried to shrug me off, but I wouldn't let him. Though I didn't have the courage to face him, he wasn't going to escape. "You need to do this, Matthew. You need to know that you can trust me."

He stood up explosively, leaving me no choice but to step back and let him go. Matthew strode away, and one hand strayed to the spot where his Bethany ampulla used to rest. Not a good sign.

"Vampires don't take warmbloods hunting, Diana."

This was not a good sign either. He was lying to me.

"Yes they do," I said softly. "You hunt with Hamish."

"That's different. I've known him for years, and I don't share a bed with him." Matthew's voice was rough, and he was staring fixedly at his bookshelves.

I started toward him, slowly. "If Hamish can hunt with you, so can I."

"No." The muscles in his shoulders stood out in sharp relief, their outlines visible under his sweater.

"Ysabeau took me with her."

The silence in the room was absolute. Matthew drew in a single, ragged breath, and the muscles in his shoulder twitched. I took another step.

"Don't," he said harshly. "I don't want you near me when I'm angry."

Reminding myself that he wasn't in charge today, I took my next steps at a much faster pace and stood directly behind him. That way he couldn't avoid my scent or the sound of my heartbeat, which was measured and steady.

"I didn't mean to make you angry."

"I'm not angry with you." He sounded bitter. "My mother, however, has a lot to answer for. She's done a great deal to try my patience over the centuries, but taking you hunting is unforgivable."

"Ysabeau asked me if I needed to come back to the château."

"You shouldn't have been given the choice," he barked, whirling around to face me. "Vampires aren't in control when they're hunting—not entirely. My mother certainly isn't to be trusted when she smells blood. For her it's all about the kill and the feeding. If the wind had caught your scent, she would have fed on you, too, without a second thought."

Matthew had reacted more negatively than I'd expected. With one of my feet firmly in the fire, however, the other one might as well go in, too.

"Your mother was only protecting you. She was concerned that I didn't understand the stakes. You would have done the same for Lucas." Once again the silence was deep and long.

"She had no right to tell you about Lucas. He belonged to me, not to her." Matthew's voice was soft, but filled with more venom than I'd ever heard in it. His eyes flickered to the shelf that held the tower.

"To you and to Blanca," I said, my voice equally soft.

"The life stories of a vampire are theirs to tell—and theirs alone. We may be outlaws, you and I, but my mother has broken a few rules herself in the past few days." He reached again for the missing Bethany ampulla.

I crossed the small distance that separated us, moving quietly and surely, as if he were a nervous animal, so as to keep him from lashing out in a way he would regret later. When I was standing no more than an inch from him, I took hold of his arms.

"Ysabeau told me other things as well. We talked about your father. She told me all of your names, and which ones you don't like, and her names as well. I don't really understand their significance, but it's not something she tells everyone. And she told me how she made you. The song she sang to make my witchwater go away was the same song she sang to you when you were first a vampire." *When you couldn't stop feeding.*

Matthew met my eyes with difficulty. They were full of pain and a vulnerability that he'd carefully hidden before now. It broke my heart.

"I can't risk it, Diana," he said. "I want you—more than anyone I've ever known. I want you physically, I want you emotionally. If my concentration shifts for an instant while we're out hunting, the deer's scent could get confused with yours, and my instinct to hunt an animal could cross with my desire to have you."

"You already have me," I said, holding on to him with my hands, my eyes, my mind, my heart. "There's no need to hunt me. I'm yours."

"It doesn't work that way," he said. "I'll never possess you completely. I'll always want more than you can give."

"You didn't in my bed this morning." My cheeks reddened at the memory of his latest rebuff. "I was more than willing to give myself to you, and you said no."

"I didn't say no—I said later."

"Is that how you hunt, too? Seduction, delay, then surrender?"

He shuddered. It was all the answer I required.

"Show me," I insisted.

"No."

"Show me!"

He growled, but I stood my ground. The sound was a warning, not a threat.

"I know you're frightened. So am I." Regret flickered in his eyes, and I made a sound of impatience. "For the last time, I am not frightened of you. It's my own power that scares me. You didn't see the witchwater, Matthew. When the water moved within me, I could have destroyed everyone and everything and not felt a drop of remorse. You're not the only dangerous creature in this room. But we have to learn how to be with each other in spite of who we are."

He gave a bitter laugh. "Maybe that's why there are rules against vampires and witches being together. Maybe it's too difficult to cross these lines after all."

"You don't believe that," I said fiercely, taking his hand in mine and holding it to my face. The shock of cold against warm sent a delicious feeling through my bones, and my heart gave its usual thump of acknowledgment. "What we feel for each other is not—cannot—be wrong."

"Diana," he began, shaking his head and drawing his fingers away.

Gripping him more tightly, I turned the palm over. His lifeline was long and smooth, and after tracing it I brought my fingers to rest on his veins. They looked black under the white skin, and Matthew shivered at my touch. There was still pain in his eyes, but he was not as furious.

"This is not wrong. You know it. Now you have to know that you can trust me, too." I laced my fingers through his and gave him time to think. But I didn't let go.

"I'll take you hunting," Matthew said at last, "provided you don't come near me and don't get down from Rakasa's back. If you get so much as a hint that I'm looking at you—that I'm even thinking about you—turn around and ride straight home to Marthe."

The decision made, Matthew stalked downstairs, waiting patiently each time he realized I was lagging behind. As he breezed past the door of the salon, Ysabeau rose from her seat.

"Come on," he said tightly, gripping my elbow and steering me downstairs.

Ysabeau was only a few feet behind us by the time we reached the kitchens, where Marthe stood in the doorway to the cold-foods larder, eyeing Matthew and me as if watching the latest drama on afternoon television. Neither needed to be told that something was wrong.

"I don't know when we'll be back," Matthew shot over his shoulder. His fingers didn't loosen, and he gave me no opportunity to do more than turn toward her with an apologetic face and mouth the word "Sorry."

"*Elle a plus de courage que j'ai pensé*," Ysabeau murmured to Marthe.

Matthew stopped abruptly, his lip curled in an unpleasant snarl.

"Yes, Mother. Diana has more courage than we deserve, you and I. And if you ever test that again, it will be the last time you see either of us. Understood?"

"Of course, Matthew," Ysabeau murmured. It was her favorite noncommittal response.

Matthew didn't speak to me on the way to the stables. Half a dozen times, he looked as though he were going to turn around and march us back to the château. At the stable door, he gripped my shoulders, searching my face and body for signs of fear. My chin went up in the air.

"Shall we?" I motioned toward the paddock.

He made a sound of exasperation and shouted for Georges. Balthasar bellowed in response and caught the apple that I tossed in his direction. Mercifully, I didn't need any help getting my boots on, though it did take me longer than it took Matthew. He watched carefully as I did up the vest's fastenings and snapped the chin strap on the helmet.

"Take this," he said, handing me a cropped whip.

"I don't need it."

"You'll take the crop, Diana."

I took it, resolved to ditch it in the brush at the first opportunity.

"And if you toss it aside when we enter the forest, we're coming home."

Did he really think I would use the crop on him? I shoved it into my boot, the handle sticking out by my knee, and stomped out into the paddock.

The horses skittered nervously when we came into view. Like Ysabeau, both knew that something was wrong. Rakasa took the apple I owed her, and I ran my fingers over her flesh and spoke to her softly in an effort to soothe her. Matthew didn't bother with Dahr. He was all business, checking the horse's tack with lightning speed. When I'd finished, Matthew tossed me onto Rakasa's back. His hands were firm around my waist, but he didn't hold on a moment longer than necessary. He didn't want any more of my scent on him.

In the forest Matthew made sure the crop was still in my boot.

"Your right stirrup needs shortening," he pointed out after we had the horses trotting. He wanted my tack in racing trim in case I needed to make a run for it. I pulled Rakasa in with a scowl and adjusted the stirrup leathers.

The now-familiar field opened up in front of me, and Matthew sniffed the air. He grabbed Rakasa's reins and brought me to a halt. He was still black with anger.

"There's a rabbit over there." Matthew nodded to the western section of the field.

"I've done rabbit," I said calmly. "And marmot, and goat, and a doe."

Matthew swore. It was concise and comprehensive, and I hoped we were out of the range of Ysabeau's keen ears.

"The phrase is 'cut to the chase,' is it not?"

"I don't hunt deer like my mother does, by frightening it to death and pouncing on it. I can kill a rabbit for you, or even a goat. But I'm not stalking a deer while you're with me." Matthew's jaw was set in an obstinate line.

"Stop pretending and trust me." I gestured at my saddlebag. "I'm prepared for the wait."

He shook his head. "Not with you at my side."

"Since I've met you," I said quietly, "you've shown me all the pleasant parts of being a vampire. You taste things I can't even imagine. You remember events and people that I can only read about in books. You smell when I change my mind or want to kiss you. You've woken me to a world of sensory possibilities I never dreamed existed."

I paused for a moment, hoping I was making progress. I wasn't.

"At the same time, you've seen me throw up, set fire to your rug, and come completely unglued when I received something unexpected in the mail. You missed the waterworks, but they weren't pretty. In return I'm asking you to let me watch you feed yourself. It's a basic thing, Matthew. If you can't bear it, then we can make the Congregation happy and call it off."

"*Dieu.* Will you never stop surprising me?" Matthew's head lifted, and he stared into the distance. His attention was caught by a young stag on the crest of the hill. The stag was cropping the grass, and the wind was blowing toward us, so he hadn't yet picked up our scent.

Thank you, I breathed silently. It was a gift from the gods for the stag to appear like that. Matthew's eyes locked on his prey, and the anger left him to make room for a preternatural awareness of his environment. I fixed my eyes on the vampire, watching for slight changes that signaled what he was thinking or feeling, but there were precious few clues.

Don't you dare move, I warned when Rakasa tensed in preparation for a fidget. She rooted her hooves into the earth and stood at attention.

Matthew smelled the wind change and took Rakasa's reins. He slowly moved both horses to the right, keeping them within the path of the downward breezes. The stag raised his head and looked down the hill, then resumed his quiet clipping of the grass. Matthew's eyes darted over the terrain, lingering momentarily on a rabbit and widening when a fox stuck his head out of a hole. A falcon swooped overhead, riding the breezes like a surfer rides the waves, and he took that in as well. I began to appreciate how he'd managed the creatures in the Bodleian. There was not a living thing in this field that he had not located, identified, and been prepared to kill after only a few minutes of observation. Matthew inched the horses toward the trees, camouflaging my presence by putting me in the midst of other animal scents and sounds.

While we moved, Matthew noted when the falcon was joined by another bird or when one rabbit disappeared down a hole and another popped up to take its place. We startled a spotted animal that looked like a cat, with a long striped tail. From the pitch of Matthew's body, it was clear he wanted to chase it, and had he been alone he would have hunted it down before turning to the stag. With difficulty he drew his eyes away from the animal's leaping form.

It took us almost an hour to make our way from the bottom of the field around the forest's edge. When we were near the top, Matthew performed his face-forward dismount. He smacked Dahr on the rump, and the horse obediently turned and headed for home.

Matthew hadn't let go of Rakasa's reins during these maneuvers, and he didn't release them now. He led her to the edge of the forest and drew in a deep breath, taking in every trace of scent. Without a sound he put us inside a small thicket of low-growing birch.

The vampire crouched, both knees bent in a position that would have been excruciating to a human after about four minutes. Matthew held it for nearly two hours. My feet fell asleep, and I woke them up by flexing my ankles in the stirrups.

Matthew had not exaggerated the difference between his way of hunting and his mother's. For Ysabeau it was primarily about filling a biological need. She needed blood, the animals had it, and she took it from them as efficiently as possible without feeling remorse that her survival required the death of another creature. For her son, however, it was clearly more complicated. He, too, needed the physical nourishment that their blood provided. But Matthew felt a kinship with his prey that reminded me of the tone of respect I'd detected in his articles about the wolves. For Matthew, hunting was primarily about strategy, about pitting his feral intelligence against something that thought and sensed the world as he did.

Remembering our play in bed that morning, my eyes closed against a sudden jolt of desire. I wanted him as badly here in the forest when he was about to kill something as I had this morning, and I began to understand what worried Matthew about hunting with me. Survival and sexuality were linked in ways I'd never appreciated until now.

He exhaled softly and left my side without warning, his body prowling through the edges of the forest. When Matthew loped across the ridge, the stag raised his head, curious to see what this strange creature was.

It took the stag only a few seconds to assess Matthew as a threat, which was longer than it would have taken me. My hair was standing on end, and I felt the same pull of concern for the stag that I had for Ysabeau's deer. The stag sprang into action, leaping down the hillside. But Matthew was faster, and he cut the animal off before it could get too close to where I was hiding. He chased it up the hill and back across the ridge. With every step, Matthew drew closer and the stag became more anxious.

I know that you're afraid, I said silently, hoping the stag could hear me. *He needs to do this. He doesn't do this for sport, or to harm you. He does it to stay alive.*

Rakasa's head swung around, and she eyed me nervously. I reached down to reassure her and kept my hand on her neck.

Be still, I urged the stag. *Stop running. Not even you are fast enough to outrun this creature.* The stag slowed, stumbling over a hole in the ground. He was running straight for me, as if he could hear my voice and was following it to its source.

Matthew reached and grabbed the stag's horns, twisting his head to one side. The stag fell on his back, his sides heaving with exertion. Matthew sank to his knees, holding its head securely, about twenty feet from the thicket. The stag tried to kick his way to his feet.

Let go, I said sadly. *It's time. This is the creature who will end your life.*

The stag gave a final kick of frustration and fear and then quieted. Matthew stared deep into the eyes of his prey, as if waiting for permission to finish the job, then moved so swiftly that there was nothing more than a blur of black and white as he battened onto the stag's neck.

As he fed, the stag's life seeped away and a surge of energy entered Matthew. There was a clean tang of iron in the air, though no drops of blood fell. When the stag's life force was gone, Matthew remained still, kneeling quietly next to the carcass with his head bowed.

I kicked Rakasa into a walk. Matthew's back stiffened at my approach. He looked up, his eyes pale gray-green and bright with satisfaction. Taking the crop out of my boot, I threw it as far as I could in the opposite direction. It sailed into the underbrush and became hopelessly entangled in the gorse. Matthew watched with interest, but the danger that he might mistake me for a doe had clearly passed.

Deliberately I took off my helmet and dismounted with my back turned. Even now I trusted him, though he didn't trust himself. Resting my hand lightly on his shoulder, I dropped to my knees and put the helmet down near the stag's staring eyes.

"I like the way you hunt better than the way Ysabeau does it. So does the deer, I think."

"How does my mother kill, that it is so different from me?" Matthew's French accent was stronger, and his voice sounded even more fluid and hypnotic than usual. He smelled different, too.

"She hunts out of biological need," I said simply. "You hunt because it makes you feel wholly alive. And you two reached an agreement." I motioned at the stag. "He was at peace, I think, in the end."

Matthew looked at me intently, snow turning to ice on my skin as he stared. "Were you talking to this stag as you talk to Balthasar and Rakasa?"

"I didn't interfere, if that's what you're worried about," I said hastily. "The kill was yours." Maybe such things mattered to vampires.

Matthew shuddered. "I don't keep score." He dragged his eyes from the stag and rose to his feet in one of those smooth movements that marked him unmistakably as a vampire. A long, slender hand reached down. "Come. You're cold kneeling on the ground."

I placed my hand in his and stood, wondering who would get rid of the stag's carcass. Some combination of Georges and Marthe would be involved. Rakasa was contentedly eating grass, unconcerned by the dead animal lying so close. Unaccountably, I was ravenous.

Rakasa, I called silently. She looked up and walked over.

"Do you mind if I eat?" I asked hesitantly, unsure what Matthew's reaction would be.

His mouth twitched. "No. Given what you've seen today, the least I can do is watch you have a sandwich."

"There's no difference, Matthew." I undid the buckle on Rakasa's saddlebag and said a silent word of thanks. Marthe, bless her, had packed cheese sandwiches. The worst of my hunger checked, I brushed the crumbs from my hands.

Matthew was watching me like a hawk. "Do you mind?" he asked quietly.

"Mind what?" I'd already told him I didn't mind about the deer.

"Blanca and Lucas. That I was married and had a child once, so long ago."

I was jealous of Blanca, but Matthew wouldn't understand how or why. I gathered my thoughts and emotions and tried to sort them into something that was both true and would make sense to him.

"I don't mind one moment of love that you've shared with any creature, living or dead," I said emphatically, "so long as you want to be with me right at this moment."

"Just at this moment?" he asked, his eyebrow arching up into a question mark.

"This is the only moment that matters." It all seemed so simple. "No one who has lived as long as you have comes without a past, Matthew. You weren't a monk, and I don't expect you to have no regrets about who you've lost along the way. How could you not have been loved before, when I love you so much?"

Matthew gathered me to his heart. I went eagerly, glad that the day's hunting had not ended in disaster and that his anger was fading. It still smoldered—it was evident in a lingering tightness in his face and shoulders—but it no longer threatened to engulf us. He cupped my chin in his long fingers and tilted my face up to his.

"Would you mind very much if I kissed you?" Matthew glanced away for a moment when he asked.

"Of course not." I stood on tiptoes so that my mouth was closer to his. Still, he hesitated, so I reached up and clasped my hands behind his neck. "Don't be idiotic. Kiss me."

He did, briefly but firmly. The final traces of blood were still on his lips, but it was neither frightening nor unpleasant. It was just Matthew.

"You know there won't be any children between us," he said while he held me close, our faces nearly touching. "Vampires can't father children the traditional way. Do you mind that?"

"There's more than one way to make a child." Children were not something I'd thought about before. "Ysabeau made you, and you belong to her no less than Lucas belonged to you and Blanca. And there are a lot of children in the world who don't have parents." I remembered the moment when Sarah and Em told me mine were gone and never coming back. "We could take them in—a whole coven of them, if we wanted to."

"I haven't made a vampire for years," he said. "I can still manage it, but I hope you don't intend that we have a large family."

"My family has doubled in the past three weeks, with you, Marthe, and Ysabeau added. I don't know how much more family I can take."

"You need to add one more to that number."

My eyes widened. "There are more of you?"

"Oh, there are always more," he said drily. "Vampire genealogies are much more complicated than witch genealogies, after all. We have blood relations on three sides, not just two. But this is a member of the family that you've already met."

"Marcus?" I asked, thinking of the young American vampire and his high-tops.

Matthew nodded. "He'll have to tell you his own story—I'm not as much of an iconoclast as my mother, despite falling in love with a witch. I made him, more than two hundred years ago. And I'm proud of him and what he's done with his life."

"But you didn't want him to take my blood in the lab," I said with a frown. "He's your son. Why couldn't you trust him with me?" Parents were supposed to trust their children.

"He was made with my blood, my darling," Matthew said, looking patient and possessive at the same time. "If I find you so irresistible, why wouldn't he? Remember, none of us is immune to the lure of blood. I might trust him more than I would a stranger, but I'll never be completely at ease when any vampire is too close to you."

"Not even Marthe?" I was aghast. I trusted Marthe completely.

"Not even Marthe," he said firmly. "You really aren't her type at all, though. She prefers her blood from far brawnier creatures."

"You don't have to worry about Marthe, or Ysabeau either." I was equally firm.

"Be careful with my mother," Matthew warned. "My father told me never to turn my back on her, and he was right. She's always been fascinated by and envious of witches. Given the right circumstances and the right mood . . . ?" He shook his head.

"And then there's what happened to Philippe."

Matthew froze.

"I'm seeing things now, Matthew. I saw Ysabeau tell you about the witches who captured your father. She has no reason to trust me, but she let me in her house anyway. The real threat is the Congregation. And there would be no danger from them if you made me into a vampire."

His face darkened. "My mother and I are going to have a long talk about appropriate topics of conversation."

"You can't keep the world of vampires—your world—away from me. I'm in it. I need to know how it works and what the rules are." My temper flared, seething down my arms and toward my nails, where it erupted into arcs of blue fire.

Matthew's eyes widened.

"You aren't the only scary creature around, are you?" I waved my fiery hands between us until the vampire shook his head. "So stop being all heroic and let me share your life. I don't want to be with Sir Lancelot. Be yourself—Matthew Clairmont. Complete with your sharp vampire teeth and your scary mother, your test tubes full of blood and your DNA, your infuriating bossiness and your maddening sense of smell."

Once I had spit all that out, the blue sparks retreated from my fingertips. They waited, somewhere around my elbows, in case I needed them again.

"If I come closer," Matthew said conversationally, as though asking for the time or the temperature, "will you turn blue again, or is that it for now?"

"I think I'm done for the time being."

"You think?" His eyebrow arched again.

"I'm perfectly under control," I said with more conviction, remembering with regret the hole in his rug in Oxford.

Matthew had his arms around me in a flash.

"Oof," I complained as he crushed my elbows into my ribs.

"And you are going to give me gray hairs—long thought impossible among vampires, by the way—with your courage, your firecracker hands, and the impossible things you say." To make sure he was safe from the last, Matthew kissed me quite thoroughly. When he was finished, I was unlikely to say much, surprising or otherwise. My ear rested against his sternum, listening patiently for his heart to thump. When it did, I gave him a satisfied squeeze, glad not to be the only one whose heart was full.

"You win, *ma vaillante fille,*" he said, cradling me against his body. "I will try—*try*—not to coddle you so much. And you must not underestimate how dangerous vampires can be."

It was hard to put "danger" and "vampire" into the same thought while pressed so firmly against him. Rakasa gazed at us indulgently, the grass sprouting out of both sides of her mouth.

"Are you finished?" I angled back my head to look at him.

"If you're asking if I need to hunt more, the answer is no."

"Rakasa is going to explode. She's been eating grass for quite some time. And she can't carry both of us." My hands took stock of Matthew's hips and buttocks.

His breath caught in his throat, making a very different kind of purring sound from the one he made when he was angry.

"You ride, and I'll walk alongside," he suggested after another very thorough kiss.

"Let's both walk." After hours in the saddle, I was not eager to get back up on Rakasa.

It was twilight when Matthew led us back through the château gates. Sept-Tours was ablaze, every lamp illuminated in silent greeting.

"Home," I said, my heart lifting at the sight.

Matthew looked at me, rather than the house, and smiled. "Home."

Chapter 28

Safely back at the château, we ate in the housekeeper's room before a blazing fire.

"Where's Ysabeau?" I asked Marthe when she brought me a fresh cup of tea.

"Out." She stalked back toward the kitchen.

"Out where?"

"Marthe," Matthew called. "We're trying not to keep things from Diana."

She turned and glared. I couldn't decide if it was directed at him, his absent mother, or me. "She went to the village to see that priest. The mayor, too." Marthe stopped, hesitated, and started again. "Then she was going to clean."

"Clean what?" I wondered.

"The woods. The hills. The caves." Marthe seemed to think this explanation was sufficient, but I looked at Matthew for clarification.

"Marthe sometimes confuses clean and clear." The light from the fire caught the facets of his heavy goblet. He was having some of the fresh wine from down the road, but he didn't drink as much as usual. "It would seem that *Maman* has gone out to make sure there are no vampires lurking around Sept-Tours."

"Is she looking for anyone in particular?"

"Domenico, of course. And one of the Congregation's other vampires, Gerbert. He's also from the Auvergne, from Aurillac. She'll look in some of his hiding places just to make sure he isn't nearby."

"Gerbert. From Aurillac? *The* Gerbert of Aurillac, the tenth-century pope who reputedly owned a brass head that spoke oracles?" The fact that Gerbert was a vampire and had once been pope was of much less interest to me than was his reputation as a student of science and magic.

"I keep forgetting how much history you know. You put even vampires to shame. Yes, that Gerbert. And," he warned, "I would like it very much if you'd stay out of his way. If you do meet him, no quizzing him about Arabic medicine or astronomy. He has always been acquisitive when it comes to witches and magic." Matthew looked at me possessively.

"Does Ysabeau know him?"

"Oh, yes. They were thick as thieves once. If he's anywhere near here, she'll find him. But you don't have to worry he'll come to the château," Matthew assured me. "He knows he's not welcome here. Stay inside the walls unless one of us is with you."

"Don't worry. I won't leave the grounds." Gerbert of Aurillac was not someone I wanted to stumble upon unexpectedly.

"I suspect she's trying to apologize for her behavior." Matthew's voice was neutral, but he was still angry.

"You're going to have to forgive her," I said again. "She didn't want you to be hurt."

"I'm not a child, Diana, and my mother needn't protect me from my own wife." He kept turning his glass this way and that. The word "wife" echoed in the room for a few moments.

"Did I miss something?" I finally asked. "When were we married?"

Matthew's eyes lifted. "The moment I came home and said I loved you. It wouldn't stand up in court perhaps, but as far as vampires are concerned, we're wed."

"Not when I said I loved you, and not when you said you loved me on the phone—it only happened when you came home and told me to my face?" This was something that demanded precision. I was planning on starting a new file on my computer with the title "Phrases That Sound One Way to Witches but Mean Something Else to Vampires."

"Vampires mate the way lions do, or wolves," he explained, sounding like a scientist in a television documentary. "The female selects her mate, and once the male has agreed, that's it. They're mated for life, and the rest of the community acknowledges their bond."

"Ah," I said faintly. We were back to the Norwegian wolves.

"I've never liked the word 'mate,' though. It always sounds impersonal, as if you're trying to match up socks, or shoes." Matthew put his goblet down and crossed his arms, resting them on the scarred surface of the table. "But you're not a vampire. Do you mind that I think of you as my wife?"

A small cyclone whipped around my brain as I tried to figure out what my love for Matthew had to do with the deadlier members of the animal kingdom and a social institution that I'd never been particularly enthusiastic about. In the whirlwind there were no warning signs or guideposts to help me find my way.

"And when two vampires mate," I inquired, when I could manage it, "is it expected that the female will obey the male, just like the rest of the pack?"

"I'm afraid so," he said, looking down at his hands.

"Hmm." I narrowed my eyes at his dark, bowed head. "What do I get out of this arrangement?"

"Love, honor, guard, and keep," he said, finally daring to meet my eyes.

"That sounds an awful lot like a medieval wedding service."

"A vampire wrote that part of the liturgy. But I'm not going to make you serve me," he assured me hastily, with a straight face. "That was put in to make the humans happy."

"The men, at least. I don't imagine it put a smile on the faces of the women."

"Probably not," he said, attempting a lopsided grin. Nerves got the better of him, and it collapsed into an anxious look instead. His gaze returned to his hands.

The past seemed gray and cold without Matthew. And the future promised to be much more interesting with him in it. No matter how brief our courtship, I certainly felt bound to him. And given vampires' pack behavior, it wasn't going to be possible to swap obedience for something more progressive, whether he called me "wife" or not.

"I feel I should point out, husband, that, strictly speaking, your mother was not protecting you from your wife." The words "husband" and "wife" felt strange on my tongue. "I wasn't your wife, under the terms laid out here, until you came home. Instead I was just some creature you left like a package with no forwarding address. Given that, I got off lightly."

A smile hovered at the corners of his mouth. "You think so? Then I suppose I should honor your wishes and forgive her." He reached for my hand and carried it to his mouth, brushing the knuckles with his lips. "I said you were mine. I meant it."

"This is why Ysabeau was so upset yesterday over our kiss in the courtyard." It explained both her anger and her abrupt surrender. "Once you were with me, there was no going back."

"Not for a vampire."

"Not for a witch either."

Matthew cut the growing thickness in the air by casting a pointed look at my empty bowl. I'd devoured three helpings of stew, insisting all the while I wasn't hungry.

"Are you finished?" he asked.

"Yes," I grumbled, annoyed at being caught out.

It was still early, but my yawns had already begun. We found Marthe rubbing down a vast wooden table with a fragrant combination of boiling water, sea salt, and lemons, and we said good night.

"Ysabeau will return soon," Matthew told her.

"She will be out all night," Marthe replied darkly, looking up from her lemons. "I will stay here."

"As you like, Marthe." He gripped her shoulder for a moment.

On the way upstairs to his study Matthew told me the story of where he bought his copy of Vesalius's anatomy book and what he thought when he first saw the illustrations. I dropped onto the sofa with the book in question and happily looked at pictures of flayed corpses, too tired to concentrate on *Aurora Consurgens,* while Matthew answered e-mail. The hidden drawer in his desk was firmly closed, I noted with relief.

"I'm going to take a bath," I said an hour later, rising and stretching my stiff muscles in preparation for climbing more stairs. I needed some time alone to think through the implications of my new status as Matthew's wife. The idea of marriage was overwhelming enough. When you factored in vampire possessiveness and my own ignorance about what was happening, it seemed an ideal time for a moment of reflection.

"I'll be up shortly," Matthew said, barely looking up from the glow of his computer screen.

The bathwater was as hot and plentiful as ever, and I sank into the tub with a groan of pleasure. Marthe had been up and had worked her magic with candles and the fire. The rooms felt cozy, if not precisely warm. I drifted through a satisfying replay of the day's accomplishments. Being in charge was better than letting random events take place.

I was still soaking in the bathtub, my hair falling over the edge in a cascade of straw, when there was a gentle knock on the door. Matthew pushed it open without waiting for me to respond. Sitting up with a start, I quickly sank back into the water when he walked in.

He grabbed one of the towels and held it out like a sail in the wind. His eyes were smoky. "Come to bed," he said, his voice gruff.

I sat in the water for a few heartbeats, trying to read his face. Matthew stood patiently during my examination, towel extended. After a deep breath, I stood, the water streaming over my naked body. Matthew's pupils dilated suddenly, his body still. Then he stood back to let me step out of the tub before he wrapped the towel around me.

Clutching it to my chest, I kept my eyes on him. When they didn't waver, I let the towel fall, the light from the candles glinting off damp skin. His eyes lingered over my body, their slow, cold progress sending a shiver of anticipation down my spine. He pulled me toward him without a word, his lips moving over my neck and shoulders. Matthew breathed in my scent, his long, cool fingers lifting the hair off my neck and back. I gasped when his thumb came to rest against the pulse in my throat.

"*Dieu,* you are beautiful," he murmured, "and so alive."

He began to kiss me again. Pulling at his T-shirt, my warm fingers moved against his cool, smooth skin. Matthew shuddered. It was much like my reaction to his first, cold touches. I smiled against his busy mouth, and he paused with a question on his face.

"It feels nice, doesn't it, when your coldness and my warmth meet?"

Matthew laughed, and the sound was as deep and smoky as his eyes. With my help, his shirt went up and over his shoulders. I started to fold it neatly. He snatched it away, balled it up, and threw it into the corner.

"Later," Matthew said impatiently, his hands moving once more over my body. Broad expanses of skin touched skin for the first time, warm and cold, in a meeting of opposites.

It was my turn to laugh, delighted by how perfectly our bodies fit. I traced his spine, my fingers sweeping up and down his back until they sent Matthew diving down to capture the hollow of my throat and the tips of my breasts with his lips.

My knees started to soften, and I grabbed his waist for support. More inequity. My hands traveled to the front of his soft pajama bottoms and undid the tie that kept them up. Matthew stopped kissing me long enough to give me a searching look. Without breaking his stare, I eased the loosened material over his hips and let it fall.

"There," I said softly. "Now we're even."

"Not even close," Matthew said, stepping out of the fabric.

I very nearly gasped but bit my lip at the last moment to keep the sound in. Nevertheless my eyes widened at the sight of him. The parts of him that hadn't been visible to me were just as perfect as those that had. Seeing Matthew, naked and gleaming, was like witnessing a classical sculpture brought to life.

Wordlessly he took my hand and led me toward the bed. Standing beside its curtained confines, he jerked the coverlet and sheets aside and lifted me onto the high mattress. Matthew climbed into bed after me. Once he'd joined me under the covers, he lay on his side with his head resting on his hand. Like his position at the end of yoga class, here was another pose that reminded me of the effigies of medieval knights in English churches.

I drew the sheets up to my chin, conscious of the parts of my own body that were far from perfect.

"What's wrong?" He frowned.

"A little nervous, that's all."

"About what?"

"I've never had sex with a vampire before."

Matthew looked genuinely shocked. "And you're not going to tonight either."

The sheet forgotten, I raised myself on my elbows. "You come into my bath, watch me get out of it naked and dripping wet, let me undress you, and then tell me we are *not* going to make love tonight?"

"I keep telling you we have no reason to rush. Modern creatures are always in such a hurry," Matthew murmured, drawing the fallen sheet down to my waist. "Call me old-fashioned if you'd like, but I want to enjoy every moment of our courtship."

I tried to snatch the edge of the bedding and cover myself with it, but his reflexes were quicker than mine. He inched the sheet lower, out of my reach, eyes keen.

"Courtship?" I cried indignantly. "You've already brought me flowers and wine. Now you're my husband, or so you tell me." I flicked the sheets off his torso. My pulse quickened once more at the sight of him.

"As a historian, you must know that scores of weddings weren't consummated immediately." His attention lingered over my hips and thighs, making them cold, then warm, in an entirely pleasant fashion. "Years of courtship were required in some cases."

"Most of those *courtships* led to bloodshed and tears." I put a slight emphasis on the word in question. Matthew grinned and stroked my breast with feather-light fingers until my gasp made him purr with satisfaction.

"I promise not to draw blood, if you promise not to weep."

It was easier to ignore his words than his fingers. "Prince Arthur and Catherine of Aragon!" I said triumphantly, pleased at my ability to recall relevant historical information under such distracting conditions. "Did you know them?"

"Not Arthur. I was in Florence. But Catherine, yes. She was nearly as brave as you are. Speaking of the past," Matthew drew the back of his hand down my arm, "what does the distinguished historian know about bundling?"

I turned on my side and slowly extended my fingertip along his jawbone. "I'm familiar with the custom. But you are neither Amish nor English. Are you telling me that—like wedding vows—the practice of getting two people into bed to talk all night but not have sex was dreamed up by vampires?"

"Modern creatures aren't only in a hurry, they're overly focused on the act of sexual intercourse. It's far too clinical and narrow a definition. Making love should be about intimacy, about knowing another's body as well as your own."

"Answer my question," I insisted, unable to think clearly now that he was kissing my shoulder. "Did vampires invent bundling?"

"No," he said softly, his eyes glittering as my fingertip rounded his chin. He nipped at it with his teeth. As promised, he drew no blood. "Once upon a time, we all did it. The Dutch and then the English came up with the variation of putting boards between the intended couple. The rest of us did it the old-fashioned way—we were just wrapped in blankets, shut into a room at dusk, and let out at dawn."

"It sounds dreadful," I said sternly. His attention drifted down my arm and across the swell of my belly. I tried to squirm away, but his free hand clamped onto my hip, keeping me still. "Matthew," I protested.

"As I recall," he said, as if I hadn't spoken, "it was a very pleasant way to spend a long winter's night. The hard part was looking innocent the next day."

His fingers played against my stomach, making my heart skip around inside my rib cage. I eyed Matthew's body with interest, picking my next target. My mouth landed on his collarbone while my hand snaked down along his flat stomach.

"I'm sure sleep was involved," I said after he found it necessary to snatch my hand and hold it away for a few minutes. My hip free, I pressed the length of my body against him. His body responded, and my face showed my satisfaction at the reaction. "No one can talk all night."

"Ah, but vampires don't need to sleep," he reminded me, just before he pulled back, bent his head, and planted a kiss below my breastbone.

I grabbed his head and lifted it. "There's only one vampire in this bed. Is this how you imagine you'll keep me awake?"

"I've been imagining little else from the first moment I saw you." Matthew's eyes shone darkly as he lowered his head. My body arched up to meet his mouth. When it did, he gently but firmly turned me onto my back, grabbing both of my wrists in his right hand and pinning them to the pillow.

Matthew shook his head. "No rushing, remember?"

I was accustomed to the kind of sex that involved a physical release without needless delay or unnecessary emotional complications. As an athlete who spent much of my time with other athletes, I was well acquainted with my body and its needs, and there was usually someone around to help me fill them. I was never casual about sex or my choice of partners, but most of my experiences had been with men who shared my frank attitude and were content to enjoy a few ardent encounters and then return to being friends again as though nothing had happened.

Matthew was making it clear that those days and nights were over. With him there would be no more straightforward sex—and I'd had no other kind. I might as well be a virgin. My deep feelings for him were becoming inextricably bound with my body's responses, his fingers and mouth tying them together in complicated, agonizing knots.

"We have all the time we need," he said stroking the undersides of my arms with his fingertips, weaving love and physical longing together until my body felt tight.

Matthew proceeded to study me with the rapt attention of a cartographer who found himself on the shores of a new world. I tried to keep up with him, wanting to discover his body while he was discovering mine, but he held my wrists firmly against the pillows. When I began to complain in earnest about the unfairness of this situation, he found an effective way to silence me. His cool fingers dipped between my legs and touched the only inches of my body that remained uncharted.

"Matthew," I breathed, "I don't think that's bundling."

"It is in France," he said complacently, a wicked gleam in his eye. He let go of my wrists, convinced quite rightly that there would be no attempts to squirm away now, and I caught his face in my hands. We kissed each other, long and deep, while my legs opened like the covers of a book. Matthew's fingers coaxed, teased, and danced between them until the pleasure was so intense it left me shaking.

He held me until the tremors subsided and my heart returned to its normal rhythm. When I finally mustered the energy to look at him, he had the self-satisfied look of a cat.

"What are the historian's thoughts on bundling now?" he asked.

"It's far less wholesome than it's been made out to be in the scholarly literature," I said, touching his lips with my fingers. "And if this is what the Amish do at night, it's no wonder they don't need television."

Matthew chuckled, the look of contentment never leaving his face. "Are you sleepy now?" he asked, trailing his fingers through my hair.

"Oh, no." I pushed him over onto his back. He folded his hands beneath his head and looked up at me with another grin. "Not in the slightest. Besides, it's my turn."

I studied him with the same intensity that he'd lavished on me. While I was inching up his hip bone, a white shadow in the shape of a triangle caught my attention. It was deep under the surface of his smooth, perfect skin. Frowning, I looked across the expanse of his chest. There were more odd marks, some shaped like snowflakes, others in crisscrossing lines. None of them were on the skin, though. They were all deep within him.

"What is this, Matthew?" I touched a particularly large snowflake under his left collarbone.

"It's just a scar," he said, craning his neck to see. "That one was made by the tip of a broadsword. The Hundred Years' War, maybe? I can't remember."

I slithered up his body to get a better look, pressing my warm skin against him, and he sighed happily.

"A scar? Turn over."

He made little sounds of pleasure while my hands swept across his back.

"Oh, Matthew." My worst fears were realized. There were dozens, if not hundreds, of marks. I knelt and pulled the sheet down to his feet. They were on his legs, too.

His head swiveled over his shoulder. "What's wrong?" The sight of my face was answer enough, and he turned over and sat up. "It's nothing, *mon coeur.* Just my vampire body, holding on to trauma."

"There are so many of them." There was another one, on the swell of muscles where his arm met his shoulders.

"I said vampires were difficult to kill. Creatures try their best to do so anyway."

"Did it hurt when you were wounded?"

"You know I feel pleasure. Why not pain, too? Yes, they hurt. But they healed quickly."

"Why haven't I seen them before?"

"The light has to be just right, and you have to look carefully. Do they bother you?" Matthew asked hesitantly.

"The scars themselves?" I shook my head. "No, of course not. I just want to hunt down all the people who gave them to you."

Like Ashmole 782, Matthew's body was a palimpsest, its bright surface obscuring the tale of him hinted at by all those scars. I shivered at the thought of the battles Matthew had already fought, in wars declared and undeclared.

"You've fought enough." My voice shook with anger and remorse. "No more."

"It's a bit late for that, Diana. I'm a warrior."

"No you're not," I said fiercely. "You're a scientist."

"I've been a warrior longer. I'm hard to kill. Here's the proof." He gestured at his long white body. As evidence of his indestructibility, the scars were strangely comforting. "Besides, most creatures who wounded me are long gone. You'll have to set that desire aside."

"Whatever will I replace it with?" I pulled the sheets over my head like a tent. Then there was silence except for an occasional gasp from Matthew, the crackle of the logs in the fireplace, and in time his own cry of pleasure. Tucking myself under his arm, I hooked my leg over his. Matthew looked down at me, one eye opened and one closed.

"Is this what they're teaching at Oxford these days?" he asked.

"It's magic. I was born knowing how to make you happy." My hand rested on his heart, pleased that I instinctively understood where and how to touch him, when to be gentle and when to leave my passion unchecked.

"If it is magic, then I'm even more delighted to be sharing the rest of my life with a witch," he said, sounding as content as I felt.

"You mean the rest of *my* life, not the rest of yours."

Matthew was suspiciously quiet, and I pushed myself up to see his expression. "Tonight I feel thirty-seven. Even more important, I believe that next year I will feel thirty-eight."

"I don't understand," I said uneasily.

He drew me back down and tucked my head under his chin. "For more than a thousand years, I've stood outside of time, watching the days and years go by. Since I've been with you, I'm aware of its passage. It's easy for vampires to forget such things. It's one of the reasons Ysabeau is so obsessed with reading the newspapers—to remind herself that there's always change, even though time doesn't alter her."

"You've never felt this way before?"

"A few times, very fleetingly. Once or twice in battle, when I feared I was about to die."

"So it's about danger, not just love." A cold wisp of fear moved through me at this matter-of-fact talk of war and death.

"My life now has a beginning, a middle, and an end. Everything before was preamble. Now I have you. One day you will be gone, and my life will be over."

"Not necessarily," I said hastily. "I've only got another handful of decades in me—you could go on forever." A world without Matthew was unthinkable.

"We'll see," he said quietly, stroking my shoulder.

Suddenly his safety was of paramount concern to me. "You will be careful?"

"No one sees as many centuries as I have without being careful. I'm always careful. Now more than ever, since I have so much more to lose."

"I would rather have had this moment with you—just this one night—than centuries with someone else," I whispered.

Matthew considered my words. "I suppose if it's taken me only a few weeks to feel thirty-seven again, I might be able to reach the point where one moment with you was enough," he said, cuddling me closer. "But this talk is too serious for a marriage bed."

"I thought conversation was the point of bundling," I said primly.

"It depends on whom you ask—the bundlers or those being bundled." He began working his mouth down from my ear to my shoulders. "Besides, I have another part of the medieval wedding service I'd like to discuss with you."

"You do, husband?" I bit his ear gently as it moved past.

"Don't do that," he said, with mock severity. "No biting in bed." I did it again anyway. "What I was referring to was the part of the ceremony where the obedient wife," he said, looking at me pointedly, "promises to be 'bonny and buxom in bed and board.' How do you intend to fulfill that promise?" He buried his face in my breasts as if he might find the answer there.

After several more hours discussing the medieval liturgy, I had a new appreciation for church ceremonies as well as folk customs. And being with him in this way was more intimate than I'd ever been with another creature.

Relaxed and at ease, I curled against Matthew's now-familiar body so that my head rested below his heart. His fingers ran through my hair again and again, until I fell asleep.

It was just before dawn when I awoke to a strange sound coming from the bed next to me, like gravel rolling around in a metal tube.

Matthew was sleeping—and snoring, too. He looked even more like the effigy of a knight on a tombstone now. All that was missing was the dog at his feet and the sword clasped at his waist.

I pulled the covers over him. He didn't stir. I smoothed his hair back, and he kept breathing deeply. I kissed him lightly on the mouth, and there was still no reaction. I smiled at my beautiful vampire, sleeping like the dead, and felt like the luckiest creature on the planet as I crept from under the covers.

Outside, the clouds were still hanging in the sky, but at the horizon they were thin enough to reveal faint traces of red behind the gray layers. It might actually clear today, I thought, stretching slightly and looking back at Matthew's recumbent form. He would be unconscious for hours. I, on the other hand, was feeling restless and oddly rejuvenated. I dressed quickly, wanting to go outside in the gardens and be by myself for a while.

When I finished dressing, Matthew was still lost in his rare, peaceful slumber. "I'll be back before you know it," I whispered, kissing him.

There was no sign of Marthe, or of Ysabeau. In the kitchen I took an apple from the bowl set aside for the horses and bit into it. The apple's crisp flesh tasted bright against my tongue.

I drifted into the garden, walking along the gravel paths, drinking in the smells of herbs and the white roses that glowed in the early-morning light. If not for my modern clothes, it could have been in the sixteenth century, with the orderly square beds and the willow fences that were supposed to keep the rabbits out—though the château's vampire occupants were no doubt a better deterrent than a scant foot of bent twigs.

Reaching down, I ran my fingers over the herbs growing at my feet. One of them was in Marthe's tea. Rue, I realized with satisfaction, pleased that the knowledge had stuck.

A gust of wind brushed past me, pulling loose the same infernal lock of hair that would not stay put. My fingers scraped it back in place, just as an arm swept me off the ground.

Ears popping, I was rocketed straight up into the sky.

The gentle tingle against my skin told me what I already knew.

When my eyes opened, I would be looking at a witch.

Chapter 29

My captor's eyes were bright blue, angled over high, strong cheekbones and topped by a shock of platinum hair. She was wearing a thick, hand-knit turtleneck and a pair of tight-fitting jeans. No black robes or brooms, but she was—unmistakably—a witch.

With a contemptuous flick of her fingers, she stopped the sound of my scream before it broke free. Her arm swept to the left, carrying us more horizontally than vertically for the first time since she'd plucked me from the garden at Sept-Tours.

Matthew would wake up and find me gone. He would never forgive himself for falling asleep, or me for going outside. *Idiot,* I told myself.

"Yes you are, Diana Bishop," the witch said in a strangely accented voice.

I slammed shut the imaginary doors behind my eyes that had always kept out the casual, invasive efforts of witches and daemons.

She laughed, a silvery sound that chilled me to the bone. Frightened, and hundreds of feet above the Auvergne, I emptied my mind in hopes of leaving nothing for her to find once she breached my inadequate defenses. Then she dropped me.

As the ground flew up, my thoughts organized themselves around a single word—Matthew.

The witch caught me up in her grip at my first whiff of earth. "You're too light to carry for one who can't fly. Why won't you, I wonder?"

Silently I recited the kings and queens of England to keep my mind blank.

She sighed. "I'm not your enemy, Diana. We are both witches."

The winds changed as the witch flew south and west, away from Sept-Tours. I quickly grew disoriented. The blaze of light in the distance might be Lyon, but we weren't headed toward it. Instead we were moving deeper into the mountains—and they didn't look like the peaks Matthew had pointed out to me earlier.

We descended toward something that looked like a crater set apart from the surrounding countryside by yawning ravines and overgrown forests. It proved to be the ruin of a medieval castle, with high walls and thick foundations that extended deep into the earth. Trees grew inside the husks of long-abandoned buildings huddled in the fortress's shadow. The castle didn't have a single graceful line or pleasing feature. There was only one reason for its existence—to keep out anyone who wished to enter. The poor dirt roads leading over the mountains were the castle's only link to the rest of the world. My heart sank.

The witch swung her feet down and pointed her toes, and when I didn't do the same, she forced mine down with another flick of her fingers. The tiny bones complained at the invisible stress. We slid along what remained of the gray tiled roofs without touching them, headed toward a small central courtyard. My feet flattened out suddenly and slammed into the stone paving, the shock reverberating through my legs.

"In time you'll learn to land more softly," the witch said matter-of-factly.

It was impossible to process my change in circumstances. Just moments ago, it seemed, I had been lying, drowsy and content, in bed with Matthew. Now I was standing in a dank castle with a strange witch.

When two pale figures detached themselves from the shadows, my confusion turned to terror. One was Domenico Michele. The other was unknown to me, but the freezing touch of his eyes told me he was a vampire, too. A wave of incense and brimstone identified him: this was Gerbert of Aurillac, the vampire-pope.

Gerbert wasn't physically intimidating, but there was evil at the core of him that made me shrink instinctively. Traces of that darkness were in brown eyes that looked out from deep sockets set over cheekbones so prominent that the skin appeared to be stretched thin over them. His nose hooked slightly, pointing down to thin lips that were curled into a cruel smile. With this vampire's dark eyes pinned on me, the threat posed by Peter Knox paled in comparison.

"Thank you for this place, Gerbert," the witch said smoothly, keeping me close by her side. "You're right—I won't be disturbed here."

"It was my pleasure, Satu. May I examine your witch?" Gerbert asked softly, walking slowly to the left and right as if searching for the best vantage point from which to view a prize. "It is difficult, when she has been with de Clermont, to tell where her scents begin and his end."

My captor glowered at the reference to Matthew. "Diana Bishop is in my care now. There is no need for your presence here any longer."

Gerbert's attention remained fixed on me as he took small, measured steps toward me. His exaggerated slowness only heightened his menace. "It is a strange book, is it not, Diana? A thousand years ago, I took it from a great wizard in Toledo. When I brought it to France, it was already bound by layers of enchantment."

"Despite your knowledge of magic, you could not discover its secrets." The scorn in the witch's voice was unmistakable. "The manuscript is no less bewitched now than it was then. Leave this to us."

He continued to advance. "I knew a witch then whose name was similar to yours—Meridiana. She didn't want to help me unlock the manuscript's secrets, of course. But my blood kept her in thrall." He was close enough now that the cold emanating from his body chilled me. "Each time I drank from her, small insights into her magic and fragments of her knowledge passed to me. They were frustratingly fleeting, though. I had to keep going back for more. She became weak, and easy to control." Gerbert's finger touched my face. "Meridiana's eyes were rather like yours, too. What did you see, Diana? Will you share it with me?"

"Enough, Gerbert." Satu's voice crackled with warning, and Domenico snarled.

"Do not think this is the last time you will see me, Diana. First the witches will bring you to heel. Then the Congregation will decide what to do with you." Gerbert's eyes bored into mine, and his finger moved down my cheek in a caress. "After that, you will be mine. For now," he said with a small bow in Satu's direction, "she is yours."

The vampires withdrew. Domenico looked back, reluctant to leave. Satu waited, her gaze vacant, until the sound of metal meeting up with wood and stone signaled that they were gone from the castle. Her blue eyes snapped to attention, and she fixed them on me. With a small gesture, she released her spell that had kept me silent.

"Who are you?" I croaked when it was possible to form words again.

"My name is Satu Järvinen," she said, walking around me in a slow circle, trailing a hand behind her. It triggered a deep memory of another hand that had moved like hers. Once Sarah had walked a similar path in the backyard in Madison when she'd tried to bind a lost dog, but the hands in my mind did not belong to her.

Sarah's talents were nothing compared to those possessed by this witch. It had been evident she was powerful from the way she flew. But she was adept at spells, too. Even now she was restraining me inside gossamer filaments of magic that stretched across the courtyard without her uttering a single word. Any hope of easy escape vanished.

"Why did you kidnap me?" I asked, trying to distract her from her work.

"We tried to make you see how dangerous Clairmont was. As witches, we didn't want to go to these lengths, but you refused to listen." Satu's words were cordial, her voice warm. "You wouldn't join us for Mabon, you ignored Peter Knox. Every day that vampire drew closer. But you're safely beyond his reach now."

Every instinct screamed danger.

"It's not your fault," Satu continued, touching me lightly on the shoulder. My skin tingled, and the witch smiled. "Vampires are so seductive, so charming. You've been caught in his thrall, just as Meridiana was caught by Gerbert. We don't blame you for this, Diana. You led such a sheltered childhood. It wasn't possible for you to see him for what he is."

"I'm not in Matthew's thrall," I insisted. Beyond the dictionary definition, I had no idea what it might involve, but Satu made it sound coercive.

"Are you quite sure?" she asked gently. "You've never tasted a drop of his blood?"

"Of course not!" My childhood might have been devoid of extensive magical training, but I wasn't a complete idiot. Vampire blood was a powerful, life-altering substance.

"No memories of a taste of concentrated salt? No unusual fatigue? You've never fallen deeply asleep when he was in your presence, even though you didn't want to close your eyes?"

On the plane to France, Matthew had touched his fingers to his own lips, then to mine. I'd tasted salt then. The next thing I knew, I was in France. My certainty wavered.

"I see. So he *has* given you his blood." Satu shook her head. "That's not good, Diana. We thought it might be the case, after he followed you back to college on Mabon and climbed through your window."

"What are you talking about?" My blood froze in my veins. Matthew would never give me his blood. Nor would he violate my territory. If he had done these things, there would have been a reason, and he would have shared it with me.

"The night you met, Clairmont hunted you down to your rooms. He crept through an open window and was there for hours. Didn't you wake up? If not, he must have used his blood to keep you asleep. How else can we explain it?"

My mouth had been full of the taste of cloves. I closed my eyes against the recollection, and the pain that accompanied it.

"This relationship has been nothing more than an elaborate deception, Diana. Matthew Clairmont has wanted only one thing: the lost manuscript.

Everything the vampire has done and every lie he's told along the way have been a means to that end."

"No." It was impossible. He couldn't have been lying to me last night. Not when we lay in each other's arms.

"Yes. I'm sorry to have to tell you these things, but you left us no other choice. We tried to keep you apart, but you are so stubborn."

Just like my father, I thought. My eyes narrowed. "How do I know that you're not lying?"

"One witch can't lie to another witch. We're sisters, after all."

"Sisters?" I demanded, my suspicions sharpening. "You're just like Gillian—pretending sisterhood while gathering information and trying to poison my mind against Matthew."

"So you know about Gillian," Satu said regretfully.

"I know she's been watching me."

"Do you know she's dead?" Satu's voice was suddenly vicious.

"What?" The floor seemed to tilt, and I felt myself sliding down the sudden incline.

"Clairmont killed her. It's why he took you away from Oxford so quickly. It's yet another innocent death we haven't been able to keep out of the press. What did the headlines say . . . ? Oh, yes: 'Young American Scholar Dies Abroad While Doing Research.'" Satu's mouth curved into a malicious smile.

"No." I shook my head. "Matthew wouldn't kill her."

"I assure you he did. No doubt he questioned her first. Apparently vampires have never learned that killing the messenger is pointless."

"The picture of my parents." Matthew might have killed whoever sent me that photo.

"It was heavy-handed for Peter to send it to you and careless of him to let Gillian deliver it," Satu continued. "Clairmont's too smart to leave evidence, though. He made it look like a suicide and left her body propped up like a calling card against Peter's door at the Randolph Hotel."

Gillian Chamberlain hadn't been a friend, but the knowledge that she would never again crouch over her glass-encased papyrus fragments was more distressing than I would have expected.

And it was Matthew who had killed her. My mind whirled. How could Matthew say he loved me and yet keep such things from me? Secrets were one thing, but murder—even under the guise of revenge and retaliation—

was something else. He kept warning me he couldn't be trusted. I'd paid no attention to him, brushing his words aside. Had that been part of his plan, too, another strategy to lure me into trusting him?

"You must let me help you." Satu's voice was gentle once more. "This has gone too far, and you are in terrible danger. I can teach you to use your power. Then you'll be able to protect yourself from Clairmont and other vampires, like Gerbert and Domenico. You will be a great witch one day, just like your mother. You can trust me, Diana. We're family."

"Family," I repeated numbly.

"Your mother and father wouldn't have wanted you to fall into a vampire's snares," Satu explained, as if I were a child. "They knew how important it was to preserve the bonds between witches."

"What did you say?" There was no whirling now. Instead my mind seemed unusually sharp and my skin was tingling all over, as if a thousand witches were staring at me. There was something I was forgetting, something about my parents that made everything Satu said a lie.

A strange sound slithered into my ears. It was a hissing and creaking, like ropes being pulled over stone. Looking down, I saw thick brown roots stretching and twisting across the floor. They crawled in my direction.

Satu seemed unaware of their approach. "Your parents would have wanted you to live up to your responsibilities as a Bishop and as a witch."

"My parents?" I drew my attention from the floor, trying to focus on Satu's words.

"You owe your loyalty and allegiance to me and your fellow witches, not to Matthew Clairmont. Think of your mother and father. Think of what this relationship would do to them, if only they knew."

A cold finger of foreboding traced my spine, and all my instincts told me that this witch was dangerous. The roots had reached my feet by then. As if they could sense my distress the roots abruptly changed direction, digging into the paving stones on either side of where I stood, before weaving themselves into a sturdy, invisible web beneath the castle floors.

"Gillian told me that witches killed my parents," I said. "Can you deny it? Tell me the truth about what happened in Nigeria."

Satu remained silent. It was as good as a confession.

"Just as I thought," I said bitterly.

A tiny motion of her wrist threw me onto my back, feet in the air, before invisible hands dragged me across the slick surface of the freezing courtyard and into a cavernous space with tall windows and only a portion of roof remaining.

My back was battered from its trip across the stones of the castle's old hall. Worse yet, my struggles against Satu's magic were inexperienced and futile. Ysabeau was right. My weakness—my ignorance of who I was and how to defend myself—had landed me in serious trouble.

"Once again you refuse to listen to reason. I don't want to hurt you, Diana, but I will if it's the only way to make you see the seriousness of this situation. You must give up Matthew Clairmont and show us what you did to call the manuscript."

"I will never give up my husband, nor will I help any of you claim Ashmole 782. It doesn't belong to us."

This remark earned me the sensation of my head splitting in two as a bloodcurdling shriek tore through the air. A cacophony of horrifying sounds followed. They were so painful I sank to my knees, and covered my head with my arms.

Satu's eyes narrowed to slits, and I found myself on my backside on the cold stone. "*Us?* You dare to think of yourself as a witch when you've come straight from the bed of a vampire?"

"I *am* a witch," I replied sharply, surprised at how much her dismissal stung.

"You're a disgrace, just like Stephen," Satu hissed. "Stubborn, argumentative, independent. And so full of secrets."

"That's right, Satu, I'm just like my father. He wouldn't have told you anything. I'm not going to either."

"Yes you will. The only way vampires can discover a witch's secrets is drop by drop." To show what she meant, Satu flicked her fingers in the direction of my right forearm. Another witch's hand had flicked at a long-ago cut on my knee, but that gesture had closed my wound better than any Band-Aid. This one sliced an invisible knife through my skin. Blood began to trickle from the gash. Satu watched the flow of blood, mesmerized.

My hand covered the cut, putting pressure on the wound. It was surprisingly painful, and my anxiety began to climb.

No, said a familiar, fierce voice. *You must not give in to the pain.* I struggled to bring myself under control.

"As a witch, I have other ways to uncover what you're hiding. I'm going to open you up, Diana, and locate every secret you possess," Satu promised. "We'll see how stubborn you are then."

All the blood left my head, making me dizzy. The familiar voice caught my attention, whispering my name. *Who do we keep our secrets from, Diana?*

Everybody, I answered, silently and automatically, as if the question were routine. Another set of far sturdier doors banged shut behind the inadequate barriers that had been all I'd ever needed to keep a curious witch out of my head.

Satu smiled, her eyes sparkling as she detected my new defenses. "There's one secret uncovered already. Let's see what else you have, besides the ability to protect your mind."

The witch muttered, and my body spun around and then flattened against the floor, facedown. The impact knocked the wind out of me. A circle of fire licked up from the cold stones, the flames green and noxious.

Something white-hot seared my back. It curved from shoulder to shoulder like a shooting star, descended to the small of my back, then curved again before climbing once again to where it had started. Satu's magic held me fast, making it impossible to wriggle away. The pain was unspeakable, but before the welcoming blackness could take me, she held off. When the darkness receded, the pain began again.

It was then that I realized with a sickening lurch of my stomach that she was opening me up, just as she'd promised. She was drawing a magical circle—onto me.

You must be very, very brave.

Through the haze of pain I followed the snaking tree roots covering the floor of the hall in the direction of the familiar voice. My mother was sitting under an apple tree just outside the line of green fire.

"Mama!" I cried weakly, reaching out for her. But Satu's magic held.

My mother's eyes—darker than I remembered, but so like my own in shape—were tenacious. She put one ghostly finger to her lips in a gesture of silence. The last of my energy was expended in a nod that acknowledged her presence. My last coherent thought was of Matthew.

After that, there was nothing but pain and fear, along with a dull desire to close my eyes and go to sleep forever.

It must have been many hours before Satu tossed me across the room in frustration. My back burned from her spell, and she'd reopened my injured forearm again and again. At some point she suspended me upside down by my ankle to weaken my resistance and taunted me about my inability to fly away and escape. Despite these efforts, Satu was no closer to understanding my magic than when she started.

She roared with anger, the low heels of her boots clicking against the stones as she paced and plotted fresh assaults. I lifted myself onto my elbow to better anticipate her next move.

Hold on. Be brave. My mother was still under the apple tree, her face shining with tears. It brought back echoes of Ysabeau telling Marthe that I had more courage than she had thought, and Matthew whispering "My brave girl" into my ear. I mustered the energy to smile, not wanting my mother to cry. My smile only made Satu more furious.

"Why won't you use your power to protect yourself? I know it's inside you!" she bellowed. Satu drew her arms together over her chest, then thrust them out with a string of words. My body rolled into a ball around a jagged pain in my abdomen. The sensation reminded me of my father's eviscerated body, the guts pulled out and lying next to him.

That's what's next. I was oddly relieved to know.

Satu's next words flung me across the floor of the ruined hall. My hands reached futilely past my head to try to stop the momentum as I skidded across the uneven stones and bumpy tree roots. My fingers flexed once as if they might reach across the Auvergne and connect to Matthew.

My mother's body had looked like this, resting inside a magic circle in Nigeria. I exhaled sharply and cried out.

Diana, you must listen to me. You will feel all alone. My mother was talking to me, and with the sound I became a child again, sitting on a swing hanging from the apple tree in the back yard of our house in Cambridge on a long-ago August afternoon. There was the smell of cut grass, fresh and green, and my mother's scent of lilies of the valley. *Can you be brave while you're alone? Can you do that for me?*

There were no soft August breezes against my skin now. Instead rough stone scraped my cheek when I nodded in reply.

Satu flipped me over, and the pointy stones cut into my back.

"We don't want to do this, sister," she said with regret. "But we must. You will understand, once Clairmont is forgotten, and forgive me for this."

Not bloody likely, I thought. *If he doesn't kill you, I'll haunt you for the rest of your life once I'm gone.*

With a few whispered words Satu lifted me from the floor and propelled me with carefully directed gusts of wind out of the hall and down a flight of curving stairs that wound into the depths of the castle. She moved me through the castle's ancient dungeons. Something rustled behind me, and I craned my neck to see what it was.

Ghosts—dozens of ghosts—were filing behind us in a spectral funeral procession, their faces sad and afraid. For all Satu's powers, she seemed unable to see the dead everywhere around us, just as she had been unable to see my mother.

The witch was attempting to raise a heavy wooden slab in the floor with her hands. I closed my eyes and braced myself for a fall. Instead Satu grabbed my hair and aimed my face into a dark hole. The smell of death rose in a noxious wave, and the ghosts shifted and moaned.

"Do you know what this is, Diana?"

I shrank back and shook my head, too frightened and exhausted to speak.

"It's an oubliette." The word rustled from ghost to ghost. A wispy woman, her face creased with age, began to weep. "Oubliettes are places of forgetting. Humans who are dropped into oubliettes go mad and then starve to death—if they survive the impact. It's a very long way down. They can't get out without help from above, and help never comes."

The ghost of a young man with a deep gash across his chest nodded in agreement with Satu's words. *Don't fall, girl*, he said in a sorrowful voice.

"But we won't forget you. I'm going for reinforcements. You might be stubborn in the face of one of the Congregation's witches, but not all three. We found that out with your father and mother, too." She tightened her grip, and we sailed more than sixty feet down to the bottom of the oubliette. The rock walls changed color and consistency as we tunneled deeper into the mountain.

"Please," I begged when Satu dropped me on the floor. "Don't leave me down here. I don't have any secrets. I don't know how to use my magic or how to recall the manuscript."

"You're Rebecca Bishop's daughter," Satu said. "You have power—I can feel it—and we'll make sure that it breaks free. If your mother were here, she would simply fly out." Satu looked into the blackness above us, then to my ankle. "But you're not really your mother's daughter, are you? Not in any way that matters."

Satu bent her knees, lifted her arms, and pushed gently against the oubliette's stone floor. She soared up and became a blur of white and blue before disappearing. Far above me the wooden door closed.

Matthew would never find me down here. By now any trail would be long gone, our scents scattered to the four winds. The only way to get out, short of being retrieved by Satu, Peter Knox, and some unknown third witch, was to get myself out.

Standing with my weight on one foot, I bent my knees, lifted my arms, and pushed against the floor as Satu had. Nothing happened. Closing my eyes, I tried to focus on the way it had felt to dance in the salon, hoping it would make me float again. All it did was make me think of Matthew, and the secrets he had kept from me. My breath turned into a sob, and when the oubliette's dank air passed into my lungs, the resulting cough brought me to my knees.

I slept a bit, but it was hard to ignore the ghosts once they started chattering. At least they provided some light in the gloom. Every time they moved, a tiny bit of phosphorescence smudged the air, linking where they had just been to where they were going. A young woman in filthy rags sat opposite me, humming quietly to herself and staring in my direction with vacant eyes. In the center of the room, a monk, a knight in full armor, and a musketeer peered into an even deeper hole that emitted a feeling of such loss that I couldn't bear to go near it. The monk muttered the mass for the dead, and the musketeer kept reaching into the pit as if looking for something he had lost.

My mind slid toward oblivion, losing its struggle against the combination of fear, pain, and cold. Frowning with concentration, I remembered the last passages I'd read in the *Aurora Consurgens* and repeated them aloud in the hope it would help me remain sane.

"'It is I who mediates the elements, bringing each into agreement,'" I mumbled through stiff lips. *"'I make what is moist dry again, and what is dry I make moist. I make what is hard soft again, and harden that which is soft. As I am the end, so my lover is the beginning. I encompass the whole work of creation, and all knowledge is hidden in me.'"* Something shimmered against the wall nearby. Here was another ghost, come to say hello, but I closed my eyes, too tired to care, and returned to my recitation.

"'Who will dare to separate me from my love? No one, for our love is as strong as death.'"

My mother interrupted me. *Won't you try to sleep, little witch?*

Behind my closed eyes, I saw my attic bedroom in Madison. It was only a few days before my parents' final trip to Africa, and I'd been brought to stay with Sarah while they were gone.

"I'm not sleepy," I replied. My voice was stubborn and childlike. I opened my eyes. The ghosts were drawing closer to the shimmer in the shadows to my right.

My mother was sitting there, propped against the oubliette's damp stone walls, holding her arms open. I inched toward her, holding my breath for fear she would disappear. She smiled in welcome, her dark eyes shining with unshed tears. My mother's ghostly arms and fingers flicked this way and that as I snuggled closer to her familiar body.

Shall I tell you a story?

"It was your hands I saw when Satu worked her magic."

Her answering laugh was gentle and made the cold stones beneath me less painful. *You were very brave.*

"I'm so tired." I sighed.

It's time for your story, then. Once upon a time, she began, *there was a little witch named Diana. When she was very small, her fairy godmother wrapped her in invisible ribbons that were every color of the rainbow.*

I remembered this tale from my childhood, when my pajamas had been purple and pink with stars on them and my hair was braided into two long pigtails that snaked down my back. Waves of memories flooded into rooms of my mind that had sat empty and unused since my parents' death.

"Why did the fairy godmother wrap her up?" I asked in my child's voice.

Because Diana loved making magic, and she was very good at it, too. But her fairy godmother knew that other witches would be jealous of her power. "When you are ready," the fairy godmother told her, "you will shrug off these ribbons. Until then you won't be able to fly, or make magic."

"That's not fair," I protested, as seven-year-olds are fond of doing. "Punish the other witches, not me."

The world isn't fair, is it? my mother asked.

I shook my head glumly.

No matter how hard Diana tried, she couldn't shake her ribbons off. In time she forgot all about them. And she forgot her magic, too.

"I would never forget my magic," I insisted.

My mother frowned. *But you have,* she said in her soft whisper. Her story continued. *One day, long after, Diana met a handsome prince who lived in the shadows between sunset and moonrise.*

This had been my favorite part. Memories of other nights flooded forth. Sometimes I had asked for his name, other times I'd proclaimed my lack of interest in a stupid prince. Mostly I wondered why anyone would want to be with a useless witch.

The prince loved Diana, despite the fact that she couldn't seem to fly. He could see the ribbons binding her, though nobody else could. He wondered what they were for and what would happen if the witch took them off. But the prince didn't think it was polite to mention them, in case she felt self-conscious. I nodded my seven-year-old head, impressed with the prince's empathy, and my much older head moved against the stone walls, too. *But he did wonder why a witch wouldn't want to fly, if she could.*

Then, my mother said, smoothing my hair, *three witches came to town. They could see the ribbons, too, and suspected that Diana was more powerful than they were. So they spirited her away to a dark castle. But the ribbons wouldn't budge, even though the witches pulled and tugged. So the witches locked her in a room, hoping she'd be so afraid she'd take the ribbons off herself.*

"Was Diana all alone?"

All alone, my mother said.

"I don't think I like this story." I pulled up my childhood bedspread, a patchwork quilt in bright colors that Sarah had bought at a Syracuse department store in anticipation of my visit, and slid down to the floor of the oubliette. My mother tucked me against the stones.

"Mama?" *Yes, Diana?*

"I did what you told me to do. I kept my secrets—from everybody."

I know it was difficult.

"Do you have any secrets?" In my mind I was running like a deer through a field, my mother chasing me.

Of course, she said, reaching out and flicking her fingers so that I soared through the air and landed in her arms.

"Will you tell me one of them?"

Yes. Her mouth was so close to my ear that it tickled. *You. You are my greatest secret.*

"But I'm right here!" I squealed, squirming free and running in the direction of the apple tree. "How can I be a secret if I'm right here?"

My mother put her fingers to her lips and smiled.

Magic.

Chapter 30

"Where is she?" Matthew slammed the keys to the Range Rover onto the table.

"We will find her, Matthew." Ysabeau was trying to be calm for her son's sake, but it had been nearly ten hours since they'd found a half-eaten apple next to a patch of rue in the garden. The two had been combing the countryside ever since, working in methodical slices of territory that Matthew divided up on a map.

After all the searching, they'd found no sign of Diana and had been unable to pick up her trail. She had simply vanished.

"It has to be a witch who took her." Matthew ran his fingers through his hair. "I told her she'd be safe as long as she stayed inside the château. I never thought the witches would dare to come here."

His mother's mouth tightened. The fact that witches had kidnapped Diana did not surprise her.

Matthew started handing out orders like a general on a battlefield. "We'll go out again. I'll drive to Brioude. Go past Aubusson, Ysabeau, and into Limousin. Marthe, wait here in case she comes back or someone calls with news."

There would be no phone calls, Ysabeau knew. If Diana had access to a phone, she would have used it before now. And though Matthew's preferred battle strategy was to chop through obstacles until he reached his goal, it was not always the best way to proceed.

"We should wait, Matthew."

"Wait?" Matthew snarled. "For what?"

"For Baldwin. He was in London and left an hour ago."

"Ysabeau, how could you tell him?" His older brother, Matthew had learned through experience, liked to destroy things. It was what he did best. Over the years he'd done it physically, mentally, and then financially, once he'd discovered that destroying people's livelihoods was almost as thrilling as flattening a village.

"When she was not in the stables or in the woods, I felt it was time. Baldwin is better at this than you are, Matthew. He can track anything."

"Yes, Baldwin's always been good at pursuing his prey. Now finding my wife is only my first task. Then I'll have to make sure she's not his next target." Matthew picked up his keys. "You wait for Baldwin. I'll go out alone."

"Once he knows that Diana belongs to you, he will not harm her. Baldwin is the head of this family. So long as this is a family matter, he has to know."

Ysabeau's words struck him as odd. She knew how much he distrusted his older brother. Matthew shrugged their strangeness aside. "They came into your home, *Maman.* It was an insult to you. If you want Baldwin involved, it's your right."

"I called Baldwin for Diana's sake—not mine. She must not be left in the hands of witches, Matthew, even if she is a witch herself."

Marthe's nose went into the air, alert to a new scent.

"Baldwin," Ysabeau said unnecessarily, her green eyes glittering.

A heavy door slammed overhead, and angry footsteps followed. Matthew stiffened, and Marthe rolled her eyes.

"Down here," Ysabeau said softly. Even in a crisis, she didn't raise her voice. They were vampires, after all, with no need for histrionics.

Baldwin Montclair, as he was known in the financial markets, strode down the hall of the ground floor. His copper-colored hair gleamed in the electric light, and his muscles twitched with the quick reflexes of a born athlete. Trained to wield a sword from childhood, he had been imposing before becoming a vampire, and after his rebirth few dared to cross him. The middle son in Philippe de Clermont's brood of three male children, Baldwin had been made a vampire in Roman times and had been Philippe's favorite. They were cut from the same cloth—fond of war, women, and wine, in that order. Despite these amiable characteristics, those who faced him in combat seldom lived to recount the experience.

Now he directed his anger at Matthew. They'd taken a dislike to each other the first time they'd met, their personalities at such odds that even Philippe had given up hope of their ever being friends. His nostrils flared as he tried to detect his brother's underlying scent of cinnamon and cloves.

"Where the hell are you, Matthew?" His deep voice echoed against the glass and stone.

Matthew stepped into his brother's path. "Here, Baldwin."

Baldwin had him by the throat before the words were out of his mouth. Their heads close together, one dark and one bright, they rocketed to the far end of the hall. Matthew's body smashed into a wooden door, splintering it with the impact.

"How could you take up with a witch, knowing what they did to Father?"

"She wasn't even born when he was captured." Matthew's voice was tight, given the pressure on his vocal cords, but he showed no fear.

"She's a witch," Baldwin spit. "They're all responsible. They knew how the Nazis were torturing him and did nothing to stop it."

"Baldwin." Ysabeau's sharp tone caught his attention. "Philippe left strict instructions that no revenge was to be taken if he came to harm." Though she had told Baldwin this repeatedly, it never lessened his anger.

"The witches helped those animals capture Philippe. Once the Nazis had him, they experimented on him to determine how much damage a vampire's body could take without dying. The witches' spells made it impossible for us to find him and free him."

"They failed to destroy Philippe's body, but they destroyed his soul." Matthew sounded hollow. "Christ, Baldwin. They could do the same to Diana."

If the witches hurt her physically, Matthew knew she might recover. But she would never be the same if the witches broke her spirit. He closed his eyes against the painful thought that Diana might not return the same stubborn, willful creature.

"So what?" Baldwin tossed his brother onto the floor in disgust and pounced on him.

A copper kettle the size of a timpani drum crashed into the wall. Both brothers leaped to their feet.

Marthe stood with gnarled hands on ample hips, glaring at them.

"She is his wife," she told Baldwin curtly.

"You *mated* with her?" Baldwin was incredulous.

"Diana is part of this family now," Ysabeau answered. "Marthe and I have accepted her. You must as well."

"Never," he said flatly. "No witch will ever be a de Clermont, or welcome in this house. Mating is a powerful instinct, but it doesn't survive death. If the witches don't kill this Bishop woman, I will."

Matthew lunged at his brother's throat. There was a sound of flesh tearing. Baldwin reeled back and howled, his hand on his neck.

"You bit me!"

"Threaten my wife again and I'll do more than that." Matthew's sides were heaving and his eyes were wild.

"Enough!" Ysabeau startled them into silence. "I have already lost my husband, a daughter, and two of my sons. I will *not* have you at each other's throats. I will *not* let witches take someone from my home without my permission." Her last words were uttered in a low hiss. "And I will *not* stand here and argue while my son's wife is in the hands of my enemies."

"In 1944 you insisted that challenging the witches wouldn't solve anything. Now look at you," Baldwin snapped, glaring at his brother.

"This is different," Matthew said tightly.

"Oh, it's different, I grant you that. You're risking the Congregation's interference in our family's affairs just so you can bed one of them."

"The decision to engage in open hostilities with the witches was not yours to make then. It was your father's—and he expressly forbade prolonging a world war." Ysabeau stopped behind Baldwin and waited until he turned to face her. "You must let this go. The power to punish such atrocities was placed in the hands of human authorities."

Baldwin looked at her sourly. "You took matters into your own hands, as I recall, Ysabeau. How many Nazis did you dine on before you were satisfied?" It was an unforgivable thing to say, but he had been pushed past his normal limits.

"As for Diana," Ysabeau continued smoothly, though her eyes sparked in warning, "if your father were alive, Lucius Sigéric Benoit Christophe Baldwin de Clermont, he would be out looking for her—witch or not. He would be ashamed of you, in here settling old scores with your brother." Every one of the names Philippe had given him over the years sounded like a slap, and Baldwin's head jerked back when they struck.

He exhaled slowly through his nose. "Thank you for the advice, Ysabeau, and the history lesson. Now, happily, it *is* my decision. Matthew will not indulge himself with this girl. End of discussion." He felt better after exercising his authority and turned to stalk out of Sept-Tours.

"Then you leave me no choice." Matthew's response stopped him in his tracks.

"Choice?" Baldwin snorted. "You'll do what I tell you to do."

"I may not be head of the family, but this is no longer a family matter." Matthew had, at last, figured out the point of Ysabeau's earlier remark.

"Fine." Baldwin shrugged. "Go on this foolish crusade, if you must. Find your witch. Take Marthe—she seems to be as enamored of her as you are. If the two of you want to pester the witches and bring the Congregation down on your heads, that's your business. To protect the family, I'll disown you."

He was on his way out the door again when his younger brother laid down his trump.

"I absolve the de Clermonts of any responsibility for sheltering Diana Bishop. The Knights of Lazarus will now see to her safety, as we have done for others in the past."

Ysabeau turned away to hide her expression of pride.

"You can't be serious," Baldwin hissed. "If you rally the brotherhood, it will be tantamount to a declaration of war."

"If that's your decision, you know the consequences. I could kill you for your disobedience, but I don't have time. Your lands and possessions are forfeit. Leave this house, and surrender your seal of office. A new French master will be appointed within the week. You are beyond the protection of the order and have seven days to find yourself a new place to live."

"Try to take Sept-Tours from me," Baldwin growled, "and you'll regret it."

"Sept-Tours isn't yours. It belongs to the Knights of Lazarus. Ysabeau lives here with the brotherhood's blessing. I'll give you one more chance to be included in that arrangement." Matthew's voice took on an indisputable tone of command. "Baldwin de Clermont, I call upon you to fulfill your sworn oath and enter the field of battle, where you will obey my commands until I release you."

He hadn't spoken or written the words for ages, but Matthew remembered each one perfectly. The Knights of Lazarus were in his blood, just as Diana was. Long-unused muscles flexed deep within him, and talents that had grown rusty began to sharpen.

"The Knights don't come to their master's aid because of a love affair gone wrong, Matthew. We fought at the Battle of Acre. We helped the Albigensian heretics resist the northerners. We survived the demise of the Templars and the English advances at Crécy and Agincourt. The Knights of Lazarus were on the ships that beat back the Ottoman Empire at Lepanto, and when we refused to fight any further, the Thirty Years' War came to an end. The brotherhood's purpose is to ensure that vampires survive in a world dominated by humans."

"We started out protecting those who could not protect themselves, Baldwin. Our heroic reputation was simply an unexpected by-product of that mission."

"Father should never have passed the order on to you when he died.

You're a soldier—and an idealist—not a commander. You don't have the stomach to make the difficult decisions." Baldwin's scorn for his brother was clear from his words, but his eyes were worried.

"Diana came to me seeking protection from her own people. I will see to it that she gets it—just as the Knights protected the citizens of Jerusalem, and Germany, and Occitania when they were under threat."

"No one will believe that this isn't personal, any more than they would have believed it in 1944. Then you said no."

"I was wrong."

Baldwin looked shocked.

Matthew drew a long, shuddering breath. "Once we would have responded immediately to such an outrage and to hell with the consequences. But a fear of divulging the family's secrets and a reluctance to raise the Congregation's ire held me back. This only encouraged our enemies to strike at this family again, and I won't make the same mistake where Diana is concerned. The witches will stop at nothing to learn about her power. They've invaded our home and snatched one of their own. It's worse than what they did to Philippe. In the witches' eyes, he was only a vampire. By taking Diana they've gone too far."

As Baldwin considered his brother's words, Matthew's anxiety grew more acute.

"Diana." Ysabeau brought Baldwin back to the matter at hand.

Baldwin nodded, once.

"Thank you," Matthew said simply. "A witch grabbed her straight up and out of the garden. Any clues there might have been about the direction they took were gone by the time we discovered she was missing." He pulled a creased map from his pocket. "Here is where we still need to search."

Baldwin looked at the areas that Ysabeau and his brother had already covered and the wide swaths of countryside that remained. "You've been searching all these places since she was taken?"

Matthew nodded. "Of course."

Baldwin couldn't conceal his irritation. "Matthew, will you never learn to stop and think before you act? Show me the garden."

Matthew and Baldwin went outdoors, leaving Marthe and Ysabeau inside so that their scents wouldn't obscure any faint traces of Diana. When the two were gone, Ysabeau began to shake from head to toe.

"It is too much, Marthe. If they have harmed her—"

"We have always known, you and I, that a day like this was coming." Marthe put a compassionate hand on her mistress's shoulder, then walked into the kitchens, leaving Ysabeau sitting pensively by the cold hearth.

In the garden Baldwin turned his preternaturally sharp eyes to the ground, where an apple lay next to a billowing patch of rue. Ysabeau had wisely insisted that they leave the fruit where they'd found it. Its location helped Baldwin see what his brother had not. The stems on the rue were slightly bent and led to another patch of herbs with ruffled leaves, then another.

"Which way was the wind blowing?" Baldwin's imagination was caught already.

"From the west," Matthew replied, trying to see what Baldwin was tracking. He gave up with a frustrated sigh. "This is taking too much time. We should split up. We can cover more ground that way. I'll go through the caves again."

"She won't be in the caves," Baldwin said, straightening his knees and brushing the scent of herbs from his hands. "Vampires use the caves, not witches. Besides, they went south."

"South? There's nothing to the south."

"Not anymore," Baldwin agreed. "But there must be something there, or the witch wouldn't have gone in that direction. We'll ask Ysabeau."

One reason the de Clermont family was so long-lived was that each member had different skills in a crisis. Philippe had always been the leader of men, a charismatic figure who could convince vampires and humans and sometimes even daemons to fight for a common cause. Their brother Hugh had been the negotiator, bringing warring sides to the bargaining table and resolving even the fiercest of conflicts. Godfrey, the youngest of Philippe's three sons, had been their conscience, teasing out the ethical implications of every decision. To Baldwin fell the battle strategies, his sharp mind quick to analyze every plan for flaws and weaknesses. Louisa had been useful as bait or as a spy, depending on the situation.

Matthew, improbably enough, had been the family's fiercest warrior. His early adventures with the sword had made his father wild with their lack of discipline, but he'd changed. Now whenever Matthew held a weapon in his hand, something in him went cold and he fought his way through obstacles with a tenacity that made him unbeatable.

Then there was Ysabeau. Everyone underestimated her except for

Philippe, who had called her either "the general" or "my secret weapon." She missed nothing and had a longer memory than Mnemosyne.

The brothers went back into the house. Baldwin shouted for Ysabeau and strode into the kitchen, grabbing a handful of flour from an open bowl and scattering it onto Marthe's worktable. He traced the outline of the Auvergne into the flour and dug his thumb into the spot where Sept-Tours stood.

"Where would a witch take another witch that is south and west of here?" he asked.

Ysabeau's forehead creased. "It would depend on the reason she was taken."

Matthew and Baldwin exchanged exasperated looks. This was the only problem with their secret weapon. Ysabeau never wanted to answer the question you posed to her—she always felt there was a more pressing one that needed to be addressed first.

"Think, *Maman*," Matthew said urgently. "The witches want to keep Diana from me."

"No, my child. You could be separated in so many ways. By coming into my home and taking my guest, the witches have done something unforgivable to this family. Hostilities such as these are like chess," Ysabeau said, touching her son's cheek with a cold hand. "The witches wanted to prove how weak we have become. You wanted Diana. Now they have taken her to make it impossible for you to ignore their challenge."

"Please, Ysabeau. Where?"

"There is nothing but barren mountains and goat tracks between here and the Cantal," Ysabeau said.

"The Cantal?" Baldwin snapped.

"Yes," she whispered, her cold blood chilled by the implications.

The Cantal was where Gerbert of Aurillac had been born. It was his home territory, and if the de Clermonts trespassed, the witches would not be the only forces gathering against them.

"If this were chess, taking her to the Cantal would put us in check," Matthew said grimly. "It's too soon for that."

Baldwin nodded approvingly. "Then we're missing something, between here and there."

"There's nothing but ruins," Ysabeau said.

Baldwin let out a frustrated sigh. "Why can't Matthew's witch defend herself?"

Marthe came into the room, wiping her hands on a towel. She and Ysabeau exchanged glances. "*Elle est enchantée*," Marthe said gruffly.

"The child is spellbound," Ysabeau agreed with reluctance. "We are certain of it."

"Spellbound?" Matthew frowned. Spellbinding put a witch in invisible shackles. It was as unforgivable among witches as trespassing was among vampires.

"Yes. It is not that she refuses her magic. She has been kept from it—deliberately." Ysabeau scowled at the idea.

"Why?" her son wondered. "It's like defanging and declawing a tiger and then returning it to the jungle. Why would you leave anyone without a way to defend herself?"

Ysabeau shrugged. "I can think of many people who might want to do such a thing—many reasons, too—and I do not know this witch well. Call her family. Ask them."

Matthew reached into his pocket and pulled out his phone. He had the house in Madison on speed dial, Baldwin noticed. The witches on the other end picked up on the first ring.

"Matthew?" The witch was frantic. "Where is she? She's in terrible pain, I can feel it."

"We know where to look for her, Sarah," Matthew said quietly, trying to soothe her. "But I need to ask you something first. Diana doesn't use her magic."

"She hasn't since her mother and father died. What does that have to do with anything?" Sarah was shouting now. Ysabeau closed her eyes against the harsh sound.

"Is there a chance, Sarah—any chance at all—that Diana is spellbound?"

The silence on the other end was absolute.

"Spellbound?" Sarah finally said, aghast. "Of course not!"

The de Clermonts heard a soft click.

"It was Rebecca," another witch said much more softly. "I promised her I wouldn't tell. And I don't know what she did or how she did it, so don't ask. Rebecca knew she and Stephen wouldn't be coming back from Africa. She'd seen something—knew something—that frightened her to death. All she would tell me was that she was going to keep Diana safe."

"Safe from what?" Sarah was horrified.

"Not 'safe from what.' Safe *until*." Em's voice dropped further. "Rebecca said she would make sure Diana was safe until her daughter was with her shadowed man."

"Her shadowed man?" Matthew repeated.

"Yes," Em whispered. "As soon as Diana told me she was spending time with a vampire, I wondered if you were the one Rebecca had foreseen. But it all happened so fast."

"Do you see anything, Emily—anything at all—that might help us?" Matthew asked.

"No. There's a darkness. Diana's in it. She's not dead," she said hastily when Matthew sucked in his breath, "but she's in pain and somehow not entirely in this world."

As Baldwin listened, he narrowed his eyes at Ysabeau. Her questions, though maddening, had been most illuminating. He uncrossed his arms and reached into his pocket for his phone. He turned away, dialed, and murmured something into it. Baldwin then looked at Matthew and drew a finger across his throat.

"I'm going for her now," Matthew said. "When we have news, we'll call you." He disconnected before Sarah or Em could pepper him with questions.

"Where are my keys?" Matthew shouted, heading for the door.

Baldwin was in front of him, barring the way.

"Calm down and think," he said roughly, kicking a stool in his brother's direction. "What were the castles between here and the Cantal? We only need to know the old castles, the ones Gerbert would be most familiar with."

"Christ, Baldwin, I can't remember. Let me through!"

"No. You need to be smart about this. The witches wouldn't have brought her into Gerbert's territory—not if they have any sense. If Diana is spellbound, then she's a mystery to them, too. It will take them some time to solve it. They'll want privacy, and no vampires interrupting them." It was the first time Baldwin had managed to say the witch's name. "In the Cantal the witches would have to answer to Gerbert, so they must be somewhere near the border. Think." Baldwin's last drop of patience evaporated. "By the gods, Matthew, you built or designed most of them."

Matthew's mind raced over the possibilities, discarding some because they were too close, others because they were too ruined. He looked up in shock. "La Pierre."

Ysabeau's mouth tightened, and Marthe looked worried. La Pierre had been the region's most forbidding castle. It was built on a foundation of basalt that couldn't be tunneled through and had walls high enough to resist any siege.

Overhead, there was a sound of air being compressed and moved.

"A helicopter," Baldwin said. "It was waiting in Clermont-Ferrand to take me back to Lyon. Your garden will need work, Ysabeau, but you no doubt think it's a small price to pay."

The two vampires streaked out of the château toward the helicopter. They jumped in and were soon flying high above the Auvergne. Nothing but blackness lay below them, punctuated here and there with a soft glow of light from a farmhouse window. It took them more than thirty minutes to arrive at the castle, and even though the brothers knew where it was, the pilot located its outlines with difficulty.

"There's nowhere to land!" the pilot shouted.

Matthew pointed to an old road that stretched away from the castle. "What about there?" he shouted back. He was already scanning the walls for signs of light or movement.

Baldwin told the pilot to put down where Matthew had indicated, and he received a dubious look in reply.

When they were still twenty feet off the ground, Matthew jumped out and set off at a dead run toward the castle's gate. Baldwin sighed and jumped after him, first directing the pilot not to move until they were both back on board.

Matthew was already inside, shouting for Diana. "Christ, she'll be terrified," he whispered when the echoes faded, running his fingers through his hair.

Baldwin caught up with him and grabbed his brother's arm. "There are two ways to do this, Matthew. We can split up and search the place from top to bottom. Or you can stop for five seconds and figure out where you would hide something in La Pierre."

"Let me go," Matthew said, baring his teeth and trying to pull his arm from his brother's grip. Baldwin's hand only tightened.

"Think," he commanded. "It will be quicker, I promise you."

Matthew went over the castle's floor plan in his mind. He started at the entrance, going up through the castle's rooms, through the tower, the sleeping apartments, the audience chambers, and the great hall. Then he worked his way from the entrance down through the kitchens, the cellars, and the dungeons. He stared at his brother in horror.

"The oubliette." He set off in the direction of the kitchens.

Baldwin's face froze. "*Dieu,*" he whispered, watching his brother's receding back. What was it about this witch that had made her own people throw her down a sixty-foot hole?

And if she were that precious, whoever had put Diana into the oubliette would be back.

Baldwin tore after Matthew, hoping it was not already too late to stop him from giving the witches not one but two hostages.

Chapter 31

Diana, it's time to wake up. My mother's voice was low but insistent.

Too exhausted to respond, I pulled the brightly colored patchwork quilt over my head, hoping that she wouldn't be able to find me. My body curled into a tight ball, and I wondered why everything hurt so much.

Wake up, sleepyhead. My father's blunt fingers gripped the fabric. A jolt of joy momentarily pushed the pain aside. He pretended he was a bear and growled. Squealing with happiness, I tightened my own hands and giggled, but when he pulled at the coverings, the cold air swept around me.

Something was wrong. I opened one eye, expecting to see the bright posters and stuffed animals that lined my room in Cambridge. But my bedroom didn't have wet, gray walls.

My father was smiling down at me with twinkling eyes. As usual, his hair was curled up at the ends and needed combing, and his collar was askew. I loved him anyway and tried to fling my arms around his neck, but they refused to work properly. He pulled me gently toward him instead, his insubstantial form clinging to me like a shield.

Fancy seeing you here, Miss Bishop. It was what he always said when I sneaked into his study at home or crept downstairs late at night for one more bedtime story.

"I'm so tired." Even though his shirt was transparent, it somehow retained the smell of stale cigarette smoke and the chocolate caramels that he kept in his pockets.

I know, my father said, his eyes no longer twinkling. *But you can't sleep anymore.*

You have to wake up. My mother's hands were on me now, trying to extricate me from my father's lap.

"Tell me the rest of the story first," I begged, "and skip the bad parts."

It doesn't work that way. My mother shook her head, and my father sadly handed me into her arms.

"But I don't feel well." My child's voice wheedled for special treatment.

My mother's sigh rustled against the stone walls. *I can't skip the bad parts. You have to face them. Can you do that, little witch?*

After considering what would be required, I nodded.

Where were we? my mother asked, sitting down next to the ghostly monk in the center of the oubliette. He looked shocked and moved a few inches away. My father stifled a smile with the back of his hand, looking at my mother the same way I looked at Matthew.

I remember, she said. *Diana was locked in a dark room, all alone. She sat hour after hour and wondered how she would ever get out. Then she heard a knocking at the window. It was the prince. "I'm trapped inside by witches!" Diana cried. The prince tried to break the window, but it was made of magic glass and he couldn't even crack it. Then the prince raced to the door and tried to open it, but it was held fast by an enchanted lock. He rattled the door in the frame, but the wood was too thick and it didn't budge.*

"Wasn't the prince strong?" I asked, slightly annoyed that he wasn't up to the task.

Very strong, said her mother solemnly, *but he was no wizard. So Diana looked around for something else for the prince to try. She spied a tiny hole in the roof. It was just big enough for a witch like her to squeeze through. Diana told the prince to fly up and lift her out. But the prince couldn't fly.*

"Because he wasn't a wizard," I repeated. The monk crossed himself every time magic or a wizard was mentioned.

That's right, my mother said. *But Diana remembered that once upon a time she had flown. She looked down and found the edge of a silver ribbon. It was wound tightly around her, but when she tugged on the end, the ribbon came loose. Diana tossed it high above her head. Then there was nothing left for her body to do except follow it up to the sky. When she got close to the hole in the roof, she put her arms together, stretched them straight, and went through into the night air. "I knew you could do it," said the prince.*

"And they lived happily ever after," I said firmly.

My mother's smile was bittersweet. *Yes, Diana.* She gave my father a long look, the kind that children don't understand until they're older.

I sighed happily, and it didn't matter so much that my back was on fire or that this was a strange place with people you could see right through.

It's time, my mother said to my father. He nodded.

Above me, heavy wood met ancient stone with a deafening crash.

"Diana?" It was Matthew. He sounded frantic. His anxiety sent a simultaneous rush of relief and adrenaline through my body.

"Matthew!" My call came out as a dull croak.

"I'm coming down." Matthew's response, echoing down all that stone, hurt my head. It was throbbing and there was something sticky on my cheek. I rubbed some of the stickiness on to my finger, but it was too dark to see what it was.

"No," said a deeper, rougher voice. "You can get down there, but I won't be able to get you out. And we need to do this fast, Matthew. They'll be back for her."

I looked up to see who was speaking, but all that was visible was a pale white ring.

"Diana, listen to me." Matthew boomed a little less now. "You need to fly. Can you do that?"

My mother nodded encouragingly. *It's time to wake up and be a witch. There's no need for secrets anymore.*

"I think so." I tried to get to my feet. My right ankle gave way underneath me, and I fell hard onto my knee. "Are you sure Satu's gone?"

"There's no one here but me and my brother, Baldwin. Fly up and we'll get you away." The other man muttered something, and Matthew replied angrily.

I didn't know who Baldwin was, and I had met enough strangers today. Not even Matthew felt entirely safe, after what Satu had said. I looked for somewhere to hide.

You can't hide from Matthew, my mother said, casting a rueful smile at my father. *He'll always find you, no matter what. You can trust him. He's the one we've been waiting for.*

My father's arms crept around her, and I remembered the feeling of Matthew's arms. Someone who held me like that couldn't be deceiving me.

"Diana, please try." Matthew couldn't keep the pleading out of his voice.

In order to fly, I needed a silver ribbon. But there wasn't one wrapped around me. Uncertain of how to proceed, I searched for my parents in the gloom. They were paler than before.

Don't you want to fly? my mother asked.

Magic is in the heart, Diana, my father said. *Don't forget.*

I shut my eyes and imagined a ribbon into place. With the end securely in my fingers, I threw it toward the white ring that flickered in the darkness. The ribbon unfurled and soared through the hole, taking my body with it.

My mother was smiling, and my father looked as proud as he had when he took the training wheels off my first bicycle. Matthew peered down, along with another face that must belong to his brother. With them were a clutch of ghosts who looked amazed that anyone, after all these years, was making it out alive.

"Thank God," Matthew breathed, stretching his long, white fingers toward me. "Take my hand."

The moment he had me in his grip, my body lost its weightlessness.

"My arm!" I cried out as the muscles pulled and the gash on my forearm gaped.

Matthew grabbed at my shoulder, assisted by another, unfamiliar hand. They lifted me out of the oubliette, and I was crushed for a moment against Matthew's chest. Grabbing handfuls of his sweater, I clung to him.

"I knew you could do it," he murmured like the prince in my mother's story, his voice full of relief.

"We don't have time for this." Matthew's brother was already running down the corridor toward the door.

Matthew gripped my shoulders and took rapid stock of my injuries. His nostrils flared at the scent of dried blood. "Can you walk?" he asked softly.

"Pick her up and get her out of here, or you'll have more to worry about than a little blood!" the other vampire shouted.

Matthew swept me up like a sack of flour and started to run, his arm tight across my lower back. I bit my lip and closed my eyes so the floor rushing underneath me wouldn't remind me of flying with Satu. A change in the air told me we were free. As my lungs filled, I began to shake.

Matthew ran even faster, carrying me toward a helicopter that was improbably parked outside the castle walls on a dirt road. He ducked his body protectively over mine and jumped into the helicopter's open door. His brother followed, the lights from the cockpit controls glinting green against his bright copper hair.

My foot brushed against Baldwin's thigh as he sat down, and he gave me a look of hatred mingled with curiosity. His face was familiar from the visions I'd seen in Matthew's study: first in light caught in the suit of armor, then again when touching the seals of the Knights of Lazarus. "I thought you were dead." I shrank toward Matthew.

Baldwin's eyes widened. "Go!" he shouted to the pilot, and we lifted into the sky.

Being airborne brought back fresh memories of Satu, and my shaking increased.

"She's gone into shock," Matthew said. "Can this thing move faster, Baldwin?"

"Knock her out," Baldwin said impatiently.

"I don't have a sedative with me."

"Yes you do." His brother's eyes glittered. "Do you want me to do it?"

Matthew looked down at me and tried to smile. My shaking subsided a little, but every time the helicopter dipped and swayed in the wind, it returned, along with my memories of Satu.

"By the gods, Matthew, she's terrified," Baldwin said angrily. "Just do it."

Matthew bit into his lip until a drop of blood beaded up on the smooth skin. He dipped his head to kiss me.

"No." I squirmed to avoid his mouth. "I know what you're doing. Satu told me. You're using your blood to keep me quiet."

"You're in shock, Diana. It's all I have. Let me help you." His face was anguished. Reaching up, I caught the drop of blood on my fingertip.

"No. I'll do it." There would be no more gossip among witches about my being in Matthew's control. I sucked the salty liquid from my numb fingertip. Lips and tongue tingled before the nerves in my mouth went dead.

The next thing I knew, there was cold air on my cheeks, perfumed with Marthe's herbs. We were in the garden at Sept-Tours. Matthew's arms were hard underneath my aching back, and he'd tucked my head into his neck. I stirred, looked around.

"We're home," he whispered, striding toward the lights of the château.

"Ysabeau and Marthe," I said, struggling to lift my head, "are they all right?"

"Perfectly all right," Matthew replied, cuddling me closer.

We passed into the kitchen corridor, which was ablaze with light. It hurt my eyes, and I turned away from it until the pain subsided. One of my eyes seemed smaller than the other, and I narrowed the larger one so they matched. A group of vampires came into view, standing down the corridor from Matthew and me. Baldwin looked curious, Ysabeau furious, Marthe grim and worried. Ysabeau took a step, and Matthew snarled.

"Matthew," she began in a patient voice, her eyes fixed on me with a look of maternal concern, "you need to call her family. Where is your phone?"

His arms tightened. My head felt too heavy for my neck. It was easier to lean it against Matthew's shoulder.

"It's in his pocket, I suppose, but he's not going to drop the witch to get it. Nor will he let you get close enough to fish it out." Baldwin handed Ysabeau his phone. "Use this."

Baldwin's gaze traveled over my battered body with such close attention that it felt as if ice packs were being applied and removed, one by one. "She certainly looks like she's been through a battle." His voice expressed reluctant admiration.

Marthe said something in Occitan, and Matthew's brother nodded. "*Òc,*" he said, eyeing me in appraisal.

"Not this time, Baldwin," Matthew rumbled.

"The number, Matthew," Ysabeau said crisply, diverting her son's attention. He rattled it off, and his mother pushed the corresponding buttons, the faint electronic tones audible.

"I'm fine," I croaked when Sarah picked up the phone. "Put me down, Matthew."

"No, this is Ysabeau de Clermont. Diana is with us."

There was more silence while Ysabeau's icicle touches swept over me. "She is hurt, but her injuries are not life-threatening. Nevertheless, Matthew should bring her home. To you."

"No. She'll follow me. Satu mustn't harm Sarah and Em," I said, struggling to break free.

"Matthew," Baldwin growled, "let Marthe see to her or keep her quiet."

"Stay out of this, Baldwin," Matthew snapped. His cool lips touched my cheeks, and my pulse slowed. His voice dropped to a murmur. "We won't do anything you don't want to do."

"We can protect her from vampires." Ysabeau sounded farther and farther away. "But not from other witches. She needs to be with those who can." The conversation faded, and a curtain of gray fog descended.

This time I came to consciousness upstairs in Matthew's tower. Every candle was lit, and the fire was roaring in the hearth. The room felt almost warm, but adrenaline and shock made me shiver. Matthew was sitting on his heels on the floor with me propped between his knees, examining my right forearm. My blood-soaked pullover had a long slit where Satu had cut me. A fresh red stain was seeping into the darker spots.

Marthe and Ysabeau stood in the doorway like a watchful pair of hawks.

"I can take care of my wife, *Maman,*" Matthew said.

"Of course, Matthew," Ysabeau murmured in her patented subservient tone.

Matthew tore the last inch of the sleeve to fully expose my flesh, and he swore. "Get my bag, Marthe."

"No," she said firmly. "She is filthy, Matthew."

"Let her take a bath," Ysabeau joined in, lending Marthe her support. "Diana is freezing, and you cannot even see her injuries. This is not helping, my child."

"No bath," he said decidedly.

"Why ever not?" Ysabeau asked impatiently. She gestured at the stairs, and Marthe departed.

"The water would be full of her blood," he said tightly. "Baldwin would smell it."

"This is not Jerusalem, Matthew," Ysabeau said. "He has never set foot in this tower, not since it was built."

"What happened in Jerusalem?" I reached for the spot where Matthew's silver coffin usually hung.

"My love, I need to look at your back."

"Okay," I whispered dully. My mind drifted, seeking an apple tree and my mother's voice.

"Lie on your stomach for me."

The cold stone floors of the castle where Satu had pinned me down were all too palpable under my chest and legs. "No, Matthew. You think I'm keeping secrets, but I don't know anything about my magic. Satu said—"

Matthew swore again. "There's no witch here, and your magic is immaterial to me." His cold hand gripped mine, as sure and firm as his gaze. "Just lean forward over my hand. I'll hold you."

Seated on his thigh, I bent from the waist, resting my chest on our clasped hands. The position stretched the skin on my back painfully, but it was better than the alternative. Underneath me, Matthew stiffened.

"Your fleece is stuck to your skin. I can't see much with it in the way. We're going to have to put you in the bath for a bit before it can be removed. Can you fill the tub, Ysabeau?"

His mother disappeared, her absence followed by the sound of running water.

"Not too hot," he called softly after her.

"What happened in Jerusalem?" I asked again.

"Later," he said, lifting me gently upright.

"The time for secrets has passed, Matthew. Tell her, and be quick about it." Ysabeau spoke sharply from the bathroom door. "She is your wife and has a right to know."

"It must be something awful, or you wouldn't have worn Lazarus's coffin." I pressed lightly on the empty spot above his heart.

With a desperate look, Matthew began his story. It came out of him in quick, staccato bursts. "I killed a woman in Jerusalem. She got between Baldwin and me. There was a great deal of blood. I loved her, and she—"

He'd killed someone else, not a witch, but a human. My finger stilled his lips. "That's enough for now. It was a long time ago." I felt calm but was shaking again, unable to bear any more revelations.

Matthew brought my left hand to his lips and kissed me hard on the knuckles. His eyes told me what he couldn't say aloud. Finally he released both my hand and my eyes and spoke. "If you're worried about Baldwin, we'll do it another way. We can soak the fleece off with compresses, or you could shower."

The mere thought of water falling on my back or the application of pressure convinced me to risk Baldwin's possible thirst. "The bath would be better."

Matthew lowered me into the lukewarm water, fully clothed right down to my running shoes. Propped in the tub, my back drawn away from the porcelain and the water wicking slowly up my fleece pullover, I began the slow process of letting go, my legs twitching and dancing under the water. Each muscle and nerve had to be told to relax, and some refused to obey.

While I soaked, Matthew tended to my face, his fingers pressing my cheekbone. He frowned in concern and called softly for Marthe. She appeared with a huge black medical bag. Matthew took out a tiny flashlight and checked my eyes, his lips pressed tightly together.

"My face hit the floor." I winced. "Is it broken?"

"I don't think so, *mon coeur,* just badly bruised."

Marthe ripped open a package, and a whiff of rubbing alcohol reached my nose. When Matthew held the pad on the sticky part of my cheek, I gripped the sides of the tub, my eyes smarting with tears. The pad came away scarlet.

"I cut it on the edge of a stone." My voice was matter-of-fact in an attempt to quiet the memories of Satu that the pain brought back.

Matthew's cool fingers traced the stinging wound to where it disappeared under my hairline. "It's superficial. You don't need stitches." He reached for a jar of ointment and smoothed some onto my skin. It smelled of mint and herbs from the garden. "Are you allergic to any medications?" he asked when he was through.

I shook my head.

He again called to Marthe, who trotted in with her arms full of towels. He rattled off a list of drugs, and Marthe nodded, jiggling a set of keys she pulled out of her pocket. Only one drug was familiar.

"Morphine?" I asked, my pulse beginning to race.

"It will alleviate the pain. The other drugs will combat swelling and infection."

The bath had lulled some of my anxiety and lessened my shock, but the pain was getting worse. The prospect of banishing it was enticing, and I reluctantly agreed to the drug in exchange for getting out of the bath. Sitting in the rusty water was making me queasy.

Before climbing out, though, Matthew insisted on looking at my right foot. He hoisted it up and out of the water, resting the sole of my shoe against his shoulder. Even that slight pressure had me gasping.

"Ysabeau. Can you come here, please?"

Like Marthe, Ysabeau was waiting patiently in the bedroom in case her son needed help. When she came in, Matthew had her stand behind me while he snapped the water-soaked shoelaces with ease and began to pry the shoe from my foot. Ysabeau held my shoulders, keeping me from thrashing my way out of the tub.

I cried during Matthew's examination—even after he stopped trying to pull the shoe off and began to rip it apart by tearing as precisely as a dressmaker cutting into fine cloth. He tore my sock off, too, and ripped along the seam of my leggings, then peeled the fabric away to reveal the ankle. It had a ring around it as though it had been closed in a manacle that had burned through the skin, leaving it black and blistered in places with odd white patches.

Matthew looked up, his eyes angry. "How was this done?"

"Satu hung me upside down. She wanted to see if I could fly." I turned away uncertainly, unable to understand why so many people were furious with me over things that weren't my fault.

Ysabeau gently took my foot. Matthew knelt beside the tub, his black hair slicked back from his forehead and his clothing ruined from water and blood. He turned my face toward him, looking at me with a mixture of fierce protectiveness and pride.

"You were born in August, yes? Under the sign of Leo?" He sounded entirely French, most of the Oxbridge accent gone.

I nodded.

"Then I will have to call you my lioness now, because only she could have fought as you did. But even *la lionne* needs her protectors." His eyes flickered toward my right arm. My gripping the tub had made the bleeding resume. "Your ankle is sprained, but it's not serious. I'll bind it later. Now let's see to your back and your arm."

Matthew scooped me out of the tub and set me down, instructing me to keep the weight off my right foot. Marthe and Ysabeau steadied me while he cut off my leggings and underclothes. The three vampires' premodern matter-of-factness about bodies left me strangely unconcerned at standing half naked in front of them. Matthew lifted the front hem of my soggy pullover, revealing a dark purple bruise that spread across my abdomen.

"Christ," he said, his fingers pushing into the stained flesh above my pubic bone. "How the hell did she do that?"

"Satu lost her temper." My teeth chattered at the memory of flying through the air and the sharp pain in my gut. Matthew tucked the towel around my waist.

"Let's get the pullover off," he said grimly. He went behind me, and there was a sting of cold metal against my back.

"What are you doing?" I twisted my head, desperate to see. Satu had kept me on my stomach for hours, and it was intolerable to have anyone—even Matthew—behind me. The trembling in my body intensified.

"Stop, Matthew," Ysabeau said urgently. "She cannot bear it."

A pair of scissors clattered to the floor.

"It's all right." Matthew nestled his body against mine like a protective shell. He crossed his arms over my chest, completely enfolding me. "I'll do it from the front."

Once the shaking subsided, he came around and resumed cutting the fabric away from my body. The cold air on my back told me that there wasn't much of it left in any case. He sliced through my bra, then got the front panel of the pullover off.

Ysabeau gasped as the last shreds fell from my back.

"*Maria, Deu maire*." Marthe sounded stunned.

"What is it? What did she do?" The room was swinging like a chandelier in an earthquake. Matthew whipped me around to face his mother. Grief and sympathy were etched on her face.

"*La sorcière est morte*," Matthew said softly.

He was already planning on killing another witch. Ice filled my veins, and there was blackness at the edges of my vision.

Matthew's hands held me upright. "Stay with me, Diana."

"Did you have to kill Gillian?" I sobbed.

"Yes." His voice was flat and dead.

"Why did you let me hear this from someone else? Satu told me you'd been in my rooms—that you were using your blood to drug me. Why, Matthew? Why didn't you tell me?"

"Because I was afraid of losing you. You know so little about me, Diana. Secrecy, the instinct to protect—to kill if I must. This is who I am."

I turned to face him, wearing nothing but a towel around my waist. My arms were crossed over my bare chest, and my emotions careened from fear to anger to something darker. "So you'll kill Satu also?"

"Yes." He made no apologies and offered no further explanation, but his eyes were full of barely controlled rage. Cold and gray, they searched my face. "You're far braver than I am. I've told you that before. Do you want to see what she did to you?" Matthew asked, gripping my elbows.

I thought for a moment, then nodded.

Ysabeau protested in rapid Occitan, and Matthew stopped her with a hiss.

"She survived the doing of it, *Maman*. The seeing of it cannot possibly be worse."

Ysabeau and Marthe went downstairs to fetch two mirrors while Matthew patted my torso with feather-light touches of a towel until it was barely damp.

"Stay with me," he repeated every time I tried to slip away from the rough fabric.

The women returned with one mirror in an ornate gilt frame from the salon and a tall cheval glass that only a vampire could have carried up to the tower. Matthew positioned the larger mirror behind me, and Ysabeau and Marthe held the other in front, angling it so that I could see both my back and Matthew, too.

But it couldn't be my back. It was someone else's—someone who had been flayed and burned until her skin was red, and blue, and black. There were strange marks on it, too—circles and symbols. The memory of fire erupted along the lesions.

"Satu said she was going to open me up," I whispered, mesmerized. "But I kept my secrets inside, Mama, just like you wanted."

Matthew's attempt to catch me was the last thing I saw reflected in the mirror before the blackness overtook me.

I awoke next to the bedroom fire again. My lower half was still wrapped up in a towel, and I was sitting on the edge of one damask-covered chair, bent over at the waist, with my torso draped across a stack of pillows on another damask-covered chair. All I could see was feet, and someone was applying ointment to my back. It was Marthe, her rough strength clearly distinguishable from Matthew's cool touches.

"Matthew?" I croaked, swiveling my head to the side to look for him.

His face appeared. "Yes, my darling?"

"Where did the pain go?"

"It's magic," he said, attempting a lopsided grin for my benefit.

"Morphine," I said slowly, remembering the list of drugs he'd given to Marthe.

"That's what I said. Everyone who has ever been in pain knows that morphine and magic are the same. Now that you're awake, we're going to wrap you up." He tossed a spool of gauze to Marthe, explaining that it would keep down the swelling and further protect my skin. It also had the benefit of binding my breasts, since I would not be wearing a bra in the near future.

The two of them unrolled miles of white surgical dressing around my torso. Thanks to the drugs, I underwent the process with a curious sense of detachment. It vanished, however, when Matthew began to rummage in his medical bag and talk about sutures. As a child I'd fallen and stuck a long fork used for toasting marshmallows into my thigh. It had required sutures, too, and my nightmares had lasted for months. I told Matthew my fears, but he was resolute.

"The cut on your arm is deep, Diana. It won't heal properly unless it's sutured."

Afterward the women got me dressed while Matthew drank some wine, his fingers shaking. I didn't have anything that fastened up the front, so Marthe disappeared once more, returning with her arms full of Matthew's clothing. They slid me into one of his fine cotton shirts. It swam on me but felt silky against my skin. Marthe carefully draped a black cashmere cardigan with leather-covered buttons—also Matthew's—around my shoulders, and she and Ysabeau snaked a pair of my own stretchy black pants up my legs and over my hips. Then Matthew lowered me into a nest of pillows on the sofa.

"Change," Marthe ordered, pushing him in the direction of the bathroom.

Matthew showered quickly and emerged from the bathroom in a fresh pair of trousers. He dried his hair roughly by the fire before pulling on the rest of his clothes.

"Will you be all right if I go downstairs for a moment?" he asked. "Marthe and Ysabeau will stay with you."

I suspected his trip downstairs involved his brother, and I nodded, still feeling the effects of the powerful drug.

While he was gone, Ysabeau muttered every now and again in a language that was neither Occitan nor French, and Marthe clucked and fussed. They'd removed most of the ruined clothes and bloody linen from the room by the time Matthew reappeared. Fallon and Hector were padding along at his side, their tongues hanging out.

Ysabeau's eyes narrowed. "Your dogs do not belong in my house."

Fallon and Hector looked from Ysabeau to Matthew with interest. Matthew clicked his fingers and pointed to the floor. The dogs sank down, their watchful faces turned to me.

"They'll stay with Diana until we leave," he said firmly, and though his mother sighed, she didn't argue with him.

Matthew picked up my feet and slid his body underneath them, his hands lightly stroking my legs. Marthe plunked down a glass of wine in front of him, then thrust a mug of tea into my hands. She and Ysabeau withdrew, leaving us alone with the watchful dogs.

My mind drifted, soothed by the morphine and the hypnotic touch of Matthew's fingers. I sorted through my memories, trying to distinguish what was real from what I'd only imagined. Had my mother's ghost really been in the oubliette, or was that a recollection of our time together before Africa? Or was it my mind's attempt to cope with stress by fracturing off into an imaginary world? I frowned.

"What is it, *ma lionne*?" Matthew asked, his voice concerned. "Are you in pain?"

"No. I'm just thinking." I focused on his face, pulling myself through the fog to his safer shores. "Where was I?"

"La Pierre. It's an old castle that no one has lived in for years."

"I met Gerbert." My brain was playing hopscotch, not wanting to linger in one place for too long.

Matthew's fingers stilled. "He was there?"

"Only in the beginning. He and Domenico were waiting when we arrived, but Satu sent them away."

"I see. Did he touch you?" Matthew's body tensed.

"On the cheek." I shivered. "He had the manuscript, Matthew, long, long ago. Gerbert boasted about how he'd taken it from Spain. It was under a spell even then. He kept a witch enthralled, hoping she would be able to break the enchantment."

"Do you want to tell me what happened?"

I thought it was too soon and was about to tell him so, but the story spilled out. When I recounted Satu's attempts to open me so that she could find the magic inside, Matthew rose and replaced the pillows supporting my back with his own body, cradling the length of me between his legs.

He held me while I spoke, and when I couldn't speak, and when I cried. Whatever Matthew's emotions when I shared Satu's revelations about him, he held them firmly in check. Even when I told him about my mother sitting under an apple tree whose roots spread across La Pierre's stone floors, he never pressed for more details, though he must have had a hundred unanswered questions.

It was not the whole tale—I left out my father's presence, my vivid memories of bedtime stories, and running through the fields behind Sarah's house in Madison. But it was a start, and the rest of it would come in time.

"What do we do now?" I asked when finished. "We can't let the Congregation harm Sarah or Em—or Marthe and Ysabeau."

"That's up to you," Matthew replied slowly. "I'll understand if you've had enough." I craned my neck to look at him, but he wouldn't meet my eyes, staring resolutely out the window into the darkness.

"You told me we were mated for life."

"Nothing will change the way I feel about you, but you aren't a vampire. What happened to you today—" Matthew stopped, started again. "If you've changed your mind about this—about me—I'll understand."

"Not even Satu could change my mind. And she tried. My mother sounded so certain when she told me that you were the one I'd been waiting for. That was when I flew." That wasn't exactly it—my mother had said that Matthew was the one *we* had been waiting for. But since it made no sense, I kept it to myself.

"You're sure?" Matthew tilted my chin up and studied my face.

"Absolutely."

His face lost some of its anguish. He bent his head to kiss me, then drew back.

"My lips are the only part of me that doesn't hurt." Besides, I needed to be reminded that there were creatures in the world who could touch me without causing pain.

He pressed his mouth gently against mine, his breath full of cloves and spice. It took away the memories of La Pierre, and for a few moments I could close my eyes and rest in his arms. But an urgent need to know what would happen next pulled me back to alertness.

"So . . . what now?" I asked again.

"Ysabeau is right. We should go to your family. Vampires can't help you learn about your magic, and the witches will keep pursuing you."

"When?" After La Pierre, I was oddly content to let him do whatever he thought best.

Matthew twitched slightly underneath me, his surprise at my compliance evident. "We'll join Baldwin and take the helicopter to Lyon. His plane is fueled and ready to leave. Satu and the Congregation's other witches won't come back here immediately, but they will be back," he said grimly.

"Ysabeau and Marthe will be safe at Sept-Tours without you?"

Matthew's laughter rumbled under me. "They've been in the thick of every major armed conflict in history. A pack of hunting vampires or a few inquisitive witches are unlikely to trouble them. I have something to see to, though, before we leave. Will you rest, if Marthe stays with you?"

"I'll need to get my things together."

"Marthe will do it. Ysabeau will help, if you'll let her."

I nodded. The idea of Ysabeau's returning to the room was surprisingly comforting.

Matthew rearranged me on the pillows, his hands tender. He called softly to Marthe and Ysabeau and gestured the dogs to the stairs, where they took up positions reminiscent of the lions at the New York Public Library.

The two women moved silently about the room, their quiet puttering and snippets of conversation providing a soothing background noise that finally lulled me to sleep. When I woke several hours later, my old duffel bag was packed and waiting by the fire and Marthe was bent over it tucking a tin inside.

"What's that?" I asked, rubbing the sleep from my eyes.

"Your tea. One cup every day. Remember?"

"Yes, Marthe." My head fell back on the pillows. "Thank you. For everything."

Marthe's gnarled hands stroked my forehead. "He loves you. You know this?" Her voice was gruffer than usual.

"I know, Marthe. I love him, too."

Hector and Fallon turned their heads, their attention caught by a sound on the stairs that was too faint for me to hear. Matthew's dark form appeared. He came to the sofa and took stock of me and nodded with approval after he felt my pulse. Then he scooped me into his arms as if I weighed nothing, the morphine ensuring that there was no more than an unpleasant tug on my back as he carried me down the stairs. Hector and Fallon brought up the rear of our little procession as we descended.

His study was lit only by firelight, and it cast shadows on the books and objects there. His eyes flickered to the wooden tower in a silent good-bye to Lucas and Blanca.

"We'll be back—as soon as we can," I promised.

Matthew smiled, but it never touched his eyes.

Baldwin was waiting for us in the hall. Hector and Fallon milled around Matthew's legs, keeping anyone from getting close. He called them off so Ysabeau could approach.

She put her cold hands on my shoulders. "Be brave, daughter, but listen to Matthew," she instructed, giving me a kiss on each check.

"I'm so sorry to have brought this trouble to your house."

"*Hein,* this house has seen worse," she replied before turning to Baldwin.

"Let me know if you need anything, Ysabeau." Baldwin brushed her cheeks with his lips.

"Of course, Baldwin. Fly safely," she murmured as he walked outside.

"There are seven letters in Father's study," Matthew told her when his brother was gone. He spoke low and very fast. "Alain will come to fetch them. He knows what to do." Ysabeau nodded, her eyes bright.

"And so it begins again," she whispered. "Your father would be proud of you, Matthew." She touched him on the arm and picked up his bags.

We made our way—a line of vampires, dogs, and witch—across the château's lawns. The helicopter's blades started moving slowly when we appeared. Matthew took me by the waist and lifted me into the cabin, then climbed in behind me.

We lifted off and hovered for a moment over the château's illuminated walls before heading east, where the lights of Lyon were visible in the dark morning sky.

Chapter 32

My eyes remained firmly closed on the way to the airport. It would be a long time before I flew without thinking of Satu.

In Lyon everything was blindingly fast and efficient. Clearly Matthew had been arranging matters from Sept-Tours and had informed the authorities that the plane was being used for medical transport. Once he'd flashed his identification and airport personnel got a good look at my face, I was whisked into a wheelchair against my objections and pushed toward the plane while an immigration officer followed behind, stamping my passport. Baldwin strode in front, and people hastily got out of our way.

The de Clermont jet was outfitted like a luxury yacht, with chairs that folded down flat to make beds, areas of upholstered seating and tables, and a small galley where a uniformed attendant waited with a bottle of red wine and some chilled mineral water. Matthew got me settled in one of the recliners, arranging pillows like bolsters to take pressure off my back. He claimed the seat nearest me. Baldwin took charge of a table large enough to hold a board meeting, where he spread out papers, logged on to two different computers, and began talking incessantly on the phone.

After takeoff Matthew ordered me to sleep. When I resisted, he threatened to give me more morphine. We were still negotiating when his phone buzzed in his pocket.

"Marcus," he said, glancing at the screen. Baldwin looked up from his table.

Matthew pushed the green button. "Hello, Marcus. I'm on a plane headed for New York with Baldwin and Diana." He spoke quickly, giving Marcus no chance to reply. His son couldn't have managed more than a few words before being disconnected.

No sooner had Matthew punched the phone's red button than lines of text began to light up his screen. Text messaging must have been a godsend for vampires in need of privacy. Matthew responded, his fingers flying over the keys. The screen went dark, and he gave me a tight smile.

"Everything all right?" I asked mildly, knowing the full story would have to wait until we were away from Baldwin.

"Yes. He was just curious where we were." This seemed doubtful, given the hour.

Drowsiness made it unnecessary for Matthew to make any further requests that I sleep. "Thank you for finding me," I said, my eyes drifting closed.

His only response was to bow his head and rest it silently on my shoulder.

I didn't wake until we landed at La Guardia, where we pulled in to the area reserved for private aircraft. Our arrival there and not at a busier, more crowded airport on the other side of town was yet another example of the magical efficiency and convenience of vampire travel. Matthew's identification worked still more magic, and the officials sped us through. Once we'd cleared customs and immigration, Baldwin surveyed us, me in my wheelchair and his brother standing grimly behind.

"You both look like hell," he commented.

"*Ta gueule*," Matthew said with a false smile, his voice acid. Even with my limited French, I knew this wasn't something you would say in front of your mother.

Baldwin smiled broadly. "That's better, Matthew. I'm glad to see you have some fight left in you. You're going to need it." He glanced at his watch. It was as masculine as he was, the type made for divers and fighter pilots, with multiple dials and the ability to survive negative G-force pressure. "I have a meeting in a few hours, but I wanted to give you some advice first."

"I've got this covered, Baldwin," Matthew said in a dangerously silky voice.

"No, you don't. Besides, I'm not talking to you." Baldwin crouched down, folding his massive body so he could lock his uncanny, light brown eyes on mine. "Do you know what a gambit is, Diana?"

"Vaguely. It's from chess."

"That's right," he replied. "A gambit lulls your opponent into a sense of false safety. You make a deliberate sacrifice in order to gain a greater advantage."

Matthew growled slightly.

"I understand the basic principles," I said.

"What happened at La Pierre feels like a gambit to me," Baldwin continued, his eyes never wavering. "The Congregation let you go for some reason of their own. Make your next move before they make theirs. Don't wait your turn like a good girl, and don't be duped into thinking your current freedom means you're safe. Decide what to do to survive, and do it."

"Thanks." He might be Matthew's brother, but Baldwin's close physical presence was unnerving. I extended my gauze-wrapped right arm to him in farewell.

"Sister, that's not how family bids each other *adieu.*" Baldwin's voice was softly mocking. He gave me no time to react but gripped my shoulders and kissed me on the cheeks. As his face passed over mine, he deliberately breathed in my scent. It felt like a threat, and I wondered if he meant it as such. He released me and stood. "Matthew, *à bientôt.*"

"Wait." Matthew followed his brother. Using his broad back to block my view, he handed Baldwin an envelope. The curved sliver of black wax on it was visible despite his efforts.

"You said you wouldn't obey my orders. After La Pierre you might have reconsidered."

Baldwin stared at the white rectangle. His face twisted sourly before falling into lines of resignation. Taking the envelope, he bowed his head and said, "*Je suis à votre commande, seigneur.*"

The words were formal, motivated by protocol rather than genuine feeling. He was a knight, and Matthew was his master. Baldwin had bowed—technically—to Matthew's authority. But just because he had followed tradition, that did not mean he liked it. He raised the envelope to his forehead in a parody of a salute.

Matthew waited until Baldwin was out of sight before returning to me. He grasped the handles of the wheelchair. "Come, let's get the car."

Somewhere over the Atlantic, Matthew had made advance arrangements for our arrival. We picked up a Range Rover at the terminal curb from a man in uniform who dropped the keys into Matthew's palm, stowed our bags in the trunk, and left without a word. Matthew reached into the backseat, plucked out a blue parka designed for arctic trekking rather than autumn in New York, and arranged it like a down-filled nest in the passenger seat.

Soon we were driving through early-morning city traffic and then out into the countryside. The navigation system had been programmed with the address of the house in Madison and informed us that we should arrive in a little more than four hours. I looked at the brightening sky and started worrying about how Sarah and Em would react to Matthew.

"We'll be home just after breakfast. That will be interesting." Sarah was not at her best before coffee—copious amounts of it—had entered her bloodstream. "We should call and let them know when to expect us."

"They already know. I called them from Sept-Tours."

Feeling thoroughly managed and slightly muzzy from morphine and fatigue, I settled back for the drive.

We passed hardscrabble farms and small houses with early-morning lights twinkling in kitchens and bedrooms. Upstate New York is at its best in October. Now the trees were on fire with red and gold foliage. After the leaves fell, Madison and the surrounding countryside would turn rusty gray and remain that way until the first snows blanketed the world in pristine white batting.

We turned down the rutted road leading to the Bishop house. Its late-eighteenth-century lines were boxy and generous, and it sat back from the road on a little knoll, surrounded by aged apple trees and lilac bushes. The white clapboard was in desperate need of repainting, and the old picket fence was falling down in places. Pale plumes rose in welcome from both chimneys, however, filling the air with the autumn scent of wood smoke.

Matthew pulled in to the driveway, which was pitted with ice-crusted potholes. The Range Rover rumbled its way over them, and he parked next to Sarah's beat-up, once-purple car. A new crop of bumper stickers adorned the back. MY OTHER CAR IS A BROOM, a perennial favorite, was stuck next to I'M PAGAN AND I VOTE. Another proclaimed WICCAN ARMY: WE WILL NOT GO SILENTLY INTO THE NIGHT. I sighed.

Matthew turned off the car and looked at me. "I'm supposed to be the nervous one."

"Aren't you?"

"Not as nervous as you are."

"Coming home always makes me behave like a teenager. All I want to do is hog the TV remote and eat ice cream." Though trying to be bright and cheerful for his sake, I was not looking forward to this homecoming.

"I'm sure we can arrange for that," he said with a frown. "Meanwhile stop pretending nothing has happened. You're not fooling me, and you won't fool your aunts either."

He left me sitting in the car while he carried our luggage to the front door. We'd amassed a surprisingly large amount of it, including two computer bags, my disreputable Yale duffel, and an elegant leather valise that might have been mistaken for a Victorian original. There was also Matthew's medical kit, his long gray coat, my bright new parka, and a case of wine. The last was a wise precaution on Matthew's part. Sarah's taste ran to harder stuff, and Em was a teetotaler.

Matthew returned and lifted me out of the car, my legs swinging. Safely on the steps, I gingerly put weight on my right ankle. We both faced the house's red, eighteenth-century door. It was flanked by tiny windows that offered a view of the front hall. Every lamp in the house was lit to welcome us.

"I smell coffee," he said, smiling down at me.

"They're up, then." The catch on the worn, familiar door latch released at my touch. "Unlocked as usual." Before losing my nerve, I warily stepped inside. "Em? Sarah?"

A note in Sarah's dark, decisive handwriting was taped to the staircase's newel post.

"*Out. Thought the house needed some time alone with you first. Move slowly. Matthew can stay in Em's old room. Your room is ready.*" There was a postscript, in Em's rounder scrawl. "*Both of you use your parents' room.*"

My eyes swept over the doors leading from the hall. They were all standing open, and there was no banging upstairs. Even the coffin doors into the keeping room were quiet, rather than swinging wildly on their hinges.

"That's a good sign."

"What? That they're out of the house?" Matthew looked confused.

"No, the silence. The house has been known to misbehave with new people."

"The house is haunted?" Matthew looked around with interest.

"We're witches—of course the house is haunted. But it's more than that. The house is . . . alive. It has its own ideas about visitors, and the more Bishops there are, the worse it acts up. That's why Em and Sarah left."

A phosphorescent smudge moved in and out of my peripheral vision. My long-dead grandmother, whom I'd never met, was sitting by the keeping room's fireplace in an unfamiliar rocking chair. She looked as young and beautiful as in her wedding picture on the landing upstairs. When she smiled, my own lips curved in response.

"Grandma?" I said tentatively.

He's a looker, isn't he? she said with a wink, her voice rustling like waxed paper.

Another head popped around the doorframe. *I'll say,* the other ghost agreed. *Should be dead, though.*

My grandmother nodded. *Suppose so, Elizabeth, but he is what he is. We'll get used to him.*

Matthew was staring in the direction of the keeping room. "Someone is there," he said, full of wonder. "I can almost smell them and hear faint sounds. But I can't see them."

"Ghosts." Reminded of the castle dungeons, I looked around for my mother and father.

Oh, they're not here, my grandmother said sadly.

Disappointed, I turned my attention from my dead family to my undead husband. "Let's go upstairs and put the bags away. That will give the house a chance to know you."

Before we could move another inch, a charcoal ball of fur rocketed out of the back of the house with a blood-chilling yowl. It stopped abruptly one foot away from me and transformed into a hissing cat. She arched her back and screeched again.

"Nice to see you too, Tabitha." Sarah's cat detested me, and the feeling was mutual.

Tabitha lowered her spine into its proper alignment and stalked toward Matthew.

"Vampires are more comfortable with dogs, as a rule," he commented as Tabitha wound around his ankles.

With unerring feline instincts, Tabitha latched on to Matthew's discomfort and was now determined to change his mind about her species. She butted her head against his shin, purring loudly.

"I'll be damned," I said. For Tabitha this was an astonishing display of affection. "She really is the most perverse cat in the history of the world."

Tabitha hissed at me and resumed her sybaritic attention to Matthew's lower legs.

"Just ignore her," I recommended, hobbling toward the stairs. Matthew swept up the bags and followed.

Gripping the banister, I made a slow ascent. Matthew took each step with me, his face alight with excitement and interest. He didn't seem at all alarmed that the house was giving him the once-over.

My body was rigid with anticipation, however. Pictures had fallen onto unsuspecting guests, doors and windows flapped open and closed, and lights went on and off without warning. I let out a sigh of relief when we made it to the landing without incident.

"Not many of my friends visited the house," I explained when he raised an eyebrow. "It was easier to see them at the mall in Syracuse."

The upstairs rooms were arranged in a square around the central staircase. Em and Sarah's room was in the front corner, overlooking the driveway. My mother and father's room was at the back of the house, with a view of the fields and a section of the old apple orchard that gradually gave way to a deeper wood of oaks and maples. The door was open, a light on inside. I stepped hesitantly toward the welcoming, golden rectangle and over the threshold.

The room was warm and comfortable, its broad bed loaded with quilts and pillows. Nothing matched, except for the plain white curtains. The floor was constructed out of wide pine planks with gaps large enough to swallow a hairbrush. A bathroom opened up to the right, and a radiator was popping and hissing inside.

"Lily of the valley," Matthew commented, his nostrils flaring at all the new scents.

"My mother's favorite perfume." An ancient bottle of Diorissimo with a faded black-and-white houndstooth ribbon wrapped around the neck still stood on the bureau.

Matthew dropped the bags onto the floor. "Is it going to bother you to be in here?" His eyes were worried. "You could have your old room, as Sarah suggested."

"No chance," I said firmly. "It's in the attic, and the bathroom is down here. Besides, there's no way we'll both fit in a single bed."

Matthew looked away. "I had thought we might—"

"We're not sleeping in separate beds. I'm no less your wife among witches than among vampires," I interrupted, drawing him toward me. The house settled on its foundations with a tiny sigh, as if bracing itself for a long conversation.

"No, but it might be easier—"

"For whom?" I interrupted again.

"For you," he finished. "You're in pain. You'd sleep more soundly in bed alone."

There would be no sleep for me at all without him at my side. Not wanting to worry him by saying so, I rested my hands on his chest in an attempt to distract him from the matter of sleeping arrangements. "Kiss me."

His mouth tightened into a no, but his eyes said yes. I pressed my body against his, and he responded with a kiss that was both sweet and gentle.

"I thought you were lost," he murmured when we parted, resting his forehead against mine, "forever. Now I'm afraid you might shatter into a thousand pieces because of what Satu did. If something had happened to you, I'd have gone mad."

My scent enveloped Matthew, and he relaxed a fraction. He relaxed further when his hands slid around my hips. They were relatively unscathed, and his touch was both comforting and electrifying. My need for him had only intensified since my ordeal with Satu.

"Can you feel it?" I took his hand in mine, pressing it against the center of my chest.

"Feel what?" Matthew's face was puzzled.

Unsure what would make an impression on his preternatural senses, I concentrated on the chain that had unfurled when he'd first kissed me. When I touched it with an imaginary finger, it emitted a low, steady hum.

Matthew gasped, a look of wonder on his face. "I can hear something. What is it?" He bent to rest his ear against my chest.

"It's you, inside me," I said. "You ground me—an anchor at the end of a long, silvery chain. It's why I'm so certain of you, I suppose." My voice dropped. "Provided I could feel you—had this connection to you—there was nothing Satu could say or do that I couldn't endure."

"It's like the sound your blood makes when you talk to Rakasa with your mind, or when you called the witchwind. Now that I know what to listen for, it's audible."

Ysabeau had mentioned she could hear my witch's blood singing. I tried to make the chain's music louder, its vibrations passing into the rest of my body.

Matthew lifted his head and gave me a glorious smile. "Amazing."

The humming grew more intense, and I lost control of the energy pulsing through me. Overhead, a score of stars burst into life and shot through the room.

"Oops." Dozens of ghostly eyes tingled against my back. The house shut the door firmly against the inquiring looks of my ancestors, who had assembled to see the fireworks display as if it were Independence Day.

"Did you do that?" Matthew stared intently at the closed door.

"No," I explained earnestly. "The sparklers were mine. That was the house. It has a thing about privacy."

"Thank God," he murmured, pulling my hips firmly to his and kissing me again in a way that had the ghosts on the other side muttering.

The fireworks fizzled out in a stream of aquamarine light over the chest of drawers.

"I love you, Matthew Clairmont," I said at the earliest opportunity.

"And I love you, Diana Bishop," he replied formally. "But your aunt and Emily must be freezing. Show me the rest of the house so that they can come inside."

Slowly we went through the other rooms on the second floor, most unused now and filled with assorted bric-a-brac from Em's yard-sale addiction and all the junk Sarah couldn't bear to throw away for fear she might need it one day.

Matthew helped me up the stairs to the attic bedroom where I'd endured my adolescence. It still had posters of musicians tacked to the walls and sported the strong shades of purple and green that were a teenager's attempt at a sophisticated color scheme.

Downstairs, we explored the big formal rooms built to receive guests—the keeping room on one side of the front door and the office and small parlor opposite. We passed through the rarely used dining room and into the heart of the house—a family room large enough to serve as TV room and eating area, with the kitchen at the far end.

"It looks like Em's taken up needlepoint—again," I said, picking up a half-finished canvas with a basket of flowers on it. "And Sarah's fallen off the wagon."

"She's a smoker?" Matthew gave the air a long sniff.

"When she's stressed. Em makes her smoke outside—but you can still smell it. Does it bother you?" I asked, acutely aware of how sensitive he might be to the odor.

"*Dieu,* Diana, I've smelled worse," he replied.

The cavernous kitchen retained its wall of brick ovens and a gigantic walk-in fireplace. There were modern appliances, too, and old stone floors that had endured two centuries of dropped pans, wet animals, muddy shoes, and other more witchy substances. I ushered him into Sarah's adjacent workroom. Originally a freestanding summer kitchen, it was now connected to the house and still equipped with cranes for holding cauldrons of stew and spits for roasting meat. Herbs hung from the ceiling, and a storage loft held drying fruits and jars of her lotions and potions. The tour over, we returned to the kitchen

"This room is so *brown.*" I studied the decor while flicking the porch light on and off again, the Bishops' long-standing signal that it was safe to enter. There was a brown refrigerator, brown wooden cabinets, warm red-brown brick, a brown rotary-dial phone, and tired brown-checked wallpaper. "What it needs is a fresh coat of white paint."

Matthew's chin lifted, and his eyes panned to the back door.

"February would be ideal for the job, if you're offering to do the work," a throaty voice said from the mudroom. Sarah rounded the corner, wearing jeans and an oversize plaid flannel shirt. Her red hair was wild and her cheeks bright with the cold.

"Hello, Sarah," I said, backing up toward the sink.

"Hello, Diana." Sarah stared fixedly at the bruise under my eye. "This is the vampire, I take it?"

"Yes." I hobbled forward again to make the introductions. Sarah's sharp gaze turned to my ankle. "Sarah, this is Matthew Clairmont. Matthew, my aunt, Sarah Bishop."

Matthew extended his right hand. "Sarah," he said, meeting her eyes without hesitation.

Sarah pursed her lips in response. Like me, she had the Bishop chin, which was slightly too long for the rest of her face. It was now jutting out even more.

"Matthew." When their hands met, Sarah flinched. "Yep," she said, turning her head slightly, "he's definitely a vampire, Em."

"Thanks for the help, Sarah," Em grumbled, walking in with an armful of small logs and an impatient expression. She was taller than me or Sarah, and her shining silver cap of hair somehow made her look younger than the color would suggest. Her narrow face broke into a delighted smile when she saw us standing in the kitchen.

Matthew jumped to take the wood away from her. Tabitha, who had been absent during the first flurry of greeting, hampered his progress to the fireplace by tracing figure eights between his feet. Miraculously, the vampire made it to the other side of the room without stepping on her.

"Thank you, Matthew. And thank you for bringing her home as well. We've been so worried." Em shook out her arms, bits of bark flying from the wool of her sweater.

"You're welcome, Emily," he said, his voice irresistibly warm and rich. Em already looked charmed. Sarah was going to be tougher, although she was studying Tabitha's efforts to scale Matthew's arm with amazement.

I tried to retreat into the shadows before Em got a clear look at my face, but I was too late. She gasped, horrified. "Oh, Diana."

Sarah pulled out a stool. "Sit," she ordered.

Matthew crossed his arms tightly, as if resisting the temptation to interfere. His wolfish need to protect me had not diminished just because we were in Madison, and his strong dislike of creatures getting too near me was not reserved for other vampires.

My aunt's eyes traveled from my face down over my collarbones. "Let's get the shirt off," she said.

I reached for the buttons dutifully.

"Maybe you should examine Diana upstairs." Em shot a worried look at Matthew.

"I don't imagine he'll get an eyeful of anything he hasn't already seen. You aren't hungry, are you?" Sarah said without a backward glance.

"No," Matthew said drily, "I ate on the plane."

My aunt's eyes tingled across my neck. So did Em's.

"Sarah! Em!" I was indignant.

"Just checking," Sarah said mildly. The shirt was off now, and she took in the gauze wrapping on my forearm, my mummified torso, and the other cuts and bruises.

"Matthew's already examined me. He's a doctor, remember?"

Her fingers probed my collarbone. I winced. "He missed this, though. It's a hairline fracture." She moved up to the cheekbone. I winced again. "What's wrong with her ankle?" As usual, I hadn't been able to conceal anything from Sarah.

"A bad sprain accompanied by superficial first- and second-degree burns." Matthew was staring at Sarah's hands, ready to haul her off if she caused me too much discomfort.

"How do you get burns and a sprain in the same place?" Sarah was treating Matthew like a first-year medical student on grand rounds.

"You get them from being hung upside down by a sadistic witch," I answered for him, squirming slightly as Sarah continued to examine my face.

"What's under that?" Sarah demanded, as if I hadn't spoken, pointing to my arm.

"An incision deep enough to require suturing," Matthew replied patiently.

"What have you got her on?"

"Painkillers, a diuretic to minimize swelling, and a broad-spectrum antibiotic." There was the barest trace of annoyance in his voice.

"Why is she wrapped up like a mummy?" Em asked, chewing on her lip.

The blood drained from my face. Sarah stopped what she was doing and gave me a probing look before she spoke.

"Let's wait on that, Em. First things first. Who did this to you, Diana?"

"A witch named Satu Järvinen. I think she's Swedish." My arms crossed protectively over my chest.

Matthew's mouth tightened, and he left my side long enough to pile more logs on the fire.

"She's not Swedish, she's Finnish," Sarah said, "and quite powerful. The next time I see her, though, she'll wish she'd never been born."

"There won't be much left of her after I'm done," Matthew murmured, "so if you want a shot at her, you'll have to reach her before I do. And I'm known for my speed."

Sarah gave him an appraising look. Her words were only a threat. Matthew's were something else entirely. They were a promise. "Who treated Diana besides you?"

"My mother and her housekeeper, Marthe."

"They know old herbal remedies. But I can do a bit more." Sarah rolled up her sleeves.

"It's a little early in the day for witchcraft. Have you had enough coffee?" I looked at Em imploringly, silently begging her to call Sarah off.

"Let Sarah fix it, honey," Em said, taking my hand and giving it a squeeze. "The sooner she does, the sooner you'll be fully healed."

Sarah's lips were already moving. Matthew edged closer, fascinated. She laid her fingertips on my face. The bone underneath tingled with electricity before the crack fused with a snap.

"Ow!" I held my cheek.

"It will only sting for a bit," Sarah said. "You were strong enough to withstand the injury—you should have no problem with the cure." She studied my cheek for a moment and nodded with satisfaction before turning to my collarbone. The electrical twinge required to mend it was more powerful, no doubt because the bones were thicker.

"Get her shoe off," she instructed Matthew, headed for the stillroom. He was the most overqualified medical assistant ever known, but he obeyed her orders without a grumble.

When Sarah returned with a pot of one of her ointments, Matthew had my foot propped up on his thigh. "There are scissors in my bag upstairs," he told my aunt, sniffing curiously as she unscrewed the pot's lid. "Shall I go get them?"

"Don't need them." Sarah muttered a few words and gestured at my ankle. The gauze began to unwind itself.

"That's handy," Matthew said enviously.

"Show-off," I said under my breath.

All eyes returned to my ankle when the gauze was finished rolling itself into a ball. It still looked nasty and was starting to ooze. Sarah calmly recited fresh spells, though the red spots on her cheeks hinted at her underlying fury. When she had finished, the black and white marks were gone, and though there was still an angry ring around my ankle, the joint itself was noticeably smaller in size.

"Thanks, Sarah." I flexed my foot while she smeared fresh ointment over the skin.

"You won't be doing any yoga for a week or so—and no running for three, Diana. It needs rest and time to fully recover." She muttered some more and beckoned to a fresh roll of gauze, which started to wind around my foot and ankle.

"Amazing," Matthew said again, shaking his head.

"Do you mind if I look at the arm?"

"Not at all." He sounded almost eager. "The muscle was slightly damaged. Can you mend that, as well as the skin?"

"Probably," Sarah said with just a hint of smugness. Fifteen minutes and a few muffled curses later, there was nothing but a thin red line running down my arm to indicate where Satu had sliced it open.

"Nice work," Matthew said, turning my arm to admire Sarah's skill.

"You, too. That was fine stitching." Sarah drank thirstily from a glass of water.

I reached for Matthew's shirt.

"You should see to her back as well."

"It can wait." I shot him an evil look. "Sarah's tired, and so am I."

Sarah's eyes moved from me to the vampire. "Matthew?" she asked, relegating me to the bottom of the pecking order.

"I want you to treat her back," he said without taking his eyes off me.

"No," I whispered, clutching his shirt to my chest.

He crouched in front of me, hands on my knees. "You've seen what Sarah can do. Your recovery will be faster if you let her help you."

Recovery? No witchcraft could help me recover from La Pierre.

"Please, *mon coeur.*" Matthew gently extricated his balled-up shirt from my hands.

Reluctantly I agreed. There was a tingle of witches' glances when Em and Sarah moved around to study my back, and my instincts urged me to run. I reached blindly for Matthew instead, and he clasped both my hands in his.

"I'm here," he assured me while Sarah muttered her first spell. The gauze wrappings parted along my spine, her words slicing through them with ease.

Em's sharp intake of breath and Sarah's silence told me when the marks were visible.

"This is an opening spell," Sarah said angrily, staring at my back. "You don't use this on living beings. She could have killed you."

"She was trying to get my magic out—like I was a piñata." With my back exposed, my emotions were swinging wildly again, and I nearly giggled at the thought of hanging from a tree while a blindfolded Satu swatted me with a stick. Matthew noticed my mounting hysteria.

"The quicker you can do this, the better, Sarah. Not to rush you, of course," he said hastily. I could easily imagine the look he'd received. "We can talk about Satu later."

Every bit of witchcraft Sarah used reminded me of Satu, and having two witches stand behind me made it impossible to keep my thoughts from returning to La Pierre. I burrowed more deeply inside myself for protection and let my mind go numb. Sarah worked more magic. But I could take no more and set my soul adrift.

"Are you almost done?" Matthew said, his voice taut with concern.

"There are two marks I can't do much with. They'll leave scars. Here," Sarah said, tracing the lines of a star between my shoulder blades, "and here." Her fingers moved down to my lower back, moving from rib to rib and scooping down to my waist in between.

My mind was no longer blank but seared with a picture to match Sarah's gestures.

A star hanging above a crescent moon.

"They suspect, Matthew!" I cried, frozen to the stool with terror. Matthew's drawerful of seals swam through my memories. They had been hidden so completely, I knew instinctively that the order of knights must be just as deeply concealed. But Satu knew about them, which meant the other witches of the Congregation probably did, too.

"My darling, what is it?" Matthew pulled me into his arms.

I pushed against his chest, trying to make him listen. "When I refused to give you up, Satu marked me—with your seal."

He turned me inside his arms, protecting as much of my exposed flesh as he could. When he'd seen what was inscribed there, Matthew went still. "They no longer suspect. At last, they know."

"What are you talking about?" demanded Sarah.

"May I have Diana's shirt, please?"

"I don't think the scars will be too bad," my aunt said somewhat defensively.

"The shirt." Matthew's voice was icy.

Em tossed it to him. Matthew pulled the sleeves gently over my arms, drawing the edges together in front. He was hiding his eyes, but the vein in his forehead was pulsing.

"I'm so sorry," I murmured.

"You have *nothing* to be sorry for." He took my face in his hands. "Any vampire would know you were mine—with or without this brand on your back. Satu wanted to make sure that every other creature knew who you belonged to as well. When I was reborn, they used to shear the hair from the heads of women who gave their bodies to the enemy. It was a crude way of exposing traitors. This is no different." He looked away. "Did Ysabeau tell you?"

"No. I was looking for paper and found the drawer."

"What the hell is going on?" Sarah snapped.

"I invaded your privacy. I shouldn't have," I whispered, clutching at his arms.

He drew away and stared at me incredulously, then crushed me to his chest without any concern for my injuries. Mercifully, Sarah's witchcraft meant that there was very little pain. "Christ, Diana. Satu told you what I did. I followed you home and broke in to your rooms. Besides, how can I blame you for finding out on your own what I should have told you myself?"

A thunderclap echoed through the kitchen, setting the pots and pans clanging.

When the sound had faded into silence, Sarah spoke. "If someone doesn't tell us what is going on *immediately,* all hell is going to break loose." A spell rose to her lips.

My fingertips tingled, and winds circled my feet. "Back off, Sarah." The wind roared through my veins, and I stepped between Sarah and Matthew. My aunt kept muttering, and my eyes narrowed.

Em put her hand on Sarah's arm in alarm. "Don't push her. She's not in control."

I could see a bow in my left hand, an arrow in my right. They felt heavy, yet strangely familiar. A few steps away, Sarah was in my sights. Without hesitation, my arms rose and drew apart in preparation to shoot.

My aunt stopped muttering in midspell. "Holy shit," she breathed, looking at Em in amazement.

"Honey, put the fire down." Em made a gesture of surrender.

Confused, I reexamined my hands. There was no fire in them.

"Not inside. If you want to unleash witchfire, we'll go outside," said Em.

"Calm down, Diana." Matthew pinned my elbows to my sides, and the heaviness associated with the bow and arrow dissolved.

"I don't like it when she threatens you." My voice sounded echoing and strange.

"Sarah wasn't threatening me. She just wanted to know what we were talking about. We need to tell her."

"But it's a secret," I said, confused. We had to keep our secrets—from everyone—whether they involved my abilities or Matthew's knights.

"No more secrets," he said firmly, his breath against my neck. "They're not good for either of us." When the winds died down, he spun me tightly against him.

"Is she always like that? Wild and out of control?" Sarah asked.

"Your niece did brilliantly," Matthew retorted, continuing to hold me.

Sarah and Matthew faced off across the kitchen floor.

"I suppose," she admitted with poor grace when their silent battle had concluded, "though you might have told us you could control witchfire, Diana. It's not exactly a run-of-the-mill ability."

"I can't *control* anything." Suddenly I was exhausted and didn't want to be standing up anymore. My legs agreed and began to buckle.

"Upstairs," he said, his tone brooking no argument. "We'll finish this conversation there."

In my parents' room, after giving me another dose of painkillers and antibiotics, Matthew tucked me into bed. Then he told my aunts more about Satu's mark. Tabitha condescended to sit on my feet as he did so in order to be closer to the sound of Matthew's voice.

"The mark Satu left on Diana's back belongs to an . . . organization that my family started many years ago. Most people have long forgotten it, and those who haven't think it doesn't exist anymore. We like to preserve that illusion. With the star and moon on her back, Satu marked your niece as my property and made it known that the witches had discovered my family's secret."

"Does this secret organization have a name?" Sarah asked.

"You don't have to tell them everything, Matthew." I reached for his hand. There was danger associated with disclosing too much about the Knights of Lazarus. I could feel it, seeping around me like a dark cloud, and I didn't want it to enfold Sarah and Em, too.

"The Knights of Lazarus of Bethany." He said it quickly, as if afraid he'd lose his resolve. "It's an old chivalric order."

Sarah snorted. "Never heard of them. Are they like the Knights of Columbus? They've got a chapter in Oneida."

"Not really." Matthew's mouth twitched. "The Knights of Lazarus date back to the Crusades."

"Didn't we watch a television program about the Crusades that had an order of knights in it?" Em asked Sarah.

"The Templars. But all those conspiracy theories are nonsense. There's no such thing as Templars now," Sarah said decidedly.

"There aren't supposed to be witches and vampires either, Sarah," I pointed out.

Matthew reached for my wrist, his fingers cool against my pulse.

"This conversation is over for the present," he said firmly. "There's plenty of time to talk about whether the Knights of Lazarus exist or not."

Matthew ushered out a reluctant Em and Sarah. Once my aunts were in the hall, the house took matters into its own hands and shut the door. The lock scraped in the frame.

"I don't have a key for that room," Sarah called to Matthew.

Unconcerned, Matthew climbed onto the bed, pulling me into the crook of his arm so that my head rested on his heart. Every time I tried to speak, he shushed me into silence.

"Later," he kept repeating.

His heart pulsed once and then, several minutes later, pulsed again.

Before it could pulse a third time, I was sound asleep.

Chapter 33

A combination of exhaustion, medication, and the familiarity of home kept me in bed for hours. I woke on my stomach, one knee bent and arm outstretched, searching vainly for Matthew.

Too groggy to sit up, I turned my head toward the door. A large key sat in the lock, and there were low voices on the other side. As the muzziness of sleep slowly gave way to awareness, the mumbling became clearer.

"It's appalling," Matthew snapped. "How could you let her go on this way?"

"We didn't know about the extent of her power—not absolutely," Sarah said, sounding equally furious. "She was bound to be different, given her parents. I never expected witchfire, though."

"How did you recognize she was trying to call it, Emily?" Matthew softened his voice.

"A witch on Cape Cod summoned it when I was a child. She must have been seventy," Em said. "I never forgot what she looked like or what it felt like to be near that kind of power."

"Witchfire is lethal. No spell can ward it off, and no witchcraft can heal the burns. My mother taught me to recognize the signs for my own protection—the smell of sulfur, the way a witch's arms moved," said Sarah. "She told me that the goddess is present when witchfire is called. I thought I'd go to my grave without witnessing it, and I certainly never expected my niece to unleash it on me in my own kitchen. Witchfire—and witchwater, too?"

"I hoped the witchfire would be recessive," Matthew confessed. "Tell me about Stephen Proctor." Until recently, the authoritative tone he adopted in moments like this had seemed a vestige of his past life as a soldier. Now that I knew about the Knights of Lazarus, I understood it as part of his present, too.

Sarah was not accustomed to having anyone use that tone with her, however, and she bristled. "Stephen was private. He didn't flaunt his power."

"No wonder the witches went digging to discover it, then."

My eyes closed tightly against the sight of my father's body, opened up from throat to groin so that other witches could understand his magic. His fate had nearly been mine.

Matthew's bulk shifted in the hall, and the house protested at the unusual weight. "He was an experienced wizard, but he was no match for them. Diana might have inherited his abilities—and Rebecca's, too, God help her. But she doesn't have their knowledge, and without it she's helpless. She might as well have a target painted on her."

I continued eavesdropping shamelessly.

"She's not a transistor radio, Matthew," Sarah said defensively. "Diana didn't come to us with batteries and an instruction manual. We did the best we could. She became a different child after Rebecca and Stephen were killed, withdrawing so far that no one could reach her. What should we have done? Forced her to face what she was so determined to deny?"

"I don't know." Matthew's exasperation was audible. "But you shouldn't have left her like this. That witch held her captive for more than twelve hours."

"We'll teach her what she needs to know."

"For her sake, it had better not take too long."

"It will take her whole life," Sarah snapped. "Magic isn't macramé. It takes time."

"We don't have time," Matthew hissed. The creaking of the floorboards told me Sarah had taken an instinctive step away from him. "The Congregation has been playing cat-and-mouse games, but the mark on Diana's back indicates those days are over."

"How dare you call what happened to my niece a *game*?" Sarah's voice rose.

"Shh," Em said. "You'll wake her."

"What might help us understand how Diana is spellbound, Emily?" Matthew was whispering now. "Can you remember anything about the days before Rebecca and Stephen left for Africa—small details, what they were worried about?"

Spellbound.

The word echoed in my mind as I slowly drew myself upright. Spellbinding was reserved for extreme circumstances—life-threatening danger, madness, pure and uncontrollable evil. Merely to threaten it earned you the censure of other witches.

Spellbound?

By the time I got to my feet, Matthew was at my side. He was frowning. "What do you need?"

"I want to talk to Em." My fingers were snapping and turning blue. So were my toes, sticking out of the bandages that protected my ankle. The gauze on my foot snagged an old nail head poking up from the floor's pine boards as I pushed past him.

Sarah and Em were waiting on the landing, trepidation on their faces.

"What's wrong with me?" I demanded.

Emily crept into the crook of Sarah's arm. "There's nothing wrong with you."

"You said I'm spellbound. That my own *mother* did it." I was some kind of monster. It was the only possible explanation.

Emily heard my thoughts as if I'd spoken them aloud. "You're not a monster, honey. Rebecca did it because she was afraid for you."

"She was afraid *of* me, you mean." My blue fingers provided an excellent reason for someone to be terrified. I tried to hide them but didn't want to singe Matthew's shirt, and resting them on the old wooden stair rail risked setting the whole house on fire.

Watch the rug, girl! The tall female ghost from the keeping room was peeking around Sarah and Em's door and pointing urgently at the floor. I lifted my toes slightly.

"No one is afraid of you." Matthew stared with frosty intensity at my back, willing me to face him.

"They are." I pointed a sparkling finger at my aunts, eyes resolutely in their direction.

So am I, confessed another dead Bishop, this one a teenage boy with slightly protruding teeth. He was carrying a berry basket and wore a pair of ripped britches.

My aunts took a step backward as I continued to glare at them.

"You have every right to be frustrated." Matthew moved so that he was standing just behind me. The wind rose, and touches of snow from his glance glazed my thighs, too. "Now the witchwind has come because you feel trapped." He crept closer, and the air around my lower legs increased slightly. "See?"

Yes, that roiling feeling might be frustration rather than anger. Distracted from the issue of spellbinding, I turned to ask him more about his theories. The color in my fingers was already fading, and the snapping sound was gone.

"You have to try to understand," Em pleaded. "Rebecca and Stephen went to Africa to protect you. They spellbound you for the same reason. All they wanted was for you to be safe."

The house moaned through its timbers and held its breath, its old wooden joists creaking.

Coldness spread through me from the inside out.

"Is it my fault they died? They went to Africa and someone killed them—because of me?" I looked at Matthew in horror.

Without waiting for an answer, I made my way blindly to the stairs, unconcerned with the pain in my ankle or anything else except fleeing.

"No, Sarah. Let her go," Matthew said sharply.

The house opened all the doors before me and slammed them behind as I went through the front hall, the dining room, the family room, and into the kitchen. A pair of Sarah's gardening boots slipped over my bare feet, their rubber surfaces cold and smooth. Once outside, I did what I'd always done when the family was too much for me and went into the woods.

My feet didn't slow until I had made it through the scraggy apple trees and into the shadows cast by the ancient white oaks and sugar maples. Out of breath and shaking with shock and exhaustion, I found myself at the foot of an enormous tree almost as wide as it was tall. Low, sprawling branches nearly touched the ground, their red and purple deeply lobed leaves standing out against the ashy bark.

All through my childhood and adolescence, I'd poured out my heartbreak and loneliness underneath its limbs. Generations of Bishops had found the same solace here and carved their initials into the tree. Mine were gouged with a penknife next to the "RB" my mother had left before me, and I traced their curves before curling up in a ball near the rough trunk and rocking myself like a child.

There was a cool touch on my hair before the blue parka settled over my shoulders. Matthew's solid frame lowered to the ground, his back scraping against the tree's bark.

"Did they tell you what's wrong with me?" My voice was muffled against my legs.

"There's nothing wrong with you, *mon coeur*."

"You have a lot to learn about witches." I rested my chin on my knees but still wouldn't look at him. "Witches don't spellbind someone without a damn good reason."

Matthew was quiet. I slid a sidelong glance in his direction. His legs were just visible from the corner of my eye—one stretched forward and the other bent—as was a long, white hand. It was draped loosely over his knee.

"Your parents had a damn good reason. They were saving their daughter's life." His voice was quiet and even, but there were stronger emotions underneath. "It's what I would have done."

"Did you know I was spellbound, too?" It wasn't possible for me to keep from sounding accusatory.

"Marthe and Ysabeau figured it out. They told me just before we left for La Pierre. Emily confirmed their suspicions. I hadn't had a chance to tell you."

"How could Em keep this from me?" I felt betrayed and alone, just as I had when Satu told me about what Matthew had done.

"You must forgive your parents and Emily. They were doing what they thought was best—for you."

"You don't understand, Matthew," I said, shaking my head stubbornly. "My mother tied me up and went to Africa as if I were an evil, deranged creature who couldn't be trusted."

"Your parents were worried about the Congregation."

"That's nonsense." My fingers tingled, and I pushed the feeling back toward my elbows, trying to control my temper. "Not everything is about the damn Congregation, Matthew."

"No, but this is. You don't have to be a witch to see it."

My white table appeared before me without warning, events past and present scattered on its surface. The puzzle pieces began to arrange themselves: my mother chasing after me while I clapped my hands and flew over the linoleum floor of our kitchen in Cambridge, my father shouting at Peter Knox in his study at home, a bedtime story about a fairy godmother and magical ribbons, both my parents standing over my bed saying spells and working magic while I lay quietly on top of the quilt. The pieces clicked into place, and the pattern emerged.

"My mother's bedtime stories," I said, turning to him in amazement. "She couldn't tell me her plans outright, so she turned it all into a story about evil witches and enchanted ribbons and a fairy godmother. Every night she told me, so that some part of me would remember."

"And do you remember anything else?"

"Before they spellbound me, Peter Knox came to see my father." I shuddered, hearing the doorbell ringing and seeing again the expression on my father's face when he opened the door. "That creature was in my house. He touched my head." Knox's hand resting on the back of my skull had produced an uncanny sensation, I recalled.

"My father sent me to my room, and the two of them fought. My mother stayed in the kitchen. It was strange that she didn't come to see what was going on. Then my father went out for a long time. My mother was frantic. She called Em that night." The memories were coming thick and fast now.

"Emily told me Rebecca's spell was cast so that it would hold until the 'shadowed man' came. Your mother thought I would be able to protect you from Knox and the Congregation." His face darkened.

"Nobody could have protected me—except me. Satu was right. I'm a sorry excuse for a witch." My head went back to my knees again. "I'm not like my mother at all."

Matthew stood, extending one hand. "Get up," he said abruptly.

I slid my hand into his, expecting him to comfort me with a hug. Instead he pushed my arms into the sleeves of the blue parka and stepped away.

"You are a witch. It's time you learned how to take care of yourself."

"Not now, Matthew."

"I wish we could let you decide, but we can't," he said brusquely. "The Congregation wants your power—or the knowledge of it at the very least. They want Ashmole 782, and you're the only creature in more than a century to see it."

"They want you and the Knights of Lazarus, too." I was desperate to make this about something besides me and my ill-understood magic.

"They could have brought down the brotherhood before. The Congregation has had plenty of chances." Matthew was obviously sizing me up and gauging my few strengths and considerable weaknesses. It made me feel vulnerable. "But they don't really care about that. They don't want me to have you or the manuscript."

"But I'm surrounded by protectors. You're with me—Sarah and Em, too."

"We can't be with you every moment, Diana. Besides, do you want Sarah and Emily to risk their lives to save yours?" It was a blunt question, and his face twisted. He backed away from me, eyes narrowed to slits.

"You're frightening me," I said as his body lowered into a crouch. The final, lingering touches of morphine drifted through my blood, chased away by the first rush of adrenaline.

"No I'm not." He shook his head slowly, looking every inch a wolf as his hair swayed around his face. "I'd smell it if you were truly frightened. You're just off balance."

A rumbling began in the back of Matthew's throat that was a far cry from the sounds he made when he felt pleasure. I took a wary step away from him.

"That's better," he purred. "At least you have a taste of fear now."

"Why are you doing this?" I whispered.

He was gone without a word.

I blinked. "Matthew?"

Two cold patches bored into the top of my skull.

Matthew was hanging like a bat between two tree limbs, his arms outstretched like wings. His feet were hooked around another branch. He watched me intently, little flickers of frost my only indication of the changes in his focus.

"I'm not a colleague you're having an argument with. This isn't an academic dispute—this is life or death."

"Come down from there," I said sharply. "You've made your point."

I didn't see him land at my side, but I felt his cold fingers at my neck and chin, twisting my head to the side and exposing my throat. "If I were Gerbert, you'd be dead already," he hissed.

"Stop it, Matthew." I struggled to break free but made no progress.

"No." His grip tightened. "Satu tried to break you, and you want to disappear because of it. But you have to fight back."

"I am." I pushed against his arms to prove my point.

"Not like a human," Matthew said contemptuously. "Fight back like a witch."

He vanished again. This time he wasn't in the tree, nor could I feel his cold eyes on me.

"I'm tired. I'm going back to the house." After I'd taken only three steps in that direction, there was a whoosh. Matthew had slung me over his shoulder, and I was moving—fast—the opposite way.

"You aren't going anywhere."

"Sarah and Em will be out here if you keep this up." One of them was bound to sense that something was wrong. And if *they* didn't, Tabitha would surely kick up a fuss.

"No they won't." Matthew set me on my feet deeper in the woods. "They promised not to leave the house—not if you screamed, no matter what danger they sensed."

I crept backward, wanting to put some distance between me and his huge black eyes. The muscles in his legs coiled to spring. When I turned to make a run for it, he was already in front of me. I turned in the opposite direction, but he was there. A breeze stirred around my feet.

"Good," he said with satisfaction. Matthew's body lowered into the same position he'd taken stalking the stag at Sept-Tours, and the menacing growl started up again.

The breeze moved around my feet in gusts, but it didn't increase. The tingling descended from my elbows into my nails. Instead of pushing back my frustration, I let the feeling mount. Arcs of blue electricity moved between my fingers.

"Use your power," he rasped. "You can't fight me any other way."

My hands waved in his direction. It didn't seem very threatening, but it was all I could think of. Matthew proved just how worthless my efforts were by pouncing on me and spinning me around before vanishing into the trees.

"You're dead—again." His voice came from somewhere to my right.

"Whatever you're trying to do isn't working!" I shouted in his direction.

"I'm right behind you," he purred into my ear.

My scream split the silence of the forest, and the winds rose around me in a cyclonic cocoon. "Stay away!" I roared.

Matthew reached for me with a determined look, his hands shooting through my windy barrier. I flung mine in his direction, instinct taking over, and a rush of air knocked him back on his heels. He looked surprised, and the predator appeared in the depths of his eyes. He came at me again in another attempt to break the wind's hold. Though I concentrated on pushing him back, the air didn't respond as I wanted it to.

"Stop trying to force it," Matthew said. He was fearless and had made his way through the cyclone, his fingers digging into my upper arms. "Your mother spellbound you so that no one could force your magic—not even you."

"Then how do I call it when needed and control it when it's not?"

"Figure it out." Matthew's snowy gaze flickered over my neck and shoulders, instinctively locating my major veins and arteries.

"I can't." A wave of panic engulfed me. "I'm not a witch."

"Stop saying that. It's not true, and you know it." He dropped me abruptly. "Close your eyes. Start walking."

"What?"

"I've watched you for weeks, Diana." The way he was moving was completely feral, the smell of cloves so overpowering that my throat closed. "You need movement and sensory deprivation so that all you can do is *feel.*" He gave me a push, and I stumbled. When I turned back, he was gone.

My eyes circled the forest. The woods were eerily silent, the animals shielding themselves from the powerful predator in their midst.

Closing my eyes, I began to breathe deeply. A breeze ruffled past me, first in one direction, then in another. It was Matthew, taunting me. I focused on my breathing, trying to be as still as the rest of the creatures in the forest, then set out.

There was a tightness between my eyes. I breathed into it, too, remembering Amira's yoga instruction and Marthe's advice to let the visions pass through me. The tightness turned to tingling and the tingling to a sense of possibility as my mind's eye—a witch's third eye—opened fully for the first time.

It took in everything that was alive in the forest—the vegetation, the energy in the earth, the water moving underneath the ground—each vital force distinct in color and shade. My mind's eye saw the rabbits crouched in the hollow of a tree, their hearts thundering in fear as they smelled the vampire. It detected the barn owls, their late-afternoon naps brought to a premature end by this creature who swung from tree limbs and jumped like a panther. The rabbits and owls knew they couldn't escape him.

"King of the beasts," I whispered.

Matthew's low chuckle sounded through the trees.

No creature in the forest could fight Matthew and win. "Except me," I breathed.

My mind's eye swept over the forest. A vampire is not fully alive, and it was hard to find him amid the dazzling energy that surrounded me. Finally I located his shape, a concentration of darkness like a black hole, the edges glowing red where his preternatural life force met the vitality of the world. Instinctively turning my face in his direction alerted him to my scrutiny and he slid away, fading into the shadows between the trees.

With both eyes closed and my mind's eye open, I started walking, hoping to lure him into following. Behind me his darkness detached from a maple tree in a gash of red and black amid the green. This time my face remained pointed in the opposite direction.

"I see you, Matthew," I said softly.

"Do you, *ma lionne*? And what will you do about it?" He chuckled again but kept stalking me, the distance between us constant.

With each step my mind's eye grew brighter, its vision more acute. There was a brushy shrub to my left, and I leaned to the right. Then there was a rock in front of me, its sharp gray edges protruding from the soil. I picked up my foot to keep from tripping.

The movement of air across my chest told me there was a small clearing. It wasn't just the life of the forest that was speaking to me now. All around me the elements were sending messages to guide my way. Earth, air, fire, and water connected with me in tiny pinpricks of awareness that were distinct from the life in the forest.

Matthew's energy focused in on itself and become darker and deeper. Then his darkness—his absence of life—arced through the air in a graceful pounce that any lion would have envied. He stretched his arms to grab me.

Fly, I thought, a second before his fingers touched my skin.

The wind rose from my body in a sudden whoosh of power. The earth released me with a gentle push upward. Just as Matthew had promised, it was easy to let my body follow where my thoughts had led. It took no more effort than following an imaginary ribbon up to the sky.

Far below, Matthew somersaulted in midair and landed lightly on his feet precisely where I'd stood a few moments before.

I soared above the treetops, my eyes wide. They felt full of the sea, as vast as the horizon, and bright with sunlight and stars. My hair floated on the currents of air, the ends of each strand turning into tongues of flame that licked my face without burning. The tendrils caressed my cheeks with warmth as the cold air swept past. A raven swooped by me in flight, amazed at this strange new creature sharing her airspace.

Matthew's pale face was turned up to me, his eyes full of wonder. When our gazes connected, he smiled.

It was the most beautiful thing I'd ever seen. There was a surge of desire, strong and visceral, and a rush of pride that he was mine.

My body dove toward him, and Matthew's face turned in an instant from wonder to wariness. He snarled, unsure of me, his instincts warning that I might attack.

Pulling back on my nosedive, I descended more slowly until our eyes were level, my feet streaming behind in Sarah's rubber boots. The wind whipped a lock of my flaming hair in his direction.

Don't harm him. My every thought was focused on his safety. Air and fire obeyed me, and my third eye drank in his darkness.

"Stay away from me," he growled, "just for a moment." Matthew was struggling to master his predatory instincts. He *wanted* to hunt me now. The king of beasts didn't like to be bested.

Paying no attention to his warning, I lowered my feet until they floated a few inches above the ground and held out my hand, palm upturned. My mind's eye filled with the image of my own energy: a shifting mass of silver and gold, green and blue, shimmering like a morning star. I scooped some of it up, watching as it rolled from my heart through my shoulder and arm.

A pulsing, swirling ball of sky, sea, earth, and fire sat in my palm. The ancient philosophers would have called it a microcosm—a little world that contained fragments of me as well as the larger universe.

"For you," I said, voice hollow. My fingers tipped toward him.

Matthew caught the ball as it fell. It moved like quicksilver, molding itself to his cold flesh. My energy came to a quivering rest in the scoop of his hand.

"What is it?" he asked, distracted from his urge to hunt by the gleaming substance.

"Me," I said simply. Matthew fixed his attention on my face, his pupils engulfing the gray-green irises in a wave of black. "You won't hurt me. I won't hurt you either."

The vampire cradled my microcosm carefully in his hand, afraid to spill a drop.

"I still don't know how to fight," I said sadly. "All I can do is fly away."

"That's the most important lesson a warrior learns, witch." Matthew's mouth turned what was usually a derogatory term among vampires into an endearment. "You learn how to pick your battles and let go of those you can't win, to fight another day."

"Are you afraid of me?" I asked, my body still hovering.

"No," he said.

My third eye tingled. He was telling the truth. "Even though I have that inside me?" My glance flickered to the glowing, twitching mass in his hand.

Matthew's face was guarded and careful. "I've seen powerful witches before. We still don't know all that's inside you, though. We have to find out."

"I never wanted to know."

"Why, Diana? Why wouldn't you want these gifts?" He drew his hand tighter, as if my magic might be snatched away and destroyed before he understood its possibilities.

"Fear? Desire?" I said softly, touching his strong cheekbones with the tips of my fingers, shocked anew at the power of my love for him. Remembering what his daemon friend Bruno had written in the sixteenth century, I quoted it again. "'*Desire urges me on, as fear bridles me.*' Doesn't that explain everything that happens in the world?"

"Everything but you," he told me, his voice thick. "There's no accounting for you."

My feet touched the ground, and I pulled my fingers from his face, slowly unfurling them. My body seemed to know the smooth movement, though my mind was quick to register its strangeness. The piece of myself that I'd given to Matthew leaped from his hand into mine. My palm closed around it, the energy quickly reabsorbed. There was the tingle of a witch's power, and I recognized it as my own. I hung my head, frightened by the creature I was becoming.

Matthew's fingertip drew aside my curtain of hair. "Nothing will hide you from this magic—not science, not willpower, not concentration. It will always find you. And you can't hide from me either."

"That's what my mother said in the oubliette. She knew about us." Frightened by the memory of La Pierre, my mind's eye closed protectively. I shivered, and Matthew drew me near. It was no warmer in his cold arms, but it felt far safer.

"Perhaps that made it easier for them, to know you wouldn't be alone," Matthew said softly. His lips were cool and firm, and my own parted to draw him closer. He buried his face in my neck, and I heard him take in my scent with a sharp inhalation. He pulled away with reluctance, smoothing my hair and tucking the parka more closely around me.

"Will you train me to fight, like one of your knights?"

Matthew's hands stilled. "They knew how to defend themselves long before coming to me. But I've trained warriors in the past—humans, vampires, daemons. Even Marcus, and God knows he was a challenge. Never a witch, though."

"Let's go home." My ankle was still throbbing, and I was ready to drop with fatigue. After a few halting steps, Matthew swung me onto his back like a child and walked through the twilight with my arms clasped around his neck. "Thank you again for finding me," I whispered when the house came into view. He knew this time I wasn't talking about La Pierre.

"I'd stopped looking long ago. But there you were in the Bodleian Library on Mabon. A historian. A witch, no less." Matthew shook his head in disbelief.

"That's what makes it magic," I said, planting a soft kiss above his collar. He was still purring when he put me down on the back porch.

Matthew went to the woodshed to get more logs for the fire, leaving me to make peace with my aunts. Both of them looked uneasy.

"I understand why you kept it secret," I explained, giving Em a hug that made her gasp with relief, "but Mom told me the time for secrets was over."

"You've seen Rebecca?" Sarah said carefully, her face white.

"In La Pierre. When Satu tried to frighten me into cooperating with her." I paused. "Daddy, too."

"Was she . . . were they happy?" Sarah had to choke out the words. My grandmother was standing behind her, watching with concern.

"They were together," I said simply, looking out the window to see if Matthew was headed back to the house.

"And they were with you," Em said firmly, her eyes full. "That means they were more than happy."

My aunt opened her mouth to say something, thought better of it, and closed it again.

"What, Sarah?" I said, putting a hand on her arm.

"Did Rebecca speak to you?" Her voice was hushed.

"She told me stories. The same stories she told me when I was a little girl—about witches and princes and a fairy godmother. Even though she and Daddy spellbound me, Mom tried to find a way to make me remember my magic. But I wanted to forget."

"That last summer, before your mom and dad went to Africa, Rebecca asked me what made the most lasting impression on children. I told her it was the stories their parents read to them at night, and all the messages about hope and strength and love that were embedded in them." Em's eyes were spilling over now, and she dashed her tears away.

"You were right," I said softly.

Though the three witches had made amends, when Matthew came into the kitchen, his arms laden with wood, Sarah pounced on him.

"Don't ever ask me to ignore Diana's cries for help, and don't you ever threaten her again—no matter what the reason. If you do, I'll put a spell on you that will make you wish you'd never been reborn. Got that, vampire?"

"Of course, Sarah," Matthew murmured blandly, in perfect imitation of Ysabeau.

We ate dinner at the table in the family room. Matthew and Sarah were in an uneasy state of détente, but open warfare threatened when my aunt saw that there wasn't a scrap of meat in sight.

"You're smoking like a chimney," Em said patiently when Sarah grumbled about the lack of "real" food. "Your arteries will thank me."

"You didn't do it for me," Sarah said, shooting Matthew an accusatory glance. "You did it so he wouldn't feel the urge to bite Diana."

Matthew smiled mildly and pulled the cork from a bottle he'd brought in from the Range Rover. "Wine, Sarah?"

She eyed the bottle suspiciously. "Is that imported?"

"It's French," he said, pouring the deep red liquid into her water tumbler.

"I don't like the French."

"Don't believe everything you read. We're much nicer than we're made out to be," he said, teasing her into a grudging smile. "Trust me, we'll grow on you." As if to prove it, Tabitha jumped onto his shoulder from the floor and sat there like a parrot for the rest of the meal.

Matthew drank his wine and chatted about the house, asking Sarah and Em about the state of the farm and the place's history. I was left with little to do but watch them—these three creatures I loved so much—and wolf down large quantities of chili and cornbread.

When at last we went up to bed, I slipped between the sheets naked, desperate to feel Matthew's cool body against mine. He joined me, drawing me toward his bare flesh.

"You're warm," he said, snuggling more tightly against me.

"Mmm. You smell good," I said, my nose pressed against his chest. The key turned itself in the lock. It had been there when I woke up that afternoon. "Was the key in the bureau?"

"The house had it." His laughter rumbled underneath me. "It shot out of the floorboards next to the bed at an angle, hit the wall over the light switch, and slid down. When I didn't pick it up straightaway, it flew across the room and landed in my lap."

I laughed while his fingers drifted around my waist. He studiously avoided Satu's marks.

"You have your battle scars," I said, hoping to soothe him. "Now I have mine."

His lips found mine unerringly in the darkness. One hand moved to the small of my back, covering the crescent moon. The other traveled between my shoulder blades, blotting out the star. No magic was necessary to understand his pain and regret. It was everywhere evident—in his gentle touch, the words he murmured in the darkness, and his body that was so solid next to mine. Gradually he let go of the worst of his fear and anger. We touched with mouths and fingers, our initial urgency slowing to prolong the joy of reunion.

Stars burst into life at the peak of my pleasure, and a few still hung beneath the ceiling, sparkling and sputtering out the remainder of their brief lives while we lay in each other's arms and waited for the morning to find us.

Chapter 34

Matthew planted a kiss on my shoulder before the sun rose, and then he slipped downstairs. My muscles were tight in an uncustomary combination of stiffness and languor. At last I dragged myself out of bed and went looking for him.

I found Sarah and Em instead. They were standing by the back window, each clutching a steaming cup of coffee. Glancing over their shoulders, I went to fill the kettle. Matthew could wait—tea could not.

"What are you looking at?" I expected them to name some rare bird.

"Matthew."

I backed up a few steps.

"He's been out there for hours. I don't think he's moved a muscle. A raven flew by. I believe she plans to perch on him," Sarah continued, taking a sip of her coffee.

Matthew was standing with his feet rooted in the earth and his arms stretched out to the sides at shoulder level, index fingers and thumbs gently touching. In his gray T-shirt and black yoga pants, he did look like an unusually well-dressed, robust scarecrow.

"Should we be worried about him? He's got nothing on his feet." Em stared at Matthew over the edge of her coffee cup. "He must be freezing."

"Vampires burn, Em. They don't freeze. He'll come in when he's ready."

After filling the kettle, I made tea and stood with my aunts, silently watching Matthew. On my second cup, he finally lowered his arms and folded over at the waist. Sarah and Em moved hastily away from the window.

"He knows we've been watching him. He's a vampire, remember?" I laughed and pushed Sarah's boots on over my wool socks and a frayed pair of leggings and clomped outside.

"Thank you for being so patient," Matthew said after he'd gathered me into his arms and soundly kissed me good morning.

I was still clutching my mug, which had been in danger of spilling tea down his back. "Meditation is the only rest you get. I'm not about to disturb it. How long have you been out here?"

"Since dawn. I needed time to think."

"The house does that to people. There are too many voices, too much going on." It was chilly, and I snuggled inside my sweatshirt with the faded maroon bobcat on the back.

Matthew touched the dark circles under my eyes. "You're still exhausted. Some meditation wouldn't do you any harm either, you know."

My sleep had been fitful, full of dreams, snatches of alchemical poetry, and mumbled tirades directed at Satu. Even my grandmother had been worried. She'd been leaning against the chest of drawers with a watchful expression while Matthew soothed me back to sleep.

"I was strictly forbidden to do anything resembling yoga for a week."

"And you obey your aunt when she sets down these rules?" Matthew's eyebrow made a question mark.

"Not usually." I laughed, grabbing him by the sleeve to pull him back inside.

Matthew had my tea out of my hands and was lifting me out of Sarah's boots in an instant. He arranged my body and stood behind me. "Are your eyes closed?"

"Now they are," I said, closing my eyes and digging my toes through my socks into the cold earth. Thoughts chased around in my mind like playful kittens.

"You're thinking," Matthew said impatiently. "Just breathe."

My mind and breath settled. Matthew came around and lifted my arms, pressing my thumbs to the tips of my ring fingers and pinkies.

"Now I look like a scarecrow, too," I said. "What am I doing with my hands?"

"Prana mudra," Matthew explained. "It encourages the life force and is good for healing."

As I stood with arms outstretched and palms facing the sky, the silence and peace worked their way through my battered body. After about five minutes, the tightness between my eyes lifted and my mind's eye opened. There was a corresponding, subtle change inside me—an ebb and flow like water lapping on the shore. With each breath I took, a drop of cold, fresh water formed in my palm. My mind remained resolutely blank, unconcerned that I might be engulfed in witchwater even as the level of water in my hands slowly rose.

My mind's eye brightened, focusing on my surroundings. When it did, I saw the fields around the house as never before. Water ran beneath the ground's surface in deep blue veins. The roots of the apple trees extended into them, and finer webs of water shimmered in the leaves as they rustled in the morning breeze. Underneath my feet the water flowed toward me, trying to understand my connection to its power.

Calmly I breathed in and out. The water level in my palms rose and fell in response to the changing tides within and underneath me. When I could control the water no longer, the mudras broke open, water cascading from my flattened palms. I was left standing in the middle of the backyard, eyes open and arms outstretched, a small puddle on the ground under each hand.

My vampire stood twelve feet away from me with a proud look on his face, his arms crossed. My aunts were on the back porch, astonished.

"That was impressive," Matthew murmured, bending to pick up the stone-cold mug of tea. "You're going to be as good at this as you are at your research, you know. Magic's not just emotional and mental—it's physical, too."

"Have you coached witches before?" I slid back into Sarah's boots, my stomach rumbling loudly.

"No. You're my one and only." Matthew laughed. "And yes, I know you're hungry. We'll talk more about this after breakfast." He held out his hand, and we walked together toward the house.

"You can make a lot of money water witching, you know," Sarah called as we approached. "Everyone in town needs a new well, and old Harry was buried with his dowsing rod when he died last year."

"I don't need a dowsing rod—I *am* a dowsing rod. And if you're thinking of digging, do it there." I pointed to a cluster of apple trees that looked less scraggy than the rest.

Inside, Matthew boiled fresh water for my tea before turning his attention to the *Syracuse Post-Standard*. It could not compete with *Le Monde,* but he seemed content. With my vampire occupied, I ate slice after slice of bread hot from the toaster. Em and Sarah refilled their coffee cups and looked warily at my hands every time I got near the electrical appliances.

"This is going to be a three-pot morning," Sarah announced, dumping the used grounds out of the coffeemaker. I looked at Em in alarm.

It's mostly decaf, she said without speaking, her lips pressed together in silent mirth. *I've been adulterating it for years.* Like text messaging, silent speech was useful if you wanted to have a private discussion in this house.

Smiling broadly, I returned my attention to the toaster. I scraped the last of the butter onto my toast and wondered idly if there was more.

A plastic tub appeared at my elbow.

I turned to thank Em, but she was on the other side of the kitchen. So was Sarah. Matthew looked up from his paper and stared at the refrigerator.

The door was open, and the jams and mustards were rearranging themselves on the top shelf. When they were in place, the door quietly closed.

"Was that the house?" Matthew asked casually.

"No," Sarah replied, looking at me with interest. "That was Diana."

"What happened?" I gasped, looking at the butter.

"You tell us," Sarah said crisply. "You were fiddling with your ninth piece of toast when the refrigerator opened and the butter sailed out."

"All I did was wonder if there was more." I picked up the empty container.

Em clapped her hands with delight at my newest sign of power, and Sarah insisted that I try to get something else out of the refrigerator. No matter what I called, it refused to come.

"Try the cabinets," Em suggested. "The doors aren't as heavy."

Matthew had been watching the activity with interest. "You just wondered about the butter because you needed it?"

I nodded.

"And when you flew yesterday, did you command the air to cooperate?"

"I thought 'Fly,' and I flew. I needed to do it more than I needed the butter, though—you were about to kill me. Again."

"Diana flew?" Sarah asked faintly.

"Is there anything you need now?" inquired Matthew.

"To sit down." My knees felt a little shaky.

A kitchen stool traveled across the floor and parked obligingly beneath my backside.

Matthew smiled with satisfaction and picked up the paper. "It's just as I thought," he murmured, returning to the headlines.

Sarah tore the paper from his hands. "Stop grinning like the Cheshire cat. What did you think?"

At the mention of another member of her species, Tabitha strutted into the house through the cat door. With a look of complete devotion, she dropped a tiny, dead field mouse at Matthew's feet.

"*Merci, ma petite,*" Matthew said gravely. "Unfortunately, I am not hungry at present."

Tabitha yowled in frustration and hauled her offering off to the corner, where she punished it by batting it between her paws for failing to please Matthew.

Undeterred, Sarah repeated her question. "What do you think?"

"The spells that Rebecca and Stephen cast ensure that nobody can force the magic from Diana. Her magic is bound up in necessity. Very clever." He smoothed out his rumpled paper and resumed reading.

"Clever and impossible," Sarah grumbled.

"Not impossible," he replied. "We just have to think like her parents. Rebecca had seen what would happen at La Pierre—not every detail, but she knew that her daughter would be held captive by a witch. Rebecca also knew that she would get away. That's why the spellbinding held fast. Diana didn't need her magic."

"How are we supposed to teach Diana how to control her power if she can't command it?" demanded my aunt.

The house gave us no chance to consider the options. There was a sound like cannon fire, followed by tap dancing.

"Oh, hell." Sarah groaned. "What does it want now?"

Matthew put down his paper. "Is something wrong?"

"The house wants us. It slams the coffin doors on the keeping room and then moves the furniture around to get our attention." I licked the butter off my fingers and padded through the family room. The lights flickered in the front hall.

"All right, all right," Sarah said testily. "We're coming."

We followed my aunts into the keeping room. The house sent a wing chair careening across the floor in my direction.

"It wants Diana," Emily said unnecessarily.

The house might have wanted me, but it didn't anticipate the interference of a protective vampire with quick reflexes. Matthew shot his foot out and stopped the chair before it hit me in the back of the knees. There was a crack of old wood on strong bones.

"Don't worry, Matthew. The house only wants me to sit down." I did so, waiting for its next move.

"The house needs to learn some manners," he retorted.

"Where did Mom's rocker come from? We got rid of it years ago," Sarah said, pursing her lips at the old chair near the front window.

"The rocking chair is back, and so is Grandma," I said. "She said hello when we arrived."

"Was Elizabeth with her?" Em sat on the uncomfortable Victorian sofa. "Tall? Serious expression?"

"Yes. I didn't get a good look, though. She was mostly behind the door."

"The ghosts don't hang around much these days," Sarah said. "We think she's some distant Bishop cousin who died in the 1870s."

A ball of green wool and two knitting needles rocketed down the chimney and rolled across the hearth.

"Does the house think I should take up knitting?" I asked.

"That's mine—I started making a sweater a few years ago, and then one day it disappeared. The house takes all sorts of things and keeps them," Em explained to Matthew as she retrieved her project. She gestured at the sofa's hideous floral upholstery. "Come sit with me. Sometimes it takes the house awhile to get to the point. And we're missing some photographs, a telephone book, the turkey platter, and my favorite winter coat."

Matthew, not surprisingly, found it difficult to relax, given that a porcelain serving dish might decapitate him, but he did his best. Sarah sat in a Windsor chair nearby, looking annoyed.

"Come on, out with it," she snapped several minutes later. "I've got things to do."

A thick brown envelope wormed its way through a crack in the green-painted paneling next to the fireplace. Once it had worked itself free, it shot across the keeping room and landed, faceup, in my lap.

"Diana" was scrawled on the front in blue ballpoint ink. My mother's small, feminine handwriting was recognizable from permission slips and birthday cards.

"It's from Mom." I looked at Sarah, amazed. "What is it?"

She was equally startled. "I have no idea."

Inside were a smaller envelope and something carefully wrapped in layers of tissue paper. The envelope was pale green, with a darker green border around the edges. My father had helped me pick it out for my mother's birthday. It had a cluster of white and green lily of the valley raised up slightly on the corner of each page. My eyes filled with tears.

"Do you want to be alone?" Matthew asked quietly, already on his feet.

"Stay. Please."

Shaking, I tore the envelope open and unfolded the papers inside. The date underneath the lily of the valley—August 13, 1983—caught my eye immediately.

My seventh birthday. It had fallen only days before my parents left for Nigeria.

I galloped through the first page of my mother's letter. The sheet fell from my fingers, drifted onto the floor, and came to rest at my feet.

Em's fear was palpable. "Diana? What is it?"

Without answering, I tucked the rest of the letter next to my thigh and picked up the brown envelope the house had been hiding for my mother. Pulling at the tissue paper, I wriggled a flat, rectangular object into the open. It was heavier than it should be, and it tingled with power.

I recognized that power and had felt it before.

Matthew heard my blood begin to sing. He came to stand behind me, his hands resting lightly on my shoulders.

I unfolded the wrappings. On top, blocking Mathew's view and separated by still more tissue from what lay beneath, was a piece of ordinary white paper, the edges brown with age. There were three lines written on it in spidery script.

"'*It begins with absence and desire,*'" I whispered around the tightness in my throat. "'*It begins with blood and fear.*'"

"'*It begins with a discovery of witches,*'" Matthew finished, looking over my shoulder.

After I'd delivered the note to Matthew's waiting fingers, he held it to his nose for a moment before passing it silently to Sarah. I lifted the top sheet of tissue paper.

Sitting in my lap was one of the missing pages from Ashmole 782.

"Christ," he breathed. "Is that what I think it is? How did your mother get it?"

"She explains in the letter," I said numbly, staring down at the brightly colored image.

Matthew bent and picked up the dropped sheet of stationery. "'*My darling Diana,*'" he read aloud. "'*Today you are seven—a magical age for a witch, when your powers should begin to stir and take shape. But your powers have been stirring since you were born. You have always been different.*'"

My knees shifted under the image's uncanny weight.

"'*That you are reading this means that your father and I succeeded. We were able to convince the Congregation that it was your father—and not you—whose power they sought. You mustn't blame yourself. It was the only decision we could possibly make. We trust that you are old enough now to understand.*'" Matthew gave my shoulder a gentle squeeze before continuing.

"'*You're old enough now, too, to take up the hunt that we began when you were born—the hunt for information about you and your magic. We received the enclosed note and drawing when you were three. It came to us in an envelope with an Israeli stamp. The department secretary told us there was no return address or signature—just the note and the picture.*

"'*We've spent much of the past four years trying to make sense of it.*

We couldn't ask too many questions. But we think the picture shows a wedding.'"

"It is a wedding—the chemical marriage of mercury and sulfur. It's a crucial step in making the philosopher's stone." My voice sounded harsh after Matthew's rich tones.

It was one of the most beautiful depictions of the chemical wedding I'd ever seen. A golden-haired woman in a pristine white gown held a white rose in one hand. It was an offering to her pale, dark-haired husband, a message that she was pure and worthy of him. He wore black-and-red robes and clasped her other hand. He, too, held a rose—but his was as red as fresh-spilled blood, a token of love and death. Behind the couple, chemicals and metals were personified as wedding guests, milling around in a landscape of trees and rocky hills. A whole menagerie of animals gathered to witness the ceremony: ravens, eagles, toads, green lions, peacocks, pelicans. A unicorn and a wolf stood side by side in the center background, behind the bride and groom. The whole scene was gathered within the outspread wings of a phoenix, its feathers flaming at the edges and its head curved down to watch the scene unfold.

"What does it mean?" Em asked.

"That someone has been waiting for Matthew and me to find each other for a long time."

"How could that picture possibly be about you and Matthew?" Sarah craned her neck to inspect it more closely.

"The queen is wearing Matthew's crest." A gleaming silver-and-gold circlet held back the bride's hair. In its midst, resting against her forehead, was a jewel in the shape of a crescent moon with a star rising above it.

Matthew reached past the picture and took up the rest of my mother's letter. "Do you mind if I continue?" he asked gently.

I shook my head, the page from the manuscript still resting on my knees. Em and Sarah, wary of its power, were exercising proper caution in the presence of an unfamiliar bewitched object and remained where they were.

"'We think the woman in white is meant to be you, Diana. We are less certain about the identity of the dark man. I've seen him in your dreams, but he's hard to place. He walks through your future, but he's in the past as well. He's always in shadows, never in the light. And though he's dangerous, the shadowed man doesn't pose a threat to you. Is he with you now? I hope so. I wish I could have known him. There is so much I would have liked to tell him about you.'" Matthew's voice stumbled over the last words.

"'We hope the two of you will be able to discover the source of this picture. Your father thinks it's from an old book. Sometimes we see text moving on the back of the page, but then the words disappear again for weeks, even months, at a time.'"

Sarah sprang out of her chair. "Give me the picture."

"It's from the book I told you about. The one in Oxford." I handed it to her reluctantly.

"It feels so heavy," she said, walking toward the window with a frown. She turned the picture over and angled the page this way and that. "But I don't see any words. Of course, it's no wonder. If this page was removed from the book it belongs to, then the magic is badly damaged."

"Is that why the words I saw were moving so fast?"

Sarah nodded. "Probably. They were searching for this page and couldn't find it."

"Pages." This was a detail I hadn't told Matthew.

"What do you mean, 'pages'?" Matthew came around the chair, flicking little shards of ice over my features.

"This isn't the only page that's missing from Ashmole 782."

"How many were removed?"

"Three," I whispered. "Three pages were missing from the front of the manuscript. I could see the stubs. It didn't seem important at the time."

"Three," Matthew repeated. His voice was flat, and it sounded as though he were about to break something apart with his bare hands.

"What does it matter whether there are three pages missing or three hundred?" Sarah was still trying to detect the hidden words. "The magic is still broken."

"Because there are three types of otherworldly creatures." Matthew touched my face to let me know he wasn't angry at me.

"And if we have one of the pages . . ." I started.

"Then who has the others?" Em finished.

"Damn it all to hell, why didn't Rebecca tell us about this?" Sarah, too, sounded like she wanted to destroy something. Emily took the picture from her hands and laid it carefully on an antique tea table.

Matthew continued reading. *"'Your father says that you will have to travel far to unlock its secrets. I won't say more, for fear this note will fall into the wrong hands. But you will figure it out, I know.'"*

He handed the sheet to me and went on to the next. *"'The house wouldn't have shared this letter if you weren't ready. That means you also know that your father and I spellbound you. Sarah will be furious, but it was the only way to protect you from the Congregation before the shadowed man was with you. He will help you with your magic. Sarah will say it's not his business because he's not a Bishop. Ignore her.'"*

Sarah snorted and looked daggers at the vampire.

"'Because you will love him as you love no one else, I tied your magic to your feelings for him. Even so, only you will have the ability to draw it into the open. I'm sorry about the panic attacks. They were the only thing I could think of. Sometimes you're too brave for your own good. Good luck learning your spells—Sarah is a perfectionist.'"

Matthew smiled. "There always was something odd about your anxiety."

"Odd how?"

"After we met in the Bodleian, it was almost impossible to provoke you into panicking."

"But I panicked when you came out of the fog by the boathouses."

"You were startled. Your instincts should have been screaming with panic whenever I was near. Instead you came closer and closer." Matthew dropped a kiss on my head and turned to the last page.

"'It's hard to know how to finish this letter when there is so much in my heart. The past seven years have been the happiest of my life. I wouldn't give up a moment of our precious time with you—not for an ocean of power or a long, safe life without you. We don't know why the goddess entrusted you to us, but not a day has passed that we didn't thank her for it.'"

I suppressed a sob but couldn't stop the tears.

"'I cannot shield you from the challenges you will face. You will know great loss and danger, but also great joy. You may doubt your instincts in the years to come, but your feet have been walking this path since the moment you were born. We knew it when you came into the world a caulbearer. You've remained between worlds ever since. It's who you are, and your destiny. Don't let anyone keep you from it.'"

"What's a caulbearer?" I whispered.

"Someone born with the amniotic sac still intact around them. It's a sign of luck," Sarah explained.

Matthew's free hand cradled the back of my skull. "Much more than luck is associated with the caul. In times past, it was thought to foretell the birth of a great seer. Some believed it was a sign you would become a vampire, a witch, or a werewolf." He gave me a lopsided grin.

"Where is it?" Em asked Sarah.

Matthew and I swung our heads in quick unison. "What?" we asked simultaneously.

"Cauls have enormous power. Stephen and Rebecca would have saved it."

We all looked at the crack in the paneling. A phonebook landed in the grate with a thud, sending a cloud of ash into the room.

"How do you save a caul?" I wondered aloud. "Do you put it in a baggie or something?"

"Traditionally, you press a piece of paper or fabric onto the baby's face and the caul sticks to it. Then you save the paper," explained Em.

All eyes swiveled to the page from Ashmole 782. Sarah picked it up and studied it closely. She muttered a few words and stared some more.

"There's something uncanny about this picture," she reported, "but it doesn't have Diana's caul attached to it."

That was a relief. It would have been one strange thing too many.

"So is that all, or does my sister have any other secrets she'd like to share with us?" Sarah asked tartly. Matthew frowned at her. "Sorry, Diana," she murmured.

"There's not much more. Can you manage it, *mon coeur*?"

I grabbed his free hand and nodded. He perched on one of the chair's padded arms, which creaked slightly under his weight.

"'Try not to be too hard on yourself as you journey into the future. Keep your wits about you, and trust your instincts. It's not much in the way of advice, but it's all that a mother can give. We can scarcely bear leaving you, but the only alternative is to risk losing you forever. Forgive us. If we have wronged you, it was because we loved you so much. Mom.'"

The room was silent, and even the house was holding its breath. A sound of loss started somewhere deep within me just before a tear fell from my eye. It swelled to the size of a softball and hit the floor with a splash. My legs felt liquid.

"Here it comes," Sarah warned.

Matthew dropped the page from the letter and swept me out of the chair and through the front door. He set me on the driveway, and my toes gripped the soil. The witchwater released harmlessly into the ground while my tears continued to flow. After a few moments, Matthew's hands slid around my waist from behind. His body shielded me from the rest of the world, and I relaxed against his chest.

"Let it all go," he murmured, his lips against my ear.

The witchwater subsided, leaving behind an aching sense of loss that would never go away completely.

"I wish they were here," I cried. "My mother and father would know what to do."

"I know you miss them. But they didn't know what to do—not really. Like all parents, they were just doing their best from moment to moment."

"My mother saw you, and what the Congregation might do. She was a great seer."

"And so will you be, one day. Until then we're going to have to manage without knowing what the future holds. But there are two of us. You don't have to do it by yourself."

We went back inside, where Sarah and Em were still scrutinizing the page from the manuscript. I announced that more tea and a fresh pot of coffee were in order, and Matthew came with me into the kitchen, though his eyes lingered on the brightly colored image.

The kitchen looked like a war zone, as usual. Every surface was covered with dishes. While the kettle came to a boil and the coffee brewed, I rolled up my sleeves to do the dishes.

Matthew's phone buzzed in his pocket. He was ignoring it, intent on putting more logs into the already overloaded fireplace.

"You should get that," I said, squirting dish liquid into the sink.

He pulled out his phone. His face revealed that this was not a call he wanted to take. *"Oui?"*

It must be Ysabeau. Something had gone wrong, someone wasn't where he or she was supposed to be—it was impossible for me to follow the particulars given their rapid exchange, but Matthew's annoyance was clear. He barked out a few orders and disconnected the phone.

"Is Ysabeau all right?" I swished my fingers through the warm water, hoping there was no new crisis.

Matthew's hands pushed my shoulders gently away from my ears, kneading the tight muscles. "She's fine. This had nothing to do with Ysabeau. It was Alain. He was doing some business for the family and ran into an unexpected situation."

"Business?" I picked up the sponge and started washing. "For the Knights of Lazarus?"

"Yes," he said shortly.

"Who is Alain?" I set the clean plate in the drainer.

"He began as my father's squire. Philippe couldn't manage without him, in war or in peace, so Marthe made him a vampire. He knows every aspect of the brotherhood's business. When my father died, Alain transferred his loyalty from Philippe to me. He called to warn me that Marcus wasn't pleased to receive my message."

I turned to meet his eyes. "Was it the same message you gave to Baldwin at La Guardia?"

He nodded.

"I'm nothing but trouble to your family."

"This isn't a de Clermont family matter anymore, Diana. The Knights of Lazarus protect those who cannot protect themselves. Marcus knew that when he accepted a place among them."

Matthew's phone buzzed again.

"And that will be Marcus," he said grimly.

"Go talk to him in private." I tilted my chin toward the door. Matthew kissed my cheek before pushing the green button on his phone and heading into the backyard.

"Hello, Marcus," he said warily, shutting the door behind him.

I continued moving the soapy water over the dishes, the repetitive motion soothing.

"Where's Matthew?" Sarah and Em were standing in the doorway, holding hands.

"Outside, talking to England," I said, nodding again in the direction of the back door.

Sarah got another clean mug out of the cabinet—the fourth she'd used that morning, by my count—and filled it with fresh coffee. Emily picked up the newspaper. Still, their eyes tingled with curiosity. The back door opened and closed. I braced for the worst.

"How is Marcus?"

"He and Miriam are on their way to New York. They have something to discuss with you." Matthew's face looked like a thundercloud.

"Me? What is it?"

"He wouldn't tell me."

"Marcus didn't want you to be on your own with only witches to keep you company." I smiled at him, and some of the tension left his face.

"They'll be here by nightfall and will check in to the inn we passed on our way through town. I'll go by and see them tonight. Whatever they need to tell you can wait until tomorrow." Matthew's worried eyes darted to Sarah and Em.

I turned to the sink again. "Call him back, Matthew. They should come straight here."

"They won't want to disturb anyone," he said smoothly. Matthew didn't want to upset Sarah and the rest of the Bishops by bringing two more vampires into the house. But my mother would never have let Marcus travel so far only to stay in a hotel.

Marcus was Matthew's son. He was my son.

My fingers prickled, and the cup I was washing slipped from my grasp. It bobbed in the water for a few moments, then sank.

"No son of mine is checking in to a hotel. He belongs in the Bishop house, with his family, and Miriam shouldn't be alone. They're both staying here, and that's final," I said firmly.

"Son?" said Sarah faintly.

"Marcus is Matthew's son, which makes him my son, too. That makes him a Bishop, and this house belongs to him as much as it does to you, or me, or Em." I turned to face them, grabbing the sleeves of my shirt tightly with my wet hands, which were shaking.

My grandmother drifted down the hallway to see what the fuss was about.

"Did you hear me, Grandma?" I called.

I believe we all heard you, Diana, she said in her rustly voice.

"Good. No acting up. And that goes for every Bishop in this house—living and dead."

The house opened its front and back doors in a premature gesture of welcome, sending a gust of chilly air through the downstairs rooms.

"Where will they sleep?" Sarah grumbled.

"They don't sleep, Sarah. They're vampires." The prickling in my fingers increased.

"Diana," Matthew said, "please step away from the sink. The electricity, *mon coeur*."

I gripped my sleeves tighter. The edges of my fingers were bright blue.

"We get the message," Sarah said hastily, eyeing my hands. "We've already got one vampire in the house."

"I'll get their rooms ready," Emily said, with a smile that looked genuine. "I'm glad we'll have a chance to meet your son, Matthew."

Matthew, who had been leaning against an ancient wooden cupboard, pulled himself upright and walked slowly toward me. "All right," he said, drawing me from the sink and tucking my head under his chin. "You've made your point. I'll call Marcus and let him know they're welcome here."

"Don't tell Marcus I called him my son. He may not want a stepmother."

"You two will have to sort that out," Matthew said, trying to suppress his amusement.

"What's so funny?" I tipped my face up to look at him.

"With all that's happened this morning, the one thing you're worried about is whether Marcus wants a stepmother. You confound me." Matthew shook his head. "Are all witches this surprising, Sarah, or is it just Bishops?"

Sarah considered her answer. "Just Bishops."

I peeked around Matthew's shoulder to give her a grateful smile.

My aunts were surrounded by a mob of ghosts, all of whom were solemnly nodding in agreement.

Chapter 35

After the dishes were done, Matthew and I gathered up my mother's letter, the mysterious note, and the page from Ashmole 782 and carried them into the dining room. We spread the papers out on the room's vast, well-worn table. These days it was seldom used, since it made no sense for two people to sit at the end of a piece of furniture designed to easily seat twelve. My aunts joined us, steaming mugs of coffee in their hands.

Sarah and Matthew crouched over the page from the alchemical manuscript.

"Why is it so heavy?" Sarah picked the page up and weighed it carefully.

"I don't feel any special weightiness," Matthew confessed, taking it from her hands, "but there's something odd about the way it smells."

Sarah gave it a long sniff. "No, it just smells old."

"It's more than that. I know what old smells like," he said sardonically.

Em and I, on the other hand, were more interested in the enigmatic note.

"What do you think it means?" I asked, pulling out a chair and sitting down.

"I'm not sure." Em hesitated. "Blood usually signifies family, war, or death. But what about absence? Does it mean this page is absent from the book? Or did it warn your parents that they wouldn't be present as you grew up?"

"Look at the last line. Did my parents discover something in Africa?"

"Or were *you* the discovery of witches?" Em suggested gently.

"The last line must be about Diana's discovery of Ashmole 782," Matthew chimed in, looking up from the chemical wedding.

"You believe that everything is about me and that manuscript," I grumbled. "The note mentions the subject of your All Souls essay—fear and desire. Don't you think that's strange?"

"No stranger than the fact that the white queen in this picture is wearing my crest." Matthew brought the illustration over to me.

"She's the embodiment of quicksilver—the principle of volatility in alchemy," I said.

"Quicksilver?" Matthew looked amused. "A metallic perpetual-motion machine?"

"You could say that." I smiled, too, thinking of the ball of energy I'd given him.

"What about the red king?"

"He's stable and grounded." I frowned. "But he's also supposed to be the sun, and he's not usually depicted wearing black and red. Usually he's just red."

"So maybe the king isn't me and the queen isn't you." He touched the white queen's face delicately with his fingertip.

"Perhaps," I said slowly, remembering a passage from Matthew's *Aurora* manuscript. *"'Attend to me, all people, and listen to me, all who inhabit the world: my beloved, who is red, has called to me. He sought, and found me. I am the flower of the field, a lily growing in the valley. I am the mother of true love, and of fear, and of understanding, and blessed hope.'"*

"What is that?" Matthew touched my face now. "It sounds biblical, but the words aren't quite right."

"It's one of the passages on the chemical wedding from the *Aurora Consurgens*." Our eyes locked, held. When the air became heavy, I changed the subject. "What did my father mean when he said we'd have to travel far to figure out the picture's significance?"

"The stamp came from Israel. Maybe Stephen meant we would have to return there."

"There are a lot of alchemical manuscripts in Jerusalem at the Hebrew University. Most of them belonged to Isaac Newton." Given Matthew's history with the place, not to mention the Knights of Lazarus, it was not a city I was eager to visit.

"Israel didn't count as 'traveling far' for your father," said Sarah, sitting opposite. Em walked around the table and joined her.

"What *did* qualify?" Matthew picked up my mother's letter and scanned the last page for further clues.

"The Australian outback. Wyoming. Mali. Those were his favorite places to timewalk."

The word cut through me with the same intensity as "spellbound" had only a few days before. I knew that some witches could move between past, present, and future, but I'd never thought to ask whether anyone in my own family had the ability. It was rare—almost as rare as witchfire.

"Stephen Proctor could travel in time?" Matthew's voice assumed the deliberate evenness it often did when magic was mentioned.

Sarah nodded. "Yes. Stephen went to the past or the future at least once a year, usually after the annual anthropologists' convention in December."

"There's something on the back of Rebecca's letter." Em bent her neck to see underneath the page.

Matthew quickly flipped it over. "I dropped the page to get you outside before the witchwater broke. I didn't see this. It's not your mother's handwriting," he said, passing it to me.

The handwriting on the penciled note had elongated loops and spiky peaks. *"Remember, Diana: 'The most beautiful experience we can have is the mysterious. It is the fundamental emotion that stands at the cradle of true art and true science. Whoever does not know it and can no longer wonder, no longer marvel, is as good as dead, and his eyes are dimmed.'"* I'd seen that hand somewhere before. In the recesses of my memory, I flipped through images trying to locate its source but without success.

"Who would have written a quote from Albert Einstein on the back of Mom's note?" I asked Sarah and Em, angling the page to face them and struck again by its familiarity.

"That looks like your dad. He took calligraphy lessons. Rebecca poked fun at him for it. It made his handwriting look so old-fashioned."

Slowly I turned the page over, scrutinizing the writing again. It did look nineteenth-century in style, like the handwriting of the clerks employed to compile the catalogs in the Bodleian back during Victoria's reign. I stiffened, looked more closely at the writing, shook my head.

"No, it's not possible." There was no way my father could have been one of those clerks, no way he could have written the nineteenth-century subtitle on Ashmole 782.

But my father could timewalk. And the message from Einstein was unquestionably meant for me. I dropped the page onto the table and put my head in my hands.

Matthew sat next to me and waited. When Sarah made an impatient sound, he silenced her with a decisive gesture. Once my mind stopped spinning, I spoke.

"There were two inscriptions on the first page of the manuscript. One was in ink, written by Elias Ashmole: '*Anthropologia, or a treatis containing a short description of Man.*' The other was in a different hand, in pencil: '*in two parts: the first Anatomical, the second Psychological.*'"

"The second inscription had to be written much later," Matthew observed. "There was no such thing as 'psychology' during Ashmole's lifetime."

"I thought it dated from the nineteenth century." I pulled my father's note toward me. "But this makes me think my father wrote it."

The room fell silent.

"Touch the words," Sarah finally suggested. "See what else they say."

My fingers passed lightly over the penciled letters. Images bloomed from the page, of my father in a dark frock coat with wide lapels and a high black cravat, crouched over a desk covered with books. There were other images, too, of him in his study at home wearing his familiar corduroy jacket, scrawling a note with a No. 2 pencil while my mother looked over his shoulder, weeping.

"It was him." My fingers lifted from the page, shaking visibly.

Matthew took my hand in his. "That's enough bravery for one day, *ma lionne*."

"But your father didn't remove the chemical wedding from the book at the Bodleian," mused Em, "so what was he doing there?"

"Stephen Proctor was bewitching Ashmole 782 so that no one but his daughter could call it from the stacks." Matthew sounded sure.

"So that's why the spell recognized me. But why didn't it behave the same way when I recalled it?"

"You didn't need it. Oh, you *wanted* it," Matthew said with a wry smile when I opened my mouth to protest, "but that's different. Remember, your parents bound your magic so that your power couldn't be forced from you. The spell on the manuscript was no different."

"When I first called Ashmole 782, all I needed was to check the next item off my to-do list. It's hard to believe that something so insignificant could trigger such a reaction."

"Your mother and father couldn't have foreseen everything—such as the fact that you would be a historian of alchemy and would regularly work at the Bodleian. Could Rebecca timewalk, too?" Matthew asked Sarah.

"No. It's rare, of course, and the most adept timewalkers are well versed in witchcraft as well. Without the right spells and precautions, you can easily end up somewhere you don't want to be, no matter how much power you have."

"Yes," Matthew said drily. "I can think of any number of times and places you would want to avoid."

"Rebecca went with Stephen sometimes, but he had to carry her." Sarah smiled at Em. "Do you remember Vienna? Stephen decided he was going to take her waltzing. He spent a full year figuring out which bonnet she should wear for the journey."

"You need three objects from the particular time and place you want to travel back to. They keep you from getting lost," Em continued. "If you want to go to the future, you have to use witchcraft, because it's the only way to direct yourself."

Sarah picked up the picture of the chemical wedding, no longer interested in timewalking. "What's the unicorn for?"

"Forget the unicorn, Sarah," I said impatiently. "Daddy couldn't have wanted me to go back in the past and get the manuscript. What did he think, that I'd timewalk and snatch it before it was bewitched? What if I ran into Matthew by accident? Surely that would mess up the time-space continuum."

"Oh, relativity." Sarah's voice was dismissive. "As an explanation that only goes so far."

"Stephen always said timewalking was like changing trains," Em said. "You get off one train, then wait at the station until there's a place for you on a different train. When you timewalk, you depart from the here and now and you're held out of time until there's room for you sometime else."

"That's similar to the way vampires change lives," Matthew mused. "We abandon one life—arrange a death, a disappearance, a change of residence—and look for another one. You'd be amazed at how easily people walk away from their homes, jobs, and families."

"Surely someone notices that the John Smith they knew last week doesn't look the same," I protested.

"That's even more amazing," Matthew admitted. "So long as you pick carefully, no one says a word. A few years in the Holy Land, a life-threatening illness, the likelihood of losing an inheritance—all provide excellent excuses for creatures and humans to turn a blind eye."

"Well, whether it's possible or not, I can't timewalk. It wasn't on the DNA report."

"Of course you can timewalk. You've been doing it since you were a child." Sarah sounded smug as she discredited Matthew's scientific findings. "The first time you were three. Your parents were scared to death, the police were called out—it was quite a scene. Four hours later they found you sitting in the kitchen high chair eating a slice of birthday cake. You must have been hungry and gone back to your own birthday party. After that, whenever you disappeared, we figured you were sometime else and you'd turn up. And you disappeared a lot."

My alarm at the thought of a toddler traveling through time gave way to the realization that I had the power to answer any historical question. I brightened considerably.

Matthew had already figured this out and was waiting patiently for me to catch up. "No matter what your father wanted, you aren't going back to 1859," he said firmly, turning the chair around so I faced him. "Time is not something you're going to meddle with. Understood?"

Even after assuring him that I would stay in the present, no one left me alone for an instant. The three of them silently passed me from one to the other in choreography worthy of Broadway. Em followed me upstairs to make sure there were towels, though I knew perfectly well where the linen closet was. When I came out of the bathroom, Matthew was lying on the bed fiddling with his phone. He stayed upstairs when I went down to make a cup of tea, knowing that Sarah and Em would be waiting for me in the family room.

Marthe's tin was in my hands, and I felt guilty for missing yesterday and breaking my promise to her. Determined to have some tea today, I filled the kettle and opened the black metal box. The smell of rue triggered a sharp recollection of being swept into the air by Satu. Gripping the lid more tightly, I focused on the other scents and happier memories of Sept-Tours. I missed its gray stone walls, the gardens, Marthe, Rakasa—even Ysabeau.

"Where did you get that, Diana?" Sarah came in the kitchen and pointed at the tin.

"Marthe and I made it."

"That's his mother's housekeeper? The one who made the medicine for your back?"

"*Marthe* is *Ysabeau's* housekeeper, yes." I put a slight emphasis on their proper names. "Vampires have names, just like witches. You need to learn them."

Sarah sniffed. "I would have thought you'd go to the doctor for a prescription, not depend on old herbal lore."

"Dr. Fowler will fit you in if you want something more reliable." Em had come in, too. "Not even Sarah is much of an advocate of herbal contraception."

I hid my confusion by plopping a tea bag into the mug, keeping my mind blank and my face hidden. "This is fine. There's no need to see Dr. Fowler."

"True. Not if you're sleeping with a vampire. They can't reproduce—not in any way that contraception is going to prevent. All you have to watch out for is teeth on your neck."

"I know, Sarah."

But I didn't. Why had Marthe taught me so carefully how to make a completely unnecessary tea? Matthew had been clear that he couldn't father children as warmbloods did. Despite my promise to Marthe, I dumped the half-steeped cup down the sink and threw the bag in the trash. The tin went on the top shelf in the cupboard, where it would be safely out of sight.

By late afternoon, in spite of many conversations about the note, the letter, and the picture, we were no closer to understanding the mystery of Ashmole 782 and my father's connection to it. My aunts started to make dinner, which meant that Em roasted a chicken while Sarah drank a glass of bourbon and criticized the quantity of vegetables being prepared. Matthew prowled around the kitchen island, uncharacteristically restless.

"Come on," he said, grabbing my hand. "You need some exercise."

It was he who needed fresh air, not I, but the prospect of going outdoors was enticing. A search in the mudroom closet revealed an old pair of my running shoes. They were worn, but they fit better than Sarah's boots.

We made it as far as the first apple trees before Matthew swung me around and pressed me between his body and one of the old, gnarled trunks. The low canopy of branches shielded us from the house's sight.

Despite my being trapped, there was no answering rush of witchwind. There were plenty of other feelings, though.

"Christ, that house is crowded," Matthew said, pausing just long enough to get the words out before refastening his lips on mine.

We'd had too little time alone since he'd returned from Oxford. It seemed a lifetime ago, but it was only days. One of his hands slid into the waistband of my jeans, his fingers cool against my bare flesh. I shivered with pleasure, and he drew me closer, his other hand locating the rounded curves of my breast. We pressed the length of our bodies against each other, but he kept looking for new ways to connect.

Finally there was only one possibility left. For a moment it seemed Matthew intended to consummate our marriage the old-fashioned way—standing up, outdoors, in a blinding rush of physical need. His control returned, however, and he pulled away.

"Not like this," he rasped, his eyes black.

"I don't care." I pulled him back against me.

"I do." There was a soft, ragged expulsion of air as Matthew breathed a vampire's sigh. "When we make love for the first time, I want you to myself—not surrounded by other people. And I'll want you for more than the few snatched moments we'd have now, believe me."

"I want you, too," I said, "and I'm not known for my patience."

His lips drew up into a smile, and he made a soft sound of agreement.

Matthew's thumb stroked the hollow in my throat, and my blood leaped. He put his lips where his thumb had been, pressing them softly against the outward sign of the vitality that pulsed beneath the surface. He traced a vein up the side of my neck toward my ear.

"I'm enjoying learning where you like to be touched. Like here." Matthew kissed behind my ear. "And here." His lips moved to my eyelids, and I made a soft sound of pleasure. "And here." He ran his thumb over my lower lip.

"Matthew," I whispered, my eyes pleading.

"What, *mon coeur*?" He watched, fascinated, as his touch drew fresh blood to the surface.

I didn't answer but pulled him to me, unconcerned with the cold, the growing darkness, and the rough bark beneath my sore back. We remained there until Sarah called from the porch.

"You didn't get very far, did you?" Her snort carried clear across the field. "That hardly qualifies as exercise."

Feeling like a schoolgirl caught necking in the driveway, I pulled my sweatshirt into the proper position and headed back to the house. Matthew chuckled and followed.

"You look pleased with yourself," Sarah said when he stepped into the kitchen. Standing under the bright lights, he was every inch a vampire—and a self-satisfied one at that. But his eyes were no longer restless, and for that I was grateful.

"Leave him alone." Em's voice was uncharacteristically sharp. She handed me the salad and pointed me to the table in the family room where we usually ate. "We saw a fair amount of that apple tree ourselves while Diana was growing up."

"Hmph," Sarah said. She picked up three wineglasses and waved them in Matthew's direction. "Got any more of that wine, Casanova?"

"I'm French, Sarah, not Italian. And I'm a vampire. I always have wine," Matthew said with a wicked smile. "There's no danger of running out. Marcus will bring more. He's not French—or Italian either, alas—but his education compensated for it."

We sat around the table, and the three witches proceeded to demolish Em's roast chicken and potatoes. Tabitha sat next to Matthew, her tail swishing flirtatiously across his feet every few minutes. He kept the wine flowing into Sarah's glass, and I sipped at my own. Em asked repeatedly if he wanted to taste anything, but Matthew declined.

"I'm not hungry, Emily, but thank you."

"Is there anything at all that you *would* eat?" Em wasn't used to people refusing her food.

"Nuts," I said firmly. "If you have to buy him food, get him nuts."

Em hesitated. "What about raw meat?"

Matthew grabbed my hand and squeezed it before I could reply. "If you want to feed me, uncooked meat would be just fine. I like broth, too—plain, no vegetables."

"Is that what your son and colleague eat, too, or are these just your favorite foods?"

Matthew's impatience with my earlier questions about his lifestyle and dining habits made sense to me now.

"It's pretty standard vampire fare when we're among warmbloods." Matthew released my hand and poured himself more wine.

"You must hang out at bars a lot, what with the wine and nuts," Sarah observed.

Em put her fork down and stared at her.

"What?" Sarah demanded.

"Sarah Bishop, if you embarrass us in front of Matthew's son, I'll never forgive you."

My resulting fit of giggles quickly turned into full-blown laughter. Sarah was the first to join in, followed by Em. Matthew sat and smiled as if he'd been dropped into a lunatic asylum but was too polite to mention it.

When the laughter subsided, he turned to Sarah. "I was wondering if I could borrow your stillroom to analyze the pigments used in the picture of the chemical wedding. Maybe they can tell us where and when it was made."

"You're not going to remove anything from that picture." The historian in me rose up in horror at the thought.

"It won't come to any harm," Matthew said mildly. "I do know how to analyze tiny pieces of evidence."

"No! We should leave it alone until we know what we're dealing with."

"Don't be so prim, Diana. Besides, it's a bit late for that when it was you who sent the book back." Sarah stood, her eyes brightening. "Let's see if the cookbook can help."

"Well, well," Em said under her breath. "You're one of the family now, Matthew."

Sarah disappeared into the stillroom and returned holding a leather-bound book the size of a family Bible. Within its covers was all the learning and lore of the Bishops, handed down from witch to witch for nearly four hundred years. The first name in the book was Rebecca, accompanied by the date 1617 in an ornate, round hand. Other names were sprawled down the first page in two columns, each one in a slightly different ink with a different date attached to it. The names continued onto the back of the sheet as well, with Susannahs, Elizabeths, Margarets, Rebeccas, and Sarahs dominating the list. My aunt never showed anybody this book—not even other witches. You had to be family to see her "cookbook."

"What is that, Sarah?" Matthew's nostrils flared at the scent of old paper, herbs, and smoke that was released as Sarah splayed its covers open.

"The Bishop grimoire." She pointed to the first name. "It first belonged to Rebecca Davies, Bridget Bishop's grandmother, then to her mother, Rebecca Playfer. Bridget handed the book down to her first daughter, born out of wedlock in England around 1650. Bridget was still in her teens at the time, and she named her daughter after her mother and grandmother. Unable to care for the girl, Bridget gave her up to a family in London. " Sarah made a soft sound of disgust. "The rumors of her immorality haunted her for the rest of her life. Later her daughter Rebecca joined her and worked in her mother's tavern. Bridget was on her second husband then, and had another daughter named Christian."

"And you're descended from Christian Bishop?" Matthew asked.

Sarah shook her head. "Christian Oliver, you mean—Bridget's daughter from her second marriage. Edward Bishop was Bridget's third husband. No, our ancestor is Rebecca. After Bridget was executed, Rebecca legally changed her name to Bishop. Rebecca was a widow, with no husband to argue with. It was an act of defiance."

Matthew gave me a long look. Defiance, it seemed to say, was clearly a genetic trait.

"Nobody remembers all of Bridget Bishop's many names anymore—she was married three times," Sarah continued. "All anyone remembers is the name she bore when she was found guilty of witchcraft and executed.

Since that time the women of the family have preserved the Bishop name, regardless of marriage or of who their father was."

"I read about Bridget's death shortly after," Matthew said softly. "It was a dark time for creatures. Even though the new science seemed to strip all the mystery from the world, humans were still convinced that unseen forces were all around them. They were right, of course."

"Well, the tension between what science promised and what their common sense told them was true resulted in the deaths of hundreds of witches." Sarah started flipping through the grimoire's pages.

"What are you looking for?" I asked, frowning. "Was one of the Bishops a manuscript conservator? If not, you won't find much help in that spell book."

"You don't know what is in this spell book, miss," Sarah said serenely. "You've never shown one bit of interest in it."

My lips pressed into a thin line. "Nobody is damaging that manuscript."

"Ah, here it is." Sarah pointed triumphantly at the grimoire. "One of Margaret Bishop's spells from the 1780s. She was a powerful witch. *'My method for perceiving obscurities in paper or fabric.'* That's where we'll start." She stood up, her finger marking the place.

"If you stain—" I began.

"I heard you the first two times, Diana. This is a spell for a vapor. Nothing but air will touch your precious manuscript page. Stop fussing."

"I'll go get it," Matthew said hastily. I shot him a filthy look.

After he returned from the dining room with the picture cradled carefully in his hands, he and Sarah went off into the stillroom together. My aunt was talking a mile a minute as Matthew listened intently.

"Who would have imagined?" said Em, shaking her head.

Em and I washed the dinner dishes and had started the process of tidying the family room, which looked like a crime scene, when a pair of headlights swept the driveway.

"They're here." My stomach tightened.

"It'll be fine, honey. They're Matthew's family." Em squeezed my arm encouragingly.

By the time I reached the front door, Marcus and Miriam were getting out of the car. Miriam looked awkward and out of place in a lightweight brown sweater with the sleeves rolled up to her elbows, a miniskirt, and ankle boots, her dark eyes taking in the farm and its surroundings with an attitude of disbelief. Marcus was observing the house's architecture and sniffing the breeze—which was no doubt redolent with coffee and witches—clothed in a short-sleeved T-shirt from a 1982 concert tour and a pair of jeans.

When the door swung open, Marcus's blue eyes met mine with a twinkle. "Hi, Mom, we're home!"

"Did he tell you?" I demanded, furious with Matthew for not obeying my wishes.

"Tell me what?" Marcus's forehead creased in puzzlement.

"Nothing," I muttered. "Hello, Marcus. Hello, Miriam."

"Diana." Miriam's fine features were drawn into their familiar look of disapproval.

"Nice house." Marcus headed up the porch stairs. He held a brown bottle in his fingers. Under the porch lights, his golden hair and polished white skin positively gleamed.

"Come in, welcome." I hurriedly pulled him inside, hoping that no one driving by the house had glimpsed the vampire on the landing.

"How are you, Diana?" There was worry in his eyes, and his nose flared to take in my scent. Matthew had told him about La Pierre.

"I'm fine." Upstairs, a door closed with a bang. "No nonsense! I am deadly serious!"

"About what?" Miriam stopped in her tracks, and her flat black curls wiggled over her shoulders like snakes.

"Nothing. Don't worry about it." Now that both vampires were safely within the walls, the house sighed.

"Nothing?" Miriam had heard the sigh, too, and her brows rose.

"The house gets a bit worried when visitors come to call, that's all."

Miriam looked up the staircase and sniffed. "How many residents does the house have?"

It was a simple question, for which there was no simple answer.

"Unsure," I said shortly, lugging a duffel bag in the direction of the stairs. "What do you have in here?"

"It's Miriam's bag. Let me." Marcus hooked it easily with his index finger.

We went upstairs so I could show them their rooms. Em had asked Matthew outright if the two would be sharing a bed. First he'd looked shocked at the impropriety of the question, and then he'd burst into gales of laughter and assured her that if they weren't separated, there would be one dead vampire by morning. Periodically throughout the day, he'd chuckled under his breath, saying "Marcus and Miriam. What an idea."

Marcus was staying in the guest bedroom that used to belong to Em, and we'd put Miriam in my old attic room. Stacks of fluffy towels were waiting on their beds, and I showed each of them where the bathroom was. There wasn't much to do to get vampire guests settled—you couldn't offer them food, or a place to lie down, or much of anything in the way of creature comforts. Happily, there'd been no spectral apparitions or falling plaster to indicate the house was displeased with their presence.

Matthew certainly knew that his son and Miriam had arrived, but the stillroom was secluded enough that Sarah remained oblivious. When I led the two vampires past the keeping room, Elizabeth peeped around the door, her eyes wide as an owl's.

"Go find Grandma." I turned to Marcus and Miriam. "Sorry, we've got ghosts."

Marcus covered his laugh with a cough. "Do all of your ancestors live with you?"

Thinking of my parents, I shook my head.

"Too bad," he murmured.

Em was waiting in the family room, her smile wide and genuine. "You must be Marcus," she said, getting to her feet and holding out her hand. "I'm Emily Mather."

"Em, this is Matthew's colleague, Miriam Shephard."

Miriam stepped forward. Though she and Em were both fine-boned, Miriam looked like a china doll in comparison.

"Welcome, Miriam," said Em, looking down with a smile. "Do either of you need something to drink? Matthew opened wine." She was entirely natural, as if vampires were always dropping by. Both Marcus and Miriam shook their heads.

"Where's Matthew?" Miriam asked, making her priorities clear. Her keen senses absorbed the details of her new environment. "I can hear him."

We led the two vampires toward the old wooden door that closed off Sarah's private sanctuary. Marcus and Miriam continued to take in all the scents of the Bishop house as we proceeded—the food, the clothes, the witches, the coffee, and the cat.

Tabitha came screeching out of the shadows by the fireplace, aiming straight for Miriam as if the two were deadly enemies.

Miriam hissed, and Tabitha froze in mid-hurtle. The two assessed each other, predator to predator. Tabitha was the first to avert her eyes when, after several long moments, the cat discovered an urgent need to groom herself. It was a silent acknowledgment that she was no longer the only female of consequence on the premises.

"That's Tabitha," I said weakly. "She's quite fond of Matthew."

In the stillroom Matthew and Sarah were crouched over a pot of something set atop an old electric burner, rapt expressions on their faces. Bunches of dried herbs swung from the rafters, and the original colonial ovens stood ready for use, their iron hooks and cranes waiting to hold heavy cauldrons over the coals.

"The eyebright is crucial," Sarah was explaining like a schoolmarm. "It clears the sight."

"That smells vile," Miriam observed, wrinkling her tiny nose and creeping closer.

Matthew's face darkened.

"Matthew," Marcus said evenly.

"Marcus," his father replied.

Sarah stood and examined the newest members of the household, both of whom glowed. The stillroom's subdued light only accentuated their unnatural paleness and the startling effect of their dilated pupils. "Goddess save us, how does anyone think you're human?"

"It's always been a mystery to me," Miriam said, studying Sarah with equal interest. "You're not exactly inconspicuous either, with all that red hair and the smell of henbane coming off you in waves. I'm Miriam Shephard."

Matthew and I exchanged a long look, wondering how Miriam and Sarah were going to coexist peacefully under the same roof.

"Welcome to the Bishop house, Miriam." Sarah's eyes narrowed, and Miriam responded in kind. My aunt turned her attention to Marcus. "So you're his kid." As usual, she had no patience with social niceties.

"I'm Matthew's son, yes." Marcus, who looked like he'd seen a ghost, slowly held out a brown bottle. "Your namesake was a healer, like you. Sarah Bishop taught me how to set a broken leg after the Battle of Bunker Hill. I still do it the way she taught me."

Two roughly shod feet dangled over the edge of the stillroom loft.

Let's hope he's got more strength now than he did then, said a woman who was the spitting image of Sarah.

"Whiskey," Sarah said, looking from the bottle to my son with new appreciation.

"She liked spirits. I thought you might, too."

Both Sarah Bishops nodded.

"You thought right," my aunt said.

"How's the potion going?" I said, trying not to sneeze in the close atmosphere.

"It needs to steep for nine hours," Sarah said. "Then we boil it again, draw the manuscript through the vapor, and see what we see." She eyed the whiskey.

"Let's take a break, then. I could open that for you," Matthew suggested, gesturing at the bottle.

"Don't mind if I do." She took the bottle from Marcus. "Thank you, Marcus."

Sarah turned off the burner and clapped a lid on the pot before we all streamed into the kitchen. Matthew poured himself some wine, offered it to Miriam and Marcus, who declined again, and got Sarah some whiskey. I made myself tea—plain Lipton's from the grocery store—while Matthew asked the vampires about their trip and the state of work at the lab.

There was no trace of warmth in Matthew's voice, or any indication he was pleased by his son's arrival. Marcus shifted uneasily from one foot to the other, knowing that he wasn't welcome. I suggested we might go into the family room and sit down in hopes that some of the awkwardness would fade.

"Let's go to the dining room instead." Sarah raised her glass to her charming great-nephew. "We'll show them the letter. Get Diana's picture, Matthew. They should see that, too."

"Marcus and Miriam won't be staying long," Matthew said with quiet reproach. "They have something to tell Diana, and then they're going back to England."

"But they're family," Sarah pointed out, seemingly oblivious to the tension in the room.

My aunt retrieved the picture herself while Matthew continued to glower at his son. Sarah led us to the front of the house. Matthew, Em, and I assembled on one side of the table. Miriam, Marcus, and Sarah sat on the other. Once settled, my aunt began chattering about the morning's events. Whenever she asked Matthew for some point of clarification, he bit out the answer without embellishment. Everyone in the room save Sarah seemed to understand that Matthew didn't want Miriam and Marcus to know the details of what had happened. My aunt blithely continued, finishing with a recitation of my mother's letter along with the postscript from my father. Matthew held firmly on to my hand while she did so.

Miriam took up the picture of the chemical wedding. She studied it carefully before turning her eyes to me. "Your mother was right. This is a picture of you. Matthew, too."

"I know," I said, meeting her gaze. "Do you know what it means?"

"Miriam?" Matthew said sharply.

"We can wait until tomorrow." Marcus looked uneasy and rose to his feet. "It's late."

"She already knows," Miriam said softly. "What comes after marriage, Diana? What's the next step in alchemical transmutation after *conjunctio*?"

The room tilted, and I smelled the herbs in my tea from Sept-Tours.

"Conceptio." My body turned to jelly, and I slid down the back of the chair as everything went black.

Chapter 36

My head was between my knees amid the utter pandemonium. Matthew's hand kept my attention glued to the pattern in the worn Oriental rug under my feet. In the background Marcus was telling Sarah that if she approached me, his father would likely rip her head off.

"It's a vampire thing," Marcus said soothingly. "We're very protective of our spouses."

"When were they married?" asked Sarah, slightly dazed.

Miriam's efforts to calm Em were far less soothing. "We call it shielding," her bell-like soprano chimed. "Ever seen a hawk with its prey? That's what Matthew's doing."

"But Diana's not his prey, is she? He's not going to . . . to bite her?" Em glanced at my neck.

"I shouldn't think so," Miriam said slowly, considering the question. "He's not hungry, and she's not bleeding. The danger is minimal."

"Knock it off, Miriam," said Marcus. "There's nothing to worry about, Emily."

"I can sit up now," I mumbled.

"Don't move. The blood flow to your head isn't back to normal yet." Matthew tried not to growl at me but couldn't manage it.

Sarah made a strangled sound, her suspicions that Matthew was constantly monitoring my blood supply now confirmed.

"Do you think he'd let me walk past Diana to get her test results?" Miriam asked Marcus.

"That depends on how pissed off he is. If you'd blindsided my wife that way, I'd poleax you and then eat you for breakfast. I'd sit tight if I were you."

Miriam's chair scraped against the floor. "I'll risk it." She darted past.

"Damn," Sarah breathed.

"She's unusually quick," Marcus reassured her, "even for a vampire."

Matthew maneuvered me into a sitting position. Even that gentle movement made my head feel like it was exploding and set the room whirling. I closed my eyes momentarily, and when I opened them again, Matthew's were looking back, full of concern.

"All right, *mon coeur*?"

"A little overwhelmed."

Matthew's fingers circled my wrist to take my pulse.

"I'm sorry, Matthew," Marcus murmured. "I had no idea Miriam would behave like this."

"You should be sorry," his father said flatly, without looking up. "Start explaining what this visit is about—quickly." The vein throbbed in Matthew's forehead.

"Miriam—" Marcus began.

"I didn't ask Miriam. I'm asking you," his father snapped.

"What's going on, Diana?" my aunt asked, looking wild. Marcus still had his arm around her shoulders.

"Miriam thinks the alchemical picture is about me and Matthew," I said cautiously. "About the stage in the making of the philosopher's stone called *conjunctio,* or marriage. The next step is *conceptio.*"

"*Conceptio*?" Sarah asked. "Does that mean what I think it does?"

"Probably. It's Latin—for conception," Matthew explained.

Sarah's eyes widened. "As in children?"

But my mind was elsewhere, flipping through the pictures in Ashmole 782.

"*Conceptio* was missing, too." I reached for Matthew. "Someone has it, just like we have *conjunctio.*"

Miriam glided into the room with impeccable timing, carrying a sheaf of papers. "Who do I give these to?"

After she'd gotten a look from Matthew that I hoped never to see again, Miriam's face went from white to pearl gray. She hastily handed him the reports.

"You've brought the wrong results, Miriam. These belong to a male," said Matthew, impatiently scanning the first two pages.

"The results do belong to Diana," Marcus said. "She's a chimera, Matthew."

"What's that?" Em asked. A chimera was a mythological beast that combined the body parts of a lioness, a dragon, and a goat. I looked down, half expecting to glimpse a tail between my legs.

"A person with cells that possess two or more different genetic profiles." Matthew was staring in disbelief at the first page.

"That's impossible." My heart gave a loud thump. Matthew circled me with his arms, holding the test results on the table in front of us.

"It's rare, but not impossible," he said grimly, his eyes moving over the gray bars.

"My guess is VTS," Miriam said, ignoring Marcus's warning frown. "Those results came from her hair. There were strands of it on the quilt we took to the Old Lodge."

"Vanishing twin syndrome," Marcus explained, turning to Sarah. "Did Rebecca have problems early in her pregnancy? Any bleeding or concerns about miscarriage?"

Sarah shook her head. "No. I don't think so. But they weren't here—Stephen and Rebecca were in Africa. They didn't come back to the States until the end of her first trimester."

Nobody had ever told me I was conceived in Africa.

"Rebecca wouldn't have known there was anything wrong." Matthew shook his head, his mouth pressed into a hard, firm line. "VTS happens before most women know they're pregnant."

"So I was a twin, and Mom miscarried my sibling?"

"Your brother," Matthew said, pointing to the test results with his free hand. "Your twin was male. In cases like yours, the viable fetus absorbs the blood and tissues of the other. It happens quite early, and in most cases there's no evidence of the vanished twin. Does Diana's hair indicate she might possess powers that didn't show up in her other DNA results?"

"A few—timewalking, shape-shifting, divination," his son replied. "Diana fully absorbed most of them."

"My brother was supposed to be the timewalker, not me," I said slowly.

A trail of phosphorescent smudges marked my grandmother's progress as she drifted into the room, touched me lightly on the shoulder, and sat at the far end of the table.

"He would have had the genetic predisposition to control witchfire, too," Marcus said, nodding. "We found only the fire marker in the hair sample—no other traces of elemental magic."

"And you don't think my mother knew about my brother?" I ran my fingertip along the bars of gray, black, and white.

"Oh, she knew." Miriam sounded confident. "You were born on the goddess's feast day. She named you Diana."

"So?" I shivered, pushing aside the memory of riding through the forest in sandals and a tunic, along with the strange feeling of holding a bow and arrow that accompanied witchfire.

"The goddess of the moon had a twin—Apollo. '*This Lion maketh the Sun so soon, / To be joined to his sister, the Moon.*'" Miriam's eyes gleamed as she recited the alchemical poem. She was up to something.

"You know 'The Hunting of the Green Lion.'"

"I know the next verses, too: '*By way of a wedding, a wondrous thing, / This Lion should cause them to beget a king.*'"

"What is she talking about?" Sarah asked testily.

When Miriam tried to answer, Matthew shook his head. The vampire fell silent.

"The sun king and moon queen—philosophical sulfur and mercury—married and conceived a child," I told Sarah. "In alchemical imagery the resulting child is a hermaphrodite, to symbolize a mixed chemical substance."

"In other words, Matthew," Miriam interjected tartly, "Ashmole 782 is not just about origins, nor is it just about evolution and extinction. It's about reproduction."

I scowled. "Nonsense."

"You may think it's nonsense, Diana, but it's clear to me. Vampires and witches may be able to have children together after all. So might other mixed partners." Miriam sat back in her chair triumphantly, silently inviting Matthew to explode.

"But vampires can't reproduce biologically," Em said. "They've never been able to. And different species can't mix like that."

"Species change, adapting to new circumstances," said Marcus. "The instinct to survive through reproduction is a powerful one—certainly powerful enough to cause genetic changes."

Sarah frowned. "You make it sound like we're going extinct."

"We might be." Matthew pushed the test results into the center of the table along with the notes and the page from Ashmole 782. "Witches are having fewer children and possess diminishing powers. Vampires are finding it harder to take a warmblood through the process of rebirth. And the daemons are more unstable than ever."

"I still don't see why that would allow vampires and witches to share children," Em said. "And if there is a change, why should it begin with Diana and Matthew?"

"Miriam began to wonder while watching them in the library," Marcus explained.

"We've seen vampires exhibit protective behavior before when they want to shield their prey or a mate. But at some point other instincts—to hunt, to feed—overwhelm the urge to protect. Matthew's protective instincts toward Diana just got stronger," said Miriam. "Then he started a vampire's equivalent of flashing his plumage, swooping and diving in the air to attract attention away from her."

"That's about protecting future children," Marcus told his father. "Nothing else makes a predator go to those lengths."

"Emily's right. Vampires and witches are too different. Diana and I can't have children," Matthew said sharply, meeting Marcus's eyes.

"We don't know that. Not absolutely. Look at the spadefoot toad." Marcus rested his elbows on the table's surface, weaving his fingers together with a loud crack of his knuckles.

"The spadefoot toad?" Sarah picked up the picture of the chemical wedding, her fingers crumpling the edge. "Wait a minute. Is Diana the lion, the toad, or the queen in this picture?"

"She's the queen. Maybe the unicorn, too." Marcus gently pried the page from my aunt's fingers and went back to amphibians. "In certain situations, the female spadefoot toad will mate with a different—though not completely unrelated—species of toad. Her offspring benefit from new traits, like faster development, that help them survive."

"Vampires and witches are not spadefoot toads, Marcus," Matthew said coldly. "And not all of the changes that result are positive."

"Why are you so resistant?" Miriam asked impatiently. "Cross-species breeding *is* the next evolutionary step."

"Genetic supercombinations—like those that would occur if a witch and a vampire were to have children—lead to accelerated evolutionary developments. All species take such leaps. It's your own findings we're reporting back to you, Matthew," said Marcus apologetically.

"You're both ignoring the high mortality associated with genetic supercombinations. And if you think we're going to test those odds with Diana, you are very much mistaken." Matthew's voice was dangerously soft.

"Because she's a chimera—and AB-positive as well—she may be less likely to reject a fetus that's half vampire. She's a universal blood recipient and has already absorbed foreign DNA into her body. Like the spadefoot toad, she might have been led to you by the pressures of survival."

"That's a hell of a lot of conjecture, Marcus."

"Diana is different, Matthew. She's not like other witches." Marcus's eyes flickered from Matthew to me. "You haven't looked at her mtDNA report."

Matthew shuffled the pages. His breath came out in a hiss.

The sheet was covered in brightly covered hoops. Miriam had written across the top in red ink *"Unknown Clan,"* accompanied by a symbol that looked like a backward *E* set at an angle with a long tail. Matthew's eyes darted over the page, and the next.

"I knew you'd question the findings, so I brought comparatives," Miriam said quietly.

"What's a clan?" I watched Matthew carefully for a sign of what he was feeling.

"A genetic lineage. Through a witch's mitochondrial DNA, we can trace descent back to one of four women who were the female ancestors of every witch we've studied."

"Except you," Marcus said to me. "You and Sarah aren't descended from any of them."

"What does this mean?" I touched the backward *E*.

"It's an ancient glyph for *heh,* the Hebrew number five." Matthew directed his next words to Miriam. "How old is it?"

Miriam considered her words carefully. "Clan Heh is old—no matter which mitochondrial-clock theory you adhere to."

"Older than Clan Gimel?" Matthew asked, referring to the Hebrew word for the number three.

"Yes." Miriam hesitated. "And to answer your next question, there are two possibilities. Clan Heh could just be another line of descent from mtLilith."

Sarah opened her mouth to ask a question, and I quieted her with a shake of my head.

"Or Clan Heh could descend from a sister of mtLilith—which would make Diana's ancestor a clan mother, but not the witches' equivalent of mtEve. In either case it's possible that without Diana's issue Clan Heh will die out in this generation."

I slid the brown envelope from my mother in Matthew's direction. "Could you draw a picture?" No one in the room was going to understand this without visual assistance.

Matthew's hand sped over the page, sketching out two sprawling diagrams. One looked like a snake, the other branched out like the brackets for a sports tournament. Matthew pointed to the snake. "These are the seven known daughters of mitochondrial Eve—mtEve for short. Scientists consider them to be the most recent common matrilineal ancestors of every human of Western European descent. Each woman appears in the DNA record at a different point in history and in a different region of the globe. They once shared a common female ancestor, though."

"That would be mtEve," I said.

"Yes." He pointed at the tournament bracket. "This is what we've uncovered about the matrilineal descent of witches. There are four lines of descent, or clans. We numbered them in the order we found them, although the woman who was mother to Clan Aleph—the first clan we discovered—lived more recently than the others."

"Define 'recently,' please," Em requested.

"Aleph lived about seven thousand years ago."

"Seven *thousand* years ago?" Sarah said incredulously. "But the Bishops can only trace our female ancestors back to 1617."

"Gimel lived about forty thousand years ago," Matthew said grimly. "So if Miriam is right, and Clan Heh is older, you'll be well beyond that."

"Damn," Sarah breathed again. "Who's Lilith?"

"The first witch." I drew Matthew's diagrams closer, remembering his cryptic response in Oxford to my asking if he was searching for the first vampire. "Or at least the first witch from whom present-day witches can claim matrilineal descent."

"Marcus is fond of the Pre-Raphaelites, and Miriam knows a lot of mythology. They picked the name," Matthew said by way of explanation.

"The Pre-Raphaelites loved Lilith. Dante Gabriel Rossetti described her as the witch Adam loved before Eve." Marcus's eyes turned dreamy. "'*So went / Thy spell through him, and left his straight neck bent / And round his heart one strangling golden hair.*'"

"That's the Song of Songs," Matthew observed. "'*You have wounded my heart, my sister, my spouse, you have wounded my heart with one of your eyes, and with one hair of your neck.*'"

"The alchemists admired the same passage," I murmured with a shake of my head. "It's in the *Aurora Consurgens,* too."

"Other accounts of Lilith are far less rapturous," Miriam said in stern tones, drawing us back to the matter at hand. "In ancient stories she was a creature of the night, goddess of the wind and the moon, and the mate of Samael, the angel of death."

"Did the goddess of the moon and the angel of death have children?" Sarah asked, looking at us sharply. Once more the similarities between old stories, alchemical texts, and my relationship with a vampire were uncanny.

"Yes." Matthew plucked the reports from my hands and put them into a tidy pile.

"So that's what the Congregation is worried about," I said softly. "They fear the birth of children that are neither vampire nor witch nor daemon, but mixed. What would they do then?"

"How many other creatures have been in the same position as you and Matthew, over the years?" wondered Marcus.

"How many are there now?" Miriam added.

"The Congregation doesn't know about these test results—and thank God for that." Matthew slid the pile of papers back into the center of the table. "But there's still no evidence that Diana can have my child."

"So why did your mother's housekeeper teach Diana how to make that tea?" Sarah asked. "She thinks it's possible."

Oh, dear, my grandmother said sympathetically. *It's going to hit the fan now.*

Matthew stiffened, and his scent became overpoweringly spicy. "I don't understand."

"That tea that Diana and what's-her-name—Marthe—made in France. It's full of abortifacients and contraceptive herbs. I smelled them the moment the tin was open."

"Did you know?" Matthew's face was white with fury.

"No," I whispered. "But no harm was done."

Matthew stood. He pulled his phone from his pocket, avoiding my eyes. "Please excuse me," he said to Em and Sarah before striding out of the room.

"Sarah, how could you?" I cried after the front door shut behind him.

"He has a right to know—and so do you. No one should take drugs without consenting to it."

"It's not your job to tell him."

"No," Miriam said with satisfaction. "It was yours."

"Stay out of this, Miriam." I was spitting mad, and my hands were twitching.

"I'm already in it, Diana. Your relationship with Matthew puts every creature in this room in danger. It's going to change *everything,* whether you two have children or not. And now he's brought the Knights of Lazarus into it." Miriam was as furious as I was. "The more creatures who sanction your relationship, the likelier it is that there will be war."

"Don't be ridiculous. War?" The marks Satu burned into my back prickled ominously. "Wars break out between nations, not because a witch and a vampire love each other."

"What Satu did to you was a challenge. Matthew responded just as they hoped he would: by calling on the brotherhood." Miriam made a sound of disgust. "Since you walked into the Bodleian, he's lost control of his senses. And the last time he lost his senses over a woman, my husband died."

The room was quiet as a tomb. Even my grandmother looked startled.

Matthew wasn't a killer, or so I told myself over and over again. But he killed to feed himself, and he killed in angry, possessive rages. I knew both of these truths and loved him anyway. What did it say about me, that I could love such a creature so completely?

"Calm down, Miriam," Marcus warned.

"No," she snarled. "This is my tale. Not yours, Marcus."

"Then tell it," I said tersely, gripping the edges of the table.

"Bertrand was Matthew's best friend. When Eleanor St. Leger was killed, Jerusalem came to the brink of war. The English and the French were at each other's throats. He called on the Knights of Lazarus to resolve the conflict. We were nearly exposed to the humans as a result." Miriam's brittle voice broke. "Someone had to pay for Eleanor's death. The St. Legers demanded justice. Eleanor died at Matthew's hands, but he was the grand master then, just as he is now. My husband took the blame—to protect Matthew as well as the order. A Saracen executioner beheaded him."

"I'm sorry, Miriam—truly sorry—about your husband's death. But I'm not Eleanor St. Leger, and this isn't Jerusalem. It was a long time ago, and Matthew's not the same creature."

"It seems like yesterday to me," Miriam said simply. "Once again Matthew de Clermont wants what he cannot have. He hasn't changed at all."

The room fell silent. Sarah looked aghast. Miriam's story had confirmed her worst suspicions about vampires in general and Matthew in particular.

"Perhaps you'll remain true to him, even after you know him better," Miriam continued, her voice dead. "But how many more creatures will Matthew destroy on your behalf? Do you think Satu Järvinen will escape Gillian Chamberlain's fate?"

"What happened to Gillian?" Em asked, her voice rising.

Miriam opened her mouth to respond, and the fingers on my right hand curled instinctively into a loose ball. The index and middle fingers released in her direction with a tiny snap. She grabbed her throat and made a gurgling sound.

That wasn't very nice, Diana, my grandmother said with a shake of her finger. *You need to watch your temper, my girl.*

"Stay out of this, Grandma—and you too, Miriam." I gave both of them withering glances and turned to Em. "Gillian's dead. She and Peter Knox sent me the picture of Mom and Dad in Nigeria. It was a threat, and Matthew felt he had to protect me. It's instinctive in him, like breathing. Please try to forgive him."

Em turned white. "Matthew killed her for *delivering a picture*?"

"Not just for that," said Marcus. "She'd been spying on Diana for years. Gillian and Knox broke in to her rooms at New College and ransacked them. They were looking for DNA evidence so they could learn more about her power. If they'd found out what we now know—"

My fate would be far worse than death if Gillian and Knox knew what was in my test results. It was devastating that Matthew hadn't told me himself, though. I hid my thoughts, trying to close the shutters behind my eyes. My aunts didn't need to know that my husband kept things from me.

But there was no keeping my grandmother out. *Oh, Diana,* she whispered. *Are you sure you know what you're doing?*

"I want you all out of my house." Sarah pushed her chair back. "You, too, Diana."

A long, slow shudder started in the house's old root cellar under the family room and spread throughout the floorboards. It climbed up the walls and shook the panes of glass in the windows. Sarah's chair shot forward, pressing her against the table. The door between the dining room and the family room slammed shut.

The house never likes it when Sarah tries to take charge, my grandmother commented.

My own chair pulled back and dumped me unceremoniously onto the floor. I used the table to haul myself up, and when I was on my feet, invisible hands spun me around and pushed me through the door toward the front entrance. The dining-room door crashed behind me, locking two witches, two vampires, and a ghost inside. There were muffled sounds of outrage.

Another ghost—one I'd never seen before—walked out of the keeping room and beckoned me forward. She wore a bodice covered with intricate embroidery atop a dark, full skirt that touched the floor. Her face was creased with age, but the stubborn chin and long nose of the Bishops was unmistakable.

Be careful, daughter. Her voice was low and husky. *You are a creature of the crossroads, neither here nor there. 'Tis a dangerous place to be.*

"Who are you?"

She looked toward the front door without answering. It opened soundlessly, its usually creaky hinges silent and smooth. *I have always known he would come—and come for you. My own mother told me so.*

I was torn between the Bishops and the de Clermonts, part of me wanting to return to the dining room, the other part needing to be with Matthew. The ghost smiled at my dilemma.

You have always been a child between, a witch apart. But there is no path forward that does not have him in it. Whichever way you go, you must choose him.

She disappeared, leaving fading traces of phosphorescence. Matthew's white face and hands were just visible through the open door, a blur of movement in the darkness at the end of the driveway. At the sight of him my decision became easy.

Outside, I drew my sleeves down over my hands to protect them from the chilly air. I picked up one foot . . . and when I put it down, Matthew was directly in front of me, his back turned. It had taken me a single step to travel the length of the driveway.

He was speaking in furiously fast Occitan. Ysabeau must be on the other end.

"Matthew." I spoke softly, not wanting to startle him.

He whipped around with a frown. "Diana. I didn't hear you."

"No, you wouldn't have. May I speak to Ysabeau, please?" I reached for the phone.

"Diana, it would be better—"

Our families were locked in the dining room, and Sarah was threatening to throw us all out. We had enough problems without severing ties with Ysabeau and Marthe.

"What was it that Abraham Lincoln said about houses?"

"'A house divided against itself cannot stand,'" Matthew said, a puzzled look on his face.

"Exactly. Give me the phone." Reluctantly he did so.

"Diana?" Ysabeau's voice had an uncharacteristic edge.

"No matter what Matthew has said, I'm not angry with you. No harm was done."

"Thank you," she breathed. "I have been trying to tell him—it was only a feeling that we had, something half remembered from very long ago. Diana was the goddess of fertility then. Your scent reminds me of those times, and of the priestesses who helped women conceive."

Matthew's eyes touched me through the darkness.

"You'll tell Marthe, too?"

"I will, Diana." She paused. "Matthew has shared your test results and Marcus's theories with me. It is a sign of how much they have startled him, that he told your tale. I do not know whether to weep with joy or sorrow at the news."

"It's early days, Ysabeau—maybe both?"

She laughed softly. "It will not be the first time my children have driven me to tears. But I wouldn't give up the sorrow if it meant giving up the joy as well."

"Is everything all right at home?" The words escaped before I thought them through, and Matthew's eyes softened.

"Home?" The significance of the word was not lost on Ysabeau either. "Yes, we are all well here. It is very . . . quiet since you both left."

My eyes filled with tears. Despite Ysabeau's sharp edges, there was something so maternal about her. "Witches are noisier than vampires, I'm afraid."

"Yes. And happiness is always louder than sadness. There hasn't been enough happiness in this house." Her voice grew brisk. "Matthew has said everything to me that he needs to say. We must hope the worst of his anger has been spent. You will take care of each other." Ysabeau's last sentence was a statement of fact. It was what the women in her family—my family—did for those they loved.

"Always." I looked at my vampire, his white skin gleaming in the dark, and pushed the red button to disconnect the line. The fields on either side of the driveway were frost-covered, the ice crystals catching the faint traces of moonlight coming through the clouds.

"Did you suspect, too? Is that why you won't make love to me?" I asked Matthew.

"I told you my reasons. Making love should be about intimacy, not just physical need." He sounded frustrated at having to repeat himself.

"If you don't want to have children with me, I *will* understand," I said firmly, though part of me quietly protested.

His hands were rough on my arms. "Christ, Diana, how can you think that I wouldn't want our children? But it might be dangerous—for you, for them."

"There's always risk with pregnancy. Not even you control nature."

"We have no idea what our children would be. What if they shared my need for blood?"

"All babies are vampires, Matthew. They're all nourished with their mother's blood."

"It's not the same, and you know it. I gave up all hope of children long ago." Our eyes met, searching for reassurance that nothing between us had changed. "But it's too soon for me to imagine losing you."

And I couldn't bear losing our children.

Matthew's unspoken words were as clear to me as an owl hooting overhead. The pain of Lucas's loss would never leave him. It cut deeper than the deaths of Blanca or Eleanor. When he lost Lucas, he lost part of himself that could never be recovered.

"So you've decided. No children. You're sure." I rested my hands on his chest, waiting for the next beat of his heart.

"I'm not sure of anything," Matthew said. "We haven't had time to discuss it."

"Then we'll take every precaution. I'll drink Marthe's tea."

"You'll do a damn sight more than that," he said grimly. "That stuff is better than nothing, but it's a far cry from modern medicine. Even so, no human form of contraception may be effective when it comes to witches and vampires."

"I'll take the pills anyway," I assured him.

"And what about you?" he asked, his fingers on my chin to keep me from avoiding his eyes. "Do you want to carry my children?"

"I never imagined myself a mother." A shadow flickered across his face. "But when I think of your children, it feels as though it was meant to be."

He dropped my chin. We stood silently in the darkness, his arms around my waist and my head on his chest. The air felt heavy, and I recognized it as the weight of responsibility. Matthew was responsible for his family, his past, the Knights of Lazarus—and now for me.

"You're worried that you couldn't protect them," I said, suddenly understanding.

"I can't even protect you," he said harshly, fingers playing over the crescent moon burned into my back.

"We don't have to decide just yet. With or without children, we already have a family to keep together." The heaviness in the air shifted, some of it settling on my shoulders. All my life I'd lived for myself alone, pushing away the obligations of family and tradition. Even now part of me wanted to return to the safety of independence and leave these new burdens behind.

His eyes traveled up the drive to the house. "What happened after I left?"

"Oh, what you'd expect. Miriam told us about Bertrand and Jerusalem—and let slip about Gillian. Marcus told us who broke in to my rooms. And then there's the fact that we might have started some kind of war."

"*Dieu*, why can't they keep their mouths shut?" He ran his fingers through his hair, his regret at concealing all this from me clear in his eyes. "At first I was sure this was about the manuscript. Then I supposed it was all about you. Now I'll be damned if I can figure out *what* it's about. Some old, powerful secret is unraveling, and we're caught up in it."

"Is Miriam right to wonder how many other creatures are tangled in it, too?" I stared at the moon as if she might answer my question. Matthew did instead.

"It's doubtful we're the first creatures to love those we should not, and we surely won't be the last." He took my arm. "Let's go inside. We have some explaining to do."

On our way up the drive, Matthew observed that explanations, like medicines, go down easier when accompanied by liquid refreshment. We entered the house through the back door to pick up the necessary supplies. While I arranged a tray, Matthew's eyes rested on me.

"What?" I looked up. "Did I forget something?"

A smile played at the corners of his mouth. "No, *ma lionne.* I'm just trying to figure out how I acquired such a fierce wife. Even putting cups on a tray, you look formidable."

"I'm not formidable," I said, tightening my ponytail self-consciously.

"Yes, you are." Matthew smiled. "Miriam wouldn't be in such a state otherwise."

When we reached the door between the dining room and the family room, we listened for sounds of a battle within, but there was nothing except quiet murmurs and low conversation. The house unlocked the door and opened it for us.

"We thought you might be thirsty," I said, putting the tray on the table.

A multitude of eyes turned in our direction—vampires, witches, ghosts. My grandmother had a whole flock of Bishops at her back, all of them rustling and shifting as they tried to adjust to having vampires in the dining room.

"Whiskey, Sarah?" Matthew asked, picking up a tumbler from the tray.

She gave him a long look. "Miriam says that by accepting your relationship we invite war. My father fought in World War II."

"So did mine," Matthew said, pouring the whiskey. So had he, no doubt, but he was silent on that point.

"He always said whiskey made it possible to close your eyes at night without hating yourself for everything you'd been ordered to do that day."

"It's no guarantee, but it helps." Matthew held out the glass.

Sarah took it. "Would you kill your own son if you thought he was a threat to Diana?"

He nodded. "Without hesitation."

"That's what he said." Sarah nodded at Marcus. "Get him a drink, too. It can't be easy, knowing your own father could kill you."

Matthew got Marcus his whiskey and poured Miriam a glass of wine. I made Em a cup of milky coffee. She'd been crying and looked more fragile than usual.

"I just don't know if I can handle this, Diana," she whispered when she took the mug. "Marcus explained what Gillian and Peter Knox had planned. But when I think of Barbara Chamberlain and what she must be feeling now that her daughter is dead—" Em shuddered to a stop.

"Gillian Chamberlain was an ambitious woman, Emily," said Matthew. "All she ever wanted was a seat at the Congregation's table."

"But you didn't have to kill her," Em insisted.

"Gillian believed absolutely that witches and vampires should remain apart. The Congregation has never been satisfied that they fully understood Stephen Proctor's power and asked her to watch Diana. She wouldn't have rested until both Ashmole 782 and Diana were in the Congregation's control."

"But it was just a picture." Em wiped at her eyes.

"It was a threat. The Congregation had to understand that I was not going to stand by and let them take Diana."

"Satu took her anyway," Em pointed out, her voice unusually sharp.

"That's enough, Em." I reached over and covered her hand with mine.

"What about this issue of children?" Sarah asked, gesturing with her glass. "Surely you two won't do something so risky?"

"That's enough," I repeated, standing and banging my hand on the table. Everyone but Matthew and my grandmother jumped in surprise. "If we are at war, we're not fighting for a bewitched alchemical manuscript, or for my safety, or for our right to marry and have children. This is about the future of all of us." I saw that future for just a moment, its bright potential spooling away in a thousand different directions. "If our children don't take the next evolutionary steps, it will be someone else's children. And whiskey isn't going to make it possible for me to close my eyes and forget that. No one else will go through this kind of hell because they love someone they're not supposed to love. I won't allow it."

My grandmother gave me a slow, sweet smile. *There's my girl. Spoken like a Bishop.*

"We don't expect anyone else to fight with us. But understand this: our army has one general. Matthew. If you don't like it, don't enlist."

In the front hall, the old case clock began to strike midnight.

The witching hour. My grandmother nodded.

Sarah looked at Em. "Well, honey? Are we going to stand with Diana and join Matthew's army or let the devil take the hindmost?"

"I don't understand what you all mean by war. Will there be battles? Will vampires and witches come here?" Em asked Matthew in a shaky voice.

"The Congregation believes Diana holds answers to their questions. They won't stop looking for her."

"But Matthew and I don't have to stay," I said. "We can be gone by morning."

"My mother always said my life wouldn't be worth living once it was tangled up with the Bishops," Em said with a wan smile.

"Thank you, Em," Sarah said simply, although her face spoke volumes.

The clock tolled a final time. Its gears whirred into place, ready to strike the next hour when it came.

"Miriam?" Matthew asked. "Are you staying here or are you going back to Oxford?"

"My place is with the de Clermonts."

"Diana is a de Clermont now." His tone was icy.

"I understand, Matthew." Miriam directed a level gaze at me. "It won't happen again."

"How strange," Marcus murmured, his eyes sweeping the room. "First it was a shared secret. Now three witches and three vampires have pledged loyalty to one another. If we had a trio of daemons, we'd be a shadow Congregation."

"We're unlikely to run into three daemons in downtown Madison," Matthew said drily. "And whatever happens, what we've talked about tonight remains among the six of us—understood? Diana's DNA is no one else's business."

There were nods all around the table as Matthew's motley army fell into line behind him, ready to face an enemy we didn't know and couldn't name.

We said our good-nights and went upstairs. Matthew kept his arm around me, guiding me through the doorframe and into the bedroom when I found it impossible to navigate the turn on my own. I slid between the icy sheets, teeth chattering. When his cool body pressed against mine, the chattering ceased.

I slept heavily, waking only once. Matthew's eyes glittered in the darkness, and he pulled me back so that we lay like spoons.

"Sleep," he said, kissing me behind the ear. "I'm here." His cold hand curved over my belly, already protecting children yet to be born.

Chapter 37

Over the next several days, Matthew's tiny army learned the first requirement of war: allies must not kill each other.

Difficult as it was for my aunts to accept vampires into their house, it was the vampires who had the real trouble adjusting. It wasn't just the ghosts and the cat. More than nuts would have to be kept in the house if vampires and warmbloods were to live in such close quarters. The very next day Marcus and Miriam had a conversation with Matthew in the driveway, then left in the Range Rover. Several hours later they returned bearing a small refrigerator marked with a red cross and enough blood and medical supplies to outfit an army field hospital. At Matthew's request, Sarah selected a corner of the stillroom to serve as the blood bank.

"It's just a precaution," Matthew assured her.

"In case Miriam gets the munchies?" Sarah picked up a bag of O-negative blood.

"I ate before I left England," Miriam said primly, her tiny bare feet slipping quietly over the stone floors as she put items away.

The deliveries also included a blister pack of birth-control pills inside a hideous yellow plastic case with a flower molded into the lid. Matthew presented them to me at bedtime.

"You can start them now or wait a few days until your period starts."

"How do you know when my period is going to start?" I'd finished my last cycle the day before Mabon—the day before I'd met Matthew.

"I know when you're planning on jumping a paddock fence. You can imagine how easy it is for me to know when you're about to bleed."

"Can you be around me while I'm menstruating?" I held the case gingerly as if it might explode.

Matthew looked surprised, then chuckled. "*Dieu,* Diana. There wouldn't be a woman alive if I couldn't." He shook his head. "It's not the same thing."

I started the pills that night.

As we adjusted to the close quarters, new patterns of activity developed in the house—many of them around me. I was never alone and never more than ten feet away from the nearest vampire. It was perfect pack behavior. The vampires were closing ranks around me.

My day was divided into zones of activity punctuated by meals, which

Matthew insisted I needed at regular intervals to fully recover from La Pierre. He joined me in yoga between breakfast and lunch, and after lunch Sarah and Em tried to teach me how to use my magic and perform spells. When I was tearing my hair out with frustration, Matthew would whisk me off for a long walk before dinner. We lingered around the table in the family room after the warmbloods had eaten, talking about current events and old movies. Marcus unearthed a chessboard, and he and his father often played together while Em and I cleaned up.

Sarah, Marcus, and Miriam shared a fondness for film noir, which now dominated the house's TV-viewing schedule. Sarah had discovered this happy coincidence when, during one of her habitual bouts of insomnia, she went downstairs in the middle of the night and found Miriam and Marcus watching *Out of the Past*. The three also shared a love of Scrabble and popcorn. By the time the rest of the house awoke, they'd transformed the family room into a cinema and everything had been swept off the coffee table save a game board, a cracked bowl full of lettered tiles, and two battered dictionaries.

Miriam proved to be a genius at remembering archaic seven-letter words.

"'Smoored'!" Sarah was exclaiming one morning when I came downstairs. "What the hell kind of word is 'smoored'? If you mean those campfire desserts with marshmallows and graham crackers, you've spelled it wrong."

"It means 'smothered,'" Miriam explained. "It's what we did to fires to keep them banked overnight. We smoored them. Look it up if you don't believe me."

Sarah grumbled and retreated to the kitchen for coffee.

"Who's winning?" I inquired.

"You need to ask?" The vampire smiled with satisfaction.

When not playing Scrabble or watching old movies, Miriam held classes covering Vampires 101. In the space of a few afternoons, she managed to teach Em the importance of names, pack behavior, possessive rituals, preternatural senses, and dining habits. Lately talk had turned to more advanced topics, such as how to slay a vampire.

"No, not even slicing our necks open is foolproof, Em," Miriam told her patiently. The two were sitting in the family room while I made tea in the kitchen. "You want to cause as much blood loss as possible. Go for the groin as well."

Matthew shook his head at the exchange and took the opportunity (since everyone else was otherwise engaged) to pin me behind the refrigerator door. My shirt was askew and my hair tumbling around my ears when our son came into the room with an armload of wood.

"Did you lose something behind the refrigerator, Matthew?" Marcus's face was the picture of innocence.

"No," Matthew purred. He buried his face in my hair so he could drink in the scent of my arousal. I swatted ineffectually at his shoulders, but he just held me tighter.

"Thanks for replenishing the firewood, Marcus," I said breathlessly.

"Should I go get more?" One blond eyebrow arched up in perfect imitation of his father.

"Good idea. It will be cold tonight." I twisted my head to reason with Matthew, but he mistook it as an invitation to kiss me again. Marcus and the wood supply faded into inconsequence.

When not lying in wait in dark corners, Matthew joined Sarah and Marcus in the most unholy trio of potion brewers since Shakespeare put three witches around a cauldron. The vapor Sarah and Matthew brewed up for the picture of the chemical wedding hadn't revealed anything, but this didn't deter them. They occupied the stillroom at all hours, consulting the Bishop grimoire and making strange concoctions that smelled bad, exploded, or both. On one occasion Em and I investigated a loud bang followed by the sound of rolling thunder.

"What are you three up to?" Em asked, hands on hips. Sarah's face was covered in gray soot, and debris was falling down the chimney.

"Nothing," Sarah grumbled. "I was trying to cleave the air and the spell got bent out of shape, that's all."

"Cleaving?" I looked at the mess, astonished.

Matthew and Marcus nodded solemnly.

"You'd better clean up this room before dinner, Sarah Bishop, or I'll show you cleaving!" Em sputtered.

Of course, not all encounters between residents were happy ones. Marcus and Matthew walked together at sunrise, leaving me to the tender care of Miriam, Sarah, and the teapot. They never went far. They were always visible from the kitchen window, their heads bent together in conversation. One morning Marcus turned on his heel and stormed back to the house, leaving his father alone in the old apple orchard.

"Diana," he growled in greeting before streaking through the family room and straight out the front door. "I'm too damn young for this!" he shouted as he left.

His engine revved—Marcus preferred sports cars to SUVs—and the tires bit into the gravel when he reversed and pulled out of the driveway.

"What's Marcus upset about?" I asked when Matthew returned, kissing his cold cheek as he reached for the paper.

"Business," he said shortly, kissing me back.

"You didn't make him seneschal?" Miriam asked incredulously.

Matthew flipped the paper open. "You must have a very high opinion of me, Miriam, if you think the brotherhood has functioned for all these years without a seneschal. That position is already occupied."

"What's a seneschal?" I put two slices of bread in the beat-up toaster. It had six slots, but only two of them worked with any reliability.

"My second in command," Matthew said briefly.

"If he's not the seneschal, why has Marcus sped out of here?" Miriam pressed.

"I appointed him marshal," Matthew said, scanning the headlines.

"He's the least likely marshal I've ever seen," she said severely. "He's a physician, for God's sake. Why not Baldwin?"

Matthew looked up from his paper and cocked his eyebrow at her. "Baldwin?"

"Okay, not Baldwin," Miriam hastily replied. "There must be someone else."

"Had I two thousand knights to choose from as I once did, there might be someone else. But there are only eight knights under my command at present—one of whom is the ninth knight and not required to fight—a handful of sergeants, and a few squires. Someone has to be marshal. I was Philippe's marshal. Now it's Marcus's turn." The terminology was so antiquated it invited giggles, but the serious look on Miriam's face kept me quiet.

"Have you told him he's to start raising banners?" Miriam and Matthew continued to speak a language of war I didn't understand.

"What's a marshal?" The toast sprang out and winged its way to the kitchen island when my stomach rumbled.

"Matthew's chief military officer." Miriam eyed the refrigerator door, which was opening without visible assistance.

"Here." Matthew neatly caught the butter as it passed over his shoulder and then handed it to me with a smile, his face serene in spite of his colleague's pestering. Matthew, though a vampire, was self-evidently a morning person.

"The banners, Matthew. Are you raising an army?"

"Of course I am, Miriam. You're the one who keeps bringing up war. If it breaks out, you don't imagine that Marcus, Baldwin, and I are going to fight the Congregation by ourselves?" Matthew shook his head. "You know better than that."

"What about Fernando? Surely he's still alive and well."

Matthew put his paper down and glowered. "I'm not going to discuss my strategy with you. Stop interfering and leave Marcus to me."

Now it was Miriam's turn to bolt. She pressed her lips tightly together and stalked out the back door, headed for the woods.

I ate my toast in silence, and Matthew returned to his paper. After a few minutes, he put it down again and made a sound of exasperation.

"Out with it, Diana. I can smell you thinking, and it's impossible for me to concentrate."

"Oh, it's nothing," I said around a mouthful of toast. "A vast military machine is swinging into action, the precise nature of which I don't understand. And you're unlikely to explain it to me, because it's some sort of brotherhood secret."

"*Dieu.*" Matthew ran his fingers through his hair until it stood on end. "Miriam causes more trouble than any creature I've ever known, with the exception of Domenico Michele and my sister Louisa. If you want to know about the Knights, I'll tell you."

Two hours later my head was spinning with information about the brotherhood. Matthew had sketched out an organizational flowchart on the back of my DNA reports. It was awesome in its complexity—and it didn't include the military side. That part of the operation was outlined on some ancient Harvard University letterhead left by my parents that we pulled out of the sideboard. I looked over Marcus's many new responsibilities.

"No wonder he's overwhelmed," I murmured, tracing the lines that connected Marcus to Matthew above him and to seven master knights below, and then to the troops of vampires each would be expected to gather.

"He'll adjust." Matthew's cold hands kneaded the tight muscles in my back, his fingers lingering on the star between my shoulder blades. "Marcus will have Baldwin and the other knights to rely upon. He can handle the responsibility, or I wouldn't have asked him."

Maybe, but he would never be the same after taking on this job for Matthew. Every new challenge would chip away a piece of his easygoing charm. It was painful to imagine the vampire Marcus would become.

"What about this Fernando? Will he help Marcus?"

Matthew's face grew secretive. "Fernando was my first choice for marshal, but he turned me down. It was he who recommended Marcus."

"Why?" From the way Miriam spoke, the vampire was a respected warrior.

"Marcus reminds Fernando of Philippe. If there is war, we'll need someone with my father's charm to convince the vampires to fight not only witches but other vampires, too." Matthew nodded thoughtfully, his eyes on the rough outlines of his empire. "Yes, Fernando will help him. And keep him from making too many mistakes."

When we returned to the kitchen—Matthew in search of his newspaper and me in pursuit of an early lunch—Sarah and Em were just back from the grocery store. They unpacked boxes of microwave popcorn as well as tins of mixed nuts and every berry available in October in upstate New York. I picked up a bag of cranberries.

"There you are." Sarah's eyes gleamed. "Time for your lessons."

"I need more tea first, and something to eat," I protested, pouring the cranberries from one hand to the other in their plastic bag. "No magic on an empty stomach."

"Give me those," Em said, grabbing the bag. "You're squashing them, and they're Marcus's favorite."

"You can eat later." Sarah pushed me in the direction of the stillroom. "Stop being such a baby and get moving."

I turned out to be as hopeless at spells now as when I was a teenager. Unable to remember how they started, and given my mind's tendency to wander, I garbled the order of the words with disastrous results.

Sarah set a candle on the stillroom's wide table. "Light it," she commanded, turning back to the indescribably stained grimoire.

It was a simple trick that even a teenage witch could manage. When the spell emerged from my mouth, however, either the candle smoked without the wick's catching light or something else burst into flames instead. This time I set a bunch of lavender on fire.

"You can't just say the words, Diana," Sarah lectured once she'd extinguished the flames. "You have to concentrate. Do it again."

I did it again—over and over. Once the candle wick sputtered with a tentative flame.

"This isn't working." My hands were tingling, the nails blue, and I was ready to scream in frustration.

"You can command witchfire and you can't light a candle."

"My arms move in a way that reminds you of someone who *could* command witchfire. That's not the same thing, and learning about magic is more important than this stuff," I said, gesturing at the grimoire.

"Magic is not the only answer," Sarah said tartly. "It's like using a chainsaw to cut bread. Sometimes a knife will do."

"You don't have a high opinion of magic, but I have a fair amount of it in me, and it wants to come out. Someone has to teach me how to control it."

"I can't." Sarah's voice was tinged with regret. "I wasn't born with the ability to summon witchfire or command witchwater. But I can damn well see to it that you can learn to light a candle with one of the simplest spells ever devised."

Sarah was right. But it took so long to master the craft, and spells would be no help if I started to spout water again.

While I returned to my candle and mumbled words, Sarah looked through the grimoire for a new challenge.

"This is a good one," she said, pointing to a page mottled with brown, green, and red residues. "It's a modified apparition spell that creates what's called an echo—an exact duplicate of someone's spoken words in another location. Very useful. Let's do that next."

"No, let's take a break." Turning away, I picked up my foot to take a step.

The apple orchard was around me when I set it down again.

In the house Sarah was shouting. "Diana? Where are you?"

Matthew rocketed out the door and down the porch steps. His sharp eyes found me easily, and he was at my side in a few rapid strides.

"What is this about?" His hand was on my elbow so that I couldn't disappear again.

"I needed to get away from Sarah. When I put my foot down, here I was. The same thing happened on the driveway the other night."

"You needed an apple, too? Walking into the kitchen wouldn't have been sufficient?" The corner of Matthew's mouth twitched in amusement.

"No," I said shortly.

"Too much all at once, *ma lionne*?"

"I'm not good at witchcraft. It's too . . ."

"Precise?" he finished.

"It takes too much patience," I confessed.

"Witchcraft and spells may not be your weapons of choice," he said softly, brushing my tense jaw with the back of his hand, "but you *will* learn to use them." The note of command was slight, but it was there. "Let's find you something to eat. That always makes you more agreeable."

"Are you managing me?" I asked darkly.

"You've just now noticed?" He chuckled. "It's been my full-time job for weeks."

Matthew continued to do so throughout the afternoon, retelling stories he'd gleaned from the paper about lost cats up trees, fire-department chili cook-offs, and impending Halloween events. By the time I'd devoured a bowl of leftovers, the food and his mindless chatter had done their work, and it was possible to face Sarah and the Bishop grimoire again. Back in the stillroom, Matthew's words came back to me whenever I threatened to abandon Sarah's detailed instructions, refocusing my attempts to conjure fire, voices, or whatever else she required.

After hours of spell casting—none of which had gone particularly well—he knocked on the stillroom door and announced it was time for our walk. In the mudroom I flung on a thick sweater, slid into my sneakers, and flew out the door. Matthew joined me at a more leisurely pace, sniffing the air appreciatively and watching the play of light on the fields around the house.

Darkness fell quickly in late October, and twilight was now my favorite time of day. Matthew might be a morning person, but his natural self-protectiveness diminished at sunset. He seemed to relax into the lengthening shadows, the fading light softening his strong bones and rendering his pale skin a touch less otherworldly.

He grabbed my hand, and we walked in companionable silence, happy to be near each other and away from our families. At the edge of the forest, Matthew sped up and I deliberately hung back, wanting to stay outdoors as long as possible.

"Come on," he said, frustrated at having to match my slow steps.

"No!" My steps became smaller and slower. "We're just a normal couple taking a walk before dinner."

"We're the least normal couple in the state of New York," Matthew said with a smile. "And this pace won't even make you break a sweat."

"What do you have in mind?" It had become clear during our previous walks that the wolflike part of Matthew enjoyed romping in the woods like an oversize puppy. He was always coming up with new ways to play with my power so that learning how to use it wouldn't seem like a chore. The dull, dutiful stuff he left to Sarah.

"Tag." He shot me a mischievous look that was impossible to resist and took off in an explosion of speed and strength. "Catch me."

I laughed and darted behind, my feet rising from the ground and my mind trying to capture a clear image of reaching his broad shoulders and touching them. My speed increased as the vision became more precise, but my agility left a lot to be desired. Simultaneously using the powers of flight and precognition at high speed made me trip over a shrub. Before I tumbled to the ground, Matthew had scooped me up.

"You smell like fresh air and wood smoke," he said, nuzzling my hair.

There was an anomaly in the forest, felt rather than seen. It was a bending of the fading light, a sense of momentum, an aura of dark intention. My head swiveled over my shoulder.

"Someone's here," I said.

The wind was blowing away from us. Matthew raised his head, trying to pick up the scent. He identified it with a sharp intake of breath.

"Vampire," he said quietly, grabbing my hand and standing. He pushed me against the trunk of a white oak.

"Friend or foe?" I asked shakily.

"Leave. *Now.*" Matthew had his phone out, pushing the single number on speed dial that connected him to Marcus. He swore at the voice-mail recording. "Someone is tracking us, Marcus. Get here—fast." He disconnected and pushed another button that brought up a text-message screen.

The wind changed, and the skin around his mouth tightened.

"Christ, no." His fingers flew over the keys, typing in two words before he flung the phone into the nearby bushes.

"SOS. Juliette."

He turned, grabbing my shoulders. "Do whatever you did in the stillroom. Pick up your feet and go back to the house. *Immediately.* I'm not asking you, Diana, I'm telling you."

My feet were frozen and refused to obey him. "I don't know how. I can't."

"You will." Matthew pushed me against the tree, his arms on either side and his back to the forest. "Gerbert introduced me to this vampire a long time ago, and she isn't to be trusted or underestimated. We spent time together in France in the eighteenth century, and in New Orleans in the nineteenth century. I'll explain everything later. Now, go."

"I'm not leaving without you." My voice was stubborn. "Who is Juliette?"

"I am Juliette Durand." The melodious voice, accented with hints of French and something else, came from above. We both looked up. "What trouble you two have caused."

A stunning vampire was perched on a thick branch of a nearby maple. Her skin was the color of milk with a splash of coffee, and her hair shone in a blend of brown and copper. Clad in the colors of autumn—brown, green, and gold—she looked like an extension of the tree. Wide hazel eyes sat atop slanted cheekbones, and her bones implied a delicacy that I knew misrepresented her strength.

"I've been watching you—listening, too. Your scents are all tangled up together." She made a quiet sound of reproof.

I didn't see her leave the branch, but Matthew did. He'd angled his body so that he would be in front of me when she landed. He faced her, lips curled in warning.

Juliette ignored him. "I have to study her." She tilted her head to the right and lifted her chin a touch, staring at me intently.

I frowned.

She frowned back.

Matthew shivered.

I glanced at him in concern, and Juliette's eyes followed mine.

She was imitating my every move. Her chin was jutting out at precisely the same angle as mine, her head was held at exactly the same incline. It was like looking into a mirror.

Panic flooded my system, filling my mouth with bitterness. I swallowed hard, and the vampire swallowed, too. Her nostrils flared, and she laughed, sharp and hard as diamonds.

"How have you resisted her, Matthew?" She took a long, slow breath. "The smell of her should drive you mad with hunger. Do you remember that frightened young woman we stalked in Rome? She smelled rather like this one, I think."

Matthew remained silent, his eyes fixed on the vampire.

Juliette took a few steps to the right, forcing him to adjust his position. "You're expecting Marcus," she observed sadly. "I'm afraid he's not coming. So handsome. I would have liked to see him again. The last time we met, he was so young and impressionable. It took us weeks to sort out the mess he'd made in New Orleans, didn't it?"

An abyss opened before me. Had she killed Marcus? Sarah and Em?

"He's on the phone," she continued. "Gerbert wanted to be sure that your son understood the risk he's taking. The Congregation's anger is directed only at the two of you—now. But if you persist, others will pay the price as well."

Marcus wasn't dead. Despite the relief, my blood ran cold at the expression on her face.

There was still no response from Matthew.

"Why so quiet, my love?" Juliette's warm voice belied the deadness of her eyes. "You should be glad to see me. I'm everything you want. Gerbert made sure of that."

He still didn't answer.

"Ah. You're silent because I've surprised you," Juliette said, her tone strangely fractured between music and malice. "You've surprised me, too. A witch?"

She feinted left, and Matthew swiveled to meet her. She somersaulted through the empty space where his head had been and landed at my side, fingers around my throat. I froze.

"I don't understand why he wants you so much." Juliette's voice was petulant. "What it is that you do? What did Gerbert fail to teach me?"

"Juliette, let her be." Matthew couldn't risk a move in my direction for fear she'd snap my neck, but his legs were rigid with the effort to stay still.

"Patience, Matthew," she said, bending her head.

I closed my eyes, expecting to feel teeth.

Instead cold lips pressed against mine. Juliette's kiss was weirdly impersonal as she teased my mouth with her tongue, trying to get me to respond. When I didn't, she made a sound of frustration.

"That should have helped me understand, but it didn't." Juliette flung me at Matthew but kept hold of one wrist, her razor-sharp nails poised above my veins. "Kiss her. I have to know how she's done it."

"Why not leave this alone, Juliette?" Matthew caught me in his cool grip.

"I must learn from my mistakes—Gerbert's been saying so since you abandoned me in New York." Juliette focused on Matthew with an avidity that made my flesh crawl.

"That was more than a hundred years ago. If you haven't learned your mistake by now, you're not going to." Though Matthew's anger was not directed at me, its power made me recoil nonetheless. He was simmering with it, the rage coming from him in waves.

Juliette's nails cut into my arm. "Kiss her, Matthew, or I will make her bleed."

Cupping my face with one careful, gentle hand, he struggled to push up the corners of his mouth into a smile. "It will be all right, *mon coeur*." Matthew's pupils were dots in a sea of gray-green. One thumb stroked my jaw as he bent nearer, his lips nearly touching mine. His kiss was slow and tender, a testament of feeling. Juliette stared at us coldly, drinking in the details. She crept closer as Matthew drew away from me.

"Ah." Her voice was blank and bitter. "You like the way she responds when you touch her. But I can't *feel* anymore."

I'd seen Ysabeau's anger and Baldwin's ruthlessness. I'd felt Domenico's desperation and smelled the unmistakable scent of evil that hung around Gerbert. But Juliette was different. Something fundamental was broken within her.

She released my arm and sprang out of Matthew's reach. His hands squeezed my elbows, and his cold fingers touched my hips. With an infinitesimal push, Matthew gave me another silent command to leave.

But I had no intention of leaving my husband alone with a psychotic vampire. Deep within, something stirred. Though neither witchwind nor witchwater would be enough to kill Juliette, they might distract her long enough for us to get away—but both refused my unspoken commands. And any spells I had learned over the past few days, no matter how imperfectly, had flown from my mind.

"Don't worry," Juliette said softly to Matthew, her eyes bright. "It will be over very quickly. I would like to linger, of course, so that we could remember what we once were to each other. But none of my touches will drive her from your mind. Therefore I must kill you and take your witch to face Gerbert and the Congregation."

"Let Diana go." Matthew raised his hands in truce. "This is between us, Juliette."

She shook her head, setting her heavy, burnished hair swaying. "I'm Gerbert's instrument, Matthew. When he made me, he left no room for my desires. I didn't want to learn philosophy or mathematics. But Gerbert insisted, so that I could please you. And I did please you, didn't I?" Juliette's attention was fixed on Matthew, and her voice was as rough as the fault lines in her broken mind.

"Yes, you pleased me."

"I thought so. But Gerbert already owned me." Juliette's eyes turned to me. They were brilliant, suggesting she had fed recently. "He will possess you, too, Diana, in ways you cannot imagine. In ways only I know. You'll be his, then, and lost to everyone else."

"No." Matthew lunged at Juliette, but she darted past.

"This is no time for games, Matthew," said Juliette.

She moved quickly—too quickly for my eyes to see—then pulled slowly away from him with a look of triumph. There was a ripping sound, and blood welled darkly at his throat.

"That will do for a start," she said with satisfaction.

There was a roaring in my head. Matthew stepped between me and Juliette. Even my imperfect warmblood nose could smell the metallic tang of his blood. It was soaking into his sweater, spreading in a dark stain across his chest.

"Don't do this, Juliette. If you ever loved me, you'll let her go. She doesn't deserve Gerbert."

Juliette answered in a blur of brown leather and muscle. Her leg swung high, and there was a crack as her foot connected with Matthew's abdomen. He bent over like a felled tree.

"I didn't *deserve* Gerbert either." There was a hysterical edge to Juliette's voice. "But I deserved *you*. You belong to me, Matthew."

My hands felt heavy, and I knew without looking that they held a bow and arrow. I backed away from the two vampires, raising my arms.

"Run!" Matthew shouted.

"No," I said in a voice that was not my own, squinting down the line of my left arm. Juliette was close to Matthew, but I could release the arrow without touching him. When my right hand flexed, Juliette would be dead. Still, I hesitated, never having killed anyone before

That moment was all Juliette needed. Her fingers punched through Matthew's chest, nails tearing through fabric and flesh as if both were paper. He gasped at the pain, and Juliette roared in victory.

All hesitation gone, my right hand tightened and opened. A ball of fire arced from the extended tips of my left fingers. Juliette heard the explosion of flame and smelled the sulfur in the air. She turned, her nails withdrawing from the hole in Matthew's chest. Disbelief showed in her eyes before the spitting ball of black, gold, and red enveloped her. Her hair caught fire first, and she reeled in panic. But I had anticipated her, and another ball of flame was waiting. She stepped right into it.

Matthew dropped to his knees, his hands pressing the blood-soaked sweater into the spot where she had punctured the skin over his heart. Screaming, Juliette reached out, trying to draw him into the inferno.

At a flick of my wrist and a word to the wind, she was picked up and carried several feet from where Matthew was collapsing into the earth. She fell onto her back, her body alight.

I wanted to run to him but continued to watch Juliette as her vampire bones and flesh resisted the flames. Her hair was gone and her skin was black and leathery, but even then she wasn't dead. Her mouth kept moving, calling Matthew's name.

My hands remained raised, ready for her to defy the odds. She lumbered to her feet once, and I released another bolt. It hit her in the middle of the chest, went through her rib cage, and came out the other side, shattering the tough skin as it passed and turning her ribs and lungs to coal. Her mouth twisted into a rictus of horror. She was beyond recovery now, no matter the strength of her vampire blood.

I rushed to Matthew's side and dropped to the ground. He could no longer keep himself upright and was lying on his back, knees bent. There was blood everywhere, pulsing out of the hole in his chest in deep purple waves and flowing more evenly from his neck, so dark it was like pitch.

"What should I do?" I frantically pressed my fingers against his throat. His white hands were still locked around the wound in his chest, but the strength was leaching out of them with each passing moment.

"Will you hold me?" he whispered.

My back to the oak tree, I pulled him between my legs.

"I'm cold," he said with dull amazement. "How strange."

"You can't leave me," I said fiercely. "I won't have it."

"There's nothing to be done about that now. Death has me in his grip." Matthew was talking in a way that had not been heard in a thousand years, his fading voice rising and falling in an ancient cadence.

"No." I fought back my tears. "You have to fight, Matthew."

"I *have* fought, Diana. And you are safe. Marcus will have you away from here before the Congregation knows what has happened."

"I won't go anywhere without you."

"You must." He struggled in my arms, shifting so that he could see my face.

"I can't lose you, Matthew. Please hold on until Marcus gets here." The chain inside me swayed, its links loosening one by one. I tried to resist by keeping him tight against my heart.

"Hush," he said softly, raising a bloody finger to touch my lips. They tingled and went numb as his freezing blood came into contact with my skin. "Marcus and Baldwin know what to do. They will see you safe to Ysabeau. Without me the Congregation will find it harder to act against you. The vampires and witches will not like it, but you are a de Clermont now, with my family's protection as well as that of the Knights of Lazarus."

"Stay with me, Matthew." I bent my head and pressed my lips against his, willing him to keep breathing. He did—barely—but his eyelids had closed.

"From birth I have searched for you," Matthew whispered with a smile, his accent strongly French. "Since finding you I have been able to hold you in my arms, have heard your heart beat against mine. It would have been a terrible thing to die without knowing what it feels like to truly love." Tiny shudders swept over him from head to toe and then subsided.

"Matthew!" I cried, but he could no longer respond. "Marcus!" I screamed into the trees, praying to the goddess all the while. By the time his son reached us, I'd already thought several times that Matthew was dead.

"Holy God," Marcus said, taking in Juliette's charred body and Matthew's bloody form.

"The bleeding won't stop," I said. "Where is it all coming from?"

"I need to examine him to know, Diana." Marcus took a tentative step toward me.

Tightening my arms around my husband, I felt my eyes turn cold. The wind began to rise where I sat.

"I'm not asking you to let go of him," Marcus said, instinctively understanding the problem, "but I have to look at his chest."

He crouched next to us and tore gently at his father's black sweater. With a horrible rending noise, the fabric gave way. A long gash crossed from Matthew's jugular vein to his heart. Next to the heart was a deep gouge where Juliette had tried to punch through to the aorta.

"The jugular is nearly severed, and the aorta has been damaged. Not even Matthew's blood can work fast enough to heal him in both places." Marcus spoke quietly, but he didn't need to speak at all. Juliette had given Matthew a death blow.

My aunts were here now, Sarah puffing slightly. Miriam appeared, white-faced, behind them. After only a glance, she turned on her heel, dashing back to the house.

"It's my fault." I sobbed, rocking Matthew like a child. "I had a clear shot, but I hesitated. I've never killed anyone before. She wouldn't have reached his heart if I'd acted sooner."

"Diana, baby," Sarah whispered. "It's not your fault. You did what you could. You're going to have to let him go."

I made a keening sound, and my hair rose up around my face. "No!" Fear bloomed in the eyes of vampire and witch as the forest grew quiet.

"Get away from her, Marcus!" shouted Em. He jumped backward just in time.

I'd become someone—something—who didn't care about these creatures, or that they were trying to help. It had been a mistake to hesitate before. Now the part of me that had killed Juliette was intent on only one thing: a knife. My right arm shot out toward my aunt.

Sarah always had two blades on her, one dull and black-handled, the other sharp and white-handled. At my call the white blade cut through her belt and flew at me point first. Sarah put up a hand to call it back, and I imagined a wall of blackness and fire between me and the surprised faces of my family. The white-handled knife sliced easily through the blackness and floated gently down near my bent right knee. Matthew's head lolled as I released him just enough to grasp the hilt.

Turning his face gently toward mine, I kissed his mouth long and hard. His eyes fluttered open. He looked so tired, and his skin was gray.

"Don't worry, my love. I'm going to fix it." I raised the knife.

Two women were standing inside the barrier of flames. One was young and wore a loose tunic, with sandals on her feet and a quiver of arrows slung across her shoulders. The strap was tangled up in her hair, which was dark and thick. The other was the old lady from the keeping room, her full skirt swaying.

"Help me," I begged.

There will be a price, the young huntress said.

"I will pay it."

Don't make a promise to the goddess lightly, daughter, the old woman murmured with a shake of her head. *You'll have to keep it.*

"Take anything—take anyone. But leave me him."

The huntress considered my offer and nodded. *He is yours.*

My eyes were on the two women as I raised the knife. Twisting Matthew closer to my body so that he couldn't see, I reached across and slashed the inside of my left elbow, the sharp blade cutting easily through fabric and flesh. My blood flowed, a trickle at first, then faster. I dropped the knife and tightened my left arm until it was in front of his mouth.

"Drink," I said, steadying his head. Matthew's eyelids flickered again, and his nostrils flared. He recognized the scent of *my* blood and struggled to get away. My arms were heavy and strong as oak branches, connected to the tree at my back. I drew my open, bleeding elbow a fraction closer to his mouth. "Drink."

The power of the tree and the earth flowed through my veins, an unexpected offering of life to a vampire on the verge of death. I smiled in gratitude at the huntress and the ghost of the old woman, nourishing Matthew with my body. I was the mother now, the third aspect of the goddess along with the maiden and the crone. With the goddess's help, my blood would heal him.

Finally Matthew succumbed to the instinct to survive. His mouth fastened onto the soft skin of my inner arm, teeth sharp. His tongue lightly probed the ragged incision, pulling the gash in my skin wider. He drew long and hard against my veins. I felt a short, sharp burst of terror.

His skin began to lose some of its pallor, but venous blood would not be enough to heal him completely. I was hoping that a taste of me would drive him beyond his normal range of control so that he would take the next step, but I felt for the white-handled knife just in case.

Giving the huntress and the witch one last look, I returned my attention to my husband. Another shock of power ran into my body as I settled more firmly against the tree.

While he fed, I began to kiss him. My hair fell around his face, mixing my familiar scent with that of his blood and mine. He turned his eyes to me, pale green and distant, as if he weren't sure of my identity. I kissed him again, tasting my own blood on his tongue.

In two fast, smooth moves that I couldn't have stopped even had I wanted to, Matthew grabbed the hair at the nape of my neck. He tilted my head back and to the side, then lowered his mouth to my throat. There was no terror then, just surrender.

"Diana," he said with complete satisfaction.

So this is how it happens, I thought. *This is where the legends come from.*

My spent, used blood had given him the strength to want something fresh and vital. Matthew's sharp upper teeth cut into his lower lip, and a bead formed there. His lips brushed my neck, sensuous and swift. I shivered, unexpectedly aroused at his touch. My skin went numb as his blood touched my flesh. He held my head firmly, his hands once again strong.

No mistakes, I prayed.

There were tiny pricks along my carotid arteries. My eyes opened wide in surprise when the first drawing pressure told me Matthew had reached the blood he sought.

Sarah turned away, unable to watch. Marcus reached for Em, and she went to him without hesitation, crying into his shoulder.

I pressed Matthew's body into mine, encouraging him to drink more deeply. His relish when he did so was evident. How he'd hungered for me, and how strong he'd been to resist.

Matthew settled into the rhythms of his feeding, pulling on my blood in waves.

Matthew, listen to me. Thanks to Gerbert, I knew that my blood would carry messages to him. My only worry was that they would be fleeting, and my power to communicate would be swallowed up.

He startled against my throat, then resumed his feeding.

I love you.

He gave another start of surprise.

This was my gift. I am inside you, giving you life.

Matthew shook his head as if to dislodge an annoying insect and kept drinking.

I am inside you, giving you life. It was harder to think, harder to see through the fire. I focused on Em and Sarah, tried to tell them with my eyes not to worry. I looked for Marcus, too, but couldn't move my eyes enough to find him.

I am inside you, giving you life. I repeated the mantra until it was no longer possible.

There was a slow pulsing, the sound of my heart starting to die.

Dying was nothing at all like I'd expected it to be.

There was a moment of bone-deep quiet.

A sense of parting and regret.

Then nothing.

Chapter 38

In my bones there was a sudden boom as of two worlds colliding.

Something stung my right arm, accompanied by the odor of latex and plastic, and Matthew was arguing with Marcus. There was cold earth below me, and the tang of leaf mold replaced the other scents. My eyes were open, but I saw nothing except blackness. With effort I was able to pick out the half-bare branches of trees crisscrossing above me.

"Use the left arm—it's already open," said Matthew with impatience.

"That arm's useless, Matthew. The tissues are full of your saliva and won't absorb anything else. The right arm is better. Her blood pressure is so low I'm having a hard time finding a vein, that's all." Marcus's voice had the unnatural quietness of the emergency-room physician who sees death regularly.

Two thick strands of spaghetti spooled onto my face. Cold fingers touched my nose, and I tried to shake them off, only to be held down.

Miriam's voice came from the darkness to my right. "Tachycardia. I'll sedate her."

"No," Matthew said roughly. "No sedatives. She's barely conscious. They could put her into a coma."

"Then keep her quiet." Miriam's tone was matter-of-fact. Tiny, cold fingers pressed against my neck with unexpected firmness. "I can't stop her from bleeding out *and* hold her still at the same time."

What was happening around me was visible only in disconcerting slices—what was directly above, what could be glimpsed from the corners of my eyes, what could be tracked through the enormous effort of swiveling them in their sockets.

"Can you do anything, Sarah?" Matthew's voice was anguished.

Sarah's face swam into view. "Witchcraft can't heal vampire bites. If it could, we'd never have had anything to fear from creatures like you."

I began drifting to somewhere peaceful, but my progress was interrupted by Em's slipping her hand into mine, holding me firmly in my own body.

"We've got no choice, then." Matthew sounded desperate. "I'll do it."

"No, Matthew," said Miriam decidedly. "You're not strong enough yet. Besides, I've done it hundreds of times." There was a tearing sound. After Juliette's attack on Matthew, I recognized that it was vampire flesh.

"Are they making me a vampire?" I whispered to Em.

"No, *mon coeur*." Matthew's voice was as decided as Miriam's had been. "You lost—I *took*—a great deal of blood. Marcus is replacing it with human blood. Now Miriam needs to see to your neck."

"Oh." It was too complicated to follow. My brain was fuzzy—almost as fuzzy as my tongue and throat. "I'm thirsty."

"You're craving vampire blood, but you're not going to get it. Lie very still," Matthew said firmly, holding my shoulders so tightly it was painful. Marcus's cold hands crept past my ears to my jaw, holding my mouth closed, too. "And, Miriam—"

"Stop fussing, Matthew," Miriam said briskly. "I was doing this to warmbloods long before you were reborn."

Something sharp cut into my neck, and the smell of blood filled the air. The cutting sensation was followed by a pain that froze and burned simultaneously. The heat and cold intensified, traveling below the surface tissues of my neck to sear the bones and muscles underneath.

I wanted to escape the icy licks, but there were two vampires holding me down. My mouth was firmly closed, too, so all I could do was let out a muffled, fearful sound.

"Her artery is obscured," Miriam said quietly. "The wound has to be cleared." She took a single, audible sip, drawing the blood away. The skin was numbed momentarily, but sensation returned full force when she withdrew.

The extreme pain sent adrenaline coursing through my system, and panic followed in its wake. The gray walls of La Pierre loomed around me, my inability to move putting me back within Satu's hands.

Matthew's fingers dug into my shoulders, returning me to the woods outside the Bishop house. "Tell her what you're doing, Miriam. That Finnish witch made her afraid of what she can't see."

"It's just drops of my blood, Diana, falling from my wrist," Miriam said calmly. "I know it hurts, but it's all we have. Vampire blood heals on contact. It will close your artery better than the sutures a surgeon would use. And you needn't worry. There's no chance such a small amount, applied topically, will make you one of us."

After her description it was possible to recognize each deliberate drop falling into my open wound. There it mingled with my witch's flesh, forcing an instantaneous buildup of scar tissue. It must require enormous control, I thought, for a vampire to undertake such a procedure without giving in to hunger. At last the drops of searing coldness came to an end.

"Done," Miriam said with a touch of relief. "All I have to do now is sew the incision." Her fingers flew over my neck, tugging and stitching the flesh back together. "I tried to neaten the wound, Diana, but Matthew tore the skin with his teeth."

"We're going to move you to the house now," Matthew said.

He cradled my head and shoulders while Marcus supported my legs. Miriam walked alongside carrying the equipment. Someone had driven the Range Rover across the fields, and it stood waiting with its rear door open. Matthew and Miriam switched places, and he disappeared into the cargo area to ready it for me.

"Miriam," I whispered. She bent toward me. "If something goes wrong—" I couldn't finish, but it was imperative she understand me. I was still a witch. But I'd rather be a vampire than dead.

She stared into my eyes, searched for a moment, then nodded. "Don't you dare die, though. He'll kill me if I do what you ask."

Matthew talked nonstop during the bumpy ride back to the house, kissing me softly whenever I tried to sleep. Despite his gentleness, it was a wrench each time.

At the house, Sarah and Em sped around collecting cushions and pillows. They made a bed in front of the keeping room's fireplace. Sarah lit the pile of logs in the grate with a few words and a gesture. A blaze began to burn, but still I shivered uncontrollably, cold to the core.

Matthew lowered me onto the cushions and covered me with quilts while Miriam pressed a bandage onto my neck. As she worked, my husband and his son muttered in the corner.

"It's what she needs, and I do know where her lungs are," Marcus said impatiently. "I won't puncture anything."

"She's strong. No central line. End of discussion. Just get rid of what's left of Juliette's body," Matthew said, his voice quiet but commanding.

"I'll see to it," Marcus replied. He turned on his heel, and the front door thudded behind him before the Range Rover sprang once more into life.

The ancient case clock in the front entrance ticked the minutes as they passed. The warmth soaked into my bones, making me drowsy. Matthew sat at my side, holding one hand tightly so that he could tug me back whenever I tried to escape into the welcome oblivion.

Finally Miriam said the magic word: "stable." Then I could give in to the blackness flitting around the edges of my consciousness. Sarah and Em kissed me and left, Miriam followed, and at last there was nothing but Matthew and the blessed quiet.

Once silence descended, however, my mind turned to Juliette.

"I killed her." My heart raced.

"You had no choice." His tone said no further discussion was required. "It was self-defense."

"No it wasn't. The witchfire . . ." It was only when he was in danger that the bow and arrow had appeared in my hands.

Matthew quieted me with a kiss. "We can talk about that tomorrow."

There was something that couldn't wait, something I wanted him to know now.

"I love you, Matthew." There hadn't been a chance to tell him before Satu snatched me away from Sept-Tours. This time I wanted to be sure it was said before something else happened.

"I love you, too." He bent his head, his lips against my ear. "Remember our dinner in Oxford? You wanted to know how you would taste."

I moved my head in acknowledgment.

"You taste of honey," he murmured. "Honey—and hope."

My lips curved, and then I slept.

But it was not restful slumber. I was caught between waking and sleeping, La Pierre and Madison, life and death. The ghostly old woman had warned me of the danger of standing at a crossroads. There were times that death seemed to be standing patiently at my side, waiting for me to choose the road I wanted to take.

I traveled countless miles that night, fleeing from place to place, never more than a step ahead of whoever was pursuing me—Gerbert, Satu, Juliette, Peter Knox. Whenever my journey brought me back to the Bishop house, Matthew was there. Sometimes Sarah was with him. Other times it was Marcus. Most often, though, Matthew was alone.

Deep in the night, someone started humming the tune we'd danced to a lifetime ago in Ysabeau's grand salon. It wasn't Marcus or Matthew—they were talking to each other—but I was too tired to figure out where the music was coming from.

"Where did she learn that old song?" Marcus asked.

"At home. Christ, even in sleep she's trying to be brave." Matthew's voice was desolate. "Baldwin is right—I'm no good at strategy. I should have foreseen this."

"Gerbert counted on your forgetting about Juliette. It had been so long. And he knew you'd be with Diana when she struck. He gloated about it on the phone."

"Yes, he knows I'm arrogant enough to think she was safe with me at her side."

"You've tried to protect her. But you can't—no one could. She's not the only one who needs to stop being brave."

There was something Marcus didn't know, something Matthew was forgetting. Snatches of half-remembered conversation came back to me. The music stopped to let me speak.

"I told you before," I said, groping for Matthew in the dark and finding only a handful of soft wool that released the scent of cloves when crushed, "I can be brave enough for both of us."

"Diana," Matthew said urgently. "Open your eyes and look at me."

His face was inches from mine. He was cradling my head with one hand, the other cool on my lower back, where a crescent moon swept from one side of my body to the other.

"There you are," I murmured. "I'm afraid we're lost."

"No, my darling, we're not lost. We're at the Bishop house. And you don't need to be brave. It's my turn."

"Will you be able to figure out which road we need to take?"

"I'll find the way. Rest and let me take care of that." Matthew's eyes were very green.

I drifted off once more, racing to elude Gerbert and Juliette, who were hard at my heels. Toward dawn my sleep deepened, and when I awoke, it was morning. A quick check revealed that my body was naked and tucked tightly under layers of quilts, like a patient in a British intensive-care ward. Tubing disappeared into my right arm, a bandage encased my left elbow, and something was stuck to my neck. Matthew was sitting nearby with knees bent and his back against the sofa.

"Matthew? Is everyone all right?" There was cotton wool wrapped around my tongue, and I was still fiercely thirsty.

"Everyone's fine." Relief washed over his face as he reached for my hand and pressed his lips to my palm. Matthew's eyes flickered to my wrist, where Juliette's fingernails had left angry red crescent moons.

The sound of our voices brought the rest of the household into the room. First there were my aunts. Sarah was lost in her thoughts, dark hollows under her eyes. Em looked tired but relieved, stroking my hair and assuring me that everything was going to be all right. Marcus came next. He examined me and talked sternly about my need to rest. Finally Miriam ordered everyone else out of the room so she could change my bandages.

"How bad was it?" I asked when we were alone.

"If you mean Matthew, it was bad. The de Clermonts don't handle loss—or the threat of it—very well. Ysabeau was worse when Philippe died. It's a good thing you lived, and not just for my sake." Miriam applied ointment to my wounds with a surprisingly delicate touch.

Her words conjured images of Matthew on a vengeful rampage. I closed my eyes to blot them out. "Tell me about Juliette."

Miriam emitted a low hiss of warning. "Juliette Durand is not my tale to tell. Ask your husband." She disconnected the IV and held out one of Sarah's old flannel shirts. After I struggled with it for a few moments, she came to my aid. Her eyes fell on the marks on my back.

"The scars don't bother me. They're just signs that I've fought and survived." I pulled the shirt over my shoulders self-consciously nonetheless.

"They don't bother him either. Loving de Clermonts always leaves a mark. Nobody knows that better than Matthew."

I buttoned up the shirt with shaking fingers, unwilling to meet her eyes. She handed over a pair of stretchy black leggings.

"Giving him your blood like that was unspeakably dangerous. He might not have been able to stop drinking." A note of admiration had crept into her voice.

"Ysabeau told me the de Clermonts fight for those they love."

"His mother will understand, but Matthew is another matter. He needs to get it out of his system—your blood, what happened last night, everything."

Juliette. The name hung unspoken in the air between us.

Miriam reconnected the IV and adjusted its flow. "Marcus will take him to Canada. It will be hours before Matthew finds someone he's willing to feed on, but it can't be helped."

"Sarah and Em will be safe with both of them gone?"

"You bought us some time. The Congregation never imagined that Juliette would fail. Gerbert is as proud as Matthew, and nearly as infallible. It will take them a few days to regroup." She froze, a guilty look on her face.

"I'd like to talk to Diana now," Matthew said quietly from the door. He looked terrible. There was hunger in the sharpened angles of his face and the lavender smudges under his eyes.

He watched silently as Miriam walked around my makeshift bed. She shut the heavy coffin doors behind her, their catches clicking together. When he turned to me, his look was concerned.

Matthew's need for blood was at war with his protective instincts.

"When are you leaving?" I asked, hoping to make my wishes clear.

"I'm not leaving."

"You need to regain your strength. Next time the Congregation won't send just one vampire or witch." I wondered how many other creatures from Matthew's past were likely to come calling at the Congregation's behest, and I struggled to sit up.

"You are so experienced with war now, *ma lionne*, that you understand their strategies?" It was impossible to judge his feelings from his features, but his voice betrayed a hint of amusement.

"We've proved we can't be beaten easily."

"Easily? You almost died." He sat next to me on the cushions.

"So did you."

"You used magic to save me. I could smell it—lady's mantle and ambergris."

"It was nothing." I didn't want him know what I'd promised in exchange for his life.

"No lies." Matthew grabbed my chin with his fingertips. "If you don't want to tell me, say so. Your secrets are your own. But no lies."

"If I do keep secrets, I won't be the only one doing so in this family. Tell me about Juliette Durand."

He let go of my chin and moved restlessly to the window. "You know that Gerbert introduced us. He kidnapped her from a Cairo brothel, brought her to the brink of death over and over again before transforming her into a vampire, and then shaped her into someone I would find appealing. I still don't know if she was insane when Gerbert found her or if her mind broke after what he did to her."

"Why?" I couldn't keep the incredulity from my voice.

"She was meant to worm her way into my heart and then into my family's affairs. Gerbert had always wanted to be included among the Knights of Lazarus, and my father refused him time and time again. Once Juliette had discovered the intricacies of the brotherhood and any other useful information about the de Clermonts, she was free to kill me. Gerbert trained her to be my assassin, as well as my lover." Matthew picked at the window frame's peeling paint. "When I first met her, she was better at hiding her illness. It took me a long time to see the signs. Baldwin and Ysabeau never trusted her, and Marcus detested her. But I—Gerbert taught her well. She reminded me of Louisa, and her emotional fragility seemed to explain her erratic behavior."

He has always liked fragile things, Ysabeau had warned me. Matthew hadn't been just sexually attracted to Juliette. The feelings had gone deeper.

"You did love her." I remembered Juliette's strange kiss and shuddered.

"Once. Long ago. For all the wrong reasons," Matthew continued. "I watched her—from a safe distance—and made sure she was cared for, since she was incapable of caring for herself. When World War I broke out, she disappeared, and I assumed she'd been killed. I never imagined she was alive somewhere."

"And all the time you were watching her, she was watching you, too." Juliette's attentive eyes had taken in my every movement. She must have observed Matthew with a similar keenness.

"If I'd known, she would never have been allowed to get near you." He stared out into the pale morning light. "But there's something else we have to discuss. You must promise me *never* to use your magic to save me. I have no wish to live longer than I'm meant to. Life and death are powerful forces. Ysabeau interfered with them on my behalf once. You aren't to do it again. And no asking Miriam—or anyone else—to make you a vampire." His voice was startling in its coldness, and he crossed the room to my side with quick, long strides. "No one—not even I—will transform you into something you're not."

"You'll have to promise me something in return."

His eyes narrowed with displeasure. "What's that?"

"Don't ever ask me to leave you when you're in danger," I said fiercely. "I won't do it."

Matthew calculated what would be required of him to keep his promise while keeping me out of harm's way. I was just as busy figuring out which of my dimly understood powers needed mastering so that I could protect him without incinerating him or drowning myself. We eyed each other warily for a few moments. Finally I touched his cheek.

"Go hunting with Marcus. We'll be fine for a few hours." His color was all wrong. I wasn't the only one who had lost a lot of blood.

"You shouldn't be alone."

"I have my aunts, not to mention Miriam. She told me at the Bodleian that her teeth are as sharp as yours. I believe her." I was more knowledgeable now about vampire teeth.

"We'll be home by dark," he said reluctantly, brushing his fingers across my cheekbone. "Is there anything you need before I go?"

"I'd like to talk to Ysabeau." Sarah had been distant that morning, and I wanted to hear a maternal voice.

"Of course," he said, hiding his surprise by reaching into his pocket for his phone. Someone had taken the time to retrieve it from the bushes. He dialed Sept-Tours with a single push of his finger.

"*Maman?*" A torrent of French erupted from the phone. "She's fine," Matthew interrupted, his voice soothing. "Diana wants—she's asked—to speak to you."

There was silence, followed by a single crisp word. "*Oui.*"

Matthew handed me the phone.

"Ysabeau?" My voice cracked, and my eyes filled with sudden tears.

"I am here, Diana." Ysabeau sounded as musical as ever.

"I almost lost him."

"You should have obeyed him and gone as far away from Juliette as you could." Ysabeau's tone was sharp before turning soft once more. "But I am glad you did not."

I cried in earnest then. Matthew stroked the hair back from my forehead, tucking my typically wayward strand behind my ear, before leaving me to my conversation.

To Ysabeau I was able to express my grief and confess my failure to kill Juliette at my first opportunity. I told her everything—about Juliette's startling appearance and her strange kiss, my terror when Matthew began to feed, about what it was like to begin to die only to return abruptly to life. Matthew's mother understood, as I'd known she would. The only time Ysabeau interrupted was during the part of my story that involved the maiden and the crone.

"So the goddess saved my son," she murmured. "She has a sense of justice, as well as humor. But that is too long a tale for today. When you are next at Sept-Tours, I will tell you."

Her mention of the château caused another sharp pang of homesickness. "I wish I were there. I'm not sure anyone in Madison can teach me all that I need to know."

"Then we must find a different teacher. Somewhere there is a creature who can help."

Ysabeau issued a series of firm instructions about obeying Matthew, taking care of him, taking care of myself, and returning to the château as soon as possible. I agreed to all of them with uncharacteristic alacrity and got off the phone.

A few tactful moments later, Matthew opened the door and stepped inside.

"Thank you," I said, sniffing and holding up his phone.

He shook his head. "Keep it. Call Marcus or Ysabeau at any time. They're numbers two and three on speed dial. You need a new phone, as well as a watch. Yours doesn't even hold a charge." Matthew settled me gently against the cushions and kissed my forehead. "Miriam's working in the dining room, but she'll hear the slightest sound."

"Sarah and Em?" I asked.

"Waiting to see you," he said with a smile.

After visiting with my aunts, I slept a few hours, until a restless yearning for Matthew had me clawing myself awake.

Em got up from my grandmother's recently returned rocker and came to me carrying a glass of water, her forehead creased in deep lines that hadn't been there a few days ago. Grandma was sitting on the sofa staring at the paneling next to the fireplace, clearly waiting for another message from the house.

"Where's Sarah?" I closed my fingers around the glass. My throat was still parched, and the water would feel divine.

"She went out for a while." Em's delicate mouth pressed into a thin line. "She blames this all on Matthew."

Em dropped down to her knees on the floor until her eyes were level with mine. "This has nothing to do with Matthew. You offered your blood to a vampire—a desperate, dying vampire." She silenced my protests with a look. "I know he's not just any vampire. Even so, Matthew could kill you. And Sarah's devastated that she can't teach you how to control your talents."

"Sarah shouldn't worry about me. Did you see what I did to Juliette?"

She nodded. "And other things as well."

My grandmother's attention was now fixed on me instead of the paneling.

"I saw the hunger in Matthew when he fed on you," Em continued quietly. "I saw the maiden and the crone, too, standing on the other side of the fire."

"Did Sarah see them?" I whispered, hoping that Miriam couldn't hear.

Em shook her head. "No. Does Matthew know?"

"No." I pushed my hair aside, relieved that Sarah was unaware of all that had happened last night.

"What did you promise the goddess in exchange for his life, Diana?"

"Anything she wanted."

"Oh, honey." Em's face crumpled. "You shouldn't have done that. There's no telling when she'll act—or what she'll take."

My grandmother was furiously rocking. Em eyed the chair's wild movements.

"I had to, Em. The goddess didn't seem surprised. It felt inevitable—right, somehow."

"Have you seen the maiden and the crone before?"

I nodded. "The maiden's been in my dreams. Sometimes it's as though I'm inside her, looking out as she rides or hunts. And the crone met me outside the keeping room."

You're in deep water now, Diana, my grandmother rustled. *I hope you can swim.*

"You mustn't call the goddess lightly," Em warned. "These are powerful forces that you don't yet understand."

"I didn't call her at all. They appeared when I decided to give Matthew my blood. They gave me their help willingly."

Maybe it wasn't your blood to give. My grandmother continued to rock back and forth, setting the floorboards creaking. *Did you ever think of that?*

"You've known Matthew for a few weeks. Yet you follow his orders so easily, and you were willing to die for him. Surely you can see why Sarah is concerned. The Diana we've known all these years is gone."

"I love him," I said fiercely. "And he loves me." Matthew's many secrets—the Knights of Lazarus, Juliette, even Marcus—I pushed to the side, along with my knowledge of his ferocious temper and his need to control everything and everyone around him.

But Em knew what I was thinking. She shook her head. "You can't ignore them, Diana. You tried that with your magic, and it found you. The parts of Matthew you don't like and don't understand are going to find you, too. You can't hide forever. Especially now."

"What do you mean?"

"There are too many creatures interested in this manuscript, and in you and Matthew. I can feel them, pressing in on the Bishop house, on you. I don't know which side of this struggle they're on, but my sixth sense tells me it won't be long before we find out."

Em tucked the quilt around me. After putting another log on the fire, she left the room.

I was awakened by my husband's distinctive, spicy scent.

"You're back," I said, rubbing my eyes.

Matthew looked rested, and his skin had returned to its normal, pearly color.

He'd fed. On human blood.

"So are you." Matthew brought my hand to his lips. "Miriam said you've been sleeping for most of the day."

"Is Sarah home?"

"Everyone's present and accounted for." He gave me a lopsided grin. "Even Tabitha."

I asked to see them, and he unhooked me from my IV without argument. When my legs were too unsteady to carry me to the family room, he simply swept me up and carried me.

Em and Marcus settled me into the sofa with great ceremony. I was quickly exhausted by nothing more strenuous than quiet conversation and watching the latest film noir selection on TV, and Matthew lifted me up once more.

"We're going upstairs," he announced. "We'll see you in the morning."

"Do you want me to bring up Diana's IV?" Miriam asked pointedly.

"No. She doesn't need it." His voice was brusque.

"Thank you for not hooking me up to all that stuff," I said as he carried me through the front hall.

"Your body is still weak, but it's remarkably resilient for a warmblood," Matthew said as he climbed the stairs. "The reward for being a perpetual-motion machine, I imagine."

Once he had turned off the light, I curled into his body with a contented sigh, my fingers splayed possessively across his chest. The moonlight streaming through the windows highlighted his new scars. They were already fading from pink to white.

Tired as I was, the gears of Matthew's mind were working so furiously that sleep proved impossible. It was plain from the set of his mouth and the bright glitter of his eyes that he was picking our road forward, just as he'd promised to do last night.

"Tell me," I said when the suspense became unbearable.

"What we need is time," he said thoughtfully.

"The Congregation isn't likely to give us that."

"We'll take it, then." His voice was almost inaudible. "We'll timewalk."

Chapter 39

We made it only halfway down the stairs the next morning before stopping to rest, but I was determined to get to the kitchen under my own steam. To my surprise, Matthew didn't try to dissuade me. We sat on the worn wooden treads in companionable silence. Pale, watery light seeped in through the wavy glass panes around the front door, hinting at a sunny day to come. From the family room came the click of Scrabble tiles.

"When will you tell them?" There wasn't much to divulge yet—he was still working on the basic outlines of the plan.

"Later," he said, leaning into me. I leaned toward him, pressing our shoulders closer.

"No amount of coffee is going to keep Sarah from freaking out when she hears." I put my hand on the banister and levered myself to my feet with a sigh. "Let's try this again."

In the family room, Em brought me my first cup of tea. I sipped it on the couch while Matthew and Marcus headed off for their walk with my silent blessing. They should spend as much time as possible together before we left.

After my tea Sarah made me her famous scrambled eggs. They were laden with onions, mushrooms, and cheese and topped with a spoonful of salsa. She put a steaming plate before me.

"Thanks, Sarah." I dove in without further ceremony.

"It's not just Matthew who needs food and rest." She glanced out the window to the orchard, where the two vampires were walking.

"I feel much better today," I said, crunching a bite of toast.

"Your appetite seems to have recovered at least." There was already a sizable dent in the mountain of eggs.

When Matthew and Marcus returned, I was on my second plate of food. They both appeared grim, but Matthew shook his head at my curious look.

Apparently they hadn't been talking about our plans to timewalk. Something else had put them into a sour mood. Matthew pulled up a stool, flapped open the paper, and concentrated on the news. I ate my eggs and toast, made more tea, and bided my time while Sarah washed and put away the dishes.

At last Matthew folded his paper and set it aside.

"I'd like to go to the woods. To where Juliette died," I announced.

He got to his feet. "I'll pull the Range Rover to the door."

"This is madness, Matthew. It's too soon." Marcus turned to Sarah for support.

"Let them go," Sarah said. "Diana should put on warmer clothes first, though. It's chilly outside."

Em appeared, a puzzled expression on her face. "Are we expecting visitors? The house thinks we are."

"You're joking!" I said. "The house hasn't added a room since the last family reunion. Where is it?"

"Between the bathroom and the junk room." Em pointed at the ceiling. *I told you this wasn't just about you and Matthew,* she said silently to me as we trooped upstairs to view the transformation. *My premonitions are seldom wrong.*

The newly materialized room held an ancient brass bed with enormous polished balls capping each corner, tatty red gingham curtains that Em insisted were coming down immediately, a hooked rug in clashing shades of maroon and plum, and a battered washstand with a chipped pink bowl and pitcher. None of us recognized a single item.

"Where did it all come from?" Miriam asked in amazement.

"Who knows where the house keeps this stuff?" Sarah sat on the bed and bounced on it vigorously. It responded with a series of outraged squeaks.

"The house's most legendary feats happened around my thirteenth birthday," I remembered with a grin. "It came up with a record four bedrooms and a Victorian parlor set."

"And twenty-four place settings of Blue Willow china," Em recalled. "We've still got some of the teacups, although most of the bigger pieces disappeared again once the family left."

After everybody had inspected the new room and the now considerably smaller storage room next door, I changed and made my halting way downstairs and into the Range Rover. When we drew close to the spot where Juliette had met her end, Matthew stopped. The heavy tires sank into the soft ground.

"Shall we walk the rest of the way?" he suggested. "We can take it slowly."

He was different this morning. He wasn't coddling me or telling me what to do.

"What's changed?" I asked as we approached the ancient oak tree.

"I've seen you fight," he said quietly. "On the battlefield the bravest men collapse in fear. They simply can't fight, even to save themselves."

"But I froze." My hair tumbled forward to conceal my face.

Matthew stopped in his tracks, his fingers tightening on my arm to make me stop, too. "Of course you did. You were about to take a life. But you don't fear death."

"No." I'd lived with death—sometimes longed for it—since I was seven.

He swung me around to face him. "After La Pierre, Satu left you broken and uncertain. All your life you've hidden from your fears. I wasn't sure you would be able to fight if you had to. Now all I have to do is keep you from taking unnecessary risks." His eyes drifted to my neck.

Matthew moved forward, towing me gently along. A smudge of blackened grass told me we'd arrived at the clearing. I stiffened, and he released my arm.

The marks left by the fire led to the dead patch where Juliette had fallen. The forest was eerily quiet, without birdcalls or other sounds of life. I gathered a bit of charred wood from the ground. It crumbled to soot in my fingers.

"I didn't know Juliette, but at that moment I hated her enough to kill her." Her brown-and-green eyes would always haunt me from shadows under the trees.

I traced the line left by the arc of conjured fire to where the maiden and the crone had agreed to help me save Matthew. I looked up into the oak tree and gasped.

"It began yesterday." Matthew followed my gaze. "Sarah says you pulled the life out of it."

Above me the branches of the tree were cracked and withered. Bare limbs forked and forked again into shapes reminiscent of a stag's horns. Brown leaves swirled at my feet. Matthew had survived because I'd pushed its vitality through my veins and into his body. The oak's rough bark had exuded such permanence, yet there was nothing now but hollowness.

"Power always exacts a price," Matthew said.

"What have I done?" The death of a tree was not going to settle my debt to the goddess. For the first time, I was afraid of the deal I'd struck.

Matthew crossed the clearing and caught me up in his arms. We hugged each other, fierce with the knowledge of all we'd almost lost.

"You promised me you would be less reckless." There was anger in his voice.

I was angry with him, too. "You were supposed to be indestructible."

He rested his forehead against mine. "I should have told you about Juliette."

"Yes, you should have. She almost took you from me." My pulse throbbed behind the bandage on my neck. Matthew's thumb settled against the spot where he'd bitten through flesh and muscle, his touch unexpectedly warm.

"It was far too close." His fingers were wrapped in my hair, and his mouth was hard on mine. Then we stood, hearts pressed together, in the quiet.

"When I took Juliette's life, it made her part of mine—forever."

Matthew stroked my hair against my skull. "Death is its own powerful magic."

Calm again, I said a silent word of thanks to the goddess, not only for Matthew's life but for my own.

We walked toward the Range Rover, but halfway there I stumbled with fatigue. Matthew swung me onto his back and carried me the rest of the way.

Sarah was bent over her desk in the office when we arrived at the house. She flew outside and pulled open the car door with speed a vampire might envy.

"Damn it, Matthew," she said, looking at my exhausted face.

Together they got me inside and back onto the family-room couch, where I rested my head in Matthew's lap. I was lulled to sleep by the quiet sounds of activity all around, and the last thing I remembered clearly was the smell of vanilla and the sound of Em's battered KitchenAid mixer.

Matthew woke me for lunch, which turned out to be vegetable soup. The look on his face suggested that I would shortly need sustenance. He was about to tell our families the plan.

"Ready, *mon coeur*?" Matthew asked. I nodded, scraping up the last of my meal. Marcus's head swiveled in our direction. "We have something to share with you," he announced.

The new household tradition was to proceed to the dining room whenever something important needed to be discussed. Once we were assembled, all eyes turned to Matthew.

"What have you decided?" Marcus asked without preamble.

Matthew took a deliberate breath and began. "We need to go where it won't be easy for the Congregation to follow, where Diana will have time and teachers who can help her master her magic."

Sarah laughed under her breath. "Where is this place, where there are powerful, patient witches who don't mind having a vampire hanging around?"

"It's not a particular place I have in mind," Matthew said cryptically. "We're going to hide Diana in time."

Everyone started shouting at once. Matthew took my hand in his.

"*Courage,*" I murmured in French, repeating his advice when I met Ysabeau.

He snorted and gave me a grim smile.

I had some sympathy for their amazed disbelief. Last night, while I was lying in bed, my own reaction had been much the same. First I'd insisted that it was impossible, and then I'd asked for a thousand details about precisely when and where we were going.

He'd explained what he could—which wasn't much.

"You want to use your magic, but now it's using you. You need a teacher, one who is more adept than Sarah or Emily. It's not their fault they can't help you. Witches in the past were different. So much of their knowledge has been lost."

"Where? When?" I'd whispered in the dark.

"Nothing too distant—though the more recent past has its own risks—but back far enough that we'll find a witch to train you. First we have to talk to Sarah about whether it can be done safely. And then we need to locate three items to steer us to the right time."

"We?" I'd asked in surprise. "Won't I just meet you there?"

"Not unless there's no alternative. I wasn't the same creature then, and I wouldn't entirely trust my past selves with you."

His mouth had softened with relief after I nodded in agreement. A few days ago, he'd rejected the idea of timewalking. Apparently the risks of staying put were even worse.

"What will the others do?"

His thumb traveled slowly over the veins on the back of my hand. "Miriam and Marcus will go back to Oxford. The Congregation will look for you here first. It would be best if Sarah and Emily went away, at least for a little while. Would they go to Ysabeau?" Matthew wondered.

On the surface it had sounded like a ridiculous idea. Sarah and Ysabeau under the same roof? The more I'd considered it, though, the less implausible it seemed.

"I don't know," I'd mused. Then a new worry had surfaced. "Marcus." I didn't fully understand the intricacies of the Knights of Lazarus, but with Matthew gone he would have to shoulder even more responsibility.

"There's no other way," Matthew had said in the darkness, quieting me with a kiss.

This was precisely the point that Em now wanted to argue.

"There must be another way," she protested.

"I tried to think of one, Emily," Matthew said apologetically.

"Where—or should I say *when*—are you planning on going? Diana won't exactly blend into the background. She's too tall." Miriam looked down at her own tiny hands.

"Regardless of whether Diana could fit in, it's too dangerous," Marcus said firmly. "You might end up in the middle of a war. Or an epidemic."

"Or a witch-hunt." Miriam didn't say it maliciously, but three heads swung around in indignation nonetheless.

"Sarah, what do you think?" asked Matthew.

Of all the creatures in the room, she was the calmest. "You'll take her to a time when she'll be with witches who will help her?"

"Yes."

Sarah closed her eyes for a moment, then opened them. "You two aren't safe here. Juliette Durand proved that. And if you aren't safe in Madison, you aren't safe anywhere."

"Thank you." Matthew opened his mouth to say something else, and Sarah held up her hand.

"Don't promise me anything," she said, voice tight. "You'll be careful for her sake, if not for your own."

"Now all we have to worry about is the timewalking." Matthew turned businesslike. "Diana will need three items from a particular time and place in order to move safely."

Sarah nodded.

"Do I count as a thing?" he asked her.

"Do you have a pulse? Of course you're not a thing!" It was one of the most positive statements Sarah had ever made about vampires.

"If you need old stuff to guide your way, you're welcome to these." Marcus pulled a thin leather cord from the neck of his shirt and lifted it over his head. It was festooned with a bizarre assortment of items, including a tooth, a coin, a lump of something that shone black and gold, and a battered silver whistle. He tossed it to Matthew.

"Didn't you get this off a yellow-fever victim?" Matthew asked, fingering the tooth.

"In New Orleans," Marcus replied. "The epidemic of 1819."

"New Orleans is out of the question," Matthew said sharply.

"I suppose so." Marcus slid a glance my way, then returned his attention to his father. "How about Paris? One of Fanny's earbobs is on there."

Matthew's fingers touched a tiny red stone set in gold filigree. "Philippe and I sent you away from Paris, and Fanny, too. They called it the Terror, remember? It's no place for Diana."

"The two of you fussed over me like old women. I'd been in one revolution already. Besides, if you're looking for a safe place in the past, you'll have a hell of a time finding one," Marcus grumbled. His face brightened. "Philadelphia?"

"I wasn't in Philadelphia with you, or in California," Matthew said hastily before his son could speak. "It would be best if we head for a time and place I know."

"Even if you know where we're going, Matthew, I'm not sure I can pull this off." My decision to stay clear of magic had caught up with me again.

"I think you can," Sarah said bluntly, "you have been doing it your whole life. When you were a baby, as a child when you played hide-and-seek with Stephen, and as an adolescent, too. Remember all those mornings we dragged you out of the woods and had to clean you up in time for school? What do you imagine you were doing then?"

"Certainly not timewalking," I said truthfully. "The science of this still worries me. Where does this body go when I'm somewhere else?"

"Who knows? But don't worry. It's happened to everybody. You drive to work and don't remember how you got there. Or the whole afternoon passes and you don't have a clue what you did. Whenever something like that happens, you can bet there's a timewalker nearby," explained Sarah. She was remarkably unfazed at the prospect.

Matthew sensed my apprehension and took my hand in his. "Einstein said that all physicists were aware that the distinctions between past, present, and future were only what he called 'a stubbornly persistent illusion.' Not only did he believe in marvels and wonders, he also believed in the elasticity of time."

There was a tentative knock at the door.

"I didn't hear a car," Miriam said warily, rising to her feet.

"It's just Sammy collecting the newspaper money." Em slid from her chair.

We waited silently while she crossed the hall, the floorboards protesting under her feet. From the way their hands were pressed flat against the table's wooden surface, Matthew and Marcus were both ready to fly to the door, too.

Cold air swept into the dining room.

"Yes?" Em asked in a puzzled voice. In an instant, Marcus and Matthew rose and joined her, accompanied by Tabitha, who was intent on supporting the leader of the pack in his important business.

"Not the paperboy," Sarah said unnecessarily, looking at the empty chair next to me.

"Are you Diana Bishop?" asked a deep male voice with a familiar foreign accent of flat vowels accompanied by a slight drawl.

"No, I'm her aunt," Em replied.

"Is there something we can do for you?" Matthew sounded cold, though polite.

"My name is Nathaniel Wilson, and this is my wife, Sophie. We were told we might find Diana Bishop here."

"Who told you that?" Matthew asked softly.

"His mother—Agatha." I stood, moving to the door.

His voice reminded me of the daemon from Blackwell's, the fashion designer from Australia with the beautiful brown eyes.

Miriam tried to bar my way into the hall but stepped aside when she saw my expression. Marcus was not so easily dealt with. He grabbed my arm and held me in the shadows by the staircase.

Nathaniel's eyes nudged gently against my face. He was in his early twenties and had familiar fair hair and chocolate-colored eyes, as well as his mother's wide mouth and fine features. Where Agatha had been compact and trim, however, he was nearly as tall as Matthew, with the broad shoulders and narrow hips of a swimmer. An enormous backpack was slung over one shoulder.

"Are you Diana Bishop?" he asked.

A woman's face peeped out from Nathaniel's side. It was sweet and round, with intelligent brown eyes and a dimpled chin. She was in her early twenties as well, and the gentle, insidious pressure of her glance indicated she, too, was a daemon.

As she studied me, a long, brown braid tumbled over her shoulder.

"That's her," the young woman said, her soft accent betraying that she was born in the South. "She looks just as she did in my dreams."

"It's all right, Matthew," I said. These two daemons posed no more danger to me than did Marthe or Ysabeau.

"So you're the vampire," Nathaniel said, giving Matthew an appraising look. "My mother warned me about you."

"You should listen to her," Matthew suggested, his voice dangerously soft.

Nathaniel seemed unimpressed. "She told me you wouldn't welcome the son of a Congregation member. But I'm not here on their behalf. I'm here because of Sophie." He drew his wife under his arm in a protective gesture, and she shivered and crept closer. Neither was dressed for autumn in New York. Nathaniel was wearing an old barn jacket, and Sophie had on nothing warmer than a turtleneck and a hand-knit cardigan that brushed her knees.

"Are they both daemons?" Matthew asked me.

"Yes," I replied, though something made me hesitate.

"Are you a vampire as well?" Nathaniel asked Marcus.

Marcus gave him a wolfish grin. "Guilty."

Sophie was still nudging me with her characteristic daemonic glance, but there was the faintest tingle on my skin. Her hand crept possessively around her belly.

"You're pregnant!" I cried.

Marcus was so surprised that he loosened his grip on me. Matthew caught me as I went by. The house, agitated by the appearance of two visitors and Matthew's sudden lunge, made its displeasure clear by banging the keeping room's doors tightly closed.

"What you feel—it's me," Sophie said, moving an inch closer to her husband. "My people were witches, but I came out wrong."

Sarah came into the hall, saw the visitors, and threw up her hands. "Here we go again. I told you daemons would be showing up in Madison before long. Still, the house usually knows our business better than we do. Now that you're here, you might as well come inside, out of the cold."

The house groaned as if it were heartily sick of us when the daemons entered.

"Don't worry," I said, trying to reassure them. "The house told us you were coming, no matter what it sounds like."

"My granny's house was just the same." Sophie smiled. "She lived in the old Norman place in Seven Devils. That's where I'm from. It's officially part of North Carolina, but my dad said that nobody bothered to tell the folks in town. We're kind of a nation unto ourselves."

The keeping-room doors opened wide, revealing my grandmother and three or four more Bishops, all of whom were watching the proceedings with interest. The boy with the berry basket waved. Sophie shyly waved back.

"Granny had ghosts, too," she said calmly.

The ghosts, combined with two unfriendly vampires and an overly expressive house, were too much for Nathaniel.

"We aren't staying longer than we have to, Sophie. You came to give something to Diana. Let's get it over with and be on our way," Nathaniel said. Miriam chose that minute to step out of the shadows by the dining room, her arms crossed over her chest. Nathaniel took a step backward.

"First vampires. Now daemons. What next?" Sarah muttered. She turned to Sophie. "So you're about five months along?"

"The baby quickened last week," Sophie replied, both hands resting on her belly. "That's when Agatha told us where we could find Diana. She didn't know about my family. I've been having dreams about you for months. And I don't know what Agatha saw that made her so scared."

"What dreams?" Matthew said, his voice quick.

"Let's have Sophie sit down before we subject her to an inquisition." Sarah quietly took charge. "Em, can you bring us some of those cookies? Milk, too?"

Em headed toward the kitchen, where we could hear the distant clatter of glasses.

"They could be my dreams, or they could be hers." Sophie gazed at her belly as Sarah led her and Nathaniel deeper into the house. She looked back over her shoulder at Matthew. "She's a witch, you see. That's probably what worried Nathaniel's mom."

All eyes dropped to the bump under Sophie's blue sweater.

"The dining room," Sarah said in a tone that brooked no nonsense. "Everybody in the dining room."

Matthew held me back. "There's something too convenient about their showing up right now. No mention of timewalking in front of them."

"They're harmless." Every instinct confirmed it.

"Nobody's harmless, and that certainly goes for Agatha Wilson's son." Tabitha, who was sitting next to Matthew, mewled in agreement.

"Are you two joining us, or do I have to drag you into this room?" Sarah called.

"We're on our way," Matthew said smoothly.

Sarah was at the head of the table. She pointed at the empty chairs to her right. "Sit."

We were facing Sophie and Nathaniel, who sat with an empty seat between them and Marcus. Matthew's son split his attention between his father and the daemons. I sat between Matthew and Miriam, both of whom never took their eyes from Nathaniel. When Em entered, she had a tray laden with wine, milk, bowls of berries and nuts, and an enormous plate of cookies.

"God, cookies make me wish like hell I was still warmblooded," Marcus said reverently, picking up one of the golden disks studded with chocolate and holding it to his nose. "They smell so good, but they taste terrible."

"Have these instead," Em said, sliding him a bowl of walnuts. "They're covered in vanilla and sugar. They're not cookies, but they're close." She passed him a bottle of wine and a corkscrew, too. "Open that and pour some for your father."

"Thanks, Em," Marcus said around a mouthful of sticky walnuts, already pulling the cork free from the bottle. "You're the best."

Sarah watched intently as Sophie drank thirstily from the glass of milk and ate a cookie. When the daemon reached for her second, my aunt turned to Nathaniel. "Now, where's your car?" Given all that had happened, it was an odd opening question.

"We came on foot." Nathaniel hadn't touched anything Em put in front of him.

"From where?" Marcus asked incredulously, handing Matthew a glass of wine. He'd seen enough of the surrounding countryside to know that there was nothing within walking distance.

"We rode with a friend from Durham to Washington," Sophie explained. "Then we caught a train from D.C. to New York. I didn't like the city much."

"We caught the train to Albany, then went on to Syracuse. The bus took us to Cazenovia." Nathaniel put a warning hand on Sophie's arm.

"He doesn't want me to tell you that we caught a ride from a stranger," Sophie confided with a smile. "The lady knew where the house was. Her kids love coming here on Halloween because you're real witches." Sophie took another sip of milk. "Not that we needed the directions. There's a lot of energy in this house. We couldn't have missed it."

"Is there a reason you took such an indirect route?" Matthew asked Nathaniel.

"Somebody followed us as far as New York, but Sophie and I got back on the train for Washington and they lost interest," Nathaniel bristled.

"Then we got off the train in New Jersey and went back to the city. The man in the station said tourists get confused all the time about which way the train is going. They didn't even charge us, did they, Nathaniel?" Sophie looked pleased at the warm reception they'd received from Amtrak.

Matthew continued with his interrogation of Nathaniel. "Where are you staying?"

"They're staying here." Em's voice had a sharp edge. "They don't have a car, and the house made room for them. Besides, Sophie needs to talk to Diana."

"I'd like that. Agatha said you'd be able to help. Something about a book for the baby," Sophie said softly. Marcus's eyes darted to the page from Ashmole 782, the edge of which was peeking from underneath the chart laying out the Knights of Lazarus's chain of command. He hastily drew the papers into a pile, moving an innocuous-looking set of DNA results to the top.

"What book, Sophie?" I asked.

"We didn't tell Agatha my people were witches. I didn't even tell Nathaniel—not until he came home to meet my dad. We'd been together for almost four years, and my dad was sick and losing control over his magic. I didn't want Nathaniel spooked. Anyway, when we got married, we thought it was best not to cause a fuss. Agatha was on the Congregation by then and was always talking about the segregation rules and what happened when folks broke them." Sophie shook her head. "It never made any sense to me."

"The book?" I repeated, gently trying to steer the conversation.

"Oh." Sophie's forehead creased with concentration, and she fell silent.

"My mother is thrilled about the baby. She said it's going to be the best-dressed child the world has ever seen." Nathaniel smiled tenderly at his wife. "Then the dreams started. Sophie felt trouble was coming. She has strong premonitions for a daemon, just like my mother. In September she started seeing Diana's face and hearing her name. Sophie said people want something from you."

Matthew's fingers touched the small of my back where Satu's scar dipped down.

"Show them her face jug, Nathaniel. It's just a picture. I wanted to bring it, but he said we couldn't carry a gallon jug from Durham to New York."

Her husband obediently took out his phone and pulled up a picture on the screen. Nathaniel handed the phone to Sarah, who gasped.

"I'm a potter, like my mama and her mother. Granny used witchfire in her kiln, but I just do it the ordinary way. All the faces from my dreams go on my jugs. Not all of them are scary. Yours wasn't."

Sarah passed the phone to Matthew. "It's beautiful, Sophie," he said sincerely.

I had to agree. Its tall, rounded shape was pale gray, and two handles curved away from its narrow spout. On the front was a face—my face, though distorted by the jug's proportions. My chin jutted out from the surface, as did my nose, my ears, and the sweep of my brow bones. Thick squiggles of clay stood in for hair. My eyes were closed, and my mouth smiled serenely, as if I were keeping a secret.

"This is for you, too." Sophie drew a small, lumpy object out of the pocket of her cardigan. It was wrapped in oilcloth secured with string. "When the baby quickened, I knew for sure it belonged to you. The baby knows, too. Maybe that's what made Agatha so worried. And of course we have to figure out what to do, since the baby is a witch. Nathaniel's mom thought you might have some ideas."

We watched in silence while Sophie picked at the knots. "Sorry," she muttered. "My dad tied it up. He was in the navy."

"Can I help you?" Marcus asked, reaching for the lump.

"No, I've got it." Sophie smiled at him sweetly and went back to her work. "It has to be wrapped up or it turns black. And it's not supposed to be black. It's supposed to be white."

Our collective curiosity was now thoroughly aroused, and there wasn't a sound in the house except for the lapping of Tabitha's tongue as she groomed her paws. The string fell away, followed by the oilcloth.

"There," Sophie whispered. "I may not be a witch, but I'm the last of the Normans. We've been keeping this for you."

It was a small figurine no more than four inches tall and made from old silver that glowed with the softly burnished light seen in museum showcases. Sophie turned the figurine so that it faced me.

"Diana," I said unnecessarily. The goddess was represented exactly, from the tips of the crescent moon on her brow to her sandaled feet. She was in motion, one foot striding forward while a hand reached over her shoulders to draw an arrow from her quiver. The other hand rested on the antlers of a stag.

"Where did you get that?" Matthew sounded strange, and his face had gone gray again.

Sophie shrugged. "Nobody knows. The Normans have always had it. It's been passed down in the family from witch to witch. 'When the time comes, give it to the one who has need of it.' That's what my granny told my father, and my father told me. It used to be written on a little piece of paper, but that was lost a long time ago."

"What is it, Matthew?" Marcus looked uneasy. So did Nathaniel.

"It's a chess piece," Matthew's voice broke. "The white queen."

"How do you know that?" Sarah looked at the figurine critically. "It's not like any chess piece I ever saw."

Matthew had to force the words out from behind tight lips. "Because it was once mine. My father gave it to me."

"How did it end up in North Carolina?" I stretched my fingers toward the silver object, and the figurine slid across the table as if it wanted to be in my possession. The stag's antlers cut into my palm as my hand closed around it, the metal quickly warming to my touch.

"I lost it in a wager," Matthew said quietly. "I have no idea how it got to North Carolina." He buried his face in his hands and murmured a single word that made no sense to me. "Kit."

"Do you remember when you last had it?" Sarah asked sharply.

"I remember precisely." Matthew lifted his head. "I was playing a game with it many years ago, on All Souls' Night. It was then that I lost my wager."

"That's next week." Miriam shifted in her seat so that she could meet Sarah's eyes. "Would timewalking be easier around the feasts of All Saints and All Souls?"

"Miriam," Matthew snarled, but it was too late.

"What's timewalking?" Nathaniel whispered to Sophie.

"Mama was a timewalker," Sophie whispered back. "She was good at it, too, and always came back from the 1700s with lots of ideas for pots and jugs."

"Your mother visited the past?" Nathaniel asked faintly. He looked around the room at the motley assortment of creatures, then at his wife's belly. "Does that run in witches' families, too, like second sight?"

Sarah answered Miriam over the daemons' whispered conversation.

"There's not much keeping the living from the dead between Halloween and All Souls. It would be easier to slip between the past and the present then."

Nathaniel looked more anxious. "The living and the dead? Sophie and I just came to deliver that statue or whatever it is so she can sleep through the night."

"Will Diana be strong enough?" Marcus asked Matthew, ignoring Nathaniel.

"This time of year, it should be much easier for Diana to timewalk," Sarah mused aloud.

Sophie looked contentedly around the table. "This reminds me of the old days when granny and her sisters got together and gossiped. They never seemed to pay attention to one another, but they always knew what had been said."

The room's many competing conversations stopped abruptly when the dining-room doors banged open and shut, followed by a booming sound produced by the heavier keeping-room doors. Nathaniel, Miriam, and Marcus shot to their feet.

"What the hell was that?" Marcus asked.

"The house," I said wearily. "I'll go see what it wants."

Matthew scooped up the figurine and followed me.

The old woman with the embroidered bodice was waiting at the keeping room's threshold.

"Hello, ma'am." Sophie had followed right behind and was nodding politely to the old woman. She scrutinized my features. "The lady looks a bit like you, doesn't she?"

So you've chosen your road, the old woman said. Her voice was fainter than before.

"We have," I said. Footsteps sounded behind me as the remaining occupants of the dining room came to see what the commotion was about.

You'll be needing something else for your journey, she replied.

The coffin doors swung open, and the press of creatures at my back was matched by the crowd of ghosts waiting by the fireplace.

This should be interesting, my grandmother said drily from her place at the head of the ghostly bunch.

There was a rumbling in the walls like bones rattling. I sat in my grandmother's rocker, my knees no longer able to hold my weight.

A crack developed in the paneling between the window and the fireplace. It stretched and widened in a diagonal slash. The old wood shuddered and squeaked. Something soft with legs and arms flew out of the gap. I flinched when it landed in my lap.

"Holy shit," Sarah said.

That paneling will never look the same, my grandmother commented, shaking her head regretfully at the cracked wood.

Whatever flew at me was made of rough-spun fabric that had faded to an indiscriminate grayish brown. In addition to its four limbs, it had a lump where the head belonged, adorned with faded tufts of hair. Someone had stitched an X where the heart should be.

"What is it?" I reached my index finger toward the uneven, rusty stitches.

"Don't touch it!" Em cried.

"I'm already touching it," I said, looking up in confusion. "It's sitting on my lap."

"I've never seen such an old poppet," said Sophie, peering down at it.

"Poppet?" Miriam frowned. "Didn't one of your ancestors get in trouble over a poppet?"

"Bridget Bishop." Sarah, Em, and I said the name at the same moment.

The old woman with the embroidered bodice was now standing next to my grandmother.

"Is this yours?" I whispered.

A smile turned up one corner of Bridget's mouth. *Remember to be canny when you find yourself at a crossroads, daughter. There's no telling what secrets are buried there.*

Looking down at the poppet, I lightly touched the X on its chest. The fabric split open, revealing a stuffing made of leaves, twigs, and dried flowers and releasing the scent of herbs into the air. "Rue," I said, recognizing it from Marthe's tea.

"Clover, broom, knotweed, and slippery elm bark, too, from the smell of it." Sarah gave the air a good sniff. "That poppet was made to draw someone—Diana, presumably—but it's got a protection spell on it, too."

You did well by her, Bridget told my grandmother with an approving nod at Sarah.

Something was gleaming through the brown. When I pulled at it gently, the poppet came apart in pieces.

And there's an end to it, Bridget said with a sigh. My grandmother put a comforting arm around her.

"It's an earring." Its intricate golden surfaces caught the light, and an enormous, teardrop-shaped pearl shone at the end.

"How the hell did one of my mother's earrings get into Bridget Bishop's poppet?" Matthew's face was back to that pasty gray color.

"Were your mother's earrings in the same place as your chess set on that long-ago night?" Miriam asked. Both the earring and the chess piece were old—older than the poppet, older than the Bishop house.

Matthew thought a moment, then nodded. "Yes. Is a week enough time? Can you be ready?" he asked me urgently.

"I don't know."

"Sure you'll be ready," Sophie crooned to her belly. "She'll make things right for you, little witch. You'll be her godmother," Sophie said with a radiant smile. "She'll like that."

"Counting the baby—and not counting the ghosts, of course," Marcus said in a deceptively conversational tone that reminded me of the way Matthew spoke when he was stressed, "there are nine of us in this room."

"Four witches, three vampires, and two daemons," Sophie said dreamily, her hands still on her belly. "But we're short a daemon. Without one we can't be a conventicle. And once Matthew and Diana leave, we'll need another vampire, too. Is Matthew's mother still alive?"

"She's tired," Nathaniel said apologetically, his hands tightening on his wife's shoulders. "It makes it difficult for her to focus."

"What did you say?" Em asked Sophie. She was struggling to keep her voice calm.

Sophie's eyes lost their dreaminess. "A conventicle. That's what they called a gathering of dissenters in the old days. Ask them." She inclined her head in the direction of Marcus and Miriam.

"I told you this wasn't about the Bishops or the de Clermonts," Em said to Sarah. "It's not even about Matthew and Diana and whether they can be together. It's about Sophie and Nathaniel, too. It's about the future, just as Diana said. This is how we'll fight the Congregation—not just as individual families but as a— What did you call it?"

"Conventicle," Miriam answered. "I always liked that word—so delightfully ominous." She settled back on her heels with a satisfied smile.

Matthew turned to Nathaniel. "It would seem your mother was right. You do belong here, with us."

"Of course they belong here," Sarah said briskly. "Your bedroom is ready, Nathaniel. It's upstairs, the second door to the right."

"Thank you," Nathaniel said, a note of cautious relief in his voice, though he still eyed Matthew warily.

"I'm Marcus." Matthew's son held out his hand to the daemon. Nathaniel clasped it firmly, barely reacting to the shocking coldness of vampire flesh.

"See? We didn't need to make reservations at that hotel, sweetie," Sophie told her husband with a beatific smile. She looked for Em in the crowd. "Are there more cookies?"

Chapter 40

A few days later, Sophie was sitting at the kitchen island with half a dozen pumpkins and a sharp knife when Matthew and I came in from our walk. The weather had turned colder, and there was a dreary hint of winter in the air.

"What do you think?" Sophie asked, turning the pumpkin. It had the hollow eyes, arched eyebrows, and gaping mouth of all Halloween pumpkins, but she had transformed the usual features into something remarkable. Lines pulled away from the mouth, and the forehead was creased, setting the eyes themselves slightly off-kilter. The overall effect was chilling.

"Amazing!" Matthew looked at the pumpkin with delight.

She bit her lip, regarding her work critically. "I'm not sure the eyes are right."

I laughed. "At least it *has* eyes. Sometimes Sarah can't be bothered and just pokes three round holes in the side with the end of a screwdriver and calls it a day."

"Halloween is a busy holiday for witches. We don't always have time for the finer details," Sarah said sharply, coming out of the stillroom to inspect Sophie's work. She nodded with approval. "But this year we'll be the envy of the neighborhood."

Sophie smiled shyly and pulled another pumpkin toward her. "I'll do a less scary one next. We don't want to make the little kids cry."

With less than a week to go until Halloween, Em and Sarah were in a flurry of activity to get ready for the Madison coven's annual fall bash. There would be food, free-flowing drink (including Em's famous punch, which had at least one July birth to its credit), and enough witchy activities to keep the sugar-high children occupied and away from the bonfire after they'd been trick-or-treating. Bobbing for apples was much more challenging when the fruit in question had been put under a spell.

My aunts hinted that they would cancel their plans, but Matthew just shook his head.

"Everyone in town would wonder if you didn't show up. This is just a typical Halloween."

We'd all looked dubious. After all, Sarah and Em weren't the only ones counting the hours to Halloween.

Last night Matthew had laid out the gradual departure of everyone in the house, starting with Nathaniel and Sophie and ending with Marcus and Miriam. It would, he believed, make our own departure less conspicuous—and it was not open to discussion.

Marcus and Nathaniel had exchanged a long look when Matthew finished his announcement, which concluded with the daemon shaking his head and pressing his lips together and the younger vampire staring fixedly at the table while a muscle in his jaw throbbed.

"But who will hand out the candy?" Em asked.

Matthew looked thoughtful. "Diana and I will do it."

The two young men had stormed out of the room when we broke up to go our separate ways, mumbling something about getting milk. They'd then climbed into Marcus's car and torn down the driveway.

"You've got to stop telling them what to do," I chided Matthew, who had joined me at the front door to watch their departure. "They're both grown men. Nathaniel has a wife, and soon he'll have a child."

"Left to their own devices, Marcus and Nathaniel would have an army of vampires on the doorstep tomorrow."

"You won't be here to order them around next week," I reminded him, watching the taillights as they turned toward town. "Your son will be in charge."

"That's what I'm worried about."

The real problem was that we were in the midst of an acute outbreak of testosterone poisoning. Nathaniel and Matthew couldn't be in the same room without sparks flying, and in the increasingly crowded house it was hard for them to avoid each other.

Their next argument occurred that afternoon when a delivery arrived. It was a box with BIOHAZARD written all over the sealing tape in large red letters.

"What the hell is this?" Marcus asked, carrying the box gingerly into the family room. Nathaniel looked up from his laptop, his brown eyes widening with alarm.

"That's for me," Matthew said smoothly, taking the box from his son.

"My wife is pregnant!" Nathaniel said furiously, snapping his laptop closed. "How could you bring that into the house?"

"It's immunizations for Diana." Matthew barely kept his annoyance in check.

I put aside my magazine. "What immunizations?"

"You're not going to the past without every possible protection from disease. Come to the stillroom," Matthew said, holding out his hand.

"Tell me what's in the box first."

"Booster vaccines—tetanus, typhoid, polio, diphtheria—as well as some vaccines you probably haven't had, like a new one-shot rabies preventive, the latest flu shots, an immunization for cholera." He paused, still holding out his hand. "And a smallpox vaccine."

"Smallpox?" They'd stopped giving smallpox vaccines to schoolchildren a few years before I was born. That meant Sophie and Nathaniel hadn't been immunized either.

Matthew reached down and hoisted me to my feet. "Let's get started," he said firmly.

"You aren't going to stick needles into me today."

"Better needles today than smallpox and lockjaw tomorrow," he countered.

"Wait a minute." Nathaniel's voice sounded in the room like a cracking whip. "The smallpox vaccine makes you contagious. What about Sophie and the baby?"

"Explain it to him, Marcus," Matthew ordered, stepping aside so I could pass.

"Not contagious with smallpox, exactly." Marcus tried to be reassuring. "It's a different strain of the disease. Sophie will be fine, provided she doesn't touch Diana's arm or anything it comes into contact with."

Sophie smiled at Marcus. "Okay. I can do that."

"Do you always do everything he tells you to do?" Nathaniel asked Marcus with contempt, unfolding from the couch. He looked down at his wife. "Sophie, we're leaving."

"Stop fussing, Nathaniel," Sophie said. "You'll upset the house—the baby, too—if you start talking about leaving. We're not going anywhere."

Nathaniel gave Matthew an evil look and sat down.

In the stillroom Matthew had me take off my sweatshirt and turtleneck and then began swabbing my left arm with alcohol. The door creaked open.

It was Sarah. She'd stood by without comment during the exchange between Matthew and Nathaniel, though her eyes had seldom left the newly delivered box.

Matthew had already sliced open the protective tape wrapped around the molded-foam container. Seven small vials were nestled within, along with a bag of pills, something that looked like a container of salt, and a two-pronged metal instrument I'd never seen before. He'd already entered the same state of clinical detachment I'd first detected in his lab in Oxford, with no time for chatter or a warm bedside manner. Sarah was welcome moral support.

"I've got some old white shirts for you to wear." Sarah momentarily distracted me from what Matthew was doing. "They'll be easy to bleach. Some white towels, too. Leave your laundry upstairs and I'll take care of it."

"Thank you, Sarah. That's one less risk of contagion to worry about." Matthew selected one of the vials. "We'll start with the tetanus booster."

Each time he stuck something in my arm, I winced. By the third shot, there was a thin sheen of sweat on my forehead and my heart was pounding. "Sarah," I said faintly. "Can you please not stand behind me?"

"Sorry." Sarah moved to stand behind Matthew instead. "I'll get you some water." She handed me a glass of ice-cold water, the outside slippery with condensation. I took it gratefully, trying to focus on holding it steady rather than on the next vial Matthew was opening.

Another needle entered my skin, and I jumped.

"That's the last shot," Matthew said. He opened the container that looked like it was filled with salt crystals and carefully added the contents to a bottle of liquid. After giving it a vigorous shake, he handed it to me. "This is the cholera vaccine. It's oral. Then there's the smallpox immunization, and some pills to take after dinner for the next few nights."

I drank it down quickly but still almost gagged at the thick texture and vile taste.

Matthew opened up the sealed pouch holding the two-pronged smallpox inoculator. "Do you know what Thomas Jefferson wrote to Edward Jenner about this vaccine?" he asked, voice hypnotic. "Jefferson said it was medicine's most useful discovery." There was a cold touch of alcohol on my right arm, then pricks as the inoculator's prongs pierced the skin. "The president dismissed Harvey's discovery of the circulation of blood as nothing more than a 'beautiful addition' to medical knowledge." Matthew moved in a circular pattern, distributing the live virus on my skin.

His diversionary tactics were working. I was too busy listening to his story to pay much attention to my arm.

"But Jefferson praised Jenner because his inoculation relegated smallpox to a disease that would be known only to historians. He'd saved the human race from one of its most deadly enemies." Matthew dumped the empty vial and the inoculator into a sealed biohazard container. "All done."

"Did you know Jefferson?" I was already fantasizing about timewalking to eighteenth-century Virginia.

"I knew Washington better. He was a soldier—a man who let his actions speak for him. Jefferson was full of words. But it wasn't easy to reach the man behind the intellect. I'd never drop by his house unannounced with a bluestocking like you in tow."

I reached for my turtleneck, but Matthew stilled my arm and carefully covered the inoculation site with a waterproof bandage. "This is a live virus, so you have to keep it covered. Sophie and Nathaniel can't come into contact with it, or with anything that touches it." He moved to the sink and vigorously washed his hands in steaming-hot water.

"For how long?"

"It will form a blister, and then the blister will scab over. No one should touch the site until the blister heals."

I pulled the old, stretched-out turtleneck over my head, taking care not to dislodge the bandage.

"Now that that's done, we need to figure out how Diana is going to carry you—and herself—to some distant time by Halloween. She may have been timewalking since she was an infant, but it's still not easy," Sarah worried, her face twisted in a frown.

Em appeared around the door. We made room for her at the table.

"I've been timewalking recently, too," I confessed.

"When?" Matthew paused for a moment in his work of clearing up what remained from the inoculations.

"First on the driveway when you were talking to Ysabeau. Then again the day Sarah was trying to make me light a candle, when I went from the stillroom to the orchard. Both times I picked up my foot, wished myself somewhere else, and put my foot down where I wanted to be."

"That sounds like timewalking," Sarah said slowly. "Of course, you didn't travel far—and you weren't carrying anything." She sized up Matthew, her expression turning doubtful.

There was a knock at the door. "Can I come in?" Sophie's call was muffled.

"Can she, Matthew?" Em asked.

"As long as she doesn't touch Diana."

When Em opened the door, Sophie was moving soothing hands around her belly. "Everything's going to be all right," she said serenely from the threshold. "As long as Matthew has a connection to the place they're going, he'll help Diana, not weigh her down."

Miriam appeared behind Sophie. "Is something interesting happening?"

"We're talking about timewalking," I said.

"How will you practice?" Miriam stepped around Sophie and pushed her firmly back toward the door when she tried to follow.

"Diana will go back in time a few hours, then a few more. We'll increase the time involved, then the distance. Then we'll add Matthew and see what happens." Sarah looked at Em. "Can you help her?"

"A bit," Em replied cautiously. "Stephen told me how he did it. He never used spells to go back in time—his power was strong enough without them. Given Diana's early experiences with timewalking and her difficulties with witchcraft, we might want to follow his example."

"Why don't you and Diana go to the barn and try?" Sarah suggested gently. "She can come straight back to the stillroom."

When Matthew started after us, Sarah put a hand out and stopped him. "Stay here."

Matthew's face had gone gray again. He didn't like me in a different room, never mind a different time.

The hop barn still held the sweet aroma of long-ago harvests. Em stood opposite and quietly issued instructions. "Stand as still as possible," she said, "and empty your mind."

"You sound like my yoga teacher," I said, arranging my limbs in the familiar lines of mountain pose.

Em smiled. "I've always thought yoga and magic had a lot in common. Now, close your eyes. Think about the stillroom you just left. You have to want to be there more than here."

Re-creating the stillroom in my mind, I furnished it with objects, scents, people. I frowned. "Where will you be?"

"It depends on when you arrive. If it's before we left, I'll be there. If not, I'll be here."

"The physics of this don't make sense." My head filled with concerns about how the universe would handle multiple Dianas and Ems—not to mention Miriams and Sarahs.

"Stop thinking about physics. What did your dad write in his note? '*Whoever can no longer wonder, no longer marvel, is as good as dead.*'"

"Close enough," I admitted reluctantly.

"It's time for you to take a big step into the mysterious, Diana. The magic and wonder that was always your birthright is waiting for you. Now, think about where you want to be."

When my mind was brimming over with images of it, I picked up my foot.

When I put it down again, there I was in the hop barn with Em.

"It didn't work," I said, panicking.

"You were too focused on the details of the room. Think about Matthew. Don't you want to be with him? Magic's in the heart, not the mind. It's not about words and following a procedure, like witchcraft. You have to *feel* it."

"Desire." I saw myself calling *Notes and Queries* from the shelf at the Bodleian, felt once more the first touch of Matthew's lips on mine in his rooms at All Souls. The barn dropped away, and Matthew was telling me the story about Thomas Jefferson and Edward Jenner.

"No," Em said, her voice steely. "Don't think about Jefferson. Think about Matthew."

"Matthew." I brought my mind back to the touch of his cool fingers against my skin, the rich sound of his voice, the sense of intense vitality when we were together.

I picked up my foot.

It landed in the corner of the stillroom, where I was squashed behind an old barrel.

"What if she gets lost?" Matthew sounded tense. "How will we get her back?"

"We don't have to worry about that," Sophie said, pointing in my direction. "She's already here."

Matthew whipped around and let out a ragged breath.

"How long have I been gone?" I felt light-headed and disoriented, but otherwise fine.

"About ninety seconds," Sarah said. "More than enough time for Matthew to have a nervous breakdown."

Matthew pulled me into his arms and tucked me under his chin. "Thank God. How soon can she take me with her?"

"Let's not get ahead of ourselves," Sarah warned. "One step at a time."

I looked around. "Where's Em?"

"In the barn." Sophie was beaming. "She'll catch up."

It took more than twenty minutes for Em to return. When she did, her cheeks were pink from concern as well as the cold, though some of the tension left her when she saw me standing with Matthew.

"You did good, Em," Sarah said, kissing her in a rare public display of affection.

"Diana started thinking about Thomas Jefferson," Em said. "She might have ended up at Monticello. Then she focused on her feelings, and her body got blurry around the edges. I blinked, and she was gone."

That afternoon, with Em's careful coaching, I took a slightly longer trip back to breakfast. Over the next few days, I went a bit farther with each timewalk. Going back in time aided by three objects was always easier than returning to the present, which required enormous concentration as well as an ability to accurately forecast where and when you wanted to arrive. Finally it was time to try carrying Matthew.

Sarah had insisted on limiting the variables to accommodate the extra effort required. "Start out wherever you want to end up," she advised. "That way all you have to worry about is thinking yourself back to a particular time. The place will take care of itself."

I took him up to the bedroom at twilight without telling him what was in store. The figure of Diana and the golden earring from Bridget Bishop's poppet were sitting on the chest of drawers in front of a photograph of my parents.

"Much as I'd like to spend a few hours with you in here—alone—dinner is almost ready," he protested, though there was a calculating gleam in his eyes.

"There's plenty of time. Sarah said I'm ready to take you timewalking. We're going back to our first night in the house."

Matthew thought for a moment, and his eyes brightened further. "Was that the night the stars came out—inside?"

I kissed him in answer.

"Oh." He looked shyly pleased. "What should I do?"

"Nothing." This would be the hardest thing about timewalking for him. "What are you always telling me? Close your eyes, relax, and let me do the rest." I grinned wickedly.

He laced his fingers through mine. "Witch."

"You won't even know it's happening," I assured him. "It's fast. Just pick up your foot and put it down again when I tell you. And don't let go."

"Not a chance," Matthew said, tightening his grip.

I thought about that night, our first alone after my encounter with Satu. I remembered his touch against my back, fierce and gentle at the same time. I felt the connection, immediate and tenacious, to that shared moment in our past.

"Now," I whispered. Our feet rose together.

But timewalking with Matthew was different. Having him along slowed us down, and for the first time I was aware of what was happening.

The past, present, and future shimmered around us in a spiderweb of light and color. Each strand in the web moved slowly, almost imperceptibly, sometimes touching another filament before moving gently away again as if caught by a breeze. Each time strands touched—and millions of strands were touching all the time—there was the soft echo of an original, inaudible sound.

Momentarily distracted by the seemingly limitless possibilities before us, we found it easy to lose sight of the twisted red-and-white strand of time we were following. I brought my concentration back to it, knowing it would take us back to our first night in Madison.

I put my foot down and felt rough floorboards against my bare skin.

"You told me it would be fast," he said hoarsely. "That didn't feel fast to me."

"No, it was different," I agreed. "Did you see the lights?"

Matthew shook his head. "There was nothing but blackness. I was falling, slowly, with only your hand keeping me from hitting bottom." He raised it to his mouth and kissed it.

There was a lingering smell of chili in the quiet house, and it was night outside. "Can you tell who's here?"

His nostrils flared, and he closed his eyes. Then he smiled and sighed with happiness. "Just Sarah and Em, and you and me. None of the children."

I giggled, drawing him closer.

"If this house gets any more crowded, it's going to burst." Matthew buried his face in my neck, then drew back. "You still have your bandage. It means that when we go back in time, we don't stop being who we are in the present or forget what happened to us here." His cold hands crept under the hem of my turtleneck. "Given your rediscovered talents as a timewalker, how accurate are you at gauging the passing of time?"

Though we happily lingered in the past, we were back in the present before Emily finished making the salad.

"Timewalking agrees with you, Matthew," Sarah said, scrutinizing his relaxed face. She rewarded him with a glass of red wine.

"Thank you, Sarah. I was in good hands." He raised his glass to me in salute.

"Glad to hear it," Sarah said drily, sounding like my ghostly grandmother. She threw some sliced radishes into the biggest salad bowl I'd ever seen.

"Where did that come from?" I peered into the bowl to hide my reddened lips.

"The house," Em said, beating the salad dressing with a whisk. "It enjoys having so many mouths to feed."

Next morning the house let us know it was anticipating yet another addition.

Sarah, Matthew, and I were discussing whether my next timewalk should be to Oxford or to Sept-Tours when Em appeared with a load of laundry in her arms. "Somebody is coming."

Matthew put down his paper and stood. "Good. I was expecting a delivery today."

"It's not a delivery, and they're not here yet. But the house is ready for them." She disappeared into the laundry room.

"Another room? Where did the house put this one?" Sarah shouted after her.

"Next to Marcus." Em's reply echoed from the depths of the washing machine.

We took bets on who it would be. The guesses ranged from Agatha Wilson to Emily's friends from Cherry Valley who liked to show up unannounced for the coven's Halloween party.

Late in the morning, there was an authoritative knock on the door. It opened to a small, dark man with intelligent eyes. He was instantly recognizable from pictures taken at celebrity parties in London and television news conferences. Any remaining doubts about his identity were erased by the familiar nudges against my cheekbones.

Our mystery houseguest was Matthew's friend Hamish Osborne.

"You must be Diana," he said without pleasure or preamble, his Scottish accent lending length to the vowels. Hamish was dressed for business, in a pin-striped charcoal suit that had been tailored to fit him exactly, a pale pink shirt with heavy silver cuff links, and a fuchsia tie embroidered with tiny black flies.

"I am. Hello, Hamish. Was Matthew expecting you?" I stepped aside to let him in.

"Probably not," Hamish said crisply, remaining on the stoop. "Where is he?"

"Hamish." Matthew was moving so quickly I felt the breeze behind me before hearing him approach. He extended his hand. "This is a surprise."

Hamish stared at the outstretched hand, then turned his eyes to its owner. "Surprise? Let's discuss surprises. When I joined your . . . 'family firm,' you swore to me this would never arrive." He brandished an envelope, its black seal broken but still clinging to the flaps.

"I did." Matthew dropped his hand and looked at Hamish warily.

"So much for your promises, then. I'm given to understand from this letter, and from my conversation with your mother, that there's some kind of trouble." Hamish's eyes flickered to me, then back to Matthew.

"Yes." Matthew's lips tightened. "But you're the ninth knight. You don't have to become involved."

"You made a *daemon* the ninth knight?" Miriam had come through the dining room with Nathaniel.

"Who's he?" Nathaniel shook a handful of Scrabble tiles in his cupped hand while surveying the new arrival.

"Hamish Osborne. And who might you be?" Hamish asked, as if addressing an impertinent employee. The last thing we needed was more testosterone in the house.

"Oh, I'm nobody," Nathaniel said airily, leaning against the dining-room door. He watched Marcus as he passed by.

"Hamish, why are you here?" Marcus looked confused, then saw the letter. "Oh."

My ancestors were congregating in the keeping room, and the house was stirring on its foundations. "Could we continue this inside? It's the house, you see. It's a little uneasy, given you're a daemon—and angry."

"Come, Hamish." Matthew tried to draw him out of the doorway. "Marcus and Sarah haven't demolished the whiskey supply yet. We'll get you a drink and sit you by the fire."

Hamish remained where he was and kept talking.

"While visiting with your mother, who was far more willing to answer my questions than you would have been, I learned that you wanted a few things from home. It seemed a shame for Alain to make such a long trip, when I was already going to come and ask you what the hell you were up to." He lifted a bulky leather briefcase with soft sides and a formidable lock, and a smaller, hard-sided case.

"Thank you, Hamish." The words were cordial enough, but Matthew was clearly displeased at having his arrangements altered.

"Speaking of explanations, it's a damn good thing the French don't care about the exportation of English national treasures. Have you any idea of the paperwork that would have been required to get this out of England? *If* they'd let me remove it at all, which I doubt."

Matthew took the briefcases from Hamish's fingers, gripped him by the elbow, and pulled his friend inside. "Later," he said hastily. "Marcus, take Hamish and introduce him to Diana's family while I put these away."

"Oh, it's you," said Sophie with delight, coming out of the dining room. The bulge of her belly showed plainly underneath a stretched University of North Carolina sweatshirt. "You're like Nathaniel, not scatterbrained like me. Your face is on one of my pots, too." She beamed at Hamish, who looked both charmed and startled.

"Are there more?" he asked me, with a cock of his head that made him resemble a tiny, bright-eyed bird.

"Many more," Sophie replied happily. "You won't see them, though."

"Come and meet my aunts," I said hastily.

"The witches?" It was impossible to know what Hamish was thinking. His sharp eyes missed nothing, and his face was nearly as impassive as Matthew's.

"Yes, the witches."

Matthew disappeared upstairs while Marcus and I introduced Hamish to Em. He seemed less annoyed with her than he was with Matthew and me, and she immediately started fussing over him. Sarah met us at the stillroom door, wondering what the commotion was about.

"We're a proper conventicle now, Sarah," Sophie observed as she reached for the pyramid of freshly baked cookies on the kitchen island. "All nine—three witches, three daemons, and three vampires—present and accounted for."

"Looks like it," Sarah agreed, sizing up Hamish. She watched her partner buzzing around the kitchen like a bewildered bee. "Em, I don't think our new guest needs tea or coffee. Is the whiskey in the dining room?"

"Diana and I call it the 'war room,'" Sophie confided, grabbing Hamish familiarly by the forearm, "though it seems unlikely we could fight a war without the humans finding out. It's the only place big enough to hold us now. Some of the ghosts manage to squeeze in, too."

"Ghosts?" Hamish reached up and loosened his tie.

"The dining room." Sarah gripped Hamish's other elbow. "Everybody in the dining room."

Matthew was already there. The aroma of hot wax filled the air. When all of us had grabbed our chosen drink and found a seat, he took charge.

"Hamish has questions," Matthew said. "Nathaniel and Sophie, too. And I suppose this is my tale to tell—mine and Diana's."

With that, Matthew took a deep breath and plunged in. He included everything—Ashmole 782, the Knights of Lazarus, the break-ins at Oxford, Satu and what happened at La Pierre, even Baldwin's fury. There were poppets and earrings and face jugs as well. Hamish looked at Matthew sharply when he discussed timewalking and the three objects I would need to travel back to a particular time and place.

"Matthew Clairmont," Hamish hissed, leaning across the table. "Is that what I brought from Sept-Tours? Does Diana know?"

"No," Matthew confessed, looking slightly uncomfortable. "She'll know on Halloween."

"Well, she'd have to know on Halloween, wouldn't she?" Hamish let out an exasperated sigh.

Though the exchange between Hamish and Matthew was heated, there were only two moments when the tension threatened to escalate into outright civil war. Both of them, not surprisingly, involved Matthew and Nathaniel.

The first was when Matthew explained to Sophie what this war would be like—the unexpected attacks, the long-simmering feuds between vampires and witches that would come to a boil, the brutal deaths that were bound to occur as creature fought creature using magic, witchcraft, brute strength, speed, and preternatural cunning.

"That's not how wars are fought anymore." Nathaniel's deep voice cut through the resulting chatter.

Matthew's eyebrow floated up, and his face took on an impatient expression. "No?"

"Wars are fought on computers. This isn't the thirteenth century. Hand-to-hand combat isn't required." He gestured at his laptop on the sideboard. "With computers you can take down your enemy without ever firing a shot or shedding a drop of blood."

"This may not be the thirteenth century, Nathaniel, but some of the combatants will have lived through those times, and they have a sentimental attachment to destroying people the old-fashioned way. Leave this to me and Marcus." Matthew thought this was the end of the matter.

Nathaniel shook his head and stared fixedly at the table.

"Do you have something else to say?" Matthew asked, an ominous purring starting in the back of his throat.

"You've made it perfectly clear you'll do what you want in any case." Nathaniel lifted his frank brown eyes in challenge, then shrugged. "Suit yourself. But you're making a mistake if you think your enemies won't use more modern methods to destroy you. There are humans to consider, after all. They'll notice if vampires and witches start fighting one another in the streets."

The second battle between Matthew and Nathaniel had to do not with war but with blood. It began innocently enough, with Matthew talking about Nathaniel's relationship to Agatha Wilson and about Sophie's witch parents.

"It's imperative that their DNA be analyzed. The baby's, too, once it's born."

Marcus and Miriam nodded, unsurprised. The rest of us were somewhat startled.

"Nathaniel and Sophie bring into question your theory that daemonic traits result from unpredictable mutations rather than heredity," I said, thinking aloud.

"We have so little data." Matthew eyed Hamish and Nathaniel with the dispassionate gaze of a scientist examining two fresh specimens. "Our current findings might be misleading."

"Sophie's case also raises the issue of whether daemons are more closely related to witches than we'd thought." Miriam directed her black eyes at the daemon's belly. "I've never heard of a witch giving birth to a daemon, never mind a daemon giving birth to a witch."

"You think I'm going to hand over Sophie's blood—and my child's blood—to a bunch of vampires?" Nathaniel looked perilously close to losing control.

"Diana isn't the only creature in this room the Congregation will want to study, Nathaniel." Matthew's words did nothing to soothe the daemon. "Your mother appreciated the danger your family was facing, or she wouldn't have sent you here. One day you might discover your wife and child gone. If you do, it's highly unlikely you'll ever see them again."

"That's enough," Sarah said sharply. "There's no need to threaten him."

"Keep your hands off my family," Nathaniel said, breathing heavily.

"I'm not a danger to them," Matthew said. "The danger comes from the Congregation, from the possibility of open hostility between the three species, and above all from pretending this isn't happening."

"They'll come for us, Nathaniel. I've seen it." Sophie's voice was purposeful, and her face had the same sudden sharpness that Agatha Wilson's had back in Oxford.

"Why didn't you tell me?" Nathaniel said.

"I started to tell Agatha, but she stopped me and ordered me not to say another word. She was so frightened. Then she gave me Diana's name and the address for the Bishop house." Sophie's face took on its characteristic fuzzy look. "I'm glad Matthew's mother is still alive. She'll like my pots. I'll put her face on one of them. And you can have my DNA whenever you want it, Matthew—the baby's, too."

Sophie's announcement effectively put an end to Nathaniel's objections. When Matthew had entertained all the questions he was willing to answer, he picked up an envelope that had been sitting unnoticed at his elbow. It was sealed with black wax.

"That leaves one piece of unfinished business." He stood and held out the letter. "Hamish, this is for you."

"Oh, no you don't." Hamish crossed his arms over his chest. "Give it to Marcus."

"You may be the ninth knight, but you're also the seneschal of the Knights of Lazarus, and my second in command. There's a protocol we must follow," Matthew said, tight-lipped.

"Matthew would know," Marcus muttered. "He's the only grand master in the history of the order who's ever resigned."

"And now I'll be the only grand master to have resigned twice," Matthew said, still holding out the envelope.

"To hell with protocol," Hamish snapped, banging his fist on the table. "Everybody out of this room except Matthew, Marcus, and Nathaniel. Please," he added as an afterthought.

"Why do we have to leave?" Sarah asked suspiciously.

Hamish studied my aunt for a moment. "You'd better stay, too."

The five of them were closeted in the dining room for the rest of the day. Once an exhausted Hamish came out and requested sandwiches. The cookies, he explained, were long gone.

"Is it me, or do you also feel that the men sent us out of the room so they could smoke cigars and talk politics?" I asked, trying to distract myself from the meeting in the dining room by flipping through a jarring mix of old movies and afternoon television. Em and Sophie were both knitting, and Miriam was doing a puzzle she'd found in a book promising *Demonically Difficult Sudoku*. She chuckled now and then and made a mark in the margins.

"What are you doing, Miriam?" Sophie asked.

"Keeping score," Miriam said, making another mark on the page.

"What are they talking about? And who's winning?" I asked, envious of her ability to hear the conversation.

"They're planning a war, Diana. As for who's winning, either Matthew or Hamish—it's too close to call," Miriam replied. "Marcus and Nathaniel managed to get in a few good shots, though, and Sarah's holding her own."

It was already dark, and Em and I were making dinner when the meeting broke up. Nathaniel and Sophie were talking quietly in the family room.

"I need to catch up on a few calls," Matthew said after he'd kissed me, his mild tone at odds with his tense face.

Seeing how tired he was, I decided my questions could wait.

"Of course," I said, touching his cheek. "Take your time. Dinner will be in an hour."

Matthew kissed me again, longer and deeper, before going out the back door.

"I need a drink," Sarah groaned, heading to the porch to sneak a cigarette.

Matthew was nothing more than a shadow through the haze of Sarah's smoke as he passed through the orchard and headed for the hop barn. Hamish came up behind me, nudging my back and neck with his eyes.

"Are you fully recovered?" he asked quietly.

"What do you think?" It had been a long day, and Hamish made no effort to hide his disapproval of me. I shook my head.

Hamish's eyes drifted away, and mine followed. We both watched as Matthew's white hands streaked through his hair before he disappeared into the barn.

"'*Tiger, tiger, burning bright / In the forests of the night*,'" Hamish said, quoting William Blake. "That poem has always reminded me of him."

I rested my knife on the cutting board and faced him. "What's on your mind, Hamish?"

"Are you certain of him, Diana?" he asked. Em wiped her hands on her apron and left the room, giving me a sad look.

"Yes." I met his eyes, trying to make my confidence in Matthew clear.

Hamish nodded, unsurprised. "I did wonder if you would take him on, once you knew who he was—who he still is. It would seem you're not afraid to have a tiger by the tail."

Wordlessly I turned back to the counter and resumed my chopping.

"Be careful." Hamish rested his hand on my forearm, forcing me to look at him. "Matthew won't be the same man where you're going."

"Yes he will." I frowned. "My Matthew is going with me. He'll be exactly the same."

"No," Hamish said grimly. "He won't."

Hamish had known Matthew far longer. And he'd pieced together where we were going based on the contents of that briefcase. I still knew nothing, except that I was headed to a time before 1976 and a place where Matthew had played chess.

Hamish joined Sarah outside, and soon two plumes of gray smoke rose into the night sky.

"Is everything all right in there?" I asked Em when she returned from the family room, where Miriam, Marcus, Nathaniel, and Sophie were talking and watching TV.

"Yes," she replied. "And here?"

"Just fine." I focused on the apple trees and waited for Matthew to come in from the dark.

Chapter 41

The day before Halloween, a fluttery feeling developed in my stomach. Still in bed, I reached for Matthew.

"I'm nervous."

He closed the book he was reading and drew me near. "I know. You were nervous before you opened your eyes."

The house was already bustling with activity. Sarah's printer was churning out page after page in the office below. The television was on, and the dryer whined faintly in the distance as it protested under another load of laundry. One sniff told me that Sarah and Em were well into the day's coffee consumption, and down the hall there was the whir of a hair dryer.

"Are we the last ones up?" I made an effort to calm my stomach.

"I think so," he said with a smile, though there was a shadow of concern in his eyes.

Downstairs, Sarah was making eggs to order while Em pulled trays of muffins out of the oven. Nathaniel was methodically plucking one after another from the tin and popping them whole into his mouth.

"Where's Hamish?" Matthew asked.

"In my office, using the printer." Sarah gave him a long look and returned to her pan.

Marcus left his Scrabble game and came to the kitchen to take a walk with his father. He grabbed a handful of nuts as he left, sniffing the muffins with a groan of frustrated desire.

"What's going on?" I asked quietly.

"Hamish is being a lawyer," Sophie replied, spreading a thick layer of butter on top of a muffin. "He says there are papers to sign."

Hamish called us into the dining room in the late morning. We straggled in carrying wineglasses and mugs. He looked as though he hadn't slept. Neat stacks of paper were arranged across the table's expanse, along with sticks of black wax and two seals belonging to the Knights of Lazarus—one small, one large. My heart hit my stomach and bounced back into my throat.

"Should we sit?" Em asked. She'd brought in a fresh pot of coffee and topped off Hamish's mug.

"Thank you, Em," Hamish said gratefully. Two empty chairs sat officiously at the head of the table. He gestured Matthew and me into them and picked up the first stack of papers. "Yesterday afternoon we went over a number of practical issues related to the situation in which we now find ourselves."

My heart sped up, and I eyed the seals again.

"A little less lawyerly, Hamish, if you please," Matthew said, his hand tightening on my back. Hamish glowered at him and continued.

"Diana and Matthew will timewalk, as planned, on Halloween. Ignore everything else Matthew told you to do." Hamish took an obvious pleasure in delivering this part of his message. "We've agreed that it would be best if everyone . . . disappeared for a little while. As of this moment, your old lives are on hold."

Hamish put a document in front of me. "This is a power of attorney, Diana. It authorizes me—or whoever occupies the position of seneschal—to act legally on your behalf."

The power of attorney gave the abstract idea of timewalking a new sense of finality. Matthew fished a pen from his pocket.

"Here," he said, placing the pen before me.

The pen's nib wasn't used to the angle and pressure of my hand, and it scratched while I put my signature on the line. When I was finished, Matthew took it and dropped a warm black blob on the bottom, then reached for his personal seal and pressed it into the wax.

Hamish picked up the next stack. "These letters are for you to sign, too. One informs your conference organizers that you cannot speak in November. The other requests a medical leave for next year. Your physician—one Dr. Marcus Whitmore—has written in support. In the event you haven't returned by April, I'll send your request to Yale."

I read the letters carefully and signed with a shaking hand, relinquishing my life in the twenty-first century.

Hamish braced his hands against the edge of the table. Clearly he was building up to something. "There is no telling when Matthew and Diana will be back with us." He didn't use the word "if," but it hovered in the room nonetheless. "Whenever any member of the firm or of the de Clermont family is preparing to take a long journey or drop out of sight for a while, it's my job to make sure their affairs are in order. Diana, you have no will."

"No." My mind was entirely blank. "But I don't have any assets—not even a car."

Hamish straightened. "That's not entirely true, is it, Matthew?"

"Give it to me," Matthew said reluctantly. Hamish handed him a thick document. "This was drawn up when I was last in Oxford."

"Before La Pierre," I said, not touching the pages.

Matthew nodded. "Essentially, it's our marriage agreement. It irrevocably settles a third of my personal assets on you. Even if you were to leave me, these assets would be yours."

It was dated before he'd come home—before we were mated for life by vampire custom.

"I'll never leave you, and I don't want this."

"You don't even know what this is," Matthew said, putting the pages in front of me.

There was too much to absorb. Staggering sums of money, a town house on an exclusive square in London, a flat in Paris, a villa outside Rome, the Old Lodge, a house in Jerusalem, still more houses in cities like Venice and Seville, jets, cars—my mind whirled.

"I have a secure job." I pushed the papers away. "This is completely unnecessary."

"It's yours nonetheless," Matthew said gruffly.

Hamish let me gather my composure before he dropped his next bombshell. "If Sarah were to die, you would inherit this house, too, on the condition that it would be Emily's home for as long as she wanted it. And you're Matthew's sole heir. So you do have assets—and I need to know your wishes."

"I'm not going to talk about this." The memories of Satu and Juliette were still fresh, and death felt all too close. I stood, ready to bolt, but Matthew grabbed my hand and held fast.

"You need to do this, *mon coeur.* We cannot leave it for Marcus and Sarah to sort out."

I sat back down and thought quietly about what to do with the inconceivable fortune and ramshackle farmhouse that might one day be mine.

"My estate should be divided equally among our children," I said finally. "And that includes *all* of Matthew's children—vampire and biological, those he made himself and any that we might have together. They're to have the Bishop house, too, when Em's through with it."

"I'll see to it," Hamish assured me.

The only remaining documents on the table were hidden inside three envelopes. Two bore Matthew's seal. The other had black-and-silver ribbon wrapped around it, a lump of sealing wax covering the knot. Hanging from the ribbon was a thick black disk as big as a dessert plate that bore the impression of the great seal of the Knights of Lazarus.

"Finally we have the brotherhood to sort out. When Matthew's father founded the Knights of Lazarus, they were known for helping to protect those who could not protect themselves. Though most creatures have forgotten about us, we still exist. And we must continue to do so even after Matthew is gone. Tomorrow, before Marcus leaves the house, Matthew will officially give up his position in the order and appoint his son grand master."

Hamish handed Matthew the two envelopes bearing his personal seal. He then handed the envelope with the larger seal to Nathaniel. Miriam's eyes widened.

"As soon as Marcus accepts his new position, which he will do *immediately,*" Hamish said, giving Marcus a stern look, "he will phone Nathaniel, who has agreed to join the firm as one of the eight provincial masters. Once Nathaniel breaks the seal on this commission, he'll be a Knight of Lazarus."

"You can't keep making daemons like Hamish and Nathaniel members of the brotherhood! How is Nathaniel going to fight?" Miriam sounded aghast.

"With these," Nathaniel said, wiggling his fingers in the air. "I know computers, and I can do my part." His voice took on a fierce edge, and he gave Sophie an equally ferocious look. "No one is going to do to my wife or daughter what they've done to Diana."

There was stunned silence.

"That's not all." Hamish pulled up a chair and sat down, knitting his fingers together before him. "Miriam believes that there will be a war. I disagree. This war has already started."

Every eye on the room was directed at Hamish. It was clear why people wanted him to play a role in government—and why Matthew had made him his second in command. He was a born leader.

"In this room we understand why such a war might be fought. It's about Diana and the appalling lengths the Congregation will go to in an effort to understand the power she's inherited. It's about the discovery of Ashmole 782 and our fear that the book's secrets might be lost forever if it falls into the witches' hands. And it's about our common belief that no one has the right to tell two creatures that they cannot love each other—no matter what their species."

Hamish surveyed the room to make sure no one's attention had wandered before he continued.

"It won't be long before the humans are aware of this conflict. They'll be forced to acknowledge that daemons, vampires, and witches are among them. When that happens, we'll need to be Sophie's conventicle in fact, not just in name. There will be casualties, hysteria, and confusion. And it will be up to us—the conventicle and the Knights of Lazarus—to help them make sense of it all and to see to it that the loss of life and destruction are minimal."

"Ysabeau is waiting for you at Sept-Tours." Matthew's voice was quiet and steady. "The castle grounds may be the only territorial boundary other vampires won't dare to cross. Sarah and Emily will try to keep the witches in check. The Bishop name should help. And the Knights of Lazarus will protect Sophie and her baby."

"So we'll scatter," Sarah said, nodding at Matthew. "Then reconvene at the de Clermont house. And when we do, we'll figure out how to proceed. Together."

"Under Marcus's leadership." Matthew raised his half-full wineglass. "To Marcus, Nathaniel, and Hamish. Honor and long life."

"It's been a long time since I've heard that," Miriam said softly.

Marcus and Nathaniel both shied away from the attention and seemed uncomfortable with their new responsibilities. Hamish merely appeared weary.

After toasting the three men—all of whom looked far too young to have to worry about a long life—Em shepherded us into the kitchen for lunch. She laid out a feast on the island, and we milled around the family room, avoiding the moment when we would have to begin our good-byes.

Finally it was time for Sophie and Nathaniel to depart. Marcus put the couple's few belongings in the trunk of his little blue sports car. Marcus and Nathaniel stood, their two blond heads close in conversation, while Sophie said good-bye to Sarah and Em. When she was finished, she turned to me. I'd been banished to the keeping room to make sure that no one inadvertently touched me.

"This isn't really good-bye," she told me from across the hall.

My third eye opened, and in the winking of the sunlight on the banister I saw myself enveloped in one of Sophie's fierce hugs.

"No," I said, surprised and comforted by the vision.

Sophie nodded as if she, too, had seen the glimpse of the future. "See, I told you. Maybe the baby will be here when you get back. Remember, you'll be her godmother."

While waiting for Sophie and Nathaniel to say their good-byes, Matthew and Miriam had positioned all the pumpkins down the driveway. With a flick of her wrist and a few mumbled words, Sarah lit them. Dusk was still hours away, but Sophie could at least get a sense of what they would look like on Halloween night. She clapped her hands and tore down the steps to fling herself into the arms of Matthew and then Miriam. Her final hug was reserved for Marcus, who exchanged a few quiet words with her before tucking her into the low-slung passenger seat.

"Thanks for the car," Sophie said, admiring the burled wood on the dashboard. "Nathaniel used to drive fast, but he drives like an old lady now on account of the baby."

"No speeding," Matthew said firmly, sounding like a father. "Call us when you get home."

We waved them off. When they were out of sight Sarah extinguished the pumpkins. Matthew put his arms around me as the remaining family drifted back inside.

"I'm ready for you, Diana," Hamish said, coming out onto the porch. He'd already put on his jacket, prepared to leave for New York before returning to London.

I signed the two copies of the will, and they were witnessed by Em and Sarah. Hamish rolled up one copy and slid it into a metal cylinder. He threaded the ends of the tube with black-and-silver ribbons and sealed it with wax bearing Matthew's mark.

Matthew waited by the black rental car while Hamish said a courteous farewell to Miriam, then kissed Em and Sarah, inviting them to stay with him on their way to Sept-Tours.

"Call me if you need anything," he told Sarah, taking her hand and giving it a single squeeze. "You have my numbers." He turned to me.

"Good-bye, Hamish." I returned his kisses, first on one cheek, then the other. "Thank you for all you did to put Matthew's mind at ease."

"Just doing my job," Hamish said with forced cheerfulness. His voice dropped. "Remember what I told you. There will be no way to call for help if you need it."

"I won't need it," I said.

A few minutes later, the car's engine turned over and Hamish, too, was gone, red taillights blinking in the gathering darkness.

The house didn't like its new emptiness and responded by banging furniture around and moaning softly whenever anyone left or entered a room.

"I'll miss them," Em confessed while making dinner. The house sighed sympathetically.

"Go," Sarah said to me, taking the knife out of Em's hand. "Take Matthew to Sept-Tours and be back here in time to make the salad."

After much discussion we'd finally decided to timewalk to the night I'd found his copy of *Origin*.

But getting Matthew to Sept-Tours was more of a challenge than I'd expected. My arms were so full of stuff to help me steer—one of his pens and two books from his study—that Matthew had to hold on to my waist. Then we got stuck.

Invisible hands seemed to hold my foot up, refusing to let me lower it into Sept-Tours. The farther back in time we went, the thicker the strands were around my feet. And time clung to Matthew in sturdy, twining vines.

At last we made it to Matthew's study. The room was just as we'd left it, with the fire lit and an unlabeled bottle of wine waiting on the table.

I dropped the books and the pen on the sofa, shaking with fatigue.

"What's wrong?" Matthew asked.

"It was as if too many pasts were coming together, and it was impossible to wade through them. I was afraid you might let go."

"Nothing felt different to me," Matthew said. "It took a bit longer than before, but I expected that, given the time and distance."

He poured us both some wine, and we discussed the pros and cons of going downstairs. Finally, our desire to see Ysabeau and Marthe won out. Matthew remembered I'd been wearing my blue sweater. Its high neckline would hide my bandage, so I went upstairs to change.

When I came back down, his face broke into a slow, appreciative smile. "Just as beautiful now as then," he said, kissing me deeply. "Maybe more so."

"Be careful," I warned him with a laugh. "You hadn't decided you loved me yet."

"Oh, I'd decided," he said, kissing me again. "I just hadn't told you."

The women were sitting right where we expected them to be, Marthe with her murder mystery and Ysabeau with her newspapers. The conversation might not have been exactly the same, but it didn't seem to matter. The most difficult part of the evening was watching Matthew dance with his mother. The bittersweet expression on his face as he twirled her was new, and he definitely hadn't caught her up in a fierce bear hug when their dance was over. When he invited me to dance, I gave his hand an extra squeeze of sympathy.

"Thank you for this," he whispered in my ear as he whirled me around. He planted a soft kiss on my neck. That definitely hadn't happened the first time.

Matthew brought the evening to a close just as he had before, by announcing that he was taking me to bed. This time we said good night knowing that it was good-bye. Our return trip was much the same, but less frightening for its familiarity. I didn't panic or lose my concentration when time resisted our passage, focusing intently on the familiar rituals of making dinner in the Bishop house. We were back in plenty of time to make the salad.

During dinner Sarah and Em regaled the vampires with tales of my adventures growing up. When my aunts ran out of stories, Matthew teased Marcus about his disastrous real-estate deals in the nineteenth century, the enormous investments he'd made in new technologies in the twentieth century that had never panned out, and his perpetual weakness for redheaded women.

"I knew I liked you." Sarah smoothed down her own unruly red mop and poured him more whiskey.

Halloween dawned clear and bright. Snow was always a possibility in this neck of the woods, but this year the weather looked encouraging. Matthew and Marcus took a longer walk than usual, and I lingered over tea and coffee with Sarah and Em.

When the phone rang, we all jumped. Sarah answered it, and we could tell from her half of the conversation that the call was unexpected.

She hung up and joined us at the table in the family room, which was once again big enough to seat all of us. "That was Faye. She and Janet are at the Hunters'. In their RV. They want to know if we'll join them on their fall trip. They're driving to Arizona, then up to Seattle."

"The goddess has been busy," Em said with a smile. The two of them had been trying for days to decide how they would extricate themselves from Madison without setting off a flurry of gossip. "I guess that settles it. We'll hit the road, then go meet Ysabeau."

We carried bags of food and other supplies to Sarah's beat-up old car. When it was fully loaded and you could barely see out the rearview mirror, they started issuing orders.

"The candy's on the counter," Em instructed. "And my costume is hanging on the back of the stillroom door. It will fit you fine. Don't forget the stockings. The kids love the stockings."

"I won't forget them," I assured her, "or the hat, though it's perfectly ridiculous."

"Of course you'll wear the hat!" Sarah said indignantly. "It's tradition. Make sure the fire is out before you leave. Tabitha is fed at four o'clock sharp. If she isn't, she'll start barfing."

"We've got this covered. You left a list," I said, patting her on the shoulder.

"Can you call us at the Hunters', let us know Miriam and Marcus have left?" Em asked.

"Here. Take this," Matthew said, handing them his phone with a lopsided smile. "You call Marcus yourself. There won't be reception where we're going."

"Are you sure?" Em asked doubtfully. We all thought of Matthew's phone as an extra limb, and it was strange to see it out of his hand.

"Absolutely. Most of the data has been erased, but I've left some contact numbers on it for you. If you need anything—anything at all—call someone. If you feel worried or if something strange happens, get in touch with Ysabeau or Hamish. They'll arrange for you to be picked up, no matter where you are."

"They have helicopters," I murmured to Em, slipping my arm through hers.

Marcus's phone rang. "Nathaniel," he said, looking at the screen. Then he stepped away to finish his call in a new gesture of privacy, one that was identical to what his father always did.

With a sad smile, Matthew watched his son. "Those two will get themselves into all kinds of trouble, but at least Marcus won't feel so alone."

"They're fine," Marcus said, turning back to us and disconnecting the phone. He smiled and ran his fingers through his hair in another gesture reminiscent of Matthew. "I should let Hamish know, so I'll say my goodbyes and call him."

Em held on to Marcus for a long time, her eyes spilling over. "Call us, too," she told him fiercely. "We'll want to know that you're both all right."

"Be safe." Sarah's eyes scrunched tight as she gathered him in her arms. "Don't doubt yourself."

Miriam's farewell to my aunts was more composed, my own far less so.

"We're very proud of you," Em said, cupping my face in her hands, tears now streaming down her face. "Your parents would be, too. Take care of each other."

"We will," I assured her, dashing the tears away.

Sarah took my hands in hers. "Listen to your teachers—whoever they are. Don't say no without hearing them out first." I nodded. "You've got more natural talent than any witch I've ever seen—maybe more than any witch who's lived for many, many years," Sarah continued. "I'm glad you're not going to waste it. Magic is a gift, Diana, just like love." She turned to Matthew. "I'm trusting you with something precious. Don't disappoint me."

"I won't, Sarah," Matthew promised.

She accepted our kisses, then bolted down the steps to the waiting car.

"Good-byes are hard for Sarah," Em explained. "We'll talk to you tomorrow, Marcus." She climbed into the front seat, waving over her shoulder. The car spluttered to life, bumped its way across the ruts in the driveway, and turned toward town.

When we went back into the house, Miriam and Marcus were waiting in the front hall, bags at their feet.

"We thought you two should have some time alone," Miriam said, handing her duffel bag to Marcus, "and I hate long good-byes." She looked around. "Well," she said briskly, heading down the porch stairs, "see you when you get back."

After shaking his head at Miriam's retreating figure, Matthew went into the dining room and returned with an envelope. "Take it," he said to Marcus, his voice gruff.

"I never wanted to be grand master," Marcus said.

"You think I did? This was my father's dream. Philippe made me promise the brotherhood wouldn't fall into Baldwin's hands. I'm asking you to do the same."

"I promise." Marcus took the envelope. "I wish you didn't have to go."

"I'm sorry, Marcus." I swallowed the lump in my throat and rested my warm fingers lightly on his cold flesh.

"For what?" His smile was bright and true. "For making my father happy?"

"For putting you in this position and leaving behind such a mess."

"I'm not afraid of war, if that's what you mean. It's following along in Matthew's wake that worries me." Marcus cracked the seal. With that deceptively insignificant snap of wax, he became the grand master of the Knights of Lazarus.

"*Je suis à votre commande, seigneur*," Matthew murmured, his head bowed. Baldwin had spoken the same words at La Guardia. They sounded so different when they were sincere.

"Then I command you to return and take back the Knights of Lazarus," Marcus said roughly, "before I make a complete hash of things. I'm not French, and I'm certainly no knight."

"You have more than a drop of French blood in you, and you're the only person I trust to do the job. Besides, you can rely on your famous American charm. And it is possible you might like being grand master in the end."

Marcus snorted and punched the number eight on his phone. "It's done," he said briefly to the person on the other end. There was a short exchange of words. "Thank you."

"Nathaniel has accepted his position," Matthew murmured, the corners of his mouth twitching. "His French is surprisingly good."

Marcus scowled at his father, walked away to say a few more words to the daemon, and returned.

Between father and son there was a long look, the clasp of hand to elbow, the press of a hand on the back—a pattern of leave-taking based on hundreds of similar farewells. For me there was a gentle kiss, a murmured "Be well," and then Marcus, too, was gone.

I reached for Matthew's hand.

We were alone.

Chapter 42

It's just us and the ghosts now." My stomach rumbled.

"What's your favorite food?" he asked.

"Pizza," I said promptly.

"You should have it while you can. Order some, and we'll pick it up."

We hadn't been beyond the immediate environs of the Bishop house since our arrival, and it felt strange to be driving around the greater Madison area in a Range Rover next to a vampire. We took the back way to Hamilton, passing south over the hills into town before swinging north again to get the pizza. During the drive I pointed out where I'd gone swimming as a child and where my first real boyfriend had lived. The town was covered with Halloween decorations—black cats, witches on brooms, even trees decorated in orange and black eggs. In this part of the world, it wasn't just witches who took the celebration seriously.

When we arrived at the pizza place, Matthew climbed out with me, seemingly unconcerned that witches or humans might see us. I stretched up to kiss him, and he returned it with a laugh that was almost lighthearted.

The college student who rang us up looked at Matthew with obvious admiration when she handed him the pie.

"Good thing she isn't a witch," I said when we got back into the car. "She would have turned me into a newt and flown off with you on her broomstick."

Fortified with pizza—pepperoni and mushroom—I tackled the mess left in the kitchen and the family room. Matthew brought out handfuls of paper from the dining room and burned them in the kitchen fireplace.

"What do we do with these?" he asked, holding up my mother's letter, the mysterious three-line epigram, and the page from Ashmole 782.

"Leave them in the keeping room," I told him. "The house will take care of them."

I continued to putter, doing laundry and straightening up Sarah's office. It was not until I went up to put our clothes away that I noticed both computers were missing. I went pounding downstairs in a panic.

"Matthew! The computers are gone!"

"Hamish has them," he said, catching me in his arms and smoothing my hair against the back of my head. "It's all right. No one's been in the house."

My shoulders sagged, heart still hammering at the idea of being surprised by another Domenico or Juliette.

He made tea, then rubbed my feet while I drank it. All the while he talked about nothing important—houses in Hamilton that had reminded him of some other place and time, his first sniff of a tomato, what he thought when he'd seen me row in Oxford—until I relaxed into the warmth and comfort.

Matthew was always different when no one else was around, but the contrast was especially marked now that our families had left. Since arriving at the Bishop house, he'd gradually taken on the responsibility for eight other lives. He'd watched over all of them, regardless of who they were or how they were related to him, with the same ferocious intensity. Now he had only one creature to manage.

"We haven't had much time to just talk," I reflected, thinking of the whirlwind of days since we'd met. "Not just the two of us."

"The past weeks have been almost biblical in their tests. I think the only thing we've escaped is a plague of locusts." He paused. "But if the universe does want to test us the old-fashioned way, this counts as the end of our trial. It will be forty days this evening."

So little time, for so much to have happened.

I put my empty mug on the table and reached for his hands. "Where are we going, Matthew?"

"Can you wait a little longer, *mon coeur*?" He looked out the window. "I want this day to last. And it will be dark soon enough."

"You like playing house with me." A piece of hair had fallen onto his forehead, and I brushed it back.

"I love playing house with you," he said, capturing my hand.

We talked quietly for another half hour, before Matthew glanced outdoors again. "Go upstairs and take a bath. Use every drop of water in the tank and take a long, hot shower, too. You may crave pizza every now and then in the days to come. But that will be nothing compared to your longing for hot water. In a few weeks, you will cheerfully commit murder for a shower."

Matthew brought up my Halloween costume while I bathed: a calf-length black dress with a high neck, sharp-toed boots, and a pointy hat.

"What, may I ask, are these?" He brandished a pair of stockings with red and white horizontal stripes.

"Those are the stockings Em mentioned." I groaned. "She'll know if I don't wear them."

"If I still had my phone, I would take a picture of you in these hideous things and blackmail you for eternity."

"Is there anything that would ensure your silence?" I sank lower into the tub.

"I'm sure there is," Matthew said, tossing the stockings behind him.

We were playful at first. As at dinner last night, and again at breakfast, we carefully avoided mentioning that this might be our last chance to be together. I was still a novice, but Em told me even the most experienced timewalkers respected the unpredictability of moving between past and future and recognized how easy it would be to wander indefinitely within the spiderweb of time.

Matthew sensed my changing mood and answered it first with greater gentleness, then with a fierce possessiveness that demanded I think of nothing but him.

Despite our obvious need for comfort and reassurance, we didn't consummate our marriage.

"When we're safe," he'd murmured, kissing me along my collarbone. "When there's more time."

Somewhere along the way, my smallpox blister burst. Matthew examined it and pronounced that it was doing nicely—an odd description for an angry open wound the size of a dime. He removed the bandage from my neck, revealing the barest trace of Miriam's sutures, and the one from my arm as well.

"You're a fast healer," he said approvingly, kissing the inside of my elbow where he'd drunk from my veins. His lips felt warm against my skin.

"How odd. My skin is cold there." I touched my neck. "Here, too."

Matthew drew his thumb across the spot where my carotid artery passed close to the surface. I shivered at his touch. The number of nerve endings there had seemingly tripled.

"Extra sensitivity," Matthew said, "as if you're part vampire." He bent and put his lips against my pulse.

"Oh," I gasped, taken aback at the intensity of feeling.

Mindful of the time, I buttoned myself into the black dress. With a braid down my back, I might have stepped out of a photograph from the turn of the nineteenth century.

"Too bad we're not timewalking to World War I," Matthew said, pulling at the sleeves of the dress. "You'd make a convincing schoolmistress circa 1912 in that getup."

"Not with these on." I sat on the bed and started pulling on the candy-striped stockings.

Matthew roared with laughter and begged me to put the hat on immediately.

"I'll set fire to myself," I protested. "Wait until the jack-o'-lanterns are lit."

We went outside with matches, thinking we could light the pumpkins the human way. A breeze had kicked up, though, which made it difficult to strike the matches and impossible to keep the candles illuminated.

"Damn it," I swore. "Sophie's work shouldn't go to waste."

"Can you use a spell?" Matthew said, already prepared to have another go at the matchbox.

"If not, then I have no business even pretending to be a witch on Halloween." The mere thought of explaining my failure to Sophie made me concentrate on the task at hand, and the wick burst into life. I lit the other eleven pumpkins that were scattered down the drive, each more amazing or terrifying than the last.

At six o'clock there was a fierce pounding on the door and muffled cries of "Trick or treat!" Matthew had never experienced an American Halloween, and he eagerly greeted our first visitors.

Whoever was outside received one of his heart-stopping smiles before Matthew grinned and beckoned me forward.

A tiny witch and a slightly larger vampire were holding hands on the front porch.

"Trick or treat," they intoned, holding out their open pillowcases.

"I'm a vampire," the boy said, baring his fangs at Matthew. He pointed to his sister. "She's a witch."

"I can see that," Matthew said gravely, taking in the black cape and white makeup. "I'm a vampire, too."

The boy examined him critically. "Your mother should have worked harder on your costume. You don't look like a vampire at all. Where's your cape?" The miniature vampire swept his arms up, a fold of his own satin cape in each fist, revealing its bat-shaped wings. "See, you need your cape to fly. Otherwise you can't turn into a bat."

"Ah. That is a problem. My cape is at home, and now I can't fly back and get it. Perhaps I can borrow yours." Matthew dumped a handful of candy into each pillowcase, the eyes of both children growing large at his generosity. I peeked around the door to wave at their parents.

"You can tell she's a witch," the girl piped up, nodding approvingly at my red-and-white-striped stockings and black boots. At their parents' urging, they shouted thank-yous as they trotted down the walk and climbed into the waiting car.

Over the next three hours, we greeted a steady stream of fairy princesses, pirates, ghosts, skeletons, mermaids, and space aliens, along with still more witches and vampires. I gently told Matthew that one piece of candy per goblin was de rigueur and that if he didn't stop distributing handfuls of goodies now, we would run out long before the trick-or-treating stopped at nine o'clock.

It was hard to criticize, however, given his obvious delight. His responses to the children who came to the door revealed a wholly new side of him. Crouching down so that he was less intimidating, he asked questions about their costumes and told every young boy purporting to be a vampire that he was the most frightening creature he'd ever beheld.

But it was his encounter with one fairy princess wearing an oversize set of wings and a gauze skirt that tugged hardest at my heart. Overwhelmed and exhausted by the occasion, she burst into tears when Matthew asked which piece of candy she wanted. Her brother, a strapping young pirate aged six, dropped her hand in horror.

"We shall ask your mother." Matthew swept the fairy princess into his arms and grabbed the pirate by the back of his bandanna. He safely delivered both children into the waiting arms of their parents. Long before reaching them, however, the fairy princess had forgotten her tears. Instead she had one sticky hand wrapped in the collar of Matthew's sweater and was tapping him lightly on the head with her wand, repeating, "Bippity, boppity, BOO!"

"When she grows up and thinks about Prince Charming, he'll look just like you," I told him after he returned to the house. A shower of silver glitter fell as he dipped his head for a kiss. "You're covered with fairy dust," I said, laughing and brushing the last of it from his hair.

Around eight o'clock, when the tide of fairy princesses and pirates turned to Gothic teenagers wearing black lipstick and leather garments festooned with chains, Matthew handed me the basket of candy and retreated to the keeping room.

"Coward," I teased, straightening my hat before answering the door to another gloomy bunch.

Only three minutes before it would be safe to turn out the porch light without ruining the Bishops' Halloween reputation, we heard another loud knock and a bellowed "Trick or treat!"

"Who can that be?" I groaned, slamming my hat back on my head.

Two young wizards stood on the front steps. One was the paperboy. He was accompanied by a lanky teenager with bad skin and a pierced nose, whom I recognized dimly as belonging to the O'Neil clan. Their costumes, such as they were, consisted of torn jeans, safety-pinned T-shirts, fake blood, plastic teeth, and lengths of dog leash.

"Aren't you a bit old for this, Sammy?"

"It'th Tham now." Sammy's voice was breaking, full of unexpected ups and downs, and his prosthetic fangs gave him a lisp.

"Hello, Sam." There were half a dozen pieces in the bottom of the candy basket. "You're welcome to what's left. We were just about to put out the lights. Shouldn't you be at the Hunters' house, bobbing for apples?"

"We heard your pumpkinth were really cool thith year." Sammy shifted from one foot to the other. "And, uh, well . . ." He flushed and took out his plastic teeth. "Rob swore he saw a vampire here the other day. I bet him twenty bucks the Bishops wouldn't let one in the house."

"What makes you so sure you'd recognize a vampire if you saw one?"

The vampire in question came out of the keeping room and stood behind me. "Gentlemen," he said quietly. Two adolescent jaws dropped.

"We'd have to be either human or really stupid not to recognize him," said Rob, awestruck. "He's the biggest vampire I've ever seen."

"Cool." Sammy grinned from ear to ear. He high-fived his friend and grabbed the candy.

"Don't forget to pay up, Sam," I said sternly.

"And, Samuel," Matthew said, his French accent unusually pronounced, "could I ask you—as a favor to me—not to tell anyone else about this?"

"Ever?" Sammy was incredulous at the notion of keeping such a juicy piece of information to himself.

Matthew's mouth twitched. "No. I see your point. Can you keep quiet until tomorrow?"

"Sure!" Sammy nodded, looking to Rob for confirmation. "That's only three hours. We can do that. No problem."

They got on their bikes and headed off.

"The roads are dark," Matthew said with a frown of concern. "We should drive them."

"They'll be fine. They're not vampires, but they can definitely find their way to town."

The two bikes skidded to a halt, sending up a shower of loose gravel.

"You want us to turn off the pumpkins?" Sammy shouted from the driveway.

"If you want to," I said. "Thanks!"

Rob O'Neil waved at the left side of the driveway and Sammy at the right, extinguishing all the jack-o'-lanterns with enviable casualness. The two boys rode off, their bikes bumping over the ruts, their progress made easier by the moon and the burgeoning sixth sense of the teenage witch.

I shut the door and leaned against it, groaning. "My feet are killing me." I unlaced my boots and kicked them off, tossing the hat onto the steps.

"The page from Ashmole 782 is gone," Matthew announced quietly, leaning against the banister post.

"Mom's letter?"

"Also gone."

"It's time, then." I pulled myself away from the old door, and the house moaned softly.

"Make yourself some tea and meet me in the family room. I'll get the bag."

He waited for me on the couch, the soft-sided briefcase sitting closed at his feet and the silver chess piece and gold earring lying on the coffee table. I handed him a glass of wine and sat alongside. "That's the last of the wine."

Matthew eyed my tea. "And that's the last of the tea for you as well." He ran his hands nervously through his hair and took a deep breath. "I would have liked to go sometime closer, when there was less death and disease," he began, sounding tentative, "and *somewhere* closer, with tea and plumbing. But I think you'll like it once you get used to it."

I still didn't know when or where "it" was.

Matthew bent down to undo the lock. When he opened the bag and saw what was on top, he let out a sigh of relief. "Thank God. I was afraid Ysabeau might have sent the wrong one."

"You haven't opened the bag yet?" I was amazed at his self-control.

"No." Matthew lifted out a book. "I didn't want to think about it too much. Just in case."

He handed me the book. It had black leather bindings with simple silver borders.

"It's beautiful," I said, running my fingers over its surface.

"Open it." Matthew looked anxious.

"Will I know where we're going once I do?" Now that the third object was in my hands, I felt strangely reluctant.

"I think so."

The front cover creaked open, and the unmistakable scent of old paper and ink rose in the air. There were no marbled endpapers, no bookplates, no additional blank sheets such as eighteenth- and nineteenth-century collectors put in their books. And the covers were heavy, indicating that wooden boards were concealed beneath the smoothly stretched leather.

Two lines were written in thick black ink on the first page, in a tight, spiky script of the late sixteenth century.

"'*To my own sweet Matt,*'" I read aloud. "'*Who ever loved, that loved not at first sight?*'"

The dedication was unsigned, but it was familiar.

"Shakespeare?" I lifted my eyes to Matthew.

"Not originally," he replied, his face tense. "Will was something of a magpie when it came to collecting other people's words."

I slowly turned the page.

It wasn't a printed book but a manuscript, written in the same bold hand as the inscription. I looked closer to make out the words.

> Settle thy studies, Faustus, and begin
> To sound the depth of that thou wilt profess.

"Jesus," I said hoarsely, clapping the book shut. My hands were shaking.

"He'll laugh like a fool when he hears that was your reaction," Matthew commented.

"Is this what I think it is?"

"Probably."

"How did you get it?"

"Kit gave it to me." Matthew touched the cover lightly. "*Faustus* was always my favorite."

Every historian of alchemy knew Christopher Marlowe's play about Dr. Faustus, who sold his soul to the devil in exchange for magical knowledge and power. I opened the book and ran my fingers over the inscription while Matthew continued.

"Kit and I were friends—good friends—in a dangerous time when there were few creatures you could trust. We raised a certain amount of hell and eyebrows. When Sophie pulled the chess piece I'd lost to him from her pocket, it seemed clear that England was our destination."

The feeling my fingertips detected in the inscription was not friendship, however. This was a lover's dedication.

"Were you in love with him, too?" I asked quietly.

"No," Matthew said shortly. "I loved Kit, but not the way you mean, and not in the way he wanted. Left to Kit, things would have been different. But it wasn't up to him, and we were never more than friends."

"Did he know what you are?" I hugged the book to my chest like a priceless treasure.

"Yes. We couldn't afford secrets. Besides, he was a daemon, and an unusually perceptive one at that. You'll soon discover it's pointless trying to keep anything from Kit."

That Christopher Marlowe was a daemon made a certain sense, based on my limited knowledge of him.

"So we're going to England," I said slowly. "When, exactly?"

"To 1590."

"Where?"

"Every year a group of us met at the Old Lodge for the old Catholic holidays of All Saints and All Souls. Few dared to celebrate them, but it made Kit feel daring and dangerous to commemorate them in some way. He would read us his latest draft of *Faustus*—he was always fiddling with it, never satisfied. We'd drink too much, play chess, and stay awake until dawn." Matthew drew the manuscript from my arms. He rested it on the table and took my hands in his. "Is this all right with you, *mon coeur*? We don't have to go. We can think of sometime else."

But it was already too late. The historian in me had started to process the opportunities of life in Elizabethan England.

"There are alchemists in England in 1590."

"Yes," he said warily. "None of them particularly pleasant to be around, given the mercury poisoning and their strange work habits. More important, Diana, there are witches—powerful witches, who can guide your magic."

"Will you take me to the playhouses?"

"Could I keep you from them?" Matthew's brows rose.

"Probably not." My imagination was caught by the prospect opening before us. "Can we walk through the Royal Exchange? After they light the lamps?"

"Yes." He drew me into his arms. "And go to St. Paul's to hear a sermon, and to Tyburn for an execution. We'll even chat about the inmates with the clerk at Bedlam." His body shook with suppressed laughter. "Good Lord, Diana. I'm taking you to a time when there was plague, few comforts, no tea, and bad dentistry, and all you can think about is what Gresham's Exchange looked like at night."

I pulled back to look at him with excitement. "Will I meet the queen?"

"Absolutely not." Matthew pressed me to him with a shudder. "The mere thought of what you might say to Elizabeth Tudor—and she to you—makes my heart falter."

"Coward," I said for the second time that night.

"You wouldn't say so if you knew her better. She eats courtiers for breakfast." Matthew paused. "Besides, there's something else we can do in 1590."

"What's that?"

"Somewhere in 1590 there's an alchemical manuscript that will one day be owned by Elias Ashmole. We might look for it."

"The manuscript might be complete then, its magic unbroken." I extricated myself from his arms and sat back against the cushions, staring in wonder at the three objects on the coffee table. "We're really going to go back in time."

"We are. Sarah told me we had to be careful not to take anything modern into the past. Marthe made you a smock and me a shirt." Matthew reached into the briefcase again and pulled out two plain linen garments with long sleeves and strings at the neck. "She had to sew them by hand, and she didn't have much time. They're not fancy, but at least we won't shock whomever we first meet."

He shook them out, and a small, black velvet bag fell from their linen folds.

Matthew frowned. "What's this?" he said, picking it up. A note was pinned to the outside. He opened it. "From Ysabeau. '*This was an anniversary gift from your father. I thought you might like to give it to Diana. It will look old-fashioned but will suit her hand.*'"

The bag held a ring made of three separate gold bands twisted together. The two outer bands were fashioned into ornate sleeves, colored with enamel and studded with small jewels to resemble embroidery. A golden hand curved out of each sleeve, perfectly executed down to the tiny bones, slender tendons, and minute fingernails.

Clasped between the two hands, on the inner ring, was a huge stone that looked like glass. It was clear and unfaceted, set in a golden bezel with a black painted background. No jeweler would put a hunk of glass in a ring so fine. It was a diamond.

"That belongs in a museum, not on my finger." I was mesmerized by the lifelike hands and tried not to think about the weight of the stone they held.

"My mother used to wear it all the time," Matthew said, picking it up between his thumb and index finger. "She called it her scribble ring because she could write on glass with the point of the diamond." His keen eyes saw some detail of the ring that mine did not. With a twist of the golden hands, the three rings fanned out in his palm. Each band was engraved, the words twining around the flat surfaces.

We peered at the tiny writing.

"They're poesies—verses that people wrote as tokens of affection. This one says '*a ma vie de coer entier,*'" Matthew said, the tip of his index finger touching the gold surface. "It's old French for 'my whole heart for my whole life.' And this, '*mon debut et ma fin,*' with an alpha and an omega."

My French was good enough to translate that—"my beginning and my end."

"What's on the inner band?"

"It's engraved on both sides." Matthew read the lines, turning the rings over as he did so. "'*Se souvenir du passe, et qu'il ya un avenir.*' 'Remember the past, and that there is a future.'"

"The poesies suit us perfectly." It was eerie that Philippe had selected verses for Ysabeau so long ago that could have meaning for Matthew and me today.

"Vampires are also timewalkers of a sort." Matthew fitted the ring together. He took my left hand and looked away, afraid of my reaction. "Will you wear it?"

I took his chin in my fingers, turning his head toward me, and nodded, quite unable to speak. Matthew's face turned shy, and his eyes dropped to my hand, still held in his. He slid the ring over my thumb so it rested just above the knuckle.

"With this ring I thee wed, and with my body I thee honor." Matthew's voice was quiet, and it shook just a bit. He moved the ring deliberately to my index finger, sliding it down until it met the middle joint. "And with all my worldly goods I thee endow." The ring skipped over my middle finger and slid home onto the fourth finger of my left hand. "In the name of the Father, and of the Son, and of the Holy Spirit." He raised my hand to his mouth and his eyes to mine once more, cold lips pressing the ring into my skin. "Amen."

"Amen," I repeated. "So now we're married in the eyes of vampires and according to church law." The ring felt heavy, but Ysabeau was right. It did suit me.

"In your eyes, too, I hope." Matthew sounded uncertain.

"Of course we're married in my eyes." Something of my happiness must have shown, because his answering smile was as broad and heartfelt as any I'd seen.

"Let's see if *Maman* sent more surprises." He dove back into the briefcase and came up with a few more books. There was another note, also from Ysabeau.

"'*These were next to the manuscript you asked for,*'" Matthew read. "'*I sent them, too—just in case.*'"

"Are they also from 1590?"

"No," Matthew said, his voice thoughtful, "none of them." He reached into the bag again. When his hand emerged, it was clutching the silver pilgrim's badge from Bethany.

There was no note to explain why it was there.

The clock in the front hall struck ten. We were due to leave—soon.

"I wish I knew why she sent these." Matthew sounded worried.

"Maybe she thought we should carry other things that were precious to you." I knew how strong his attachment was to the tiny silver coffin.

"Not if it makes it harder for you to concentrate on 1590." He glanced at the ring on my left hand, and I closed my fingers. There was no way he was taking it off, whether it was from 1590 or not.

"We could call Sarah and ask her what she thinks."

Matthew shook his head. "No. Let's not trouble her. We know what we need to do—take three objects and nothing else from the past or present that might get in the way. We'll make an exception for the ring, now that it's on your finger." He opened the top book and froze.

"What is it?"

"My annotations are in this book—and I don't remember putting them there."

"It's more than four hundred years old. Maybe you forgot." In spite of my words, a cold finger ran up my spine.

Matthew flipped through a few more pages and inhaled sharply. "If we leave these books in the keeping room, along with the pilgrim's badge, will the house take care of them?"

"It will if we ask it to," I said. "Matthew, what's going on?"

"I'll tell you later. We should go. These," he said, lifting the books and Lazarus's coffin, "need to stay here."

We changed in silence. I took off everything down to my bare skin, shivering as the linen smock slipped over my shoulders. The cuffs skimmed my wrists as it fell to my ankles, and the wide neck drew closed when I tugged on the string.

Matthew was out of his clothes and into his shirt quickly. It nearly reached his knees, and his long white legs stuck out below. While I collected our clothes, Matthew went to the dining room and came out with stationery and one of his favorite pens. His hand sped across the page, and he folded the single sheet and tucked it into the waiting envelope.

"A note for Sarah," he explained. "We'll ask the house to take care of that, too."

We carried the extra books, the note, and the pilgrim's badge to the keeping room. Mathew put them carefully on the sofa.

"Shall we leave the lights on?" Matthew asked.

"No," I said. "Just the porch light, in case it's still dark when they come home."

There was a smudge of green when we turned off the lamps. It was my grandmother, rocking in her chair.

"Good-bye, Grandma." Neither Bridget Bishop nor Elizabeth was with her.

Good-bye, Diana.

"The house needs to take care of those." I pointed to the pile of objects on the sofa.

Don't worry about a thing except for where you're going.

Slowly we walked the length of the house to the back door, shutting off lights as we went. In the family room, Matthew picked up *Doctor Faustus,* the earring, and the chess piece.

I looked around one last time at the familiar brown kitchen. "Good-bye, house."

Tabitha heard my voice and ran screeching from the stillroom. She came to an abrupt halt and stared at us without blinking.

"Good-bye, *ma petite,*" Matthew said, stooping to scratch her ears.

We'd decided to leave from the hop barn. It was quiet, with no vestiges of modern life to serve as distractions. We moved through the apple orchard and over the frost-covered grass in our bare feet, the cold quickening our steps. When Matthew pulled open the barn door, my breath was visible in the chilly air.

"It's freezing." I drew my smock closer, teeth chattering.

"There will be a fire when we arrive at the Old Lodge," he said, handing me the earring.

I put the thin wire through the hole in my ear and held my hand out for the goddess. Matthew dropped her into my palm.

"What else?"

"Wine, of course—red wine." Matthew handed me the book and folded me into his arms, planting a firm kiss on my forehead.

"Where are your rooms?" I shut my eyes, remembering the Old Lodge.

"Upstairs, on the western side of the courtyard, overlooking the deer park."

"And what will it smell like?"

"Like home," he said. "Wood smoke and roasted meat from the servants' dinner, beeswax from the candles, and the lavender used to keep the linens fresh."

"Can you hear anything special?"

"Nothing at all. Just the bells from St. Mary's and St. Michael's, the crackle of the fires, and the dogs snoring on the stairs."

"How do you feel when you're there?" I asked, concentrating on his words and the way they in turn made me feel.

"I've always felt . . . ordinary at the Old Lodge," Matthew said softly. "It's a place where I can be myself."

A whiff of lavender swirled through the air, out of time and place in a Madison hop barn in October. I marveled at the scent and thought of my father's note. My eyes were fully open to the possibilities of magic now.

"What will we do tomorrow?"

"We'll walk in the park," he said, his voice a murmur and his arms iron bands around my ribs. "If the weather's fine, we'll go riding. There won't be much in the gardens this time of year. There must be a lute somewhere. I'll teach you to play, if you'd like."

Another scent—spicy and sweet—joined with the lavender, and I saw a tree laden with heavy, golden fruit. A hand stretched up, and a diamond winked in the sunlight, but the fruit was out of reach. I felt frustration and the keen edge of desire, and I was reminded of Emily's telling me that magic was in the heart as well as the mind.

"Is there a quince in the garden?"

"Yes," Matthew said, his mouth against my hair. "The fruit will be ripe now."

The tree dissolved, though the honeyed scent remained. Now I saw a shallow silver dish sitting on a long wooden table. Candles and firelight were reflected in its burnished surface. Piled inside the dish were the bright yellow quinces that were the source of the scent. My fingers flexed on the cover of the book I held in the present, but in my mind they closed on a piece of fruit in the past.

"I can smell the quinces." Our new life in the Old Lodge was already calling to me. "Remember, don't let go—no matter what." With the past everywhere around me, the possibility of losing him was all that was frightening.

"Never," he said firmly.

"And lift up your foot and then put it down again when I tell you."

He chuckled. "I love you, *ma lionne*." It was an unusual response, but it was enough.

Home, I thought.

My heart tugged with longing.

An unfamiliar bell tolled the hour.

There was a warm touch of fire against my skin.

The air filled with scents of lavender, beeswax, and ripe quince.

"It's time." Together we lifted our feet and stepped into the unknown.

Chapter 43

The house was unnaturally quiet.

For Sarah it wasn't just the absence of chatter or the removal of seven active minds that made it seem so empty.

It was not knowing.

They'd come home earlier than usual from the coven's gathering, claiming they needed to pack for Faye and Janet's road trip. Em had found the empty briefcase sitting by the family-room couch, and Sarah had discovered the clothes bundled up on top of the washing machine.

"They're gone," Em had said.

Sarah went straight into her arms, her shoulders shaking.

"Are they all right?" she'd whispered.

"They're together," Em had replied. It wasn't the answer Sarah wanted, but it was honest, just like Em.

They'd thrown their own clothes into duffel bags, paying little attention to what they were doing. Now Tabitha and Em were already in the RV, and Faye and Janet were waiting patiently for Sarah to close up the house.

Sarah and the vampire had talked for hours in the stillroom on their last night in the house, sharing a bottle of red wine. Matthew had told her something of his past and shared his fears for the future. Sarah had listened, making an effort not to show her own shock and surprise at some of the tales he told. Though she was pagan, Sarah understood he wanted to make confession and had cast her in the role of priest. She had given him the absolution she could, knowing all the while that some deeds could never be forgiven or forgotten.

But there was one secret he'd refused to share, and Sarah still knew nothing of where and when her niece had gone.

The floorboards of the Bishop house creaked a chorus of groans and wheezes as Sarah walked through the familiar, darkened rooms. She closed the keeping-room doors and turned to bid farewell to the only home she'd ever known.

The keeping-room doors opened with a sharp bang. One of the floorboards near the fireplace sprang up, revealing a small, black-bound book and a creamy envelope. It was the brightest thing in the room, and it gleamed in the moonlight.

Sarah muffled a cry and held out her hand. The cream square flew easily into it, landed with a slight smack, and flipped over. A single word was written on it.

"Sarah."

She touched the letters lightly and saw Matthew's long white fingers. She tore at the paper, her heart beating fast.

"Sarah," it said. *"Don't worry. We made it."*

Her heart rate calmed.

Sarah put the single sheet of paper on her mother's rocking chair and gestured for the book. Once the house delivered it, the floorboard returned to its normal resting place with a groan of old wood and the shriek of old nails.

She flipped to the first page. *The Shadow of Night, Containing Two Poeticall Hymnes devised by G. C. gent. 1594.* The book smelled old but not unpleasant, like incense in a dusty cathedral.

Just like Matthew, Sarah thought with a smile.

A slip of paper stuck out of the top. It led her to the dedication page. *"To my deare and most worthy friend Matthew Roydon."* Sarah peered more closely and saw a tiny, faded drawing of a hand with a ruffled cuff pointing imperiously to the name, with the number *"29"* written underneath in ancient brown ink.

She turned obediently to page twenty-nine, struggling through tears as she read the underlined passage:

She hunters makes: and of that substance hounds
Whose mouths deafe heaven, and furrow earth with wounds,
And marvaile not a Nimphe so rich in grace
To hounds rude pursuits should be given in chase.
For she could turne her selfe to everie shape
Of swiftest beasts, and at her pleasure scape.

The words conjured up the image of Diana—clear, bright, unbidden—her face framed with gauzy wings and her throat thickly encircled with silver and diamonds. A single tear-shaped ruby quivered on her skin like a drop of blood, nestled into the notch between her collarbones.

In the stillroom, as the sun was rising, he had promised to find some way to let her know Diana was safe.

"Thank you, Matthew." Sarah kissed the book and the note and threw them into the cavernous fireplace. She said the words to conjure a white-hot fire. The paper caught quickly, and the book's edges began to curl.

Sarah watched the fire burn for a few moments. Then she walked out the front door, leaving it unlocked, and didn't look back.

Once the door closed, a worn silver coffin shot down the chimney and landed on the burning paper. Two gobbets of blood and mercury, released from the hollow chambers inside the ampulla by the heat of the fire, chased each other around the surface of the book before falling into the grate. There they seeped into the soft old mortar of the fireplace and traveled into the heart of the house. When they reached it, the house sighed with relief and released a forgotten, forbidden scent.

Sarah drank in the cool night air as she climbed into the RV. Her senses were not sharp enough to catch the cinnamon and blackthorn, honeysuckle and chamomile dancing in the air.

"Okay?" Em asked, her voice serene.

Sarah leaned across the cat carrier that held Tabitha and squeezed Em's knee. "Just fine."

Faye turned the key in the ignition and pulled down the driveway and onto the county road that would take them to the interstate, chattering about where they could stop for breakfast.

The four witches were too far away to perceive the shift in atmosphere around the house as hundreds of night creatures detected the unusual aroma of commingled vampire and witch, or to see the pale green smudges of the two ghosts in the keeping-room window.

Bridget Bishop and Diana's grandmother watched the vehicle's departure.

What will we do now? Diana's grandmother asked.

What we've always done, Joanna, Bridget replied. *Remember the past—and await the future.*

ACKNOWLEDGMENTS

My greatest debt is to the friends and family who read this book, chapter by chapter, as it was written: Cara, Karen, Lisa, Margaret, and my mom, Olive. Peg and Lynn, as always, provided excellent meals, warm companionship, and wise counsel. And I am especially appreciative of the editorial work that Lisa Halttunen did to prepare the manuscript for submission.

Colleagues generously lent me their expertise as I wandered far from my own area of specialization. Philippa Levine, Andrés Reséndez, Vanessa Schwartz, and Patrick Wyman steered me in the right direction whenever I took a misstep. Any errors that remain are, of course, my own.

I will always be grateful that Sam Stoloff of the Frances Goldin Literary Agency took the news that I had written a novel, and not another work of history, with grace and good humor. He also read the early drafts with a keen eye. Additional thanks to the agency's Ellen Geiger, for her inspired choice of dinner companions!

The team at Viking has become a second family to me. My editor, Carole DeSanti, represents what every author hopes for when they are writing a book: someone who will not only appreciate what you have put on the page but can envision what story those words could tell if they were tweaked just so. Maureen Sugden, copy editor extraordinaire, polished the book in record time. Thank you also to Clare Ferraro, Leigh Butler, Hal Fessenden, and the rights group; Nancy Sheppard, Carolyn Coleburn, and the marketing and sales team; Victoria Klose, Christopher Russell, and everyone who has helped transform this work from a stack of paper into a book.

Because this is a book *about* books, I consulted a substantial number of texts as I wrote. Curious readers can find some of them by consulting the Douay-Rheims translation of the Bible, Marie-Louise von Franz's critical edition and translation of *Aurora Consurgens* (Pantheon Books, 1966), and Paul Eugene Memmo's translation of Giordano Bruno's *Heroic Frenzies* (University of North Carolina Press, 1964). Those readers who do go exploring should know that the translations here are my own and therefore have their idiosyncrasies. Anyone who wants to delve further into the mind of Charles Darwin has the ideal place to start in Janet Browne's *Charles Darwin: A Biography* (2 vols., Alfred Knopf, 1995 and 2002). And for a lucid introduction to mtDNA and its application to the problems of human history consult Brian Sykes, *The Seven Daughters of Eve* (W. W. Norton, 2001).